Contents

CW00361948

The Comprehensive Guide to The UK Music Industry and Associated Service Companies

Published annually: Number 39
ISSN: 0267-3290
ISBN: 0 86213 159 6

Database Manager:
Nick Tesco
t 020 7921 8353
e nick@musicweek.com
w musicweekdirectory.com

Editor: Martin Talbot
Project Manager: Nicky Hembra
Group Production Manager: Desrae Procos
Deputy Production Manager: Mark Saunders

Business Development Manager:
Matthew Tyrrell

Sales Manager: Matt Slade
t 020 7921 8340 **f** 020 7921 8372
e matt@musicweek.com
Senior Sales Executive: Billy Fahey
Sales Executive: Dwaine Tyndale
Logo Sales Executive: Maria Edwards

Circulation Development Manager:
David Pagendam
t 020 7921 8320 **f** 020 7921 8404
e dpagendam@cmpi.biz

Publisher: Ajax Scott

Published by Music Week
CMP Information Ltd
1st Floor, Ludgate House
245 Blackfriars Road
London SE1 9UR
w musicweek.com

Database Typesetting and Printing by:
MPG Impressions Ltd, Units E1-E4 Barwell
Business Park, Leatherhead Road, Chessington,
Surrey KT9 2NY

Additional Copies are available by contacting:
Tower Publishing Services **t** 01858 438893
UK & Northern Ireland - **£40** Europe & Eire - **£45**
Rest of World 1 - **£50** Rest of World 2 - **£60**
Cheques should be made payable
to CMP Information Ltd

All material copyright © Music Week 2007

From the Editor

Welcome to the latest Music Week Directory, the essential contacts book for the modern day music industry – and the only directory worth having in 2007.

There are plenty of guides to the music industry, for newcomers looking for the right connections to make their way in the business, or for established, experienced players looking for the most up to date contact data. The book you hold in your hand is the most established of the lot; it is the daddy of them all.

It has the highest standing and the best reputation, dating back more than two decades. That counts for a lot.

The Music Week Directory has that deserved reputation because people who work in the business put it together and it has the most accurate contact data there is – spanning some 10,000 companies. It is the music industry's directory and that is reflected in the authority which is held in every line, every contact name, every telephone number and email address.

It is a directory that combines reliability with a continuing drive to update with new sections, enhanced areas of content. This year we have improved our coverage of the digital world, while also improving our studio listings with additional data on the technical spec offered by the cream of the sector.

The other development to our service has been to make this directory live and breathe, on a monthly, weekly and daily basis. Its sister website – musicweekdirectory.com – is the definitive online directory of the UK music industry, updated throughout the year and free-to-access for anyone who wants to.

It is another innovation that spells out our determination to remain ahead of the game.

Enjoy the 2007 Music Week Directory.

Mart

Kind regards,

Martin Talbot,
Editor, Music Week.

Section Index

The Music Week Directory 2007

Licensing recorded music on behalf of
record companies and performers

PPL

Record Companies:

International Hqs

EMI GROUP PLC

27 Wrights Lane, London W8 5SW **t** 020 7795 7000
f 020 7795 7001 **e** firstname.lastname@emimusic.com
w emigroup.com. Chairman& CEO, EMI Group: Eric Nicoli.
Chairman & CEO, EMI Music: Alain Levy. Vice Chairman, EMI
Music: David Munns. COO & Regional Director, EMI Music: Stuart
Ells. General Counsel, EMI Music & EMI Group plc: Charles
Ashcroft. Chairman & CEO, EMI Music Continental Europe: Jean-
Francois Cecillon. President EMI Classics: Costa Pilavachi. Senior
Vice President Global Marketing, EMI Music: Matthieu Lauriot-
Prevost. Head of Digital: Barney Wragg.

SONY BMG MUSIC ENTERTAINMENT (INTERNATIONAL) LTD

Bedford House, 69-79 Fulham High St, London SW6 3JW
t +44 20 7384 7500 **e** firstname.lastname@sonybmg.com
w sonybmg.com. President, Continental Europe: Maarten
Steinkamp. SVP, Global Marketing, Europe: Tim Delaney. SVP,
Human Resources, Continental Europe: Greg Lockhart. SVP &
European Counsel: Jonathan Sternberg. SVP, Worldwide A&R:
Martin Dodd. SVP, Digital Operations: Matt Carpenter. VP, Global
Marketing Europe: Laura Bartlett. VP, International Catalogue
Marketing: Tim Fraser-Harding. VP, Continental Europe: Soeren
Hinsch. VP, Finance Europe: William Rowe. VP, IS&T Europe:
Charles Soobroy. VP, Commercial Affairs, Continental Europe:
Wolfgang Orthmayr.

UNIVERSAL MUSIC GROUP INTERNATIONAL

UNIVERSAL MUSIC GROUP INTERNATIONAL
364-366 Kensington High Street, London W14 8NS
t 020 7471 5000 **f** 020 7471 5001
e firstname.lastname@umusic.com **w** umusic.com. Chairman &
CEO: Lucian Grainge. Chief Financial Officer: Boyd Muir.
President, Asia Pacific Region/Executive Vice President,
Marketing and A&R: Max Hole. President, Mediterranean, South
America, Middle East/President, Universal Music France: Pascal
Negre. Senior Vice President, Human Resources: Malcolm
Swatton.

WARNER MUSIC INTERNATIONAL

WARNER MUSIC INTERNATIONAL
28 Kensington Church St, London W8 4EP **t** 020 7368 2500
f 020 7368 2734 **e** firstname.lastname@warnermusic.com
w wmg.com. Chairman/CEO: Patrick Vien. Vice-Chairman/COO:
Gero Caccia. Vice-Chairman, Music, Content and Marketing: John
Reid. SVP/CFO: Jos de Raaij. SVP Business Affairs: John Watson.
SVP Law and Corporate Affairs: Anne Mansbridge. VP Human
Resources: Maria Osherova. SVP Business Development and
Strategic Partnerships, EMEA: Jay Durgan. VP A&R: Ric Salmon.
VP, Corporate Communications: Mel Fox.

Record Companies and Labels

020 Records (see Above The Sky Records / Lunastate Ltd)

2NV Records 1 Canada Sq, 29th Floor Canary Wharf Tower,
London E14 5DY **t** 0870 220 0237 **f** 0870 220 0238
e info@2nvrecords.com **w** 2nvrecords.com MD: Chris Nathaniel.

2Point9 Records PO Box 44607, London N16 0YP
t 07801 033 741 **e** Office@2point9.com **w** 2point9.com
Dirs: Billy Grant, Rob Stuart.

3 Beat Label Management 5 Slater St, Liverpool
L1 4BW **t** 0151 709 2323 **f** 0151 709 3707
e 3blm@3beat.co.uk **w** 3beat.co.uk MD: Andy Jarrod.

3 Beat Music 5 Slater St, Liverpool, Merseyside L1 4BW
t 0151 709 3355 **f** 0151 709 3707 **e** mike@3beat.co.uk
w 3beat.co.uk Label Mgr: Mike Miller.

3kHz 54 Pentney Rd, London SW12 0NY **t** 020 8772 0108
f 020 8675 1636 **e** info@3khz.com **w** 3khz.com
MD: Mike Hedges.

3rd Stone Records (see Adasam Limited)

4 Zero Records 27 Arden Mhor, Pinner, Middlesex HA5 2HR
t 020 8868 5279 **e** dave@4zerorcords.co.uk
w 4zerorecords.co.uk Founder: Dave Weller.

4AD

17-19 Alma Road, London SW18 1AA **t** 020 8870 9724
f 020 8877 9109 **e** 4ad@4ad.com **w** 4ad.com MD: Chris Sharp.
A&R Manager: Ed Horrox. A&R Scout : Jane Abernethy.

>4 Music PO Box 47163, London W6 6AS **t** 020 8748 4997
or 07885 512 721 **e** info@morethan4.com **w** morethan4.com
MD: Anthony Hamer-Hodges.

4Real Records Myrtle Cottage, Rye Rd, Hawkhurst, Kent
TN18 5DW **t** 01580 754 771 **f** 01580 754 771
e scully4real@yahoo.co.uk **w** 4realrecords.com MD: Terry Scully.

5.15 Records PO Box 3062, Brighton, E Sussex BN50 9EA
t 01273 779944 **f** 01273 748829
e info@fivefifteenrecords.co.uk **w** fivefifteenrecords.co.uk
Dirs: John Reid, Phil Barton.

7Hz Recordings 4 Margaret St, London W1W 8RF
t 020 7462 1269 **f** 020 7436 5431 **e** barry@7hzrecordings.com
w 7hzrecordings.com GM: Barry Campbell.

7Ts (see Cherry Red Records)

10 Kilo (see Tip World)

11c Recordings 25 Heathmans Rd, London SW6 4TJ
t 020 7371 5756 **f** 020 7371 7731 **e** office@pureuk.com
w pureuk.com/11c CEO: Evros Stakis.

13 Amp (see Mercury Music Group)

13th Moon Records PO Box 79, Bridgend, Mid Glamorgan
CF32 8ZR **t** 01656 872582 **f** 01656 872582
e liz@asf-13thmoon.demon.co.uk **w** asf-13thmoon.demon.co.uk
Mgr: Liz Howell.

14TH FLOOR RECORDS

Electric Lighting Station, 46 Kensington Court, London W8 5DA
t 020 7938 5500 **f** 020 7368 4928
e firstname.lastname@warnermusic.com. MD: Christian
Tattersfield. Head of Press: Peter Hall. Marketing Manager: Elkie
Brooks. A&R Manager: Alex Gilbert. Label Co-ordinator: Jess
Barratt.

16 Tons Ltd Devlin House, 36 St. George St, Mayfair, London
W1S 2FW **t** 020 7871 4755 or 07951 406 938
e archer@16tons.com **w** 16tons.com MD: Archer Adams.

21st Century Generation (see Plaza Records)

21st Century Soul 28 Tooting High St, London SW17 0RG
t 020 8333 5400 **f** 020 8333 5401
e info@21stCenturySoul.com **w** 21stCenturySoul.com
MD: Tom Hayes.

23rd Precinct (see Limbo Records)

33 Jazz Records The Hat Factory, 65-67 Bute St, Luton
LU1 2EY **t** 01582 419584 **f** 01582 459401
e 33jazz@compuserve.com **w** 33jazz.com Dir: Paul Jolly.

37 Music Mare Street Studios, 203-213 Mare St, Hackney,
London E8 3QE **t** 020 8525 1188 **f** 020 8525 1188
e info@37music.com **w** 37music.com MD: Jermaine Fagan.

99 Degrees (see Higher State)

99 North (see Higher State)

162a Records First floor, 8-9 Rivington Pl, London
EC2A 3BA **t** 020 7691 7940 or 07803 131 646
f 020 7691 7940 **e** jan@162a.com **w** 162a.com
MD: Jan Sodderland.

500 Rekords PO Box 9499, London E5 0UG
t 020 8806 9500 or 07966 194346 **f** 020 8806 9500
e paul@500rekords.freeserve.co.uk MD: Paul C.

679 RECORDINGS

Second Floor, 172a Arlington Road, London NW1 7HL
t 020 7284 5780 **f** 020 7284 5795
e firstname.lastname@679recordings.com **w** 679recordings.com.
MD: Nick Worthington. Label Manager: Simon Rose. A&R
Manager: Dan Stacey. Product Manager: Katie Holland. Label Co-
ordinator: Nina Dufmats.

1-2-3-4 Records 27 Cowper St, London EC2A 4AP
t 020 7684 1126 **f** 020 7613 5917 **e** info@1234records.com
w 1234records.com Dirs: Sean McLusky, James Mullord.

1965 RECORDS

2nd floor, Hammer House, 117 Wardour Street, London
W1F 0UN **t** 020 7734 5861 **f** 020 7434 1511
e info@1965records.com **w** 1965records.com A&R: Raf Rundell.
MD: James Endeacott.

A&G Records 1st Floor, 5 Ching Court, 61-63 Monmouth St,
London WC2H 9EY **t** 020 7845 9880 **f** 020 7845 9884
e firstname@aegweb.com **w** agrecords.co.uk MD: Roy Jackson.

The A Label (see Numinous Music Group)

A LIST RECORDS LTD

500 Chiswick High Rd, London W4 5RG **t** 020 8956 2615
f 020 8956 2614 **e** mail@alistrecords.com **w** alistrecords.com
Chairman: Cary George.
A List Records are an innovative entertainment company
who pride themselves on delivering to the world truly top
quality music from all music genres & progressing top artists
from around the world. Artists include Attica, Blind Pew, The
Passenger and The Stremes.

A3 Music PO Box 1345, Worthing, W Sussex BN14 7FB
t 01903 202426 **f** 01903 202426 **e** music@A3music.co.uk
w A3music.co.uk Dir: John Ginger.

Aardvark Records 75 Alderwood Parc, Penryn, Cornwall
TR10 8RL **t** 01326 376 707 **f** 01326 376 707
e musicman@aardvarkrecords.co.uk **w** aardvarkrecords.co.uk
Chairman: Andrew Reeve.

Abbey Records (SCS Music Ltd) PO Box 197, Beckley,
Oxford OX3 9YJ **t** 01865 358282 **e** info@scsmusic.co.uk
MD: Steve C Smith.

Above The Sky Records / Lunastate Ltd Studio 211,
24-28 Hatton Wall, Clerkenwell, London EC1N 8JH
t 020 7404 1005 **e** info@abovethesky.com **w** abovethesky.com
Dir: A J Burt.

Absolute (see Absolute Records)

Absolute Records Craig Gowan, Carrbridge, Inverness-shire
PH23 3AX **t** 01479 841771 **e** absolutemuse@hotmail.com
w absoluterecords.co.uk MD: Sue Moss.

Absolution Records The Old Lamp Works, Rodney Pl,
Merton, London SW19 2LQ **t** 020 8540 4242
f 020 8540 6056 **e** simon@absolutemarketing.co.uk
w absolutemarketing.co.uk MD: Simon Wills.

Abstract Sounds 10 Tiverton Rd, London NW10 3HL
t 020 7286 1106 **f** 020 7289 8679
e abstractsounds@btclick.com
w abstractsounds.co.uk; candlelightrecords.co.uk
MD: Edward Christie.

Accidental Records Suite 210, Bon Marche Building, 241-
251 Ferndale Rd, London SW9 8BJ **t** 020 7737 6464
f 020 7978 9514 **e** info@accidentalrecords.com
w magicandaccident.com Label Mgr: Pepe Jansz.

Ace (see Ace Records)

Ace Eyed Records (see Blue Melon Records Ltd)

ACE RECORDS

42-50 Steele Rd, London NW10 7AS **t** 020 8453 1311
f 020 8961 8725 **e** sales@acerecords.co.uk **w** acerecords.co.uk
Sales & Marketing Dir: Phil Stoker.

Acid Jazz Records 146 Bethnal Green Rd, London E2 6DG
t 020 7613 1100 **e** info@acidjazz.co.uk **w** acidjazz.co.uk
Label Manager: Danny Corr.

ACL Records PO Box 31, Potters Bar, Herts EN6 1XR
t 01707 644706 **f** 01707 644706 **e** WMD644706@aol.com
Contact: David Thomas.

Acorn Records 1 Tylney View, London Rd, Hook, Hants
RG27 9LJ **t** 078083 77350 **e** acornrecords@hotmail.com
MD: Mark Olrog.

Acoustics Records PO Box 350, Reading, Berks RG6 7DQ
t 0118 926 8615 **e** mail@AcousticsRecords.co.uk
w AcousticsRecords.co.uk MD: HA Jones.

Acrobat Music Ltd 30a Green Lane, Northwood, Middx
HA6 2QB **t** 01923 821559 **f** 01923 821296
e enquiries@acrobatmusic.net **w** acrobatmusic.net
MD: John Cooper.

Action Records 46 Church St, Preston, Lancs PR1 3DH
t 01772 884 772 or 01772 258809 **f** 01772 252 255
e sales@actionrecords.co.uk **w** actionrecords.co.uk
Mgr: Gordon Gibson.

Activa (see 4Real Records)

Activation (see ATCR: Trance Communication)

AD Music 5 Albion Rd, Bungay, Suffolk NR35 1LQ
t 01986 894712 **f** 01986 894712 **e** admin@admusiconline.com
w admusiconline.com Label Owner: Elaine Wright.

Adage Music 22 Gravesend Rd, London W12 0SZ
t 07973 295113 **e** Dobs@adagemusic.co.uk
w publicsymphony.com Mgr: Dobs Vye.

Adasam Limited PO Box 8, Corby, Northants NN17 2XZ
t 01536 202295 **f** 01536 266246 **e** adasam@adasam.co.uk
w adasam.co.uk Label Mgr: Steve Kalidoski.

Additive EMI House, 43 Brook Green, London W6 7EF
t 020 7605 5000 **f** 020 7605 5050
e firstname.lastname@emimusic.com **w** additiverecords.co.uk
Dir: Jason Ellis. Label Co-ordinator: Nathan Taylor.

Adept (see Avex Inc)

Adventure Records PO Box 261, Wallingford, Oxon
OX10 0XY **t** 01491 832 183 **e** info@adventuresin-music.com
w adventure-records.com Label Manager: Katie Conroy.

Afro Art Recordings 109 Dukes Ave, Muswell Hill, London
N10 2QD **t** 020 8374 4412 **f** 020 8374 4410
e simonebeedle@afroartrecords.com **w** afroartrecords.com
Dir: Simone Beedle.

Afrolution Records 85 Fourth Ave, Manor Pk, London E12 6DP **t** 020 7095 1218 **e** hello@blackmangomusic.com **w** blackmangomusic.com Label Manager: Trenton Birch.

Aftermath (see Hi-Note Music)

Against the Grain 29 Kensington Gardens, Brighton BN1 4AL **t** 01273 628 181 **f** 01273 670 444 **e** lloyd@superchargedmusic.com **w** superchargedmusic.com Label Manager: Lloyd Seymour.

Agenda Music (see Peacefrog Records)

Ainm Music Unit C10, Wicklow Enterprise Pk, The Murrough, Wicklow Town, Co Wicklow, Ireland **t** +353 404 62527 **f** +353 404 62527 **e** fstubbs@ainm-music.com **w** ainm-music.com MD: Frank Stubbs.

Airplay Records The Sound Foundation, PO Box 4900, Earley, Berks RG10 0GA **t** 0118 934 9600 or 07973 559 203 **e** info@soundfoundation.co.uk **w** airplayrecords.co.uk Label Mgr: Hadyn Wood.

Albert Productions Unit 29, Cygnus Business Centre, Dalmeyer Rd, London NW10 2XA **t** 020 8830 0330 **f** 020 8830 0220 **e** james@alberts.co.uk **w** albertmusic.co.uk Head of A&R: James Cassidy.

All Action Figure Records Unit 9, Darvells Works, Common Rd, Chorleywood, Herts WD3 5LP **t** 01923 286010 **f** 01923 286070 **e** info@allactionfigure.co.uk **w** bigsur.co.uk MD: Steve Lowes.

All Around The World 9-13 Penny St, Blackburn, Lancs BB1 6HJ **t** 01254 264120 **f** 01254 693768 **e** info@aatw.com **w** aatw.com GM: Matt Cadman.

All Good Vinyl (see Copasetik Recordings Ltd)

Almighty (see Almighty Records)

Almighty Records PO Box 40069, London N6 5uj **t** 020 8341 0101 **f** 020 8340 9494 **e** info@almightyrecords.com **w** almightyrecords.com MD: Martyn Norris.

Almost Anonymous (see 3 Beat Label Management)

Alpha Engineering Records Ltd 6 Waterloo Park Industrial Est, Wellington Rd, Bidford on Avon, Warcs B50 4JG **e** alphaengine@hotmail.com **w** alphaengineeringrecords.co.uk Contact: Paul Townend.

Altarus Inc (UK Office) Easton Dene, Bailbrook Lane, Bath BA1 7AA **t** 01225 852323 **f** 01225 852523 **e** sorabji-archive@lineone.net **w** altarusrecords.com UK Office Manager: Alistair Hinton.

A&M (see Polydor Records)

Amalie (see Loose Tie Records)

Amazing Feet (see Rotator Records)

Amazon Records Ltd PO Box 5109, Hove, E Sussex BN52 9EA **t** 01273 726 414 **f** 01273 726 414 **e** info@amazonrecords.co.uk **w** amazonrecords.co.uk MD: Frank Sansom.

American Activities 29 St Michaels Rd, Leeds, West Yorks LS6 3BG **t** 0113 274 2106 **f** 0113 278 6291 **e** dave@bluescat.com **w** bluescat.com MD: Dave Foster.

Amethyst (see Rainbow Quartz Records)

Amphion (see Priory Records)

Anagram (see Cherry Red Records)

Analogue Baroque (see Cherry Red Records)

Angel Air (see Angel Air Records)

Angel Air Records Unicorn House, Station Road West, Stowmarket, Suffolk IP14 1ES **t** 01449 770139 **f** 01449 770133 **e** sales@angelair.co.uk **w** angelair.co.uk MD: Peter Purnell.

ANGEL MUSIC GROUP

Angel Music Group

Crown House, 72 Hammersmith Road, London W14 8UD **t** 020 7605 5000 **f** 020 7605 5050 **e** firstname.lastname@emimusic.com **w** emimusic.co.uk Director: Mark Poston. A&R: Elias Christidis. Director, Artist Development: Sara Freeman. Head of Marketing Strategy: Elin Falk.

Anjunabeats Fortress Studios, 34-38 Provost St, London N1 7NG **t** 020 7608 1567 **f** 020 7253 9825 **e** info@anjunabeats.com **w** anjunabeats.com Label Manager: Soraya Sobh.

Ankst Musik Records The Old Police Station, The Square, Pentraeth, Anglesey LL75 8AZ **t** 01248 450 155 **f** 01248 450 155 **e** emyr@ankst.co.uk **w** ankst.co.uk MD: Emyr Glyn Williams.

Annie Records 39 Ivygreen Rd, Chorlton, Manchester M21 9AG **t** 0161 860 4133 **e** annie.records@ntlworld.com **w** annierecords.com CEO: Ann Louttit.

Anno Domini (see Talking Elephant)

Antara (see Line-Up PMC)

Antilles (see Island Records Group)

Apace Music Ltd Unit LG4, Shepherds Central, Charecroft Way, London W14 0EH **t** 020 7471 9270 **f** 020 7471 9383 **e** sales@apacemusic.co.uk **w** apacemusic.co.uk MD: Tim Millington.

Apartment 22 19 Tewkesbury Rd, Bristol BS2 9UL **t** 0117 955 6615 **f** 0117 955 6616 **e** caretaker@apartment22.com MD: Andy Morgan.

Ape City (see Primaudial Recordings)

APL Oddfellows Hall, London Rd, Chipping Norton, Oxon OX7 5AR **t** 01608 641592 **f** 01608 641969 **e** help@aitkenproductions.co.uk.

Apocalypse (see Snapper Music)

Apollo Sound 32 Ellerdale Rd, London NW3 6BB **t** 020 7435 5255 **f** 020 7431 0621 **e** info@apollosound.com **w** apollosound.com MD: Toby Herschmann.

Apropos (see Siren Music Ltd)

ARC Music Productions International PO Box 111, East Grinstead, W Sussex RH19 4LZ **t** 01342 328567 **f** 01342 315958 **e** info@arcmusic.co.uk **w** arcmusic.co.uk Sales & Mktg Dir: Robert Graves.

Archangel Recordings PO Box 1013, Woking GU22 7ZD
t 01483 729 447 **e** info@archangelrecordings.co.uk
w archangelrecordings.co.uk A&R: Bruce Elliott-Smith.

Archive Recordings Lower Grd Floor, 12, Thicket Rd,
London SE20 8DD **t** 07944 667 281 **e** mrwrightis@yahoo.co.uk
MD: Morris Wright.

Are We Mad? (see Ariwa Sounds Ltd)

Arista (see Sony BMG Music Entertainment UK & Ireland)

Ariwa Sounds Ltd 34 Whitehorse Lane, London SE25 6RE
t 020 8653 7744 **f** 020 8771 1911 **e** ariwastudios@aol.com
w ariwa.com Label Manager: Holly Fraser.

Ark 21 1 Water Lane, London NW1 8NZ **t** 020 7267 1101
f 020 7267 7466 **e** info@ark21.com **w** ark21.com
Label Mgr: Roisin Murphy.

Ark Records Fetcham Park House, Lower Rd, Leatherhead,
Surrey KT22 9HD **t** 01372 360300 **f** 01372 360878
e info@arkrecords.com **w** arkrecords.com MD: Greg Walsh.

Arriba Records 156-158 Gray's Inn Rd, London WC1X 8ED
t 020 7713 0998 **f** 020 7713 1132 **e** info@arriba-records.com
w arriba-records.com Dir: S-J Henry.

Arrivederci Baby! (see Cherry Red Records)

Artfield 5 Grosvenor Sq, London W1K 4AF **t** 020 7499 9941
f 020 7499 5519 **e** info@artfieldmusic.com **w** bbcooper.com
MD: BB Cooper.

Artful Records Ltd Unit 7 Grand Union Centre, West Row,
Ladbroke Grove, London W10 5AS **t** 020 8968 1545
f 020 8964 1181 **e** info@artfulrecords.co.uk
w artfulrecords.co.uk Contact: Danielle Chambers.

Artisan (see Snapper Music)

ARC - Artist Record Company 1 North Worple Way,
Mortlake, London SW14 8QG **t** 020 8876 2533
f 020 8878 4229 **e** artistrec@aol.com **w** arcarc.co.uk
Dir of Promotions: Geraldine Perry.

Arvee (see Everest Copyrights)

ASB Ltd (see Vanquish Music Group)

Ash International (see Touch)

Ash Records Hillside Farm, Hassocky Lane, Temple
Normanton, Chesterfield, Derbyshire S42 5DH **t** 01246 231762
e ash_music36@hotmail.com Head of A&R: Paul Townsend.

Associate (see Silverword Music Group)

Astounding Sounds, Amazing Music (see Voiceprint)

Astralwerks Kensal House, 553-579 Harrow Rd, London
W10 4RH **t** 020 8964 6220 **f** 020 8964 6221
e (through website) **w** astralwerks.com.

ASV (see Sanctuary Classics)

ATCR: Trance Communication PO Box 272, Headington,
Oxford OX3 8PL **t** 01865 764568 **f** 01865 744056
e info@atcr.co.uk **w** atcr.org.uk Mgr: Tim Stark.

ATG Records Kontakt Productions, 44b Whifflet St,
Coatbridge ML5 4EL **t** 01236 434 083 **f** 01236 434 083
e fraser@kontaktproductions.com **w** kontaktproductions.com
Label Manager: Fraser Grieve.

Athene (see Priory Records)

Atlantic Jaxx (see Accidental Records)

ATLANTIC RECORDS UK

Electric Lighting Station, 46 Kensington Court, London W8 5DA
t 020 7938 5500 **e** firstname.lastname@atlanticrecords.co.uk
w atlanticrecords.co.uk. MD: Max Lousada. Director of Business
Affairs: Rachel Evers. Director of Promotions: Damian Christian.
Director of Marketing: Richard Hinkley. Creative Director: Richard
Skinner. Head of A&R: Steve Sasse. A&R: Hugo Bedford, Joel
De'ath, Thomas Haimovici. A&R Scout: Steve Proud.

Atomic 133 Longacre, Covent Garden, London WC2E 9DT
t 020 7379 3010 **f** 020 7379 5583 **e** mn@atomic-london.com
w atomic.co.uk Dir: Mick Newton.

Attaboy Records Unit 4 The Pavilions, 2 East Rd, S.
Wimbledon, London SW19 1UW **t** 020 8545 8580
f 020 8545 8581 **e** mikel@simplyvinyl.com **w** simplyvinyl.com
Label Mgr: Mike Loveday.

Audio Bug 3 Buck St, Camden, London NW1 8NJ
t 020 7267 1526 **e** info@audiobugrecords.co.uk
w audiobugrecords.co.uk Contact: Martin Audio.

Audio Freaks (see 3 Beat Label Management)

Audio Therapy 52a High Pavement, The Lace Market,
Nottingham NG1 1HW **t** 0115 943 7901 **f** 0115 950 1121
e info@therapymusic.co.uk **w** therapymusic.co.uk
Label Manager: Scott Dawson.

Audiorec Ltd 21B Silicon Business Centre, 26-28 Wadsworth
Rd, Greenford, Middlesex UB6 7JZ **t** 020 8810 7779
f 020 8810 7773 **e** info@audiorec.co.uk **w** audiorec.co.uk
Dir: Jyotindra Patel.

Audiorec Premium (see Audiorec Ltd)

Authentic Media 9 Holdom Ave, Bletchley, Milton Keynes,
Bucks MK1 1QR **t** 01908 364 200 **f** 01908 648 592
e info@authenticmedia.co.uk **w** authenticmedia.co.uk
MD: David Withers.

Automatic Records Unit 5 Waldo Works, Waldo Rd,
London NW10 6AW **t** 020 8964 8890 **f** 020 8960 5741
e russel@digitalstores.co.uk **w** automaticsongs.com
MD: Russel Coultart.

Automatic Records. The Old Vicarage, Pickering, N Yorks
YO18 7AW **t** 01751 475 502 **f** 01751 475 502
e organised@ukonline.co.uk MD: Francis Ward.

Aux Delux (see Supreme Music)

Avalanche Records 17 West Nicolson St, Edinburgh, Lothian EH8 9DA **t** 0131 668 2374 **f** 0131 668 3234 **e** avalanche.records@virgin.net **w** avalancherecords.co.uk MD: Kevin Buckle.

Avalon Records PO Box 929, Ferndown, Dorset BH22 9YF **t** 01202 870 084 **e** info@galahadonline.com **w** galahadonline.com Mgr: Stuart Nicholson.

Avex Inc The Heals Building, Unit A3, 3rd Floor, 22-24 Torrington Pl, London WC1E 7HJ **t** 020 7323 6420 **f** 020 7323 6413 **e** song@avex-inc.com **w** avex.co.jp General Mgr: S.C.Song.

Avid Entertainment 10 Metro Centre, Dwight Rd, Tolpits Lane, Watford, Herts WD18 9UF **t** 01923 281 281 **f** 01923 281 200 **e** info@avidgroup.co.uk **w** avidgroup.co.uk MD: Richard Lim.

Avie Records 1 Rose Alley, London SE1 9AS **t** 020 7921 9233 **f** 020 7261 1058 **e** musicco@musicco.f9.co.uk **w** avierecords.com Executive Director: Simon Foster.

Axtone Records Ltd 12 St Davids Close, Farnham, Surrey GU9 9DR **t** 01252 330 894 or 07775 515 025 **f** 01252 330 894 **e** james@axtone.com **w** axtone.com MD: James Sefton.

Azuli Records 25 D'Arblay St, London W1V 8ES **t** 020 7287 1932 **f** 020 7439 2490 **e** info@azuli.com **w** azuli.com Mktg: Sean Brosnan.

B-Unique Records 1A Cranbrook Rd, London W4 2LH **t** 020 8987 0393 **f** 020 8995 9917 **e** info@b-uniquerecords.com **w** b-uniquerecords.com MDs: Mark Lewis, Martin Toher.

Back Alley Records (see Nikt Records)

Back Yard Recordings 24 Oppidans Rd, Primrose Hill, London NW3 3AG **t** 020 7722 7522 **f** 020 7722 7622 **e** sam.richardson@back-yard.co.uk **w** back-yard.co.uk Dir: Gil Goldberg.

Backbone (see Flair Records)

Background Records (see Hi-Note Music)

Backs Recording Company St Mary's Works, St Mary's Plain, Norwich, Norfolk NR3 3AF **t** 01603 624290 or 01603 626221 **f** 01603 619999 **e** info@backsrecords.co.uk MD: Jonathan Appel.

Back2Basics Recordings Ltd PO Box 41, Tipton, W Midlands DY4 7YT **t** 0121 520 1150 **f** 0121 520 1150 **e** info@back2basicsrecords.co.uk **w** back2basicsrecords.co.uk Dirs: Jason Ball & Anamaria Gibbons.

Baktabak (see Baktabak Records)

Baktabak Records Network House, 29-39 Stirling Rd, London W3 8DJ **t** 020 8993 5966 **f** 020 8992 0340 **e** chris@arab.co.uk **w** baktabak Dir: Chris Leaning.

Bamaco Vine Cottage, 255 Lower Rd, Great Bookham, Leatherhead, Surrey KT23 4DX **t** 01372 450 752 **e** barrymurrayents@aol.com Contact: Barry Murray.

Banana Recordings Leroy House, Unit 2L, 436 Essex Rd, London N1 3QP **t** 020 7354 7353 **f** 020 7288 2958 **e** infobanana@btconnect.com **w** bananarecordings.co.uk Dir: Richard Hermitage.

Bandleader Recordings Unit 3, Faraday Way, St. Mary Cray, Kent BR5 3QW **t** 01689 879090 **f** 01689 879091 **e** janice@modernpublicity.co.uk GM: Janice Whybrow.

Bandwagon Records Studio 507 Enterprise House, 1-2 Hatfields, London SE1 9PG **t** 020 7993 1221 **e** support@bandwagon.co.uk **w** bandwagon.co.uk Dirs: Owen Farrington, Huw Thomas.

Barely Breaking Even Records PO Box 25896, London N5 1WE **t** 020 7607 0597 **f** 020 7607 4696 **e** leeb@bbemusic.demon.co.uk **w** bbemusic.com Co Sec: Lee Bright.

Baria Records Start Building, 25 Barnes Wallis Rd, Fareham, Hants PO15 5TT **t** 01489 889 823 **e** info@bariarecords.com **w** bariarecords.com Contact: Eugene Bari, Marcus Coles.

BBC Audio Books St James House, Lower Bristol Rd, Bath BA2 3SB **t** 01225 335 336 **f** 01225 448 005 **e** info@audiobookcollection.com **w** audiobookcollection.com MD: Paul Dempsey.

BBC Music Room A2036, Woodlands, 80 Wood Lane, London W12 0TT **t** 020 8433 1711 **f** 020 8433 1743 **e** jim.reid.01@bbc.co.uk Label Manager: Jim Reid.

Bear Family (see Rollercoaster Records)

Bearcat (see Bearcat Records)

Bearcat Records PO Box 94, Derby, Derbyshire DE22 1XA **t** 01332 332336 or 07702 564804 **f** 01332 332336 **e** chrishall@swampmusic.co.uk **w** swampmusic.co.uk Dir: Chris Hall.

Beat Goes On Records (BGO) 7 St. Andrews St North, Bury St Edmunds, Suffolk IP33 1TZ **t** 01284 724406 **f** 01284 762245 **e** andy@bgo-records.com **w** bgo-records.com MD: Andy Gray.

Beathut 13 Greenwich Centre Business Pk, Norman Rd, Greenwich, London SE10 9PY **t** 020 8858 7700 **e** info@beathutonline.com **w** beathutonline.com Mgr: Caroline Hemingway.

Beatz (see Valve)

Beautiful Jo Records PO Box 1039, Oxford OX1 4UA **t** 01865 249 194 **f** 01865 792 765 **e** tim@bejo.co.uk **w** bejo.co.uk MD: Tim Healey.

Because Music Ltd 8 Kensington Park Rd, London W11 3BU **t** 020 7313 3302 or 07979 238 142 **f** 020 7221 8899 **e** jenny@adlington30.freeserve.co.uk **w** amadou-mariam.com Label Manager: Jenny Adlington.

Beckmann Visual Publishing 1 The Courtyard, Court Row, Ramsey, Isle of Man IM8 1AS **t** 01624 816585 **f** 01624 816589 **e** sales@beckmandirect.com **w** beckmandirect.com MD: Jo White.

Bedrock Records Reverb House, Bennett St, London W4 2AH **t** 020 8742 7670 **f** 020 8994 8617 **e** info@bedrock.uk.net **w** bedrock.org.uk Label Manager: Nick Bates.

Beggars Banquet Records 17-19 Alma Rd, London SW18 1AA **t** 020 8870 9912 **f** 020 8871 1766 **e** beggars@almaroad.co.uk **w** beggars.com Contact: Ann Wilson.

The Beggars Group 17-19 Alma Rd, London SW18 1AA **t** 020 8870 9912 **f** 020 8871 1766 **e** postmaster@beggars.com **w** beggars.com.

Bell Records (see Sony BMG Music Entertainment UK & Ireland)

Bella Union 14 Church St, Twickenham, Middx TW1 3NJ **t** 020 8744 2777 **f** 020 8891 1895 **e** info@bellaunion.com **w** bellaunion.com Label Mgr: Fiona Glyn-Jones.

Berlin Records Caxton House, Caxton Ave, Blackpool, Lancs FY2 9AP **t** 01253 591 169 **f** 01253 508 670 **e** info@berlinstudios.co.uk **w** berlinstudios.co.uk MD: Ron Sharples.

Better The Devil Records PO Box 292, Adversane, Billingshurst, W Sussex RH14 9XY **t** 01403 784 920 **f** 01403 783 245 **e** info@btdrecords.com **w** betterthedevilrecords.com MD: Graham Stokes.

Beulah (see Priory Records)

Beyer (see Priory Records)

BGP (see Ace Records)

BHI Records 21b Mitcham Lane, London SW16 6LQ **t** 020 8677 4651 **f** 020 8677 4651 **e** admin@bhirecords.co.uk **w** bhirecords.co.uk Label Mgrs: Paul Harris, Lanre Bombata.

Biff Bang Pow Records 12 Denyer Court, Fradley, Nr Lichfield, Staffs WS13 8TQ **t** 01543 444261 **f** 01543 444261 **e** info@biffbangpow.org.uk **w** biffbangpow.org.uk MD: Paul Hooper-Keeley.

Big Bear Records PO Box 944, Birmingham, W Midlands B16 8UT **t** 0121 454 7020 **f** 0121 454 9996 **e** records@bigbearmusic.com **w** bigbearmusic.com MD: Jim Simpson.

Big Beat (see Ace Records)

Big Cat (UK) Records PO Box 34449, London W6 0RT **t** 020 7751 0199 **f** 020 7751 0199 **e** info@bigcatrecords.com MD: Abbo.

Big Chill Recordings PO Box 52707, London EC2P 2WE **t** 020 7684 1172 **f** 020 7684 2022 **e** eugenie@bigchill.net **w** bigchill.net Label Mgr: Eugenie Arrowsmith.

Big City (see Candid Productions)

Big Dada PO Box 4296, London SE11 4WW **t** 020 7820 3555 **f** 020 7820 3434 **e** info@bigdada.com **w** bigdada.com Lbl Mgr: Will Ashon.

Big Dada (see Ninja Tune)

Big Deal Records 83 Dartmouth Park Rd, London NW5 1SL **t** 020 7681 0585 **f** 020 7681 0585 **e** Lew@Bigdealrecords.net MD: Lew Wernick.

Big Fish Audio (see 3 Beat Label Management)

Big Moon Records PO Box 347, Weybridge, Surrey KT13 9WZ **t** 01932 590169 **f** 01932 889802 **e** info@tzuke.com **w** tzuke.com Label Head: Jamie Muggleton.

Binliner (see Detour Records Ltd)

Biondi Records 33 Lamb Court, 69 Narrow St, London E14 8EJ **t** 020 7538 5749 **e** info@biondi.co.uk **w** biondi.co.uk Label Manager: Marc Andrewes.

Bitch Records (see Automatic Records)

BKO Productions The Old Truman Brewery, 91 Brick Lane, London E1 6QL **t** 020 7377 9373 **f** 020 7377 6523 **e** byron@bko-alarcon.co.uk Dir: Byron K. Orme.

Black (see Revolver Music Ltd)

Black Box Music (see Sanctuary Classics)

Black Burst Records (see Rough Trade Records)

Black Hole UK (see New State Entertainment)

Black Jesus (see Quiet Riot Records)

Black Magic Records 296 Earls Court Rd, London SW5 9BA **t** 020 7565 0806 **f** 020 7565 0806 **e** blackmagicrecords@talk21.com **w** blackmagicrecords.com MD: Mataya Clifford.

Black Mango Music 85 Fourth Ave, Manor Pk, London E12 6DP **t** 020 7095 1218 **e** hello@blackmangomusic.com **w** blackmangomusic.com Label Manager: Trenton Birch.

Black Mountain Recordings 1 Squire Court, The Marina, Swansea SA1 3XB **t** 01792 301 500 **f** 01792 301 500 **e** info@blackmountainmobile.co.uk **w** blackmountainmobile.co.uk MD: Michael Evans.

Black Records (see Bedrock Records)

Blackend (see Plastic Head Records Ltd)

BLACKLIST ENTERTAINMENT

Fulham Palace, Bishops Avenue, London SW6 6EA **t** 020 7751 0175 **f** 020 7736 0606 **e** firstname@blacklistent.com **w** blacklistent.com Chairman: Clive Black.

Blackmoon Records (see BMR Entertainment Ltd)

Blakamix International Records Garvey House, 42 Margetts Rd, Bedford, Beds MK42 8DS **t** 01234 856164 or 01234 302115 **f** 01234 854344 **e** blakamix@aol.com **w** blakamix.co.uk MD: Dennis Bedeau.

Blaktrax Records (see Shaboom Records)

Blanco Y Negro 66 Golborne Rd, London W10 5PS **t** 020 8960 9888 **f** 020 8968 6715 **e** pru@roughtraderecords.com MD: Bob Harding.

Blast First (see Mute Records Ltd)

Bleach Records Eltime House, Hall Rd, Maldon, Essex CM9 4NF **t** 01621 856 943 **f** 01621 855 335 **e** info@bleachrecords.co.uk Artist Dir: Mark Hurst.

Blix Street Records PO Box 5174, Hove BN52 9HG
t 01273 206509 **f** 01273 206579 **e** info@blixstreet.co.uk
w blixstreet.co.uk Dir: Tom Norrell.

Blood and Fire Room 105, Ducie House, 37, Ducie St,
Manchester M1 2JW **t** 0161 228 3034 **f** 0161 228 3036
e info@bloodandfire.co.uk **w** bloodandfire.co.uk MD: Bob Harding.

Blow Up Records Limited PO Box 4961, London
W1A 7ZX **t** 020 7636 7744 **f** 020 7636 7755
e webmaster@blowup.co.uk **w** blowup.co.uk MD: Paul Tunkin.

Blu Bamboo Records Ltd 32 Ransomes Dock, 35-37
Parkgate Rd, London SW11 4NP **t** 020 7801 1919
f 020 7738 1819 **e** info@blu-bamboo.com **w** blu-bamboo.com
Dirs/A&R: Alister Jamieson, Stuart Muff.

Blue Banana Records (see Blue Melon Records Ltd)

Blue Juice Music Ltd Hobbs Barn, Wick End, Stagsden,
Beds MK43 8TS **t** 01234 823452 **f** 01234 823452
e bluejuicemusic@aol.com MD: Rob Butterfield.

Blue Melon Records Ltd 240A High Rd, Harrow Weald,
Middx HA3 7BB **t** 020 8863 2520 **f** 020 8863 2520
e steve@bluemelon.co.uk MD: Steven Glen.

Blue Note EMI House, 43 Brook Green, London W6 7EF
t 020 7605 5000 **f** 020 7605 5050
e firstname.lastname@emimusic.com **w** emimusic.co.uk.

Blue Planet Records (see Blue Melon Records Ltd)

Blue Star (see East Central One Ltd)

Blue Thumb (see Universal Music Classics & Jazz (UK))

Blueprint (see Voiceprint)

Blueprint Recording Corporation PO Box 593, Woking,
Surrey GU23 7YF **t** 01483 715336 **f** 01483 757490
e blueprint@lineone.net **w** blueprint-records.net MD: John Glover.

Blues Matters Records PO Box 18, Bridgend CF33 6YW
t 01656 743406 **e** alan@bluesmatters.com **w** bluesmatters.com
MD: Alan Pearce.

Blunted Vinyl (see Island Records Group)

BMR Entertainment Ltd PO Box 14535, London
N17 0WG **t** 020 8376 1650 **f** 020 8376 8622
e JefQ1@aol.com A&R Mgr: Jef Q.

Bolshi Records Studio 11, 25 Denmark St, London
WC2H 8NJ **t** 020 7240 2248 **f** 0870 420 4392
e sarah@bolshi.com **w** bolshi.com MD: Sarah Bolshi.

Bonaire Recordings (see Blue Melon Records Ltd)

Booo! (see Direct Heat Records)

Border Community (see 3 Beat Label Management)

Border Community Recordings PO Box 38846, London
W12 8YT **t** 020 8746 0407 **f** 020 8746 0407
e info@bordercommunity.com **w** bordercommunity.com
A&R: James Holden.

Born to Dance Records PO Box 50, Brighton BN2 6YP
t 01273 301555 **f** 01273 305266 **e** info@borntodance.com
w borntodance.com Lbl Mgr: Natasha Brown.

Boss Records (see 3 Beat Label Management)

Boss Sounds (see Cherry Red Records)

Botchit & Scarper/eMotif Recordings 134-146
Curtain Rd, London EC2A 3AR **t** 020 7729 8030
f 020 7729 8121 **e** info@botchit.com **w** botchit.com
Dir: Martin Love.

Boulevard (see Silverword Music Group)

Bowmans Capsule PO Box 30466, London NW6 1GJ
t 020 7431 3129 **f** 020 7431 3129
e sugar@bowmanscapsule.co.uk **w** bowmanscapsule.co.uk
Dir: Richard Burdett.

Box Out Records PO Box 697, Wembley HA9 8WQ
t 020 8904 6670 or 07956 583 221 **f** 020 8681 1007
e info@boxoutrecords.com **w** boxoutrecords.com
CEO: Harold Anthony.

Brainlove Records 8b Cecilia Rd, London E8 2EP
t 07939 583 089 **e** info@brainloverecords.com
w brainloverecords.com Dir: John Brainlove.

Breakin' Loose 32 Quadrant House, Burrell St, London
SE1 0UW **t** 020 7633 9576 or 07721 065 618
e sjbbreakinloose@aol.com MD: Steve Bingham.

Breathless Records Alexandra House, 6 Little Portland St,
London W1W 7JE **t** 020 7907 1733 **f** 020 7907 1734
e email@breathlessrecords.com **w** breathlessrecords.com
Label Manager: Louis Mears.

Brewhouse Music Breeds Farm, 57 High St, Wicken, Ely,
Cambs CB7 5XR **t** 01353 720309 **f** 01353 723364
e info@brewhousemusic.co.uk **w** brewhousemusic.co.uk
MD: Eric Cowell.

Brickyard (see Loose Records)

Bright Star Recordings Suite 5, Emerson House, 14b
Ballynahinch Rd, Carryduff, Belfast BT8 8DN **t** 028 90 817111
f 028 90 817444 **e** brightstarrec@musicni.co.uk
w brightstarrecordings.com MD: Johnny Davis.

BRIGHTSIDE RECORDINGS

BRIGHTSIDE ®
RECORDINGS

Bedford House, 69-79 Fulham High St, London SW6 3JW
t 020 7384 7500 **f** 020 7371 9298
e firstname.lastname@sonybmg.com MD: Hugh Goldsmith. GM:
Justine Bell. Snr A&R Manager: James Roberts.

Brille Records Ltd. North Studio, Ground Floor, Walker
House, Boundary St, London E2 7JE **t** 020 7324 7260 or
020 7324 7268 **f** 020 7324 7261 **e** info@brillerecords.com
w brillerecords.com Marketing Assistant: Victoria Hunt.

Bristol Archive (see Sugar Shack Records Ltd)

British Steel (see Cherry Red Records)

Broadley Records Broadley House, 48 Broadley Terrace,
London NW1 6LG **t** 020 7258 0324 **f** 020 7724 2361
e admin@broadleystudios.com **w** broadleystudios.com
MD: Ellis Elias.

Brodsky Records (see Sanctuary Classics)

Bronze Records Unit 1, 73 Maygrove Rd, London NW6 2EG
t 020 7209 4666 **f** 020 7209 2334 **e** info@bronzerecords.com
w bronzerecords.com GM: Chris Knowles.

Bronze Records Ltd 17 Priory Rd, London NW6 4NN
t 020 7209 2766 **f** 020 7813 2766
e gerrybron@bronzerecords.co.uk **w** bronzerecords.co.uk
MD: Gerry Bron.

Brownswood Recordings Unit 212, The Saga Centre, 326
Kensal Rd, London W10 5BZ **t** 020 8968 0111
f 020 8968 0110 **e** info@brownswoodrecordings.com
w brownswoodrecordings.com
MDs: Simon Goffe & Gilles Peterson.

BTM (see Gotham Records)

Bubblin' (see Gut Recordings)

Bugged Out! Recordings 15 Holywell Row, London
EC2A 4JB **t** 020 7684 5228 **f** 020 7684 5230
e paul@buggedout.net **w** buggedout.net
Dirs: Paul Benney, John Burgess.

Bulletproof (see Mohawk Records)

Burning Ice Records PO Box 48, Dorking, Surrey RH4 1YE
t 01306 877692 **e** info@objayda.co.uk **w** objayda.co.uk
Dir: Tim Howe.

Burning Shed c/o Windsor House, 74 Thorpe Rd, Norwich,
Norfolk NR1 1QH **t** 01603 767726 **f** 01603 767746
e info@burningshed.com **w** burningshed.com
Prod'n: Pete Morgan.

Bushranger Records Station Lodge, 196 Rayleigh Rd,
Hutton, Brentwood, Essex CM13 1PN **t** 01277 222095
e bushrangermusic@aol.com Lbl Mgr: Kathy Lister.

But! Records Walsingham Cottage, 7 Sussex Sq, Brighton, E.
Sussex BN2 1FJ **t** 01273 680799 **e** allan.james1@virgin.net
w butgroup.com MD: Allan James.

Buttercuts Limited 5 Hasker St, London SW3 2LE
t 020 7225 2780 or 07957 420 492 **f** 020 7589 2278
e management@buttercuts.co.uk **w** Buttercuts.co.uk
MD: Andrew Oury.

Butterfly Recordings (see Dragonfly Records)

Buyhear.Com 240 High Rd, Harrow Weald, Middlesex
HA3 7BB **t** 020 8863 2520 **f** 020 8863 2520
e steve@buyhear.com **w** buyhear.com Dir: Steven Robert Glen.

Buzz Records 32 Priory Pl, Perth, Perthshire PH2 0DT
t 01738 638140 **f** 01738 638140 **e** info@thebuzzgroup.co.uk
w thebuzzgroup.co.uk MD: Dave Arcari.

Buzz To It Records PO Box 33849, London N8 9XJ
t 07092 047 780 **e** info@buzztoitrecords.co.uk
MD: Michael Bukowski.

Buzzin' Fly Records 31 Camden Lock Pl, London NW1 8AL
t 020 7284 9940 **f** 020 7284 9941 **e** info@buzzinfly.com
w buzzinfly.com Label Manager: Marianne Frederick.

BXR UK (see Media Records Ltd)

Cacophonous (see Visible Noise)

Cadence Recordings (see Within Records)

Cafe de Soul 2nd Floor, 62 Belgrave Gate, Leicester LE1 3GQ
t 0116 299 0700 **f** 0116 299 0077 **e** cafedesoul@hotmail.com
w cafedesoul.co.uk Label Managers: Nigel Bird, Vijay Mistry.

Cala Records 17 Shakespeare Gardens, London N2 9LJ
t 020 8883 7306 **f** 020 8365 3388 **e** jeremy@calarecords.com
w calarecords.com
Sales & Marketing Manager: Jeremy Swerling.

Calig (see Priory Records)

Calliope-Muse-Ic Ltd The Fold, Waggon Lane, Upton, W
Yorks WF9 1JS **t** 0845 056 0238 **f** 01977 651391
e info@calliope-muse-ic.com **w** calliope-muse-ic.com
MD: Andrea Meadows.

Camino Records Crown Studios, 16-18 Crown Rd,
Twickenham, Middx TW1 3EE **t** 020 8891 4233
f 020 8891 2339 **e** mail@camino.co.uk **w** camino.co.uk
Marketing Manager: John Wood.

Candid Productions 16 Castelnau, London SW13 9RU
t 020 8741 3608 **f** 020 8563 0013 **e** info@candidrecords.com
w candidrecords.com MD: Alan Bates.

Candlelight Records (see Abstract Sounds)

Candy Records (see PlayLouder Recordings)

Canned Fruit 78 Alcester Rd, Moseley, Birmingham, W
Midlands B13 8BB **t** 0121 256 1304 **f** 0121 256 1302
e john@music.mercia.org Contact: John Hemming.

Cantankerous (see Quiet Riot Records)

Capitol (see EMI Music UK & Ireland)

Caprio (see Silverword Music Group)

Captain Oi! PO Box 501, High Wycombe, Bucks HP10 8QA
t 01494 813031 **f** 01494 816712 **e** oi@captainoi.com
w captainoi.com MD: Mark Brennan.

Captured Music (see Above The Sky Records / Lunastate
Ltd)

Caragan Music Agency 5 The Meadows, Worlington,
Suffolk IP28 8SH **t** 01638 717 390 **e** daren@caragan.com
w caragan.com Head of A&R: Daren Walder.

Cargo Records 17 Heathmans Rd, London SW6 4TJ
t 020 7731 5125 **f** 020 7731 3866 **e** phil@cargorecords.co.uk
MD: Philip Hill.

Carioca (see 3 Beat Label Management)

Caritas Records Achmore, Moss Rd, Ullapool IV26 2TF
t 01854 612 938 **f** 01854 612 938
e caritas-records@caritas-music.co.uk **w** caritas-music.co.uk
Professional Mgr: Katharine H Douglas.

Carlton Video The Waterfront, Elstree Rd, Elstree, Herts
WD6 3BS **t** 020 8207 6207 **f** 020 8207 5789
e gerry.donohoe@carltonvideo.co.uk **w** carltonvideo.co.uk
MD: Gerry Donohoe.

Casa Nostra (see Wyze Recordings)

Casual Records Arch 462, 83 Rivington St, London
EC2A 3AY **t** 020 7613 7746 **f** 020 7613 7740
e info@casuallondon.com **w** casual-london.com
Label Manager: Kim St.Martin.

Catch Records (see One Step Music Ltd)

Catskills Records PO Box 3365, Brighton BN1 1WQ **t** 01273 626245 **f** 01273 626246 **e** info@catskillsrecords.com **w** catskillsrecords.com Dirs: Khalid, Amr or Jonny.

Catskills:Projects (see Catskills Records)

Cavalcade Records Ltd 18 Pindock Mews, London W9 2PY **t** 020 7289 7281 **f** 020 7289 2648 **e** songs@mindermusic.com **w** mindermusic.com MD: John Fogarty.

The CD Card Company 29-39 Stirling House, London W3 8DJ **t** 020 8993 5966 **f** 020 8992 0340 or 020 8992 0098 **e** cdcard@arab.co.uk **w** cdcard.com Sales Mgr: Greg Warrington.

Cello Classics (see Naxos AudioBooks)

Celtic Collections Ltd 30-32 Sir John Rogersons Quay, Dublin 2, Ireland **t** +353 1 679 0667 **f** +353 1 679 0668 **e** info@celtic-collections.com **w** celtic-collections.com MD: Sharon Browne.

Celtic Heritage Series (see Ainm Music)

Cent Records Melbourne House, Chamberlain St, Wells BA5 2PJ **t** 01749 689 074 **f** 01749 670 315 **e** iain@centrecords.com **w** centrecords.com MD: Kevin Newton.

Centaur Discs 40-42 Brantwood Ave, Dundee DD3 6EW **t** 01382 776595 **f** 01382 736702 **e** info@cd-services.com **w** cd-services.com MD: Dave Shoesmith.

Century Media Records 6 Water Lane, Camden, London NW1 8NZ **t** 020 7482 0161 **f** 020 7482 3165 **e** andy@centurymedia.net **w** centurymedia.net Label Mgr: Andy Turner.

Certificate18 Records Battersea Business Centre, Unit 36, 99-109 Lavender Hill, London SW11 5QL **t** 020 7924 1333 **f** 020 7924 1833 **e** info@certificate18.com **w** certificate18.com MD: Paul Arnold.

Champion Records Ltd 181 High St, Harlesden, London NW10 4TE **t** 020 8961 5202 **f** 020 8961 6665 **e** mel@championrecords.co.uk **w** championrecords.co.uk Owner: Mel Medalie.

Chandos Records Chandos House, 1 Commerce Pk, Commerce Way, Colchester, Essex CO2 8HX **t** 01206 225200 **f** 01206 225201 **e** enquiries@chandos.net **w** chandos.net Mktg: Becky Lees.

Change of Weather Records Ltd 29 Gladwell Rd, London N8 9AA **t** 020 8245 2136 or 07974 070 880 **e** pcarmichael@changeofweather.com **w** changeofweather.com MD: Paul Carmichael.

Channel 4 Recordings 124 Horseferry Rd, London SW1P 2TX **t** 020 7396 4444 **f** 020 7306 8044 **e** c4recordings@channel4.co.uk **w** channel4.com Music Manager: Liz Edmunds.

Charlie (see Snapper Music)

Charly Acquisitions Ltd. The Old Station, The Avenue, Sark, via Guernsey, Channel Islands GY9 0SB **t** 01481 832794 **f** 01481 832795 **e** firstname.lastname@Charly-acquisitions.com International Affairs: Jan Friedmann.

Chateau (see Silverword Music Group)

Cheeky (see Sony BMG Music Entertainment UK & Ireland)

Chemikal Underground Records PO Box 3609, Glasgow G42 9TP **t** 0141 550 1919 **f** 0141 550 1918 **e** stewart@chemikal.co.uk **w** chemikal.co.uk Dir: Stewart Henderson.

Cherry Red Records 3a Long Island House, Warple Way, London W3 0RG **t** 020 8740 4110 **f** 020 8740 4208 **e** infonet@cherryred.co.uk **w** cherryred.co.uk Chairman: Iain McNay.

Chewin' Gum Records PO Box 13301, Tividale, Oldbury, W Midlands B69 9BA **t** 07957 692 398 **e** kev@chewin-gumrecords.co.uk **w** chewin-gumrecords.co.uk Label Manager: Kev Bennison.

Chillifunk Records 2 Park Cottages, The Oaks, Ruislip, Middx HA4 7LF **t** 01895 639195 **f** 01895 639239 **e** mm@chillifunk.com **w** chillifunk.com MD: Lofty.

Choice (see Millennium Records Ltd)

Chrysalis (see EMI Music UK & Ireland)

Chunk Records 139 Whitfield St, London W1T 5EN **t** 020 7380 1000 **e** info@chunkrecords.com **w** chunkrecords.com Label Mgr: Neil Stainton.

Circulation Recordings 7C Lingfield Point, McMullen Rd, Darlington, Co Durham DL1 1RW **t** 01325 255 252 or 07917 690 223 **f** 01325 255 252 **e** Graeme.circ@ntlworld.com **w** virtual-venue.net MD: Graeme Robinson.

City Rockers First Floor Rear, 3 Plough Yard, London EC2A 3LP **t** 020 7377 1210 **f** 020 7655 4984 **e** info@city-rockers.com **w** city-rockers.com MD: Phil Howells, Charlie Lexton.

City Rollaz Inc 78 Alcester Rd, Moseley, Birmingham, W Midlands B13 8BB **t** 0121 256 1311 **f** 0121 256 1318 **e** del@music.mercia.org **w** cityrollazinc.co.uk Label Manager: Del Edwards.

City Slang (see V2)

Ciwdod Unit 8, 24 Norbury Rd, Fairwater, Cardiff CF5 3AU **t** 029 2083 8060 **f** 029 2056 6573 **e** prosiectcymraeg@communitymusicwales.org.uk Co-ordinator: Esyllt Williams.

Clarinet Classics (see Naxos AudioBooks)

Classic Pictures Shepperton Int'l Film Studios, Studios Rd, Shepperton, Middx TW17 0QD **t** 01932 592016 **f** 01932 592046 **e** Jo.garofalo@classicpictures.co.uk **w** classicpictures.co.uk Sales & Marketing Dir: Jo Garofalo.

Claudio Records Ltd Studio 17, The Promenade, Peacehaven, E. Sussex BN10 8PU **t** 01273 580 250 **f** 01273 583 530 **e** Info@ClaudioRecords.com **w** ClaudioRecords.com MD: Colin Attwell.

Clay Records (see Sanctuary Records Group)

Clean Up (see One Little Indian Records)

Clear Vision 36 Queensway, Ponders End, Enfield, Middlesex EN3 4SA **t** 020 8805 1354 **f** 020 8805 9987 **e** info@clearvision.co.uk **w** silvervision.co.uk Contact: Ian Allan.

Cleveland City Records 52A Clifton St, Chapel Ash, Wolverhampton, W Midlands WV3 0QT **t** 01902 838 500 **f** 01902 839 500 **e** info@clevelandcity.co.uk **w** clevelandcity.co.uk Contact: Mike Evans, Lee Glover.

Climax Recordings Summit Studio, 3 Osborne Ave, Jesmond, Newcastle-upon-Tyne NE2 1JQ **t** 0191 212 0854 **f** 0191 281 5789 **e** james_climax@hotmail.com **w** climaxrecordings.co.uk Label Manager: James Wilson.

Clovelly Recordings Ltd 1 The Old Cannery, Hengist Rd, Deal, Kent CT14 6WY **t** 01304 239356 **f** 01304 239356 **e** clovellyrecordings@hotmail.com **w** clovellyrecordings.com MD: John Perkins.

Clown Records P.O Box 20432, London SE17 3WT **t** 07986 359 568 **e** office@clownrecords.co.uk **w** clownrecords.co.uk A&R: Stephen Adams.

Club AC30 Records 19 Daisy Rd, South Woodford, London E18 1EA **t** 020 85308381 **e** nick@clubac30.com **w** clubac30.com Label Manager: Nick Allport.

Clubscene PO Box 26723, Glasgow G1 4YY **t** 0870 922 0941 or 07785 222 205 **f** 0141 552 1184 **e** mail@clubscene.co.uk **w** clubscene.co.uk Contact: Bill Grainger.

CMP (see Silva Screen Records)

COE Records (see Sanctuary Classics)

Collecting Records LLP 21A Clifftown Rd, Southend-On-Sea, Essex SS1 1AB **t** 01702 330005 **f** 01702 333309 **e** bcollent@aol.com **w** barrycollings.co.uk MD: Barry Collings.

Collective Music Ltd 5 Henchley Dene, Guildford, Surrey GU4 7BH **t** 01483 431 803 **f** 01483 431 803 **e** info@collective.mu **w** collective.mu MD: Phil Hardy.

Collegium Records PO Box 172, Whittlesford, Cambridge CB2 4QZ **t** 01223 832474 **f** 01223 836723 **e** info@collegium.co.uk **w** collegium.co.uk Sales & Marketing: Michael Stevens.

COLUMBIA RECORDS LABEL GROUP

Bedford House, 69 - 79 Fulham High Street, London SW6 3JW **t** 020 7384 7500 **f** 020 7371 9298 **e** firstname.lastname@sonybmg.com **w** columbia.co.uk MD: Mike Smith. VP A&R: Mike Pickering. VP A&R Development: Mark Pinder. VP Marketing: Richard Connell. VP Legal & Business Affairs: Simon Jenkins. Director TV: Deirdre Moran. Director Radio: Joanne Kennet. Head Of Press: Jakub Blackman. Head Of Digital Marketing: Dan Ayers. Sales: Arvato.

Comet Records 5 Cope St, Temple Bar, Dublin 2, Ireland **t** +353 87 2441 874 **f** +353 1 2891 074 **e** comet@indigo.ie **w** cometrecords.eu MD: Brian O'Kelly.

Commercial Recordings 12 Lisnagleer Rd, Dungannon, Co Tyrone BT70 3LN **t** 028 8776 1995 **f** 028 8776 1995 **e** info@commercialrecordings.com **w** commercialrecordings.com MD: Raymond Stewart.

Communiqque' Records Ltd Longfield House, Bury Ave, Ruislip, Middx HA4 7RT **t** 01895 477522 **f** 01895 477522 **e** tomdoherty@supanet.com **w** communiquerecords.com Dir: Tom Doherty.

Complete Control Music Unit 8, 24 Norbury Rd, Cardiff CF5 3AU **t** 029 2083 8060 **f** 029 2056 6573 **e** touring@communitymusicwales.org.uk **w** completecontrolmusic.com Label Manager: Simon Dancey.

Completist (see Siren Music Ltd)

Composure Records 20 Churchward Drive, Frome, Somerset BA11 2XL **t** 07816 285809 **e** composurerecords@btinternet.com **w** composurerecords.co.uk MD: Paul Davies.

Concept Music Shepherds Building, Charecroft Way, London W14 0EE **t** 020 7751 1755 or 020 7751 1744 **f** 020 7751 1566 **e** info@conceptmusic.com **w** conceptmusic.com MD: Max Bloom.

Concrete Plastic Records PO Box 5019, Brighton BN50 9JW **t** 01273 572 235 or 07949 266 495 **e** info@concreteplastic.co.uk **w** concreteplastic.co.uk Label Manager: Steve Hyland.

Concrete Recordings Ltd 35 Beech Rd, Chorlton, Manchester M21 8BX **t** 0161 881 2332 **f** 0161 860 7283 **e** ms@concreterecordings.co.uk **w** concreterecordings.co.uk Dir: Sarah Purcell.

Congo Music Ltd 17A Craven Park Rd, Harlsden, London NW10 8SE **t** 020 8961 5461 **f** 020 8961 5461 **e** byron@congomusic.freeserve.co.uk **w** congomusic.com A&R Director: Root Jackson.

Constellation (see Southern Records)

Contra Music 13 Cotswold Mews, 30 Battersea Sq, London SW11 3RA **t** 020 7978 7888 **f** 020 7978 7808 **e** auto@automan.co.uk **w** genenet.co.uk MD: Jerry Smith.

Cookin' (see Good Looking Records)

Cooking Vinyl 10 Allied Way, London W3 0RQ **t** 020 8600 9200 **f** 020 8743 7448 **e** info@cookingvinyl.com **w** cookingvinyl.com MD: Martin Goldschmidt.

Copasetik Recordings Ltd 9 Spedan Close, London NW3 7XF **t** 07855 551 024 **e** copasetik1@aol.com **w** copasetik.com MD/Head of A&R: Jon Sexton.

Corban Recordings PO Box 2, Glasgow G44 3LB **t** 0141 637 5277 **f** 0141 637 5277 **e** alastair@corbanrecordings.com **w** corbanrecordings.co.uk Contact: Alastair McDonald.

Cowboy Records (see Amazon Records Ltd)

Cowgirl Records 27 Old Gloucester St, London WC1N 3XX **t** 07973 221 690 or 07949 839 852 **e** info@cowgirlrecords.com **w** cowgirlrecords.com Dirs: Peter Gold, Laurence Jones.

Cr2 Records PO Box 718, Richmond, Surrey TW9 4XR **t** 020 8288 7438 **f** 020 8332 1171 **e** info@cr2records.co.uk **w** cr2records.co.uk MD: Mark Brown.

Cramer (see Priory Records)

Crapola Records PO Box 808, Hook, Hants RG29 1TA
t 01256 862865 **f** 01256 862182 **e** feedback@crapola.com
w crapolarecords.com Head of A&R: Martin Curtis.

Craze Productions 14 Tottenham Ct Rd. 119, London
W1T 1JY **t** 020 7993 8548 or 07711 253 726
e Doctorofdance@gmail.com **w** crazedigital.com
Dir: Sam Kleinman.

Creamy Groove Machine Recordings (see Copasetik
Recordings Ltd)

Creative World The Croft, Deanslade Farm, Claypit Lane,
Lichfield WS14 0AG **t** 01543 253576 or 07885 341745
f 01543 253576 **e** info@creative-world-entertainment.co.uk
w creative-world-entertainment.co.uk MD: Mervyn Spence.

Creature Music (see East Central One Ltd)

Creole (see Sanctuary Records Group)

Crimson Productions Holden House, 57 Rathbone Pl,
London W1T 1JU **t** 020 7396 8899 **f** 020 7470 6655
e info@demonmusicgroup.co.uk **w** vci.co.uk
GM: Colin Auchterlonie.

Critical Mass (see Heat Recordings)

Crocodile Records 431 Linen Hall, 162-168 Regent St,
London W1B 5TE **t** 020 7580 0080 **f** 020 7637 0097
e music@crocodilemusic.com **w** crocodilemusic.com
Contact: Malcolm Ironton, Ray Tattle.

Crossover Urban (see Heavenly Dance)

CSA Word (Audio Books) 6a Archway Mews, 241a
Putney Bridge Rd, London SW15 2PE **t** 020 8871 0220
f 020 8877 0712 **e** info@csaword.co.uk **w** csaword.co.uk
Audio Manager: Victoria Williams.

THE LABEL THAT BROUGHT YOU:

TOM MCRAE
ELECTRIC SOFT PARADE

db records
PO Box 19318
Bath BA1 6ZS

db records

T. 01225 782322
W. www.dbrecords.co.uk
E. info@dbrecords.co.uk

Cube Soundtracks Onward House, 11 Uxbridge St, London
W8 7TQ **t** 020 7221 4275 **f** 020 7229 6893
e cube@bucksmusicgroup.co.uk **w** cubesoundtracks.co.uk
Label Manager: Ronen Guha.

Culburnie (see Greentrax Recordings Ltd)

Cultural Foundation Hollin Bush, Dalehead, Rosedale, N
Yorks YO18 8RL **t** 0845 458 4699 or 01751 417 147
f 01751 417 804 **e** info@cultfound.org **w** cultfound.org
MD: Peter Bell.

Curb Records Ltd 45 Great Guildford St, London SE1 0ES
t 020 7401 8877 **f** 020 7928 8590 **e** firstname@curb-uk.com
w curb.com MD: Phil Cokell.

Cursery Rhymes (see Klone UK)

Cycle Records 50 Stroud Green Rd, London N4 3ES
t 01923 444440 **f** 01923 444440 **e** info@cyclerecords.co.uk
w cyclerecords.co.uk MD: Buzz Aldrin.

Cyclops Records 33A Tolworth Park Rd, Tolworth, Surrey
KT6 7RL **t** 020 8339 9965 **f** 020 8399 0070
e postmaster@gft-cyclops.co.uk **w** gft-cyclops.co.uk
MD: Malcolm Parker.

D-Mak Records 2A Downing St, Ashton-under-Lyne, Lancs
OL7 9LR **t** 0161 292 9493 **f** 0161 344 1673
e d.murphy@easynet.co.uk **w** pincermetal.com MD: Dale Murphy.

d Records 35 Brompton Rd, London SW3 1DE
t 020 7368 6311 **f** 020 7823 9553 **e** d@35bromptonroad.com
w drecords.co.uk MD: Douglas Mew.

Da Doo Ron Ron Records 5 Mayfield Court, Victoria Rd,
Freshfield, Liverpool, Merseyside L37 7JL **t** 01704 834105
f 01704 834105 **e** ronellis50@hotmail.com **w** ronellis.co.uk
MD: Ron Ellis.

The Daisy Label Unit 2 Carriglea, Naas Rd, Dublin 12, Ireland
t +353 1 429 8600 **f** +353 1 429 8602
e daithi@daisydiscs.com **w** daisydiscs.com MD: John Dunford.

Dance Paradise UK 207 Muirfield Rd, Watford, Herts
WD19 6HZ **t** 020 8421 3817 **f** 020 8387 4299
e info@dance-paradise.co.uk **w** dance-paradise.com
MD: Andrei Riazanski.

Dangerous Records Sandwell Manor, Totnes, Devon
TQ9 7LL **t** 01803 867 850 or 07738 543 746
f 01803 867 850 **e** info@dangerousrecords.co.uk
w dangerousrecords.co.uk Label Manager: Liam Smith.

The Daniel Azure Music Group 72 New Bond St,
London W1S 1RR **t** 07894 702 007 **f** 020 8240 8787
e info@jvpr.net **w** danielazure.com CEO: Daniel Azure.

Dara (see Dolphin Music)

Dark Beat (see Smexi Playaz Records)

Data 103 Gaunt St, London SE1 6DP **t** 020 7740 8600
f 020 7403 5348 **e** initial+lastname@ministryofsound.com
w datarecords.co.uk A&R Dir: Ben Cooke.

Datum (see Priory Records)

Day Release Records (see Fire Records)

db records PO Box 19318, Bath, Somerset BA1 6ZS
t 01225 782 322 **e** demo@dbrecords.co.uk **w** dbrecords.co.uk
A&R: David Bates.

De Angelis Records Power Road Studios, 114 Power Rd,
London W4 5PY **t** 020 8994 4600 **f** 020 8994 4446
e voices@de-angelisrecords.com **w** de-angelisrecords.com
Product Manager: Martine McLean.

de Wolfe Music Shropshire House, 11-20 Capper St, London
WC1E 6JA **t** 020 7631 3600 **f** 020 7631 3700
e info@dewolfemusic.co.uk **w** dewolfemusic.co.uk
MD: Warren De Wolfe.

Dead Earnest PO Box 10170, Dundee, Tayside DD4 8WW
t 01382 776 595 or 07795 273 274
e deadearnest@btopenworld.com **w** deadearnest.btinternet.co.uk
Owner: Andy Garibaldi.

Dead Happy Records 3B Castledown Ave, Hastings, E
Sussex TN34 3RJ **t** 01424 434778 **e** Vibezone@excite.com
w deadhappyrecords.co.uk Dir: David Arnold.

Debonair Records & Tapes Ltd Eaton House, 39 Lower
Richmond Rd, Putney, London SW15 1ET **t** 020 8788 4557
f 020 8780 9711 **e** info@eatonmusic.com
w debonairrecords.co.uk MD: Terry Oates.

Decadent Records 6Q Atlas Business Centre, Oxgate Lane,
London NW2 7HU **t** 020 8452 2255 **f** 020 8452 4242
e info@decadentrecords.co.uk **w** decadentrecords.co.uk
Label Manager: Nick Bennett.

The Decca Music Group 8 St James's Sq, London
SW1Y 4JU **t** 020 7747 4000 **f** 020 7747 4599
e firstname.lastname@umusic.com **w** deccaclassics.com
Pres: Bogdan Rošcic.

Decca UK 364-366 Kensington High St, London W14 8NS
t 020 7471 5096 **e** firstname.lastname@umusic.com
w universalclassics.com GM: Dickon Stainer.

Deceptive Records PO Box 288, St Albans, Herts AL4 9YU
t 01727 834 130 MD: Tony Smith.

Decipher Recordings 101 Salisbury Rd, Farnborough,
Hants. GU14 7AE **t** 0771 289 9665 **f** 020 8995 1133
e decipher@decipher-recordings.com **w** decipher-recordings.com
MD: Brendan Byrne.

Deep (see 3 Beat Label Management)

Deep Focus (see 3 Beat Label Management)

Def Jam (see Mercury Music Group)

Defected Records Ltd 8 Charterhouse Buildings, Goswell
Rd, London EC1M 7AN **t** 020 7549 2970 **f** 020 7250 0449
e firstname@defected.com **w** defected.com MD: Hector Dewar.

Delicious Records 78 Church Path, London W4 5BJ
t 020 8994 3142 **f** 020 8994 3142
e delicious@elenaonline.com **w** deliciousrecords.co.uk
MD: Kris Gray.

Delta Music PLC 222 Cray Ave, Orpington, Kent BR5 3PZ
t 01689 888888 **f** 01689 888800 **e** info@deltamusic.co.uk
w deltamusic.co.uk MD: Laurie Adams.

DELTASONIC RECORDS

102 Rose Lane, Mossley Hill, Liverpool L18 8AG
t 0151 724 4760 **f** 0151 724 6286 **e** firstname@deltasonic.co.uk
w deltasonic.co.uk Label Manager: Sean Atkins. MD: Alan Wills.
Dir: Ann Heston. Creative Director/A&R: Joe Fearon. Financial
Manager: Karin Struyk. Label Co-ordinator: Nikki Harris. A&R
Assistant: Marc Jones.

Demi Monde Records Llanfair Caereinion, Powys, Wales
SY21 0DS **t** 01938 810 758 **f** 01938 810 758
e demimonde@dial.pipex.com **w** demimonde.co.uk
MD: Dave Anderson.

DEMON MUSIC GROUP

33 Foley Street, London W1W 7TL **t** 020 7612 3300
f 020 7612 3301 **e** firstname.lastname@demonmusicgroup.co.uk
w demonmusicgroup.co.uk MD: Neela Ebbett. Commercial
Director: Adrian Sear. Sales & Marketing Director: Danny Keene.
Director of Catalogue and TV: Colin Auchterlonie.

Demon Records Ltd (see Demon Music Group)

DEP International 1 Andover St, Birmingham, W Midlands
B5 5RG **t** 0121 633 4742 **f** 0121 643 4904
e enquiries@ub40.co.uk **w** ub40.co.uk
Business Mgr: Lanval Storrod.

Department of Sound Building 348a, Westcott Venture
Pk, Westcott, Aylesbury, Bucks HP18 0XB **t** 01296 655 880
e enquiries@departmentofsound.com **w** departmentofsound.com
MD: Adrienne Aiken.

Desoto (see Southern Records)

Destined Records (see Back Yard Recordings)

Destiny Music Iron Bridge House, 3 Bridge Approach,
London NW1 8BD **t** 020 7734 3251 **f** 020 7439 2391
e nick@destinymusic.co.uk **w** carlinmusic.co.uk MD: Nick Farries.

Detour Records Ltd PO Box 18, Midhurst, W Sussex
GU29 9YU **t** 01730 815422 **f** 01730 815422
e detour@btinternet.com **w** detour-records.co.uk
Dirs: David Holmes & Tania Holmes.

Deutsche Grammophon (see Universal Music Classics &
Jazz (UK))

Deviant 12 Southam St, London W10 5PH **t** 020 8969 0666
f 020 8968 6128 **e** whoever@deviant.co.uk
w deviantrecords.com MD: Rob Deacon.

Devolution Recordings Ltd 25 Pinehurst Court, Colville Gardens, London W11 2BH **t** 020 7229 5021 **f** 020 7229 5021 **e** info@devolution.freeserve.co.uk **w** devolutionrecordings.com MD: Geremy O'Mahony.

Dew Process Records Unit 70, 3-6 Banister Rd, London W10 4AR **t** 07896 163 003 **e** megan@dew-process.com **w** dew-process.com Publicity and Promotions Manager: Megan Reeder.

Diamond Life Entertainment Ltd 6 Cheyne Walk, Hornsea, East Yorks HU18 1BX **t** 01964 536193 **e** info@diamondlifeentertainment.com **w** diamondlifeentertainment.com MD: Paul Cook.

Different Drummer Ltd PO Box 2571, Birmingham B30 1BZ **t** 0121 603 0033 **e** info@differentdrummer.co.uk **w** differentdrummer.co.uk MD: Richard Whittingham.

Digimix Records Sovereign House, 12 Trewartha Rd, Praa Sands, Penzance, Cornwall TR20 9ST **t** 01736 762 826 **f** 01736 763 328 **e** info@digimixrecords.com **w** digimixrecords.com CEO: Roderick Jones.

Digital Plastic Ltd 22 Rutland Gardens, Hove, E Sussex BN3 5PB **t** 01273 779 793 **f** 01273 779 820 **e** enzo@plastic-music.co.uk **w** plastic-music.co.uk MD: Enzo (Vincent Amico).

Direct Heat Records PO Box 1345, Worthing, W Sussex BN14 7FB **t** 01903 202426 **f** 01903 202426 **e** dhr@happyvibes.co.uk **w** happyvibes.co.uk MD: Mike Pailthorpe.

Dis-funktional Recordings (see Nocturnal Recordings)

Dischord (see Southern Records)

Discipline (see Vinyl Japan)

Discover (see Supreme Music)

Discovery Records PO Box 10896, Birmingham B13 0ZU **t** 0121 247 6981 or 07976 215 719 **f** 0121 247 6981 **e** rod@fruitionmusic.co.uk MD: Rod Thomson.

Discovery Records Ltd Nursteed Rd, Devizes, Wilts SN10 3DY **t** 01380 728000 **f** 01380 722244 **e** info@discovery-records.com **w** discovery-records.com MD: Mike Cox.

Disky Communications Ltd Connaught House, 112-120 High Rd, Loughton, Essex IG10 4HJ **t** 020 8508 3723 **f** 020 8508 0432 **e** disky.uk@disky.nl MD: Alan Byron.

Disorient Recordings (see Mr Bongo)

Distinct'ive Breaks (see Distinct'ive Records)

Distinct'ive Records 35 Drury Lane, Covent Garden, London WC2B 5RH **t** 020 7240 1399 **f** 020 7240 1261 **e** richard@distinctiverecords.com **w** distinctiverecords.com Head of A&R: Richard Ford.

Divine Art Record Company 8 The Beeches, East Harlsey, Northallerton, North Yorks DL6 2DJ **t** 01609 882062 or 07811 479151 **e** info@divine-art.com **w** divine-art.com MD: Stephen Sutton.

DK House Records (see 3 Beat Label Management)

DK Records (see 3 Beat Label Management)

DMC Ltd PO Box 89, Slough, Berks SL1 8NA **t** 01628 667124 **f** 01628 605246 **e** info@dmcworld.com **w** dmcworld.com Label Manager: Nick Derby.

DMI Arch 25, Kings Cross Freight Depot, York Way, London N1 0EZ **t** 020 7713 8130 **f** 020 7713 8247 **e** info@dmirecords.com **w** dmirecords.com Dirs: Massimo Bonaddio/Dan Carey.

DND Produtions Reverb House, Bennett St, London W4 2AH **t** 020 8747 0660 ext224 **f** 020 8747 0880 **e** andy.rutherford@reverbxl.com Label Manager: Andy Rutherford.

Dolphin Music Unit 4, 3-4 Great Ship St, Dublin 8, Ireland **t** +353 1 478 3455 **f** +353 1 478 2143 **e** irishmus@iol.ie **w** irelandcd.com Export Manager: Paul Heffernan.

Dolphine Records (see 3 Beat Label Management)

Dome Records Ltd PO Box 3274, East Preston, W Sussex BN16 9BD **t** 01903 771 027 **f** 01903 779 565 **e** info@domerecords.co.uk **w** domerecords.co.uk MD: Peter Robinson.

Domino Recording Company PO Box 47029, London SW18 1WD **t** 020 8875 1390 **f** 020 8875 1391 **e** info@dominorecordco.com **w** dominorecordco.com A&R: Paul Sandell.

D.O.R. PO Box 1797, London E1 4TX **t** 020 7702 7842 **e** info@dor.co.uk **w** dor.co.uk Contact: Martin Parker.

Dorado Records 76 Brewer St, London W1F 9TX **t** 020 7287 1689 **f** 020 7287 1684 **e** ollie@dorado.net **w** dorado.net MD: Ollie Buckwell.

Dorian (see Priory Records)

Dorigen Music Unit 12, Lodge Bank Industrial Estate, Off Crown Lane, Horwich, Bolton BL6 5HY **t** 01204 675500 **f** 01204 479005 **e** simonb@uniquedist.co.uk **w** uniquedist.co.uk Label Mgr: Simon Blade.

Double Dragon Music 120-124 Curtain Rd, London EC2A 3SQ **t** 020 7739 6903 **f** 020 7613 2715 **e** tav@outthere.co.uk MD: Stephen Taverner.

Dovehouse Records Crabtree Cottage, Mill Lane, Kidmore End, Oxon RG4 9HB **t** 0118 972 4356 or 0118 972 4809 **w** doverecords@btconnect.com Pres: Thomas Pemberton.

Down By Law Records PO Box 20242, London NW1 7FL **t** 020 7485 1113 **e** info@proofsongs.co.uk.

Dragonfly Records 67-69 Chalton St, London NW1 1HY **t** 020 7554 2100 **f** 020 7554 2154 **e** info@dragonflyrecords.com **w** dragonflyrecords.com Label Mgr: Nick Jones.

Dramatico Entertainment Box 214, Farnham, Surrey GU10 5XZ **t** 01252 850421 **e** mail@dramatico.com **w** dramatico.com Contact: Pete or Roseanna.

Dream Catcher Records Goodsoal Farm, Burwash Common, E Sussex TN19 7LX **t** 01435 883197 **f** 01435 883833 **e** info@dreamcatcher-records.com **w** dreamcatcher-records.com MD: Gem Howard-Kemp.

DreamWorks (see Polydor Records)

Dreamy Records PO Box 30427, London NW6 3FF
t 079 6133 6121 **e** info@dreamyrecords.com
w dreamyrecords.com MD: Tracy Lee Jackson.

Drowned in Sound Recordings 1 Chilworth Mews,
London W2 3RG **t** 020 7087 8880 **f** 020 7087 8899
e info@disrecords.com **w** disrecords.com
Label Mgr: Sean Adams.

Dtox Records Ltd 33 Alexander Rd, Aylesbury, Bucks
HP20 2NR **t** 01296 434731 **f** 01296 422530 **e** fmluk@aol.com
w dtox.co.uk Label Manager: Joseph Stopps.

DTPM Recordings First floor, 40A Gt Eastern St, London
EC2A 3EP **t** 020 7749 1199 **f** 020 7749 1188
e guy@blue-cube.net **w** dtpmrecordings.net
Label Mgr: Guy Williams.

Dulcima Records 39 Tadorne Rd, Tadworth, Surrey
KT20 5TF **t** 01737 812922 **f** 01737 812922
e dulcima@ukgateway.net **w** dulcimarecords.com
Dir: Norma Camby.

Dune Records 1st Floor, 73 Canning Rd, Harrow, Middx
HA3 7SP **t** 020 8424 2807 **f** 020 8861 5371
e info@dune-music.com **w** dune-music.com MD: Janine Irons.

Duophonic UHF PO Box 3787, London SE22 9DZ
t 020 8299 1650 **f** 020 8693 5514
e duophonic@btopenworld.com **w** duophonic.com
Dir: Martin Pike.

Dusk Fire Records Market House, Market Sq, Winslow,
Bucks MK18 3AF **t** 01296 715 228 **f** 01296 715 486
e info@duskfire.co.uk **w** duskfire.co.uk MD: Peter Muir.

Duty Free Recordings Courtsyard Office, 68-69 Chalk
Farm Rd, London NW1 8AN **t** 020 7424 0774
f 020 7424 9094 **e** info@dutyfreerecordings.co.uk
w dutyfreerecordings.co.uk MD: Steffan Chandler.

Dynamic (see Priory Records)

EAGLE RECORDS

eagle records

Eagle House, 22 Armoury Way, London SW18 1EZ
t 020 8870 5670 **f** 020 8874 2333 **e** mail@eagle-rock.com
w eagle-rock.com Executive Chairman: Terry Shand. Chief
Operating Officer: Geoff Kempin. MD, Worldwide: Lindsay Brown.
Artist Liaison/Repertoire Manager: Andy McIntyre. Press &
Promotions: Darren Edwards.

Ealing Records Timperley House, 11 St.Albans Rd, Skircoat
Green, Halifax, W.Yorks HX3 0ND **t** 01422 367040
MD: Bill Byford.

Ear Candy Records 79-89 Pentonville Rd, London N1 9LG
t 020 7993 3316 or 3317 **e** info@transmissionmanagement.com
Contact: Adrian Bell, Will Williams.

Earache Records Ltd Suite 1-3 Westminster Building,
Theatre Sq, Nottingham NG1 6LG **t** 0115 950 6400
f 0115 950 8585 **e** mail@earache.com **w** earache.com
MD: Digby Pearson.

Earthworks (see Stern's Records)

East Central One Ltd Creeting House, All Saints Rd,
Creeting St Mary, Ipswich, Suffolk IP6 8PR **t** 01449 723 244
f 01449 726 067 **e** enquiries@eastcentralone.com
w eastcentralone.com Co-Dir: Steve Fernie.

East West (see Atlantic Records UK)

Eastern Bloc Underground 5 & 6 Central Buildings,
Oldham St, Manchester M1 1JT **t** 0161 228 6432
f 0161 228 6728 **e** info@easternblocrecords.co.uk
w easternblocrecords.co.uk MD: John Berry.

Eastside Records Ltd Top Floor, Outset Building, 2 Grange
Rd, London E17 8AH **t** 020 8509 6070 **f** 020 8509 6021
e info@eastside-records.co.uk **w** eastside-records.co.uk
Dir: Alexis Michaelides.

Easy Street Music 333 Millbrook Rd, Southampton, Hants
S015 0HW **t** 023 8078 0088 **f** 023 8078 0099
e info@easyst.co.uk **w** easyst.co.uk Dir: Jason Thomas.

Easyaccess (see Silver Planet Records)

Eat Sleep Records (see Full Time Hobby Records)

The Echo Label Ltd The Chrysalis Building, 13 Bramley Rd,
London W10 6SP **t** 020 7229 1616 **f** 020 7465 6296
e firstname.lastname@chrysalis.com **w** echo.co.uk
CEO, Chrysalis Music Div: Jeremy Lascelles.

Edel (see Blacklist Entertainment)

Edgy (see Metal Nation)

Edition (see Loose Records)

EG Records PO Box 606, London WC2E 7YT
t 020 8540 9935 A&R: Chris Kettle.

Electric Music People (see 3 Beat Label Management)

Electrix Records (see Tortured Records)

Electronic Alchemy Records Ltd PO Box 197, Bexhill on
Sea TN40 9BF **t** 01424 844 411 **f** 01424 844 466
e jenny@ea-records.com **w** ea-records.com
Head of A&R: Jenny Strickson.

Electronic Projects (see Certificate18 Records)

Elektra (see Atlantic Records UK)

Elemental (see One Little Indian Records)

Elusive (see Genius Records Ltd)

Emerald Music (Ireland) Ltd. 120A Coach Rd,
Templepatrick, Co Antrim BT39 0HB **t** 028 9443 2619
f 028 9446 2162 **e** info@emeraldmusic.co.uk
w emeraldmusiconline.com MD: George Doherty.

The Emergency Broadcast System PO Box 6131,
London W3 8ZR **t** 020 8993 8436 **f** 020 8896 1778
e star_rat@hawkwind.com **w** hawkwind.com/ Contact: Eve Carr.

EMI Catalogue/EMI Gold/EMI Liberty EMI House,
43 Brook Green, London W6 7EF **t** 020 7605 5000
f 020 7605 5050 **e** firstname.lastname@emimusic.com
w emimusic.co.uk

EMI CLASSICS INTERNATIONAL

27 Wrights Lane, London W8 5SW **t** 020 7795 7000
e firstname.lastname@emic.co.uk **w** emiclassics.com President,
EMI Classics: Costa Pilavachi. VP, A&R & Int'l Mktg: Theo Lap.
VP Finance & Business Affairs : John King. Snr Dir Int'l Mktg:
Polly Miller. Int'l Press and Promotions Dir: Sophie Jefferies.

EMI CLASSICS UK

43 Brook Green, London W6 7EF **t** 020 7605 5000
f 020 7605 5050 **e** firstname.lastname@emic.co.uk
w emiclassics.com MD, EMI Classics UK: Thomas Kaurich.
Marketing Manager: Lee Woolard. Head of Press & PR: Alexa
Pentecost.

EMI Gold (see EMI Catalogue/EMI Gold/EMI Liberty)

EMI Music Commercial Marketing and Catalogue
EMI House, 43 Brook Green, London W6 7EF **t** 020 7605 5000
f 020 7605 5050 **e** firstname.lastname@emimusic.com
w emimusic.co.uk.

EMI MUSIC IRELAND

EMI **Music Ireland**

EMI House, 1 Ailesbury Road, Dublin 4, Ireland
t +353 1 203 9900 **f** +353 1 269 6341
e firstname.lastname@emimusic.com **w** emimusic.co.uk. MD:
Willie Kavanagh. Sales & Mktg Dir: David Gogan. Head of
Promotions: Gillian Waters. Finance Dir: Harry Finney.

EMI MUSIC UK & IRELAND

EMI **Music UK and Ireland**

EMI House, 43 Brook Green, London W6 7EF **t** 020 7605 5000
f 020 7605 5050 **e** firstname.lastname@emimusic.com
w emimusic.co.uk. Chairman & CEO: Tony Wadsworth. President,
Capitol Music UK: Keith Wozencroft. SVP, EMI Music UK: Mark
Collen. Director, Angel Music Group: Mark Poston. MD, EMI
Records: Terry Felgate. MD, Parlophone: Miles Leonard. MD,
Virgin Records: Ferdy Unger-Hamilton. MD, EMI Music Ireland:
Willie Kavanagh. Co-MDs, EMI Comm. Mktg & Catalogue: Peter
Duckworth and Steve Pritchard. MD, Studios Group: David Holley.
Director Comms: Cathy Cremer. Director HR: Michelle Emmerson.
Director Business Affairs: Julian French. CFO: Justin Morris. SVP
Commercial & Digital Media: Mike McMahon. SVP International
Marketing: Mike Allen. Head of DVD & Audiovisual: Stefan
Demetriou.

EMI Music UK & Ireland DVD Dept. EMI House, 43
Brook Green, London W6 7EF **t** 020 7605 5332
f 020 7605 2526 **e** stefan.demetriou@emimusic.com
DVD & New Formats Mgr: Stefan Demetriou.

EMI RECORDS

EMI House, 43 Brook Green, London W6 7EF **t** 020 7605 5000
f 020 7605 5050 **e** firstname.lastname@emimusic.com
w emirecords.co.uk. MD: Terry Felgate. Head of A&R: Matt
Edwards. Mktg & Creative Director: John Leahy. Media Director:
Rebecca Coates. Business Affairs Director: James Mullan.

Emit Records U4C Studios, The Old Knows Factory, St
Anne's Hill Rd, Nottingham NG3 4GP **t** 0115 847 0899
e matthall@emitrecords.com **w** emitrecords.com
Label Manager: Matt Hall.

EM:T Records Unit 4C Studios, The Old Knows Factory, St
Anns Hill Rd, Nottingham NG3 4GP **t** 0115 847 0897
e matt@emitrecords.net **w** emitrecords.net Contact: Matt Hall.

Enable Music Ltd 54 Baldry Gardens, London SW16 3DJ
t 020 8144 0616 or 07775 737 281 **e** mike@enablemusic.co.uk
w enablemusic.co.uk MD: Mike Andrews.

English Garden (see Hi-Note Music)

Erato (see Warner Classics)

Erra Records Ltd 45 Kenwood Gardens, Gants Hill, Essex
IG2 6YQ **t** 07725 551 746 **e** Olu@strykemusic.com
w errarecords.com Dir: Benji Olufowobi.

Essence Records 10 Trevelyan Gardens, London NW10 3JY
t 020 8930 4760 **f** 020 8451 3380
e info@essencerecords.co.uk **w** essencerecords.co.uk
MD: Phil Cheeseman.

Estereo (see Skint Records)

Ether Music Broadway Studios, 28 Tooting High St, London
SW17 0RG **t** 020 8378 6956 **f** 020 8378 6959
e contact@etheruk.com **w** ethermusic.net Dir: Adrian Harley.

Ethereal Records 68 Seabrook Rd, Hythe, Kent CT21 5QA
t 01303 267509 **e** Robertmdrury@aol.com
w etherealrecords.com MD: Bob Drury.

Euphoric (see Almighty Records)

Eureka Music Ltd 4 Yeomans Keep, Rickmansworth Rd,
Chorleywood, Herts WD3 5RU **t** 01923 284171
e p.summerfield@virgin.net MD: Peter Summerfield.

Evangeline Recorded Works Ltd The Old School House,
Knowstone, South Molton, Devon EX36 4YW **t** 01398 341465
f 01398 341677 **e** evangelinemusic@aol.com **w** evangeline.co.uk
Label Manager: Sarah Lock.

Evasive Records Unit 18-19 Croydon House, 1 Peall Rd,
Croydon, Surrey CR0 3EX **t** 020 8287 8585 **f** 020 8287 0220
e info@evasive.co.uk **w** evasive.co.uk MD: Rob Pearson.

Eve (see Supreme Music)

Eve Nova (see Supreme Music)

Eventide Music PO Box 27, Baldock, Herts SG7 6UH
t 01462 893995 **f** 01462 893995
e eventide.music@ntlworld.com MD: Kevin Kendle.

Everest Copyrights The Studios, The Park, Newtown,
Powys SY16 2NZ **t** 01686 623555 **f** 01686 623666
e info@everestcopyrights.net Contact: Austin Powell.

Everlasting Records 71a Sutton Rd, London N10 1HH
t 020 8444 8190 **f** 020 8444 9565
e info@everlastingmusic.co.uk **w** everlastingmusic.co.uk
MD: Danny Parnes.

Everybodywantsit Music Label 1st Floor, 27 Lexington
St, London W1F 9AQ **t** 020 7287 9601 **f** 020 7287 9602
e info@everybodywantsit.co.uk **w** everybodywantsit.co.uk
Contact: Rufus Stone.

Evolve Records The Courtyard, 42 Colwith Rd, London
W6 9EY **t** 020 8741 1419 **f** 020 8741 3289
e firstname@evolverecords.co.uk **w** evolverecords.co.uk
Chairman: Oliver Smallman.

Excalibur Records (see Satellite Music Ltd)

Exceptional Records PO Box 16208, London W4 1ZU
t 020 8995 8738 **f** 020 8995 8738
e info@exceptionalrecords.co.uk **w** exceptionalrecords.co.uk
MD: Bob Fisher.

Exotica Records 49 Belvoir Rd, London SE22 0QY
t 020 8299 2342 **f** 020 8693 9006
e jim@exoticarecords.co.uk **w** exoticarecords.co.uk
MD: Jim Phelan.

Expansion Records 20 Blyth Rd, Hayes, Middlesex
UB3 1BY **t** 020 8848 8767 **f** 020 8848 8768
e ralph@expansion-records.co.uk **w** expansionrecords.com
MD: Ralph Tee.

Explicit Records 29 Oakroyd Ave, Potters Bar, Herts
EN6 2EL **t** 01707 651439 **f** 01707 651439
e constantine@steveconstantine.freeserve.co.uk
MD: Steve Constantine.

Extrema (see 3 Beat Label Management)

Extreme Action Records (see Digimix Records)

F Communications (UK) (see PIAS Wall of Sound
Recordings Ltd)

Fabric 12 Greenhill Rents, London EC1M 6BN
t 020 7336 8898 **f** 020 7253 3932 **e** cds@fabriclondon.com
w fabriclondon.com Label Manager: Geoff Muncey.

Fabulous (see Acrobat Music Ltd)

Face 2 Face (see Adasam Limited)

Faculty Music Media Innovation Labs, Watford Rd,
Harrow, Middx HA1 3TP **t** 020 7193 8036
e facultyoffice@facultymusic.com **w** facultymusic.com
MD: Tony Martin.

Fairy Cake Universe 35 Playfield Crescent, London
SE22 8QR **t** 020 8299 1645 **e** aquamanda@skyfruit.com
w aquamanda.net MD: Amanda Greatorex.

Faith & Hope Records 23 New Mount St, Manchester
M4 4DE **t** 0161 839 4445 **f** 0161 839 1060
e email@faithandhope.co.uk **w** faithandhope.co.uk
Contact: Neil Claxton.

Fall Out (see Jungle Records)

Falling A Records 22 Frating Crescent, Woodford Green,
Essex IG8 0DW **t** 020 8505 6606 **e** info@dynamitevision.com
w dynamitevision.com MD: Barry Lamb.

Fantastic Plastic The Church, Archway Close, London
N19 3TD **t** 020 7263 2267 **f** 020 7263 2268
e enquire@fantasticplasticrecords.com
w fantasticplasticrecords.com MD: Darrin Robson.

Fantasy (see Ace Records)

Far Out Recordings TBC **t** 020 8758 1233
f 020 8758 1244 **e** joe@faroutrecordings.com
w faroutrecordings.com MD: Joe Davis.

Fashion Records 17 Davids Rd, London SE23 3EP
t 020 8291 6253 **f** 020 8291 1097
e chrislane@dubvendor.co.uk **w** dubvendor.co.uk
Studio Manager: Chris Lane.

Fast Western Group Ltd Bank Top Cottage, Meadow
Lane, Millers Dale, Derbyshire SK17 8SN **t** 01298 872462
f 01298 872461 **e** fast.west@virgin.net MD: Ric Lee.

Fastforward Music Ltd 1 Sorrel Horse Mews, Ipswich,
Suffolk IP4 1LN **t** 01473 210 555 **f** 01473 210 500
e sales@fastforwardmusic.co.uk Sales Director: Neil Read.

Fat Cat Records 14 Regent Hill, Brighton, E Sussex
BN1 3ED **t** 01273 747 433 **f** 01273 777 718 **e** info@fat-cat.co.uk
w fat-cat.co.uk Label Managers: Dave, Alex.

Fat City Recordings Third Floor, Habib House, 9 Stevenson
Sq, Manchester M1 1DB **t** 0161 228 7884 **f** 0161 228 7266
e label@fatcity.co.uk **w** fatcity.co.uk Label Manager: Matt Triggs.

Fat Fox Records 24a Radley Mews, off Stratford Rd,
London W8 6JP **t** 020 7376 9555 **f** 020 7937 6246
e felix@fatfox.co.uk **w** fatfox.co.uk Dir: Felix Bechtolsheimer.

Fat! Records Battersea Business Centre, Unit 36, 99-109
Lavender Hill, London SW11 5QL **t** 020 7924 1333
f 020 7924 1833 **e** info@thefatclub.com **w** thefatclub.com
MD: Paul Arnold.

FDM Records 15 Woodcote Rd, Leamington Spa, Warcs
CV32 4PX **t** 01926 833 460 **f** 01926 426 393
e info@fdmrecords.com Label Dir: Kieron Concannon.

Feed Me Records (see 3 Beat Label Management)

Fellside Recordings Ltd PO Box 40, Workington, Cumbria
CA14 3GJ **t** 01900 61556 **e** info@fellside.com **w** fellside.com
Dir: Paul Adams.

Fencat Music (see East Central One Ltd)

Fenetik (see Soma Recordings Ltd)

Festivo (see Priory Records)

FF Vinyl Records 1st Floor, Warwick Hall, Off Banastre Ave,
Cardiff CF14 3NR **t** 029 2069 4450 **f** 029 2069 4338
e enquiries@ffvinyl.com **w** ffvinyl.com MD: Martin Bowen.

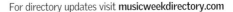

F.I. (see Hot Lead Records)

Fierce Panda 39 Tollington Rd, London N7 6PB
t 020 7609 2789 **f** 020 7609 8034 **e** mrbongopanda@aol.com
w fiercepanda.co.uk MD: Simon Williams.

Fifth Avenue Films 14 South Ave, Hullbridge, Hockley, Essex
SS5 6HA **t** 01702 232396 **f** 01702 230944
e fifthavenuefilms@supanet.com **w** fifthavenuefilms.co.uk
Contact: Dave Harris.

Filthy Pretty Records (see A&G Records)

Fine Style (see Fashion Records)

Finger Lickin' Records 2nd Floor Rear, 20 Great Portland
St, London W1W 8QR **t** 020 7255 2660 **f** 020 7637 2903
e info@fingerlickin.co.uk **w** fingerlickin.co.uk
MD: Justin Rushmore.

Fire Records The Vicarage, Windmill Lane, Nottingham
NG2 4QB **t** 0115 950 9590 **f** 0115 950 9590
e james@firerecords.com **w** firerecords.com
Creative Director: James Nicholls.

Firetraxx (see ATCR: Trance Communication)

First Night Records Ltd 3 Warren Mews, London
W1T 6AN **t** 020 7383 7767 **f** 020 7383 3020
e info@firstnightrecords.com **w** first-night-records.com
MD: John Craig.

First Records 201-205 Hackney Rd, London E2 8JL
t 020 7729 7593 **f** 020 7739 5600
e info@premises.demon.co.uk **w** premises.demon.co.uk
MD: Viv Broughton.

First Time Records 31 Saltburn Rd, St. Budeaux, Plymouth,
Devon PL5 1PA **t** 01752 350785 or 07956 392237
e firsttimerecords@btinternet.com **w** firsttimerecords.co.uk
MD: George Thomas.

Flair Records 15 Tabbs Lane, Scholes, Cleckheaton, West
Yorks BD19 6DY **t** 01274 851365 **f** 01274 874329
e john@now-music.com **w** now-music.com MD: John Wagstaff.

Flapper (see Pavilion Records Ltd)

Flat Records 5 Doods Rd, Reigate, Surrey RH2 0NT
t 01737 210848 **f** 01737 210848 **e** flatrecords@dial.pipex.com
w netlink.co.uk/users/sonic/flat.htm MD: Richard Coppen.

Flo Records (see Nation Records Ltd)

Fly Records (see Cube Soundtracks)

FM (see Revolver Music Ltd)

FM Dance (see Revolver Music Ltd)

FM Jazz (see Revolver Music Ltd)

FM-Revolver (see Revolver Music Ltd)

Focus Music International Ltd 10 Dukes Court, 77
Mortlake High St, London SW14 8HS **t** 020 8876 7111
f 020 8878 0331 **e** info@focus-music.com **w** focus-music.com
MD: Don Reedman.

Fokused Records (see 3 Beat Label Management)

Folkprint (see Voiceprint)

Folktrax Heritage House, 16 Brunswick Sq, Gloucester, Gloucs
GL1 1UG **t** 01452 415110 **f** 01452 503643
e folktrax@blueyonder.co.uk **w** folktrax.org Mgr: Peter Kennedy.

Fontana (see Mercury Music Group)

Fony Records Cambridge House, Card Hill, Forest Row, E.
Sussex RH18 5BA **t** 01342 822619 **f** 01342 822619
e mickey.modernwood@virgin.net MD: Mickey Modern.

Food (see Parlophone)

Formation Records 1st Floor, 38 Charles St, Leicester
LE1 1FB **t** 01162 530048 **f** 01162 621080
e promotions@formationsrecords.com **w** formationrecords.co.uk.

Formula One Records 71 Alan Moss Rd, Loughborough,
Leics LE11 5LR **t** 01509 213632 MD: Ian Barker.

Fortune and Glory Osmond House, 78 Alcester Rd, Moseley,
Birmingham, W Midlands B13 8BB **t** 0121 256 1310
f 0121 256 1318 **e** hendricks@fortuneandglory.co.uk
w fortuneandglory.co.uk MD: Hendricks.

four:twenty (see Hope Music Group)

Fox Records Ltd 62 Lake Rise, Romford, Essex RM1 4EE
t 01708 760544 **f** 01708 760563 **e** foxrecords@talk21.com
w foxrecordsltd.co.uk Dir: Colin Brewer.

Fragile Records Unit 3, 1 St Mary Rd, London E17 9RG
t 020 8520 4442 **f** 020 8520 2514 **e** info@fragilerecords.co.uk
MD: Dave Thompson.

Frank Records (see Hepcat Records)

Fred Label Ltd 45 Vyner St, London E2 9DQ
t 020 8981 2987 **f** 020 8981 9912 **e** info@fred-london.com
w fred-label.com Dir: Fred Mann.

Fredag Records Ltd 39 Palmerston Pl, Edinburgh
EH12 5AU **t** 0131 202 6236 **f** 0131 202 6238
e info@fredagrecords.com **w** fredagrecords.com
Managing Consultant: David Murray.

Free Construction Records 4 Canalot Studios, 222
Kensal Rd, London W10 5BN **t** 020 8960 4443
f 020 8960 9889 **e** martyn@freeconstuction.co.uk
w freeconstuction.co.uk MD: Martyn Barter.

free2air recordings Fulham Palace, Bishops Ave, London
SW6 6EA **t** 020 7751 0175 **f** 020 7736 0606
e info@free2airrecordings.com **w** free2airrecordings.com
Contact: Craig Dimech.

Freedom Records PO Box 283, Manchester M14 4WY
t 0161 227 9727 or 07811 326 200 **e** info@calebstorkey.com
w freedom.cd MD: Caleb Storkey.

Freemaison Records 36 Brunswick St West, Hove, E
Sussex BN3 1EL **t** 07979 757 033 **f** 01273 325 935
e info@freemaison.com **w** freemaison.com
Label Mgrs: Russell Small, James Wiltshire.

Freestyle Records 77 Fortess Rd, London NW5 1AG
t 020 7482 4555 **f** 020 7482 4551
e info@freestylerecords.co.uk **w** freestylerecords.co.uk
Label Manager: Jon Sheppard.

Freshly Squeezed (Music Ltd) 116 Stanford Ave, Brighton BN1 6FE **t** 01273 563201 **f** 01273 563201 **e** info@freshlysqueezedmusic.com **w** freshlysqueezedmusic.com MD: Nick Perring.

Full Cycle Records Unit 23, Easton Business Centre, Felix Rd, Bristol BS5 0HE **t** 0117 941 5824 **f** 0117 941 5823 **e** info@fullcycle.co.uk **w** fullcycle.co.uk Label Manager: Gerard Cantwell.

Full Fat Records (see Rumour Records Ltd)

Full Time Hobby Records 3rd Floor, 1A Adpar St, London W2 1DE **t** 020 7535 6740 **f** 020 7563 7283 **e** info@FullTimeHobby.co.uk **w** fulltimehobby.co.uk GM: Nigel Adams.

Fullfill LLC UK Ltd Unit 41, 249-251 Kensal Rd, London W10 5DB **t** 020 8968 1231 **f** 020 8964 1181 **e** info@fullfill.co.uk **w** fullfill.co.uk Office Manager: Savanna Sparkes.

Fume Recordings 92 Camden Mews, Camden, London NW1 9AG **t** 020 7424 8665 **f** 020 7482 2210 **e** info@fume.co.uk **w** fume.co.uk MD: Seamus Morley.

FUN (see Future Underground Nation)

Functional Breaks (see Future Underground Nation)

Funky Inc 206 Golden House, 29 Great Pulteney St, London W1R 3DD **t** 020 7434 0779 **f** 020 7434 0710 **e** funkyinc@funkyinc.com **w** funkyinc.com Contact: Brendan Donohoe.

Furious? (see Furious? Records)

Furious? Records PO Box 40, Arundel, W Sussex BN18 0UQ **t** 01243 558444 **f** 01243 558455 **e** info@furiousrecords.co.uk **w** furiousrecords.co.uk Mgr: Tony Patoto.

Furry Tongue Records (see Jackpot Records)

Fury Records PO Box 7187, Ringstead, Kettering NN16 6DJ **t** 01933 626 945 **e** furyrecords@btconnect.com **w** fury-records.com Owner: Dell Richardson.

Future Earth Records 59 Fitzwilliam St, Wath Upon Dearne, Rotherham, South Yorks S63 7HG **t** 01709 872875 **e** records@future-earth.co.uk **w** future-earth.co.uk MD: David Moffitt.

Future Underground Nation 80 Monks Rd, Exeter, Devon EX4 7BE **t** 01392 490064 **f** 01392 420580 **e** fun@fun-1.com **w** fun-1.com Label Mgr: Colin Mitchell.

Futureproof Records Ltd 330 Westbourne Park Rd, London W11 1EQ **t** 020 7792 8597 **f** 020 7221 3694 **e** info@futureproofrecords.com **w** futureproofrecords.com MD: Phil Legg.

G2 (see Greentrax Recordings Ltd)

Gallic (see Silverword Music Group)

Gammer (see Annie Records)

Gargleblast Records 8 Dornoch Court, Bellshill, Lanarkshire ML4 1HN **t** 01698 842 899 or 07716 167 979 **e** info@gargleblastrecords.com **w** gargleblastrecords.com Label Manager: Shaun Tallamy.

GAS Records 10 St John's Sq, Glastonbury, Somerset BA6 9LJ **t** 01458 833040 **f** 01458 833958 **e** info@planetgong.co.uk **w** planetgong.co.uk Contact: Johnny Greene.

Gaudeamus (see Sanctuary Classics)

Geffen (see Polydor Records)

Genepool Records 34 Windsor Rd, Teddington, Middlesex TW11 0SF **t** n/a **f** n/a **e** contact@genepoolrecords.com **w** genepoolrecords.com Dir: Peter Ward-Edwards.

Genetic Records Rivington House, 82 Great Eastern St, London EC2A 3JF **t** 020 8695 6959 **f** 020 8698 6600 **e** info@geneticrecords.co.uk **w** geneticrecords.co.uk Project Manager: Bhavna Patel.

Genius Records Ltd PO Box 22949, London N10 3ZH **t** 020 8444 0987 **e** genius@brmmusic.com **w** brmmusic.com A&R: Phillip Rose.

Genuine Recordings (see PIAS Wall of Sound Recordings Ltd)

Georgian (see Divine Art Record Company)

Get Back (see Abstract Sounds)

Giant Pitch (see ATCR: Trance Communication)

Giant Records Woking, Surrey GU21 6NS **t** 01483 859 849 **e** mark.studio@ntlworld.com 57 Kingsway: Mark Taylor.

Giants Of Jazz (see Hasmick Promotions)

Gig Records UK (see Wayward Records)

Gimell Records PO Box 197, Beckley, Oxford, Oxon OX3 9YJ **t** 01865 358282 **e** info@gimell.com **w** gimell.com MD: Steve C Smith.

Glasgow Records Ltd Lovat House, Gavell Rd, Glasgow G65 9BS **t** 01236 826555 **f** 01236 825560 **e** sasha@glasgowrecords.com **w** glasgowrecords.com MD: Tessa Hartmann.

Gliss Records (see GAS Records)

Glitterhouse Records 123c Cadogan Terrace, London E9 5HP **t** 020 8533 3577 or 07958 564 624 **e** tris@glitterhouserecords.co.uk **w** glitterhouserecords.co.uk MD: Tris Dickin.

Global Music Development Ltd Global House, 7 Fernbank Drive, Bingley, W Yorks BD16 4HB **t** 0113 2256 707 or 07887 852 393 **e** Kirk@globalmusicdevelopment.com **w** globalmusicdevelopment.com Label Director: Kirk Worley.

Global Talent Records 2nd Floor, 53 Frith St, London W1D 4SN **t** 020 7292 9600 **f** 020 7292 9611 **e** email@globaltalentgroup.com **w** globaltalentgroup.com MDs: Ashley Tabor, David Forecast.

Global Underground Kings House, Forth Banks, Newcastle upon Tyne NE1 3PA **t** 0191 232 4064 **f** 0191 232 5766 **e** firstname@globalunderground.co.uk **w** globalunderground.co.uk MD: Colin Tierney.

Global Warming Ltd PO Box 5192, Hatfield Peveral, Chelmsford, Essex CM3 2QH **t** 07785 231 741 or 07939 631 390 **e** johnp@susanshouse.demon.co.uk **w** globalwarmingrecords.com MD: John Pearson, Trevor Holden.

Globe Records (see Universal Music TV)

G-Man Entertainment Dalton House, 60 Windsor Ave, London SW19 2RR **t** 0845 057 3739 **f** 020 7787 8788 **e** grant.music@btconnect.com MD: John Watson-Grant.

Go Beat (see Island Records Group)

Go Disc (see Island Records Group)

Going for a Song Ltd Chiltern House, 184 High St, Berkhamsted, Herts HP4 3AP **t** 01442 877417 **f** 01442 870944 **e** sales@goingforasong.com **w** goingforasong.com Sales & Logistics C'tor: Luke White.

Gold Top Records (see Rumour Records Ltd)

Goldrush Records 9 Kinnoull St, Perth, Scotland PH1 5EN **t** 01738 629730 **f** 01738 629730 **e** sales@goldrushrecords.co.uk **w** goldrushrecords.co.uk MD: John S. Thomson.

Goldsoul Entertainment Hartford House, Common Rd, Thorpe Salvin, Notts. S80 3JJ **t** 0870 446 0196 **e** sales@goldsoul.co.uk **w** goldsoul.co.uk Sales Manager: Ann Roberts.

Good Behaviour (see Fony Records)

Good Looking Records 84 Queens Rd, Watford, Herts WD17 2LA **t** 01923 690700 **f** 01923 249495 **e** info@goodlookingrecords.co.uk **w** goodlookingrecords.co.uk MD: Tony Fordham.

Gorgeous Music Suite D, 67 Abbey Rd, London NW8 0AE **t** 020 7724 2635 **f** 020 7724 2635 **e** velliott@gorgeousmusic.net **w** gorgeousmusic.net Label Manager: Victoria Elliott.

Gotham Records PO Box 6003, Birmingham, W Midlands B45 0AR **t** 0121 477 9553 **f** 0121 693 2954 **e** Barry@gotham-records.com **w** gotham-records.com Prop: Barry Tomes.

Grace Records PO Box 19558, Greenock PA15 9AL **t** 01475 798 869 **e** info@gracerecords.co.uk MD, UK Music: Stuart Clark.

Graduate Records PO Box 388, Holt Heath, Worcester, Worcs WR6 6WQ **t** 01905 620786 **e** davidrobertvirr@aol.com **w** graduaterecords.com MD: David Virr.

Gramavision (see Palm Pictures)

Gramophone Records Unit X, 37 Hamilton Rd, Twickenham, Middx. TW2 6SN **t** 020 8894 2169 **e** woo@attglobal.net Dirs: Bruce Woolley, Andy Visser.

Granada Ventures 48 Leicester Sq, London WC2H 7FB **t** 020 7389 8555 **e** Mark.hurry@ITV.com **w** granadaventures.tv Commercial Affairs Director: Mark Hurry.

Grapevine Music Group 17 Blenheim Rd, Wakefield, West Yorks WF1 3JZ **t** 01924 299461 **e** info@grapevine-soul.com **w** grapevine-soul.com MD: Garry J Cape.

Grateful Dead (see Ace Records)

Great Western Records (see Rollercoaster Records)

The Green Label Music Company Ltd PO Box 133, Leatherhead KT24 6WQ **t** 01483 281 300 and 01708 444 282 **f** 01483 281 811 **e** john@greenlabelmusic.co.uk Dirs: John Boyden and Andrew Humphries.

Greensleeves Records Unit 14 Metro Centre, St John's Rd, Isleworth, Middlesex TW7 6NJ **t** 020 8758 0564 **f** 020 8758 0811 **e** marcus@greensleeves.net **w** greensleeves.net FD: Marcus Lee.

Greentrax Recordings Ltd Cockenzie Business Centre, Edinburgh Rd, Cockenzie, East Lothian EH32 0HL **t** 01875 814 155 or 01875 815 888 **f** 01875 813 545 **e** greentrax@aol.com **w** greentrax.com MD: Ian D Green.

Grey Mause Records 155 Regents Park Rd, London NW1 8BB **t** 0871 900 8410 **e** info@greymause.com **w** GreyMause.com.

Gridlockaz Records Unit S14, Shakespeare Business Centre, 245a Coldharbour Lane, London SW9 8RR **t** 020 7501 9339 **f** 020 7501 9339 **e** info@gridlockaz.com **w** gridlockaz.com Label Mgr: Victor Omosevwerha.

Griffin & Co Church House, St.Mary's Gate, 96 Church St, Lancaster LA1 1TD **t** 01524 844399 **f** 01524 844335 **e** sales@griffinrecords.co.uk **w** griffinrecords.co.uk GM: Ian Murray.

GRONLAND RECORDS

9-10 Domingo Street, London EC1Y 0TA **t** 020 7553 9166 **f** 020 7553 9198 **e** thebear@groenland.com **w** gronland.co.uk MD: Rene Renner. A&R: Robert Hoile.

Groovefinder Records 30, Havelock Rd, Southsea, Portsmouth PO5 1RU **t** 07831 450 241 **e** jeff@groovefinderproductions.com **w** groovefinderproductions.com MD: Jeff Powell.

Groovetech Records 10 Latimer Industrial Estate, Latimer Rd, London W10 6RQ **t** 020 8962 3350 **f** 020 8962 3355 **e** groovetechrecords@groovetech.com **w** groovetech.com Label Mgr: Ana Saskia Adang.

Groovin' Records Hoylake CH47 2HP **t** 0845 458 0037 **e** groovin.records@virgin.net **w** groovinrecords.co.uk PO Box 39: AL Willard Peterson.

Ground Groove (see Headzone Ltd)

GRP (see Universal Music Classics & Jazz (UK))

GTV RECORDS

Byron House, 112A Shirland Road, London W9 2EQ
t 020 7266 0777 f 020 7266 7734 e general@gutrecords.com
w gutrecords.com. Chairman: Guy Holmes. MD: Karen Meekings.
Compilations and branded releases.

Guild (see Priory Records)

Gull Records (see Q Zone Ltd)

GUSTO RECORDINGS

Byron House, 112A Shirland Road, London W9 2EQ
t 020 7266 0777 f 020 7266 7734 e general@gutrecords.com
w gutrecords.com. Chairman: Guy Holmes. MD: Steve Tandy.
Director of Marketing/International: Fraser Ealey. A&R: Julian
Hargreaves, Lucy Francis, Simon Hills, Sean Denny.
Gusto

GUT RECORDINGS

Byron House, 112A Shirland Road, London W9 2EQ
t 020 7266 0777 f 020 7266 7734 e general@gutrecords.com
w gutrecords.com. Chairman: Guy Holmes. MD: Steve Tandy.
Director of Marketing/International: Fraser Ealey. A&R: Julian
Hargreaves, Lucy Francis.

Gutta (Sweden) (see Plankton Records)

GVC (see Highnote Ltd)

Hallé (see Sanctuary Classics)

Halo UK Records 88 Church Lane, London N2 0TB
t 020 8444 0049 or 07711 062 309
e halomanagement@hotmail.com w halo-uk.net
Dir: Mike Karl Maslen.

Handspun Records 64 Harbour St, Whitstable, Kent
CT5 1AG t 07973 149 333 e handspun@haveaniceday.ws
w haveaniceday.ws Owner: Anthony Cooper.

Hannibal (see Palm Pictures)

Harbourtown Records PO Box 25, Ulverston, Cumbria
LA12 7UN t 01229 588290 f 01229 588290
e records@hartown.demon.co.uk w harbourtownrecords.com
MD: Gordon Jones.

Hardleaders (see Kickin Music Ltd)

Harkit Records PO Box 617, Bushey Heath, Herts.
WD23 1SX t 020 8385 7771 f 020 8421 8463
e sales@harkitrecords.com w harkitrecords.com
MD: Michael Fishberg.

Harmless Recordings (see Demon Music Group)

Harper Collins Audio Books 77-85 Fulham Palace Rd,
Hammersmith, London W6 8JB t 020 8741 7070 or
020 8307 4618 f 020 8307 4517 or 020 8307 4440
e rosalie.george@harpercollins.co.uk w fireandwater.com
Publishing Manager: Rosalie George.

Hasmick Promotions Unit 8, Forest Hill Trading Estate,
London SE23 2LX t 020 8291 6777 f 020 8291 0081
e jasmine@hasmick.co.uk w hasmick.co.uk
Contact: Carl Hazeldine.

Hassle Records (see Full Time Hobby Records)

Haven Records St Mary's Works, St Mary's Plain, Norwich,
Norfolk NR3 3AF t 01603 624290 or 01603 626221
f 01603 619999 e derek@backsrecords.co.uk
w havenrecords.co.uk A&R: Derek Chapman/Boo Hewerdine.

Headline (see Hi-Note Music)

Headscope Headrest, Broadoak, Heathfield, E Sussex
TN21 8TU t 01435 863994 f 01435 867027
e headscope@geesin.demon.co.uk w rongeesin.com
Ptnr: Ron Geesin.

Headstone Records 46 Tintagel Way, Woking, Surrey
GU22 7DG t 01483 856 760 or 07811 387220
e colinfwspencer@hotmail.com MD: Colin Spencer.

Headwrecker Records 21 Lancaster Rd, Seven Dials,
Brighton BN1 5DG t 07810 658 764 or 07748 110 853
e info@headwreckerrecords.com w headwreckerrecords.com
Dirs: Luke Bevans, Sarah Sherry.

Headzone Ltd 43 Canham Rd, London W3 7SR
t 020 8749 8860 f 020 8742 9462 e info@intergroove.co.uk
w intergroove.co.uk MD: Andy Howarth.

Heat Recordings 63 Hartland Rd, London NW6 6BH
t 020 7625 5552 f 020 7625 5553 e info@heatrecordings.com
w heatrecordings.com MD/A&R: Alex Payne.

Heavenly Recordings 47 Frith St, London W1D 4SE
t 020 7494 2998 f 020 7437 3317
e info@heavenlyrecordings.com w heavenly100.com
MD: Jeff Barrett.

Heavenly Dance PO Box 640, Bromley BR1 4XZ
t 07985 439 453 f 020 8290 4589
e Heavenlydance1@aol.com Head A&R: Minister ID.

Heavy Metal Records 152 Goldthorn Hill, Penn,
Wolverhampton WV2 3JA t 01902 345345 f 01902 345155
e Paul.Birch@revolver-e.com w HeavyMetalRecords.com
MD: Paul Birch.

Heavy Rotation Recordings PO Box 516, London HA8 7XL **t** 07905 888 865 **e** info@heavyrotation.co.uk **w** heavyrotation.co.uk Label Mgr: Simon Ross.

Hectic (see 3 Beat Label Management)

Hed Kandi (see Ministry Of Sound Recordings)

Hellsquad Records PO Box 54319, London W2 7AZ **t** 020 77929494 **e** enquiries@hellsquadrecords.com **w** hellsquadrecords.com MD: Thomas Dalton.

Hens Teeth Records Millham Lane, Dulverton, Somerset TA22 9HQ **t** 01398 324114 **f** 01398 324114 **e** hens.teeth@bigfoot.com MD: Andrew Quarrie.

Hepcat Records Sovereign House, 12 Trewartha Rd, Praa Sands, Penzance, Cornwall TR20 9ST **t** 01736 762 826 or 07721 449 477 **f** 01736 763 328 **e** panamus@aol.com **w** panamamusic.co.uk MD: Roderick Jones.

Heraldic Records (see First Time Records)

Heraldic Vintage (see First Time Records)

Hex Unit (see Gut Recordings)

HHO Ltd Suite 1, 1-13 Britannia Business Centre, Cricklewood Lane, London NW2 1ET **t** 020 8830 8813 **f** 020 8830 8801 **e** info@hho.co.uk **w** hho.co.uk MD: Henry Hadaway.

Hi-Fi (see Everest Copyrights)

Hi-Note Music PO Box 26, Windsor, Berks SL4 2YX **t** 01784 432 868 **f** 01784 477 702 **e** info@hinotemusic.com **w** hinotemusic.com MD: Graham Brook.

Hidden Art Recordings (see Adasam Limited)

Hidden Art Recordings PO Box 8, Corby, Nothants. NN17 2XZ **t** 01536 202295 **f** 01536 266246 **e** steve@adasam.demon.co.uk **w** hiddenartrecordings.com Label Manager: Steve Kalidoski.

High Barn Records The Bardfield Centre, Great Bardfield, Braintree, Essex CM7 4SL **t** 01371 811 291 **f** 01371 811 404 **e** info@high-barn.com **w** high-barn.com MD: Chris Bullen.

Higher State 95-99 North St, London SW4 0HF **t** 020 7627 5656 **f** 020 7627 5757 **e** info@higherstate.co.uk **w** higherstate.co.uk A&R Mgr: Jamie Pierce.

Highnote Ltd Studio 65, Shepperton Film Studio, Shepperton, Middx TW17 0QD **t** 01932 592949 **f** 01932 592269 **e** info@highnote.co.uk **w** highnote.co.uk MD: Mark Rye.

Hip Bop (see Silva Screen Records)

Hit Mania Ltd 6, Albemarle St, London W1S 4HA **t** 020 7499 7451 **f** 020 7499 7452 **e** info@hitmania.co.uk **w** hitmania.com Office Manager: Laura Fasser.

The Hit Music Company Shepperton Film Studios, Studios Rd, Shepperton, Middx TW17 0QD **t** 01932 593 634 **e** chet@thehitmusiccompany.com **w** thehitmusiccompany.com Chief: Chet Selwood.

HMV Classics (see EMI Classics International)

Hoax Records PO Box 23604, London E7 0YT **t** 0870 910 6666 **e** hoax@hoaxrecords.com **w** hoaxrecords.com MD: Ben Angwin.

Holier Than Thou Records Ltd 46 Rother St, Stratford on Avon, Warcs CV37 6LT **t** 01789 268661 **e** httrecords@aol.com **w** holierthanthourecords.com A&R Director: David Begg.

HomeFront Productions 47 Sydney Rd, Ealing, London W13 9EZ **t** 020 8579 4782 or 07980 822 517 **e** roland@rolandchadwick.com **w** rolandchadwick.com Dir: Roland Chadwick.

Honchos Music (see NRK Sound Division Ltd)

Honey Records 85-89 Duke St, Liverpool L1 5AP **t** 0151 708 7722 **e** info@honeyrecords.co.uk **w** honeyrecords.co.uk Dirs: Mat Flynn, Keith Mullin.

Honeypot Records 1 Victoria Bank, Robin Bank Rd, Darwen, Blackburn BB3 0DF **t** 01254 771 658 **f** 01254 771 658 **e** natashahoneypot@hotmail.com **w** natashajones.org Label Mgr: Julie Jones.

Hope Music Group Loft 5, The Tobacco Factory, Raleigh Rd, Southville, Bristol BS3 1TF **t** 0117 953 5566 **f** 0117 953 7733 **e** info@hoperecordings.com **w** hoperecordings.com MD: Leon Alexander.

Hope Recordings (see Hope Music Group)

Hope Records (see Music Fusion Ltd)

Horatio Nelson PO Box 1123, London SW1P 1HB **t** 020 7828 6533 **f** 020 7828 1271 MD: Derek Boulton.

Hospital Records 182-184 Dartmouth Rd, Sydenham, London SE26 4QZ **t** 020 8613 0400 **f** 020 8613 0401 **e** info@hospitalrecords.com **w** hospitalrecords.com Marketing & Promotions: Tom Kelsey.

Hot Dog (see The Store For Music)

Hot Lead Records 2, Laurel Bank, Lowestwood, Huddersfield, Yorks HD7 4ER **t** 01484 846333 **f** 01484 846333 **e** HotLeadRecords@btopenworld.com **w** fimusic.co.uk MD: Ian R. Smith.

Hot Records PO Box 333, Brighton, Sussex BN1 2EH **t** 01403 740 260 **f** 01403 740 261 **e** info@hotrecords.uk.com **w** hotrecords.uk.com MD: Martin Jennings.

Hotshot Records (see American Activities)

The House of Wax (see Global Warming Ltd)

Household Name Records PO Box 12286, London SW9 6BT **t** 020 7582 9972 **f** 020 7840 0383 **e** info@householdnamerecords.co.uk **w** householdnamerecords.co.uk Label Manager: David Giles.

Housexy (see Ministry Of Sound Recordings)

Human Condition (see Human Condition Records)

Human Condition Records 120A West Granton Rd, Edinburgh EH5 1PF **t** 0131 551 6632 **f** 0131 551 6632 **e** mail@humancondition.co.uk **w** humancondition.co.uk Dir: Jamie Watson.

Hungry Audio 7 Elwyn Rd, Norwich NR1 2RX **t** 01603 632 466 or 07909 920 574 **e** contact@hungryaudio.co.uk **w** hungryaudio.co.uk MD: Adrian Cooke.

Hustle Music (see 37 Music)

Hux Records PO Box 12647, London SE18 8ZF
t 07939 529772 **f** 01253 796 492 **e** info@huxrecords.com
w huxrecords.com Contact: Brian O'Reilly.

Hwyl 2 The Square, Yapham, York, N Yorks YO42 1PJ
t 01759 304514 **f** 01759 304514 **e** stevejparry@yahoo.co.uk
w hwylnofio.com Dir: Steve Parry.

Hydraulix (see Truelove Records)

Hydrogen Dukebox 89 Borough High St, London SE1 1NL
t 020 7357 9799 **e** hydrogen@dukebox.demon.co.uk
w hydrogendukebox.com Contact: Doug Hart.

Hyperion Records Ltd PO Box 25, London SE9 1AX
t 020 8318 1234 **f** 020 8463 1230
e info@hyperion-records.co.uk **w** hyperion-records.co.uk
Dir: Simon Perry.

I-Anka PO Box 917, London W10 5FA **t** 020 8968 6221
f 020 8968 7500 **e** ianka.records@boltblue.com
w bobandy.com MD: Janis Punford.

IDJ (see Incentive Music Ltd)

Iffy Biffa Records Welland House Farm, Spalding Marsh,
Spalding, Lincs PE12 6HF **t** 07711 513791 **f** 01406 370478
e mark@iffybiffa.co.uk **w** iffybiffa.co.uk MD: Mark Bunn.

Ignition 54 Linhope St, London NW1 6HL **t** 020 7298 6000
f 020 7258 0962 **e** mail@ignition-man.co.uk MD: Alec McKinlay.

IHT Records Unit 2D, Clapham North Arts Centre, 26-32
Voltaire Rd, London SW4 6DH **t** 020 7720 7411
f 020 7720 8095 **e** rob@ihtrecords.com **w** davidgray.com
Contact: Rob Holden.

Ikon (see Priory Records)

Illegal Beats Unit 11, Impress House, Mansell Rd, London
W3 7QH **t** 020 8743 5218 **f** 020 7681 3949
e info@jalapenorecords.com **w** jalapenorecords.com
Label Mgr: Trevor McNamee.

Illicit Recordings PO Box 51871, London NW2 9BR
t 020 8830 7831 **f** 020 8830 7859 **e** ian@mumbojumbo.co.uk
w illicitrecordings.com MD: Ian Clifford.

Imagemaker Sound & Vision PO Box 69, Launceston,
Cornwall PL15 7YA **t** 01566 86308 **f** 01566 86308
e mail@timwheater.com **w** timwheater.com MD: Olive Lister.

Imaginary Music 2 Monument Cottages, Warpsgrove Lane,
Chalgrove, Oxon OX44 7RW **t** 01865 400286 **f** 01865 400286
e halls@dialin.net **w** soft.net.uk/gphall/ Contact: GP Hall.

Immaterial Records PO Box 706, Ilford, Essex IG2 6ED
t 07973 676160 **f** 020 7323 9008 **e** bij@btinternet.com
Owner: Bijal Dodhia.

Immoral Recordings (see JPS Recordings)

Imprint (see D.O.R.)

Imprint Music Unit 17C Raines Court, Northwold Rd, London
N16 7DH **t** 020 7275 8682 **f** 020 7275 0791
e paul@ignitemarketing.co.uk **w** ignitemarketing.co.uk
MD: Paul West.

Impulse Records & Distribution 1 Romborough Way,
London SE13 6NS **t** 020 8488 0158 or 07931 590005
e neilpaulmarch@aol.com Dir: Neil March.

In Jeopardy Records 3 Fleece Yard, Market Hill,
Buckingham MK18 1JX **t** 01280 821170 **f** 01280 821840
e injeopardy@reactstudios.co.uk **w** injeopardy.co.uk
Lbl Mgr: Sarah Hodgetts.

In Music Ltd 2 The Hall, Turners Green Rd, Wadhurst, E
Sussex TN5 6TR **t** 01892 785005 **f** 01892 785023
e info@inmusicltd.co.uk **w** inmusicltd.co.uk MD: Alex Branson.

Incentive Music Ltd Unit 21, Grand Union Centre, West
Row, London W10 5AS **t** 020 8964 2555 **f** 020 8964 8778
e incentive@incentivemusic.co.uk **w** incentivemusic.com
MD: Nick Halkes.

Independent Records Ltd (see Wayward Records).

INDEPENDIENTE LTD

independiente

The Drill Hall, 3 Heathfield Terrace, Chiswick, London W4 4JE
t 020 8747 8111 **f** 020 8747 8113
e firstname@independiente.co.uk **w** independiente.co.uk.
Chairman: Andy Macdonald. A&R Dir: Dave Boyd. Director of
Finance & Business Affairs: Neville Acaster. A&R Fax: 020 8400
5399. Legal Fax: 020 8995 5907. Andy's Fax: 020 8400 5509.

Indie 500 (see New Leaf Records)

Indigo Records (see Sanctuary Records Group)

Indipop Records P.O.Box 369, Glastonbury, Somerset
BA6 8YN **t** 01749 831 674 **f** 01749 831 674 MD: Steve Coe.

Industry (see Resist Music)

Industry Recordings (see 3 Beat Label Management)

Infectious (see Atlantic Records UK)

Inferno Cool (see Inferno Records)

Inferno Records 32-36 Telford Way, London W3 7XS
t 020 8742 9300 **f** 020 8742 9097 **e** pat@infernorecords.co.uk
w infernorecords.co.uk Heaf of A&R: Pat Travers.

Infinite Bloom Recordings Ltd 41 Walters Workshop,
249 Kensal Rd, London W10 5DB **t** 020 8969 5347
e gordon@infinitebloom.com **w** infinitebloom.com
Contact: Gordon Biggins.

Infur (see Seriously Groovy Music)

INFX Records Buckinghamshire Chilterns Uni., Wellesbourne
Campus, Kingshill Rd, High Wycombe, Bucks HP13 5BB
t 01494 52214 ex 4020 **f** 01494 465432
e fmacke01@bcuc.ac.uk **w** bcuc.ac.uk HoM: Frazer Mackenzie.

Inigo Recordings Label Group 642 Wandsworth Rd,
London SW8 3JW **t** 020 7168 9118 **f** 020 7168 9118
e info@inigorecordings.com **w** inigo-online.com
MD: Alex Harriman.

Ink (see Distinct'ive Records)

Inner Rhythm (see Born to Dance Records)

Inner Sanctum Recordings (see Adasam Limited)

Innerground Records 8 Roland Mews, Stepney Green, London E1 3JT **t** 020 7929 3333 **f** 020 7929 3222 **e** info@innergroundrecords.com **w** innergroundrecords.com MD: Oliver J. Brown.

Innocent Records Crown House, 72 Hammersmith Rd, London W14 8UD **t** 020 7605 5000 **f** 020 7605 5050 **e** firstname.lastname@emimusic.com **w** emimusic.com Director of A&R: Elias Christides.

Instant Karma PO Box 50668, London SW6 3UY **e** zen@instantkarma.co.uk **w** instantkarma.co.uk Chairman: Rob Dickins.

INSTITUTE RECORDINGS

Byron House, 112A Shirland Road, London W9 2EQ **t** 020 7266 0777 **f** 020 7266 7734 **e** general@gutrecords.com **w** gutrecords.com. Chairman: Guy Holmes. MD: Steve Tandy. Director of Marketing/International: Fraser Ealey. A&R: Julian Hargreaves, Lucy Francis.

Intec Records Reverb House, Bennett St, London W4 2AH **t** 020 8742 7693 **f** 020 8994 8617 **e** intec@intecrecords.com **w** intecrecords.com Label Manager: Tintin Chambers.

Integrity Records Ltd 40 Mill St, Bedford MK40 3HD **t** 01234 267459 **f** 01234 212864 **e** david@plutonik.com Dir: David R Twigden.

Interactive Music Ltd 2 Carriglea, Naas Rd, Dublin 12, Ireland **t** +353 1 419 5039 **f** +353 1 429 3850 **e** info@interactive-music.com **w** interactive-music.com Dir: Suriya Moodliar.

Intercom Recordings PO Box 32, Beccles NR34 9XJ **t** 01502 501414 **f** 01502 501414 **e** inter.comrecordings@virgin.net **w** intercomrecordings.com Label Manager: Jay Hurren.

Interscope (see Polydor Records)

Introducing (see World Music Network (UK) Ltd)

Intruder Records PO Box 22949, London N10 3ZH **t** 020 8444 0987 **e** intruder@brmmusic.com **w** brmmusic.com A&R: Simon Kay.

Invicta Hi-Fi Records Limited Liverpool Palace, 6-10 Slater St, Liverpool L1 4BT **t** 0151 709 5264 **f** 0151 709 8439 **e** invictahifi@dial.pipex.com **w** invictahifi.co.uk Contact: Jules Bennett.

Invisible Hands Music 15 Chalk Farm Rd, London NW1 8AG **t** 020 7284 3322 **f** 020 7284 4455 **e** info@invisiblehands.co.uk **w** invisiblehands.co.uk MD: Charles Kennedy.

Iodine Records (see Wayward Records)

Iona Records (see Lismor Recordings)

Ipecac (see Southern Records)

Iris Light Records 9 Station Walk, Highbridge, Somerset TA9 3HQ **t** 01278 780904 **f** 01278 780904 **e** iLIGHT@irislight.co.uk **w** irislight.co.uk MD: Adam Sykes.

IRL PO Box 30884, London W12 9AZ **t** 020 8746 7461 **f** 020 8749 7441 **e** info@independentrecordsltd.com **w** independentrecordsltd.com Dirs: David Jaymes & Tom Haxell.

Iron Man Records PO Box 9121, Birmingham B13 8AU **t** 08712 260910 **e** info@ironmanrecords.co.uk **w** ironmanrecords.co.uk Label Manager: Mark Badger.

ISLAND RECORDS GROUP

364-366 Kensington High St, London W14 8NS **t** 020 7471 5300 **f** 020 7471 5001 **e** firstname.lastname@umusic.com **w** islandrecords.co.uk President: Nick Gatfield. MD Island Label: Dan Keeling. GM, Finance & Commercial Affairs: David Sharpe. Legal & Business Affairs Director: Claire Sugrue. GM Island Label: Jon Turner. GM Universal Label: Ted Cockle. Press Director: Ted Cummings. Promotions Director: Ruth Parrish.

Isobar Records 56 Gloucester Pl, London W1U 8HJ **t** 020 7486 3297 or 07956 493 692 **f** 020 7486 3297 **e** info@isobarrecords.com **w** isobarrecords.com MD: Peter Morris.

J & S Construction (see Taste Media Ltd)

Jackpot Records PO Box 2272, Rottingdean, Brighton BN2 8XD **t** 01273 304681 **f** 01273 308120 **e** steveb@a7music.com **w** a7music.com Label Manager: Steve B.

Jalapeno Records Unit 11, Impress House, Mansell Rd, London W3 7QH **t** 020 8743 5218 **f** 020 7681 3949 **e** info@jalapenorecords.com **w** jalapenorecords.com Label Mgr: Trevor McNamee.

Jam Central Records PO Box 230, Aylesbury, Bucks HP21 9WA **t** 07765 258 225 **e** admin@jamcentralrecords.co.uk **w** jamcentralrecords.co.uk MD: Stuart Robb.

Jasmine Records (see Hasmick Promotions)

Jaygee Cassettes 5 Woodfield, Burnham on Sea, Somerset TA8 1QL **t** 01278 789352 **f** 01278 789352 **e** roger@jaygeecassettes.co.uk **w** babysooth.com Snr Partners: Roger & Patricia Wannell.

Jeepster Recordings Ltd 2nd Floor, 11 Hillgate Pl, London SW12 9ER **t** 0845 126 0621 **f** 020 8772 1092 **e** info@jeepster.co.uk **w** jeepster.co.uk Label Manager: Kay Heath.

JESSICA RECORDS LTD

jessica records ltd

Suite 10, 42 Brunswick Terrace, Hove, East Sussex BN3 1HA **t** 01273 220 604 **f** 01273 220 604 **e** jappla@o2.co.uk **w** jessica-records.com Label Manager: Jessica Appla. Independent record label, covering mainly pop, dance. indie, rock and RnB. Interested in all genres. CD demos accepted only.

Jewish Music Heritage Recordings PO Box 232, Harrow, Middlesex HA1 2NN **t** 020 8909 2445 **f** 020 8909 1030 **e** jewishmusic@jmi.org.uk **w** jmi.org.uk MD: Geraldine Auerbach MBE.

JFM Records 11 Alexander House, Tiller Rd, London E14 8PT **t** 020 7987 8596 **f** 020 7987 8596 **e** burdlawrence@btinternet.com MD: Julius Pemberton Maynard.

Jive (see Sony BMG Music Entertainment UK & Ireland)

JML Productions Ltd Redloh House, 2 Michael Rd, London SW6 2AD **t** 020 7736 3377 **f** 020 7731 0567 **e** tash@jjdm.net Contact: Jeremy Marsh, Tash Courage.

JOOF Recordings Unit 5 Waldo Works, Waldo Rd, London NW10 6AW **t** 020 8964 8890 **f** 020 8960 5741 **e** mail@joof.uk.com **w** joof.uk.com A&R: John Fleming.

JPS Recordings PO Box 2643, Reading, Berks RG5 4GF **t** 0118 969 9269 or 07885 058 911 **f** 0118 969 9264 **e** johnjpsuk@aol.com MD: John Saunderson.

JSP Records PO Box 1584, London N3 3NW **t** 020 8346 8663 **f** 020 8346 8848 **e** john@jsprecords.com **w** jpsrecords.com MD: John Stedman.

Jukebox In The Sky (see 3 Beat Label Management)

Jumpin' & Pumpin' (see Passion Music)

Jungle (see Jungle Records)

Jungle Records Old Dairy Mews, 62 Chalk Farm Rd, London NW1 8AN **t** 020 7267 0171 **f** 020 7267 0912 **e** enquiries@jungle-records.com **w** jungle-records.com Dirs: Alan Hauser, Graham Combi.

Jus Listen (see RF Records)

Just Music Hope House, 40 St Peters Rd, London W6 9BD **t** 020 8741 6020 **f** 020 8741 8362 **e** justmusic@justmusic.co.uk **w** justmusic.co.uk Dirs: Serena & John Benedict.

K (see Southern Records)

K-Scope (see Snapper Music)

K-Tel Entertainment (UK) K-tel House, 12 Fairway Drive, Greenford, Middlesex UB6 8PW **t** 020 8747 7550 **f** 020 8575 2264 **e** sales@k-tel.com **w** k-tel.com GM: Janie Webber.

Kabuki 23 Weavers Way, Camden Town, London NW1 0XF **t** 020 7916 2142 **e** email@kabuki.co.uk **w** kabuki.co.uk Mgr: Sheila Naujoks.

Kamaflage Records (see Dragonfly Records)

Kamaric (see Fury Records)

Kamera Shy (see Gotham Records)

Kamikaze (see Superglider Records)

Karon Records 20 Radstone Court, Hillview Rd, Woking, Surrey GU22 7NB **t** 01483 755 153 **e** ron.roker@ntlworld.com MD: Ron Roker.

Keda Records The Sight And Sound Centre, Priory Way, Southall, Middlesex UB2 5EB **t** 020 8843 1546 **f** 020 8574 4243 **e** kuljit@compuserve.com **w** keda.co.uk Owner: Kuljit Bhamra.

Kennel Records Unit One, 25a Blue Anchor Lane, London SE16 3UL **t** 020 7231 1393 **f** 020 7232 1373 **e** info@kennelrecords.com **w** kennelrecords.com Contact: Jo.

KENNINGTON RECORDINGS

44 Norwood Park Road, London SE27 9UA **t** 020 8670 4082 **e** corporatecommunications@kenningtonrecordings.com **w** kenningtonrecordings.com Contact: Mister L, Commissioner Gordon or The Chief.

Kent (see Ace Records)

Keswick (see Loose Records)

Kevin Mayhew (see Priory Records)

Keystone Records Ltd 13 Alliance Court, Aliance Rd, London W3 0RB **t** 020 8993 7441 **f** 020 8992 9993 **e** keystone@dorm.co.uk **w** keystone-records.co.uk GM: John O'Reilly.

Kickin Music Ltd 282 Westbourne Park Rd, London W11 1EH **t** 020 7985 0700 **f** 020 7985 0701 **e** info@kickinmusic.com **w** kickinmusic.com MD: Peter Harris.

Kila Records Charlemont House, 33 Charlemont St, Dublin 2 **t** +353 1 476 0627 **f** +353 1 476 0627 **e** info@kilarecords.com **w** kila.ie Dir: Colm O'Snodaigh.

Kingsize Records The Old Bakehouse, Hale St, Staines, Middx TW18 4UW **t** 01784 458700 **f** 01784 458333 **e** info@kingsize.co.uk **w** kingsize.co.uk Lbl Mgr: Julian Shay.

Kingsway Music 26-28 Lottbridge Drove, Eastbourne, E Sussex BN23 6NT **t** 01323 437700 **f** 01323 411970 **e** music@kingsway.co.uk **w** kingsway.co.uk A&R Mgr: Caroline Bonnett.

Kinkyred (see Zedfunk)

Kismet Records 91 Saffron Hill, London EC1N 8PT **t** 020 7404 3333 **e** info@kismetrecords.com **w** kismetrecords.com Dir: Gilly Da Silva.

Kitchenware Records 7 The Stables, Saint Thomas St, Newcastle upon Tyne, Tyne and Wear NE1 4LE **t** 0191 230 1970 **f** 0191 232 0262 **e** info@kware.demon.co.uk **w** kitchenwarerecords.com Administration: Nicki Turner.

Klone Records (see Rumour Records Ltd)

Klone UK 1 Melville Rd, Sidcup, Kent DA14 4LU **t** 020 8300 7020 **f** 020 8300 7022 **e** info@kloneuk.com **w** kloneuk.com MD: George Kimpton.

Klubbed (see 3 Beat Label Management)

Kom (see Genius Records Ltd)

Kontakt Records (see ATG Records)

Kooba Cuts 6 Westleigh Court, 28 Birdhurst Rd, South Croydon, Surrey CR2 7EA **t** 020 8667 1982 **e** simon@koobarecords.com **w** koobarecords.com Head of A&R: Simon King.

KOROVA

The Warner Building, 28a Kensington Church Street, London W8 4EP **t** 020 7368 2500 **f** 020 7368 2773 **e** firstname.lastname@warnermusic.com **w** korovarecords.com. Label Manager: Johnny Hudson. Product Manager: Lara Marshall. Business Affairs: Jonathan Cross. Financial Planning Manager: Sarah Hammond.

Kranky (see Southern Records)

KRL 9 Watt Rd, Hillington, Glasgow G52 4RY **t** 0141 882 9060 **f** 0141 883 3686 **e** krl@krl.co.uk **w** krl.co.uk MD: Gus McDonald.

Krome Recordings Ltd (London) Sub Base Studios, 107 Holland Rd, London NW10 5AT **t** 020 8961 0427 or 07958 143 966 **f** 020 8961 0427 **e** info@kromerecordings.plus.com **w** kromerecordings.org MD: Andrew Radix.

Krypton Records 31 Fife St, St James, Northampton NN5 5BH **t** 01604 752800 **f** 01604 752800 **e** ray@thejets.co.uk **w** thejets.co.uk Contact: Ray Cotton.

Kudos Records Ltd 77 Fortess Rd, Kentish Town, London NW5 1AG **t** 020 7482 4555 **f** 020 7482 4551 **e** info@kudosrecords.co.uk **w** kudosrecords.co.uk MD: Danny Ryan.

La Cooka Ratcha (see Voiceprint)

Lab Recordings (see 3 Beat Label Management)

Lager Records 10 Barley Rise, Baldock, Herts SG7 6RT **t** 01462 636799 **f** 01462 636799 **e** dan@Lockupmusic.co.uk Dir: Steve Knight.

Lake (see Fellside Recordings Ltd)

Lakeview Records 158 Upland Rd, London SE22 0DQ **t** 020 8693 5991 **f** 020 8693 5991 **e** simon@kickhorns.com **w** kickhorns.com MD: Simon Clarke.

Lakota Records 43 Donnybrook Manor, Donnybrook, Dublin 4, Ireland **t** +353 1 283 9071 **f** +353 1 283 9071 **e** info@lakotarecords.com **w** lakotarecords.com MD: Conor Brooks.

Lammas Records 118 The Mount, York YO24 1AS **t** 01904 624132 **f** 01904 624132 **e** enquiries@lammas.co.uk **w** lammas.co.uk Prop: Lance Andrews.

Landscape Channel Landscape Studios, Crowhurst, E Sussex TN33 9BX **t** 01424 830900 **f** 01424 830680 **e** info@cablenet.net **w** landscapetv.com.

LAS Records UK PO Box 14303, London SE26 4ZH **t** 07000 472572 or 07956 446 342 **f** 07000 472572 or 020 8291 9236 **e** info@latinartsgroup.com **w** latinartsgroup.com Dir: Hector Rosquete.

Laughing Outlaw Records (UK) Cambrian Cottage, 3, Trimpley St, Ellesmere, Shropshire SY12 0AD **t** 07855 724 798 or 01691 622 356 **e** laughingoutlaw@talk21.com **w** laughingoutlaw.com.au Label Mgr: Geraint Jones.

Laughing Stock Productions. 32 Percy St, London W1T 2DE **t** 020 7637 7943 **f** 020 7436 1666 **e** mike@laughingstock.co.uk **w** laughingstock.co.uk Dir: Mike O'Brien.

Lavolta Records Unit F2, Shepherds Building, Rockley Rd, London W14 0DA **t** 020 7371 1311 **f** 020 7371 1312 **e** info@lavoltarecords.com **w** lavoltarecords.com Dirs: Ben Durling & Siona Ryan.

The Leaf Label PO Box 272, Leeds LS19 9BP **t** 0113 216 1021 **f** 0870 912 8322 **e** contact@theleaflabel.com **w** theleaflabel.com MD: Tony Morley.

Leap Masters Ltd 60 Kingly St, London W1B 5DS **t** 020 7453 4011 **f** 020 7453 4242 **e** richard@leapmusic.com **w** leapmusic.com MD: Richard Kirstein.

Leningrad Masters (see Priory Records)

Lewis Recordings PO Box 37163, London E4 7DR **t** 020 8523 9578 **f** 020 8523 9601 **e** info@LewisRecordings.com **w** LewisRecordings.com Dir: Mike Lewis.

Lex (see Warp)

Liberty (see EMI Music UK & Ireland)

LibertyTRAX PO Box 451, Macclesfield, Cheshire SK10 3FR **t** 07921 626 900 **e** darren.eager@libertytrax.co.uk **w** libertytrax.co.uk Contact: Darren Eager.

Lick Records (see Automatic Records)

Lifetime Vision 11 St. James Sq, London SW1Y 4LB **t** 020 7389 0790 **f** 020 7389 0791 **e** lifetimevision@dial.pipex.com MD: Robert Page.

Limbo Records 23rd Precinct Music Ltd., 23 Bath St, Glasgow G2 1HU **t** 0141 332 4806 **f** 0141 353 3039 **e** billy@23rdprecinct.co.uk **w** 23rdprecinct.co.uk MD: Billy Kiltie.

Lindenburg (see Priory Records)

Lineage Recordings P.O. Box 1034, Maidstone, Kent ME15 0WZ **t** 07821 357 713 **e** lineage@toucansurf.com MD: CJ Jammer.

Line-Up PMC 9A Tankerville Pl, Newcastle-upon-Tyne, Tyne and Wear NE2 3AT **t** 0191 281 6449 **f** 0191 212 0913 **e** chrismurtagh@line-up.co.uk **w** line-up.co.uk Owner: Christopher Murtagh.

Linn Records Glasgow Rd, Waterfoot, Eaglesham G76 0EQ **t** 0141 303 5026 **f** 0141 303 5007 **e** info@linnrecords.co.uk **w** linnrecords.com Business Manager: Caroline Dooley.

Liquid Asset Recordings (see Tailormade Music Ltd)

Liquid Sound (see Dragonfly Records)

Lismor Recordings PO Box 7264, Glasgow, Strathclyde G46 6YE **t** 0141 637 6010 **f** 0141 637 6010 **e** lismor@lismor.com **w** allcelticmusic.com MD: Ronnie Simpson.

Little Acorn Records Ltd PO Box 238, Witney, Oxon OX8 6FZ **e** tod@acornrecords.co.uk **w** acornrecords.co.uk.

Little Piece of Jamaica (LPOJ) 55 Finsbury Park Rd, Highbury, London N4 2JY **t** 020 7359 0788 or 07973 630 729 **e** paulhuelpoj@yahoo.co.uk Dir: Paul Hue.

Livewire (see K-Tel Entertainment (UK))

Living Era (see Sanctuary Classics)

Loaded (see Skint Records)

Lock The Coachhouse, Mansion Farm, Liverton Hill, Sandway, Maidstone, Kent ME17 2NJ **t** 01622 858300 **f** 01622 858300 **e** info@eddielock.com **w** eddielock.co.uk A&R Mgr: Eddie Lock.

Locked On Records 679 Holloway Rd, London N19 5SE **t** 020 7263 4660 **f** 020 7263 9669 **e** stevehill@puregroove.co.uk **w** puregroove.co.uk MD: Tarik Nashnush.

Lockjaw Records 1 Oaklands, Cradley, Malvern, Worcs WR13 5LA **t** 01886 880035 **f** 01886 880135 **e** info@lockjawrecords.co.uk **w** lockjawrecords.co.uk Business Affs Mgr: Jack Turner.

LOE Records LOE House, 159 Broadhurst Gardens, London NW6 3AU **t** 020 7328 6100 **f** 020 7624 6384 **e** watanabe@loe.uk.net Creative Mgr: Jonny Wilson.

Lo-Five 22 Herbert St, Glasgow G20 6NB **t** 0141 560 2748 or 0141 337 1199 **f** 0141 357 0655 **e** info@lo-fiverecords.com **w** lo-fiverecords.com Dir: Robin Morton.

London Independent Records Suite F33, Waterfront Studios, 1 Dock Rd, London E16 1AG **t** 020 3203 0003 **e** info@london-independent.co.uk **w** london-independent.co.uk Dir: Jan Hart.

London Records (see Warner Bros Records)

London Records (see WEA London Records).

LongMan (see LongMan Records)

LongMan Records West House, Forthaven, Shoreham-by-Sea, W. Sussex BN43 5HY **t** 01273 453422 **f** 01273 452914 **e** richard@longman-records.com **w** longman-records.com Dir: Richard Durrant.

Longshot 81 Tuam Rd, London SE18 2QY **t** 020 8316 1884 **f** 08701 246920 **e** info@longshotrecords.co.uk **w** longshotrecords.co.uk Contact: Peter Wilkins.

Loog Records 130a Wigmore St, (entrance on Seymour Mews), London W1U 3SB **t** 020 7224 0222 **f** 020 7935 7476 **e** info@loogrecords.co.uk **w** loogrecords.co.uk MD: James Oldham.

Loose PO Box 67, Runcorn, Cheshire WA7 4NL **t** 01928 566 261 **e** jaki.florek@virgin.net Mgr: Jaki Florek.

Loose Music Unit 205, 5-10 Eastman Rd, London W3 7YG **t** 020 8749 9330 **f** 020 8749 2230 **e** info@loosemusic.com **w** loosemusic.com MD/A&R: Tom Bridgewater.

Loose Records Pinery Building, Highmoor, Wigton, Cumbria CA7 9LW **t** 016973 45422 **f** 016973 45422 **e** edwards@looserecords.com **w** looserecords.com A&R: Tim Edwards.

Loose Tie Records 15 Stanhope Rd, London N6 5NE **t** 020 8340 7797 **f** 020 8340 6923 **e** paul@paulrodriguezmus.demon.co.uk MD: Paul Rodriguez.

Loriana Music PO Box 2731, Romford RM7 1AD **t** 01708 750 185 or 07748 343 363 **f** 01708 750 185 **e** info@lorianamusic.com **w** lorianamusic.com Owner: Jean-Louis Fargier.

Lost Highway (see Mercury Music Group)

Love Triangle Music (see 3 Beat Label Management)

Lovechild Records (see Big Cat (UK) Records)

Lovers Leap (see Ariwa Sounds Ltd)

Low Quality Accident 71 Lansdowne Rd, Purley, Surrey CR8 2PD **t** 020 8645 0013 **e** flamingofleece@yahoo.com **w** geocities.com/flamingofleece MD: Alvin LeDup.

Lowered Recordings Ltd The Dairy, Porters End, Kimpton, Hitchin, Herts SG4 8ER **t** 01438 831 065 **f** 01438 833 500 **e** enquiries@loweredrecordings.com **w** loweredrecordings.com MD: Jules Spinner.

LPMusic 14 Bellfield St, Edinburgh EH15 2BP **t** 0131 468 1716 **e** admin@lpmusic.org.uk **w** lpmusic.org.uk MD: Lee Patterson.

Lucky 7's (see Tip World)

Lucky Number PO Box 45080, London N4 4XD **t** 07909 532 723 **e** contact@luckynumbermusic.com **w** luckynumbermusic.com Dirs: Steve Richards, Mike Morley.

Luggage (see Silverword Music Group)

Luminous Records P.O Box 341, Deal, Kent CT14 6AZ **t** 01304 369 053 **e** luminousrecords@hotmail.com **w** luminousrecords.co.uk MD: Howard Werth.

Lunar Records 5-6 Lombard St, East, Dublin 2, Ireland **t** +353 1 677 4229 **f** +353 1 671 0421 **e** lunar@indigo.ie GM: Judy Cardiff.

M60 Recordings 24 Derby St, Edgeley, Stockport, Cheshire SK3 9HF **t** 0161 476 1172 or 07950 119 151 **e** andylacallen@yahoo.co.uk A&R Director: Andy Callen.

Macjaz (see Corban Recordings)

Macmeanmna Gladstone Buildings, Quay Brae, Portree, Isle Of Skye IV51 9DB **t** 01478 612990 **f** 01478 613263 **e** info@gaelicmusic.com **w** gaelicmusic.com Ptnr: Arthur Cormack.

Mad As Toast 3 Broomlands St, Paisley PA1 2LS **t** 07717 437 148 **f** 0141 887 8888 **e** info@madastoast.com **w** madastoast.com Dirs: John Richardson, George Watson.

Madacy Entertainment Group (GB) Ltd 39-41 Chase Side, Southgate, London N14 5BP **t** 020 8242 5570 **f** 020 8242 5571 **e** madacyuk@aol.com **w** madacyuk.com Operations Dir: Karen Moran.

Madam Music Ltd Studio 26, 24-28 St Leonards Rd, Windsor, Berks SL4 3BB **t** 0870 7503755 **f** 0871 9941280 **e** mm@madammusic.com **w** madammusicrecords.com MD: Deborah Collier.

Madfish (see Snapper Music)

Madrigal Records Guy Hall, Awre, Gloucs GL14 1EL
t 01594 510512 **f** 01594 510512 **e** artists@madrigalmusic.co.uk
w madrigalmusic.co.uk MD: Nick Ford.

Maelstrom (see New State Entertainment)

Maestro Records PO Box 2255, Mitcham, Surrey CR4 3BG
t 020 8687 2008 **f** 020 8687 1998
e music@maestrorecords.com **w** maestrorecords.com
MD: Tommy Sanderson.

Magick Eye Records PO Box 3037, Wokingham, Berks
RG40 4GR **t** 0118 932 8320 **f** 0118 932 8237
e info@magickeye.com **w** magickeye.com MD: Chris Hillman.

Magik Muzik UK (see New State Entertainment)

Magnolia Label 2 Townfield Rd, West Kirby, Merseyside
CH48 7EZ **t** 0151 625 6737 or 07760 170 990
e dave@magnoliamam.co.uk **w** magnoliamam.co.uk
MD: Dave Wibberley.

Magnum Music Magnum House, High St, Lane End, Bucks
HP14 3JG **t** 01494 882858 **f** 01494 883792
e synergielogistics@btconnect.com CEO: Nigel Molden.

Main Spring Recordings PO Box 38648, London
W13 9WJ **t** 020 8567 1376 **e** blair@main-spring.com
w main-spring.com MD: Blair McDonald.

Majic Music PO Box 66, Manchester M12 4XJ
t 0161 225 9991 **e** info@majicmusic.co.uk **w** sirenstorm.com
Dir: Mike Coppock.

Make Some Noise Records PO Box 792, Maidstone, Kent
ME14 5LG **t** 01622 691 106 **f** 01622 691 106
e info@makesomenoiserecords.com
w makesomenoiserecords.com Mgr: Clive Austen.

Mango (see Island Records Group)

Manifesto (see Universal Music Dance)

Mantra (see Beggars Banquet Records)

MAP Records 27 Abercorn Pl, London NW8 9DX
t 07905 116 455 **f** 020 7624 7219 **e** info@mapmusic.co.uk
w mapmusic.co.uk Head of A&R: Anthony Pringle.

Marine Parade Records Loft 5, Tobacco Factory, Raleigh
Rd, Bristol BS3 1TF **t** 0117 953 5566 **f** 0117 953 7733
e luke@marineparade.co.uk **w** marineparade.net
Label Manager: Luke Allen.

Market Square Records Market House, Market Sq,
Winslow, Bucks MK18 3AF **t** 01296 715 228 **f** 01296 715 486
e peter@marketsquarerecords.co.uk
w marketsquarerecords.co.uk MD: Peter Muir.

Matador Records Ltd 17-19 Alma Rd, London SW18 1AA
t 020 8870 9912 **f** 020 8871 1766 **e** info@matadoreurope.com
w matadoreurope.com GM: Mike Holdsworth.

Maximum Boost Recordings 1 Andover St, Digbeth,
Birmingham B5 5RG **t** 0121 633 4742 **f** 0121 249 1826
e enquiries@maximum-boost.co.uk **w** maximum-boost.co.uk
Contact: Carole Beirne.

Maximum Minimum (see Truelove Records)

Mazaruni (see Ariwa Sounds Ltd)

MCA (see Island Records Group)

MCI (see Demon Music Group)

MCI - Music Collection International (see Demon
Music Group)

Measured Records Ltd. Studio 19, St. George's Studios,
93-97 St. George's Rd, Glasgow G3 6JA **t** 0141 331 9888
f 0141 331 9889 **e** mr@measuredrecords.com
w measuredrecords.com MD: Dougie Souness.

Media Records Ltd Units 1-2 Pepys Court, 84-86 The
Chase, Clapham Common, London SW4 0NF **t** 020 7720 7266
f 020 7720 7255 **e** info@nukleuz.co.uk **w** nukleuz.com
MD: Peter Pritchard.

Medical Records PO Box 488, Rochdale OL16 9AG
t 07711 040 036 **e** andy@akcreativemanagement.co.uk
w medicalrecords.org.uk Contact: Andy Barrow.

Mega Hit Records (UK) PO Box 56, Boston, Lincs
PE22 8JL **t** 07976 553624
e chrisdunn@megahitrecordsuk.co.uk **w** megahitrecordsuk.co.uk
Contact: Chris Kamara.

Megabop Records 34 Great James St, London WC1N 3HB
t 020 7404 1050 **f** 0870 922 3582 **e** info@megabop.plus.com
w Megabop.com Dir: Paul Ballance.

Mellow Monkey Records 2 Stucley Pl, Camden, London
NW1 8NS **t** 020 7482 6660 **f** 020 7482 6606
e art@mainartery.co.uk MD: Jo Mirowski.

Melodic 4th Floor, 20 Dale St, Manchester M1 1EZ
t 0161 228 3070 **f** 0161 228 3070 **e** david@melodic.co.uk
w melodic.co.uk MD: David Cooper.

Memnon Entertainment (UK) Ltd Habib House, 3rd
Floor, 9 Stevenson Sq, Piccadilly, Manchester M1 1DB
t 0161 238 8516 **f** 0161 236 6717 **e** memnon@btconnect.com
w memnonentertainment.com Dir of Business Affairs: Rudi Kidd.

Memoir Records PO Box 66, Pinner, Middlesex HA5 2SA
t 020 8866 4865 **f** 020 8866 7804
e mor@memoir.demon.co.uk **w** memoir.demon.co.uk
MD: Gordon Gray.

MERCURY MUSIC GROUP

MERCURY **MUSIC** GROUP
364-366 Kensington High Street, London W14 8NS
t 020 7471 5333 **f** 020 7471 5306
e firstname.lastname@umusic.com **w** mercuryrecords.com.
President: Jason Iley. Senior Dir A&R: Paul Adam. Promotions
Dir: Bruno Morelli. Marketing Dir: Charlotte Soussan. Dir of Legal
& Business Affairs: Adam Barker. Dir of Communications: Regine
Moylett. Finance Dir: Kirsty Andrew. Creative Dir: Tom Bird.
Senior National Account Manager: Brian Regan. Hd of Digital:
Luke Bevans. Hd of Press: Rachel Hendry.

Meridian Records PO Box 317, Eltham, London SE9 4SF
t 020 8857 3213 **f** 020 8857 0731
e mail@meridian-records.co.uk **w** meridian-records.co.uk
Dir: Richard Hughes.

Mesmobeat (see Stretchy Records Ltd)

Messy Productions Ltd Studio 2, Soho Recording Studios, 22-24 Torrington Pl, London WC1E 7HJ **t** 020 7813 7202 **f** 020 7419 2333 **e** info@messypro.com **w** messypro.com MD: Zak Vracelli.

Metal Nation 2 Whitehouse Mews, The Green, Wallsend, Tyne & Wear NE28 7EP **f** 0191 263 8382 **e** metalnation1@hotmail.com **w** metalnationrecords.co.uk MD: Jess Cox.

Metier (see Priory Records)

MIA Video Emtertainment Ltd 4th Floor, 72-75 Marylebone High St, London W1U 5JW **t** 020 7935 9225 **f** 020 7935 9565 **e** miavid@aol.com GM: Vanessa Chinn.

Microbe 22 The Nursery, Sutton Courtenay, Oxon OX14 4UA **t** 01235 845800 **f** 01235 847692 **e** john@cyard.com **w** courtyardmusic.net A&R Mgr: John Bennett.

Microphonic Limited Unit G25 Waterfront Studios, 1 Dock Rd, London E16 1AG **t** 020 7474 6696 **e** info@microphonic.biz **w** microphonic.biz Dir: Colin Bird.

Midnight Rock (see Fury Records)

Mighty Atom Records Dylan Thomas House, 32 Alexander Rd, Swansea SA1 5DT **t** 01792 476567 **f** 01792 476564 **e** info@mightyatom.co.uk **w** mightyatom.co.uk MD: Dave Simpson.

Mike Lewis Entertainment Ltd (see Lewis Recordings)

Millbrand Enterprises PO Box 357, Middlesbrough, Cleveland TS1 4WZ **t** 01642 806 795 or 01642 218 057 **f** 01642 800 986 **e** info@millbrand **w** millbrand.com MD: Paul Mooney.

Millennium Records Ltd 6 Water Lane, Camden, London NW1 8NZ **t** 020 7482 0272 **f** 020 7267 4908 **e** ben@millenniumrecords.com **w** millenniumrecords.com MD: Ben Recknagel.

Mimi Entertainment 26-Hammersmith Grove, Hammersmith, London W6 7BA **t** 020 8834 1085 **f** 020 8834 1185 **e** info@mimi-music.com **w** mimi-music.com Label Manager: Nicola S.

Mindlab Recordings PO Box 50045, London SE6 2ZB **t** 07765 440 031 or 020 8695 2682 **f** 020 8695 2682 **e** info@mindlabrecordings.com **w** mindlabrecordings.com Contact: Harry Pitters Jnr.

Ministry Of Sound Recordings 103 Gaunt St, London SE1 6DP **t** 0870 0600 010 **f** 020 7403 5348 **e** initial+lastname@ministryofsound.com **w** ministryofsound.com MD: Lohan Presencer.

Mint (see Jungle Records)

Minta (see Plum Projects)

Mirabeau (see Silverword Music Group)

Miss Moneypenny's Music (see K-Tel Entertainment (UK))

MK Music Ltd PO Box 43312, Highbury, London N5 2XS **t** 07939 080 524 **e** debi@mickkarn.net **w** mickkarn.net Dir: Debi Zornes.

Mob (see New State Entertainment)

Mobb Rule Records PO Box 26335, London N8 9ZA **t** 020 8340 8050 **e** info@mobbrule.com **w** mobbrule.com MDs: Stewart Pettey, Wayne Clements.

Mogul Records 21 Bedford Sq, London WC1B 3HH **t** 020 7637 4444 **f** 020 7323 2857 **e** guy@fspg.co.uk MD: Guy Rippon.

Mohawk Records Unit 3, Westmoreland House, Scrubs Lane, London NW10 6RE **t** 020 8960 4777 **f** 020 8960 7266 **e** info@alpha-magic.com **w** alpha-magic.com Label Mgr: Lee Stacy.

Mohican Records 99 Rochester Ave, Feltham, Middlesex TW13 4EF **t** 020 8751 2244 **e** David.hughes55@btinternet.com **w** mohicanrecords.co.uk MD: David Hughes.

Mohock Records (see Hepcat Records)

Moist Records Ltd PO Box 528, Enfield, Middx EN3 7ZP **t** 070 107 107 24 **f** 0870 137 3787 **e** info@moistrecords.com **w** moistrecords.com MD: Rodney Lewis.

Moksha Recordings Ltd PO Box 102, London E15 2HH **t** 020 8555 5423 **f** 020 8519 6834 **e** info@moksha.co.uk **w** moksha.co.uk MD: Charles Cosh.

Mona Records 144 Warren House, Beckford Close, Warwick Rd, London W14 8TW **t** 020 7348 9161 or 020 7348 9195 **f** 020 7348 9165 **e** info@mona-records.co.uk **w** mona-records.co.uk Label Co-ordinator: Kevin Clark.

Monarch (see KRL)

Mook Records PO Box 155, Leeds, W Yorks LS7 2XN **t** 0113 230 4008 **f** 0113 230 4008 **e** mail@mookhouse.ndo.co.uk **w** mookhouse.ndo.co.uk Label Manager: Phil Mayne.

Moon Records UK PO Box 2061, Ilford, Essex IG1 9GU **t** 020 8551 1011 **f** 020 8553 4954 **e** moonrecordsuk@aol.com **w** moonrecords.co.uk MD: Howard Berlin.

Mooncrest Records (see Sanctuary Records Group)

Moor Records Ltd Suite 52, Chancel House, Neasden Lane, London NW10 2TU **t** 020 8214 1430 **f** 020 8214 1431 **e** moorinfo@moor-records.com **w** moor-records.com A&R Director: Fresh de Moor.

Moshi Moshi Premises Studios, 201-205 Hackney Rd, London E2 8JL **e** hello@moshimoshimusic.com **w** moshimoshimusic.com GM: Michael McClatchey.

Mosquito Media 64a Warwick Ave, Little Venice, London W9 2PU **t** 07813 174 185 **e** mosquitomedia@aol.com **w** mosquito-media.co.uk Contact: Richard Abbott.

Motown (see Island Records Group)

Mottete Ursina (see Priory Records)

Move (see Divine Art Record Company)

Moving Shadow Ltd PO Box 2251, London SE1 2FH **t** 020 7252 2661 **f** 0870 0512594 **e** info2004@movingshadow.com **w** movingshadow.com MD: Rob Playford.

Mo'Wax Labels Ltd 1 Codrington Mews, London W11 2EH
t 020 8870 7511 **f** 020 8871 4178 **e** mowax@almaroad.co.uk
w mowax.com Label Head: Toby Feltwell.

MP2 (see Multiply Records)

MPRecords 124 Sunny Bank, Spring Bank West, Hull
HU3 1LE **t** 01482 343352 **f** 01482 343038
e rod@backtobase.demon.co.uk **w** backtobase.co.uk
MD: Barbara Ray.

Mr Bongo 2nd Floor, 24 Old Steine, Brighton BN1 1EL
t 01273 600 546 **f** 01273 600 578 **e** info@mrbongo.com
w mrbongo.com MD: Dave Buttle.

MRR 11 Gt George St, Bristol BS1 5RR **t** 0117 929 2393
f 0117 929 2696 **e** craigg.williams@virgin.net
Label Manager: Craig Williams.

Multi Vision (see Headzone Ltd)

Multiply (see Multiply Records)

Multiply Records 107 Mortlake High St, London SW14 8HQ
t 020 8878 7888 **e** info@multiply.co.uk **w** multiply.co.uk
MD: Mike Hall.

Multisonic (see Priory Records)

Mushroom (see Atlantic Records UK)

Music At Monumental Unit B44A, Eurolink Business
Centre, Effra Rd, London SW2 1BZ **t** 020 7871 2803
e info@monumentalmanagement.co.uk
w MusicAtMonumental.co.uk MD: Brett Leboff.

Music Factory Mastermix Hawthorne House, Fitzwilliam
St, Parkgate, Rotherham, South Yorks S62 6EP **t** 01709 710022
f 01709 523141 **e** info@mastermixdj.com **w** mastermixdj.com
MD: Rob Moore.

Music For Dreams (see Reverb Records Ltd)

Music For Pleasure (MFP) (see EMI Catalogue/EMI
Gold/EMI Liberty)

Music From Another Room Ltd The Penthouse, 20
Bulstrode St, London W1U 2JW **t** 020 7224 4442
f 020 7224 7226 **e** patrick@julianlennon.com
w julianlennon.com Mgr: Patrick Cousins.

Music Fusion Ltd Shepperton Studios, Studio Rd,
Shepperton, Middx TW17 0QD **t** 01932 592016
f 01932 592046 **e** ben.williams@classicpictures.co.uk
w rwcc.com Mktg Mgr: Ben Williams.

Music Mercia (see Fortune and Glory)

Music Of Life Records Unit 9B, Wingbury Business Village,
Upper Wingbury Farm, Wingrave, Bucks HP22 4LW
t 07770 364 268 **e** chris@musicoflife.com **w** musicoflife.com
MD: Chris France.

Music With Attitude (MWA) 20 Middle Row, Ladbroke
Grove, London W10 5AT **t** 020 8964 4555 **f** 020 8964 4666
e morgan@musicwithattitude.com **w** musicwithattitude.com
MD: Morgan Khan.

Musketeer Records 56 Castle Bank, Stafford, Staffs
ST16 1DW **t** 01785 258746 **f** 01785 255367
e p.halliwell@tesco.net MD: Paul Halliwell.

Must Destroy Music 7 Jeffreys Pl, London NW1 9PP
e tremendousmike@mustdestroymusic.com
w mustdestroymusic.com Contact: Tremendous Mike.

Mutant Disc 36 Brunswick St West, Hove, E Sussex BN3 1EL
t 07979 757 033 **f** 01273 325 935 **e** info@phatsandsmall.com
Label Mgrs: Russell Small, Jason Hayward.

Mute Records Ltd 429 Harrow Rd, London W10 4RE
t 020 8964 2001 **f** 020 8968 4977 **e** info@mutehq.co.uk
w mute.com Chairman: Daniel Miller.

MVM Records 35 Alma Rd, Reigate, Surrey RH2 0DN
t 01737 224151 **f** 01737 241481 MD: Maryetta Midgley.

My Dad Recordings 39 Barnfield Rd, Hyde, Cheshire
SK14 4EL **t** 07967 732 616 **e** label@mydadrecordings.com
w mydadrecordings.com MD: Paul Vella.

My Kung Fu The Coal Exchange, Mount Stuart Sq, Cardiff
Bay, Cardiff CF10 5ED **t** 029 2019 0153
e carl@my-kung-fu.com **w** my-kung-fu.com
Label Mgr: Carl Morris.

N2 Records (see Evolve Records)

Nachural Records PO Box 2656, Smethwick, Warley, W
Midlands B66 4JF **t** 0121 505 6500 **f** 0121 505 6515
e info@nachural.co.uk **w** nachural.co.uk MD: Ninder Johal.

Nagashi 98A Penwith Rd, London SW18 4QE
t 020 8870 5727 **f** 0208 870 5727 **e** boomtang@msn.com
w antiatlas.co.uk Label Manager: Geoff Kite.

Nascente (see Demon Music Group)

Nasha Records PO Box 42545, London E1 6WZ
t 07904 145 743 **f** 020 7709 0097 **e** music@nasha.co.uk
w nasha.co.uk Label Manager: Sobur Ahmed.

Nation Records Ltd 19 All Saints Rd, Notting Hill, London
W11 1HE **t** 020 7792 8167 **f** 020 7792 2854
e info@nationrecords.co.uk **w** nationrecords.co.uk
MD: Aki Nawaz.

Natural Grooves 3 Tannsfeld Rd, Sydenham, London
SE26 5DQ **t** 020 8488 3677 **f** 020 8473 6539
e jon@naturalgrooves.co.uk **w** naturalgrooves.co.uk
MD: Jonathan Sharif.

Naxos (see Naxos AudioBooks)

Naxos AudioBooks 40a High St, Wellwyn, Herts AL6 9EQ
t 01438 717 808 **f** 01438 717 809
e naxos_audiobooks@compuserve.com **w** naxosaudiobooks.com
MD: Nicholas Soames.

Ncompass Suite 1, 92 King George Rd, Ware, Herts SG12 7DT
t 01920 461 000 **e** silverscope@btconnect.com
MD: Richard Rogers.

Neat Records 71 High Street East, Wallsend, Tyne and Wear
NE28 7RJ **t** 0191 262 4999 **f** 0191 263 7082
e offices@neatrecords.freeserve.co.uk **w** neatrecords.com
MD: Jess Cox.

Nebula Music (see New State Entertainment)

Nemesis Records Nemesis House, 1 Oxford Court,
Bishopsgate, Manchester M2 3WQ **t** 0161 228 6465
e nigel@nmsmanagement.co.uk MD: Nigel Martin-Smith.

Neon Records Studio Two, 19 Marine Crescent, Kinning Pk, Glasgow G51 1HD **t** 0141 429 6366 **f** 0141 429 6377 **e** mail@go2neon.com **w** go2neon.com Contact: Robert Noakes.

Nero Schwarz (see East Central One Ltd)

Nettwerk Productions UK Clearwater Yard, 35 Inverness St, London NW1 7HB **t** 020 7424 7500 **f** 020 7424 7501 **e** eleanor@nettwerk.com **w** nettwerk.com Dir: Gary Levermore.

Neuropa 60 Baronald Drive, Glasgow G12 0HW **t** 0141 339 9894 **e** neuropa@talk21.com Administrator: Alexander Macpherson.

New Age Music Ltd 17 Priory Rd, London NW6 4NN **t** 020 7209 2766 **f** 020 7813 2766 **e** gerrybron@bronzerecords.co.uk **w** bronzerecords.co.uk MD: Gerry Bron.

New Christian Music (NCM Records) (see New Music Records)

New Dawn Records Box 1-2, 191 Greenhead St, Glasgow G40 1HX **t** 0141 554 6475 **f** 0141 554 6475 **e** newdawnrecords@talk21.com **w** belles.demon.co.uk Contact: Admin Dept.

A New Day Records 75 Wren Way, Farnborough, Hants GU14 8TA **t** 01252 540270 or 07889 797482 **f** 01252 372001 **e** DAVIDREES1@compuserve.com **w** anewdayrecords.co.uk MD: Dave Rees.

New Leaf Records 9 Church Rd, Conington, Peterborough, Cambs PE7 3QJ **t** 01487 830778 **e** indie500@madasafish.com **w** indie500.co.uk Prop: Andrew Clifton.

New Music Records Meredale, The Dell, Reach Lane, Heath and Reach, Leighton Buzzard, Beds LU7 0AL **t** 01525 237700 **f** 01525 237700 **e** enq@newmusicenterprises.com **w** newmusicenterprises.com Prop: Paul Davis.

New Religion 740 Alaska Buildings, Grange Rd, London SE1 3BD **t** 020 7237 9985 **e** sarah@newreligionmusic.com Label Manager: Sarah Pearson.

New State Entertainment Unit 2A Queens Studios, 121 Salusbury Rd, London NW6 6RG **t** 020 7372 4474 **f** 020 7372 4484 or 020 7328 4447 **e** info@newstate.co.uk **w** newstate.co.uk MD: Tom Parkinson.

New World Music Harmony House, Hillside Road East, Bungay, Suffolk NR35 1RX **t** 01986 891600 **f** 01986 891601 **e** info@newworldmusic.co.uk **w** newworldmusic.com MD: Jeff Stewart.

NGM Records North Glasgow College, 110 Flemington St, Glasgow G21 4BX **t** 0141 558 6440 or 0141 558 9001 x 249 **f** 0141 558 9905 **e** hbrankin@north-gla.ac.uk **w** north-gla.ac.uk Senior Lecturer Music: Hugh Brankin.

Nice 'N' Ripe Records FX Promotions, Unit 30, Grenville Workshops, 502 Hornsey Rd, London N19 4EF **t** 020 7281 8363 **f** 020 7281 7663 **e** nicenripe@fxpromotions.demon.co.uk **w** fxpromotions.demon.co.uk/nicenripe MD: George Power.

NiceTunes 111 Holden Rd, London N12 7DF **t** 020 8445 8766 **e** Luke@ntunes.co.uk **w** ntunes.co.uk A&R Dir: Luke Simons.

Night & Day (see BMR Entertainment Ltd)

Nightbreed Recordings PO Box 6242, Nottingham NG1 5HY **t** 01623 401207 **f** 01623 401207 **e** trev@nightbreedmusic.co.uk **w** nightbreedmusic.co.uk Label Mgr: Trev.

Nikt Records Cadillac Ranch, Pencraig Uchaf, Cwm Bach, Whitland, Dyfed SA34 0DT **t** 01994 484294 **f** 01994 484294 **e** cadillacranch@telco4u.net **w** nikturner.com Dir: Nik Turner.

Wyastone Estate Limited t/a Nimbus Records Wyastone Leys, Monmouth, Monmouthshire NP25 3SR **t** 01600 890 007 **f** 01600 891 052 **e** antony@wyastone.co.uk **w** wyastone.co.uk Dir: Antony Smith.

1967 28 Kensington Church St, London W8 4EP **t** 020 7368 2500 **f** 020 7368 2788 **e** firstname.lastname@warnermusic.com MD: Christian Tattersfield.

Ninja Tune PO Box 4296, London SE11 4WW **t** 020 7820 3535 **f** 020 7820 3434 **e** ninja@ninjatune.net **w** ninjatune.net MD: Peter Quicke.

NMC Recordings 18-20 Southwark St, London SE1 1TJ **t** 020 7403 9445 **f** 020 7403 9446 **e** nmc@nmcrec.co.uk **w** nmcrec.co.uk Label Mgr: Hannah Vlcek.

No Dancing Records PO Box 125, Belfast BT7 3WE **t** 07887 915 112 **e** info@nodancing.co.uk **w** nodancing.co.uk Label Manager: Jimmy Devlin.

Nocturnal Groove 45A Warwick Ave, London W9 2PR **t** 020 7266 1382 **f** 020 7266 1382 **e** info@nocturnalgroove.co.uk **w** nocturnalgroove.co.uk Label Manager: Lola Marlin.

Nocturnal Recordings 103 Rossetti Pl, 2 Lower Byrom St, Manchester M3 4AN **t** 07790 909 896 **e** jmw@bulldoghome.com Director/A&R: Jonathan M Waller.

Noise Music (see Innerground Records)

Nomadic Music Unit 18, Farm Lane Trading Estate, 101 Farm Lane, London SW6 1QJ **t** 020 7386 6800 or 07779 257 577 **f** 020 7386 2401 **e** info@nomadicmusic.net **w** nomadicmusic.net Label Head: Paul Flanagan.

NONESUCH RECORDS UK

NONESUCH

12 Lancer Square, London W8 4EH **t** 020 7368 3536 **f** 020 7368 3761 **e** firstname.lastname@warnermusic.com **w** nonesuch-uk.com Label & Publicity Manager: Matthew Rankin. Marketing & Publicity Officer: Katie Havelock.

North South (see Abstract Sounds)

Nova Mute (see Mute Records Ltd)

Now And Then Productions 208 Wigan Rd, Ashton In Makerfield, Wigan, Lancs WN4 9SX **t** 01942 513298 **e** info@nowandthen.co.uk **w** nowandthen.co.uk Label Mgr: Mark Ashton.

NoWHere Records 30 Tweedholm Ave East, Walkerburn, Peeblesshire EH43 6AR **t** 01896 870 284 or 07812 818 183 **e** michaelwild@btopenworld.com MD: Michael Wild.

NRK Sound Division Ltd Unit 5.3 Paintworks, Bath Rd, Bristol BS4 3EH **t** 0117 300 5497 **f** 0117 300 5498 **e** info@nrkmusic.com **w** nrkmusic.com Dir: Nick Harris.

NSMA Records PO Box 5413, Bournemouth BH1 4UJ **t** 0870 040 6767 **e** info@nsma.com **w** nsma.com MD: Chris Jenkins.

Ntone (see Ninja Tune)

Nu Directions PO Box 1668, Wolverhampton, W Midlands WV3 0AE **t** 01902 423 627 **f** 01902 423 627 **e** info@nudirections.net **w** nudirections.net Label Mgr: Neil Hutchinson.

nu-republic (see 3 Beat Label Management)

Nucool Records 34 Beaumont Rd, London W4 5AP **t** 020 8248 2157 **e** smiles@richardniles.demon.co.uk **w** richardniles.com Dir: Richard Niles.

Nude Records 120 -124 Curtain Rd, London EC2A 3SQ **t** 020 7426 5151/3 **f** 020 7426 5102 **e** info@nuderecords.com **w** nuderecords.com MD: Saul Galpern, Ben James.

Nukleuz (see Media Records Ltd)

NuLife (see Sony BMG Music Entertainment UK & Ireland)

Numa Records 86 Staines Rd, Wraybury, Middlesex TW19 5AA **t** 01784 483589 **f** 01784 483211 **e** tonywebb@numan.co.uk **w** numan.co.uk/ MD: Tony Webb.

Numinous Music Group Figment House, Church St, Ware, Herts SG12 9EN **t** 01273 680799 **f** 01920 463883 **e** jhbee@numinous.biz **w** numinous.biz Dir. A&R/Marketing/Promo: John Bee.

Nut Records 17 Barons Court Rd, West Kensington, London W14 9DP **t** 020 7384 5961 **e** info@nutrecords.com **w** nutrecords.com Label Manager: James Merritt.

NYJO Records 11 Victor Rd, Harrow, Middlesex HA2 6PT **t** 020 8863 2717 **f** 020 8863 8685 **e** bill.ashton@virgin.net **w** NYJO.org.uk Dir: Bill Ashton.

Oblong Records (see Plank Records)

Obsessive (see Sony BMG Music Entertainment UK & Ireland)

Ochre Records PO Box 155, Cheltenham, Glos. GL51 0YS **t** 01242 514332 **f** 01242 514332 **e** ochre@talbot.force9.co.uk **w** ochre.co.uk Prop: Talbot.

Odyssey Video Regal Chambers, 51 Bancroft, Hitchin, Herts SG5 1LL **t** 01462 421818 **f** 01462 420393 **e** adrian_munsey@msn.com MD: Adrian Munsey.

Offbeat Scotland 107 High St, Royal Mile, Edinburgh EH1 1SW **t** 0131 556 4882 **f** 0131 558 7019 **e** iain@offbeat.co.uk **w** offbeat.co.uk MD: Iain McKinna.

OffDaWallMusic 4 Cliveden Close, Ferndown, Dorset BH22 9UL **t** 01202 873708 or 07776 258802 **e** info@offdawallmusic.com **w** offdawallmusic.com Co-MD: James Crompton.

Offslip Productions 3 Lion Court, Studio Way, Borehamwood WD6 5NJ **t** 07789 955 059 **e** danfeel@offslip.com **w** offslip.com Dir: Daniel Roberts.

Ohmy Recordings PO Box 52284, London SW16 5XR **t** 07005 98 18 38 **e** info@ohmyrecordings.com **w** ohmyrecordings.com Dirs: Sophie McAdam, Elliott J Brown.

Olympia (see Priory Records)

On-Line-Records (see Line-Up PMC)

One Little Indian Records 34 Trinity Crescent, London SW17 7AE **t** 020 8772 7600 **f** 020 8772 7601 **e** info@indian.co.uk **w** indian.co.uk GM: Paul Johannes.

One Step Music Ltd Independent House, 54 Larkshall Rd, London E4 6PD **t** 020 8523 9000 **f** 020 8523 8888 **e** erich@independentmusicgroup.com **w** independentmusicgroup.com CEO: Ellis Rich.

One Trak Records 67-69 Chalton St, London NW1 1HY **t** 020 7554 2100 **f** 020 7554 2154 **e** Paul@biglifemanagement.com MD: Paul Kennedy.

Opal (see Pavilion Records Ltd)

Opera Rara 134-146 Curtain Rd, London EC2A 3AR **t** 020 7613 2858 **f** 020 7613 2261 **e** info@opera-rara.com **w** opera-rara.com MD: Stephen Revell.

Ophidian (see Rotator Records)

Optimum (see Silverword Music Group)

Or (see Touch)

Orbison Records Covetous Corner, Hudnall Common, Little Gaddesden, Herts HP4 1QW **t** 01442 842039 **f** 01442 842082 **e** mhaynes@orbison.com **w** orbison.com European Consultant: Mandy Haynes.

Orbit (see Collecting Records LLP)

Orbit (see Everest Copyrights)

Ore (see Beggars Banquet Records)

Org Records Suite 212, The Old Gramophone Works, 326 Kensal Rd, London W10 5BZ **t** 020 8964 3066 **e** organ@organart.demon.co.uk **w** organart.com MD: Sean Worrall.

Organ Grinder Records 29 Chelsea Crescent, Chelsea Harbour, London SW10 0XB **t** 020 7351 9385 **f** 020 7351 9385 **e** info@organgrinderrecords.com **w** organgrinderrecords.com Dir: James Lesslie.

Orgy Records PO Box 8245, Sawbridgeworth, Herts CM21 9WU **t** 01279 600081 **e** info@orgyrecords.com **w** orgyrecords.com Contact: Nic Ward.

Oriental Star Agency 548-550 Moseley Rd, Birmingham, W Midlands B12 9AD **t** 0121 449 6437 **f** 0121 449 5404 **e** info@osa.co.uk **w** osa.co.uk Dir: Mohammed Farooq.

Osceola Records PO Box 38805, London W12 7XL **t** 020 8740 8898 **e** info@osceolarecords.com **w** osceolarecords.com Prop: Jimmy Thomas.

Ottavo (see Priory Records)

Outafocus Recordings 146 Bethnal Green Rd, London E2 6DG **t** 020 7613 1100 **e** info@outafocus.co.uk **w** outafocus.co.uk Label Manager: Danny Corr.

Outback Productions PO Box 381, Great Missenden, Bucks HP16 9BE **t** 01494 890086 **f** 0870 054 8130 **e** nigelrush@appletreesongs.com Dir: Nigel Rush.

Outcaste Records Limited 43 Brook Green, London W6 7EF **t** 020 7605 5808 **f** 020 7605 5188 **e** firstname@mvillage.co.uk **w** outcaste.com Co-MDs: Paul Franklyn and Shabs Jobanputra.

Outdigo Records (see Shifty Disco Ltd)

Outer Recordings PO Box 18888, London SW7 4FQ **t** 020 7373 1614 **f** 020 7373 8376 **e** danny@outer-recordings.co.uk **w** outer-recordings.co.uk Label Mgr: Danny Jones.

Outerglobe Records 113 Cheesemans Terrace, London W14 9XH **t** 020 7385 5447 **f** 020 7385 5447 **e** debbie@outerglobe.com **w** outerglobe.com MD: Debbie Golt.

Outstanding Records 7 Pelham Crescent, Hastings, E Sussex TN34 3AF **t** 020 7871 4564 **e** outstanding.records@ntlworld.com **w** outstandingrecords.com A&R Co-ordinator: Mark Randall.

Oval Records 326 Brixton Rd, London SW9 7AA **t** 020 7622 0111 **e** charlie@ovalmusic.co.uk **w** ovalmusic.co.uk Dir: Charlie Gillett.

Ovation Recordings (see Adasam Limited)

OVC Ltd 88 Berkeley Court, Baker St, London NW1 5ND **t** 020 7402 9111 **f** 020 7723 3064 **e** Joanne.ovc@virgin.net MD: Joanne Cohen.

Overground Records PO Box 1NW, Newcastle-upon-Tyne NE99 1NW **t** 0191 266 3802 **f** 0191 266 6073 **e** john@overgroundrecords.co.uk **w** overgroundrecords.co.uk MD: John Esplen.

Owl Records International Limited 1 Stanaway Drive, Crumlin, Dublin 12, Ireland **t** 00 353 1 455 7750 **f** 00 353 1 455 7782 **e** owl@eircom.net **w** owlrecords.com MD: Reg Keating.

Oyster Music Limited Oakwood Manor, Oakwood Hill, Ockley, Surrey RH5 5PU **t** 01306 627277 **f** 01306 627277 **e** info@oystermusic.com **w** oystermusic.com Dirs: Chris Cooke, Adrian Fitt.

P3 Music Ltd 4 St Andrew St, Alyth, Perthshire PH11 8AT **t** 01828 633790 **f** 01828 633798 **e** records@p3music.com **w** p3music.com Dir: Alison Burns.

Pablo (see Ace Records)

Pagan (see Ark 21)

Palm Pictures 8 Kensington Park Rd, Notting Hill Gate, London W11 3BU **t** 020 7229 3000 **f** 020 7229 0897 **e** firstname@palmpictures.co.uk **w** palmpictures.com MD: Andy Childs.

Panton (see Prestige Elite Records Ltd)

Parachute Music (see Creative World)

Park Lane (see The Hit Music Company)

Park Records PO Box 651, Oxford, Oxon OX2 9RB **t** 01865 241717 **f** 01865 204556 **e** info@parkrecords.com **w** parkrecords.com MD: John Dagnell.

PARLOPHONE

 **Parlophone**

EMI House, 43 Brook Green, London W6 7EF **t** 020 7605 5000 **f** 020 7605 5050 **e** firstname.lastname@emimusic.com **w** parlophone.co.uk. MD: Miles Leonard. Head of A&R: Nigel Coxon. Marketing Dir: Mandy Plumb. Director of Promotions: Steve Hayes. Business Affairs Director: James Mullan. Director of Press: Murray Chalmers.

Parlophone Rhythm Series (see Parlophone)

Partisan Recordings c/o Mute Song, 429 Harrow Rd, London W19 4RE **t** 020 8964 2001 **f** 020 8968 8437 **e** mamapimp@btopenworld.com **w** emusic.com MD: Caroline Butler.

Pasadena Records Priors Hall, Tye Green, Elsenham, Bishop Stortford, Herts CM22 6DY **t** 01279 813 240 or 01279 815 593 **f** 01279 815 895 **e** procentral@aol.com **w** pasadena.co.uk Dir: David Curtis.

Passion Music 20 Blyth Rd, Hayes, Middlesex UB3 1BY **t** 020 8848 8767 **f** 020 8848 8768 **e** les@passionmusic.co.uk **w** passionmusic.co.uk MD: Les McCutcheon.

Past & Present Records 11 Hatherley Mews, Walthamstow, London E17 4QP **t** 020 8521 2211 **f** 020 8521 6911 **e** spencer@megaworld.co.uk **w** megaworld.com Label Mgr: Spencer Kelly.

Past Perfect Lower Farm Barns, Bainton Rd, Bucknell, Oxon OX27 7LT **t** 01869 325052 **f** 01869 325072 **e** info@pastperfect.com **w** pastperfect.com Sales & Marketing Mgr: Jonothan Draper.

Pavilion Records Ltd Sparrows Green, Wadhurst, E Sussex TN5 6SJ **t** 01892 783591 **f** 01892 784156 **e** pearl@pavilionrecords.com **w** pavilionrecords.com MD: John Waite.

Peacefrog Records PO Box 38171, London W10 5WU **t** 020 7575 3045 **f** 020 7575 3047 **e** info@peacefrog.com **w** peacefrog.com Label Manager: Phil Vernol.

Peaceville (see Snapper Music)

Peaceville Records PO Box 101, Cleckheaton, West Yorks BD19 4YF **t** 01274 878101 **f** 01274 874313 **e** hammy@peaceville.com **w** peaceville.com A&R Director: Hammy Halmshaw.

Pearl (see Pavilion Records Ltd)

Penguin Music Classics (see Decca UK)

People Music Adela Street Studio, The Saga Centre, 326 Kensal Rd, London W10 5BZ **t** 020 8968 9666 **f** 020 8969 9558 **e** info@goyamusic.com **w** goyamusic.com Dir: Mike Slocombe.

Personal Records (see Baria Records)

Pet Sounds PO Box 158, Twickenham, Middlesex TW2 6RW **t** 07976 577 773 **f** 0871 733 3401 **e** robinhill@soundpets.freeserve.co.uk Dir: Robin Hill.

PHAB Records High Notes, Sheerwater Ave, Woodham, Weybridge, Surrey KT15 3DS **t** 019323 48174 **f** 019323 40921 MD: Philip HA Bailey.

Phantasm Records Unit B140-141, Riverside Business Centre, Bendon Valley, London SW18 4UQ **t** 020 8870 4484 **f** 020 8870 4483 **e** john@phantasm-uk.demon.co.uk **w** phantasm-uk.demon.co.uk MD: John Ford.

Philips (see Universal Music Classics & Jazz (UK))

Philips Classics (see Universal Music Classics & Jazz (UK))

Phonetic Recordings PO Box 172, Hampton, Middx TW12 1BT **t** 020 8255 3158 or 07989 564 293 **e** phonetic@blueyonder.co.uk Head of A&R: Rob Roar.

PHONOGENIC

Bedford House, 69-79 Fulham High Street, London SW6 3JW **t** 020 7384 7500 **f** 020 7371 9298 **e** firstname.lastname@sonybmg.com **w** phonogenic.net Directors: Paul Lisberg, Tops Henderson.

Piano (see Voiceprint)

PIAS Wall of Sound Recordings Ltd 338A Ladbroke Grove, London W10 5AH **t** 020 8324 2500 **f** 020 8324 0010 **e** info@piasrecordings.com **w** pias.com/uk MD: Mark Jones.

Pickled Egg Records PO Box 6944, Leicester LE2 0WL **e** info@pickled-egg.co.uk **w** pickled-egg.co.uk Owner: Nigel Turner.

Pickwick Group Ltd 230 Centennial Pk, Elstree Hill South, Elstree, Borehamwood, Herts WD6 3SN **t** 020 8236 2310 **f** 020 8236 2312 **e** info@pickwickgroup.com **w** pickwickgroup.com GM: Mark Lawton.

Picnic 22 Herbert St, Glasgow G20 6NB **t** 0141 560 2748 or 0141 337 1199 **f** 0141 357 0655 **e** info@picnicrecords.com **w** picnicrecords.com Dir: Robin Morton.

Picture Music International 30 Gloucester Pl, London W1H 4AJ **t** 020 7467 2000 **f** 020 7224 5927 Director of Sales: Dawn Stevenson.

Pier (see Wooden Hill Recordings Ltd)

Pilgrim's Star (see Divine Art Record Company)

Pinball Records (see Amazon Records Ltd)

Pinkpenny Records PO Box 244, Newton Abbot, Devon TQ12 1TH **t** 01626 201 818 or 07977 268 306 **e** sales@pinkpennyrecords.com **w** pinkpennyrecords.com A&R: Matt Vinyl.

Piranha (see Star-Write Ltd)

Planet Records 2nd Floor, 11 Newmarket St, Colne, Lancs BB8 9BJ **t** 01282 866 317 **f** 01282 866 317 **e** info@pendlehawkmusic.co.uk **w** pendlehawkmusic.co.uk MD: Adrian Melling.

Planet1 Music PO Box 44377, London SW19 1WB **t** 01227 733 701 **f** 01227 733 701 **e** info@planet1music.com **w** planet1music.com MD: John Pepper, Sarah H.C.

Plank Records 9 Shaftesbury Centre, 85 Barlby Rd, London W10 6BN **t** 020 8962 6244 **e** bushwacka@plank.co.uk **w** plank.co.uk Lbl Mgr: Matthew Bushwacka.

Plankton Records PO Box 13533, London E7 0SG **t** 020 8534 8500 **e** plankton.records@virgin.net Ptnr: Keith Dixon.

Plastic Head Records Ltd Avtech House, Hithercroft Rd, Wallingford, Oxon OX10 9DA **t** 01491 825029 **f** 01491 826320 **e** tom@plastichead.com **w** plastichead.com Dir: Tom Doherty.

Platipus Records Unit 206, Old Gramophone Works, 326 Kensal Rd, London W10 5BZ **t** 020 8969 9009 **f** 020 8969 8044 **e** geremy@platipus.com **w** platipus.com Lbl Mgr: Geremy O'Mahony.

Playaville Records Imperial House, 64 Willoughby Lane, London N17 0SP **t** 0870 766 8303 **f** 0870 766 9851 **e** info@playaville.com **w** playaville.com Contact: Stevie Nash.

Player Records Regents Park House, Regent St, Leeds LS2 7QJ **t** 0113 223 7665 **f** 0113 223 7514 **e** info@playerrecords.com **w** playerrecords.com Label Manager: Sarah Flay.

PlayLouder Recordings 8-10 Rhoda St, London E2 7EF **t** 020 7729 4797 **f** 020 7739 8571 **e** paul.hitchman@playlouder.com MDs: Paul Hitchman & Jim Gottlieb.

Plaza Records PO Box 726, London NW11 7XQ **t** 020 8458 6200 **f** 020 8458 6200 **e** roberto@plazarecords.co.uk **w** plazarecords.co.uk MD: Roberto Danova.

Pleasuredome PO Box 425, London SW6 3TX **f** 020 7736 9212 **e** getdown@thepleasuredome.demon.co.uk **w** pleasuredome.co.uk Chairman: Holly Johnson.

Plum Projects 8 Perseverance Pl, Richmond, Surrey TW9 2PN **t** 020 8288 0531 **f** 020 8288 0531 **e** info@plumprojects.com **w** plumprojects.com.

Point Classics (see Priory Records)

Point4 Records Unit 16 Talina Centre,, Bagleys Lane, London SW6 2BW **e** info@point4music.com **w** point4music.com Dirs: Paul Newton, Peter Day.

Pollytone (see Pollytone Records)

Pollytone Records PO Box 124, Ruislip, Middx HA4 9BB **t** 01895 638584 **f** 01895 624793 **e** val@pollyton.demon.co.uk **w** pollytone.com MD: Val Bird.

Polo Records (see Champion Records Ltd)

POLYDOR RECORDS

364-366 Kensington High Street, London W14 8NS
t 020 7471 5400 **f** 020 7471 5401
e firstname.lastname@umusic.com **w** polydor.co.uk. Joint Presidents: David Joseph & Colin Barlow. Senior Dir, Legal & Business Affairs: James Radice. GM, Marketing: Karen Simmonds. Senior Finance Dir: Geoff Harris. Dir of Marketing, PUK: Joe Munns. Dir of Marketing, PUK: Orla Lee. Dir of Press & Communications: Selina Webb. Dir of Promotions: Neil Hughes. Dir of International: Greg Sambrook. GM, Fascination: Peter Loraine. Head of Fiction: Jim Chancellor. Head of A&M: Simon Gavin. Head of Press: Sundraj Sreenivasan.

Polyphonic Reproductions Ltd PO Box 19292, London NW10 9WP **t** 020 8459 6194 **f** 020 8451 6470 **e** sales@studio-music.co.uk MD: Stan Kitchen.

Poptones 2 Berkley Grove, London NW1 8XY **t** 020 7483 2541 **f** 020 7722 8412 **e** info@creationmngt.com **w** poptones.co.uk Label Mgr: Gideon Mountford.

Positiva EMI House, 43 Brook Green, London W6 7EF **t** 020 7605 5000 **f** 020 7605 5050 **e** firstname.lastname@emimusic.com **w** positivarecords.com Dir: Jason Ellis.

Positive Records (see Evolve Records)

Possessed Records Ltd PO Box 35064, London NW1Y 9YX **t** 07890 877 913 **e** info@possessedrecords.com **w** possessedrecords.com Contact: Abigail Hopkins.

Power Records 29 Riversdale Rd, Thames Ditton, Surrey KT7 0QN **t** 020 8398 5236 **f** 020 8398 7901 MD: Barry Evans.

President Records Ltd Units 6 & 7, 11 Wyfold Rd, Fulham, London SW6 6SE **t** 020 7385 7700 **f** 020 7385 3402 **e** hits@president-records.co.uk **w** president-records.co.uk MD: David Kassner.

Prestige (see Ace Records)

Prestige Elite Records Ltd 34 Great James St, London WC1N 3HB **t** 020 7405 3786 **f** 020 7405 5245 **e** info@prestige-elite.com **w** prestige-elite.com Chairman: Keith C Thomas.

Pretap Music PO Box 31890, London SE17 1XG **t** 020 7708 2098 **f** 020 7564 4406 **e** ikeleo@pretap.com **w** pretap.com A&R: Ike Leo.

Priestess Records Ground Floor Flat, 30 Kenilworth Rd, St Leonards on Sea, E Sussex TN38 0JL **t** 01424 203 991 or 07814 659 729 **e** kat.leeryan@btinternet.com **w** nakedangel.co.uk MD: Kat Lee-Ryan.

Primaudial Recordings Flat 3, 157, Church Walk, Stoke Newington, London N16 8QA **t** 020 7241 5283 **f** 0870 130 2469 **e** skioakenfull@gmail.com **w** skioakenfull.com Label Manager: Ski Oakenfull.

Priory Records 3 Eden Court, Eden Way, Leighton Buzzard, Beds LU7 4FY **t** 01525 377566 **f** 01525 371477 **e** sales@priory.org.uk **w** priory.org.uk MD: Neil Collier.

Prison Records 13 Sandys Rd, Worcester WR1 3HE **t** 01905 29 809 **f** 01905 613 023 **e** info@prison-records.com **w** prison-records.com Co-MDs: Chris Warren, Ian Orkin.

Private & Confidential Group Ltd Fairlight Mews, 15 St. Johns Rd, Kingston upon Thames, Surrey KT1 4AN **t** 0208 977 0632 **f** 0870 770 8669 **e** info@pncmusic.com **w** pncrecords.com MD: Sir Harry.

Probation Records (see FF Vinyl Records)

Profile (see Silverword Music Group)

Prolific Recordings PO Box 282, Tadworth, Surrey KT20 5WA **t** 07770 874 282 **e** andy@prolificrecordings.co.uk **w** prolificrecordings.co.uk Label Manager: Andy Lewis.

Prolifica Records Unit 101, Saga Land, 326 Kensal Rd, London W10 5BZ **t** 020 8964 1917 **f** 020 8960 9971 **e** Gavino@btclick.com **w** Prolifica.net Label Manager: Gavino Prunas.

Proof Records (see Down By Law Records)

Proper Records Unit 1, Gateway Business Centre, Kangley Bridge Rd, London SE26 5AN **t** 020 8676 5180 **f** 020 8676 5190 **e** malc@proper.uk.com **w** proper.uk.com MD: Malcolm Mills.

Props Records Ltd 7 Croxley Rd, London W9 3HH **t** 020 8960 1115 **e** info@props.co.uk **w** props.co.uk Dir: Martin Lascelles.

Protest Recordings Ltd Truman Brewery, 91 Brick Lane, London E1 6QL **t** 020 7770 6115/6116 or 07786 680 316 **e** mon@protestrecordings.com **w** protestrecordings.com Dir: Monica Stephen.

Prototype Recordings (see Virus Recordings)

Providence Music Ward Industries Ltd, Providence House, Brooks Rd, Raunds, Northants NN9 6NS **t** 01933 624963 **f** 01933 625458 **e** Wardind1@aol.com **w** pamelaward.co.uk Mkting Dir: Paul Cherrington.

Provocateur Records Friendly Hall, 31 Fordwich Rd, Fordwich, Kent CT2 0BW **t** 01227 711008 **f** 01227 712021 **e** info@provocateurrecords.co.uk **w** provocateurrecords.co.uk MD: Jane Lindsey.

Psychic Deli (see Phantasm Records)

Public Records 84A Strand On The Green, London W4 3PU **t** 020 8995 0989 **f** 020 8995 0878 **e** jcmusic@dial.pipex.com MD: John Campbell.

Pucka (see Highnote Ltd)

Pulse Records Cammell Lairds Waterfront Pk, Campbeltown Rd, Wirral, Merseyside CH41 9HP **t** 0151 649 0427 **f** 0151 649 0894 **e** info@pulse-records.co.uk **w** pulse-records.co.uk MDs: Rob Fennah, Alan Fennah.

Pure Gold Records (see Hepcat Records)

Pure Mint Recordings The Old Post Office, 31 Penrose St, London SE17 3DW **t** 020 7703 1239 **f** 020 7703 1239 **e** info@pure-mint.com **w** pure-mint.com MD: Anthony Hall.

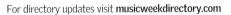

Pure Motion Muzik Ltd 226 Seven Sisters Rd, London N4 3GG **t** 020 7372 6806 **f** 020 7372 0969 **e** info@pmmuzik.com **w** pmmuzik.com Dir: Plucky.

Pure Records PO Box 174, Penistone, Sheffield S36 8XB **t** 0870 240 5058 **f** 0870 240 5058 **e** info@purerecords.net **w** purerecords.net.

Pure Silk (see Broadley Records)

PureUK Recordings (see Stirling Music Group)

PURPLE CITY LTD

PO Box 31, Bushey, Herts WD23 2PT **t** 01923 244 673 **f** 01923 244 693 **e** info@purplecitymusic.com **w** purplecitymusic.com MD: Barry Blue. Promo Director: Lynda West. PA: Taryn Israelsohn.

Purple Records Aizlewood Mill, Nursery St, Sheffield, S Yorks S3 8GG **t** 0114 233 3024 **f** 0114 234 7326 **e** ann@darkerthanblue.fsnet.co.uk **w** purplerecords.net MD: Simon Robinson.

Purr Records 70 The Hollow, Southdown, Bath BA2 1LZ **t** 01225 443 844 **e** info@purr.org.uk **w** purr.org.uk Contact: Dave Tinkham, Tim Orchard.

Q Music Recordings (see Suburban Soul (Music))

Q Zone Ltd 21C Heathmans Rd, Parsons Green, London SW6 4TJ **t** 020 7731 9313 **f** 020 7731 9314 **e** mail@darah.co.uk MD: David Howells.

Qnote Records (see Cube Soundtracks)

Quannum Projects (see Ninja Tune)

Quarterstick (see Southern Records)

Quiet Riot Records 130A Plough Rd, Battersea, London SW11 2AA **t** 020 7924 1948 **f** 020 7924 6069 **e** adam@grlondon.com Label Manager: Adam Records.

Quixotic Records PO Box 27947, London SE7 8WN **t** 020 8269 0352 or 07778 049 706 **f** 020 8269 0353 **e** suzanne@quixoticrecords.com **w** quixoticrecords.com Dir: Suzanne Hunt.

R2 Records PO Box 100, Moreton-in-Marsh, Gloucs GL56 0ZX **t** 01608 651 802 **f** 01608 652 814 **e** editor@jacobsladder.org.uk **w** jacobsladder.org.uk MD: Robb Eden.

Racing Junior (see Glitterhouse Records)

Radiate (see Virgin Records)

Radioactive (see Island Records Group)

Radiotone Records PO Box 43103, London E17 8WD **t** 07989 301910 **e** info@radiotone.co.uk **w** radiotone.co.uk Dir: Steve Cooper.

Rage (see Avex Inc)

Ragtag Music (see Fastforward Music Ltd)

Rainbow Quartz Records 74 Riverside 3, Sir Thomas Longley Rd, Rochester, Kent ME2 4BH **t** +212 385 8000 **f** +212 385 7845 **e** rainbowqtz@aol.com **w** rainbowquartz.com Founder: Jim McGarry.

Rainy Day Records (see Hepcat Records)

Raise the Roof (see Collecting Records LLP)

Ram Records Ltd PO Box 70, Hornchurch, Essex RM11 3NR **t** 01708 445851 **f** 01708 441270 **e** info@ramrecords.com **w** ramrecords.com Label Mgr: Scott Bourne.

Randan 52 Osborne St, Glasgow G1 5QH **t** 0141 552 0375 **e** horse@randan.fsworld.co.uk **w** horse-randan.com Business Affairs: Bill Matthews.

RandM Records 72 Marylebone Lane, London W1U 2PL **t** 020 7486 7458 **f** 020 8467 6997 **e** mike@randm.co.uk; roy@randm.co.uk **w** randm.co.uk MDs: Mike Andrews & Roy Eldridge.

Rat Records 76 Brewer St, London W1F 9TX **t** 08707 501 379 **f** 020 7287 1684 **e** info@ratrecords.info **w** ratrecords.info Contact: DJ Deekline.

Ravishing Rhymes PO Box 241, Hitchin SG4 0WS **t** 07815 163 070 **e** info@ravishingrhymes.co.uk **w** ravishingrhymes.co.uk Contact: Michelle Hoskin.

Raw Strings (see RF Records)

Rawkus Entertainment (see Island Records Group)

Rayman Recordings (see Adasam Limited)

RCA LABEL GROUP

Bedford House, 69-79 Fulham High St, London SW6 3JW **t** 020 7384 7500 **f** 020 7371 9298 **e** firstname.lastname@sonybmg.com **w** rca-records.co.uk MD: Craig Logan. SVP Media: Alex Crass. VP Marketing: Louise Hart. VP A&R and Business Development: Marvyn Lyn. VP Of Legal & Business Affairs: David Tunrbull. Director Of A&R: Celia Gilmour. Director Of Radio: Leighton Woods. Director Of TV: Jacqui Quaife. Head Of Press: Kate Head. Head Of Digital: Seb Weller. Sales: Arvato.

RDL Music (see Savant Records)

RDL Records 132 Chase Way, London N14 5DH **t** 020 8361 5002 or 07050 055167 **f** 0870 741 5252 **e** atlanticcrossingartists@yahoo.com **w** mkentertainments.8k.com Dir: Colin Jacques.

React (see Resist Music)

Ready, Steady, Go! (see Graduate Records)

Real World Records Box Mill, Mill Lane, Box, Corsham, Wilts SN13 8PL **t** 01225 743188 **f** 01225 743787 **e** records@realworld.co.uk **w** realworldrecords.com Label Mgr: Amanda Jones.

Really Free Solutions Ichthus House, 1 Northfield Rd, Aylesbury, Bucks HP20 1PB **t** 01296 583700 **e** info@reallyfreemusic.co.uk **w** reallyfreemusic.co.uk Contact: Peter Wheeler.

Really Useful Records 22 Tower St, London WC2H 9TW **t** 020 7240 0880 **f** 020 7240 8922 **e** querymaster@reallyuseful.co.uk **w** reallyuseful.com MD (Music Division): Tristram Penna.

Receiver Records (see Sanctuary Records Group)

Recharge (see Supreme Music)

The Record Label The Old Schoolhouse, 138 Lower Mortlake Rd, Richmond, Surrey TW9 2JZ **t** 020 8332 7245 **f** 020 8948 6982 **e** info@recordlabel.co.uk **w** recordlabel.co.uk MD: Matt Nicholson.

Recoup Recordings Suite B, 2 Tunstall Rd, London SW9 8DA **t** 020 7733 5400 **f** 020 7733 4449 **e** recouprecordings@westburymusic.net **w** westburymusic.net.

Recover (see Supreme Music)

Red Admiral Records The Cedars, Elvington Lane, Hawkinge., Nr. Folkestone, Kent CT18 7AD **t** 01303 893472 **f** 01303 893833 **e** info@redadmiralrecords.com **w** redadmiralrecords.com MD: Chris Ashman.

Red Balloon (see 4Real Records)

Red Cat (see The Store For Music)

Red Chord (see Born to Dance Records)

Red Egyptian Records 35 Britannia Row, London N1 8QH **t** 020 7704 8080 **f** 020 7704 1616 **e** tony@headonmanagement.co.uk Label Manager: Tony Higgins.

The Red Flag Recording Company 1 Star St, London W2 1QD **t** 020 7258 0093 **f** 020 7402 9238 **e** info@redflagrecords.com **w** redflagrecords.com Contact: Sophie Young.

Red Hot Records 105 Emlyn Rd, London W12 9TG **t** 020 8749 3730 **e** redhotrecs@aol.com MD: Brian Leafe.

RED INK

1st floor, 20 Fulham Broadway, London SW6 1AH **t** 020 7835 5200 **f** 020 7835 5342 **e** firstname.lastname@redinkmusic.com **w** redinkmusic.com. General Manager: Angie Somerside. Head of Marketing: Murray Rose. Head of International: Helen Hampson. A&R: Sara Leathem.

Red Kite Records Cwmargenau, Llanwrda, Carms SA19 8AP **t** 01550 722 000 **f** 01550 722 022 **e** info@redkiterecords.co.uk **w** redkiterecords.co.uk Contact: Ron Dukelow.

Red Records 412 Beersbridge Rd, Belfast BT5 5EB **t** 08707 454640 **f** 08707 454650 **e** michael@machtwo.co.uk **w** red-records.com MD: Michael Taylor.

Red Sky Records PO Box 27, Stroud, Gloucs GL6 0YQ **t** 0845 644 1447 **f** 01453 836877 **e** info@redskyrecords.co.uk **w** redskyrecords.co.uk MD: Johnny Coppin.

Redemption 516 Queslett Rd, Great Barr, Birmingham B43 7EJ **t** 0121 605 4791 **f** 0121 605 4791 **e** bhaskar@redemption.co.uk **w** redemption.co.uk MD/Head A&R: Bhaskar Dandona.

Redemption Records PO Box 8045, Reading RG30 9AZ **t** 020 7384 0938 or 07866 626 946 **f** 020 7384 0934 **e** info@redemption-records.com **w** redemption-records.com MD: Phil Knox-Roberts.

Reel Track Records PO Box 1099, London SE5 9HT **t** 020 7326 4824 **f** 020 7535 5901 **e** gamesmaster@chartmoves.com **w** chartmoves.com A&R Manager: Dave Mombasa.

Regal Recordings EMI House, 43 Brook Green, London W6 7EF **t** 020 7605 5000 **f** 020 7605 5050 **e** firstname.lastname@emimusic.com **w** regal.co.uk Head of Label: Miles Leonard.

Regis Records Ltd Southover House, Tolpuddle, Dorset DT2 7HF **t** 01305 848983 **f** 01305 848516 **e** info@regisrecords.co.uk **w** regisrecords.co.uk GM: Robin Vaughan.

Rekids Ltd PO Box 42769, London N2 0YY **t** 020 8883 4092 **e** james@rekids.co.uk **w** rekids.co.uk Label Manager: James Masters.

REL Records 86 Causewayside, Edinburgh EH9 1PY **t** 0131 668 3366 **f** 0131 662 4463 **e** neil@holyroodproductions.com MD: Neil Ross.

Release Records 7 North Parade, Bath, Somerset BA2 4DD **t** 01225 428284 **f** 01225 400090 **e** aca_aba@freenet.co.uk MD: Harry Finegold.

Relentless Records EMI House, 43 Brook Green, Hammersmith, London W6 7EF **t** 020 7605 5000 **f** 020 7605 5050 **e** firstname@mvillage.co.uk **w** relentless-records.net Co-MD: Shabs, Paul Franklyn..

Religion Music 36 Fitzwilliam Sq, Dublin 2, Ireland **t** +353 1 207 0508 **f** +353 1 207 0418 **e** info@religionmusic.com **w** religionmusic.com MD: Glenn Herlihy.

Remote (see Locked On Records)

Renaissance Recordings 1st Floor, 24 Regent St, Nottingham NG1 5BQ **t** 0115 910 1111 **f** 0115 910 1071 **e** marcus@renaissanceuk.com **w** renaissanceuk.com Label Manager: Marcus James.

Renegade Hardware (see TOV Music Group Ltd (Trouble on Vinyl))

Renegade Recordings (see TOV Music Group Ltd (Trouble on Vinyl))

Renk Records 189 Upton Lane, Forest Gate, London E7 9PJ **t** 020 8985 0091 **e** renkrecords@msn.com **w** renkrecords.com MD: Junior Hart.

Rephlex PO Box 2676, London N11 1AZ **t** 020 8368 5903 **f** 020 8361 2811 **e** info@rephlex.com **w** rephlex.com Press/Distrib: Marcus Scott.

ReprinT Records 9 The Causeway, Downend, Fareham, Hants PO16 8RN **t** 023 9257 0632 **e** water.fall@virgin.net Dir: Jo Womar.

Resist Music 131-151 Great Titchfield St, London W1W 5BB **t** 020 3008 2355 **f** 020 3008 2351 **e** mailbox@resist-music.co.uk **w** resist-music.co.uk MD: James Horrocks.

Resonance (see Sanctuary Classics)

Resurgence (see Voiceprint)

Retch Records 49 Rose Crescent, Woodvale, Southport, Merseyside PR8 3RZ **t** 01704 577835 or 07951 201407 **e** retchrecords@aol.com **w** hometown.aol.co.uk/retchrecords Owner: M Hines.

Retek (see Supreme Music)

Rev-Ola (see Cherry Red Records)

Reveal Records 63 St Peters St, Derby, Derbyshire DE1 2AB **t** 01332 349 242 **f** 01332 349 141 **e** tomreveal@mac.com **w** revealrecords.com MD: Tom Rose.

Reverb Records Ltd Reverb House, Bennett St, London W4 2AH **t** 020 8747 0660 **f** 020 8747 0880 **e** records@reverbxl.com **w** reverbxl.com Label Manager: Mark Lusty.

Revolver Music Ltd 152 Goldthorn Hill, Penn, Wolverhampton, W Midlands WV2 3JA **t** 01902 345345 **f** 01902 345155 **e** Paul.Birch@revolver-e.com **w** revolver-records.com MD: Paul Birch.

Rex (see XL Recordings)

Rexx (see Highnote Ltd)

RF (see RF Records)

RF Records Room A30, City College, Chorlton St, Manchester M1 3HB **t** 0161 279 7302 or 07909 907 089 **f** 0161 279 7225 **e** pellis@ccm.ac.uk **w** rfrecords.com Label Mgr: Phil Ellis.

RHINO UK

The Warner Building, 28A Kensington Church Street, London W8 4EP **t** 020 7368 2500 **f** 020 7368 2773 **e** firstname.lastname@warnermusic.com Director: Nick Stewart. General Manager: Phil Penman. Head of Warner Music Catalogue: Erik James. Licensing Manager: Tonia Andrew. Catalogue Marketing Manager: Rick Conrad. Senior Product Manager: Florence Halfon. Platinum Manager: Joe Arditti. Asset Library Manager: James Rose. Business Affairs: Jonathan Cross. Financial Planning Manager: Sarah Hammond.

Rhythmbank Records 8 Upper Grosvenor St, London W1K 2LY **t** 020 7495 8333 **f** 020 7495 7833 **w** rhythmbank.com Contact: Vicki Wickham.

Richmond (see Cherry Red Records)

Riddle (see Nikt Records)

Rideout Records Lillie House, 1A Conduit St, Leicester, Leics LE2 0JN **t** 0116 223 0318 **f** 0116 223 0302 **e** rideout@stayfree.co.uk **w** music.stayfree.co.uk/rideout Mkt Promo Mgr: Darren Nockles.

Ridge Records 1 York St, Aberdeen AB11 5DL **t** 01224 573100 **f** 01224 572598 **e** office@ridge-records.com **w** ridge-records.com Mgr: Mike Smith.

Right Recordings Ltd 177 High St, Harlesden, London NW10 4TE **t** 020 8961 3889 **f** 020 8951 9955 **e** info@rightrecordings.com **w** rightrecordings.com Dirs: David Landau, John Kaufman.

Ring-pull Records 241A East Barnet Rd, East Barnet, Herts EN4 8SS **t** 020 8449 0766 **e** info@ringpullrecords.com **w** ringpullrecords.com Label Mgr: Angelique Ekart.

Riot Club Records Unit 4, 27a Spring Grove Rd, Hounslow, Middx TW3 4BE **t** 020 8570 8100 **f** 020 8572 9590 **e** lee@riotclub.co.uk **w** riotclubrecords.co.uk MD: Lee Farrow.

Rise & Shine (see Wyze Recordings)

Riverbank Media Limited 34 Meadowside, Cambridge Pk, Twickenham TW1 2JQ **t** 020 8404 8307 **f** 020 8404 8307 **e** info@riverbankmedia.com MD: Nicholas Dicker.

Riverboat Records (see World Music Network (UK) Ltd)

Riverman Records Top Floor, George House, Brecon Rd, London W6 8PY **t** 020 7381 4000 **f** 020 7381 9666 **e** info@riverman.co.uk **w** riverman.co.uk Dir: David McLean.

Riviera Music & Publishing 83 Dolphin Crescent, Paignton, Devon TQ3 1JZ **t** 07071 226078 **f** 01803 665728 **e** Info@rivieramusic.net **w** rivieramusic.net MD: Kevin Jarvis.

RL-2 15 Boulevard Aristide Briand, Pouzolles, France 34480 **t** +33 4 67 24 77 72 **e** info9@rl-2.com **w** rl-2.com GM: Paul Lilly.

RMO/Chill-out Music & Film 5a Tonbridge Rd, Maidstone, Kent ME16 8RL **t** 01622 768 668 **f** 01622 768 667 Dir: Reg McLean.

Road Train Recordings (see Shout Out Records)

Roadrunner Records Ealing Studios, Ealing Green, London W5 5EP **t** 020 8567 6762 **f** 020 8567 6793 **e** rrguest@roadrunnerrecords.co.uk **w** roadrunnerrecords.co.uk MD: Mark Palmer.

Rock Action Records PO Box 15107, Glasgow G1 1US **e** info@rockactionrecords.co.uk **w** rockactionrecords.co.uk Label Manager: Craig Hargrave.

Rocstar Recordings PO Box 113, Hove BN32YQ **t** 01273 329528 **f** 01273 329528 **e** info@rocstar.com **w** rocstar.com MD: Marco Distefano.

Rogue Records Ltd PO Box 337, London N4 1TW **t** 020 8340 9651 **f** 020 8348 5626 **e** rogue@frootsmag.com **w** frootsmag.com/beatnik MD: Ian Anderson.

Rollercoaster Records Rock House, London Rd, St Mary's, Chalford, Gloucs GL6 8PU **t** 0845 456 9759 or 01453 886 252 **f** 0845 456 9760 or 01453 885 361 **e** info@rollercoasterrecords.com **w** rollercoasterrecords.com Dir: John Beecher.

Ronco 107 Mortlake St, London SW14 8HQ **t** 020 8392 6876 **f** 020 8392 6829 **e** ray.levy@telstar.co.uk Label Manager: Ray Levy.

Rosette Records 43-51 Wembley Hill Rd, Wembley, Middx HA9 8AU **t** 020 8733 1440 **f** 020 8903 5859 **e** info@rosetterecords.com **w** rosetterecords.com MD: David Smith.

Ross Records (Turriff) Ltd 30 Main St, Turriff, Aberdeenshire AB53 4AB **t** 01888 568 899 **f** 01888 568 890 **e** gibson@rossrecords.com **w** rossrecords.com MD: Gibson Ross.

Rotator Records Interzone House, 74-77 Magdalen Rd, Oxford OX4 1RE **t** 01865 205600 **f** 01865 205700 **e** info@rotator.co.uk **w** rotator.co.uk A&R: Richard Cotton.

Rough Trade Records 66 Golborne Rd, London W10 5PS **t** 020 8960 9888 **f** 020 8968 6715 **e** pru@roughtraderecords.com **w** roughtraderecords.com Contact: Pru Harris.

RPM (see Cherry Red Records)

RPM Productions PO Box 158, Chipping Norton, Oxon OX7 5ZL **t** 01608 643 738 **e** info@rpmrecords.co.uk **w** rpmrecords.co.uk MD: Mark Stratford.

Rubber Road Records 4-10 Lamb Walk, London SE1 3TT **t** 020 7921 8353 **e** rubber_road_records@yahoo.co.uk Head of A&R: Nick Lightowlers.

Rubicon Records 59 Park View Rd, London NW10 1AJ **t** 020 8450 5154 **f** 020 8452 0187 **e** rubiconrecords@btopenworld.com **w** rubiconrecords.co.uk Founder: Graham Le Fevre.

Rubyworks Records 6 Park Rd, Dun Laoghaire, County Dublin, Ireland **t** +353 1 284 1747 **f** +353 1 284 1767 **e** info@rubyworks.com **w** rubyworks.com Dir: Niall Muckian.

Rumour Records Ltd PO BOX 54127, London W5 9BE **t** 020 8997 7893 **f** 020 8997 7901 **e** post@rumour.demon.co.uk **w** rumourrecords.com MD: Anne Plaxton.

Rump Ltd PO Box 53512, London SE19 2ZW **t** 07973 360 960 **e** rump.ltd@hotmail.com MD: Paul Eldon.

Running Man Records PO Box 32100, London N1 1GR **f** 020 8374 5054 **e** runningman@oysterband.co.uk **w** oysterband.co.uk Label Manager: Colin Clowtt.

Ryko Latin (see Rykodisc)

Rykodisc 329 Latimer Rd, London W10 6RA **t** 020 8960 3311 **f** 020 8960 1177 **e** info@rykodisc.co.uk **w** rykodisc.com Sales & Distribution Dir: Andy Childs.

S Records (see Sony BMG Music Entertainment UK & Ireland)

S12 (see Simply Vinyl)

Sacred Records 187 Freston Rd, London W10 6TH **t** 020 8969 1323 **f** 020 8969 1363 **e** info@sacred-music.com Label Manager: Adjei Amaning.

Saddle Creek Records PO Box 34254, London NW5 3XA **t** 020 7281 6979 **f** 020 7272 2969 **e** europe@saddle-creek.com **w** saddle-creek.com Label Managers: Thomas Davies, Gillian Pittaway.

Safehouse Recordings Fulham Palace, Bishop's Ave, London SW6 6EA **t** 020 7751 0175 **f** 020 7736 0606 **e** info@safehouserecordings.com **w** safehouserecordings.com Chairman: Clive Black.

Sakay (see Rogue Records Ltd)

Salsoul UK (see suss'd! records - the home of Salsoul UK)

Salt Hill Recordings (see Whole 9 Yards)

S:Alt Records Ltd PO Box 34140, London NW10 2WW **t** 020 8830 3355 **f** 020 8830 4466 **e** info@saltrecords.com **w** saltrecords.com Label Mgr: Sandra Ceschia.

Sanctuary Classics Sanctuary House, 45-53 Sinclair Rd, London W14 0NS **t** 020 7300 1888 **f** 020 7300 1306 **e** info@sanctuaryclassics.com **w** sanctuaryclassics.com A&R & Label Manager: Pollyanna Gunning.

Sanctuary Records Group Sanctuary House, 45-53 Sinclair Rd, London W14 0NS **t** 020 7602 6351 **f** 020 7603 5941 **e** info@sanctuaryrecords.com **w** sanctuaryrecords.co.uk CEO: Joe Cokell.

Sandman Records Ltd 57 Albert Rd, London N22 7AA **t** 020 8881 4235 or 07961 126 990 **e** sandmandave57@hotmail.com A&R: Dave Bolton.

Sangraal (see Science Friction)

Sargasso Records PO Box 10565, London N1 8SR **t** 020 8731 1998 **f** 020 8141 9592 **e** info@sargasso.com **w** sargasso.com Dir: Daniel Biro.

Satellite Music Ltd 34 Salisbury St, London NW8 8QE **t** 020 7402 9111 **f** 020 7723 3064 **e** satellite_artists@hotmail.com MD: Eliot Cohen.

Saucer (see Seriously Groovy Music)

SavageTrax Suite 147, 77 Beak St, London W1F 9BD **t** 020 7000 3146 or 07778 645 239 **f** 020 7000 3146 **e** kevin@savagetrax.com **w** savagetrax.com Contact: Kevin Savage.

Savant Records 132 Chase Way, London N14 5DH **t** 07050 055168 **f** 0870 741 5252 **e** teleryngg@msn.com **w** teleryngg.com MD: Richard Struple.

Savoy Records PO Box 271, Coulsdon, Surrey CR5 3YZ **t** 01737 554 739 **f** 01737 556 737 **e** admin@savoymusic.com **w** savoymusic.com MD: Wendy Smith.

Saydisc Records The Barton, Inglestone Common, Badminton, Gloucs GL9 1BX **f** 01454 299 858 **e** saydisc@aol.com **w** saydisc.com MD: Gef Lucena.

SBS Records PO Box 37, Blackwood, Gwent NP12 2YQ **t** 01495 201116 or 07711 984651 **f** 01495 201190 **e** enquiry@sbsrecords.co.uk **w** sbsrecords.co.uk MD: Glenn Powell.

Scarlet Records Southview, 68 Siltside, Gosberton Risegate, Lincs PE11 4ET **t** 01755 841750 **f** 01755 841750 **e** info@scarletrecording.co.uk **w** scarletrecording.co.uk MD: Liz Lenten.

Schnitzel Records PO Box 51389, 2 Nevitt House, London N1 6YD **t** 020 7684 1129 **f** 020 7684 1129 **e** info@schnitzel.co.uk **w** schnitzel.co.uk MD: Oliver Geywitz.

Science (see Virgin Records)

Science Friction 21 Stupton Rd, Sheffield, South Yorks S9 1BQ **t** 0114 261 1649 **f** 0114 261 1649 **e** dc@cprod.win-uk.net **w** royharper.co.uk Label Manager: Darren Crisp.

Scotdisc - BGS Productions Ltd Newtown St, Kilsyth, Glasgow, Strathclyde G65 0LY **t** 01236 821081 **f** 01236 826900 **e** info@scotdisc.co.uk **w** scotdisc.co.uk MD: Dougie Stevenson.

Scratch (see The Store For Music)

Screen Edge 102a St Annes House, 329 Clifton Drive South, Lytham St Annes, Lancs FY8 1LP **t** 01253 781994 **f** 01253 712453 **e** johnb@outlaw23.com **w** screenedge.com MD: John Bentham.

Scribendum (see SilverOak Music Entertainment Ltd)

Sea Dream (see Plankton Records)

Seal Records 72 Coolfin Rd, Custom House, London E16 3BE **t** 020 7474 2801 **f** 020 7473 5271 **e** info@sealrecords.com **w** sealrecords.com Owner: Thomas St.John.

Seamless Recordings 192-194 Clapham High St, London SW4 7UD **t** 020 7498 5551 **f** 020 7498 2333 **e** amber@bargrooves.com **w** seamlessrecordings.com Label Mgr: Amber Spencer-Holmes.

Season Records Ltd 17 Hardman Rd, Kingston Upon Thames, Kingston Upon Thames, Surrey KT2 6RH **t** 07779 126 694 **e** daniel@seasonrecords.com **w** seasonrecords.com CEO: Daniel Godding.

Secret Planet Recordings 185 Ladbroke Grove, London W10 6HH **t** 020 8964 3551 **f** 020 8964 3550 **e** info@secretplanetrecordings.com **w** secretplanetrecordings.com Contact: Henriette Amiel.

Secret Records Regent House, 1 Pratt Mews, London NW1 0AD **t** 020 7267 6899 **f** 020 7267 6746 **e** partners@newman-and.co.uk MD: Colin Newman.

Sedna Records 10 Barley Mow Passage, Chiswick, London W4 4PH **t** 020 8747 4534 **e** info@sednarecords.com **w** sednarecords.com MD: Jonathan Wild.

Seeca Records Bridge House, 11, Creek Rd, Hampton Court, Surrey KT8 9BE **t** 020 8979 1313 or 07970 094 257 **f** 020 8979 9891 **e** info@seeca.co.uk **w** seeca.co.uk Dir: Louise Martins.

Select Music and Video Ltd. 3 Wells Pl, Redhill, Surrey RH1 3SL **t** 01737 645600 **f** 01737 644065 **e** BHolden@selectmusic.co.uk **w** naxos.com Naxos Label Mgr/Mktg Mgr: Barry Holden.

Selecta Records (see Millbrand Enterprises)

Sema (see Flat Records)

Sense World Music 93, Belgrave Rd, Leicester, Leics LE4 6AS **t** 0116 266 7046 **f** 0116 261 0480 **e** alpesh@senseworldmusic.com **w** senseworldmusic.com MD: Alpesh Patel.

Sensory Education Records PO Box 317, West Malling, Kent ME19 6WZ **t** 01622 204808 **f** 01622 204808 **e** info@sensoryeducation.com **w** sensoryeducation.com Dir: Claire Wright.

Serengeti Records 43A Old Woking Rd, West Byfleet, Surrey KT14 6LG **t** 01932 351925 **f** 01932 336431 **e** info@serengeti-records.com MD: Martin Howell.

Serious (see Renk Records)

Seriously Groovy Music 3rd Floor, 28 D'Arblay St, Soho, London W1F 8EW **t** 020 7439 1947 **f** 020 7734 7540 **e** admin@seriouslygroovy.com **w** seriouslygroovy.com Dirs: Dave Holmes, Lorraine Snape.

Setanta Records 174 Camden Rd, London NW1 9HJ **t** 020 7284 4877 **f** 020 7284 4577 **e** info@setantarecords.com **w** setantarecords.com MD: Keith Cullen

Sexy Records Ltd PO Box 421, Aylesbury, Bucks HP17 8BS **t** 01844 290528 **f** 01844 290528 **e** unie@sexyrecords.co.uk **w** sexyrecords.com MD: Unie Moller.

Shaboom Records PO Box 38, South Shore, Blackpool FY1 6GH **t** 01253 620039 **f** 01253 620756 **e** mail@shaboom.co.uk **w** shaboom.co.uk Co Owner: Dick Johnson.

Shade Factor Productions Ltd 4 Cleveland Sq, London W2 6DH **t** 020 7402 6477 **f** 020 7402 7144 **e** mail@shadefactor.com **w** shadefactor.com MD: Ann Symonds.

Shadow Cryptic (see Moving Shadow Ltd)

Shamtown Records 13 St Mary's Terrace, Galway, Ireland **t** +353 91 521309 **f** +353 91 526341 **e** sawdoc@eircom.net **w** sawdoctors.com MD: Ollie Jennings.

Shaping The Invisible Mulberry House, The Ridings, Shotover, Headington, Oxford OX3 8TB **t** 07585 4989800 **f** 01993 779030 **e** charlie@bsdr.com Contact: Charles Seaward.

Shark Records 23 Rollscourt Ave, Herne Hill, London SE24 0EA **t** 020 7737 4580 **f** 020 7737 4580 **e** mellor@organix.fsbusiness.co.uk MD: Mr MH Mellor.

Sharpe Music 9A Irish St, Dungannon, Co Tyrone BT70 3LN **t** 028 8772 4621 **f** 028 8775 2195 **e** info@sharpemusicireland.com **w** sharpemusicireland.com MD: Raymond Stewart.

Shatterproof Records 1st Floor, St Andrew's House, 62 Bridge St, Manchester M3 BW **t** 0161 838 9180 **f** 0161 838 9189 **e** caroline@shatterproofrecords.com **w** shatterproofrecords.com Head of A&R: Caroline Elleray.

Sheepfold 43 Broadleaf Ave, Bishop's Stortford, Herts CM23 3JF **t** 01279 835067 **f** 01920 461187 **e** pauljamesburrell@aol.com Mgr: Paul Burrell.

Sheer Bravado Records East Garth, Far Lane, Waddington, Lincs LN5 9QG **t** 01522 722837 **e** v.ford@sheerbravado.com **w** sheerbravado.com MD: Vince Ford.

Shellwood Productions (see Priory Records)

Shifty Disco Ltd Oxford Music Central, 1st Floor, 9 Park End St, Oxford OX1 1HH **t** 01865 798 791 **f** 01865 798 792 **e** info@shiftydisco.co.uk **w** shiftydisco.co.uk MD: Dave Newton.

Shinkansen Recordings PO Box 14274, London SE11 6ZG
t 020 7582 2877 **f** 020 7582 3342 **e** shink@dircon.co.uk
w shink.dircon.co.uk MD: Matt Haynes.

Shock Records PO Box 301, Torquay, Devon TQ2 7TB
t 01803 614392 **f** 01803 616271 **e** info@shockrecords.co.uk
w shockrecords.co.uk A&R Manager: Graham Eden.

Shoeshine Records PO Box 15193, Glasgow G2 6LB
t 0141 204 5654 **f** 0141 204 5654 **e** info@shoeshine.co.uk
w shoeshine.co.uk Prop: Francis Macdonald.

Shotgun Records (see Millbrand Enterprises)

Shout Out Records 51 Clarkegrove Rd, Sheffield S10 2NH
t 0114 268 5665 **f** 0114 268 4161 **e** entsuk@aol.com
MD: John Roddison.

Sidewalk 7 154 New Kings Rd, London SW6 4LZ
t 020 7731 3350 **e** info@sidewalk7.com **w** sidewalk7.com
MD: Rocco Gardner.

Silva Classics (see Silva Screen Records)

Silva Screen Records 3 Prowse Pl, London NW1 9PH
t 020 7428 5500 **f** 020 7482 2385 **e** info@silvascreen.co.uk
w silvascreen.co.uk MD: Reynold da Silva.

Silva Treasury (see Silva Screen Records)

Silver Planet Records 16 Stratford Rd, London W8 6QD
t 020 7937 6246 **f** 020 7937 6246
e info@silverplanetrecordings.com **w** silverplanetrecordings.com
A&R Mgr: David Conway.

SilverOak Music Entertainment Ltd Silver Oaks Farm,
Waldron, E Sussex TN210RS **t** 01435 810020 **f** 01435 810026
e mail@silveroak.biz **w** silveroak.biz MD: Giorgio Cuppini.

Silverscope Music Suite 1, 92 King George Rd, Ware, Herts
SG12 7DT **t** 01920 461 000 **e** silverscope@btconnect.com
MD: Richard Rogers.

Silverword Music Group 16 Limetrees, Llangattock,
Crickhowell, Powys NP8 1LB **t** 01873 810142 **f** 01873 811557
e silvergb@aol.com **w** silverword.co.uk MD: Kevin Holland-King.

Simple Records First Floor, 75 Abbeville Rd SW4 9JN
t 020 8673 1818 **f** 020 8673 6751 **e** info@simplerecords.co.uk
A&R Director: Will Saul.

Simply Music (see Simply Vinyl)

Simply Recordings (see Simply Vinyl)

Simply Vinyl Unit 4, The Pavilions, 2 East Rd, South
Wimbledon, London SW19 1UW **t** 020 8545 8580
f 020 8545 8581 **e** info@simplyvinyl.com **w** simplyvinyl.com
MD: Mike Loveday.

Sinister Recordings 22 Upper Grosvenor St, London
W1K 7PE **t** 020 7495 3885 **f** 020 7495 3885
e info@sinister-recordings.com **w** sinister-recordings.com
Label Manager: Alex Lee.

Sink And Stove PO Box 992, Bristol BS99 5ZN
t 0117 907 6931 **f** 0117 907 6931 **e** info@sinkandstove.co.uk
w sinkandstove.co.uk Label Mgr: Benjamin Shillabeer.

Sire (see Warner Bros Records)

Siren Music Ltd PO Box 166, Hartlepool, Cleveland
TS26 9JA **t** 01429 424 603 or 07951 679 666
e daveianhill@yahoo.co.uk **w** tenacitymusicpr.co.uk Dir: Dave Hill.

Six Armed Man Records (see Falling A Records)

Six Degrees Records (see Collective Music Ltd)

Skindependent Leacroft, Chertion Cross, Cheriton Bishop,
Exeter, Devon EX6 6JH **t** 01647 24502 **f** 01647 24502
e charlie35@supanet.com **w** lizardsun-music.co.uk
MD: Charles Salt.

Skint Records PO Box 174, Brighton, E Sussex BN1 4BA
t 01273 738527 **f** 01273 208766 **e** mail@skint.net **w** skint.net
Dir: Damian Harris.

Skyline (see New State Entertainment)

Slalom Recordings Ltd 12 Farleigh Wick, Bradford on
Avon, Wilts BA15 2PU **t** 01225 864860 **f** 08453 339305
e info@slalom.co.uk **w** slalom.co.uk MD: James Reade.

Slam Productions 3 Thesiger Rd, Abingdon, Oxon
OX14 2DX **t** 01235 529 012 **f** 01235 529 012
e slamprods@aol.com **w** slamproductions.net
Prop: George Haslam.

Slate Records PO Box 173, New Malden, Surrey KT3 3YR
t 020 8949 7730 **f** 020 8949 7798
e john.osb1@btinternet.com Prop: John Osborne.

Slave Records PO Box 200, South Shore, Blackpool, Lancs
FY1 6GR **t** 07714 910257 **e** sploj3@yahoo.co.uk
Contact: Rob Powell.

Sleeper Music Ltd Block 2, 6 Erskine Rd, Primrose Hill,
London NW3 3AJ **t** 020 7580 3995 **f** 020 7900 6244
e info@sleepermusic.co.uk **w** guychambers.com
Contact: Dylan Chambers, Louise Jeremy.

Slick Slut Recordings Brewmasters House, 91 Brick Lane,
London E1 6QL **t** 020 7375 2332 **f** 020 7375 2442
e info@essentialdirect.co.uk **w** essentialdirect.co.uk
A&R: Gary Dedman.

Slinky Music Ltd PO Box 3344, Bournemouth, Dorset
BH1 4YB **t** 01202 652100 **f** 01202 652036 **e** info@slinky.co.uk
w slinky.co.uk Label Manager: Dave Lea.

Slip 'N' Slide (see Kickin Music Ltd)

Slow Graffiti 149 Albany Rd, Roath, Cardiff CF24 3NT
t 07813 069 739 **e** buymore@slowgraffiti.com
w slowgraffiti.com MD: Andy Davidson.

Small Pond (see East Central One Ltd)

Smexi Playaz Records PO Box 2035, Blackpool
FY4 1WW **t** 01253 347329 **f** 01253 347329
e glenn@outlet-promotions.com **w** outlet-promotions.com
MD: Glenn Wilson.

Smiled Records RGA Studio, 209 Goldhawk Rd, London
W12 8EP **t** 020 8746 7000 or 07776 188 191
f 020 8746 7700 **e** info@smiled.net **w** smiled.net
MD: James Barton.

Snapper Music 1 Star St, London W2 1QD
t 020 7563 5500 **f** 020 7563 5599
e sales@snappermusic.co.uk **w** snappermusic.co.uk
CEO: Jon Beecher.

So Real Records (see East Central One Ltd)

Sobriety Records (see Shout Out Records)

Soda (see Seriously Groovy Music)

Sofa (see Seriously Groovy Music)

Solarise Records PO Box 31104, London E16 4NS
t 07980 453 628 or 07790 865 199
e info@solariserecords.com **w** solariserecords.com
Owners: Paul/Lee.

Solent Records 68-70 Lugley St, Newport, Isle Of Wight
PO30 5ET **t** 01983 524110 **f** 0870 1640388
e md@solentrecords.co.uk **w** solentrecords.co.uk
Owner: John Waterman.

Soma Recordings Ltd 2nd Floor, 342 Argyle St, Glasgow
G2 8LY **t** 0141 229 6220 **f** 0141 226 4383
e info@somarecords.com **w** somarecords.com MD: Dave Clarke.

Sombrero 33 Riding House St, London W1W 7DZ
t 020 7636 3939 **f** 020 7636 0033 **e** info@sonic360.com
w sonic360.com Creative Director: Hana Miya.

Some (see Southern Records)

Some Bizarre (see Some Bizzare)

Some Bizzare 14 Tottenham Court Rd, London W1T 1JY
t 020 7836 9995 **f** 020 8348 2526 **e** info@somebizarre.com
w somebizarre.com MD: Stevo.

Somerset Entertainment International Ltd 3D Moss
Rd, Witham, Essex CM8 3UW **t** 01376 521527 **f** 01376 521528
e uk@somersetent.com **w** somersetent.com
Marketing Manager: Caren Pearce.

Something In Construction Unit 2B, Westpoint, 39-40
Warple Way, London W3 0RG **t** 020 8746 0666
f 020 8746 7676 **e** info@somethinginconstruction.com
w somethinginconstruction.com Joint MD: David Laurie.

Sonar Records 82 London Rd, Coventry, W Midlands
CV1 2JT **t** 024 7622 0749 **e** office@sonar-records.demon.co.uk
w cabinstudio.co.uk GM: Jon Lord.

Songphonic Records PO Box 250, Chertsey KT16 6AG
t 01932 568 969 **e** info@songphonic.com **w** songphonic.com
CEO: Osman Kent.

SonRise Records Western House, Richardson St, Swansea
SA1 3JF **t** 01792 642849 **e** info@sonriserecords.co.uk
w sonriserecords.co.uk Contact: Darren Pullin.

Sony BMG Music Entertainment Ireland Embassy
House, Ballsbridge, Dublin 4 **t** +353 1 647 3400
f +353 1 647 3430 **e** firstname.lastname@sonybmg.com.

SONY BMG MUSIC ENTERTAINMENT UK & IRELAND

Bedford House, 69-79 Fulham High Street, London SW6 3JW
t 020 7384 7500 **f** 020 7371 9298
e firstname.lastname@sonybmg.com **w** sonybmg.com. Chairman
and CEO: Ged Doherty. SVP Commercial Division: Richard Story.
SVP Finance, IT & Operations: David Pearce. SVP Legal And
Business Affairs: Michael Smith. MD Ireland: Annette Donnelly.
SVP Sales: Nicola Tuer. VP Human Resources: Sally Shields.
Director Of Communications: Paul Bursche. MD, RCA Label
Group: Craig Logan. MD, Columbia Label Group: Mike Smith.

Sorepoint (see Full Time Hobby Records)

Sorepoint Records 103 Gaunt St, London SE1 6DP
t 020 7740 8624 **f** 020 7740 8806
e info@sorepointrecords.com **w** sorepointrecords.com
MD: Ian Westley.

Sorted Records PO Box 5922, Leicester LE1 6XU
t 0116 291 1580 or 0771 128 0098 **f** 0116 291 1580
e sortedrecords@Hotmail.com **w** sorted-records.org.uk
MD: Dave Dixey.

SOSL Recordings (see Tuff Street - SOSL Recordings)

Soul 2 Soul Recordings 36-38 Rochester Pl, London
NW1 9JX **t** 020 7284 0293 **f** 020 7284 2290
e info@soul2soul.co.uk **w** soul2soul.co.uk MD: Jazzie B.

Soul Brother (see Expansion Records)

Soul Jazz Records 7 Broadwick St, London W1F 0DA
t 020 7734 3341 **f** 020 7494 1035
e info@soundsoftheuniverse.com **w** souljazzrecords.co.uk
Publicity & Production: Angela Scott.

Soul Junction (see Grapevine Music Group)

Sound & Video Gems Ltd Quaker's Coppice, Crewe,
Cheshire CW1 6EY **t** 01270 589321 **f** 01270 587438
MD: M Bates.

Soundscape Music 4 Bridgefield, Farnham, Surrey
GU9 8AN **t** 01252 721 096 **f** 01252 733 909
e bobholroyd@soundscapemusic.co.uk **w** soundscapemusic.co.uk
Dir: Bob Holroyd.

S.O.U.R. Recordings (see Tuff Street - SOSL Recordings)

Source (see Virgin Records).

Southbound (see Ace Records)

Southern Fried Records Fulham Palace, Bishops Ave,
London SW6 6EA **t** 020 7384 7373 **f** 020 7384 7392
e nathan@southernfriedrecords.com **w** southernfriedrecords.com
A&R Manager: Nathan Thursting.

Southern Lord (see Southern Records)

Southern Records Unit 3, Cranford Way, London N8 9DG
t 020 8348 4640 **f** 020 8348 9156 **e** info@southern.com
w southern.net GM: Allison Schnackenberg.

Sovereign (see Hot Lead Records)

Sovereign Lifestyle Records PO Box 356, Leighton Buzzard, Beds LU7 3WP **t** 01525 385578 **f** 01525 372743 **e** sovereignmusic@aol.com MD: Robert Lamont.

Soviet Union Records Musicdash, PO Box 1977, Manchester M26 2YB **t** 0787 0727 075 **e** sovrec@yahoo.co.uk **w** sovietunion.co.uk Dir: Jon Ashley.

SP Groove (see Truelove Records)

Space Age Recordings (see Adasam Limited)

Special Fried (see New State Entertainment)

Spit and Polish Records (see Shoeshine Records)

Splash Records 29 Manor House, 250 Marylebone Rd, London NW1 5NP **t** 020 7723 7177 **f** 020 7262 0775 **e** splashrecords.uk@btconnect.com **w** splashrecords.com Dir: Chas Peate.

Splinter Recordings Terminal Studios, Lamb Walk, London SE1 3TT **t** 020 7357 8416 **f** 020 7357 8437 **e** parmesanchic@aol.com **w** sneakerpimps.com MD: Caroline Butler.

Sprawl Imprint 63 Windmill Rd, Brentford, Middlesex TW8 0QQ **t** 0208 568 3145 **e** sprawl@benfo.demon.co.uk **w** sprawl.org.uk MD: Douglas Benford.

Spring Recordings Dargan House, Duncairn Terrace, Bray, Co. Wicklow, Ireland **t** +353 12 861514 **f** +353 12 861514 **e** kosi@mrspring.net **w** mrspring.net MD: Mr Spring.

Springthyme Records Balmalcolm House, Balmalcolm, Cupar, Fife KY15 7TJ **t** 01337 830773 **e** music@springthyme.co.uk **w** springthyme.co.uk Dir: Peter Shepheard.

Square Biz Records 65A Beresford Rd, London N5 2HR **t** 020 7354 0841 **f** 020 7503 6457 **e** sujiro.gray@btinternet.com MD: Mr J Gray.

Squarepeg Records Studio 201, Westbourne Studios, 242 Acklam Rd, London W10 5JJ **t** 020 7575 3325 **f** 020 7575 3326 **e** info@squarepeg-uk.com **w** squarepeg-uk.com MD: Matt Fisher.

Squeaky Records Ltd. 37 Baldock Rd, Royston, Herts. SG8 5BJ **t** 01763 243 603 **f** 01763 243 603 **e** info@squeakyrecords.com **w** squeakyrecords.com Dir: Helen Gregorios-Pippas.

Squint Entertainment (see Collective Music Ltd)

Star-Write Ltd PO Box 16715, London NW4 1WN **t** 020 8203 5062 **f** 020 8202 3746 **e** starwrite@btinternet.com Dir: John Lisners.

Starshaped Records PO Box 28424, Edinburgh EH4 5YH **t** 0131 336 2776 or 07931 595 285 **e** info@starshaped.co.uk **w** starshaped.co.uk Label Manager: Ian White.

Start Entertainments Ltd 3 Warmair House, Green Lane, Northwood, Middx HA6 2QB **t** 01923 841 414 **f** 01923 842 223 **e** info@startentertainments.com **w** startentertainments.com GM: Nicholas Dicker.

State Art The Basement, 3 Eaton Pl, Brighton, E Sussex BN2 1EH **t** 01273 572090 **f** 01273 572090 **e** stateart@mexone.co.uk **w** mexonerecordings.co.uk Creative Partner: Paul Mex.

State Records 67 Upper Berkeley St, London W1H 7QX **t** 020 7563 7028 **f** 020 7563 7029 **e** recordings@staterecords.co.uk **w** staterecords.co.uk MD: Dr Wayne Bickerton.

Stax (see Ace Records)

Stay Up Forever (see Truelove Records)

Sterling (see Priory Records)

Stern's Records 74-75 Warren St, London W1T 5PF **t** 020 7387 5550 or 020 7388 5533 **f** 020 7388 2756 **e** info@sternsmusic.com **w** sternsmusic.com MD: Don Bay.

Sticky Music PO Box 176, Glasgow G11 5YJ **t** 01698 207230 **f** 0141 576 8431 **e** info@stickymusic.co.uk **w** stickymusic.co.uk Ptnr: Charlie Irvine.

Stiff Records (see ZTT Records Ltd)

Stirling Music Group 25, Heathmans Rd, London SW6 4TJ **t** 020 7371 5756 **f** 020 7371 7731 **e** office@pureuk.com **w** pureuk.com CEO: Evros Stakis.

Stockholm (see Polydor Records)

Stompatime (see Fury Records)

Stoned Asia Music (see Kickin Music Ltd)

The Store For Music Hatch Farm Studios, Chertsey Rd, Addlestone, Surrey KT15 2EH **t** 01932 828715 **f** 01932 828717 **e** brian.adams@dial.pipex.com **w** thestoreformusic.com MD: Brian Adams.

Storm Music 2nd Floor, 1 Ridgefield, Manchester M2 6EG **t** 0161 839 5111 **f** 0161 839 7898 **e** info@storm-music.com **w** storm-music.com Contact: Mike Ball.

Stradivarius (see Priory Records)

Strathan Music Canisp House, Roster, Caithness KW3 6BD **t** 0870 241 2094 **f** 01593 721758 **e** mail@strathan.com **w** strathan.com Dir: Karen Brimm.

Stretchy Records Ltd PO Box 5520, Bishops Stortford, Herts CM23 3WH **t** 01279 865070 **f** 01279 834268 **e** simon@ozrics.com **w** ozrics.com GM: Simon Baker.

Strictly Rhythm (see Warner Bros Records)

Strike Back Records 271 Royal College St, Camden Town, London NW1 9LU **t** 020 7482 0115 **f** 020 7267 1169 **e** maurice@baconempire.com MD: Maurice Bacon.

Strong Records Unit 212, The Saga Centre, 326 Kensal Rd, London W10 5BZ **t** 020 8968 0111 **f** 020 8968 0110 **e** emily@heavyweightman.com Label Mgr: Emily Moxon.

Sublime Music 211 Piccadilly, London W1J 9HF **t** 020 7917 2948 **e** mw@sublime-music.co.uk **w** sublime-music.co.uk Mgr: Nick Grant.

Sublime Recordings Brighton Media Centre, 21/22 Old Steyne, Brighton, E Sussex BN1 1EL **t** 01273 648 330 **f** 01273 648 332 **e** info@sublimemusic.co.uk **w** sublimemusic.co.uk MD: Patrick Spinks.

Suburban Soul (Music) PO Box 415, Bromley, Kent BR1 2XR **t** 020 8402 1984 or 0798 406 1954 **f** 020 8325 0708 **e** urban_music@msn.com Dir: RT Brown.

Subversive Records Old House, 154 Prince Consort Rd, Gateshead NE8 4DU **t** 0191 469 0100 **f** 0191 469 0001 **e** info@subversiverecords.co.uk **w** subversiverecords.co.uk Dir: Martin Jones.

Sugar Shack Records Ltd PO Box 73, Fishponds, Bristol BS16 7EZ **t** 01179 855092 **f** 01179 855092 **e** info@sugarshackrecords.co.uk **w** sugarshackrecords.co.uk Dir: Mike Darby, Adrian Stiff.

Sugar Sound 130 Shaftesbury Ave, London W1D 5EU **t** 020 7031 0971 **e** simon@thesugargroup.com **w** thesugargroup.com Label Manager: Simon Omer.

Sugarstar Ltd IT Centre, York Science Pk, York YO10 5DG **t** 08456 448 424 **f** 0709 222 8681 **e** Info@sugarstar.com **w** sugarstar.com MD: Mark Fordyce.

Summerhouse Records PO Box 34601, London E17 6GA **t** 020 8520 2650 **e** office@summerhouserecordsltd.co.uk **w** summerhouserecordsltd.co.uk MD: William Jones.

Sumo Records 38 Burnfoot Rd, Hawick, Scottish Borders TD9 8EN **t** 01450 378212 **e** info@orbital-productions.com **w** orbital-productions.com MD: Jacqui Gresswell.

Sunday Best Studio 10, 25 Denmark St, London WC2H 8NJ **t** 020 7240 2248 **f** 0870 420 4392 **e** info@sundaybest.net **w** sundaybest.net MD: Rob Da Bank.

Sundissential (see Mohawk Records)

Sunny Records Ltd 29 Fife Rd, East Sheen, London SW14 7EJ **t** 020 8876 9871 **f** 020 8392 2371 **e** getcarter.sunny29@amserve.com Contact: John Carter.

Sunrise Records Silverdene, Scaleby Hill, Carlisle CA6 4LU **t** 01228 675822 **f** 01228 675822 **e** info@sunriserecords.co.uk **w** sunriserecords.co.uk MD: Martin Smith.

SuperCharged Music 29 Kensington Gardens, Brighton BN1 4AL **t** 01273 628 181 **f** 01273 670 444 **e** lloyd@superchargedmusic.com **w** superchargedmusic.com Label Manager: Lloyd Seymour.

Superglider Records First Floor, 123 Old Christchurch Rd, Bournemouth, Dorset BH1 1EP **t** 07968 345173 **e** mail@superglider.com **w** superglider.com Contact: Griff.

Supersonic Records (see New State Entertainment)

Supertone 15 Carrick Court, 137 Stockwell St, Glasgow G1 7LR **t** 07904 113 034 **e** iaininm@aol.com MD: Iain MacDonald.

Supertron Music 19-23 Fosse Way, London W13 0BZ **t** 020 8998 6372 or 020 8998 4372 **e** mikinvent@aol.com(DO NOT PUBLISH) MD: Michael Rodriguez.

Supreme Music PO Box 184, Hove, E Sussex BN3 6UY **t** 01273 556321 **f** 01273 503333 **e** info@recoverworld.com **w** recoverworld.com MD: Chris Hampshire.

Supremo Recordings PO Box 8679, Dublin 7, Ireland **t** +353 1 671 7393 **f** +353 1 671 7393 **e** info@supremorecordings.com **w** supremorecordings.com MD: Philip Cartin.

Surface2Air Ltd 28C Kilburn Lane, London W10 4AH **t** 07960 957 939 **e** info@surface2air.net **w** surface2air.net Head of A&R: Tom Nicolson.

Surfdog Records (see Collective Music Ltd)

Sursagar (see Sense World Music)

Survival Records PO Box 2502, Devizes, Wilts SN10 3ZN **t** 01380 860 500 **f** 01380 860 596 **e** AnneMarie@survivalrecords.co.uk **w** survivalrecords.co.uk Dir: David Rome.

Suspect Records 58 Greenfell Mansions, Glaisher St, London SE8 3EU **t** 07764 159175 **e** info@suspectrecords.com **w** suspectrecords.com MD: Stephen Davison.

suss'd! records - the home of Salsoul UK 35 Britannia Row, Islington, London N1 8QH **t** 020 7359 6998 **f** 020 7354 8661 **e** info@sussd.com **w** salsoul.co.uk Contact: Rob Horrocks.

Susu (see Concept Music)

Sweet Nothing (see Cargo Records)

Swing Cafe 32 Willesden Lane, London NW6 7ST **t** 020 7625 0231 **f** 020 372 5439 **e** lauriejay@btconnect.com Head of A&R: Chas White.

Swing City (see Wyze Recordings)

Switchflicker 3rd Floor, 24 Lever St, Northern Quarter, Manchester M1 1DX **t** 07803 601 885 **e** jayne@switchflicker.com **w** switchflicker.com A&R: Jayne Compton.

Swordmaker Records PO Box 55, Consett, Co Durham DH8 0UX **t** 01207 509365 **f** 01207 509365 **e** enquiries@swordmaker.co.uk **w** swordmaker.co.uk A&R: Jonny Rye.

SYCO

Bedford House, 69-79 Fulham High Street, London SW6 3JW **t** 020 7384 7500 **f** 020 7973 0332 **e** firstname.lastname@sonybmg.com. MD: Simon Cowell. Syco Music: Sonny Takhar. Syco TV: Nigel Hall, Siobhan Greene.

Sylvantone Records 11 Saunton Ave, Redcar, N Yorks TS10 2RL **t** 01642 479898 **f** 0709 235 9333 **e** sylvantone@hotmail.com **w** countrymusic.org.uk/tony-goodacre/index.html Prop: Tony Goodacre.

Symposium Records 110 Derwent Ave, East Barnet, Herts EN4 8LZ **t** 020 8368 8667 **f** 020 8368 8667 **e** symposium@cwcom.net **w** symposiumrecords.co.uk

Taciturn Records PO Box 36202, London SE19 3YW **t** 020 8653 6318 **f** 020 8653 6318 **e** taciturn@chrisshields.com **w** chrisshields.com Dir: Chris Shields.

Tahra (see Priory Records)

Tailormade Music Ltd PO Box 2311, Romford, Essex
RM5 2DZ **t** 01708 734670 **f** 01708 734671
e info@dancelabel.com **w** dancelabel.com Dir: Dan Donnelly.

Talking Elephant 8 Martin Dene, Bexleyheath, Kent
DA6 8NA **t** 020 8301 2828 **f** 020 8301 2424
e talkelephant@aol.com **w** talkingelephant.com
Ptnr: Barry Riddington.

Tall Pop (see Adasam Limited)

Tanty Records PO Box 557, Harrow, Middlesex HA2 6ZX
t 020 8421 4004 **f** 020 8933 1027 **e** kelvin.r@tantyrecord.com
w tantyrecord.com Owner: Kelvin Richard.

Tara Music Company Basement, 18 Upper Mount St,
Dublin 2, Ireland **t** +353 1 678 7871 **f** +353 1 678 7873
e info@taramusic.com **w** taramusic.com MD: John Cook.

Taste Media Ltd 263 Putney Bridge Rd, London SW15 2PU
t 020 8780 3311 **f** 020 8785 9894 **e** laurie@tastemedia.com
w tastemedia.com Creative Manager: Laurie Latham Jnr.

TCM Music Ltd 18 Bramley Rd, Ealing, London W5 4SS
t 0208 840 6008 **f** 0208 840 6008 **e** ted@tcmmusic.co.uk
w tcmmusic.co.uk Dir: Ted Carfrae.

TeC (see Truelove Records)

Teldec (see Warner Classics)

Teleryngg (see Savant Records)

Telica Communications (see Supreme Music)

Tenor Vossa Records Ltd 1 Colville Pl, London W1T 2BG
t 020 7221 0511 **f** 020 7221 0511 **e** tenor.vossa@virgin.net
w tenorvossa.co.uk MD: Ari Neufeld.

Terminus Records (see Collective Music Ltd)

Test Recordings (see Valve)

The Hallowe'en Society (see Adasam Limited)

The White (see Jessica Records Ltd)

Them's Good Records (see Adasam Limited)

There's A Riot Going On Records PO Box 1977,
Salisbury SP3 5ZW **t** 01722 716716 **f** 01722 716413
e targo.entscorps@virgin.net MD: Mathew Priest.

The Thin Man 38 Oakford Rd, London NW5 1AH
t 07966 046621 **e** hello@thethinman.co.uk **w** thethinman.co.uk
MD: Toby Kidd.

13th Hour (see Mute Records Ltd)

Thirty-Seven Records 28 St. Albans Gdns, Stranmillis Rd,
Belfast, Co. Antrim BT9 5DR **t** 07736 548 969
e sean@thirtysevenrecords.com **w** thirtysevenrecords.com
Label Mgr: Sean Douglas.

Thunder (see Rollercoaster Records)

Thunderbird Records (see RPM Productions)

Thursday Club Recordings Ltd 310 King St, London
W6 0RR **t** 0208 748 9480 **f** 0208 748 9489
e info@tcr.uk.com **w** tcr.uk.com MD: Rennie Pilgrem.

Tickety-Boo Ltd The Boat House, Crabtree Lane, London
SW6 6TY **t** 020 7610 0122 **f** 020 7610 0133
e tickety-boo@tickety-boo.com **w** tickety-boo.com
Mgr: Steve Brown.

Tiger Trax PO Box 204, Alton, Hants GU34 1YA
t 07838 111 026 **e** info@tigertrax.co.uk **w** tigertrax.co.uk
Business Affairs: Sam Radford.

Tiny Dog Records 9 Park Rd, Wells-next-the-Sea, Norfolk
NR23 1DQ **t** 01328 711 115 **f** 01328 711 115
e info@tinydog.co.uk **w** tinydog.co.uk MD: Pete Jennison.

Tip World PO Box 18157, London NW6 7FF
t 020 8537 2675 **f** 020 8537 2671 **e** info@tipworld.co.uk
w tipworld.co.uk Label Manager: Richard Bloor.

Tolotta (see Southern Records)

Tongue Master Records PO Box 38621, London
W13 8WG **t** 020 8723 4985 **f** 020 7371 4884
e info@tonguemaster.co.uk **w** tonguemaster.co.uk
MD: Theodore Vlassopulos.

Too Pure 17-19 Alma Rd, London SW18 1AA
t 020 8875 6208 **f** 020 8875 1205 **e** toopure@toopure.co.uk
w toopure.com Label Head: Jason White.

Too Young To Die Records Unit 14, Buspace Studios,
Conlan St, London W10 5AR **t** 020 8560 8402
e info@tooyoungtodierecords.com **w** tooyoungtodierecords.com
MDs: Pete Hobbs, Jonathan Owen.

Top Notch (see Fashion Records)

Topaz (see Pavilion Records Ltd)

Topic Records 50 Stroud Green Rd, London N4 3ES
t 020 7263 1240 **f** 020 7281 5671 **e** info@topicrecords.co.uk
w topicrecords.co.uk MD: Tony Engle.

Tortured Records PO Box 32, Beckenham BR3 6ZP
t 01273 779 515 **e** billy@torturedrecords.co.uk
w torturedrecords.co.uk MD: Billy Nasty.

Total Control Records PO Box 1345, Ilford, Essex
IG4 5FX **t** 07050 333 555 **f** 07020 923 292
e info@ArtistDevelopment.org A&R Director: Wendy Kickes.

Touch 13 Osward Rd, London SW17 7SS **t** 020 8355 9672
f 020 8355 9672 **e** info@touchmusic.org.uk **w** touchmusic.org.uk
Dirs: Jon Wozencroft, Michael Harding.

Touch And Go (see Southern Records)

Tough Cookie Ltd 3rd Floor, 24 Denmark St, London
WC2H 8NJ **t** 020 8870 9233 or 07977 248 646
f 0871 242 2442 **e** office@tough-cookie.co.uk
w myspace.com/toughcookiemusic Dir: Andy Wood.

TOV Music Group Ltd (Trouble on Vinyl) 120
Wandsworth Rd, London SW8 2LB **t** 020 7498 3888
f 020 7622 1030 **e** info@tovmusic.com **w** tovmusic.com
MD: Clayton Hines.

Town Hill Records Ty Cefn, Rectory Rd, Canton, Cardiff
CF5 1QL **t** 029 2022 7993 **f** 029 2039 9400
e huwwilliams@townhillmusic.com **w** townhillmusic.com
Dir: Huw Williams.

Track Records PO Box 107, South Godstone, Redhill, Surrey RH9 8YS **t** 01342 892 178 or 01342 892 074 **f** 01342 893 411 **e** ian.grant@trackrecords.co.uk **w** trackrecords.co.uk MD: Ian Grant.

Tradition (see Palm Pictures)

Transcopic Records Nettwerk, Clearwater Yard, 35 Inverness St, London NW1 7HB **t** 020 7424 7522 **e** jamie@transcopic.com **w** transcopic.com MD: Jamie Davis.

Transgressive Records 3a Highbury Crescent, Islington, London N5 1RN **t** 020 7700 4464 **e** toby@transgressiverecords.co.uk **w** transgressiverecords.co.uk Label Manager: Toby L.

Transient Records (see Automatic Records)

Transistor Records (see RPM Productions)

Transmission Recordings Ltd Bedford House, 8B Berkeley Gardens, London W8 4AP **t** 020 7243 2921 **f** 020 7243 2894 **e** peter.chalcraft@nottinghillmusic.com Dir: Peter Chalcraft.

Trial and Error Recordings 274 Caledonian Rd, London N1 1BA **t** 07867 552 931 **e** info@trialanderrorrecordings.com **w** trialanderrorrecordings.com Co-manager: JeanGa.

Triangle Records 66c Chalk Farm Rd, London NW1 8AN **t** 020 8482 6945 **f** 020 8485 9244 **e** info@triangle-records.co.uk **w** triangle-records.co.uk MD: Chris Lock.

Tribe Recordings 30 Watermore Close, Bristol BS36 2NH **t** 07976 751 781 **e** triberecordings@hotmail.com Dir: David Cridge.

Trinity Records Company 72 New Bond St, London W1S 1RR **t** 020 7499 4141 **e** info@trinitymediagroup.net **w** trinitymediagroup.net MD: Peter Murray.

Triple A Records Ltd GMC Studio, Hollingbourne, Kent ME17 1UQ **t** 01622 880599 **f** 01622 880020 **e** records@triple-a.uk.com **w** triple-a.uk.com CEO: Terry Armstrong.

Tripoli Trax (see Locked On Records)

TRL PO Box 20, Banbury, OX17 3YT **t** 0129 581 4995 **e** music@therecordlabel.co.uk **w** therecordlabel.co.uk Dirs: Steve Betts, Phil Knox-Roberts.

Trojan Records (see Sanctuary Records Group)

Tropical Fish Music 1 Pauntley House, Pauntley St, London N19 3TG **t** 0870 444 5462 or 07973 386 279 **f** 0870 132 3318 **e** info@tropicalfishmusic.com **w** tropicalfishmusic.com MD: Grishma Jashapara.

Tru Thoughts PO Box 2818, Brighton, E Sussex BN1 4RL **t** 01273 694617 **f** 01273 694589 **e** info@tru-thoughts.co.uk **w** tru-thoughts.co.uk Label Mgr: Paul Jonas.

Truck Records 15 Percy St, Oxford OX4 3AA **t** 01865 722333 **e** paul@truckrecords.com **w** truckrecords.com MD: Paul Bonham.

Truelove Records 19F Tower Workshops, Riley Rd, London SE1 3DG **t** 020 7252 2900 **f** 020 7252 2890 **e** business@truelove.co.uk **w** truelove.co.uk Contact: John Truelove, Brian Roach.

Trust Me I'm A Thief 31 Oxmantown Rd, Stoneybatter, Dublin 7, Ireland **t** +353 87 6364206 **e** info@trustmeimathief.com **w** trustmeimathief.com Dir: Brian Mooney.

TrustTheDJ Records White Horse Yard, 78 Liverpool Rd, London N1 0QD **t** 020 7288 9814 **f** 020 7288 9817 **e** contact@trustthedj.com **w** trustthedj.com Label Managers: Matt Bullamore, Cam MacPhail.

Tuff Gong (see Island Records Group)

Tuff Street Recordings (see Tuff Street - SOSL Recordings)

Tuff Street - SOSL Recordings PO Box 7874, London SW20 9XD **t** 07050 605219 **f** 07050 605239 **e** sam@pan-africa.org **w** umengroup.com CEO: Oscar Sam Carrol Jnr.

Tugboat Records (see Rough Trade Records)

TV Records Ltd (see Tenor Vossa Records Ltd)

TVT Records UK Unit 226, Canalot Studios, 222 Kensal Rd, London W10 5BN **t** 020 8968 9700 **f** 020 8968 9732 **e** info@tvtrecords.co.uk **w** tvtrecords.co.uk MD: Jonathan Green.

Twisted Nerve Records 6 Fleet St, Hyde, Cheshire SK14 2LF **t** 07967 732 616 **e** info@twistednerve.co.uk **w** twistednerve.co.uk Label Manager: Paul Vella.

Tyrant 4a Scampston Mews, Cambridge Gardens, London W10 6HX **t** 020 8968 6815 **f** 020 8969 1728 **e** info@tyrant.co.uk **w** tyrant.co.uk Dirs: Craig Richards/Amanda Eastwood.

Tyst Music UK Ltd 35 Albany Rd, Chorlton, Manchester M21 0BH **t** 0161 882 0058 **f** 0161 882 0058 **e** info@tsytdigital.com **w** tsytdigital.com Dir: David Wheawill.

Udiscs Monk's Retreat, 33 Dumbreck Rd, Glasgow, Glasgow G41 5LJ **t** 0141 427 3707 **f** 0141 427 3707 **e** info@udiscs.com **w** udiscs.com Label Mgr: Steve Bonellie.

U4ria (see Flat Records)

Ugly Records (see Fume Recordings)

UGR (see Urban Gospel Records)

Ultimate Dilemma (see Atlantic Records UK)

Ultrafunk (see Truelove Records)

Underground Music Movement (UMM) (see Media Records Ltd)

Underwater Records (see Southern Fried Records)

Union Records (see 37 Music)

Union Square Music Unit 11 Shepherds Studios, Rockley Rd, London W14 0DA **t** 020 7471 7940 **f** 020 7471 7941 **e** info@unionsquaremusic.co.uk **w** unionsquaremusic.co.uk MD: Peter Stack.

Unique Corp 15 Shaftesbury Centre, 85 Barlby Rd, London W10 6BN **t** 020 8964 9333 **f** 020 8964 9888 **e** info@uniquecorp.co.uk **w** uniquecorp.co.uk MD: Alan Bellman.

United Nations Records (see Down By Law Records)

UNIVERSAL MUSIC CLASSICS & JAZZ (UK)

364-366 Kensington High St, London W14 8NS
t 020 7471 5000 **f** 020 7471 5001
e firstname.lastname@umusic.com **w** universalclassics.com. MD:
Bill Holland. General Manager: Dickon Stainer. Marketing Director:
Mark Wilkinson. Head of Legal & Business Affairs: Jackie Joseph.
Senior Finance Director: Geoff Harris. Head of Press &
Promotions: Rebecca Allen. Head of A&R: Tom Lewis.

Universal Music Catalogue 1st Floor, 364-366
Kensington High St, London W14 8NS **t** 020 7471 5000
f 020 7471 5001 **e** silvia.montello@umusic.com **w** umusic.co.uk
Head of Catalogue: Silvia Montello.

Universal Music Dance 364-366 Kensington High St,
London W14 8NS **t** 020 7471 5000 **f** 020 7471 5138
e firstname.lastname@umusic.com **w** manifesto-records.com
Head of A&R: Eddie Ruffett.

UNIVERSAL MUSIC IRELAND

9 Whitefriars, Aungier Street, Dublin 2, Ireland
t +353 1 402 2600 **f** +353 1 475 7860
e firstname.lastname@umusic.com **w** universalmusic.com MD:
Dave Pennefather. Chairman/CEO: Lucian Grainge. Dir of Finance:
Cathy McMorrow. Dir of Sales: Freddie Blake. Product Mgr
(Classics/Jazz): Catherine Hughes. Promotions & Mktg Executive:
Anne Pennefather. Promotions & Mktg Co-ordinator: Laura
Fitzgerald.

UNIVERSAL MUSIC TV

UNIVERSAL MUSIC TV

364-366 Kensington High St, London W14 8NS
t 020 7471 5000 **f** 020 7471 5001
e firstname.lastname@umusic.com MD: Brian Berg. Sales &
Marketing Dir: Paul Chisnall. Head of Legal & Business Affairs:
Jackie Joseph. Senior Finance Director: Geoff Harris. Head of
Licensing & Business Development: Kevin Phelan.

UNIVERSAL MUSIC (UK) LTD

UNIVERSAL MUSIC UK

364-366 Kensington High St, London W14 8NS
t 020 7471 5000 **f** 020 7471 5001
e firstname.lastname@umusic.com **w** umusic.com CEO &
Chairman: Lucian Grainge. Executive VP: Clive Fisher. CFO: David
Bryant. Commercial Dir: Brian Rose. President, Universal Music
Operations: David Joseph. Distribution Dir: Russell Richards. Dir,
HR Operations: Michael Pye. Divisional Dir, New Media & Digital:
Rob Wells. Snr VP International Marketing: Hassan Choudhury.
Dir of Communications: Selina Webb.

Universal Pictures Video Prospect House, 80-110 New
Oxford St, London WC1A 1HB **t** 020 7079 6000
f 020 7079 6500 **e** firstname.lastname@nbcuni.com
w universalpictures.co.uk MDs: Johnny Fewings, Helen Parker.

Universal Pictures Visual Programming Prospect
House, 80-110 New Oxford St, London WC1A 1HB
t 020 7079 6331 **f** 020 7079 6521
e vanessa.schneider@nbcuni.com **w** universalstudios.com
Pres: Hugh Rees-Parnall.

Untalented Artist Inc. (see Low Quality Accident)

Unyque Artists PO Box 1257, London E5 0UD
t 020 8986 1984 **e** mal@jastoy.co.uk MD: Tee.

Up North Records Ltd. 67 McDonald Rd, Edinburgh
EH7 4NA **t** 0131 4778693 **e** admin@upnorthrecords.co.uk
w upnorthrecords.co.uk MD: Tony Lyons.

Upbeat Classics (see Upbeat Recordings Ltd)

Upbeat Jazz (see Upbeat Recordings Ltd)

Upbeat Recordings Ltd PO Box 63, Wallington, Surrey
SM6 9YP **t** 020 8773 1223 **f** 020 8669 6752
e liz@upbeat.co.uk **w** upbeat.co.uk MD, Exec Prod: Liz Biddle.

Upbeat Showbiz (see Upbeat Recordings Ltd)

Upside Records 14 Clarence Mews, Balham, London
SW12 9SR. **t** 020 8673 8549 or 07786 066 665
f 020 8673 8498 **e** simon@upsideuk.com MD: Simon Jones.

Urban Dubz Recordings PO Box 12275, Birmingham
B23 3AB **t** 07931 139 806 **e** info@urbandubz.com
w urbandubz.com Prop: Jeremy Sylvester.

Urban Gospel Records PO Box 178, Sutton, Surrey
SM2 6XG **t** 020 8643 6403 or 07904 255 244
f 020 8643 6403 **e** info@urbangospelrecords.com
w urbangospelrecords.com Head of A&R: P Mac.

Urban Precinct 34 Wroxham Ave, Hemel Hempstead, Herts
HP3 9HF **t** 01442 265 415 **f** 01442 265 415
e da3rd@3rdprecinct.co.uk **w** urbanprecinct.com
MD: Floyd Adams.

Urbanstar Records Global House, 92 De Beauvoir Rd,
London N1 4EN **t** 020 7288 2239 **f** 0870 429 2493
e info@urbanstarrecords.com **w** urbanstarrecords.com
Dir: Nick Sellors.

Record Companies: Record Companies and Labels

URP (see Urban Gospel Records)

US Everest (see Everest Copyrights)

Usk Recordings 26 Caterham Rd, London SE13 5AR
t 020 7274 5610 or 020 8318 2031 **f** 020 7737 0063
e info@uskrecordings.com **w** uskrecordings.com
Dir: Rosemary Lindsay.

V Ram Discs UK Nestlingdown, Chapel Hill, Pothtowan,
Truro, Cornwall TR4 8AS **t** 01209 890606 Dir: John Bowyer.

V2
Unit 24, 101 Farm Lane, Fulham, London SW6 1QJ
t 020 7471 3000 **e** firstname.lastname@v2music.com
w v2music.com Group CEO: Tony Harlow. Business Affairs:
Charlie Wale. Head of New Media and Business Development:
Beth Appleton. UK MD: David Steele. FD: Andrew Parker.
Director A&R: Charlie Pinder. Head of Marketing: Jason Rackham.

VA Recordings (see Finger Lickin' Records)

Vagabond (see Silverword Music Group)

Vagrant (see Full Time Hobby Records)

Valve Unit 24 Ropery Business Pk, Anchor & Hope Lane,
London SE7 7RX **t** 020 8853 4900 **f** 020 8853 4908
e info@valverecordings.com **w** valverecordings.com
Label Manager: Josephine Serieux.

Vane Recordings P.O. Box 70, Witney, Oxon OX29 4GA
t 01865 883671 or 07939 228435 **f** 01865 883671
e jerry@vane-recordings.com **w** vane-recordings.com
Prop: Jerry Butson.

Vanquish Music Group 5 Gartons Way, London
SW11 3SX **t** 020 3238 0033 **f** 0870 288 7181
e info@vanquish-musicgroup.co.uk **w** vanquish-musicgroup.co.uk
Head of A&R: Adjei.

Vapour (see 3 Beat Label Management)

VC Recordings (see Virgin Records)

Veesik Records Back Charlotte Lane, Lerwick, Shetland
ZE1 0JD **t** 01595 696622 **f** 01595 696622
e alan@veesikrecords.co.uk **w** veesikrecords.co.uk
MD: Alan Longmuir.

Velvel (see Fire Records)

Venus Music & Records Ltd 13 Fernhurst Gardens,
Edgware, Middx HA8 7PQ **t** 020 8952 1924 or 07956 064 019
f 020 8952 3496 **e** kamalmmalak@onetel.net.uk
w venusmusicandrecords.co.uk MD: Kamal M Malak.

Vertigo (see Mercury Music Group)

Verve (see Universal Music Classics & Jazz (UK))

Vibe Entertainment (see Taste Media Ltd)

Vibezone (see Dead Happy Records)

Victoria Music Ltd Unit 215, Old Gramophone Works, 326
Kensal Rd, London W10 5BZ **t** 020 7565 8193
f 020 8960 3834 **e** info@victoria-music.com
w victoria-music.com Dir: Charlie Hall.

Video Collection International 76 Dean St, London
W1D 3SQ **t** 020 7396 8888 **f** 020 7396 8996 or
020 7396 8997 **e** info@vci.co.uk **w** vciplc.co.uk
Contact: Amanda Morgan.

The Video Pool 99A Linden Gardens, London W2 4EX
t 020 7221 3803 or 020 7229 1723 **f** 020 7221 3280
e roz@videopool.com **w** videopool.com MD: Roz Bea.

Viktor Records The Saga Centre, 326 Kensal Rd, London
W10 5BZ **t** 020 8969 3370 **f** 020 8969 3374
e info@streetfeat.demon.co.uk MD: Colin Schaverien.

Vintage (see Collecting Records LLP)

Vinyl Japan 98 Camden Rd, London NW1 9EA
t 020 7284 0359 **f** 020 7267 5186 **e** office@vinyljapan.com
w vinyljapan.com Label Mgr: Claire Munro.

VIRGIN RECORDS

Crown House, 72 Hammersmith Road, London W14 8UD
t 020 7605 5000 **f** 020 7605 5050
e firstname.lastname@emimusic.com **w** virginrecords.co.uk MD:
Ferdy Unger-Hamilton. GM: Mark Terry. Head of Press: Susie
Ember.

Virus Recordings Unit 125 Safestore, 5-10 Eastman Rd,
Acton, London W3 7YG **t** 07971 798 393 **f** 0709 200 4055
e ellise@sirenproductions.freeserve.co.uk
Label Manager: Ellise Fleming.

Visceral Thrill Recordings 8 Deronda Rd, London
SE24 9BG **t** 020 8674 7990 or 07775 806 288
f 020 8671 5548 MD: Dave Massey.

Visible Noise 231 Portobello Rd, London W11 1LT
t 020 7792 9791 **f** 020 7792 9871 **e** julie@visiblenoise.com
w visiblenoise.com MD: Julie Weir.

Vision Video Ltd 1 Sussex Pl, Hammersmith, London
W6 9XS **t** 020 8910 5000 **f** 020 8910 5404
e firstname.lastname@unistudios.com A&R Manager: Tim Payne.

Visionary Communications 329 Clifton Drive South,
Lytham St Annes, Lancs FY8 1LP **t** 01253 712453
f 01253 712362 **e** nicky@visionary.co.uk **w** outlaw23.com
Dir: Nicky O'Toole.

Visionquest (see Loose Tie Records)

Vixen Records (Ireland) Glenmundar House, Ballyman Rd,
Bray, Co. Wicklow, Ireland **t** +353 86 257 6244
f +353 1 282 0508 **e** picket@iol.ie Dir: Deke O'Brien.

Vocaphone Records Stanley House, Stanley Rd, Acton,
London W3 7SY **t** 020 8735 0284 **e** vocaphone@bigupjazz.com
w neilpyzer.com Label Manager: Cole Parker.

Voiceprint PO Box 50, Houghton-le-Spring, Tyne & Wear
DH4 5YP **t** 0191 512 1103 **f** 0191 512 1104
e info@voiceprint.co.uk **w** voiceprint.co.uk MD: Rob Ayling.

Voltage (see New State Entertainment)

Voluptuous Records 26 Top Rd, Frodsham, Cheshire WA6 6SW **t** 07939 140 774 **e** carl@formidable-mgmt.com **w** formidable-mgmt.com Dir: Carl Marcantonio.

VP Records UK Ltd Unit 12B, Shaftsbury Centre, 85 Barlby Rd, London W10 6BN **t** 020 8962 2760 **f** 020 8968 6791 **e** joye@vprecords.com **w** vprecords.com Mktg Mgr: Joy Ellington.

VX Records (see Planet1 Music)

W14 MUSIC

364-366 Kensington High Street, London W14 8NS **t** 020 7471 5000 **f** 020 7471 5001 **e** firstname.lastname@umusic.com MD: John Williams. Consultant: John Knowles. Director Legal & Business Affairs: Jackie Joseph. Commercial Director: Brian Rose. Head of Marketing: Silvia Montello.

Wagram Music Unit 203, Westbourne Studios, 242 Acklam Rd, London W10 5YG **t** 020 8968 8800 **f** 020 8968 8877 **e** wagrammusic@btclick.com MD: Peter Walmsley.

Wah Wah 45s Flat 12, St. Luke's Church, 38 Mayfield Rd, London N8 9LP **t** 07775 657 578 or 07812 089 629 **e** info@wahwah45s.com **w** wahwah45s.com Label Mgrs, A&R: Dom Servini & Simon Goss.

Walt Disney Records 3 Queen Caroline St, London W6 9PE **t** 020 8222 2281 **f** 020 8222 2283 **e** firstname.lastname@disney.com Exec Dir: Hilary Stebbings.

WARNER BROS RECORDS

RECORDS

12 Lancer Square, London W8 4EH **t** 020 7368 3500 **f** 020 7368 3760 **e** firstname.lastname@warnermusic.com **w** warnerbrosrecords.com. MD: Korda Marshall. Dir of Bus Affs: Gez Orakwusi. General Manager: Adam Hollywood. Mktg Dir (Domestic): Matt Thomas. Press Director: Andy Prevezer. Promotions Dir: Sarah Adams. Heads of A&R: James Dowdall & Rose Noone. A&R Managers: Neil Ridley & Paul Brown.

WARNER CLASSICS

 WarnerClassics

3rd Floor, Griffin House, 161 Hammersmith Road, London W6 8BS **t** 020 8563 5100 **f** 020 8563 6226 **e** firstname.lastname@warnermusic.com **w** warnerclassics.com. Director: Nick Stewart. General Manager: Stefan Bown. Classics Paralegal: Emily Koti.

Warner Home DVD Warner House, 98 Theobald's Rd, London WC1X 8WB **t** 020 7984 6400 **f** 020 7984 5001 **e** neil.mcewan@warnerbros.com **w** warnerbros.com MD: Neil McEwan.

WARNER MUSIC (UK)

WARNER MUSIC
UNITED KINGDOM

The Warner Building, 28A Kensington Church Street, London W8 4EP **t** 020 7368 2500 **f** 020 7368 2770 **e** firstname.lastname@warnermusic.com **w** warnermusic.co.uk. Chairman: Nick Phillips. Commercial Director: Alan Young. Senior VP Business Affairs WMI: John Watson. Finance Director: Mike Saunter. MD Atlantic Records UK: Max Lousada. MD Warner Bros Records: Korda Marshall. MD 679 Recordings: Nick Worthington. MD 14th Floor Records: Christian Tattersfield. Director Rhino UK & Warner Classics: Nick Stewart. Head of HR: Gill Tacchi. Communications and Artist Relations Director: Jason Morais. PA to Chairman: Liz Marshall.

Warner Music (Ireland) 2nd Floor, Skylab, 2, Exchange St Upper, Dublin 8, Ireland **t** +353 1 881 4500 **f** +353 1 881 4599 **e** firstname.lastname@warnermusic.com **w** warnermusic.com GM: Pat Creed.

Warner Vision International The Electric Lighting Station, 46 Kensington Court, London W8 5DA **t** 020 7938 5500 **f** 020 7368 4931 **e** julia.fiske@warnermusic.com Pres: Ray Still.

Warp Spectrum House, 32-34 Gordon House Rd, London NW5 1LP **t** 020 7284 8350 **f** 020 7284 8360 **e** info@warprecords.com **w** warprecords.com GM: Kevin Flemming.

Way Out West Records 69 Hampton Rd, Teddington, Middx TW11 0LA **t** 020 8977 6509 **f** 020 8977 6400 **e** wowrecco@aol.com **w** wowrecords.co.uk MD: Simon Davies.

Wayward (see IRL)

Wayward Records PO Box 30884, London W12 9AZ **t** 020 8746 7461 **f** 020 8749 7441 **e** wayward@spiritmm.com Label Manager: Tom Haxell.

WEA London (see Warner Bros Records)

Weekend Beatnik (see Rogue Records Ltd)

Welsh Gold (see Silverword Music Group)

What Records Ltd. PO Box 10387, Birmingham B16 8WB **t** 0121 455 6034 or 01895 824674 **f** 0121 456 5122 or 01895 822994 **e** whatrecords@blueyonder.co.uk Dirs: Mick Cater/David Harper.

Whirlie Records 14 Broughton Pl, Edinburgh EH1 3RX **t** 0131 557 9099 **f** 0131 557 6519 **e** info@whirlierecords.co.uk **w** whirlierecords.co.uk MD: George Brown.

White Line (see Sanctuary Classics)

White Noise The Motor Museum, 1 Hesketh St, Liverpool L17 8XJ **t** 0151 222 2760 **e** office@whitenoiseuk.com **w** whitenoiseuk.com Label Manager: Eric Mackay.

Whole 9 Yards PO Box 435, Walton on Thames, Surrey KT12 4XR **t** 01932 230088 **f** 01932 223796 **e** info@w9y.co.uk **w** w9y.co.uk Label Mgr: Mark Pember.

Wichita Recordings 120 Curtain Rd, London EC2A 3SQ **t** 020 7729 3371 **e** info@wichita-recordings.com **w** wichita-recordings.com Contact: Dick Green/Mark Bowen.

Wide-Eyed Music 24A Camden Rd, London NW1 9DP **t** 020 7482 5277 **f** 020 7267 3430 **e** wem@pierconnection.co.uk Prop: Vid Lakhani.

Wienerworld Ltd Unit 7 Freetrade House, Lowther Rd, Stanmore, Middx HA7 1EP **t** 020 8206 1177 **f** 020 8206 2757 **e** wworld@wienerworld.com **w** wienerworld.com MD: Anthony Broza.

Wiiija (see 4AD)

Wild Card (see Polydor Records)

Wildloops 5, Link Rd, Sale, Cheshire M33 4HW **t** 07801 454187 **e** info@wildloops.com **w** wildloops.com Label Manager: Kevin Gorman.

John Williams Productions Burnfield Rd, Giffnock, Glasgow, Strathclyde G46 7TH **t** 0141 637 2244 **f** 0141 637 2231 **e** jwp.sbl@virgin.net Production Manager: Karen McKay.

Within Records 21 Higher Audley Ave, Torquay, Devon TQ2 7PG **t** 07849 199 613 or 07835 773 338 **e** within@movementinsound.com **w** movementinsound.com Dirs: Chris Clark, Stephen Gould.

Wizard Records PO Box 6779, Birmingham B13 9RZ **t** 0121 778 2218 or 07956 984 754 **f** 0121 778 1856 **e** pk.sharma@ukonline.co.uk **w** wizardrecords.co.uk MD: Mambo Sharma.

WMTV

WARNER MUSIC TV

The Warner Building, 28a Kensington Church Street, London W8 4EP **t** 020 7368 2500 **f** 020 7368 2773 **e** firstname.lastname@warnermusic.com Director: Nick Stewart. General Manager: James Harris. Marketing Manager: Elena Bello. Head of Licensing: Kathy Kelly. Product Manager: Lucy Beacon.

Wolftown Recordings PO Box 1668, Wolverhampton, W Midlands WV2 3WG **t** 07968 295 913 **f** 01902 423 627 **e** info@wolftownrecordings.com **w** wolftownrecordings.com Dirs: Tricksta & Late.

Wonderland Media Ltd 23 London Rd, Aston Clinton, Aylesbury, Bucks HP22 5HG **t** 01296 631 003 **e** nick@wonderlandmedia.net **w** wonderlandmedia.net Contact: Nick Hindle.

Wooden Hill Recordings Ltd Lister House, 117 Milton Rd, Weston-super-Mare, Somerset BS23 2UX **t** 01934 644309 **f** 01934 644402 **e** cliffdane@tiscali.co.uk **w** mediaresearchpublishing.com Chairman: Cliff Dane.

Workers Playtime Music Co. 204 Crescent House, Goswell Rd, London EC1Y 0SL **t** 020 7490 7346 **e** bill@workersplaytime.co.uk **w** workersplaytime.co.uk MD: Bill Gilliam.

Working Class Records 22 Upper Brook St, Mayfair, London W1K 7PZ **t** 020 7491 1060 **f** 020 7491 9996 **e** workingclassmusic@btinternet.com **w** workingclassrecords.co.uk Contact: Matt Crossey, Lisa Barker.

World Circuit 138 Kingsland Rd, London E2 8DY **t** 020 7749 3222 **f** 020 7749 3232 **e** post@worldcircuit.co.uk **w** worldcircuit.co.uk MD: Nick Gold.

World Music Network (UK) Ltd 6 Abbeville Mews, 88 Clapham Park Rd, London SW4 7BX **t** 020 7498 5252 **f** 020 7498 5353 **e** post@worldmusic.net **w** worldmusic.net MD: Phil Stanton.

Worst Case Scenario Records Global House, Bridge St, Guildford, Surrey GU1 4SB **t** 01483 501 218 **f** 01483 501 201 **e** wcs@wcsrecords.com **w** wcsrecords.com Label Manager: Brendan Byrne.

Wrasse Records Wrasse House, The Drive, Tyrrells Wood, Leatherhead KT22 8QW **t** 01372 376 266 **f** 01372 370 281 **e** jo.ashbridge@wrasserecords.com **w** wrasserecords.com Joint MDs: Jo & Ian Ashbridge.

Wrench Records BCM Box 4049, London WC1N 3XX **f** 020 7700 3855 **e** mail@wrench.org **w** wrench.org MD: Charlie Chainsaw.

Wundaland & Boogy Limited 65, Hazelwood Rd, Bush Hill Pk, Middx. EN1 1JG **t** 020 8245 6573 **f** 020 8254 6573 **e** jemgant@yahoo.co.uk MD: Jem Gant.

Wyze Recordings PO Box 847, Camberley, Surrey GU15 3ZZ **t** 01276 671441 **f** 01276 684460 **e** info@wyze.com **w** wyze.com MD: Kate Ross.

XL Recordings 1 Codrington Mews, London W11 2EH **t** 020 8870 7511 **f** 020 8871 4178 **e** xl@xl-recordings.com **w** xl-recordings.com Contact: Jo Bagenal.

Xplosive Records 33/37 Hatherley Mews, Walthamstow, London E17 4QP **t** 020 8521 9227 **f** 020 8520 5553 **e** postmaster@xplosiverecords.co.uk **w** xplosiverecords.co.uk Partners: Terry McLeod/Tapps Bandawe.

Xtra Mile Recordings 5-7 Vernon Yard, off Portobello Rd, London W11 2DX **t** 020 7792 9400 **f** 020 7243 2262 **e** Charlie@presscounsel.com **w** xtramilerecordings.com MD: Charlie Caplowe.

Y2K (see Locked On Records)

Yolk (see High Barn Records)

York Ambisonic PO Box 66, Lancaster, Lancs LA2 6HS **t** 01524 823020 **f** 01524 824420 **e** yorkambisonic@aol.com MD: Brendan Hearne.

You Clash! Recordings PO Box 21469, Highgate, London N6 4ZG **t** 020 8340 5151 **f** 020 8340 5159 **e** james@topdrawmusic.biz Dirs: Paul Masterson/James Hamilton.

Zane Records 162 Castle Hill, Reading, Berks RG1 7RP **t** 0118 957 4567 **f** 0118 956 1261 **e** info@zanerecords.com **w** zanerecords.com MD: Peter Thompson.

Zebra (see Cherry Red Records)

Zebra 3 Records 26 Smithy Drive, Ashford, Kent TN23 3NS
t 07970 185 443 **e** zebra3records@aol.com **w** zebra3.co.uk
MD: Ben Watson.

Zebra Traffic (see Tru Thoughts)

Zedfunk PO Box 7497, London N21 2DX **t** 07050 657 465
e info@zedfunk.com **w** zedfunk.com MD: Paul Z.

Zero Tolerance (see 3 Beat Label Management)

Zest Music Ltd 29-30 St James's St, London SW1A 1HB
t 0870 389 6999 **f** 0870 389 6998 **e** steve@zestmusic.com
w zestmusic.com Chief Exec: Steve Weltman.

Zeus Records Helions Farm, Sages End Rd, Helions
Bumpstead, Suffolk CB9 7AW **t** 01440 730 795 or
07984 468 415 or 01440 730 752 **e** info@zeusrecords.com
w zeusrecords.com Dirs: Ash White, Darren King.

Zomba Records Ltd (see Jive Records).

Zone 5 Records (see Megabop Records)

Zopf Ltd 52 King Henry's Walk, London N1 4NN
t 020 7503 3546 **f** 020 7503 3546
e joanna.stephenson@penguincafe.com **w** penguincafe.com
Business Affairs Mgr: Joanna Stephenson.

ZTT Records Ltd The Blue Building, 8-10 Basing St, London
W11 1ET **t** 020 7221 5101 **f** 020 7221 9247 **e** info@ztt.com
w ztt.com International & Licensing: Pete Gardiner.

Video and DVD Companies

Acorn Media UK 16, Welmar Mews, Ivy Works, 154,
Clapham Park Rd, London SW4 7DE **t** 020 7627 7200
f 020 7627 2501 **e** customerservices@acornmediauk.com
w acornmediauk.com MD: Paul Holland.

Artificial Eye Video 14 King St, London WC2E 8HR
t 020 7240 5353 **f** 020 7240 5242 **e** info@artificial-eye.com
w artificial-eye.com Video/DVD Mgr: Steve Lewis.

Sony Pictures Home Entertainment 25 Golden Sq,
London W1R 6LU **t** 020 7533 1000 **f** 020 7533 1172
e firstname_lastname@fpe.sony.com **w** sphe.co.uk.

Contender Home Entertainment 48 Margaret St,
London W1W 8SE **t** 020 7907 3773 **f** 020 7907 3777
e enquiries@contendergroup.com **w** contendergroup.com
Marketing Manager: Matt Brightwell.

Eagle Rock Entertainment Ltd. Eagle House, 22
Armoury Way, London SW18 1EZ **t** 020 8870 5670
f 020 8874 2333 **e** mail@eagle-rock.com **w** eagle-rock.com
Executive Chairman: Terry Shand.

EAGLE VISION

Eagle House, 22 Armoury Way, London SW18 1EZ
t 020 8870 5670 **f** 020 8874 2333 **e** mail@eagle-rock.com
w eagle-rock.com Executive Chairman: Terry Shand. Chief
Operating Officer: Geoff Kempin. Group Finance Director: Simon
Hosken. Dir. Of Business Affairs: Martin Dacre. Dir. Of Intl.Sales
and Marketing: Lindsay Brown. MD of Intl. Television and New
Media: Peter Worsley. Dir. Of Intl.TV Sales and New Media:
Andrew Winter. Int'l DVD and New Media Licensing Director:
Lesley Wilsdon. UK Marketing Manager: Ian Rowe. Intl. Product
Manager: Nicola Munns.

GALA Productions 25 Stamford Brook Rd, London
W6 0XJ **t** 020 8741 4200 or 07768 078 865
f 020 8741 2323 **e** beata@galaproductions.co.uk
w galaproductions.co.uk Executive Producer: Beata Romanowski.

Granada Ventures 48 Leicester Sq, London WC2H 7FB
t 020 7389 8555 **e** Mark.hurry@ITV.com **w** granadaventures.tv
Commercial Affairs Director: Mark Hurry.

GUT VISION

VISION

Byron House, 112A Shirland Road, London W9 2EQ
t 020 7266 0777 **f** 020 7266 7734 **e** general@gut-vision.com
w gut-vision.com. Chairman: Guy Holmes. Creative Director:
Fraser Ealey.

IQ Media (Bracknell) Ltd 2 Venture House, Arlington Sq,
Bracknell, Berks RG12 1WA **t** 01344 422 551 or
07884 262 755 **f** 01344 453 355
e information@iqmedia-uk.com **w** iqmedia-uk.com
MD: Tony Bellamy.

Prism Leisure Corporation plc Unit 1, 1 Dundee Way,
Enfield, Middlesex EN3 7SX **t** 020 8804 8100
f 020 8216 6645 **e** prism@prismleisure.com **w** prismleisure.com
Head Of Sales: Adrian Ball.

Sanctuary Visual Entertainment Sanctuary House, 45-
53 Sinclair Rd, London W14 0NS **t** 020 7602 6351
f 020 7603 5941 **e** info@sanctuaryrecords.co.uk
w sanctuaryrecords.co.uk Label Mgr: Claire White.

Urban Edge Entertainment Ltd Unit 7 Freetrade House,
Lowther Rd, Stanmore, Middx HA7 1EP **t** 020 8206 1177
f 020 8206 2757 **e** urbanedge@wienerworld.com
w wienerworld.com MD: Anthony Broza.

The Valentine Music Group 7 Garrick St, London
WC2E 9AR **t** 020 7240 1628 **f** 020 7497 9242
e pat@valentinemusic.co.uk **w** valentinemusic.co.uk
MD: John Nice.

Vital DVD 338a Ladbroke Grove, London W10 5AH
t 020 8324 2400 or 020 8324 2429 **f** 020 8324 0001
e firstname.lastname@vitaluk.com **w** vitaluk.com
DVD Sales Mgr: James Akerman.

Wienerworld Ltd Unit 7 Freetrade House, Lowther Rd,
Stanmore, Middx HA7 1EP **t** 020 8206 1177 **f** 020 8206 2757
e wworld@wienerworld.com **w** wienerworld.com
MD: Anthony Broza.

**For all the latest
directory listings visit
www.musicweekdirectory.com**

Publishers

Pro Sound News Europe – since 1986 PSNE has remained Europe's leading news-based publication for the professional audio industry. Its comprehensive, independent editorial content is written by some of the finest journalists in Europe, focusing on Recording & Post Production, Audio for Broadcast, Live and Installed Sound.

Installation Europe – Europe's only magazine dedicated to audio, video and lighting in the built environment. For systems designers, integrators, consultants and contractors.

PSN Live is Pro Sound News Europe's new launch dedicated exclusively to the European Live Sound market! PSN Live provides market information never previously published, quantifying and analysing market trends whilst looking at developments in technology within this growing sector.

Look out for the next edition early in 2007.

Advertising sales contact: **Steve Connolly** tel: **+44(0)20 7921 8316**

Publishers:

Publishers and Affiliates

2NV Publishing 1 Canada Sq, 29th Floor Canary Wharf Tower, London E14 5DY **t** 0870 220 0237 **f** 0870 220 0238 **e** info@2nvpublishing.com **w** 2nvpublishing.com Co-MDs: Kevin Black, Deon Burton.

3rd Stone (see Heavy Truth Music Publishing Ltd)

4 Liberty Music (see Notting Hill Music (UK) Ltd)

5HQ (see Paul Rodriguez Music Ltd)

7Hz Music 4 Margaret St, London W1W 8RF **t** 020 7462 1269 **f** 020 7436 5431 **e** barry@7hz.co.uk **w** 7hzmusic.co.uk GM: Barry Campbell.

7pm Music (see A7 Music)

19 Music 33 Ransomes Dock, 35-37 Parkgate Rd, London SW11 4NP **t** 020 7801 1919 **f** 020 7801 1920 **e** reception@19.co.uk **w** 19.co.uk MD: Simon Fuller.

23rd Precinct Music (see Notting Hill Music (UK) Ltd)

A LIST MUSIC LTD

500 Chiswick High Road, London W4 5RG **t** 020 8956 2615 **f** 020 8956 2614 **e** mail@alistmusic.com **w** alistmusic.com Contact: Deon Sharma.
A List Music looks after the rights of various titles and artists in all forms and genres from around the world, creating a one stop, hassle free music solution for future music partnership opportunities. Writers include James Berryman, Andy Mcgregor, Paul McGranaghan and Wayne Pauli.

A Songs/Anglo Plugging Music Fulham Palace, Bishops Ave, London SW6 6EA **t** 020 7384 7373 **f** 020 7384 7374 **e** johnny@asongs.co.uk Dir: Johnny Matthews.

A Train Management (see Bucks Music Group)

A&G Publishing 1st Floor, 5 Ching Court, 61-63 Monmouth St, London WC2H 9EY **t** 020 7845 9880 **f** 020 7845 9884 **e** firstname@aegweb.com **w** agrecords.co.uk MD: Roy Jackson.

Abacus (see Carlin Music Corporation)

Abigail London (see Warner Chappell Music Ltd)

Abood Music (see Jamdown Music Ltd)

ABRSM Publishing (see Oxford University Press)

A&C Black (Publishers) 37 Soho Sq, London W1D 3QZ **t** 020 7758 0200 **f** 020 7758 0222 or 020 7758 0333 **e** educationalsales@acblack.com Educational Music Ed: Sheena Hodge.

Accolade Music 250 Earlsdon Avenue North, Coventry, W Midlands CV5 6GX **t** 02476 711935 **f** 02476 711191 **e** rootsrecs@btclick.com MD: Graham Bradshaw.

Acorn Publishing 1, Tylney View, London Rd, Hook, Hants RG27 9LJ **t** 07808 377 350 **e** publishingacorn@hotmail.com MD: Mark Olrog.

Acrobat Music Publishing 30a Green Lane, Northwood, Middx HA6 2QB **t** 01923 821559 **f** 01923 821296 **e** enquiries@acrobatmusic.net **w** acrobatmusic.net MD: John Cooper.

Active (see Mute Song)

Acton Green (see EMI Music Publishing)

Acuff-Rose Music (see Sony/ATV Music Publishing)

Ad-Chorel Music 86 Causewayside, Edinburgh EH9 1PY **t** 0131 668 3366 **f** 0131 662 4463 **e** neil@ad-chorelmusic.com MD: Neil Ross.

Addington State (see The Valentine Music Group)

ADN Creation Music Library (see Panama Music Library)

Adventures in Music PO Box 261, Wallingford, Oxon OX10 0XY **t** 01491 832 183 **e** info@adventuresin-music.com **w** adventure-records.com MD: Paul Conroy.

AE Copyrights (see Air-Edel Associates)

Afrikan Cowboy 33 Colomb St, London SE10 9HA **t** 07957 391 418 or 020 8305 2448 **e** info@afrikancowboy.com **w** afrikancowboy.com Dir: Dean Hart.

Ainm Music Unit C10, Wicklow Enterprise Pk, The Murrough, Wicklow Town, Co Wicklow, Ireland **t** +353 404 62527 **f** +353 404 62527 **e** fstubbs@ainm-music.com **w** ainm-music.com MD: Frank Stubbs.

Air-Edel Associates 18 Rodmarton St, London W1U 8BJ **t** 020 7486 6466 **f** 020 7224 0344 **e** susan@air-edel.co.uk **w** air-edel.co.uk Publishing Manager: Susan Arnison.

Air (London) (see Chrysalis Music Ltd)

Air Music and Media Group Limited Chiltern House, 184 High St, Berkhamsted, Herts HP4 3AP **t** 01442 877018 **f** 01442 877015 **e** info@airmusicandmedia.com **w** airmusicandmedia.com Contact: Michael Infante.

Air Traffic Control Music Publishing 29 Harley St, London W1G 9QR **t** 0870 20 200 20 or 07973 270 963 **e** mark@airtrafficcontrolhq.com Dir: Mark Barker.

Airdog Music (see Notting Hill Music (UK) Ltd)

AJ (see Kassner Associated Publishers)

Alan Price (see Carlin Music Corporation)

Alarcon Music Ltd The Old Truman Brewery, 91 Brick Lane, London E1 6QL **t** 020 7377 9373 **f** 020 7377 6523 **e** byron@bko-alarcon.co.uk Dir: Byron Orme.

Alaw 4 Tyfila Rd, Pontypridd, Rhondda Cynon Taf CF37 2DA **t** 01443 402178 **f** 01443 402178 **e** sales@alawmusic.com **w** alawmusic.com Dir: Brian Raby.

J Albert & Son (UK) Ltd Unit 29, Cygnus Business Centre, Dalmeyer Rd, London NW10 2XA **t** 020 8830 0330 **f** 020 8830 0220 **e** james@alberts.co.uk **w** albertmusic.co.uk Head of A&R: James Cassidy.

Albion (see BMG Music Publishing Ltd)

Alexscar (see Menace Music)

Alfred Lengnick & Co (see BMG Music Publishing Ltd)

Alfred Publishing Co (UK) Ltd Burnt Mill, Elizabeth Way, Harlow, Essex CM20 2HX **t** 01279 828 960 **f** 01279 828 961 **e** music@alfreduk.com **w** alfreduk.com Mktg Mgr: Andrew Higgins.

All Action Figure Music Unit 9 Darvells Works, Common Rd, Chorleywood, Herts WD3 5LP **t** 01923 286010 **f** 01923 286070 **e** songs@allactionfigure.co.uk MD: Steve Lowes.

All Around The World Music Munro House, High Close, Rawdon, nr Leeds, W Yorks LS19 6HF **t** 01132 503338 **f** 01132 507343 **e** stewart@artandmusic.co.uk MD: Stewart Coxhead.

All Boys Music Ltd 222-224 Borough High St, London SE1 1JX **t** 020 7403 0007 **f** 020 7403 8202 **e** helen@pwl-studios.com Mgr: Helen Dann.

All Good Music Group (see Copasetik Music)

All Media Music (see Paul Rodriguez Music Ltd)

All Zakatek Music 3 Purley Hill, Purley, Surrey CR8 1AP **t** 020 8660 0861 **f** 020 8660 0861 **e** allzakatekmusic@aol.com MD: Lenny Zakatek.

Alola Music (see Westbury Music Ltd)

Alon Music (see Charly Publishing Ltd)

Alpadon Music Shenandoah, Manor Pk, Chislehurst, Kent BR7 5QD **t** 020 8295 0310 **e** donpercival@freenet.co.uk MD: Don Percival.

Amazing Feet Publishing Interzone House, 74-77 Magdalen Rd, Oxford OX4 1RE **t** 01865 205600 **f** 01865 205700 **e** amazing@rotator.co.uk **w** rotator.co.uk/amazingfeet MD: Richard Cotton.

Amazon Music Ltd (see Peermusic (UK))

Ambassador Music (see Hornall Brothers Music Ltd)

Amco Music Publishing 2 Gawsworth Rd, Macclesfield, Cheshire SK11 8UE **t** 01625 420 163 **f** 01625 420 168 **e** amco@cottagegroup.co.uk **w** cottagegroup.co.uk MD: Roger Boden.

Amigos De Musica (see Menace Music)

Amokshasong (see Tairona Songs Ltd)

Amos Barr Music (see Bucks Music Group)

Amphonic Music Ltd. Kerchesters, Waterhouse Lane, Kingswood, Surrey KT20 6HT **t** 01737 832837 **f** 01737 833812 **e** info@amphonic.co.uk **w** amphonic.co.uk MD: Ian Dale.

Anew Music (see Crashed Music)

Anglia Music Company 39 Tadorne Rd, Tadworth, Surrey KT20 5TF **t** 01737 812922 **f** 01737 812922 **e** angliamusic@ukgateway.net Dir/Co Sec: Norma Camby.

Anglia TV (see Carlin Music Corporation)

Angus Publications 14 Graham Terrace, Belgravia, London SW1W 8JH **t** 07850 845 280 **f** 020 7730 3368 **e** bill.puppetmartin@virgin.net **w** billmartinsongwriter.com Chairman: Bill Martin.

Anna (see Miriamusic)

Annie Reed Music Ltd 3 Crossways House, Box Hill, Corsham, Wilts SN13 8ES **t** 0845 159 7639 or 07770 623 110 **e** annie@anniereedmusic.com Dir: Annie Havard.

Anxious Music (see Universal Music Publishing Ltd)

Appleseed Music (see Bucks Music Group)

AppleTreeSongs Ltd PO Box 381, Great Missenden, Bucks HP16 9BE **t** 01494 890086 **f** 0870 054 8130 **e** nigelrush@appletreesongs.com Dir: Nigel Rush.

Applied Music (see Bucks Music Group)

Arcadia Production Music (UK) Greenlands, Payhembury, Devon EX14 3HY **t** 01404 841601 **f** 01404 841687 **e** admin@arcadiamusic.tv **w** arcadiamusic.tv Prop: John Brett.

Ardmore & Beechwood (see EMI Music Publishing)

Arena Music Co Ltd Hatch Farm Studios, Chertsey Rd, Addlestone, Surrey KT15 2EH **t** 01932 828715 **f** 01932 828717 **e** brian.adams@dial.pipex.com MD: Brian Adams.

Arhelger (see New Music Enterprises)

Ariel Music Malvern House, Sibford Ferris, Banbury, Oxon OX15 5RG **t** 01295 780679 **f** 01295 788630 **e** jane@arielmusic.co.uk **w** arielmusic.co.uk Managing Partner: Jane Woolfenden.

Aristocrat Music Ltd Bournemouth Business Centre, 1052-54 Christchurch Rd, Bournemouth, Dorset BH7 6DS **t** 020 8441 6996 **f** 08708 362 339 **e** AristocratMusic@aol.com MD: Terry King.

Arketek Music 53 Edge St, Nutgrove, St Helens, Merseyside WA9 5JX **t** 0151 430 6290 **e** info@arketek.com **w** arketek.com MD: Alan Ferreira.

ARL (see TMR Publishing)

Arloco Music (see Bucks Music Group)

Arnakata Music Ltd (see Astwood Music Ltd)

Arnisongs Unit A, The Courtyard, 42 Colwith Rd, London W6 9EY **t** 020 8846 3737 **f** 020 8846 3738 **e** john@terraartists.com MD: John Arnison.

Arpeggio Music Bell Farm House, Eton Wick, Windsor, Berks SL4 6LH **t** 01753 864910 **f** 01753 884810 MD: Beverley Campion.

Art Music (see Paul Rodriguez Music Ltd)

Artfield 5 Grosvenor Sq, London W1K 4AF **t** 020 7499 9941 **f** 020 7499 5519 **e** info@artfieldmusic.com **w** bbcooper.com MD: BB Cooper.

Arthur's Mother (see The Valentine Music Group)

Arts Music Publishing 185 Upton Lane, Forest Gate, London E7 9PJ **t** 020 8985 0091 **e** renkrecords@msn.com MD: Junior Hart.

Artwork (see Bucks Music Group)

Ascherberg, Hopwood & Crew (see Warner Chappell Music Ltd)

A7 Music PO Box 2272, Brighton BN2 8XD **t** 01273 304681 **f** 01273 308120 **e** info@a7music.com **w** a7music.com Dir: Seven Webster.

Ash Music (GB) Hillside Farm, Hassocky Lane, Temple Normanton, Chesterfield, Derbyshire S42 5DH **t** 01246 231762 **e** ash_music36@hotmail.com Head of A&R: Paul Townsend.

Ashley Mark Publishing Company 1-2 Vance Court, Trans Britannia Enterprise Pk, Blaydon on Tyne, Tyne & Wear NE21 5NH **t** 0191 414 9000 **f** 0191 414 9001 **e** mail@ashleymark.co.uk **w** ashleymark.co.uk MD: Simon Turnbull.

Asongs Publishing (see A Songs/Anglo Plugging Music)

Assoc. Board of the Royal Schools of Music (Pub'g) 24 Portland Pl, London W1B 1LU **t** 020 7636 5400 **f** 020 7637 0234 **e** publishing@abrsm.ac.uk **w** abrsmpublishing.co.uk Director of Publishing: Leslie East.

Associated (see Music Sales Ltd)

Associated Music International Ltd 34 Salisbury St, London NW8 8QE **t** 020 7402 9111 **f** 020 7723 3064 **e** eliot@amimedia.co.uk **w** amimedia.co.uk MD: Eliot Cohen.

Asterisk Music Rock House, London Rd, St Marys, Stroud, Gloucs GL6 8PU **t** 01453 886252 or 0845 456 9759 **f** 01453 885361 or 0845 456 9760 **e** asterisk@rollercoasterrecords.com MD: John Beecher.

Astwood Music Ltd Latimer Studios, West Kington, Wilts SN14 7JQ **t** 01249 783 599 **f** 0870 169 8433 **e** Dolan@metro-associates.co.uk **w** media-print.co.uk CEO: Mike Dolan.

Asylum Songs PO Box 121, Hove, E Sussex BN3 4YY **t** 01273 774 468 **f** 08709 223 099 **e** info@AsylumGroup.com **w** AsylumGroup.com Dirs: Bob James, Scott Chester.

Atham (see Asterisk Music)

Atlantic Seven Productions/Music Library Ltd 52 Lancaster Rd, London N4 4PR **t** 020 7263 4435 **f** 020 7436 9233 or 020 8374 9774 **e** musiclibrary@atlanticseven.com MD: Patrick Shart.

Atmosphere Music (see BMG Zomba Production Music)

Attic Music PO Box 38805, London W12 7XL **t** 020 8740 8898 **e** atticmusic@btinternet.com **w** atticmusic.co.uk Prop: Jimmy Thomas.

Audio-Visual Media Music Library (see Panama Music Library)

Authentic Media 9 Holdom Ave, Bletchley, Milton Keynes, Bucks MK1 1QR **t** 01908 364 200 **f** 01908 648 592 **e** info@authenticmedia.co.uk **w** authenticmedia.co.uk MD: David Withers.

Automatic Songs Ltd Unit 5 Waldo Works, Waldo Rd, London NW10 6AW **t** 020 8964 8890 **f** 020 8960 5741 **e** russel@digitalstores.co.uk **w** automaticsongs.com MD: Russel Coultart.

Autonomy Music Publishing (see Bucks Music Group)

AV Music (see The Valentine Music Group)

Avatar Music (see Notting Hill Music (UK) Ltd)

Aviation Music Ltd (see Maxwood Music)

Aviva (see Music Sales Ltd)

B Feldman & Co (see EMI Music Publishing)

B-Unique Music 1A Cranbrook Rd, London W4 2LH **t** 020 8987 0393 **f** 020 8995 9917 **e** info@b-uniquerecords.com **w** b-uniquerecords.com MDs: Mark Lewis, Martin Toher.

The Bacon Empire Publishing 271 Royal College St, Camden Town, London NW1 9LU **t** 020 7482 0115 **f** 020 7267 1169 **e** maurice@baconempire.com MD: Maurice Bacon.

Bad B Music (see Cheeky Music)

Bados Music (see Paul Rodriguez Music Ltd)

Baerenreiter Ltd Burnt Mill, Elizabeth Way, Harlow, Essex CM20 2HX **t** 01279 828930 **f** 01279 828931 **e** baerenreiter@dial.pipex.com **w** baerenreiter.com MD: Christopher Jackson.

Bamaco Vine Cottage, 255 Lower Rd, Great Bookham, Leatherhead, Surrey KT23 4DX **t** 01372 450 752 **e** barrymurrayents@aol.com Contact: Barry Murray.

Bandleader Music Co. 7 Garrick St, London WC2E 9AR **t** 020 7240 1628 **f** 020 7497 9242 **e** valentine@bandleader.co.uk MD: John Nice.

Bandleader Publications (see Kirklees Music)

Banks Music Publications The Old Forge, Sand Hutton, York, N Yorks YO41 1LB **t** 01904 468472 **f** 01904 468679 **e** banksmusic@tiscali.co.uk **w** banksmusicpublications.co.uk Prop: Margaret Silver.

Barbera Music 102 Dean St, London W1D 3TQ **t** 020 7758 1494 **e** hgadsdon@barberamusic.co.uk Contact: Hugh Gadsdon, Mel Stephenson.

Bardell Smith (see EMI Music Publishing)

Bardic Edition 6 Fairfax Crescent, Aylesbury, Bucks HP20 2ES **t** 0870 950 3493 **f** 0870 950 3494 **e** info@bardic-music.com **w** bardic-music.com Prop: Barry Peter Ould.

Bardis Music Co. Ltd CPG House, Glenageary Office Pk, Glenageary, Co Dublin, Ireland **t** +353 1 285 8711 **f** +353 1 285 8928 **e** info@bardis.ie **w** bardis.ie MD: Peter Bardon.

Barking Green Music 19 Ashford Carbonell, Ludlow, Shropshire SY8 4DB **t** 01584 831 475 **f** 01584 831 294 **e** peterstretton@barkinggreenmusic.co.uk Dir: Peter J. Stretton.

Barn Dance Publications Ltd 62 Beechwood Rd, South Croydon, Surrey CR2 0AA **t** 020 8657 2813 **f** 020 8651 6080 **e** info@barndancepublications.co.uk **w** barndancepublications.co.uk MD: Derek Jones.

Barn Publishing (Slade) Ltd 1 Pratt Mews, London NW1 0AD **t** 020 7267 6899 **f** 020 7267 6746 **e** partners@newman-and.co.uk Pub: Colin Newman.

Basement Music Ltd. 20 Cyprus Gardens, London N3 1SP **t** 020 8922 4908 **f** 020 8922 4908 **e** basementmusic@btinternet.com Business Manager: John Cefai.

Batoni (see Notting Hill Music (UK) Ltd)

BBC (see BMG Music Publishing Ltd)

BBC Music Publishing A2033 Woodlands, 80 Wood Lane, London W12 0TT **t** 020 8433 1723 **f** 020 8433 1741 **e** victoria.watkins@bbc.co.uk Catalogue Manager: Victoria Watkins.

B&C Music Publishing (see Maxwood Music)

BDI Music Ltd Onward House, 11 Uxbridge St, London W8 7TQ **t** 020 7243 4101 **f** 020 7243 4131 **e** sarah@bdimusic.com **w** bdimusic.com MD: Sarah Liversedge.

Beacon Music (see Paul Rodriguez Music Ltd)

Publishers: Publishers and Affiliates

Beamlink (see Paul Rodriguez Music Ltd)

Bearsongs PO Box 944, Birmingham, W Midlands B16 8UT
t 0121 454 7020 **f** 0121 454 9996
e bigbearmusic@compuserve.com **w** bigbearmusic.com
MD: Jim Simpson.

Beat Music (see Paul Rodriguez Music Ltd)

Beat That Music Ltd (see Independent Music Group Ltd)

Beautiful (see Kassner Associated Publishers)

Bed & Breakfast Publishing 211 Piccadilly, London
W1J 9HF **t** 020 7917 2948 **e** mw@sublime-music.co.uk
w sublime-music.co.uk MD: Nick Grant.

Beez (see Paul Rodriguez Music Ltd)

Beggars Banquet (see 4AD Music)

Beijing Publishing 105 Emlyn Rd, London W12 9TG
t 020 8749 3730 **e** brianleafe@aol.com Owner: Brian Leafe.

Belsize Music Ltd 29 Manor House, 250 Marylebone Rd,
London NW1 5NP **t** 020 7723 7177 **f** 020 7262 0775
e belsizemusic@btconnect.com Dir: Chas Peate.

Belwin Mills (see EMI Music Publishing)

Berkley (see Bucks Music Group)

Best Sounds (see Paul Rodriguez Music Ltd)

Bicameral (see Menace Music)

Big City Triumph Music 3 St Andrews St, Lincoln, Lincs
LN5 7NE **t** 01522 539883 **f** 01522 528964
e steve.hawkins@easynet.co.uk **w** icegroup.co.uk
MD: Steve Hawkins.

Big Life Music 67-69 Chalton St, London NW1 1HY
t 020 7554 2100 **f** 020 7554 2154
e reception@biglifemanagement.com **w** biglifemanagement.com
MD: Tim Parry.

Big Note Music Limited Comforts Pl, Tandridge Lane,
Lingfield, Surrey RH7 6LW **t** 01342 893046 **f** 01342 893562
e ahillesq@aol.com Contact: Deborah Beaton.

Big One (see Big World Publishing)

Big Shot Music Ltd PO Box 14535, London N17 0WG
t 020 8376 1650 **f** 020 8376 8622 **e** Pingramc2@aol.com
Contact: P Ingram.

Big Spliff (see Paul Rodriguez Music Ltd)

Big World Publishing 9 Bloomsbury Pl, East Hill,
Wandsworth, London SW18 2JB **t** 020 8877 1335
f 020 8877 1335 **e** songs@bigworldpublishing.com
w bigworldpublishing.com MD: Patrick Meads.

Bigtime Music Publishing 86 Marlborough Rd, Oxford
OX1 4LS **t** 01865 249 194 **f** 01865 792 765 **e** info@bejo.co.uk
w bejo.co.uk Administrator: Tim Healey.

Billym (see Menace Music)

Billymac (see Paul Rodriguez Music Ltd)

Biswas Music 21 Bedford Sq, London WC1B 3HH
t 020 7637 4444 **f** 020 7323 2857 **e** guy@fspg.co.uk
MD: Guy Rippon.

Black Heat Music 13a Filey Ave, London N16 6JL
t 020 8806 4193 **e** tmorgan@ntlworld.com Dir: Tony Morgan.

Blow Up Songs PO Box 4961, London W1A 7ZX
t 020 7636 7744 **f** 020 7636 7755 **e** webmaster@blowup.co.uk
w blowup.co.uk MD: Paul Tunkin.

Blue Banana Music (see Blue Melon Publishing)

Blue Cat (see Asterisk Music)

Blue Dot Music (see PXM Publishing)

Blue Melon Publishing 240A High Rd, Harrow Weald,
Middx HA3 7BB **t** 020 8863 2520 **f** 020 8863 2520
e steve@bluemelon.co.uk MD: Steven Glen.

Blue Mountain Music Ltd 8 Kensington Park Rd, London
W11 3BU **t** 020 7229 3000 **f** 020 7221 8899
e bluemountain@islandlife.co.uk **w** bluemountainmusic.tv
MD: Alistair Norbury.

Blue Planet Music (see Blue Melon Publishing)

Blue Ribbon Music Ltd (see Hornall Brothers Music).

Blue Ribbon Music Ltd (see Hornall Brothers Music Ltd)

Blujay Music 55 Loudoun Rd, St Johns Wood, London
NW8 0DL **t** 020 7604 3633 **f** 020 7604 3639
e info@blujay.co.uk Dirs: Steve Tannett, Carly Martin.

BMG MUSIC PUBLISHING LTD

MUSIC PUBLISHING
UNITED KINGDOM

20 Fulham Broadway, London SW6 1AH **t** 020 7835 5200
f 020 7835 5394 **e** firstname.lastname@bmg.com
w bmgmusicsearch.com. Chairman: Paul Curran. **t** 020 7835
5333. General Manager: Ian Ramage. **t** 020 7835 5244. Head Of
Global Marketing: Steve Levy. **t** 020 7835 5386. Dir Of Business
& Commercial Affairs: Jackie Alway. **t** 020 7835 5277. Finance
Dir: Will Downs. **t** 020 7835 5299.

BMG Music Publishing International 20 Fulham
Broadway, London SW6 1AH **t** 020 7835 5200
f 020 7835 5201 **e** firstname.lastname@bmg.co.uk
Pres: Andrew Jenkins.

BMG Music Publishing Manchester First Floor, 62
Bridge St, Manchester M3 3BW **t** 0161 838 9180
f 0161 838 9189 **e** caroline.elleray@bmg.co.uk
Contact: Caroline Elleray.

BMG Zomba Production Music 20 Fulham Broadway,
London SW6 1AH **t** 020 7835 5300 **f** 020 7835 5318
e musicresearch@bmgzomba.com **w** bmgzomba.com
Senior Promotions Exec: Julia Dean.

BMP - Broken Music Publishing Riverbank House, 1
Putney Bridge Approach, London SW6 3JD **t** 020 7371 0022
f 020 7371 0099 **e** ripe@compuserve.com
Dirs: Sharon Brooks, Jurgen Dramm.

Bob Ltd (see Notting Hill Music (UK) Ltd)

BobbySox (see Castle Hill Music)

Bobnal Music Inc (see Bucks Music Group)

Bocu Music Ltd 1 Wyndham Yard, Wyndham Pl, London
W1H 1AR **t** 020 7402 7433 **f** 020 7402 2833
Dir: Carole Broughton.

Bolland & Bolland (see Menace Music)

Bollywood (see Notting Hill Music (UK) Ltd)

Bomber Music Publishing 18 Highfield Ave, London NW11 9ET **t** 020 8731 7951 or 07941 560 343 **e** donagh@bombermusic.com MD: Donagh O'Leary.

Boneless (see Menace Music)

Bonney (see Kassner Associated Publishers)

Boosey & Hawkes Music Publishers Ltd Aldwych House, 71-91 Aldwych, London WC2B 4HN **t** 020 7054 7200 **f** 020 7054 7293 **e** marketing.uk@boosey.com **w** boosey.com Hd of Publicity & Mktg: David Allenby.

BOP Music (see The Valentine Music Group)

Boulevard Music Publishing (see Kevin King Music Publishing)

Bourne Music 2nd Floor, 207/209 Regent St, London W1B 4ND **t** 020 7734 3454 **f** 020 7734 3385 **e** bournemusic@supanet.com Office Manager: John Woodward.

Bramsdene (see Music Sales Ltd)

Brass Wind Publications 4 St Mary's Rd, Manton, Oakham, Rutland LE15 8SU **t** 01572 737409 **f** 01572 737409 **e** info@brasswindpublications.co.uk **w** brasswindpublications.co.uk.

Breakin' Loose 32 Quadrant House, Burrell St, London SE1 0UW **t** 020 7633 9576 or 07721 065 618 **e** sjbbreakinloose@aol.com MD: Steve Bingham.

Breakloose (see Bucks Music Group)

Breezy Tunes (see Jonsongs Music)

Breitkopf & Hartel Broome Cottage, The Street, Suffield, Norwich NR11 7EQ **t** 01263 768732 **f** 01263 768733 **e** sales@breitkopf.com **w** breitkopf.com Sales Rep: Robin Winter.

Brenda Brooker Enterprises 9 Cork St, Mayfair, London W1S 3LL **t** 020 7544 2893 **e** BrookerB@aol.com MD: Brenda Brooker.

Brentwood Benson Music (see Bucks Music Group)

Briar Music 5-6 Lombard St, Dublin 2, Ireland **t** +353 1 677 4229 or +353 1 677 9762 **f** +353 1 671 0421 **e** lunar@indigo.ie MD: Brian Molloy.

Bright Music Ltd 21c Heathmans Rd, Parsons Green, London SW6 4TJ **t** 020 7751 9935 **f** 020 7731 9314 **e** brightmusic@aol.com **w** brightmusic.co.uk MD: Martin Wyatt.

Brightly Music 231 Lower Clapton Rd, London E5 8EG **t** 020 8533 7994 or 07973 616342 **f** 020 8986 4035 **e** abrightly@yahoo.com **w** brightly.freeserve.co.uk MD: Anthony Brightly.

Briter Music (see Asterisk Music)

Brm Music Publishing Ltd. PO Box 22949, London N10 3ZH **t** 0208 444 0987 **e** info@brmmusic.com **w** brmmusic.com MD: Bruce Ruffin.

Broadbent & Dunn 66 Nursery Lane, Dover, Kent CT16 3EX **t** 01304 825 604 **f** 0870 135 3567 **e** bd.music@broadbent-dunn.com **w** broadbent-dunn.com Company Secretary: William Dunn.

Broadley Music (Int) Ltd Broadley House, 48 Bradley Terrace, London NW1 6LG **t** 020 7258 0324 **f** 020 7724 2361 **e** admin@broadleystudios.com **w** broadleystudios.com MD: Ellis Elias.

Broadley Music Library (see Broadley Music (Int) Ltd)

Broadley Studios Ltd (see Broadley Music (Int) Ltd)

Brookside (see Asterisk Music)

Broughton Park Music Kennedy House, 31 Stamford St, Altrincham, Cheshire WA14 1ES **f** 0161 980 7100 **e** harveylisberg@aol.com MD: Harvey Lisberg.

Bruco (see Menace Music)

Bryter Music Marlinspike Hall, Walpole Halesworth, Suffolk IP19 9AR **t** 01986 784 664 **f** 01986 784 664 **e** cally@brytermusic.com **w** brytermusic.com Prop: Cally.

Bs In Trees (see Menace Music)

Bill Buckley Music Saunders, Wood & Co, The White House, 140A Tatchbrook St, London SW1V 2NE **t** 020 7821 0455 **f** 020 7821 6196 **e** nigel@s-wood.dircon.co.uk Ptnr: Nigel J Wood.

Bucks Music Group Onward House, 11 Uxbridge St, London W8 7TQ **t** 020 7221 4275 **f** 020 7229 6893 **e** info@bucksmusicgroup.co.uk **w** bucksmusicgroup.com MD: Simon Platz.

Buffalo Music Ltd PO Box 586, Rickmansworth WD3 6ZQ **t** 01923 266664 **f** 01923 261761 **e** info@buffalomusic.co.uk **w** buffalomusic.co.uk Office Manager: Janet LeSage.

Bug Music Ltd Long Island House, Unit GB, 1-4 Warple Way, London W3 0RG **t** 020 8735 1868 **f** 020 8743 1551 **e** info@bugmusic.co.uk **w** bugmusic.com MD/VP International: Mark Anders.

Bugle Publishing Group Second Floor, 81 Rivington St, London EC2A 3AY **t** 020 7012 1416 **f** 020 7012 1419 **e** tcgleg@aol.com **w** milescopeland.com.

Bulk Music Ltd 9 Watt Rd, Hillington Pk, Glasgow, Strathclyde G52 4RY **t** 0141 882 9986 **f** 0141 883 3686 **e** krl@krl.co.uk **w** krl.co.uk MD: Gus McDonald.

Bull-Sheet Music 18 The Bramblings, London E4 6LU **t** 020 8529 5807 **f** 020 8529 5807 **e** irene.bull@btinternet.com **w** bull-sheetmusic.co.uk; bandmemberswanted.co.uk MD: Irene Bull.

Bullish Music Inc (see Bucks Music Group)

Burlington (see Warner Chappell Music Ltd)

Burning Petals Music 5 Clover Ground, Shepton Mallet, Somerset BA4 4AS **t** 0870 749 1117 **e** enquiries@burning-petals.com **w** burning-petals.com MD: Richard Jay.

Burnt Puppy (see Bucks Music Group)

Burnt Toast Music Publishing 12 Denyer Court, Fradley, Nr Lichfield, Staffs WS13 8TQ **t** 01543 444261 **f** 01543 444261 **e** phooper-keeley@softhome.net MD: Paul Hooper-Keeley.

Burton Way (see Universal Music Publishing Ltd)

Bushranger Music Station Lodge, 196 Rayleigh Rd, Hutton, Brentwood, Essex CM13 1PN **t** 01277 222095 **e** bushrangermusic@aol.com MD: Kathy Lister.

Buyhear.Com 240 High Rd, Harrow Weald, Middlesex HA3 7BB **t** 020 8863 2520 **f** 020 8863 2520 **e** steve@buyhear.com **w** buyhear.com Dir: Steven Robert Glen.

Cactus (see Creole Music Ltd)

Cala Music Publishing 17 Shakespeare Gardens, London N2 9LJ **t** 020 8883 7306 **f** 020 8365 3388 **e** paul@calarecords.com **w** calarecords.com Sales & Marketing Manager: Paul Sarcich.

Caleche (see Castle Hill Music)

California Phase (see Menace Music)

Campbell Connelly & Co (see Music Sales Ltd)

Candid Music 16 Castelnau, London SW13 9RU **t** 020 8741 3608 **f** 020 8563 0013 **e** info@candidrecords.com **w** candidrecords.com MD: Alan Bates.

Candle Music Ltd 44 Southern Row, London W10 5AN **t** 020 8960 0111 or 07860 912 192 **f** 020 8968 7008 **e** email@candle.org.uk **w** candle.org.uk MD: Tony Satchell.

Candor Music (see TMR Publishing)

Cara Music The Studio, R.O. 63 Station Rd, Winchmore Hill, London N21 3NB **t** 020 8364 3121 **f** 020 8364 3090 **e** caramusicltd@dial.pipex.com Dir: Michael McDonagh.

Cardinal (see Carlin Music Corporation)

Cargo Music Publishing 39 Clitterhouse Crescent, Cricklewood, London NW2 1DB **t** 020 8458 1020 **f** 020 8458 1020 **e** mike@mikecarr.co.uk **w** mikecarr.co.uk MD: Mike Carr.

Caribbean Music (see Paul Rodriguez Music Ltd)

Caribbean Music Library Sovereign House, 12 Trewartha Rd, Praa Sands, Penzance, Cornwall TR20 9ST **t** 01736 762 826 or 07721 449 477 **f** 01736 763 328 **e** panamus@aol.com **w** panamamusic.co.uk Dir: Roderick Jones.

Carlin Music Corporation Iron Bridge House, 3 Bridge Approach, London NW1 8BD **t** 020 7734 3251 **f** 020 7916 8759 **e** davidjapp@carlinmusic.com **w** carlinmusic.com MD: David Japp.

Carnaby Music 78 Portland Rd, London W11 4LQ **t** 020 7727 2063 **f** 020 7229 4188 **e** negfan@aol.com Dir: Charles Negus-Fancey.

Carte Blanche (see Fay Gibbs Music Services)

Castle Hill Music PO Box 7, Huddersfield, W Yorks HD7 4YA **t** 01484 846333 **f** 01484 846333 **e** HotLeadRecords@btopenworld.com **w** fimusic.co.uk MD: Ian R Smith.

Catalyst Music Publishing Ltd 171 Southgate Rd, London N1 3LE **t** 020 7704 8542 **f** 020 7704 2028 **e** peterknightjr@btinternet.com MD: Peter Knight Jr..

Cathedral Music King Charles Cottage, Racton, Chichester, W Sussex PO18 9DT **t** 01243 379968 **f** 01243 379859 **e** enquiries@cathedral-music.co.uk Prop: Richard Barnes.

Cat's Eye Music (see Multiplay Music)

Catskills Music Publishing PO Box 3365, Brighton BN1 1WQ **t** 01273 626245 **f** 01273 626246 **e** info@catskillsrecords.com **w** catskillsrecords.com Dirs: Khalid, Amr or Jonny.

Cauliflower (see Bucks Music Group)

Cavendish Music (see Boosey & Hawkes Music Publishers Ltd)

Cecil Lennox (see Kassner Associated Publishers)

Cee Cee (see Asterisk Music)

Celtic Songs Unit 4, Great Ship St, Dublin 8, Ireland **t** +353 1 478 3455 **f** +353 1 478 2143 **e** irishmus@iol.ie **w** irelandcd.com GM: Paul O'Reilly.

CF Kahnt (see Peters Edition)

Chain Music 24 Cornwall Rd, Cheam, Surrey SM2 6DT **t** 020 8643 3353 **f** 020 8643 9423 **e** gchurchill@c-h-a-ltd.demon.co.uk Chairman: Carole Howells.

Chain Of Love (see Sea Dream Music)

Chalumeau (see Paul Rodriguez Music Ltd)

Champion Music (see Cheeky Music)

Chandos Music Ltd Chandos House, Commerce Way, Colchester, Essex CO2 8HQ **t** 01206 225200 **f** 01206 225201 **e** shogger@chandos.net **w** chandos.net Music/Copyright Admin: Stephen Hogger.

Chapala Productions Rectory House, Church Lane, Warfield, Berks RG12 6EE **t** 01344 890001 **f** 01344 885323 Contact: Alan Bown.

Chappell (see Warner Chappell Music Ltd)

Chappell Morris (see Warner Chappell Music Ltd)

Charisma Music Publishing (see EMI Music Publishing)

Charjan Music (see Paul Rodriguez Music Ltd)

Charlena (see Menace Music)

Charly Publishing Ltd Suite 379, 37 Store St, London WC1E 7BS **t** 07050 136143 **f** 07050 136144 Contact: Jan Friedmann.

Chart Music Company Ltd Island Cottage, Rod Eyot, Wargrave Rd, Henley-on-Thames, Oxon RG9 3JD **t** 01491 412946 **e** mail@islandmusicjf.co.uk Dir: JW Farmer.

Chartel (see Bucks Music Group)

Chatwise Music (see Bucks Music Group)

Cheeky Music 181 High St, Harlesden, London NW10 4TE **t** 020 8961 5202 **f** 020 8965 3948 **e** eddie@championrecords.co.uk **w** championrecords.co.uk Business Affairs: Eddie Seago.

Chelsea Music Publishing Co 124 Great Portland St, London W1W 6PP **t** 020 7580 0044 **f** 020 7580 0045 **e** eddie@chelseamusicpublishing.com **w** chelseamusicpublishing.com MD: Eddie Levy.

Cherry Lane Music (see Catalyst Music Publishing Ltd)

Cherry Red Music (see BMG Music Publishing Ltd)

Cherry Red Songs 3a Long Island House, Warple Way, London W3 0RG **t** 020 8740 4110 **f** 020 8740 4208 **e** matt@cherryred.co.uk **w** cherryred.co.uk Dir of Business Affairs: Matt Bristow.

Chester Music 8-9 Frith St, London W1D 3JB **t** 020 7434 0066 **f** 020 7287 6329 **e** promotion@musicsales.co.uk **w** chesternovello.com MD: James Rushton.

Chestnut Music Smoke Tree House, Tilford Rd, Farnham, Surrey GU10 2EN **t** 01252 794253 **f** 01252 792642 **e** admin@keynoteaudio.co.uk MD: Tim Wheatley.

Chick-A-Boom Music (see Asterisk Music)

Chipglow (see Asterisk Music)

Chisholm Songs 36 Follingham Court, Drysdale Pl, London N1 6LZ **t** 020 7684 8594 **f** 020 7684 8740 **e** deschisholm@hotmail.com Prop: Desmond Chisholm.

Christabel Music 32 High Ash Drive, Alwoodley, Leeds, W Yorks LS17 8RA **t** 0113 268 5528 **f** 0113 266 5954 MD: Jeff Christie.

Christian Music Ministries (see Sovereign Music UK)

Chrome Dreams PO Box 230, New Malden, Surrey KT3 6YY **t** 020 8715 9781 **f** 020 8241 1426 **e** mail@chromedreams.co.uk **w** chromedreams.co.uk GM: Andy Walker.

Chrys-A-Lee (see Chrysalis Music Ltd)

CHRYSALIS MUSIC LTD

The Chrysalis Building, 13 Bramley Rd, London W10 6SP **t** 020 7221 2213 **f** 020 7465 6178 **e** firstname.lastname@chrysalis.com **w** chrysalis.com MD: Alison Donald. CEO, Chrysalis Music Division: Jeremy Lascelles. Chief Operating Officer, Chrysalis Music Division: Neil Fenton. Dir of A&R, Europe: Paul Kinder. International Head of Royalties: Janet Anderson. Dir of Legal & Business Affairs: Simon Harvey. Head of Copyright: Andy Godfrey. Head of A&R: Ben Bodie. Creative Director: Kate Sweetsur. Dir of Synchronisation: Gary Downing. A&R Scout: Craig Michie.

Chuckle Music 6 Northend Gardens, Kingswood, Bristol BS15 1UA **t** 0117 783 7586 or 0789 994 8199 **e** ply501@netscapeonline.co.uk MD: Peter Michaels.

CIC UK (see Universal Music Publishing Ltd)

Cicada (see Paul Rodriguez Music Ltd)

Cinephonie Co (see Music Sales Ltd)

Cinque Port Music (see The Valentine Music Group)

Citybeat (see 4AD Music)

Class 52 Music Ltd (see Paternoster Music)

Classic Editions (see Wilson Editions)

CLM 153 Vauxhall St, The Barbican, Plymouth, Devon PL4 0DF **t** 01752 510710 **f** 01752 224281 **e** robhancock@lineone.net Ptnr: Rob Hancock.

Clouseau (see SGO Music Publishing)

Clown Songs PO Box 20432, London SE17 3WT **t** 07986 359 568 **e** office@clownmediagroup.co.uk **w** clownmediagroup.co.uk A&R: Stephen Adams.

Coda (see Bucks Music Group)

Cold Harbour Recording Company Ltd 1 York St, London W1U 6PA **t** 01449 720988 **e** enquiries@eastcentralone.com **w** eastcentralone.com MD: Steve Fernie.

Collegium Music Publications PO Box 172, Whittlesford, Cambridge CB2 4QZ **t** 01223 832474 **f** 01223 836723 **e** info@collegium.co.uk **w** collegium.co.uk Sales & Marketing: Michael Stevens.

Barry Collings Entertainments 21A Clifftown Rd, Southend-On-Sea, Essex SS1 1AB **t** 01702 330005 **f** 01702 333309 **e** bcollent@aol.com **w** barrycollings.co.uk Prop: Barry Collings.

Collingwood O'Hare (see Bucks Music Group)

Columbia Publishing Wales Ltd Glen More, 6 Cwrt y Camden, Brecon, Powys LD3 7RR **t** 01874 625270 **f** 01874 625270 **e** dng@columbiawales.fsnet.co.uk **w** columbiapublishing.co.uk MD: Dafydd Gittins.

Come Again Music (see Broadley Music (Int) Ltd)

Cometmarket (see Notting Hill Music (UK) Ltd)

Comma Music (see Paul Rodriguez Music Ltd)

Complete Music 3rd Floor, Bishops Park House, 25-29 Fulham High St, London SW6 3JH **t** 020 7731 8595 **f** 020 7371 5665 **e** info@complete-music.co.uk **w** complete-music.co.uk A&R: Kareem Taylor.

Complete Music (see BMG Music Publishing Ltd)

Concord (see The Essex Music Group)

Concord Music Hire Library (see Maecenas Music)

The Concord Partnership 5 Bushey Close, Old Barn Lane, Kenley, Surrey CR8 5AU **t** 020 8660 4766 or 020 8660 3914 **f** 020 8668 5273 **e** concordptnrship@aol.com Ptnr: Malcolm Binney.

Congo Music Ltd 17A Craven Park Rd, Harlsden, London NW10 8SE **t** 020 8961 5461 **f** 020 8961 5461 **e** byron@congomusic.freeserve.co.uk **w** congomusic.com A&R Director: Root Jackson.

Connect 2 Music (see Zomba Music Publishers)

Connoisseur Music (see Crashed Music)

Consentrated Music (see Bucks Music Group)

Console Sounds PO Box 7515, Glasgow G41 3ZW **t** 0141 636 6336 **f** 0141 636 6336 **e** info@solemusic.co.uk **w** consolesounds.co.uk Dir: Stevie Middleton.

Constant In Opal Music Publishing Sovereign House, 12 Trewartha Rd, Praa Sands, Penzance, Cornwall TR20 9ST **t** 01736 762826 **f** 01736 763328 **e** panamus@aol.com **w** panamamusic.co.uk MD: Roderick Jones.

The Contemporary Music Centre 19 Fishamble St, Temple Bar, Dublin 8, Ireland **t** +353 1 673 1922 **f** +353 1 648 9100 **e** info@cmc.ie **w** cmc.ie Dir: Eve O'Kelly.

Cooking Vinyl Ltd 10 Allied Way, London W3 0RQ **t** 020 8600 9200 **f** 020 8743 7448 **e** info@cookingvinyl.com **w** cookingvinyl.com MD: Martin Goldschmidt.

Copasetik Music 9 Spedan Close, Branch Hill, London NW3 7XF **t** 07855 551 024 **e** copasetik1@aol.com **w** copasetik.com MD/Head of A&R: Jon Sexton.

Copeberg (see Bugle Publishing Group)

Copperplate Music (see Bardic Edition)

Cordella Music Alhambra, High St, Shirrell Heath, Southampton, Hants SO32 2JH **t** 08450 616 616 **f** 01329 833 433 **e** barry@cordellamusic.co.uk **w** cordellamusic.co.uk MD: Barry Upton.

Corelia Music Library (see Panama Music Library)

Corner Stone (see The Valentine Music Group)

Cornerways Music Ty'r Craig, Longleat Ave, Craigside, Llandudno LL30 3AE **t** 01492 549759 **f** 01492 541482 **e** gordonlorenz@compuserve.com Contact: Gordon Lorenz.

C.O.R.S. Ltd (see MCS Plc).

C.O.R.S. Ltd (see MCS Music Ltd)

Cot Valley Music (see Scamp Music)

CPP (see International Music Publications (IMP))

Cramer Music 23 Garrick St, London WC2E 9RY **t** 020 7240 1612 **f** 020 7240 2639 **e** enquiries@cramermusic.co.uk MD: Peter Maxwell.

Cranford Summer School Of Music (see The Concord Partnership)

Crashed Music 162 Church Rd, East Wall, Dublin 3, Ireland **t** +353 1 888 1188 **f** +353 1 856 1122 **e** shay@crashedmusic.com **w** crashedmusic.com MD: Shay Hennessy.

Creative Minds (see Bucks Music Group)

Creative World Entertainment Ltd The Croft, Deanslade Farm, Claypit Lane, Lichfield, Staffs WS14 0AG **t** 01543 253576 or 07885 341745 **f** 01543 255185 **e** info@creative-world-entertainment.co.uk **w** creative-world-entertainment.co.uk MD: Mervyn Spence.

Creole Music Ltd The Chilterns, France Hill Drive, Camberley, Surrey GU15 3QA **t** 01276 686077 **f** 01276 686055 **e** creole@clara.net MD: Bruce White.

Crimson Flame (see Sea Dream Music)

Cringe Music (Publishing) The Cedars, Elvington Lane, Hawkinge, Nr. Folkestone, Kent CT18 7AD **t** 01303 893472 **f** 01303 893833 **e** info@cringemusic.co.uk **w** cringemusic.co.uk MD: Chris Ashman.

Cromwell Music (see The Essex Music Group)

Cross Music (see Music Sales Ltd)

Crumbs Music The Stable Lodge, Lime Ave, Kingwood, Henley-on-Thames, Oxon RG9 5WB **t** 01491 628 111 or 07813 696 999 **f** 01491 629 668 **e** crumbsmusic@btopenworld.com **w** raywilliamsmusic.com MD: Ray Williams.

Crystal City (see Sea Dream Music)

CSA Word 6a Archway Mews, 241a Putney Bridge Rd, London SW15 2PE **t** 020 8871 0220 **f** 020 8877 0712 **e** info@csaword.co.uk **w** csaword.co.uk Audio Manager: Victoria Williams.

CTV Music The Television Centre, St Helier, Jersey, Channel Islands JE1 3ZD **t** 01534 816816 **f** 01534 816778 **e** broadcast@channeltv.co.uk **w** channeltv.co.uk Dir Sales/Mktg: Gordon de Ste. Croix.

Cultural Foundation Hollin Bush, Dalehead, Rosedale, N Yorks YO18 8RL **t** 0845 458 4699 or 01751 417 147 **f** 01751 417 804 **e** info@cultfound.org **w** cultfound.org MD: Peter Bell.

David Cunningham Music 17 Kirkland Lane, Penkhull, Stoke on Trent, Staffs ST4 5DJ **t** 01782 410237 or 07754 170541 **f** 01782 410237 **e** davidcunninghammusic@yahoo.co.uk Contact: David Cunningham.

Curious (see Bucks Music Group)

Cutting Edge Music Ltd Ground Floor, 36 King St, London WC2E 8JS **t** 020 7759 8550 **f** 020 7759 8549 **e** philipm@cutting-edge.uk.com **w** cutting-edge.uk.com MD: Philip Moross.

Cutting Records Music (see Dejamus Ltd)

Cwmni Cyhoeddi Gwynn (see Cyhoeddiadau Sain)

Cwmni Cyhoeddi Gwynn Cyf 28 Heol-y-Dwr, Penygroes, Caernarfon, Gwynedd LL54 6LR **t** 01286 881797 **f** 01286 882634 **e** info@gwynn.co.uk **w** gwynn.co.uk Administrator: Wendy Jones.

Cyclo Music (see Bucks Music Group)

Cyhoeddiadau Sain Canolfan Sain, Llandwrog, Caernarfon, Gwynedd LL54 5TG **t** 01286 831111 **f** 01286 831497 **e** rhian@sain.wales.com **w** sain.wales.com Contact: Rhian Eleri.

CYP Music Limited The Fairway, Bush Fair, Harlow, Essex CM18 6LY **t** 01279 444707 **f** 01279 445570 **e** sales@cyp.co.uk **w** cyp.co.uk Nat'l Accounts Mgr: Gary Wilmot.

Cznin Music (see Menace Music)

D-Jon Music (see Menace Music)

d Music 35 Brompton Rd, London SW3 1DE **t** 020 7368 6311 **f** 020 7823 9553 **e** d@35bromptonroad.com **w** drecords.co.uk MD: Douglas Mew.

DA Licensing Osmond House, 78 Alcester Rd, Moseley Village, Birmingham B13 8BB **t** 0121 449 3814 **e** rod@darecordings.com **w** emusu.com Head of Licensing: Rod Thompson.

Dacara Music (see Menace Music)

Daisy Publishing Unit 2 Carriglea, Naas Rd, Dublin 12, Ireland **t** +353 1 429 8600 **f** +353 1 429 8602 **e** daithi@daisydiscs.com **w** daisydiscs.com MD: John Dunford.

Daisynook (see Notting Hill Music (UK) Ltd)

Dalmatian Songs Ltd PO Box 49155, London SW20 0YL **t** 020 8946 7242 **f** 020 8946 7242 **e** w.stonebridge@btopenworld.com Dirs: Bill Stonebridge, Marc Fox.

Damani Songs (see Darah Music)

The Daniel Azure Music Group 72 New Bond St, London W1S 1RR **t** 07894 702 007 **f** 020 8240 8787 **e** info@jvpr.net **w** danielazure.com CEO: Daniel Azure.

Danny Thompson Music (see SGO Music Publishing)

Darah Music 21C Heathmans Rd, Parsons Green, London SW6 4TJ **t** 020 7731 9313 **f** 020 7731 9314 **e** mail@darah.co.uk MD: David Howells.

Toby Darling Ltd 37/39 Southgate St, Winchester, Hants SO23 9EH **t** 01962 844480 **f** 01962 854400 **e** info@tobydarling.com **w** tobydarling.com MD: Toby Darling.

Dartsongs (see Asterisk Music)

Dash Music (see Music Sales Ltd)

Datsmaboy Music (see Menace Music)

David Paramor Publishing (see Kassner Associated Publishers)

DCI Video (see International Music Publications (IMP))

De Haske Music (UK) Ltd Fleming Rd, Earlstrees, Corby, Northants NN17 4SN **t** 01536 260981 or 0800 616415 **f** 01536 401075 or 0800 616415 **e** music@dehaske.co.uk Sales & Marketing Mgr: Mark Coull.

Decentric Music PO Box 241, Harrow, Middx HA2 8YX **t** 020 8977 4616 **f** 020 8977 4616 **e** decentricjb@waitrose.com Dir: James Bedbrook.

Deceptive Music PO Box 288, St Albans, Herts AL4 9YU **t** 01727 834 130 MD: Tony Smith.

Deconstruction Songs (see BMG Music Publishing Ltd)

Deekers (see Eaton Music Ltd)

Deep Blue Music (see Bucks Music Group)

Deep Blue Publishing (see Sovereign Music UK)

Dejamus Ltd Suite 11, Accurist House, 44 Baker St, London W1U 7AZ **t** 020 7486 5838 **f** 020 7487 2634 **e** firstname+lastname@dejamus.co.uk MD: Stephen James.

Delerium Music Ltd PO Box 1288, Gerrards Cross, Bucks SL9 9YB **t** 01753 890635 **f** 01753 892289 **e** firstname.lastname@delerium.co.uk MD: Richard Allen.

Delfont Music (see Warner Chappell Music Ltd)

Delicious Publishing Suite GB, 39-40 Warple Way, Acton, London W3 0RG **t** 020 8749 7272 **f** 020 8749 7474 **e** info@deliciousdigital.com **w** deliciousdigital.com MD: Ollie Raphael.

Demi Monde Publishing Llanfair Caereinion, Powys, Wales SY21 0DS **t** 01938 810 758 **f** 01938 810 758 **e** demimonde@dial.pipex.com **w** demimonde.co.uk MD: Dave Anderson.

Denker Music (see Kassner Associated Publishers)

Design Music (see Carlin Music Corporation)

Destiny Music (see Carlin Music Corporation)

Deutscher Verlag Fur Musik, Leipzig (see Breitkopf & Hartel)

Dharma Music PO Box 50668, London SW6 3UY **e** zen@instantkarma.co.uk Chairman: Rob Dickins.

Dick Music (see Tabitha Music Ltd)

Digger Music 21 Bedford Sq, London WC1B 3HH **t** 020 7637 4444 **f** 020 7323 2857 **e** tills@globalnet.co.uk CEO: Tilly Rutherford.

Dinosaur Music Publishing 5 Heyburn Crescent, Westport Gardens, Stoke On Trent, Staffs ST6 4DL **t** 01782 824 051 **f** 01782 761 752 **e** music@dinosaurmusic.co.uk **w** dinosaurmusic.co.uk MD: Alan Dutton.

Diverse Music Ltd Creeting House, All Saints Rd, Creeting St Mary, Ipswich, Suffolk IP6 8PR **t** 01449 720 988 **f** 01449 726 067 **e** diversemusicltd@compuserve.com MD: Diana Graham.

DJL Music (see Catalyst Music Publishing Ltd)

DL Songs (see Kassner Associated Publishers)

DMX Music Ltd Forest Lodge, Westerham Rd, Keston, Kent BR2 6HE **t** 01689 882 200 **f** 01689 882 288 **e** vanessa.warren@dmxmusic.com **w** dmxmusic.co.uk Marketing Manager: Vanessa Warren.

Do It Yourself Music (see Bucks Music Group)

Doctor Snuggles Music (see Roedean Music Ltd)

Dog Music (see Crashed Music)

Dome Music Publishing PO Box 3274, East Preston, W Sussex BN16 9BD **t** 01903 771 027 **f** 01903 779 565 **e** info@domerecords.co.uk **w** domerecords.co.uk MD: Peter Robinson.

Domino Music (see Tabitha Music Ltd)

Domino Publishing Co Ltd Unit 3 Delta Pk, Smugglers Way, London SW18 1EG **t** 020 8875 1390 **f** 020 8875 1391 **e** publishing@dominorecordco.com GM: Paul Lambden.

Donna (see EMI Music Publishing)

D.O.R Encryption PO Box 1797, London E1 4TX **t** 020 7702 7842 **e** Encryption@dor.co.uk **w** dor.co.uk/artists MD: Martin Parker.

Dorsey Brothers Music (see Music Sales Ltd)

Douglas Music (see Anglia Music Company)

Douglas Sahm Music (see Menace Music)

Dr Watson Music (see Sherlock Holmes Music)

Dread Music (see Bucks Music Group)

Dreambase Music PO Box 13383, London NW3 5ZR **t** 020 7794 2540 **f** 020 7794 7393 **e** hitman@popstar.com A&R: Tony Strong.

Drumblade Music (see Bardic Edition)

Dub Plate Music (see Greensleeves Publishing Ltd)

Dune Music 1st Floor, 73 Canning Rd, Harrow, Middx HA3 7SP **t** 020 8424 2807 **f** 020 8861 5371 **e** info@dune-music.com **w** dune-music.com MD: Janine Irons.

Durham Music (see Bucks Music Group)

Eagle (see Bucks Music Group)

Earache Songs UK Ltd Suite 1-3 Westminster Building, Theatre Sq, Nottingham NG1 6LG **t** 0115 950 6400 **f** 0115 950 8585 **e** mail@earache.com **w** earache.com MD: Digby Pearson.

Earlham Press (see De Haske Music (UK) Ltd)

Earthsongs (see Bucks Music Group)

Eaton Music Ltd Eaton House, 39 Lower Richmond Rd, Putney, London SW15 1ET **t** 020 8788 4557 **f** 020 8780 9711 **e** info@eatonmusic.com **w** eatonmusic.com Dir: Mandy Oates.

Eclectic Dance Music (see Westbury Music Ltd)

Eddie Trevett Music (see Carlin Music Corporation)

Edition (see Loose Music (UK))

Edition Kunzelmann (see Obelisk Music)

Edition Schwann (see Peters Edition)

Editions Penguin Cafe Ltd 52 King Henry's Walk, London N1 4NN **t** 020 7503 3546 **f** 020 7503 3546 **e** joanna.stephenson@penguincafe.com **w** penguincafe.com Business Affairs Manager: Joanna Stephenson.

Edwin Ashdown (see Music Sales Ltd)

EG Music Ltd PO Box 606, London WC2E 7YT **t** 020 8540 9935 **e** CK@egmusic.demon.co.uk MD: Sam Alder.

Egleg Music (see Asterisk Music)

ELA MUSIC

Argentum, 2 Queen Caroline Street, London W6 9DX **t** 020 8323 8013 **f** 020 8323 8080 **e** ela@ela.co.uk **w** ela.co.uk MD: John Giacobbi.

Eldorado Music Publishing (see Future Earth Music Publishing)

Eleven East Music Inc. (see Bucks Music Group)

William Elkin Music Services Station Road Industrial Estate, Salhouse, Norwich, Norfolk NR13 6NS **t** 01603 721302 **f** 01603 721801 **e** sales@elkinmusic.co.uk **w** elkinmusic.co.uk Ptnr: Richard Elkin.

Embassy Music (see Music Sales Ltd)

Emerson Edition Ltd Windmill Farm, Ampleforth, N Yorks Y062 4HF **t** 01439 788324 **f** 01439 788715 **e** JuneEmerson@compuserve.com MD: June Emerson.

EMI Film & Theatre Music (see EMI Music Publishing)

EMI Music (see Kingsway Music)

EMI MUSIC PUBLISHING

127 Charing Cross Road, London WC2H 0QY **t** 020 7434 2131 **f** 020 7434 3531 **e** firstinitial+lastname@emimusicpub.com **w** emimusicpub.com. MD: Guy Moot. EVP, General Manager: William Booth. Dir of Legal & Business Aff: Antony Bebawi. SVP, Media & Business Dev't: Jonathan Channon. Dir KPM Music: Peter Cox. Finance Dir: Andy Mollett. Dir, Operations and A&R Administration: Fran Malyan.

EMI Music Publishing Continental Europe Publishing House, 127 Charing Cross Rd, London WC2H 0QY **t** 020 7434 2131 **f** 020 7287 5254 **e** firstinitial+lastname@emimusicpub.com **w** emimusicpub.co.uk. Chief Operating Officer Continental European: Claudia Palmer. Dir of Fin & Admin Continental European Operations: Kevin Pallent.

Emusic Pty Ltd (see SGO Music Publishing)

Endomorph Music Publishing 29 St Michael's Rd, Leeds, W Yorks LS6 3BG **t** 0113 274 2106 **f** 0113 278 6291 **e** dave@bluescat.com **w** bluescat.com MD: Dave Foster.

English West Coast Music The Old Bakehouse, 150 High St, Honiton, Devon EX14 8JX **t** 01404 42234 **f** 07767 869029 **e** Studio@ewcm.co.uk **w** ewcm.co.uk Studio Manager: Sean Brown.

Ensign Music (see Famous Music Publishing)

ERA Music (see Express Music (UK) Ltd)

Ernst Eulenburg (see Schott Music Limited)

Ernvik Musik (Sweden) (see Sea Dream Music)

Eschenbach Editions Achmore, Moss Rd, Ullapool IV26 2TF **t** 01854 612 938 **f** 01854 612 938 **e** eschenbach@caritas-music.co.uk **w** caritas-music.co.uk MD: James Douglas.

Esoterica Music Ltd 20 Station Rd, Eckington Rd, Sheffield, S Yorks S21 4FX **t** 01246 432507 or 07785 232176 **f** 01246 432507 **e** richardcory@lineone.net MD: Richard Cory.

Esquire Music Company 185A Newmarket Rd, Norwich, Norfolk NR4 6AP **t** 01603 451139 MD: Peter Newbrook.

The Essex Music Group Suite 207, Plaza 535, Kings Rd, London SW10 0SZ **t** 020 7823 3773 **f** 020 7351 3615 **e** sx@essexmusic.co.uk MD: Frank D Richmond.

Euterpe Music (see Paul Rodriguez Music Ltd)

EV-Web (see Bucks Music Group)

Eventide Music (see Panama Music Library)

Evergreen Music (see Music Sales Ltd)

Evita Music (see Universal Music Publishing Ltd)

Evocative Music (see G2 Music)

Evolve Music Ltd The Courtyard, 42 Colwith Rd, London W6 9EY **t** 020 8741 1419 **f** 020 8741 3289 **e** firstname@evolverecords.co.uk Co-MD: Oliver Smallman.

Ewan McColl Music (see Bucks Music Group)

Express Music (UK) Ltd Matlock, Brady Rd, Lyminge, Kent CT18 8HA **t** 01303 863185 **f** 01303 863185 **e** siggyjackson@onetel.net.uk MD: Siggy Jackson.

Extra Slick Music (see Menace Music)

Faber Music 3 Queen Sq, London WC1N 3AU **t** 020 7833 7900 **f** 020 7833 7939 **e** information@fabermusic.com **w** fabermusic.com.

Fabulous Music (see The Essex Music Group)

Fairwood Music (UK) Ltd 72 Marylebone Lane, London W1U 2PL **t** 020 7487 5044 **f** 020 7935 2270 **e** betul@fairwoodmusic.com **w** fairwoodmusic.com GM: Betul Al-Bassam.

Faith & Hope Publishing 23 New Mount St, Manchester M4 4DE **t** 0161 839 4445 **f** 0161 839 1060 **e** email@faithandhope.co.uk **w** faithandhope.co.uk Contact: Neil Claxton.

Fall River Music (see Bucks Music Group)

Famous Music Publishing 20 Fulham Broadway, London SW6 1AH **t** 020 7385 9429 **f** 020 7385 3261 **e** luke.famousmusic@btconnect.com **w** famousmusic.com A&R Director: Luke McGrellis.

Far Out Music (see Westbury Music Ltd)

Fast Western Ltd. Bank Top Cottage, Meadow Lane, Millers Dale, Derbyshire SK17 8SN **t** 01298 872462 **f** 01298 872461 **e** fast.west@virgin.net MD: Ric Lee.

Fastforward Music Publishing Ltd 1 Sorrel Horse Mews, Ipswich, Suffolk IP4 1LN **t** 01473 210555 **f** 01473 210500 **e** sales@fastforwardmusic.co.uk Sales Dir: Neil Read.

Fat Fox Music 24a Radley Mews, off Stratford Rd, London W8 6JP **t** 020 7376 9555 **f** 020 7937 6246 **e** nick@fatfox.co.uk **w** fatfox.co.uk Dir: Nick Wilde.

Favored Nations Music Publishing Ltd PO Box 31, Bushey, Herts WD23 2PT **t** 01923 244 673 **f** 01923 244 693 **e** info@favorednationsmusic.com **w** favorednationsmusic.com MD: Barry Blue.

Fenette Music (see De Haske Music (UK) Ltd)

FI Music 2 Laurel Bank, Lowestwood, Huddersfield, W Yorks HD7 4ER **t** 01484 846 333 **f** 01484 846 333 **e** HotLeadRecords@btopenworld.com **w** fimusic.co.uk Co-Director: Ian R Smith.

John Fiddy Music Unit 3, Moorgate Business Centre, South Green, Dereham NR19 1PT **t** 01362 697922 **f** 01362 697923 **e** info@johnfiddymusic.co.uk **w** johnfiddymusic.co.uk Prop: John Fiddy.

Fintage Music Flat 7 UP, 1 Lexington St, London W1F 9AF **t** 020 7727 9126 **f** 020 7220 2945 **e** firstname.lastname@fintagehouse.com **w** fintagehouse.com Contact: Bruce Lampcov, Suzanne Plesman.

Fireworks Music 8 Berwick St, Soho, London W1F 0PH **t** 020 7292 0011 **f** 020 7292 0016 **e** fwx@fireworksmusic.co.uk **w** fireworksmusic.co.uk Mgr: Lizzie Prior.

First Time Music (Publishing) UK Sovereign House, 12 Trewartha Rd, Praa Sands, Penzance, Cornwall TR20 9ST **t** 01736 762 826 or 07721 449 477 **f** 01736 763 328 **e** panamas@aol.com **w** songwriters-guild.co.uk MD: Roderick Jones.

Flip Flop Music (see Asterisk Music)

The Flying Music Company Ltd FM House, 110 Clarendon Rd, London W11 2HR **t** 020 7221 7799 **f** 020 7221 5016 **e** info@flyingmusic.com **w** flyingmusic.com Dirs: Paul Walden, Derek Nicol.

Focus Music Library (see Focus Music (Publishing) Ltd)

Focus Music (Publishing) Ltd 4 Pilgrims Lane, London NW3 1SL **t** 020 7435 8266 **f** 020 7435 1505 **e** info@focusmusic.com **w** focusmusic.com MD: Paul Greedus.

Folktrax & Soundpost Publications Heritage House, 16 Brunswick Sq, Gloucester, Gloucs GL1 1UG **t** 01452 415110 **f** 01452 503643 **e** folktrax@blueyonder.co.uk **w** folktrax.org Mgr: Peter Kennedy.

FON Music (see Universal Music Publishing Ltd)

Forsyth Brothers Ltd 126 Deansgate, Manchester M3 2GR **t** 0161 834 3281 **f** 0161 834 0630 **e** info@forsyths.co.uk **w** forsyths.co.uk Publishing Division Mgr: Stewart Inchliffe.

Fortissimo Music 78 Portland Rd, London W11 4LQ **t** 020 7727 2063 **f** 020 7229 4188 **e** negfan@aol.com.

Fortunes Fading Music Unit 1, Pepys Court, 84-86 The Chase, London SW4 0NF **t** 020 7720 7266 **f** 020 7720 7255 **e** ffading@btinternet.com MD: Peter Pritchard.

Four Seasons Music Ltd Killarney House, Killarney Rd, Bray, Co. Wicklow, Ireland **t** +353 1 286 9944 **f** +353 1 286 9945 **e** coulter@indigo.ie **w** philcoulter.com PA to MD: Moira Winget.

4AD Music 17-19 Alma Rd, London SW18 1AA **t** 020 8871 2121 **f** 020 8871 2745 **e** postmaster@almaroad.co.uk MD: Andy Heath.

FourFives Music 21d Heathman's Rd, London SW6 4TJ **t** 020 7731 6555 **f** 020 7371 5005 **e** mp@fourfives-music.com **w** fourfives-music.com MD: Neil Duckworth.

Fox Publishing (see EMI Music Publishing)

Francis Day & Hunter (see EMI Music Publishing)

Francis Dreyfus Music (see Catalyst Music Publishing Ltd)

Frank Chacksfield Music (see Music Sales Ltd)

Freak'n See Music Ltd Suite C, 19 Heathmans Rd, London SW6 4TJ **t** 020 7384 2429 **f** 020 7384 2429 **e** firstname@freaknsee.com **w** freaknsee.com MD: Jimmy Mikaoui.

Freddy Bienstock Music (see Carlin Music Corporation)

Freedom Songs Ltd PO Box 272, London N20 0BY **t** 020 8368 0340 **f** 020 8361 3370 **e** freedom@jt-management.demon.co.uk MD: John Taylor.

Friendly Overtures Walkers Cottage, Aston Lane, Henley-on-Thames, Oxon RG9 3EJ **t** 01491 574 457 **f** 01491 574 457 Creative Dir: Michael Batory.

Frontline Music (see Shanna Music Ltd)

Frontline Music Publishing Ltd (see Purple City Ltd).

Frooty Music (see No Known Cure Publishing)

Full Cycle Music (see Bucks Music Group)

Fundamental Music Ltd The Old Lampworks, Rodney Pl, London SW19 2LQ **t** 020 8542 4222 **f** 020 8542 9934 **e** info@fundamental.co.uk MD: Tim Prior.

Fundit (see Fundamental Music Ltd)

Fungus (see Paul Rodriguez Music Ltd)

Funtastik Music 43 Seaforth Gardens, Stoneleigh, Surrey KT19 0LR **t** 020 8393 1970 **f** 020 8393 2428 **e** info@funtastikmusic.com **w** funtastikmusic.com Contact: John Burns.

Future Earth Music Publishing 59 Fitzwilliam St, Wath Upon Dearne, Rotherham, South Yorks S63 7HG **t** 01709 872875 **e** david@future-earth.co.uk **w** future-earth.co.uk MD: David Moffitt.

Future Stars Publishing Company (see Bucks Music Group)

FX Media Publishing (see Notting Hill Music (UK) Ltd)

G Whitty Music (see Bucks Music Group)

G2 Music 33 Bournehall Ave, Bushey, Herts WD23 3AU **t** 08707 605 714 **f** 020 8950 1294 **e** hitsongs@g2-music.com **w** g2-music.com CEO: Helen Gammons.

Gabsongs (see Arnisongs)

Gael Linn Music (see Crashed Music)

Garron Music Newtown St, Kilsyth, Glasgow, Strathclyde G65 0LY **t** 01236 821081 **f** 01236 826900 **e** info@scotdisc.co.uk **w** scotdisc.co.uk MD: Bill Garden.

Gazell Publishing International PO Box 370, Newquay, Cornwall TR8 5YZ **t** 01637 831011 **f** 01637 831037 **e** dianamelbourne@aol.com Mgr: Di Melbourne.

GDR Music Publishing Ltd 7C Lingfield Point, McMullen Rd, Darlington, Co Durham DL1 1RW **t** 01325 255 252 or 07917 690 223 **f** 01325 255 252 **e** Graeme.circ@ntlworld.com **w** virtual-venue.net MD: Graeme Robinson.

Gerig, Cologne (see Breitkopf & Hartel)

Getaway Music (see BMG Music Publishing Ltd)

Ghost Music Ltd. (see Freedom Songs Ltd)

Fay Gibbs Music Services Warwick Lodge, 37 Telford Ave, London SW2 4XL **t** 020 8671 9699 **f** 020 8674 8558 **e** faygibbs@fgmusicservice.demon.co.uk **w** fgmusicservice.co.uk MD: Fay Gibbs.

Gill Music 40 Highfield Park Rd, Bredbury, Stockport, Cheshire SK6 2PG **t** 0161 494 2098 **e** a1.entertainment@btdigitaltv.com **w** a1entertainmentshowbiz.com Contact: Mrs Gill Cragen.

Ginn Millbrand Group (see Millbrand Copyright Management Ltd)

Glad Music (see Music Sales Ltd)

Glendale Music (see Music Sales Ltd)

Global Journey Ltd Unit 3 Boston Court, Salford Quays, Manchester M50 2GN **t** 0870 264 7484 **f** 0870 264 6444 **e** psamuels@global-journey.com **w** global-journey.com Head of A&R: Peter Samuels.

Global Talent Publishing 2nd Floor, 53 Frith St, London W1D 4SN **t** 020 7292 9640 **f** 020 7292 9611 **e** email@globaltalentgroup.com **w** globaltalentgroup.com MD: Miller Williams.

G&M Brand Publications PO Box 367, Aylesbury, Bucks HP22 4LJ **t** 01296 682220 **f** 01296 681989 **e** orders@rsmith.co.uk MD: Michael Brand.

GMW (see Bucks Music Group)

Go Ahead Music Ltd Kerchesters, Waterhouse Lane, Kingswood, Tadworth, Surrey KT20 6HT **t** 01737 832 837 **f** 01737 833 812 **e** info@amphonic.co.uk MD: Ian Dale.

Gol-Don Publishing 3 Heronwood Rd, Aldershot, Hants. GU12 4AJ **t** 01252 312 382 or 07904 232 292 **e** gol-don.music@ntlworld.com **w** goforit-promotions.com Partners: Golly Gallagher & Don Leach.

Golden Apple Productions (see Music Sales Ltd)

Golden Cornflake Music (see Menace Music)

Golden Mountain Music (see Catalyst Music Publishing Ltd)

Good Groove Songs Ltd Unit 217 Buspace Studios, Conlan St, London W10 5AP **t** 020 7565 0050 **f** 020 7565 0049 **e** gary@goodgroove.co.uk Contact: Gary Davies.

Goodmusic Publishing PO Box 100, Tewkesbury, Gloucs GL20 7YQ **t** 01684 773883 **f** 01684 773884 **e** sales@goodmusic-uk.com **w** goodmusic-uk.com.

Graduate Music PO Box 388, Holt Heath, Worcester, Worcs WR6 6WQ **t** 01905 620786 **e** davidrobertvirr@aol.com **w** graduaterecords.com MD: David Virr.

Grainger Society Edition (see Bardic Edition)

Grand Central Music Publishing Ltd Habib House, 3rd Floor, 9 Stevenson Sq, Piccadilly, Manchester M1 1DB **t** 0161 237 3360 or 07711 269 939 **f** 0161 236 6717 **e** grandcentral01@btconnect.com Dir: Rudi Kidd.

Grapedime Music 28 Hurst Crescent, Barrowby, Grantham, Lincs NG32 1TE **t** 01476 560 241 **f** 01476 560 241 **e** grapedime@pjbray.globalnet.co.uk A&R Manager: Phil Bray.

Grapevine Music Ltd 1 York St, London W1U 6PA **t** 01449 720988 **e** enquiries@eastcentralone.com **w** eastcentralone.com MD: Steve Fernie.

Grass Roots Music Publishing 29 Love Lane, Rayleigh, Essex SS6 7DL **t** 01268 747 077 MD: Gerald Mahlowe.

Greensleeves Publishing Ltd Unit 14, Metro Centre, St John's Rd, Isleworth, Middlesex TW7 6NJ **t** 020 8758 0564 **f** 020 8758 0811 **e** clare@greensleeves.net **w** greensleeves.net Publishing Manager: Clare Ram.

GRG Music (see PXM Publishing)

Grin Music Hurston Mill, Pulborough, W Sussex RH20 2EW **t** 01903 741502 **f** 01903 741502 Copyright Mgr: Patrick Davis.

Groove Consortium Studio 13, The Old Truman Brewery, 91 Brick Lane, London E1 6QL **t** 020 7053 2091 or 07989 340 593 **e** brian@thelemongroup.com **w** thelemongroup.com MD: Brian Allen.

Gull Songs (see Darah Music)

Gut Music Byron House, 112A Shirland Rd, London W9 2EQ **t** 020 7266 0777 **f** 020 7266 7734 **e** admin@gutrecords.com **w** gutrecords.com Chairman: Guy Holmes.

Gwynn Publishing (see Cwmni Cyhoeddi Gwynn Cyf)

Habana Music Publishing (see Gazell Publishing International)

Hal Carter Organisation 72 Borough Way, Potters Bar, Herts EN6 3HB **t** 01707 649 700 or 07958 252 906 **f** 01707 657 822 **e** artistes@halcarterorg.com **w** halcarterorg.com MD: Abbie Carter.

Halcyon Music 233 Regents Park Rd, Finchley, London N3 3LF **t** 07000 783633 **f** 07000 783634 MD: Alan Williams.

Hallin Music Ltd 70A Totteridge Rd, High Wycombe, Bucks HP13 6EX **t** 01494 528 665 **e** b.hallin@virgin.net MD: Brian Hallin.

Halo Publishing 88 Church Lane, London N2 0TB **t** 020 8444 0049 or 07711 062 309 **e** halomanagement@hotmail.com **w** halo-uk.net Dir: Mike Karl Maslen.

Hamburger Publishing PO Box 51389, 2 Nevitt House, London N1 6YD **t** 020 7684 1129 **f** 020 7684 1129 **e** info@schnitzel.co.uk **w** schnitzel.co.uk MD: Oliver Geywitz.

Hammer Musik (see Bucks Music Group)

Hammerhead Music Suite 237, 78 Marylebone High St, London W1U 5AP **t** 07973 129068 **f** 07971 402973 **e** hammer007@jerseymail.co.uk Director A&R: Bob Miller.

Hand Picked Songs (see Catalyst Music Publishing Ltd)

Harbrook Music (see Thames Music)

Hardmonic Music Unit 29, Cygnus Business Center, Dalmeyer Rd, London NW10 2XA **t** 020 8830 0077 **f** 020 8830 0220 **e** info@hardmonic.com **w** hardmonic.com Mgr: Sandra Ceschia.

Haripa Publishing 282 Westbourne Park Rd, London W11 1EH **t** 020 7985 0700 **f** 020 7985 0701 **e** info@kickinmusic.com **w** kickinmusic.com Repertoire & Acquisitions: Alistair Wells.

Harmony Music (see Bucks Music Group)

Harrison Music (see Music Sales Ltd)

Harvard Music (see Bucks Music Group)

Hatton & Rose Publishers 46 Northcourt Ave, Reading, Berks RG2 7HQ **t** 0118 987 4938 **f** 0118 987 4938 Contact: Graham Hatton.

Haynestorm (see Menace Music)

Hazell Dean Music (see Chelsea Music Publishing Co)

H&B Webman & Co (see Chelsea Music Publishing Co)

HBF Music (see Menace Music)

Heart2Heart Music 8 Bicton Pl, Exeter, Devon EX8 2SU **t** 01395 276 414 **f** 01395 276 413 **e** info@heart2heartmusic.co.uk MD: Brian Oliver.

Heartbeat Music (see SGO Music Publishing)

Heartsongs (see Bucks Music Group)

Heaven Music PO Box 92, Gloucester GL4 8HW **t** 01452 814321 **f** 01452 812106 **e** vic_coppersmith@hotmail.com MD: Vic Coppersmith-Heaven.

Heavenly Music (see Paul Rodriguez Music Ltd)

Heavenly Songs 47 Frith St, London W1D 4SE **t** 020 7494 2998 **f** 020 7437 3317 **e** info@heavenlyrecordings.com **w** heavenly100.com MDs: Jeff Barrett, Martin Kelly.

Heavy Harmony Music (see Menace Music)

Heavy Truth Music Publishing Ltd PO Box 8, Corby, Northants NN17 2XZ **t** 01536 202295 **f** 01536 266246 **e** skalidoski@heavytruth.com **w** heavytruth.com Label Mgr: Steve Kalidoski.

Hedgecock Music (see Menace Music)

Heinrichshofen (see Peters Edition)

Hello Cutie/Heru Xuti Publishing Cadillac Ranch, Pencraig Uchaf, Cwm Bach, Whitland, Carms. SA34 0DT **t** 01994 484466 **f** 01994 484294 **e** cadillacranch@telco4u.net **w** nikturner.com Dir: Mendy Menendes.

Hened Music (see Menace Music)

Heraldic Production Music (see Panama Music Library)

HHO Music Suite 1, 1-13 Britannia Business Centre, Cricklewood Lane, London NW2 1ET **t** 020 8830 8813 **f** 020 8830 8801 **e** info@hho.co.uk **w** hho.co.uk MD: Henry Hadaway.

High-Fye Music (see Music Sales Ltd)

Hilltop Publishing Ltd. PO Box 429, Aylesbury, Bucks. HP18 9XY **t** 01844 238692 **f** 01844 238692 **e** info@hilltoppublishing.co.uk **w** brillsongs.com Dir: Catherine Croydon.

Hit & Run (see EMI Music Publishing)

HMP Publishing UK PO Box 14303, London SE26 4ZH **t** 07000 472 572 or 07956 446 342 **f** 07000 472 572 or 020 8291 9236 **e** info@latinartsgroup.com **w** latinartsgroup.com Dir: Hector Rosquete.

Hoax Music Publishing PO Box 23604, London E7 0YT **t** 0870 910 6666 **e** hoax@hoaxmusic.com **w** hoaxmusic.com MD: Ben Angwin.

Honeyhill Music (see Bucks Music Group)

Hooj Choons (see Mute Song)

Hornall Brothers Music Ltd 1 Northfields Prospect, Putney Bridge Rd, London SW18 1PE **t** 020 8877 3366 **f** 020 8874 3131 **e** stuart@hobro.co.uk **w** hobro.co.uk MD: Stuart Hornall.

Hot Melt Music (see Universal Music Publishing Ltd)

Hournew Music (see Music Sales Ltd)

Howard Beach Music Inc. (see Bucks Music Group)

Howlin' Music Ltd 114 Lower Park Rd, Loughton, Essex IG10 4NE **t** 020 8508 4564 or 07831 430080 **e** djone@howardmarks.freeserve.co.uk Prop/A&R: Howard Marks.

Hub Music (see Universal Music Publishing Ltd)

Hubris Music (see BDI Music Ltd)

Hucks Productions (see Bucks Music Group)

Hummingbird Productions (see Bucks Music Group)

Humph Music (see Paul Rodriguez Music Ltd)

Hunka Lisa Marie Music (see SGO Music Publishing)

Hunter Bond Music (see Millbrand Copyright Management Ltd)

Huntley Music (see Bucks Music Group)

Hyde Park Music 110 Westbourne Terrace Mews, London W2 6QG **t** 020 7402 8419 **f** 020 7723 6104 **e** tony@tonyhiller.com Chairman: Tony Hiller.

Hydrogen Duke Box Music Publishing (see Reverb Music Ltd)

I.L.C Music Ltd The Old Props Building, Pinewood Studios, Pinewood Rd, Iver Heath, Bucks SL0 0NH **t** 01753 785 631 **f** 01753 785 632 **e** Nigelwood@ilcgroup.co.uk Dirs: Nigel Wood & Ellis Elias.

Illicit Entertainment PO Box 51871, London NW2 9BR **t** 020 8830 7831 **f** 020 8830 7859 **e** ian@illicit.tv **w** mumbojumbo.co.uk MD: Ian Clifford.

Ilona Sekacz Music (see Bucks Music Group)

Imma Play Jason Music (see Notting Hill Music (UK) Ltd)

Immortal Music Ltd (see Independent Music Group).

In The Frame Music 42 Winsford Gardens, Westcliff On Sea, Essex SS0 0DP **t** 01702 390353 **f** 01702 390355 **e** will@willbirch.com Prop: Will Birch.

Inair Musikverlag (see BMP - Broken Music Publishing)

Incentive Music Ltd Unit 21, Grand Union Centre, West Row, London W10 5AS **t** 020 8964 2555 **f** 020 8964 8778 **e** incentive@incentivemusic.co.uk **w** incentivemusic.com MD: Nick Halkes.

Incredible Music (see Notting Hill Music (UK) Ltd)

Independent Music Group Ltd Independent House, 54 Larkshall Rd, London E4 6PD **t** 020 8523 9000 **f** 020 8523 8888 **e** erich@independentmusicgroup.com **w** independentmusicgroup.com CEO: Ellis Rich.

Indian Hill Music (see Menace Music)

Indipop Music P.O. Box 369, Glastonbury, Somerset BA6 8YN **t** 01749 831 674 **f** 01749 831 674 MD: Steve Coe.

Industrial Music (see Bucks Music Group)

Infectious Music (see 4AD Music)

Infernal Music (see Notting Hill Music (UK) Ltd)

Inky Blackness Music Ltd PO Box 32089, Camden Town, London NW1 0NX **t** 07958 520580 **e** inky@inkyblackness.co.uk **w** inkyblackness.co.uk MD: Ian Tregoning.

International Music Network Ltd (see Independent Music Group Ltd)

International Music Publications (IMP) Griffin House, 161 Hammersmith Rd, London W6 8BS **t** 020 8222 9200 **f** 020 8222 9260 **e** imp.info@warnerchappell.com **w** wbpdealers.com Sales Manager: Chris Statham.

International Songwriters' Music PO Box 46, Limerick City, Ireland **t** +353 61 228837 **f** +353 61 2288379 **e** jliddane@songwriter.iol.ie **w** songwriter.co.uk MD: James D Liddane.

Intersate (see Paul Rodriguez Music Ltd)

IQ Music Commercial House, 52 Perrymount Rd, Haywards Heath, W Sussex RH16 3DT **t** 01444 452 807 **f** 01444 451 739 **e** kathie@iqmusic.co.uk Dir: Kathie Iqbal.

IRMA UK Unit 21, Isabel House, 46 Victoria Rd, Surbiton, Surrey KT6 4JL **t** 020 8390 6708 **f** 020 8399 2534 **e** corrado@irmagroup.com **w** irmagroup.com MD: Corrado Dierna.

IRS Music/IRS Songs (see Bugle Publishing Group)

Isa Music 260 St.Vincent St, Glasgow G2 5RL **t** 0141 248 2266 **f** 0141 248 4333 **e** admin@isa-music.com **w** isa-music.com MD: Ronnie Simpson.

Isobar Music 56 Gloucester Pl, London W1U 8HJ **t** 020 7486 3297 or 07956 493 692 **f** 020 7486 3297 **e** info@isobarrecords.com MD: Peter Morris.

Ivy Music (see Music Sales Ltd)

Ixion (see Eaton Music Ltd)

J Curwen & Sons (see Music Sales Ltd)

Jack Good Music (see Carlin Music Corporation)

Jacobs Ladder Music Ltd 11 Claremont Crescent, Croxley Green, Rickmansworth, Herts WD3 3QP **t** 01923 220 628 **e** allen.jacobs@virgin.net MD: Allen Jacobs.

Jacquinabox Music Ltd (see Independent Music Group).

Jamdown Music Ltd Stanley House Studios, 39 Stanley Gardens, London W3 7SY **t** 020 8735 0280 **f** 07970 574924 **e** othman@jamdown-music.com **w** jamdown-music.com MD: Othman Mukhlis.

Jap Songs (see Proof Songs)

Jarb Publishing (see Charly Publishing Ltd)

Jay Nick Enterprises (see Menace Music)

Jaykay Music (see Bucks Music Group)

Jazid Music (see Paul Rodriguez Music Ltd)

Jazz Art Music (see Bucks Music Group)

JB Max Music 142 New Cavendish St, London W1W 6YF **t** 020 7323 2420 **f** 020 7580 7776 **e** jbmax.co.uk Dirs: Adrian Bullock, Paul Moore.

Jeff Wayne Music Group Oliver House, 8-9 Ivor Pl, London NW1 6BY **t** 020 7724 2471 **f** 020 7724 6245 **e** info@jeffwaynemusic.com **w** jeffwaynemusic.com Group Dir: Jane Jones.

Jenjo Music Publishing 68 Wharton Ave, Sheffield, S Yorks S26 3SA **t** 0114 287 9882 **f** 0114 287 9882 Contact: Mike Ward.

Jester Song 78 Gladstone Rd, London SW19 1QT **t** 020 8543 4056 **f** 020 8542 8225 **e** jestersong@msn.com MD: R B Rogers.

Jetstar Publishers (see Carlin Music Corporation)

Jewel Music Co (see Warner Chappell Music Ltd)

Jewel Music Publishing Ltd (see Hornall Brothers Music).

J&H Publishing (see Dejamus Ltd)

Jiving Brothers (see G&M Brand Publications)

JKMC Publishing (see Dejamus Ltd)

J&M Music Publishing (see Paul Rodriguez Music Ltd)

JML Publishing Ltd Redloh House, 2 Michael Rd, London SW6 2AD **t** 020 7736 3377 **f** 020 7731 0567 **e** tash@jjdm.net Contact: Jeremy Marsh, Tash Courage.

Jobete Music (UK) Ltd (see EMI Music Publishing)

Joe Gibb (see Westbury Music Ltd)

Johi Music (see Dejamus Ltd)

John Rubie (see Paul Rodriguez Music Ltd)

John Stedman Music Publishing PO Box 1584, London N3 3NW **t** 020 8346 8663 **f** 020 8346 8848 **e** john@jsprecords.com **w** jsprecords.com Contact: John Stedman.

Johnsongs (see Universal Music Publishing Ltd)

Jonalco Music (see Halcyon Music)

Jonathan Music (see Catalyst Music Publishing Ltd)

Jonjo Music (see Bocu Music Ltd)

Jonsongs Music 3 Farrers Pl, Croydon, Surrey CR0 5HB **t** 020 8654 5829 **f** 020 8656 3313 **e** jonsongsuk@yahoo.co.uk GM: Patricia Bancroft.

Josef Weinberger 12-14 Mortimer St, London W1T 3JJ **t** 020 7580 2827 **f** 020 7436 9616 **e** general.info@jwmail.co.uk **w** josef-weinberger.co.uk Promotion: Lewis Mitchell.

Joustwise Myrtle Cottage, Rye Rd, Hawkhurst, Kent TN18 5DW **t** 01580 754 771 **f** 01580 754 771 **e** scully4real@yahoo.co.uk **w** 4realrecords.com MD: Terry Scully.

JSE Music Publishing Ltd (see Independent Music Group Ltd)

Ju-Ju Bee Music (see Dejamus Ltd)

Jubilee Music Ltd (see IQ Music)

David Julius Publishing 11 Alexander House, Tiller Rd, London E14 8PT **t** 020 7987 8596 **f** 020 7987 8596 **e** burdlawrence@btinternet.com MD: David Maynard.

June Songs (see Chelsea Music Publishing Co)

Jupiter 2000 (see Crumbs Music)

Just Isn't Music PO Box 4296, London SE11 4WW **t** 020 7820 3535 **f** 020 7820 3434 **e** adrian@ninjatune.net **w** ninjatune.net Contact: Adrian Kemp.

Just Music Publishing Hope House, 40 St Peters Rd, London W6 9BD **t** 020 8741 6020 **f** 020 8741 8362 **e** justmusic@justmusic.co.uk **w** justmusic.co.uk Dirs: Serena & John Benedict.

Justice Music (see Bucks Music Group)

K7 Publishing (see Bucks Music Group)

Kaleidoscope Publishing Ltd Suite 215, 535 King's Rd, London SW10 0SZ **t** 020 7351 4877 **f** 020 7351 4848 **e** ross.fitzsimons@btopenworld.com Contact: Ross Fitzsimons.

Kalmann Music (see Carlin Music Corporation)

Kamara Music Publishing PO Box 56, Boston, Lincs PE22 8JL **t** 07976 553624 **e** chrisdunn@kamaramusic.fsnet.co.uk **w** megahitrecordsuk.co.uk MD: Chris Dunn.

Karonsongs 20 Radstone Court, Hillview Rd, Woking, Surrey GU22 7NB **t** 01483 755 153 **e** ron.roker@ntlworld.com MD: Ron Roker.

Kassner Associated Publishers Units 6 & 7, 11 Wyfold Rd, Fulham, London SW6 6SE **t** 020 7385 7700 **f** 020 7385 3402 **e** songs@kassner-music.co.uk **w** president-records.co.uk MD: David Kassner.

Katsback (see Menace Music)

Kaplan Kaye Music 95 Gloucester Rd, Hampton, Middlesex TW12 2UW **t** 020 8783 0039 **f** 020 8979 6487 **e** kaplan222@aol.com Contact: Kaplan Kaye.

Kayenne Music (see The Valentine Music Group)

Kenny Lynch Music (see Carlin Music Corporation)

Kensington Music (see The Essex Music Group)

Kensongs (see Paul Rodriguez Music Ltd)

Kerroy Music Publishing 2 Queensmead, St John's Wood Pk, London NW8 6RE **t** 020 7722 9828 **f** 020 7722 9886 **e** kerroy@btinternet.com CEO: Iain Kerr.

Keswick (see Loose Music (UK))

Kevin King Music Publishing 16 Limetrees, Llangattock, Crickhowell, Powys NP8 1LB **t** 01873 810142 **f** 01873 811557 **e** kevinkinggb@aol.com **w** silverword.co.uk MD: Kevin King.

Key Music (see Bucks Music Group)

Kickin Music (see Haripa Publishing)

Kickstart Music 12 Port House, Square Rigger Row, Plantation Wharf, London SW11 3TY **t** 020 7223 8666 **f** 020 7223 8777 **e** info@kickstart.uk.net Dir: Frank Clark.

Kila Music Publishing Charlemont House, 33 Charlemont St, Dublin 2, Ireland **t** +353 1 476 0627 **f** +353 1 476 0627 **e** info@kilarecords.com **w** kila.ie Dir: Colm O'Snodaigh.

Killer Trax (see BMG Zomba Production Music)

King Jam Music (see Paul Rodriguez Music Ltd)

King Of Spades (see Paul Rodriguez Music Ltd)

Kingstreet Media Group G12 Shepherds Studio, Rockley Rd, London W14 0DA **t** 020 7751 1155 **f** 07092 315 184 **e** info@kingstreetgroup.co.uk **w** kingstreetgroup.co.uk GM - Music Publishing: Andy Spacey.

Kingsway Music Lottbridge Drove, Eastbourne, E Sussex BN23 6NT **t** 01323 437700 **f** 01323 411970 **e** music@kingsway.co.uk **w** kingsway.co.uk Label Mgr: Stephen Doherty.

Kinsella Music 68 Schools Hill, Cheadle, Cheshire SK8 1JD **t** 0161 491 5776 **f** 0161 491 6600 **e** kevkinsella@aol.com MD: Kevin Kinsella Snr.

Kirklees Music 609 Bradford Rd, Bailiff Bridge, Brighouse, W Yorkshire HD6 4DN **t** 01484 722855 **f** 01484 723591 **e** sales@kirkleesmusic.co.uk **w** kirkleesmusic.co.uk Ptnr: Graham Horsfield.

Kirschner-Warner Bros Music (see Warner Chappell Music Ltd)

Kite Music Ltd Binny Estate, Ecclesmachan, Edinburgh EH52 6NL **t** 01506 858885 **f** 01506 858155 **e** kitemusic@aol.com MD: Billy Russell.

Knox Music (see Carlin Music Corporation)

Koala Publishing (see Music Exchange (Manchester) Ltd)

Kobalt Music Group 4 Valentine Pl, London SE1 8QH **t** 020 7401 5500 **f** 020 7401 5501 **e** firstname@kobaltmusic.com **w** kobaltmusic.com Exec VP: Sas Metcalfe.

Kojam Music (see Kobalt Music Group)

Koka Media (see BMG Zomba Production Music)

KPM Music (see EMI Music Publishing)

KPM MusicHouse 127 Charing Cross Rd, London WC2H 0EA **t** 020 7412 9126 **f** 020 7413 0061 **e** elaine@kpmmusichouse.com **w** kpmmusichouse.com Creative Dir: Elaine Van Der Schoot.

Kudos Film and TV (see BDI Music Ltd)

Kunzelmann (see Peters Edition)

Lady's Gold Mercedes (see Bucks Music Group)

Lakes Music Wakefield Pl, Sandgate, Kendal, Cumbria LA9 6HT **t** 01539 724433 **f** 01539 724499 **e** info@ensign.uk.com Dir: Neil Clark.

Lakeview Music Pub Co (see The Essex Music Group)

Lantern Music 34 Batchelor St, London N1 0EG **t** 020 7278 4288 **e** rgoldmff@aol.com Contact: Rob Gold.

Lark Music (see Carlin Music Corporation)

Latino Buggerveil Music (see Notting Hill Music (UK) Ltd)

Laurel Music (see EMI Music Publishing)

Laurie Johnson Music (see Bucks Music Group)

Laws Of Motion Publishing (see Westbury Music Ltd)

Leaf Songs Reverb House, Bennett St, London W4 2AH
t 020 8747 0660 **f** 020 8747 0880 **e** liam@leafsongs.com
w leafsongs.com MD: Liam Teeling.

Dick Leahy Music Ltd 1 Star St, London W2 1QD
t 020 7258 0093 **f** 020 7402 9238 **e** info@playwrite.uk.com
Office Manager: Nicky McDermott.

Leap Music Ltd 60 Kingly St, London W1B 5DS
t 020 7453 4011 **f** 020 7453 4242 **e** richard@leapmusic.com
w leapmusic.com MD: Richard Kirstein.

Legend Music Highridge, Bath Rd, Farmborough, Nr. Bath
BA2 0BG **t** 07161 470023 **e** davidrees55@aol.com
MD: David Rees.

Leonard, Gould & Butler (see Music Exchange
(Manchester) Ltd)

LEOPARD MUSIC PUBLISHING

LEOPARD
music publishing

PO Box 45, Cleckheaton, West Yorkshire BD19 4YX
t 05601 480 068 or 07738 882 264 **f** 01274 879 594
e leopardmusic@btinternet.com **w** leopardmusicgroup.com
Managing Director: Brian Williams. Creative Director: Teresa
Coultard.
Leopard Music is an independent publisher with a catalogue
of pop music for worldwide exploitation available for the
music industry.

Leosong Copyright Service Ltd (see MCS Plc).

Les Etoiles de la Musique (see Menace Music)

Les Molloy 27 Willesden Lane, London NW6 7RD
t 07860 389 598 or 07860 389 598 **f** 020 7625 1199
e lmolloy@dircon.co.uk Contact: Les Molloy.

Leslie Veale Music (see Scamp Music)

The Licensing Team Ltd 23 Capel Rd, Watford
WD19 4FE **t** 01923 234 021 **f** 020 8421 6590
e Info@TheLicensingTeam.com **w** thelicensingteam.com
Dir: Lucy Winch.

Lindsay Music 23 Hitchin St, Biggleswade, Beds SG18 8AX
t 01767 316521 **f** 01767 317221 **e** office@lindsaymusic.co.uk
w lindsaymusic.co.uk Ptnr: Carole Lindsay-Douglas.

Linvoy Music (see Carlin Music Corporation)

Lionrich Music (see Menace Music)

Little Diva (see Menace Music)

Little Dragon Music (see Bucks Music Group)

Little Rox Music (see Celtic Songs)

Little Venice (see Bucks Music Group)

Little Victory Music (see Menace Music)

Littlechap (see Jeff Wayne Music Group)

Livingsting Music (see Greensleeves Publishing Ltd)

LOE Music LOE House, 159 Broadhurst Gardens, London
NW6 3AU **t** 020 7328 6100 **f** 020 7624 6384
e watanabe@loe.uk.net MD: Hiroshi Kato.

Logo Songs (see Hornall Brothers Music Ltd)

Lomond Music 32 Bankton Pk, Kingskettle, Fife KY15 7PY
t 01337 830974 **f** 01337 830653 **e** bruce.fraser@zetnet.co.uk
w lomondmusic.com Partners: Bruce & Pat Fraser.

Longstop Productions (see Bucks Music Group)

Loose Music (UK) Pinery Building, Highmoor, Wigton,
Cumbria CA7 9LW **t** 016973 45422 **f** 016973 45422
e edwards@looserecords.com **w** looserecords.com
A&R: Tim Edwards.

Lorna Music (see EMI Music Publishing)

Louise Music (see Menace Music)

Love-Ly-N-Divine (see Menace Music)

Love Music (see Crashed Music)

Ludix Music (see Carlin Music Corporation)

Ludwig Van Music Ltd PO Box 30884, London W12 9XA
t 020 8746 7461 **f** 020 8749 7441 **e** info@spiritmm.com
Dir: David Jaymes.

Lupus Music 1 Star St, London W2 1QD **t** 020 7706 7304
f 020 7706 8197 **e** lupusmusic@btconnect.com
MD: Cora Barnes.

Lynton Muir Music Ltd 1 Oakwood Parade, London
N14 4HY **t** 020 8950 8732 **f** 020 8950 6648
e paul.lynton@btopenworld.com MD: Paul Lynton.

Lynwood Music 2 Church St, West Hagley, W Midlands
DY9 0NA **t** 01562 886625 **f** 01562 886625
e downlyn@globalnet.co.uk
w users.globalnet.co.uk/~downlyn/index.html
Mgr: Rosemary Cooper.

M2 Music (see Bucks Music Group)

Machola Music (see Darah Music)

Madena (see Eaton Music Ltd)

Madrigal Music Guy Hall, Awre, Glocs GL14 1EL
t 01594 510512 **f** 01594 510512 **e** artists@madrigalmusic.co.uk
w madrigalmusic.co.uk MD: Nick Ford.

Maecenas Contemporary Composers Ltd (see
Maecenas Music)

Maecenas Music 5 Bushey Close, Old Barn Lane, Kenley,
Surrey CR8 5AU **t** 020 8660 4766 or 020 8660 3914
f 020 8668 5273 **e** maecenasmusicltd@aol.com
w maecenasmusic.co.uk Trade Mgr: Bill Burnett.

Magic Frog Music (see Focus Music (Publishing) Ltd)

Magick Eye Publishing PO Box 3037, Wokingham, Berks
RG40 4GR **t** 0118 932 8320 **f** 0118 932 8237
e info@magickeye.com **w** magickeye.com MD: Chris Hillman.

Magneil Publishing (see Bugle Publishing Group)

Magnet Music (see Warner Chappell Music Ltd)

Main Spring Music PO Box 38648, London W13 9WJ
t 020 8567 1376 **e** blair@main-spring.com **w** main-spring.com
MD: Blair McDonald.

Main Street (see Greensleeves Publishing Ltd)

Make Some Noise Publishing PO Box 792, Maidstone, Kent ME14 5LG **t** 01622 691 106 **f** 01622 691 106 **e** info@makesomenoiserecords.com **w** makesomenoiserecords.com Mgr: Clive Austen.

Malahat (see Menace Music)

MAM Music (see Chrysalis Music Ltd)

Man in the Street Publishing The Old Chapel, Hardwick, Aylesbury, Bucks HP22 4DZ **t** 0845 644 1839 **e** manstreetpub@aol.com Prop: Derik Timms.

Mann Music Ltd (see Paternoster Music)

Mansem Music (see Wilson Editions)

Marlyn Music (see Carlin Music Corporation)

Marmalade Music (see Warner Chappell Music Ltd)

Marquis Music (see Bocu Music Ltd)

George Martin Music /o CA Management, Southpark Studios, 88 Peterborough Rd, London SW6 3HH **t** 020 7384 9575 **e** information@georgemartinmusic.com **w** georgemartinmusic.com A&R: Adam Sharp.

Marzique Music (see Menace Music)

Match Production Music (see BMG Zomba Production Music)

Mattapan Music (see Bucks Music Group)

Matthews Music (see SGO Music Publishing)

Mautoglade Music (see Hornall Brothers Music Ltd)

Max-Hill Music (see Notting Hill Music (UK) Ltd)

Maximum Music (see Paul Rodriguez Music Ltd)

Maxwood Music Regent House, 1 Pratt Mews, London NW1 0AD **t** 020 7267 6899 **f** 020 7267 6746 **e** partners@newman-and.co.uk MD: Colin Newman.

Mayhew Music (see Kassner Associated Publishers)

Mcasso Music Publishing 32-34 Great Marlborough St, London W1F 7JB **t** 020 7734 3664 **f** 020 7439 2375 **e** music@mcasso.com **w** mcasso.com Professional Manager: Lisa McCaffery.

McGuinness Whelan 30-32 Sir John Rogersons Quay, Dublin 2, Ireland **t** +353 1 677 7330 **f** +353 1 677 7276 MD: Paul McGuinness.

MCI Music Publishing Ltd 4th Floor, Holden House, 57 Rathbone Pl, London W1T 1JU **t** 020 7396 8899 **f** 020 7470 6659 **e** info@mcimusic.co.uk Creative Manager: James Bedbrook.

MCS Music Ltd (A Division of Music Copyright, Solutions Plc), 32 Lexington St, London W1F 0LQ **t** 020 7255 8777 **f** 020 7255 8778 **e** info@mcsmusic.com **w** mcsmusic.com.

Measured Music Ltd. Studio 19, St. George's Studios, 93-97 St. George's Rd, Glasgow G3 6JA **t** 0141 331 9888 **f** 0141 331 9889 **e** mr@measuredrecords.com **w** measuredrecords.com MD: Dougie Souness.

Mediant Music (see Kassner Associated Publishers)

Melody First Music (see Panama Music Library)

Melody Lauren Music Unit 7 Freetrade House, Lowther Rd, Stanmore, Middlesex HA7 1EP **t** 020 8206 1177 **f** 020 8206 2757 **e** wworld@wienerworld.com **w** wienerworld.com MD: Anthony Broza.

Memnon Music Habib House, 3rd Floor, 9 Stevenson Sq, Piccadilly, Manchester M1 1DB **t** 0161 238 8516 **f** 0161 236 6717 **e** memnon@btconnect.com **w** memnonentertainment.com Dir of Business Affairs: Rudi Kidd.

Memory Lane Music Ltd Independent House, 54 Larkshall Rd, London E4 6PD **t** 020 8523 9000 **f** 020 8523 8888 **e** erich@independentmusicgroup.com **w** independentmusicgroup.com CEO: Ellis Rich.

Menace Music 2 Park Rd, Radlett, Herts WD7 8EQ **t** 01923 853789 **f** 01923 853318 **e** menacemusicmanagement@btopenworld.com MD: Dennis Collopy.

Menace USA (see Menace Music)

Menlo Music (see International Songwriters' Music)

Mercury Music (see EMI Music Publishing)

Meriden Music (Classical) The Studio Barn, Silverwood House, Woolaston, Nr Lydney, Gloucs GL15 6PJ **t** 01594 529026 **f** 01594 529027 **e** info@meridenmusic.co.uk **w** meridenmusic.co.uk Contact: The Secretary.

Meringue Productions Ltd 37 Church St, Twickenham, Middlesex TW1 3NR **t** 020 8744 2277 **f** 020 8744 9333 **e** meringue@meringue.co.uk **w** meringue.co.uk Dir: Lynn Earnshaw.

Mesh Music 13 Sandys Rd, Worcester WR1 3HE **t** 01905 613 023 **e** meshmusic@prison-records.com MD: Chris Warren.

Mesmerizing Music 1 Glenthorne Mews, 115a Glenthorne Rd, London W6 0LJ **t** 020 8741 9365 **e** howard.berman@mesmermusic.com MD: Howard Berman.

Messer Music (see Bucks Music Group)

Metric Music (see Bugle Publishing Group)

Metro Music Library (see Amphonic Music Ltd.)

Metrophonic Tithebarns, Tithebarns Lane, Send, Surrey GU23 7LE **t** 01483 225 226 **f** 01483 479 606 **e** mail@metrophonic.com **w** metrophonic.com MD: Brian Rawling.

Michael Batory Music (see Friendly Overtures)

Middle Eight Music (see Cramer Music)

Miggins Music (UK) 33 Mandarin Pl, Grove, Oxon OX12 0QH **t** 01235 771577 **f** 01235 767171 **e** migginsmusic3@yahoo.com Creative Director: Des Leyton.

Mighty Iron Music (see Asterisk Music)

Mike Music Ltd Freshwater House, Outdowns, Effingham, Surrey KT24 5QR **t** 01483 281500 or 01483 281501 **f** 01483 281502 **e** yellowbal@aol.com MD: Mike Smith.

Mikosa Music 9-10 Regent Sq, London WC1H 8HZ **t** 020 7837 9648 **f** 020 7837 9648 **e** mikosapanin@hotmail.com MD: Mike Osapanin.

Millbrand Copyright Management Ltd PO Box 357, Middlesbrough, Cleveland TS1 4WZ **t** 01642 806 795 or 01642 218 057 **f** 01642 800 986 **e** info@millbrand.com **w** millbrand.com MD: Paul Mooney.

Millbrand Music (see Millbrand Copyright Management Ltd)

Millennium Songs 6 Water Lane, Camden, London NW1 8NZ **t** 020 7482 0272 **f** 020 7267 4908 **e** mail@millenniumrecords.com MD: Ben Recknagel.

Milstein Music (see Dejamus Ltd)

MINDER MUSIC LTD

18 Pindock Mews, London W9 2PY **t** 020 7289 7281 **f** 020 7289 2648 **e** songs@mindermusic.com **w** mindermusic.com. Dirs: John Fogarty, Beth Clough. Administration: Jenny Clough. Business Affairs: Roger Nickson. A&R: S Boy. Security: Jack Russell.

Minerva Vision Music (see Paul Rodriguez Music Ltd)

Mio Fratello (see Dejamus Ltd)

Miracle Music (see Carlin Music Corporation)

Miriamusic 1 Glanleam Rd, Stanmore, Middlesex HA7 4NW **t** 020 8954 2025 MD: Zack Laurence.

Mistletoe Melodies (see Bocu Music Ltd)

Misty River Music (see Bucks Music Group)

Mix Music PO Box 89, Slough, Berks SL1 6DQ **t** 01628 667124 **f** 01628 605246 **e** simon@dmcworld.com **w** dmcworld.com Business Affairs Mgr: Simon Gurney.

Mizmo International (see Notting Hill Music (UK) Ltd)

MMV Music 4 Heathgate Pl, 75-83 Agincourt Rd, London NW3 2NU **t** 020 7424 8688 **f** 020 7424 8699 **e** info@mmvmusic.com Contact: Björn Hall.

Model Music (see Kassner Associated Publishers)

Moggie Music Ltd 101 Hazelwood Lane, London N13 5HQ **t** 020 8886 2801 **f** 020 8882 7380 **e** artistes@halcarterorg.com **w** halcarterorg.com Owner: Hal Carter.

Moist Music Ltd PO Box 528, Enfield, Middx EN3 7ZP **t** 070 107 107 24 **f** 0870 137 3787 **e** info@moistrecords.com **w** moistrecords.com MD: Rodney Lewis.

Moncur Street Music Ltd PO Box 16114, London SW3 4WG **t** 020 7349 9909 **f** 020 7376 8532 **e** mail@moncurstreet.com **w** moncurstreet.com MD: Jonathan Simon.

Monument Music (see Diverse Music Ltd)

MoonRock Music PO Box 883, Liverpool L69 4RH **t** 0151 922 5657 **f** 0151 922 5657 **e** bstratt@mersinet.co.uk **w** mersinet.co.uk Publishing Manager: Billy Stratton.

Moonsung Music PO Box 369, Glastonbury, Somerset BA6 8YN **t** 01749 831 674 **f** 01749 831 674 Contact: Sheila Chandra.

Morgan Music Co Ltd (see Maxwood Music)

Bryan Morrison Music 1 Star St, London W2 1QD **t** 020 7706 7304 **f** 020 7706 8197 **e** bryanmorrisonmusic@btconnect.com MD: Bryan Morrison.

Morrison Evans Music (see Bryan Morrison Music)

Morrison Leahy Music 1 Star St, London W2 1QD **t** 020 7258 0093 **f** 020 7402 9238 **e** nicky@playwrite.uk.com Contact: Nicky McDermott.

Moss Music 7 Dennis Rd, Corfe Mullen, Wimborne, Dorset BH21 3NF **t** 01202 695965 **f** 01202 695965 **e** petermossmusic@onetel.net.uk MD: Peter Moss.

Mostyn Music 8 Milvil Court, Milvil Rd, Lee on the Solent, Hants PO13 9LY **t** 023 9255 0566 **f** 023 9255 0566 **e** Maureen@mostynmusic.com **w** mostynmusic.com Ptnr: Maureen Cresswell.

Mother Music (see McGuinness Whelan)

Mother Tongue 35 Marsden St, London NW5 3HE **t** 07973 137 554 **e** Julian@mothertongue.tv **w** mothertongue.tv MD: Julian de Takats.

Moving Shadow Music PO Box 2551, London SE1 2FH **t** 020 7252 2661 **f** 0870 051 2594 **e** info2004@movingshadow.com **w** movingshadow.com MD: Rob Playford.

MP Belaieff (see Peters Edition)

Mr & Mrs Music Suite 11, Accurist House, 44 Baker St, London W1U 7AZ **t** 020 7224 2280 **f** 020 7224 2290 **e** lesburgess45@aol.com MD: Les Burgess.

Mr Sunshine (see Menace Music)

MRM Ltd Cedar House, Vine Lane, Hillingdon, Middx UB10 0BX **t** 01895 251515 **f** 01895 251616 **e** mail@mrmltd.co.uk MD: Mark Rowles.

MSM (see Music Exchange (Manchester) Ltd)

Muirhead Music Anchor House, 2nd Floor, 15-19 Britten St, London SW3 3TY **t** 020 7351 5167 or 07785 226 542 **f** 020 7000 1227 **e** info@muirheadmanagement.co.uk **w** muirheadmanagement.co.uk CEO: Dennis Muirhead.

Mule UK Music PO Box 77, Leeds LS13 2WZ **t** 08709 905 078 **f** 0113 256 1315 **e** katherine@full360ltd.com MD: Katherine Canoville.

Multiplay Music 19 Eagle Way, Harrold, Bedford MK43 7EW **t** 01234 720 785 or 07971 885 375 **f** 01234 720 664 **e** kevin@multiplaymusic.com **w** multiplaymusic.com MD: Kevin White.

Mumbo Jumbo Publishing Contact: Illicit Entertainment.

Mummer Music 38 Grovelands Rd, London N13 4RH **t** 020 8350 0613 **f** 020 8350 0613 **e** jim@jcook21.freeserve.co.uk Dir: Jim Cook.

Mummy Dust Music (see Catalyst Music Publishing Ltd)

Munka (see Paul Rodriguez Music Ltd)

Munnycroft (see Darah Music)

Murfin Music International 1 Post Office Lane, Kempsey, Worcester WR5 3NS **t** 01905 820659 **f** 01905 820015 **e** muffmurfin@btconnect.com MD: Muff Murfin.

Music 1 Ltd. (see Independent Music Group Ltd)

Music Box Publications (see Paul Rodriguez Music Ltd)

Music By Design 5th Floor, Film House, 142 Wardour St, London W1F 8ZU **t** 020 7434 3244 **f** 020 7434 1064 **e** rosa@musicbydesign.co.uk **w** musicbydesign.co.uk Production Manager & Music Consultant: Rosa Martinez.

Music Exchange (Manchester) Ltd Claverton Rd, Wythenshawe, Greater Manchester M23 9ZA **t** 0161 946 1234 **f** 0161 946 1195 **e** sales@music-exchange.co.uk **w** musicx.co.uk (Trade Only) Sales Director: Gerald Burns.

Music For Films (see Lantern Music)

Music Funtime (see G&M Brand Publications)

Music House (International) 2nd Floor, 143 Charing Cross Rd, London WC2H 0EH **t** 020 7434 9678 **f** 020 7434 1470 **w** playmusichouse.com GM: Simon James.

Music Like Dirt 9 Bloomsbury Pl, East Hill, Wandsworth, London SW18 2JB **t** 020 8877 1335 **f** 020 8877 1335 **e** mld@bigworldpublishing.com **w** bigworldpublishing.com MD: Patrick Meads.

Music Music (see Paul Rodriguez Music Ltd)

Music Partner (see Peters Edition)

Music Sales Ltd 8-9 Frith St, London W1D 3JB **t** 020 7434 0066 **f** 020 7734 8416 **e** music@musicsales.co.uk **w** musicsales.com GM: Chris Butler.

Music To Picture (see The Valentine Music Group)

Music 4/Music4 41-42 Berners St, London W1T 3NB **t** 020 7016 2000 **e** studios@music4.com **w** music4.com MD: Sandy Beech.

Musica Oscura (see Paul Rodriguez Music Ltd)

Musica Rara (see Breitkopf & Hartel)

Musicalities Limited Snows Ride Farm, Snows Ride, Windlesham, Surrey GU20 6LA **t** 01276 474181 **f** 01276 452227 **e** ivan@musicalities.co.uk **w** musicalities.co.uk MD: Ivan Chandler.

Musicare Ltd 60 Huntstown Wood, Clonsilla, Dublin 15, Ireland **t** +353 1 820 6483 **e** musicare@eircom.net Dir: Brian Barker.

Musicland (see Peters Edition)

Musik'Image Music Library (see Panama Music Library)

Musisca Publishing 34 Strand, Topsham, Exeter, Devon EX3 0AY **t** 01392 877737 **f** 01453 751911 **e** info@musisca-publishing.co.uk **w** musisca-publishing.co.uk Prop: Philippe Oboussier.

MusiWorks Services Ltd 8 Whitehouse Lane, Wooburn Moor, Bucks HP10 0NR **t** 01494 730 143 **f** 01494 730 143 **e** mark@musiworks.com **w** musiworks.com Dir: Mark Mumford.

Mute Song 429 Harrow Rd, London W10 4RE **t** 020 8964 2001 **f** 020 8968 4977 **e** info@mutehq.co.uk **w** mute.com MD: Daniel Miller.

My Ears! My Ears! (see Mute Song)

Myers Music (see Kassner Associated Publishers)

Myra Music (see Bucks Music Group)

N2 Music Ltd (see Evolve Music Ltd)

N2K Publishing Ltd The Studios, 8 Hornton Pl, Kensington, London W8 4LZ **t** 020 7937 0272 **f** 020 7368 6573 **e** marketing@n2kltd.com **w** n2k.ltd.uk Dir: Marcus Shelton.

Native Songs Unit 32 Ransome's Dock, 35-37 Parkgate Rd, London SW11 4NP **t** 020 7801 1919 **f** 020 7738 1819 **e** info@nativemanagement.com **w** nativemanagement.com Contact: Anna Carpenter.

Ncompass Suite 1, 92 King George Rd, Ware, Herts SG12 7DT **t** 01920 461 000 **e** silverscope@btconnect.com MD: Richard Rogers.

Neon Music Studio Two, 19 Marine Crescent, Kinning Pk, Glasgow G51 1HD **t** 0141 429 6366 **f** 0141 429 6377 **e** mail@go2neon.com **w** go2neon.com Contact: Robert Noakes.

Nervous Publishing 5 Sussex Crescent, Northolt, Middlesex UB5 4DL **t** 020 8423 7373 **f** 020 8423 7773 **e** info@nervous.co.uk **w** nervous.co.uk MD: Roy Williams.

Nettwerk Songs Publishing (U.K.) Ltd. Clearwater Yard, 35 Inverness St, London NW1 7HB **t** 020 7424 7500 **f** 020 7424 7501 **e** mark@nettwerk.com **w** nettwerksongspublishing.com MD: Mark Jowett.

New Claims Music (see Graduate Music)

New Ikon Music (see The Essex Music Group)

New Music Enterprises Meredale, Reach Lane, Heath And Reach, Leighton Buzzard, Beds LU7 0AL **t** 01525 237700 **f** 01525 237700 **e** Pauldavis@newmusic28.freeserve.co.uk Prop: Paul Davis.

New Music West (see The Concord Partnership)

New State Publishing Ltd Unit 2A, Queens Studios, 121 Salusbury Rd, London NW6 6RG **t** 020 7372 4474 **f** 020 7328 4447 or 020 7372 4484 **e** info@newstate.co.uk **w** newstate.co.uk MD: Tom Parkinson.

New Town Sound Ltd (see Maxwood Music)

Newquay Music (see Bucks Music Group)

Next Century (see Bucks Music Group)

Nice 'n' Ripe Music (see Westbury Music Ltd)

Nicklewhistle Music (see Menace Music)

Niles Productions 34 Beaumont Rd, London W4 5AP **t** 020 8248 2157 **e** r.niles@richardniles.com **w** richardniles.com Dir: Richard Niles.

NKS Publishing (see Westbury Music Ltd)

No Known Cure Publishing 45 Kings Rd, Dover Court, Harwich, Essex CO12 4DS **t** 07760 427306 **e** tomsong1@hotmail.com MD: TF McCarthy.

Noeland Productions (see Bucks Music Group)

Nomadic Music Unit 18, Farm Lane Trading Estate, 101 Farm Lane, London SW6 1QJ **t** 020 7386 6800 or 07779 257 577 **f** 020 7386 2401 **e** info@nomadicmusic.net **w** nomadicmusic.net Label Head: Paul Flanagan.

Northern Light Music Noyna Lodge, Manor Rd, Colne, Lancs BB8 7AS **t** 07970 728 210 **e** ajjh@freenetname.co.uk Dir: Andrew Hall.

NorthStar Music Publishing Ltd PO Box 868, Cambridge CB1 6SJ **t** 01787 278256 **f** 01787 279069 **e** info@northstarmusic.co.uk **w** northstarmusic.co.uk MD: Grahame Maclean.

Not S'bad Music (see Crashed Music)

Notting Dale Songs (see Notting Hill Music (UK) Ltd)

NOTTING HILL MUSIC (UK) LTD

NOTTING HILL
music

Bedford House, 8B Berkeley Gardens, London W8 4AP
t 020 7243 2921 **f** 020 7243 2894
e info@nottinghillmusic.com **w** nottinghillmusic.com MD: David
Loader. Chair: Andy McQueen. Int Dir: Peter Chalcraft.
Professional Manager: Leo Whiteley. Royalty Manager: Liz Davey.
Head of Administration: Charles Garside.

Novello & Co Ltd 8-9 Frith St, London W1D 3JB
t 020 7434 0066 **f** 020 7287 6329
e firstname.lastname@musicsales.co.uk **w** chesternovello.com
MD: James Rushton.

Nowhere Publishing 30 Tweedholm Ave East, Walkerburn,
Peeblesshire EH43 6AR **t** 01896 870284
e michaelwild@btopenworld.com MD: Michael Wild.

Numinous Music Figment House, Church St, Ware, Herts
SG12 9EN **t** 01273 680799 **f** 01920 463883
e jhbee@numinous.biz **w** numinous.biz
Dir. A&R/Marketing/Promo: John Bee.

Nu-Song 106 Canalot Production Studios, 222 Kensal Rd,
London W10 5BN **t** 020 8964 4778 **f** 020 8960 8907
e info@north-nusong.com **w** north-nusong.com
MD: John MacLennan.

Nuthouse Music (see Notting Hill Music (UK) Ltd)

Obelisk Music 32 Ellerdale Rd, London NW3 6BB
t 020 7435 5255 **f** 020 7431 0621 MD: Mr H Herschmann.

Oblivion Music (see Accolade Music)

Ocean Music (see Express Music (UK) Ltd)

Odyssey Music (see Reliable Source Music)

Off The Peg Songs (see In The Frame Music)

Old Bridge Music PO Box 7, Ilkley, West Yorks LS29 9RY
t 01943 602203 **f** 01943 435472 **e** mail@oldbridgemusic.com
w oldbridgemusic.com Ptnr: Chris Newman.

Old School Songs (see SGO Music Publishing)

Old Strains (see Paul Rodriguez Music Ltd)

Olrac Songs (see Asterisk Music)

One Note Music (see Asterisk Music)

Onion Music Unit 29, Cygnus Business Centre, Dalmeyer Rd,
London NW10 2XA **t** 020 8830 4466 **f** 020 8830 0220
e barry@7hz.co.uk **w** 7hz.co.uk/onionmusic.htm
MD: Barry Campbell.

Online Music Unit 18, Croydon House, 1 Peall Rd, Croydon,
Surrey CR0 3EX **t** 020 8287 8585 **f** 020 8287 0220
e publishing@onlinestudios.co.uk **w** onlinestudios.co.uk
MD: Rob Pearson.

Onward Music (see Bucks Music Group)

Opal Music Studio 1, 223A Portobello Rd, London W11 1LU
t 020 7221 7239 **f** 020 7727 5404 **e** opal@opaloffice.com
Dir: Jane Geerts.

Openchoice (see Roedean Music Ltd)

Optimum Publishing Unit 3, 1 St Mary Rd, London E17 9RG
t 020 8520 1188 **f** 020 8520 2514
e info@optimumpublishing.co.uk MD: Debra Thompson.

Orange Songs Ltd 2nd Floor, 28 Denmark St, London
WC2H 8NA **t** 020 7240 7696 **f** 020 7379 3398
e cliff.cooper@omec.com MD: Cliff Cooper.

Orestes Music Publishing 13 Alliance Court, Aliance Rd,
London W3 0RB **t** 020 8993 7441 **e** orestes@dorm.co.uk
w orestesmusic.com GM: John O'Reilly.

Orgy Music Publishing PO Box 8245, Sawbridgeworth,
Herts CM21 9WU **t** 01279 600081 **e** info@orgyrecords.com
w orgyrecords.com Contact: Martin Hayter.

Ossian (see Music Exchange (Manchester) Ltd)

Our Music (see Associated Music International Ltd)

Outcaste Music Publishing 43 Brook Green, London
W6 7EF **t** 020 7605 5808 **f** 020 7605 5188
e firstname@mvillage.co.uk **w** outcaste.com
Co-MDs: Paul Franklyn and Shabs Jobanputra.

Oval Music 326 Brixton Rd, London SW9 7AA
t 020 7622 0111 **e** charlie@ovalmusic.co.uk **w** ovalmusic.co.uk
Dir: Charlie Gillett.

Oxford Film Co. (see Paul Rodriguez Music Ltd)

Oxford University Press Music Department, Great
Clarendon St, Oxford, Oxon OX2 6DP **t** 01865 353349
f 01865 353749 **e** music.enquiry.uk@oup.com
w oup.com/uk/music Music Sales & Mktng: Suzy Gooch.

Oyster Songs Ltd Oakwood Manor, Oakwood Hill, Ockley,
Surrey RH5 5PU **t** 01306 627277 **f** 01306 627277
e info@oystermusic.com Dirs: Adrian Fitt, Chris Cooke.

P3 Music 4 St Andrew St, Alyth, Perthshire PH11 8AT
t 01828 633790 **f** 01828 633798 **e** publishing@p3music.com
w p3music.com MD: James Taylor.

Page One Music (see Kassner Associated Publishers)

Painted Desert Music Corp. (see Shapiro, Bernstein & Co
Ltd)

Palace Music (see Warner Chappell Music Ltd)

Palan Music Publishing (see Kingstreet Media Group)

Pan Musik (see Kassner Associated Publishers)

Panache Music Ltd (see Maxwood Music)

PANAMA MUSIC LIBRARY

PANAMA MUSIC LIBRARY

Sovereign House, 12 Trewartha Rd, Praa Sands, Penzance,
Cornwall TR20 9ST **t** 01736 762 826 or 07721 449 477
f 01736 763 328 **e** panamus@aol.com **w** panamamusic.co.uk
MD: Roderick Jones. Copyright & Royalties: Carole Jones. Prod
Dir: Colin Eade. Business Affairs: Anne Eade.

Panganai Music 296 Earls Court Rd, London SW5 9BA
t 020 7565 0806 **f** 020 7565 0806
e blackmagicrecords@talk21.com **w** blackmagicrecords.com
MD: Mataya Clifford.

Pao Pao Publishing S.A. c/o Fetcham Park House, Lower
Rd, Leatherhead, Surrey KT22 9HD **t** 01372 360300
f 01372 360878 **e** info@paopao-publishing.com
w paopao-publishing.com.

Paper Publishing (see Westbury Music Ltd)

Par Entertainment (see Charly Publishing Ltd)

Paradise Line Music (see Blue Melon Publishing)

Parliament Music Ltd PO Box 6328, London N2 0UN **t** 020 8444 9841 **f** 020 8442 1973 **e** info@parliament-management.com Dir: David Woolfson.

Partisan Songs c/o Mute Song, 429 Harrow Rd, London W10 4RE **t** 020 8964 2001 **f** 020 8968 8437 **e** mamapimp@btopenworld.com MD: Caroline Butler.

Pasadena Music (see Paul Rodriguez Music Ltd)

Patch Music (see SGO Music Publishing)

Paternoster Music 16 Thorpewood Ave, London SE26 4BX **t** 020 8699 1245 **f** 020 8291 5584 **e** peterfilleul@compuserve.com MD: Peter Filleul, Sian Wynne.

Patricia Music (see Warner Chappell Music Ltd)

Paul Ballance Music PO Box 72, Beckenham, Kent BR3 5UR **t** 020 8650 2976 **f** 0870 922 3582 **e** info@megabop.plus.com **w** megabop.com MD: Paul Ballance.

Paul Cooke Music 6 Cheyne Walk, Hornsea, E Yorks HU18 1BX **t** 01964 536 193 **e** paulcookemusic@btinternet.com **w** paulcookemusic.com MD: Paul Cooke.

Paul Rodriguez Music Ltd 15 Stanhope Rd, London N6 5NE **t** 020 8340 7797 **f** 020 8340 6923 **e** paul@paulrodriguezmus.demon.co.uk MD: Paul Rodriguez.

Peacefrog Music PO Box 38171, London W10 5WU **t** 020 7575 3045 **f** 020 7575 3047 **e** info@peacefrog.com **w** peacefrog.com MD: Phil Vernol.

Pearl Music (see Asterisk Music)

PEERMUSIC (UK)

Peer House, 8-14 Verulam Street, London WC1X 8LZ **t** 020 7404 7200 **f** 020 7404 7004 **e** peermusic@peermusic.com **w** peermusic.com MD: Nigel Elderton. Financial Director: Keith Wiggins. Business Affairs Manager: Allan Dann. Creative Manager: Richard Holley. Synch/Copyright Mgr: Samantha Stevens.

Penkiln Burn (see Bryter Music)

Penny St Music (see Bucks Music Group)

Perfect Songs The Blue Building, 8-10 Basing St, London W11 1ET **t** 020 7229 1229 **f** 020 7221 9247 **e** firstname@spz.com MD: Emma Kamen.

Perfect Space Music Publishing Ichthus House, 1 Northfield Rd, Aylesbury, Bucks HP20 1PB **t** 01296 583700 **e** info@reallyfreemusic.co.uk **w** reallyfreemusic.co.uk Contact: Peter Wheeler.

Performance Music (see Kassner Associated Publishers)

Perpetuity Music (Urban Division) 69 Neal St, London WC2H 9PJ **t** 020 7240 7666 **e** info@perpetuity.biz **w** perpetuity.biz MD: Michael Gordon.

Pete Allen Music (see Paul Rodriguez Music Ltd)

Peter Maurice (see EMI Music Publishing)

Peterman & Co (see Carlin Music Corporation)

Peters Edition Hinrichsen House, 10-12 Baches St, London N1 6DN **t** 020 7553 4000 or 020 7553 4020 (Hire) **f** 020 7490 4921 **e** sales@editionpeters.com **w** editionpeters.com Marketing Manager: Linda Hawken.

PHAB Music High Notes, Sheerwater Ave, Woodham, Surrey KT15 3DS **t** 019323 48174 **f** 019323 40921 MD: Philip HA Bailey.

Phillday (see Menace Music)

Phoenix Music Bryn Golau, Saron, Denbighshire LL16 4TH **t** 01745 550 317 **f** 01745 550 560 **e** sales@phoenix-music.com **w** phoenix-music.com Prop: Kath Banks.

Phonetic Music Publishing Ltd 12 St Davids Close, Farnham, Surrey GU9 9DR **t** 01252 330 894 or 07775 515 025 **f** 01252 330 894 **e** james@phoneticmusic.com **w** phoneticmusic.com MD: James Sefton.

PI34 Music (see Notting Hill Music (UK) Ltd)

Pinera Music (see Menace Music)

Pink Floyd Music Publishers Ltd (see Plangent Visions Music Ltd)

Pipefish Media UK The Bunk House, The Forest Inn, Hexworthy, Princetown, Devon PL20 6SD **t** 01364 631 143 or 07739 796 770 **f** 01364 631 143 **e** info@pipefishmedia.com **w** pipefishmedia.com Contact: Steve and Sarah Simpson.

Pisces Publishing Limited 20 Middle Row, Ladbroke Grove, London W10 5AT **t** 020 8964 4555 **f** 020 8964 4666 **e** morgan@musicwithattitude.com **w** musicwithattitude.com MD: Morgan Khan.

Plan C Music Ltd Covetous Corner, Hudnall Common, Little Gaddesden, Herts HP4 1QW **t** 01442 842851 **f** 01442 842082 **e** christian.ulf@virgin.net **w** plancmusic.com MD: Christian Ulf-Hansen.

Plangent Visions Music Ltd 27 Noel St, London W1F 8GZ **t** 020 7734 6892 **f** 020 7439 4613 **e** info@noelstreet.com MD: Peter Barnes.

Plantation Music Pub (see Independent Music Group Ltd)

Platinum Status (see Notting Hill Music (UK) Ltd)

Platypus Music Unit 3 Home Farm, Welford, Newbury, Berks RG20 8HR **t** 01488 657200 **f** 01488 657222 MD: John Brand.

Playwrite Music Limited The Penthouse, 1 Star St, London W2 1QD **t** 020 7258 0093 **f** 020 7402 9238 **e** info@playwrite.uk.com Mgr: Nicky McDermott.

Plaza Music (see Express Music (UK) Ltd)

Plus 8 Music Benelux (see Independent Music Group Ltd)

Plus 8 Music Europe (see Independent Music Group Ltd)

Plus Music Publishing 36 Follingham Court, Drysdale Pl, London N1 6LZ **t** 020 7684 8594 **f** 020 7684 8740 **e** info@plusmusic.co.uk **w** plusmusic.co.uk Prop: Desmond Chisholm.

PM Muzik Publishing Ltd 226 Seven Sisters Rd, London N4 3GG **t** 020 7372 6806 **f** 020 7372 0969 **e** info@pmmuzik.com **w** pmmuzik.com Dir: Plucky.

Pod Publishing 11 Lindal Rd, Crofton Pk, London SE4 1EJ **t** 020 8691 1564 **f** 020 8691 1564 **e** music@podpublishing.biz Dir: Natalie Cummings.

Point4 Music Unit 16 Talina Centre, Bagleys Lane, Fulham, London SW6 2BW **e** info@point4music.com **w** point4music.com Dirs: Peter Day, Paul Newton.

Pollination Music 92 Camden Mews, Camden, London NW1 9AG **t** 020 7424 8665 **f** 020 7482 2210 **e** info@pollinationmusic.co.uk **w** pollinationmusic.co.uk A&R Dir: Seamus Morley.

Pollytone Music PO Box 124, Ruislip, Middx HA4 9BB **t** 01895 638584 **f** 01895 624793 **e** val@pollyton.demon.co.uk **w** pollytone.com MD: Val Bird.

Pop Anarchy Music 98 Camden Rd, London NW1 9EA **t** 020 7284 0359 **f** 020 7267 5186 **e** office@vinyljapan.com **w** vinyljapan.com Contact: Claire Munro.

Pop Muzik Haslemere, 40 Broomfield Rd, Henfield, W. Sussex BN5 9UA **t** 01273 491 416 **f** 01273 491 417 **e** robin@robinscott.org **w** robinscott.org Dir: Robin Scott.

Porpete Music (see Menace Music)

Portland Productions (see Cramer Music)

Possie Music (see Independent Music Group Ltd)

Post House Music Fairways, Benover Rd, Yalding, Kent ME18 6ES **t** 01622 814 154 **e** phmusic@onetel.com Contact: Pauline Southcombe.

Powdermill Music Aka Ray Pillow Music (see Independent Music Group Ltd)

Power Music 29 Riversdale Rd, Thames Ditton, Surrey KT7 0QN **t** 020 8398 5236 **f** 020 8398 7901 MD: Barry Evans.

Power Music Company (see Music Sales Ltd)

P&P Songs Ltd Hope House, 40 St Peter's Rd, London W6 9BD **t** 020 8237 8400 **f** 020 8741 0825 **e** firstname@pandpsongs.com **w** pandpsongs.com Contact: Peter McCamley, Paul Flynn, Indi Chawla.

Preshus Child Music (see Independent Music Group Ltd)

Prestige Music (see Bocu Music Ltd)

Primo Music 39 Bettespol Meadows, Redbourn, Herts AL3 7EN **t** 01582 626 015 or 07740 645 628 **e** tony@primomusic.co.uk MD: Tony Peters.

Private & Confidential Music Ltd Fairlight Mews, 15 St. Johns Rd, Kingston upon Thames, Surrey KT1 4AN **t** 0208 977 0632 **f** 0870 770 8669 **e** info@pncmusic.com **w** pncrecords.com MD: Sir Harry.

Producer's Workshop Music (see Carlin Music Corporation)

Promo Sonor International (SARL) Sovereign House, 12 Trewartha Rd, Praa Sands, Penzance, Cornwall TR20 9ST **t** 01736 762 826 **f** 01736 763 328 **e** panamus@aol.com **w** panamamusic.co.uk Dir: Roderick Jones.

Proof Songs PO Box 20242, London NW1 7FL **t** 020 7485 1113 **e** info@proofsongs.co.uk.

Proper Music Publishing Ltd Unit 1, Gateway Business Centre, Kangley Bridge Rd, London SE26 5AN **t** 020 8676 5152 **f** 020 8676 5190 **e** malc@proper.uk.com MD: Malcolm Mills.

PS Songs (see Bucks Music Group)

PSI Music Library (see Panama Music Library)

Psychedelic Research Lab Songs (see Independent Music Group Ltd)

PUBLISHED BY PATRICK

PUBLISHED BY PATRICK

18 Pindock Mews, London W9 2PY **t** 020 7289 7281 **f** 020 7289 2648 **e** songs@mindermusic.com **w** mindermusic.com MD: John Fogarty. Administration: Jenny Clough. Business Affairs: Roger Nickson. A&R: Patrick Fogarty. Security: Jack Russell.

Puppet Music (see Paul Rodriguez Music Ltd)

Pure Groove Music 679 Holloway Rd, London N19 5SE **t** 020 7263 4660 **f** 020 7263 5590 **e** mickshiner@puregroove.co.uk **w** puregroove.co.uk Head of A&R: Mick Shiner.

Pure Silk Music The Old Props Building, Pinewood Studios, Pinewood Rd, Iver Heath, Bucks SL0 0NH **t** 01753 785 631 **f** 01753 785 632 **e** Elliselias@ilcgroup.com MD: Ellis Elias.

Purple Patch Music (see Editions Penguin Cafe Ltd)

Pushcart Music (see Independent Music Group Ltd)

PXM Publishing 68 Cranston Ave, Bexhill On Sea, E Sussex TN39 3NN **t** 01424 215 617 or 01424 215 617 **e** pxm.publishing@virgin.net **w** pxmpublishing.com Director/Admin: Carolyne Rodgers.

Quaife Music Publishing 9 Carroll Hill, Loughton, Essex IG10 1NL **t** 020 8508 3639 **e** Qmusic@carrollhill.freeserve.co.uk MD: Alan Quaife.

Quick Step Music (see Lomond Music)

Radical UK Music (see Sovereign Music UK)

Raeworks (see Independent Music Group Ltd)

RAK Publishing Ltd 42-48 Charlbert St, London NW8 7BU **t** 020 7586 2012 **f** 020 7722 5823 **e** rakpublishing@yahoo.com GM: Nathalie Hayes.

Rakeway Music (see Kirklees Music)

Ralphie Dee Music (see Independent Music Group Ltd)

RandM Music 72 Marylebone Lane, London W1U 2PL **t** 020 7486 7458 **f** 020 8467 6997 **e** roy@randm.co.uk MDs: Roy Eldridge, Mike Andrews.

Randscape Music (see Menace Music)

Rapido Music (see Bucks Music Group)

RBT Publications PO Box 640, Bromley BR1 4XZ **t** 07985 439 453 **f** 020 8290 4589 Mgr: Roy MacPepple.

R&E Music (see Independent Music Group Ltd)

Reach Global, Inc. (PRS/ASCAP) (see Reach Global (UK) Ltd)

Reach Global Songs (BMI) (see Reach Global (UK) Ltd)

Reach Global (UK) Ltd 4F Shirland Mews, London W9 3DY **t** 020 7854 2836 **e** info@reachglobal.com **w** reachglobal.com Pres: Michael Closter.

React Music Publishing 138b West Hill, London SW15 2UE **t** 020 8780 0305 **f** 020 8788 2889 **e** mailbox@react-music.co.uk **w** resist-music.co.uk MD: James Horrocks.

Real Magic Publishing (see Bucks Music Group)

Real World Music Ltd Box Mill, Mill Lane, Box, Corsham, Wilts SN13 8PL **t** 01225 743188 **f** 01225 744369 **e** publishing@realworld.co.uk **w** realworld.co.uk/publishing Publishing Manager: Rob Bozas.

Really Free Music (see Sea Dream Music)

The Really Useful Group 22 Tower St, London WC2H 9TW **t** 020 7240 0880 **f** 020 7240 8977 **e** robinsond@reallyuseful.co.uk **w** reallyuseful.com Head Of Music Licensing: David Robinson.

Rebecca Music Ltd Terwick Pl, Rogate, Petersfield, Hants GU31 5BY **t** 01730 821644 **f** 01730 821597 **e** donna@lesreed.com **w** lesreed.com Dir: Donna Reed.

Recent Future Music (see Universal Music Publishing Ltd)

Red Cherry Music (see SGO Music Publishing)

Red House Music (see Bucks Music Group)

Red Kite Music Cwmargenau, Llanwrda, Carms SA19 8AP **t** 01550 722 000 **f** 01550 722 022 **e** info@redkiterecords.co.uk **w** redkiterecords.co.uk Contact: Ron Dukelow.

Red Songs (see Bucks Music Group)

Redwood Music (see Carlin Music Corporation)

Reggae Giant Music (see Castle Hill Music)

Regina Music (see Music Exchange (Manchester) Ltd)

Reinforced Music (see Westbury Music Ltd)

Reliable Source Music 67 Upper Berkeley St, London W1H 7QX **t** 020 7563 7028 **f** 020 7563 7029 **e** library@reliable-source.co.uk **w** reliable-source.co.uk MD: Dr Wayne Bickerton.

Religion Music 36 Fitzwilliam Sq, Dublin 2, Ireland **t** +353 1 207 0508 **f** +353 1 207 0418 **e** info@religionmusic.com **w** religionmusic.com MD: Glenn Herlihy.

Remission Music (see Sovereign Music UK)

Repetoire (see Bucks Music Group)

Respect Music Suite 2, 11 Sylvan Hill, London SE19 2QB **t** 07919 533 244 or 07900 528 692 **e** firstname@respectmusic.co.uk **w** respectmusic.co.uk Dirs: Sharon Dean, Terry McDonald.

Restoration Music Ltd (see Sovereign Music UK)

Reverb 2 Music Ltd (see Reverb Music Ltd)

Reverb 3 Music Ltd (see Reverb Music Ltd)

Reverb Music Ltd Reverb House, Bennett St, London W4 2AH **t** 020 8747 0660 **f** 020 8747 0880 **e** publishing@reverbxl.com **w** reverbxl.com MD: Annette Barrett.

Revolver Music Ltd 152 Goldthorn Hill, Penn, Wolverhampton, W Midlands WV2 3JA **t** 01902 345345 **f** 01902 345155 **e** Paul.Birch@revolver-e.com **w** revolver-records.com MD: Paul Birch.

Revue Music (see Creole Music Ltd)

Reyshell Music (see Menace Music)

Rhiannon Music (see SGO Music Publishing)

Richmond Music (see Paul Rodriguez Music Ltd)

Rickim Music Publishing Company Thatched Rest, Queen Hoo Lane, Tewin, Herts AL6 0LT **t** 01438 798305 **f** 01438 798395 **e** joyce@bigmgroup.freeserve.co.uk **w** martywilde.com MD: Joyce Wilde.

Riderwood Music (see Carlin Music Corporation)

RIGHT BANK MUSIC UK

Home Park House, Hampton Court Road, Kingston upon Thames, Surrey KT1 4AE **t** 020 8977 0666 **f** 020 8977 0600 **e** rightbankmusicuk@rightbankmusicuk.com **w** rightbankmusicuk.com Vice President: Ian Mack.

Right Key Music (see Independent Music Group Ltd)

Right Music 177 High St, Harlesden, London NW10 4TE **t** 020 8961 3889 **f** 020 8951 9955 **e** info@rightrecordings.com **w** rightrecordings.com Dirs: David Landau, John Kaufman.

Rights Worldwide Ltd (see Faber Music)

Rinsin Music (see Bucks Music Group)

Rita (Publishing) Ltd 12 Pound Court, The Marld, Ashtead, Surrey KT21 1RN **t** 01372 276293 **f** 01372 276328 **e** thebestmusicis@ritapublishing.com **w** ritapublishing.com MD: Ralph Norton.

Riverboat (UK) Music 6 Abbeville Mews, 88 Clapham Park Rd, London SW4 7BX **t** 020 7498 5252 **f** 020 7498 5353 **e** phil@worldmusic.net **w** worldmusic.net MD: Phil Stanton.

Riverhorse Songs (see MCS Music Ltd)

Rivers Music (see Independent Music Group Ltd)

RL2 Music 15 Boulevard Aristide Briand, Pouzolles, France 34480 **t** +33 4 67 24 77 72 **e** info9@rl-2.com **w** rl-2.com GM: Paul Lilly.

Roba Music (see Independent Music Group Ltd)

Robbins Music Corp (see EMI Music Publishing)

Robert Forberg (see Peters Edition)

Robert Lienau (see Peters Edition)

Roberton Publications (see Goodmusic Publishing)

Robroy West Music (see Independent Music Group Ltd)

Rock Music Company Ltd (see Plangent Visions Music Ltd)

Roedean Music Ltd Suite 7, 54 Broadwick St, London W1F 7AH **t** 020 7434 7286 **f** 020 7434 7288 **e** tonyhall@btconnect.com MD: Tony Hall.

Rokstone Music Ltd (see Darah Music)

Roky Erickson (see Menace Music)

Roland Robinson Music (see Menace Music)

Rolf Baierle Music Limited (see Independent Music Group Ltd)

Rollercoaster Music (see Asterisk Music)

Rondercrest (see Loose Music (UK))

Rondor Music Publishing (see Universal Music Publishing Ltd)

Ronster Music (see Independent Music Group Ltd)

Rose Rouge International AWS House, Trinity Sq, St Peter Port, Guernsey, Channel Islands GY1 1LX **t** 01481 728 283 **f** 01481 714 118 **e** awsgroup@cwgsy.net Director/Producer: Steve Free.

Rosette Music (see The Valentine Music Group)

The Rosewood Music Company PO Box 6754, Dublin 13, Ireland **t** +353 1 843 9713 **f** +353 1 843 9713 **e** rosewood@iol.ie **w** rosewoodmusic.ie Professional Mgr: Greg Rogers.

Rough Trade Publishing 81 Wallingford Rd, Goring, Reading, Berks RG8 OHL **t** 01491 873612 **f** 01491 872744 **e** info@rough-trade.com **w** rough-trade.com MD: Matt Wilkinson.

The Royal School Of Church Music (RSCM) 19 The Close, Salisbury, Wilts SP1 2EB **t** 01722 424 848 **f** 01722 424 849 **e** press@rscm.com **w** rscm.com Mgr, Press/Music Direct: Tim Ruffer.

RT Music (see Asterisk Music)

Rubber Road Music 4-10 Lamb Walk, London SE1 3TT **t** 020 7921 8353 **f** 020 7579 4171 **e** rubber_road_records@yahoo.co.uk **w** rubberroadmusic.com Creative Manager: Nick Lightowlers.

Ruben Blades (see Dejamus Ltd)

Rumour Music Publishing Ltd PO BOX 54127, London W5 9BE **t** 020 8997 7893 **f** 020 8997 7901 **e** post@rumour.demon.co.uk **w** rumourrecords.com MD: Anne Plaxton.

Rustomatic Music (see Menace Music)

Rybar Music (see Paul Rodriguez Music Ltd)

Rydim Music (see Blue Mountain Music Ltd)

Rykomusic Ltd 329 Latimer Rd, London W10 6RA **t** 020 8960 3311 **f** 020 8960 1177 **e** info@rykodisc.co.uk **w** rykomusic.com GM: Paul Lambden.

SA Rodger & SD Jones Publishing (see Westbury Music Ltd)

Sabre Music (see Eaton Music Ltd)

Safe (see Bucks Music Group)

St James Music 34 Great James St, London WC1N 3HB **t** 020 7405 3786 **f** 020 7405 5245 **e** info@prestige-elite.com **w** prestige-elite.com MD: Keith Thomas.

Salsoul Music Publish (see Independent Music Group Ltd)

Salvo West Ltd t/a Union Square (see Bucks Music Group)

Sanctuary Music Publishing Ltd Sanctuary House, 45-53 Sinclair Rd, London W14 0NS **t** 020 7602 6351 **f** 020 7603 5941 **e** info@sanctuaryrecords.co.uk **w** sanctuaryrecords.co.uk.

Sands Music (see Independent Music Group Ltd)

Sanga Music (see Bucks Music Group)

Sarah Music Cherry Tree Lodge, Copmanthorpe, York, North Yorks YO23 3SH **t** 01904 703764 **f** 01904 702312 **e** suespence@aol.com MD: Mal Spence.

Satellite Music (see Associated Music International Ltd)

Scamp Music Sovereign House, 12 Trewartha Rd, Praa Sands, Penzance, Cornwall TR20 9ST **t** 01736 762 826 or 07721 449 477 **f** 01736 763 328 **e** panamus@aol.com **w** panamamusic.co.uk MD: Roderick Jones.

Scaramanga Music (see Menace Music)

Scarf Music Publishing (see Sea Dream Music)

Schaeffers-Kassner Music (see Kassner Associated Publishers)

Schauer & May (see Boosey & Hawkes Music Publishers Ltd)

Schott Music Limited 48 Great Marlborough St, London W1F 7BB **t** 020 7534 0700 **f** 020 7534 0719 **e** info@schott-music.com **w** schott-music.com Dir: Sally Groves.

SCO Music 29 Oakroyd Ave, Potters Bar, Herts EN6 2EL **t** 01707 651439 **f** 01707 651439 **e** constantine@steveconstantine.freeserve.co.uk MD: Steve Constantine.

Screen Gems-EMI Music (see EMI Music Publishing)

Screen Music Services (see MCS Music Ltd)

Screwbox (see Menace Music)

Sea Dream Music Sandcastle Productions, PO Box 13533, London E7 0SG **t** 020 8534 8500 **e** sea.dream@virgin.net Snr Partner: Simon Law.

Second Skin Music (see Reverb Music Ltd)

Seeca Music Publishing Bridge House, 11, Creek Rd, Hampton Court, Surrey KT8 9BE **t** 020 8979 1313 or 07970 094 257 **f** 020 8979 9891 **e** info@seeca.co.uk **w** seeca.co.uk Dir: Louise Martins.

Semprini Music (see Carlin Music Corporation)

Sepia (see Bucks Music Group)

Serious Worldwide Publishing PO Box 13143, London N6 5BG **t** 020 8815 5550 **f** 020 8815 5559 **e** sam@seriousworld.com **w** seriousworld.com MD: Sam O'Riordan.

Seriously Groovy Music 3rd Floor, 28 D'Arblay St, Soho, London W1F 8EW **t** 020 7439 1947 **f** 020 7734 7540 **e** admin@seriouslygroovy.com **w** seriouslygroovy.com Dirs: Dave Holmes, Lorraine Snape.

Seriously Wonderful Music (see Bucks Music Group)

Seven B Music (see Charly Publishing Ltd)

Seventh House Music (see Bucks Music Group)

Sexy Music Ltd PO Box 421, Aylesbury, Bucks HP17 8BS **t** 01844 290528 **f** 01844 290528 **e** unie@redd-angel.com MD: Unie Moller.

SGO Music Publishing PO Box 2015, Salisbury SP2 7WU **t** 01264 811 154 **f** 01264 811 172 **e** sgomusic@sgomusic.com **w** sgomusic.com MD: Stuart Ongley.

Shade Factor Productions Limited 4 Cleveland Sq, London W2 6DH **t** 020 7402 6477 **f** 020 7402 7144 **e** mail@shadefactor.com **w** shadefactor.com MD: Ann Symonds.

Shadows Music (see Carlin Music Corporation)

Shaftesbury (see Chrysalis Music Ltd)

Shak Music (see SGO Music Publishing)

Shake Up Music Ickenham Manor, Ickenham, Uxbridge, Middx UB10 8QT **t** 01895 672994 **f** 01895 633264 **e** mail@shakeupmusic.co.uk Dir: Joanna Tizard.

Shalit Global Music 7 Moor St, Soho, London W1D 5NB **t** 020 7851 9155 **f** 020 7851 9156 **e** info@shalitglobal.com MD: Jonathan Shalit.

Shanna Music Ltd (see Purple City Ltd).

Shapiro Bernstein & Company Inc (see Shapiro, Bernstein & Co Ltd)

Shapiro, Bernstein & Co Ltd 12th Floor, 488 Madison Ave, New York, New York, 10022 USA **t** 020 7247 2001 **e** sbinfo@shapirobernstein.com **w** shapiroberstein.com Pres: Michael Brettler.

Shaun Davey Music (see Bucks Music Group)

Shay Songs (see Crashed Music)

Shed Publishing (see Scamp Music)

Sheila Music (see Creole Music Ltd)

Shepsongs Inc (see Independent Music Group Ltd)

Sherlock Holmes Music Unit 1 Chapel Rd, Portslade, Brighton BN1 1PF **t** 01273 424703 **f** 01273 418856 **e** mail@sherlockholmesmusic.co.uk **w** sherlockholmesmusic.co.uk MD: Vernon Rossiter.

Shipston Music (see Independent Music Group Ltd)

Shogun Music (see Eaton Music Ltd)

Shrub Music (see Menace Music)

Signia Music 44 Edith Rd, London W14 9BB **t** 020 7371 2137 **e** dee@signiamusic.com **w** signiamusic.com MD: Dee Harrington.

Silence Music (see Independent Music Group Ltd)

Silhouette Music (see New Music Enterprises)

Silk Music (see Independent Music Group Ltd)

Silktone Songs Inc (see Independent Music Group Ltd)

Silva Screen Publishing 3 Prowse Pl, London NW1 9PH **t** 020 7428 5500 **f** 020 7482 2385 **e** info@silvascreen.co.uk **w** silvascreen.co.uk MD: Reynold da Silva.

Silver Cradle Music (see Independent Music Group Ltd)

Silverscope Music Suite 1, 92 King George Rd, Ware, Herts SG12 7DT **t** 01920 461 000 **e** silverscope@btconnect.com MD: Richard Rogers.

Alan Simmons Music PO Box 7, Scissett, Huddersfield, W Yorks HD8 9YZ **t** 01924 848888 **f** 01924 849999 **e** mail@alansimmonsmusic.com **w** alansimmonsmusic.com MD: Alan Simmons.

Simon Rights Music (see Eaton Music Ltd)

Single Minded Music 11 Cambridge Court, 210 Shepherd's Bush Rd, London W6 7NJ **t** 0870 011 3748 **f** 0870 011 3749 **e** tony@singleminded.com **w** singleminded.com MD: Tony Byrne.

Singletree Music (see Independent Music Group Ltd)

Sixteen Stars Music (see Independent Music Group Ltd)

Size: Music PO Box 798, London EN1 1ZP **t** 07977 181 121 **e** simon@size-music.com **w** size-music.com Contact: Simon Nicholls.

SJ Music 23 Leys Rd, Cambridge CB4 2AP **t** 01223 314771 **w** printed-music.com/sjmusic Principle: Judith Rattenbury.

Skidmore Music Co Ltd (see Shapiro, Bernstein & Co Ltd)

Sky Blue Recordings 164D Albion Rd, London N16 9JS **t** 020 7503 2258 or 0781 372 4854 **f** 020 7503 2258 **e** alyson@skybluerecordings.com **w** skybluerecordings.com MD: Alyson Gilliland.

Slam Dunk Music (see Independent Music Group Ltd)

Slamina Music (see Carlin Music Corporation)

Sleeping Giant Music International (see St James Music)

SLI Music (see Asterisk Music)

SLNB 143 Westmead Rd, Sutton, Surrey SM1 4JP **t** 020 8395 3045 **f** 020 8395 3046 **e** smac143@tesco.net **w** slnb.co.uk MD: Steve McIntosh.

Smackin' Music (see Universal Music Publishing Ltd)

Smirk (see Bucks Music Group)

SMK Publishing (see Independent Music Group Ltd)

SMV Schacht Musikvalage (see Bucks Music Group)

Snapper Music Publishing 1 Star St, London W2 1QD **t** 020 7706 7304 **f** 020 7706 8197 **e** snappermusicpublishing@btconnect.com Dir: Bryan Morrison.

Snappersongs (see Asterisk Music)

So Good Music (see Independent Music Group Ltd)

S'Od Music (see Bucks Music Group)

Solent Songs 68-70 Lugley St, Newport, Isle Of Wight PO30 5ET **t** 01983 524110 **f** 0870 1640388 **e** songs@solentrecords.co.uk **w** solentrecords.co.uk Owner: John Waterman.

Solid Air Music 18 Drayton Grove, London W13 0LA **t** 020 8566 9824 **f** 020 8566 9824 **e** nathan@solidairproductions.com **w** solidairproductions.com Dirs: Nathan Graves, Grant Calton.

Solida-Soulville Music (see Urban Music Entertainment Network (U-Men))

Songlines Ltd PO Box 20206, London NW1 7FF **t** 020 7284 3970 **f** 020 7485 0511 **e** doug@songlines.demon.co.uk **w** songlines.co.uk MD: Doug D'Arcy.

Songphonic Music PO Box 250, Chertsey KT16 6AG **t** 01932 568 969 **e** info@songphonic.com **w** songphonic.com CEO: Osman Kent.

Songs For Real (see Bucks Music Group)

Songs In The Key Of Knife Red Corner Door, 17 Barons Court Rd, London W14 9DP **t** 020 7386 8760 **f** 020 7381 8014 **e** info@hospitalrecords.com **w** hospitalrecords.com MD: Tony Colman.

Songstream Music Nestlingdown, Chapel Hill, Porthtowan, Truro, Cornwall TR4 8AS **t** 01209 890606 MD: Roger Bourne.

Songwriter Music (see International Songwriters' Music)

Songwriters' Showcase (see First Time Music (Publishing) UK)

Sonic Arts Network Jerwood Space, 171 Union St, London SE1 0LN **t** 020 7928 7337 **e** phil@sonicartsnetwork.org **w** sonicartsnetwork.org Chief Exec: Phil Hallett.

Sonic Sheet (see Menace Music)

sonic360music 33 Riding House St, London W1W 7DZ **t** 020 7636 3939 **f** 020 7636 0033 **e** info@sonic360.com **w** sonic360.com Publishing Mgr: Zen Grisdale.

SONY/ATV MUSIC PUBLISHING

Sony/ATV Music Publishing (UK) Limited

13 Great Marlborough Street, London W1F 7LP **e** firstname_lastname@uk.sonymusic.com **w** sonyatv.com MD: Rakesh Sanghvi t 020 7911 8466. Head of Business Affairs: Mark Waring **t** 020 7911 8292 Senior Repertoire Manager: Simon Aldridge **t** 020 7911 8256 Head of Synchronisation & Marketing: Karina Masters **t** 020 7911 8805 Senior Administration Manager: Gary Bhupsingh **t** 020 7911 8135 Senior Finance Manager: Brenda McGimpsey **t** 020 7911 8567 International Human Resources Manager: Ian Budhu **t** 020 7911 8213

The Sorabji Archive Easton Dene, Bailbrook Lane, Bath BA1 7AA **t** 01225 852323 **f** 01225 852523 **e** sorabji-archive@lineone.net **w** sorabji-archive.co.uk Curator/Director: Alistair Hinton.

Soul II Soul Mad Music Ltd 36-38 Rochester Pl, London NW1 9JX **t** 020 7284 0393 **f** 020 7284 2290 **e** info@soul2soul.co.uk MD: Jazzie B.

Souls Kitchens Music 7 The Stables, Saint Thomas St, Newcastle upon Tyne, Tyne and Wear NE1 4LE **t** 0191 230 1970 **f** 0191 232 0262 **e** info@kware.demon.co.uk **w** kitchenwarerecords.com Administration: Nicki Turner.

Soulstreet Music Publishing Inc (see Independent Music Group Ltd)

Sound Of Jupiter Music (see Carlin Music Corporation)

Sound Songs First Floor, 32 Brighton Rd, Shoreham-By-Sea, W Sussex BN43 6RG **t** 01273 248978 **e** info@thesoundgroup.com **w** thesoundgroup.com CEO: Paula Greenwood.

Sound Stage Production Music (see Amphonic Music Ltd.)

Sounds Like A Hit Ltd 48 Shelvers Way, Tadworth, Surrey KT20 5QF **t** 01737 218899 **f** 01737 355443 **e** steve@soundslikeahit.com **w** soundslikeahit.com Dir: Steve Crosby.

Soundslike Music (see Bucks Music Group)

Sovereign Music UK PO Box 356, Leighton Buzzard, Beds LU7 3WP **t** 01525 385578 **f** 01525 372743 **e** sovereignmusic@aol.com MD: Robert Lamont.

Sovereign Lifestyle Music (see Sovereign Music UK)

SP2 Music (USA & Canada) (see Perfect Songs)

Spadesongs (see Asterisk Music)

Spielman Music (see Independent Music Group Ltd)

Split Music (see Mesh Music)

Spoon Music (see Bucks Music Group)

Spring River Music (see Independent Music Group Ltd)

Springthyme Music Balmalcolm House, Balmalcolm, Cupar, Fife KY15 7TJ **t** 01337 830773 **e** music@springthyme.co.uk **w** springthyme.co.uk MD: Peter Shepheard.

Sprint Music Ltd High Jarmany Farm, Jarmany Hill, Barton St David, Somerton, Somerset TA11 6DA **t** 01458 851 010 **f** 01458 851 029 **e** info@sprintmusic.co.uk **w** sprintmusic.co.uk Industry Consultant, Producer, Writer: John Ratcliff.

Squarepeg Publishing Studio 201, Westbourne Studios, 242 Acklam Rd, London W10 5JJ **t** 020 7575 3325 **f** 020 7575 3326 **e** info@squarepeg-uk.com **w** squarepeg-uk.com MD: Matt Fisher.

Squaw Peak Music (see Independent Music Group Ltd)

Squirrel (see Briar Music)

St Annes Music Ltd Kennedy House, 31 Stamford St, Altrincham, Cheshire WA14 1ES **t** 0161 941 5151 **f** 0161 928 9491 **e** kse@kennedystreet.com Dir: Danny Betesh.

Stage Three Music Ltd. 13a Hillgate St, London W8 7SP **t** 020 7792 6060 **f** 020 7792 6061 **e** info@stagethreemusic.com **w** stagethreemusic.com MD: Steve Lewis.

Stagecoach Music (see Barry Collings Entertainments)

Standard Music Library (see Bucks Music Group)

Stanley House Music (see Jamdown Music Ltd)

Stanza Music 11 Victor Rd, Harrow, Middlesex HA2 6PT **t** 020 8863 2717 **f** 020 8863 8685 **e** bill.ashton@virgin.net **w** nyjo.org.uk Dir: Bill Ashton.

Star Street Music Ltd PO Box 375, Chorleywood, Herts WD3 5ZZ **t** 01923 440608 **e** starstreet.uk@ntlworld.com MD: Nick Battle.

Star-Write Music PO Box 16715, London NW4 1WN **t** 020 8203 5062 **f** 020 8202 3746 **e** starwrite@btinternet.com Dir: John Lisners.

State Music (see Reliable Source Music)

Stave & Nickelodeon (see Blue Melon Publishing)

Steam Power Music (see The Really Useful Group)

Steelchest Music (see Menace Music)

Steelworks Songs 4 Canalot Studios, 222 Kensal Rd, London W10 5BN **t** 020 8960 4443 **f** 020 8960 9889 **e** freedom@frdm.co.uk MD: Martyn Barter.

Step by Step Music (see Independent Music Group Ltd)

Steve Dan Mills Music (see Independent Music Group Ltd)

Steve Glen Music (see Blue Melon Publishing)

Steve Marriott Licensing Ltd. Unit 9B, Wingbury Business Village, Upper Wingbury Farm, Wingrave, Bucks HP22 4LW **t** 07770 364 268 **e** chris@stevemarriott.co.uk **w** stevemarriott.co.uk MD: Chris France.

Steve Warner Music (see Independent Music Group Ltd)

Stevensong Music (see Ash Music (GB))

Stickysongs 33 Trewince Rd, Wimbledon, London SW20 8RD **t** 020 8739 0928 **e** stickysongs@hotmail.com MD: Peter Gosling.

Still Working Music Covetous Corner, Hudnall Common, Little Gaddesden, Herts HP4 1QW **t** 01442 842039 **f** 01442 842082 **e** mhaynes@orbison.com **w** orbison.com European Consultant: Mandy Haynes.

Stinkhorn Music (see Asterisk Music)

Stomp Off Music (see Paul Rodriguez Music Ltd)

Stop Drop & Roll Music Colbury Manor, Jacobs Gutter Lane, Eling, Southampton SO40 9FY **t** 0845 658 5006 **f** 0845 658 5009 **e** frontdesk@stopdroproll.com **w** stopdroproll.com Publishing Executive: Emma Curtis.

Stormking Music (see Bucks Music Group)

Strada 2 Publishing 25 Heathmans Rd, London SW6 4TJ **t** 020 7371 5756 **f** 020 7371 7731 **e** office@pureuk.com **w** pureuk.com Creative Dir: Billy Royal.

Strange Art Music (see Miggins Music (UK))

Strathmere Music (see Independent Music Group Ltd)

Stratsong (see Carlin Music Corporation)

Strictly Confidential UK 338A Ladbroke Grove, London W10 5AH **t** 020 8365 3367 **f** 020 8374 5967 **e** mike@strictly-confidential.co.uk MD: Pierre Mossiat.

Strongsongs Publishing 107 Mortlake High St, London SW14 8HQ **t** 020 8392 6839 **f** 020 8878 7886 **e** anna.jolley@strongsongs.com MD: Anna Jolley.

Structure Music PO Box 26273, London W3 6FN **t** 0870 207 7720 **f** 0870 208 8820 **e** sound@structure.co.uk **w** structure.co.uk Contact: Olly Groves.

Studio G Cedar Tree House, Main St, Farthingstone, Northants N12 8EZ **t** 01327 360820 **f** 01327 360821 **e** library@studiog.co.uk **w** studiog.co.uk MD: John Gale.

Studio Music Company PO Box 19292, London NW10 9WP **t** 020 8830 0110 **f** 020 8451 6470 **e** sales@studio-music.co.uk **w** studio-music.co.uk Ptnr: Stan Kitchen.

Sublime Music Publishing Brighton Media Centre, 21/22 Old Steyne, Brighton, E Sussex BN1 1EL **t** 01273 648 330 **f** 01273 648 332 **e** info@sublimemusic.co.uk **w** sublimemusic.co.uk MD: Patrick Spinks.

Suburban Base Music (see Bryan Morrison Music)

Success Music (see Kassner Associated Publishers)

Sugar Bottom Publishing (see Independent Music Group Ltd)

Sugar Songs UK (see Chelsea Music Publishing Co)

Sugarcane Music 32 Blackmore Ave, Southall, Middlesex UB1 3ES **t** 020 8574 2130 **f** 020 8574 2130 MD: Astrid Pringsheim.

Sugarfree Music (see Bucks Music Group)

Sugarmusic (see Universal Music Publishing Ltd)

Sugarstar Music Ltd IT Centre, York Science Pk, York YO10 5DG **t** 08456 448424 **f** 0709 222 8681 **e** info@sugarstar.com **w** sugarstar.com MD: Mark J. Fordyce.

Suggsongs (see Menace Music)

Sun-Pacific Music (London) Ltd PO Box 5, Hastings, E. Sussex TN34 IHR **t** 01424 721196 **f** 01424 717704 **e** aquarius.lib@clara.net MD: Gilbert Gibson.

Sun Star Songs (BMI) (see Independent Music Group Ltd)

Sunflower Music (see John Fiddy Music)

Supreme Songs Ltd (see Independent Music Group).

Survival Music PO Box 2502, Devizes, Wilts SN10 3ZN **t** 01380 860 500 **f** 01380 860 596 **e** annemarie@survivalrecords.co.uk **w** survivalrecords.co.uk Dir: Anne-Marie Heighway.

Survivor Records (see Kingsway Music)

Susan May Music (see Paul Rodriguez Music Ltd)

Sutjujo Music (see Independent Music Group Ltd)

Suzuki (see International Music Publications (IMP))

Sweet Glenn Music Inc (see Independent Music Group Ltd)

Sweet Karol Music Inc (see Independent Music Group Ltd)

Sweet 'n' Sour Songs 2-3 Fitzroy Mews, London W1T 6DF **t** 020 7383 7767 **f** 020 7383 3020 MD: John Craig.

Swiggeroux Music (see SGO Music Publishing)

Swivel Publishing (see Independent Music Group Ltd)

Sylvantone Music 11 Saunton Ave, Redcar, N Yorks TS10 2RL **t** 01642 479898 **f** 0709 235 9333 **e** sylvantone@hotmail.com **w** countrymusic.org.uk/tony-goodacre/index.html Prop: Tony Goodacre.

T H Music (see Chelsea Music Publishing Co)

Tabitha Music Ltd 39 Cordery Rd, Exeter, Devon EX2 9DJ **t** 01392 499889 **e** graham@tabithamusic.com **w** tabithamusic.com MD: Graham Sclater.

Tabraylah (see Menace Music)

Tafari Music (see Greensleeves Publishing Ltd)

Tairona Songs Ltd PO Box 102, London E15 2HH **t** 020 8555 5423 **f** 020 8519 6834 **e** tairona@moksha.co.uk **w** moksha.co.uk MD: Charles Cosh.

Take It Quick Music (see Bucks Music Group)

Takes On Music (see Eaton Music Ltd)

Tales from Forever Publishing (see Independent Music Group Ltd)

Tancott Music (see Independent Music Group Ltd)

Tanspan Music (see Asterisk Music)

Tapadero Music (see Independent Music Group Ltd)

Tapestry Music (see Bucks Music Group)

Tapier Music (see Charly Publishing Ltd)

Tarantula Productions (see Bucks Music Group)

Taste Music Ltd 263 Putney Bridge Rd, London SW15 2PU
t 020 8780 3311 **f** 020 8785 9894 **e** laurie@tastemedia.com
w tastemedia.com Creative Manager: Laurie Latham Jnr.

Tayborn Publishing (see Music Exchange (Manchester) Ltd)

TBM International (see Independent Music Group Ltd)

TCB Music (see Independent Music Group Ltd)

TCR Music (see Westbury Music Ltd)

Teleny Music (see Miriamusic)

Television Music Ltd Yorkshire Television, TV Centre,
Leeds, W Yorks LS3 1JS **t** 0113 243 8283 **f** 0113 222 7166
e sue.clark@granadamedia.com Contact: Sue Clark.

Tema International 151 Nork Way, Banstead, Surrey
SM7 1HR **t** 01737 219607 **f** 01737 219609
e music@tema-intl.demon.co.uk **w** temadance.com
Production Manager: Amanda Harris.

Temple Records & Publishing Shillinghill, Temple,
Midlothian EH23 4SH **t** 01875 830328 **f** 01875 825390
e robin@templerecords.co.uk **w** templerecords.co.uk
Prop: Robin Morton.

Termidor Music (see Editions Penguin Cafe Ltd)

Texas Red Songs (see Independent Music Group Ltd)

TGM Hammer (see Bucks Music Group)

Thames Music 445 Russell Court, Woburn Pl, London
WC1H ONJ **t** 020 7837 6240 **f** 020 7833 4043
MD: C W Adams.

Thank You Music (see Kingsway Music)

The First Composers Company (see Carlin Music
Corporation)

The Music Factor (see Paul Rodriguez Music Ltd)

The Music Trunk Publishing Co. Ltd (see Broughton
Park Music)

The Royalty Network (see Notting Hill Music (UK) Ltd)

The Sparta Florida Music Group (see Music Sales Ltd)

Third Tier Music (see Catalyst Music Publishing Ltd)

Third World (see Paul Rodriguez Music Ltd)

Thomas & Taylor Music Works (see Independent Music
Group Ltd)

Thompson Station Music (see Independent Music Group
Ltd)

Three 4 Music (see Bucks Music Group)

Three Saints Music (see Millbrand Copyright Management
Ltd)

Three Two Music (see Crashed Music)

Throat Music (see Warner Chappell Music Ltd)

Thrust Magnum Inc (see Bucks Music Group)

Thumpin' Publishing (see Independent Music Group Ltd)

Tia Music Publishing (see SGO Music Publishing)

Tic-Toc Music (UK) Ltd 1 Wicklesham Farm Cottages,
Faringdon, Oxon SN7 7PJ **t** 01367 243895 **f** 01367 241858
e tictoc@nildram.co.uk **w** toallmylovedones.com
Director of Administration: Ruth Stephens.

Tidy Trax Hawthorne House, Fitzwilliam St, Parkgate,
Rotherham, South Yorks S62 6EP **t** 01709 710022
f 01709 523141 **e** firstname.lastname@tidy.com **w** tidy.com
MD: Andy Pickles.

Tiger Trax Limited (see Independent Music Group Ltd)

Timbuk One Music (see Independent Music Group Ltd)

Timewarp (see Paul Rodriguez Music Ltd)

Tin Whistle Music (see Bucks Music Group)

Tinrib (see Paul Rodriguez Music Ltd)

Tiparm Music Publishers Inc (see Bucks Music Group)

TM Music (see Carlin Music Corporation)

TMC Publishing (see Triad Publishing).

TMR Publishing PO Box 3775, London SE18 3QR
t 020 8316 4690 **f** 020 8316 4690
e marc@wufog.freeserve.co.uk **w** Braindead-Studios.com
MD: Marc Bell.

TNR Music 5B Oakleigh Mews, Whetstone, London N20 9HQ
t 020 8343 9971 **f** 020 8445 9258
e tnrmusic@thenextroom.com **w** thenextroom.com
MD: Richard Burton.

Todo Music (see Paul Rodriguez Music Ltd)

Tomake Music (see Independent Music Group Ltd)

Tomeja Music (see Independent Music Group Ltd)

Tomi Girl Music (see Independent Music Group Ltd)

Tomi Music Co (see Westbury Music Ltd)

Tonecolor Music (see Express Music (UK) Ltd)

Tony Carlisle Music (see Independent Music Group Ltd)

Tony Randolph (see Paul Rodriguez Music Ltd)

Too Pure Music (see 4AD Music)

Torgrimson Music (see Independent Music Group Ltd)

Tosca Music (see Bucks Music Group)

Trace Elements (see Menace Music)

Track Music PO Box 107, South Godstone, Redhill, Surrey
RH9 8YS **t** 01342 892 178 or 01342 892 074
f 01342 893 411 **e** ian.grant@trackrecords.co.uk
w trackrecords.co.uk MD: Ian Grant.

Trackdown Music Ickenham Manor, Ickenham, Uxbridge,
Middx UB10 8QT **t** 01895 672994 **f** 01895 633264
e mail@trackdownmusic.co.uk **w** trackdownmusic.co.uk
Dir: Joanna Tizard.

Trailvine Publishing Ltd Unit 4C, Eggerton St, Nottingham
NG3 4GP **t** 0115 847 0899 **e** info@emitrecords.com
w emitrecords.com MD: John Bagguley.

Trax On Wax Music Publishers Glenmundar House,
Ballyman Rd, Bray, Co. Wicklow, Ireland **t** +353 86 257 6244
f +353 1 216 4395 **e** picket@iol.ie Dir: Deke O'Brien.

Tree Music (see Sony/ATV Music Publishing)

Trevor Fung (see Independent Music Group Ltd)

Treyball Music (see Notting Hill Music (UK) Ltd)

Triad Publishing PO Box 150, Chesterfield S40 0YT
t 0870 746 8478 **e** traid@themanagementcompany.biz
w themanagementcompany.biz MD: Tony Hedley.

Trinity Music (see The Valentine Music Group)

Trinity Publishing Company 72 New Bond St, London
W1S 1RR **t** 020 7499 4141 **e** info@trinitymediagroup.net
w trinitymediagroup.net MD: Peter Murray.

Triple A Publishing Ltd GMC Studio, Hollingbourne, Kent
ME17 1UQ **t** 01622 880599 **f** 01622 880020
e publishing@triple-a.uk.com **w** triple-a.uk.com
CEO: Terry Armstrong.

Tristan Music Ltd (see Hornall Brothers Music).

TRO Essex Music (see The Essex Music Group)

Truck Publishing 15 Percy St, Oxford OX4 3AA
t 01865 722333 **e** paul@truckrecords.com **w** truckrecords.com
MD: Paul Bonham.

True Playaz Music Publishing (see Bucks Music Group)

Truelove Music 19F Tower Workshops, Riley Rd, London
SE1 3DG **t** 020 7252 2900 **f** 020 7252 2890
e business@truelove.co.uk **w** truelove.co.uk
Contact: John Truelove, Brian Roach.

Tsunami Sounds Muscott House, Meadrow, Godalming,
Surrey GU7 3HN **t** 01483 410100 **f** 01483 410100
e info@tsunami.co.uk **w** tsunami.co.uk Dir: Ken Easter.

Tuesday Music (see PXM Publishing)

Tuesday Productions (see Bucks Music Group)

Tumi Music (Editorial) Ltd 8-9 New Bond St. Pl, Bath,
Somerset BA1 1BH **t** 01225 464736 **f** 01225 444870
e info@tumimusic.com **w** tumimusic.com MD: Mo Fini.

Tune Kel Publishing (see Charly Publishing Ltd)

TVS Music (see Bucks Music Group)

Twangy Music (see Music Sales Ltd)

Two Guys Who Are Publishers (see Independent Music
Group Ltd)

Two Song (see Menace Music)

TwoPointNine Publishing Ltd PO Box 44607, London
N16 0YP **t** 07801 033 741 **e** Office@2point9.com
w 2point9.com Dirs: Billy Grant, Rob Stuart.

Tyler Music (see The Essex Music Group)

Ubiquitunes (see Bucks Music Group)

UGR Publishing PO Box 178, Sutton, Surrey SM2 6XG
t 020 8643 6403 or 07904 255 244 **f** 020 8643 6403
e info@ugrpublishing.com **w** ugrpublishing.com
Head of A&R: P Mac.

Ultimate Dilemma Music (see Westbury Music Ltd)

Ultimate Musical Publishing Co (see The Bacon Empire
Publishing)

Ultramodern Music (see Bucks Music Group)

Under The Counter Music (see Westbury Music Ltd)

Unforgettable Songs (see Perfect Songs)

Unique Corp. 15 Shaftesbury Centre, 85 Barlby Rd, London
W10 6BN **t** 020 8964 9333 or 07768 065661
f 020 8964 9888 **e** info@uniquecorp.co.uk **w** uniquecorp.co.uk
MD: Alan Bellman.

Unique Publishing (see Bucks Music Group)

Unit 11 Publishing Ltd (see Independent Music Group Ltd)

United Music GBMH (see Independent Music Group Ltd)

United Music Publishers Ltd 42 Rivington St, London
EC2A 3BN **t** 020 7729 4700 **f** 020 7739 6549
e info@ump.co.uk **w** ump.co.uk MD: Shirley Ranger.

United Songwriters Music (see International
Songwriters' Music)

Universal Edition (London) 48 Gt Marlborough St,
London W1F 7BB **t** 020 7439 6678 **f** 020 7437 6115
e connell@universaledition.com **w** universaledition.com
Sales/Mktng Mgr: Adrian Connell.

UNIVERSAL MUSIC PUBLISHING LTD

**UNIVERSAL MUSIC
PUBLISHING GROUP**

136-144 New Kings Rd, London SW6 4LZ **t** 020 8752 2600
f 020 8752 2601 **e** firstname.lastname@umusic.com MD UK &
Pres. Europe: Paul Connolly. Deputy Managing Director: Mike
McCormack. European Finance Dir: Simon Baker. VP,
International: Kim Frankiewicz. General Manager / Head of Legal
& Business Affairs: Sarah Levin. Head of UK Finance: Rob Morris.
Head of Film & TV: Barbara Zamoyska. UK Licensing Manager:
Ross Pelling. Creative Services Manager: Karina Masters. A&R:
Willi Morrison, Claire Walters, Andy Thompson, Frank Tope,
Darryl Watts, Dougie Bruce. UK Admin: UK Copyright Mgr: David
Livermore. UK Royalty Mgr: Simon Lindquist.

Upright Music 204 Crescent House, Goswell Rd, London
EC1Y 0SL **t** 020 7490 7346 **e** bill@workersplaytime.co.uk
w workersplaytime.co.uk MD: Bill Gilliam.

Upright Songs (see Independent Music Group Ltd)

Urban Music Entertainment Network (U-Men) PO
Box 7874, London SW20 9XD **t** 07050 605219
f 07050 605239 **e** sam@pan-africa.org **w** umengroup.com
CEO: Oscar Sam-Carrol Jnr.

Urbanstar Music Global House, 92 De Beauvoir Rd, London
N1 4EN **t** 020 7288 2239 **f** 0870 429 2493
e info@urbanstarrecords.com **w** urbanstarrecords.com
Dirs: Steve Wren, Nick Sellors.

Utopia Publishing Utopia Village, 7 Chalcot Rd, London
NW1 8LH **t** 020 7586 3434 **f** 020 7586 3438
e utopiarec@aol.com MD: Phil Wainman.

V2 Music Publishing Ltd Unit 24, 101 Farm Lane, Fulham,
London SW6 1QJ **t** 020 7471 3000
e firstname.lastname@v2music.com **w** V2music.com.

The Valentine Music Group 7 Garrick St, London
WC2E 9AR **t** 020 7240 1628 **f** 020 7497 9242
e pat@valentinemusic.co.uk **w** valentinemusic.co.uk
MD: John Nice.

Valley Music Ltd. 11 Cedar Court, Fairmile, Henley-on-Thames, Oxon RG9 2JR **t** 01491 845 840 **f** 01491 413 667 **e** info@valleymusicuk.com **w** tomjones.com MD: Mark Woodward.

Valliant Publishing (see Charly Publishing Ltd)

Value Added Tunes (see Independent Music Group).

Van Steene Music Publishing 23 Anthony Rd, Borehamwood, Herts WD6 4NF **t** 020 8905 2878 **f** 020 8905 2879 **e** guyvansteene@macunlimited.net MD: Guy Van Steene.

Vanderbeek & Imrie Ltd 15 Marvig, Lochs, Isle Of Lewis, Scotland HS2 9QP **t** 01851 880216 **f** 01851 880216 **e** mapamundi@aol.com MD: M Imrie.

Vanessa Music Co 35 Tower Way, Dunkeswell, Devon EX14 4XH **t** 01404 891598 MD: Don Todd MBE.

Vanwarmer Music (see Independent Music Group Ltd)

Vaughan Williams Memorial Library (Sound Archive) Cecil Sharp House, 2 Regent's Park Rd, Camden, London NW1 7AY **t** 020 7485 2206 **f** 020 7284 0534 **e** info@efdss.org **w** efdss.org Publications Manager: Felicity Greenland.

Vector Music (see Independent Music Group Ltd)

Veltone Music (see Independent Music Group Ltd)

Venus Music 13 Fernhurst Gardens, Edgware, Middx HA8 7PQ **t** 020 8952 1924 or 07956 064 019 **f** 020 8952 3496 **e** kamalmmalak@onetel.net.uk **w** venusmusicandrecords.co.uk MD: Kamal M Malak.

Verge Music (see Asterisk Music)

Veronica Music (see Music Sales Ltd)

Verulam Music (see Bocu Music Ltd)

Vicki Music (see Carlin Music Corporation)

Victor Hugo Salsa PO Box 14303, London SE26 4ZH **t** 07000 472572 **f** 07000 472572 **e** victorhugo@victorhugosalsa.com **w** victorhugosalsa.com Mgr: Hector Rosquete.

Victoria Kay Music (see Independent Music Group Ltd)

Vidor Publications (see Independent Music Group Ltd)

Ville de Beest (see Asterisk Music)

Vince Barranco Music (see Independent Music Group Ltd)

Virgin Music (see EMI Music Publishing)

Visual Music Publishing West House, Forthaven, Shoreham-by-Sea, W. Sussex BN43 5HY **t** 01273 453 422 **f** 01273 452 914 **e** richard@longman-records.com **w** richard-durrant.com Dir: Richard Durrant.

Vital Spark Music 1 Waterloo, Breakish, Isle Of Skye IV42 8QE **t** 01471 822 484 or 07768 031 060 **e** chris@vitalsparkmusic.demon.co.uk **w** hi-arts.co.uk/studios1.htm Mgr: Chris Harley.

Vitamin V Music 1 Sekforde St, London EC1R 0BE **t** 020 7075 6080 **f** 020 7075 6081 **e** firstname@vitaminv.tv Dir: Les Mear.

VLS Music Inc (see Independent Music Group Ltd)

Voiceprint Publishing PO Box 50, Houghton-le-Spring, Tyne and Wear DH4 5YP **t** 0191 512 1103 **f** 0191 512 1104 **e** info@voiceprint.co.uk **w** voiceprint.co.uk MD: Rob Ayling.

W Bessel, London (see Breitkopf & Hartel)

Waif Productions 1 North Worple Way, London SW14 8QG **t** 020 8876 2533 **f** 020 8878 4229 **e** artistrec@aol.com **w** arcarc.co.uk GM: Marie Hourihan.

Walden Creek Music (see Independent Music Group Ltd)

Walk on the Wild Side 8 Deronda Rd, London SE24 9BG **t** 020 8674 7990 or 07775 806288 **f** 020 8671 5548 MD: Dave Massey.

Wall Of Sound Music 338A Ladbroke Grove, London W10 5AH **t** 020 8324 2500 **f** 020 8324 0010 **e** info@piaswos.com **w** wallofsound.net MD: Marc Jones.

Walter Neal Music (see Asterisk Music)

W.A.M. Music Ltd. (see Broadley Music (Int) Ltd)

Wardlaw Banks Ltd Studio 2, Shepperton Film Studios, Shepperton, Middx TW17 0QD **t** 0845 299 0150 or 07852 320 736 **f** 020 7117 3171 **e** info@wardlawbanks.com **w** wardlawbanks.com Dir: Stanley Banks.

Wardo Music (see Bucks Music Group)

Wardour Music (see Express Music (UK) Ltd)

Warlock Music (see Rykomusic Ltd)

Warner Chappell Hire Library (see The Concord Partnership)

WARNER CHAPPELL MUSIC LTD

The Warner Building, 28 Kensington Church St, London W8 4EP **t** 020 7938 0000 **f** 020 7368 2777 **e** firstname.surname@warnerchappell.com **w** warnerchappell.com. MD: Richard Manners. Fin Dir: Mike Lavin. SVP, International Legal & Business Affairs: Jane Dyball. Head of Legal & Business Affairs: Honey Onile-Ere. Snr A&R Manager: David Donald. A&R Mgr: Kehinde Olarinmoye. A&R Mgr: Jane Rees. Scout: Mike Lightford. Head of Film & TV: Jim Reid. Standard Repertoire Mgr: Caroline Underwood. Mgr UK & Int'l Services: Lesley Hatch. Head of European Administration (Copyright, Royalties and Tracking): Stephen Clark. UK Copyright Mgr: Glenn Stokes. UK Royalty Mgr: Barry McKee. European Copyright Mgr: Julie Kenealy. European Royalty Processing Mgr: Alex Mackintosh. **Please note that Royalties and Copyright Administration operate from Griffin House, 161 Hammersmith Road, London W6 8BS. t 020 8563 5800. f 020 8563 5801.**

Warner Chappell Music International (see Warner Chappell Music Ltd)

Water House Music (see Greensleeves Publishing Ltd)

Water Music Productions 6 Erskine Rd, London NW3 3AJ **t** 020 7722 3478 **f** 020 7722 6605 **e** splash@watermusic.co.uk Producer: Tessa Lawlor.

Websongs The Troupe Studio, 106 Thetford Rd, New Malden, Surrey KT3 5DZ **t** 020 8949 0928 **f** 020 8605 0238 **e** kip@websongs.co.uk **w** websongs.co.uk MD: Kip Trevor.

Welsh Media Music Gorwelion, Llanfynydd, Carmarthen, Dyfed SA32 7TG **t** 01558 668525 **f** 01558 668750 **e** dpierce@fsmail.net MD: Dave Pierce.

WESTBURY MUSIC LTD

Suite B, 2 Tunstall Rd, London SW9 8DA **t** 020 7733 5400 **f** 020 7733 4449 **e** info@westburymusic.net **w** westburymusic.net General Manager: Paulette Long. Business Affairs: Jon Handle. A&R: Felix Hines.

Westminster Music (see The Essex Music Group)

WGS Music (see Bardic Edition)

Whacker Music (see Independent Music Group Ltd)

Whispering Wings Music (see Independent Music Group Ltd)

White Noise The Motor Museum, 1 Hesketh St, Liverpool L17 8XJ **t** 0151 222 2760 **e** office@whitenoiseuk.com **w** whitenoiseuk.com Label Manager: Eric Mackay.

Whitman (see Eaton Music Ltd)

Whole Earth Music (see Independent Music Group Ltd)

Wienerworld (see Melody Lauren Music)

Wiiija Music (see 4AD Music)

Wild Bouquet Music (see Independent Music Group Ltd)

Wildwood Music (see The Essex Music Group)

Wilhelm Music (see New Music Enterprises)

Wilson Editions Magnus House, 8 Ashfield Rd, Cheadle, Cheshire SK8 1BB **t** 0161 491 6655 **f** 0161 491 6688 **e** dimus@aol.com **w** dimusic.co.uk MD: Alan Wilson.

Windfall (see Bucks Music Group)

Window Music (see Independent Music Group Ltd)

Windswept Music (London) (see P&P Songs Ltd)

Wintrup Songs 31 Buckingham St, Brighton, E Sussex BN1 3LT **t** 01273 880439 **e** allan@allanmcgowan.com Contact: Allan McGowan.

Winwood Music Unit 7 Fieldside Farm, Quainton, Bucks HP22 4DQ **t** 01296 655777 **f** 01296 655778 **e** sales@winwoodmusic.com **w** winwoodmusic.com MD: Eric Wilson.

Wipe Out Music PO Box 1NW, Newcastle-Upon-Tyne NE99 1NW **t** 0191 266 3802 **f** 0191 266 6073 **e** johnesplen@btconnect.com Mgr: John Esplen.

WOMAD Music Ltd Box Mill, Mill Lane, Box, Wilts SN13 8PL **t** 01225 743188 **f** 01225 744369 **e** publishing@realworld.co.uk **w** realworld.co.uk/publishing Publisher: Annie Reed.

Wooden (see Bucks Music Group)

Woody Guthrie Publications (see Bucks Music Group)

World Music Press (see Lindsay Music)

WW Music (see Paul Rodriguez Music Ltd)

WW Norton (see Peters Edition)

Wyze Music PO Box 847, Camberley, Surrey GU15 3ZZ **t** 01276 671441 **f** 01276 684460 **e** info@wyze.com **w** wyze.com MD: Kate Ross.

Yancey Music (see Asterisk Music)

Yard Dog Music (see Independent Music Group Ltd)

Year Zero Music (see Bucks Music Group)

Yell Music PO Box 46301, London W5 3UX **t** 020 8579 8300 or 07779 852 418 **e** jana.yell@yellmusic.com **w** yellmusic.com MD: Jana Yell.

Yesterday's Music (see Multiplay Music)

Yok Music (see Bucks Music Group)

Yorke Edition Grove Cottage, Southgate, Fakenham, Norfolk NR21 9PA **t** 01328 823 501 **f** 01328 823 502 **e** info@yorkedition.co.uk **w** yorkedition.co.uk Prop: Rodney Slatford.

Young Beau Music (see Independent Music Group Ltd)

Young Man Moving (see Independent Music Group Ltd)

The Yukon Music Utopia Village, Chalcot Rd, Primrose Hill, London NW1 8LH **t** 020 7242 8408 **e** music@theyukonmusic.com MD: Andrew Maurice.

Zagora Editions (see Independent Music Group Ltd)

Zamalama Music (see Independent Music Group Ltd)

Zane Music 162 Castle Hill, Reading, Berks RG1 7RP **t** 0118 957 4567 **f** 0118 956 1261 **e** info@zaneproductions.demon.co.uk **w** zanerecords.com Contact: Peter Thompson.

Zedfunk PO Box 7497, London N21 2DX **t** 07050 657 465 **e** info@zedfunk.com **w** zedfunk.com MD: Paul Z.

Zest Songs Ltd 29-30 St James's St, London SW1A 1HB **t** 0870 389 6999 **f** 0870 389 6998 **e** steve@zestmusic.com **w** zestmusic.com Chief Exec: Steve Weltman.

Zok Music (see Bucks Music Group)

Zomba Music Publishers 20 Fulham Broadway, London SW6 1AH **t** 020 7835 5260 **f** 020 7835 5261 **e** firstname.lastname@zomba.com GM: Tim Smith.

Zonic Music (see Creole Music Ltd)

Zoo-Bee Music (see SGO Music Publishing)

Zorch Music (see Nervous Publishing)

Sheet Music Suppliers

A&C Black Howard Rd, Eaton Socon, Cambs PE19 8EZ **t** 01480 212666 **f** 01480 405014 **e** custser@acblack.com Educational Support Mgr: Hilary While.

Alker & Askem Arrangements and Transcriptions The Coach House, Market Sq, Bicester, Oxon OX26 6AG **t** 01869 250647 **f** 01869 321552 **e** aaa@groovecompany.co.uk **w** aaarrangements.co.uk MD: Martin Alker.

Boosey & Hawkes Music Publishers Ltd Aldwych House, 71-91 Aldwych, London WC2B 4HN **t** 020 7054 7200 **f** 020 7054 7293 **e** marketing.uk@boosey.com **w** boosey.com Hd of Publicity & Mktg: David Allenby.

Faber Music Burnt Mill, Elizabeth Way, Harlow, Essex CM20 2HX **t** 01279 828989 or 01279 828900 **f** 01279 828990 or 01279 828901 **e** sales@fabermusic.com **w** fabermusic.com Sales & Mktg Dir: Phillip Littlemore.

Jazzwise 2B Gleneagle Mews, Ambleside Ave, London SW16 6AE **t** 020 8769 7725 **f** 020 8677 7128 **e** admin@jazzwise.com **w** jazzwise.com MD: Charles Alexander.

Alfred A Kalmus/Universal Edition (London) 48 Gt Marlborough St, London W1F 7BB **t** 020 7437 5203 **f** 020 7437 6115 **e** andrew.knowles@uemusic.co.uk Sales Promo Mgr: Andrew Knowles.

London Orchestrations (c/o Jazzwise).

Lookmusic 21 Presley Way, Crownhill, Milton Keynes, Bucks MK8 0ES **t** 0870 333 0091 **f** 01908 263301 **e** sales@lookmusic.com **w** lookmusic.com Head of IT: Philip Evans.

MakeMusic! Inc 8 Whitehouse Lane, Wooburn Moor, Bucks HP10 0NR **t** 01494 730 143 **f** 01494 730 143 **e** mark@musiworks.com **w** musiworks.com Dir: Mark Mumford.

Music Exchange (Manchester) Ltd. Claverton Rd, Wythenshawe, Manchester M23 9ZA **t** 0161 946 1234 **f** 0161 946 1195 **e** sales@music-exchange.co.uk **w** musicx.co.uk (Trade Only) Sales Director: Gerald Burns.

Music Sales Ltd 8/9 Frith St, London W1V 5TZ **t** 020 7434 0066 **f** 020 7734 8416 **e** music@musicsales.co.uk **w** musicsales.com GM: Chris Butler.

Musicroom.com 14-15 Berners St, London W1T 3LJ **t** 020 7612 7400 **f** 020 7836 4810 **e** info@musicroom.com **w** musicroom.com Dir, Internet Operations: Tomas Wise.

RSCM Music Direct c/o SCM-Canterbury Press, St Mary's Works, St Mary's Plain, Norwich NR3 3BH **t** 0845 021 7726 **f** 0845 021 8826 **e** musicdirect@rscm.com **w** rscm.com.

Stainer & Bell PO Box 110, Victoria House, 23 Gruneisen Rd, London N3 1DZ **t** 020 8343 3303 **f** 020 8343 3024 **e** post@stainer.co.uk **w** stainer.co.uk Joint MD: Carol Wakefield.

Studio Music Company (Sheet Music Distributors) PO Box 19292, London NW10 9WP **t** 020 8830 0110 **f** 020 8451 6470 **e** sales@studio-music.co.uk Ptnr: Stan Kitchen.

United Music Publishers 42 Rivington St, London EC2A 3BN **t** 020 7729 4700 **f** 020 7739 6549 **e** info@ump.co.uk **w** ump.co.uk Mktng Mgr: James Perkins.

Production Music

Adage Music 22 Gravesend Rd, London W12 0SZ **t** 07973 295 113 **e** dobs@adagemusic.co.uk **w** adagemusic.com MD: Dobs Vye.

Adelphoi Music Ltd 26 Litchfield St, Covent Garden, London WC2H 9TZ **t** 020 7240 7250 **f** 020 7240 7260 **e** info@adelphoi.com **w** adelphoimusic.com Hd, Product'n & Bus. Dev.: Paul Reynolds.

Admax Music 25 Heathmans RD, London SW6 4TJ **t** 020 7371 5756 **f** 020 7371 7731 **e** stirling@stakis.com **w** pureuk.com Contact: Ian Ferguson Brown.

Air-Edel Associates 18 Rodmarton St, London W1U 8BJ **t** 020 7486 6466 **f** 020 7224 0344 **e** mrodford@air-edel.co.uk **w** air-edel.co.uk MD: Maggie Rodford.

Arcadia Production Music (UK) Greenlands, Payhembury, Devon EX14 3HY **t** 01404 841601 **f** 01404 841687 **e** admin@arcadiamusic.tv **w** arcadiamusic.tv Prop: John Brett.

Arclite Productions The Grove Music Studios, Unit 10.Latimer Ind. Est, Latimer Rd, London W10 6RQ **t** 020 8964 9047 **e** info@arcliteproductions.com **w** arcliteproductions.com Prod: Alan Bleay.

David Arnold Music Ltd Unit 9, Dry Drayton Industries, Dry Drayton, Cambridge CB3 8AT **t** 01954 212020 **f** 01954 212222 **e** alex@davidarnoldmusic.com **w** davidarnoldmusic.com.

Atmosphere Music (see BMG Production Music).

Barefoot Communications 24 Coronet St, London N1 6HD **t** 020 7613 4697 **f** 020 7729 6613 **e** alex@barefootuk.co.uk **w** barefootuk.co.uk Dir: Alex Gover.

Bazza Productions 1 Chemin de la Sini, 66130 Ille-sur-Tet, France **t** +33(0)4 68 84 17 26 **e** bsguard@aol.com **w** barrieguard.com MD: Barrie Guard.

Beatsuite.com Music Library Suite 45, 7-15 Pink Lane, Newcastle, Tyne & Wear NE1 5DW **t** 0845 094 1512 **e** info@beatsuite.com **w** beatsuite.com Marketing Manager: Mark Malekpour.

Beetroot Music Newlands House, 40 Berners St, London W1T 3NA **t** 020 7255 2408 **e** info@beetrootmusic.com **w** beetrootmusic.com Co MD: Tish Lord.

Big George and Sons PO Box 7094, Kiln Farm MK11 1LL **t** 01908 566 453 **e** big.george@btinternet.com **w** biggeorge.co.uk Mgr: Big George Webley.

Blossom Audiomedia Station Rd, Blaina, Gwent NP13 3PW **t** 01495 290 960 or 07932 377 109 **e** info@blossomstudio.co.uk **w** blossomstudio.co.uk Proprietor & Engineer: Noel Watson.

Blue Sky Radio Mixes Wisteria House, 56 Cole Park Rd, Twickenham, Middx TW1 1HS **t** 020 8891 3333 **f** 020 8891 3222 **e** julian@redshadow.co.uk Dir: Julian Spear.

BMG Zomba Production Music 20 Fulham Broadway, London SW6 1AH **t** 020 7835 5300 **f** 020 7835 5318 **e** musicresearch@bmgzomba.com **w** bmgzomba.com Senior Promotions Exec: Julia Dean.

BOB Ltd 62 New Cavendish St, London W1G 8TA **t** 020 7580 9373 **f** 020 7580 9375 **e** boblimited@aol.com Dir: Alex White.

Boom! Music Ltd 16 Blackwood Close, West Byfleet, Surrey KT14 6PP **t** 01932 336212 **e** Phil@music4media.tv **w** music4media.tv Composer: Phil Binding.

Boosey Media Aldwych House, 71-91 Aldwych, London WC2B 4HN **t** 020 7054 7200 **f** 020 7054 7293 **e** booseymedia@boosey **w** booseymedia.com Media Manager: Ann Dawson.

Burning Petals Production Music 5 Clover Ground, Shepton Mallet BA4 4AS **t** 0870 749 1117 **e** enquiries@burning-petals.com **w** burning-petals.com Contact: Richard Jay.

Buzz-erk Music 17 Villiers Rd, Kingston Upon Thames, Surrey KT1 3AP **t** 020 8931 1044 **e** info@buzz-erk.com **w** Buzz-erk.com Dir: Niraj Chag.

Caleche Studios 175 Roundhay Rd, Leeds LS8 5AN **t** 0113 219 4941 **f** 0113 249 4941 **e** calechestudios@ntlworld.com MD: Leslie Coleman.

Candle 44 Southern Row, London W10 5AN **t** 020 8960 0111 or 07860 912 192 **f** 020 8968 7008 or (ISDN) 020 8960 4370 **e** email@candle.org.uk **w** candle.org.uk MD: Tony Satchell.

Capitol Studios 6 The White House, 42 The Terrace, Torquay, Devon TQ1 1DE **t** 01803 201918 **f** 01803 292323 **e** derek@radiojingles.com **w** radiojingles.com Commercial Prod: Julian Sharp.

Caritas Media Music (inc Caritas Music Library) Achmore, Moss Rd, Ullapool IV26 2TF **t** 01854 612 938 **f** 01854 612 938 **e** media@caritas-music.co.uk **w** caritas-music.co.uk Publishing Manager: Katharine Douglas.

Chantelle Music 3A Ashheld Parade, London N14 5EH **t** 020 8886 6236 **e** info@chantellemusic.co.uk **w** chantellemusic.co.uk MD: Riss Chantelle.

Chicken Sounds PO Box 43829, London NW6 1WN **t** 020 7209 2586 **f** 020 7209 2586 **e** mail@whitehousemanagement.com Dir: Sue Whitehouse.

Crocodile Music 431 Linen Hall, 162-168 Regent St, London W1B 5TE **t** 020 7580 0080 **f** 020 7637 0097 **e** music@crocodilemusic.com **w** crocodilemusic.com Contact: Malcolm Ironton, Ray Tattle.

CYP The Fairway, Bush Fair, Harlow, Essex CM18 6LY **t** 01279 444707 **f** 01279 445570 **e** sales@cypmusic.co.uk **w** kidsmusic.co.uk Sales Manager: Gary Wilmot.

delicious digital Suite GB, 39-40 Warple Way, Acton, London W3 0RG **t** 020 8749 7272 **f** 020 8749 7474 **e** info@deliciousdigital.com **w** deliciousdigital.com Dirs: Ollie Raphael, Ed Moris.

Doodlehums 30 Cullesden Rd, Kenley, Surrey CR8 5LR **t** 020 8668 4833 **f** 020 8668 4833 **e** oswinf@lineone.net Prop: Mr O Falquero.

Dreamscape Music 36 Eastcastle St, London W1W 8DP **t** 020 7631 1799 or 07767 771 157 **f** 020 7631 1720 **e** lester@lesterbarnes.com **w** lesterbarnes.com Composer: Lester Barnes.

Eagle Eye Productions Eagle House, 22 Armoury Way, London SW18 1EZ **t** 020 8870 5670 **f** 020 8874 2333 **e** mail@eagle-rock.com **w** eagle-rock.com Supervising Producer: Alan Ravenscroft.

Everyday Productions 33 Mandarin Pl, Grove, Oxon OX12 0QH **t** 01235 767171 **e** smi_everyday_productions@yahoo.com VP Special Proj: David Wareham.

Liz Gallacher Music Supervision Suite 1, Buidling 500, Shepperton Studios, Studios Rd, Shepperton, Middlesex TW17 0QD **t** 01932 577 880 **f** 01932 569 371 **e** kay@lizg.com **w** lizg.com Music Supervisor: Liz Gallacher.

Gecko Music Ltd The Studio, 1 Tanworth Close, Northwood, Middx HA6 2GF **t** 01923 450 972 or 07904 546 729 **e** macwell@geckomusic.com Contact: Stuart Macwell.

Geezers (Song Sourcing & Music Supervision) (see Beetroot Music).

G3 Music 13 Hales Prior, Calshot St, London N1 9JW **t** 020 8361 2170 **f** 020 8361 2170 **e** g3music@g3music.com **w** g3music.com Creative Dir: Greg Heath.

Hear No Evil 6 Lillie Yard, London SW6 1UB **t** 020 7385 8244 **f** 020 7385 0700 **e** info@hearnoevil.net **w** hearnoevil.net MD: Sharon Rose-Parr.

Higher Ground Music Productions The Stables, Albury Lodge, Albury, Ware, Herts SG11 2LH **t** 01279 776 019 **e** info@highergrounduk.com **w** highergrounduk.com Creative & Commercial Dir: Greg Newman.

HotHouse Music Greenland Pl, 115-123 Bayham St, London NW1 0AG **t** 020 7446 7446 **f** 020 7446 7448 **e** info@hot-house-music.com **w** hot-house-music.com Co-MDs: Becky Bentham, Karen Elliott.

Howarth & Johnston 61 Timber Bush, Leith, Edinburgh, Lothian EH6 6QH **t** 0131 555 2288 **f** 0131 555 0088 **e** doit@redfacilities.com **w** redfacilities.com Ptnr: Max Howarth.

HUM 31 Oval Rd, London NW1 7EA **t** 020 7482 2345 **f** 020 7482 6242 **e** firstname@hum.co.uk **w** hum.co.uk Prod: Daniel Simmons.

Instant Music 14 Moorend Crescent, Cheltenham, Gloucs GL53 0EL **t** 01242 523304 or 07957 355630 **f** 01242 523304 **e** info@instantmusic.co.uk **w** instantmusic.co.uk MD: Martin Mitchell.

Jeff Wayne Music Group Oliver House, 8-9 Ivor Pl, London NW1 6BY **t** 020 7724 2471 **f** 020 7724 6245 **e** info@jeffwaynemusic.com **w** jeffwaynemusic.com Group Dir: Jane Jones.

Jingle Jangles The Strand, 156 Holywood Rd, Belfast, Co Antrim BT4 1NY **t** 028 9065 6769 **f** 028 9067 3771 **e** steve@jinglejangles.tv **w** jinglejangles.tv MD: Steve Martin.

Joe & Co (Music) 59 Dean St, London W1D 6AN **t** 020 7439 1272 **f** 020 7437 5504 **e** justine@joeandco.com **w** joeandco.com Office Mgr: Justine Campbell.

Killer Tracks (see BMG Production Music).

Carl Kingston 557 Street Lane, Leeds, W Yorks LS17 6JA **t** 0113 268 7886 or 07836 568888 **f** 0113 266 0045 **e** carl@carlkingston.co.uk **w** carlkingston.co.uk Contact: Carl Kingston.

Knifedge 57b Riding House St, London W1W 7EF **t** 020 7436 5434 **f** 020 7436 5431 **e** info@knifedge.net **w** knifedge.net Dir: Jonathan Brigden.

Koka Media (see BMG Production Music).

Dave Langer Creative Services 27 Cavendish Rd, Salford, Manchester M7 4WP **t** 0161 740 7171 **f** 0161 792 9595 **e** info@jingle.org **w** jingle.org MD: Dave Langer.

LBS Manchester 11-13 Bamford St, Stockport, Cheshire SK1 3NZ **t** 0161 477 2710 **f** 0161 480 9497 **e** info@lbs.co.uk **w** lbs.co.uk Prod: Adders.

LBS Music **t** 01865 725521 or 07071 225625 **e** richard@lbsmusic.demon.co.uk **w** lbsmusic.demon.co.uk MD: Richard Lewis.

Publishers: Production Music

Living Productions 39 Tadorne Rd, Tadworth, Surrey KT20 5TF **t** 01737 812922 **f** 01737 812922 **e** Livingprods@ukgateway.net Dir/Co Sec: Norma Camby.

Loriana Music PO Box 2731, Romford RM7 1AD **t** 01708 750 185 or 07748 343 363 **f** 01708 750 185 **e** info@lorianamusic.com **w** lorianamusic.com Owner: Jean-Louis Fargier.

Mad Hat Studios The Upper Hattons Media Centre, The Upper Hattons, Pendeford Hall Lane, Coven, Nr Wolverhampton WV9 5BD **t** 01902 840440 **f** 01902 840448 **e** studio@madhat.co.uk **w** madhat.co.uk Dir: Claire Swan.

Pete Martin Productions 305 Canalot Studios, 222 Kensal Rd, London W10 5BN **t** 020 8960 0700 **f** 020 8960 0762 **e** info@frontierrecordings.com **w** frontierrecordings.com Dir: Pete Martin.

Match Production Music (see BMG Production Music).

Mcasso Music Production 32-34 Great Marlborough St, London W1F 7JB **t** 020 7734 3664 **f** 020 7439 2375 **e** music@mcasso.com **w** mcasso.com Producer: Dan Hancock.

Meringue Productions 37 Church St, Twickenham, Middx TW1 3NR **t** 020 8744 2277 **f** 020 8744 9333 **e** enquiries@meringue.co.uk **w** meringue.co.uk Dir: Lynn Earnshaw.

Mike Stevens Music Canalot Studios, 222 Kensal Rd, London W10 5BN **t** 020 8960 5069 **e** sue@msmusic.demon.co.uk MD: Mike Stevens.

The Morrighan PO Box 23066, London W11 3FR **t** 07956 311810 **e** the@morrighan.com **w** morrighan.com Dir: Jon Crosse.

Music By Design 5th Floor, Film House, 142 Wardour St, London W1F 8ZU **t** 020 7434 3244 **f** 020 7434 1064 **e** rosa@musicbydesign.co.uk **w** musicbydesign.co.uk Production Manager & Music Consultant: Rosa Martinez.

North Star Music Publishing Ltd PO Box 868, Cambridge CB1 6SJ **t** 01787 278256 **f** 01787 279069 **e** info@northstarmusic.co.uk **w** northstarmusic.co.uk MD: Grahame Maclean.

Orbital Productions 38 Burnfoot Rd, Hawick, Scottish Borders TD9 8EN **t** 01450 378212 **e** info@orbital-productions.com **w** orbital-productions.com MD: Jacqui Gresswell.

Panama Productions Sovereign House, 12 Trewartha Rd, Praa Sands, Penzance, Cornwall TR20 9ST **t** 01736 762 826 or 07721 449477 **f** 01736 763 328 **e** panamus@aol.com **w** panamamusic.co.uk MD: Roderick Jones.

Pluto Music Hulgrave Hall, Tiverton, Tarporley, Cheshire CW6 9UQ **t** 01829 732427 **f** 01829 733802 **e** info@plutomusic.com **w** plutomusic.com MD: Keith Hopwood.

Pond-Life **t** 07973 759146 **e** cchesney@hotmail.com **w** chrischesney.co.uk Dir: Chris Chesney.

Poportunity Highridge, Bath Rd, Farmborough, Nr Bath BA2 0BG **t** 01761 470023 **e** davidrees@poportunity.co.uk **w** poportunity.co.uk Dir: David Rees.

Primrose Music Publishing 1 Leitrim House, 36 Worple Rd, London SW19 4EQ **t** 020 8946 7808 **f** 020 8946 3392 **e** jestersong@msn.com **w** primrosemusic.com Dir: R B Rogers.

The Product Exchange Ltd 68 Cranston Ave, Bexhill On Sea, E Sussex TN39 3NN **t** 01424 215 617 or 01424 215 617 **e** music@productexchange.co.uk **w** productexchange.co.uk MD: Frank Rodgers.

Quince Productions 62a Balcombe St, Marylebone, London NW1 6NE **t** 020 7723 4196 or 07810 752 765 **f** 020 7723 1010 **e** info@quincestudios.co.uk **w** quincestudios.co.uk Dir: Matt Walters.

RBM Composers Churchwood Studios, 1 Woodchurch Rd, London NW6 3PL **t** 020 7372 2229 **f** 020 7372 3339 **e** rbm@easynet.co.uk MD: Ronnie Bond.

Resonant Matrix 10 Unity Wharf, London SE1 2BH **t** 020 7252 2661 **f** 0870 051 2594 **e** gav@movingshadow.com **w** movingshadow.com Business Manager: Gavin Johnson.

Ricall Limited First Floor, 14 Buckingham Palace Rd, London SW1W 0QP **t** 020 7592 1710 **f** 020 7592 1713 **e** marketing@ricall.com **w** ricall.com MD, Investor Relations: Richard Corbett.

Savin Productions 19 Woodlea Drive, Solihull, Birmingham, W Midlands B91 1PG **t** 0121 240 1100 **f** 0121 240 4042 **e** info@savinproductions.com **w** savinproductions.com Prop: Brian Savin.

Select Music & Video Distribution Ltd. 3 Wells Pl, Redhill, Surrey RH1 3SL **t** 01737 645600 ext 306 or 01635 871338 **f** 01737 644065 **e** GBartholomew@selectmusic.co.uk **w** naxos.com Licensing Mgr: Graham Bartholomew.

Skyblue Recordings PO Box 44616, London N16 9WH **t** 0781 372 4854 **e** alyson@skybluerecordings.com **w** skybluerecordings.com Dir: Alyson Gilliland.

Somethin' Else Sound Direction Unit 1-4, 1A Old Nichol St, London E2 7HR **t** 020 7613 3211 **f** 020 7739 9799 **e** info@somethin-else.com **w** somethin-else.com Dir: Steve Ackerman.

Sound Service Hill View, 93 Pointout Rd, Bassett, Southampton, Hants SO16 7DL **t** 023 8070 1682 **f** 023 8079 0130 **e** colin@sound-service.co.uk **w** sound-service.co.uk Prop: Colin Willsher.

Soundbytes Promotions PO Box 1209, Stafford ST16 1XW **t** 01785 222382 **f** 0871 277 3060 **e** soundbytes@btinternet.com Creative Dir: Robert L Hicks.

Soundtree Music Unit 124, Canalot Studios, 222 Kensal Rd, London W10 5BN **t** 020 8968 1449 **f** 020 8968 1500 **e** post@soundtree.co.uk **w** soundtree.co.uk GM: Jay James.

Space City Productions 77 Blythe Rd, London W14 0HP **t** 020 7371 4000 **f** 020 7371 4001 **e** info@spacecity.co.uk **w** spacecity.co.uk MD: Claire Rimmer.

Street Level Management Ltd 1st Floor, 17 Bowater Rd, Westminster Industrial Estate, Woolwich, London SE18 5TF **t** 07886 260 686 **e** ceo@streetlevelenterprises.co.uk **w** streetlevelenterprises.com MD: Sam Crawford.

Ten21 Little Milgate, Otham Lane, Bearsted, Maidstone, Kent ME15 8SJ **t** 01622 735 200 **f** 01622 735 200 **e** info@ten21.biz **w** ten21.biz Owner: Sean Kenny.

Tom Dick and Debbie Productions 43a Botley Rd, Oxford OX2 0BN **t** 01865 201564 **f** 01865 201935 **e** info@tomdickanddebbie.com **w** tomdickanddebbie.com Dir: Richard Lewis.

Torchlight Music 34 Wycombe Gardens, London NW11 8AL **t** 020 8731 9858 **f** 020 8731 9858 **e** tony@torchlightmusic.com Dir: Tony Orchudesch.

Tough Cookie Ltd 3rd Floor, 24 Denmark St, London WC2H 8NJ **t** 020 8870 9233 or 07977 248 646 **f** 0871 242 2442 **e** office@tough-cookie.co.uk **w** myspace.com/toughcookiemusic Dir: Andy Wood.

Townend Music 44 Eastwick Crescent, Rickmansworth, Herts WD3 8YJ **t** 01923 720083 or 07974 048955 **f** 01923 710587 **e** townendmus@aol.com MD: Mike Townend.

Trimmer Music 13 Outram Rd, London N22 7AB **t** 020 8881 7510 **e** trimmer@thejazzangels.fsnet.co.uk MD: Akane Abe.

Triple M Productions 31 Elmar Rd, Aigburth, Liverpool L17 0DA **t** 0151 727 7405 or 07800 993 192 **f** 0151 727 7405 **e** mike.moran@thevocalbooth.com **w** triplemproductions.mersinet.co.uk Producer/Composer: Mike Moarn.

Tsunami Sounds Ltd. Muscott House, Meadrow, Godalming, Surrey GU7 3HN **t** 01483 410100 **f** 01483 410100 **e** info@tsunami.co.uk **w** tsunami.co.uk Dir: Ken Easter.

Ultimate Unit 6 Belfont Trading Estate, Mucklow Hill, Halesowen, W Midlands B62 8DR **t** 0121 585 8001 **f** 0121 585 8003 **e** info@ultimate1.co.uk **w** ultimate1.co.uk Mgr: Andy Tain.

V-THE PRODUCTION LIBRARY

c/o Music 4 Ltd, Lower Ground, 41-42 Berners Street, London W1T 3NB **t** 020 7016 2010 **e** office@v-theproductionlibrary.com **w** v-theproductionlibrary.com. **Contemporary music library produced to commercial release standards.**

Visual Music West House, Forthaven, Shoreham-by-Sea, W. Sussex BN43 5HY **t** 01273 453 422 **f** 01273 452 914 **e** richard@longman-records.com **w** richard-durrant.com Dir: Richard Durrant.

Wavsub Music Penvose Cottage, Summers St, Lostwithiel, Cornwall PL22 0DH **t** 08700 702 265 **e** info@wavsub.com **w** wavsub.com Projects Manager: Lisa Baker.

Music Supervisors & Consultants

Abi Leland Music Supervision 1 Lonsdale Rd, London NW6 6RA **t** 020 7625 5757 or 07961 369 830 **f** 020 7625 0200 **e** abi@lelandnightingale.com MD: Abi Leland.

Air-Edel Music Supervision 18 Rodmarton St, London W1U 8BJ **t** 020 7486 6466 **f** 020 7224 0344 **e** air-edel@air-edel.co.uk Contact: Maggie Rodford & Matt Biffa.

Alice Kendall - Synch Consultant Address on request. **t** 07801 179 586 **e** alice.kendall@mac.com MD: Alice Kendall.

Anthem Ltd Long Ridge, Arrow Lane, Hartley Wintney, Hants RG27 8LR **t** 07834 766 077 **e** info@anthemltd.co.uk **w** anthemltd.co.uk Creative Director: Jonathan Painter.

CouchLife Ltd Devonshire House, 223 Upper Richmond Rd, London SW15 6SQ **t** 020 8780 0612 **f** 020 8789 8668 **e** info@couchlife.co.uk **w** couchlife.com Music Director: Rob Sawyer.

FKM PO Box 242, Haslemere, Surrey GU26 6ZT **t** 01428 608 149 **e** fken10353@aol.com Chairman: Fraser Kennedy.

Liz Gallacher Music Supervision Suite 1, Buidling 500, Shepperton Studios, Studios Rd, Shepperton, Middlesex TW17 0QD **t** 01932 577 880 **f** 01932 569 371 **e** kay@lizg.com **w** lizg.com Music Supervisor: Liz Gallacher.

Gas Music Tracking (GMT) OMC, 1st Floor, 9 Park End St, Oxford OX1 1HH **t** 01865 798791 **f** 01865 798792 **e** gmt@oxfordmusic.net Master Tracker: Dave Newton.

Graphite Media PO Box 605, Richmond TW9 2YE **t** 020 8948 8629 **e** info@graphitemedia.net **w** graphitemedia.net Dir: Ben Turner.

Green Bandana Productions / JLH Music 7 Iron Bridge House, Bridge Approach, London NW1 8BD **t** 020 7722 1081 **f** 020 7483 0028 **e** james.hyman@virgin.net **w** jameshyman.com MD: James Hyman.

Jester Song 78 Gladstone Rd, London SW19 1QT **t** 020 8543 4056 **f** 020 8542 8225 **e** jestersong@msn.com MD: R B Rogers.

Leap Music Ltd 60 Kingly St, London W1B 5DS **t** 020 7453 4011 **f** 020 7453 4242 **e** richard@leapmusic.com **w** leapmusic.com MD: Richard Kirstein.

The Music & Media Partnership Sanctuary House, 45-53 Sinclair Rd, London W14 0NS **t** 020 7300 6652 **f** 020 7300 1884 **e** firstname@tmmp.co.uk MD: Rick Blaskey.

Music Data Tracking (MDT) 282 Westbourne Park Rd, London W11 1EH **t** 020 7985 0700 **f** 020 7985 0701 **e** info@kickinmusic.com **w** kickinmusic.com Repertoire & Acquisitions: Alistair Wells.

NiceMan Productions (Licensing & Repertoire Mgmt) 111 Holden Rd, London N12 7DF **t** 020 8445 8766 **e** scott@nicemanproductions.com **w** nicemanproductions.com Licensing Dir: Scott Simons.

Pipefish Media UK The Bunk House, The Forest Inn, Hexworthy, Princetown, Devon PL20 6SD **t** 01364 631 143 or 07739 796 770 **f** 01364 631 143 **e** info@pipefishmedia.com **w** pipefishmedia.com Contact: Steve and Sarah Simpson.

The Product Exchange Ltd 68 Cranston Ave, Bexhill On Sea, E Sussex TN39 3NN **t** 01424 215 617 or 01424 215 617 **e** music@productexchange.co.uk **w** productexchange.co.uk MD: Frank Rodgers.

Record-Play Consultants Studio 203, 45-46 Charlotte Rd, London EC2A 3PD **t** 020 7193 9792 or 07753 388 275 **e** info@record-play.com **w** record-play.com Prop: Daniel Cross.

RICALL LIMITED

ricall
music. we get it.

First Floor, 14 Buckingham Palace Road, London SW1W 0QP **t** 020 7592 1710 **f** 020 7592 1713 **e** marketing@ricall.com **w** ricall.com MD, Investor Relations: Richard Corbett. Account Support: Kate Carne-Ross (accountsupport@ricall.com). Music Research: Lou Rigolli (research@ricall.com). Music Licensing: Joan Eades (licensing@ricall.com). Copyright Acquisition: Paul Lynton (copyright@ricall.com). Media Relations: Jennifer Kersis (pr@ricall.com). **Ricall is the world's leading music marketplace for synch licensing connecting more than 3,500 record companies and 22,000 publishers directly to over 1,500 companies representing over 10,000 brands.**

Richard Thomas - Music Consultant 42 Geraldine Rd, London SW18 2NT **t** 020 8870 2701 **e** richtt123@yahoo.co.uk Contact: Richard Thomas.

Right Music Old Church Cottage, Wilby, Suffolk IP21 5LE **t** 01379 388 365 **f** 01379 384 731 **e** kirsten@rightmusic.co.uk **w** rightmusic.co.uk MD: Kirsten Lane.

Search (a division of Jeff Wayne Music Group) Oliver House, 8-9 Ivor Pl, London NW1 6BY **t** 020 7724 2471 **f** 020 7724 6245 **e** info@jeffwaynemusic.com **w** jeffwaynemusic.com Group Dir: Jane Jones.

searchtheyukon.com Utopia Village, Chalcot Rd, Primrose Hill, London NW1 8LH **t** 020 7242 8408 **e** music@theyukonmusic.com MD: Andrew Maurice.

Soundtree Music Unit 124, Canalot Studios, 222 Kensal Rd, London W10 5BN **t** 020 8968 1449 **f** 020 8968 1500 **e** post@soundtree.co.uk **w** soundtree.co.uk GM: Jay James.

Spark Marketing Entertainment 16 Winton Ave, London N11 2AT **t** 0870 460 5439 **e** mbauss@spark-me.com **w** spark-me.com Executive Director: Matthias Bauss.

Squarepeg Music Consultancy Studio 201, Westbourne Studios, 242 Acklam Rd, London W10 5JJ **t** 020 7575 3325 **f** 020 7575 3326 **e** info@squarepeg-uk.com **w** squarepeg-uk.com MD: Matt Fisher.

Synchronicity 28 Howard House, 161 Cleveland St, London W1T 6QP **t** 020 7388 2099 or 07976 743 081 **e** jp@synchronicity.uk.com **w** synchronicity.uk.com MD: Joanna Pearson.

Upside Productions (Music Consultancy) 14 Clarence Mews, Balham, London SW12 9SR **t** 020 8673 8549 **f** 020 8673 8498 **e** simon@upsideuk.com Co MDs: Simon Jones & Denise Beighton.

Urban Consultants 51A Woodville Rd, Thornton Heath, Surrey CR7 8LN **t** 07956 368 680 **e** R.Pascoe@RPMan.co.uk **w** myspace.com/rpmanagement Contact: Richard Pascoe.

Ray Williams Music Consultant The Stable Lodge, Lime Ave, Kingwood, Henley-on-Thames, Oxon RG9 5WB **t** 01491 628 111 or 07813 696 999 **f** 01491 629 668 **e** crumbsmusic@btopenworld.com **w** raywilliamsmusic.com MD: Ray Williams.

Retail

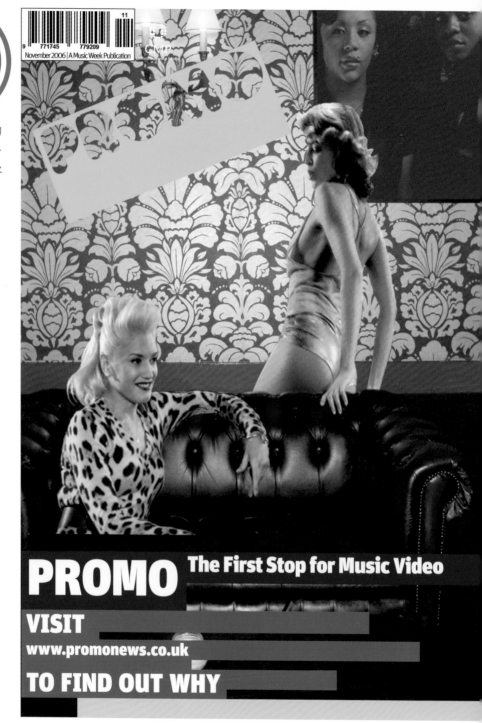

November 2006 | A Music Week Publication

Retail

PROMO The First Stop for Music Video

VISIT

www.promonews.co.uk

TO FIND OUT WHY

Retail:

Retailers

2Funky 62 Belgrave Gate, Leicester LE1 3GQ
t 0116 299 0700 **f** 0116 299 0077 **e** shop@2-funky.co.uk
w 2-funky.co.uk Mgr: Vijay Mistry.

3 Beat Records 5 Slater St, Liverpool L1 4BW
t 0151 709 3355 **f** 0151 709 3707 **e** info@3beat.co.uk
w 3beat.co.uk Shop Mgr: Pezz.

8 Ball 18 Queen St, Southwell, Notts NG25 0AA
t 01636 813040 **f** 01636 813141 **e** info@8ball.ltd.uk
w 8ball.ltd.uk Prop: Tim Allsopp.

23rd Precinct 23 Bath St, Glasgow G2 1HU
t 0141 332 4806 **f** 0141 353 3039 **e** billy@23rdprecinct.co.uk
w 23rdprecinct.co.uk Dirs: Billy Kiltie, David Yeats.

A&A Music 15 Bridge St, Congleton, Cheshire CW12 1AS
t 01260 280778 **f** 01260 298311 **e** mail@aamusic.co.uk
w aamusic.co.uk Owner: Alan Farrar.

Aardvark Music Compton House, 9 Totnes Rd, Paignton,
Devon TQ2 5BY **t** 01803 664481 **f** 01803 664481
e cj@torrerecords.freeserve.co.uk Co-owner: Clive Jones.

Abergavenny Music 23 Cross St, Abergavenny, Gwent
NP7 5EW **t** 01873 853394 **e** service@abergavennymusic.com
w abergavennymusic.com Owner: James Joseph.

Acorn Music 3 Glovers Walk, Yeovil, Somerset BA20 1LH
t 01935 425 503 Owner: Chris Lowe.

Action Records 46 Church St, Preston, Lancs PR1 3DH
t 01772 884 772 or 01772 258809 **f** 01772 252 255
e sales@actionrecords.co.uk **w** actionrecords.co.uk
Mgr: Gordon Gibson.

Action Replay 24 Lake Rd, Bowness-on-Windermere,
Cumbria LA23 3AP **t** 01539 445 089
e davidsnaith@actionreplay.wanadoo.co.uk Owner: David Snaith.

Adrians 36-38 High St, Wickford, Essex SS12 9AZ
t 01268 733 318 or 01268 733 319 **f** 01268 764 507
e sales@adrians.co.uk **w** adrians.co.uk Contact: Adrian Rondeau.

AG Kemble Ltd 63 Leicester Rd, Wigston, Leics. LE18 1NR
t 0116 288 1557 **f** 0116 288 3949
e kembles-records@btconnect.com
Owners: Paul Watkins & Fiona Nicholls.

All Ages Records 27a Pratt St, London NW1 0BG
t 020 7267 0393 **e** shop@allagesrecords.com
w allagesrecords.com GM: Nick Collins.

Andy Cash Music 596 Kingsbury Rd, Erdington,
Birmingham B24 9PJ **t** 0121 384 1424
e andy.cash@btconnect.com Owner: Andy Cash.

Asda Southbank, Great Wilson St, Leeds, W Yorks LS11 5AD
t 0113 241 8470 or 0113 243 5435 **f** 0113 241 8785
e tbrunto@asda.co.uk **w** asda.co.uk
Marketing Manager: Tracy Brunton.

Audiosonic 6 College St, Gloucester, Glos. GL1 2NE
t 01452 302 280 **f** 01452 302 202 **e** music@audiosonic.co.uk
w audiosonic.uk.com Owner: Sylvia Parker.

Avalanche Records (Head Office) 63 Cockburn St,
Edinburgh EH1 1BS **t** 0131 225 3939 **f** 0131 225 3939
e avalanche634reps@btconnect.com **w** avalancherecords.co.uk
Owner: Kevin Buckle.

Avid Records 32-33 The Triangle, Bournemouth BH2 5SE
t 01202 295465 **f** 01202 295465 **e** paul@avidrecords-uk.com
w avidrecords-uk.com Owner: Martin Howes.

Badlands 11 St George's Pl, Cheltenham, Glos GL50 3LA
t 01242 227724 **f** 01242 227393 **e** shop@badlands.co.uk
w badlands.co.uk MD: Philip Jump.

Bailey's Records 40 Bull Ring Indoor Market, Edgbaston St,
Birmingham, W Midlands B5 4RQ **t** 0121 622 6899
f 0121 622 6899 **w** birminghamindoormarket.co.uk
Mgr: David Rock.

Banquet Records 52 Eden St, Kingston-upon-Thames
KT1 1EE **t** 020 8549 5871 **e** info@banquetrecords.com
w banquetrecords.com Owner: Dave Jarvis.

Barneys 21A Cross Keys, Market Sq, St Neots PE19 2AR
t 01480 406270 **f** 01480 406270
e keith.barnes2@btinternet.com Contact: Keith Barnes.

The Basement 7 North St, Carrickfergus, Co Antrim
BT38 7AQ **t** 028 9336 3678 **e** carrick@basementni.com
w basementni.com Owner: Phil Barnhill.

Bath Compact Discs 11 Broad St, Bath BA1 5LJ
t 01225 464766 **f** 01225 482275 **e** Bathcds@btinternet.com
w bathcds.btinternet.co.uk Co-owner: Steve Macallister.

Beanos Ltd 7 Middle St, Croydon, Surrey CR0 1RE
t 020 8680 1202 **f** 020 8680 1203 **e** david@beanos.co.uk
w beanos.co.uk MD: David Lashmar.

Beatin Rhythm Records 42 Tib St, Manchester M4 1LA
t 0161 834 7783 **e** music@beatinrhythm.com
w beatinrhythm.com Dir: Tom Smith.

The Beatmuseum Block 130, Unit 4, Nasmyth Rd South,
Hillington, Glasgow G52 4RE **t** 0141 882 4445
f 0141 882 8563 **e** james@beatmuseum.com
w beatmuseum.com Contact: James Rennie.

Bigshot Records 53a Harpur St, Bedford, Beds. MK40 2SR
t 01234 355542 **f** 01234 355542 **e** info@bigshotrecords.com
w bigshotrecords.com Mgr: Hayley Syratt.

Bim Bam Records Chalfont House, Botley Rd, Horton Heath,
Eastleigh SO50 7DN **t** 02380 600329 **f** 02380 600329
e bob@bim-bam.com **w** bim-bam.com Owner: Bob Thomas.

Black Market Records 25 D'Arblay St, London W1F 8EJ
t 020 7287 1932 or 020 7437 0478 **f** 020 7494 1303
e shop@blackmarket.co.uk MD: David Piccioni.

Blackwell's Music Shop Beaver House, Hythe Bridge St,
Oxford OX1 2ET **t** 01865 333580 **f** 01865 790937
e vanessa.williams@blackwell.co.uk **w** blackwell.co.uk
Music Manager: Vanessa Williams.

Boogietimes Records 3 Old Mill Parade, Victoria Rd, Romford, Essex RM1 2HU **t** 01708 727029 **f** 01708 740424 **e** info@boogietimes-records.co.uk **w** boogietimes-records.co.uk Mgr: Andy James.

Borders Books, Music & Video 4th Floor, 122 Charing Cross Rd, London WC2 0JR **t** 020 7379 7313 **f** 020 7836 0373 **w** bordersstores.co.uk.

Bridport Record Centre 33A South St, Bridport, Dorset DT6 3NY **t** 01308 425707 **f** 01308 458271 **e** bridrec@btinternet.com **w** bridportrecordcentre.co.uk Owners: Piers & Stephanie Garner.

Carbon Music 33-38 Kensington High St, London W8 4PF **t** 020 7373 9911 **f** 020 7938 2952 **e** info@carbonmusic.com **w** carbonmusic.com CEO: Jan Mehmet.

Catapult 100% Vinyl 22, High Street Arcade, Cardiff CF10 1BB **t** 029 2022 8990 or 029 2034 2322 **f** 029 2023 1690 **e** enquiries@catapult.co.uk **w** catapult.co.uk Prop: Lucy Squire.

Chalky's 78 High St, Banbury, Oxon. OX16 5JG **t** 01295 271190 **f** 01295 262221 **e** richard@chalkys.com MD: Richard White.

Changes One 58 Denham Drive, Seaton Delaval, Whitley Bay, Tyne & Wear NE25 0JY **t** 0191 237 0251 **f** 0191 298 0903 **e** ian@changesone.co.uk **w** changesone.co.uk Owner: Ian Tunstall.

Citysounds Ltd 5 Kirby St, London EC1N 8TS **t** 020 7405 5454 **f** 020 7242 1863 **e** sales@city-sounds.co.uk **w** city-sounds.co.uk Owners: Tom & Dave.

Clerkenwell Music 27 Exmouth Market, London EC1R 4QL **t** 020 7833 9757 **e** jeremy@clerkenwellmusic.co.uk Owner: Jeremy Brill.

CODA Music 12 Bank St, Edinburgh EH1 2LN **t** 0131 622 7246 **f** 0131 622 7245 **e** enquiries@codamusic.demon.co.uk **w** codamusic.co.uk Co-owner: Dougie Anderson.

Compact Discounts 258-260 Lavender Hill, Battersea, London SW11 1LJ **t** 020 7978 5560 **f** 020 7978 5931 **e** info@compactdiscounts.co.uk **w** compactdiscounts.co.uk Dir: Mark Canavan.

Concepts 4A Framwellgate Bridge, Durham DH1 4SJ **t** 0191 383 0745 **f** 0191 383 0112 **e** dave-murray@lineone.net **w** concepts-durham.co.uk Owner: Dave Murray.

Connect Records 18 Badger Rd, Coventry CV3 2PU **t** 024 7626 5400 **e** info@connect-records.com **w** connect-records.com Mgr: Matt Green.

Coolwax Music Unit 13, The Craft Centre, Orchard Sq Shopping Centre, Sheffield S1 2FB **t** 0114 279 5878 **e** staff@coolwax.co.uk **w** coolwax.co.uk Mgr: Corey Mahoney.

Counter Culture 130 Desborough Rd, High Wycombe, Bucks HP11 2PU **t** 01494 463 366 **f** 01494 463 366 **e** counterculture1@btconnect.com Owner: Cheryl Evans.

Crash Records 35 The Headrow, Leeds, W Yorks LS1 6PU **t** 0113 243 6743 **f** 0113 234 0421 **e** store@crashrecords.co.uk **w** crashrecords.co.uk Prop: Ian De-Whytell.

Crazy Beat Records 87 Corbets Tey Rd, Upminster, Essex RM14 2AH **t** 01708 228678 **f** 01708 640946 **e** sales@crazybeat.co.uk **w** crazybeat.co.uk Owner: Gary Dennis.

Crucial Music Pinery Buildings, Highmoor, Wigton, Cumbria CA7 9LW **t** 016973 45422 **f** 016973 45422 **e** simon@crucialmusic.co.uk **w** crucialmusic.co.uk MD: Simon James.

Cruisin' Records 132 Welling High St, Welling, Kent DA16 1TJ **t** 020 8304 5853 **f** 020 8304 0429 **e** john@cruisin-records.fsnet.co.uk **w** cruisinrecords.com Owner: John Setford.

Dance 2 Records 9 Woodbridge Rd, Guildford, Surrey GU1 4PU **t** 01483 451002 **f** 01483 451006 **e** in2dance2@hotmail.com **w** dance2.co.uk MD: Hans Vind.

Disc-N-Tape 17 Gloucester Rd, Bishopston, Bristol BS7 8AA **t** 0117 942 2227 **f** 0117 942 2227 **e** graeme@disc-n-tape.co.uk **w** disc-n-tape.co.uk Owner: Graeme Cornish.

Discount Disc 21 Percy St, Hanley, Stoke-on-Trent, Staffs ST1 1NA **t** 01782 266888 **f** 01782 266888 **e** discountdisc@talk21.com **w** discountdisc.co.uk Mgr: Ian Trigg.

Discurio Unit 3, Faraday Way, St Mary's Cray, Kent BR5 3QW **t** 01689 879101 **f** 01689 879101 **e** discurio1@aol.com **w** discurio.com Mgr: Jonathan Mitchell.

Diskits 7 Outram St, Sutton-in-Ashfield, Notts NG17 4BA **t** 01623 441413 or 01623 466220 **f** 01623 441413 **e** shop@diskits.co.uk **w** diskits.co.uk Ptnr: Mel Vickers.

Disky.com 3 York St, St. Helier, Jersey, Channel Islands JE2 3RQ **t** 01534 509 687 **e** music.online@disky.com **w** disky.com MD: Robert Bisson.

Disque Ltd 11 Chapel Market, Islington, London N1 9EZ **t** 020 7833 1104 **f** 020 7278 4895 **e** info@disque.co.uk **w** disque.co.uk MD: Ed Davies.

Dixons Stores Group Maylands Ave, Hemel Hempstead, Herts HP2 7TG **t** 01442 888653 **f** 01442 353127 **e** dave.poulter@dixons.co.uk **w** dixons.co.uk Cat Mgr, DVD Software: Dave Poulter.

Dolphin Discs 56 Moore St, Dublin 1, Ireland **t** +353 1 872 9364 **f** +353 1 872 0405 **e** irishmus@iol.ie **w** irelandcd.com GM: Paul Heffernan.

Dub Vendor Records 17 Davids Rd, London SE23 3EP **t** 020 8291 6253 **f** 020 8291 1097 **e** distribution@dubvendor.co.uk **w** dubvendor.co.uk MD: John MacGillivray.

Earwaves Records 9/11 Paton St, Piccadilly, Manchester M1 2BA **t** 0161 236 4022 **f** 0161 237 5932 **e** info@earwavesrecords.co.uk **w** earwavesrecords.co.uk Prop: Alan Lacy.

Eastern Bloc Records 5-6 Central Buildings, Oldham St, Manchester M1 1JQ **t** 0161 228 6432 **f** 0161 228 6728 **e** info@easternblocrecords.co.uk **w** easternblocrecords.co.uk Mgr: John Berry.

The Energy 106 Store 63 High St, Belfast, Co Antrim BT1 2JZ **t** 028 9033 3122 or 028 9032 07780 **f** 028 9033 3122 **e** cd.heaven@btclick.com Mgr: Paul Chapman.

Esprit International Limited Esprit House, 5 Railway Sidings, Meopham, Kent DA13 0YS **t** 01474 815010 or 01474 815099 **f** 01474 815030 or 01474 814414 **e** sales@eil.com **w** eil.com MD: Robert Croydon.

Essential Music 16 The Market, Greenwich, London SE10 9HZ **t** 020 8293 4982 **f** 020 8293 4982 **e** essmusco@aol.com Owner: Neil Williams.

Eukatech Records 49 Endell St, Covent Garden, London WC2H 9AJ **t** 020 7240 8060 **f** 020 7379 4939 **e** shop@eukatechrecords.com **w** eukatechrecords.com Mgr: Rory Viggers.

FAB Music 55 The Broadway, Crouch End, London N8 8DT **t** 020 8347 6767 **f** 020 8348 3270 **e** fab@fabmusic.co.uk Dirs: Mal Page, Kevin Payne.

Fat City Records 20 Oldham St, Manchester M1 1JN **t** 0161 237 1181 **f** 0161 236 9304 **e** shop@fatcity.co.uk **w** fatcity.co.uk Mgr: Paul Watson.

Fives 22 Broadway, Leigh-On-Sea, Essex SS9 1AW **t** 01702 711629 **f** 01702 712737 **e** peter@fives-records.co.uk **w** fives-records.co.uk Mgr: Pete Taylor.

Flashback 50 Essex Rd, London N1 8LR **t** 020 7354 9356 **f** 020 7354 9358 **e** mark@flashback.co.uk **w** flashback.co.uk Owner: Mark Burgess.

Flip Records 2 Mardol, Shrewsbury SY1 1PY **t** 01743 244 469 **f** 01743 260 985 **e** sales@fliprecords.co.uk **w** fliprecords.co.uk Owner: Duncan Morris.

Flying Records 94 Dean St, London W1D 3TA **t** 020 7734 0172 **f** 020 7287 0766 **e** info@flyingrecords.com **w** flyingrecords.com Mgr: Anthony Cox.

Fopp Ltd Head Office, 19 Union St, Glasgow G1 3RB **t** 0141 222 2128 **e** info@fopp.co.uk **w** fopp.co.uk.

Forest Records 7, Earley Court, High St, Lymington, Hampshire SO41 9EP **t** 01590 676 588 **f** 01590 612 162 **e** forestrec@btconnect.com Buyer: Neil Hutson.

Forsyth Brothers 126 Deansgate, Manchester M3 2GR **t** 0161 834 3281 **f** 0161 834 0630 **e** info@forsyths.co.uk **w** forsyths.co.uk Dept. Mgr, Recorded Music: Audrey Wilson.

45s Record Shop 64 Northgate St, Gloucester GL1 1SL **t** 01452 309445 **f** 01452 309445 **e** chrismanna@onetel.net.uk Contact: Chris Manna.

Gatefield Sounds 70 High St, Whitstable, Kent CT5 1BB **t** 01227 263 337 MD: Mike Winch.

Gee CDs 5 Home St, Tollcross, Edinburgh EH3 9LZ **t** 0131 228 2022 **e** sales@geecds.co.uk **w** gee-cds.co.uk.

Global Groove Records Global House, 13 Bucknall New Rd, Hanley, Stoke-on-Trent, Staffs ST1 2BA **t** 01782 215 554 or 01782 207 234 **f** 01782 201 698 **e** mail@globalgroove.co.uk **w** globalgroove.co.uk Mgr: Dan.

Golden Disc Group 11 Windsor Pl, Pembroke St, Dublin 2 **t** +353 1 676 8444 **f** +353 1 676 8565 **e** info@goldendiscs.ie **w** goldendiscs.ie.

Good Vibrations Records 54 Howard St, Belfast, Co Antrim BT1 6PG **t** 028 9058 2250 **f** 028 9058 2252 **w** goodvibrations.ie MD: Terri Hooley.

Hits 10 The Arcade, Station Rd, Redhill, Surrey RH1 1PA **t** 01737 773565 **f** 01737 773565 Contact: Brian Hawkins.

HMV Group plc Shelley House, 2-4 York Rd, Maidenhead, Berks SL6 1SR **t** 01628 818300 **f** 01628 818301 **e** firstname.lastname@hmvgroup.com **w** hmv.co.uk CEO: Alan Giles.

HMV UK Ltd Film House, 142 Wardour St, London W1F 8LN **t** 020 7432 2000 **f** 020 7434 1090 **e** firstname.lastname@hmv.co.uk **w** hmv.co.uk.

Honest Jon's Records 278 Portobello Rd, London W10 5TE **t** 020 8969 9822 **f** 020 8969 5395 **e** mail@honestjons.com **w** honestjons.com.

HW Audio (Sound & Lighting) 180-198 St Georges Rd, Bolton, Lancs BL1 2PH **t** 01204 385199 **f** 01204 364057 **e** sales@hwaudio.co.uk **w** hwaudio.co.uk Sales Dir: Richard Harfield.

Impulse Music Travel Ltd Unit 3, Campus Five, Letchworth, Herts SG6 2JF **t** 01462 677227 **f** 01462 480169 **e** firstname.lastname@imtl.co.uk **w** impulseonline.co.uk Audio Buyer: Andy Lazarewicz.

J Sainsbury 33 Holborn, London EC1N 2HT **t** 020 7695 4295 **f** 020 7695 4295 **e** julian.monaghan@sainsburys.co.uk **w** sainsbury.co.uk Music Manager: Julian Monaghan.

Jacks Records Unit 1, Aberdeen Court, 95-97 Division St, Sheffield S1 4GE **t** 0114 276 6356 **e** sales@jacksrecords.idps.co.uk **w** jacksrecords.free-online.co.uk Owner: Ian Gadsby.

Jibbering Records 136 Alcester Rd, Moseley, Birmingham B13 8EE **t** 0121 449 4551 **e** contact@jibberingrecords.com **w** jibberingrecords.com Owner: Dan Raffety.

JMF Records 86 High St, Invergordon, Ross-shire IV18 0DL **t** 01349 853369 **f** 01349 853369 **e** jmfrecords@hotmail.com **w** jmfrecords.co.uk Mgr: James Fraser.

Jumbo Records 5-6 St Johns Centre, Leeds, W Yorks LS2 8LQ **t** 0113 245 5570 **f** 0113 242 5019 **e** hunter@jumborecords.fsnet.co.uk **w** jumborecords.co.uk Partners: Hunter Smith, Lornette Smith.

June Emerson Wind Music Windmill Farm, Ampleforth, York YO62 4HF **t** 01439 788324 **f** 01439 788715 **e** JuneEmerson@compuserve.com Prop: June Emerson.

Kane's Records 14 Kendrick St, Stroud, Glocs. GL5 1AA **t** 01453 766 886 **f** 01453 755 377 **e** sales@kanesrecords.com **w** kanesrecords.com Owner: Kane Jones.

Kingbee Records 519 Wilbraham Rd, Chorlton-Cum-Hardy, Manchester M21 0UF **t** 0161 860 4762 **f** 0161 860 4762 **e** kingbeerecords@lycos.co.uk Contact: Les Hare.

Know How Records 3 Buck St, London NW1 8NJ **t** 020 7267 1526 **f** 020 7267 1526 **e** info@knowhowrecords.co.uk **w** knowhowrecords.co.uk Buyer/Owner: Martin Audio.

Langland Records 2 Bell St, Wellington, Shropshire TF1 1LS **t** 01952 244 845 Owner: Ian Bridgewater.

The Left Legged Pineapple 24-25 Churchgate, Loughborough, Leics. LE11 1UD **t** 01509 210130 or 01509 236791 **f** 01509 210106 **e** pineapple@left-legged.com **w** left-legged.com Owner: Jason White.

Lewks Music & Movies 3 Wales Court, Downham Market, Norfolk PE38 9JZ **t** 01366 383762 **f** 01366 383544 **e** admin@lewks.co.uk **w** lewks.co.uk.

Loco Records 5 Church St, Chatham, Kent ME4 4BS **t** 01634 818330 **f** 01634 880321 **e** info@locomusic.co.uk **w** locomusic.co.uk Owner: Gary Turner.

Longplayer 3 Grosvenor Rd, Tunbridge Wells, Kent TN1 2AH **t** 01892 539273 **f** 01892 516770 **e** shop@longplayer.fsnet.co.uk **w** longplayer.co.uk Owner: Ali Furmidge.

Main Street Music 11 Smithfield Centre, Leek, Staffs ST13 5JW **t** 01538 384 315 **e** mike@demon655.freeserve.co.uk.

Malcolm's Musicland Baptist Chapel, Chapel St, Chorley, Lancs PR7 1BW **t** 01257 264 362 **f** 01257 267 636 **e** sales@cdvideo.co.uk **w** cdvideo.co.uk Prop: Malcolm Allen.

MDC Classic Music Ltd 124 Camden High St, London NW1 0LU **t** 020 7485 4777 **f** 020 7482 6888 **e** info@mdcmusic.co.uk **w** mdcmusic.co.uk Dir: Alan Goulden.

Millenium Music 16-18 The Arcade, Oakhampton, Devon EX20 1EX **t** 01837 659249 **e** milleniummusic@btopenworld.com **w** millenium-music.net Owner: Richard Appleby.

Mixmaster Records Market Sq, Castlebar, Co Mayo, Ireland **t** +353 94 23732 **f** +353 94 23732 **e** mixmaster@eircom.net Owner: Pat Concannon.

Morning After Music Llyfnant House Shop, 22 Penrallt St, Machynlleth, Powys SY20 8AJ **t** 01654 703767 Propietor: Malcolm Hume.

WM Morrisons Supermarkets plc Wakefield 41 Industrial Est., Wakefield, W Yorks WF2 0XF **t** 01924 870000 **f** 01924 875300 Home & Leisure Dir: Andrew Pleasance.

Mr Redeye Unit 66, 4th Ave, Brixton Village, London SW9 8PS **t** 020 7737 0800 **e** info@mrredeye.com **w** mrredeye.com Co-owner: Carlos Northon.

MSM Recordstore 1st Floor, 17 Chalk Farm Rd, London NW1 8AG **t** 020 7284 2527 **f** 020 7284 2504 **e** info@msmrecordstore.co.uk **w** msmrecordstore.co.uk MD: Des Carr.

The Music AID Store **e** retail@musicaid.org **w** musicaid.org.

The Music Box 13 Market Pl, Wallingford, Oxon OX10 0AD **t** 01491 836269 **e** info@themusicbox.net Owner: Richard Strange.

Music City Ltd 122 New Cross Rd, London SE14 5BA **t** 020 7277 9657 **f** 0870 7572004 **e** info@musiccity.co.uk **w** musiccity.co.uk Store Mgr: Nick Kemp.

Music Room 8 North St, Sandwich, Isle of Lewis, Outer Hebrides HS2 0AD **t** 07754 614498 **e** karen@celticmusicroom.com **w** celticmusicroom.com Contact: John Clarke.

The Music Room St.John's Works, St. John's Pl, Cleckheaton, W Yorks BD19 3RR **t** 01274 879 768 **f** 01274 852 280 **e** info@the-music-room.com **w** the-music-room.com Shop Mgr: Terry Evans.

Music World The Old Armistice, 31 Hart St, Henley-On-Thames, Oxon RG9 2AR **t** 01491 572700 **e** musicworldhenley@aol.com Owner: Dave Smith.

Music Zone Direct Music Zone House, Heapriding Business Pk, Ford St, Chestergate, Stockport, Cheshire SK3 0BT **t** 0161 477 5088 **f** 0161 477 5082 **e** enquiries@musiczone.co.uk **w** musiczone.co.uk Head of Buying: Andy Flint.

Musicbank 5 Station Way, Cheam Village, Surrey SM3 8SD **t** 020 8643 2869 **f** 020 8643 3092 Contact: Robert Bush.

Noise Annoys 53 Howard St, Sheffield S1 2LW **t** 0114 276 9177 **f** 0114 276 9177 **e** sales@noise-annoys.co.uk **w** noise-annoys.co.uk Mgr: Simon Baxter.

One Up 17 Belmont St, Aberdeen AB10 1JR **t** 01224 642662 **f** 01224 646560 **e** office@oneupmusic.com Ptnr: Raymond Bird.

Pelicanneck Records 74-76 High St, Manchester M4 1ES **t** 0161 834 2569 **f** 0161 236 3351 **e** mailboy@boomkat.com **w** boomkat.com Owner: Shlom Sviri.

Pendulum Records 34 Market Pl, Melton Mowbray, Leics LE13 1XD **t** 01664 565025 **f** 01664 560310 **e** mw@pendulum-records.co.uk **w** pendulum-records.co.uk Owner: Mike Eden.

Phonica Records 51 Poland St, London W1F 7NG **t** 020 7025 6070 **e** simon@vinylfactory.co.uk **w** phonicarecords.co.uk Mgr: Simon Rigg.

Piccadilly Records Unit G9, Smithfield Buildings, 53 Oldham St, Manchester M1 1JR **t** 0161 834 8888 or 0161 834 8789 **f** 0161 839 8008 **e** mail@piccadillyrecords.com **w** piccadillyrecords.com MD: John Kerfoot.

Pied Piper Records 293 Wellingborough Rd, Northampton NN1 4EW **t** 01604 624777 **f** 01604 624777 **e** piedpiperrecords@aol.com **w** pied-piper-records.co.uk Prop: Nick Hamlyn.

Pinpoint Music 44a Market St, Eastleigh, Hants SO50 5RA **t** 023 8064 2559 **f** 023 8032 6100 **e** cdsales@pinpoint-music.co.uk **w** pinpoint-music.co.uk Mgr: Drew.

Planet of Sound (Scotland) 236 High St, Ayr, South Ayrshire KA7 1RN **t** 01292 265913 **f** 01292 265493 **e** planet-of-sound@btconnect.com Mgr: Ian Hollins.

Popscene 97 High St, Cosham, Hants PO6 3AZ **t** 023 9242 8042 **f** 023 9279 2355 **e** enquiries@popsceneuk.com **w** popsceneuk.com Owner: Chris Lovett.

Prelude Records 25B Giles St, Norwich NR2 1JN **t** 01603 628319 **f** 01603 620170 **e** admin@preluderecords.co.uk **w** preluderecords.co.uk Ptnr: Andrew Cane.

Premier Record Stores 3-5 Smithfield Sq, Belfast, Co Antrim BT1 1JE **t** 028 9024 0896 **f** 028 9027 8868 Contact: Ciarna McBurney.

Probe Records 9 Slater St, Liverpool, Merseyside L1 4BW
t 0151 708 8815 **f** 0151 709 7121
e probe-records@btconnect.com **w** probe-records.com
Owner: Anne Davies.

Providence Music 1 St Georges Rd, Bristol BS1 5UL
t 0117 9276536 **f** 0117 9276680
e shop@providencemusic.co.uk **w** providencemusic.co.uk
Mgr: Ruth Hopton.

Pure Groove Records 649 Holloway Rd, London N19 5SE
t 020 7281 4877 **f** 020 7263 5590 **e** info@puregroove.co.uk
w puregroove.co.uk Buyers: Ziad Nashnush / Paul Christian.

Quirk's Records 29 Church St, Ormskirk, Lancs L39 3AG
t 01695 570570 **f** 01695 570519 **e** quirks@email.com
w quirks.co.uk Ptnr: Paul Quirk.

Range Records & Tapes 61 High St, Brownhills, W
Midlands WS8 6HH **t** 01543 374299 **f** 01543 374299
e paul@rangerecords.com **w** rangerecords.com
Prop: Paul Whitehouse.

Rapture Records 37-38 St John's St, Colchester, Essex
CO2 7AD **t** 01206 542541 **f** 01206 542546
e john@rapturerecords.com **w** rapturerecords.com
Prop: John Parkhurst.

Ray's Jazz at Foyles 1st Floor, 113-119 Charing Cross Rd,
London WC2H 0EB **t** 020 7440 3205 **e** paul@foyles.co.uk
w foyles.com Mgr: Paul Pace.

Record Corner Pound Lane, Godalming, Surrey GU7 1BX
t 01483 422006 **e** info@therecordcorner.co.uk
w therecordcorner.co.uk Prop: Tom Briggs.

Record Sleeve Longwalk Shopping Centre, Dundalk, Co
Louth, Ireland **t** +353 42 932 7374 **f** +353 42 933 2404
e enquiries@therecordsleeve.com **w** therecordsleeve.com.

Record Village 8 Cole St, Scunthorpe, North Lincs.
DN15 6QZ **t** 01724 851048 **f** 01724 280582
e sales@recordvillage.co.uk **w** recordvillage.co.uk
Prop.: Dave Greaves.

Recordstore.co.uk Unit 5, Waldo Works, Waldo Rd, London
NW10 6AW **t** 020 8964 9020 **f** 020 8964 9090
e simon.coates@recordstore.co.uk **w** recordstore.co.uk
GM: Simon Coates.

Reflex 23 Nun St, Newcastle upon Tyne NE1 5AG
t 0191 260 3246 **f** 0191 260 3245 **e** info@reflexcd.co.uk
w reflexcd.co.uk Owner: Alan Jourdan.

Reform Ltd Easton Buildings, Little Castle St, Exeter, Devon
EX4 3PX **t** 01392 435577 **f** 01392 435577
e enquiries@reform-records.co.uk **w** reform-records.co.uk.

Release The Groove Records 20 Denman St, London
W1D 7HR **t** 020 7734 7712 **f** 020 7734 7713
e sales@easyvinyl.com **w** easyvinyl.com
Managing Directors: Gary Dillon, Dean Savonne.

Replay Records Stall 18 Indoor Market, Tunstall, Stoke On
Trent, Staffs ST6 5TP **t** 01782 823456
e mack937@btinternet.com Prop: Brian Mack.

Replay 73 Park St, Bristol BS1 5PF **t** 0117 904 1134 or
0117 904 1135 **e** bristol@replay.co.uk **w** replay.co.uk
Mgr: Bob Jones.

**For all the latest
directory listings visit
www.musicweekdirectory.com**

Retail: Retailers

Reveal Records 63 St Peters St, Derby, Derbyshire DE1 2AB
t 01332 349 242 **f** 01332 349 141 **e** tomreveal@mac.com
w revealrecords.com MD: Tom Rose.

Rhythm & Rhyme Records 9 High St, Launceston,
Cornwall PL15 8ER **t** 01566 772774 **f** 01566 775668
e chris@rrrecords.co.uk **w** rrrecords.co.uk Owner: Chris Parsons.

R&K Records 8 Clinton Arms Court, Newark, Notts
NG24 1EB **t** 01636 702653 **f** 01636 702653
e rkrecords@hotmail.com Prop: Richard Young.

Roadkill Records 89 Oldham St, Manchester M4 1LW
t 0161 832 4444 **e** info@roadkill-records.com
w roadkill-records.com Mgr: Liam Stewart.

Rock Box 151 London Rd, Camberley, Surrey GU15 3JY
t 01276 26628 **f** 01276 678776 **e** mailorder@rockbox.co.uk
w rockbox.co.uk Owner: Alan Bush.

Rough Trade 130 Talbot Rd, London W11 1JA
t 020 7229 8541 or 020 7221 3066 **f** 020 7221 1146
e shop@roughtrade.com **w** roughtrade.com Contact: Nigel House.

Rounder Records 19 Brighton Sq, Brighton, E Sussex
BN1 1HD **t** 01273 325 440 **f** 01273 776 991
e philshop@btconnect.com Mgr: Johnny Hartford.

Rub A Dub 35 Howard St, Glasgow, Lanarkshire G1 4BA
t 0141 221 9657 **f** 0141 221 9650 **e** info@rubadub.co.uk
w rubadub.co.uk Ptnr: Dan Lurinsky.

Seaford Music 24 Pevensey Rd, Eastbourne, E. Sussex
BN21 3HP **t** 01323 732553 **f** 01323 417455
e mail@seaford-music.co.uk **w** seaford-music.co.uk.

Seeds Records 7 Oxton Rd, Charing Cross, Birkenhead
CH41 2QQ **t** 0151 653 4224 **f** 0151 653 3223
e lee@seedsrecords.co.uk **w** seedsrecords.co.uk Mgr: Lee Hessler.

Selectadisc 21 Market St, Nottingham NG1 6HX
t 0115 947 5420 **f** 0115 941 4261 Owner: Brian Selby.

Sellanby 245 Northolt Rd, South Harrow, Middx. HA2 8HR
t 020 8864 2622 Owners: David & Peter Smith.

Sho'nuff...Beatz Workin' 86 Main St, Bangor, Co. Down
BT20 4AG **t** 028 9147 7926 **f** 028 9147 7927
e steve@shonuff.co.uk **w** shonuff.co.uk Owner: Steve McDowell.

Silverback Records 40 Bloomsbury Way, London
WC1A 2SA **t** 020 7404 9456 **e** info@silverbackrecords.co.uk
w silverbackrecords.co.uk Owners: Ben Addison, Mike Oxley.

Sister Ray 34-35 Berwick St, London W1V 8RP
t 020 7734 3297 **f** 020 7734 3298 **e** sales@sisterray.co.uk
w sisterray.co.uk Admin: Nick Harrison.

Slough Record Centre 241-243 Farnham Rd, Slough,
Berks SL2 1DE **t** 01753 528194 or 01753 572272
f 01753 692110 **e** sloughrecords@btconnect.com
w sloughrecords.co.uk Sales: Terry & Simon.

Smallfish Records 372 Old St, London EC1V 9LT
t 020 7739 2252 **f** 020 7739 7502 **e** justusfish@smallfish.co.uk
w smallfish.co.uk Mgr: Nick Turner.

WH Smith High Street Greenbridge Rd, Swindon, Wilts
SN3 3LD **t** 01793 616161 **f** 01793 562570
e firstname.lastname@whsmith.co.uk **w** whsmithgroup.com
Music Buyer: Chris Davies.

Smyths Musique 12 Railway St, Newcastle, Co Down
BT33 0AL **t** 028 4372 2831 **e** musique@smyths.biz
w smyths.biz.

Snv Music 8 Gammon Walk, Barnstaple, Devon EX31 1DJ
t 01271 323382 **f** 01271 327017 **e** snv@snv2000.com.

Solo Music 22a Market Arcade, Guildhall Shopping Centre,
Exeter EX4 3HW **t** 01392 496564 **f** 01392 491785
e admin@solomusic.freeserve.co.uk **w** solomusic.co.uk
Co-Owner: Penny Keen, Maggie Garrett.

Soul Brother Records 1, Keswick Rd, London SW15 2HL
t 020 8875 1018 **f** 020 8871 0180
e soulbrother@btinternet.com **w** soulbrother.com
Ptnr: Laurence Prangell.

Sound Fusion Records 209 High St, Bromley, Kent
BR1 1NY **t** 020 8464 8123 **f** 020 8466 9514
e mail@sfrecords.co.uk **w** sfrecords.co.uk
Owner: Martyn Thomas.

Soundclash 28 St Benedicts St, Norwich, Norfolk NR2 4AQ
t 01603 761004 **f** 01603 762248 **e** soundclash@btinternet.com
w run.to/soundclash MD: Paul Mills.

Sounds Good 26 Clarence St, Cheltenham, Gloucs GL50 3NU
t 01242 234 604 **f** 01242 253 030
e cds@soundsgoodonline.co.uk **w** soundsgoodonline.co.uk
Partners: John & Diana Ross.

Sounds of the Universe 7 Broadwick St, London
W1F 0DA **t** 020 7494 2004 **f** 020 7494 2004
e info@soundsoftheuniverse.com **w** souljazzrecords.co.uk
Contact: Karl Shale.

Sounds To Go 130 Holloway Rd, London N7 8JE
t 020 7609 3851 **f** 020 7609 3851
e sounds_to_go@hotmail.com **w** gem.co.uk Owner: Alex Isaacs.

Speed Music PLC 195 Caerleon Rd, Newport, South Wales
NP19 7HA **t** 01633 215577 **f** 01633 213214
e info@speedmusic.co.uk **w** speedmusic.co.uk Dir: Nick Fowler.

Spillers Records 36, The Hayes, Cardiff CF10 1AJ
t 029 2022 4905 **f** 029 2034 0358 **e** info@spillersrecords.com
w spillersrecords.com.

Spin Compact Discs 8 High Bridge, Newcastle-upon-Tyne
NE1 1EN **t** 0191 261 4741 or 0191 261 4742 **f** 0191 261 4747
e info@spincds.com **w** spincds.com Owner: Dave Dodds.

Spin It Records 13 High Rd, Willesden Green, London
NW10 2TE **t** 020 8459 0761 **f** 020 8459 7464
e sales@spinitrecords.co.uk **w** spinitrecords.co.uk
Sales Manager: Tony.

Spiral Classics Classical LPs 52 Herbert St,
Loughborough LE11 1NX **t** 01509 557 846 **f** 01509 557 847
e sophia@spiralclassics.co.uk **w** spiralclassics.co.uk
Owner: Sophia Singer.

Stand-Out 23 Fisherton St, Salisbury, Wilts SP2 7SU
t 01722 411344 **f** 01722 421505 **e** stand-out@totalise.co.uk
Owners: Colin Mundy, Andy Bennett.

Stern's African Record Centre 293 Euston Rd, London
NW1 3AD **t** 020 7387 5550 or 020 7388 5533
f 020 7388 2756 **e** fred@sternsmusic.com **w** sternsmusic.com
Mgrs: Fred Hines, Dom Raymond-Barker.

Streetwise Music 76 King St, Cambridge, Cambs CB1 1LD **t** 01223 300 496 **f** 01223 300 496 **e** info@streetwisemusic.co.uk **w** streetwisemusic.co.uk Owner: Simon Ryan.

Swordfish 14 Temple St, Birmingham B2 5BG **t** 0121 6334859 **f** n/a Owner: Mike Caddick.

Teeshirtstore.co.uk Unit 5, Waldo Works, Waldo Rd, London NW10 6AW **t** 020 8964 9020 **f** 020 8964 9090 **e** simon.coates@recordstore.co.uk **w** recordstore.co.uk GM: Simon Coates.

Tempest Records 83 Bull St, City Centre, Birmingham B4 6AD **t** 0121 236 9170 **f** 0121 236 9270 **e** info@tempest-records.co.uk Mgr: Mark Thornton.

Tesco Stores Ltd PO Box 44, Cirrus Building C, Shire Pk, Welwyn Garden City, Herts AL7 1ZR **t** 01992 632222 **f** 01707 297690 **w** tesco.com Snr Buying Mgr, Music: Alan Hunt.

Three Shades Records 16 Needless Alley, off New St, Birmingham City Centre, W Midlands B2 5AE **t** 0121 687 2772 **e** info@threeshades.com **w** threeshades.com Shop Manager: Martin Banks.

Threshold Records 53 High St, Cobham, Surrey KT11 3DP **t** 01932 865678 **f** 01932 865678 **e** sales@threshold-cd.co.uk Mgr: Phil Pavling.

Time Life Music Brettenham House, Lancaster Pl, London WC2E 7TL **t** 020 7499 4080 **e** info@timelife.co.uk **w** timelife.co.uk.

Torre Records 240 Union St, Torquay, Devon TQ2 5BY **t** 01803 291506 **f** 01803 291506 **e** cj@torrerecords.freeserve.co.uk Co-owner: Lee Jones.

Totem Records 168 Stoke Newington Church St, London N16 0JL **t** 020 7275 0234 **f** 020 7275 0111 **e** sales@totemrecords.com **w** totemrecords.com MD: Tony Fischetti.

Tower Records Ireland 6-8 Wicklow St, Dublin 2, Rep Of Ireland **t** +353 1 671 3250 **f** +353 1 671 3260 **e** cliveb@towerrecords.ie **w** towerrecords.ie Store Mgr: Clive Branagan.

Townsend Records 30 Queen St, Great Harwood, Lancs BB6 7QQ **t** 01254 885995 **f** 01254 887835 **e** admin@townsend-records.co.uk **w** townsend-records.co.uk MD: Steve Bamber.

Townsend Records (2) 117 Market St, Chorley, Lancs PR7 1SQ **t** 01257 264727 **f** 01257 264727 **e** sales@townsend-records.co.uk Mgr: Adrian Crook.

Track Records 50 Goodramgate, York, N Yorks YO1 7LF **t** 01904 629 022 **f** 01904 610 637 **e** trackrecords@btinternet.com **w** trackrecordsuk.com Owner: Keith Howe.

Tracks 14 Railway St, Hertford SG14 1BG **t** 01992 589294 **f** 01992 587090 **e** enquiries@tracks.sonnet.co.uk **w** tracks.org.uk Buyer: Dennis Osborne.

Trading Post 23 Nelson St, Stroud, Glos **t** 01453 759116 **f** 01453 756455 **e** simon@tradingpost.freeserve.co.uk **w** the-tradingpost.co.uk.

Tudor Tunes 7 Tudor Row, Lichfield WS13 6HH **t** 01543 257627 **f** 01543 257627 **e** tudortunes@williams3291.fsnet.co.uk Owners: Dave & Janice Williams.

UDM Records 30 Southbury Rd, Enfield, Middx EN1 1SA **t** 020 8366 5422 **f** 020 8366 5422 **e** info@ultimatedancemusic.co.uk **w** ultimatedancemusic.co.uk Owner: Neil Stamp.

Upbeat Trevelver, Belle Vue, Bude, Cornwall EX23 8JL **t** 01288 355763 **f** 01288 355763 Owner: Keith Shepherd.

Uptown Records 3 D'Arblay St, London W1F 8DH **t** 020 7434 3639 **f** 020 7434 3649 **e** izzy@uptownrecords.com **w** uptownrecords.com.

Vinyl Addiction Record Shop 6 Inverness St, Camden, London NW1 7HJ **t** 020 7482 1114 **f** 020 7681 6039 **e** music@vinyladdiction.co.uk **w** vinyladdiction.co.uk MD: Justin Rushmore.

Virgin Entertainment Group Ltd The School House, 50 Brook Green, London W6 7RR **t** 020 8752 9000 **f** 020 8752 9001 **e** firstname.lastname@virginmega.com **w** virgin.com CEO, Virgin Ent. Group: Simon Wright.

Vox Pop 53-55 Thomas St, Manchester M4 1NA **e** enquiries@voxpopmusic.com **w** voxpopmusic.com Mgr: Tim Giles.

Waterside Music 1 Waterside House, The Plains, Totnes, Devon TQ9 5DW **t** 01803 867947 Prop: John Cooper.

What Records Unit 40, Abbeygate Shopping Centre, Nuneaton, Warickshire CV11 4EH **t** 02476 352904 **f** 02476 320805 **e** whatuk@aol.com **w** whatrecords.co.uk Owner: Tim Ellis.

Whitelabel Records 4, Colomberie, St Helier, Jersey, Channel Islands JE2 4QB **t** 01534 725 256 **f** 01534 780 956 **e** info@whitelabelrecords.co.uk **w** whitelabelrecords.co.uk Owner: Mal White.

The Woods 6 The Arcade, Bognor Regis, W Sussex PO21 1LH **t** 01243 827 712 **f** 01243 842 615 **e** sales@the-woods.co.uk **w** the-woods.co.uk Prop: Trevor Flack.

Woolworths plc Woolworth House, 242-246 Marylebone Rd, London NW1 6JL **t** 020 7262 1222 **f** 020 7706 5975 **e** firstname.lastname@woolworths.co.uk **w** woolworths.co.uk.

WS::Records 3 Mill St, Bedford MK40 3EU **t** 01234 266244 **e** wsrcrds@aol.com **w** wsrecords.com Mgr: Paul Willsher.

WyldPytch Records 51 Lexington St, London W1F 9HL **t** 020 7434 3472 **f** 020 7287 1403 **e** contact@wyldpytch.com **w** wyldpytch.com Owner: Digger Elias.

X-Records 44 Bridge St, Bolton, Lancs BL1 2EG **t** 01204 524018 **f** 01204 370214 **e** xrecords@xrecords.co.uk **w** xrecords.co.uk.

Zhivago Sound And Vision 5-6 Shop St, Galway, Ireland **t** +353 91 564198 **f** +353 91 509951 **e** info@musicireland.com **w** musicireland.com GM: Des Hubbard.

The Zone PO Box 57, Radlett, Herts WD7 8BU **t** 01923 850650 **f** 01923 859903 **e** feedback@thezone.co.uk **w** thezone.co.uk MD: Carey Budnick.

Retail Services

Airplay The Manse, 39 Northenden Rd, Sale, Cheshire M33 2DH **t** 0161 962 2002 **f** 0161 962 2112 **e** mailbox@airplay.co.uk **w** airplay.co.uk HoM: Paul Maunder.

Blueprint Digital Unit 1, 73 Maygrove Rd, London NW6 2EG **t** 020 7209 4224 **f** 020 7209 2334 **e** info@blueprint.net **w** blueprint.net SVP, Products & Services: Mike Pears.

C-Burn Systems Ltd 33 Sekforde St, London EC1R 0HH **t** 020 7250 1133 **f** 020 7253 8553 **e** info@c-burn.com **w** c-burn.com Sales & Marketing: Neil Phillips.

Cardiff M Light & Sound Units 9/10, Tarran Buildings, Freeschool Court, Bridgend, Mid Glamorgan CF31 3AG **t** 01656 648170 **f** 01656 648412 **e** info@cardiffm.co.uk **w** cardiffm.co.uk MD: Philip Evans.

Colorset Graphics 2-3 Black Swan Yard, Bermondsey St, London SE1 3XW **t** 020 7234 0300 **f** 020 7234 0118 **e** mail@colorsetgraphics.co.uk **w** colorsetgraphics.co.uk Dir: Frank Baptiste.

Creative Retail Entertainment 2 Pincents Kiln, Calcot, Reading, Berks RG31 7SD **t** 0118 930 5599 **f** 0118 930 3369 **e** info@cre.co.uk **w** cre.co.uk Mktg: Iona Hood.

Cube Music The Albany Boathouse, Lower Ham Rd, Kingston upon Thames, Surrey KT2 6BB **t** 020 8547 1543 **f** 020 8547 1544 **e** info@cube-music.com **w** cube-music.com Music & Promotions Dir: Mick Hilton.

Digital DJ Ltd 22 The Ropery, Newcastle upon Tyne NE6 1TY **t** 0191 276 2791 **f** 0191 224 0148 **e** info@digitaldjsystems.com **w** digitaldjsystems.com Dir: Paul Rogers.

Essanby Ltd Riverside Works, Amwell Lane, Ware, Herts SG12 8EB **t** 01920 870596 **f** 01920 871553 **e** shatcher@essanby.co.uk **w** essanby.co.uk MD: Steve Hatcher.

International Displays Stonehill, Stukeley Meadows Ind Estate, Huntingdon, Cambs PE29 6ED **t** 01480 414204 **f** 01480 414205 **e** info@internationaldisplays.co.uk **w** internationaldisplays.co.uk Sales & Marketing Dir.: Carl Jenkin.

Kempner Distribution Ltd 498-500 Honeypot Lane, Stanmore, MIddlesex HA7 1JZ **t** 020 8952 5262 **f** 020 8952 8061 **e** info@kempner.co.uk **w** kempner.co.uk Mkting Mgr: Eddie Rollinson.

KPD London Ltd 297 Haydons Rd, London SW19 8TX **t** 020 8542 9535 **f** 020 8543 9406 **e** reception@kpd.co.uk **w** kpd.co.uk MD: Ivor Heller.

Lift (UK) 42 Edison Rd, Rabans Land Industrial Estate, Aylesbury, Bucks HP19 8TE **t** 01296 468 790 **f** 01296 468 791 **e** info@lift-uk.co.uk **w** liftsystems.com Business Manager: Gudrun Heidenbauer.

Masson Seeley & Co Ltd Howdale, Downham Market, Norfolk PE38 9AL **t** 01366 388000 **f** 01366 385222 or 01366 388025 **e** admin@masson-seeley.co.uk **w** masson-seeley.co.uk Contact: Martin Potten.

Micro Video Services 24 Cobham Rd, Ferndown Industrial Estate, Wimborne, Dorset BH21 7NP **t** 01202 861 696 **f** 01202 654 919 **e** av.sales@mvsav.co.uk **w** microvideoservices.com Contact: Sales Department.

MRIB Heckfield Pl, 530 Fulham Rd, London SW6 5NR **t** 020 7731 3555 **f** 020 7731 8545 **e** contactus@mrib.co.uk **w** mrib.co.uk MD: Paul Basford.

Musonic (UK) Unit 13, Wenta Business Centre, Colne Way, Watford, Herts WD24 7ND **t** 01923 213344 **f** 01923 213355 **e** sales@musonic.co.uk **w** musonic.co.uk Dir: Stephen Blank.

MUZE EUROPE

muze®

Muze Drives the Media Experience™

Paulton House, 8 Shepherdess Walk, London N1 7LB **t** 020 7566 8216 **f** 020 7566 8259 **e** dsass@muzeeurope.com **w** muzeeurope.com Head of European Sales and Client Services: Deborah Sass.

Pentonville Rubber Products Ltd 104-106 Pentonville Rd, London N1 9JB **t** 020 7837 4582 **f** 020 7278 7392 **e** queries@pentonvillerubber.co.uk **w** pentonvillerubber.co.uk.

pre.vu Sales Office Queens Wharf, Queen Caroline St, Hammersmith, London W6 9RJ **t** 020 8600 2657 **e** sales@origgio.co.uk **w** pre.vu Sales & Marketing Dir: Andy Lown.

Pro.Loc Europe Royal Albert House, Sheet St, Windsor, Berks SL4 1BE **t** 01753 705030 **f** 01753 831541 **e** proloc@proloc.co.uk **w** proloc-online.com GM: Mike Vickers.

Pro.Loc UK Ltd Northgate Business Centre, 38 Northgate, Newark on Trent, Notts NG24 1EZ **t** 01636 642827 **f** 01636 642865 **e** sales@proloc.co.uk **w** proloc-online.com Sales: Sam Jessop.

Retail Entertainment Displays Ltd (RED) 27-28 Stapledon Rd, Orton Southgate, Peterborough, Cambs PE2 6TD **t** 01733 239001 **f** 01733 239002 **e** info@reddisplays.com **w** reddisplays.com MD: John Findlay.

Retail Management Solutions Bloxham Mill, Barford Rd, Bloxham, Banbury OX15 4FF **t** 01295 724568 **f** 01295 722801 **e** info@rmsepos.com **w** rmsepos.com Contact: Robert Collier.

Sarem & Co 43A Old Woking Rd, West Byfleet, Surrey KT14 6LG **t** 01932 352535 **f** 01932 336431 **e** info@sarem-co.com **w** sarem-co.com Ptnr: Adrian Connelly.

Sounds Wholesale Unit 2, Park St, Burton on Trent, Staffs DE14 3SE **t** 01283 566823 **f** 01283 568631 **e** matpriest@aol.com **w** soundswholesaleltd.co.uk Dir: Matt Priest.

Mike Thorn Display & Design 30 Muswell Ave, London N10 2EG **t** 020 8442 0279 **f** 020 8442 0496 **e** info@bear-art.com MD: Mike Thorn.

Walsh & Jenkins plc Power House, Powerscroft Rd, Sidcup, Kent DA14 5EA **t** 020 8308 6300 **f** 020 8308 6340 **e** sales@walsh-jenkins.co.uk **w** walsh-jenkins.co.uk Sales Office Co-ordiantor: Jackie Read.

West 4 Tapes And Records 105 Stocks Lane, Bracklesham Bay, W Sussex PO20 8NU **t** 01243 671238 Sales Dir: Kenneth G Roe.

Wilton of London Stanhope House, 4-8 Highgate High St, London N6 5JL **t** 020 8341 7070 **f** 020 8341 1176 **w** wilton-of-london.co.uk Contact: The Managing Director.

Mail Order Companies

3 Beat Records 5 Slater St, Liverpool L1 4BW **t** 0151 709 3355 **f** 0151 709 3707 **e** info@3beat.co.uk **w** 3beat.co.uk Shop Mgr: Pezz.

Action Replay 24 Lake Rd, Bowness-on-Windermere, Cumbria LA23 3AP **t** 01539 445 089 **e** davidsnaith@actionreplay.wanadoo.co.uk Owner: David Snaith.

Alma Road Mail Order PO Box 3813, London SW18 1XE **t** 020 8870 9912 **f** 020 8871 1766 **e** mailorder@almaroad.co.uk **w** beggars.com Mail Order Manager: Jo.

Badlands Mail Order 11 St George's Pl, Cheltenham, Gloucs GL50 3LA **t** 01242 227724 **f** 01242 227393 **e** shop@badlands.co.uk **w** badlands.co.uk MD: Philip Jump.

The Basement 7 North St, Carrickfergus, Co Antrim BT38 7AQ **t** 028 9336 3678 **e** carrick@basementni.com **w** basementni.com Owner: Phil Barnhill.

BMG Direct Bedford House, 69-79 Fulham High St, London SW6 3JW **t** 020 7384 7500 **f** 020 7973 0345 Special Markets Mgr: Dom Higgins.

Bus Stop Mail Order Ltd 42-50 Steele Rd, London NW10 7AS **t** 020 8453 1311 **f** 020 8961 8725 **e** info@busstop.co.uk **w** acerecords.co.uk Dir: Yvette DeRoy.

Carbon Disks PO Box 28, Cromer, Norfolk NR27 9RG **t** 01263 515963 **f** 01263 515963 **e** data@carbondisks.com **w** carbondisks.com Contact: Barry Fry.

Catapult 100% Vinyl 22 High Street Arcade, Cardiff CF10 2BB **t** 029 2022 8990 or 029 2034 2322 **f** 029 2023 1690 **e** enquiries@catapult.co.uk **w** catapult.co.uk MD: Lucy Squire.

CDX Music By Mail The Olde Coach House, Windsor Cresent, Radyr, South Glamorgan CF4 8AG **t** 029 2084 3604 or 029 2084 2878 **f** 029 2084 2184 **e** sales@cdx.co.uk **w** cdx.co.uk MD: Paul Karamouzis.

CeeDee Mail Ltd PO Box 14, Stowmarket, Suffolk IP14 1ED **t** 01449 770138 **f** 01449 770133 **e** CeeDeeMail@aol.com Contact: Tobias Wilcox.

Celtic Music Room 8 North St, Sandwich, Isle of Lewis HS2 0AD **t** 01851 706741 **e** info@celticmusicroom.com **w** celticmusicroom.com Contact: John Clarke.

City Sounds 5 Kirby St, London EC1N 8TS **t** 020 7404 1800 or 020 7405 5454 **f** 020 7242 1863 **e** sales@city-sounds.co.uk **w** city-sounds.co.uk Contact: Tom Henneby.

The Compact Disc Club 6 The Arcade, Bognor Regis, W Sussex PO21 1LH **t** 01243 827 712 **f** 01243 842 615 **e** sales@the-woods.co.uk **w** the-woods.co.uk Prop: Trevor Flack.

Compact Disc Services 40-42 Brantwood Ave, Dundee DD3 6EW **t** 01382 776595 **f** 01382 736702 **e** cdser@aol.com **w** cd-services.com Snr Partner: Dave Shoesmith.

Cooking Vinyl Mail Order PO Box 1845, London W3 0BR **t** 020 8600 9200 **f** 020 8743 7534 **e** bob@cookingvinyl.com **w** cookingvinyl.com Direct Mktg Mgr: Bob Allan.

Copperplate Mail Order 68, Belleville Rd, London SW11 6PP **t** 020 7585 0357 **f** 020 7585 0357 **e** copperplate2000@yahoo.com **w** copperplatemailorder.com MD: Alan O'Leary.

Cyclops 33A Tolworth Park Rd, Tolworth, Surrey KT6 7RL **t** 020 8339 9965 **f** 020 8399 0070 **e** postmaster@gft-cyclops.co.uk **w** gft-cyclops.co.uk MD: Malcolm Parker.

Didgeridoo PO Box 333, Brighton, E Sussex BN1 2EH **t** 01403 740 289 **f** 01403 740 261 **e** ukorders@didgerecords.com **w** didgerecords.com Head of Mail Order: Sarah Clark.

Dub Vendor Mail Order 17 Davids Rd, London SE23 3EP **t** 020 8291 8950 **f** 020 8291 1097 **e** mailorder@dubvendor.co.uk **w** dubvendor.co.uk MD: John MacGillivray.

For all the latest directory listings visit www.musicweekdirectory.com

Fair Oaks Entertainments 7 Tower St, Ulverston, Cumbria LA12 9AN **t** 01229 581766 **f** 01229 581766 **e** fairoaksorderline@hotmail.com **w** anglefire.com/music5/roots2rockmusic Contact: JG Livingstone.

Fast Forward Units 9-10 Sutherland Court, Tolpits Lane, Watford, Herts WD18 9SP **t** 01923 897080 **f** 01923 896263 **e** sales@fast-forward.co.uk MD: Ken Hill.

Freak Emporium Mail-Order PO Box 1288, Gerrards Cross, Bucks SL9 9YB **t** 01753 893008 **f** 01753 892879 **e** sales@freakemporium.com **w** freakemporium.com MD: Richard Allen.

GFT Ltd (see Cyclops).

Greensleeves Mail Order Unit 14 Metro Centre, St John's Rd, Isleworth, Middlesex TW7 6NJ **t** 020 8758 2301 **f** 020 8758 0811 **e** mailorder@greensleeves.net **w** greensleeves.net Mail Order Manager: Chris O'Brien.

Hard To Find Record Vinyl House, 10 Upper Gough St, Birmingham, W Midlands B1 1JG **t** 0121 687 7777 **f** 0121 687 7774 **e** sales@htfr.com **w** htfr.com Contact: Jason Kirby.

Jim Stewart, Motown, Soul & Sixties CD Specialist 37 Main Rd, Hextable, Swanley, Kent BR8 7RA **t** 01322 613883 **f** 01322 613883 **e** jstew79431@aol.com **w** soulsearchingplus.co.uk Contact: Jim Stewart.

Magpie Direct Music Studio 65, Shepperton Film Studio, Shepperton, Middx TW17 0QD **t** 01932 592949 **f** 01932 592269 **e** editor@highnote.co.uk **w** magpiedirect.com MD: Mark Rye.

Mostly Music 28 Carlisle Close, Mobberley, Knutsford, Cheshire WA16 7HD **t** 01565 872650 **f** 01565 872650 **e** mostlymusic@btinternet.com **w** mostlymusic.co.uk Prop: Roger Wilkes.

Music Exchange (Manchester) Ltd Mail Order Dept., Claverton Rd, Wythenshawe, Manchester M23 9ZA **t** 0161 946 9301 **f** 0161 946 1195 **e** mail@music-exchange.co.uk **w** music-exchange.co.uk Mail Order Mgr: Elizabeth Howarth.

Mute Bank 429 Harrow Rd, London W10 4RE **t** 020 8964 0029 **f** 020 8964 3722 **e** info@mutebank.co.uk **w** mutebank.co.uk Head of Mailorder: Michael Lopatis.

Nostalgia Direct 11 St Nicholas Chambers, Newcastle-upon-Tyne NE1 1PE **t** 0191 233 1200 **f** 0191 233 1215 Contact: George Carr.

Open Ear Productions Ltd. Main St, Oughterard, Co.Galway, Ireland **t** +353 91 552816 **f** +353 91 557967 **e** info@openear.ie **w** openear.ie MD: Bruno Staehelin.

Pendulum Direct 34 Market Pl, Melton Mowbray, Leics LE13 1XD **t** 01664 566246 **f** 01664 560310 **e** mw@pendulum-direct.com **w** pendulum-direct.com MD: Mike Eden.

Posteverything Suite 216, Bon Marche Buliding, 241 Ferndale Rd, London SW9 8BJ **t** 020 7733 2344 **f** 020 7733 5818 **e** feedback@posteverything.com **w** posteverything.com Contact: Duncan Moore.

Red Lick Records Porthmadog, Gwynedd LL49 9DJ **t** 01766 512151 **f** 01766 512851 **e** sales@redlick.com **w** redlick.com MD: Ann Smith.

Reggae Revive 27 Thamesgate, St. Edmund's Rd, Dartford, Kent DA1 5ND **t** 01322 271 634 **e** reggae.revive@virgin.net **w** reggaerevive.com Owner: Bob Brooks.

Rocking Chair PO Box 296, Matlock, Derbyshire DE4 3XU **t** 01629 827013 **f** 01629 821874 **e** rc@mrscasey.co.uk **w** mrscasey.co.uk/rockingchair MD: Steve Heap.

Rugby Songs Unlimited Whitwell, Colyford, Colyton, Devon EX24 6HS **t** 01297 553803 **e** very_funny@compuserve.com **w** rugby-songs.co.uk MD: Mike Williams.

Selections Dorchester, Dorset DT2 7YG **t** 0845 644 1560 **f** 01305 848516 **e** sales@cdselections.com **w** cdselections.com Contact: Michael Slocock.

Soul Brother Records 1 Keswick Rd, London SW15 2HL **t** 020 8875 1018 **f** 020 8871 0180 **e** SoulBrother@btinternet.com **w** SoulBrother.com Ptnr: Laurence Prangell.

Soundtracks Direct 3 Prowse Pl, London NW1 9PH **t** 020 7428 5500 **f** 020 7482 2385 **e** info@silvascreen.co.uk **w** soundtracksdirect.co.uk MD: Reynold D'Silva.

Spin It Records 13 High Rd, London NW10 2TE **t** 020 8459 0761 **f** 020 8459 7464 **e** sales@spinitrecords.co.uk **w** spinitrecords.co.uk.

Sterns Postal 293 Euston Rd, London NW1 3AD **t** 020 7387 5550 **f** 020 7388 2756 **e** info@sternsmusic.com **w** sternsmusic.com Retail Mgr: Dominic Raymond Barker.

Thirdwave Music Direct PO Box 19, Orpington, Kent BR6 9ZF **t** 01689 609481 **f** 01689 609481 **e** info@thirdwavemusic.com **w** thirdwavemusic.com MD: Matt Gall.

Track Records 50 Goodramgate, York, N Yorks YO1 7LF **t** 01904 629 022 **f** 01904 610 637 **e** trackrecords@btinternet.com **w** trackrecordsuk.com Owner: Keith Howe.

Tracks PO Box 117, Chorley, Lancs PR6 0UU **t** 01257 269726 **f** 01257 231340 **e** sales@tracks.co.uk **w** tracks.co.uk Contact: Paul Wane.

Universal Group Direct Ltd 76 Oxford St, London W1D 1BS **t** 020 8910 6012 **f** 020 8553 9613 **e** linda.porter@umusic.com **w** bclub.co.uk MD: Ford Ennals.

Vinyl Tap Mail Order Music 1 Minerva Works, Crossley Lane, Kirkheaton, Huddersfield, W Yorks HD5 0QP **t** 01484 421446 **f** 01484 531019 **e** sales@vinyltap.demon.co.uk **w** vinyltap.co.uk Contact: Dan Browning.

Vivante Music Ltd Unit 6, Fontigarry Business Pk, Reigate Rd, Sidlow Nr Reigate, Surrey RG2 8QH **t** 01293 822186 **f** 01293 821965 **e** sales@vivante.co.uk **w** vivante.co.uk MD: Steven Carr.

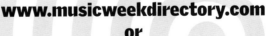
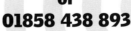

ully automated web & WAP mobile & digital store solutions
for the music industry...

Digital

fully automated & internationalised web & WAP based stores
advanced content management & real time reporting systems
international billing across key territories (P-SMS, Bango & credit card)
mobile marketing consultancy & campaign management
full client and consumser facing support services

mobiq

(t) +44 (0)121 311 9980   (email) sales@mobiq.tv   (web) www.mobiq.tv

Digital

- **Vinyl Mastering**
- **SACD/DVD-A Mastering**
- **CD Duplication**
- **Voice Recording**
- **Sync-to-Picture**

Alchemy Mastering Ltd,
29th Floor, Centre Point,
103 New Oxford Street,
London WC1A 1DD

T: 020 7420 8000
E: info@alchemysoho.com
W: www.alchemysoho.com
F: 020 7420 8001

alchemy
great views, great coffee, great sound

SOHO

Digital:

Music Portals and Online Magazines

Amazon.co.uk Patriot Court, The Grove, Slough SL1 1QP **t** 020 8636 9200 **f** 020 8636 9400 **e** info@amazon.co.uk **w** amazon.co.uk Contact: Judith Catton.

Band Family Tree 2 Oakfield Terrace, Childer Thornton, Wirral CH66 7NY **t** 0870 011 6289 **e** admin@bandfamilytree.com **w** bandfamilytree.com MD: Rob Cowley.

Bandname.com 21 Market Pl, Blandford Forum, Devon DT11 7AF **e** information@bandname.com **w** bandname.com Mgr: Crystal Beaubien.

Base.ad PO Box 56374, London SE1 3WF **t** 0207 357 8066 **f** 0207 357 8166 **e** london@base.ad **w** base.ad Ed: Tanya Mannar.

borderevents.com Ltd 2 Heatherlie Pk, Selkirk, Selkirkshire TD7 5AL **t** 01750 725 480 **e** info@borderevents.com **w** borderevents.com Sales Manager: Andrew Lang.

Classical World Ltd. trading as Classical.com 18 Denbigh Rd, London W11 2SN **t** 020 8816 8848 **f** 0870 762 0010 **e** conductor@classical.com **w** classical.com Dir: Roger Press.

Clickmusic Ltd 58-60 Fitzroy St, London W1T 5BU **t** 020 7383 3038 **f** 0870 458 4183 **e** editor@clickmusic.co.uk **w** clickmusic.co.uk Ed: Stephen Ackroyd.

Cliff Chart Site.co.uk 17, Podsmead Rd, Tuffley, Glos GL1 5PB **t** 01452 306104 **f** 01452 306104 **e** william@cliffchartsite.co.uk **w** cliffchartsite.co.uk Ed: William Hooper.

The DAW Buyers Guide 216A Gipsy Rd, London SE27 9RB **t** 020 8761 1042 **e** sypha@syphaonline.com **w** http://DAWguide.com Group Editor: Yasmin Hashmi.

Drowned in Sound 1 Chilworth Mews, London W2 3RG **t** 020 7087 8880 **f** 020 7087 8899 **e** editor@drownedinsound.com **w** drownedinsound.com Ed: Colin Roberts.

Drum & Bass Arena Brincliffe House, 861 Ecclesall Rd, Sheffield S11 7AE **t** 0114 281 4470 **f** 0114 292 3020 **e** editorial@lists.breakbeat.co.uk **w** breakbeat.co.uk MD: Del Dias.

FirstForMusic.com 23 New Mount St, Manchester M4 4DE **t** 0161 953 4081 **f** 0161 953 4091 **e** info@FirstForMusic.com **w** FirstForMusic.com Contact: Steven Oakes.

Fmagazine.com 9 Cambridge Court, Earlham St, Covent Garden, London WC2H 9RZ **t** 020 7379 4466 or 07979 905015 **e** chrissie@fmagazine.com **w** fmagazine.com MD: Chrissie Adams.

garageband.com USA **e** artistmanager@garageband.com **w** garageband.com.

GBOB International (Global Battle of the Bands) 21 Denmark St, London WC2H 8NA **t** 020 7379 3777 **f** 020 7379 4888 **e** music@gbob.com **w** gbob.com Int'l Director: Matt Walker.

God Is In The TV 36 Loftus St, Canton, Cardiff CF5 1HL **t** 029 2019 1692 **e** godisinthetvzine2003@yahoo.co.uk **w** godisinthetvzine.co.uk Ed: Bill Cummings.

Jukebox 3 Gray Pl, Wokingham Rd, Bracknell, Berks RG42 1QA **t** 01344 428 308 **f** 07043 018 674 **e** vikki@jukebo.cx **w** jukebo.cx Ed: Vikki Roberts.

Kent Gigs (One Kent) The Cedars, Elvington Lane, Hawkinge, Nr. Folkestone, Kent CT18 7AD **t** 01303 893472 **f** 01303 893833 **e** Chris@kentgigs.com **w** kentgigs.com MD: Chris Ashman.

KinDups Ltd PO Box 711, Godalming GU7 9BE **t** 07760 128 024 **e** info@kindups.com **w** kindups.com Dir: Dominic Graham-Hyde.

Let's Talk Music The Dog House, 32 Sullivan Crescent, Harefield, Middlesex UB9 6NL **t** 01895 825 757 **e** Bill@letstalkmusic.com **w** letstalkmusic.com Contact: Bill Smith.

livegigguide ltd The Windsor Centre, 15-29 Windsor St, London N1 8QG **t** 020 7359 2927 **f** 020 7359 7212 **e** info@livegigguide.com **w** livegigguide.com Director of Operations: Olivier de Peretti Clark.

The Living Tradition PO Box 1026, Kilmarnock, Ayrshire, Scotland KA2 0LG **t** 01563 571220 **f** 01563 544855 **e** admin@livingtradition.co.uk **w** folkmusic.net Ed: Pete Heywood.

Manchestermusic.co.uk Musicdash, PO Box 1977, Manchester M26 2YB **t** 0787 0727 075 **e** mancmusic@hotmail.com **w** manchestermusic.co.uk Ed: Jon Ashley.

Music Hurts Ramp Industry, 3rd Floor, 20 Flaxman Terrace, London WC1H 9AT **t** 020 7388 0709 **e** hello@musichurts.com **w** musichurts.com Editorial Dir: Andy Crysell.

MUSIC WEEK DIRECTORY

MUSICWEEK

Directory

CMP Information, Ludgate House, 245 Blackfriars Road, London SE1 9UR **t** 020 7921 8353 **f** 020 7921 8327 **e** mwdirectory@cmpi.biz **w** musicweekdirectory.com Database Manager: Nick Tesco. Publisher: Ajax Scott. Business Development Manager: Matthew Tyrrell. Advertising Manager: Matt Slade. Senior Advertising Sales Executive: Billy Fahey. Advertising Sales Executive: Dwaine Tyndale. Logo Sales Executive: Maria Edwards. **The definitive contacts directory for the UK music industry.**

Musiqtrader Ltd 260 Horns Rd, Barkingside, Ilford, Essex IG61BS **t** 07738 421 972 **e** ngohil@musiqtrader.co.uk **w** musiqtrader.co.uk MD: Naimish Gohil.

New CD Weekly 56 Manston Rd, Exeter, Devon EX1 2QA **t** 01392 432 630 **f** 01392 432 630 **e** rod@newcdweekly.com **w** newcdweekly.com MD: Rod Walsom.

NME.COM IPC Music Magazines, Kingsreach Tower, Stamford St, London SE1 9LS **t** 020 7261 5000 **f** 020 7261 6022 **e** news@nme.com **w** nme.com Ed: Ben Perreau.

Noise Festival Ltd P.O. Box 4106, Manchester M60 1WW **t** 0161 237 9009 **e** enq@noisefestival.com **w** noisefestival.com Executive Producer: Denise Proctor.

Odyssey.fm PO Box 18888, London SW7 4FQ **t** 020 7373 1614 **f** 020 7373 1614 **e** info@outer-media.co.uk **w** odyssey.fm Dir: Gregory Mihalcheon.

Online Classics Gnd & 1st Floors, 31 Eastcastle St, London W1W 8DL **t** 020 7636 1400 **f** 020 7637 1355 **e** team@onlineclassics.com **w** onlineclassics.com CEO: Christopher Hunt.

OnlineConcerts.com 2 Valentine Cottages, Petworth Rd, Witley, Godalming, Surrey GU8 5LS **t** 01428 684537 **e** jdoukas@onlineconcerts.com **w** onlineconcerts.com Founder: John Doukas.

Oxfordmusic.net Suite 1, 2nd Floor, 65 George St, Oxford OX1 2BE **t** 01865 798796 **f** 01865 798792 **e** info@oxfordmusic.net **w** oxfordmusic.net MD: Andy Clyde.

Playlouder 8-10 Rhoda St, London E2 7EF **t** 020 7729 4797 **f** 020 7739 8571 **e** site@playlouder.com **w** playlouder.com MDs: Paul Hitchman, Jim Gottlieb.

Popjustice.com 31 Chelsea Wharf, Lots Rd, London SW10 0QJ **t** 020 7352 9444 **e** contact@popjustice.com **w** popjustice.com Ed: Peter Robinson.

POPWORLD LTD.

popworld

14 Ransome's Dock, 35 Parkgate Road, London SW11 4NP **t** 020 7350 5500 **f** 020 7350 5501 **e** firstname@popworld.com **w** popworld.com CEO: Martin Lowde. Creative: Will Allen. Editorial: Stef Dicembre.

Primal Sounds.com PO Box 5, Alton, Hants GU34 2EN **t** 07967 155542 **e** mail@primalsounds.com **w** primalsounds.com Owner: Carl Saunders.

Record of the Day PO Box 49554, London E17 9WB **t** 020 8520 2130 (PS) 020 7095 1500 (DB) **f** 020 8520 2130 **e** info@recordoftheday.com **w** recordoftheday.com Eds: Paul Scaife, David Balfour.

Record-Play Studio 203, 45-46 Charlotte Rd, London EC2A 3PD **t** 020 7193 9792 or 07753 388 275 **e** info@record-play.com **w** record-play.com Prop: Daniel Cross.

Revolution 211 Western Rd, London SW19 2QD **t** 020 8646 7094 **f** 020 8646 7094 **e** info@revolutionsuk.com **w** revolutionuk.com Ed: John Lonergan.

Rockarama Radio Network 2nd Floor, 145-157 St John St, London EC1V 4PY **t** 07732 213917 **e** news@rockaramaradionetwork.com **w** rockaramaradionetwork.com Managing Editor: Kevin Gover.

Rockfeedback.com 3a Highbury Crescent, Islington, London N5 1RN **t** 020 7700 4464 **e** tobyl@rockfeedback.com **w** rockfeedback.com Ed: Toby L.

Roomthirteen.com 55 Cranleigh Dr, Cheadle, Cheshire SK8 2DH **t** 07745 632 529 **f** 0845 280 7575 **e** guy.powell@roomthirteen.com **w** roomthirteen.com Ed: Guy Powell.

RWD Magazine Suite B3 Lafone House, Leathermarket St, London SE1 3HN **t** 020 7367 4136 or 07932 636 615 **f** 020 7367 6184 **e** editor@rwdmag.com **w** rwdmag.com Ed: Hattie Collins.

Skrufff-E and Skrufff.com Available on request. **t** 020 7792 4537 **e** jonty@skrufff.com **w** skrufff.com MD/DJ: Skrufff.

thewhitelabel.com limited 1-3 Croft Lane, Henfield, W. Sussex BN5 9TT **t** 01273 492620 **e** contact@thewhitelabel.com **w** thewhitelabel.com GM: Nic Vine.

Thisdayinmusic.com Hazelhurst Barn, Valley Rd, Hayfield, Derbyshire SK22 2JP **t** 01663 747 970 or 07768 652 899 **e** neil@thisdayinmusic.com **w** Thisdayinmusic.com Ed: Neil Cossar.

Tiscali UK 20 Broadwick St, London W1F 8HT **t** 020 7087 2000 **e** firstname.lastname@uk.tiscali.com **w** tiscali.co.uk/music Head of Music and Mobile: Dave Castell.

TotalRock 1-6 Denmark Pl, London WC2H 8NL **t** 020 7240 6665 **e** info@totalrock.com **w** totalrock.com HoM: Tony Wilson.

Turnround Multi-Media 16 Berkeley Mews, 29 High St, Cheltenham, Gloucs GL50 1DY **t** 01242 224360 **f** 01242 226566 **e** studio@turnround.co.uk **w** turnround.co.uk MD: Ross Lammas.

Twistedear.com 8 Stirling Close, Ash Vale, Surrey GU12 5SD **t** 01252 890013 **e** beck@twistedear.com **w** twistedear.com Ed: Beck Kingsnorth.

UKMusic.com PO Box 50703, London NW6 6XG **t** 07834 351 690 **e** management@ukmusic.com **w** ukmusic.com MD: Doug Cooper.

Umusic.co.uk Universal UK, 364-366 Kensington High St, London W14 8NS **t** 020 7471 5000 **f** 020 7471 5001 **e** firstname.lastname@umusic.com **w** umusic.co.uk Divisional Dir, New Media & Digital: Rob Wells.

Video-C 1 Bayham St, London NW1 0ER **t** 020 7916 5483 **f** 020 7916 5482 **e** info@video-c.co.uk **w** video-c.co.uk MD: Karl Badger.

VidZone Digital Media The Limes, 123 Mortlake High St, London SW14 8SN **t** 020 8487 5880 **f** 020 8487 9683 **e** adrian@vidzone.tv **w** vidzone.tv CEO: Adrian Workman.

Virgin.net The Communications Bld, 48 Leicester Sq, London WC2H 7LT **t** 020 7664 6069 **f** 020 7664 6006 **e** virgincontact@london.virgin.net **w** virgin.net Head of Content: Caroline Hugh.

Virtual Festivals.com 4 Rowan Court, 56 High St, Wimbledon, London SW19 5EE **t** 020 8605 2691 **f** 020 8605 2255 **e** steve@virtualfestivals.com **w** virtualfestivals.com MD: Steve Jenner.

wildplum Live PO Box 999, Enfield, London EN1 9AD **t** 0777 1777 998 **e** info@wildplum.co.uk **w** wildplum.co.uk Artist Development and Events Manager: AL Douglas.

Yahoo! UK & Ireland 10 Ebury Bridge Rd, London WC2H 8AD **t** 020 7131 1000 **f** 020 7808 4203 **e** mccraw@uk.yahoo-inc.com **w** yahoo.co.uk European Mktg Mgr, Mobile: Beth McCraw.

Download and Mail Order Websites

1 Off Wax PO Box 5139, Glasgow G76 8WF
t 0141 585 7354 **f** 0141 585 7354 **e** sales@1offwax.co.uk
w 1offwax.co.uk Sales Director: Theresa Talbot.

101cd.com PO Box 103, Jersey, Channel Islands JEF 8QX
t 020 8680 5282 **f** 01534 481 360 **e** service@101cd.com
w 101cd.com Commercial Dir: Hanif Virani.

abovethesky.com Studio 211, 24-28 Hatton Wall,
Clerkenwell, London EC1N 8JH **t** 020 7404 1005
e info@abovethesky.com **w** abovethesky.com Dir: A J Burt.

Action Records 46 Church St, Preston, Lancs PR1 3DH
t 01772 884 772 or 01772 258809 **f** 01772 252 255
e sales@actionrecords.co.uk **w** actionrecords.co.uk
Mgr: Gordon Gibson.

The All Celtic Music Store PO Box 7264, Glasgow
G46 6YE **t** 0141 637 6010 **f** 0141 637 6010
e sales@allcelticmusic.com **w** allcelticmusic.com
MD: Ronnie Simpson.

Arkade Fetcham Park House, Lower Rd, Leatherhead, Surrey
KT22 9HD **t** 01372 360300 **f** 01372 360878
e info@arkade.com **w** arkade.com.

Atomic Sounds PO Box 2074, Lancing, W Sussex
BN15 8YA **t** 01903 754 341 **e** atomic1@fastnet.co.uk
w atomicsounds.co.uk Owner: Tony Grist.

Audiojelly.com 80 Hadley Rd, Barnet, Herts EN5 5QS
t 020 8440 0710 **f** 020 8441 8522 **e** ricky@audiojelly.com
w audiojelly.com Mgr: Ricky Simmonds.

Bandwagon Ltd Studio 507 Enterprise House, 1-2 Hatfields,
London SE1 9PG **t** 020 7993 1221 **e** support@bandwagon.co.uk
w bandwagon.co.uk Dirs: Owen Farrington, Huw Thomas.

BBC Shop BBC Worldwide, 80 Wood Lane, London
W12 0TT **t** 020 8433 1303 **f** 020 8225 7877
e bbcshop@bbc.co.uk **w** bbcshop.com
Executive Producer: Greg Jarvis.

Beathut.com PO Box 3365, Brighton BN1 1WQ
t 01273 626245 **f** 01273 626246 **e** info@catskillsrecords.com
w beathut.com Dirs: Khalid, Amr or Jonny.

Buyhear.Com 240 High Rd, Harrow Weald, Middlesex
HA3 7BB **t** 020 8863 2520 **f** 020 8863 2520
e steve@buyhear.com **w** buyhear.com Dir: Steven Robert Glen.

Cardiff Music 1 St Georges Rd, Bristol BS1 5UL
t 02920 229 700 **f** 0117 9276 680 **e** shop@cardiffmusic.com
w cardiffmusic.com Mgr: Paul Skyrme.

Cargo Records (UK) Ltd 17 Heathmans Rd, Parsons
Green, London SW6 4TJ **t** 020 7731 5125 **f** 020 7731 3866
e info@cargorecords.co.uk **w** cargorecords.co.uk MD: Philip Hill.

CDJShop.com Festival House, Suite 3.19, Jessop Ave,
Cheltenham GL50 3SH **t** 01242 633 613 **f** 01242 633 615
e info@cdjshop.com **w** cdjshop.com Dir: Simon Brisk.

DAW Buyers Guide Gipsy Rd, London SE27 9RB
t 020 8761 1042 **e** info@syphaonline.com **w** syphaonline.com
Ptnr: Yasmin Hashmi.

Disky.com 3 York St, St. Helier, Jersey, Channel Islands
JE2 3RQ **t** 01534 509 687 **e** music.online@disky.com
w disky.com MD: Robert Bisson.

DJdownload.com 31 Mysore Rd, Battersea, London
SW11 5RY **t** 020 7924 2329 **f** 020 7924 2329
e info@djdownload.com **w** djdownload.com
Contact: Guy Osborne, Justin Pearse.

EBTM Plc Unit A1, Riverside Business Centre, Haldane Pl,
London SW18 4UQ **t** 020 8704 0034 or 07713 404 101
f 020 8704 0086 **e** grant@EBTM.com **w** EBTM.com
Dir: Grant Calton.

eil.com Esprit House, Railway Sidings, Meopham, Kent
DA13 0YS **t** 01474 815010 **f** 01474 815030 **e** sales@eil.com
w eil.com Marketing Manager: Simon Wright.

Elevate 3rd Floor, 7 Holyrood St, London SE1 2EL
t 020 7378 5818 **f** 020 7378 4761 **e** info@elevateuk.com
Contact: Mark Hutton.

eMusic Europe 48 Charlotte St, London W1T 2NS
t 0203 008 4610 **f** 020 7067 9731 **e** Emusic-uk@emusic.com
w emusic.com GM: Madeleine Milne.

Flip Records 2 Mardol, Shrewsbury SY1 1PY
t 01743 244 469 **f** 01743 260 985 **e** sales@fliprecords.com
w fliprecords.co.uk Owner: Duncan Morris.

The Fly 59-61 Farringdon Rd, London EC1M 3JB
t 020 7691 4555 **f** 020 7691 4666 **e** editorial@channelfly.com
w channelfly.com Ed: Will Kinsman.

HMV.co.uk Film House, 142 Wardour St, London W1F 8LN
t 020 7432 2000 **f** 020 7534 8113
e firstname.lastname@hmv.co.uk **w** hmv.co.uk
Head of Digital: Mark Bennett.

IntoMusic Unit 8, 6 Bloom Grove, London SE27 0HZ
t 020 8676 4850 **e** info@intomusic.co.uk **w** intomusic.co.uk
CEO: Gavin Moulton.

iTunes Europe 1 Hanover St, London W1S 1YZ
t 020 7184 1440 **f** 020 7184 1184
e lastname.initial@euro.apple.com **w** itunes.com.

Jansmusic PO Box 3136, Barnet, Herts EN5 1DY
t 020 8447 3862 **f** 020 8447 3862 **e** jan@jansmusic.co.uk
w jansmusic.co.uk Dir: Jan Hart.

Lost Dog Recordings 1103 Argyle St, Glasgow G3 8ND
t 0141 243 2439 **e** info@lostdogrecordings.com
w lostdogrecordings.com A&R: Jonathan Stone.

The Music Index 34 Coniston Rd, Neston, Cheshire
CH64 0TD **t** 0151 336 6199 **f** 0151 336 6199
e info@themusicindex.com **w** themusicindex.com
Sales Director: Christine Randall.

Music Village PO Box 8922, Maldon, Essex CM9 6ZW
e info@music-village.com **w** music-village.com Dir: John Carnell.

Musicroom.com 14-15 Berners St, London W1T 3LJ
t 020 7612 7400 **f** 020 7836 4810 **e** info@musicroom.com
w musicroom.com Dir, Internet Operations: Tomas Wise.

Musoswire PO Box 100, Gainsborough, Lincs DN21 3XH
t 01427 629184 **f** 01427 629184 **e** helpdesk@musoswire.com
w musoswire.com Prop: Dan Nash.

Napster UK 57-61 Mortimer St, London W1W 8HS
t 020 7101 7275 **f** 020 7101 7120
e firstname.lastname@napster.co.uk **w** napster.co.uk
Dir, UK & Int'l Prog'ing: Jeff Smith.

Netsounds Music PO Box 3007, Church Stretton SY6 7XH
t 0871 474 0564 **e** enquiries@netsoundsmusic.com
w netsoundsmusic.com.

Nu Urban Music Unit 3, Rivermead Industrial Estate,
Pipersway, Thatcham, Berks RG19 4EP **t** 01635 587900
f 01635 292314 **e** kevin@nu-urbanmusic.co.uk
w nu-urbanmusic.co.uk A&R Manager: Kevin Broome.

Oxfordmusic.net ltd 65 George St, Oxford OX1 2BE
t 01865 798796 **f** 01865 798792 **e** info@oxfordmusic.net
w oxfordmusic.net MD: Andy Clyde.

peoplesound.com 20 Orange St, London WC2H 7NN
t 020 7766 4000 **f** 020 7766 4001
e enquiries@peoplesound.com **w** peoplesound.com
Office Mgr: Arabella Edwards.

Plastic Music Ltd 22 Rutland Gardens, Hove, E Sussex
BN3 5PB **t** 01273 779 793 **f** 01273 779 820
e enzo@plastic-music.co.uk **w** plastic-music.co.uk
MD: Enzo (Vincent Amico).

PostEverything Suite 216, Bon Marché Centre, 241 Ferndale
Rd, London SW9 8BJ **t** 020 7733 2344 **f** 020 7733 5818
e feedback@posteverything.com **w** posteverything.com
Contact: Duncan Moore.

Pulse Rated Enterprise House, Wood Green Industrial Estate,
Salhouse, Norwich NR13 6NY **t** 0870 142 3456
f 01603 735 160 **e** business@pulserated.com **w** pulserated.com
Business Development: Peter Davis.

Rap and Soul Box 37163, London E4 7WR
t 020 8523 9578 **f** 020 8523 9601
e James@RapAndSoulMailOrder.com
w RapAndSoulMailOrder.com Dir: Mike Lewis.

Recordstore.co.uk Unit 5, Waldo Works, Waldo Rd, London
NW10 6AW **t** 020 8964 9020 **f** 020 8964 9090
e simon.coates@recordstore.co.uk **w** recordstore.co.uk
GM: Simon Coates.

Secondsounds.com PO Box 570, Amersham, Bucks
HP6 5ZP **t** 01494 875759 **e** information@secondsounds.com
w secondsounds.com Mkt Director: Kevin Rockett.

Shetland Music Distribution Ltd Griesta, Tingwall,
Shetland ZE2 9QB **t** 01595 840670 **f** 01595 840671
e enquiries@shetlandmusicdistribution.co.uk
w shetlandmusicdistribution.co.uk Dir: Alan Longmuir.

Simbiotic Dir, Argyle Court, 1103 Argyle St, Glasgow G3 8ND
t 0141 243 2439 **e** graham@simbiotic.co.uk **w** simbiotic.co.uk
Project Manager: Graham Collins.

sonic360 33 Riding House St, London W1W 7DZ
t 020 7636 3939 **f** 020 7636 0033 **e** info@sonic360.com
w sonic360.com Creative Director: Marc Raue.

Streetsonline.co.uk Overline House, Station Way, Crawley,
W Sussex RH10 1JA **t** 01293 402040 **f** 01293 402050
e nick.coquet@streetsonline.co.uk **w** streetsonline.co.uk
Content Mgr: Nick Coquet.

Tanty Records - The Dub Shop PO Box 557, Harrow,
Middlesex HA2 6ZX **t** 07802 463 154 **f** 020 8933 1027
e store@tantyrecordshop.com **w** tantyrecordshop.com
Owner: Kelvin Richard.

Ticketmaster UK 48 Leicester Sq, London WC2H 7LR
t 020 7344 4000 **f** 020 7915 0411 **e** sales@ticketmaster.co.uk
w ticketmaster.co.uk MD: Chris Edmonds.

TicketWeb UK 48 Leicester Sq, London WC2H 7LR
t 020 7344 4000 **f** 020 7915 0411 or c
e clients@ticketweb.co.uk **w** ticketweb.co.uk GM: Sam Arnold.

Toughshed.com 72 Rosebank Rd, Hanwell, London W7 2EN
t 07976 372 032 **f** 07092 272 032 **e** orders@toughshed.com
w toughshed.com MD: Neato.

Tower Records Ireland 6-8 Wicklow St, Dublin 2, Rep Of
Ireland **t** +353 1 671 3250 **f** +353 1 671 3260
e cliveb@towerrecords.ie **w** towerrecords.ie
Store Mgr: Clive Branagan.

Trax2burn Suite 201, Homelife House, 26 - 32 Oxford Rd,
Bournemouth BH8 8EZ **t** 01202 315333 **f** 01202 315600
e info@trax2burn.com **w** trax2burn.com Dir: Cliff Lay.

Tribal2Go.co.uk 11 Hillgate Pl, London SW12 9ER
t 020 8673 4343 **f** 020 8675 8562 **e** sales@tribal2go.co.uk
w tribal2go.co.uk Dirs: Alison Wilson, Terry Woolner.

Trustthedj.com White Horse Yard, 78 Liverpool Rd, London
N1 0QD **t** 020 7288 9810 **f** 020 7288 9817
e info@trustthedj.com **w** trustthedj.com Ops Mgr: Gab Rolph.

Tumi Music Ltd 8-9 New Bond Street Pl, Bath BA1 1BH
t 01225 464736 **f** 01225 444870 **e** info@tumi.co.uk
w tumimusic.com E Commerce: Damien Doherty.

TuneTribe 50-52 Paul St, London EC2A 4LB
t 020 7613 8260 **f** 020 7613 8360 **e** info@tunetribe.com
w tunetribe.com COO: Ronnie Traynor.

Tystdigital.com 35 Albany Rd, Chorlton, Manchester
M21 0BH **t** 0161 882 0058 **f** 0161 882 0058
e info@tsytdigital.com **w** tsytdigital.com Dir: David Wheawill.

UKSounds.com PO Box 36, Nantwich, Cheshire CW5 5FQ
t 01270 627264 **e** info@uksounds.com **w** uksounds.com
MD: Russ Walton.

UN Records Mare Street Studios, 203-213 Mare St, Hackney,
London E8 3QE **t** 020 8525 1188 **f** 020 8525 1188
e info@unrecords.co.uk **w** unrecords.co.uk MD: Jermaine Fagan.

Universal Group Direct Ltd 76 Oxford St, London
W1D 1BS **t** 020 8910 6012 **f** 020 8553 9613
e linda.porter@umusic.com **w** bclub.co.uk MD: Ford Ennals.

Upbeat Mail Order PO Box 63, Wallington, Surrey
SM6 9YP **t** 020 8773 1223 **f** 020 8669 6752
e info@upbeat.co.uk **w** upbeat.co.uk MD: Liz Biddle.

VidZone Digital Media The Limes, 123 Mortlake High St,
London SW14 8SN **t** 020 8487 5880 **f** 020 8487 9683
e adrian@vidzone.tv **w** vidzone.tv CEO: Adrian Workman.

Vinyl Tap 1 Minerva Works, Crossley Lane, Kirkheaton,
Huddersfiled, W Yorks HD5 0QP **t** 01484 421446
f 01484 531019 **e** sales@vinyltap.demon.co.uk **w** vinyltap.co.uk
Dir: Tony Boothroyd.

Virgin Retail School House, 50 Brook Green, Hammersmith,
London W6 7RR **t** 020 8752 9000 **f** 020 8752 9001
w virginmega.co.uk.

Vivante Music Ltd Unit 6, Fontigarry Business Pk, Reigate
Rd, Sidlow, Surrey RG2 8QH **t** 01293 822816 **f** 01293 821956
e sales@vivante.co.uk **w** vivante.co.uk MD: Steven Carr.

WeGotTickets.com 9 Park End St, Oxford OX1 1HH
t 01865 798 797 **f** 01865 798 792 **e** info@wegottickets.com
w WeGotTickets.com Marketing Dir: Laura Kramer.

WH Smith Online 1 Ashville Way, Cowley, Oxford OX4 6TS
t 01865 771772 **f** 01865 711766
e support@whsmithonline.co.uk **w** whsmith.co.uk
Mkting: Rowan Sadler.

Wippit 116 Gloucester Pl, London W1U 6HZ **t** 0870 737 1100
f 0870 737 1120 **e** info@wippit.com **w** wippit.com
MD: Paul Myers.

Xpressbeats.com Devonshire House, 223 Upper Richmond
Rd, London SW15 6SQ **t** 020 8780 0612 **f** 020 8789 8668
e admin@xpressbeats.com **w** xpressbeats.com
Contact: Rob Sawyer.

Online Delivery and Distribution

7 Digital Media Unit 3c, Zetland House, 5-25 Scrutton St,
London EC2A 4HJ **t** 020 7135 7777 **f** 0871 733 4149
e info@7digital.com **w** 7digital.com Contact: Ben Drury.

24-7 MusicShop 76 Hammersmith Rd, London W14 8UD
t 020 8243 4026 **f** 020 7610 5031 **e** js@247ms.com
w 247ms.com VP UK: Jonathan Smith.

Art Empire Industries Ltd Brincliffe House, 861 Ecclesall
Rd, Sheffield S11 7AE **t** 0114 281 4470 **f** 0114 292 3020
e sheffield@artempireindustries.com **w** artempireindustries.com
MD: Del Dias.

Astream Limited 25 Denmark St, London WC2H 8NJ
t 020 7628 9063 **f** 020 7638 2913 **e** info@astream.co.uk
w astream.net Comm Dir: Mark Wilson.

Awal (UK) Limited PO Box 183, Sheffield S2 4WX
t 0114 221 1906 **e** info@awal.co.uk **w** awal.co.uk
Label Manager: Paul Bower.

Blueprint Digital Unit 1, 73 Maygrove Rd, London NW6 2EG
t 020 7209 4224 **f** 020 7209 2334 **e** info@blueprint.net
w blueprint.net SVP, Products & Services: Mike Pears.

Broadchart Limited Shelana House, 31-32 Eastcastle St,
London W1W 8DW **t** 020 7637 8800 **f** 020 7436 8558
e info@broadchart.com **w** broadchart.com CEO: Andy Hill.

Cadiz Digital Ltd 2 Greenwich Quay, Clarence Rd, London
SE8 3EY **t** 020 8692 4691 **f** 020 8469 3300
e info@cadizdigital.net **w** cadizdigital.net MD: Richard England.

Consolidated Independent 8-10 Rhoda St, London
E2 7EF **t** 020 7729 8493 **e** info@ci-info.com **w** ci-info.com
MD: Gavin Starks.

CoullMedia The Television Centre, Bath Rd, Bristol BS4 3HG
t 0117 373 0470 **f** 0117 373 0471 **e** info@coullmedia.com
w coullmedia.com Sales Dir: Alastair Newing.

DA Recordings Ltd Osmond House, 78 Alcester Rd, Moseley
Village, Birmingham B13 8BB **t** 0121 449 3814
e info@darecordings.com **w** emusu.com MD: Chris Thompson.

Digital Pressure Inc. (Europe) The Peer House, 12
Lower Pembroke St, Dublin 2, Ireland **t** +353 1 662 9337
f +353 1 662 9339 **e** Darragh@digitalpressure.com
w digitalpressure.com VP: Darragh M. Kettle.

Unit 5, Waldo Works, Waldo Rd, London NW10 6AW
t 020 8964 9020 **f** 020 8964 9090
e Firstname+surname initial@digitalstores.co.uk
w digitalstores.co.uk Sales Dir: Simon Moxon. CEO: Russel
Coultart. New Business: Gary Pitt.
**Online Retail, E-commerce and fulfilment for physical and
digital products.**

Ditto Music 96 Ferncliffe Rd, Harborne, Birmingham B17 0QH
t 0121 420 1473 **f** 0121 420 1473 **e** info@dittomusic.com
w dittomusic.com MD: Matt Parsons.

DX3 3rd Floor, Clydesdale Bank House, 33 Regent St, London
SW1Y 4ZT **t** 0870 22 55 265 or 020 3105 2800
e info@dx3.net **w** dx3.net Dir: Tim Newmarch.

Dynamic Distribution - Massive Digital Unit 1, Crooks
Industrial Estate, Croft St, Leckhampton, Cheltenham, Glos
GL53 0ED **t** 01242 237 755 **f** 01242 237 755
e info@dynamic-distribution.net **w** dynamic-distribution.net
Dir: Joanna Massive.

Entertainment UK Direct Auriol Drive, Greenford Pk,
Greenford, Middx UB6 0DS **t** 020 8833 2888
f 020 8833 2967 **e** enquiriesdirect@entuk.co.uk **w** entuk.co.uk
GM: Graham Lambdon.

ePM Online Unit 204, Saga Centre, 326 Kensal Rd, London
W10 5BZ **t** 020 8964 4900 **f** 020 8964 3600
e melle@epm-musiconline.com **w** epm-musiconline.com
Ptnr: Melle Boels.

Fastrax Allan House, 10 John Prince's St, London W1G 0JW
t 020 7468 6888 **f** 020 7468 6889 **e** info@fastrax.co.uk
w fastrax.co.uk Contact: Ross Priestley, Sam Bailey, Karina Howe.

Flowphonics Ltd Argyle House, 1103 Argyle St, Glasgow
G3 8ND **t** 0141 221 2221 **e** info@flowphonics.com
w flowphonics.com MD: Gavin Robertson.

Indiestore.com Unit 3c, Zetland House, 5-25 Scrutton St,
London EC2A 4HJ **t** 020 7135 7777 **e** info@indiestore.com
w indiestore.com MD: Ben Drury.

Interactive Web Solutions 10 Parker Court, Dyson Way,
Staffordshire Technology Pk, Stafford, Staffs ST18 0WP
t 01785 279 920 **f** 01785 223 514
e services@iwebsolutions.co.uk **w** iwebsolutions.co.uk
Business Dev't Dir: Ian Gordon.

Digital: Download and Mail Order Websites; Online Delivery and Distribution

INTEROUTE

interoute⁺

Walbrook Building, 195 Marsh Wall, London E14 9SG
t 020 7025 9000 **f** 020 7025 9858 **e** info@interoute.com
w interoute.com Product Manager, Media Services: Oisin Lunny.
Head of Media Sales: Tim Daly. Head of Media Software
Development: Mark Lewis. Media Account Manager: Liza Cook.
Media Sales Manager: William Morrish. Media Platform
Architect: Russell Albert.
**From Podcasts, watermarking and DRM to video streaming,
Interoute's media CDN platform enables leading companies
to outsource digital infrastructure with confidence.**

Ioda 10 Allied Way, London W3 0RQ **t** 020 8600 9207
e info@iodalliance.com **w** iodalliance.com MD: Pete Dodge.

Key Production Digital Services 8 Jeffrey's Pl, Camden,
London NW1 9PP **t** 020 7284 8831 **f** 020 7284 8844
e mail@keyproduction.co.uk **w** keyproduction.co.uk
Sales & Marketing: Wendy Wood.

Radio Magnetic Argyle House, 16 Argyle Court, 1103 Argyle
St, Glasgow G3 8ND **t** 0141 226 8808 **f** 0141 226 8818
e dougal@radiomagnetic.com **w** radiomagnetic.com
Programme Director: Dougal Perman.

Matinee Sound & Vision Ltd 132-134 Oxford Rd,
Reading, Berks RG1 7NL **t** 0118 958 4934 **f** 0118 959 4936
e info@matinee.co.uk **w** matinee.co.uk
Marketing Co-ordinator: Miranda Harley.

MusicNet 109 Talbot Rd, #4,, London W11 2AT
t 07940 554 981 **e** markm@musicnet.com **w** musicnet.com
Snr Dir, Bus Dev't: Mark Mooradian.

Musicpoint Andrews House, College Rd, Guildford, Surrey
GU1 4QB **t** 01483 510 910 **f** 01483 510 911
e info@musicpointuk.com **w** musicpointuk.com
Business Development Mgr: Jeremy Wood.

Musoswire PO Box 100, Gainsborough, Lincs DN21 3XH
t 01427 629184 **f** 01427 629184 **e** helpdesk@musoswire.com
w musoswire.com Prop: Dan Nash.

MUZE EUROPE

Muze Drives the Media Experience™

Paulton House, 8 Shepherdess Walk, London N1 7LB
t 020 7566 8216 **f** 020 7566 8259 **e** dsass@muzeeurope.com
w muzeeurope.com Head of European Sales and Client Services:
Deborah Sass.
**International switchboard: +44 (0)20 7566 8216 Fax: +44
(0)20 7566 8259 www.searchmuze.co.uk**

On Demand Distribution (OD2) Macmillan House, 96
Kensington High St, London W8 4SG **t** 020 7082 0850
f 020 7082 0847 **e** info@ondemanddistribution.com
w ondemanddistribution.com UK Sales Dir: Paul Smith.

Pinnacle Digital Heather Court, 6 Maidstone Rd, Sidcup,
Kent DA14 5HH **t** 020 8309 3600 **f** 020 8309 3908
e info@pinnacle-records.co.uk **w** pinnacle-entertainment.co.uk
Head Of New Media: Dominic Jones.

Stream UK Ltd Studio 522, Highgate Studio, 53-79 Highgate
Rd, London NW5 1TL **t** 020 7387 6090 **f** 020 7419 1819
e enquiries@streamuk.com **w** streamuk.com
Sales Dir: Alfie Dennen.

Symbios Group 25 Barnes Wallis Rd, Segensworth East,
Fareham PO15 5TT **t** 0870 490 0000 **f** 0870 478 1530
e info@symbiosgroup.co.uk **w** symbiosgroup.co.uk
Marketing Dir: Gavin White.

THE (TOTAL HOME ENTERTAINMENT)

Committed to growing your business

London Commercial Office: 3.1 Shepherds West, Rockley Road,
Shepherds Bush, London W14 0DA **t** 020 8600 3500
f 020 8600 3519 **e** firstname.lastname@the.co.uk **w** the.co.uk
Commercial Dir: David Hollander. Audio General Manager: Andy
Adamson. Audio Buying Manager: Matt Rooke. Audio Marketing
Manager: Mike Ashton. Audio Marketing Assistant: Christian San
Martin. Audio Buyer: Melvyn Phillips. Export & Import Manager:
Luke Smith. Exclusive Labels & Export Manager: Mike Fay. Head
of Digital: Mark Headley.

TRIBAL2GO.CO.UK

TRIBAL2GO

11 Hillgate Place, London SW12 9ER **t** 020 8673 4343
f 020 8675 8562 **e** sales@tribal2go.co.uk **w** tribal2go.co.uk
Directors: Alison Wilson, Terry Woolner.
**For a secure on line service to customers via your own web
site for physical & digital product delivery.**

Universal Music Operations Ltd New Media And Digital
Services, 364-366 Kensington High St, London W14 8NS
t 020 7471 5000 or 020 7471 5077 **f** 020 7471 5001
e firstname.lastname@umusic.co.uk **w** umusic.co.uk
Head of Operations: PJ Dulay.

**Valuflik, Inc - Direct Choice TV Communications
Ltd** Suite 10, 3rd Floor, Macmillan House, 96 Kensington High
St, London W8 4SG **t** 020 7082 3928 or 07884 268 082
f 020 7082 0880 **e** jthomas@directchoicetv.com **w** valuflik.com
Business Dev't Manager: Johanna Thomas.

VidZone Digital Media The Limes, 123 Mortlake High St,
London SW14 8SN **t** 020 8487 5880 **f** 020 8487 9683
e adrian@vidzone.tv **w** vidzone.tv CEO: Adrian Workman.

VITAL:PIAS DIGITAL

[VITAL:PIAS]
DIGITAL

338a Ladbroke Grove, London W10 5AH **t** 020 8324 2400
f 020 8324 0001 **e** firstname.lastname@vitaluk.com
w vitaluk.com Head of Vital:Pias Digital: Adrian Pope. Vital:PIAS
Digital Manager: Will Cooper. **Direct Line: 020 8324 2447.**
Vital:PIAS Digital (Mobile): Richard Willis. **Direct Line: 020
8324 2436.**

WAM TV (Worldart Media Television Ltd) 1 High
St, Lasswade, Midlothian EH18 1NA **t** 0131 654 2372
e contact@wam.tv **w** wam.tv MD: Paul Blyth.

Mobile Delivery and Distribution

3 Star House, 20 Grenfell Rd, Maidenhead, Berks SL6 1EH **t** 01628 765 000 **f** 01628 767 031 **e** firstname.lastname@three.co.uk **w** three.co.uk Hd of Music & Entertain't: Andrew Parker.

7 Digital Media Unit 3c, Zetland House, 5-25 Scrutton St, London EC2A 4HJ **t** 020 7135 7777 **f** 0871 733 4149 **e** info@7digital.com **w** 7digital.com Contact: Ben Drury.

24-7 MUSICSHOP

76 Hammersmith Rd, London W14 8UD **t** 020 8243 4026 **f** 020 7610 5031 **e** js@247ms.com **w** 247ms.com VP UK: Jonathan Smith. CEO: Frank Taubert. CTO: Carl Nielsen. 24-7 provides an end-to-end solution for the legal sale of music and related digital assets over internet and mobile.

AEI Mobile Brincliffe House, 861 Ecclesall Rd, Sheffield S11 7AE **t** 0114 2814 470 **f** 01142 923 020 **e** info@aeimobile.com **w** aeimobile.com MD: Del Dias.

Awal (UK) Limited PO Box 183, Sheffield S2 4WX **t** 0114 221 1906 **e** info@awal.co.uk **w** awal.co.uk Label Manager: Paul Bower.

Bandwagon Ltd Studio 507 Enterprise House, 1-2 Hatfields, London SE1 9PG **t** 020 7993 1221 **e** support@bandwagon.co.uk **w** bandwagon.co.uk Dirs: Owen Farrington, Huw Thomas.

Blueprint Digital Unit 1, 73 Maygrove Rd, London NW6 2EG **t** 020 7209 4224 **f** 020 7209 2334 **e** info@blueprint.net **w** blueprint.net SVP, Products & Services: Mike Pears.

DX3 3rd Floor, Clydesdale Bank House, 33 Regent St, London SW1Y 4ZT **t** 0870 22 55 265 or 020 3105 2800 **e** info@dx3.net **w** dx3.net Dir: Tim Newmarch.

Flowphonics Ltd Argyle House, 1103 Argyle St, Glasgow G3 8ND **t** 0141 221 2221 **e** info@flowphonics.com **w** flowphonics.com MD: Gavin Robertson.

Inventa Productions 3rd Floor, Centro 3, 19 Mandela St, London NW1 0DU **t** 020 7387 2000 **f** 020 7529 8700 **e** theteam@inventa.co.uk **w** inventa.co.uk MD: Youssef Hammad.

Key Production Digital Services 8 Jeffrey's Pl, Camden, London NW1 9PP **t** 020 7284 8831 **f** 020 7284 8844 **e** mail@keyproduction.co.uk **w** keyproduction.co.uk Sales & Marketing: Wendy Wood.

Kodime 39 The Woodlands, Esher, Surrey KT10 8DD **t** 0870 787 4652 **f** 020 8224 0033 **e** info@kodime.com **w** kodime.com MD: Nico Kopke.

Look Media Queen's Wharf, Queen Caroline St, London W6 9RJ **t** 020 8600 2615 **f** 020 8600 2501 **e** dedmonds@lookmediauk.com **w** lookmediauk.com Contact: Damien Edmonds.

M2Y-Siemens UK 90 Long Acre, London WC2E 9RZ **t** 07730 426 310 **e** leslie.golding@siemens.com **w** siemens.com/m2y Hd of Content: Leslie Golding.

Masterpiece Unit 14 The Talina Centre, Bagleys Lane, London SW6 2BW **t** 020 7731 5758 **f** 020 7384 1750 **e** leena.bhatti@masterpiecelondon.com **w** masterpiecelondon.com Sales & Marketing Manager: Leena Bhatti.

MELODI

Ringtone House, 8 Wade Street, Lichfield, Staffordshire WS13 6HL **t** 0870 0622 900 **f** 01543 255 718 **e** info@melodimedia.co.uk **w** melodimedia.co.uk MD: Iain Kerr.

Mobiletones.com Unit 4, Handford Court, Garston Lane, Watford WD25 9EJ **t** 0870 444 7110 **f** 01923 675 299 **e** info@mobiletones.com **w** mobiletones.com Music Development Manager: Dominic Bignall.

MOBIQ

Tech House, Reddicap Trading Estate, Coleshill Road, Sutton Coldfield B75 7BU **t** 0121 311 9980 **f** 0121 311 9981 **e** info@mobiq.tv **w** mobiq.tv Commercial Dir: John Plant.

Mobiqa 111 George St, Edinburgh EH2 4JN **t** 0131 225 3141 **f** 0131 220 5353 **e** info@mobiqa.com **w** mobiqa.com CEO: Iain McCready.

MonsterMob Group Plc 52 Berkeley Sq, London W1J 5BT **t** 020 7408 4732 **f** 020 7491 3794 **e** david.bloomfield@monstermob.com **w** mob.tv HoM: David Bloomfield.

MusicNet 109 Talbot Rd, #4,, London W11 2AT **t** 07940 554 981 **e** markm@musicnet.com **w** musicnet.com Snr Dir, Bus Dev't: Mark Mooradian.

Indie Mobile 1st floor, Temple Gate Dojo, Templemeads, Bristol BS1 6QS **t** 0870 909 0500 **f** 0870 622 1314 **e** info@indie-mobile.com **w** indie-mobile.com MD: Seth Jackson.

MusiWave UK 77 Oxford St, London W1D 2ES **t** 020 7659 2053 **f** 020 7659 2100 **e** noel@musicwave.com **w** musiwave.com Business Dev't Mgr: Noel Penzer.

NoMoreMusic Ltd PO Box 44139, London SW6 7XR **t** 020 7386 2692 **f** 08707 060 024 **e** contact@nomoremusic.com **w** nomoremusic.com Dirs: Bobby M, Julian Lai-Hung.

O2 Music O2 UK, 260 Bath Rd, Slough, Berks SL1 4DX **t** 01132 722 000 **f** 01753 565 010 **e** firstname.lastname@o2.com **w** o2.co.uk/music Head of Content (Music, TV/Film and Sport): Grahame Riddell.

Pocket Group Unit 62/63, Pall Mall Depositry, 124-128 Barlby Rd, London W10 6BL **t** 0870 241 1827 **f** 0870 241 1829 **e** info@pocketgroup.co.uk **w** pocketgroup.co.uk MD: Andrew Hull.

Digital: Mobile Delivery and Distribution

pvNS - Alcatel Voyager Pl, Shoppenhangers Rd, Maidenhead, Berks SL6 2PJ **t** 01633 413600 **e** firstname.lastname@alcatel.co.uk **w** alcatel.com Contact: Patrick Parodi.

Qpass Golden Cross House, 8 Duncannon St, London WC2N 4JF **t** 020 7484 5031 **f** 020 7484 4958 **e** cpoepperl@qpass.com **w** qpass.com Marketing Dir: Claudia Poepperl.

Que Pasa Communications Ltd Coppergate House, 16 Brune St, London E1 7NJ **t** 020 7953 7700 **f** 020 7953 7709 **e** hugh@quepasacomms.co.uk **w** que-pasa.co.uk Commercial Dir: Hugh Burrows.

Rightsrouter 11 Sandyford Pl, Glasgow G3 7NB **t** 0141 222 1790 **f** 0141 221 4047 **e** info@rightsrouter.co.uk **w** rightsrouter.com CEO: Gavin Robinson.

ScreenFX Dudley House, 36-38 Southampton St, Covent Garden, London WC1E 7HE **t** 020 7240 0123 **f** 020 7240 0611 **e** info@screenfx.com **w** screenfx.com Sales Dir: Billy Howard.

SMS MusicMaker P.O. Box 44197, Fulham, London SW6 2XP **t** 07947 370 056 **e** info@smsmusicmaker.com **w** smsmusicmaker.com Dir: Barney Cordell.

Symbios Group 25 Barnes Wallis Rd, Segensworth East, Fareham PO15 5TT **t** 0870 490 0000 **f** 0870 478 1530 **e** info@symbiosgroup.co.uk **w** symbiosgroup.co.uk Marketing Dir: Gavin White.

T-Mobile International UK Hatfield Business Pk, Hatfield, Herts AL10 9BW **t** 01707 315000 or 01707 319000 **e** firstname.lastname@t-mobile.net **w** t-mobile.co.uk Snr Mgr, Content & Media: Keston Smith.

Tao Group Ltd 62 Suttons Business Pk, Reading, Berks RG6 1AZ **t** 0118 901 2999 **f** 0118 901 2963 **e** info@tao-group.com **w** tao-group.com Head of Audio: Tim Cole.

Toryumon 22 Upper Grosvenor St, London W1K 7PE **t** 020 7495 7794 **f** 020 7495 3885 **e** info@toryumon.co.uk **w** toryumon.co.uk UK Manager: Paul Kiernan.

Universal Music Operations Ltd New Media And Digital Services, 364-366 Kensington High St, London W14 8NS **t** 020 7471 5000 or 020 7471 5077 **f** 020 7471 5001 **e** firstname.lastname@umusic.com **w** umusic.co.uk Head of Operations: PJ Dulay.

Valuflik, Inc - Direct Choice TV Communications Ltd Suite 10, 3rd Floor, Macmillan House, 96 Kensington High St, London W8 4SG **t** 020 7082 3928 or 07884 268 082 **f** 020 7082 0880 **e** jthomas@directchoicetv.com **w** valuflik.com Business Dev't Manager: Johanna Thomas.

Victoria Real Ltd Shepherds Building Central, Charecroft Way, London W14 0EE **t** 020 8222 4170 **f** 020 8222 4415 **e** susan.doherty@victoriareal.com **w** victoriareal.com Hd of Business Dev't: Susan Doherty.

VIDZONE DIGITAL MEDIA

The Limes, 123 Mortlake High Street, London SW14 8SN **t** 020 8487 5880 **f** 020 8487 9683 **e** adrian@vidzone.tv **w** vidzone.tv CEO: Adrian Workman. CTO: Michael Russo. Head of Marketing: Louisa Jackson. Operations Manager: Jon Pike. Web Manager: Ben Speas.

Vodafone Group Services 80 Strand, London WC2R 0RJ **t** 020 7212 0000 **f** 020 7212 0701 **e** firstname.lastname@vodafone.com **w** via.vodafone.com HoM.

WIN 1 Cliveden Office Village, Lancaster Rd, High Wycombe, Bucks HP12 3YZ **t** 01494 750500 **f** 01494 750800 **e** businessdevelopment@winplc.com **w** winplc.com Marketing Manager: Ben King.

Xbox - Europe, Middle East & Africa Microsoft House, 10 Great Pulteney St, London W1F 9NB **t** 020 7434 6172 **f** 020 7434 6495 **e** markcad@microsoft.com Hd, Strategic P'tnerships: Mark Cadogan.

Web Design and Digital Services

7 Digital Media Unit 3c, Zetland House, 5-25 Scrutton St, London EC2A 4HJ **t** 020 7135 7777 **f** 0871 733 4149 **e** info@7digital.com **w** 7digital.com Contact: Ben Drury.

Agitprop Design & Communications 19 Links Yard, 29a Spelman St, London E1 5LX **t** 07989 586 272 **e** musicweek@agitprop.co.uk **w** agitprop.co.uk Creative Dir: Jim Holt.

Airside 24 Cross St, London N1 2BG **t** 020 7354 9912 **f** 020 7354 5529 **e** studio@airside.co.uk **w** airside.co.uk Studio Manager: Anne Brassier.

All of Music Design PO Box 2361, Romford, Essex RM2 6EZ **t** 01708 688 088 **f** 020 7691 9508 **e** michelle@allofmusic.co.uk **w** allofmusic.co.uk MD: Danielle Barnett.

AMP Online Marketing 8-10 Rhoda St, London E2 7EF **t** 020 7739 0100 **f** 020 7739 8571 **e** info@ampunited.com **w** ampunited.com Dir: Jim Gottlieb.

Amplifeye 5 Pendarves Rd, Camborne, Cornwall TR14 7QB **t** 0871 789 4219 or 07886 923 821 **e** dan@amplifeye.com **w** amplifeye.net Dir: Daniel Mitchell.

AOL 80 Hammersmith Rd, London W14 8UD **t** 020 7348 8000 **f** 020 7348 8002 **w** aol.com.

ArtScience Limited 3-5 Hardwidge St, London SE1 3SY **t** 020 7939 9500 **f** 020 7939 9499 **e** lab5@artscience.net **w** artscience.net Dirs: Douglas Coates, Pete Rope.

Atari Landmark House, Hammersmith Bridge Rd, London W6 9DP **t** 020 8222 9700 **e** firstname.lastname@atari.com **w** atari.com UK Marketing Director: Richard Orr.

Backbeat Solutions 24 Annandale Rd, Greenwich, London SE10 0DA **t** 020 8858 6241 **e** info@backbeatsolutions.com **w** backbeatsolutions.com CEO: Chris Chambers.

Bang On - Online PR 41B Ferntower Rd, London N5 2JE **t** 020 7503 4778 **e** info@bangonpr.com **w** bangonpr.com Online Publicists: Leanne Mison, Katie Riding.

Beatwax Communications 91 Berwick St, London W1F ONE **t** 020 7734 1965 **f** 020 7292 8333 **e** michael@beatwax.com **w** beatwax.com MD: Michael Brown.

Big Picture Interactive Ltd 9 Parade, Leamington Spa, Warcs CV32 4DG **t** 01926 422002 **f** 01926 450945 **e** enquiries@bigpictureinteractive.co.uk **w** thebigpic.co.uk PA: Sarah Pannell.

Bite IT Ltd Atrium House, 574 Manchester Rd, Bury BL9 9SW **t** 0845 052 2875 **f** 0870 490 2327 **e** declan@biteit.net **w** biteit.net MD: Declan Cosgrove.

Bloc Media Ltd 61 Charlotte Rd, London EC2A 3QT **t** 020 7739 1718 **f** 020 7739 9494 **e** contact@blocmedia.com **w** blocmedia.com MD: Rick Palmer.

Blue Source Ltd. Lower Ground Floor, 49-51 Central St, London EC1V 8AB **t** 020 7553 7950 **e** seb@bluesource.com **w** bluesource.com Company Director: Seb Marling.

Bomdigi Productions 37 Snowsfields, London SE1 3SU **t** 07949 617863 **f** 0207 4074615 **e** jo@bomdigi.com **w** bomdigi.com Multimedia Producer & Director: Jo Roach.

C-Burn Systems Ltd 33 Sekforde St, London EC1R 0HH **t** 020 7250 1133 **f** 020 7253 8553 **e** info@c-burn.com **w** c-burn.com Sales & Marketing: Neil Phillips.

Cake Group Ltd 10 Stephen Mews, London W1T 1AG **t** 020 7307 3100 **f** 020 7307 3101 **e** andrea@cakegroup.com **w** cakegroup.com Head of Marketing: Andrea Ledsham.

Cannonball PR 695 High Rd, Seven Kings, Ilford, Essex IG3 8RH **t** 020 8590 0022 or 07885 670 294 **f** 020 8599 2870 **e** jamie@cannonballpr.com **w** cannonballpr.com MD: Jamie Danan.

Chieftain Music 17 Maidavale Crescent, Styvechale, Coventry CV3 6FZ **t** 07811 469 888 **e** chiefdave@gmail.com MD: Dave Robinson.

Clear Sound And Vision Ltd CSV House, 51 Marlborough Rd, London E18 1AR **t** 020 8989 8777 **f** 020 8989 9777 **e** sales@c-s-v.co.uk **w** c-s-v.co.uk MD: Clive Robins.

Clevercherry.com Victoria Works, Birmingham B1 3PE **t** 0121 236 1060 **e** ineedhelp@clevercherry.com **w** clevercherry.com MD: Ian Allen.

ColBrowne.co.uk St 4, Fl 4, The Old Truman Brewery, 91-95 Brick Lane, London E1 6QL **t** 07802 824 001 **e** me@colbrowne.co.uk **w** colbrowne.co.uk MD: Col Browne.

CopyMaster International Ltd 8 Arundel Rd, Uxbridge Trading Estate, Uxbridge, Middlesex UB8 2RR **t** 01895 814 813 **f** 01895 814 999 **e** firstname@copymaster.co.uk **w** copymaster.co.uk Sales Mgr: Ron Boucaud.

Counterpoint Systems 74-80 Camden St, London NW1 0EG **t** 020 7543 7500 **f** 020 7543 7600 **e** info@counterp.com **w** counterp.com CEO: Amos Biegun.

The Creative Corporation Magpie Studios, 2a Leconfield Rd, London N5 2SN **t** 020 7704 9234 or 07779 615 217 **e** contact@thecreativecorporation.co.uk **w** thecreativecorporation.co.uk Contact: Dave Stansbie.

D-Fuse 13-14 Gt.Sutton St, London EC1V 0BX **t** 020 7253 3462 **e** info@dfuse.com **w** dfuse.com Dir: Michael Faulkner.

Demon Imaging 4th Floor, 23 Charlotte Rd, London EC2A 3PB **t** 020 7739 9697 **e** info@demonimaging.com **w** demonimaging.com Dir: Jamie Baker.

Design Esti First Floor, St. Andrews House, 62 Bridge St, Manchester M3 3BW **t** 0161 838 9183 **f** 0161 838 9189 **e** Hello@DesignEsti.com **w** designesti.com Marketing Director: Steven Oakes.

Design Lab Studio 336, Stratford Workshops, Burford Rd, London E15 2SP **t** 020 8555 5540 or 07841 196 787 **f** 0208 5555540 **e** info@design-lab.tv **w** design-lab.tv Art Director: Matthew James.

Digital Press Kit 11 St. Bede's Terrace, Christchurch, Sunderland SR3 8HS **t** 0191 565 2429 **e** info@martinjames.demon.co.uk **w** digitalpresskit.co.uk MD: Martin James.

Digital Stores Unit 5, Waldo Works, Waldo Rd, London NW10 6AW **t** 020 8964 9020 **f** 020 8964 9090 **e** Firstname+surname initial@digitalstores.co.uk **w** digitalstores.co.uk Sales Dir: Simon Moxon.

Diverse Interactive 6 Gorleston St, London W14 8XS **t** 020 7603 4567 **f** 020 7603 2148 **e** info@diverse.tv **w** diverse.co.uk Interactive Prod Mgr: Nicola Wells.

Division 100 Unit Two, 34 Charlotte Rd, London EC2A 3PB **t** 020 7033 0000 **f** 020 7033 0001 **e** designers@division100.com **w** division100.com Dir: Terence Chisholm.

DMCC - Online Marketing and Search Engines 34 Hereford Rd, London W2 5AJ **t** 07092 047 348 **f** 07092 047 348 **e** SearchFindUse@DMCC.net **w** dmcc.net Projects Director: Fiona Austin.

Dreamcatcher Studios Ltd 3, Merryman Drive, Crowthorne, Berks RG45 6TW **t** 07771 818 111 **f** 01344 779 677 **e** leeault@dreamcatcherstudios.co.uk **w** dreamcatcherstudios.co.uk Creative Director: Lee Ault.

DS Emotion Ltd Chantry House, Victoria Rd, Leeds, W Yorks LS5 3JB **t** 0113 225 7100 **f** 0113 225 7200 **e** info@dsemotion.com **w** dsemotion.com.

eJay Empire Interactive Europe Ltd., The Spires, 677 High Rd, North Finchley, London N12 0DA **t** 020 8492 1049 **f** 020 8343 7447 **e** cate@empire.co.uk **w** eJay.com Brand Manager: Cate Swift.

Epic 52 Old Steine, Brighton, E Sussex BN1 1NH **t** 01273 728 686 **f** 01273 821 567 **e** marketing@epic.co.uk **w** epic.co.uk Marketing Manager: Ericka Newton.

Fastchanges 15 Barlby Gardens, London W10 5LW **t** 020 7870 8159 **e** info@fastchanges.com **w** fastchanges.com Design Director: Jude Samuel.

Firebrand 3 Wish Rd, Eastbourne, E Sussex BN21 4NX **t** 01323 430700 **f** 01323 430223 **e** enq@firebrand.co.uk **w** firebrand.co.uk Creative Director: Michael Dale.

Four23 Films The Apex, 6 Southern St, Castlefield, Manchester M3 4NN **t** 0161 835 9466 **f** 0161 835 9468 **e** mailman@four23.net **w** four23.net Dir: Warren Bramley.

Fourmiles Media Services PO Box 5571, Milton Keynes MK3 5YN **t** 0709 222 3643 **f** 0705 069 8195 **e** enquiries@fourmiles.com **w** fourmiles.com MD: David Wright.

Freehand Limited Unit 52, Dunsfold Pk, Cranleigh, Surrey GU6 8TB **t** 01483 200 111 **f** 01483 200 101 **e** phil.kerby@freehand.co.uk **w** freehand.co.uk/production Contact: Phil Kerby.

Glasseye Unit 20A, Iliffe Yard, Crampton St, London SE17 3QA **t** 020 7701 4300 **e** info@glasseyeltd.com **w** glasseyeltd.com Dir: James Jefferson.

Good Technology 15-19 Gt Titchfield St, London W1W 8AZ **t** 020 7299 7000 **f** 020 7299 7070 **e** info@goodtechnology.com **w** goodtechnology.com MD: Xanthe Arvanitakis.

Graphico Goldwell House, Old Bath Rd, Newbury, Berks RG14 1JH **t** 01635 522810 **f** 01635 580621 **e** solutions@graphico.co.uk **w** graphico.co.uk Strategic Partner: Graham Darracott.

Greenroom Digital PR 87A Worship St, London EC2A 2BE **t** 020 7426 5700 **f** 020 7377 8616 **e** emily@greenroom-digital.com **w** greenroom-digital.com Office Manager: Emily Eades.

Hyperlaunch New Media Mardyke House, 16-22 Hotwell Rd, Bristol BS8 4UD **t** 0117 914 0070 **f** 0117 914 0071 **e** don@hyperlaunch.com **w** hyperlaunch.com MD: Don Jenkins.

iCast UK Ltd 7 Charteris Rd, London NW6 7EU **t** 020 7624 4605 or 07970 488 179 **e** gill@icast.uk.com **w** icast.uk.com Dir: Gill Mills.

ID Interactive 5 Rolls Crescent, Manchester M15 5JX **t** 0161 232 9314 **f** 0161 232 9514 **e** info@idinteractive.co.uk **w** idinteractive.net Mgr: Azmat Mohammed.

Ignite Marketing Unit 17C Raines Court, Northwold Rd, London N16 7DH **t** 020 7275 8682 **f** 020 7275 0791 **e** paul@ignitemarketing.co.uk **w** ignitemarketing.co.uk MD: Paul West.

iMastering Online Mastering Services Metropolis Group, The Powerhouse, 70 Chiswick High Rd, London W4 1SY **t** 020 8742 1111 **f** 020 8742 2626 **e** imaster@metropolis-group.co.uk **w** imastering.co.uk Mastering Mgr: Michele Conroy.

Indiestore.com Unit 3c, Zetland House, 5-25 Scrutton St, London EC2A 4HJ **t** 020 7135 7777 **e** info@indiestore.com **w** indiestore.com MD: Ben Drury.

Inner Ear Ltd Argyle House, 16 Argyle Court, 1103 Argyle St, Glasgow G3 8ND **t** 0141 226 8808 **f** 0141 226 8818 **e** dougal@radiomagnetic.com **w** radiomagnetic.com Programme Director: Dougal Perman.

Interactive Web Solutions 10 Parker Court, Dyson Way, Staffordshire Technology Pk, Stafford, Staffs ST18 0WP **t** 01785 279 920 **f** 01785 223 514 **e** services@iwebsolutions.co.uk **w** iwebsolutions.co.uk Business Dev't Dir: Ian Gordon.

Interface New Media 20A Brownlow Mews, London WC1N 2LA **t** 020 7416 0702 **f** 020 7416 0700 **e** info@interface-newmedia.com **w** interface-newmedia.com Dir: Neil Jones.

iomart Lister Pavilion, Kelvin Campus, West of Scotland Science Pk, Glasgow, Scotland G20 0SP **t** 0141 931 6400 **f** 0141 931 6401 **e** forrest@iomart.com **w** iomart.com Sales: Forrest Duncan.

IQ Media (Bracknell) Ltd 2 Venture House, Arlington Sq, Bracknell, Berks RG12 1WA **t** 01344 422 551 or 07884 262 755 **f** 01344 453 355 **e** information@iqmedia-uk.com **w** iqmedia-uk.com MD: Tony Bellamy.

Key Production Digital Services 8 Jeffrey's Pl, Camden, London NW1 9PP **t** 020 7284 8831 **f** 020 7284 8844 **e** mail@keyproduction.co.uk **w** keyproduction.co.uk Sales & Marketing: Wendy Wood.

Lateral Net Ltd Charlotte House, 47-49 Charlotte Rd, London EC2A 3QT **t** 020 7613 4449 **f** 020 7613 4645 **e** studio@lateral.net **w** lateral.net Client Services Dir: David Hart.

LoFly Web Technology Unit 2A Queens Studios, 121 Salusbury Rd, London NW6 6RG **t** 020 7372 4474 **f** 020 7328 4447 **e** info@lofly.co.uk **w** lofly.co.uk New Media Programmers: Peter Gill, Tom Parkinson.

Luna Internet Ltd 8 Triumph Way, Woburn Road Industrial Estate, Kempston, Bedford MK42 7QB **t** 0845 345 0175 **f** 01234 299 009 **e** info@luna.co.uk **w** luna.co.uk Sales & Mktg Dir: Spencer Ecclestone.

Mackerel Design Ltd 15-17 Middle St, Brighton, W Sussex BN1 1AL **t** 01273 201313 **e** info@mackerel.co.uk **w** mackerel.co.uk Dir: Mark Davis.

Magex Limited 4th Floor, 32 Lombard St, London EC3V 9BQ **t** 020 7070 4000 **f** 020 7070 4999 **e** ask@magex.com **w** magex.com Pres: Alexander Grous.

Mando Group 30-32 Faraday Rd, Wavertree Tech Pk, Liverpool L13 1EH **t** 0151 281 4040 **f** 0151 281 0060 **e** liverpool@mandogroup.com **w** mandogroup.com

Martello Media Limited 4 Islington Ave, Sandycove, Co Dublin, Ireland **t** +353 1 284 4668 **f** +353 1 280 3195 **e** info@martellomedia.com **w** martellomedia.com Mkting Mgr: Edel Peppard.

MasteringWorld.com Hafod, St Hilary, Cowbridge, Wales CF71 7DP **t** 01446 771789 **f** 01446 775512 **e** enquiries@masteringworld.com **w** masteringworld.com Dir: Donal Whelan.

Matinée Sound & Vision Ltd 132-134 Oxford Rd, Reading, Berks RG1 7NL **t** 0118 957 5876 **f** 0118 959 4936 **e** info@matinee.co.uk **w** matinee.co.uk Marketing Co-ordinator: Miranda Harley.

!MediaTank First Floor, 63 Allington Rd, Bristol BS3 1PT **t** 020 7193 5559 **e** mark@mediatank.co.uk **w** mediatank.co.uk Contact: Mark Panay.

Mekon Ltd Mekon House, 31-35 St Nicholas Way, Sutton, Surrey SM1 1JN **t** 020 8722 8400 **f** 020 8722 8500 **e** info@mekon.com **w** mekon.com Sales Dir: Julian Murfitt.

Microsoft - MSN Microsoft House, 10 Great Pulteney St, London W1R 3TG **t** 0870 60 10 100 **w** mircrosoft.com/uk/info.

Midas Multimedia 11 Ashley Park South, Aberdeen AB10 6RP **t** 07808 725 362 **f** 01224 580 113 **e** info@midas-multimedia.com **w** midas-multimedia.com Ptnr: Scott Brown.

Million 3 Brook St, Twyford RG10 9NX **t** 07855 449 845
e neil@1-000-000.com **w** 1-000-000.com MD: Neil Cartwright.

Moonfish Ltd 43 Hulme St, Manchester M15 6AW
t 08700 70 4321 **f** 08707 41 8931
e fish.market@moonfish.com **w** moonfish.com
Creative Dir: Bill Croson.

Motion 8-10 Rhoda St, London E2 7EF **t** 020 7739 0100
f 020 7739 8571 **e** steven@motiongroup.co.uk
w motiongroup.co.uk
New Media Marketing Manager: Steven Colborne.

**Musicalc Systems Ltd. (Royalty Accounting
Software)** 24 Grove Lane, Kingston-upon-Thames, Surrey
KT1 2ST **t** 020 8541 5135 or 07881 913 279 **f** 020 8541 1885
e info@musicalc.com **w** musicalc.com
Marketing Manager: Asa Palmer.

Musically Ltd Davina House, 137-149 Goswell Rd, London
EC1V 7ET **t** 020 7490 5444 or 07956 579 642
f 0870 160 6572 **e** paul@musically.com **w** musically.com
MD: Paul Brindley.

Mystery Ltd 2nd Floor, 79 Parkway, Camden, London
NW1 7PP **t** 020 7424 1900 **f** 020 7267 0191
e will@mystery.co.uk **w** mystery.co.uk
Studio Manager: Will Watts.

Nile-On Online PR & Marketing 24 Porden Rd, London
SW2 5RT **t** 020 7737 1433 **e** serena@nile-on.com **w** nile-on.com
Online Press Director: Serena Wilson.

ntl: 90 Long Acre, London WC2E 9RA **t** 020 7909 2100
f 020 7909 2101 **e** firstname.surname@ntl.com **w** ntl.co.uk
Contact: Mark James.

onedotzero Unit 212C, Curtain House, 134-146 Curtain Rd,
London EC2A 3AR **t** 020 7729 0072 **f** 020 7729 0057
e info@onedotzero.com **w** onedotzero.com Dir: Shane Walter.

OR Multimedia Ltd Unit 5 Elm Court, 156-170 Bermondsey
St, London SE1 3TQ **t** 020 7939 9540 **f** 020 7939 9541
e info@or-media.com **w** or-media.com Dir: Peter Gough.

Outpost Unit 20, Acklam Workspace, 10 Acklam Rd, London
W10 5QZ **t** 020 8964 8541 **f** 020 8968 7725
e david@outpostmedia.co.uk **w** outpostmedia.co.uk
Dir: David Silverman.

Outside Line Butler House, 177-178 Tottenham Court Rd,
London W1T 7NY **t** 020 7636 5511 **f** 020 7636 1155
e ant@outsideline.co.uk **w** outsideline.co.uk Dir: Anthony Cauchi.

Phoenix Video Ltd Global House, Denham, North Orbital Rd,
Uxbridge, Middlesex UB9 5HL **t** 01895 837000
f 01895 833085 **e** sales@phoenix-video.co.uk
w phoenix-video.co.uk MD: Terry Young.

Poptel Technology Ltd 2nd Floor, 13 Swan Yard, London
N1 1SD **t** 0845 899 1001 **f** 0845 899 0180
e info@poptech.coop **w** poptech.coop
Business Development: Paul Evans.

Prezence 35 Denby Buildings, Regent Grove, Leamington Spa,
Warcs CV32 4NY **t** 01926 422004 **f** 01926 422005
e tim@prezence.co.uk **w** prezence.co.uk MD: Tim Bishop.

Proactive PR Suite 201, Homelife House, 26 - 32 Oxford Rd,
Bournemouth BH8 8EZ **t** 01202 315 333 **f** 01202 315 600
e info@proactivepr.org **w** proactivepr.org Dir: Cliff Lay.

Probe Media 2nd Floor, The Hogarth Centre, Hogarth Lane,
London W4 2QN **t** 020 8742 3636 **f** 020 8995 1350
e sanjay@probemedia.co.uk **w** probemedia.co.uk
Account Director: Sanjay Vadher.

Real Time The Unit, 2 Manor Gardens, London N7 6ER
t 020 7561 6700 **f** 020 7561 6701 **e** hq@realtimeinfo.co.uk
w realtimeinfo.co.uk Dir: Simon Edwards.

Real World Multimedia Box Mill, Millside, Mill Lane, Box,
Wilts SN13 8PL **t** 01225 743188 **f** 01225 744369
e york.tillyer@realworld.co.uk **w** realworld.co.uk
Interactive Dir: York Tillyer.

RealNetworks Europe Ltd. 1st Floor, 233 High Holborn,
London WC1V 7DN **t** 020 7618 4000 **f** 020 7618 4001
e initial+lastname@real.com **w** realnetworks.com
Sales Director: David Smith.

Rednet Ltd 6 Cliveden Office Village, Lancaster Rd, High
Wycombe, Bucks HP12 3YZ **t** 01494 513 333 **f** 01494 443 374
e contactus@red.net **w** red.net Mktg Mgr: Zoe Marrett.

rehabstudio Ltd 1st Floor, Oaklands, 64-66 Redchurch St,
London E2 7DP **t** 0203 222 0080
e newbusiness@rehabstudio.com **w** rehabstudio.com
Creative Director: Tim Rodgers.

Ricall Limited First Floor, 14 Buckingham Palace Rd, London
SW1W 0QP **t** 020 7592 1710 **f** 020 7592 1713
e marketing@ricall.com **w** ricall.com
MD, Investor Relations: Richard Corbett.

Rightsrouter 11 Sandyford Pl, Glasgow G3 7NB
t 0141 222 1790 **f** 0141 221 4047 **e** info@rightsrouter.co.uk
w rightsrouter.com CEO: Gavin Robinson.

Rootsmusic.com 22 Oregon Ave, Manor Pk, London
E12 5TD **t** 020 8553 1435 **f** 020 8553 1435
e info@rootsmusic.co.uk **w** rootsmusic.co.uk MD: Ayo Bamidele.

Sandbag Ltd 59/61 Milford Rd, Reading RG1 8LG
t 0118 9505812 **f** 0118 9505813 **e** mungo@sandbag.uk.com
w sandbag.uk.com Contact: Christiaan Munro.

Sign-Up Technologies (E-Marketing) 60 Maltings Pl,
London SW6 2BX **t** 0845 644 4184 **e** solutions@sign-up.to
w sign-up.to MD: Matt McNeill.

Simbiotic Mercat House, Argyle Court, 1103 Argyle St,
Glasgow G3 8ND **t** 0141 243 2439 **e** graham@simbiotic.co.uk
w simbiotic.co.uk Dir: Graham Collins.

Single Minded Productions 11 Cambridge Court, 210
Shepherd's Bush Rd, London W6 7NJ **t** 0870 011 3748
f 0870 011 3749 **e** tony@singleminded.com **w** singleminded.com
MD: Tony Byrne.

Skinny 4th Floor, 11 D'Arblay St, London W1F 8DT
t 020 7287 1888 **e** sonya@fullfatskinny.com **w** fullfatskinny.com
Dir: Sonya Skinner.

Solaris Media 20 Damien St, London E1 2HX
t 020 7791 1555 **f** 020 7791 1545
e musicweek.email@solarismedia.com **w** solarismedia.com
MD: Rob Davis.

Sonic Arts The Shaftesbury Centre, 85 Barlby Rd, London
W10 6BN **t** 020 8962 3000 **f** 020 8962 6200
e avi@sonic-arts.com **w** sonic-arts.com
Contact: Miranda Webster.

Sony Psygnosis Ltd Napier Court, Wavertree Technology Pk, Liverpool, Merseyside L13 1HD **t** 0151 282 3000 **f** 0151 282 3001 **e** (firstname)_(surname)@scee.net **w** playstation.com.

Soundengineer.co.uk 49 Liddington Rd, London E15 3PL **t** 020 8536 0649 **f** 07092 022897 **e** ian@soundengineer.co.uk **w** soundengineer.co.uk Sound Engineer: Ian Hasell.

state51 8-10 Rhoda St, London E2 7EF **t** 020 7729 4343 **f** 020 7729 8494 **e** intouch@state51.co.uk **w** state51.co.uk Dir: Paul Sanders.

Storm Interactive Entertainment c/o Sloane & Co, 36-38 Westbourne Grove, Newton Rd, London W2 5SH **t** 020 7099 8849 **f** 020 7099 8850 **e** info@storminteractive.com **w** storminteractive.com MD: Stephen Bayley-Johnston.

Stream UK Studio 522, Highgate Studio, 53-79 Highgate Rd, London NW5 1TL **t** 020 7387 6090 **f** 020 7419 1819 **e** enquiries@streamuk.com **w** streamuk.com Sales Dir: Alfie Dennen.

Telepathy Interactive Media Hardy House, High St, Box, Wilts SN13 8NF **t** 01225 744225 **f** 01225 744554 **e** info@telepathy.co.uk **w** telepathy.co.uk Dir: Nigel Milk.

TheFireFactory.com 3-5 High Pavement, The Lace Market, Nottingham NG1 1HF **t** 0115 989 7389 **f** 0870 131 4234 **e** info@thefirefactory.com **w** thefirefactory.com Producer: Jake Shaw.

Tomorrow Never Knows 15 Hopkin Close, Queen Elizabeth Pk, Guildford, Surrey GU2 9LS **t** 01483 234428 **f** 01483 234428 **e** ritch@tomorrowneverknows.co.uk **w** tomorrowneverknows.co.uk MD: Ritch Ames.

TWO:design London Studio 20, The Arches, Hartland Rd, Camden, London NW1 8HR **t** 020 7267 1118 **f** 020 7482 0221 **e** studio@twodesign.net **w** twodesign.net Creative Director: Graham Peake.

UnLimited Digital Fl 3, Grampian House, Meridian Gate, London E14 9YT **t** 0870 744 2643 **f** 070 9231 4982 **e** chris@unlimitedmedia.co.uk **w** unlimitedmedia.co.uk MD: Chris Cooke.

Version 15 Holywell Row, London EC2A 4JB **t** 020 7684 5470 **f** 020 7684 5472 **e** info@versioncreative.com **w** versioncreative.com Dirs: Anthony Oram, Mo Chicharro.

Version Industries Ltd 47 Lower End, Swaffham Prior, Cambridge CB5 0HT **t** 07903 886 471 **f** 020 8374 4021 **e** team@versionindustries.com **w** versionindustries.com Lead Designer/Developer: Gavin Singleton.

VidZone Digital Media The Limes, 123 Mortlake High St, London SW14 8SN **t** 020 8487 5880 **f** 020 8487 9683 **e** adrian@vidzone.tv **w** vidzone.tv CEO: Adrian Workman.

Virgin Interactive Entertainment 74A Charlotte St, London W1T 4QN **t** 020 7551 4236 **f** 020 7551 4267 **e** clifford_harry@hotmail.com **w** vie.co.uk Tech Support Rep.: Clifford Harry.

Virgin Net The Communications Building, 48 Leicester Sq, London WC2H 7LT **t** 020 7664 6000 **f** 020 7664 6006 **e** media@london.virgin.net **w** virgin.net.

Visualeyes Imaging Services 11 West St, Covent Garden, London WC2H 9NE **t** 020 7836 3004 **f** 020 7240 0079 **e** imaging@visphoto.co.uk **w** visphoto.co.uk Sales & Marketing Manager: Fergal O'Regan.

WayOutWebs.co.uk PO Box 1345, Ilford, Essex IG4 5FX **t** 07050 333 555 **e** info@wayoutwebs.co.uk **w** wayoutwebs.co.uk Business Devt Director: Paul Booth.

WEB SHERIFF

Argentum, 2 Queen Caroline Street, London W6 9DX **t** 020 8323 8013 **f** 020 8323 8080 **e** websheriff@websheriff.com **w** websheriff.com MD: John Giacobbi.

Web User IPC Media, Kings Reach Tower, Stamford St, London SE1 9LS **t** 020 7261 6597 **f** 020 7261 7878 **e** nicola_ponting@ipcmedia.com **w** web-user.co.uk Advertising and Sponsorship Manager: Nicola Ponting.

Wheel Beaumont House, Kensington Village, Avonmore Rd, London W14 8TS **t** 020 7348 1000 **f** 020 7348 1111 **e** jillian.cross@wheel.co.uk **w** wheel.co.uk Business Dev't Mgr: Jillian Cross.

White Label Productions Ltd Power Road Studios, 114 Power Rd, London W4 5PY **t** 020 8987 7070 **f** 020 8987 7090 **e** c.grant@whitelabelproductions.co.uk **w** whitelabelproductions.co.uk MD: Cheryl Grant.

x! Artwork: Music Art Design + Direction London Studio, Suite VP, PO Box 43128, London E17 6WS **t** 020 8925 6542 or 07753 755 353 **f** 020 8925 6542 **e** services@xartwork.co.uk **w** xartwork.co.uk Creative Director: William Frank.

ZDNet UK Ltd International House, 1 St Katharine's Way, London E1W 1XQ **t** 020 7903 6800 **f** 020 7903 6000 **e** firstname.lastname@zdnet.co.uk **w** zdnet.co.uk Ops Dir: Jill Hourston.

bands, singers, artists, businesses
what are you waiting for?

photos

images

music

documents

ac copydi

cd and dvd duplication,
booklets, cases,
overwrapping,
full mastering service
full design service

working wit

bands
singers
artists
businesses

Whether you need 10 cd/dvds or
10,000 - we can provide a full service
from start to finish...

please give
a call on:

0191 275 50

...and you thought there
were only 4 ACES?

email: info@acecopydisc.co.uk
website: www.acecopydisc.co.uk

Design, Pressing & Distribution:

*	APRS members (PAD group)
CD	Compact Disc
CDi	Compact Disc Interactive
CDR	Compact Disc Read Only
DAT	Digital Audio Tape
DVD	Digital Versatile Disc
MC	Music Cassette
MD	MiniDisc
MP3	MP3
V	Vinyl
VC	Video Cassette

Pressers and Duplicators

Accurate Disc Duplication Queniborough Industrial Estate, Melton Rd, Queniborough, Leics LE7 8FP **t** 0870 774 1112 **f** 0870 774 1113 **e** info@accuratedisc.com **w** accuratedisc.com MD. [CD CDR DAT DVD]

ACS Media Ltd 37 Bartholomew St, Newbury, Berks RG14 5LL **t** 01635 552237 or 01635 580448 **f** 01635 34179 **e** sales@acsmedia.co.uk **w** acsmedia.co.uk MD: Wilber Craik. [CD CDR DAT DCC DVD MD Video Vinyl]

AGR MANUFACTURING LTD

The Stables, 44, Stortford Rd, Great Dunmow, Essex CM6 1DL **t** 01371 859 393 **f** 01371 859 375 **e** info@agrm.co.uk **w** agrm.co.uk Quotations and Prices: Martyn Hewitt. Artwork, Audio and Technical: Ed Jones. [CD CDR DVD Vinyl] Complete Record Pressing and CD/DVD replication service. Experienced, friendly with loads of capacity. Call for a quote or chat.

Alfasound Duplication Old School House, 1 Green Lane, Ashton On Mersey, Sale, Cheshire M33 5PN **t** 0161 905 1361 **f** 0161 282 1360 **e** garry.adl@btinternet.com MD: Garry Bowen. [CD CDR DAT MD]

AND Press (Manufacturing Agents) Westfield Cottage, Scragged Oak Rd, Maidstone, Kent ME14 3HA **t** 01622 632 634 **f** 01622 632 634 **e** info@andpress.co.uk **w** andpress.co.uk MD: Andy Rutherford. [CD Vinyl]

Armco Units 1 & 2, Forest Ind Pk, Forest Rd, Hainault, Essex IG6 3HL **t** 020 8500 1981 **f** 020 8501 1319 **e** armco@globalnet.co.uk **w** armco.co.uk MD: Jan Fonseca. [CD CDR]

Ascent Media Ltd Film House, 142 Wardour St, London W1F 8DD **t** 020 7878 0000 **f** 020 7878 7870 **e** firstname.lastname@ascentmedia.co.uk **w** ascentmedia.co.uk Head of Sales & Mktg: Sally Reid. [CDR DAT DVD Video]

AWL Compact Disc Company 356 Scraptoft Lane, Leicester LE5 1PB **t** 0116 241 3979 **f** 0116 243 3760 Dir: Andrew Lipinski. [CD Vinyl]

Bluecrest International Ltd 272 Field End Rd, Eastcote, Ruislip, Middx HA4 9NA **t** 020 8582 0230 **f** 020 8582 0232 **e** info@bluecrest.com **w** bluecrest.com. [CD CDR DVD]

C2 Productions Ltd Cromer House, Caxton Way, Stevenage, Herts SG1 2DF **t** 01438 317333 **f** 01438 317555 **e** info@c2productions.co.uk **w** c2productions.co.uk Dir: Carlos Buhagiar. [CD CDR DVD Video]

Canon Video (UK) Ltd 15 Main Drive, East Lane Business Pk, Wembley, Middlesex HA9 7FF **t** 020 8385 4455 **f** 020 8385 0722 **e** nathan@canonvideo.co.uk **w** canonvideo.co.uk Sales Dir: Mr Nathan. [CD DVD Video]

CD and Cassette Duplication Ltd. 77 Barlow Rd, Stannington, Sheffield, S Yorks S6 5HR **t** 0114 233 0033 **f** 0114 233 0033 MD: Ian Stead. [CD DAT]

CD Industries Units 7-10, Sovereign Pk, Coronation Rd, London NW10 7QP **t** 020 8961 8898 **f** 020 8961 8688 Prod'n: Ms ME Tan. [CD CDR Video]

CDA Disc Ltd Abbey House, 450 Bath Rd, Longford, Heathrow UB7 0EB **t** 020 8757 8966 **f** 020 8757 8972 **e** sales@cdadisc.com **w** cdadisc.com Sales Manager: Ian Mackay. [CD CDR DVD]

Chameleon Developments Ltd 71 Rampton Drift, Longstanton, Cambridge CB4 5EW **t** 0845 456 2144 **f** 01223 528449 **e** chameleon-d@btconnect.com **w** chameleon-developments.com MD: Tash Cox. [CD]

Cine Wessex Westway House, St Thomas St, Winchester, Hants SO23 9HJ **t** 01962 865 454 **f** 01962 842 017 **e** info@cinewessex.co.uk **w** cinewessex.co.uk Duplication Manager: Ema Branton. [Video]

Cinram Europe 3, Shortlands, Hammersmith, London W6 8RX **t** 020 8735 9494 **f** 020 8735 9499 **e** uk.sales@cinram.com **w** cinram.com UK Sales Director: Jonathan Beddows. [CD CDR DVD Video]

CLEAR SOUND AND VISION LTD

CSV House, 51 Marlborough Rd, London E18 1AR **t** 020 8989 8777 **f** 020 8989 9777 **e** sales@c-s-v.co.uk **w** c-s-v.co.uk Managing Director: Clive Robins. Sales Manager: Danny Sperling - danny@c-s-v.co.uk Sales Manager: Will Appleyard - will@c-s-v.co.uk Sales Manager: James Hobbs - james@c-s-v.co.uk General Manager: Laura Evans - laura@c-s-v.co.uk [CD CDR DVD MD Video Vinyl] Project Management, In-house Design Studio, Reprographics, CD, DVD & Authoring, Comprehensive Print & Special Packaging & Vinyl pressing service.

CopyMaster International Ltd 8 Arundel Rd, Uxbridge Trading Estate, Uxbridge, Middlesex UB8 2RR **t** 01895 814 813 **f** 01895 814 999 **e** firstname@copymaster.co.uk **w** copymaster.co.uk Sales Mgr: Ron Boucaud. [CD CDR DVD]

Copysound 3 Bowdens Business Centre, Hambridge, Somerset TA10 0BP **t** 01458 259 280 **f** 01458 259 280 **e** sales@copysound.co.uk **w** copysound.co.uk Duplication Manager: Nigel Neill. [CD Cdi CDR DAT DVD]

The Cottage Group 2 Gawsworth Rd, Macclesfield, Cheshire SK11 8UE **t** 01625 420 163 **f** 01625 420 168 **e** info@cottagegroup.co.uk **w** cottagegroup.co.uk MD: Roger Boden. [CD]

Cutgroove Ltd (Vinyl Pressing Agency) 101 Bashley Rd, Park Royal, London NW10 6TE **t** 020 8838 8270 **f** 020 8838 2012 **e** nikki@cutgroove.com **w** intergroove.co.uk Mgr: Nikki Howarth. [CD Vinyl]

CVB Duplication 179A Bilton Rd, Perivale, Middlesex UB6 7HQ **t** 020 8991 2610 **f** 020 8997 0180 **e** sales@cvbduplication.co.uk **w** cvbduplication.co.uk Sales & Marketing: Phil Stringer. [CD CDR DAT DCC DVD MD Video]

Damont Audio 20 Blyth Rd, Hayes, Middlesex UB3 1BY **t** 020 8573 5122 **f** 020 8561 0979 or 020 8813 6692 **e** sales@damontaudio.com **w** damontaudio.com Commercial Dir: Chris Seymour. [CD Vinyl]

Diamond Black Ltd The Old Bancroft Buildings, Kingham Way, Luton, Beds LU2 7RG **t** 01582 425 555 **f** 01582 725 900 **e** diamondblack@btconnect.com Dir: Perri D'Cruz. [Vinyl]

Disc Makers 15-16 Raynham Rd Trading Est., Bishop's Stortford, Herts CM23 5PD **t** 0845 130 2200 **f** 01279 657 115 **e** ben@discmakers.co.uk **w** discmakers.co.uk UK Sales Mgr: Ben Bull. [CD CDR DVD Vinyl]

DOCdata UK Ltd Halesfield 14, Telford, Shropshire TF7 4QX **t** 01952 680131 **f** 01952 583501 **e** uksales@docdata.com **w** docdata.co.uk Contact: Tina Buttery. [CD DVD]

Downsoft Ltd Downsway House, Epsom Rd, Ashtead, Surrey KT21 1HA **t** 01372 272422 **f** 01372 276122 **e** work@downsoft.co.uk **w** downsoft.co.uk Mgr: Martin Dare. [DAT]

EDC BLACKBURN LTD

ENTERTAINMENT DISTRIBUTION COMPANY

Philips Road, Blackburn, Lancs BB1 5RZ **t** 01254 505 300 **f** 01254 505 421 **e** firstname.surname@edcllc.com **w** edcllc.com Sales: Martin Bignall, Simon Papworth & Angela Kaye. Customer Services: Andrew Dixon. Director: Andrew Lloyd-Jones. [CD CDR DVD]

Combining the best of tradition and innovation, EDC delivers capacity, experience and expertise whilst providing a truly independent perspective.

EMS Audio Ltd Dir, 12 Balloo Ave, Bangor, Co. Down BT19 7QT **t** 028 9127 4411 **f** 028 9127 4412 **e** info@musicshop.to **w** musicshop.to William Thompson: EMS. [CD]

Eurodisc Manufacturing Ltd 1st Floor, Howard House, The Runway, South Ruislip, Middx HA4 6SE **t** 020 8839 0060 **f** 020 8845 6679 **e** info@euro-disc.co.uk **w** euro-disc.co.uk [CD CDR DVD Video Vinyl]

Fairview Music Cavewood Grange Farm, Common Lane, North Cave, Brough, East Yorks HU15 2PE **t** 01430 425546 **f** 01430 425547 **e** sales@fairviewstudios.co.uk **w** fairviewstudios.co.uk Graphics Manager: Dave Beauchamp. [CD CDR DAT DCC MD Video]

Filterbond Ltd 19 Sadlers Way, Hertford, Herts SG14 2DZ **t** 01992 500101 **f** 01992 500101 **e** jbsrecords.filterbondltd@virgin.net MD: John B Schefel. [DAT]

First Choice Media Unit 1, Murray Business Centre, Murray Rd, Orpington, Kent **t** 01689 828 182 or 07980 728 106 **f** 01689 899 369 **e** dudley.perrin@firstchoiceltd.co.uk **w** firstchoiceltd.co.uk HoM: Dudley Perrin. [CD CDR DVD]

GZ Digital Media UK PO Box 37860, London SE23 3WT **t** 020 8291 3175 **f** 020 8181 4555 **e** paul@gzcd.co.uk **w** gzcd.cz Sales Dir: Paul Bibby. [CD DVD Vinyl]

Heathmans 7 Heathmans Rd, London SW6 4TJ **t** 020 7371 0978 **f** 020 7371 9360 **e** susana@heathmans.co.uk **w** heathmans.co.uk MD: Ronnie Garrity. [CD CDR DAT MD Vinyl]

Hiltongrove Mastering Hiltongrove Business Centre, Hatherley Mews, London E17 4QP **t** 020 8509 2244 **f** 020 8509 1155 **e** theteam@hiltongrovemastering.com **w** hiltongrovemastering.com MD: David Blackman. [CDR Vinyl]

Hiltongrove Multimedia Hiltongrove Business Centre, Hatherley Mews, London E17 4QP **t** 020 8521 2424 **f** 020 8521 4343 **e** info@hiltongrove.com **w** hiltongrove.com MD: Guy Davis. [CD DVD]

ICC Duplication Regency Mews, Silverdale Rd, Eastbourne, E Sussex BN20 7AB **t** 01323 647 880 **f** 01323 643 095 **e** info@iccduplication.co.uk **w** iccduplication.co.uk Operations Dir: Andy Thorpe. [CD CDR DVD MD Video]

Icon Marketing Ltd Park House, 27 South Ave, Thorpe St Andrew, Norwich NR7 0EZ **t** 01603 708050 **f** 01603 708005 **e** Icon@dircon.co.uk **w** icon-marketing.co.uk Production Manager: Sarah Neve. [CD CDR DVD MD Vinyl]

Ideal Mastering Ltd Ground Floor Shop, 696 Holloway Rd, London N19 3NL **t** 020 7263 3346 **f** 020 7263 3396 **e** mark@idealmastering.co.uk **w** idealmastering.co.uk Dir: Mark Saunders. [CD CDR DAT MD]

IMPRESS MUSIC LTD

Unit 5C, Northfield Industrial Estate, Beresford Avenue, Wembley, Middx HA0 1NW **t** 020 8795 0101 **f** 020 8795 0303 **e** firstname@impressmusic-uk.com **w** impressmusic-uk.com Chairman: Alastair Bloom. Director of Production: Simon Cass. Managing Director: Richard Stern. Warehouse: Peter Bon. Artwork: Sui Yin Chan Tam Chan. Sales: Andreea Ciorbeea. Production: Laurent Corneille. Sales: Morley Ham. Artwork: Eric Hung. Sales: Ros Hyman. Burns: Ni Cuu Lieu - burns@impressmusic-uk.com Production: Ivano Nocivelli. Finance: Yashoda Pindoria. IT: Sid Ralph. Finance: Monika Skwierczynska. [CD Cdi CDR DAT DVD Video Vinyl]
Manufacturers of CD, DVD, Short Run CD & DVD Burns, Vinyl & MC, Posters & Postcards, T-Shirts & assorted merchandise. For all Sales enquiries please email quotes@impressmusic-uk.com

Isis Duplicating Co - Head Office Unit 11 Shaftesbury Ind Centre, The Runnings, Cheltenham, Gloucs GL51 9NH **t** 01242 571 818 **f** 01242 571 315 **e** john@isis-uk.com **w** isis-uk.com Divisional Mgr: John Fairclough. [CD CDR]

ITD Cassettes Ltd 31 Angelvale, Buckingham Industrial Pk, Buckingham, Bucks MK18 1TH **t** 01280 821177 **f** 01280 821188 **e** ITDcassets@aol.com **w** ITDcassettes.com MD: Mike McLoughlin. [CD CDR]

KDG UK Ltd Unit 5 Triangle Business Pk, Pentrebach, Merthyr Tydfil, Mid Galmorgan SF48 4TQ **t** 01685 354700 **f** 01685 354701 **e** sales@kdguk.com **w** kdg-mt.com Sales Mgr: Ian Browning.

8 Jeffreys Place, London NW1 9PP **t** 020 7284 8800 **f** 020 7284 8844 **e** mail@keyproduction.co.uk **w** keyproduction.co.uk Sales & Marketing: Wendy Wood. Sales Executive: Amy Bevil. [CD CDR DAT DCC DVD MD Video Vinyl] **16 years experience in CD, DVD, Vinyl manufacturing; specialist packaging, including in-house design and reprographics; excellent quality and competitive rates.**

Keynote Audio Services Ltd Smoke Tree House, Tilford Rd, Farnham, Surrey GU10 2EN **t** 01252 794 253 **f** 01252 792 642 **e** admin@keynoteaudio.co.uk **w** keynoteaudio.co.uk MD: Tim Wheatley. [CD CDR DAT]

Lemon Media Ltd The Hub, Warne Rd, Weston-super-Mare, Somerset BS23 3UU **t** 01934 423 022 or 07966 311 058 **e** Stuart@LemonMedia.co.uk **w** lemonmedia.co.uk Sales Mgr: Stuart Timmis. [CD Cdi CDR DAT DVD Video Vinyl]

Logicom Sound And Vision Portland House, 1 Portland Drive, Willen, Milton Keynes, Bucks MK15 9JW **t** 01908 663848 **f** 01908 666654 **e** grayham.amos@luk.net **w** luk.net Bus Dev Mgr: Grayham Amos. [CD CDR DAT MD Video]

MacTrak Duplicating 3/2 Inveresk Industrial Estate, Musselburgh, Edinburgh EH21 7UL **t** 0131 665 5377 **f** 0131 653 6905 **e** mactrak@ednet.co.uk **w** mactrak.co.uk Prop: MD MacGregor. [CD CDR]

MAP Music Ltd 46 Grafton Rd, London NW5 3DU **t** 020 7916 0545 or 020 7916 0544 **f** 020 7284 4232 **e** info@mapmusic.net **w** mapmusic.net MD: Chris Townsend. [CD]

Meltones Media 3 King Edward Drive, Chessington, Surrey KT9 1DW **t** 020 8391 9406 **f** 020 8391 8924 **e** tony@meltones.com **w** meltones-media.co.uk Sales/Mkt Dir: Tony Fernandez. [CD]

Metro Broadcast Ltd 5-7 Great Chapel St, London W1F 8FF **t** 020 7434 7700 **f** 020 7434 7701 **e** info@metrobroadcast.com **w** metrobroadcast.com Business Development Dir: Paul Beale. [CDR Video]

Modo Production Ltd 14 Regent Hill, Brighton, E Sussex BN1 3ED **t** 01273 779 030 **f** 01273 777 718 **e** tim@modo.co.uk **w** modo.co.uk MD: Tim Bevan. [CD DVD]

MPO Ireland Ltd Blanchardstown Industrial Est, Snugborough Rd, Blanchardstown, Dublin 15, Ireland **t** +353 1 822 1363 **f** +353 1 806 6064 **e** swalsh@mpo.ie **w** mpo.fr Sales Director: Sharon Walsh. [CD CDR DVD LD Vinyl]

MPO UK Ltd Unit 3-4, Nucleus Central Way, Park Royal, London NW10 7XT **t** 020 8963 6888 or 07714 676 925 **f** 020 8963 8693 **e** matt@mpo.co.uk **w** MPO.co.uk Audio Sales Executive: Matt Shoults. [CD CDR DVD Video Vinyl]

Multi Media Replication Ltd Unit 4 Balksbury Estate, Upper Clatford, Andover, Hants SP11 7LW **t** 01264 336 330 **f** 01264 336 694 **e** info@replication.com **w** replication.com MD: Philip Hall. [CD DVD]

Design, Pressing & Distribution: Pressers and Duplicators

MUSICBASE MUSIC PRESSING

3 Greenwich Quay, Clarence Road, London SE8 3EY
t 020 8469 4495 **e** info@musicbase.uk.com
w musicbase.uk.com Contact: Kevin Jamieson. [CD CDR DVD Vinyl]
Specialists in pressing Vinyl, DVD, CD and creative packaging. Our products include 7", 10" and 12" vinyl, enhanced CD, DVD 5, 9 & 10, picture discs, etched or coloured vinyl and all associated printed parts.

Noisebox Digital Media Ltd Windsor House, 74 Thorpe Rd, Norwich NR1 1BA **t** 01603 767726 **f** 01603 767746 **e** info@noisebox.co.uk **w** noisebox.co.uk MD: Pete Morgan. [CD CDR Video]

Offside Management Unit A, 16-24 Brewery Rd, London N7 9NH **t** 020 7700 2662 **f** 020 7700 2882 **e** info@bsimerch.com **w** bsimerch.com Sales Director: Richard Cassar. [CD CDR DVD]

Open Ear Productions Ltd. Kinarva, Co. Galway, Ireland **t** +353 91 635810 **f** +353 87 58575588 **e** info@openear.ie **w** openear.ie MD: Bruno Staehelin. [CD]

OPTIMAL MEDIA UK LTD. T/A

Unit 109, Tent Street, London E1 5DZ **t** 020 7392 8900 **f** 020 7392 8868 **e** asl@audio-services.co.uk **w** audio-services.co.uk Director: Mel Gale. [CD CDR DVD Vinyl]

Orbis Digital Ltd Unit 52E, Sunnyside Rd, Coatbridge ML5 3DG **t** 0845 60 76 123 or 01236 44 96 99 **e** alan@orbisdigital.co.uk **w** orbisdigital.co.uk Optical Media Consultant: Alan Mann. [CD DVD]

Orlake Records (Vinyl Specialists) Sterling Industrial Estate, Rainham Road South, Dagenham, Essex RM10 8HP **t** 020 8592 0242 **f** 020 8595 8182 **e** info@orlakerecords.com **w** orlakerecords.co.uk Production Controller: Paula Pearl. [Vinyl]

Portalspace Records Apollo House, 120 Blyth Rd, Hayes, Middx UB3 1SY **t** 020 8756 0826 **f** 020 8756 0936 **e** info@portalspacerecords.com **w** portalspacerecords.co.uk Commercial Mgr: Bob Bailey. [Vinyl]

Pozzoli Ltd 100 New Kings Rd, London SW6 4LX **t** 020 7384 3283 **f** 020 7384 3067 **e** julian.malin@pozzoli.co.uk **w** pozzolispa.com Sales Dir: Julian Malin. [CD DVD]

PR Records Hamilton House, Endeavour Way, London SW19 8UH **t** 01423 541020 **f** 01423 540970 **e** pr@celtic-music.co.uk Cust Liason: Ruth Bulmer. [CD CDR DAT MD Vinyl]

Professional Magnetics Ltd Cassette House, 329 Hunslet Rd, Leeds, W Yorks LS10 1NJ **t** 0113 270 6066 **f** 0113 271 8106 **e** promags@aol.com **w** promags.freeserve.co.uk Dir: Hilary Rhodes. [CD CDR DAT DCC MD Video]

Reflex Media Services Ltd Unit 5, Cirrus, Glebe Rd, Huntingdon PE29 7DL **t** 01480 412 222 **f** 01480 411 441 **e** sally@reflex-media.co.uk **w** reflex-media.co.uk Factory Manager: Sally Houghton.

Repeat Performance RPM Unit 6, Grand Union Centre, West Row, London W10 5AS **t** 020 8960 7222 **f** 020 8968 1378 **e** info@rpmuk.com **w** rpmuk.com MD: Robin Springall. [CD CDR DAT DCC]

Replica North Works, Hookstone Pk, Harrogate, N Yorks HG2 7DB **t** 01423 888979 or 01423 541020 **f** 01423 540970 **e** replica@northworks.co.uk Dir: David Bulmer. [CDR Vinyl]

RMS Studios 43-45 Clifton Rd, London, London SE25 6PX **t** 020 8653 4965 **f** 020 8653 4965 **e** rmsstudios@blueyonder.co.uk **w** rms-studios.co.uk Bookings Mgr: Alan Jones. [CD DAT MD]

SKM Europe Charlotte Cottage, 73 Leighton Rd, Wing, Leighton Buzzard, Beds LU7 0NN **t** 01296 681 535 **f** 01296 689 428 **e** anita@skmeurope.co.uk **w** skm.co.kr Sales Dir: Steve Castle.

SONOPRESS (UK)

Wednesbury One Business Park, Black Country New Rd, Wednesbury, West Midlands WS10 7NY **t** 0121 502 7800 **f** 0121 502 7811 **e** sales@sonopress.co.uk **w** sonopress.co.uk Sales Dir - Music: Anthony Daly. MD: John Shervey. [CD CDR DAT DVD Vinyl]

Sony DADC UK Ltd Southwater Business Pk, Worthing Rd, Southwater, W Sussex RH13 9YT **t** 01403 739 600 **f** 01403 739 601 **e** firstname.lastname@sonydadc.com **w** sonydadc.com Dir, Sales & Client Services: Siegfried Obermayr. [CD Cdi CDR DVD]

Sound and Video Services UK Ltd Shentonfield Rd, Sharston Industrial Estate, Manchester M22 4RW **t** 0161 491 6660 **f** 0161 491 6669 **e** sales@svsmedia.com **w** svsmedia.com Dir: Mike Glasspole. [CD DVD]

Sound Discs Ltd. Unit 10 Linen House, 253 Kilburn Lane, London W10 4BQ **t** 020 8968 7080 or 07721 624 868 **f** 020 8968 7475 **e** info@sound-discs.co.uk **w** sound-discs.co.uk Production Director: Peter Bullick. [CD CDR DAT DVD MD Vinyl]

SOUND PERFORMANCE

3 Greenwich Quay, Clarence Road, London SE8 3EY **t** 020 8691 2121 **f** 020 8691 3144 **e** sales@soundperformance.co.uk **w** soundperformance.co.uk Contact: Sales. [CD CDR DVD Video Vinyl]
CD, DVD & Vinyl Manufacturing & all associated printing & packaging, including special packaging. Dedicated customer service, excellent quality & competitive rates.

Design, Pressing & Distribution: Pressers and Duplicators

Sounds Good Ltd 12 Chiltern Enterprise Centre, Station Rd, Theale, Reading, Berks RG7 4AA **t** 0118 930 1700 **f** 0118 930 1709 **e** sales-info@sounds-good.co.uk **w** sounds-good.co.uk Dir: Martin Maynard.

Sponge Multimedia Ltd Sponge Studios, Cross Chancellor St, Leeds, W Yorks LS6 2TG **t** 0113 234 0004 **f** 0113 242 4296 **e** damian@spongestudios.demon.co.uk **w** spongestudios.demon.co.uk Dir: Damian McLean-Brown. [CD CDR DCC DVD Video Vinyl]

Tapemaster (Europe) Ltd King George's Pl, 764 Eastern Ave, Newbury Pk, Ilford, Essex IG2 7HU **t** 020 8518 4202 **f** 020 8518 4203 **e** tapemaster@msn.com **w** tapemaster.co.uk MD: Laji Lalli. [CD CDR DVD Video]

TC Video Wembley Commercial Centre, East Lane, Wembley, Middx HA9 7UU **t** 020 8904 6271 **f** 020 8904 0172 **e** info@tcvideo.co.uk **w** tcvideo.co.uk Marketing Manager: Lissandra Xavier. [CD CDR DVD Video]

Technicolor Llantarnam Pk, Cwmbran, Gwent NP44 3AB **t** 01633 465259 **f** 01633 867799 **e** technicolor.europe@thomson.net **w** technicolor.com Dir, Optical Disc: Emil Dudek. [CD CDR DVD Video]

Thames Valley Video 660 Ajax Ave, Slough, Berks SL1 4BG **t** 01753 553131 **f** 01753 554505 **e** tvv@netcomuk.co.uk MD: Nigel Morris. [Video]

Thamesdown SDC Frankland Rd, Blagrove, Swindon, Wilts SN5 8YG **t** 01793 421300 **f** 01793 511125 **e** sales@thamesdownsdc.com **w** thamesdownsdc.com New Business Mgr: Dave Johnson. [CD CDR DVD]

TOTAL VINYL

Unit 31-32, Atlas Business Centre, Oxgate Lane, London NW2 7HU **t** 020 8452 5544 **f** 020 8452 4242 **e** Totalvinylsales@aol.com **w** totalvinyl.net Dir: Bob Kane. [Vinyl] See how vinyl is made at www.myspace.com/totalvinyl

Townhouse Studios (Mastering) 150 Goldhawk Rd, London W12 8HH **t** 020 8932 3200 **f** 020 8932 3207 **e** info@townhousestudios.co.uk **w** townhousestudios.co.uk Bookings: Gay Marshall or Lavinia Burrell. [CD CDR]

Transition Mastering Studios Kemble House, Kemble Rd, London SE23 2DJ **t** 020 8699 7888 **f** 020 8699 9441 **e** info@transition-studios.co.uk **w** transition-studios.co.uk Mgr: Jason Goz. [CD Vinyl]

Trend Studios A2 Canal Bank, Park West Industrial Pk, Dublin 12, Ireland **t** +353 1 6160 600 **f** +353 1 6160 601 **e** muswk@trendstudios.com **w** trendstudios.com Tech Dir: Paul Waldron. [CD Cdi CDR DAT]

TRIBAL MANUFACTURING LTD.

11 Hillgate Place, London SW12 9ER **t** 020 8673 0610 **f** 020 8675 8562 **e** sales@tribal.co.uk **w** tribal.co.uk Directors: Alison Wilson, Terry Woolner. [CD CDE CDR DVD DVDR UMD Vinyl] An independent company supplying manufacturing & print across the industry. Standard and special packaging & point of sale solutions . Tribal – making sense of manufacturing.

Vanderquest 7 Latimer Rd, Teddington, Middlesex TW11 8QA **t** 020 8977 1743 **f** 020 8943 2818 **e** nick@vanderquest.co.uk MD: Nick Maingay. [Video]

Vinyl Factory Productions (One Stop Service) Sterling Industrial Est, Rainham Rd South, Dagenham, Essex RM10 8HP **t** 020 8526 8070 **e** paula.pearl@vinylfactory.co.uk **w** vinylfactory.co.uk Production Mgr: Paula Pearl. [CD Vinyl]

Vinyl Pressing 308 High St, London E15 1AJ **t** 020 8519 4260 **f** 020 8519 5187 MD: Terence Murphy. [CD Cdi Vinyl]

Warren Recordings 59 Hendale Ave, London NW4 4LP **t** 020 8203 0306 **f** 020 8203 0306 **e** stanley@warrenworld.fsnet.co.uk Dir: Stanley Warren. [CD DAT Video Vinyl]

Wyastone Estate Limited Wyastone Leys, Monmouth NP25 3SR **t** 01600 890 007 **f** 01600 891 052 **e** sales@wyastone.co.uk **w** wyastone.co.uk Business Dir: Antony Smith. [CD]

Mastering and Post Production

10th Planet 68-70 Wardour St, London W1F OTB **t** 020 7434 2345 **f** 020 7637 9599 **e** studio@10thplanet.net **w** 10thplanet.net MD: Ben Wooley. [CD CDR DVD]

360 Mastering Ltd 18A Farm Lane Trading Centre, 101 Farm Lane, London SW6 1QJ **t** 020 7385 6161 **f** 020 7386 0473 **e** studio@360mastering.co.uk **w** 360mastering.co.uk MD: Dick Beetham. [CD Digital Audio Tape DVD MD Vinyl]

The 400 Company B3, The Workshops, 2A, Askew Crescent, London W12 9DP **t** 020 8746 1400 **f** 020 8746 0847 **e** info@the400.co.uk **w** the400.co.uk Production manager: Christian Riou. [DVD]

Abbey Road Studios 3 Abbey Rd, London NW8 9AY **t** 020 7266 7000 **f** 020 7266 7250 **e** bookings@abbeyroad.com **w** abbeyroad.com Post Prod Mgr: Lucy Launder. [CD Digital Audio Tape MD Video Vinyl]

AGR Manufacturing Ltd The Stables, 44, Stortford Rd, Great Dunmow, Essex CM6 1DL **t** 01371 859 393 **f** 01371 859 375 **e** info@agrm.co.uk **w** agrm.co.uk Quotations and Prices: Martyn Hewitt. [CD DVD Vinyl]

Airtight Productions - DVD Authoring Unit 16, Albany Rd Trading Estate, Albany Rd, Chorlton M21 0AZ **t** 0161 881 5157 **e** info@airtightproductions.co.uk **w** airtightproductions.co.uk Dir: Anthony Davey. [DVD]

Alchemy SoHo 29th Floor, Centre Point, 103 New Oxford St, London WC1A 1DD **t** 020 7420 8000 **f** 020 7420 8001 **e** info@alchemysoho.com **w** alchemysoho.com Vinyl & CD Bookings: Natasha Bicknell. [CD CDR Digital Audio Tape MD Vinyl]

ADS (Audio Duplication Services) 54, Woodview Estate, Castlebridge, Wexford, Ireland. **t** +353 53 59370 **f** +353 53 59371 **e** sales@duplication.ie **w** duplication.ie Dir: Tom Byrne. [CD CDR Digital Audio Tape Vinyl]

Audio Sorcery Little Wold, Station Rd, Groombridge, E Sussex TN3 9NE **t** 01892 862489 **e** info@tgas.co.uk **w** tgas.co.uk Contact: Paul Midcalf. [CD]

B&H Sound Services Ltd The Old School Studio, Crowland Rd, Eye, Peterborough PE6 7TN **t** 01733 223535 **f** 01733 223545 **e** sound@bhsound.co.uk **w** bhsound.co.uk Recording Manager: Nicola Seager.

Blue Post Production 58 Old Compton St, London W1D 4UF **t** 020 7437 2626 **f** 020 7439 2477 **e** info@bluepp.co.uk **w** bluepp.co.uk Facilities Mgr: Ashley Ranson. [DVD Video]

Boomtown (ProTools) Studio Valetta Rd, London W3 7TG **t** 020 8723 9548 or 07961 405 140 **e** info@boomtownstudio.co.uk **w** boomtownstudio.co.uk Contact: Simon Wilkinson.

Chapelmedia The Studios, 8 Hornton Pl, Kensington, London W8 4LZ **t** 020 7937 8485 **f** 020 7937 4326 **e** sales@chapelmedia.biz **w** chapelmedia.biz Technical Director: Ian Higson. [DVD]

The Classical Recording Company Ltd. 16-17 Wolsey Mews, Kentish Town, London NW5 2DX **t** 020 7482 2303 **f** 020 7482 2302 **e** info@classicalrecording.com **w** classicalrecording.com Senior Producer: Simon Weir. [CD Video Vinyl]

Close To The Edge 2 The Embankment, Twickenham, Middlesex TW1 3DU **t** 01225 311661 **f** 01225 482013 **e** info@positivebiz.com **w** positivebiz.com Mgr: Carole Davies. [CD Digital Audio Tape DVD]

CopyMaster International Ltd 8 Arundel Rd, Uxbridge Trading Estate, Uxbridge, Middlesex UB8 2RR **t** 01895 814 813 **f** 01895 814 999 **e** firstname@copymaster.co.uk **w** copymaster.co.uk Sales Mgr: Ron Boucaud. [CD CDR DVD]

Cottage Media Mastering 2 Gawsworth Rd, Macclesfield, Cheshire SK11 8UE **t** 01625 420 163 **f** 01625 420 168 **e** cmm@cottagegroup.co.uk **w** cottagegroup.co.uk MD: Roger Boden. [CD]

Diverse Media PO Box 3, South Croydon, Surrey CR2 0YW **t** 0870 765 4343 **f** 0870 765 4344 **e** firstname.lastname@diversemedia.com **w** audiomastering.co.uk Sales Dir: Debra Jacobs. [CD]

Edit Videos Audely House, 9 Margaret St, London W1W 8RH **t** 020 7637 2288 **f** 020 7637 2299 **e** mail@editvideo.co.uk **w** editvideo.co.uk MD/Editor: Henry Stein. [DVD Video]

Electric Mastering 308 Westbourne Studios, 242 Acklam Rd, London W10 5JJ **t** 020 7524 7547 **f** 020 7524 7558 **e** info@electricmastering.com **w** electricmastering.com Studio Mgr: Lily May. [CD CDR Vinyl]

The Exchange 42 Bruges Pl, Randolph St, London NW1 0TX
t 020 7485 0530 **f** 020 7482 4588
e studio@exchangemastering.co.uk **w** exchangemastering.co.uk
MD: Graeme Durham. [CD Digital Audio Tape MD Vinyl]

Figment DVD 341-345 Old St, London EC1V 9LL
t 020 7729 1969 **f** 020 7739 1969 **e** mail@figment-media.com
w figment-media.com MD: Andrew Huffer. [DVD]

Finesplice Ltd 1 Summerhouse Lane, Harmondsworth, West
Drayton, Middlesex UB7 0AT **t** 020 8564 7839
f 020 8759 9629 **e** info@finesplice.co.uk **w** finesplice.co.uk
MD: Ben Turner. [CD CDR Digital Audio Tape MD]

Firebird Suite 11 Osram Rd, East Lane Business Pk,
Wembley, Middx HA9 7NG **t** 020 8904 4422 **f** 020 8904 3777
e info@thefirebirdsuite.com **w** thefirebirdsuite.com.

Flare DVD Ingestre Court, Ingestre Pl, London W1F 0JL
t 020 7343 6565 **f** 020 7343 6555 **e** darrell@flare-dvd.com
w flare-dvd.com Designer: Darrell de Vries. [DVD]

Fleetwood Post Denham Media Pk, North Orbital Rd,
Denham, Bucks UB9 5HQ **t** 08700 771071 **f** 08700 771068
e ian.d@fleetwoodmobiles.com **w** fleetwoodmobiles.com
MD: Ian Dyckhoff. [CD DVD]

Floating Earth Unit 14, 21 Wadsworth Rd, Perivale, Middx
UB6 7JD **t** 020 8997 4000 **f** 020 8998 5767
e record@floatingearth.com **w** floatingearth.com Dir: Steve Long.
[CD Digital Audio Tape]

Flow Mastering 83 Brixton Water Lane, London SW2 1PH
t 020 7733 8088 **f** 020 7326 4016 **e** brethes@mac.com
w flowmastering.co.uk Dir: Dominique Brethes. [CD Mp3 Vinyl]

Flying Ace Productions Walders, Oldbury Lane, Ightham,
Sevenoaks TN15 9DD **t** 01732 887 056 or 07778 165931
f 01732 887 056 **e** reiddick@netmatters.co.uk
Dir: Will Reid Dick. [CD CDR Digital Audio Tape MD]

Freehand Limited Unit 52, Dunsfold Pk, Cranleigh, Surrey
GU6 8TB **t** 01483 200 111 **f** 01483 200 101
e phil.kerby@freehand.co.uk **w** freehand.co.uk/production
Contact: Phil Kerby. [DVD]

Hafod Mastering Hafod, St Hilary, Cowbridge, Wales
CF71 7DP **t** 01446 775512 **f** 01446 775512
e studio@hafodmastering.co.uk **w** hafodmastering.co.uk
Dir: Donal Whelan. [CD Vinyl]

Hangman Studios 111 Frithville Gardens, London W12 7JQ
t 020 8600 3440 **f** 020 8600 3401
e danielle@hangmanstudios.com **w** hangmanstudios.com
Studio Mgr: Danielle Edwards. [DVD Video]

Happybeat 101 Greenway Rd, Higher Tranmere, Merseyside
CH42 0NE **t** 0151 653 3463 **e** happybeatstudios@yahoo.co.uk
w happybeat.net Contact: Fran Ashcroft. [CD]

Heathmans Mastering Ltd 7 Heathmans Rd, London
SW6 4TJ **t** 020 7371 0978 **f** 020 7371 9360
e susana@heathmans.co.uk **w** heathmans.co.uk
MD: Ronnie Garrity. [CD Digital Audio Tape MD Vinyl]

Hiltongrove Mastering Hiltongrove Business Centre,
Hatherley Mews, London E17 4QP **t** 020 8509 2244
f 020 8509 1155 **e** theteam@hiltongrovemastering.com
w hiltongrovemastering.com MD: David Blackman. [CDR Vinyl]

Hiltongrove Multimedia Hiltongrove Business Centre,
Hatherley Mews, London E17 4QP **t** 020 8521 2424
f 020 8521 4343 **e** info@hiltongrove.com **w** hiltongrove.com
MD: Guy Davis. [CD DVD]

Ideal Mastering Ground Floor Shop, 696 Holloway Rd,
London N19 3NL **t** 020 7263 3346 **f** 020 7263 3396
e mark@idealmastering.co.uk **w** idealmastering.co.uk
Dir: Mark Saunders. [CD Digital Audio Tape DVD Vinyl]

International Broadcast Facilities 15 Monmouth St,
London WC2H 9DA **t** 020 7497 1515 **f** 020 7379 8562
e post@ibf.co.uk **w** ibf.co.uk Head of Audio: Martin Reekie.
[Digital Audio Tape Video]

Intimate Recording Studios The Smokehouse, 120
Pennington St, London E1 9BB **t** 07860 109 612 or
020 7702 0789 **e** paul.madden47@ntlworld.com
w intimatestudios.com Contact: Paul Madden. [CD Vinyl]

ISIS Duplicating Company Sales & Production, Unit M2
Albany Rd, Prescot, Merseyside L34 2UP **t** 0151 430 9001 or
07799 030 500 **f** 0151 430 7441 **e** john@isis-uk.com
w isis-uk.com Divisional Mgr: John Fairclough. [CD CDR DVD
Video]

JRP Music Services Empire House, Hereford Rd, Southsea,
Hants PO5 2DH **t** 023 9229 7839
e James.Perrett@soc.soton.ac.uk **w** jrpmusic.fsnet.co.uk
Senior Engineer: James Perrett. [CD Vinyl]

JTS 73 Digby Rd, London E9 6HX **t** 020 8985 3000
f 020 8986 7688 **e** sales@jts-uk.com **w** jts-uk.com
Studio Mgr: Keith Jeffrey. [CD Vinyl]

Keynote Audio Services Ltd Smoke Tree House, Tilford
Rd, Farnham, Surrey GU10 2EN **t** 01252 794 253
f 01252 792 642 **e** admin@keynoteaudio.co.uk
w keynoteaudio.co.uk MD: Tim Wheatley. [CD CDR Digital Audio
Tape MD Vinyl]

Lansdowne Studios Rickmansworth Rd, Watford
WD17 3JN **t** 020 8846 9444 **f** 05601 155 009
e info@cts-lansdowne.co.uk **w** cts-lansdowne.co.uk
Bookings Enquiries: Sharon Rose. [CD Digital Audio Tape MD]

Liquid Mastering Unit 6Q, Atlas Business Centre, Oxgate
Lane, London NW2 7HU **t** 020 8452 2255 **f** 020 8422 4242
e sales@liquidmastering.co.uk **w** liquidmastering.co.uk
Dir: Bob Kane. [CD Video Vinyl]

Locomotion 1-8 Bateman's Building, Soho Sq, London
W1D 3EN **t** 020 7304 4403 **f** 020 7304 4400
e info@locomotion.co.uk **w** locomotion.co.uk. [DVD Video]

LOUD MASTERING & LOUD INDEPENDENT

2-3 Windsor Place, Whitehall, Taunton, Somerset TA1 1PG
t 01823 353 123 **f** 01823 353 055
e enquiries@loudmastering.com **w** loudmastering.com Bookings
Manager: John Wilkins. Proprietor & Engineer: John Dent.
Engineer: Jason Mitchell. [CD Vinyl]

The Lynic Group 645 Ajax Ave, Slough, Berks SL1 4BG
t 01753 786 200 **f** 01753 786 201 **e** sales@lynic.com
w lynic.com Sales Dir: Simon Notton. [CD Cdi CDR DVD]

The Machine Room 54-58 Wardour St, London W1D 4JQ
t 020 7734 3433 **f** 020 7287 3773
e paul.willey@themachineroom.co.uk **w** themachineroom.co.uk
Contact: Paul Willey. [DVD Video]

Masterpiece Media Unit 14 The Talina Centre, Bagleys Lane, London SW6 2BW **t** 020 7731 5758 **f** 020 7384 1750 **e** leena.bhatti@masterpiecelondon.com **w** masterpiecelondon.com Sales & Marketing Manager: Leena Bhatti. [CD CDR Digital Audio Tape DVD MD Video]

Mediadisc Unit 4C, Farm Lane Trading Centre, 101 Farm Lane, Fulham, London SW6 1QJ **t** 020 7385 2299 **f** 020 7385 4888 **e** studio@mediadisc.co.uk **w** mediadisc.co.uk MD: Simon Payne.

Metropolis Group The Power House, 70 Chiswick High Rd, London W4 1SY **t** 020 8742 1111 **f** 020 8742 2626 **e** reception@metropolis-group.co.uk **w** metropolis-group.co.uk Digital Media Manager: Katy Deegan. [DVD]

Metropolis Mastering The Power House, 70 Chiswick High Rd, London W4 1SY **t** 020 8742 1111 **f** 020 8742 3777 **e** mastering@metropolis-group.co.uk **w** metropolis-group.co.uk Mastering Bookings: Jo Buckley, Dan Baldwin. [CD CDR Digital Audio Tape DVD MD Vinyl]

Molinare 34 Fouberts Pl, London W1F 7PX **t** 020 7478 7000 **f** 020 7478 7299 **e** bookings@molinare.co.uk **w** molinare.co.uk. [CD CDR Digital Audio Tape Video]

M2 Facilities Group (TV Post Production only) The Forum, 74-80 Camden St, London NW1 0EG **t** 020 7387 5001 **f** 020 7343 6777 **e** info@m2tv.com **w** m2tv.com Mgr: Simon Partington.

optimal media UK Ltd. t/a Unit 109, Tent St, London E1 5DZ **t** 020 7392 8900 **f** 020 7392 8868 **e** asl@audio-services.co.uk **w** audio-services.co.uk Dir: Mel Gale. [CD CDR DVD Mp3 Vinyl]

OPTIMUM MASTERING

Unit 5.4, The Paintworks, Bath Road, Bristol BS4 3EH **t** 0117 971 6901 **f** 0117 971 0700 **e** info@optimum-mastering.com **w** optimum-mastering.com Engineers: Shawn Joseph, Matt Colton. Bookings: San Phillips-Acharya. [CD Vinyl]

The Pavement 4a Burbage House, 83 Curtain Rd, London EC2A 3BS **t** 020 7749 4300 **f** 020 7749 4301 **e** info@the-pavement.com **w** the-pavement.com Sales: Guy Goodger. [DVD]

The Picture House (Edit Suites) Ltd The Strand, 156 Holywood Rd, Belfast, Co Antrim BT4 1NY **t** 028 9065 1111 **f** 028 9067 3771 **e** stephen@thepicturehouse.tv **w** thepicturehouse.tv Studio Manager: Stephen Petticrew. [DVD Video]

PMC Studios Ltd 21-24 St Johns Rd, Plymouth PL4 0PA **t** 01752 201275 **e** info@pmc.uk.net **w** pmc.uk.net MD: Dave Summers. [CD DVD]

Pulse Post 36 Berwick St, London W1F 8RR **t** 020 7437 5518 **f** 020 7287 6505 **e** marisa@pulsefilms.co.uk **w** pulsefilms.co.uk Producer: Marisa Clifford. [DVD]

Red Facilities 61 Timberbush, Leith, Edinburgh EH6 6QH **t** 0131 555 2288 **f** 0131 555 0088 **e** doit@redfacilities.com **w** redfacilities.com Ptnr: Max Howarth.

Red Light Mastering 27 Lexington St, London W1F 9AQ **t** 020 7287 7373 or 07796 958 115 **e** craig@red-light.co.uk **w** red-light.co.uk Contact: Craig Dormer. [CD CDR Digital Audio Tape MD Video]

Redwood Studios 20 Great Chapel St, London W1F 8FW **t** 020 7287 3799 **e** andrestudios@yahoo.co.uk **w** sound-design.net MD/Producer: Andre Jacquemin. [CD Digital Audio Tape]

Reflex Media Services Ltd Unit 5, Cirrus, Glebe Rd, Huntingdon PE29 7DL **t** 01480 412 222 **f** 01480 411 441 **e** sally@reflex-media.co.uk **w** reflex-media.co.uk Factory Manager: Sally Houghton.

Repeat Performance RPM 6 Grand Union Centre, West Row, London W10 5AS **t** 020 8960 7222 **f** 020 8968 1378 **e** info@rpmuk.com **w** rpmuk.com MD: Robin Springall. [CD CDR DCC Digital Audio Tape MD]

Revolution Digital 1st Floor, 34 Lexington St, London W1F 0LH **t** 020 7439 3332 **e** laura@rdigital.co.uk **w** rdigital.co.uk MD: Laura Gate-Eastley. [CD CDR DVD]

Reynolds Mastering PO Box 5092, Colchester, Essex CO1 1FN **t** 01206 562655 **f** 01206 761936 **e** reynolds.mastering@virgin.net(DO NOT PUBLISH) MD: Peter Reynolds. [CD Digital Audio Tape MD Vinyl]

Sanctuary Archives 32-36 Telford Way, East Acton, London W3 7XS **t** 020 8600 3916 **f** 020 8749 9683 **e** mike.mastrangelo@sanctuarygroup.com **w** sanctuaryrecords.co.uk Head Of Archives: Mike Mastrangelo.

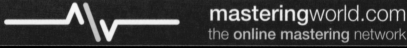

The Sanctuary (Soho) 53 Frith St, London W1D 4SN
t 020 7734 4480 **f** 020 7439 7394 **e** info@thesanctuary.tv
w thesanctuary.tv Joint MDs: Maryan Kennedy, Daniel Stracey.
[DVD Video]

Scopitone Ltd Tower Bridge Business Complex, Block J -
Suite 212, 100 Clements Rd, London SE16 4DG
t 020 7193 6528 **e** info@scopitone.co.uk **w** scopitone.co.uk
Producer: Alex Piot. [DVD]

Silk Recordings 65 High St, Kings Langley, Herts. WD4 9HU
t 01923 270 852 or 07812 602 535 **e** info@silkrecordings.com
w silkrecordings.com MD: Bob Whitney. [CD]

Sonic Arts The Shaftesbury Centre, 85 Barlby Rd, London
W10 6BN **t** 020 8962 3000 **f** 020 8962 6200
e avi@sonic-arts.com **w** sonic-arts.com
Contact: Miranda Webster. [CD CDR DVD MD Vinyl]

Sonic Union PO Box 357, Middlesbrough, Cleveland TS1 4WZ
t 01642 806 795 or 01642 218 057 **f** 01642 800 986
e info@millbrand.com **w** millbrand.com MD: Paul Mooney.

Sound Discs CD Mastering & Manufacturing Ltd
Unit 10 The Linen House, 253 Kilburn Lane, London W10 4BQ
t 020 8968 7080 or 07721 624 868 **f** 020 8968 7475
e info@sound-discs.co.uk **w** sound-discs.co.uk
Production Director: Peter Bullick. [CD CDR Digital Audio Tape
DVD MD Video]

Sound Generation Unit 3, Clarence Rd, Greenwich, London
SE8 3EY **t** 020 8691 2121 **f** 020 8691 3144
e at@soundperformance.co.uk **w** soundperformance.co.uk
Studio Mgr: Andrew Thompson. [CD]

Sound Mastering 48-50 Steele Rd, London NW10 7AS
t 020 8961 1741 **f** 020 8838 2824
e info@soundmastering.com MD: Duncan Cowell. [CD]

Sound Performance 3 Greenwich Quay, Clarence Rd,
London SE8 3EY **t** 020 8691 2121 **f** 020 8691 3144
e sales@soundperformance.co.uk **w** soundperformance.co.uk
Contact: Sales. [CD CDR DVD Video Vinyl]

Sound Recording Technology Audio House, Edison Rd,
St Ives, Cambridge, Cambs PE27 3LF **t** 01480 461880
f 01480 496100 **e** srt@btinternet.com
w soundrecordingtechnology.co.uk
Dirs: Sarah Pownall, Karen Kenney. [CD CDR DCC Digital Audio
Tape MD]

The Soundmasters International Ltd The New
Boathouse, 136-142 Bramley Rd, London W10 6SR
t 020 7565 3020 **f** 020 7565 3021
e amie@soundmasters.co.uk **w** soundmasters.co.uk
Post Production Coordinator: Amie Nedwell. [CD Digital Audio
Tape DVD Vinyl]

Sounds Good Ltd 12 Chiltern Enterprise Centre, Station Rd,
Theale, Reading, Berks RG7 4AA **t** 0118 930 1700
f 0118 930 1709 **e** sales-info@sounds-good.co.uk
w sounds-good.co.uk Dir: Martin Maynard. [CD CDR DVD Video]

Stream Digital Media Ltd 61 Charlotte St, London
W1P 1LA **t** 020 7208 1567 **f** 020 7208 1555
e info@streamdm.co.uk **w** streamdm.co.uk
Head of Stream: Paul Kind. [DVD Video]

SUPER AUDIO MASTERING

Monks Withecombe, Chagford, Devon TQ13 8JY
t 01647 432858 or 07721 613145 **f** 01647 432308
e info@superaudiomastering.com **w** superaudiomastering.com
MD: Simon Heyworth. [CD Cdi CDR DVD]

SVC 142 Wardour St, London W1F 8ZU **t** 020 7734 1600
f 020 7437 1854 **e** post@svc.co.uk **w** svc.co.uk
Facilities Mgr: Jon Murray. [CD CDR Digital Audio Tape DVD
Video]

Tangerine Dreams Riverside Studios, Crisp Rd,
Hammersmith, London W6 9RL **t** 0800 085 6732 or
01189 89 2306 **f** 020 8237 1220
e prodvd@tangerinedreams.co.uk **w** tangerinedreams.co.uk. [CD
CDR DVD]

The Tape Gallery 28 Lexington St, London W1F 0LF
t 020 7439 3325 **f** 020 7734 9417 **e** info@tape-gallery.co.uk
w tape-gallery.co.uk Studio Mgrs: David Croft & Tara Simpson.

Town House Mastering Sanctuary Town House, 140
Goldhawk Rd, London W12 8HH **t** 020 8932 3200
f 020 8932 3209 **e** mastering@sanctuarystudios.co.uk
w sanctuarystudios.co.uk Mastering Mgr: Sophie Nathan. [CD
CDR DCC Digital Audio Tape DVD MD Vinyl]

Townhouse Studios (Mastering) 150 Goldhawk Rd,
London W12 8HH **t** 020 8932 3200 **f** 020 8932 3207
e info@townhousestudios.co.uk **w** townhousestudios.co.uk
Bookings: Gay Marshall or Lavinia Burrell. [CD Mp3 Vinyl]

Transfermation Ltd 63 Lant St, London SE1 1QN
t 020 7417 7021 **f** 020 7378 0516 **e** trace@transfermation.com
w transfermation.com Co-ordinator: Tracey Roper. [CD Digital
Audio Tape MD Vinyl]

Transition Mastering Kemble House, Kemble Rd, London
SE23 2DJ **t** 020 8699 7888 **f** 020 8699 9441
e info@transition-studios.co.uk **w** transition-studios.com
Mastering Eng: Jason Goz. [CD Digital Audio Tape Vinyl]

Trend A2 Canal Bank, Park West Industrial Pk, Dublin 12,
Ireland **t** +353 1 6060 600 **f** +353 1 6060 601
e muswk@trendstudios.com **w** trendstudios.com
Tech Dir: Paul Waldron. [CD Digital Audio Tape MD]

VDC Group VDC House, South Way, Wembley, Middx
HA9 0HB **t** 020 8903 3345 **f** 020 8900 1427
e enquiries@vdcgroup.com **w** vdcgroup.com
Sales Executive: Aaron Williamson. [CD CDR DVD Video]

Videosonics 13 Hawley Crescent, London NW1 8NP
t 020 7209 0209 **f** 020 7419 4460 **e** info@videosonics.com
w videosonics.com Studio Mgr: Peter Hoskins.

Waterfall Studios 2 Silver Rd, London W12 7SG
t 020 8746 2000 **f** 020 8746 0180
e info@waterfall-studios.com **w** waterfall-studios.com
Facilities Mgr: Samantha Leese. [DVD Video]

Wolf Mastering Studios 83 Brixton Water Lane, London
SW2 1PH **t** 020 7733 8088 **f** 020 7326 4016
e brethes@mac.com **w** wolfstudios.co.uk Dir: Dominique Brethes.
[CD Mp3 Vinyl]

Design, Pressing & Distribution: Mastering and Post Production

Printers & Packaging

ACS Media Ltd (Printers) 37 Bartholomew St, Newbury, Berks RG14 5LL **t** 01635 552237 or 01635 580448 **f** 01635 34179 **e** sales@acsmedia.co.uk Contact: Wilber Craik.

After Dark Media Unit 29, Scott Business Pk, Beacom Park Rd, Plymouth PL2 2PB **t** 01752 294130 **f** 01752 257320 **e** nigel@afterdarkmedia.net **w** afterdarkmedia.net Mgr: Nigel Muntz.

AGI Amaray Amaray House, Arkwright Rd, Corby NN17 5AE **t** 01536 263653 **f** 01536 274899 **e** amaraysales@uk.agimedia.com **w** amaray.com; agimedia.com Customer Services Manager: William Millen.

AGI Media Berghem Mews, Blythe Rd, London W14 0HN **t** 020 7605 1940 **f** 020 7605 1941 **e** sales@uk.agimedia.com **w** agimedia.com Contact: Jonathan Rogers.

AGR Manufacturing Ltd The Stables, 44, Stortford Rd, Great Dunmow, Essex CM6 1DL **t** 01371 859 393 **f** 01371 859 375 **e** info@agrm.co.uk **w** agrm.co.uk Quotations and Prices: Martyn Hewitt.

Audioprint Wolseley Court, Wolseley Road Ind Estate, Kempston, Bedford, Beds MK42 7AY **t** 01234 857566 **f** 01234 841700 **e** audio.print@virgin.net **w** audioprint.co.uk Dir/General Manager: Peter Hull.

Bernard Kaymar Trout St, Preston, Lancs PR1 4AL **t** 01772 562211 **f** 01772 257813 **e** sales@bernard-kaymar.co.uk **w** bernard-kaymar.co.uk MD: Mrs J Stead.

Blackgate Security Print & Promotions Ltd PO Box 2696, Ascot SL5 8ZQ **t** 01344 891 500 or 01344 891 500 **f** 01344 891 500 **e** info@bspp.biz **w** bspp.biz Sales & Marketing Director: Vicky Butcher.

Capital Repro Suite G, Tech West House, Warple Way, London W3 0UE **t** 020 8743 0111 **f** 020 8743 0112 **e** ian@caprep.co.uk **w** caprep.co.uk Sales Director: Ian Part.

Clear Sound And Vision Ltd CSV House, 51 Marlborough Rd, London E18 1AR **t** 020 8989 8777 **f** 020 8989 9777 **e** sales@c-s-v.co.uk **w** c-s-v.co.uk MD: Clive Robins.

CMCS Group Plc 1, Kennet Rd, Dartford, Kent DA1 4QN **t** 020 8308 5000 **f** 020 8308 5005 **e** sales@cmcs.co.uk **w** cmcs.co.uk MD: Adam Teskey.

CMJ Print Services (Poster Specialists) **e** jcomic@indigo.ie.

Compac Print Unit 6, The Greenbridge Centre, Greenbridge Rd, Swindon, Wilts SN3 3JQ **t** 01793 421242 **f** 01793 421252 **e** adam.teskey@cmcs.co.uk Contact: Adam Teskey.

Delga Group Seaplane House, Riverside Est., Sir Thomas Longley Rd, Medway City Estate, Rochester, Kent ME2 4BH **t** 01634 227 000 **e** info@delga.co.uk **w** delga.co.uk Sales: Greg Barden.

Gemini Print & Display Europa House, Denmark St, Maidenhead, Berks SL6 7BN **t** 01628 410068 **f** 01628 412128 **e** kevingemini@netscapeonline.co.uk Contact: Kevin Hill.

GM Printing Ltd Buttermere House, Clyde Rd, Wallington, Surrey SM6 8PZ **t** 0800 216620 **f** 020 8286 4646 **e** info@gmprinting.co.uk **w** gmprinting.co.uk Contact: Steven Lo Presti.

Go Digital Print Ltd 21 Wates Way, Mitcham, Surrey CR4 4HR **t** 020 8648 7060 **f** 020 8241 0989 **e** godigital@stjames.org.uk **w** godigitalprint.co.uk Production Manager: Steve Hill.

Ingersoll Printers Second Way, Wembley, Middlesex HA9 0YJ **t** 020 8903 1355 **f** 020 8795 1381 **e** tcarney@ingersoll-printers.co.uk **w** ingersoll-printers.co.uk Marketing Dir: Terry Carney.

Jourdans Kestral Way, Sowton Industrial Estate, Exeter, Devon EX2 7LA **t** 01392 445524 **f** 01392 445526 **e** rhino@jourdans.co.uk Mktg Dir: David Gargrave.

Key Production (London) Ltd 8 Jeffreys Pl, London NW1 9PP **t** 020 7284 8800 **f** 020 7284 8844 **e** mail@keyproduction.co.uk **w** keyproduction.co.uk Sales & Marketing: Wendy Wood.

Keyprint (Printers) Research House, Fraser Rd, Greenford, Middlesex UB6 7AQ **t** 020 8566 7246 or 01992 553193 **f** 020 8566 7247 **e** sales@keyprinters.co.uk **w** keyprinters.co.uk MD: Mike Keyworth.

Lexon Group Park Rd, Risca, Gwent NP11 6YJ **t** 01633 613444 **f** 01633 601333 **e** print@lexongroup.com **w** lexongroup.com Contact: Sales Dept.

Leyprint Leyland Lane, Leyland, Preston, Lancs PR25 1UT **t** 01772 425000 **f** 01772 425001 **e** edward@leyprint.co.uk **w** leyprint.co.uk Sales & Mktg Dir: Edward Mould.

London Fancy Box Co Ltd Poulton Close, Dover, Kent CT17 0XB **t** 01304 242001 **f** 01304 240229 **e** castle@londonfancybox.co.uk **w** londonfancybox.co.uk Contact: Drew Dixon.

MODO PRODUCTIONS LTD

MODO

14 Regent Hill, Brighton, E Sussex BN1 3ED **t** 01273 779 030 **f** 01273 777 718, **e** tim@modo.co.uk **w** modo.co.uk MD: Tim Bevan. Creative Director: Henry Lavelle. Sales Manager: Mike Hicks.
Bespoke and creative packaging; CD, DVD, Vinyl duplication; full print service; design. Proven track record with prestigious clients; competitive rates.

MPO UK Ltd Units 3-4, Nucleus Central Way, Park Royal, London NW10 7XT **t** 020 8963 6888 **f** 020 8963 8693 **e** matt@MPO.co.uk **w** MPO.co.uk
Audio Sales Exec: Matt Shoults.

MPT Colour Graphics Unit 9 Thame Park Bus.Cen., Wenman Rd, Thame, Oxon OX9 3XA **t** 01844 216888 **f** 01844 218999 **e** sales@mptcolour.co.uk **w** mptcolour.co.uk GM: Gary Pople.

Nuleaf Graphics Ltd 37-42 Compton St., London EC1V 0AP **t** 020 7250 3558 **f** 020 7251 6981 **e** peter@nuleaf-group.co.uk Contact: Keith Morgan, Peter Moran.

Panmer Plastics (UK) Ltd. Unit 4-5, Delta Centre, Mount Pleasant, Wembley, Middx. HA0 1UX **t** 020 8903 7733 **f** 020 8903 3036 **e** info@panmer.com **w** panmer.com MD: Nimesh Shah.

Paul Linard Print 57-63 Brownfields, Welwyn Garden City, Herts AL7 1AN **t** 01707 333716 **f** 01707 334211 **e** Pat@linards.co.uk **w** linards.co.uk MD: Patrick Leighton.

Pollard Boxes Ltd 193 Gloucester Crescent, South Wigston, Leics LE18 4YH **t** 0116 277 2999 **f** 0116 277 3888 **e** sales@pollardboxes.co.uk Dir: Peter Conner.

Proactive PR Suite 201, Homelife House, 26 - 32 Oxford Rd, Bournemouth BH8 8EZ **t** 01202 315 333 **f** 01202 315 600 **e** info@proactivepr.org **w** proactivepr.org Dir: Cliff Lay.

RAD Printing Ltd Unit 10, Block F, Northfleet Industrial Estate, Kent DA11 9SW **t** 01322 380775 **f** 01322 380647 **e** info@radprint.com **w** radprint.com Production Manager: Emilie Bish.

Reflex Media Services Ltd Unit 5, Cirrus, Glebe Rd, Huntingdon PE29 7DL **t** 01480 412 222 **f** 01480 411 441 **e** sally@reflex-media.co.uk **w** reflex-media.co.uk Factory Manager: Sally Houghton.

Senol Printing 6 Sandiford Rd, Kimpton Road Trading Estate, Sutton, Surrey SM3 9RD **t** 020 8641 3890 **f** 020 8641 3486 **e** info@senolprinting.co.uk **w** senolprinting.co.uk Contact: Jacqui Gunn.

Shellway Press 42-44 Telford Way, Westway Estate, London W3 7XS **t** 020 8749 8191 **f** 020 8749 8721 **e** stuart@shellway.co.uk MD: Stuart Shelbourn.

SMP Group Plc 2 Swan Rd, Woolwich, London SE18 5TT **t** 020 8855 5535 or 07808 909 292 **f** 020 8855 5367 **e** John.Leahy@smpgroup.co.uk **w** smpgroup.co.uk MD: John Leahy.

Sounds Good Ltd 12 Chiltern Enterprise Centre, Station Rd, Theale, Reading, Berks RG7 4AA **t** 0118 930 1700 **f** 0118 930 1709 **e** sales-info@sounds-good.co.uk **w** sounds-good.co.uk Dir: Martin Maynard.

St Ives Print & Display (Blackburn) Ltd Greenbank Technology Pk, Challenge Way, Blackburn, Lancs BB1 5QB **t** 01254 278 800 **f** 01254 278 811 **e** salesbl@stivespd.co.uk **w** stivespd.co.uk MD: Mark Ord.

St Ives Print & Display Ltd Optima Pk, Thames Rd, Crayford, Kent TN2 3EY **t** 01322 621 560 **f** 01322 625 060 **e** sales@stivespd.co.uk **w** stivespd.co.uk Sales Director: Mark Vincent.

St James Litho 21 Wates Way, Mitcham, Surrey CR4 4HR **t** 020 8640 9438 **f** 020 8241 0989 **e** production@stjames.org.uk **w** stjames.org.uk Production Manager: Vince Lowe.

The Standard Press Ltd Standard House, 7/9 Burnham St, Kingston Upon Thames, Surrey KT2 6QR **t** 020 8549 1990 **f** 020 8549 6500 or 020 8547 3358(ISDN) **e** sales@standardpress.co.uk **w** standardpress.co.uk Production Manager: Paul Williams.

Total Spectrum Ltd 11 Intec 2, Wade Rd, Basingstoke, Hants RG24 8NE **t** 01256 814114 **f** 01256 814115 **e** sales@totalspectrum.co.uk **w** totalspectrum.co.uk Contact: Sales.

Vycon Products Ltd Units 1&2, Crathie Rd, off Western Rd, Kilmarnock, Ayrshire KA3 1NG **t** 01563 574481 **f** 01563 533537 **e** sales@vycon.co.uk **w** vycon.co.uk Sales Dir: Morag Belford.

Design, Pressing & Distribution: Printers & Packaging

Art and Creative Studios

Abbey Road Interactive Abbey Road Studios, 3 Abbey Rd, London NW8 9AY **t** 020 7266 7282 **f** 020 7266 7321 **e** interactive@abbeyroad.com **w** abbeyroadinteractive.com Studio Manager: Trish McGregor.

After Dark Media Unit 29, Scott Business Pk, Beacom Park Rd, Plymouth PL2 2PB **t** 01752 294130 **f** 01752 257320 **e** nigel@afterdarkmedia.net **w** afterdarkmedia.net Mgr: Nigel Muntz.

Agitprop Design & Communications 19 Links Yard, 29a Spelman St, London E1 5LX **t** 07989 586 272 **e** musicweek@agitprop.co.uk **w** agitprop.co.uk Creative Dir: Jim Holt.

Airside 24 Cross St, London N1 2BG **t** 020 7354 9912 **f** 020 7354 5529 **e** studio@airside.co.uk **w** airside.co.uk Studio Manager: Anne Brassier.

Antar Marlinspike Hall, Walpole Halesworth, Suffolk IP19 9AR **t** 01986 784 664 **f** 01986 784 664 **e** cally@antar.cc **w** antar.cc MD: Cally.

Art Goes Boom Weir Bank, Bray-on-Thames, Maidenhead, Berks SL6 2ED **t** 01628 762651 **f** 01628 762650 **e** jayne@artgoesboom.co.uk **w** artgoesboom.co.uk Contact: Jayne Holt.

ArtScience Limited 3-5 Hardwidge St, London SE1 3SY **t** 020 7939 9500 **f** 020 7939 9499 **e** lab5@artscience.net **w** artscience.net Dirs: Douglas Coates, Pete Rope.

Barnes Music Engraving Ltd 26 St Anthony's Ave, Eastbourne, E Sussex BN23 6LP **t** 01323 434 979 **f** 01323 434 979 **e** info@barnes.co.uk Mgr: Julia Bovee.

Big Active Ltd (Art Direction & Design) Unit D4, Metropolitan Wharf, Wapping Wall, London E1W 3SS **t** 020 7702 9365 **f** 020 7702 9366 **e** contact@bigactive.com **w** bigactive.com Creative Dir: Gerard Saint.

Bijoux Graphics 10 L Peabody Bldgs, Clerkenwell Close, London EC1R 0AY **t** 020 7608 1316 or 07947 896 775 **f** 020 7608 0525 **e** davies@bijouxgraphics.co.uk **w** bijouxgraphics.co.uk Dir: David Davies.

BLADE DESIGN LTD

Unit 4, 101 Pentonville Rd, Islington, London N1 9LG **t** 020 3119 1022 **f** 020 3119 1033 **e** steve@bladeweb.co.uk **w** bladeweb.co.uk Director: Steve Knee.

Blue Source Ltd. Lower Ground Floor, 49-51 Central St, London EC1V 8AB **t** 020 7553 7950 **e** seb@bluesource.com **w** bluesource.com Company Director: Seb Marling.

Brian Burrows Ind Illustration & Graphic Design Enterprise House, 133 Blyth Rd, Hayes, Middlesex UB3 1DD **t** 020 8573 8761 **f** 020 8561 9114 **e** bburrows@btinternet.com MD: Brian Burrows.

Century Displays 75, Park Rd, Kingston Upon Thames, Surrey KT2 6DE **t** 020 8974 8950 **f** 020 8546 3689 **e** info@centurydisplays.co.uk **w** centurydisplays.co.uk GM: Neil Wicks.

Colors 42-44 Hanway St, London W1T 1UT **t** 020 7637 1842 **f** 020 7637 5568 **e** studio@colors.co.uk **w** colors.co.uk Dir: Chris Green.

Coloset Graphics 3 Black Swan Yard, Bermondsey St, London SE1 3XW **t** 020 7234 0300 **f** 020 7234 0118 **e** info@colorsetgraphics.co.uk **w** colorsetgraphics.co.uk Dir: Frank Baptiste.

The Creative Corporation Magpie Studios, 2a Leconfield Rd, London N5 2SN **t** 020 7704 9234 or 07779 615 217 **e** contact@thecreativecorporation.co.uk **w** thecreativecorporation.co.uk Contact: Dave Stansbie.

Crush Design & Art Direction 6 Gloucester St, Brighton BN1 4EW **t** 01273 606058 **e** info@crushed.co.uk **w** crushed.co.uk Dir: Carl.

D-Face Unit 104, 326 Kensal Rd, London W10 5BZ **t** 020 8959 3125 or 07817 806 011 **f** 020 8959 3125 **e** design@d-face.co.uk **w** d-face.co.uk Creative Director: Donna Pickup.

D-Fuse 13-14 Gt.Sutton St, London EC1V 0BX **t** 020 7253 3462 **e** info@dfuse.com **w** dfuse.com Dir: Michael Faulkner.

Darkwaveart 3 Spalding Rd, Nottingham NG3 2AY **t** 07775 506 479 **e** darkwaveart@hotmail.com **w** darkwaveart.co.uk Designer: Matt Vickerstaff.

Delga Group Seaplane House, Riverside Est., Sir Thomas Longley Rd, Medway City Estate, Rochester, Kent ME2 4BH **t** 01634 227 000 **e** info@delga.co.uk **w** delga.co.uk Sales: Greg Barden.

The Design & Advertising Resource 7 Kings Wharf, 301 Kingsland Rd, Hoxton, London E8 4DS **t** 020 7254 3191 **f** 0870 442 5297 **e** info@your-resource.co.uk **w** your-resource.co.uk Account Director: Richard Fearn.

THE DESIGN CORPORATION LTD

design4music.com

7 Portland Mews, Soho, London W1F 8JQ **t** 020 7734 5676 or 07974 144 830 **e** us@design4music.com **w** design4music.com MD: Nigel Pearce.

The Design Dell 13a Newnham St, Ely, Cambs CB7 4PG **t** 01353 659911 **f** 01353 650011 **e** dan@design-dell.com **w** design-dell.com Creative Director: Dan Donovan.

Design Lab Studio 336, Stratford Workshops, Burford Rd, London E15 2SP **t** 020 8555 5540 or 07841 196 787 **f** 0208 5555540 **e** info@design-lab.tv **w** design-lab.tv Art Director: Matthew James.

Designers Republic Work Station, Unit 415, Paternoster Row, Sheffield, S Yorks S1 2BX **t** 0114 275 4982 **e** disinfo@thedesignersrepublic.com **w** thedesignersrepublic.com Creative Dir: Ian Anderson.

Division 100 Unit Two, 34 Charlotte Rd, London EC2A 3PB **t** 020 7033 0000 **f** 020 7033 0001 **e** designers@division100.com **w** division100.com Dir: Terence Chisholm.

Dreamcatcher Studios Ltd 3, Merryman Drive, Crowthorne, Berks RG45 6TW **t** 07771 818 111 **f** 01344 779 677 **e** leeault@dreamcatcherstudios.co.uk **w** dreamcatcherstudios.co.uk Creative Director: Lee Ault.

DS Emotion Ltd Chantry House, Victoria Rd, Leeds, W Yorks LS5 3JB **t** 0113 225 7100 **f** 0113 225 7200 **e** info@dsemotion.com **w** dsemotion.com.

Eject Limited 5 Green Dragon Court, Borough Market, London SE1 9AW **t** 020 7407 3003 **f** 020 7407 3012 **e** studio@eject.it **w** eject.it Dir: Lee Murrell.

Eldamar Ltd 157 Oxford Rd, Cowley, Oxford OX4 2ES **t** 01865 77 99 44 **e** ideas@eldamar.co.uk **w** eldamar.co.uk Creative Director: Ayd Instone.

expdesign.co.uk 1st Floor, 23 Charlotte Rd, London EC2A 3PB **t** 020 7729 8255 **f** 020 7729 8258 **e** creative@expdesign.co.uk **w** expdesign.co.uk Creative Director: Mark Bailey.

Eyetoeye Digital 6H Sloane Sq, London SW1W 8EE **t** 020 7730 8946 **e** drew@eyetoeye.com **w** eyetoeye.com Creative Director: Andrew W. Ellis.

Farrow Design Ltd 23-24 Great James St, London WC1N 3ES **t** 020 7404 4225 or 020 7831 4976 ISDN **f** 020 7404 4223 **e** studio@farrowdesign.com **w** farrowdesign.com Contact: Mark Farrow.

Firebird.com Ltd Kyrle House Studios, Edde Cross St, Ross-on-Wye, Herefordshire HR9 7BZ **t** 01989 762269 **e** info@firebird.com **w** firebird.com CEO: Peter Martin.

Fluid Graphic Design Ltd Fluid Studios, 12 Tenby St, Birmingham B1 3AJ **t** 0121 212 0121 **f** 0121 212 0202 **e** james@fluidesign.co.uk **w** fluidesign.co.uk Dir: James Glover.

Form 47 Tabernacle St, London EC2A 4AA **t** 020 7014 1430 **f** 020 7014 1431 or 020 7014 1432 ISDN **e** studio@form.uk.com **w** form.uk.com Partners: Paula Benson, Paul West.

Four23 Films The Apex, 6 Southern St, Castlefield, Manchester M3 4NN **t** 0161 835 9466 **f** 0161 835 9468 **e** mailman@four23.net **w** four23.net Dir: Warren Bramley.

Framous Unit 12/13 Impress House, Mansell Rd, Acton, London W3 7QH **t** 020 8735 0047 **f** 020 8735 0048 **e** lucy@framous.ltd.uk **w** framous.ltd.uk Office Manager: Lucy Walker.

Glasseye Unit 20A, Iliffe Yard, Crampton St, London SE17 3QA **t** 020 7701 4300 **e** info@glasseyeltd.com **w** glasseyeltd.com Dir: James Jefferson.

Graphite Media PO Box 605, Richmond TW9 2YE **t** 020 8948 8629 **e** info@graphitemedia.net **w** graphitemedia.net Dir: Ben Turner.

Green Ink 28 Hanbury St, Spitalfields, London E1 6QR **t** 020 7247 7248 **f** 020 7247 7293 **e** design@green-ink.co.uk **w** green-ink.co.uk MD: Bruce Gill.

Hiltongrove Multimedia Hiltongrove Business Centre, Hatherley Mews, London E17 4QP **t** 020 8521 2424 **f** 020 8521 4343 **e** chris@hiltongrove.com **w** hiltongrove.com Creative Director: Chris Watson.

Tom Hingston Studio 76 Brewer St, London W1F 9TX **t** 020 7287 6044 **f** 020 7287 6048 **e** info@hingston.net **w** hingston.net Contact: Tom Hingston.

How Splendid 54-62 Regent St, London W1B 5RE **t** 020 7287 4442 **f** 020 7287 5557 **e** dan@howsplendid.com **w** howsplendid.com Account Dir: Dan Morris.

Hutch 19, Nelson Ave, Tonbridge, Kent TN9 1XA **t** 020 7252 0147 or 07952 751614 **e** info@willhutchinson.co.uk **w** willhutchinson.co.uk MD: Will Hutchinson.

icoico.com 22 Jamaica St, Glasgow G1 4QD **t** 0141 221 4171 **f** 0141 221 4172 **e** info@icoico.co.uk **w** icoico.co.uk MD: Lee McLean.

ID Interactive 5 Rolls Crescent, Manchester M15 5JX **t** 0161 232 9314 **f** 0161 232 9514 **e** info@idinteractive.co.uk **w** idinteractive.net Mgr: Azmat Mohammed.

Ideas Redding House, Redding, Falkirk FK2 9TR **t** 01324 716827 **f** 01324 716827 **e** inquiries@ideas.co.uk **w** ideas.co.uk Creative Director: Don Jack.

Ignite Marketing Unit 17C Raines Court, Northwold Rd, London N16 7DH **t** 020 7275 8682 **f** 020 7275 0791 **e** paul@ignitemarketing.co.uk **w** ignitemarketing.co.uk MD: Paul West.

Impac Associates Ltd Grafton House, 2-3 Golden Sq, London W1F 9HR **t** 020 7734 1134 **f** 020 7734 1135 **e** impac.tom@virgin.net Contact: Tom Heron.

Intro 42 St John St, London EC1M 4DL **t** 020 7324 3244 **f** 020 7324 3245 **e** intro@intro-uk.com **w** introwebsite.com New Business Mgr: Jo Marsh.

Jeff Cummins Design 125, High Oak Rd, Ware, Herts SG12 7PA **t** 01920 411434 or 07751 549098 **f** 01920 411434 **e** info@jeffcummins.com **w** jeffcummins.com Art Director: Jeff Cummins.

Joel Harrison Design c/o Addiction, 2 Moray House, 23-31 Great Titchfield St, London W1W 7PA **t** 020 7291 5827 or 07968 773 972 **f** 020 7637 8185 **e** info@joelharrisondesign.com **w** joelharrisondesign.com Art Director: Joel Harrison.

JP3 Studio 3, 3A Brackenbury Rd, London W6 0BE **t** 020 8762 9153 **f** 020 8740 0200 **e** info@jp3.co.uk **w** jp3.co.uk MD: Paul McGarvey.

Chris Kay (UK) Ltd 158 Station Rd, Witham, Essex CM8 3YS **t** 01376 500566 **f** 01376 500578 **e** sales@chriskay.com **w** chriskay.com Contact: Eddie Clark.

Lewis Creative Consultants 4 Quayside Mills, Leith, Edinburgh EH6 6EX **t** 0131 554 1286 **e** postman@lewis.co.uk **w** lewis.co.uk Dir: Alan Hepburn.

LGD Ltd 180 Corporation St, Birmingham B4 6UD **t** 0121 212 3450 **f** 0121 212 3455 **e** info@lgdgroup.co.uk **w** lgdgroup.co.uk Ptnr: Phil Jolly.

P Linard Marketing & Advertising 57-63 Brownfields, Welwyn Garden City, Herts AL7 1AN **t** 01707 333716 **f** 01707 334211 **e** neil@linards.co.uk **w** linards.co.uk Contact: Neil Smith.

Mackerel Design Ltd 15-17 Middle St, Brighton, W Sussex BN1 1AL **t** 01273 201313 **e** info@mackerel.co.uk **w** mackerel.co.uk Dir: Mark Davis.

Mainartery Design 2 Stucley Pl, London NW1 8NS **t** 020 7482 6660 **f** 020 7482 6606 **e** art@mainartery.co.uk **w** mainartery.co.uk Creative Dir: Jo Mirowski.

Design, Pressing & Distribution: Art and Creative Studios

Design, Pressing & Distribution: Art and Creative Studios

Me Company 14 Apollo Studios, Charlton Kings Rd, London NW5 2SA **t** 020 7482 4262 **f** 020 7284 0402 **e** meco@mecompany.com **w** mecompany.com Art Dir: Paul White.

Mental Block Unit 2, Archway Mews, Putney Bridge Rd, London SW15 2PE **t** 020 8877 0085 **e** laurence@mentalblockdesign.com **w** mentalblockdesign.com MD: Laurence Smith.

Modo Production Ltd 14 Regent Hill, Brighton, E Sussex BN1 3ED **t** 01273 779 030 **f** 01273 777 718 **e** henry@modo.co.uk **w** modo.co.uk Creative Manager: Henry Lavelle.

Mystery Ltd 2nd Floor, 79 Parkway, Camden, London NW1 7PP **t** 020 7424 1900 **f** 020 7267 0191 **e** will@mystery.co.uk **w** mystery.co.uk Studio Manager: Will Watts.

Navig8 Basement, 36 Charlotte St, Fitzrovia, London W1T 2NA **t** 020 7813 0373 **f** 020 7436 8996 **e** enquiries@navig8.co.uk **w** navig8.co.uk Contact: Drew Corps.

Nu Urban Design Unit 3, Rivermead Industrial Estate, Pipersway, Thatcham, Berks RG149 4EP **t** 01635 587900 **f** 01635 292314 **e** kevin@nu-urbanmusic.co.uk **w** nu-urbandesign.co.uk Head of Design: Kevin Broome.

The Nuclear Family 149 Defoe House, London EC2Y 8ND **t** 07979 848 754 **e** red@thenuclearfamily.co.uk **w** thenuclearfamily.co.uk Creative Dir: Red James.

One Hand Clapping Design Studio 125, 77 Beak St, London W1F 9DB **t** 020 8348 6607 or 07956 967 288 **e** heidi@ohcdesign.com **w** ohcdesign.com Contact: Heidi Ng.

Oort Ltd 62 Sprules Rd, London SE4 2NN **t** 020 7635 6765 **e** emma@oortmedia.net **w** oortmedia.net Creative Director: Emma Peters.

OR Multimedia Ltd Unit 5 Elm Court, 156-170 Bermondsey St, London SE1 3TQ **t** 020 7939 9540 **f** 020 7939 9541 **e** info@or-media.com **w** or-media.com Dir: Peter Gough.

Peacock Design 34 Percy St, London W1T 2DG **t** 020 7580 8868 **f** 020 7323 9780 **e** mailus@peacockdesign.com **w** peacockdesign.com MD: Keith Peacock.

Playground Creative Services 21 Wates Way, Mitcham, Surrey CR4 4HR **t** 020 8685 9453 **f** 020 8241 0989 **e** playground@stjames.org.uk **w** playgroundcreative.com Art Director: Tim Bridle.

Plus Two Studio 153 Hagley Rd, Oldswinford, Stourbridge, W Midlands DY8 2JB **t** 01384 393311 **f** 01384 393232 **e** studio@plustwo.co.uk **w** plustwostudio.com Art Dir: Andrew Higginbotham.

Proactive PR Suite 201, Homelife House, 26 - 32 Oxford Rd, Bournemouth BH8 8EZ **t** 01202 315 333 **f** 01202 315 600 **e** info@proactivepr.org **w** proactivepr.org Dir: Cliff Lay.

Purple Frog Studios Ltd The Byre, Manor Farm, Aston Sandford, Aylesbury, Bucks HP17 8LP **t** 01844 295170 **f** 01844 292981 **e** sales@purplefrog.co.uk **w** purplefrog.co.uk Creative Dir: Marcus Marsh.

Qd 93 Great Titchfield, London W1P 7FP **t** 020 7462 1700 **f** 020 7636 0652 **e** info@qotd.co.uk **w** qotd.co.uk Contact: Dave Wharin.

Quite Great Design Unit D, Magog Court, Shelford Bttm, Cambridge CB2 4AD **t** 01223 410 000 **e** Harvey@quitegreat.co.uk **w** quitegreat.co.uk MD: Mark Lovell.

Raw-Paw Graphics 13-14 Great Sutton St, London EC1 0BX **t** 020 7253 3462 **f** 020 7253 3463 **e** mike@dfuse.com **w** raw-paw.net MD: Michael Faulkner.

Real World Design Mill Lane, Box, Corsham, Wilts SN13 8PN **t** 01225 743188 **f** 01225 744369 **e** york.tillyer@realworld.co.uk **w** realworld.co.uk Interactive Director: York Tillyer.

Red James London EC2 **t** 020 7628 7853 **e** red@redjam.com **w** redjam.com Dir: Red James.

Red Sky Media 12 Austral Way, Althorne, Essex CM3 6UP **t** 01621 743 979 or 07957 297 872 **e** dan@redskymedia.co.uk **w** redskymedia.co.uk Mgr: Daniel Raynham.

rehabstudio Ltd 1st Floor, Oaklands, 64-66 Redchurch St, London E2 7DP **t** 0203 222 0080 **e** newbusiness@rehabstudio.com **w** rehabstudio.com Creative Director: Tim Rodgers.

The Reptile House 69-70 Long Lane, Smithfield, London EC1A 9EJ **t** 020 7796 3545 **f** 020 7796 3561 **e** matt@the-reptile-house.co.uk **w** the-reptile-house.co.uk Creative Director: Matt Hughes.

Root Associates Ground Floor, 4 Ravey St, London EC2A 4QP **t** 020 7739 2277 **f** 020 7613 0342 **e** martin@rootdesign.co.uk **w** rootdesign.co.uk Creative Director: Martin Root.

Ryan Art 48A Southern Row, London W10 5AN **t** 020 8968 0966 **f** 020 8968 6418 **e** info@ryanart.com **w** ryanart.com Contact: Niamh McGovern.

Seed Software The Seed Warehouse, Maidenhead Yard, The Wash, Herts SG14 1PX **t** 01992 558 881 **f** 01992 558 465 **e** info@seedsoftware.co.uk **w** seedsoftware.co.uk MD: Andrew W Ellis.

Sirenstorm Media/Majic Design PO Box 66, Manchester M12 4XJ **t** 0161 225 9991 **e** info@sirenstorm.com **w** sirenstorm.com Dir: Tony Spalding.

Skinny 4th Floor, 11 D'Arblay St, London W1F 8DT **t** 020 7287 1888 **e** sonya@fullfatskinny.com **w** fullfatskinny.com Dir: Sonya Skinner.

Sounds Good Ltd 12 Chiltern Enterprise Centre, Station Rd, Theale, Reading, Berks RG7 4AA **t** 0118 930 1700 **f** 0118 930 1709 **e** sales-info@sounds-good.co.uk **w** sounds-good.co.uk Dir: Martin Maynard.

Storm Media 134 Godstone Rd, Caterham, Surrey CR3 6RB **t** 01883 372639 **f** 01883 372639 **e** enquiries@stormmedia.uk.com **w** stormmedia.uk.com MD: Stephen Bailey-Johnston.

Studio Lobster & Design The Foundry, Forth Banks, Newcastle upon Tyne, Tyne & Wear NE1 3PA **t** 0191 261 2101 **f** 0191 230 0707 **e** shorty@studiolobster.com **w** studiolobster.com MD: Richard Short.

Studio Plum 39 Belgrade Rd, London N16 8DH **t** 0207 249 8198 **e** jonnie@studioplum.co.uk **w** studioplum.co.uk Producer: Jonnie Pound.

StudioMix 3rd Floor, Mayfair House, 11 Lurke St, Bedford MK40 3HZ **t** 01234 272347 **f** 01234 272327 **e** design@studiomix.co.uk **w** studiomix.co.uk Senior Designer: Mick Lowe.

Stylorouge 57/60 Charlotte Rd, London EC2A 3QT **t** 020 7729 1005 **f** 020 7739 7124 **e** rob@stylorouge.co.uk **w** stylorouge.co.uk Dir: Rob O'Connor.

Superdead Graphics 42 Neale Rd, Chorlton, Manchester M21 9DQ **t** 0161 232 0031 **e** ed@superdead.com **w** superdead.com Designer: Ed Syder.

thelongdrop Studio 12, Atlas Works, Foundry Lane, Earls Colne, Essex CO6 2TE **t** 01787 224 464 **f** 01787 220 055 **e** studio@thelongdrop.com **w** thelongdrop.com Creative Dir: Andy Carne.

TMCA 13 John Prince's St, London W1G 0JR **t** 020 7493 9197 **f** 020 7493 9092 **e** info@tmca.uk.com **w** tmca.uk.com Ptnr: Jean-Marc Rathe.

Tourist 1 Willow St, Shoreditch, London EC2A 4BH **t** 020 7739 3011 **f** 020 7739 3033 **e** info@wearetourist.com **w** wearetourist.com Dirs: Rob Chenery, Keith White.

Traffic Design 3 Astrop Mews, Hammersmith, London W6 7HR **t** 020 8742 9559 **e** jeremy@traffic-design.com **w** traffic-design.com Contact: Jeremy Plumb.

Tumbling Dice Creative Management PO Box 6234, Leighton Buzzard LU7 2WX **t** 01525 217727 **e** enquiries@wearetumblingdice.com **w** wearetumblingdice.com MD: Duncan Illing.

TWO:design Studio 20, The Arches, Hartland Rd, Camden, London NW1 8HR **t** 020 7267 1118 **f** 020 7482 0221 or 020 7424 9147(ISDN) **e** studio@twodesign.net **w** twodesign.net Art Dir: Graham Peake.

Undertow Design No7, 9-10 College Terrace, London E3 5EP **t** 020 8983 4718 or 07966170109 **f** 020 8983 4718 **e** info@undertow-design.co.uk **w** undertow-design.co.uk Art Director: Steve Wilkins.

UnLimited Creative Fl 3 Grampian House, Meridian Gate, London E14 9YT **t** 0870 744 2643 **f** 070 9231 4982 **e** creative@unlimitedmedia.co.uk **w** unlimitedmedia.co.uk Dirs: Chris Cooke, Alan Ogilvie.

Version 15 Holywell Row, London EC2A 4JB **t** 020 7684 5470 **f** 020 7684 5472 **e** info@versioncreative.com **w** versioncreative.com Dirs: Anthony Oram, Mo Chicharro.

Version Industries Ltd 47 Lower End, Swaffham Prior, Cambridge CB5 0HT **t** 07903 886 471 **f** 020 8374 4021 **e** team@versionindustries.com **w** versionindustries.com Lead Designer/Developer: Gavin Singleton.

Vivid Design Consultants 138 Cherry Orchard Rd, Croydon, Surrey CR0 6BB **t** 020 8649 8825 **f** 020 8667 1682 **e** paul@vividdesignconsultants.com **w** vividdesignconsultants.com Owner: Paul Jukes.

Wherefore Art? 8 Primrose Mews, Sharpleshall St, London NW1 8YW **t** 020 7586 8866 **f** 020 7586 8800 or 020 7586 8008 (ISDN) **e** info@whereforeart.com **w** whereforeart.com Creative Director: David Costa.

White Label Productions Ltd Power Road Studios, 114 Power Rd, London W4 5PY **t** 020 8987 7070 **f** 020 8987 7090 **e** c.grant@whitelabelproductions.co.uk **w** whitelabelproductions.co.uk MD: Cheryl Grant.

Wolf Graphics 49 Belvoir Rd, London SE22 0QY **t** 020 8299 2342 **f** 020 8693 9006 **e** jim@exoticarecords.co.uk **w** exoticarecords.co.uk MD: Jim Phelan.

X! ARTWORK: MUSIC ART DESIGN + DIRECTION

London Studio, Suite VP, PO Box 43128, London E17 6WS **t** 020 8925 6542 or 07753 755 353 **f** 020 8925 6542 **e** services@xartwork.co.uk **w** xartwork.co.uk Creative Director: William Frank. Services : Graphic Art Design / Direction; Illustration; Website Design; Project Management.

ZiP Design Ltd Unit 2A Queens Studios, 121 Salusbury Rd, London NW6 6RG **t** 020 7372 4474 **f** 020 7372 4484 or 020 7328 4447 **e** info@zipdesign.co.uk **w** zipdesign.co.uk Art Director: Peter Chadwick.

Merchandise Companies

ABC Shirts Unit 16, Greenwich Centre Business Pk, 53 Norman Rd, London SE10 9QF **t** 020 8853 1103 **f** 020 8293 1746 **e** sales@abcshirts.com **w** abcshirts.com Contact: Jane Cheese.

Action Jacket Company PO Box 1180, Stourbridge, W Midlands DY9 0LX **t** 01562 887096 **f** 01562 882010 **e** info@actionjacket.co.uk Prop: Brian Smith.

Active Merchandising (T Shirts) 58, Overn Ave, Buckingham MK18 1LT **t** 01280 814510 **f** 01280 814519 **e** leonprice@lineone.net MD: Leon Price.

Adrenalin Merchandising Unit 5, Church House, Church St, London E15 3JA **t** 020 8503 0634 **f** 020 8221 2528 **e** scott@adrenalin-merch.demon.co.uk **w** adrenalin-merch.demon.co.uk Contact: Scott Cooper.

Airborne Packaging Pegasus House, Beatrice Rd, Leicester LE3 9FH **t** 0116 253 6136 **f** 0116 251 4485 **e** sales@airbornebags.co.uk **w** airbornebags.co.uk Sales Manager: Gary Newby.

Alchemy Carta Ltd The Alembic, Hazel Drive, Narborough Road South, Leicester LE3 2JE **t** 0116 282 4824 **f** 0116 282 5202 **e** info@alchemygroup.co.uk **w** alcemygroup.co.uk Sales Dir: Sandra Philipson.

Alex Co 94 Guildford Rd, Croydon, Surrey CR0 2HJ **t** 020 8683 0546 **f** 020 8689 4749 **e** alexco@btinternet.com MD: Stuart Alexander.

Alister Reid Ties 9 Applegate House, Applegate, Brentwood, Essex CM14 5PL **t** 01277 375329 **f** 01277 375331 **e** colin@arties.fsbusiness.co.uk Sales Manager: Colin Stoddart.

Backstreet International Merchandise Ltd. Unit A, 1st Floor, 16-24 Brewery Rd, London N7 9NH **t** 020 7700 2662 **f** 020 7700 2882 **e** sales@bsimerch.com **w** bsimerch.com Senior Account Manager: Richard Cassar.

Baskind Promotions Ltd 54 Otley Rd, Headingley, Leeds, W Yorks LS6 2AL **t** 0113 389 4100 **f** 0113 389 4101 or 0113 278 8307 ISDN **e** simon@baskind.com **w** baskind.com MD: Simon Baskind.

Blowfish U.V. 29 Granville St, Loughborough, Leics. LE11 3BL **t** 07900 262 052 **f** 01509 560 221 **e** anna@blowfishuv.co.uk **w** blowfishuv.co.uk MD: Anna Sandiford.

Blue Grape Tech West House, 4 Warple Way, London W3 0UE **t** 020 8740 5398 **f** 020 8749 5897 **e** wclarke@bluegrape.co.uk **w** bluegrape.gb.com Contact: Wayne Clarke.

BRAVADO INTERNATIONAL GROUP

12 Deer Park Road, Wimbledon, London SW19 3FB **t** 020 8545 8100 **f** 020 8542 1807 **e** jackie.phillimore@bravado.com **w** bravado.com A&R: Jackie Phillimore. A&R: Keith Drinkwater, Barry Drinkwater, Benny Lindstrom. Retail: Peter Palmer. Promotions: Ken Brudenell.

Caterprint Ltd Unit 3, Chaseside Works,, Chelmsford Rd, Southgate, London N14 4JN **t** 020 8886 1600 **f** 020 8886 1636 **e** info@caterprint.co.uk **w** caterprint.co.uk Contact: Leonard.

Century Displays 75, Park Rd, Kingston Upon Thames, Surrey KT2 6DE **t** 020 8974 8950 **f** 020 8546 3689 **e** info@centurydisplays.co.uk **w** centurydisplays.co.uk GM: Neil Wicks.

Charitees 37 Barnfield Ave, Kingston upon Thames, Surrey KT2 5RD **t** 020 8549 8653 **f** 020 8404 7368 **e** info@charitees.co.uk **w** charitees.co.uk Proprieter: Don Chetland.

Chester Hopkins International PO Box 536, Headington, Oxford OX3 7LR **t** 01865 766 766 or 020 8441 1555 **f** 01865 769 736 **e** office@chesterhopkins.co.uk **w** chesterhopkins.co.uk MDs: Adrian Hopkins, Jo Chester.

De-lux Merchandise Co Zetland House, 5/25 Scrutton St, London EC2A 4HJ **t** 020 7613 3550 **f** 020 7613 3555 **e** info@de-lux.net **w** de-lux.net MD: Jeremy Joseph.

Dynamic Distribution Unit 1, Crooks Industrial Estate, Croft St, Leckhampton, Cheltenham, Glos GL53 0ED **t** 01242 237 755 **f** 01242 237 755 **e** info@dynamic-distribution.net **w** dynamic-distribution.net Dir: Joanna Massive.

EBTM Plc Unit A1, Riverside Business Centre, Haldane Pl, London SW18 4UQ **t** 020 8704 0034 or 07713 404 101 **f** 020 8704 0086 **e** grant@EBTM.com **w** EBTM.com Dir: Grant Calton.

EMC Advertising Gifts Derwent House, 1064 High Rd, Whetstone, London N20 0YY **t** 020 8492 2200 **f** 020 8445 9347 **e** sales@emcadgifts.co.uk **w** emcadgifts.co.uk Sales Dir: John Kay.

Epona Fairtrade and Organic Cotton Clothing Unit 5, 61 Lilford Rd, London SE5 9HR **t** 020 7095 1222 **f** 020 7095 9888 **e** info@eponasport.com **w** eponasport.com Dir: Tom Andrews.

Event Merchandising Unit 11, The Edge, Humber Rd, London NW2 6EW **t** 020 8208 1166 **f** 020 8208 4477 **e** event@eventmerch.com **w** eventmerchandising.com MD: Jeremy Goldsmith.

Fair Oaks Entertainments 7 Towers St, Ulverston, Cumbria LA12 9AN **t** 01229 581766 **f** 01229 581766 **e** fairoaksonline@audiohighway.net **w** ahwy.net/fairoaksonline/files/mainpage.doc Contact: JG Livingstone.

FEZBOROUGH LIMITED

Manor Farm Studio, Cleveley, Oxfordshire OX7 4DY **t** 01608 677 100 or 07889 787 600 **f** 01608 677 101 **e** kellogs@fezbro.com **w** fezbro.com Promot'nl Merchandise Dir: John Kalinowski.

Fifth Column T Shirt Design & Print 276 Kentish Town Rd, London NW5 2AA **t** 020 7485 8599 **f** 020 7267 3718 **e** info@fifthcolumn.co.uk **w** fifthcolumn.co.uk MD: Rodney Adams.

Finally Fan-Fair PO Box 153, Stanmore, Middx HA7 2HF **t** 01923 896 975 **f** 01923 896 985 **e** hrano@fan-fair.freeserve.co.uk MD: Mike Hrano.

Flag Standards Compass House, Waldron, E Sussex TN21 0RE **t** 01435 810080 **f** 01435 810082 **e** sales@flagstandards.co.uk **w** flagstandards.co.uk Owner: Tim Eustace.

GB Posters 1 Russell St, Kelham Island, Sheffield S3 8RW **t** 0114 276 7454 **f** 0114 272 9599 **e** enquiries@gbposters.com **w** businessgbposters.com Licensing Director: Robert G Edwards.

GMerch 2 Glenthorne Mews, London W6 0LJ **t** 020 8741 7100 **f** 020 8741 1170 **e** Paula.Campbell@gmerch.com **w** gmerch.com MD: Mark Stredwick.

Green Island Promotions Ltd Unit 31, 56 Gloucester Rd, Kensington, London SW7 4UB **t** 0870 789 3377 **f** 0870 789 3414 **e** greenisland@btinternet.com Dir: Steve Lucas.

IDD Enterprises Ltd The Old Boat House, 66 London Rd, Sheffield, S Yorks S2 4HL **t** 0114 273 9848 **f** 0114 278 7855 **e** ian@iddltd.co.uk **w** iddltd.co.uk Sales Director: Ian Bell.

Idle Eyes Printshop 81 Sheen Court, Richmond, Surrey TW10 5DF **t** 020 8876 0099 **f** 020 8876 0099 **e** IdleEyes@gmail.com **w** idleeyesprintshop.com Mgr: Jonathan Rees.

Independent Posters PO Box 7259, Brentwood, Essex CM14 5ZA **t** 01277 372000 **f** 01277 375333 **e** info@independentposters.co.uk Publishing Manager: Kim Miller.

Inkorporate 10A Lower Mall, Hammersmith, London W6 9DJ **t** 020 8748 3311 **f** 020 8563 7999 **e** sales@inkorporate.co.uk **w** inkorporate.co.uk Sales Director: Melvyn de Villiers.

Iris Unit 8a, Southam St, London W10 5PH **t** 0208 969 4761 **e** info@irisprinting.co.uk **w** irisprinting.co.uk Dir: Tim.

ITV Worldwide 48 Leicester Sq, London WC2H 7FB **t** 020 7389 8555 **e** Mark.hurry@ITV.com **w** granadaventures.tv Commercial Affairs Director: Mark Hurry.

JTL Printed And Embroided Leisurewear Unit 12, Worcester Road Industrial Est, Chipping Norton, Oxon OX7 5XW **t** 0845 2250725 **f** 01608 645529 **e** sales@jtlembroidery.co.uk Sales Director: Mike Yallop.

Klobber Ltd 443 Streatham High Rd, London SW16 3PH **t** 020 8679 9289 **f** 020 679 9775 **e** info@fruitpiemusic.com **w** fruitpiemusic.com Dir: Kumar Kamalagharan.

LOGO Promotional Merchandise Ltd 10 Crescent Terrace, Ilkley, W Yorks LS29 8DL **t** 01943 817 238 **f** 01943 605 259 **e** alan@logomerchandising.co.uk **w** logomerchandising.co.uk Dir: Alan Strachan.

Masons Music Dept. 260, Drury Lane, Ponswood Industrial Est, St Leonards On Sea, E Sussex TN38 9BA **t** 01424 427562 **f** 01424 434362 **e** sales@masonsmusic.co.uk **w** masonsmusic.co.uk Sales Admin: Alastair Sutton.

Metro Merchandising Ltd The Warehouse, 60 Queen St, Desborough, Northants NN14 2RE **t** 01536 763100 **f** 01536 763200 **e** mailbox@metro-ltd.co.uk **w** metro-ltd.co.uk MD: Martin Stowe.

Mick Wright Merchandising 185 Weedon Rd, Northampton NN5 5DA **t** 07000 226397 or 07802 500054 **f** 08701 372735 **e** tshirts@mickwright.com **w** mickwright.com CEO: Mick Wright.

Olympus Designs Unit 3, Balthane, Ballasalla, Isle of Man IM9 2AJ **t** 01624 825396 **e** enquiries@olympusdesigns.com **w** olympusdesigns.com MD: Chris Beards.

Pagan 1A Kirk Lane, Ruddington, Notts NG11 6NN **t** 0115 984 4224 **f** 0115 984 3227 **e** PAGAN.BYH@btinternet.com Contact: Garry Sharpe-Young.

PINK! Brand Solutions Ltd 565 24/28 St Leonards Rd, Windsor, Berks SL4 3BB **t** 01753 622555 **f** 01753 622557 **e** stuff@pink-brand.co.uk **w** pink-brand.co.uk Dir: Stuart Bailey.

PKA Promotions 6 South Folds Rd, Oakley Hay Industrial Estate, Corby, Northants NN18 9EU **t** 01536 461122 **f** 01536 744668 **e** PKaPromotions@aol.com MD: Mr D Dias.

Promotional Condom Co PO Box 111, Croydon, Surrey CR9 6WS **t** 0033 29751 2950 **f** 0033 29739 3306 **e** promotionalcondoms@btopenworld.com Dir: Andrew Kennedy.

Propaganda Symal House, 423 Edgware Rd, London NW9 0HU **t** 020 8200 1000 **f** 020 8200 4929 **e** sales@propa.net **w** propa.net Sales Manager: Jason Stevens.

Pyramid Posters The Works, Park Rd, Blaby, Leicester LE8 4EF **t** 0116 264 2642 **f** 0116 264 2640 **e** mordy.benaiah@pyramidposters.com **w** pyramidposters.com Licensing Director: Mordy Benaiah.

Razamataz 4 Derby St, Colne, Lancs BB8 9AA **t** 01282 861099 **f** 01282 861327 **e** sales@razamataz.com **w** razamataz.com Contact: Simon Hartley, Rachel Redfearn.

Rock-It! Promotions Old Employment Exchange, East Grove, (off Rectory Rd), Rushden, Northants NN10 0AR **t** 0800 980 4660 **f** 01933 413279 **e** rock-it@easynet.co.uk **w** promoclothing.com Sales Manager: Andy Campen.

RTG Branded Apparel The Old Dispensary, 36 The Millfields, Plymouth, Devon PL1 3JB **t** 01752 253888 **f** 01752 255663 **e** sales@rtg.co.uk **w** rtg.co.uk Sales Dir: Andy Moulding.

Sandbag Ltd 59/61 Milford Rd, Reading RG1 8LG **t** 0118 9505812 **f** 0118 9505813 **e** mungo@sandbag.uk.com **w** sandbag.uk.com Contact: Christiaan Munro.

Screen Machine UK Ltd Valley Farm Way, Wakefield Rd, Leeds LS10 1SE **t** 0113 276 0445 **f** 0113 277 0869 **e** sales@screen-machine.co.uk **w** printwear.co.uk Works Manager: Tony de Whytell.

Shirty Shirts 144 Algernon Rd, London SE13 7AW **t** 020 8690 7658 **f** 020 7692 9258 **e** justin@shirtyshirts.screaming.net Ops Dir: Justin Simpson.

SMP Group Plc 2 Swan Rd, Woolwich, London SE18 5TT **t** 020 8855 5535 or 07808 909 292 **f** 020 8855 5367 **e** John.Leahy@smpgroup.co.uk **w** smpgroup.co.uk MD: John Leahy.

SRL Group PO Box 74, Middlesbrough TS7 0WX **t** 01642 318 926 **f** 01642 318 927 **e** sales@srleisure.freeserve.co.uk **w** srlgroup.co.uk Contact: Roy Sunley.

STARWORLD

Starworld

4A Stretton Distribution Centre, Grappenhall Lane, Appleton, Warrington, Cheshire WA4 4QT **t** 01925 210018 **f** 01925 210028 **e** sales@starworlduk.com **w** starworldonline.com Sales Manager: Chris Burrows.

Stop Press Screen Printing 38 Torquay Gardens, Redbridge, Ilford, Essex IG4 5PT **t** 020 8551 9005 **f** 020 8551 9005 **e** g4gql@aol.com.uk Contact: Alan Shipman.

Sweet Concepts Symal House, 423 Edgware Rd, London NW9 0HU **t** 020 8200 5000 **f** 020 8200 4929 **e** sales@sweetconcepts.com **w** sweetconcepts.com MD: Stephen Taylor.

Tabak Marketing Ltd Network House, 29-39 Stirling Rd, London W3 8DJ **t** 020 8993 5966 **f** 020 8992 0340 or 020 8893 1396 **e** tabak@arab.co.uk Mgr: Chris Leaning.

Target Transfers Ltd Anglia Way, Chapel Hill, Braintree, Essex CM7 3RG **t** 01376 326351 **f** 01376 345876 **e** info@targettransfers.com **w** targettransfers.com MD: Robin Bull.

TCB Inc Merchandise Unit C1, Mint Business Pk, 41 Butchers Rd, London E16 1PH **t** 020 7511 5775 **e** guy@tcbinc.co.uk **w** tcbinc.co.uk MD: Guy Gillam.

TDC Neckwear 34 Chandlers Rd, St Albans, Herts AL4 9RS
t 01727 840548 **f** 01727 840552 **e** djt@tieman.co.uk
w tieman.co.uk MD: David Taylor.

Teeshirtstore.co.uk Unit 5, Waldo Works, Waldo Rd,
London NW10 6AW **t** 020 8964 9020 **f** 020 8964 9090
e simon.coates@recordstore.co.uk **w** recordstore.co.uk
GM: Simon Coates.

Tie Rack Corporate Neckwear Capital Interchange
Way, Brentford, Middlesex TW8 0EX **t** 020 8230 2345
f 020 8230 2350 **e** corp.sales@tie-rack.co.uk
w tierackcorporate.com MD: Peter Hirsch.

T.O.T. Shirts 14B Banksia Rd, Eley Estate, Edmonton, London
N18 3BH **t** 020 8807 8083 **f** 020 8345 6095
e sales@t-o-t-shirts.co.uk **w** t-o-t-shirts.co.uk
Snr Account Dir: Paul Whiskin.

The Tradewinds Merchandising Company Ltd
Cranford Way, London N8 9DG **t** 0208 341 9700
f 0208 341 6295 **e** sales@tradewinds.eu.com
w tradewinds.eu.com Sales Manager: Les Deacon.

T-Shirts 4 Less Ltd 12 Barnet Rd, Arkley, Herts EN5 3HB
t 020 8441 2244 **f** 020 8440 0394
e tshirts4less@btconnect.com **w** tshirts4less.co.uk
Sales Director: Varn Lykourgos.

UNDER THE SUN

Unit 3 Currendon Farm Building, Currendon Hill, Swanage, Dorset
BH19 3BB **t** 01929 450 090 **f** 01929 450 058
e enquiries@under-the-sun.co.uk **w** under-the-sun.co.uk Sales:
Phaedra, Neil and Simon.
We pride ourselves in sourcing different and unusual
merchandise from printed T-shirts and apparel to cutting
edge novelty ideas - give us your next brief...

West Country Marketing & Advertising Kyre Pk,
Kyre, Tenbury Wells, Worcs WR15 8RP **t** 01885 410247
f 01885 410398 **e** info@wcma.co.uk **w** wcma.co.uk
Sales Director: Simon Adam.

Wyrd Sects 1A Kirk Lane, Ruddington, Notts NG11 6NN
t 0115 984 4224 or 0800 3281382 **f** 0115 984 3227
e PAGAN.BYH@btinternet.com Contact: Garry Sharpe-Young.

Zephyr Flags And Banners Midland Rd, Thrapston,
Northants NN14 4LX **t** 01832 734484 **f** 01832 733064
e sskey@zephyrflags.com **w** zephyrflags.com
Sales Mgr: Simon Skey.

Distributors

ABSOLUTE MARKETING & DISTRIBUTION LTD.

The Old Lamp Works, Rodney Place, Wimbledon, London
SW19 2LQ **t** 020 8540 4242 **f** 020 8540 6056
e info@absolutemarketing.co.uk **w** absolutemarketing.co.uk MD:
Henry Semmence. Director: Simon Wills. Manufacturing: Rob
Dwyer. Product Manager: Mark Dowling. Digital: Seb Robert.
Accounts: Fran O'Donnell.
Label management, consultancy, sales, manufacturing,
distribution, marketing, international licensing,
synchronisation, copyright management, administration,
mobile and digital downloads.

ACTIVE MEDIA DISTRIBUTION LTD

Lower Farmhouse, Church Hill, East Ilsley, Newbury, Berks
RG20 7LP **t** 01635 281 358 or 281 377 **f** 01635 281 607
e firstname@amdist.com **w** amdist.com Directors: Nigel Reveler,
Colin Jennings.
National Sales Representation, Export, Licensing, Project
Management - fulfilment through Universal or THE.
Representing The Waterboys, Runrig, Thea Gilmore, among
others.

ADA UK

12 Lancer Square, London W8 4EH **t** 020 7368 3640
f 020 7368 3770 **e** firstname.lastname@ada-music.co.uk
w ada-music.co.uk. Managing Director: Susan Rush. Business
Manager: Ian Harmon. Label Manager: Lisa Bardsley. Repertoire
Manager: Nick Roden.

African Caribbean Asian Entertainment Stars
Building, 10 Silverhill Close, Nottingham NG8 6QL
t 0870 830 0683 **f** 0115 951 9874
e acts@african-caribbean-ents.com **w** african-caribbean-ents.com
Contact: Mr Sackey.

Altered Ego 230 Centennial Pk, Elstree Hill South, Elstree,
Borehamwood, Herts. WD6 3SN **t** 020 8236 2310
f 020 8236 2312 **e** info@alteredegomusic.com
w alteredegomusic.com GM: Mark Lawton.

Alternative Music Distribution Unit 29 Cygnus Business
Centre, Dalmeyer Rd, London NW10 2XA **t** 020 8830 4401
f 020 8830 4466 **e** Info@altmusic-dist.com **w** altmusic-dist.com
Sales Dir: Matt Stoddart.

Amato Distribution 4, Minerva Business Centre, 58-60, Minerva Rd, London NW10 6HJ **t** 020 8838 8330 **f** 020 8838 8331 **e** info@amatodistribution.co.uk **w** amatodistribution.co.uk MD: Mario Forsyth.

APEX Home Entertainment Ltd Unit 3 & 4, Albert St, Droylsden, Manchester M43 7BA **t** 0161 370 6908 **f** 0161 371 8207 **e** sales@apexhomeentertainment.com **w** apexhomeentertainment.com MD: Bill White.

Arabesque Distribution Network House, 29-39 Stirling Rd, London W3 8DJ **t** 020 8992 7732 or 020 8992 0098 **f** 020 8992 0340 **e** sales@arab.co.uk **w** arab.co.uk MD: Brian Horn.

ARC Music Distribution UK Ltd PO Box 111, East Grinstead, W Sussex RH19 4FZ **t** 01342 312161 **f** 01342 325209 **e** info@arcmusic.co.uk **w** arcmusic.co.uk Executive Director: Phil Collinson.

Arvato Entertainment Services 24 Crystal Drive, Sandwell Business Pk, Warley, W Midlands B66 1QG **t** 0121 543 4000 **f** 0121 543 4399 **e** firstname.lastname@arvatoentertainment.co.uk **w** arvatoentertainment.co.uk Head of New Business: Paul Hazlewood.

Authentic Media 9 Holdom Ave, Bletchley, Milton Keynes, Bucks MK1 1QR **t** 01908 364 200 **f** 01908 648 592 **e** info@authenticmedia.co.uk **w** authenticmedia.co.uk MD: David Withers.

Avanti Records Unit 11, Airlinks Ind Estate, Spitfire Way, Heston, Middlesex TW5 9NR **t** 020 8848 9800 **f** 020 8756 1883 **e** sales@avanti-records.com Hd of Sales: Charlie Paulinski.

Avid Entertainment 10 Metro Centre, Dwight Rd, Tolpits Lane, Watford, Herts WD18 9UF **t** 01923 281 281 **f** 01923 281 200 **e** info@avidgroup.co.uk **w** avidgroup.co.uk MD: Richard Lim.

Backs Distribution St Mary's Works, St Mary's Plain, Norwich, Norfolk NR3 3AF **t** 01603 624290 or 01603 626221 **f** 01603 619999 **e** info@backsrecords.co.uk Distribution Manager: Derek Chapman.

Baked Goods Distribution Ducie House, 37 Ducie St, Manchester M1 2JW **t** 0161 236 3233 **f** 0161 236 3351 **e** simon@baked-goods.com **w** baked-goods.com Sales Director: Simon Tonkinson.

Beathut Distribution 13 Greenwich Centre Business Pk, Norman Rd, Greenwich, London SE10 9PY **t** 020 8858 7700 **e** info@beathutonline.com **w** beathutonline.com Mgr: Caroline Hemingway.

Blackhole Distribution 35 Howard St, Glasgow G1 4BA **t** 0141 553 2600 **e** sales@blackholedistribution.com **w** blackholedistribution.com Ptnr: Martin McKay.

Cadiz Music Ltd 2 Greenwich Quay, Clarence Rd, London SE8 3EY **t** 020 8692 4691 or 020 8692 3555 **f** 020 8469 3300 **e** richard@cadizmusic.co.uk **w** cadizmusic.co.uk MD: Richard England.

Candid Productions Ltd 16 Castelnau, London SW13 9RU **t** 020 8741 3608 **f** 020 8563 0013 **e** info@candidrecords.com **w** candidrecords.com MD: Alan Bates.

Cargo Records Distribution (UK) Ltd 17 Heathmans Rd, Parsons Green, London SW6 4TJ **t** 020 7731 5125 **f** 020 7731 3866 **e** info@cargorecords.co.uk **w** cargorecords.co.uk MD: Philip Hill.

Chandos Records Chandos House, 1 Commerce Pk, Commerce Way, Colchester, Essex CO2 8HX **t** 01206 225200 **f** 01206 225201 **e** enquiries@chandos.net **w** chandos.net Mktg: Becky Lees.

Changing World Distribution Willow Croft, Wagg Drove, Huish Episcopi, Near Langport, Somerset TA10 9ER **t** 01458 253838 **f** 01458 250317 **e** enquiries@changing-world.com **w** changing-world.com Owner: David Hatfield.

Chart Records 5-6 Lombard Street East, Westland Row, Dublin 2, Ireland **t** 00 353 1 671 3426 or 00 353 1 677 9914 **f** 00 353 1 671 0237 **e** sales@chart.ie MD: Noel Cusack.

Cisco Europe 144 Princes Ave, London W3 8LT **t** 020 8992 7351 **f** 020 8400 4931 **e** info@ciscoeurope.co.uk MD: Mimi Kobayashi.

Claddagh Records Dame House, Dame St, Dublin 2, Ireland **t** +353 1 677 8943 **f** +353 1 679 3664 **e** wholesale@crl.ie **w** claddaghrecords.com Co Mgr: Jane Bolton.

Classical International Ltd 3rd Floor, 82-84 Clerkenwell Rd, London EC1M 5RF **t** 020 7689 1080 **f** 020 7689 1180 **e** info@classical.com **w** classical.com VP Content & Business: Roger Press.

CM Distribution North Works, Hook Stone Pk, Harrogate, N Yorks HG2 7DB **t** 01423 888979 **f** 01423 540970 **e** info@northworks.co.uk MD: DR Bulmer.

Code 7 Music 23 London Rd, Aston Clinton, Aylesbury, Bucks HP22 5HG **t** 01296 631 003 **e** info@code7music.com **w** code7music.com Contact: Nick Hindle.

Contact (UK) Research House, Fraser Rd, Greenford, Middlesex UB6 7AQ **t** 020 8997 5662 **f** 020 8997 5664 **e** contactukltd@btinternet.com **w** contactmusic.co.uk Dir: Michael Lo Bianco.

Copperplate Distribution 68 Belleville Rd, London SW11 6PP **t** 020 7585 0357 **f** 020 7585 0357 **e** copperplate2000@yahoo.com **w** copperplatedistribution.com CEO: Alan O'Leary.

CYP Children's Audio The Fairway, Bush Fair, Harlow, Essex CM18 6LY **t** 01279 444707 **f** 01279 445570 **e** sales@cypmusic.co.uk **w** kidsmusic.co.uk Sales Manager: Gary Wilmot.

D2J Distribution Unit 4, Templefields Enterprise Centre, South Rd, Harlow, Essex CM20 2AR **t** 01279 431 161 **e** demos@d2jstudios.co.uk **w** d2jstudios.co.uk/distribution/index2.htm A&R: Michael Donoghue.

DA Tape & Records 56 Castle Bank, Stafford ST16 1DW **t** 01785 258746 **f** 01785 255367 **e** p.halliwell@tesco.net MD: Paul Halliwell.

Delta Music PLC 222 Cray Ave, Orpington, Kent BR5 3PZ **t** 01689 888888 **f** 01689 888040 **e** info@deltamusic.co.uk **w** deltamusic.co.uk MD: Laurie Adams.

Digital Classics Distribution Ltd 31 Eastcastle St, London W1W 8DL **t** 020 7636 1400 **f** 020 7299 8190 **e** nb@digitalclassics.co.uk **w** digitalclassics.co.uk Head of Sales: Rick Barker.

Digital Import Software Co The Old Coach House, Windsor Crescent, Radyr, South Glamorgan CF15 8AE **t** 029 2084 3334 **f** 029 2084 2184 **e** digitaldisc@ision.co.uk Prop: Paul Kay.

Disc Imports Ltd Magnus House, 8 Ashfield Rd, Cheadle, Cheshire SK8 1BB **t** 0161 491 6655 **f** 0161 491 6688 **e** dimus@aol.com **w** dimusic.co.uk MD: Alan Wilson.

Discovery Records Nursteed Rd, Devizes, Wilts SN10 3DY **t** 01380 728000 **f** 01380 722244 **e** info@discovery-records.com **w** discovery-records.com MD: Mike Cox.

Gordon Duncan Distributions 20 Newtown St, Kilsyth, Glasgow, Lanarkshire G65 0LY **t** 01236 827550 **f** 01236 827560 **e** gordon-duncan@sol.co.uk Contact: Jack Scott, Senga Gregor.

Dynamic Distribution - Massive Digital Unit 1, Crooks Industrial Estate, Croft St, Leckhampton, Cheltenham, Glos GL53 0ED **t** 01242 237 755 **f** 01242 237 755 **e** info@dynamic-distribution.net **w** dynamic-distribution.net Dir: Joanna Massive.

Dynamic Entertainment Unit 22 Acton Park Estate, The Vale, London W3 7QE **t** 020 8746 9500 **f** 020 8746 9501 **e** info@dynamicentertainment.co.uk MD: Beverley King.

Dynamite Vision 22 Frating Crescent, Woodford Green, Essex IG8 0DW **t** 020 8505 6606 **e** info@dynamitevision.com **w** dynamitevision.com MD: Barry Lamb.

Elap UK Ltd 42 Keswick Close, Tilehurst, Reading, Berks RG30 4SD **t** 01189 452999 **f** 01189 451313 **e** chris.wickens@elap.com **w** elap.com GM: Chris Wickens.

EMI Distribution Hermes Close, Tachbrook Pk, Leamington Spa, Warcs CV34 6RP **t** 01926 466300 **f** 01926 466392 **e** john.williams@emimusic.com Ops Dir: John Williams.

EMI Records (Ireland) EMI House, 1 Ailesbury Rd, Dublin 4, Ireland **t** +353 1 203 9900 **f** +353 1 269 6341 **e** firstname.lastname@emimusic.com **w** emirecords.ie MD: Willie Kavanagh.

Empathy Records PO Box 3439, Brighton BN50 9JG **t** 01273 623 117 **f** 01273 602 870 **e** info@empathyrecords.co.uk **w** empathyrecords.co.uk Dir: Cat Gahan.

TEN (The Entertainment Network) Rabans Lane, Aylesbury, Bucks HP19 7TS **t** 01296 426151 **f** 01296 481009 **e** firstname_lastname@ten-distribution.com **w** ten-net.com MD: Shaun Plunkett.

Entertainment UK Ltd 243 Blyth Rd, Hayes, Middlesex UB3 1DN **t** 020 8848 7511 **f** 020 8754 6600 **e** enquiries@entuk.co.uk **w** entuk.com MD: Lloyd Wigglesworth.

Ernie B's Reggae 74-75 Warren St, London W1T 5PF **t** 020 7387 5550 **f** 020 7387 2756 **e** zep@sternsmusic.com **w** ebreggae.com Contact: Zep.

Essential Direct Ltd Brewmaster House, 91 Brick Lane, London E1 6QL **t** 020 7375 2332 **f** 020 7375 2442 **e** info@essentialdirect.co.uk **w** essentialdirect.co.uk A&R/Dir: Gary Dedman.

Essential Exports Brewmaster House, 91 Brick Lane, London E1 6QL **t** 020 7375 2332 **f** 020 7375 2442 **e** info@essentialdirect.co.uk **w** essentialdirect.co.uk A&R/Dir: Gary Dedman.

Excel Marketing Services Ltd 151 Valley Rd, Rickmansworth, Herts WD3 4BR **t** 01923 721 004 or 07860 800 808 **f** 01923 721 004 **e** excelms@aol.com MD: Vinoth Kumar.

EXO Ltd Unit 23 Cannon Wharf, 35 Evelyn St, London SE8 5RT **t** 020 7394 7234 **f** 020 7394 7239 **e** davidwest@exoltd.fsnet.co.uk MD: David West.

F Minor Ltd Unit 8, Commercial Mews North, 45A, Commercial Rd, Eastbourne, E Sussex BN21 3XF **t** 01323 736598 **f** 01323 738763 **e** sales@fminor.com **w** fminor.com MD: Paul Callaghan.

FAT CAT INTERNATIONAL LTD

20 Liddell Road Estate, Maygrove Road, London NW6 2EW **t** 020 7624 4335 **f** 020 7624 4866 **e** info@fatcatint.co.uk **w** fatcatint.co.uk Buyer - CD & DVD: Trevor Reidy. Sales - Overstock CD & DVD: Simon Checketts. Sales - DVD, Games & Books: Dan Thomas. Label Manager: Glenn Gretlund. Accounts: Julia Kyriacou.

Fat Shadow Records Ltd Unit 23, Cygnus Business Centre, Dalmeyer Rd, London NW10 2XA **t** 020 8830 2233 **f** 020 8830 2244 **e** mikekirk@fatshad.co.uk **w** fatshadowrecords.com MD: Michael Kirkman.

Fierce! Distribution PO Box 40, Arundel, W Sussex BN18 0UQ **t** 01243 558444 **f** 01243 558455 **e** info@fiercedistribution.com **w** fiercedistribution.com Dir: Jonathan Brown.

Fopp Ltd Unit 1, Eldonwall Trading Estate, Brislington, Bristol BS4 3QE **t** 0117 972 7130 **f** 0117 941 8724 **e** info@fopp.co.uk; firstname.lastname@fopp.co.uk **w** fopp.co.uk Dist. & Mkt'g Mgr: Ryan Latham.

Forte Music Distribution Ltd Unit 5g, Ramsden Rd, Rotherwas Industrial Estate, Hereford, Herefordshire HR2 6NP **t** 08707 622 864 or 01432 272 777 **f** 08707 626 015 **e** info@fortedistribution.co.uk **w** fortedistribution.co.uk MDs: Simon Keeler, Scott Stewart.

Fullfill LLC UK Ltd Unit 41, 249-251 Kensal Rd, London W10 5DB **t** 020 8968 1231 **f** 020 8964 1181 **e** info@fullfill.co.uk **w** fullfill.co.uk Office Manager: Savanna Sparkes.

Futureproof Distribution 330 Westbourne Park Rd, London W11 1EQ **t** 020 7792 8597 **f** 020 7221 3694 **e** info@futureproofrecords.com **w** futureproofrecords.com MD: Phil Legg.

Golds Uplands Business Pk, Blackhorse Lane, Walthamstow, London E17 5QJ **t** 020 8501 9600 or 020 8527 1035 **f** 020 8527 3232 **e** sales@sgolds.co.uk **w** sgolds.co.uk Marketing Manager: Lance Hamilton.

Goya Music Distribution Ltd The Saga Centre, 326 Kensal Rd, London W10 5BZ **t** 020 8968 9666 **f** 020 8969 9558 **e** info@goyamusic.com **w** goyamusic.com Dirs: Mike Slocombe, Spencer Weekes.

GR London Ltd 130A Plough Rd, Battersea, London SW11 2AA **t** 020 7924 1948 or 020 7924 2254 **f** 020 7924 6069 **e** info@grlondon.com **w** grlondon.com Dir: John Wright.

Griffin & Co. Ltd Church House, 96 Church St, St Mary's Gate, Lancaster LA1 1TD **t** 01524 844399 **f** 01524 844335 **e** sales@griffinrecords.co.uk **w** griffinrecords.co.uk GM: Ian Murray.

Handleman UK Ltd 27 Leacroft Rd, Birchwood, Warrington, Cheshire WA3 6PJ **t** 0870 4445844 **f** 0870 4445944 **e** robsalter@handleman.co.uk **w** handleman.co.uk Head of Purchasing: John Misra.

Harmonia Mundi (UK) Ltd 45 Vyner St, London E2 9DQ **t** 020 8709 9509 **f** 020 8709 9501 **e** info.uk@harmoniamundi.com **w** harmoniamundi.com MD: Serge Rousset.

Hermanex Ltd Connaught House, 112-120 High Rd, Loughton, Essex IG10 4HJ **t** 020 8508 3723 **f** 020 8508 0432 **e** uk@hermanex.nl Dir: Dave Harmer.

HHO Distribution Suite 1, Brittania Business Centre, London NW2 1ET **t** 020 8830 8813 **f** 020 8830 8801 **e** info@hho.co.uk **w** hho.co.uk MD: Henry Hadaway.

Hot Records PO Box 333, Brighton, Sussex BN1 2EH **t** 01403 740 260 **f** 01403 740 261 **e** info@hotrecords.uk.com **w** hotrecords.uk.com MD: Martin Jennings.

Hot Shot Records 29 St Michaels Rd, Leeds, W Yorks LS6 3BG **t** 0113 274 2106 **f** 0113 278 6291 **e** sales@bluescat.com **w** bluescat.com MD: Dave Foster.

Impetus Distribution Ltd 10 High St, Skigersta, Ness, Isle of Lewis, Outer Hebrides HS2 0TS **t** 01851 810 808 **f** 01851 810 809 **e** mpetusrecs@aol.com MD: Paul Acott-Stephens.

IMS (Interactive Management Services) Unit 4C, The Odyssey Centre, Corporation Rd, Birkenhead, Merseyside CH41 1LB **t** 0845 644 1580 **f** 0845 644 1580 **e** daveims@compuserve.com **w** heritagevideo.co.uk MD: David MacWilliam.

Independent Thinking 4 Hall Farm Barns, Fornham All Saints, Bury St Edmunds, Suffolk IP28 6JJ **t** 07795 516 065 or 020 7368 2596 **f** 01284 756320 **e** jacqui@indie-thinking.co.uk MD: Jacqui Sinclair.

InterGroove Ltd 101 Bashley Rd, Park Royal, London NW10 6TE **t** 020 8838 2000 **f** 020 8838 2003 **e** info@intergroove.co.uk **w** intergroove.co.uk MD: Andy Howarth.

Jazz Music Glenview, Moylegrove, Cardigan, Dyfed SA43 3BW **t** 01239 881278 **f** 01239 881296 **e** jazz.music@btinternet.com Sales Mgr: Jutta Greaves.

Jed-Eye Distribution Ltd Enterprise House, 113-115 George Lane, London E18 1AB **t** 020 8262 6277 **f** 020 8262 6361 **e** info@jed-eye.com **w** jed-eye.com MD: Adrian Smith.

Jet Star Phonographics 155 Acton Lane, Park Royal, London NW10 7NJ **t** 020 8961 5818 **f** 020 8965 7008 **e** sales@jetstar.co.uk **w** jetstar.co.uk MD: Carl Palmer.

Kelso Entertainment Ltd 592 London Rd, Isleworth TW7 4EY **t** 020 8758 1635 **f** 020 8758 1635 **e** info@kelsoent.co.uk **w** kelsoent.co.uk MD: Oliver Comberti.

Kila Records & Distribution Charlemont House, 33 Charlemont St, Dublin 2 **t** +353 1 476 0627 **f** +353 1 476 0627 **e** info@kilarecords.com **w** kila.ie Dir: Colm O'Snodaigh.

KRD 81-82 Stour St, Birmingham B18 7AJ **t** 0121 248 2548 **f** 0121 248 2549 **e** krd1@supanet.com MD: Pat Ward.

Kudos Records Ltd 77 Fortess Rd, Kentish Town, London NW5 1AG **t** 020 7482 4555 **f** 020 7482 4551 **e** info@kudosrecords.co.uk **w** kudosrecords.co.uk MD: Danny Ryan.

Lasgo Chrysalis

Units 2/3/4, Chapmans Park Industrial Estate, 378-388 High Road, Willesden, London NW10 2DY **t** 020 8459 8800 **f** 020 8451 5555 **e** info@lasgo.co.uk **w** lasgo.co.uk Sales Manager: Paul Burrows. MD: Peter Lassman. Director: Nick Lassman. Financial Director: Steve Digby. Audio Sales Manager: Martin O'Donnell. UK & Ireland Business Manager: Glenn Baker. Audio Campaigns Manager: Franco Passaniti. DVD Manager: Robert Klein. Senior Audio Buyer: Alan Kemp. Dance Department Manager: Martin Clench.

Lightning Export First Floor, 141 High St, Southgate, London N14 6BX **t** 020 8920 1250 **f** 020 8920 1252 **e** Export.Information@the.co.uk **w** the.co.uk GM: Bill Brightley.

Load Media Green Lane, Burghfield Bridge, Burghfield, Reading RG30 3XN **t** 01189 599 944 **f** 01189 587 416 **e** info@load-media.co.uk **w** load-media.co.uk A&R & Production: Brillo.

Love Da Records 20/F New Victory House, 93-103 Wing Lok St, Hong Kong **t** +852 2264 1025 **f** +852 2264 1211 **e** tommy@love-da-records.com **w** love-da-records.com Dir: Tommy Chan.

Magnum Distribution Magnum House, High St, Lane End, Bucks HP14 3JG **t** 01494 882858 **f** 01494 883792 **e** synergielogistics@btconnect.com CEO: Nigel Molden.

Media UK Distribution Sovereign House, 12 Trewartha Rd, Praa Sands, Penzance, Cornwall TR20 9ST **t** 01736 762 826 or 07721 449 477 **f** 01736 763 328 **e** panamus@aol.com **w** songwriters-guild.co.uk MD: Roderick Jones.

Metrodome Distribution 110 Park St, London W1K 6NX **t** 020 7408 2121 **f** 020 7409 1935 **e** video@metrodomegroup.com **w** metrodomegroup.com Head Of Marketing: Jane Lawson.

Metronome Distribution Singleton Court, Wonastow Rd, Monmouth NP25 5JA **t** 01600 775 395 **f** 01600 775 396 **e** info@metronome.co.uk **w** metronomedistribution.co.uk Label Manager: Colin Chambers.

MIA Video Entertainment Ltd MIA Video, 4th Floor, 72-75 Marylebone High St, London W1U 5JW **t** 020 7935 9225 **f** 020 7935 9565 **e** miavid@aol.com Prod Mgr: Vanessa Chinn.

Midland Records Chase Rd, Brownhills, W Midlands WS8 6JT **t** 01543 378222 or 01543 378225 **f** 01543 360988 Dir: Ms Wendy Creffield.

Moon Distribution (UK) PO Box 2061, Ilford, Essex IG1 9GU **t** 020 8551 1011 **f** 020 8553 4954 **e** moonrecordsuk@aol.com **w** moonrecords.co.uk MD: Howard Berlin.

Movementinsound 21 Higher Audley Ave, Torquay, Devon TQ2 7PG **t** 07849 199 613 or 07835 773 338 **e** info@movementinsound.com **w** movementinsound.com Dirs: Chris Clark, Stephen Gould.

Multiple Sounds Distribution Units 1 - 2 Bay Close, Port of Heysham Ind Estate, Heysham, Lancs LA3 2XS **t** 01524 851177 **f** 01524 851188 **e** info@multiplesounds.com **w** multiplesounds.com MD: Mike Hargreaves.

Design, Pressing & Distribution: Distributors

Music Box Leisure Ltd Unit 9, Enterprise Court, Lancashire Enterprise Bus Pk, Centurion Way, Leyland PR26 6TZ **t** 01772 455000 **f** 01772 331199 **e** enquiries@musicboxleisure.com Sales Director: Jan Beer.

Music Express Ltd Sheepscar House, Sheepscar Street South, Leeds, W Yorks LS7 1AD **t** 0113 234 4112 **f** 0113 234 4113 **e** office@music-express.co.uk Dir: Christopher Lane.

Music Sales (Northern Ireland) 224B Shore Rd, Lower Greenisland, Carrickfergus, Co Antrim BT38 8TX **t** 028 9086 5422 **f** 028 9086 2902 **e** musicsales@dnet.co.uk **w** musicsalesni.co.uk Dir: Eddie Graham.

Musical Memories Ltd 11 Riverside, Wraysbury, Nr Staines TW19 5JN **t** 01784 483217 **f** 01784 483210 **e** Info@musicalmemories.co.uk **w** musicalmemories.co.uk MD: Jimmy Devlin.

Nervous Records 5 Sussex Crescent, Northolt, Middlesex UB5 4DL **t** 020 8423 7373 **f** 020 8423 7773 **e** info@nervous.co.uk **w** nervous.co.uk MD: Roy Williams.

New Note Distribution Ltd Electron House, Cray Ave, Orpington, Kent BR5 3RJ **t** 01689 877884 **f** 01689 877891 **e** mail@newnote.com **w** newnote.com Joint MD (Distrib/Admin): Graham Griffiths.

Northern Record Supplies Ltd Star Works, Wham St, Heywood, Lancs OL10 4QU **t** 01706 367 412 or 01706 620 842 **e** nrs99@ukonline.co.uk MD: Simon Jones.

NOVA SALES AND DISTRIBUTION (UK) LTD

Isabel House, 46 Victoria Road, Surbiton, Surrey KT6 4JL **t** 020 8390 3322 or 020 8390 6639 (Telesales) **f** 020 8390 3338 **e** info@novadist.net **w** novadist.net MD: Wilf Mann.

Nu Urban Music Unit 3, Rivermead Industrial Estate, Pipersway, Thatcham, Berks RG19 4EP **t** 01635 587900 **f** 01635 292314 **e** kevin@nu-urbanmusic.co.uk **w** nu-urbanmusic.co.uk A&R Manager: Kevin Broome.

One Nation Exports Units G11/G10, Belgravia Workshops, 159-163 Marlborough Rd, London N19 4NP **t** 020 7263 3100 **f** 020 7263 3002 **e** barry@onenation.co.uk MD: Barry Milligan.

One Shot Music (Wholesale Only) The Forge, Water Lane, Roydon, Essex CM19 5DR **t** 01279 792 985 **e** vinylmo@btinternet.com MD: Morris Cszechowicz.

The Orchard 25 Floral St, Covent Garden, London WC2E 9DS **t** 020 7031 8278 or 0788 438 1970 **e** jason@theorchard.com **w** theorchard.com MD: Jason Ojalvo.

Pendle Hawk Music 2nd Floor, 11 Newmarket St, Colne, Lancs BB8 9BJ **t** 01282 866 317 **f** 01282 866 317 **e** info@pendlehawkmusic.co.uk **w** pendlehawkmusic.co.uk MD: Adrian Melling.

Pickwick Group Ltd 230 Centennial Pk, Elstree Hill South, Elstree, Borehamwood, Herts WD6 3SN **t** 020 8236 2310 **f** 020 8236 2312 **e** info@pickwickgroup.com **w** pickwickgroup.com GM: Mark Lawton.

PINNACLE RECORDS

Heather Court, 6 Maidstone Road, Sidcup, Kent DA14 5HH **t** 020 8309 3600 or Customer Service Telephone: 020 8309 3925 **f** 020 8309 3892 or **Tele-Ordering Fax: 020 8309 3894** **e** firstname.lastname@pinnacle-records.co.uk **w** pinnacle-entertainment.co.uk. Chairman: Sean Sullivan. Commercial Director: Chris Maskery. Operations Director: Alan King. Head of Label Management: Stuart Meikle. Head of New Media: Dominic Jones. Tele-Ordering Telephone: 020 8309 3926. Tele-Ordering Email: orders@pinnacle-records.co.ukThe UK's largest distributor of independent music, Pinnacle have exclusive responsibility for the sales, marketing and distribution of over 200 record labels. Also representing: Apace Music, Cadiz, Kudos, New Note, Nova, Putumayo, Shellshock, Weatherbox & Zeit Distribution.

Plastic Head Music Distribution Ltd Avtech House, Hithercroft Rd, Wallingford, Oxon OX10 9DA **t** 01491 825029 **f** 01491 826320 admin **e** info@plastichead.com **w** plastichead.com Dir: Steve Beatty.

Play Right Distribution Crabtree Cottage, Mill Lane, Kidmore End, Oxon RG4 9HB **t** 0118 972 4356 **f** 0118 972 4809 **e** ppmusicint@aol.com **w** dovehouserecords.com Head of Sales: Lara Pavey.

Priory Records Ltd 3 Eden Court, Eden Way, Leighton Buzzard, Beds LU7 4FY **t** 01525 377566 **f** 01525 371477 **e** sales@priory.org.uk **w** priory.org.uk MD: Neil Collier.

Prism Leisure Corporation plc Unit 1, 1 Dundee Way, Enfield, Middlesex EN3 7SX **t** 020 8804 8100 **f** 020 8216 6645 **e** prism@prismleisure.com **w** prismleisure.com Head Of Sales: Adrian Ball.

Proper Music Distribution Ltd Unit 1, Gateway Business Centre, Kangley Bridge Rd, London SE26 5AN **t** 0870 444 0800 **f** 0870 444 0801 **e** info@proper.uk.com **w** proper.uk.com MD: Malcolm Mills.

Rare Beatz Distribution PO Box 20176, London SE19 1DN **t** 020 8670 5338 **f** 0871 781 9364 **e** info@groovechronicles.net **w** groovechronicles.net Label Manager: Noodles.

Red Lightnin' The White House, The Street, North Lopham, Diss, Norfolk IP22 2LU **t** 01379 687693 **f** 01379 687559 **e** peter@redlightnin.com **w** redlightnin.com MD: Pete Shertser.

Regis Records Ltd Southover House, Tolpuddle, Dorset DT2 7HF **t** 01305 848983 **f** 01305 848516 **e** info@regisrecords.co.uk **w** regisrecords.co.uk GM: Robin Vaughan.

Revolver Music Distribution 152 Goldthorn Hill, Penn, Wolverhampton, W Midlands WV2 3JA **t** 01902 345345 **f** 01902 345155 **e** Paul.Birch@revolver-e.com **w** revolver-records.com MD: Paul Birch.

RIGHT TRACK DISTRIBUTION

42 Adelaide Road, Surbiton, Surrey KT6 4SS **t** 020 8786 2121
f 020 8786 2123 **e** info@righttrackdistribution.com
w righttrackdistribution.com Contact: Colin Peter, Neil Smith.

RMG Chart Entertainment Ltd. 2, Carriglea, Naas Rd,
Dublin 12 **t** +353 1 419 5000 **f** +353 1 419 5016
e info@rmgchart.ie **w** rmgchart.ie MD: Peter Kenny.

Rolica Music Distribution 7 Towers St, Ulverston,
Cumbria LA12 9AN **t** 01229 581766 **f** 01229 581766
e fairoaksorderline@hotmail.com **w** hmpge.com/roots2rockmusic
Prop: John Graeme Livingstone.

Roots Records 250 Earlsdon Avenue North, Coventry, W
Midlands CV5 6GX **t** 02476 711935 **f** 02476 7 1191
e rootsrecs@btclick.com MD: Graham Bradshaw.

Rose Records 1B Ellington St, Islington, London N7 8PP
t 020 7609 8288 **f** 020 7607 7851 **e** rose.records@lineone.net
MD: John Butcher.

Ross Record Distribution 29 Main St, Turriff,
Aberdeenshire AB53 4AB **t** 01888 568899 **f** 01888 568890
e info@rossrecords.com **w** rossrecords.com MD: Gibson Ross.

Route 1 Unit F34, Third Floor, Park Hall Rd Trading Estate, 40
Martell Rd, London SE21 8EN **t** 020 8670 9433
f 020 8670 8452 **e** steve@directdance.co.uk MD: Steve Bradley.

RS Sound & Vision Unit C2, M4 Business Pk, Maynooth Rd,
Celbridge, Co.Kildare, Ireland **t** +353 1 627 4110
f +353 1 627 4107 **e** rsirl@indigo.ie **w** recordservices.biz
MD: Brian Wynne.

RSK ENTERTAINMENT LTD

Units 4&5, Home Farm, Welford, Newbury, Berks RG20 8HR
t 01488 608 900 **f** 01488 608 901
e info@rskentertainment.co.uk **w** rskentertainment.co.uk Joint
MDs: Rashmi Patani, Simon Carver. Senior Label Manager: Bill
Edwards. Classical Product Manager: Matt Groom.

Sain (Recordiau) Cyf Canolfan Sain, Llandwrog,
Caernarfon, Gwynedd LL54 5TG **t** 01286 831111
f 01286 831497 **e** music@sain.wales.com **w** sain.wales.com
MD: Daffydd Iwan.

Savoy Strict Tempo Distributors PO Box 271,
Coulsdon, Surrey CR5 3TR **t** 01737 554 739 **f** 01737 556 737
e admin@savoymusic.com **w** savoymusic.com Dir: Wendy Smith.

SBI Global Ltd Oak Lodge, Leighams Rd, Bicknacre,
Chelmsford, Essex CM3 4HF **t** 01245 328683 **f** 020 7504 8242
e sales@sbiglobal.com **w** sbiglobal.com GM: Keith Page.

Securicor Omega Express Sutton Park House, 15
Carshalton Rd, Sutton, Surrey SM1 4LD **t** 020 8770 7000
f 020 8722 2974 **e** marketing@soe.securicor.co.uk
w securicor.com/euroexpress
Director of Sales: Jonathan Simpson.

Select Music & Video Distribution 3 Wells Pl, Redhill,
Surrey RH1 3SL **t** 01737 645600 **f** 01737 644065
e cds@selectmusic.co.uk **w** selectmusic.co.uk
MD: Anthony Anderson.

Shellshock Distribution 23A Collingwood Rd, London
N15 4LD **t** 020 8800 8110 **f** 020 8800 8140
e info@shellshock.co.uk **w** shellshock.co.uk MD: Garreth Ryan.

SMG Distribution 16 Limetrees, Llangattock, Crickhowell,
Powys NP8 1LB **t** 01873 810142 **f** 01873 811557
e smgdistribution@aol.com **w** silverword.co.uk
MD: Kevin Holland King.

Snapper Music plc 1 Star St, London W2 1QD
t 020 7563 5500 **f** 020 7563 5599
e sales@snappermusic.co.uk **w** snappermusic.com
Head of Int'l Sales: Tony Harris.

Soul Trader Unit 43, Imex-Spaces Business Centre, Ingate Pl,
London SW8 3NS **t** 020 7498 0732 **f** 020 7498 0737
e soultrader@btconnect.com MD: Marc Lessner.

Sound & Video Gems Ltd Quakers Coppice, Crewe,
Cheshire CW1 6EY **t** 01270 589321 **f** 01270 587438
MD: Michael Bates.

Sound And Media Ltd Unit 4, Coomber Way, Croydon,
Surrey CR0 4TQ **t** 020 8684 4286 **f** 020 8684 4173
e info@soundandmedia.co.uk **w** soundandmedia.co.uk
Ops Dir: Rob Worsfold.

Sound Entertainment Ltd The Music Village, 11B Osiers
Rd, London SW18 1NL **t** 020 8874 8444 **f** 020 8874 0337
e info@soundentertainment.co.uk Dir: Bob Nolan.

SRD (Southern Record Distribution) 70 Lawrence Rd,
London N15 4EG **t** 020 8802 3000 or 020 8802 4444
f 020 8802 2222 **e** info@southern.com **w** southern.com
MD: John Knight.

ST Holdings Ltd Unit 2 Old Forge Rd, Ferndown Industrial
Estate, Wimborne, Dorset BH21 7RR **t** 01202 890889
f 01202 890886 **e** andrew@stholdings.co.uk **w** stholdings.co.uk
Contact: Chris Parkinson.

Stern's Distribution 74-75 Warren St, London W1T 5PF
t 020 7388 5533 or 020 7387 5550 **f** 020 7388 2756
e sales@sternsmusic.com **w** sternsmusic.com
UK Sales Mgr: Ian Thomas.

Streets Ahead Record Distribution PO Box 208,
Bangor, Co Down, N.Ireland BT20 3WB **t** 028 9147 4116
f 028 9147 4116 **e** streets.ahead@business.ntl.com
MD: Paul Wyness.

Swift Record Distributors Units 8 & 9 Phoenix Works,
R/O 93 Windsor Rd, Bexhill-on-Sea, E Sussex TN39 3PE
t 01424 220028 **f** 01424 213440 **e** swiftrd@btinternet.com
w swiftrd.btinternet.co.uk GM: Robin L Gosden.

Talking Books Ltd 11 Wigmore St, London W1U 1PE
t 020 7491 4117 **f** 020 7629 1966
e support@talkingbooks.co.uk **w** talkingbooks.co.uk
Dir: Stanley Simmonds.

Design, Pressing & Distribution: Distributors

Technicolor Distribution Services Ltd Unit 8, Northfield Industrial Estate, Beresford Ave, Wembley, Middlesex HA0 1NW **t** 020 8900 1122 **f** 020 8900 1658 **e** sales@technicolor.com **w** technicolor.com Dir: Tony Brown.

Thames Distributors Ltd Unit 12, Millfarm Business Pk, Millfield Rd, Hounslow, Middlesex TW4 5PY **t** 020 8898 2227 **f** 020 8898 2228 **e** gibbon_roger@hotmail.com **w** thamesworldmusic.com Dir: Roger Gibbon.

THE (TOTAL HOME ENTERTAINMENT)

Committed to growing your business

London Commercial Office: 3.1 Shepherds West, Rockley Road, Shepherds Bush, London W14 0DA **t** 020 8600 3500 **f** 020 8600 3519 **e** firstname.lastname@the.co.uk **w** the.co.uk Commercial Dir: David Hollander. Audio General Manager: Andy Adamson. Audio Buying Manager: Matt Rooke. Audio Marketing Manager: Mike Ashton. Audio Marketing Assistant: Christian San Martin. Audio Buyer: Melvyn Phillips. Export & Import Manager: Luke Smith. Exclusive Labels & Export Manager: Mike Fay. Head of Digital: Mark Headley.

Timewarp Distribution GFM House, Cox Lane, Chessington, Surrey KT9 1SD **t** 020 8397 4466 **f** 020 8397 1950 **e** info@timewarpdis.com **w** timewarpdis.com MD: Bill Shannon.

Tuned Distribution Unit 26 Acklam Workshops, 10 Acklam Rd, London W10 5QZ **t** 020 8964 1355 **f** 020 8969 1342 **e** info@tuned-distribution.co.uk **w** tuned-distribution.co.uk MD: Lee Muspratt.

UgGR Distributions PO Box 178, Surrey SM2 6XG **t** 020 8643 6403 or 07904 255 244 **f** 020 8643 6403 **e** ugrrecords@hotmail.com **w** ugrrecords.com Hd of Marketing & Sales: P. Mac.

Unique Distribution Unit 12, Lodge Bank Industrial Estate, Off Crown Lane, Horwich, Bolton BL6 5HY **t** 01204 675500 **f** 01204 479005 **e** hi@uniquedist.co.uk **w** uniquedist.co.uk Dir: James Waddicker.

Universal Music Operations Chippenham Drive, Kingston, Milton Keynes, Bucks MK10 0AT **t** 020 8910 5000 or 08705 310310(orders) **f** 01908 452600 **e** information.centre@umusic.com **w** distribution.umusic.co.uk Commercial/Logistics Mgr: Clive Smith.

Vinyl UK 59-61 Milford Rd, Reading, Berks RG1 8LG **t** 0118 960 5700 **f** 0118 960 6800 **e** info@vinyl.nu Owner: Lance Phipps.

Vision Video PO Box 1420, Sussex Pl, London W6 9XS **t** 020 8910 5000 **f** 020 8910 5404 **e** firstname.lastname@unistudios.com A&R Manager: Tim Payne.

Vital Ireland Space 28, North Lotts, Dublin 1 **t** +353 1 872 1936 **f** +353 1 872 1938 **e** Sales@vitalireland.com GM: Jay Ahern.

VITAL SALES & MARKETING

VITAL:

338A Ladbroke Grove, London W10 5AH **t** 020 8324 2400 **f** 020 8324 0001 **e** firstname.lastname@vitaluk.com **w** vitaluk.com MD: Peter Thompson. Product Director: Ian Dutt. Head of Vital:PIAS Digital: Adrian Pope. Vital:PIAS Digital Manager: Will Cooper. **Direct Line: 020 8324 2447.** Head of Label Management: Craig Caukill. Sales & Marketing Director: Richard Sefton. **Direct Line: 020 8324 2424.** Head Of International: Adrian Hughes. **Direct Line +44 20 8324 2492.** Vital:PIAS Digital (Mobile): Richard Willis. **Direct Line: 020 8324 2436.** Marketing Manager: Luke Selby – Integral. **Direct Line 020 8324 2466.** Head of DVD Sales: James Akerman. Vital:PIAS CEO: Nick Hartley.

Vivante Music Ltd 32 The Netherlands, Coulsdon, Surrey CR5 1ND **t** 01737 559 357 **f** 01737 559 503 **e** sales@vivante.co.uk **w** vivante.co.uk MD: Steven Carr.

Windsong International Heather Court, 6 Maidstone Rd, Sidcup, Kent DA14 5HH **t** 020 8309 3867 **f** 020 8309 3905 **e** enquiries@windsong.co.uk **w** windsong.co.uk Hd Of International Sales: David Gadsby.

The Woods 6 The Arcade, Bognor Regis, W Sussex PO21 1LH **t** 01243 864923 **f** 01243 842615 **e** twiddi@yahoo.co.uk **w** twiddi.co.uk Prop: Trevor Flack.

WRD Worldwide Music 282 Camden Rd, London NW1 9AB **t** 020 7267 6762 **f** 020 7482 4029 **e** info@wrdmusic.com **w** wrdmusic.com MD: Steve Johanson.

Wwwatt CD Gregory House, Harlaxton Rd, Grantham, Lincs NG31 7JX **t** 01476 577734 **f** 01476 579309 **e** malcolm@wwwatt.co.uk **w** wwwatt.com Ops Mgr: Malcolm Mclean.

Zander Exports 34 Sapcote Trading Centre, 374 High Rd, Willesden, London NW10 2DJ **t** 020 8451 5955 **f** 020 8451 4940 **e** zander@btinternet.com **w** zanderman.co.uk Dir: John Yorke.

Zeit Distribution PO Box 50, Houghton-le-Spring, Tyne & Wear DH4 5YP **t** 0191 512 1103 **f** 0191 512 1104 **e** info@voiceprint.co.uk **w** voiceprint.co.uk MD: Rob Ayling.

Zenith Sales & Marketing Ltd 70 Wellsway, Bath BA2 4SB **t** 01225 329806 **f** 01225 329650 **e** info@zenithltd.fsbusiness.co.uk **w** zenithlimited.com MD: Andy Richmond.

Design, Pressing & Distribution: Distributors

Distributed Labels

2 Sinners ST Holdings Ltd
4 Real Empathy Records
4 Zero Records Forte Music Distribution Ltd
4AD Vital Sales & Marketing
7 Bridges Timewarp Distribution
10 Kilo InterGroove Ltd
13 Music Load Media
13th Moon Records Nova Sales and Distribution (UK) Ltd
16 Tons Ltd Pinnacle Records
211b Pinnacle Records
441 Records The Woods
482 Music The Woods
541 Timewarp Distribution
2000 Black Goya Music Distribution Ltd
A Proper Music Distribution Ltd
A List Records Ltd Absolute Marketing & Distribution Ltd.
A One Gordon Duncan Distributions
A Touch Of Class Cargo Records Distribution (UK) Ltd
A Touch of Music Jazz Music
AAA Arvato Entertainment Services
Aarde Proper Music Distribution Ltd
Abacabe Hot Shot Records
Abaco Pinnacle Records
abCDs New Note Distribution Ltd, Pinnacle Records
ABL Nova Sales and Distribution (UK) Ltd
ABM Pickwick Group Ltd
Abokadisc Proper Music Distribution Ltd
Absolute Arvato Entertainment Services, Essential Direct Ltd
Abstract Sounds Plastic Head Music Distribution Ltd
Abuse Your Friends Pinnacle Records
Accidental Records Vital Sales & Marketing
Accolade EMI Distribution, Roots Records
Accurate Proper Music Distribution Ltd
Ace Jazz Music, New Note Distribution Ltd, Pinnacle Records
Ace Records Pinnacle Records
Acetone Cargo Records Distribution (UK) Ltd
Acid Stings Plastic Head Music Distribution Ltd
Acme F Minor Ltd
Acoustics Records RSK Entertainment Ltd
Acruacree Pinnacle Records
Act New Note Distribution Ltd, Pinnacle Records
Action Records Shellshock Distribution
Active Suspension Baked Goods Distribution
AD Music Golds
Addis SRD (Southern Record Distribution)
Additive EMI Distribution
Adeline Plastic Head Music Distribution Ltd
Adept Pinnacle Records
ADN Creation Music Library Media UK Distribution
Adrenaline Plastic Head Music Distribution Ltd
ADSR Pinnacle Records
Advanced Bio Systems SRD (Southern Record Distribution)
Advisory Load Media
Aegean Pinnacle Records
Aerospace Jazz Music
Aesthetics Shellshock Distribution
AFM Records Plastic Head Music Distribution Ltd
African Love Jet Star Phonographics
African Music Stern's Distribution
Afrolution Records Proper Music Distribution Ltd
After Dark Arvato Entertainment Services
Afternoon Focus Cargo Records Distribution (UK) Ltd
Against the Grain SRD (Southern Record Distribution)
Age Of Panik Arvato Entertainment Services
Age Of Venus Shellshock Distribution
Aggro Proper Music Distribution Ltd

Agram Hot Shot Records
Ahum New Note Distribution Ltd
AIM Proper Music Distribution Ltd
Air Mail Harmonia Mundi (UK) Ltd
Air Movement Universal Music Operations
Air Raid Pinnacle Records
Airtight Vital Sales & Marketing
Airwave Records RSK Entertainment Ltd
Akarma Cargo Records Distribution (UK) Ltd, F Minor Ltd
Akashic Cargo Records Distribution (UK) Ltd
AKT/Seventh Harmonia Mundi (UK) Ltd
Al Segno New Note Distribution Ltd
Al Sur Discovery Records
Alam Madina Proper Music Distribution Ltd
Alba Pinnacle Records
Alchemy New Note Distribution Ltd, Pinnacle Records
Aleph RSK Entertainment Ltd
Alia Vox Select Music & Video Distribution
Alien Trax Amato Distribution, Pinnacle Records
Alient Recordings SRD (Southern Record Distribution)
Alive Pinnacle Records
All Around The World Universal Music Operations
All City Cargo Records Distribution (UK) Ltd
All Good Vinyl Vital Sales & Marketing
All Natural Cargo Records Distribution (UK) Ltd
All Saints Vital Sales & Marketing
All Star Collection Pinnacle Records
All That Records New Note Distribution Ltd
Alladin Avid Entertainment
Allez-Hop Cargo Records Distribution (UK) Ltd
Alliance EMI Distribution
Alligator Proper Music Distribution Ltd
Alltone New Note Distribution Ltd
Alma Latina Discovery Records
Almafame Absolute Marketing & Distribution Ltd., Pinnacle Records
Almighty Arvato Entertainment Services
Almo Sounds Pinnacle Records
Alola Amato Distribution
Alopecia Pinnacle Records
Alpaca Park Pinnacle Records
Alpha Pinnacle Records
Alpha & Omega SRD (Southern Record Distribution)
Alpha Park Pinnacle Records
Alphabet. SRD (Southern Record Distribution)
Alphabet Records Plastic Head Music Distribution Ltd
Alphaphone Pinnacle Records
Al's Vital Sales & Marketing
Alter Ego Vital Sales & Marketing
Altered Ego Music Pickwick Group Ltd
Altered Vibes Cargo Records Distribution (UK) Ltd
Alternative Tentacles Plastic Head Music Distribution Ltd
A&M Universal Music Operations
Amate Jet Star Phonographics
Amazing Feet Nova Sales and Distribution (UK) Ltd, Pinnacle Records
Amazon Records Ltd Absolute Marketing & Distribution Ltd.
Ambassador Jazz Music
Amber Vital Sales & Marketing
Amberley Cargo Records Distribution (UK) Ltd
Ambient EMI Distribution
Ambition RSK Entertainment Ltd
Ambush Pinnacle Records
American Recordings Arvato Entertainment Services
American Clave New Note Distribution Ltd, Proper Music Distribution Ltd
American Music The Woods
American Pop Project Cargo Records Distribution (UK) Ltd
American Primitive Cargo Records Distribution (UK) Ltd
Amiata Universal Music Operations

Design, Pressing & Distribution: Distributed Labels

Amos Recordings SRD (Southern Record Distribution)
Amphetamine Reptile USA Plastic Head Music Distribution Ltd
AM:PM Universal Music Operations
Anagram Pinnacle Records
Anansi Pinnacle Records
Andmoresound Cargo Records Distribution (UK) Ltd
Angel Air Proper Music Distribution Ltd
Angella Jet Star Phonographics
AniManga New Note Distribution Ltd, Pinnacle Records
Anjunabeats Amato Distribution
Ankst Musik Records Shellshock Distribution
Another Planet Pinnacle Records, Plastic Head Music Distribution Ltd
Antigua Sun Universal Music Operations
Antilles Universal Music Operations
Antiphon Vital Sales & Marketing
Antipop Pinnacle Records
Antones Proper Music Distribution Ltd
Anty Vital Sales & Marketing
Anuna Teo Proper Music Distribution Ltd
AnXious TEN (The Entertainment Network)
Anything Goze Nova Sales and Distribution (UK) Ltd
Anyway Cargo Records Distribution (UK) Ltd
Apace Music Pinnacle Records
Apace Music Ltd Pinnacle Records
Apartment Cargo Records Distribution (UK) Ltd
Apartment B Baked Goods Distribution
Apartment 22 Kudos Records Ltd
Apati The Woods
Ape City Soul Trader
Aphrodite Pinnacle Records
Apollo Pinnacle Records
Apollo Sound Backs Distribution
Appaloosa Amato Distribution
April Pinnacle Records
Aqua Pinnacle Records
Aquarius Pinnacle Records
Arabesque Arabesque Distribution
ARC Music ARC Music Distribution UK Ltd
Arcade Discovery Records
Arcadia Vital Sales & Marketing
Arcanum Empathy Records
Archangel Recordings Pinnacle Records
Architex Pinnacle Records
Arctic Pinnacle Records
Ardo Gordon Duncan Distributions
Arena Rock Cargo Records Distribution (UK) Ltd
Arf Arf F Minor Ltd
Arg Arvato Entertainment Services
Arhoolie Proper Music Distribution Ltd
Arion Discovery Records
Arista Arvato Entertainment Services
Arka Sound SRD (Southern Record Distribution)
Arkadia Jazz Magnum Distribution
Armed Cargo Records Distribution (UK) Ltd
Aromasound Vital Sales & Marketing
Arrow Jet Star Phonographics
ARS Produktion Vivante Music Ltd
Art & Soul Pinnacle Records
Art Monk Construction SRD (Southern Record Distribution)
Art-Tek Baked Goods Distribution
Artbus Pinnacle Records
Artefact Cargo Records Distribution (UK) Ltd
Artelier New Note Distribution Ltd, Pinnacle Records
Artful Records Arvato Entertainment Services
Arthaus Musik (DVD) Select Music & Video Distribution
Arthur Mix Vital Sales & Marketing
Artificial Universal Music Operations
Artisan Pinnacle Records

Artlos Pinnacle Records
Artrocker Shellshock Distribution
Artus Pinnacle Records
ASC Records New Note Distribution Ltd
Ascendant Grooves Vital Sales & Marketing
Ascension Load Media
Asian Man Plastic Head Music Distribution Ltd
Aspect ST Holdings Ltd
Asphodel Pinnacle Records, Shellshock Distribution
ASPIC Harmonia Mundi (UK) Ltd
Assembly Active Media Distribution Ltd
Astor Place New Note Distribution Ltd, Pinnacle Records
Astral Gordon Duncan Distributions, Vital Sales & Marketing
Astralwerks Pinnacle Records
Astree Harmonia Mundi (UK) Ltd
ASV Select Music & Video Distribution
Atavistic Forte Music Distribution Ltd
ATCR: Trance Communication Amato Distribution
Athletico Vital Sales & Marketing
Atlantic Records UK THE (Total Home Entertainment)
Atlas Load Media
ATMA Classique Metronome Distribution
Atoll Stern's Distribution
Atomic Arvato Entertainment Services
Atomic Theory Proper Music Distribution Ltd
Attic Gordon Duncan Distributions
A2 Universal Music Operations
Au Go Go Cargo Records Distribution (UK) Ltd
Audio Archive F Minor Ltd
Audio Bug InterGroove Ltd
Audio Couture SRD (Southern Record Distribution)
Audio Therapy Amato Distribution
Audioglobe Plastic Head Music Distribution Ltd
Audiopharm Timewarp Distribution
Audiophile Delta Music PLC, Jazz Music, The Woods
Audioquest Vivante Music Ltd
Audioview Cargo Records Distribution (UK) Ltd
Augogo Cargo Records Distribution (UK) Ltd
August Vital Sales & Marketing
Aum Fidelity Cargo Records Distribution (UK) Ltd
Auracle Recordings Arvato Entertainment Services, Essential Direct Ltd
Autonomy EMI Distribution
Autpilot Excel Marketing Services Ltd
Auvidis Astree Harmonia Mundi (UK) Ltd
Auvidis Ethnic Harmonia Mundi (UK) Ltd
Auvidis Silex Harmonia Mundi (UK) Ltd
Auvidis Tempo Harmonia Mundi (UK) Ltd
Auvidis Textes Harmonia Mundi (UK) Ltd
Avant Harmonia Mundi (UK) Ltd
Avant Garde Amato Distribution, Shellshock Distribution
Avid Avid Entertainment
Axe Killer Cargo Records Distribution (UK) Ltd
Axiomatic Vital Sales & Marketing
Axis Records Rare Beatz Distribution
Azra Empathy Records
Azuli Records TEN (The Entertainment Network)
Azure Jazz Music
Ba Da Bing Cargo Records Distribution (UK) Ltd
Babel Harmonia Mundi (UK) Ltd
Babi-Yaga Cargo Records Distribution (UK) Ltd
Babushka Records Amato Distribution
Bacchus Archives F Minor Ltd
Back Bone Vital Sales & Marketing
Back Door Pinnacle Records
Back 2 Front Arvato Entertainment Services, Essential Direct Ltd
Back Yard Recordings Amato Distribution
Back2Basics Recordings Ltd SRD (Southern Record Distribution)

Backbone Arvato Entertainment Services, Essential Direct Ltd
Background Records F Minor Ltd
Backstreet Cargo Records Distribution (UK) Ltd
Backyard Brew Vital Sales & Marketing
Backyard Movement SRD (Southern Record Distribution)
Bacteria Pinnacle Records
Bad Acid Records Plastic Head Music Distribution Ltd
Bad Afro Cargo Records Distribution (UK) Ltd
Bad Boy Cargo Records Distribution (UK) Ltd
Bad Dog Cargo Records Distribution (UK) Ltd
Bad Habits Arvato Entertainment Services
Bad Jazz Cargo Records Distribution (UK) Ltd
Bad Magic Vital Sales & Marketing
Bad Parents Cargo Records Distribution (UK) Ltd
Bad Taste Cargo Records Distribution (UK) Ltd, RSK Entertainment Ltd
Badman Recording Co Shellshock Distribution
Bag Arvato Entertainment Services
Baktabak Arabesque Distribution
Ball Product Vital Sales & Marketing
Baltic SRD (Southern Record Distribution)
Banana Pinnacle Records
Banana Juice Nervous Records
Bandstand Hot Shot Records
Bandwagon Records Shellshock Distribution
Bankylous Jet Star Phonographics
Baraka Cargo Records Distribution (UK) Ltd
Barbarity Stern's Distribution
Barber's Itch Cargo Records Distribution (UK) Ltd
Barclay France Discovery Records
Barely Breaking Even Records Pinnacle Records
Barend Video Plastic Head Music Distribution Ltd
Baria Records Shellshock Distribution
Barracuda Amato Distribution
Bartrax Jazz Music
Basstard Recordings Load Media
Basswerk Pinnacle Records
Basta F Minor Ltd, Proper Music Distribution Ltd
Bastardized Shellshock Distribution
Bay City Recordings Pinnacle Records
BBC Audio Collection Technicolor Distribution Services Ltd
BBC CLASSIC COLLECTION New Note Distribution Ltd
BBC Jazz Legends New Note Distribution Ltd
BBC Legends/Britten New Note Distribution Ltd
BBC Proms New Note Distribution Ltd
BBC Video Technicolor Distribution Services Ltd
BCR International Jet Star Phonographics
Bear Family Swift Record Distributors
Bear Necessities SRD (Southern Record Distribution)
Bearcat Proper Music Distribution Ltd
Beard Of Stars F Minor Ltd
Bearos Cargo Records Distribution (UK) Ltd
Beat Freak ST Holdings Ltd
Beat Goes On Records (BGO) Universal Music Operations
Beat Rocket F Minor Ltd
Beat Service Pinnacle Records
Beatific Pinnacle Records
Beatnik Pinnacle Records
Beatservice Pinnacle Records
Beau Monde Kudos Records Ltd, Vital Sales & Marketing
Beau Range Cargo Records Distribution (UK) Ltd
Beautiful Jo Records Proper Music Distribution Ltd
Beautiful Noise Pinnacle Records
Beautiful Place Vital Sales & Marketing
Because Music Ltd ADA UK
Bedrock Vital Sales & Marketing
Beebees Nervous Records
Beechwood Arvato Entertainment Services
Beeswax SRD (Southern Record Distribution)
Beggars Banquet Records Vital Sales & Marketing

Bella Union Pinnacle Records
Bella Voce Arvato Entertainment Services
Bellaphon Pinnacle Records, Plastic Head Music Distribution Ltd
Bellboy InterGroove Ltd
Beltane Gordon Duncan Distributions
Benbecula Baked Goods Distribution
Bentley Welcomes Careful Drivers Cargo Records Distribution (UK) Ltd
Bespoke Sound Entertainment Ltd
Best Of Jazz Discovery Records
Best Test Pinnacle Records
Beta SRD (Southern Record Distribution)
Better Vital Sales & Marketing
Better Looking Records Shellshock Distribution
Beyongolia Vital Sales & Marketing
BGO Pinnacle Records
BGP Pinnacle Records
BGS Records Metronome Distribution
Biddulph Harmonia Mundi (UK) Ltd
Bieler Bros. Records ADA UK
Biff Bang Pow F Minor Ltd
Big & Complex World Pinnacle Records
Big Balls Cargo Records Distribution (UK) Ltd
Big Banana Arvato Entertainment Services
Big Bang Arvato Entertainment Services
Big Barber Cargo Records Distribution (UK) Ltd
Big Boss Hot Shot Records
Big Brother Pinnacle Records
Big City Candid Productions Ltd, Proper Music Distribution Ltd
Big Deal Cargo Records Distribution (UK) Ltd
Big Drum Jet Star Phonographics
Big Musik The Woods
Big Scary Monsters Shellshock Distribution
Big Ship Jet Star Phonographics
Big Star Universal Music Operations
Big Sur Timewarp Distribution
Big Yard Jet Star Phonographics
Biograph Jazz Music
Birdland New Note Distribution Ltd, Pinnacle Records
Birdman Cargo Records Distribution (UK) Ltd
Bird's Eye Jet Star Phonographics
Birdsnest Cargo Records Distribution (UK) Ltd
BIS Select Music & Video Distribution
Bistro Pinnacle Records
Bitch Vinyl Pinnacle Records
Bittersweet Vital Sales & Marketing
Bitzcore Records GMBH Plastic Head Music Distribution Ltd
BKO Absolute Marketing & Distribution Ltd.
Black Jet Star Phonographics
Black & Tan Hot Shot Records
Black Arc Vital Sales & Marketing
Black Box Music Select Music & Video Distribution
Black Burst Records Pinnacle Records
Black Flag Cargo Records Distribution (UK) Ltd
Black Gold Recordings Vital Sales & Marketing
Black Hoodz SRD (Southern Record Distribution)
Black Jack Arvato Entertainment Services, Essential Direct Ltd
Black Jam Vital Sales & Marketing
Black Jesus GR London Ltd
Black Label Jet Star Phonographics
Black Mango Music Proper Music Distribution Ltd
Black Market Activities Shellshock Distribution
Black Market International Vital Sales & Marketing
Black No Sugar ST Holdings Ltd
Black Roots SRD (Southern Record Distribution)
Black Saint Harmonia Mundi (UK) Ltd
Black Scorpio Jet Star Phonographics
Black Solidarity SRD (Southern Record Distribution)
Black Sunshine Vital Sales & Marketing
Black Swan Jazz Music, The Woods

Black Top Proper Music Distribution Ltd
Black Up Arvato Entertainment Services, Essential Direct Ltd
Black Widow F Minor Ltd, Plastic Head Music Distribution Ltd
Blackberry Cargo Records Distribution (UK) Ltd
Blackbox Pinnacle Records
Blackend Plastic Head Music Distribution Ltd
Blacker Dread Jet Star Phonographics
Blackfish Plastic Head Music Distribution Ltd
Blackhood SRD (Southern Record Distribution)
Blacklabel Jet Star Phonographics
Blackout Vital Sales & Marketing
Blackplastic Pinnacle Records
Blacktop Hot Shot Records
Blade Load Media
Blakamix SRD (Southern Record Distribution)
Blanco Y Negro TEN (The Entertainment Network)
Blank Canvas Shellshock Distribution
Blapps! Vital Sales & Marketing
Blast Pinnacle Records
Blast First Vital Sales & Marketing
Blaster Vital Sales & Marketing
Blatant Arvato Entertainment Services
Bleeding Hearts Pinnacle Records
Blind Pig Proper Music Distribution Ltd
Blindside Pinnacle Records
Bliss Pinnacle Records
Blissfulmusic Metronome Distribution
Blix Street Records Pinnacle Records
Blokshok Pinnacle Records
Blood SRD (Southern Record Distribution)
Blood And Fire Universal Music Operations, Vital Sales & Marketing
Blood Lust Vital Sales & Marketing
Bloodshot Proper Music Distribution Ltd, Shellshock Distribution
Blow The Fuse New Note Distribution Ltd, Pinnacle Records
BLS Jet Star Phonographics
Blu Bamboo Records Ltd Nova Sales and Distribution (UK) Ltd
Blu Violet Records Rare Beatz Distribution
Blue Universal Music Operations
Blue August Backs Distribution, Pinnacle Records
Blue Chicago Proper Music Distribution Ltd
Blue Dog Pinnacle Records
Blue Gorilla Universal Music Operations
Blue Harlem Hot Shot Records
Blue Horizon Hot Shot Records
Blue House Jet Star Phonographics
Blue Jackel New Note Distribution Ltd, Pinnacle Records
Blue Moon Discovery Records
Blue Music New Note Distribution Ltd
Blue Nite Delta Music PLC
Blue Plate Proper Music Distribution Ltd
Blue Ray Hot Shot Records
Blue Rhythm Nova Sales and Distribution (UK) Ltd
Blue Room Pinnacle Records
Blue Rose Pinnacle Records, Shellshock Distribution
Blue Sanct Cargo Records Distribution (UK) Ltd
Blue Silver Stern's Distribution
Blue Sting Hot Shot Records
Blue Suit Hot Shot Records
Blue Sun Hot Shot Records
Blue Thumb Arvato Entertainment Services
Bluebell Jazz Music, Pinnacle Records
Blueblood Hot Shot Records
Blueloon Hot Shot Records
Blueprint Pinnacle Records
Blues Alliance New Note Distribution Ltd, Pinnacle Records
Blues Archives Discovery Records
Blues Beacon New Note Distribution Ltd, Pinnacle Records
Blues Collection Discovery Records

Blues Document Hot Shot Records
Blues Factory Arvato Entertainment Services
Blues Works Hot Shot Records
Bluesanct Cargo Records Distribution (UK) Ltd
Bluesrock Hot Shot Records
Bluesting Hot Shot Records
Bluestone Cargo Records Distribution (UK) Ltd
Bluetrak Hot Shot Records
Blunt Pinnacle Records
Blunted Vinyl Vital Sales & Marketing
Blut Pinnacle Records
BMG Europe Discovery Records
BNA Arvato Entertainment Services
BNE Shellshock Distribution
B9 Pinnacle Records
Bobsled Cargo Records Distribution (UK) Ltd
Body & Soul New Note Distribution Ltd
Boiler House! Vital Sales & Marketing
Boka Proper Music Distribution Ltd
Bomb Basic Cargo Records Distribution (UK) Ltd
Bomb Hiphop Cargo Records Distribution (UK) Ltd
Bombed Out Shellshock Distribution
Bombtraxx Load Media
Bomp F Minor Ltd, Vital Sales & Marketing
Bomp! Backs Distribution
Bon Cargo Records Distribution (UK) Ltd
Bonaire Recordings Arvato Entertainment Services, Essential Direct Ltd
Bond Girl Pinnacle Records
Bone Voyage Shellshock Distribution
Bongload Cargo Records Distribution (UK) Ltd
Boo KRD
Boogie Back Vital Sales & Marketing
Boogie Wonderland SRD (Southern Record Distribution)
Book Jazz Music
Boom Pinnacle Records
Boom! Records Shellshock Distribution
Boom Shacka Lacka Pinnacle Records
Boomba Records Plastic Head Music Distribution Ltd
Boomtang Arvato Entertainment Services
Boot Amato Distribution
Bootleg Net Pinnacle Records
Booze Nervous Records
Boplicity Jazz Music
Borderline F Minor Ltd
Bosca Beats SRD (Southern Record Distribution)
Bosh Arvato Entertainment Services
Boston Skyline Metronome Distribution
Botchit & Scarper SRD (Southern Record Distribution)
The Bottom Line Pinnacle Records
Bottrop-Boy Baked Goods Distribution
Bounce!! Arvato Entertainment Services
Bovinyl Vital Sales & Marketing
Bowstone Jazz Music
Box In Records Rare Beatz Distribution
Boys Arvato Entertainment Services
Boys of the Lough Gordon Duncan Distributions
BPitch Control Baked Goods Distribution
Brambus Pendle Hawk Music
Branded Pinnacle Records
Break Butt Pinnacle Records
Break Records 2000 Arvato Entertainment Services
Breakbeat Culture SRD (Southern Record Distribution)
Breakdown Pinnacle Records
Breaker Breaks ST Holdings Ltd
Breakin' Beats Pinnacle Records
Breakin Even Load Media
Breathe Arvato Entertainment Services
Breeze Arvato Entertainment Services
Brian Houston Songs Active Media Distribution Ltd

Brick Wall Jet Star Phonographics
Bridge RSK Entertainment Ltd
Bright Choice RMG Chart Entertainment Ltd.
Bright Star Recordings Vital Sales & Marketing
Brille Records Ltd. Vital Sales & Marketing
Brinkman Cargo Records Distribution (UK) Ltd
Broadstar Vital Sales & Marketing
Broken. Pinnacle Records
Broken Rekids Cargo Records Distribution (UK) Ltd
Bronze SRD (Southern Record Distribution)
Bronze Records Ltd Pinnacle Records
Brown Sugar F Minor Ltd, Timewarp Distribution
Brownswood Recordings Universal Music Operations
Bubble Core SRD (Southern Record Distribution)
Bubblin' Vital Sales & Marketing
Bud Universal Music Operations
Buda Discovery Records
Budapest Music Centre (BMC) Metronome Distribution
Buena Vista Home Video Technicolor Distribution Services Ltd
Bullion Pinnacle Records
Bulls Eye Blues Munich Hot Shot Records
Bulls Eye Rounder Hot Shot Records
Bullseye Proper Music Distribution Ltd
Bullseye Blues Proper Music Distribution Ltd
Bungalow Cargo Records Distribution (UK) Ltd, Shellshock Distribution
Burial Mix SRD (Southern Record Distribution)
Burning Airliner Excel Marketing Services Ltd, Pinnacle Records
Burning Rome Vital Sales & Marketing
Burning Sounds Universal Music Operations
Burnt Hair Cargo Records Distribution (UK) Ltd
Bush Arvato Entertainment Services, KRD
Bushranger Pinnacle Records
Business Jet Star Phonographics
But! Records Proper Music Distribution Ltd
Butcher's Wig Pinnacle Records
Buzzin' Fly Records Amato Distribution
BYG Actuel F Minor Ltd
BYO Records Plastic Head Music Distribution Ltd
Cabal SRD (Southern Record Distribution)
Caber Proper Music Distribution Ltd
Cacophonous Vital Sales & Marketing
Cactus Island Baked Goods Distribution
Cadillac Jazz Music
Cadiz Pinnacle Records
Caipirinha Pinnacle Records
Calligraph Jazz Music, New Note Distribution Ltd
Calliope Harmonia Mundi (UK) Ltd
Cam Original Soundtracks Hot Records
Cambrian Sain (Recordiau) Cyf
Camden Arvato Entertainment Services
Camel Pinnacle Records
Cameo Arvato Entertainment Services, Disc Imports Ltd
Camera Obscura Cargo Records Distribution (UK) Ltd
Camp Fabulous Arvato Entertainment Services, Pinnacle Records
Campion Records Disc Imports Ltd
Can Jet Star Phonographics
Can Can Vital Sales & Marketing
Candid Candid Productions Ltd, Jazz Music, Proper Music Distribution Ltd
Candle Hot Records
Candlelight Records Plastic Head Music Distribution Ltd
Candy Ass Vital Sales & Marketing
Caney Discovery Records
Cantankerous GR London Ltd
Canzona New Note Distribution Ltd, Pinnacle Records
Capitol EMI Distribution

Capitol Jazz EMI Distribution
Capri Records The Woods
Capriccio Arvato Entertainment Services
Capricorn Universal Music Operations
Capstack Cargo Records Distribution (UK) Ltd
Captain Oi! Plastic Head Music Distribution Ltd
Captain Trip F Minor Ltd
Cardas Vivante Music Ltd
Cardina TEN (The Entertainment Network)
Cargogold New Note Distribution Ltd
Caribbean Jet Star Phonographics
Caribbean Music Library Media UK Distribution
Cariwak Jet Star Phonographics
Carlton Video Technicolor Distribution Services Ltd
Carmo New Note Distribution Ltd
Caroline Vital Sales & Marketing
Carrack UK Absolute Marketing & Distribution Ltd.
Carrera Pinnacle Records
Carzy Love Nervous Records
Casa Nostra Amato Distribution
Casa Trax Pinnacle Records
Cascade Hot Shot Records
Case Invaders SRD (Southern Record Distribution)
Casino Pinnacle Records
Castle Home Video Pinnacle Records
Castle Music Pinnacle Records
Casualty Vital Sales & Marketing
Catalyst Arvato Entertainment Services
Catcall Vital Sales & Marketing
Catfish Pinnacle Records
Catskills Vital Sales & Marketing
Cause4Concern Load Media
The CD Card Company Arabesque Distribution
Cedille Metronome Distribution
Cee 22 Vital Sales & Marketing
Celebrity Candid Productions Ltd
Celtic Music CM Distribution
Celtic Pride Delta Music PLC
Celtophile Proper Music Distribution Ltd
Centaur F Minor Ltd, Pinnacle Records
Central Control International Forte Music Distribution Ltd
Central Hill Arvato Entertainment Services
Central Station Arvato Entertainment Services, Essential Direct Ltd
Centric Pinnacle Records
Century Media RSK Entertainment Ltd
Chain Reaction SRD (Southern Record Distribution)
Challenge Jazz Music, Proper Music Distribution Ltd
Champagne Lake Pinnacle Records
Champion Arvato Entertainment Services
Changing World Changing World Distribution
Channel Classics RSK Entertainment Ltd
Channel 4 Universal Music Operations
Channel One SRD (Southern Record Distribution)
Chant du Monde Harmonia Mundi (UK) Ltd
Chapter 22 Vital Sales & Marketing
Charm Jet Star Phonographics
Charnel Harmonia Mundi (UK) Ltd
Chase Arvato Entertainment Services
Chatback Universal Music Operations
Chaucer Nova Sales and Distribution (UK) Ltd
Che Cargo Records Distribution (UK) Ltd
Checkered Past Proper Music Distribution Ltd
Checkpoint Vital Sales & Marketing
Cheeky Arvato Entertainment Services
Cheeky Junior Arvato Entertainment Services
Cheese International Vital Sales & Marketing
Cherokee Nervous Records
Cherry Red Records Pinnacle Records
Chesky Discovery Records, Vivante Music Ltd

Chess Arvato Entertainment Services
Chiarascuro Jazz Music
Chili Funk Absolute Marketing & Distribution Ltd.
Chillifunk Records Pinnacle Records
China Pinnacle Records, TEN (The Entertainment Network)
Choice Candid Productions Ltd
Choo Choo InterGroove Ltd, Unique Distribution
Chris Barber Collection New Note Distribution Ltd
Christel Deesk Vital Sales & Marketing
Chrome Dreams Nova Sales and Distribution (UK) Ltd
Chrome Dreams Media Nova Sales and Distribution (UK) Ltd
Chronicles Universal Music Operations
Chrysalis EMI Distribution
Chug & Bump KRD
Chunk Records Proper Music Distribution Ltd
Chute Cargo Records Distribution (UK) Ltd
Ciano Pinnacle Records
CIC Claddagh Records
Cinedelic F Minor Ltd
Circa EMI Distribution
Circle F Minor Ltd, Jazz Music, The Woods
Circulation Pinnacle Records
Citadel Hot Records, Proper Music Distribution Ltd
Citrus Pinnacle Records
City Centre Offices Baked Goods Distribution
City Slang Vital Sales & Marketing
Citywax Arvato Entertainment Services, Essential Direct Ltd
Claddagh Proper Music Distribution Ltd
Claire Cargo Records Distribution (UK) Ltd
Clarinet Classics Select Music & Video Distribution
Clarion Swift Record Distributors
Clarity Magnum Distribution, Vivante Music Ltd
Clarke & BL Jet Star Phonographics
Classic FM Arvato Entertainment Services
Classic Records F Minor Ltd
Classic Rock Nova Sales and Distribution (UK) Ltd
Classics Discovery Records, Jazz Music
Classified Vital Sales & Marketing
Claudio Records Ltd Metronome Distribution
Claytwins Cargo Records Distribution (UK) Ltd
Clean Up Pinnacle Records
Clear Vital Sales & Marketing
Clearspot Pinnacle Records
Cleopatra Cargo Records Distribution (UK) Ltd
Clifford Jazz Music
Climax Arvato Entertainment Services
Clinkscale Gordon Duncan Distributions
Clive Mulcahy Hot Shot Records
Clo Iar Chonnachta Copperplate Distribution
Cloak And Dagger Vital Sales & Marketing
Cloud Nine New Note Distribution Ltd
Club Spangle Pinnacle Records
Club Tools Vital Sales & Marketing
Club Tracks SRD (Southern Record Distribution)
Clubscene Universal Music Operations
Clubstar Timewarp Distribution
Clued SRD (Southern Record Distribution)
CMC Arvato Entertainment Services
CML Gordon Duncan Distributions
C&N Universal Music Operations
CNN Vital Sales & Marketing
Coalition Plastic Head Music Distribution Ltd, Shellshock Distribution
Coast SRD (Southern Record Distribution)
Cocaine SRD (Southern Record Distribution)
Code666 Shellshock Distribution
Codex Pinnacle Records
Cog Sinister Pinnacle Records
Cohesion Active Media Distribution Ltd
Cold Blue RSK Entertainment Ltd

Cold Meat Industry Shellshock Distribution, Vital Sales & Marketing
Cold Spring Shellshock Distribution, Vital Sales & Marketing
Colin Campbell Gordon Duncan Distributions
Colin Fat Jet Star Phonographics
Collection Delta Music PLC
Collector Magnum Distribution
Collectors Choice RSK Entertainment Ltd
Collector's Classics Arvato Entertainment Services, Jazz Music
Collector's Edition Pinnacle Records
Collegium Select Music & Video Distribution
Collins Classics Pinnacle Records
Collision Vital Sales & Marketing
Colombe d'Or Arvato Entertainment Services
Colony Baked Goods Distribution
Colosseum Pinnacle Records
Colour Blind Arvato Entertainment Services, Essential Direct Ltd
Colour Of House Records Rare Beatz Distribution
Columbia Records Label Group Arvato Entertainment Services
Combination Shellshock Distribution
Comet F Minor Ltd, Music Express Ltd
Communion Cargo Records Distribution (UK) Ltd
Communique Records Plastic Head Music Distribution Ltd
Community Cargo Records Distribution (UK) Ltd, Plastic Head Music Distribution Ltd
The Compact Organization Pinnacle Records
Complex Universal Music Operations
Compose SRD (Southern Record Distribution)
Compost SRD (Southern Record Distribution)
Concept Absolute Marketing & Distribution Ltd.
Concord New Note Distribution Ltd, Pinnacle Records
Concord Concerto New Note Distribution Ltd, Pinnacle Records
Concord Crossover New Note Distribution Ltd
Concord Jazz New Note Distribution Ltd, Pinnacle Records
Concord Picante New Note Distribution Ltd, Pinnacle Records
Concord Vista New Note Distribution Ltd, Pinnacle Records
Concrete Vital Sales & Marketing
Concrete Plastic Records Cargo Records Distribution (UK) Ltd
Concrete Productions Arvato Entertainment Services
Congo Pinnacle Records
Connoisseur Collection Pinnacle Records
Conqueror Universal Music Operations
Conquistador Pinnacle Records
Conscious Sounds SRD (Southern Record Distribution)
Constellation Cargo Records Distribution (UK) Ltd
Contemporary Jazz Music, New Note Distribution Ltd
Continental Song City Proper Music Distribution Ltd
Control Vital Sales & Marketing
Cooker Arvato Entertainment Services
Cooking Vinyl Vital Sales & Marketing
Cool D:Vision Timewarp Distribution
Cool Guy Cargo Records Distribution (UK) Ltd
Cooler Cargo Records Distribution (UK) Ltd
Cooltempo EMI Distribution
Coop Pinnacle Records
Cop International Cargo Records Distribution (UK) Ltd
Copasetik Vital Sales & Marketing
Copro Records Plastic Head Music Distribution Ltd
Coral Jet Star Phonographics
Corban Gordon Duncan Distributions
Corduroy F Minor Ltd
Core-Tex Records Plastic Head Music Distribution Ltd
Cornerstone Records The Woods
Corntreeper Jet Star Phonographics
Corporate Image Vital Sales & Marketing
Corpus Christi SRD (Southern Record Distribution)
Corpus Hermeticum Cargo Records Distribution (UK) Ltd

The Corries Ross Record Distribution
Cortical Harmonia Mundi (UK) Ltd
Couchblip Baked Goods Distribution
Country Routes Hot Shot Records, Jazz Music
County Proper Music Distribution Ltd
Cousin Jet Star Phonographics
Cousins Jet Star Phonographics
Cowards Cargo Records Distribution (UK) Ltd
Cowboy Records Absolute Marketing & Distribution Ltd.
Cowsong Proper Music Distribution Ltd
CPO Select Music & Video Distribution
Crackle Plastic Head Music Distribution Ltd
Crai Proper Music Distribution Ltd, Sain (Recordiau) Cyf
Cramboy New Note Distribution Ltd
Crammed Discs New Note Distribution Ltd
Cramworld New Note Distribution Ltd, Pinnacle Records
Crazy Love Nervous Records
Crazy Rhythm Nervous Records
CRD Regis Records Ltd
Cream New Note Distribution Ltd
Cream Records New Note Distribution Ltd
Creative Entertainment Pinnacle Records
Creative Man Cargo Records Distribution (UK) Ltd
Creative Souls Shellshock Distribution
Creative Wax Vital Sales & Marketing
Creeping Bent SRD (Southern Record Distribution)
Creole Universal Music Operations
Crepuscule Discovery Records
Criminal Records Active Media Distribution Ltd
Crippled Dick SRD (Southern Record Distribution)
Crippled Dick Hot Wax Shellshock Distribution
Crisis Nova Sales and Distribution (UK) Ltd
Criss Cross Jazz Proper Music Distribution Ltd
Critical Mass Amato Distribution
Crocodile Bites SRD (Southern Record Distribution)
Crosby's Jet Star Phonographics
Cross Baked Goods Distribution
Cross Section ST Holdings Ltd
Crosscut Proper Music Distribution Ltd
Crossroads Jet Star Phonographics
Crosstown Arvato Entertainment Services, Essential Direct Ltd
Crosstrax Amato Distribution
CRS Jet Star Phonographics
Cruise Jet Star Phonographics
Cruise International Arvato Entertainment Services, Essential Direct Ltd
Crunch Melody Vital Sales & Marketing
Crunk ST Holdings Ltd
Crypt Pinnacle Records, Shellshock Distribution
CSA Telltapes Universal Music Operations
Cube Metier The Woods
Cubop New Note Distribution Ltd, Pinnacle Records
Culburnie Gordon Duncan Distributions, Proper Music Distribution Ltd
Cuneiform Shellshock Distribution
Cup Of Tea Vital Sales & Marketing
Curlique Timewarp Distribution
Curve Pinnacle Records
Cyanide Load Media, Vital Sales & Marketing
Cyberchotik SRD (Southern Record Distribution)
Cyclops Pinnacle Records
d Records Universal Music Operations
Da Lick SRD (Southern Record Distribution)
Da Music RSK Entertainment Ltd
Da Poison EMI Distribution
DAD International Cargo Records Distribution (UK) Ltd
Daddy Amato Distribution
Dagored F Minor Ltd, RSK Entertainment Ltd
Dallas Blues Society Hot Shot Records
Damaged Goods Pinnacle Records

Dambuster CM Distribution
Damnation Vital Sales & Marketing
Dance Mix Vital Sales & Marketing
Dance Naked Arvato Entertainment Services, Essential Direct Ltd
Dance Planet SRD (Southern Record Distribution)
Dance Pool TEN (The Entertainment Network)
Dance Reaction Arvato Entertainment Services
Dance Rock Load Media
Dance 2 Essential Direct Ltd
Dancecop Discovery Records
Dangerous Records Pinnacle Records
Dangerzone Hot Shot Records
Dara Universal Music Operations
Dare Dare Cargo Records Distribution (UK) Ltd
Daring Jazz Music, Proper Music Distribution Ltd
Dark Beat Arvato Entertainment Services
Dark Beloved Cargo Records Distribution (UK) Ltd
Dark Dungeon Vital Sales & Marketing
Dark House Pinnacle Records
Dark Matter Vital Sales & Marketing
Dark Sea Pinnacle Records
Dark Trinity Vital Sales & Marketing
Darla Cargo Records Distribution (UK) Ltd
Data Error Shellshock Distribution
Dave Cooper Jazz Music
DBM SRD (Southern Record Distribution)
DBX Pinnacle Records
DC Recordings Vital Sales & Marketing
DCC Vivante Music Ltd
De Angelis Records Nova Sales and Distribution (UK) Ltd
De La Haye SRD (Southern Record Distribution)
De Soto SRD (Southern Record Distribution)
De Underground SRD (Southern Record Distribution)
Dead Dead Good Pinnacle Records
Dead Reckoning Proper Music Distribution Ltd
Deadly Records Load Media
Deadly Systems Pinnacle Records
Deansville CM Distribution
Death Becomes Me SRD (Southern Record Distribution)
Death Row Universal Music Operations
Deathwish Inc Shellshock Distribution
Debt Vital Sales & Marketing
Debutante Universal Music Operations
Decca UK Universal Music Operations
Deceptive Records Vital Sales & Marketing
Decipher Amato Distribution
Decision Arvato Entertainment Services
Deconstruction Arvato Entertainment Services
Decor Records Shellshock Distribution
Decoy Vital Sales & Marketing
Dedicated Vital Sales & Marketing
Dee Jay SRD (Southern Record Distribution)
Deeay Gordon Duncan Distributions
Deep Beats Pinnacle Records
Deep Elm Records Plastic Head Music Distribution Ltd, Shellshock Distribution
Deep End Arvato Entertainment Services, Essential Direct Ltd
Deep Root SRD (Southern Record Distribution)
Def Jam Universal Music Operations
Def Soul Universal Music Operations
Defected Records Ltd Vital Sales & Marketing
Defender Arvato Entertainment Services, Essential Direct Ltd
Defiant Pinnacle Records
DeFocus ST Holdings Ltd
Defunked ST Holdings Ltd
Del-Fi Cargo Records Distribution (UK) Ltd
Delabel Cargo Records Distribution (UK) Ltd
Delancey Street Vital Sales & Marketing
Delerium RSK Entertainment Ltd

Delicious Vinyl Pinnacle Records
Delikatessan Baked Goods Distribution
Delinquent Cargo Records Distribution (UK) Ltd
Delirious Pinnacle Records
Delmark Proper Music Distribution Ltd
Delos Metronome Distribution
Delta Delta Music PLC
Demerara Nova Sales and Distribution (UK) Ltd
Demi Monde Records Shellshock Distribution
Demon Records Ltd Arvato Entertainment Services
Demonic ST Holdings Ltd
DEP International EMI Distribution
Depth Pinnacle Records
Depth Of Field Proper Music Distribution Ltd
Deram Universal Music Operations
Derivative Cargo Records Distribution (UK) Ltd
Derock Cargo Records Distribution (UK) Ltd
Desco Cargo Records Distribution (UK) Ltd
Destiny Arvato Entertainment Services
Detour F Minor Ltd, Plastic Head Music Distribution Ltd
Detox Vital Sales & Marketing
Deutsche Grammophon Universal Music Operations
Deux-Elles RSK Entertainment Ltd
Deux Z/Nato Harmonia Mundi (UK) Ltd
Deva Vital Sales & Marketing
Deviant Vital Sales & Marketing
Deviation Vital Sales & Marketing
Device Electronic Entertainment Baked Goods Distribution
Devil May Care Amato Distribution
Devious Jet Star Phonographics
Devon Pinnacle Records
Dexter's Cigar Cargo Records Distribution (UK) Ltd
DHR Vital Sales & Marketing
Diablo Arvato Entertainment Services
Diablo Fuel Pinnacle Records
Diagonal Nova Sales and Distribution (UK) Ltd
Diamond Plastic Head Music Distribution Ltd
Diamond Classics Pinnacle Records
Diamond Range Jet Star Phonographics
Diamond Recordings Pinnacle Records
Dice Magnum Distribution
Die Hard Shellshock Distribution
Diesel Jet Star Phonographics
Different Drummer Kudos Records Ltd, Pinnacle Records
Different Recordings Vital Sales & Marketing
Diffusion Universal Music Operations
Dig The Fuzz Cargo Records Distribution (UK) Ltd, F Minor Ltd
Diggler F Minor Ltd
Digi Dub Pinnacle Records
Digital B Jet Star Phonographics
Digital Hardcore Recordings Forte Music Distribution Ltd
Dill Cargo Records Distribution (UK) Ltd
Dimension Jet Star Phonographics
Din SRD (Southern Record Distribution)
Dionysus Cargo Records Distribution (UK) Ltd, F Minor Ltd
Direct Disco Unique Distribution
Dirt Pinnacle Records
Dirter Pinnacle Records
Dirtnap Shellshock Distribution
Dischord SRD (Southern Record Distribution)
Discipline Pinnacle Records
Discipline Global Mobile Pinnacle Records
Discipline Records Plastic Head Music Distribution Ltd
Disco 2000 Arvato Entertainment Services, Essential Direct Ltd
Disco Volante TEN (The Entertainment Network)
Discocaine Production# Amato Distribution
Discography Pinnacle Records
Discordant Pinnacle Records
Discotex Jet Star Phonographics
Discribe Jet Star Phonographics

Dishy SRD (Southern Record Distribution)
Diskono Baked Goods Distribution, Cargo Records Distribution (UK) Ltd
Disorient Recordings Vital Sales & Marketing
Displeased Records Plastic Head Music Distribution Ltd, Shellshock Distribution
Disque Arabe Harmonia Mundi (UK) Ltd
Disques Solid Vital Sales & Marketing
Distance Pinnacle Records
Distinct'ive Breaks Pinnacle Records
Distinct'ive Records Amato Distribution
Distortions F Minor Ltd
Diverse F Minor Ltd, Pinnacle Records
Diverse Products Load Media
Diversity. SRD (Southern Record Distribution)
Divine Art CM Distribution
Dixiefrog Proper Music Distribution Ltd
Django Jet Star Phonographics
Djenne Stern's Distribution
DJT Vital Sales & Marketing
DMC Pinnacle Records
DMP Vivante Music Ltd
DNA Records New Note Distribution Ltd
DNM Timewarp Distribution
Document Hot Shot Records, Jazz Music
Dodge Pinnacle Records
Dodgem Discs New Note Distribution Ltd
Dog Eat Cat Arvato Entertainment Services
Doghouse Plastic Head Music Distribution Ltd
Dolores Records Plastic Head Music Distribution Ltd
Domination ST Holdings Ltd
Domino Vital Sales & Marketing
Domino Recording Company Vital Sales & Marketing
Domo Pinnacle Records
Don Q SRD (Southern Record Distribution)
Done SRD (Southern Record Distribution)
Donside Gordon Duncan Distributions
Doolittle Proper Music Distribution Ltd
Doop Pinnacle Records
Doorstep Vinyl Cargo Records Distribution (UK) Ltd
Dope On Plastic Vital Sales & Marketing
Dope Wax Universal Music Operations
Dopesmoker Cargo Records Distribution (UK) Ltd
Doppelganger Arvato Entertainment Services
Dorado Pinnacle Records
Dorian Metronome Distribution, Pinnacle Records
Dorigen Unique Distribution
Dot Pinnacle Records
Double Gold Arvato Entertainment Services
Double Scoop New Note Distribution Ltd
Douglas Music Pinnacle Records
Down Boy Arvato Entertainment Services
Downbeat Cargo Records Distribution (UK) Ltd
Downsall Plastics Pinnacle Records
Downsound Jet Star Phonographics
Downwards Plastic Head Music Distribution Ltd
Doxa Shellshock Distribution
Doyen Arvato Entertainment Services
DPR Records Rare Beatz Distribution
Drag City Cargo Records Distribution (UK) Ltd
Dragonfly Vital Sales & Marketing
Dreadbeat Proper Music Distribution Ltd
Dream Circle Cargo Records Distribution (UK) Ltd
DreamWorks Universal Music Operations
Dressed To Kill Arvato Entertainment Services, Avanti Records
Dreyfus New Note Distribution Ltd, Pinnacle Records
DRG New Note Distribution Ltd, Pinnacle Records, RSK Entertainment Ltd
DRG Records New Note Distribution Ltd
Drive-In Cargo Records Distribution (UK) Ltd

Drive Thru Plastic Head Music Distribution Ltd
Droffig Pinnacle Records
Drop Beat Cargo Records Distribution (UK) Ltd
Drop Music InterGroove Ltd
Dropload Records Rare Beatz Distribution
Drought SRD (Southern Record Distribution)
Drug Squad Vital Sales & Marketing
Drugracer Cargo Records Distribution (UK) Ltd
Drunkabilly Nervous Records
Drunken Fish Cargo Records Distribution (UK) Ltd
Dry Run Recordings Shellshock Distribution
DSS69 Plastic Head Music Distribution Ltd
D3 RSK Entertainment Ltd
Dtox Universal Music Operations
DTR Metronome Distribution
DTS Vivante Music Ltd
Duality Universal Music Operations
Dualtone Proper Music Distribution Ltd
Dub Mission SRD (Southern Record Distribution)
Dub Organiser SRD (Southern Record Distribution)
Dubhead SRD (Southern Record Distribution)
Dublin One SRD (Southern Record Distribution)
Dubmission SRD (Southern Record Distribution)
Dubology SRD (Southern Record Distribution)
Dubplates Load Media
Duckdown RSK Entertainment Ltd
Dulcima Records Avid Entertainment
Dunkeld Gordon Duncan Distributions, Proper Music Distribution Ltd
Duophonic UHF Vital Sales & Marketing
Duplikate Records Rare Beatz Distribution
Dusk Fire Records Proper Music Distribution Ltd
Dust F Minor Ltd, SRD (Southern Record Distribution)
Duty Free Vital Sales & Marketing
DV8 Universal Music Operations
Dwell Plastic Head Music Distribution Ltd
Dyad New Note Distribution Ltd
Dynamic Jet Star Phonographics
Dynosupreme SRD (Southern Record Distribution)
Dysfunctional Cargo Records Distribution (UK) Ltd
Eagle Arvato Entertainment Services
Earache Records Ltd ADA UK
Earful Timewarp Distribution
Earth Pinnacle Records
Earth Connection SRD (Southern Record Distribution)
Earthnoise Vital Sales & Marketing
Earthsounds Vital Sales & Marketing
Earthworks Stern's Distribution
Earworm Cargo Records Distribution (UK) Ltd
East Central One Ltd Active Media Distribution Ltd
East Coast SRD (Southern Record Distribution)
East Coast Empire Plastic Head Music Distribution Ltd
East Edge Vital Sales & Marketing
East Side Digital SRD (Southern Record Distribution)
East Side Load Media
East West TEN (The Entertainment Network)
Eastern Developments Baked Goods Distribution
Eastworld Plastic Head Music Distribution Ltd
Easy DB Vital Sales & Marketing
Easy Jam Universal Music Operations
Easy Star Empathy Records
Easydisc Proper Music Distribution Ltd
Easy!Tiger Pinnacle Records
Eat Raw Cargo Records Distribution (UK) Ltd
Ebony SRD (Southern Record Distribution)
EBS Arvato Entertainment Services
Ecco.Chamber Timewarp Distribution
Echo Beach Records Pinnacle Records, Shellshock Distribution
Echo Drop Vital Sales & Marketing
Eclectic Pinnacle Records

Eclipse Gordon Duncan Distributions
ECM New Note Distribution Ltd, Pinnacle Records
ECM Books New Note Distribution Ltd
ECM New Series New Note Distribution Ltd
ECM Works New Note Distribution Ltd
Ecstatic SRD (Southern Record Distribution)
Ecstatic Peace Cargo Records Distribution (UK) Ltd
Edel Vital Sales & Marketing
Eden Gordon Duncan Distributions
Eden Productions The Woods
Edgar Music Pinnacle Records
Edgy Proper Music Distribution Ltd
Edinburgh Tattoo Gordon Duncan Distributions
Edsel Arvato Entertainment Services
Eerie Materials Cargo Records Distribution (UK) Ltd
EFA SRD (Southern Record Distribution)
Ego Vital Sales & Marketing
Eidechse Arvato Entertainment Services, Essential Direct Ltd
18th Street Lounge Cargo Records Distribution (UK) Ltd
Eighth Day Amato Distribution
El Bandoneon Discovery Records
El Cortez Records Shellshock Distribution
Elastic Cargo Records Distribution (UK) Ltd
Electric Lounge Timewarp Distribution
Electric Melt Amato Distribution
Electro Bunker Cologne SRD (Southern Record Distribution)
Electro-Fi Hot Shot Records
Electro Soul Records Rare Beatz Distribution
Electron Industries Vital Sales & Marketing
Electronic Alchemy Records Ltd The Orchard
Eledethorn Pinnacle Records
Elefant Records Shellshock Distribution, SRD (Southern Record Distribution)
Elegy Plastic Head Music Distribution Ltd
Elektra TEN (The Entertainment Network)
Elektrik Orgasm Pinnacle Records
Elemental Pinnacle Records
Elements Of Sound Arvato Entertainment Services, Essential Direct Ltd
Elevator Music Plastic Head Music Distribution Ltd
Elf Cut Pinnacle Records
Elite Cargo Records Distribution (UK) Ltd
Elleffe Universal Music Operations
Elliesis Arts Stern's Distribution
Elstree Hill Entertainment Pickwick Group Ltd
Elypsia Vital Sales & Marketing
Emanem Harmonia Mundi (UK) Ltd
Emarcy Universal Music Operations
Ember Pinnacle Records
Emerald Hour Proper Music Distribution Ltd
Emergency Broadcast System Ltd Plastic Head Music Distribution Ltd
EMI EMI Distribution
EMI Brazil Stern's Distribution
EMI Classics UK EMI Distribution
EMI Gold EMI Distribution
EMI South Africa Stern's Distribution
Emissions Vital Sales & Marketing
Emix Records Rare Beatz Distribution
Emocion New Note Distribution Ltd
Emoticon Baked Goods Distribution
Emotif SRD (Southern Record Distribution)
Emperor Jones Cargo Records Distribution (UK) Ltd
Empreinte DIG Harmonia Mundi (UK) Ltd
Empress RSK Entertainment Ltd
Empty Cargo Records Distribution (UK) Ltd
En Seine Amato Distribution
Enable Music Ltd Active Media Distribution Ltd
Endorphin Cargo Records Distribution (UK) Ltd
Energetic SRD (Southern Record Distribution)

Design, Pressing & Distribution: Distributed Labels

Engine Vital Sales & Marketing
English Muffin Baked Goods Distribution
Enja New Note Distribution Ltd, Pinnacle Records
Enraptured Cargo Records Distribution (UK) Ltd
Enriched Pinnacle Records
Entertainment In Video TEN (The Entertainment Network)
Entracte Hot Records
Entropica Changing World Distribution
Entropy Productions Vital Sales & Marketing
Enviken Nervous Records
Environ Shellshock Distribution, Vital Sales & Marketing
Epic TEN (The Entertainment Network)
Epidemic Universal Music Operations
Epigram Cargo Records Distribution (UK) Ltd
Episode Universal Music Operations
Epitaph Pinnacle Records
EPM Discovery Records
Erato TEN (The Entertainment Network)
Ermitage Metronome Distribution
Ernie Smith Jet Star Phonographics
Erra Records Ltd Timewarp Distribution
Eruption Pinnacle Records
ESC Records New Note Distribution Ltd
Escapade Cargo Records Distribution (UK) Ltd
Escape Cargo Records Distribution (UK) Ltd, RSK Entertainment Ltd
Escape Artist Records Shellshock Distribution
Escape Music Cargo Records Distribution (UK) Ltd
Eskimo Recordings Timewarp Distribution
ESL Cargo Records Distribution (UK) Ltd
Esoteric Load Media
ESP Disk F Minor Ltd
Essay Recordings Cargo Records Distribution (UK) Ltd, Shellshock Distribution
Essential Pinnacle Records
Essential Music African Caribbean Asian Entertainment
Estrus Cargo Records Distribution (UK) Ltd
Eternal TEN (The Entertainment Network)
Ethbo Kudos Records Ltd
Ethnic-Flamenco Vivo Harmonia Mundi (UK) Ltd
Ethnic Flight Arvato Entertainment Services, Essential Direct Ltd
Euphonious Vital Sales & Marketing
Euphoria F Minor Ltd
Euphoric Arvato Entertainment Services
Eureka Arvato Entertainment Services
Euro Ralph Cargo Records Distribution (UK) Ltd
Europress Pinnacle Records
Evans World Of Music Harmonia Mundi (UK) Ltd
Eve Amato Distribution
Eve Nova Amato Distribution
Event Cargo Records Distribution (UK) Ltd
Eventide Music Media UK Distribution
Everlasting Records The Orchard
Evil SRD (Southern Record Distribution)
Evocative Pinnacle Records
Evol Intent Load Media
Evolution Gold Arvato Entertainment Services
Excession Vital Sales & Marketing
Exil Proper Music Distribution Ltd
Exoteric Arvato Entertainment Services, Essential Direct Ltd
Exotica SRD (Southern Record Distribution)
Expanding Baked Goods Distribution
Experience Jet Star Phonographics
Explicit Load Media
Exploding Plastic Arvato Entertainment Services, Essential Direct Ltd
Explosive Arvato Entertainment Services
Expression Pinnacle Records
Extatique Vital Sales & Marketing

Exterminator Jet Star Phonographics
Extreme Vital Sales & Marketing
Eye Q Vital Sales & Marketing
Eyesofsound Shellshock Distribution
F Communications (UK) Vital Sales & Marketing
F O D Nova Sales and Distribution (UK) Ltd
Fabric KRD
Fabric Of Life Amato Distribution
Factory Too Pinnacle Records
Falasha SRD (Southern Record Distribution)
Falcone Pinnacle Records
Fantastic Plastic Vital Sales & Marketing
Fantasy Pinnacle Records
Fantasy Jazz New Note Distribution Ltd
Far Out KRD, New Note Distribution Ltd, Pinnacle Records
Farside Timewarp Distribution
Fast Music Plastic Head Music Distribution Ltd
Fat Records InterGroove Ltd
Fat Beats Pinnacle Records
Fat Cat Records Vital Sales & Marketing
Fat Eyes Jet Star Phonographics
Fat Fox Records Active Media Distribution Ltd
Fat Man SRD (Southern Record Distribution)
Fat 'n' Round Pinnacle Records
Fat Wreck Plastic Head Music Distribution Ltd
Fatlip Vital Sales & Marketing
Fauve Vital Sales & Marketing
Faze 2 Records Absolute Marketing & Distribution Ltd.
FDM Records Nova Sales and Distribution (UK) Ltd
Fear Of Music SRD (Southern Record Distribution)
Federation Universal Music Operations
Fedora Proper Music Distribution Ltd
Feedback Arvato Entertainment Services
Fellside Gordon Duncan Distributions, Proper Music Distribution Ltd
Fen Cat Universal Music Operations
Fenetik Kudos Records Ltd
Ferocious Vital Sales & Marketing
Ferric Mordant Pinnacle Records
Festival Cargo Records Distribution (UK) Ltd
FF Vinyl Shellshock Distribution
Ffrench Production Jet Star Phonographics
ffrr TEN (The Entertainment Network)
Fiasco Kudos Records Ltd, Pinnacle Records
Fie! Vital Sales & Marketing
Fierce SRD (Southern Record Distribution)
1500 Cargo Records Distribution (UK) Ltd
Fifth Freedom Vital Sales & Marketing
Fifty First Recordings Pinnacle Records
Film Four Technicolor Distribution Services Ltd
Film 2000 TEN (The Entertainment Network)
FilmGuerrero Shellshock Distribution
Filter Pinnacle Records
Filth Pinnacle Records
Filthy Sonnix Pinnacle Records
Fine Art Vital Sales & Marketing
Fine Balance SRD (Southern Record Distribution)
Finest Gramophone Shellshock Distribution
Fingal Gordon Duncan Distributions
Finger Cargo Records Distribution (UK) Ltd
Finlandia TEN (The Entertainment Network)
Fire Inc Cargo Records Distribution (UK) Ltd
Fire Island Universal Music Operations
Fire Recordings Pinnacle Records
Fireball Excel Marketing Services Ltd, Proper Music Distribution Ltd
Firm Music Pinnacle Records
First Edition Jet Star Phonographics
First Impressions Vivante Music Ltd
First Love Cargo Records Distribution (UK) Ltd

First Night Records Ltd Pinnacle Records
First Time Media UK Distribution
Fisheye Cargo Records Distribution (UK) Ltd
Fishtail Hot Shot Records
555 Recordings Cargo Records Distribution (UK) Ltd
500 Arvato Entertainment Services, Essential Direct Ltd
504 Proper Music Distribution Ltd
Five O Four Jazz Music
Five Trees Absolute Marketing & Distribution Ltd., Pinnacle Records
5HQ SRD (Southern Record Distribution)
FJ Entertainment Jet Star Phonographics
Flair Absolute Marketing & Distribution Ltd., Arvato Entertainment Services
Flameshovel Forte Music Distribution Ltd
Flamingo West The Woods
Flapper Pinnacle Records
Flapping Jet Cargo Records Distribution (UK) Ltd
Flarenasch Discovery Records
Flashlight Magnum Distribution
Flat Earth Cargo Records Distribution (UK) Ltd
Flat Rock Proper Music Distribution Ltd
Flaw Vital Sales & Marketing
Fledg'ling Proper Music Distribution Ltd
Flex Jet Star Phonographics
Flin Flak Records Rare Beatz Distribution
Flintwood Jet Star Phonographics
Flipside Pinnacle Records
Fliptop Records Plastic Head Music Distribution Ltd
Flittchen Pinnacle Records
Flo Records SRD (Southern Record Distribution)
Flotsam & Jetsam SRD (Southern Record Distribution)
Fluffy Pinnacle Records
Fluffy Bunny Pinnacle Records
Fluid Amato Distribution
Fluid Ounce Cargo Records Distribution (UK) Ltd
Flute Arvato Entertainment Services
Flux Vital Sales & Marketing
Fly Casual Cargo Records Distribution (UK) Ltd
Flydaddy Pinnacle Records
Flying Fish Proper Music Distribution Ltd
Flying Rhino SRD (Southern Record Distribution)
Flying Thorn Proper Music Distribution Ltd
Flyright Hot Shot Records, Jazz Music
Fog Area Pinnacle Records
Folk Corporation Pinnacle Records
Folk Era Rolica Music Distribution
Folksound CM Distribution, Roots Records
F1 TEN (The Entertainment Network)
Fontana Universal Music Operations
Food EMI Distribution
Food For Thought Pinnacle Records
For All The Right Reasons Pinnacle Records
For Real Amato Distribution
Force Inc SRD (Southern Record Distribution)
Forever Forward Arvato Entertainment Services
Formacentric DisK Cargo Records Distribution (UK) Ltd
Format Supremacy Cargo Records Distribution (UK) Ltd
Formation SRD (Southern Record Distribution)
Forsaken Plastic Head Music Distribution Ltd
Fortress ST Holdings Ltd
Fortuna Pop Pinnacle Records
Fortunate Pinnacle Records
Fortune & Glory Shellshock Distribution
49th Parallel Vital Sales & Marketing
Forum Regis Records Ltd
Forward Jet Star Phonographics
Fotofone Jet Star Phonographics
Foundation Sound Works Vital Sales & Marketing
Foundry Band Gordon Duncan Distributions

Four D Amato Distribution
4 Liberty Pinnacle Records
4 Men With Beards F Minor Ltd
Fourbeat Pinnacle Records
4M Pinnacle Records
4most Pinnacle Records
four:twenty InterGroove Ltd
Fractured Transmitter Shellshock Distribution
Fragments SRD (Southern Record Distribution)
Frances Court Jazz Music
Frank Records Media UK Distribution
Frantic Vital Sales & Marketing
Freak Load Media, Pinnacle Records
FreakStreet Pinnacle Records
Fred Label Ltd Absolute Marketing & Distribution Ltd.
Free F Minor Ltd, Pinnacle Records
Free Booze Pinnacle Records
Free Range Kudos Records Ltd
Free Reed CM Distribution
Free World SRD (Southern Record Distribution)
free2air recordings Vital Sales & Marketing
Freebass Amato Distribution
Freeform Pinnacle Records
Freek Cargo Records Distribution (UK) Ltd
Freemaison Records Jed-Eye Distribution Ltd
Freestyle Records Kudos Records Ltd
Fremeaux Discovery Records
Frenchkiss Forte Music Distribution Ltd
Frequency Factory Load Media
Frequent Soundz Timewarp Distribution
Fresh Pinnacle Records
Fresh Ear Pinnacle Records
Fresh Kutt SRD (Southern Record Distribution)
Fresh Sound Discovery Records
Freshly Squeezed (Music Ltd) Kudos Records Ltd
Freskanova Pinnacle Records
Fret New Note Distribution Ltd, Pendle Hawk Music
Frog Jazz Music
Fromage Rouge Vital Sales & Marketing
Frontiers Cargo Records Distribution (UK) Ltd
Fruit Tree F Minor Ltd
Fruitbeard Kudos Records Ltd
Fruition Pinnacle Records
Fuel Pinnacle Records
Fueled By Ramen Plastic Head Music Distribution Ltd
Fuju Amato Distribution
Fuk Amato Distribution
Full Blown Arvato Entertainment Services
Full Circle Vital Sales & Marketing
Full Moon Plastic Head Music Distribution Ltd
FUN Pinnacle Records
Funakasaurus Vital Sales & Marketing
Function Load Media
Function 8 Cargo Records Distribution (UK) Ltd
Fundamental Pinnacle Records, Shellshock Distribution
Funfundvierzig Shellshock Distribution
Funky Beats Universal Music Operations
Funky Frequency Records Rare Beatz Distribution
Furious? Vital Sales & Marketing
Fury Records Windsong International
Fuse Proper Music Distribution Ltd
Fused & Bruised SRD (Southern Record Distribution)
Fusion Arvato Entertainment Services
Future Legend Pinnacle Records
Future Primitive Cargo Records Distribution (UK) Ltd
Future Sound & Vision Arvato Entertainment Services
Future Tense Vital Sales & Marketing
Future Underground Nation Amato Distribution
Futurus Pinnacle Records
G-Spot Arvato Entertainment Services, Essential Direct Ltd

Gail Davies Proper Music Distribution Ltd
Gailo Stern's Distribution
Gala Arvato Entertainment Services
Galaktic Sound Lab Proper Music Distribution Ltd
Galaxia Cargo Records Distribution (UK) Ltd
Gale Metronome Distribution
Game Arvato Entertainment Services
Game Two Records Shellshock Distribution
Gamp Pinnacle Records
Gannet Jazz Music
Garage Nation Pinnacle Records
Garden Pinnacle Records
Gargleblast Records Shellshock Distribution
Gazmo Universal Music Operations
GC Records Rare Beatz Distribution
GDI Nova Sales and Distribution (UK) Ltd
Gear Fab F Minor Ltd
Gear Head F Minor Ltd
Gecko Pinnacle Records
Gee Street Pinnacle Records
Geffen Arvato Entertainment Services
Geist Vital Sales & Marketing
Generations Vital Sales & Marketing
Generic Pinnacle Records
Genetic Records Universal Music Operations
Genetic Stress SRD (Southern Record Distribution)
Genius Avid Entertainment
Gentilly The Woods
Gentlemen Music Shellshock Distribution
Germstore Baked Goods Distribution
Gern Blandsten Forte Music Distribution Ltd
Gern Blansten SRD (Southern Record Distribution)
Get Back Cargo Records Distribution (UK) Ltd, F Minor Ltd
Get Hip F Minor Ltd
Get Real Productions Proper Music Distribution Ltd
GHB Jazz Music
GHB Jazz Foundation The Woods
Ghetto Safari Cargo Records Distribution (UK) Ltd
Giant Arvato Entertainment Services
Giant Claw Cargo Records Distribution (UK) Ltd
Giant Electric Pea Pinnacle Records
Giants Of Jazz Arvato Entertainment Services, Delta Music PLC, Jazz Music, Swift Record Distributors
Gift Of Life Cargo Records Distribution (UK) Ltd
Giga Arvato Entertainment Services
Giglo SRD (Southern Record Distribution)
Gigolo SRD (Southern Record Distribution)
Ginga EMI Distribution
Ginger Cargo Records Distribution (UK) Ltd
Girl Vital Sales & Marketing
Girl Dependence Pinnacle Records
Glamma Jet Star Phonographics
Glasgow Absolute Marketing & Distribution Ltd., Universal Music Operations
The Glass Gramophone Co Swift Record Distributors
Glencoe Gordon Duncan Distributions
Glenda Leigh Lewis Jet Star Phonographics
Gliss Records Pinnacle Records
Glitterhouse Records Shellshock Distribution
Global Harmony Amato Distribution
Global Headz Vital Sales & Marketing
Global Labels Vital Sales & Marketing
Global Mobile Pinnacle Records
Global Nite Life Pinnacle Records
Global Talent Records Pinnacle Records
Global TV Arvato Entertainment Services
Global Warming Cargo Records Distribution (UK) Ltd
Globestyle New Note Distribution Ltd, Pinnacle Records, Stern's Distribution
Glossa Harmonia Mundi (UK) Ltd

GM Recordings Metronome Distribution
GMM Cargo Records Distribution (UK) Ltd, Plastic Head Music Distribution Ltd
GNP Pinnacle Records
Go Clubland New Note Distribution Ltd
Go For It InterGroove Ltd
Go-Go Girl SRD (Southern Record Distribution)
Go Jazz New Note Distribution Ltd, Vital Sales & Marketing
Go Kart Pinnacle Records, Plastic Head Music Distribution Ltd
Go.Beat Universal Music Operations
God Bless Cargo Records Distribution (UK) Ltd
Go!Discs Universal Music Operations
God's Pop Pinnacle Records
Gogo Girl SRD (Southern Record Distribution)
Going For A Song Magnum Distribution
Golden Triangle Pinnacle Records
Goldmine Vital Sales & Marketing
Golf Plastic Head Music Distribution Ltd
Gone Clear Jet Star Phonographics
Gonzo Circus Pinnacle Records
Goo! Pinnacle Records
Good As Amato Distribution
Good Life Cargo Records Distribution (UK) Ltd
Good Sounds TEN (The Entertainment Network)
Good Time Jazz Jazz Music
Good Vibe Cargo Records Distribution (UK) Ltd
Goodfellow Records Shellshock Distribution
Goodlife Cargo Records Distribution (UK) Ltd
Goodtime Jazz New Note Distribution Ltd
Goofin Magnum Distribution, Nervous Records
Gosh Pinnacle Records
GPR Vital Sales & Marketing
Gracethril Jet Star Phonographics
Grade Cargo Records Distribution (UK) Ltd
Grainne Arvato Entertainment Services
Gramavision Vital Sales & Marketing
Gran Kru SRD (Southern Record Distribution)
Grand Recordings Proper Music Distribution Ltd, Shellshock Distribution
Grand Larceny SRD (Southern Record Distribution)
Grand Royal EMI Distribution, Vital Sales & Marketing
Grasmere Arvato Entertainment Services, Delta Music PLC, Gordon Duncan Distributions
Grateful Dead Pinnacle Records
Grave News Ltd Plastic Head Music Distribution Ltd
Gravitate Cargo Records Distribution (UK) Ltd
Gravitation Pinnacle Records
Gravity Dip Shellshock Distribution
Graylan Universal Music Operations
Great British Techno Arvato Entertainment Services
Great Movie Themes Arvato Entertainment Services
Green Light Vital Sales & Marketing
Green Linnet Claddagh Records, Proper Music Distribution Ltd
Green Tea SRD (Southern Record Distribution)
Green Vinyl Pinnacle Records
Greentrax Recordings Ltd Pendle Hawk Music
Grilled Cheese Cargo Records Distribution (UK) Ltd
Grilli Universal Music Operations
Grimm Records Plastic Head Music Distribution Ltd
Gringo Pinnacle Records
Groove SRD (Southern Record Distribution)
Groove Attack Pinnacle Records
Groove Kissing Vital Sales & Marketing
Groovenote Vivante Music Ltd
Grooves Magazine Baked Goods Distribution
Gross National Product Pinnacle Records
Ground Vital Sales & Marketing
Ground Control Cargo Records Distribution (UK) Ltd
Grover Plastic Head Music Distribution Ltd
GRP Arvato Entertainment Services

G2 Proper Music Distribution Ltd
Guess What Jet Star Phonographics
Guidance Cargo Records Distribution (UK) Ltd
Guided Missile Pinnacle Records
Guild Pinnacle Records
Gun Plastic Head Music Distribution Ltd
Gussie P Jet Star Phonographics
Gut Recordings Pinnacle Records
Gut Vision Pinnacle Records
Gwynfryn Sain (Recordiau) Cyf
Gyration Pinnacle Records
Habit Load Media
Hades Vital Sales & Marketing
Hairball 8 Cargo Records Distribution (UK) Ltd
Halcyon Jazz Music
Halesouth Pinnacle Records
Half-A-Cow Cargo Records Distribution (UK) Ltd
Half Moon Arvato Entertainment Services
Hall Of Sermon Plastic Head Music Distribution Ltd
Hallmark Pickwick Group Ltd
The Hallowe'en Society Cargo Records Distribution (UK) Ltd
Halo Nova Sales and Distribution (UK) Ltd, Pinnacle Records
Hana Universal Music Operations
H&H Music Fat Cat International Ltd
Hands On Pinnacle Records
Handsome Devil Load Media
Hangdog Cargo Records Distribution (UK) Ltd
Hangman's Daughter Pinnacle Records
Hannibal Vital Sales & Marketing
Hansome Vital Sales & Marketing
Hanssler Select Music & Video Distribution
Happy Accident Pinnacle Records
Happy Days Arvato Entertainment Services
Happy Gang Gordon Duncan Distributions
Happy Go Lucky Cargo Records Distribution (UK) Ltd
Happy Trax Universal Music Operations
Harbinger Pinnacle Records
Hard Times Vital Sales & Marketing
Hardleaders SRD (Southern Record Distribution)
Hardward Records Plastic Head Music Distribution Ltd
Harkit Pinnacle Records
Harlequin Hot Shot Records, Jazz Music, Stern's Distribution
Harmonia Mundi Harmonia Mundi (UK) Ltd
Harp Gordon Duncan Distributions
Harper Collins Pinnacle Records, Sound Entertainment Ltd
Harthouse Vital Sales & Marketing
Harvest SRD (Southern Record Distribution)
Harzfein Pinnacle Records
Hash SRD (Southern Record Distribution)
Hat Hut Harmonia Mundi (UK) Ltd
Hat Now Harmonia Mundi (UK) Ltd
Hate Arvato Entertainment Services, Essential Direct Ltd
Hatology Harmonia Mundi (UK) Ltd
Hausmusic Cargo Records Distribution (UK) Ltd
Hausmusik Baked Goods Distribution
Havana SRD (Southern Record Distribution)
Hawkeye SRD (Southern Record Distribution)
Head Hunter Cargo Records Distribution (UK) Ltd
Header Vital Sales & Marketing
Headhunter Cargo Records Distribution (UK) Ltd
Headroom Shellshock Distribution
Headspace Vital Sales & Marketing
Heard Vital Sales & Marketing
Hearpen Vital Sales & Marketing
Heart Beat Jet Star Phonographics
Heartbeat Proper Music Distribution Ltd
Heat Recordings Vital Sales & Marketing
Heaven Universal Music Operations
Heaven Hotel Cargo Records Distribution (UK) Ltd

Heavenly Arvato Entertainment Services, Pinnacle Records, Vital Sales & Marketing
Heavy Truth Vital Sales & Marketing
Heavyweight Universal Music Operations
Hefty Baked Goods Distribution, Cargo Records Distribution (UK) Ltd
Heiro Imperium Cargo Records Distribution (UK) Ltd
Helix SRD (Southern Record Distribution)
Hell Yeah Cargo Records Distribution (UK) Ltd
Hellcat Pinnacle Records
Helter Skelter Pinnacle Records, Plastic Head Music Distribution Ltd
Hemiola Vital Sales & Marketing
Hendricks Arvato Entertainment Services
Henry Street Proper Music Distribution Ltd
HEP Jazz Music, New Note Distribution Ltd, Pinnacle Records
Hep Records New Note Distribution Ltd
Heraldic Records Media UK Distribution
Heraldic Jester Media UK Distribution
Heraldic Vintage Media UK Distribution
Heritage Hot Shot Records, Jazz Music
Hey Presto Music Express Ltd
Hi Arvato Entertainment Services
Hi Fashion SRD (Southern Record Distribution)
Hi-Life Universal Music Operations
Hibiscus Cargo Records Distribution (UK) Ltd
Hidden Agenda Cargo Records Distribution (UK) Ltd
Hideaway Blues Band Hot Shot Records
High Action Hot Shot Records
High Barn Records Backs Distribution
High Coin Cadiz Music Ltd
High Gain Records Plastic Head Music Distribution Ltd
High Noon SRD (Southern Record Distribution)
High Note Proper Music Distribution Ltd
High Octane Cargo Records Distribution (UK) Ltd
High On Hope Pinnacle Records
High Society International Plastic Head Music Distribution Ltd
Higher Ground TEN (The Entertainment Network)
Higher Limits Arvato Entertainment Services
Higher Octave EMI Distribution
Higher Plane Hot Shot Records
Higher State Essential Direct Ltd
Highlander Ross Record Distribution
HighTone Proper Music Distribution Ltd
Hightone/HMG Proper Music Distribution Ltd
Hillside Music RSK Entertainment Ltd
Hindsight Arvato Entertainment Services, Jazz Music
Hip-No Arvato Entertainment Services
HIT LABEL Technicolor Distribution Services Ltd, Universal Music Operations
The Hit Label Pinnacle Records
Hitback Pinnacle Records
Hitbound SRD (Southern Record Distribution)
Hitchcock Media Metronome Distribution
Hitop Records Timewarp Distribution
HMV Classics EMI Distribution
Hocus Pocus Universal Music Operations
Hodder Headline Pinnacle Records
Hoe Down City SRD (Southern Record Distribution)
Hole In The Floor Pinnacle Records
Holistic Pinnacle Records
Hollow Planet Pinnacle Records
Hollywood Vital Sales & Marketing
Holy Moly Amato Distribution
Holy Records Plastic Head Music Distribution Ltd
Hom-Mega Pinnacle Records
Hombre SRD (Southern Record Distribution)
Hombre Mapache Brand SRD (Southern Record Distribution)

Home Alone Arvato Entertainment Services, Essential Direct Ltd
Home Entertainment Cargo Records Distribution (UK) Ltd
Homelife Kudos Records Ltd
Homemade Records New Note Distribution Ltd
Homer Pinnacle Records
Homesleep Shellshock Distribution
Homework Pinnacle Records
Honey Bear Cargo Records Distribution (UK) Ltd
Honibokum Vital Sales & Marketing
Hooj Choons Vital Sales & Marketing
Hook InterGroove Ltd
Hooley Gordon Duncan Distributions
Hooligan Universal Music Operations
Hope Records Pinnacle Records
Hope Recordings Vital Sales & Marketing
Hopeless Cargo Records Distribution (UK) Ltd
Horseback Pinnacle Records
Horseplay Hot Shot Records
Hostile Load Media
Hot Hot Records, Vital Sales & Marketing
Hot Air Baked Goods Distribution, Cargo Records Distribution (UK) Ltd
Hot Classics Cargo Records Distribution (UK) Ltd
Hot House Records Harmonia Mundi (UK) Ltd
Hot Vinyl Jet Star Phonographics
Hottis Jet Star Phonographics
House Of God Cargo Records Distribution (UK) Ltd
Household Name Records Plastic Head Music Distribution Ltd, The Orchard
Howling Duck Pinnacle Records
HPT Independent Arvato Entertainment Services, Essential Direct Ltd
HRL Arvato Entertainment Services
HTD Pinnacle Records
H2OH Recordings Universal Music Operations
Hubbcap Universal Music Operations
Human Roots Records
Human Imprint Load Media
Hungry Audio Pinnacle Records, Shellshock Distribution
Hungry Dog Active Media Distribution Ltd
Hustler Z Active Media Distribution Ltd
Hut EMI Distribution
Hwyl Cargo Records Distribution (UK) Ltd
Hydrahead Shellshock Distribution
Hydration Universal Music Operations
Hydrogen Dukebox Pinnacle Records
Hydroponic SRD (Southern Record Distribution)
Hyper Pinnacle Records
Hyperspace Cargo Records Distribution (UK) Ltd
Hypertension Proper Music Distribution Ltd
Hypnotic Vital Sales & Marketing
Hypnotize Nova Sales and Distribution (UK) Ltd
I Scream Records Plastic Head Music Distribution Ltd, Shellshock Distribution
Iajrc Jazz Music
Ice Rink Vital Sales & Marketing
ID Identity SRD (Southern Record Distribution)
Idiot Savant Cargo Records Distribution (UK) Ltd
IE Music Universal Music Operations
Ignition Vital Sales & Marketing
Igus Discovery Records
Ikef F Minor Ltd
Ill Recordings Vital Sales & Marketing
Illastate Records SRD (Southern Record Distribution)
Illegal Jet Star Phonographics
Illegal Beats Amato Distribution
Illusion Arvato Entertainment Services
Imaginary Music Harmonia Mundi (UK) Ltd
Imago Proper Music Distribution Ltd

Imani Jet Star Phonographics
Immaterial Vital Sales & Marketing
IMP Discovery Records
Impact Records Plastic Head Music Distribution Ltd
Imperial Dub Pinnacle Records
Important Vital Sales & Marketing
Impulse Arvato Entertainment Services
In & Out Vital Sales & Marketing
In At The Deep End Shellshock Distribution
In-Tec Pinnacle Records, SRD (Southern Record Distribution)
In The Red Cargo Records Distribution (UK) Ltd
Inakustic Proper Music Distribution Ltd
Incentive Music Ltd Universal Music Operations
Incoming! Pinnacle Records
INCredible TEN (The Entertainment Network)
Independent Dealers Vital Sales & Marketing
Independiente Ltd Arvato Entertainment Services
India Navigation Discovery Records
Indie 500 Backs Distribution, Pinnacle Records
Indigo Records Jazz Music, New Note Distribution Ltd, Proper Music Distribution Ltd
Indochina Pinnacle Records
Industrial Strength Vital Sales & Marketing
Industry Standard Amato Distribution
Inertia SRD (Southern Record Distribution)
Infernal Pinnacle Records
Inferno Cool Vital Sales & Marketing
Infiltration Pinnacle Records
Infinite Bloom Recordings Ltd Fullfill LLC UK Ltd
Infinity Pinnacle Records
Influential Pinnacle Records
Infonet Vital Sales & Marketing
Infracom SRD (Southern Record Distribution), Timewarp Distribution
Infrared Pinnacle Records
Infur Pinnacle Records
Infusion Vital Sales & Marketing
Innocent Records EMI Distribution
Inside Out TEN (The Entertainment Network)
Instant Karma TEN (The Entertainment Network)
Instant Mayhem Vital Sales & Marketing
Instinct Cargo Records Distribution (UK) Ltd
Instinctive TEN (The Entertainment Network)
Insurrection Cargo Records Distribution (UK) Ltd
Intasound Load Media
Integral SRD (Southern Record Distribution)
Integrity SRD (Southern Record Distribution)
Inter City Vital Sales & Marketing
Intercom SRD (Southern Record Distribution)
Intermusic Nervous Records
International Deejay Gigolos SRD (Southern Record Distribution)
International Playboy Gigolos SRD (Southern Record Distribution)
Internazionale Pinnacle Records
Interra Arvato Entertainment Services
Interscope Arvato Entertainment Services
Intersound Jazz Music
Intruder Arvato Entertainment Services, Essential Direct Ltd
Invicta Hi-Fi Vital Sales & Marketing
Invisible Pinnacle Records
Invisible Hands Records Pinnacle Records
Invisible Records Plastic Head Music Distribution Ltd
Involve Baked Goods Distribution
Ion Cargo Records Distribution (UK) Ltd
Irdial Baked Goods Distribution
Iris Light Records Shellshock Distribution
Irish Arvato Entertainment Services
Irma Arvato Entertainment Services, Essential Direct Ltd, Nova Sales and Distribution (UK) Ltd

Irma On Canvas Timewarp Distribution
Iron Man Cargo Records Distribution (UK) Ltd
Irregular Proper Music Distribution Ltd
Island Universal Music Operations
Island Black Music Universal Music Operations
Island Jamaica Universal Music Operations, Vital Sales & Marketing
Island Masters Universal Music Operations
Isobar Records Pinnacle Records
It Records Vital Sales & Marketing
Itchy Teeth Cargo Records Distribution (UK) Ltd
ITN Corporation Plastic Head Music Distribution Ltd
It's Fabulous SRD (Southern Record Distribution)
It's Music Pinnacle Records
IVL Videos Excel Marketing Services Ltd
Ivory SRD (Southern Record Distribution)
IVP Gordon Duncan Distributions
Ivy Vital Sales & Marketing
J7 Active Media Distribution Ltd
Jab Gordon Duncan Distributions
Jade Tree Forte Music Distribution Ltd
Jagjaguwar Cargo Records Distribution (UK) Ltd
JAGZ The Woods
Jah Warrior SRD (Southern Record Distribution)
Jah Works SRD (Southern Record Distribution)
Jahmani Jet Star Phonographics
Jal Premium SRD (Southern Record Distribution)
Jam Jah Absolute Marketing & Distribution Ltd.
Jamaica Jet Star Phonographics
Jamal Pinnacle Records
Jamazima Jet Star Phonographics
Jamixal Jet Star Phonographics
Jammys Jet Star Phonographics
Jamnic Absolute Marketing & Distribution Ltd.
Japo New Note Distribution Ltd
Jardis The Woods
Jas SRD (Southern Record Distribution)
Jasmine Records Proper Music Distribution Ltd
Jasper Pinnacle Records
Javelin THE (Total Home Entertainment)
Jazz & Blues Arvato Entertainment Services, Delta Music PLC
Jazz Academy New Note Distribution Ltd
Jazz Alliance New Note Distribution Ltd, Pinnacle Records
Jazz Archives Discovery Records, Jazz Music
Jazz Arena The Woods
Jazz Base The Woods
Jazz Cat New Note Distribution Ltd
Jazz Classics Proper Music Distribution Ltd
Jazz Compass The Woods
Jazz Hour Jazz Music
Jazz House Magnum Distribution, New Note Distribution Ltd
Jazz Monkey Cargo Records Distribution (UK) Ltd
Jazz Oracle Jazz Music
Jazz Perspective Hot Shot Records, Jazz Music
Jazz Unlimited Jazz Music, Proper Music Distribution Ltd
Jazzanova SRD (Southern Record Distribution)
Jazzband Hot Shot Records, Jazz Music
Jazzheads The Woods
Jazzizit New Note Distribution Ltd
Jazzizzit Pinnacle Records
Jazzman Timewarp Distribution
Jazzology Jazz Music, The Woods
JB Records The Woods
JBO Pinnacle Records
JDJ Pinnacle Records
Jealous Forte Music Distribution Ltd
Jeepster Recordings Ltd Pinnacle Records
Jeity Music Pinnacle Records
Jelly Street Arvato Entertainment Services
Jesper Pinnacle Records

Jet Proper Music Distribution Ltd
Jetstar Jet Star Phonographics
Jika New Note Distribution Ltd
Jimmi Kidd Pinnacle Records
Jive Pinnacle Records
Jive House Pinnacle Records
J&M Recordings Jazz Music
JMC Jet Star Phonographics
JMS New Note Distribution Ltd
JMY/Moon/IAI/Red Harmonia Mundi (UK) Ltd
Jockey Slut Vital Sales & Marketing
Joe Frasier Jet Star Phonographics
Joe Gibbs SRD (Southern Record Distribution)
Joe G's Jet Star Phonographics
Johanna Proper Music Distribution Ltd
Johann's Face Cargo Records Distribution (UK) Ltd
John Holt Jet Star Phonographics
John John Jet Star Phonographics
Johnny Ferreira Hot Shot Records
Joke Productions SRD (Southern Record Distribution)
Joker SRD (Southern Record Distribution)
Jonson Family Cargo Records Distribution (UK) Ltd
Joss House Kudos Records Ltd
Journeys By DJ Pinnacle Records
Jowonio Productions Baked Goods Distribution
Joy Jazz Music
JR Productions Jet Star Phonographics
JR Records Jazz Music
JRB Metronome Distribution
JTC Music Group The Woods
Juice SRD (Southern Record Distribution), Timewarp Distribution
Juice Box SRD (Southern Record Distribution)
Juicy Cuts Universal Music Operations
Jukebox Jazz Jazz Music
Jump Up Cargo Records Distribution (UK) Ltd
Jump Wax Vital Sales & Marketing
Jumpin' & Pumpin' TEN (The Entertainment Network)
Jungle SRD (Southern Record Distribution)
Jungle Growers Pinnacle Records
Jungle Sky Cargo Records Distribution (UK) Ltd
Junior Amato Distribution
Junior Productions Jet Star Phonographics
Junior Recordings Amato Distribution
Junk Cargo Records Distribution (UK) Ltd
Just A Memory Pinnacle Records
Just Another Bootleg SRD (Southern Record Distribution)
Just Another Label SRD (Southern Record Distribution)
Just Frienz Jet Star Phonographics
Justin Time New Note Distribution Ltd, Pinnacle Records
Justine Vital Sales & Marketing
JVC Proper Music Distribution Ltd, Vivante Music Ltd
JW Productions Jet Star Phonographics
JZ & Arkh - MCMLXV Productions Baked Goods Distribution
Kamera Shy THE (Total Home Entertainment)
Kanzleramt Shellshock Distribution
Karaoke Kalk SRD (Southern Record Distribution)
Karmagiraffe SRD (Southern Record Distribution)
Karonte Discovery Records
Kartoonz SRD (Southern Record Distribution)
Kat Cargo Records Distribution (UK) Ltd
Katsweb Active Media Distribution Ltd
Katt Pie CM Distribution
Kay Video Jazz Music
Kayak Cargo Records Distribution (UK) Ltd
K'Boro Pinnacle Records
Kbox Magnum Distribution
KC Hot Shot Records
KDC Pendle Hawk Music

Keltia Discovery Records
Kemet Jet Star Phonographics
Ken Colyer Trust Jazz Music
Kenneth Jazz Music
Kent Pinnacle Records
Kent Duchaine Hot Shot Records
Kettle Gordon Duncan Distributions
Key Proper Music Distribution Ltd
Keynote Load Media
K422 Vital Sales & Marketing
Kick On Pinnacle Records
Kicking Mule Pinnacle Records
Kid Rhino Pinnacle Records
Kiff SM Vital Sales & Marketing
Kila Proper Music Distribution Ltd
Kill Rock Stars Forte Music Distribution Ltd
Killing Sheep Load Media
Kin Baked Goods Distribution
Kindercore Cargo Records Distribution (UK) Ltd
Kindness Vital Sales & Marketing
Kinetic Load Media
Kinetix Pinnacle Records
King Arvato Entertainment Services
King Biscuit Flower Pinnacle Records
King Edwards Jet Star Phonographics
King Mob TEN (The Entertainment Network)
King Pin SRD (Southern Record Distribution)
King Super Analogue Vivante Music Ltd
King Syndrome Sounds Soul Trader
Kingpin Amato Distribution
Kings Cross Harmonia Mundi (UK) Ltd
Kings Of Kings Jet Star Phonographics
Kiss Kidee Jet Star Phonographics
Kissing Spell F Minor Ltd
Kitchenware Vital Sales & Marketing
Kitty Kitty Corporation SRD (Southern Record Distribution)
Kitty Yo Cargo Records Distribution (UK) Ltd, SRD (Southern Record Distribution)
K&K Jet Star Phonographics
KK Traxx Cargo Records Distribution (UK) Ltd
Kleptomania Cargo Records Distribution (UK) Ltd
Knite Force Universal Music Operations
Knitebreed Universal Music Operations
Knitting Factory New Note Distribution Ltd, Pinnacle Records
Knock On Wood Discovery Records
Knock Out Cargo Records Distribution (UK) Ltd
Knoy Cargo Records Distribution (UK) Ltd
Koala Pinnacle Records
Kollaps Cargo Records Distribution (UK) Ltd
Kompakt SRD (Southern Record Distribution)
Konkurrent SRD (Southern Record Distribution)
Konter Pinnacle Records
Kooky Cargo Records Distribution (UK) Ltd
Koolworld Vital Sales & Marketing
Korova TEN (The Entertainment Network)
Koyote Pinnacle Records
Krazy Kat Hot Shot Records, Jazz Music
KRL Gordon Duncan Distributions, Ross Record Distribution, Vital Sales & Marketing
Krunch SRD (Southern Record Distribution)
Krunchie Pinnacle Records
Krush Grooves SRD (Southern Record Distribution)
K7 Vital Sales & Marketing
Kudos Pinnacle Records
Kufe Jet Star Phonographics
Kuff EMI Distribution
Kuku Pinnacle Records
Kultbox Cargo Records Distribution (UK) Ltd
Kung Fu Pinnacle Records
Kurbel SRD (Southern Record Distribution)

Kus SRD (Southern Record Distribution)
KWR Arvato Entertainment Services, Essential Direct Ltd
KYO Shellshock Distribution
La La The Woods
La La Land Vital Sales & Marketing
La Lichere Discovery Records
Label Bleu New Note Distribution Ltd, Pinnacle Records
Label X Hot Records
Labyrinth Vital Sales & Marketing
Lacerated Baked Goods Distribution
Lacerba TEN (The Entertainment Network)
LaFace Arvato Entertainment Services
Lagoon Jet Star Phonographics
Lake Delta Music PLC
Lammas Music New Note Distribution Ltd
Lance Rock Cargo Records Distribution (UK) Ltd
Land Speed Cargo Records Distribution (UK) Ltd
Language Vital Sales & Marketing
Lapwing CM Distribution
Large Club Amato Distribution
Laserlight Arvato Entertainment Services, Delta Music PLC
Laserlight Celtic Arvato Entertainment Services
Last Call Proper Music Distribution Ltd
Last Days Hot Shot Records
Last Visible Dog Forte Music Distribution Ltd
Latent Talent Proper Music Distribution Ltd
L'Attitude Vital Sales & Marketing
Laughing Outlaw Records (UK) Shellshock Distribution
Laughing Stock Vital Sales & Marketing
Lava. SRD (Southern Record Distribution)
LD Vital Sales & Marketing
Le Chant Du Monde Harmonia Mundi (UK) Ltd
Le Club Du Disque Arabe Harmonia Mundi (UK) Ltd
Le Village Vert Pinnacle Records
LEA Timewarp Distribution
Leader CM Distribution
Leadhead Active Media Distribution Ltd
Leadmill Vital Sales & Marketing
Left Hand Pinnacle Records
Leo Pendle Hawk Music
Liberation Cargo Records Distribution (UK) Ltd
Liberation Records Plastic Head Music Distribution Ltd
Lidocaine Pinnacle Records
Lifelike Baked Goods Distribution
Liftin' Spirit SRD (Southern Record Distribution)
Light In The Attic Timewarp Distribution
Light Town Cargo Records Distribution (UK) Ltd
Lightning Rock SRD (Southern Record Distribution)
Limbo Pinnacle Records
Lime Street Pinnacle Records
Limetree New Note Distribution Ltd
Linn Records Universal Music Operations
Lino Vinyl Vital Sales & Marketing
Lion & Roots SRD (Southern Record Distribution)
Lion Dub Load Media
Lipstick Pinnacle Records
Liquefaction Cargo Records Distribution (UK) Ltd
Liquid SRD (Southern Record Distribution)
Lissy's Cargo Records Distribution (UK) Ltd
Listenable Records Plastic Head Music Distribution Ltd, Shellshock Distribution
Litte Arthur Jazz Music
Little Boy Lost Universal Music Operations
Little Brother Vital Sales & Marketing
Little Fish Pinnacle Records
Little Teddy Pinnacle Records
Little Tykes Arvato Entertainment Services, Essential Direct Ltd
Live SRD (Southern Record Distribution)
Live & Learn Jet Star Phonographics
Live & Love Jet Star Phonographics

Livid Meercat Vital Sales & Marketing
Living Beat Universal Music Operations
Living Tradition Gordon Duncan Distributions
Lizard Proper Music Distribution Ltd
LKJ Jet Star Phonographics
Lo Fi Hi Baked Goods Distribution
Lo-Five Shellshock Distribution
Lo Recordings SRD (Southern Record Distribution)
Load Forte Music Distribution Ltd
Lobster Records Plastic Head Music Distribution Ltd
Lochshore Proper Music Distribution Ltd
Lock Records Essential Direct Ltd, Unique Distribution
Locust F Minor Ltd
Logic Records Arvato Entertainment Services
Logistic Cargo Records Distribution (UK) Ltd
Londisc Jet Star Phonographics
London Records TEN (The Entertainment Network)
London Dub Plates Arvato Entertainment Services, Essential Direct Ltd
London Ragtime Orchestra Jazz Music
London Somet'ing SRD (Southern Record Distribution)
Long Distance Discovery Records
Long Hair F Minor Ltd
Long Lost Brother Vital Sales & Marketing
Lookout Records Pinnacle Records, Shellshock Distribution
Looney Tunes Plastic Head Music Distribution Ltd
Loose Tie Records Arvato Entertainment Services
Lord Of The Wing Active Media Distribution Ltd
Lost & Found Plastic Head Music Distribution Ltd
Lost Dog Recordings Vital Sales & Marketing
Lost House Pinnacle Records
Lost Vegas Pinnacle Records
Loud Arvato Entertainment Services
Loud & Slow Amato Distribution
Lough Claddagh Records
Louisville Records Shellshock Distribution
Lounge Cargo Records Distribution (UK) Ltd
Love Jet Star Phonographics
Love Train SRD (Southern Record Distribution)
Low Pressings InterGroove Ltd
Lowlands Pinnacle Records
Lowlife Vital Sales & Marketing
Lowri Records RSK Entertainment Ltd
Lowspeak Pinnacle Records
L Plates Load Media
LS Diezel Vital Sales & Marketing
LSD Cargo Records Distribution (UK) Ltd
LSO Live Harmonia Mundi (UK) Ltd
Luaka Bop Stern's Distribution
Lucertola Media SRD (Southern Record Distribution)
Lumberjack Vital Sales & Marketing
Lumenessence Recordings Shellshock Distribution
Lunar Vital Sales & Marketing
Lunatec Pinnacle Records
Lusafrica Discovery Records, New Note Distribution Ltd
Luscious Peach Pinnacle Records
Luv N Haight New Note Distribution Ltd
Lux Nigra Baked Goods Distribution
Lypsoland Jet Star Phonographics
M-Net Magnum Distribution
M People Arvato Entertainment Services
Mac Developments RSK Entertainment Ltd
Macca SRD (Southern Record Distribution)
Macdada Jet Star Phonographics
Macmeannma Gordon Duncan Distributions
Macmillan Pinnacle Records
Mad Pinnacle Records
Mad Cat Vital Sales & Marketing
Mad Dog Unique Distribution
Mad Entropic Pinnacle Records

Mad 4 It Amato Distribution
Mad Mob Cargo Records Distribution (UK) Ltd
Mad Promotions Cargo Records Distribution (UK) Ltd
Made To Measure New Note Distribution Ltd, Pinnacle Records
Madfish Pinnacle Records
Madhouse Nervous Records
Maelstrom Vital Sales & Marketing
Mag Wheel Cargo Records Distribution (UK) Ltd
Magic F Minor Ltd, Jazz Music
Magic Carpet F Minor Ltd
Magic Talent Arvato Entertainment Services
Magnetic Proper Music Distribution Ltd
Magneto Recordings Cargo Records Distribution (UK) Ltd
Magnum Magnum Distribution
Magnum Force Magnum Distribution
Magnum Opus Magnum Distribution
Magpie Hot Shot Records, Jazz Music
Main Squeeze Goya Music Distribution Ltd
Main Street Jet Star Phonographics
Mainframe Universal Music Operations
Mainstreet Jet Star Phonographics
Majestic Reggae Proper Music Distribution Ltd
Major League Productions RSK Entertainment Ltd
Mako Music Pinnacle Records
Malandro Metronome Distribution
Malarky Vital Sales & Marketing
Malawi Universal Music Operations
Mama Pinnacle Records
Mammoth Cargo Records Distribution (UK) Ltd
Man Recordings Shellshock Distribution
Manchester Pinnacle Records
Mandala Harmonia Mundi (UK) Ltd
Manga TEN (The Entertainment Network)
Mangled Kudos Records Ltd
Mango Universal Music Operations
Manifesto Universal Music Operations
Manifesto Records Inc Plastic Head Music Distribution Ltd
Manikin F Minor Ltd
Man's Ruin Cargo Records Distribution (UK) Ltd
Manteca New Note Distribution Ltd
Mantra Vital Sales & Marketing
Mapleshade Vivante Music Ltd
Marble Arch Arvato Entertainment Services
Marble Bar EMI Distribution, Vital Sales & Marketing
Marco Polo Select Music & Video Distribution
Maree Records Copperplate Distribution
Marginal Talent Pinnacle Records
Mariposa CM Distribution
Marlboro Music Arvato Entertainment Services
Marquis Metronome Distribution
Martians Go Home Cargo Records Distribution (UK) Ltd
Mascot Plastic Head Music Distribution Ltd
Mask Vital Sales & Marketing
Mass Of Black Vital Sales & Marketing
Massacre Records Plastic Head Music Distribution Ltd
Massive Pinnacle Records
Massive Music Pinnacle Records
Massman Cargo Records Distribution (UK) Ltd
Master Detective Pinnacle Records
Master Mix New Note Distribution Ltd
Mastercuts Arvato Entertainment Services
MasterTone Multimedia Pinnacle Records
Matchbox Hot Shot Records, Jazz Music
Materiali Sonori Cargo Records Distribution (UK) Ltd
Matrix Amato Distribution
Matsuri Productions SRD (Southern Record Distribution)
Mau Mau Arvato Entertainment Services
Maverick TEN (The Entertainment Network)
Mawson & Wareham CM Distribution

Design, Pressing & Distribution: Distributed Labels

Max Picou Cargo Records Distribution (UK) Ltd
Max.Ernst Shellshock Distribution
Maybe Records Shellshock Distribution
Mayhem Pinnacle Records
Mayker Gordon Duncan Distributions
Mazaruni SRD (Southern Record Distribution)
Mazzo Proper Music Distribution Ltd
MC Proper Music Distribution Ltd
MC Projects Pinnacle Records
MC Records RSK Entertainment Ltd
MCA Universal Music Operations
MCG - Medien Nervous Records
MCG-Medien Nervous Records
McQueen Vital Sales & Marketing
MDG Chandos Records
Me & My Proper Music Distribution Ltd
Me & My Blues Proper Music Distribution Ltd
Mean Vital Sales & Marketing
Meantime New Note Distribution Ltd, Pinnacle Records
Measured Records Ltd. Pinnacle Records
Mecca Pinnacle Records
Med Fly SRD (Southern Record Distribution)
Medcom Universal Music Operations
Media Arvato Entertainment Services
Media Records Ltd Amato Distribution
Medium Pinnacle Records
Medium Cool Vital Sales & Marketing
Medusa TEN (The Entertainment Network)
Mega Universal Music Operations
Megaworld Universal Music Operations
Mei Mei Pinnacle Records
Melange Baked Goods Distribution
Melankolic EMI Distribution
Melljazz The Woods
Mellowvibe Jet Star Phonographics
Melodie Discovery Records, Stern's Distribution
Melt Pinnacle Records
Memoir Arvato Entertainment Services, Delta Music PLC
Memory Man Cargo Records Distribution (UK) Ltd
Memphis Industries Kudos Records Ltd
Menace Pinnacle Records
Menlo Park Cargo Records Distribution (UK) Ltd
Mentiras Amato Distribution
Mephisto Amato Distribution
Merciful Release Vital Sales & Marketing
Merciless Records Plastic Head Music Distribution Ltd
Mercury Universal Music Operations
Merge Amato Distribution
Merrymakers Jazz Music
Mesmer Pinnacle Records
Mess Media Baked Goods Distribution
Metal Blade Pinnacle Records
Metalimbo New Note Distribution Ltd
Metamorphic Vital Sales & Marketing
Metech Recordings Plastic Head Music Distribution Ltd
Meteosound Shellshock Distribution
Metro New Note Distribution Ltd
Metro Independent Arvato Entertainment Services, Essential Direct Ltd
Metrodome Technicolor Distribution Services Ltd
Metronome Metronome Distribution
Metropolis Universal Music Operations
M&F Jet Star Phonographics
Mic Mac Vital Sales & Marketing
Michael Burks Hot Shot Records
Microbe Pinnacle Records
Middle Class Pig Plastic Head Music Distribution Ltd
Middle Earth SRD (Southern Record Distribution)
Midnight Creeper Hot Shot Records

Midnite Jazz Regis Records Ltd
Miguel Cargo Records Distribution (UK) Ltd
Milan Arvato Entertainment Services
Miles Music New Note Distribution Ltd
Milestone New Note Distribution Ltd
Milestones Jazz Music
Militant Funk Pinnacle Records
Milk SRD (Southern Record Distribution)
Mill Gordon Duncan Distributions
Millennium SRD (Southern Record Distribution)
Millennium Classics Arvato Entertainment Services
Millionaire's Bookshelf Pinnacle Records
Milltown Universal Music Operations
Milo Pinnacle Records
Mind Expansion Cargo Records Distribution (UK) Ltd
Mind The Gap SRD (Southern Record Distribution)
Minimal Communication Cargo Records Distribution (UK) Ltd
Ministry Of Sound TEN (The Entertainment Network)
Minor Music Vital Sales & Marketing
Mint SRD (Southern Record Distribution)
Minta Pinnacle Records
Minus Cargo Records Distribution (UK) Ltd, Shellshock Distribution
Mir Cargo Records Distribution (UK) Ltd
Miracle Pinnacle Records
Miramar New Note Distribution Ltd
Misanthropy Vital Sales & Marketing
Missile SRD (Southern Record Distribution)
Mission Control Cargo Records Distribution (UK) Ltd
Mission Hall Cargo Records Distribution (UK) Ltd
Mitek Shellshock Distribution
Mixmag Live! Vital Sales & Marketing
Mixman Pinnacle Records
Mixology Arvato Entertainment Services
MJJ TEN (The Entertainment Network)
MK Ultra Cargo Records Distribution (UK) Ltd
MMP New Note Distribution Ltd
Mo Wax Vital Sales & Marketing
Mob Vital Sales & Marketing
Mobile Fidelity Vivante Music Ltd
Mock Rock Pinnacle Records
Mode Harmonia Mundi (UK) Ltd
Modern Invasion Music & T Shir Plastic Head Music Distribution Ltd
Modern Love Baked Goods Distribution
Mog Cargo Records Distribution (UK) Ltd
Mogul Absolute Marketing & Distribution Ltd., Shellshock Distribution
Mohock Records Media UK Distribution
Moidart Arvato Entertainment Services, Gordon Duncan Distributions
Mokum Universal Music Operations
Mole In The Ground Cargo Records Distribution (UK) Ltd
Moll SRD (Southern Record Distribution)
Moll-Selekta Shellshock Distribution
Moll Seleta SRD (Southern Record Distribution)
Monarch Gordon Duncan Distributions, Proper Music Distribution Ltd
Money Jet Star Phonographics
Mongo Cargo Records Distribution (UK) Ltd
Mono Pinnacle Records
Monolake/Imbalance Computer Shellshock Distribution
Monoplize Universal Music Operations
Mons Pinnacle Records
Montaigne Harmonia Mundi (UK) Ltd
Montana Essential Direct Ltd
Montpellier Jazz Music
Mood Food Cargo Records Distribution (UK) Ltd
Mook Records Shellshock Distribution

Moon Ska Europe Plastic Head Music Distribution Ltd
Moon Wave Jet Star Phonographics
Moonbeam Gordon Duncan Distributions
Mooncrest Records Proper Music Distribution Ltd
Moonshine Cargo Records Distribution (UK) Ltd
Moonska Plastic Head Music Distribution Ltd
Moonwave SRD (Southern Record Distribution)
Morbid Vital Sales & Marketing
More Protein Pinnacle Records
More Rockers Vital Sales & Marketing
Morning Arvato Entertainment Services
Morpheus Vital Sales & Marketing
Mosaic Vivante Music Ltd
Mosaic Movies TEN (The Entertainment Network)
Moshi Moshi SRD (Southern Record Distribution)
Mosquito SRD (Southern Record Distribution)
Most Famous Hits Fat Cat International Ltd
Moteer Baked Goods Distribution
Motel F Minor Ltd
Motel Kings Hot Shot Records
Mother. Universal Music Operations
Mother Stoat Pinnacle Records
Motion Cargo Records Distribution (UK) Ltd
Motor Cargo Records Distribution (UK) Ltd
Motor Music Universal Music Operations
Motorama Pinnacle Records
Motorway Cargo Records Distribution (UK) Ltd
Motown Universal Music Operations
Mount Ararat Jet Star Phonographics
Mouse Universal Music Operations
Mouthpiece Proper Music Distribution Ltd
Movement (Movement London Ltd.) SRD (Southern Record Distribution)
Movieplay Gold Delta Music PLC
Movin' House Essential Direct Ltd
Moving Shadow SRD (Southern Record Distribution)
MPS Universal Music Operations
Mr Bongo Vital Sales & Marketing
Mr Punch Pinnacle Records
MRR&B Hot Shot Records
Mrs Ackroyd Proper Music Distribution Ltd
MTM Music RSK Entertainment Ltd
Mud Cargo Records Distribution (UK) Ltd
Muddy Waters Jazz Music
Muff Ugga Hot Shot Records
Multicultural Media Proper Music Distribution Ltd
Multimedia Cargo Records Distribution (UK) Ltd
Multiplex Pinnacle Records
Multiply TEN (The Entertainment Network)
Multiply White Vital Sales & Marketing
Munich Proper Music Distribution Ltd
Munster Cargo Records Distribution (UK) Ltd, F Minor Ltd, Shellshock Distribution
Murena Records Kudos Records Ltd
Murgatroid Pinnacle Records
Musea Nova Sales and Distribution (UK) Ltd
Mushroom Pinnacle Records
Music Arvato Entertainment Services
Music & Arts Harmonia Mundi (UK) Ltd
Music And Words Discovery Records
Music Avenue Universal Music Operations
Music Base Universal Music Operations
Music Choice New Note Distribution Ltd
Music City Jet Star Phonographics
Music Collection International New Note Distribution Ltd
A Music Company Pinnacle Records
Music For Freaks Pinnacle Records
Music For Nations Pinnacle Records
Music For Pleasure (MFP) EMI Distribution

Music From Another Room Pinnacle Records
Music Fusion Pinnacle Records
Music Lab Jet Star Phonographics
Music Man Arvato Entertainment Services
Music Maniac Cargo Records Distribution (UK) Ltd
Music Mecca Jazz Music
Music Mountain Jet Star Phonographics
Music Of The World Arvato Entertainment Services
Music Unites Pinnacle Records
Music Vision Active Media Distribution Ltd
Musica Latina Arvato Entertainment Services, Delta Music PLC
Musica Omnia Metronome Distribution
Musicbase Pinnacle Records
Musicsysytem Baked Goods Distribution
Musidisc Universal Music Operations
Musik'Image Music Library Media UK Distribution
Mutant Sound System Cargo Records Distribution (UK) Ltd
Mutt Records RSK Entertainment Ltd
Muzik Release Arvato Entertainment Services, Essential Direct Ltd
Muzikzone Records Rare Beatz Distribution
Muzique Tropique Vital Sales & Marketing
MVG Cargo Records Distribution (UK) Ltd
MVP Pinnacle Records
My Own Planet Pinnacle Records
Mystic Pinnacle Records
Mystic Man Jet Star Phonographics
Mystic Productions Plastic Head Music Distribution Ltd
Mysty Lane F Minor Ltd
N-Coded New Note Distribution Ltd
Nail Vital Sales & Marketing
Naim Audio RSK Entertainment Ltd
Naive Cargo Records Distribution (UK) Ltd
Naked Arvato Entertainment Services, Essential Direct Ltd
Napalm Records Plastic Head Music Distribution Ltd, Shellshock Distribution
Narada EMI Distribution
Narcotix Lounge SRD (Southern Record Distribution)
Natasha Imports Jazz Music
Nation Vital Sales & Marketing
Natural History Museum Pinnacle Records
Navras New Note Distribution Ltd, Pinnacle Records
Navras Records New Note Distribution Ltd
Naxos Select Music & Video Distribution
Naxos AudioBooks Select Music & Video Distribution
Naxos Historical Select Music & Video Distribution
Naxos Jazz Select Music & Video Distribution
Naxos Nostalgia Select Music & Video Distribution
Naxos World Select Music & Video Distribution
NC Jet Star Phonographics
Nebula Music Amato Distribution
Necropolis Plastic Head Music Distribution Ltd
Necropolis - Trade Plastic Head Music Distribution Ltd
Necropolis Records Plastic Head Music Distribution Ltd
Necrosis Vital Sales & Marketing
Nectah Vital Sales & Marketing
Needlework SRD (Southern Record Distribution)
Needs Timewarp Distribution
Negative Progression Cargo Records Distribution (UK) Ltd
Negus Nagast SRD (Southern Record Distribution)
Nemesis Load Media
Neo Ouija Baked Goods Distribution
Neon Records Proper Music Distribution Ltd
Neoteric Arvato Entertainment Services
Nepenta Pinnacle Records
Nervous Nervous Records
Nettwerk Pinnacle Records
Network Harmonia Mundi (UK) Ltd, Sound And Media Ltd
The Network Arvato Entertainment Services

Neurot Plastic Head Music Distribution Ltd
New Albion Harmonia Mundi (UK) Ltd
New Beats Pinnacle Records
New Blue Hot Shot Records
New Classical Metronome Distribution
A New Day Proper Music Distribution Ltd
New Earth ARC Music Distribution UK Ltd
New Electronica Arvato Entertainment Services
New Emissions Vital Sales & Marketing
New Identity SRD (Southern Record Distribution)
New Millenium Pinnacle Records
New Moon Hot Shot Records
New Note Pinnacle Records
New Red Archives Plastic Head Music Distribution Ltd
New World Music Harmonia Mundi (UK) Ltd
Next Century SRD (Southern Record Distribution)
Next Music Stern's Distribution
Next Plateau Pinnacle Records
Next Step SRD (Southern Record Distribution)
Nexus Vital Sales & Marketing
Ngovart Stern's Distribution
Nice Vital Sales & Marketing
Niche Amato Distribution
Nickel & Dime Cargo Records Distribution (UK) Ltd
Nif Nuff The Woods
Night & Day Discovery Records
Nightbreed Plastic Head Music Distribution Ltd
Nightingale RSK Entertainment Ltd
Nightvision Vital Sales & Marketing
Nil By Mouth Pinnacle Records
9 AM Arvato Entertainment Services, Essential Direct Ltd
Ninebar SRD (Southern Record Distribution)
99 North Essential Direct Ltd
Ninety Six Backs Distribution
99 Degrees Essential Direct Ltd
Ninja Toolz Vital Sales & Marketing
Ninja Tune Vital Sales & Marketing
Nitedance Arvato Entertainment Services, Essential Direct Ltd
Nitro Pinnacle Records
NMC RSK Entertainment Ltd
NMG/Pavement Music Plastic Head Music Distribution Ltd
No Bones Pinnacle Records
No Choice Jet Star Phonographics
No Dancing Records Shellshock Distribution
No Fashion Cargo Records Distribution (UK) Ltd
No Idea Plastic Head Music Distribution Ltd
No Interference Pinnacle Records
No Label Cargo Records Distribution (UK) Ltd
No Master's Cooperative Proper Music Distribution Ltd
No More Heroes Plastic Head Music Distribution Ltd
No U Turn SRD (Southern Record Distribution)
Nocturnal Cargo Records Distribution (UK) Ltd
Nocturnal Art Manufacturing Plastic Head Music Distribution Ltd
Nocturnal Art Productions Plastic Head Music Distribution Ltd
Nocturnal Groove Amato Distribution
Nocturne Discovery Records
Noid Recordings Kudos Records Ltd
Noise Factory Vital Sales & Marketing
Noise Museum Vital Sales & Marketing
The Nominal Recording Company Vital Sales & Marketing
Nonesuch Records UK TEN (The Entertainment Network)
Nonplace Shellshock Distribution
Nons Pinnacle Records
Noodles SRD (Southern Record Distribution)
Normal Proper Music Distribution Ltd, Shellshock Distribution
North East West Jet Star Phonographics
North Pole Sound Lab Pinnacle Records

North South Pinnacle Records
Northern Heights Cargo Records Distribution (UK) Ltd
Northern Sky Proper Music Distribution Ltd
Northwest 10 Vital Sales & Marketing
Northwestside Arvato Entertainment Services
Norton F Minor Ltd
Not Lame Cargo Records Distribution (UK) Ltd
Not Now Music Fat Cat International Ltd
Note Music The Woods
Nova Pinnacle Records
Nova Mute Vital Sales & Marketing
Nova Tekk Pinnacle Records
Nova Zembla Cargo Records Distribution (UK) Ltd
Now Absolute Marketing & Distribution Ltd., Pinnacle Records
NOW Music Pinnacle Records
NRK Vital Sales & Marketing
NRK Sound Division Vital Sales & Marketing
NSM Records Plastic Head Music Distribution Ltd
Ntone Vital Sales & Marketing
Nu Direction Load Media
Nu Image TEN (The Entertainment Network)
Nu Recordings SRD (Southern Record Distribution)
Nuba Discovery Records
Nubian Vital Sales & Marketing
NuCamp Vital Sales & Marketing
Nuclear Blast Pinnacle Records
Nucool New Note Distribution Ltd
Nuenergy SRD (Southern Record Distribution)
Nukleuz Amato Distribution
Nuova Era Metronome Distribution
Nuphonic Vital Sales & Marketing
NV Records Hot Shot Records
NVQ Jet Star Phonographics
NYC New Note Distribution Ltd, Pinnacle Records
NYC Records New Note Distribution Ltd
Obliqsound Timewarp Distribution
Oblong Records InterGroove Ltd
Obscene Load Media
Observer SRD (Southern Record Distribution)
Obzaki Arvato Entertainment Services, Essential Direct Ltd
Oceandeep Universal Music Operations
Ocho New Note Distribution Ltd
Ocora Harmonia Mundi (UK) Ltd
Octagon Amato Distribution
Octopus Pinnacle Records
Odeon SRD (Southern Record Distribution)
Odyssey TEN (The Entertainment Network)
Off Beat Gordon Duncan Distributions, Pinnacle Records
Off The Wall SRD (Southern Record Distribution)
Offtime Cargo Records Distribution (UK) Ltd
Offyerface Backs Distribution
Oggum Cargo Records Distribution (UK) Ltd
Ogun Jazz Music
Oh Boy Proper Music Distribution Ltd
Ohn.Cet Pinnacle Records
Old Bean Jazz Music
Old Bridge Claddagh Records, Pendle Hawk Music, Proper Music Distribution Ltd
Old Eagle Vital Sales & Marketing
Old Hat Forte Music Distribution Ltd
Old Tramp Hot Shot Records
Oldie Blues Proper Music Distribution Ltd
Om Pinnacle Records
On Delancey Street Vital Sales & Marketing
On Line Pinnacle Records
On The Air Arvato Entertainment Services
On-U Sound SRD (Southern Record Distribution)
One Big Cowboy Pinnacle Records
One Fifteen Arvato Entertainment Services

One Foot Plastic Head Music Distribution Ltd
100 Guitar Mania Cargo Records Distribution (UK) Ltd
One Louder Pinnacle Records
One Step Pinnacle Records
One Stop RSK Entertainment Ltd
One To One Arvato Entertainment Services, Essential Direct Ltd
One Way F Minor Ltd
Onedaysaviour Recordings Shellshock Distribution
1+2 Cargo Records Distribution (UK) Ltd
Ongaku Metronome Distribution
Onwards Jet Star Phonographics
Ooh Amato Distribution
Opaque Pinnacle Records
Opaz Pinnacle Records
Opera House Jet Star Phonographics
Opera Rara Select Music & Video Distribution
Opus III Select Music & Video Distribution
Opus Kura Metronome Distribution
Opus 3 Harmonia Mundi (UK) Ltd, Jazz Music, Proper Music Distribution Ltd, Vivante Music Ltd
Orange Egg Pinnacle Records
Orange Street Excel Marketing Services Ltd, Proper Music Distribution Ltd
Orange Tree Arvato Entertainment Services, Essential Direct Ltd
Orbit Vital Sales & Marketing
Orbiter Pinnacle Records
Ore Vital Sales & Marketing
Orfeo Chandos Records
Organic Vital Sales & Marketing
Organic Music The Woods
Orgasm Cargo Records Distribution (UK) Ltd
Orgone Discovery Records
Orient SRD (Southern Record Distribution)
Origin Music Pinnacle Records
Original Blues Classics Jazz Music
Original Jazz Classics Jazz Music, New Note Distribution Ltd, Pinnacle Records
Ornament (CMA Music Production) Hot Shot Records
Orphange Cargo Records Distribution (UK) Ltd
Orpheus Amato Distribution
Oscar Arvato Entertainment Services
Osiris Pinnacle Records
Osk Arvato Entertainment Services, Essential Direct Ltd
Oska Cargo Records Distribution (UK) Ltd
Osmose Productions Plastic Head Music Distribution Ltd, Shellshock Distribution
Osmosys Proper Music Distribution Ltd, RSK Entertainment Ltd
Ossian Claddagh Records, Proper Music Distribution Ltd
Other Pinnacle Records
Other People's Music Cargo Records Distribution (UK) Ltd
Otherworld Vital Sales & Marketing
Our Time Baked Goods Distribution
Out Of Time Proper Music Distribution Ltd
Outcaste Records Limited Pinnacle Records
Outdigo Records Vital Sales & Marketing
Outer Music Pinnacle Records
Outlaw Arvato Entertainment Services, Essential Direct Ltd
Outlet Records Ltd Proper Music Distribution Ltd
Outlet Gordon Duncan Distributions
Outpost Arvato Entertainment Services
Output SRD (Southern Record Distribution)
Outsider Load Media
Outstanding Records Proper Music Distribution Ltd
Overcoat Forte Music Distribution Ltd
Overground Pinnacle Records
Ovni Pinnacle Records
Own Pinnacle Records
Oxingale Metronome Distribution

Oxygen Music Works Pinnacle Records
Ozit Cargo Records Distribution (UK) Ltd
Pablo Jazz Music, New Note Distribution Ltd
Pacific Jazz EMI Distribution
Pagan Universal Music Operations, Vital Sales & Marketing
Pagoda Universal Music Operations
Palm Pictures TEN (The Entertainment Network)
Pan Vital Sales & Marketing
Panama Music (Library) Media UK Distribution
Pandemonium Pinnacle Records
Panic Cargo Records Distribution (UK) Ltd
Panorama Pinnacle Records
Panther International Amato Distribution
Paper Vital Sales & Marketing
Paperbag Records Shellshock Distribution
PAR Jazz Music
Parachute Music Pinnacle Records
Parade Cargo Records Distribution (UK) Ltd
Paradox Vital Sales & Marketing
Parasol Cargo Records Distribution (UK) Ltd
Park Pinnacle Records
Parlophone EMI Distribution
Parlophone Rhythm Series EMI Distribution
Parnassus Pinnacle Records, Regis Records Ltd
Parousia Arvato Entertainment Services, Pinnacle Records
Parrot Jazz Music
Part Nervous Records
Partisan Pinnacle Records
Pasadena Records New Note Distribution Ltd
Passenger Pinnacle Records
Passion Jazz TEN (The Entertainment Network)
Past & Present F Minor Ltd
Past Perfect Swift Record Distributors
Pati Pami Avid Entertainment
Pattern 25 Forte Music Distribution Ltd
Pause'n'break Records Rare Beatz Distribution
Pavement Music Plastic Head Music Distribution Ltd
Pavilion Pinnacle Records
PCP Vital Sales & Marketing
Peace Feast Kudos Records Ltd, Vital Sales & Marketing
Peace Frog Vital Sales & Marketing
Peace Not War Shellshock Distribution
Peacemaker Jet Star Phonographics
Peaceman Pinnacle Records
Peaceville Pinnacle Records
Peach Pinnacle Records
Peak New Note Distribution Ltd
Michael Peavy Music Hot Shot Records
Pebble Beach Nova Sales and Distribution (UK) Ltd
Pee Wee Pinnacle Records
Peek A Boo Cargo Records Distribution (UK) Ltd
Peerless Hot Shot Records
PEK Jazz Music
Pelican Vital Sales & Marketing
Penalty Recordings Pinnacle Records
Pendulum Hot Shot Records
Penetration Load Media
Peng Timewarp Distribution
Penguin Pinnacle Records
Penny Black Pinnacle Records, ST Holdings Ltd
Penthouse Jet Star Phonographics
People Goya Music Distribution Ltd
People Of Rhythm Cargo Records Distribution (UK) Ltd
Pepper Pinnacle Records
Perceptive Universal Music Operations
Perfect Toy Timewarp Distribution
Perishable Cargo Records Distribution (UK) Ltd
Persevere Records RSK Entertainment Ltd
Perspective Universal Music Operations

Pessimiser Cargo Records Distribution (UK) Ltd
Pet Sounds Pinnacle Records
Phantom Hot Records
Phantom Audio Load Media
Pharm Pinnacle Records
Pharma SRD (Southern Record Distribution)
Phase 4 Cargo Records Distribution (UK) Ltd
Pheroes Entertainment Arvato Entertainment Services, Essential Direct Ltd
Philips Universal Music Operations
Philips Classics Universal Music Operations
Philly Blunt SRD (Southern Record Distribution)
Philo Proper Music Distribution Ltd
Phoenix Universal Music Operations
Phonographe Metronome Distribution
Phonography Vital Sales & Marketing
Phonokol Pinnacle Records
Phontastic Jazz Music
Phuzion Load Media
Phuzz Amato Distribution
Piano Pinnacle Records
Piao! SRD (Southern Record Distribution)
Pick Your Own Proper Music Distribution Ltd
Pickninny Cargo Records Distribution (UK) Ltd
Pickout Jet Star Phonographics
Pickwick Pickwick Group Ltd
Picnic Shellshock Distribution
Pied Piper Amato Distribution
Pier Proper Music Distribution Ltd
Pig's Whiskers Proper Music Distribution Ltd
Piknmix SRD (Southern Record Distribution)
Pimp SRD (Southern Record Distribution)
Pin Up Vital Sales & Marketing
Pinhead Pinnacle Records
Pinkerton Vital Sales & Marketing
Pinkpenny Records Unique Distribution
Pipe Active Media Distribution Ltd
Piperman Jet Star Phonographics
Piranha New Note Distribution Ltd, Stern's Distribution
Pivotal ST Holdings Ltd
Placid Casual Pinnacle Records, Sain (Recordiau) Cyf
Plain F Minor Ltd
Planet Dog Pinnacle Records, Vital Sales & Marketing
Planet Nice Pinnacle Records
Planet Of Drums SRD (Southern Record Distribution)
Planet Records Pendle Hawk Music
Planet 3 Pinnacle Records
Planet U Vital Sales & Marketing
Planetary Consciousness InterGroove Ltd
Plantagenet Harmonia Mundi (UK) Ltd
Plastic Pinnacle Records
Plastica InterGroove Ltd
Plastica Red InterGroove Ltd
Plastique Pinnacle Records
Play Avid Entertainment
Play It Again Sam Vital Sales & Marketing
Playasound Harmonia Mundi (UK) Ltd
Playback Pinnacle Records
Playtime Pinnacle Records
Pleasure Pinnacle Records
Pleasuredome Vital Sales & Marketing
PLR Pinnacle Records
Plum Projects Pinnacle Records
PMM Vital Sales & Marketing
A PMS Plan Soul Trader
Pohjola Proper Music Distribution Ltd
Point Entertaiinment Cargo Records Distribution (UK) Ltd
Point Music Universal Music Operations
Pointblank EMI Distribution

Pointy Records Pinnacle Records, Shellshock Distribution
Polestar Cargo Records Distribution (UK) Ltd
Polydor Records Universal Music Operations
Polyester Amato Distribution
PolyGram Brazil Stern's Distribution
Polygram (Norway) Rolica Music Distribution
Polyvinyl Forte Music Distribution Ltd
Pomme Discovery Records
Pony Vital Sales & Marketing
Pony Canyon Cargo Records Distribution (UK) Ltd
Pop Fiction Shellshock Distribution
Pop God Vital Sales & Marketing
Pop Llama Vital Sales & Marketing
Popmafia Cargo Records Distribution (UK) Ltd
Poppy Pinnacle Records
Poptones Vital Sales & Marketing
Populuxe Pinnacle Records
Pork Kudos Records Ltd, Pinnacle Records
Pork Pie Plastic Head Music Distribution Ltd
Position Chrome SRD (Southern Record Distribution)
Positiva EMI Distribution
Possessed Nova Sales and Distribution (UK) Ltd
Postar Cargo Records Distribution (UK) Ltd
Postcard Vital Sales & Marketing
Potlatch Harmonia Mundi (UK) Ltd
Pow! Pinnacle Records
Power Bros Harmonia Mundi (UK) Ltd
Powerage Plastic Head Music Distribution Ltd
Powerhouse New Note Distribution Ltd
Powertool Pinnacle Records
Praga Harmonia Mundi (UK) Ltd
Prague Jazz The Woods
Prank Cargo Records Distribution (UK) Ltd
Prawn Song Vital Sales & Marketing
Preamble Hot Records
Precious Organisation Universal Music Operations
Precision SRD (Southern Record Distribution)
Preiser Harmonia Mundi (UK) Ltd
Premier Soundtracks EMI Distribution
Preponderance SRD (Southern Record Distribution)
Pressure Sounds Empathy Records
Prestige Jazz Music, New Note Distribution Ltd, Nova Sales and Distribution (UK) Ltd, THE (Total Home Entertainment)
Prestige Elite Pinnacle Records
Pricepoint Proper Music Distribution Ltd
Prima Proper Music Distribution Ltd
Primavera Pinnacle Records
Primrose Discovery Records
Prince Buster Jet Star Phonographics
Priority EMI Distribution
Prism Leisure Prism Leisure Corporation plc
Prism Leisure Classics Prism Leisure Corporation plc
Pro-Activ Arvato Entertainment Services
Pro-Jex Pinnacle Records
Pro Logic Arvato Entertainment Services
Profile Pinnacle Records
Progression SRD (Southern Record Distribution)
Progressive Jazz Music, The Woods
Progressive Form Baked Goods Distribution
Prohibited Records Shellshock Distribution
Prohibition Pinnacle Records
Project SRD (Southern Record Distribution)
Project Blowed Cargo Records Distribution (UK) Ltd
Prolekult Vital Sales & Marketing
Promo SRD (Southern Record Distribution)
Promo Sonor International Music Library Media UK Distribution
Pronoia Nova Sales and Distribution (UK) Ltd
Proper Records Proper Music Distribution Ltd

Proper Talent Vital Sales & Marketing
Prophecy Productions Shellshock Distribution
Proprius Jazz Music
Protected Pinnacle Records
Prototype Harmonia Mundi (UK) Ltd
Protractor Vital Sales & Marketing
Proud Cargo Records Distribution (UK) Ltd
Provogue Pinnacle Records
Pseudonym F Minor Ltd
PSF Harmonia Mundi (UK) Ltd
Psi Fi F Minor Ltd
PSI Music Library Media UK Distribution
PSI Piano Bar Library Media UK Distribution
Psychic Vital Sales & Marketing
Psychomat SRD (Southern Record Distribution)
Psychonavigation Baked Goods Distribution
Pub Rock Pendle Hawk Music
Public Domain Backs Distribution
Puck Active Media Distribution Ltd
Puff Daddy Arvato Entertainment Services
Puffin Audio Pinnacle Records
Pugwash Proper Music Distribution Ltd
Pulsar Magnum Distribution
Pulse-8 Pinnacle Records
Pulver Timewarp Distribution
Pulverised Vital Sales & Marketing
Pump Pinnacle Records
Punch SRD (Southern Record Distribution)
Punisher Universal Music Operations
Punt Rock SRD (Southern Record Distribution)
P.U.P Metal Mind Productions Plastic Head Music
Distribution Ltd
Pure Amato Distribution
Pure Gold Records Media UK Distribution
Pure Plastic Cargo Records Distribution (UK) Ltd
Pure Silk Absolute Marketing & Distribution Ltd., Pinnacle
Records
Purple Pinnacle Records
Purpose Maker Cargo Records Distribution (UK) Ltd
Purr Records Shellshock Distribution
Push SRD (Southern Record Distribution)
Pussyfoot SRD (Southern Record Distribution)
Putamayo Universal Music Operations
Putumayo World Music New Note Distribution Ltd, Pinnacle
Records, Universal Music Operations
PVC Vital Sales & Marketing
PWL TEN (The Entertainment Network)
Pylon Baked Goods Distribution
Pyssy Soul Trader
QDK Media Proper Music Distribution Ltd
Quaint Proper Music Distribution Ltd
Quality Control Amato Distribution
Quality Umlaut SRD (Southern Record Distribution)
Quality Words Pinnacle Records
Quango Universal Music Operations
Quark Vital Sales & Marketing
Quartz Jet Star Phonographics, One Nation Exports
Quatermass Shellshock Distribution
Queen Arvato Entertainment Services, Essential Direct Ltd
Queen Bee Brand Hot Shot Records
Quench Arvato Entertainment Services, Essential Direct Ltd
Quiet Riot GR London Ltd
Quinlan Road Claddagh Records, Proper Music Distribution Ltd
Quixotic Records Active Media Distribution Ltd
Raceway Pinnacle Records
Radarscope Pinnacle Records
Radial Vital Sales & Marketing
Radiate Pinnacle Records
Radical Plastic Head Music Distribution Ltd

Radical Ambient Cargo Records Distribution (UK) Ltd
Radikal Fear Vital Sales & Marketing
Radio Blast Cargo Records Distribution (UK) Ltd
Radio France Harmonia Mundi (UK) Ltd
Radiotone Cargo Records Distribution (UK) Ltd
Radius SRD (Southern Record Distribution)
RAFR Cargo Records Distribution (UK) Ltd
Rafting Dog Proper Music Distribution Ltd
Rage Nervous Records, Pinnacle Records
Rage of Achilles Shellshock Distribution
Raging Bull Arvato Entertainment Services
Raid Pinnacle Records
Railway Records New Note Distribution Ltd
Rainlight Proper Music Distribution Ltd
Rainy Day Records Media UK Distribution
randan Pinnacle Records
Random Load Media
Random House Pinnacle Records
Randy's Pinnacle Records
Rapido Cargo Records Distribution (UK) Ltd
Raputation Pinnacle Records
Rare SRD (Southern Record Distribution)
RAS Proper Music Distribution Ltd
Rashaan Arvato Entertainment Services, Essential Direct Ltd
Rat Records SRD (Southern Record Distribution)
Ratio ST Holdings Ltd
Raucous Nervous Records
Raven Cargo Records Distribution (UK) Ltd, Proper Music
Distribution Ltd
Raw Elements SRD (Southern Record Distribution)
Raw Power Pinnacle Records
Raw Talent Jet Star Phonographics
Rawkus Entertainment Pinnacle Records
Rayman Recordings Cargo Records Distribution (UK) Ltd
RB Music Jet Star Phonographics
RBN Recordings Plastic Head Music Distribution Ltd
RCA Classics Arvato Entertainment Services
RCA International Series Arvato Entertainment Services
RCA Label Group Arvato Entertainment Services
RCA Victor Arvato Entertainment Services
RCA Victor Gold Seal Arvato Entertainment Services
RCR Pinnacle Records
R&D Vital Sales & Marketing
Reach Out International Pinnacle Records
React Vital Sales & Marketing
Reactor Vital Sales & Marketing
Readers Digest Talking Books Ltd
Real Authentic Sound Proper Music Distribution Ltd
Real Life RSK Entertainment Ltd
Real Music Universal Music Operations
Real World EMI Distribution
Really Useful Universal Music Operations
Realsound Metronome Distribution
Realty Jazz Music
Rebel Proper Music Distribution Ltd
Rebound Load Media
Rec 90 Absolute Marketing & Distribution Ltd., Shellshock
Distribution
Recall 2CD Pinnacle Records
Receiver Records Proper Music Distribution Ltd
Reception Vital Sales & Marketing
Rec90 Cargo Records Distribution (UK) Ltd
Recognition Universal Music Operations
Recon Pinnacle Records
Record Factory Jet Star Phonographics
The Record Label Pinnacle Records
Recordhead Pinnacle Records
Recordings Of Substance Pinnacle Records
Recycle Or Die Vital Sales & Marketing

Red Balloon RSK Entertainment Ltd
Red Bullet F Minor Ltd
Red Dot Pinnacle Records
Red Egyptian Jazz Timewarp Distribution
Red House RSK Entertainment Ltd
Red Ink Pinnacle Records
Red Light Vital Sales & Marketing
Red Lightnin' Hot Shot Records, Magnum Distribution, Swift Record Distributors
Red 'n Raw Unique Distribution
Red Pajamas Proper Music Distribution Ltd
Red Parrot Amato Distribution
Red Rose Vivante Music Ltd
Red Sky Records Proper Music Distribution Ltd
Red Square Arvato Entertainment Services, Essential Direct Ltd
Red Steel Pinnacle Records, RSK Entertainment Ltd
Red Telephone Box Vital Sales & Marketing
Red Weed SRD (Southern Record Distribution)
Redcliffe Pinnacle Records
Redhouse Absolute Marketing & Distribution Ltd.
Redial Universal Music Operations
Redwing Proper Music Distribution Ltd
Reekie Gordon Duncan Distributions
Reel Music Vital Sales & Marketing
Reference Jazz Music, Vivante Music Ltd
Refined The Woods
Reflections Plastic Head Music Distribution Ltd, Shellshock Distribution
Regal Vital Sales & Marketing
Regency Sound Proper Music Distribution Ltd
Reggae On Top SRD (Southern Record Distribution)
Reggae Retro SRD (Southern Record Distribution)
Regis Regis Records Ltd
Rehab SRD (Southern Record Distribution)
Reinforced Load Media
Rejected Cargo Records Distribution (UK) Ltd, Plastic Head Music Distribution Ltd
Rekids Ltd Amato Distribution
REL Gordon Duncan Distributions, Proper Music Distribution Ltd
Relapse Pinnacle Records
Relapse Records Plastic Head Music Distribution Ltd
Related Recordings Pinnacle Records
Relativity Cargo Records Distribution (UK) Ltd, TEN (The Entertainment Network)
Relaxation Co Stern's Distribution
Remedy Pinnacle Records
Renaissance TEN (The Entertainment Network)
Renaissance Music Amato Distribution
Renascent Shellshock Distribution, Vital Sales & Marketing
Renegade Hardware SRD (Southern Record Distribution)
Renegade Recordings SRD (Southern Record Distribution)
Renella Records The Woods
Repap Vital Sales & Marketing
R*E*P*E*A*T Records Shellshock Distribution
Repellent Vital Sales & Marketing
Repertoire RSK Entertainment Ltd
Rephlex SRD (Southern Record Distribution), Vital Sales & Marketing
Replay Music Cargo Records Distribution (UK) Ltd
Replicant Universal Music Operations
Reprise TEN (The Entertainment Network)
ReR Vital Sales & Marketing
ReR Megacorp Shellshock Distribution
Reservoir Pinnacle Records
Resolve Vital Sales & Marketing
Resource Pinnacle Records
Response Pinnacle Records
Restless Vital Sales & Marketing
Resurgence Pinnacle Records

Resurrection Records Plastic Head Music Distribution Ltd
Retrieval Proper Music Distribution Ltd
Retro Afric Stern's Distribution
Retrograde Hot Records
Retrowrek Proper Music Distribution Ltd
Return To Sender Proper Music Distribution Ltd
Return To The Source Changing World Distribution
Rev-Ola Pinnacle Records
Reveal Records Vital Sales & Marketing
Revelation Plastic Head Music Distribution Ltd
Revenant Cargo Records Distribution (UK) Ltd
Reverb Records Ltd Pinnacle Records
Revolution Arvato Entertainment Services
Rewika Shellshock Distribution
RGF Proper Music Distribution Ltd
RH Records Pinnacle Records
Rhiannon Records Proper Music Distribution Ltd
Rhythm & Freakquencies Vital Sales & Marketing
Rhythm Division Arvato Entertainment Services, Essential Direct Ltd
Rhythm King Arvato Entertainment Services
Rhythm of Life Inc Shellshock Distribution
Rhythm Robbers Amato Distribution
Rhythm Syndicate Amato Distribution
Rhythm Vicar Plastic Head Music Distribution Ltd
Rialto Proper Music Distribution Ltd
Ricky-Tick Timewarp Distribution
Riddim SRD (Southern Record Distribution)
Ridge Records Active Media Distribution Ltd
Right Pinnacle Records
Right Now Pinnacle Records
Righteous Arvato Entertainment Services, Vital Sales & Marketing
Righteous Babe RSK Entertainment Ltd
Rinse Out SRD (Southern Record Distribution)
Ripe Recordings Pinnacle Records
Ripe 'n' Ready Jet Star Phonographics
Rise Above Pinnacle Records
Rising Sun Productions Plastic Head Music Distribution Ltd
Rising Tide Arvato Entertainment Services
Ritornell SRD (Southern Record Distribution)
Ritz Gordon Duncan Distributions, Universal Music Operations
River Horse TEN (The Entertainment Network)
Riverboat Records New Note Distribution Ltd
Riverman Records Vital Sales & Marketing
Riverrun Metronome Distribution
Riverside Jazz Music, New Note Distribution Ltd, Nova Sales and Distribution (UK) Ltd
Riverwalk Jazz The Woods
Riviera Arvato Entertainment Services
RMD Nervous Records
Road Cone Cargo Records Distribution (UK) Ltd
Road Goes On Forever Proper Music Distribution Ltd
Road Trip Hot Records
Robert Parker Jazz Classics New Note Distribution Ltd, Pinnacle Records
Robert Parker Metronome Distribution
Robert Parker's Jazz Classics New Note Distribution Ltd
Robinwood Productions The Woods
Robot Pinnacle Records
Robotic Empire Shellshock Distribution
Robs Pinnacle Records
Roc & Presta Recordings Universal Music Operations
Roch Proper Music Distribution Ltd
Rock Action Vital Sales & Marketing
Rock Docs Plastic Head Music Distribution Ltd
Rock Hard Cargo Records Distribution (UK) Ltd
Rockadillo Proper Music Distribution Ltd
Rockers Jet Star Phonographics

Rocket Universal Music Operations
Rocket Girl Cargo Records Distribution (UK) Ltd
Rocket Racer Cargo Records Distribution (UK) Ltd
Rockhouse Nervous Records, RSK Entertainment Ltd
Rockstar Nervous Records
Rockville Gordon Duncan Distributions
Rocky One SRD (Southern Record Distribution)
Roesch Hot Shot Records
Rogue Proper Music Distribution Ltd
R.O.I.R. Inc. Shellshock Distribution
Rolling Acres Vital Sales & Marketing
Rolling Thunder RSK Entertainment Ltd
Rollin'Rock Nervous Records
Ronin Soul Trader
Ronnie Scott's Jazz House Magnum Distribution
rooArt Cargo Records Distribution (UK) Ltd
Rooster Proper Music Distribution Ltd
Ros Dubh Gordon Duncan Distributions
Ross CM Distribution, Gordon Duncan Distributions, Ross Record Distribution
Rotation SRD (Southern Record Distribution)
Rough Guides New Note Distribution Ltd
Rough Trade Records Pinnacle Records
Roulette EMI Distribution
Round SRD (Southern Record Distribution)
Round Tower Arvato Entertainment Services, Avid Entertainment
Rounder Proper Music Distribution Ltd
Roundtrip Jet Star Phonographics
Rowdy Arvato Entertainment Services
Royal Jazz Jazz Music
Royal Mint Vital Sales & Marketing
Royal Palm Kudos Records Ltd, Pinnacle Records
RP Media Nova Sales and Distribution (UK) Ltd
RPM Pinnacle Records
RRE Vital Sales & Marketing
R&S Pinnacle Records
RSR Universal Music Operations
RST Hot Shot Records, Jazz Music
RST (Austria) Hot Shot Records
Rubber Cargo Records Distribution (UK) Ltd
Rubyworks Records Vital Sales & Marketing
Ruf Proper Music Distribution Ltd
Ruf Beat SRD (Southern Record Distribution)
Ruff Beat SRD (Southern Record Distribution)
Ruff Cut Jet Star Phonographics
Ruffhouse TEN (The Entertainment Network)
Rufige Load Media
Rugger Bugger Pinnacle Records
Rum Baked Goods Distribution
Rumble Cargo Records Distribution (UK) Ltd, Nervous Records
Rumblestrip Pinnacle Records
Rumour Records Ltd Pinnacle Records
Runegrammofon New Note Distribution Ltd
Runn Jet Star Phonographics
Runnetherlands Jet Star Phonographics
Runningz SRD (Southern Record Distribution)
Runt Cargo Records Distribution (UK) Ltd
Rupie Jet Star Phonographics
Russian Season Harmonia Mundi (UK) Ltd
Rutland Pinnacle Records
Rykodisc Pinnacle Records
S Records Amato Distribution
Sabotage SRD (Southern Record Distribution)
Sackville Jazz Music
Sacred Vital Sales & Marketing
Safe House Plastic Head Music Distribution Ltd
Saigon SRD (Southern Record Distribution)
Sain Sain (Recordiau) Cyf

Sakay Proper Music Distribution Ltd
Saludos Amigos Delta Music PLC
Sandman Cargo Records Distribution (UK) Ltd
Sandy Pinnacle Records
Sano Pinnacle Records
Sapphire Vital Sales & Marketing
Sarge Jet Star Phonographics
Saskris Avid Entertainment
Satellite City Pinnacle Records
Satis Jet Star Phonographics
Satisfaction SRD (Southern Record Distribution)
Sativae SRD (Southern Record Distribution)
Sativa Recordings Load Media
Satori Vital Sales & Marketing
Satril Pinnacle Records
Satyricon Vital Sales & Marketing
Savage Bee Cargo Records Distribution (UK) Ltd
Savant Proper Music Distribution Ltd
Saxon Jet Star Phonographics
SBK EMI Distribution
Scandinavia SRD (Southern Record Distribution)
Scared Hitless Vital Sales & Marketing
Scared Of Girls Vital Sales & Marketing
Scarlet Pinnacle Records
Scat Pinnacle Records
Scenario Pinnacle Records
Scenescoff F Minor Ltd
Schema Jet Star Phonographics, Timewarp Distribution
Schism Pinnacle Records
Schizophonic Vital Sales & Marketing
Science EMI Distribution
Science Fiction Load Media
Science Friction Pinnacle Records
Scooch Pooch F Minor Ltd, Pinnacle Records
Scorcher SRD (Southern Record Distribution)
Scorchio Amato Distribution
Scorpio Arvato Entertainment Services
Scotdisc Gordon Duncan Distributions, Ross Record Distribution
Scottish Harp Gordon Duncan Distributions
Scratch Cargo Records Distribution (UK) Ltd
Scratchy Pinnacle Records
Screwgun New Note Distribution Ltd, Pinnacle Records
SCSI Av Baked Goods Distribution
Sea Breeze Jazz The Woods
Sea Records Shellshock Distribution
Seal Jet Star Phonographics
Second Battle F Minor Ltd
Second Skin Pinnacle Records
2nd Movement SRD (Southern Record Distribution)
Secret Pinnacle Records
Secret Agent SRD (Southern Record Distribution)
Secret Operations Load Media
Secret Service Pinnacle Records
Secretly Canadian Cargo Records Distribution (UK) Ltd
See For Miles RSK Entertainment Ltd
See Thru Nova Sales and Distribution (UK) Ltd
Seeca Records Cargo Records Distribution (UK) Ltd
Seed Baked Goods Distribution
Seil Gordon Duncan Distributions
Seismic SRD (Southern Record Distribution)
Select Arvato Entertainment Services
Selection Club Cargo Records Distribution (UK) Ltd
Selector Vital Sales & Marketing
Self-Indulgent Music Cargo Records Distribution (UK) Ltd
Sense UK Amato Distribution
Sense World Music Stern's Distribution
Sensor Load Media
Senton Baked Goods Distribution
Sequel Pinnacle Records

Sequential Arvato Entertainment Services, Essential Direct Ltd
Series 500 Vital Sales & Marketing
Serious Vital Sales & Marketing
Seriously Groovy Music Shellshock Distribution
Sessions Cargo Records Distribution (UK) Ltd
720 Degrees Vital Sales & Marketing
Severn Hot Shot Records
SFDB Records Shellshock Distribution
SFRI F Minor Ltd
Shadbury And Duxbury Nova Sales and Distribution (UK) Ltd
Shadow Cargo Records Distribution (UK) Ltd
Shadow Law Load Media
Shady Acorns Pinnacle Records
Shagadelic F Minor Ltd
Shagpile Cargo Records Distribution (UK) Ltd
Shake The Record Label Cargo Records Distribution (UK) Ltd
Shanachie Jet Star Phonographics
Shang Jet Star Phonographics
Shaping The Invisible Proper Music Distribution Ltd
Sharma Productions Jet Star Phonographics
Sharp Vital Sales & Marketing
Sharp End Universal Music Operations
Sharp Nine The Woods
Sharpe Arvato Entertainment Services, Delta Music PLC, Gordon Duncan Distributions
Shatterproof Records Vital Sales & Marketing
She Wolf Pendle Hawk Music
Shedcentral ST Holdings Ltd
Shelflife Essential Direct Ltd
Shell Nova Sales and Distribution (UK) Ltd
Shellshock Pinnacle Records
Shellwood Priory Records Ltd
Shielburn Gordon Duncan Distributions
Shield Vital Sales & Marketing
Shifty Disco Ltd Pinnacle Records
Shimmy Disc Pinnacle Records
Shine Pinnacle Records
Shining Path Vital Sales & Marketing
Shinkansen SRD (Southern Record Distribution)
Shitkatapult Shellshock Distribution
Shiva Nova Nova Sales and Distribution (UK) Ltd
Shiver SRD (Southern Record Distribution)
Shocking Vibes Jet Star Phonographics
Shoebox Pinnacle Records
Shoeshine Pinnacle Records, Proper Music Distribution Ltd
Shongolo Arvato Entertainment Services, Essential Direct Ltd
Shore Jet Star Phonographics
Shot Arvato Entertainment Services, Essential Direct Ltd
Shout Load Media
Shrimper Cargo Records Distribution (UK) Ltd
Shut Up And Dance Vital Sales & Marketing
SI Projects Cargo Records Distribution (UK) Ltd
Siam New Note Distribution Ltd
Side One Dummy Plastic Head Music Distribution Ltd
Siesta Records Pinnacle Records, Shellshock Distribution
Significant Music Pinnacle Records
Siltbreeze Vital Sales & Marketing
Silva Classics Arvato Entertainment Services
Silva CMP RSK Entertainment Ltd
Silva Productions RSK Entertainment Ltd
Silvertone Pinnacle Records
Simax Chandos Records
Simba Pinnacle Records
Simon & Schuster Pinnacle Records
Simpleton Pinnacle Records
Simply Vinyl F Minor Ltd
Sincere Sounds Vital Sales & Marketing
Sing, Eunuchs! Cargo Records Distribution (UK) Ltd
Sing Sing Vital Sales & Marketing

Sioux Pinnacle Records
Sir Peter Jet Star Phonographics
Sire TEN (The Entertainment Network)
Siren Music Zeit Distribution
Sirkus Vital Sales & Marketing
Sirocco Jazz New Note Distribution Ltd, Pinnacle Records
Six & Seven Jet Star Phonographics
60 Degrees North Pinnacle Records
Size 8 Pinnacle Records
SJP Pinnacle Records
Skam SRD (Southern Record Distribution)
Skerries Gordon Duncan Distributions
Skiff-A-Billy Nervous Records
Skingraft Shellshock Distribution
Skinnydog Shellshock Distribution
Skint Pinnacle Records
Skint Under 5s Pinnacle Records
Skratch Music TEN (The Entertainment Network)
Sky Ranch Discovery Records
Skycap Cargo Records Distribution (UK) Ltd
Skyline Vital Sales & Marketing
Skyranch Discovery Records
Skyride Pinnacle Records
Skyway Pinnacle Records
S.L. Records Shellshock Distribution
Slalom SRD (Southern Record Distribution)
SLAM Jazz Music, Pendle Hawk Music
Slam City Jet Star Phonographics
Slamm Vital Sales & Marketing
Slap A Ham Cargo Records Distribution (UK) Ltd
Slappa Pinnacle Records
Slash Universal Music Operations
Sleepin' Corporation Cargo Records Distribution (UK) Ltd
Sleepytown Gordon Duncan Distributions, Ross Record Distribution
Sliced Vital Sales & Marketing
Slick Sluts Arvato Entertainment Services, Essential Direct Ltd
Slider Music The Woods
Slip Discs Proper Music Distribution Ltd
Slip 'N' Slide Vital Sales & Marketing
Slip'd By Arvato Entertainment Services, Essential Direct Ltd
Slow River Vital Sales & Marketing
Slumberland Cargo Records Distribution (UK) Ltd
Slut Trax Vital Sales & Marketing
Small Stone Cargo Records Distribution (UK) Ltd
Small Wonder Pinnacle Records
Smalltown Supersound Cargo Records Distribution (UK) Ltd
Smallworld Proper Music Distribution Ltd
Sm:)e Pinnacle Records
Smells Like Cargo Records Distribution (UK) Ltd
Smiddymade Gordon Duncan Distributions
Smitten SRD (Southern Record Distribution)
Smoke Pinnacle Records
Smokers Inc SRD (Southern Record Distribution)
Smugg Vital Sales & Marketing
Snapper Pinnacle Records
Snatch Backs Distribution
SND / Premium Leisure Baked Goods Distribution
Snowblind SRD (Southern Record Distribution)
Soap Dodja Pinnacle Records
Sockett SRD (Southern Record Distribution)
Sofa Baked Goods Distribution
SoleSides Universal Music Operations
Solid Vital Sales & Marketing
Solistic Discovery Records
Solistitium Records Plastic Head Music Distribution Ltd
Solistium Vital Sales & Marketing
Solo Art Jazz Music, The Woods
Some Bizarre Pinnacle Records

Something Else Pinnacle Records
Son Kudos Records Ltd
Son Of Soundclash Vital Sales & Marketing
Sona Rupa New Note Distribution Ltd
Sonar Kollektiv Timewarp Distribution
Sonic Art Union Pinnacle Records
Sonic Images Cargo Records Distribution (UK) Ltd
Sonic Rendezvous Plastic Head Music Distribution Ltd
Sonic Wave Pinnacle Records
Sonig Shellshock Distribution
Sonix ST Holdings Ltd
Sons of Sound The Woods
Sony BMG Music Entertainment UK & Ireland Arvato Entertainment Services
Sony Brazil Stern's Distribution
Sony Classical TEN (The Entertainment Network)
Sony Computer Entertainment (SCE) TEN (The Entertainment Network)
Sony Jazz TEN (The Entertainment Network)
Sony Music TV TEN (The Entertainment Network)
Sony Music Video (SMV) TEN (The Entertainment Network)
Sony S2 TEN (The Entertainment Network)
Sony South Africa Stern's Distribution
Sony S3 TEN (The Entertainment Network)
Soothsayer Load Media
Sophisticat New Note Distribution Ltd
Sophisticuts Pinnacle Records
Sore Thumb Records Proper Music Distribution Ltd
SOS Plastic Head Music Distribution Ltd
Soul Beat SRD (Southern Record Distribution)
Soul Brother New Note Distribution Ltd, Pinnacle Records
Soul Fire F Minor Ltd
Soul Note Harmonia Mundi (UK) Ltd
Soul On Wax Vital Sales & Marketing
Soul Static Sound SRD (Southern Record Distribution)
Soul Supply Vital Sales & Marketing
Soulciety Pinnacle Records
Soulja Essential Direct Ltd
Sound Box Jet Star Phonographics
Sound Chamber Pinnacle Records
Sound Clash SRD (Southern Record Distribution)
Sound Corporation Amato Distribution
Sound Design Vital Sales & Marketing
Sound Dimension Arvato Entertainment Services
Sound Hills Harmonia Mundi (UK) Ltd
Sound Information Vital Sales & Marketing
Sound Proof Arvato Entertainment Services
Sound Riot Plastic Head Music Distribution Ltd
Soundalive Metronome Distribution
Soundbites Universal Music Operations
Soundboy Vital Sales & Marketing
Soundclash SRD (Southern Record Distribution)
Soundclash. Backs Distribution
Soundfx Pinnacle Records
Soundings Talking Books Ltd
Soundjam Universal Music Operations
Sounds Of The World Arvato Entertainment Services
Soundsational Cargo Records Distribution (UK) Ltd
Soundslike Baked Goods Distribution
Soundwaves Delta Music PLC
Soundway Timewarp Distribution
Source EMI Distribution
Soussol Timewarp Distribution
South Circular Pinnacle Records
South Of Sanity Vital Sales & Marketing
South West F Minor Ltd
Southbound Universal Music Operations
Southern Cross Hot Records
Southland Jazz Music

Southland Records The Woods
Southpaw Recordings Vital Sales & Marketing
Southside Production SRD (Southern Record Distribution)
Sow & Reap Jet Star Phonographics
Space Age Recordings Cargo Records Distribution (UK) Ltd
Spalax Cargo Records Distribution (UK) Ltd, F Minor Ltd
Spank Shellshock Distribution
Spanking Herman Cargo Records Distribution (UK) Ltd
Spa:rk Baked Goods Distribution
Spawn Load Media
Speakers Corner Vinyl Vivante Music Ltd
Special Emissions Vital Sales & Marketing
Special Fried Amato Distribution
Spectrum Universal Music Operations
Spectrum. Kudos Records Ltd
Speedowax Cargo Records Distribution (UK) Ltd
Spezial Material Baked Goods Distribution
Spinart Cargo Records Distribution (UK) Ltd, Plastic Head Music Distribution Ltd
Spindle Jet Star Phonographics
Spindrift Nervous Records
Spinefarm Pinnacle Records, Plastic Head Music Distribution Ltd
Spinning Wheel Cargo Records Distribution (UK) Ltd
Spira SRD (Southern Record Distribution)
Spiral F Minor Ltd
Spiral Grooves Amato Distribution
Spiral Trax Pinnacle Records
Spirit Amato Distribution, Vital Sales & Marketing
Spirit Of Orr Pinnacle Records
Spirit Zone Pinnacle Records
Spit and Polish Records Pinnacle Records, Proper Music Distribution Ltd
Spoilt For Choice Pinnacle Records
Spoilt Records SRD (Southern Record Distribution)
Spoon Vital Sales & Marketing
Spot On Amato Distribution
Spotlite Jazz Music, New Note Distribution Ltd, Pinnacle Records
Sprawl SRD (Southern Record Distribution)
Sprint Jet Star Phonographics
SPV RSK Entertainment Ltd
Spyda Pinnacle Records
Spymania Vital Sales & Marketing
Square Pinnacle Records
Squarepeg Records Absolute Marketing & Distribution Ltd.
Squeaky Records Ltd. Absolute Marketing & Distribution Ltd.
Squealer Cargo Records Distribution (UK) Ltd
Squire Excel Marketing Services Ltd
SSR SRD (Southern Record Distribution)
SST Records Plastic Head Music Distribution Ltd
Staalplaat Vital Sales & Marketing
Stable Gordon Duncan Distributions
Stadium Arvato Entertainment Services, Essential Direct Ltd
Standard Cargo Records Distribution (UK) Ltd
Standback Cargo Records Distribution (UK) Ltd
Starburst Pinnacle Records
Start RSK Entertainment Ltd
Stash Jazz Music
Static Caravan Cargo Records Distribution (UK) Ltd
Static Sound SRD (Southern Record Distribution)
Status Jazz Music
Staubgold Shellshock Distribution
Stayfree Vital Sales & Marketing
Steady On New Note Distribution Ltd
Steel Fish Amato Distribution
Steelcage Records Shellshock Distribution
Step 1 Music Plastic Head Music Distribution Ltd
Step One Cargo Records Distribution (UK) Ltd

Steppin' Out Pinnacle Records
Stereo Deluxe Timewarp Distribution
Sterling Circle The Woods
Sterndale Arvato Entertainment Services, Metronome Distribution
Sterns Stern's Distribution
Stewardess SRD (Southern Record Distribution)
Stickman Records Cargo Records Distribution (UK) Ltd, Shellshock Distribution
Sticky Label Pinnacle Records
Stiff Weapon Nova Sales and Distribution (UK) Ltd
StiKKi TiMeS MuSiC Harmonia Mundi (UK) Ltd
Stillwater Rolica Music Distribution
Stim Pinnacle Records
Stimulant Amato Distribution
Stingray Jet Star Phonographics
Stockwell Park Vital Sales & Marketing
Stomp Universal Music Operations
Stomp Off Jazz Music, The Woods
Stomper Time Nervous Records
Stone Island Arvato Entertainment Services, Essential Direct Ltd
Stone Love Jet Star Phonographics
Stoned Heights Vital Sales & Marketing
Stonedrive Arvato Entertainment Services, Essential Direct Ltd
Stonelove Jet Star Phonographics
Stoner Shit SRD (Southern Record Distribution)
Stone's Throw Cargo Records Distribution (UK) Ltd
Storyville Jazz Music, Proper Music Distribution Ltd
Straker's Jet Star Phonographics
Strange & Beautiful Music New Note Distribution Ltd
Strange Fruit Pinnacle Records
Strategy Arvato Entertainment Services, Essential Direct Ltd
Strawberry Sundae SRD (Southern Record Distribution)
Streamline EMI Distribution
Street Beat Cargo Records Distribution (UK) Ltd
Street Corner Amato Distribution
Street Vibes Jet Star Phonographics
Stretch New Note Distribution Ltd, Pinnacle Records
Strictly Country Proper Music Distribution Ltd
Strictly Rhythm TEN (The Entertainment Network)
Stringbean Jet Star Phonographics
Striving For Togetherness Cargo Records Distribution (UK) Ltd
Strong Like Sitting Bull Active Media Distribution Ltd
Stronghouse Amato Distribution
Strongjazz Amato Distribution
Strut Vital Sales & Marketing
Stubborn Nova Sales and Distribution (UK) Ltd
Studio 1 SRD (Southern Record Distribution)
Stupid Cat Pinnacle Records
STW Pinnacle Records
Sub Dub Hot Records
Sub Pop Records Shellshock Distribution
Sub Rosa Shellshock Distribution
Sub Tub Players Timewarp Distribution
Subkrauts Pinnacle Records
Subliminal F Minor Ltd
Subtitles ST Holdings Ltd
Suburban Home Plastic Head Music Distribution Ltd
Subvert Vital Sales & Marketing
Subvoice Pinnacle Records
Suckapunch Plastic Head Music Distribution Ltd
Sudden Death Records Shellshock Distribution
Sudden Def Load Media, Pinnacle Records
Sugar Free Cargo Records Distribution (UK) Ltd
Sugar Hill Proper Music Distribution Ltd
Sugarcube Pinnacle Records

SugarDaddy Absolute Marketing & Distribution Ltd., Pinnacle Records
Sugarlicks Records Shellshock Distribution
Suicide Squeeze Forte Music Distribution Ltd
Sulphuric Nova Sales and Distribution (UK) Ltd
Sum Arvato Entertainment Services
Summershine Cargo Records Distribution (UK) Ltd
Summit Metronome Distribution, Sound And Media Ltd
Sunbird Records Shellshock Distribution
Sundazed Cargo Records Distribution (UK) Ltd, F Minor Ltd
Sundown Magnum Distribution
Sunflower Amato Distribution
Sunjay Magnum Distribution
Sunshine Enterprises Timewarp Distribution
Sunshot (Japan) SRD (Southern Record Distribution)
Sunspot F Minor Ltd
Super Discount Vital Sales & Marketing
Super Electro Cargo Records Distribution (UK) Ltd
Super Power Jet Star Phonographics
SuperCharged Music InterGroove Ltd
Superior Quality Vital Sales & Marketing
Supernal Vital Sales & Marketing
Supertone Absolute Marketing & Distribution Ltd., Universal Music Operations
Supple Pipe Vital Sales & Marketing
Supraphon RSK Entertainment Ltd
Supreme Underground Pinnacle Records
Supremo Pinnacle Records
Sure Shot Proper Music Distribution Ltd
Surehand Plastic Head Music Distribution Ltd
Surface Cargo Records Distribution (UK) Ltd
Surface2Air Ltd RSK Entertainment Ltd
Surgury Vital Sales & Marketing
SurroundedBy Vivante Music Ltd
Survival Records Pinnacle Records
SUS SRD (Southern Record Distribution)
Susan Lawly Cargo Records Distribution (UK) Ltd
Swaggie Jazz Music
Swami Forte Music Distribution Ltd
Swank SRD (Southern Record Distribution)
Swansong TEN (The Entertainment Network)
Swarf Finger Cargo Records Distribution (UK) Ltd
Swashbuckle Nova Sales and Distribution (UK) Ltd
Sweat Pinnacle Records, Universal Music Operations
Sweet Pinnacle Records
Sweet Nothing Cargo Records Distribution (UK) Ltd
Swim Cargo Records Distribution (UK) Ltd
Swirl Timewarp Distribution
Switch SRD (Southern Record Distribution), ST Holdings Ltd
Switchflicker Baked Goods Distribution
Swordmaker Records (SMK) Universal Music Operations
SWS Jet Star Phonographics
Sylem Records Pinnacle Records, Shellshock Distribution
Symbol Records The Woods
Sympathy For The Record Industry Cargo Records Distribution (UK) Ltd
Syncom SRD (Southern Record Distribution)
Syrous ST Holdings Ltd
System Shock Load Media
TAA New Note Distribution Ltd
Taang Records Plastic Head Music Distribution Ltd
Table Of Elements Cargo Records Distribution (UK) Ltd
Tabu Universal Music Operations
Tacet Vivante Music Ltd
Tacklebox Cargo Records Distribution (UK) Ltd
Tailormade Pinnacle Records
Takoma Pinnacle Records
Talitres Shellshock Distribution
Talkin Loud Universal Music Operations

Tall Guy Hot Shot Records
Tall Pop Cargo Records Distribution (UK) Ltd
Tamoki Wambesi SRD (Southern Record Distribution)
Tangible Pendle Hawk Music
Tango Mi Amor Arvato Entertainment Services
Tank Amato Distribution
Tantara Productions Inc The Woods
Tanty Records Shellshock Distribution
Tapestry The Woods
Tara Claddagh Records, Proper Music Distribution Ltd
Taratn Tapes Gordon Duncan Distributions
Target Vital Sales & Marketing
Tartan Tapes Pendle Hawk Music
Tatra Productions Ltd Plastic Head Music Distribution Ltd
Tax Jazz Music
TB/Peacefrog Vital Sales & Marketing
TCB New Note Distribution Ltd, Pinnacle Records
TCR SRD (Southern Record Distribution)
TDK Nova Sales and Distribution (UK) Ltd
TDV Vital Sales & Marketing
Tea Leaf Records Plastic Head Music Distribution Ltd
TeC SRD (Southern Record Distribution)
Technical Freak Load Media
Technical Itch Load Media
Tee Hee Sound Entertainment Ltd
Teem SRD (Southern Record Distribution)
Teenage Shutdown Pinnacle Records
Teenbeat Vital Sales & Marketing
Telarc New Note Distribution Ltd
Teldec TEN (The Entertainment Network)
Telebender Proper Music Distribution Ltd
Telica Amato Distribution
Telica Communications Amato Distribution
Telstar Arvato Entertainment Services
Tema Northern Record Supplies Ltd, Savoy Strict Tempo Distributors
Tempa Essential Direct Ltd
Temple Gordon Duncan Distributions
Tempo Toons SRD (Southern Record Distribution)
Temptation Universal Music Operations
Ten Lovers Unique Distribution
10 To 4 Pinnacle Records
Ten To Ten The Woods
Ten Years After Nova Sales and Distribution (UK) Ltd
Tenacious Pinnacle Records
Tenor Vossa Records Ltd Pinnacle Records, Shellshock Distribution
Tenth Planet F Minor Ltd
Terra Nova Proper Music Distribution Ltd
Terrascape Arvato Entertainment Services
Tess Vital Sales & Marketing
Test Recordings Load Media
Testament Proper Music Distribution Ltd
Textone Nervous Records
Thang Plastic Head Music Distribution Ltd
Thats Entertainment RSK Entertainment Ltd
The Daisy Label RMG Chart Entertainment Ltd.
The Echo Label Ltd Pinnacle Records
Thee Blak Label Vital Sales & Marketing
Them's Good Records Plastic Head Music Distribution Ltd
Themsgood Records Plastic Head Music Distribution Ltd
Theologian Records Plastic Head Music Distribution Ltd
Theory Cargo Records Distribution (UK) Ltd
Thick Cargo Records Distribution (UK) Ltd
Things To Come Pinnacle Records
Think Progressive SRD (Southern Record Distribution)
Third Eye SRD (Southern Record Distribution)
3rd Stone Records Cargo Records Distribution (UK) Ltd
Thirdwave Amato Distribution

Thirsty Ear Vital Sales & Marketing
Thirteen Recording Cargo Records Distribution (UK) Ltd
30 Hertz Empathy Records
30Hz Vital Sales & Marketing
33 Jazz New Note Distribution Ltd
32 Records Hot Records
This Way Up Universal Music Operations
Thoofa Cargo Records Distribution (UK) Ltd
Three Cord Trick Nervous Records
Threeman Pinnacle Records
304 SRD (Southern Record Distribution)
Threshold Pinnacle Records
Thrill Jockey Vital Sales & Marketing
Thriving Underground Pinnacle Records
Thumpin' Vinyl SRD (Southern Record Distribution)
Thunderbird Records Proper Music Distribution Ltd
Thunderbolt Magnum Distribution
Tidy Trax Amato Distribution
Timebomb Cargo Records Distribution (UK) Ltd
Timeless Jazz Music, Load Media, New Note Distribution Ltd, Pinnacle Records
Timeless Historical New Note Distribution Ltd
Timeless Traditional New Note Distribution Ltd
Timewave Vital Sales & Marketing
Tin Can Arvato Entertainment Services
Tinseltones Cargo Records Distribution (UK) Ltd
Tiny Dog Cargo Records Distribution (UK) Ltd
Tiny Superhero Cargo Records Distribution (UK) Ltd
Tiptoe New Note Distribution Ltd, Pinnacle Records
T.I.P.World Arabesque Distribution
Titan Sounds ST Holdings Ltd
Tivoli Pinnacle Records
TKM New Note Distribution Ltd
TKO Magnum Pinnacle Records
TKO Records Plastic Head Music Distribution Ltd
Tolerance Vital Sales & Marketing
Tolerance Records Plastic Head Music Distribution Ltd
Tomato Vital Sales & Marketing
Tombstone Nervous Records
Tommy Boy Pinnacle Records
Tone Casualties Cargo Records Distribution (UK) Ltd
Tone-Cool Proper Music Distribution Ltd
Tone Cool Proper Music Distribution Ltd
Tone King Hot Shot Records
Tongue And Groove Vital Sales & Marketing
Tonka Arvato Entertainment Services, Essential Direct Ltd
Too Pure Vital Sales & Marketing
Tooth & Nail Plastic Head Music Distribution Ltd
Top Banana Vital Sales & Marketing
Top Deck SRD (Southern Record Distribution)
Topaz Pinnacle Records
Topaz Jazz Pinnacle Records
Torment Arvato Entertainment Services
Torn Cargo Records Distribution (UK) Ltd
Torrance Gordon Duncan Distributions
Tortuga Shellshock Distribution
Total Arvato Entertainment Services
Total Energy F Minor Ltd
Touch Kudos Records Ltd
Touch And Go Cargo Records Distribution (UK) Ltd
Town Crier The Woods
Track Records Active Media Distribution Ltd
Trade 2 Vital Sales & Marketing
Tradition Vital Sales & Marketing
Tradition & Moderne Proper Music Distribution Ltd
Traditional Crossroads Stern's Distribution
Train Wreck Proper Music Distribution Ltd
Traktor SRD (Southern Record Distribution)
Trance SRD (Southern Record Distribution)

Trans Solar Shellshock Distribution
Transatlantic Pinnacle Records
Transformed Dreams Shellshock Distribution
Transglobal Vital Sales & Marketing
Transgressive Records ADA UK
Transmat Vital Sales & Marketing
Transmission F Minor Ltd
Transmute Load Media
Transparent Load Media
Trauma Arvato Entertainment Services
Travellin' Man Jazz Music
Trax Pinnacle Records
Tree Roots Jet Star Phonographics
Trelik Pinnacle Records
Trial and Error Recordings Cargo Records Distribution (UK) Ltd
Tribal UK Vital Sales & Marketing
Tribe SRD (Southern Record Distribution)
Tribesman Jet Star Phonographics
Trick Arvato Entertainment Services, Essential Direct Ltd
Trident Universal Music Operations
Triefeelin Jet Star Phonographics
Trifekta Cargo Records Distribution (UK) Ltd
Trikont Shellshock Distribution
Trinidad & Tobago Jet Star Phonographics
Trinity Cargo Records Distribution (UK) Ltd
Trinity Records Plastic Head Music Distribution Ltd
Trio EMI Distribution, The Woods
Trip The Woods
Triple Crown Plastic Head Music Distribution Ltd
Triple X Plastic Head Music Distribution Ltd
Triple XXX SRD (Southern Record Distribution)
Tripoli Trax Vital Sales & Marketing
Tripsichord Nova Sales and Distribution (UK) Ltd
Trocadero Pinnacle Records
Trojan Records Proper Music Distribution Ltd
Tropical Discovery Records
Trouble Man F Minor Ltd
Trouble On Vinyl SRD (Southern Record Distribution)
Troubleman Utd Cargo Records Distribution (UK) Ltd
TRS Jet Star Phonographics
Tru 2 Da Game Universal Music Operations
Truckadelic Cargo Records Distribution (UK) Ltd
Truckstop Cargo Records Distribution (UK) Ltd
True Playaz SRD (Southern Record Distribution)
TrueTone Load Media
Trunk SRD (Southern Record Distribution)
Trybute SRD (Southern Record Distribution)
Tryfan Sain (Recordiau) Cyf
Tsk Tsk Shellshock Distribution
TSM Records New Note Distribution Ltd
Tu Pierdes Proper Music Distribution Ltd
Tuff City Cargo Records Distribution (UK) Ltd
Tuff Gong Universal Music Operations
Tugboat Records Pinnacle Records
Tuition Shellshock Distribution
Tumbao Discovery Records
Tumi Universal Music Operations
Tummy Touch Pinnacle Records
Turmoil Pinnacle Records
Turnbuckle Cargo Records Distribution (UK) Ltd
Turning Point F Minor Ltd
TVD Entertainment Arvato Entertainment Services
TVT Cargo Records Distribution (UK) Ltd, F Minor Ltd
TVT Records UK Vital Sales & Marketing
Twah! Pinnacle Records
Tweak Cargo Records Distribution (UK) Ltd
Tweed Vital Sales & Marketing
23rd Precinct Pinnacle Records

2012 Vital Sales & Marketing
Twilight Shellshock Distribution
Twin Arrows Universal Music Operations
Twin Tone Vital Sales & Marketing
Twist F Minor Ltd, SRD (Southern Record Distribution)
Twist And Shout Pinnacle Records
Twisted Nerve Vital Sales & Marketing
Twisted UK Arvato Entertainment Services, Vital Sales & Marketing
Twisted Village Cargo Records Distribution (UK) Ltd
2 Bob Sounds Pinnacle Records
2/4 Spoke Pinnacle Records
2 Kool Pinnacle Records
2.13.61 Pinnacle Records
Two To Tango Universal Music Operations
242 Vital Sales & Marketing
Tycoon Pinnacle Records
Tzadik Cargo Records Distribution (UK) Ltd
U-Star Pinnacle Records
U Star Records Kudos Records Ltd
UBC Pinnacle Records
Ubiquity New Note Distribution Ltd, Timewarp Distribution
Ufcro Cargo Records Distribution (UK) Ltd
UFO F Minor Ltd, Pinnacle Records
UG InterGroove Ltd
Ugly Bug SRD (Southern Record Distribution)
Ugly Things Empathy Records
UK Reggae Performers Jet Star Phonographics
UK Roses Jet Star Phonographics
Ulftone Proper Music Distribution Ltd
Ultimate Pinnacle Records
Ultimate Dilemma Pinnacle Records
Ultimate Groove Universal Music Operations
Ultra Cargo Records Distribution (UK) Ltd
Ultra Violet SRD (Southern Record Distribution)
Ultrapop Pinnacle Records
Umbrella Active Media Distribution Ltd
Un-Disputed Pinnacle Records
Unaware Collection Universal Music Operations
Uncle Sam's Vinyl Arvato Entertainment Services, Essential Direct Ltd
Unda-Vybe Vital Sales & Marketing
Under One Sun Proper Music Distribution Ltd
Under The Counter Vital Sales & Marketing
Undercover Cargo Records Distribution (UK) Ltd
Undergroove Shellshock Distribution
Underground Classics SRD (Southern Record Distribution)
Underground Vibe Pinnacle Records
Undervybe Arvato Entertainment Services, Essential Direct Ltd
Underware Vital Sales & Marketing
Unexplored Beats Pinnacle Records
Unforscene Pinnacle Records
Ungleich Shellshock Distribution
Unicorn Records Plastic Head Music Distribution Ltd
Union Jack Amato Distribution
Union Square New Note Distribution Ltd
Unique Pinnacle Records
Unique Gravity Proper Music Distribution Ltd
Unique 2 Rhythm Amato Distribution
Unisound Records International Plastic Head Music Distribution Ltd
United Pinnacle Records
United DJs Of America Pinnacle Records
United Recordings Timewarp Distribution
Unity Pinnacle Records
Universe F Minor Ltd
Universal Language Vital Sales & Marketing
Universal Sound Vital Sales & Marketing
Universal TV Universal Music Operations

Unknown ST Holdings Ltd, Vital Sales & Marketing
Unknown Territory Vital Sales & Marketing
Unreleased Project Amato Distribution
Unsigned Talent Jet Star Phonographics
Untertainment TEN (The Entertainment Network)
Untidy Trax Pinnacle Records
Up & Running Nervous Records
Up Beat Jazz Music
Up North Records Ltd. Proper Music Distribution Ltd
Upbeat Arvato Entertainment Services, Delta Music PLC
Upfront SRD (Southern Record Distribution)
Uppercut Vital Sales & Marketing
Uprising Load Media
Upstart Proper Music Distribution Ltd
Uptempo Jet Star Phonographics
Urban Universal Music Operations
Urban Beat Collection Arvato Entertainment Services,
Essential Direct Ltd
Urban Collective Vital Sales & Marketing
Urban Dance Universal Music Operations
Urban Groove Vital Sales & Marketing
Urban House Universal Music Operations
Urgent Arvato Entertainment Services
Urningsou Jet Star Phonographics
USG Cargo Records Distribution (UK) Ltd
USR Universal Music Operations
Uwe Nova Sales and Distribution (UK) Ltd
Uxbridge Street Amato Distribution
V Recordings SRD (Southern Record Distribution)
V2 Universal Music Operations
VA Recordings InterGroove Ltd
Vaclav Vital Sales & Marketing
Vagrant Cargo Records Distribution (UK) Ltd, F Minor Ltd
Vagrant Records Plastic Head Music Distribution Ltd
Vague Cargo Records Distribution (UK) Ltd
Vampirella Nervous Records, Plastic Head Music Distribution
Ltd
Vampisoul Timewarp Distribution
Van Der Linden Hot Shot Records
Vandeleur Universal Music Operations
Vanguard F Minor Ltd, New Note Distribution Ltd, Pinnacle
Records
Vanquish Music Group Pinnacle Records
Vapours Pinnacle Records
Varese Saraband Pinnacle Records
Varrick Proper Music Distribution Ltd
Varup Active Media Distribution Ltd
Vasco Cargo Records Distribution (UK) Ltd
VC Recordings EMI Distribution
Vee Jay Discovery Records
Velvel Pinnacle Records
Vendome Pinnacle Records
Venture EMI Distribution
VeraBra Pinnacle Records
Verbatim Magnum Distribution
Verge New Note Distribution Ltd
Verglas Pinnacle Records
Vermiform Cargo Records Distribution (UK) Ltd
Vernon Yard EMI Distribution, Vital Sales & Marketing
Vertigo Universal Music Operations
Verve Universal Music Operations
Verve Forecast Universal Music Operations
VESK Cargo Records Distribution (UK) Ltd
Vespertine Cargo Records Distribution (UK) Ltd
Vesuvius SRD (Southern Record Distribution)
VHF Cargo Records Distribution (UK) Ltd
Via Pinnacle Records
Via Satellite Cargo Records Distribution (UK) Ltd
Vibez Load Media

Vibrations From The Backs Distribution
Viceroy Arvato Entertainment Services
Vicious Vinyl Unique Distribution
Victory Records Plastic Head Music Distribution Ltd
Vigilante Nova Sales and Distribution (UK) Ltd
Vigilantes Of Love Cargo Records Distribution (UK) Ltd
Viking Discovery Records
Vine Gate Music New Note Distribution Ltd
Vintage Jazz Band Jazz Music
Vintage Jazz Classics Jazz Music
Vintage Music Company Arvato Entertainment Services
Vinyl Communications Cargo Records Distribution (UK) Ltd
Vinyl Japan Plastic Head Music Distribution Ltd
Vinyl Junkie Vital Sales & Marketing
Vinyl Syndicate ST Holdings Ltd
Viper Pinnacle Records
Vipers Nest Proper Music Distribution Ltd
Virgin EMI Distribution
Virgin America EMI Distribution
Virgin Classics EMI Distribution
Virgin/EMI TV EMI Distribution
Visible Noise Vital Sales & Marketing
Visionary Pinnacle Records
Visions Inc Goya Music Distribution Ltd
Vital Cog Cargo Records Distribution (UK) Ltd
Viva Voce Copperplate Distribution
Volatile Pendle Hawk Music
Voltage Amato Distribution
Voodoo Proper Music Distribution Ltd, Vital Sales & Marketing
Voodoo Records Kudos Records Ltd
Vortex Arvato Entertainment Services, Essential Direct Ltd
Vox Pop 45s Timewarp Distribution
Voyager Discovery Records
Voyageur Pinnacle Records
VP Jet Star Phonographics
Waako Universal Music Operations
Wabana Pinnacle Records
Wackies Jet Star Phonographics
Wag Absolute Marketing & Distribution Ltd.
Wagram Plastic Head Music Distribution Ltd
Wah Wah Cargo Records Distribution (UK) Ltd, F Minor Ltd,
Kudos Records Ltd
Wah'tup Proper Music Distribution Ltd
Walt Disney Vital Sales & Marketing
Walzwerk Cargo Records Distribution (UK) Ltd
Walzwerk Records Plastic Head Music Distribution Ltd
Wambesi Pinnacle Records
Waqt Recordings Amato Distribution
War Music AB Plastic Head Music Distribution Ltd
Ware Shellshock Distribution
Warner Bros Records TEN (The Entertainment Network)
Warner Classics THE (Total Home Entertainment)
Warner Home Video (WHV) TEN (The Entertainment
Network)
Warner Vision (WVI) TEN (The Entertainment Network)
Water F Minor Ltd
Watercolour Gordon Duncan Distributions
Waterlily Proper Music Distribution Ltd, Vivante Music Ltd
Watermelon Proper Music Distribution Ltd
Watt New Note Distribution Ltd, Pinnacle Records
Waulk Elektrik Proper Music Distribution Ltd
Wave Records New Note Distribution Ltd
Wax Arvato Entertainment Services
Wax Trax Cargo Records Distribution (UK) Ltd
Way Out West Proper Music Distribution Ltd
Wayward Arvato Entertainment Services, Essential Direct Ltd
We Love You Vital Sales & Marketing
WEA London TEN (The Entertainment Network)
Wearhouse Music Co Load Media

Design, Pressing & Distribution: Distributed Labels

Weatherbox Pinnacle Records
Weekend Beatnik Proper Music Distribution Ltd
Weird Neighbourhood Pinnacle Records
Well Charged Arvato Entertainment Services, Essential Direct Ltd
Welsh Teldisc Sain (Recordiau) Cyf
The Wenlock Label Cargo Records Distribution (UK) Ltd
Wergo Harmonia Mundi (UK) Ltd
West Ten SRD (Southern Record Distribution)
West 2 Recordings Vital Sales & Marketing
Westbound Pinnacle Records
Western Arvato Entertainment Services, Essential Direct Ltd
Westmoor Arvato Entertainment Services
Westpoint SRD (Southern Record Distribution)
Westway Amato Distribution
What Else? Cargo Records Distribution (UK) Ltd
Whatever Pinnacle Records
Whatsoever Arvato Entertainment Services
When! Pinnacle Records
Where It's At Is Where You Are Pinnacle Records, Shellshock Distribution
Whipcord Pinnacle Records
Whippa Snappa Plastic Head Music Distribution Ltd
Whippet Pinnacle Records
Whirl-y-Gig Changing World Distribution
Whirlie Gordon Duncan Distributions
Whirlybird Cargo Records Distribution (UK) Ltd
White TEN (The Entertainment Network)
White Dragon Cargo Records Distribution (UK) Ltd
White Jazz Cargo Records Distribution (UK) Ltd
White Label Music Shellshock Distribution
White Lines Vital Sales & Marketing
White Noise Vital Sales & Marketing
White Water TEN (The Entertainment Network)
The Whole Nine Yards SRD (Southern Record Distribution)
Whoop! InterGroove Ltd
Who's The Daddy Now? Shellshock Distribution
WHV/BBC Superbudget Technicolor Distribution Services Ltd
Why Not Candid Productions Ltd
Wicked Worlds Vital Sales & Marketing
Wigwam Pinnacle Records
Wiiija Vital Sales & Marketing
Wikkid Nova Sales and Distribution (UK) Ltd
Wild Bunch EMI Distribution
Wild Card Universal Music Operations
Wild England Arvato Entertainment Services, Essential Direct Ltd
Wildcat Hot Shot Records
Wildloops InterGroove Ltd
Wildwood Acoustic Pendle Hawk Music
Windsong Pinnacle Records
Winter & Winter Harmonia Mundi (UK) Ltd
The Wire Editions Harmonia Mundi (UK) Ltd
Wirl Music Jet Star Phonographics
Witness Pinnacle Records
WMD Discovery Records
WMO Vital Sales & Marketing
Wolf Hot Shot Records, RSK Entertainment Ltd
Wolfrilla F Minor Ltd
WOMAD Select Proper Music Distribution Ltd
Wonder Shellshock Distribution
Wonderboy Universal Music Operations
Won't Stop Pinnacle Records
Woo Me SRD (Southern Record Distribution)
Wooded Hill Recordings Pinnacle Records
Wooden Hill Proper Music Distribution Ltd
Woodland Timewarp Distribution
Woof! Pinnacle Records
Wooligan Jet Star Phonographics

Word Sound SRD (Southern Record Distribution)
Words Of Warning SRD (Southern Record Distribution)
Words On Music Shellshock Distribution
Wordsound SRD (Southern Record Distribution)
Worker's Playtime Pinnacle Records
World Gordon Duncan Distributions, Plastic Head Music Distribution Ltd, Proper Music Distribution Ltd
World Connection Proper Music Distribution Ltd
World Domination Cargo Records Distribution (UK) Ltd
World In Sound F Minor Ltd
World Music Network (UK) Ltd New Note Distribution Ltd
World Service Vital Sales & Marketing
World Village Harmonia Mundi (UK) Ltd
Worm Interface Pinnacle Records
Wotre Music Discovery Records
Wounded Bird F Minor Ltd
Wrath Records Shellshock Distribution
Wreckage Plastic Head Music Distribution Ltd
Wrong Again Records Plastic Head Music Distribution Ltd
Wu-Tang Vital Sales & Marketing
Wurlitzer Jukebox Cargo Records Distribution (UK) Ltd
X-Clusive Vital Sales & Marketing
Xacca Sounds Nova Sales and Distribution (UK) Ltd
Xenophile Proper Music Distribution Ltd
XL Recordings Vital Sales & Marketing
Xplicit Vinyl Vital Sales & Marketing
Xterminator Jet Star Phonographics
Xtra Large Productions Jet Star Phonographics
Xtravaganza TEN (The Entertainment Network)
Xtreme TEN (The Entertainment Network)
Y Vital Sales & Marketing
Yard Beat Jet Star Phonographics
Yard Face Jet Star Phonographics
Yard High New Note Distribution Ltd
Yard Music SRD (Southern Record Distribution)
Yassaba Pinnacle Records
Yazoo Proper Music Distribution Ltd
Ye Gods Pinnacle Records
Yeaah Absolute Marketing & Distribution Ltd.
Yep Roc Shellshock Distribution
York Ambisonic Metronome Distribution
Yoshiko Vital Sales & Marketing
Young God Forte Music Distribution Ltd
Your Mum Arvato Entertainment Services, Essential Direct Ltd
YR 3000 Plastic Head Music Distribution Ltd
Yunx Recordings Baked Goods Distribution
Yush Pinnacle Records
Yush Recordings Kudos Records Ltd
Zane Records Pinnacle Records
Zarnak Pinnacle Records
Zebra Pinnacle Records
Zebra 3 Records Proper Music Distribution Ltd
Zeit Pinnacle Records
Zephyr New Note Distribution Ltd, Pinnacle Records
Zero Hour Pinnacle Records
Zero House Pinnacle Records
Zerox Vital Sales & Marketing
Zest ST Holdings Ltd
Zev Vital Sales & Marketing
Zhark Pinnacle Records
Zimbob Stern's Distribution
Zip Records Shellshock Distribution
Ziriguiboom New Note Distribution Ltd
Zok Arvato Entertainment Services
Zomart Arvato Entertainment Services
Zone Recordings Pinnacle Records
Zoom Club Plastic Head Music Distribution Ltd
ZTT Pinnacle Records
ZZZ Cargo Records Distribution (UK) Ltd

WEB SHERIFF®

PROTECTING YOUR RIGHTS
ON THE INTERNET
ASSOCIATED WORLDWIDE

Web Sheriff is Europe's leading internet policing specialist and acts for numerous media organisations, newspapers, broadcasters, film companies, record companies, artists and celebrities.

Web Sheriff's services include :-

 Pre-Release Protection - Protecting new films and albums against the damaging effects of internet piracy in the crucial run-up period to commercial release.

 Internet Auditing - Analysing the entire internet in relation to a client's IP portfolio and advising upon all aspects from anti-piracy to on-line licensing.

 Global Brand Protection - 365 day, 24/7 anti-piracy and internet auditing functions, to protect global brands, image rights, catalogues and other high-value IP rights.

 Digital Rights Management - All elements of DRM, from watermarking and secure delivery, to web-site hosting and management.

 On-Line Investigations - From investigative assignments for newspapers and broadcasters, to tackling the commercial piracy of merchandising, music and films.

Web Sheriff has been extensively featured in the media, including the BBC, ITV, Sky News, Channel 5, the Sunday Times, the Mail On Sunday, The Guardian, Music Week and Hi-Fi & Computer World.

Web Sheriff's motto is **"Prevention Is Better Than Cure"** ... ... feel free to contact us to discuss your on-line rights.

Tel : 00-44-(0)208-323 8013
E-Mail : websheriff@websheriff.com
www.websheriff.com

Business Services

MUSICIANS
BENEVOLENT FUND

listening to musicians – responding to their needs

For people in the music business there is always help at hand from the Musicians Benevolent Fund

- Help with stress and health problems

- Help and advice with financial problems

- Help that's given in strict confidence

- Help given to outstanding young musicians

We operate throughout England, Scotland, Wales and the whole of Ireland

If you or someone you know needs our help, please contact:

Musicians Benevolent Fund
16 Ogle Street
London W1W 6JA

Telephone: 020 7636 4481
Facsimile: 020 7637 4307

email: info@mbf.org.uk
website: www.mbf.org.uk

Reg. Charity No. 228089

Business Services:

Industry Organisations

The Agents' Association (Great Britain) 54 Keyes House, Dolphin Sq, London SW1V 3NA **t** 020 7834 0515 **f** 020 7821 0261 **e** association@agents-uk.com **w** agents-uk.com Administrator: Carol Richards.

AIM (THE ASSOCIATION OF INDEPENDENT MUSIC)

Lamb House, Church Street, Chiswick, London W4 2PD **t** 020 8994 5599 **f** 020 8994 5222 **e** info@musicindie.com **w** musicindie.com Chief Executive: Alison Wenham. Legal & Business Affairs: Michael Fuller. Special Projects: Remi Harris. Membership & Communications: Lara Baker. International and Friends of AIM: Judith Govey. Association Administrator: Ellie Mules. Press Office: Sam Shemtob.
British association of independent record companies and distributors with over 900 members. General enquiries to info@musicindie.com.

APRS (Assoc. of Professional Recording Services) PO Box 22, Totnes, Devon TQ9 7YZ **t** 01803 868 600 **f** 01803 868 444 **e** info@aprs.co.uk **w** aprs.co.uk Exec Director: Peter Filleul.

Arthur Doodson (Brokers) Ltd 219 - 225 Slade Lane, Manchester M19 2EX **t** 0161 225 9060 **f** 0161 224 6150 **e** info@arthurdoodson.co.uk **w** arthurdoodson.co.uk Dir: Richard Doodson & David Leech.

Arts Council of England 14 Great Peter St, London SW1P 3NQ **t** 020 7333 0100 or 020 7973 6784 **f** 020 7973 6590 **e** alan.james@artscouncil.org.uk **w** artscouncil.org.uk Head of Contemp Music: Alan James.

Arts Council of Ireland 70 Merrion Sq, Dublin 2, Ireland **t** +353 1 618 0200 **f** +353 1 676 1302 **e** info@artscouncil.ie **w** artscouncil.ie Dir: Mary Cloake.

Association of British Jazz Musicians First Floor, 132 Southwark St, London SE1 0SW **t** 020 7928 9089 **f** 020 7401 6870 **e** info@jazzservices.org.uk **w** jazzservices.org.uk Hon Sec: Chris Hodgkins.

ASCAP (AMERICAN SOCIETY OF COMPOSERS AUTHORS & PUBLISHERS)

8 Cork Street, London W1S 3LJ **t** 020 7439 0909 **f** 020 7434 0073 **e** initial+lastname@ascap.com **w** ascap.com Contact: Karen Hewson. Snr Vice President, Int: Roger Greenaway. VP Membership: Sean Devine. Membership: Ross Gautreau.
The only American performing right society created and controlled by songwriters and publishers. The industry leader in the USA since 1914.

Association of Festival Organisers PO Box 296, Matlock, Derbyshire DE4 3XU **t** 01629 827014 **f** 01629 821874 **e** info@afouk.org **w** afouk.org Administrator: Frances Watt.

Attitude is Everything c/o Artsline, 54 Chalton St, London NW1 1HS **t** 020 7388 2227 **f** 020 7383 2653 **e** business.aie@artsline.org.uk **w** attitude-is-everything.co.uk Business Manager: Paul Bonham.

AURA (The featured performers society) 1 York St, London W1U 6PA **t** 020 7487 5640 **f** 0870 8505 201 **e** info@aurauk.com **w** aurauk.com General Secretary: Peter Horrey.

Bloc Music Industry Network Ltd Ty Cefn, Rectory Rd, Canton, Cardiff, South Glamorgan CF5 1QL **t** 029 2066 8127 **f** 029 2034 1622 **e** bloc@welshmusicfoundation.com **w** welshmusicfoundation.com/bloc Music Development Mgr: Claire Heat.

BMI (BROADCAST MUSIC INCORPORATED)

84 Harley House, Marylebone Road, London NW1 5HN **t** 020 7486 2036 **f** 020 7224 1046 **e** London@bmi.com **w** bmi.com. Senior Executive European Writer-Publisher Relations: Brandon Bakshi. Executive Writer-Publisher Relations: Nick Robinson. Writer-Publisher Relations: Tabitha Capaldi. Administrative Assistant: Briar McIntyre. Writer-Publisher Relations: Jon Miller.
BMI is the premier U.S. performing rights organisation which represents approximately 300,000 songwriters, composers and music publishers in all genres of music.

BPI - THE BRITISH RECORDED MUSIC INDUSTRY

The British Recorded Music Industry

Riverside Building, County Hall, Westminster Bridge Rd, London SE1 7JA **t** 020 7803 1300 **f** 020 7803 1310 **e** general@bpi.co.uk **w** bpi.co.uk Executive Chairman: Peter Jamieson. Director of Communications & Development: Steve Redmond. Director of Independent Member Services: Jon Webster. Director of Anti-Piracy: David Martin. Director of Charities & Events: Maggie Crowe.

Bristol Music Foundation 11 Great George St, Bristol BS1 5RR **t** 01395 576 690 **f** 01395 576 690 **e** matt@bristolmusicfoundation.com **w** bristolmusicfoundation.com Dir: Matt Booth.

Brit Awards c/o BPI, Riverside Building, County Hall, Westminster Bridge Rd, London SE1 7JA **t** 020 7803 1300 **f** 020 7803 1310 **e** brits@bpi.co.uk **w** brits.co.uk Dir, Events & Charity: Maggie Crowe.

Brit Trust c/o BPI, Riverside Building, County Hall, Westminster Bridge Rd, London SE1 7JA **t** 020 7803 1300 **f** 020 7803 1310 **e** brittrust@bpi.co.uk **w** brittrust.co.uk Dir, Events & Charity: Maggie Crowe.

THE BRITISH ACADEMY OF COMPOSERS & SONGWRITERS

British Music House, 26 Berners Street, London W1T 3LR **t** 020 7636 2929 **f** 020 7636 2212 **e** firstname@britishacademy.com **w** britishacademy.com Membership Manager: Fran Matthews. Chief Executive: Chris Green. Chairman: David Ferguson. Ivor Novello Awards & Events: Amanda McCarthy & Fergal Kilroy. Financial Controller: Vick Bain. Policy Coordinator: Lucy Weston.

British Country Music Association PO Box 240, Harrow, Middlesex HA3 7PH **t** 01273 559750 **f** 01273 559750 **e** theBCMA@yahoo.com **w** britishcountrymusicassociation.co.uk Chairman: Jim Marshall.

British Federation Of Audio PO Box 365, Farnham, Surrey GU10 2BD **t** 01428 714616 **f** 01428 717599 **e** chrisc@british-audio.org.uk **w** british-audio.org.uk Secretary: Chris Cowan.

British Interactive Media Association Briarlea, Southend Rd, South Green, Billericay, Essex CM11 2PR **t** 01277 658107 **f** 0870 051 7842 **e** info@bima.co.uk **w** bima.co.uk Office Administrator: Janice Cable.

British Library Sound Archive 96 Euston Rd, London NW1 2DB **t** 020 7412 7676 **e** sound-archive@bl.uk **w** bl.uk/soundarchive Contact: Director.

BRITISH MUSIC RIGHTS LTD

BRITISH MUSIC RIGHTS:

British Music House, 26 Berners Street, London W1T 3LR **t** 020 7306 4446 **f** 020 7306 4449 **e** britishmusic@bmr.org **w** bmr.org Chief Executive: Emma Pike.
Promoting the interests of British music composers, songwriters and publishers through lobbying to UK government and EU institutions, education, PR and events. Members: BAC&S, MPA & the MCPS-PRS Alliance.

Broadcasting Commission of Ireland 2/5 Warrington Pl, Dublin 2, Ireland **t** +353 1 676 0966 **f** +353 1 676 0948 **e** info@bci.ie **w** bci.ie CEO: Michael O'Keeffe.

BVA (British Video Association) 167 Great Portland St, London W1W 5PE **t** 020 7436 0041 **f** 020 7436 0043 **e** general@bva.org.uk **w** bva.org.uk Dir Gen: Lavinia Carey.

CATCO

1 Upper James Street, London W1F 9DE **t** 020 7534 1331 **f** 020 7535 1383 **e** info@catcouk.com **w** catcouk.com. Chairman & CEO: Fran Nevrkla. Director of Business Development: Clive Bishop. Director of Member and Performer Services: Sue Carty. Director of Licensing: Tony Clark. Director of HR and Facilities: Janice Davies. Finance Director: Ben Lambert. Director of Legal & Business Affairs and Rights Negotiation: Peter Leathem. Director of Government Relations: Dominic McGonigal. Director of Public Relations and Corporate Communications: Jonathan Morrish. Director of Public Performance Operations: Sally Stevens.
The Record Industry's track level sound recording database, providing the 'one-stop-drop' for all sound recording data needs.

Christian Copyright Licencing (Europe) Ltd PO Box 1339, Eastbourne, E Sussex BN21 4YF **t** 01323 417711 **f** 01323 417722 **e** info@ccli.co.uk **w** ccli.co.uk Sales Mgr: Chris Williams.

Community Media Association 15 Paternoster Row, Sheffield, S Yorks S1 2BX **t** 0114 279 5219 **f** 0114 279 8976 **e** cma@commedia.org.uk **w** commedia.org.uk Dir: Diane Reid.

Community Music Wales Unit 8, 24 Norbury Rd, Fairwater, Cardiff CF5 3AU **t** 029 2083 8060 **f** 029 2056 6573 **e** admin@communitymusicwales.org.uk **w** communitymusicwales.org.uk Music Director: Simon Dancey.

Copyright Advice and Anti-Piracy Hotline **t** 0845 603 4567.

Coventry Music Network 223 Four Pounds Ave, Coventry CV5 8JS **t** 07791 500 705 **e** richelms.cmn@tiscali.co.uk **w** myspace.com/coventrymusicnetwork Project Manager: Richard Elms.

CPA (Concert Promoters Association) 6 St Mark's Rd, Henley-on-Thames, Oxon RG9 1LJ **t** 01491 575060 **f** 01491 414082 **e** carolesmith.cpa@virgin.net Secretary: Carole Smith.

Department for Culture, Media and Sport 2-4
Cockspur St, London SW1Y 5DH **t** 020 7211 6200
f 020 7211 6032 **e** enquiries@culture.gov.uk **w** culture.gov.uk
Contact: Public Enquiries.

EDiMA (European Digital Media Association) Friars
House, Office 118, 157-168 Blackfriars Rd, London SE1 8EZ
t 020 7401 2661 **f** 020 7928 5850 **e** info@edima.org
w edima.org Dir: Wes Himes.

English Folk Dance & Song Society Cecil Sharp House,
2 Regent's Park Rd, Camden, London NW1 7AY
t 020 7485 2206 **f** 020 7284 0534 **e** info@efdss.org
w efdss.org Publications Manager: Felicity Greenland.

Enterprise Ireland Merrion Hall, Strand Rd, Sandymont,
Dublin 4, Ireland **t** +353 1 206 6000 **f** +353 1 206 6400
e client.service@enterprise-ireland.com **w** enterprise-ireland.com.

ERA (Entertainment Retailers Association) 1st
Floor, Colonnade House, 2 Westover Rd, Bournemouth, Dorset
BH1 2BY **t** 01202 292 063 **f** 01202 292 067
e admin@eraltd.org **w** eraltd.org Secretary General: Kim Bayley.

Federation Against Copyright Theft (FACT) 7
Victory Business Centre, Worton Rd, Isleworth, Middx TW7 6DB
t 020 8568 6646 **f** 020 8560 6364 **e** contact@fact-uk.org.uk
w fact-uk.org.uk Dir General: Raymond Leinster.

Folk Arts Network PO BOx 296, Matlock, Derbyshire
DE4 3XU **t** 01629 827014 **f** 01629 821874
e admin@folkartsnetwork.org.uk **w** folkartsnetwork.org.uk
Administrator: Frances Watt.

Folktrax Heritage House, 16 Brunswick Sq, Gloucester, Gloucs
GL1 1UG **t** 01452 415110 **f** 01452 503643
e folktrax@blueyonder.co.uk **w** folktrax.org Mgr: Peter Kennedy.

French Music Bureau Institut Francais, 17 Queensberry Pl,
London SW7 2DT **t** 020 7073 1301 **f** 020 7073 1359
e uk@french-music.org **w** french-music.org/uk
Dir: Corinne Micaelli.

GS1 UK

10 Maltravers Street, London WC2R 3BX **t** 020 7655 9001
f 020 7681 2290 **e** info@gs1uk.org **w** gs1uk.org Contact: Help
Desk.
GS1 UK adds value to members' businesses by delivering and
supporting the adoption of cross sector, global supply chain
standards. Using GS1 standards for bar coding, electronic
business messaging, data synchronisation and through the
EPCglobal Network, radio frequency identification
technology, members can enhance product visibility, reduce
costs, increase stock availability and improve customer
safety.

**GUILD OF INTERNATIONAL SONGWRITERS &
COMPOSERS**

Sovereign House, 12 Trewartha Road, Praa Sands, Penzance,
Cornwall TR20 9ST **t** 01736 762 826 **f** 01736 763 328
e songmag@aol.com **w** songwriters-guild.co.uk Membership Sec:
Carole A Jones.
International songwriters' organisation representing
songwriters, composers, lyricists, artistes, musicians,
publishers etc. Music industry consultants. Publishers of
Songwriting and Composing magazine.

Hospital Broadcasting Association 50 Neale St,
Fulwell, Sunderland, Tyne & Wear SR6 9EZ **t** 0870 321 6017
e info@hbauk.com **w** hbauk.com
Contact: Executive Administrator.

**IFPI (Int Federation of the Phonographic
Industry)** IFPI Secretariat, 54-62 Regent St, London
W1B 5RE **t** 020 7878 7900 **f** 020 7878 7950 **e** info@ifpi.org
w ifpi.org Dir of Comms: Adrian Strain.

IMRO (Irish Music Rights Organisation) Copyright
House, Pembroke Row, Lower Baggot St, Dublin 2, Ireland
t +353 1 661 4844 **f** +353 1 676 3125 **e** info@imro.ie **w** imro.ie
Chief Exec: Adrian Gaffney.

Interactive Media in Retail Group 5 Dryden St, London
WC2E 9BN **t** 07000 464674 **f** 07000 394674
e market@imrg.org **w** imrg.org MD: Jo Tucker.

**International Association of Professional
Creators** 6 Cheyne Walk, Hornsea, East Yorks HU18 1BX
t 01964 533982 **f** 01964 536193 **e** paul@digitaldomain.org
w digitaldomain.org Administrator: Paul Cook.

International Music Managers Forum (IMMF) 1
York St, London W1U 6PA **t** 020 7935 2446 **f** 020 7486 6045
e davids@immf.net **w** immf.net Exec Dir: David Stopps.

IRMA IRMA House, 1 Corrig Ave, Dun Laoghaire, Co Dublin,
Ireland **t** +353 1 280 6571 **f** +353 1 280 6579 **e** info@irma.ie
w irma.ie Dir Gen: Dick Doyle.

**ISA (INTERNATIONAL SONGWRITERS'
ASSOCIATION)**

PO Box 46, Limerick City, Limerick, Ireland **t** +353 61 228837
f +353 61 2288379 **e** jliddane@songwriter.iol.ie
w songwriter.co.uk CEO: James D Liddane. Contacts: Anna M
Sinden, Bill Miller.

ISM (The Incorporated Society Of Musicians) 10
Stratford Pl, London W1C 1AA **t** 020 7629 4413
f 020 7408 1538 **e** membership@ism.org **w** ism.org
Chief Exec: Neil Hoyle.

ITC (Independent Television Commission) (see Ofcom).

Jazz Services 1st Floor, 132 Southwark St, London SE1 0SW t 020 7928 9089 f 020 7401 6870 e info@jazzservices.org.uk w jazzservices.org.uk Dir: Chris Hodgkins.

Making Music (The Nat'l Fed. Of Music Societies) 7-15 Rosebery Ave, London EC1R 4SP t 0870 872 3300 f 0870 903 3785 e info@makingmusic.org.uk w makingmusic.org.uk Chief Executive: Robin Osterley.

Manchester City Music Network 14b Turner St, Manchester M4 1DZ t 0161 839 7007 f 0161 839 6970 e network@manchester-music.org.uk w manchester-music.org.uk Project Director: Stuart Worthington.

MCPS (Ireland) Pembroke Row, Lower Baggot St, Dublin 2, Ireland t +353 1 676 6940 f +353 1 661 1316 e victor.finn@mcps.ie w mcps.ie MD: Victor Finn.

MCPS (Mechanical Copyright Protection Society Ltd) Copyright House, 29-33 Berners St, London W1T 3AB t 020 7580 5544 f 020 7306 4455 e admissions@mcps-prs-alliance.co.uk w mcps.co.uk MD: Steve Porter.

Mercury Prize 3 Grand Union Centre, London W10 5AS t 020 8964 9964 f 020 8969 7249 e km@nationwidemercuryprize.com w nationwidemercurys.com Dir: Kevin Milburn.

Merseyside Music Development Agency (MMDA) Level C, 70 Hope St, Liverpool L1 9EB t 0151 709 2202 f 0151 709 2005 e info@mmda.org.uk w mmda.org.uk.

Millward Brown UK Olympus Ave, Tachbrook Pk, Warwick CV34 6RJ t 01926 826610 f 01926 826209 e bob.barnes@uk.millwardbrown.com w millwardbrown.com Charts Dir: Bob Barnes.

MMF (MUSIC MANAGERS FORUM)

British Music House, 26 Berners Street, London W1T 3LR t 0870 8507 800 f 0870 8507 801 e info@musicmanagersforum.co.uk w musicmanagersforum.co.uk General Secretary: James Sellar. Chairman: Jazz Summers. Vice Chairman: Gary McClarnan. Treasurer: Charlie Carne. Dir, Training & Education: Stuart Worthington.

MMF Training 14b Turner St, Manchester M4 1DZ t 0161 839 7007 f 0161 839 6970 e admin@mmf-training.com w mmf-training.com Head of Training & Education: Stuart Worthington.

Mobile Entertainment Forum (MEF) 313 Westbourne Studios, 242 Acklam Rd, London W10 5JJ t 020 7524 7878 f 020 7524 7879 e info@m-e-f.org w m-e-f.org Executive Director: Rimma Perelmuter.

Music Of Black Origin - Mobo Awards 22 Stephenson Way, London NW1 2HD t 020 7419 1800 f 020 7419 1600 e info@mobo.com w mobo.com Founder: Kanya King MBE.

MPA (Music Publishers Association) 6th Floor, British Music House, 26 Berners St, London W1T 3LR t 020 7580 0126 f 020 7637 3929 e info@mpaonline.org.uk w mpaonline.org.uk Communications Manager: Felix Taylor. CEO: Stephen Navin.

Music Industries Association Ivy Cottage Offices, Finch's Yard, Eastwick Rd, Great Bookham, Surrey KT23 4BA t 01372 750600 f 01372 750515 e office@mia.org.uk w mia.org.uk Chief Executive: Paul McManus.

Music Preserved Hillside Cottage, Hill Brow Rd, Liss, Hants GU33 7 t 01730 892148 f 01730 894264 e musicpreserved@dial.pipex.com w musicpreserved.org Chairman: Basil Tschaikov.

MPG (The Music Producers Guild Ltd) PO Box 32, Harrow HA2 7ZX t 020 8993 5504 f 020 8992 1195 e office@mpg.org.uk w mpg.org.uk Chairman: Mike Howlett.

musicaid.org Please, visit website for more deatils e mail@musicaid.org w musicaid.org.

Musicians Benevolent Fund 16 Ogle St, London W1W 6JA t 020 7636 4481 f 020 7637 4307 e info@mbf.org.uk w mbf.org.uk Chief Executive: Rosanna Preston.

MUSICIANS UNION

musicians union

60-62 Clapham Road, London SW9 0JJ t 020 7582 5566 f 020 7582 9805 e info@musiciansunion.org.uk w musiciansunion.org.uk Gen Sec: John F Smith. Asst Gen Sec (Music Industry): Horace Trubridge. National Organiser - Media: Nigel McCune. In House Solicitor: David Fenton. Comms Official: Keith Ames. Session Organiser: Pete Thoms. **The Musicians' Union represents the rights and interests of over 32,000 musicians working in all sectors of the music business.**

National Association of Youth Orchestras Central Hall, West Tollcross, Edinburgh EH3 9BP t 0131 221 1927 f 0131 229 2921 e admin@nayo.org.uk w nayo.org.uk GM: Susan White.

National Entertainment Agents Council PO Box 112, Seaford, E Sussex BN25 2DQ t 0870 755 7612 f 0870 755 7613 e info@neac.org.uk w neac.org.uk Gen Sec: Chris Bray.

National Foundation for Youth Music (Youth Music) One America St, London SE1 0NE t 020 7902 1060 f 020 7902 1061 e info@youthmusic.org.uk w youthmusic.org.uk Chief Executive: Christina Coker.

National Student Music Awards PO Box 5413, Bournemouth BH1 4UJ t 0870 040 6767 e info@nsma.com w nsma.com MD: Chris Jenkins.

NEMIS (New Music In Scotland) 2nd Floor, 22 Jamaica St, Glasgow G1 4QD t 07803 752 913 e alec@nemis.org w nemis.org Development Officer: Alec Downie.

Nordoff-Robbins Music Therapy Studio A2, 1927 Building, 2 Michael Rd, London SW6 2AD t 020 7371 8404 f 020 7371 8206 e lindamac@nrfr.co.uk w silverclef.com Appeals Manager: Linda McLean.

Ofcom Riverside House, 2a Southwark Bridge Rd, London SE1 9HA **t** 020 7981 3000 **f** 020 7981 3333 **e** contact@ofcom.org.uk **w** ofcom.org.uk.

The Official UK Charts Company Ltd 4th Floor, 58/59 Great Marlborough St, London W1F 7JY **t** 020 7478 8500 **f** 020 7478 8519 **e** info@theofficialcharts.com **w** theofficialcharts.com Chart Dir: Omar Maskatiya.

PAMRA (Performing Artists Media Rights Assoc.) 161 Borough High St, London SE1 1HR **t** 020 7940 0410 **f** 020 7407 2008 **e** office@pamra.org.uk **w** pamra.org.uk.

The Patent Office Concept House, Cardiff Rd, Newport, Gwent NP10 8QQ **t** 01633 814000 or 08459 500505 **f** 01633 813600 **e** enquiries@patent.gov.uk **w** patent.gov.uk.

PLASA (Professional Lighting & Sound Association) 38 St Leonards Rd, Eastbourne, E Sussex BN21 3UT **t** 01323 410335 **f** 01323 646905 **e** info@plasa.org **w** plasa.org Executive Dir: Ruth Rossington.

PPI (Phonographic Performance Ireland) PPI House, 1 Corrig Ave, Dun Laoghaire, Co Dublin, Ireland **t** +353 1 280 6571 **f** +353 1 280 6579 **e** info@ppiltd.com **w** ppiltd.com CEO: Dick Doyle.

PPL (PHONOGRAPHIC PERFORMANCE LTD)

1 Upper James Street, London W1F 9DE **t** 020 7534 1000 **f** 020 7534 1111 **e** info@ppluk.com **w** ppluk.com. Chairman & CEO: Fran Nevrkla. Director of Business Development: Clive Bishop. Director of Member and Performer Services: Sue Carty. Director of Licensing: Tony Clark. Director of HR and Facilities: Janice Davies. Finance Director: Ben Lambert. Director of Legal & Business Affairs and Rights Negotiation: Peter Leathem. Director of Government Relations: Dominic McGonigal. Director of Public Relations and Corporate Communications: Jonathan Morrish. Director of Public Performance Operations: Sally Stevens. **PPL is a music entertainment service company collecting and distributing broadcast and public performance royalties in the UK on behalf of over 3,500 record companies and 40,000 performers.**

PRC (Performer Registration Centre) 1 Upper James St, London W1F 9DE **t** 020 7534 1234 **f** 020 7534 1383 **e** PRC.info@ppluk.com **w** performersmoney.ppluk.com.

The Prince's Trust 18 Park Square East, London NW1 4LH **t** 020 7543 1234 or 0800 842 842 **f** 020 7543 1200 **e** info@princes-trust.org.uk **w** princes-trust.org.uk Chief Executive: Martina Milburn.

Production Services Association PO Box 2709, Bath BA1 3YS **t** 01225 332 668 **f** 01225 332 701 **e** gm@psa.org.uk **w** psa.org.uk GM: Andy Lenthall.

PRS (Performing Right Society) Copyright House, 29-33 Berners St, London W1T 3AB **t** 020 7580 5544 **f** 020 7306 4455 **e** admissions@mcps-prs-alliance.co.uk **w** mcps.co.uk MD: Steve Porter.

The Radio Academy 5 Market Pl, London W1W 8AE **t** 020 7255 2010 **f** 020 7255 2029 **e** info@radioacademy.org **w** radioacademy.org Dir: Trevor Dann.

RadioCentre 77 Shaftesbury Ave, London W1D 5DU **t** 020 7306 2603 **f** 020 7470 0062 **e** info@radiocentre.org **w** radiocentre.org Chairman: Paul Brown.

Radiocommunications Agency Wyndham House, 189 Marsh Wall, London E14 9SX **t** 020 7211 0211 **f** 020 7211 0507 **e** library@ra.gsi.gov.uk **w** radio.gov.uk.

Rajar (Radio Joint Audience Research) Paramount House, 162-170 Wardour St, London W1F 8ZX **t** 020 7292 9040 **e** info@rajar.co.uk **w** rajar.co.uk MD: Sally de la Bedoyere.

Scottish Arts Council 12 Manor Pl, Edinburgh EH3 7DD **t** 0845 603 6000 **f** 0131 225 9833 **e** help.desk@scottisharts.org.uk **w** scottisharts.org.uk.

Scottish Music Centre 1 Bowmont Gardens, Glasgow G12 9LR **t** 0141 334 6393 **f** 0141 337 1161 **e** info@scottishmusiccentre.com **w** scottishmusiccentre.com MD: Gill Maxwell.

SESAC (Society of European Songwriters & Composers 67 Upper Berkeley St, London W1H 7QX **t** 020 7616 9284 **f** 020 7563 7029 **e** rights@sesac.co.uk **w** sesac.co.uk Chairman: Wayne Bickerton.

Sound Sense 7, Tavern St, Stowmarket, Suffolk IP14 1PJ **t** 01449 673990 **f** 01449 673994 **e** info@soundsense.org **w** soundsense.org Central Services Manager: Kati Wakefield.

South West Association of Promoters 143A East Reach, Taunton, Somerset TA1 3HN **t** 01823 332335 **f** 01823 332335 **e** weekenderlive@btopenworld.com **w** swapuk.co.uk Regional Secretary: Martin Brice.

Variety & Light Entertainment Council 54 Keyes House, Dolphin Sq, London SW1V 3NA **t** 020 7834 0515 **f** 020 7821 0261 Joint Secretary: Kenneth Earle.

Variety Club Of Great Britain 93 Bayham St, London NW1 0AG **t** 020 7428 8100 **f** 020 7482 8123 **e** press@varietyclub.org.uk **w** varietyclub.org.uk The Chief Barker: Tony Frame.

VPL (VIDEO PERFORMANCE LTD)

1 Upper James St, London W1F 9DE **t** 020 7534 1400 **f** 020 7534 1414 **e** info@vpluk.com **w** vpluk.com. Chairman & CEO: Fran Nevrkla. Director of Business Development: Clive Bishop. Director of Member and Performer Services: Sue Carty. Director of Licensing: Tony Clark. Director of HR and Facilities: Janice Davies. Finance Director: Ben Lambert. Director of Legal & Business Affairs and Rights Negotiation: Peter Leathem. Director of Government Relations: Dominic McGonigal. Director of Public Relations and Corporate Communications: Jonathan Morrish. Director of Public Performance Operations: Sally Stevens. **VPL is a music entertainment service company collecting and distributing broadcast and public performance royalties in the UK on behalf of 1,200 record company members.**

Welsh Music Foundation Ty Cefn, Rectory Rd, Canton, Cardiff CF5 1QL **t** 029 2066 8127 **f** 029 2034 1622 **e** enquiries@welshmusicfoundation.com **w** welshmusicfoundation.com Chief Executive: Elliot Reuben.

Women In Music 7 Tavern St, Stowmarket, Suffolk IP14 1PJ **t** 01449 673990 **f** 01449 673994 **e** info@womeninmusic.org.uk **w** womeninmusic.org.uk Admin Officer: Louise Fiddaman.

The Worshipful Company Of Musicians 6th Floor, 2 London Wall Buildings, London EC2M 5PP **t** 020 7496 8980 **f** 020 7588 3633 **e** deputyclerk@wcom.org.uk **w** wcom.org.uk Dept Clerk: Margaret Alford.

Accountants

A & Co (Part of BKL LLP) 7 Ivebury Court, 325 Latimer Rd, London W10 6RA **t** 020 8960 6644 **f** 020 8960 8437 **e** lesley.alexander@bkl.co.uk **w** bkl.co.uk Ptnr: Lesley E Alexander.

Addis & Co Emery House, 192 Heaton Moor Rd, Stockport, Cheshire SK4 4DU **t** 0161 432 3307 **f** 0161 432 3376 **e** enquiries@a-addis.co.uk **w** a-addis.co.uk Ptnr: Anthony Addis.

Alan Heywood & Company 78 Mill Lane, London NW6 1JZ **t** 020 7435 0101 **f** 020 7431 5410 **e** alan@alanheywood.co.uk **w** alanheywood.co.uk Contact: Alan Heywood FCA.

BackOffice Babies LLP 380 Longbanks, Harlow, Essex CM18 7PG **t** 01279 304 526 **f** 01279 304 526 **e** jpweston@ntlworld.com Manager/Consultant: John Weston ACCA.

Baker Tilly 2 Bloomsbury St, London WC1B 3ST **t** 020 7413 5100 **f** 020 7413 5101 **e** david.blacher@bakertilly.co.uk **w** bakertilly.co.uk Head of Media Group: David Blacher.

BDO Stoy Hayward 8 Baker St, London W1U 3LL **t** 020 7486 5888 **f** 020 7487 3686 **e** chris.maddock@bdo.co.uk **w** bdo.co.uk Ptnr: Chris Maddock.

BERG KAPROW LEWIS LLP

Berg Kaprow Lewis

35 Ballards Lane, London N3 1XW **t** 020 8922 9222 **f** 020 8922 9223 **e** firstname.lastname@bkl.co.uk **w** bkl.co.uk Partner: Lesley Alexander. Partner: Steven Hocking Robinson.

Bettersounds Consultancy Little Orchards, Sandyhurst Lane, Ashford, Kent TN25 4NT **t** 01233 643325 **f** 01233 645570 **e** Bettersounds@btconnect.com Contact: Bernard Symonds.

BEVIS & CO

Apex House, 6 West Street, Epsom, Surrey KT18 7RG **t** 01372 840 280 **f** 01372 840 282 **e** chris@bevisandco.co.uk **w** bevisandco.co.uk Partner: Chris Bevis.

BKR Haines Watts Sterling House, 177-181 Farnham Rd, Slough, Berks SL1 4XP **t** 01753 530333 **f** 01753 576606 **e** slough@hwca.com **w** hwca.com Ptnr: Michael Davidson.

Blackstone Franks LLP 26-34 Old St, London EC1V 9QR **t** 020 7250 3300 **f** 020 7250 1402 **e** RMaas@blackstones.co.uk **w** blackstonefranks.com Ptnr: Robert Maas.

Blinkhorns Business & Taxation Advisers 27 Mortimer St, London W1T 3BL **t** 020 7636 3702 **f** 020 7636 0335 **e** Joel.Trott@blinkhorns.co.uk **w** blinkhorns.co.uk Senior Manager: Joel Trott.

Alan Boddy & Co Chartered Accountants Damer House, Meadoway, Wickford, Essex SS12 9HA **t** 01268 571466 **f** 01268 570638 **e** alan@albodd.freeserve.co.uk **w** alanboddy.co.uk Principal: Alan Boddy FCA.

Bowker Orford 15-19 Cavendish Pl, London W1G 0DD **t** 020 7636 6391 **f** 020 7580 3909 **e** mail@bowkerorford.com Ptnr: Michael Orford.

Bradney & Co South House, 21-37 South St, Dorking, Surrey RH4 2JZ **t** 01306 743939 **f** 01306 740253 **e** mail@bradney.co.uk **w** bradney.co.uk MD: John Bradney.

Brebner, Allen & Trapp The Quadrangle, 180 Wardour St, London W1F 8LB **t** 020 7734 2244 **f** 020 7287 5315 **e** partners@brebner.co.uk **w** brebner.co.uk Ptnr: Jose Goumal.

Brett Adams-Chartered Accountants 25 Manchester Sq, London W1U 3PY **t** 020 7486 8985 **f** 020 7486 8991 **e** Info@brettadams.co.uk Music Partner: Steven Davidson.

Bright Grahame Murray Chartered Accountants 124-130 Seymour Pl, London W1H 1BG **t** 020 7402 5201 **f** 020 7402 6659 **e** post@bgm.co.uk **w** bgm.co.uk Auditor: Shailesh Gor/Kevin Levine.

Brighten Jeffrey James 421a Finchley Rd, Hampstead, London NW3 6HJ **t** 020 7794 7373 **f** 020 7431 5566 **e** info@brightenjeffreyjames.co.uk **w** brightenjeffreyjames.com Ptnr: Roger Brighten.

BROWN MCLEOD LTD.

51 Clarkegrove Rd, Sheffield, South Yorks S10 2NH **t** 0114 268 4747 **f** 0114 268 4161 **e** john@brownmcleod.co.uk **w** brownmcleod.co.uk MD: John Roddison. London office: 10 Three Kings Yard, Mayfair, London W1K 4JR Tel: 020 7495 7429

From record labels and publishing to management or recording studios, WMF is on hand to provide help and support on all aspects of the music industry:

WELSH MUSIC

BUSINESS - Supporting the economic development of the music industry in Wales.

DIRECTORY - Over 1700 entries in 65 categories, a comprehensive guide to Welsh music businesses.

ADVICE - For SMEs, start ups or any music related organisation, WMF is the first place to call.

EDUCATION - Seminars, courses and workshops on all aspects of the industry.

STAKEHOLDERS - Representing the interests of the key Welsh music businesses.

FOUNDATION

For more about the support we offer or to become a stakeholder contact us:

WELSH MUSIC FOUNDATION:
33-35 WEST BUTE STREET: CARDIFF BAY:
CARDIFF: CF10 5LH
Tel: 029 2049 4110 / email: enquiries@welshmusicfoundation.com

Llywodraeth Cynulliad Cymru
Welsh Assembly Government

Bullocks Ltd 142 New Cavendish St, London W1W 6YF
t 020 7323 2417 **f** 020 7580 7776 **e** abullock@bullocks.co.uk
w bullocks.co.uk MD: Adrian Bullock.

Carnmores Royalties Consultants Ltd Chelsea
Business Centre, 73-77 Britannia Rd, London SW6 2JR
t 020 7384 3216 **e** richard@carnmores.co.uk
Dir: Richard Jackson-Bass.

Conroy & Company 27 Beaumont Ave, St. Albans, Herts
AL1 4TL **t** 01727 858 589
e conroyandcompany@btconnect.com
Snr Partner: A Conroy FCA, FSCA.

Coombes Wales Quinnell 100 Baker St, London
W1U 6WG **t** 020 7486 9798 **f** 020 7486 0092
e advice@cwq.co.uk Ptnr: Ian Coombes.

Cousins Brett 20 Bulstrode St, London W1U 2JW
t 020 7486 5791 **f** 020 7224 7226
e johncousins@cousinsbrett.com Ptnr: John Cousins.

DALES EVANS & CO LTD CHARTERED ACCOUNTANTS

DALES EVANS
CHArTEREd
ACCOUNTANTS

4th Floor, 88/90 Baker St, London W1U 6TQ **t** 020 7298 1899
f 020 7298 1871 Dirs: Lester Dales, Paul Makin.
Email: LesterDales@dalesevans.co.uk or
PaulMakin@dalesevans.co.uk

W John Daniel FCCA The Beam House, 14 Winkfield Rd,
Windsor, Berks SL4 4BG **t** 01753 852924 **f** 01753 852924
e johndaniel@btconnect.com Snr Partner: John Daniel.

dBM Ltd 8 The Glasshouse, 49A Goldhawk Rd, London
W12 8QP **t** 020 8222 6628 **f** 020 8222 6629
e david@dbmltd.co.uk MD: David Hitchcock.

De La Haye Royalty Services 76 High St, Stony
Stratford, Bucks MK11 1AH **t** 01908 568800 **f** 01908 568890
e royalties@delahaye.co.uk **w** delahaye.co.uk MD: Roger La Haye.

Deloitte & Touche 180 Strand, London WC2R 1BL
t 020 7936 3000 **f** 020 7303 4766
e cbradbrook@deloitte.co.uk **w** deloitte.co.uk
Tax Partner, Music/Media: Charles Bradbrook.

DPC Media Holed Stone Barn, Stisted Cottage Fm, Hollies Rd,
Bradwell, Braintree, Essex CM77 8DZ **t** 01376 551426
f 01376 551787 **e** info@dpcmedia.demon.co.uk
Business Mgr: Dave Clark.

EMTACS-Entertainers & Musicians Tax & Accountancy 69 Loughborough Rd, West Bridgford,
Nottingham NG2 7LA **t** 0115 981 5001 **f** 0115 981 5005
e emtacs@aol.com **w** emtacs.com Ptnr: Geoff Challinger.

Entertainment Accounting International 26a
Winders Rd, Battersea, London SW11 3HB **t** 020 7978 4488
f 020 7978 4492 **e** contact@eai.uk.com Prop: Mike Donovan.

Entertainment Audit Services Northumberland House,
11 The Pavement, Popes Lane, Ealing, London W5 4NG
t 020 8832 7393 **f** 020 8832 7394 **e** easltd@btinternet.com
Contact: Tony Hughes.

Ernst & Young 1 More London Pl, London SE1 2AF
t 020 7951 2000 **f** 020 7951 9336 **e** aflitcroft@uk.ey.com
w ey.com Ptnr: Alan Flitcroft.

HW Fisher & Company Acre House, 11-15 William Rd,
London NW1 3ER **t** 020 7388 7000 **f** 020 7380 4900
e info@hwfisher.co.uk **w** hwfisher.co.uk Ptnr: Martin Taylor.

Freedman Frankl & Taylor Reedham House, 31 King
Street West, Manchester M3 2PJ **t** 0161 834 2574
f 0161 831 7608 **e** mail@fft.co.uk **w** fft.co.uk.

FSPG CHARTERED ACCOUNTANTS

CHARTERED ACCOUNTANTS

21 Bedford Square, London WC1B 3HH **t** 020 7637 4444
f 020 7323 2857 **e** jon@fspg.co.uk Partner: Jon Glasner.

Gelfand Rennert Feldman & Brown Langham House,
1b Portland Pl, London W1B 1GR **t** 020 7636 1776
f 020 7636 6331 **e** info@grfb-uk.com
Contact: Stephen Marks, Robert Perez.

GRANT THORNTON UK LLP

Grant Thornton

Media & Entertainment Group, Grant Thornton House, Melton
Street, London NW1 2EP **t** 020 7383 5100 **f** 020 7383 4715
e terry.a.back@gtuk.com **w** grant-thornton.co.uk Head of Media
& Entertainment: Terry Back. Head of Media Tax: Liz Brion -
liz.a.brion@gtuk.com; Consultant: Harry Hicks -
harry.hicks@gtuk.com; Manager: Steven Leith -
steven.leith@gtuk.com.

Guy Rippon Organisation 21 Bedford Sq, London
WC1B 3HH **t** 020 7637 4444 **f** 020 7323 2857
e guyrippon@mobileemail.vodafone.net Principal: Guy Rippon.

Hardwick & Morris 4 New Burlington St, London W1S 2JG
t 020 7287 9940 **f** 08707 065 204
e stephanie@hardwickandmorris.co.uk
w hardwickandmorris.co.uk Ptnr: Stephanie Hardwick.

Harold Everett Wreford, Chartered Accountants
32 Wigmore St, London W1U 2RP **t** 020 7535 5900
f 020 7535 5901 **e** mail@hew.co.uk
Partner, Entertainment: Jeffrey Sloneem.

HARRIS & TROTTER

65 New Cavendish Street, London W1G 7LS **t** 020 7467 6300
f 020 7467 6363 **e** mail@harrisandtrotter.co.uk
w harrisandtrotter.co.uk Senior Partner: Ronnie Harris. Partners:
Russell Selwyn, Hugh Lask, Jason Boas.

George Hay & Co 83 Cambridge St, London SW1V 4PS
t 020 7630 0582 **f** 020 7630 1502 **e** george.hay@virgin.net
Contact: The Snr Partner.

Immediate Business Management 61 Birch Green,
Hertford, Herts SG14 2LR **t** 01992 550573 **f** 01992 550573
e immediate@onetel.com Ptnr: Derek Jones.

Jeffrey James Chartered Accountants 421a Finchley Rd, Hampstead, London NW3 6HJ **t** 020 7794 7373 **f** 020 7431 5566 **e** info@jeffreyjames.co.uk Ptnr: Jeffrey Kaye.

JER 4 Crescent Stables, 139 Upper Richmond Rd, London SW15 2TN **t** 020 8704 5407 **f** 020 8785 1969 **e** julieeyre@btinternet.com **w** jeroyalties.com Royalty Auditor: Julie Eyre.

Johnsons Chartered Accountants Lancashire House, 217 Uxbridge Rd, London W13 9AA **t** 020 8567 3451 **f** 020 8840 6823 **e** mail@johnsonsca.com **w** johnsonsca.com Ptnr: Shaukat Murad.

Jon Child & Co 202 Ducie House, Ducie St, Manchester M1 2JW **t** 0161 228 1314 **f** 0161 228 3134 **e** jonchild@msn.com Ptnr: Jon Child.

OJ Kilkenny & Company 6 Lansdowne Mews, London W11 3BH **t** 020 7792 9494 **f** 020 7792 1722 **e** mail@ojkilkenny.co.uk Contact: Patrick Savage.

K.M.Malak & Co Ltd 1st Floor Rear Office, 11 The Quadrant, Edgware, Middx HA8 7LU **t** 020 8952 9500 **f** 020 8952 3496 **e** kamalmmalak@onetel.com Principal: Kamal M Malak.

KPMG LLP Aquis Court, 31 Fishpool St, St Albans AL3 4RF **t** 01727 733063 **f** 01727 733001 **e** charles.lestrangemeakin@kpmg.co.uk **w** kpmg.com Dir: Charles Le Strange Meakin.

Leigh Philip & Partners 1-6 Clay St, London W1U 6DA **t** 020 7486 4889 **f** 020 7486 4885 **e** mail@lpplondon.co.uk Snr Partner: Leigh Genis.

Lloyd Piggott Blackfriars House, Parsonage, Manchester M3 2JA **t** 0161 833 0346 **f** 0161 832 0045 **e** info@lloydpiggott.co.uk **w** lloydpiggott.co.uk Tax Associate: Paula Abbott.

Lubbock Fine Russell Bedford House, City Forum, 250 City Rd, London EC1V 2QQ **t** 020 7490 7766 **f** 020 7490 5102 **e** post@lubbockfine.co.uk **w** lubbockfine.co.uk Ptnr: Jeff Gitter.

Macnair Mason St Clare House, 30-33 Minories, London EC3N 1DD **t** 020 7767 3500 **f** 020 7767 3600 **e** mm@macmas.co.uk **w** macmas.co.uk Ptnr: Anton Luck.

Mansfield & Co, Chartered Accountants 55 Kentish Town Rd, Camden Town, London NW1 8NX **t** 020 7482 2022 **f** 020 7482 2025 **e** mco@mansfields.co.uk **w** mansfields.co.uk Snr Partner: David FL Mansfield.

MMG @ MGR (MARTIN GREENE RAVDEN)

Media Management Group

55 Loudoun Road, St John's Wood, London NW8 0DL **t** 020 7625 4545 **f** 020 7625 5265 **e** info@mmguk.com **w** mmguk.com. Contact: David Ravden, Steve Daniel, Ed Grossman & Lionel Martin.

Morris & Shah 31 Paddington St, London W1U 4HD **t** 020 7486 9554 **f** 020 7486 9557 **e** MorrisandShah@aol.com Partners: Jonathan Morris, Kewal Shah.

Music Business Associates Ltd Apex House, 6 West St, Epsom, Surrey KT18 7RG **t** 01372 840 281 **f** 01372 840 282 **e** johnw@musicbusinessassociates.com **w** musicbusinessassociates.com Contact: Chris or John.

Music Business Services 3 Marlborough Rd, Lancing, W Sussex BN15 8UF **t** 01903 530 005 or 07950 274 224 **e** ray@rowlesmusic.co.uk **w** rowlesmusic.co.uk Contact: Ray Rowles.

Music Royalties Ltd 26 Pavilion Way, Eastcote, Middlesex HA4 9JN **t** 07855 411 983 **e** david@musicroyalties.co.uk **w** musicroyalties.co.uk Dir: David Rayment.

MWM Chartered Accountants & Business Advisers 11 Great George St, Bristol BS1 5RR **t** 0117 929 2393 **f** 0117 929 2696 **e** office@mwmuk.com Dir: Craig Williams.

Neill & Co 25 Hill Rd, Theydon Bois, Epping, Essex CM16 7LX **t** 01992 812211 **f** 01992 812299 **e** info@neill.co.uk **w** neill.co.uk Principal: Keith Neill.

Newman & Co Regent House, 1 Pratt Mews, London NW1 0AD **t** 020 7267 6899 **f** 020 7267 6746 **e** partners@newman-and.co.uk **w** newman-and.co.uk Snr Partner: Colin Newman.

Nieman Walters Niman Rosewood Suite, Teresa Gavin House, Woodford Ave, Woodford Green, Essex IG8 8FH **t** 020 8550 3131 **f** 020 8550 6020 **e** info@nwnaccounts.com **w** nwnaccounts.com Ptnr: Edmund Niman.

Note for Note 15 Marroway, Weston Turville, Aylesbury, Bucks HP22 5TQ **t** 01296 614966 **f** 01296 614651 **e** Chris@note-for-note.co.uk Prop: Chris Turner.

Nyman Libson Paul Regina House, 124 Finchley Rd, London NW3 5JS **t** 020 7433 2400 **f** 020 7433 2401 **e** mail@nlpca.co.uk **w** nlpca.co.uk Ptnr: Amin Saleh.

Pearson & Co 113 Smug Oak Business Centre, Lye Lane, Bricket Wood, St Albans, Herts AL2 3UG **t** 01923 894404 **f** 01923 894990 **e** richard@stantonpearson.co.uk Ptnr: Richard Pearson.

PKF (UK) LLP Farringdon Pl, 20 Farringdon Rd, London EC1M 3AP **t** 020 7065 0000 **f** 020 7065 0650 **e** info.london@uk.pkf.com **w** pkf.co.uk.

Portman Music Services Ltd 38 Osnaburgh St, London NW1 3ND **t** 01962 732033 or 07971 455 920 **f** 01962 732032 **e** maria@portmanmusicservices.net **w** portmanmusicservices.co.uk Royalty & Copyright Mgr: Maria Comiskey.

Positive Accounting Solutions 22 Denewood Close, Watford, Herts WD17 4SZ **t** 07836 694 462 **e** simon@positiveaccounting.co.uk MD: Simon Durban.

Prager and Fenton Midway House, 27-29 Cursitor St, London EC4A 1LT **t** 020 7831 4200 **f** 020 7831 5080 **e** mgoldberg@pragerfenton.co.uk **w** pragerfenton.com.

PricewaterhouseCoopers 1 Embankment Pl, London WC2N 6RH **t** 020 7583 5000 **f** 020 7822 4652 **e** firstname.lastname@uk.pwc.com **w** pwc.com Head of UK E&M: Robert W Boyle.

RCO - Royalty Compliance Organisation 4 Crescent Stables, 139 Upper Richmond Rd, London SW15 2TN **t** 020 8789 6444 **f** 020 8785 1960 **e** ask@TheRcO.co.uk **w** rcoonline.com Partners: Mike Skeet, Gill Sharp.

Reeds Copperfields, Mount Pleasant, Crowborough, E Sussex TN6 2NF **t** 01892 668676 **f** 01892 668678 Principle: Chris Reed.

ROSS BENNET-SMITH

112 Jermyn Street, London SW1Y 6LS **t** 020 7930 6000 **f** 020 7930 7070 **e** info@rossbennetsmith.com **w** rossbennetsmith.com Partner: Daniel Ross. Representing many of the worlds' most prominent recording artists, bands, producers, labels, industry executives and new talent. Associate Offices: New York, Los Angeles.

RSM Robson Rhodes LLP 186 City Rd, London EC1V 2NU **t** 020 7251 1644 **f** 020 7250 0801 **e** enquiries@rsmi.co.uk **w** rsmi.co.uk Contact: Dir of Communications.

Ryan & Co 4F, Shirland Mews, London W9 3DY **t** 020 8960 0961 **f** 020 8960 0963 **e** ryan@ryanandco.com **w** ryanandco.com Chartered Accountant: Cliff Ryan.

SAFFERY CHAMPNESS

Saffery Champness

CHARTERED   ACCOUNTANTS

Lion House, Red Lion Street, London WC1R 4GB **t** 020 7841 4000 **f** 020 7841 4100 **e** nick.kelsey@saffery.com **w** saffery.com Partners: Nick Kelsey, Nick Gaskell.

Reeds ...

S.C. Song (Accountants) 50 Eaton Drive, Kingston-Upon-Thames, Surrey KT2 7QX **t** 07770 816 015 **f** 020 8241 8309 **e** scsong403@msn.com Accountant: SC Song.

SEDLEY RICHARD LAURENCE VOULTERS

SEDLEY RICHARD LAURENCE VOULTERS
IN ASSOCIATION WITH GELFANDS

Kendal House, 1 Conduit Street, London W1S 2XA **t** 020 7287 9595 **f** 020 7287 9696 **e** general@srlv.co.uk **w** srlv.co.uk Contact: Richard Rosenberg, Steve Jeffery, Stephen Marks.

Neville Shulman CBE FCA 35A Huntsworth Mews, Gloucester Pl, London NW1 6DB **t** 020 7616 0777 **f** 020 7724 8266 **e** 888@shulman.co.uk **w** shulman.co.uk Principal: Neville Shulman.

Sloane & Co 36-38 Westbourne Grove, Newton Rd, London W2 5SH **t** 020 7221 3292 **f** 020 7229 4810 **e** mail@sloane.co.uk **w** sloane.co.uk Contact: David Sloane.

Ivan Sopher & Company 5 Elstree Gate, Elstree Way, Borehamwood, Herts WD6 1JD **t** 020 8207 0602 **f** 020 8207 6758 **e** accountants@ivansopher.co.uk **w** ivansopher.co.uk Prop: Ivan Sopher.

Synergy Business Management 143 Syon Lane, Osterley, Middlesex TW7 5PZ **t** 020 8568 0609 **f** 020 8568 6968 **e** synergy143@aol.com Ptnr: Eddie Bull.

TENON MEDIA

Tenon media

66 Chiltern St, London W1U 4JT **t** 020 7535 1400 **f** 020 7535 1401 **e** julian.hedley@tenongroup.com **w** tenongroup.com MD: Julian Hedley. Music Group Manager: Kathy Johnson (kathy.johnson@tenongroup.com). Accounting Services Manager: Darren Drake (darren.drake@tenongroup.com).

CR Thomas & Co The 1929 Building, Merton Abbey Mills, Wimbledon, London SW19 2RD **t** 020 8542 4262 **f** 020 8545 0662 **e** ah@thomas-harris.com Snr Partner: Chris Thomas.

Anthony Tiscoe & Company Brentmead House, Britannia Rd, London N12 9RU **t** 020 8343 8749 or 07976 661 217 **f** 020 8492 0159 **e** tony@tiscoe.fsnet.co.uk Chartered Accountant: Anthony Tiscoe.

Vantis plc 66 Wigmore St, London W1U 2SB **t** 020 7467 4000 **f** 020 7467 4040 **e** media@vantisplc.com **w** vantisplc.com Contact: Sarf Malik.

Warley & Warley Chartered Accountants 76 Cambridge Rd, Kingston-Upon-Thames, Surrey KT1 3NA **t** 020 8549 5137 **f** 020 8546 3022 **e** info@warleyandwarley.co.uk **w** warleyandwarley.co.uk Ptnr: Andrew Wordingham.

Westbury Schotness 145-157 St John St, London EC1V 4PY **t** 020 7253 7272 **f** 020 7253 0814 **e** Keithg@westbury.co.uk **w** westbury.co.uk Ptnr: Keith Graham.

William Evans & Partners 20 Harcourt St, London
W1H 4HG **t** 020 7563 8390 **f** 020 7569 8700
e wep@williamevans.co.uk Senior Partner: Stephen Evans.

Willott Kingston Smith 141 Wardour St, London
W1F 0UT **t** 020 7304 4646 **f** 020 7304 4647
e ghowells@kingstonsmith.co.uk **w** kingstonsmith.co.uk/wks
Ptnr: Geraint Howells.

Wingrave Yeats Ltd (Chartered Accountants) 65
Duke St, London W1K 5AJ **t** 020 7495 2244 **f** 020 7499 9442
e wyl@wingrave.co.uk **w** wingrave.co.uk Dir: Philip Hedges.

Winters 29 Ludgate Hill, London EC4M 7JE **t** 020 7919 9100
f 020 7919 9019 **e** info@winters.co.uk **w** winters.co.uk
Ptnr: Roy Bristow.

Wyndhams 177 High St, Harlesden, London NW10 4TE
t 020 8961 3889 **f** 020 8961 4620
e wyndhams@btopenworld.com Ptnr: David Landau.

Yellocello 49 Windmill Rd, London W4 1RN
t 020 8742 2001 **e** info@yellocello.com **w** yellocello.com
Chartered Accountant: Charlie Carne.

CC YOUNG & CO

1st Floor, 48 Poland Street, London W1F 7ND **t** 020 7494 5680
f 020 7494 5690 **e** ccy@ccyoung.co.uk Contact: Colin Young,
Chris Chapman or Kate Dosanjh.

Legal

Addleshaw Goddard 150 Aldersgate St, London EC1A 4EJ
t 020 7606 8855 **f** 020 7606 4390
e paddy.graftongreen@addleshawgoddard.com
w addleshawgoddard.com Ptnr: Paddy Grafton Green.

ADR Chambers - Mediators City Point, 1 Ropemaker St,
London EC2Y 9HT **t** 0845 072 0111 **f** 0845 072 0112
e duggan@adrchambers.co.uk **w** adrchambers.co.uk
Mediator: Dennis Muirhead.

Alastair Nicholas Music and Entertainment Law
89A Leathwaite Rd, London SW11 6RN **t** 020 7924 1904
f 020 7738 1764 **e** awnicholas@btinternet.com
Ptnr: Alastair Nicholas.

Angel & Co 1 Green St, Mayfair, London W1K 6RG
t 020 7495 0555 **f** 020 7495 7550 **e** mail@legalangel-uk.com
Contact: Nigel Angel.

Baxter McKay Schoenfeld LLP Suite 208 Panther
House, 38 Mount Pleasant, London WC1X 0AN
t 020 7833 9191 **f** 020 7833 9494 **e** gb@baxtermckay.com
Ptnr: Gill Baxter.

Benedicts (Solicitors) LLP Hope House, 40 St Peters Rd,
London W6 9BD **t** 020 8741 6020 **f** 020 8741 8362
e john@benedicts.biz Ptnr: John Benedict.

SJ Berwin & Co 222 Grays Inn Rd, London WC1X 8XF
t 020 7533 2222 **f** 020 7533 2000 **e** info@sjberwin.com
w sjberwin.com Solicitor: Nora Mullally.

Brabners Chaffe Street 1 Dale St, Liverpool L2 2ET
t 0151 600 3000 **f** 0151 600 3009
e francis.mcentegart@brabnerscs.com
w brabnerschaffestreet.com Solicitor, Media: Francis McEntegart.

Bray and Krais Solicitors Suite 10, Fulham Business
Exchange, The Boulevard, Imperial Wharf, London SW6 2TL
t 020 7384 3050 **f** 020 7384 3051 **e** bandk@brayandkrais.com
Senior Partner: Richard Bray.

Briffa Business Design Centre, Upper St, Islington, London
N1 0QH **t** 020 7288 6003 **f** 020 7288 6004
e margaret@briffa.com **w** briffa.com
Snr Partner: Margaret Briffa.

BrookStreet Des Roches 1 Des Roches Sq, Witan Way,
Witney, Oxon OX28 4LF **t** 01993 771616 **f** 01993 779030
e charlie.seaward@bsdr.com Ptnr: Charlie Seaward.

John Byrne & Co Sheraton House, Castle Pk, Cambridge
CB3 0AX **t** 01223 370063 **f** 01223 370065
e JB@johnbyrne.co.uk Principal: John Byrne.

CALVERT SOLICITORS

77 Weston Street, London Bridge, London SE1 3RS
t 020 7234 0707 **f** 020 7234 0909
e mail@calvertsolicitors.co.uk **w** calvertsolicitors.co.uk Contact:
Nigel Calvert.

Cambridge Civil Mediation Sheraton House, Castle Pk,
Cambridge CB3 0AX **t** 01223 370063 **f** 01223 370065
e jb@johnbyrne.co.uk Mediator: John Byrne.

Charles Russell Solicitors 8-10 New Fetter Lane, London
EC4A 1RS **t** 020 7203 5075 **f** 020 7203 5002
e firstname.lastname@charlesrussell.co.uk **w** charlesrussell.co.uk
Ptnr: Michael Cover.

CLINTONS

Clintons ©

55 Drury Lane, London WC2B 5RZ **t** 020 7379 6080
f 020 7240 9310 **e** amyers@clintons.co.uk **w** clintons.co.uk
Contact: Andrew Myers, Peter Button.

Cobbetts 39 Newhall St, Birmingham B3 3DY
t 0121 236 4477 **f** 0121 236 0774
e frances.anderson@cobbetts.co.uk **w** cobbetts.co.uk
Ptnr: Frances Anderson.

Collins Long Solicitors 24 Pepper St, London SE1 0EB
t 020 7401 9800 **f** 020 7401 9850 **e** info@collinslong.com
w collinslong.com Partners: James Collins & Simon Long.

COLLYER BRISTOW LLP SOLICITORS

Collyer Bristow

4 Bedford Row, London WC1R 4DF **t** 020 7242 7363
f 020 7405 0555 **e** cblaw@collyerbristow.com
w collyerbristow.com Partner: Howard Ricklow. Music
Consultant: Nick Kanaar.

Jim Cook 38 Grovelands Rd, London N13 4RH
t 020 8350 0613 **f** 020 8350 0613
e jim@jcook21.freeserve.co.uk Solicitor: Jim Cook.

Davenport Lyons 30 Old Burlington St, London W1S 3NL
t 020 7468 2600 **f** 020 7437 8216
e rsprawfon@davenportlyons.com **w** davenportlyons.com
Ptnr: Rupert Sprawfon.

DAVID WINEMAN SOLICITORS

Craven House, 121 Kingsway, London WC2B 6NX
t 020 7400 7800 **f** 020 7400 7890
e irving.david@davidwineman.co.uk **w** davidwineman.co.uk
Contact: Irving David.
Please see our full page advertisement for details of our services.

DEAN MARSH & CO

Dean Marsh & Co Solicitors

73A Middle Street, Brighton BN1 1AL **t** 01273 823 770
f 01273 823 771 **e** dean@deanmarsh.com **w** deanmarsh.com
Principal: Dean Marsh.
London office: 1892 Building, Sans Walk, London EC1R 0LU
t 020 7553 4400 **f** 020 7553 4414

DLA Piper Rudnick Gray Cary 3 Noble St, London
EC2V 7EE **t** 08700 111 111 **e** firstname.lastname@dlapiper.com
w dlapiper.com Head of TMC: Simon Levine.

Edmonds Bowen 4 Old Park Lane, London W1K 1QW
t 020 7629 8000 **f** 020 7221 9334
e info@edmondsbowen.co.uk **w** edmondsbowen.co.uk
Consultant: Nick Pedgrift.

Effective Legal Services 185 Ladbroke Grove, London
W10 6HH **t** 020 8964 3551 or 07808 741 277
f 020 8964 3550 **e** henriette@effectivemusicservices.com
w effectivemusicservices.com Solicitor: Henriette Amiel.

ENGEL MONJACK SOLICITORS

16-18 Berners St, London W1T 3LN **t** 020 7291 3838
f 020 7291 3839 **e** info@engelmonjack.com
w engelmonjack.com Contact: Jonathan Monjack and Lawrence
Engel.

Ent-Law Solicitors 3 Grange Farm Business Pk, Shedfield,
Southampton, Hants SO32 2HD **t** 01329 834100
f 01329 834448 **e** paul@ent-law.co.uk
Contact: Paul Lambeth LLB.

Entertainment Advice Ltd. 31 Penrose St, London
SE17 3DW **t** 020 7708 8822 **f** 020 7703 1239
e info@entertainmentadvice.co.uk **w** entertainmentadvice.co.uk
Consultants: Len Bendel, Anthony Hall.

ENTERTAINMENT LAW ASSOCIATES

Argentum, 2 Queen Caroline Street, London W6 9DX
t 020 8323 8013 **f** 020 8323 8080 **e** ela@ela.co.uk **w** ela.co.uk
MD: John Giacobbi.

Field Fisher Waterhouse 35 Vine St, London EC3N 2AA
t 020 7861 4000 **f** 020 7488 0084 **e** info@ffw.com
w ffw.com.

Finers Stephens Innocent 179 Great Portland St, London
W1W 5LF **t** 020 7323 4000 **f** 020 7580 7069
e marketing@fsilaw.co.uk **w** fsilaw.com Ptnr: Robert Lands.

FORBES ANDERSON FREE

16-18 Berners Street, London W1T 3LN **t** 020 7291 3500
f 020 7291 3511 **e** info@forbesanderson.com Partners: Andrew
Forbes, Dominic Free & Martyn Bailey.

Fox Williams Ten Dominion St, London EC2M 2EE
t 020 7628 2000 **f** 020 7628 2100 **e** mail@foxwilliams.com
w foxwilliams.com Senior Associate: Jane Elliot.

P Ganz & Co 88 Calvert Rd, Greenwich, London SE10 0DF
t 020 8293 9103 **f** 020 8355 9328
e penny.ganz@ganzlegal.com Solicitor: Penny Ganz.

Goldkorn Mathias Gentle 6 Coptic St, London
WC1A 1NW **t** 020 7631 1811 **f** 020 7631 0431
e davidgentle@gmglegal.com Ptnr: David Gentle.

Gray & Co Habib House, 3rd Floor, 9 Stevenson Sq, Manchester M1 1DB **t** 0161 237 3360 **f** 0161 236 6717 **e** grayco@grayand.co.uk **w** grayand.co.uk Ptnr: Rudi Kidd.

GSC Solicitors 31-32 Ely Pl, London EC1N 6TD **t** 020 7822 2222 **f** 020 7822 2211 **e** info@gscsolicitors.com **w** gscsolicitors.com Managing Partner: Saleem Sheikh.

H2O Law 40-43 Chancery Lane, London WC2A 1JQ **t** 020 7405 4700 **e** enquiries@h2o-law.com **w** h2o-law.com.

Hamlins Roxburghe House, 273-287 Regent St, London W1B 2AD **t** 020 7355 6000 **f** 020 7518 9100 **e** ent-law@hamlins.co.uk **w** hamlins.co.uk Managing Partner: Laurence Gilmore.

Harbottle and Lewis Hanover House, 14 Hanover Sq, London W1S 1HP **t** 020 7667 5000 **f** 020 7667 5100 **e** info@harbottle.com **w** harbottle.com Head of Music Group: Paul Jones.

Harrisons Entertainment Law Ltd Suite 4, 19-21 Crawford St, London W1H 1PJ **t** 020 7486 2586 **f** 020 7486 2786 **e** info@annharrison.co.uk **w** annharrison.co.uk Principal: Ann Harrison.

Haynes Phillips Solicitors 113-117 Farringdon Rd, London EC1R 3BX **t** 020 7841 0123 **f** 020 7841 0124 **e** chris@haynesphillips.com **w** haynesphillips.com Ptnr: Chris Phillips.

Helen Searle - Legal & Business Adviser Shortbridge Mill Barn, Piltdown, E Sussex TN22 3XA **t** 01825 769356 **f** 01825 769357 **e** helen@helensearle.com Ptnr: Helen Searle.

Howard Livingstone, Solicitor 37 Trinity Rd, E.Finchley, London N2 8JJ **t** 020 8365 2962 **f** 020 8365 2484 **e** howard@hlivingstone.fsnet.co.uk **w** musicattorney.co.uk Music Lawyer: Howard Livingstone.

HOWELL-JONES PARTNERSHIP

HOWELL - JONES
PARTNERSHIP
—— *Solicitors* ——

Flint House, 52 High St, Leatherhead, Surrey KT22 8AJ **t** 01372 860650 **f** 01372 860659 **e** leatherhead@hjplaw.co.uk **w** hjplaw.co.uk Snr Partner: Peter Scott. **25 years advising the music industry.**

Howletts 60 Grays Inn Rd, London WC1X 8LA **t** 020 7404 5612 **f** 020 7831 0635 **e** howletts@zoom.co.uk Ptnr: David Semmens.

INDEPENDENT LABEL SCHEME

Independent LabelScheme

73A Middle Street, Brighton BN1 1AL **t** 01273 823 770 **f** 01273 823 771 **e** dean@indielabelscheme.com **w** indielabelscheme.com Principal: Dean Marsh. **London office: 1892 Building, Sans Walk, Clerkenwell, London EC1R 0LU t 020 7553 4400 f 020 7553 4414**

John Ireland & Co 57 Elgin Crescent, London W11 2JU **t** 020 7792 1666 **f** 08700 516 570 **e** john@johnirelandandco.net **w** johnirelandandco.net Contact: John Ireland.

James Chapman & Co Solicitors 76, King St, Manchester M2 4NH **t** 0161 828 8000 **f** 0161 828 8012 **e** firstname.lastname@james-chapman.co.uk **w** james-chapman.co.uk Contact: John Cullen, Mike Blood.

Jane Clemetson 85 Charing Cross Rd, London WC2H 0AA **t** 020 7287 1380 **f** 020 7734 3394 **e** jclemetson@btconnect.com Contact: Jane Clemetson.

JAYES & PAGE

JAYES & PAGE

Universal House, 251 Tottenham Court Rd, London W1T 7JY **t** 020 7291 9111 **f** 020 7291 9119 **e** enquiries@jayesandpage.com **w** jayesandpage.com Partners: Anthony Jayes and Bob Page. **Specialist music and media solicitors experienced in undertaking non-contentious and contentious work for corporate and individual clients.**

Jens Hills & Co Northburgh House, 10 Northburgh St, London EC1V 0AT **t** 020 7490 8160 **f** 020 7490 8140 **e** info@jenshills.com Principal: Jens Hills.

KIRKPATRICK & LOCKHART NICHOLSON GRAHAM LLP

K&L® *Challenge us.*®

Kirkpatrick & Lockhart Nicholson Graham LLP

110 Cannon St, London EC4N 6AR **t** 020 7648 9000 **f** 020 7648 9001 **e** ndavies@klng.com **w** klng.com Partner: Nigel Davies.

MC Kirton & Co 83 St Albans Ave, London W4 5JS **t** 020 8987 8880 **f** 020 8932 7908 **e** michael@mckirton.com Snr Partner: Michael Kirton.

Peter Last 75 Holland Rd, Kensington, London W14 8HL **t** 020 7603 4245 **e** prlast@aol.com Lawyer: Peter Last (LL.B, LL.M).

Lawrence Harrison Limited 60 Redston Rd, London N8 7HE **t** 020 8348 1616 **e** info@lawrenceharrison.co.uk **w** lawrenceharrison.co.uk Dir: Lawrence Harrison.

Laytons Solicitors 22 St John St, Manchester M3 4EB **t** 0161 834 2100 **f** 0161 834 6862 **e** music@laytons.com Music Law Department: Eleanor Brody or David Sefton.

Lazarus Consulting Ltd Cydale House, 249A West End Lane, London NW6 1XN **t** 020 7794 1666 or 07976 239 140 **f** 020 7794 1666 **e** info@lazarusconsulting.net **w** lazarusconsulting.net MD: Steve Lazarus.

Lea & Company Solicitors Bank Chambers, Market Pl, Stockport, Cheshire SK1 1UN **t** 0161 480 6691 **f** 0161 480 0904 **e** mail@lealaw.com **w** lealaw.com Ptnr: Stephen Lea.

Lee & Thompson Greengarden House, 15-22 St Christopher's Pl, London W1U 1NL **t** 020 7935 4665 **f** 020 7563 4949 **e** mail@leeandthompson.com **w** leeandthompson.com Ptnr: Andrew Thompson.

The Legal Side Limited 14 Birchlands Ave, London SW12 8ND **t** 020 8675 5747 **f** 020 8675 9101 **e** sally@legalside.co.uk Principal: Sally Bevan.

Lewis Davis Shapiro & Lewit see Smiths.

Lipkin Gorman 61 Grosvenor St, Mayfair, London W1K 3JE **t** 020 7493 4010 **f** 020 7409 1734 Ptnr: Charles Gorman.

Lovells Atlantic House, Holborn Viaduct, London EC1A 2FGlo **t** 020 7296 2000 **f** 020 7296 2001 **e** lindy.golding@lovells.com **w** lovells.com Ptnr: Lindy Golding.

Leonard Lowy & Co 500 Chiswick High Rd, London W4 5RG **t** 020 8956 2785 **f** 020 8956 2786 **e** lowy@leonardlowy.co.uk **w** leonardlowy.co.uk Principal: Leonard Lowy.

Maclay, Murray & Spens 151 St Vincent St, Glasgow G2 5NJ **t** 0141 248 5011 **f** 0141 248 5819 **e** murray.buchanan@mms.co.uk **w** mms.co.uk Consultant: Murray J. Buchanan.

Maclay, Murray & Spens, London 10 Foster Lane, London EC2V 6HR **t** 020 7606 6130 **f** 020 7600 0992 **e** murray.buchanan@mms.co.uk **w** mms.co.uk Consultant: Murray J. Buchanan.

Magrath & Co 52-54 Maddox St, London W1S 1PA **t** 020 7495 3003 **f** 020 7409 1745 **e** alexis.grower@magrath.co.uk **w** magrath.co.uk Consultant: Alexis Grower.

Manches Aldwych House, 81 Aldwych, London WC2B 4RP **t** 020 7404 4433 **f** 020 7430 1133 **e** manches@manches.co.uk **w** manches.co.uk.

Marriott Harrison 12 Great James St, London WC1N 3DR **t** 020 7209 2000 or 020 7209 2093 **f** 020 7209 2001 **e** tony.morris@marriottharrison.co.uk **w** marriottharrison.com Partner & Head of Media: Tony Morris.

McClure Naismith 292 St Vincent St, Glasgow, Lanarkshire G2 5TQ **t** 0141 204 2700 **f** 0141 248 3998 **e** glasgow@mcclurenaismith.com **w** mcclurenaismith.com Associate: Euan Duncan.

Metcalfes Solicitors 46-48 Queen Sq, Bristol BS1 4LY **t** 0117 929 0451 **f** 0117 929 9551 **e** mburgess@metcalfes.co.uk **w** metcalfes.co.uk Entertainment Lawyer: Martino Burgess.

MICHAEL SIMKINS LLP

Michael Simkins LLP
SOLICITORS

45-51 Whitfield Street, London W1T 4HB **t** 020 7907 3000 **f** 020 7907 3111 **e** info@simkins.com **w** simkins.com Music Group: David Franks, Richard Taylor, Paddy Grafton Green, James Harman, Euan Lawson, Alan Lander, Alexi Cory-Smith, Ed Baden–Powell, Catherine Fehler and Roger Billins.
One of the largest and most experienced teams of music lawyers in Europe handling transactional work, litigation and business affairs.

Mishcon de Reya Summit House, 12, Red Lion Sq, London WC1R 4QD **t** 020 7440 7000 **f** 020 7404 5982 **e** feedback@mishcon.co.uk **w** mishcon.co.uk Ptnr: Martin Dacre.

Robin Morton, Solicitor 22 Herbert St, Glasgow G20 6NB **t** 0141 560 2748 or 0141 337 1199 or 07870 590 909 **f** 0141 357 0655 **e** robinmorto@aol.com Contact: Robin Morton.

Moss & Coleman 170-180 High St, Hornchurch, Essex RM12 6JP **t** 01708 446 781 **f** 01708 470 341 **e** d.beeson@mosco.co.uk **w** mosco.co.uk Contact: Dale Beeson.

Multiplay Music Consultants 19 Eagle Way, Harrold, Bedford MK43 7EW **t** 01234 720 785 or 07971 885 375 **f** 01234 720 664 **e** kevin@multiplaymusic.com **w** multiplaymusic.com MD: Kevin White.

Nicolaou Solicitors The Barn Studios, Burnt Farm Ride, Goffs Oak, Herts EN7 5JA **t** 01707 877707 or 07785 933377 **f** 01707 877708 **e** niclaw@tiscali.co.uk Solicitor: Constantina Nicolaou.

Nigel Dewar Gibb & Co Solicitors 43 St John St, London EC1M 4AN **t** 020 7608 1091 **f** 020 7608 1092 **e** ndg@e-legaluk.co.uk **w** e-legaluk.co.uk Principal: Nigel Dewar Gibb.

NORTHROP MCNAUGHTAN DELLER

solicitors

18c Pindock Mews, Little Venice, London W9 2PY **t** 020 7289 7300 **f** 020 7286 9555 **e** nmd@nmdsolicitors.com **w** nmdsolicitors.com Partners: Tim Northrop, Christy McNaughtan, Martin Deller.

Olswang 90 Long Acre, London WC2E 9TT **t** 020 7208 8888 **f** 020 7208 8800 **e** olsmail@olswang.com **w** olswang.com Ptnr: John Enser.

Pinsent Curtis Biddle 1 Gresham St, London EC2V 7BU **t** 020 7606 9301 **f** 020 7606 3305 **e** martin.lane@pinsents.com **w** pinsents.com Managing Ptnr: Martin Lane.

Quastels Avery Midgen LLP 74 Wimpole St, London W1G 9RR **t** 020 7908 2525 **f** 020 7908 2626 **e** sconroy@quastels.com **w** quastels.com Ptnr: Simon Conroy.

ROHAN & CO SOLICITORS

ROHAN & C°
SOLICITORS

Aviation House, 1-7 Sussex Road, Haywards Heath, West Sussex RH16 1RX **t** 01444 450 901 **f** 01444 440 437 **e** partners@rohansolicitors.co.uk **w** rohansolicitors.co.uk Contact: Rupert Rohan.

Ross & Craig 12A Upper Berkeley St, London W1H 7QE **t** 020 7262 3077 **f** 020 7724 6427 **e** david.leadercramer@rosscraig.com **w** rosscraig.com MD: David Leadercramer.

James Rubinstein & Co 149 Cholmley Gardens, Mill Lane, London NW6 1AB **t** 020 7431 5500 **f** 020 7431 5600 **e** help@jamesrubinstein.co.uk **w** jamesrubinstein.co.uk Senior Partner: James Rubinstein.

Russell-Cooke 8 Bedford Row, London WC1R 4BX
t 020 7440 4843 **f** 020 7611 1721
e surname@russell-cooke.co.uk **w** russell-cooke.co.uk
Ptnr: Lawrence Harrison.

P Russell & Co, Solicitors Suite 48, London House, 271
King St, London W6 9LZ **t** 020 8233 2943 **f** 020 8233 2944
e info@prcsolicitors.com Ptnr: Paul Russell.

Russells Regency House, 1-4 Warwick St, London W1R 6LJ
t 020 7439 8692 **f** 020 7494 3582 **e** media@russells.co.uk
Contact: Mr R Page.

Sample 1 Ltd 10 Crystal Palace Rd, London SE22 9HB
t 020 8637 9795 **f** 020 8516 5572 **e** info@sample1.co.uk
w sample1.co.uk MD: Mark Pearse.

Sample Clearance Services Ltd 73A Middle St,
Brighton, E Sussex BN1 1AL **t** 01273 326999 **f** 01273 328999
e saranne@sampleclearance.com **w** sampleclearance.com
MD: Saranne Reid.

Schillings Royalty House, 72-74 Dean St, London W1D 3TL
t 020 7453 2500 **f** 020 7453 2600 **e** legal@schillings.co.uk
w schillings.co.uk Office Mgr: Shelley Vincent.

Search (a division of Jeff Wayne Music Group)
Oliver House, 8-9 Ivor Pl, London NW1 6BY **t** 020 7724 2471
f 020 7724 6245 **e** info@jeffwaynemusic.com
w jeffwaynemusic.com Group Dir: Jane Jones.

SEDDONS

5 Portman Square, London W1H 6NT **t** 020 7725 8000
f 020 7725 5235 **e** media@seddons.co.uk **w** seddons.co.uk
Partner: David Kent. Solicitor: Hannah Shield.
**For further information about our entertainment & media
work, please contact David Kent or Hannah Shield on +44
(0) 20 7725 8000 or email them at media@seddons.co.uk**

Sheridans Whittington House, Alfred Pl, London WC1E 7EA
t 020 7079 0100 **f** 020 7079 0200
e entertainment@sheridans.co.uk **w** sheridans.co.uk
Ptnr: Stephen Luckman.

Simons Muirhead & Burton 50 Broadwick St, London
W1F 7AG **t** 020 7734 4499 **f** 020 7734 3263
e info@smab.co.uk **w** smab.co.uk Ptnr: Simon Goldberg.

SK Sport and Entertainment 50a Kingsway Pl, London
EC1R 0LU **t** 020 7253 7333 **f** 020 7253 7222
e info@sk-se.com **w** sk-se.com
Solicitor: Nigel Gibb, Jeremy Summers.

Smiths 17 Shorts Gardens, Covent Garden, London WC2H 9AT
t 020 7395 8630 **f** 020 7395 8639 **e** lewis@smiths-law.com
w smiths-law.com Ptnr: Andrew Lewis.

Spraggon Stennett Brabyn Matrix Complex, 91
Peterborough Rd, London SW6 3BU **t** 020 7348 7630
f 020 7348 7631 **e** legal@ssb.co.uk **w** ssb.co.uk
Office Manager: Chris Weller.

Statham Gill Davies 52 Welbeck St, London W1G 9XP
t 020 7317 3210 **f** 020 7487 5925
e john.statham@stathamgilldavies.com
Solicitor/Partner: John Statham.

Steeles Law LLP 11 Guilford St, London WC1N 1DT
t 020 7421 1720 **f** 020 7421 1749 **e** music@steeleslaw.co.uk
w steeleslaw.co.uk Consultant: Patrick Rackow.

Swan Turton 68a Neal St, Covent Garden, London
WC2H 9PA **t** 020 7520 9555 **f** 020 7520 9556
e info@swanturton.com **w** swanturton.com
Head of Music Group: Julian Turton.

Tarlo Lyons Watchmaker Court, 33 St John's Lane, London
EC1M 4DB **t** 020 7405 2000 **f** 020 7814 9421
e info@tarlolyons.com **w** tarlolyons.com
Partners: Stanley Munson, D Michael Rose.

Taylor Wessing Carmelite, 50 Victoria Embankment, London
EC4Y 0DX **t** 020 7300 7000 **f** 020 7300 7100
e london@taylorwessing.com **w** taylorwessing.com
Ptnr: Paul Mitchell.

Teacher Stern Selby 37-41 Bedford Row, London
WC1R 4JH **t** 020 7242 3191 **f** 020 7405 2964
e g.shear@tsslaw.co.uk **w** tsslaw.co.uk
Snr Partner: Graham Shear.

TODS MURRAY LLP

TODS MURRAY LLP
SOLICITORS

Edinburgh Quay, 133 Fountainbridge, Edinburgh EH3 9AG
t 0131 656 2000 **f** 0131 656 2020
e firstname.lastname@todsmurray.com **w** todsmurray.com
Contact: Andy Harris or Richard Findlay.
**With offices in Edinburgh and Glasgow, we advise clients
throughout Scotland and beyond on all aspects of the music
industry.**

Tods Murray LLP (Glasgow) 33 Bothwell St, Glasgow
G2 6NL **t** 0141 275 4771 **f** 0141 275 4781
e firstname.lastname@todsmurray.com **w** todsmurray.com
Contact: Richard Findlay or Andy Harris.

Turner Parkinson Hollins Chambers, 64a Bridge St,
Manchester M3 3BA **t** 0161 833 1212 **f** 0161 834 9098
e andrew.booth@tp.co.uk **w** tp.co.uk Ptnr: Andy Booth.

WEB SHERIFF

Argentum, 2 Queen Caroline Street, London W6 9DX
t 020 8323 8013 **f** 020 8323 8080
e websheriff@websheriff.com **w** websheriff.com MD: John
Giacobbi.
Protecting your rights on the internet.

WGS Solicitors 133 Praed St, London W2 1RN
t 020 7723 1656 **f** 020 7724 6936 **e** cl@wgs.co.uk **w** wgs.co.uk
Ptnr: Charles Law.

Wiggin LLP 95 The Promenade, Cheltenham, Glocs GL50 1WG **t** 01242 224114 **f** 01242 224223 **e** alexander.ross@wiggin.co.uk **w** wiggin.co.uk Ptnr: Alexander Ross.

Zimmers Solicitors Rechtsanwälte 32 Corringham Rd, London NW11 7BU **t** 0870 770 0171 or 020 8457 8850 **f** 0870 770 0172 **e** hanna.weber@zimmerslaw.com European Registered Lawy.: Hanna Weber.

Insurance

Albemarle Insurance Brokers Ltd 10B Printing House Yard, Shoreditch, London E2 7PR **t** 020 7613 5919 **f** 020 7613 5839 **e** ruth@albemarleinsurance.com **w** albemarleinsurance.com MD: Ruth Sandler.

NW Brown Insurance Brokers Ltd Richmond House, 16-20 Regent St, Cambridge CB2 1DB **t** 01223 720310 **f** 01223 353705 **e** richard.rampley@nwbrown.co.uk **w** nwbrown.co.uk Account Exec: Richard Rampley.

ESR Insurance Services Ltd 4 Langthorne St, London SW6 6JY **t** 020 7385 4001 or 07920 293 898 **f** 020 7385 4151 **e** mgoebbels@esrinsurance.co.uk **w** esrinsurance.co.uk Contact: Martin Goebbels.

FMW Risk Services Ltd FMW House, Inworth Rd, Feering, Essex CO5 9SE **t** 01376 574 200 **f** 01376 574 222 **e** d.macmahon@fmw.co.uk **w** fmw.co.uk Dir: Dominic MacMahon.

HCF Partnership Star House, 6 Garland Rd, Stanmore, Middlesex HA7 1NR **t** 020 8731 5151 **f** 020 8951 3081 **e** enquiries@hcfltd.co.uk **w** hcf.co.uk Ptnr: Steven Gordon.

Honour Point Ltd 88 Hagley Rd, Edgbaston, Birmingham B16 8LU **t** 0121 454 8388 **f** 0121 454 6685 **e** info@honour-point.co.uk Dir: Matthew Stephens.

La Playa The Stables, Manor Farm, Milton Rd, Impington, Cambridge CB4 9NF **t** 01223 522411 **f** 01223 237942 **e** media@laplaya.co.uk **w** laplaya.co.uk MD: Mark Boon.

Musicguard (Pavilion Insurance Management Ltd) Pavilion House, Mercia Business Village, Westwood Business Pk, Coventry CV4 8HX **t** 02476 851000 **f** 02476 851080 **e** sales@musicguard.co.uk **w** musicguard.co.uk Sales Dir: Sarah Gow.

Robertson Taylor Insurance Brokers Ltd 5 Plato Pl, 72-74 St Dionis Rd, London SW6 4TU **t** 020 7510 1234 **f** 020 7510 1134 **e** enquiries@rtib.net **w** robertson-taylor.co.uk Dir: John Silcock.

Stafford Knight Entertainment Insurance Brokers 55 Aldgate High St, London EC3N 1AL **t** 020 7481 6262 **f** 020 7481 7638 **e** tony.crawford@towergate.co.uk Divisional Dir: Tony Crawford.

Swinglehurst Ltd St Clare House, 30-33 Minories, London EC3N 2DD **t** 020 7480 6969 **f** 020 7480 6996 **e** lastname@swinglehurst.co.uk **w** swinglehurst.co.uk Ptnr: Gordon Devlin.

Financial Advisors

Aaron Knight Saili & Associates 27 Lynwood Ave, Langley, Berks SL3 7BJ **t** 01753 676300 **f** 01753 676301 **e** aksaili@btinternet.com Principal: Arun Saili.

Albemarle Insurance 7 Hodgkinson Farm, Boot Lane, Heaton, Bolton BL1 5ST **t** 01204 840444 **f** 01204 841411 Contact: Ruth Sandler.

Chelver Media Finance First Floor, Kendal House, 1 Conduit St, London W1S 2XA **t** 020 7287 7087 **f** 020 7287 9696 **e** steve@ccdb.cc **w** ccdb.cc Contact: Steve Cherry.

Collins Financial Consultants Ltd Allum Gate House, Theobald St, Borehamwood, Herts WD6 4RS **t** 020 8823 0316 **f** 020 8823 0305 **e** CFC@sjpp.co.uk Dir: Paul Collins.

Craig Ryle Financial Ltd 62 Lake Rise, Romford, Essex RM1 4EE **t** 01708 760 544 **f** 01708 760 563 **e** mail@craigryle.fsnet.co.uk Dir: Linda Ryle.

Ents. & Musicians Tax. and Accounts. Services 69 Loughborough Rd, West Bridgford, Nottingham NG2 7LA **t** 0115 9815001 **f** 0115 9815005 **e** info@emtacs.com **w** emtacs.com Mgr: Geoff Challinger.

Kingston Smith Financial Services Ltd 105 St Peter's St, St Albans, Herts AL1 3EJ **t** 01727 896000 **f** 01727 896001 **e** ksfs@kingstonsmith.co.uk **w** kingstonsmith.co.uk Dir: Derek Prentice.

LGI Consulting - Professional Mortgage Advice 2nd Floor, 41a Church St, Weybridge, Surrey KT13 8DG **t** 01932 856 699 **f** 01932 856 685 **e** info@lgiconsulting.co.uk **w** lgiconsulting.co.uk Contact: Giuseppe Iannelli.

MMG @ MGR (MARTIN GREENE RAVDEN)

Media Management Group

55 Loudoun Road, St John's Wood, London NW8 0DL **t** 020 7625 4545 **f** 020 7625 5265 **e** info@mmguk.com **w** mmguk.com. Contact: David Ravden, Steve Daniel, Ed Grossman & Lionel Martin.

Music Media IFA Ltd Bright Cook House, 139 Upper Richmond Rd, London SW15 2TX **t** 020 8780 0988 **f** 020 8780 1594 **e** post@musicmedia.co.uk **w** musicmedia.co.uk Planning Dir: Malcolm Lyons.

Smith & Williamson 30 Queen Sq, Bristol BS1 4ND **t** 0117 925 7603 **f** 0117 922 5105 **e** ttl@smith.williamson.co.uk **w** smith.williamson.co.uk Senior Consultant: Tony Thorpe.

TMP Financial Planning Colbury Manor, Eling, Southampton SO40 9FY **t** 023 8042 7750 **f** 023 8042 7761 **e** howard.lucas@tmpfinancial.co.uk **w** themanorpartnership.com Dir: Howard Lucas.

WTK Wealth Management Limited Regus House, Manchester Business Pk, 3000 Aviator Way, Manchester M22 5TG **t** 01625 599 944 **f** 01625 599 001 **e** info@wtkltd.com **w** wtkltd.com.

Artist Management

1 2 ONE ENTERTAINMENT

67-69 Chalton Street, London NW1 1HY **t** 020 7554 2100
f 020 7554 2154 **e** Paul@12one.net **w** 12one.net MD: Paul
Kennedy.
See also www.myspace.com/12oneent

2Point9 Management PO Box 44607, London N16 0YP
t 07801 033 741 **e** Office@2point9.com **w** 2point9.com
Dirs: Billy Grant, Rob Stuart.

3cord Management 54 Portobello Rd, London W11 3DL
t 020 7229 9218 **e** simon@3cord.net Mgr: Simon Hicks.

3rd Precinct 34 Wroxham Ave, Hemel Hempstead, Herts
HP3 9HF **t** 01442 265 415 **f** 01442 265 415
e charlotte@3rdprecinct.co.uk **w** 3rdprecinct.co.uk
CEO: Charlotte Roel.

3rd Stone PO Box 8, Corby, Northants NN17 2XZ
t 01536 202295 **f** 01536 266246 **e** steve@adasam.co.uk
w adasam.co.uk Label Mgr: Steve Kalidoski.

>4 Management PO Box 47163, London W6 6AS
t 020 8748 4997 or 07885 512 721 **e** info@morethan4.com
w morethan4.com MD: Anthony Hamer-Hodges.

4 Tunes Management PO Box 36534, London W4 3XE
t 020 8293 0999 **f** 020 8293 9525 **e** andy@4-tunes.com
w 4-tunes.com MD: Andy Murray.

7pm Management PO Box 2272, Rottingdean, Brighton
BN2 8XD **t** 01273 304681 **f** 01273 308120
e info@a7music.com **w** a7music.com Dir: Seven Webster.

10 Management 29 Lansdowne Crescent, Notting Hill,
London W11 2NS **t** 020 7467 0622
e jonathan@10management.com Contact: Jonathan Wild.

13th Moon Management PO Box 79, Bridgend, Mid
Glamorgan CF32 8ZR **t** 01656 872582 **f** 01656 872582
e liz@asf-13thmoon.demon.co.uk **w** asf-13thmoon.demon.co.uk
Mgr: Liz Howell.

19 Management 33 Ransomes Dock, 35-37 Parkgate Rd,
London SW11 4NP **t** 020 7801 1919 **f** 020 7801 1920
e reception@19.co.uk **w** 19.co.uk MD: Simon Fuller.

21st Artist 1 Blythe Rd, London W14 0HG **t** 020 7348 4800
f 020 7348 4801 **w** eltonjohn.com
Dir: Frank Presland, Clive Banks.

162a Music First floor, 8-9 Rivington Pl, London EC2A 3BA
t 020 7691 7940 or 07803 131 646 **f** 020 7691 7940
e jan@162a.com **w** 162a.com MD: Jan Sodderland.

365 Artists Ltd 91 Peterborough Rd, London SW6 3BU
t 020 7384 6500 **f** 020 7384 6504 **e** info@365artists.com
w 365artists.com Dir: Adam Clough.

A1 Entertainment 40 Highfield Park Rd, Bredbury,
Stockport, Cheshire SK6 2PG **t** 0161 494 2098
e a1.entertainment@btdigitaltv.com
w a1entertainmentshowbiz.com MD: Gill Cragen.

ACA Music Management Blenheim House, Henry St,
Bath, Somerset BA1 1TAR **t** 01225 428284 **f** 01225 400090
e aca_aba@freenet.co.uk MD: Harry Finegold.

Active Music Management Suite 401, 29 Margaret St,
London W1B 3HH **t** 0870 120 7668 **f** 0870 120 9880
e activemm@btopenworld.com **w** activemm.co.uk
MD: Mark Winters.

Adventures in Music PO Box 261, Wallingford, Oxon
OX10 0XY **t** 01491 832 183 **e** info@adventuresin-music.com
w adventure-records.com MD: Paul Conroy.

Aire International 2a Ferry Rd, London SW13 9RX
t 020 8834 7373 **f** 020 8834 7474 **e** info@airmtm.com
w airmtm.com Dir: Marc Connor.

AK Creative Management PO Box 488, Rochdale
OL16 9AG **t** 07711 040 036
e andy@akcreativemanagement.co.uk
w akcreativemanagement.co.uk Contact: Andy Barrow.

AKlass Artist Management PO Box 42371, London
N12 0WS **t** 020 8368 7760 **e** info@aklass.biz **w** aklass.biz
Contact: Patsy McKay.

Albert Samuel Management 42 City Business Centre,
Lower Rd, London SE16 2XB **t** 020 7740 1600
f 020 7740 1700 **e** asm@missioncontrol.net
w asmanagement.co.uk Dir: Albert & David Samuel.

**Vern Allen Entertainments & Management
Agency** P.O Box 135, Exeter, Devon EX2 9WA
t 01392 273305 **f** 01392 426421 **e** vern@vernallen.co.uk
w vernallen.co.uk Dir: Vernon Winteridge.

Amber PO Box 1, Chipping Ongar, Essex CM5 9HZ
t 01277 362916 or 01277 365046
e management@amberartists.com **w** amberartists.com
MD: Paul Tage.

Ambush Management 32 Ransome's Dock, 35-37
Parkgate Rd, London SW11 4NP **t** 020 7801 1919
f 020 7738 1819 **e** alambush.native@19.co.uk
w ambushgroup.co.uk MD: Alister Jamieson.

A.M.P./TBA 13-14 Margaret St, London W1W 8RN
t 020 7224 1992 **f** 020 7224 0111
e mail@harveygoldsmith.com MD: Harvey Goldsmith CBE.

Amusico Limited Fides House, 10 Chertsey Rd, Woking,
Surrey GU21 5AB **t** 07966 438 376 **e** ed@amusico.com
w amusico.com Contact: Ed Weidman.

Nita Anderson Entertainments 165 Wolverhampton Rd,
Sedgley, Dudley, W Midlands DY3 1QR **t** 01902 882211
f 01902 883356 **e** nitaandersonagency@hotmail.com
w nitaanderson.co.uk Contact: Juanita Anderson.

The Animal Farm Atomic Studios, Block B, Tower Bridge
Business Complex, 100 Clements Rd, London SE16 4DG
t 020 7237 8768 **e** ville@theanimalfarm.co.uk
w theanimalfarm.co.uk MD: Ville Leppanen.

Apollo Management 40A Old Compton St, London
W1D 4TU **t** 020 7434 9919 **f** 020 7439 0794
e Apollo.Mgmt@mediajunction.co.uk MD: Giles Cooper.

ARB Music Management F5 157 Wells Rd, Bristol
BS4 2BU **t** 0117 977 9917 or 07768 905238 **f** 0117 977 9917
e anthony.braine@arbmusic.co.uk Mgr: Anthony Braine.

Archangel Management PO Box 1013, Woking
GU22 7ZD **t** 01483 729 447
e info@archangelmanagement.co.uk
w archangelmanagement.co.uk A&R: Bruce Elliott-Smith.

Archetype Management 91 Clarendon Rd, London
W11 4JG **t** 020 7221 5543 **f** 020 7691 7002
e jon@archetype.cc **w** archetype.cc MD: Jon Terry.

Ardent Music PO Box 20078, London NW2 3FA
t 020 7435 7706 **f** 020 7435 7712 **e** info@ardentmusic.co.uk
MD: Ian Blackaby.

Arketek Management 53 Edge St, Nutgrove, St Helens,
Merseyside WA9 5JX **t** 0151 430 6290 **e** info@arketek.com
w arketek.com MD: Alan Ferreira.

Armstrong Academy Artist Management Ltd GMC
Studio, Hollingbourne, Kent ME17 1UQ **t** 01622 880599
f 01622 880020 **e** management@triple-a.uk.com
w triple-a.uk.com MD: Scott Armstrong.

The Art & Music Corporation Munro House, High Close,
Rawdon, Leeds, W Yorks LS19 6HF **t** 0113 250 3338
f 0113 250 7343 **e** stewart@artandmusic.demon.co.uk
w acoustic-alchemy.net MD: Stewart Coxhead.

Artists & Media Ltd Devlin House, 36 St George St,
Mayfair, London W1R 9FA **t** 07951 406 938
e andrian@msn.com MD: Andrian Adams.

Askonas Holt Ltd (classical artists only) Lonsdale
Chambers, 27 Chancery Lane, London WC2A 1PF
t 020 7400 1700 **f** 020 7400 1799 **e** info@askonasholt.co.uk
w askonasholt.co.uk Joint Chief Executive: Robert Rattray.

Asylum Artists PO Box 121, Hove, E Sussex BN3 4YY
t 01273 774 468 **f** 08709 223 099 **e** info@AsylumGroup.com
w AsylumGroup.com Dirs: Bob James, Scott Chester.

ATC Management 142 New Cavendish St, London
W1W 6YF **t** 020 7323 2430 or 07833 641 484
f 020 7580 7776 **e** ollie@atcmanagement.com
Contact: Ollie Slaney.

Atomic Management Elme House, 133 Long Acre, Covent
Garden, London WC2H 9DT **t** 020 7379 3010
f 020 7240 8272 **e** info@atomic-london.com
Contact: Mick Newton.

Atrium Music PO Box 278, Wavertree, Liverpool L15 8WY
t 0151 737 1886 or 07786 537 866
e query@atrium-music.co.uk **w** atrium-music.co.uk
MD: Paula McCool.

Audio Authority Management 1, Sherwood Oaks,
Frensham Rd, Kenley, Surrey CR8 5NS **t** 020 7101 2880 or
07980 607 808 **e** tim.hole@audioauthority.co.uk
w audioauthority.co.uk Contact: Tim Hole.

AUTOMATIC MANAGEMENT

AUTOMATIC MANAGEMENT

13 Cotswold Mews, 30 Battersea Square, London SW11 3RA
t 020 7978 7888 **f** 020 7978 7808 **e** auto@automan.co.uk
w automaticmanagement.co.uk MD: Jerry Smith.
See also: www.soundsoftheunderground.net

Autonomy Music Unit 212 The Gramophone Works, 326
Kensal Rd, London W10 5BZ **t** 020 8969 9111
f 020 8969 9955 **e** info@autonomy-music.co.uk
w autonomy-music.co.uk MD: Grant Bishop.

Avalon Management Group Ltd 4a Exmoor St, London
W10 6BD **t** 020 7598 8000 **f** 020 7598 7300
e sarahb@avalonuk.com **w** avalonuk.com HoM: Sarah Bowden.

Axis Management 42 Ferry Rd, Barnes, London
SW13 9PW **t** 020 7751 0199 **f** 020 7751 0199
e jeremy.pearce@axismanagement.net MD: Jeremy Pearce.

azoffmusic management 22 Gordon Ave, St Margarets,
Twickenham, Middx TW1 1NQ **t** 020 8744 2404
f 020 8744 2406 **e** sarahfj2@aol.com
UK Representative: Sarah Ferguson-Jones.

Back Yard Management 24 Oppidans Rd, Primrose Hill,
London NW3 3AG **t** 020 7722 7522 **f** 020 7722 7622
e info@back-yard.co.uk **w** back-yard.co.uk Mgr: Gil Goldberg.

Badger Management 4 Ormonde Gardens, Belfast
BT6 9FL **t** 028 9079 1666 **e** steve@badger-management.com
Contact: Stephen Orr.

Bamn Management Unit 123 Buspace Studios, Conlan St,
London W10 5AP **t** 0208 964 0770 **f** 0208 964 0620
e steve@bamn.co.uk Dirs: Fran O'Connor, Steve Finan.

Banchory Management PO Box 25074, Glasgow G3 8TT
t 0141 204 2269 **f** 0141 226 3181 **e** info@banchory.net
w banchory.net Mgr: Neil Robertson, Katrina House.

Bandana Management 100 Golborne Rd, London
W10 5PS **t** 020 8969 0606 **f** 020 8969 0505
e info@banman.co.uk **w** banman.co.uk MD: Brian Lane.

Joe Bangay Enterprises River House, Riverwoods,
Marlow, Bucks SL7 1QY **t** 01628 486 193 **f** 01628 890 239
e william.b@btclick.com **w** joebangay.com MD: Joe Bangay.

Paul Barrett (Rock 'n Roll Enterprises) 21 Grove
Terrace, Penarth, South Glamorgan CF64 2NG **t** 029 2070 4279
f 029 2070 9989 **e** barrettrocknroll@ntlworld.com
MD: Paul Barrett.

Barrington Pheloung Management Andrew's, off Rand
Rd, High Roding, Great Dunmow CM6 1NQ **t** 01371 874 022
f 01371 874 110 **e** info@pheloung.co.uk
Composer: Barrington Pheloung.

Bastard Management 22 Charmouth House, Dorset Rd,
London SW8 1EU **t** 020 7582 5532
e bastardmgt@hotmail.com MD: Alex Holland.

Bedlam Management PO Box 34449, London W6 0RT
t 07974 355 078 **e** info@bedlammanagement.com
MD: Steven Abbott.

Beetroot Management Newlands House, 40 Berners St,
London W1T 3NA **t** 020 7255 2408 **e** info@beetrootmusic.com
w beetrootmusic.com Assistant Manager: Annabel Burn.

Bermuda Management Matrix Complex, 91 Peterborough
Rd, London SW6 3BU **t** 020 7371 5444 **f** 020 7371 5454
e paul@crownmusic.co.uk MD: Paul Samuels.

B&H Management PO Box 1162, Bovingdon, Herts.
HP1 9DE **t** 01442 832 010 **f** 01442 834 910
e simon@bandhmanagement.demon.co.uk
w myspace.com/bandhmanagement MD: Simon Harrison.

Big Blue Music Windy Ridge, 39-41 Buck Lane, London
NW9 0AP **t** 020 8205 2990 **f** 020 8205 2990
e info@bigbluemusic.biz **w** bigbluemusic.biz
Mgr/Producer: Steve Ancliffe.

Big Brother Management. PO Box 1288, Gerrards Cross, Bucks SL9 9YB **t** 01753 880873 **f** 01753 892879 **e** richard.allen@delerium.co.uk Mgr: Richard Allen.

Big Dipper Productions 3rd Floor, 29-31 Cowper St, London EC2A 4AT **t** 020 7608 4591 **f** 020 7608 4599 **e** john@bestest.co.uk Dirs: John Best, Dean O'Connor.

Big Help Music Deppers Bridge Farm, Southam, Warwicks CV47 2SZ **t** 01926 614640 or 07782 172 101 **e** dutch@bighelpmusic.com **w** bighelpmusic.com MD: Dutch Van Spall.

Big Life Management 67-69 Chalton St, London NW1 1HY **t** 020 7554 2100 **f** 020 7554 2154 **e** reception@biglifemanagement.com **w** biglifemanagement.com MD: Jazz Summers. Tim Parry, Tony Beard..

Big M Productions Thatched Rest, Queen Hoo Lane, Tewin, Herts AL6 0LT **t** 01438 798 395 **f** 01438 798 395 **e** joyce@bigmgroup.freeserve.co.uk **w** martywilde.com MD: Joyce Wilde.

Bizarre Management 29 Halifax Rd, Enfield, Middlesex EN2 0PP **t** 020 8351 0872 **f** 020 8351 0872 **e** info@bizarremanagement.com **w** bizarremanagement.com MD: Matthias Siefert.

BK 40 Management 14 Molasses Row, Plantation Wharf, York Rd, London SW11 3UX **t** 020 8133 1109 or 07843 500 935 **f** 020 7228 3447 **e** glynnsmith55@hotmail.com **w** bk40.com Dirs: Glynn Smith, Barrie Knight.

BLACK LYCETT

BLACK|LYCETT
MANAGEMENT

Fulham Palace, Bishop's Avenue, London SW6 6EA **t** 020 7751 0175 **f** 020 7736 0606 **e** info@blacklycett.com **w** blacklycett.com Directors: Clive Black, Daniel Lycett.

Black Magic Management 296 Earls Court Rd, London SW5 9BA **t** 020 7565 0806 **f** 020 7565 0806 **e** blackmagicrecords@talk21.com **w** blackmagicrecords.com MD: Mataya Clifford.

Blacklist Management Fulham Palace, Bishop's Ave, London SW6 6EA **t** 020 7751 0175 **f** 020 7736 0606 **e** firstname@blacklistent.com **w** blacklistent.com Chairman: Clive Black.

Terry Blamey Management PO Box 13196, London SW6 4WF **t** 020 7371 7627 **f** 020 7731 7578 **e** info@TerryBlamey.com Assistant Manager: Alli MacGregor.

Blind Faith Management 1 Allevard, Blackrock Rd, Cork, Ireland **t** +353 87 2269 273 **f** +353 21 453 7478 **e** blindfaith@iol.ie **w** junofalls.com MD: Gerald O'Leary.

Blue Hippo Management Studio 308-310, Custard Factory, Gibb St, Birmingham B9 4AA **t** 0121 687 1404 or 07710 836 471 **f** 0121 475 7452 **e** rob@bluehippomedia.com **w** bluehippomedia.com Dir: Rob Taylor.

Blue Sky Entertainment PO Box 314, Bristol BS9 1XY **t** 07771 934 624 **e** firstname.lastname@blue-sky.uk.com Mgr: Gordon Biggins.

Blujay Management 55 Loudoun Rd, St Johns Wood, London NW8 0DL **t** 020 7604 3633 **f** 020 7604 3639 **e** info@blujay.co.uk Mgrs: Steve Tannett, Carly Martin.

Roger Boden Management 2 Gawsworth Rd, Macclesfield, Cheshire SK11 8UE **t** 01625 420 163 **f** 01625 420 168 **e** rbm@cottagegroup.co.uk **w** cottagegroup.co.uk MD: Roger Boden.

Bodo Music Co Ashley Rd, Hale, Altrincham, Cheshire WA15 9SF **t** 07939 521 465 **f** 0161 928 8136 **e** fgarcia777@hotmail.com(DO NOT PUBLISH) MD: FL Marshall.

Bond Management 500 Chiswick High Rd, London W4 5RG **t** 020 8956 2785 **f** 020 8956 2786 **e** bondmgt@dial.pipex.com Dirs: Jon Barlow, Leonard Lowe.

Boom Management & Consultancy 42 Adelaide Rd, Surbiton, Surrey KT6 4SS **t** 020 8786 2121 **f** 020 8786 2123 **e** info@boommanagement.com **w** boommanagement.com Dir: Ian Titchener.

The Bootleg Beatles Suite 46, Aaron House, 6 Bardolph Rd, Richmond, Surrey TW9 2LS **t** 020 8948 8308 **f** 020 8332 7183 **e** info@bootlegbeatles.com **w** bootlegbeatles.com Company Manager: Raj Patel.

Boss Music 7 Jeffrey's Pl, Camden, London NW1 9PP **t** 020 7284 2554 **f** 020 7284 2560 **e** info@bossmusic.net **w** bossmusic.net MD: Andy Ross.

BossMedia Cashmere House, 180 Kensington Church St, Notting Hill, London W8 4DP **t** 020 7727 2727 **e** info@bossmedia.co.uk **w** bossmedia.co.uk Dir: Taharqa Daniel-Rashid.

Derek Boulton Management 76 Carlisle Mansions, Carlisle Pl, London SW1P 1HZ **t** 020 7828 6533 **f** 020 7828 1271 MD: Derek Boulton.

Braw Management 31 Hartington Pl, Edinburgh EH10 4LF **t** 0131 221 0011 **f** 0131 221 1313 **e** kenny@brawmusic.com Mgr: Kenny MacDonald.

Brenda Brooker Enterprises 9 Cork St, Mayfair, London W1S 3LL **t** 020 7544 2893 **e** BrookerB@aol.com MD: Brenda Brooker.

Brian Gannon Management PO Box 106, Rochdale, Lancs OL15 0HY **t** 01706 374411 **f** 01706 377303 **e** brian@briangannon.co.uk **w** briangannon.co.uk Owner: Brian Gannon.

Brilliant! Castlett House, Guiting Power, Glos GL54 5US **t** 07990 513 555 or 01451 851 101 **e** neil@brilpr.co.uk **w** brilpr.co.uk Contact: Neil Ferris and Jill Ferris.

Brilliant 19 Ltd 32 Ransomes Dock, 35-37 Parkgate Rd, London SW11 4NP **t** 020 7801 1919 **f** 020 7738 1819 **e** reception@19.co.uk MD: Nick Godwyn.

Brilliant Entertainment Management Ltd The Old Truman Brewery, 91-95 Brick Lane, London E1 6QL **t** 020 7247 4750 **f** 020 7247 4712 **e** anita@brilliantmanagement.co.uk **w** brilliantmanagement.co.uk MDs: Anita Heryet, Richard Brown.

Brotherhood Of Man Management Westfield, 75 Burkes Rd, Beaconsfield, Bucks HP9 1PP **t** 01494 673073 **f** 01494 680920 **e** agency@brotherhoodofman.co.uk **w** brotherhoodofman.co.uk

Brown McLeod Ltd. 51 Clarkegrove Rd, Sheffield, South Yorks S10 2NH **t** 0114 268 4747 **f** 0114 268 4161 **e** john@brownmcleod.co.uk **w** brownmcleod.co.uk MD: John Roddison.

BTM PO Box 6003, Birmingham, W Midlands B45 0AR **t** 0121 477 9553 **f** 0121 693 2954 **e** barry@barrytomes.com **w** gotham-records.com Prop: Barry Tomes.

Bulldozer Management 8 Roland Mews, Stepney Green, London E1 3JT **t** 020 7929 3333 **f** 020 7929 3222 **e** oliver@bulldozermedia.com **w** bulldozermedia.com MD: Oliver J. Brown.

Burning Candle Music 151 Bookerhill Rd, High Wycombe, Bucks HP12 4EU **t** 01494 445673 **e** chris.bradford@burningcandlemusic.co.uk **w** burningcandlemusic.co.uk Creative Manager: Chris Bradford.

But! Management Walsingham Cottage, 7 Sussex Sq, Brighton, E. Sussex BN2 1FJ **t** 01273 680799 **e** allan.james1@virgin.net **w** butgroup.com MD: Allan James.

Buzz Artist Management 32 Priory Pl, Perth PH2 0DT **t** 01738 638140 **f** 01738 638140 **e** info@thebuzzgroup.co.uk **w** thebuzzgroup.co.uk MD: Dave Arcari.

CA Management Southpark Studios, 88 Peterborough Rd, London SW6 3HH **t** 0207 384 9575 **e** adam@camanagement.co.uk **w** camanagement.co.uk MD: Adam Sharp.

Cambrian Entertainments International 24 Titan Court, Laporte Way, Luton LU4 8EF **t** 0870 200 5000 **f** 01582 488877 **e** mailbox@cambrian.tv **w** cambrian.tv Dir: Robin Breese-Davies.

Carol & Associates 57 Meadowbank, Bushy Park Rd, Dublin 6, Ireland **t** +353 1 490 9339 **f** +353 1 492 1100 **e** carolh@indigo.ie **w** carolandassociates.com MD: Carol Hanna.

CEC Management 65-69 White Lion St, London N1 9PP **t** 020 7837 2517 **f** 020 7278 5915 **e** jit@cecmanagement.com MD: Peter Felstead.

Cent Management Melbourne House, Chamberlain St, Wells BA5 2PJ **t** 01749 689 074 **f** 01749 670 315 **e** iain@centrecords.com **w** centrecords.com MD: Kevin Newton.

Chantelle Music 3A Ashfield Parade, London N14 5EH **t** 020 8886 6236 **e** info@chantellemusic.co.uk **w** chantellemusic.co.uk MD: Riss Chantelle.

Charabanc Music Management 18 Sparkle St, Manchester M1 2NA **t** 0161 273 5554 **f** 0161 273 5554 **e** charabanc@btconnect.com **w** charabanc.net MD: Richard Lynch.

Charmenko Email for details. **e** nick@charmenko.net **w** charmenko.net MD: Nick Hobbs.

Choir Connexion & London Community Gospel Choir Brookdale House, 75 Brookdale Rd, Walthamstow, London E17 6QH **t** 020 8509 7288 **f** 020 8509 7299 **e** choirconnexion@btconnect.com **w** lcgc.org.uk Principle: Bazil Meade.

Chris Griffin Management 69 Shakespeare Rd, London W7 1LU **t** 07973 883 159 **f** 020 8357 9047 **e** chris@crgriffin.demon.co.uk Contact: Chris Griffin.

Chuffmedia Unit 29 Cygnus Business Centre, Dalmeyer Rd, London NW10 2XA **t** 020 8830 0330 or 07762 130 510 **f** 020 8830 0220 **e** warren@chuffmedia.com **w** chuffmedia.com Dir: Warren Higgins.

Chunk Management 97a Scrubs Lane, London NW10 6QU **t** 020 8960 1331 **f** 020 8968 3377 **e** info@chunkmanagement.com **w** chunkmanagement.com MD: Mike Nelson.

Chute P.O. Box 211, Dundee DD1 9PH **t** 07941 286 555 **e** jan.burnett10@ntlworld.com Mgr: Jan D Burnett.

Cigale Entertainment Ltd PO Box 38115, London W10 6XG **t** 020 8932 2860 **f** 020 8960 0787 **e** info@cigale-ent.com **w** cigale-ent.com MD: Luc Vergier.

Clarion/Seven Muses (Classical Artist Management) 47 Whitehall Pk, London N19 3TW **t** 020 7272 4413 or 020 7272 5125 **f** 020 7281 9687 **e** admin@c7m.co.uk **w** c7m.co.uk Partners: Caroline Oakes, Nicholas Curry.

Clown Management P.O Box 20432, London SE17 3WT **t** 07986 359 568 **e** office@clownmediagroup.co.uk **w** clownmediagroup.co.uk A&R: Stephen Adams.

CMO Management International Ltd Studio 2.6, Shepherds East, Richmond Way, London W14 0DQ **t** 020 7316 6969 **f** 020 7316 6970 **e** reception@cmomanagement.co.uk **w** cmomanagement.co.uk MD: Chris Morrison.

Coalition Management Devonshire House, 12 Barley Mow Passage, London W4 4PH **t** 020 8987 0123 **f** 020 8987 0345 **e** management@coalitiongroup.co.uk Contact: Tim Vigon, Tony Perrin.

Raymond Coffer Management Ltd PO Box 595, Bushey, Herts WD23 1PZ **t** 020 8420 4430 **f** 020 8950 7617 **e** raymond.coffer@btopenworld.com Contact: Raymond Coffer.

Coldplay Management Clearwater Yard, 35 Inverness St, London NW1 7HB **t** 020 7424 7513 **f** 020 7424 7551 **e** ewilkinson@dcmhq.com; htickett@dcmhq.com Mgr: Estelle Wilkinson.

Collaboration 33 Montpellier St, Brighton, E Sussex BN1 3DL **t** 01273 730744 **f** 01273 775134 **e** nikki@collaborationuk.com **w** collaborationuk.com MD: Nikki Neave.

Conception Artist Management 36 Percy St, London W1T 2DH **t** 020 7580 4424 **f** 020 7323 1695 **e** info@conception.gb.com MD: Jean-Nicol Chelmiah.

Congo Music Ltd 17A Craven Park Rd, Harlsden, London NW10 8SE **t** 020 8961 5461 **f** 020 8961 5461 **e** byron@congomusic.freeserve.co.uk **w** congomusic.com A&R Director: Root Jackson.

Connected Artists P.O.Box 46758, London SW17 9YE **t** 020 8682 2460 **f** 020 8682 2460 **e** paul@connectedartists.com MD: Paul McDonald.

Consigliari Ltd Langdale House, 11 Marshalsea Rd, London SE1 1EN **t** 020 7089 2608 **f** 020 7940 5642 **e** holly@consigliari.com Contact: Mark Melton, Holly Goodchild.

Martin Coull Management 65A Dundas St, Edinburgh EH3 6RS **t** 0131 557 5330 or 07803 137509 **f** 0131 557 1050 **e** marticoull@aol.com Prop: Martin Coull.

Courtyard Management 21 The Nursery, Sutton Courtenay, Oxon OX14 4UA **t** 01235 845800 **f** 01235 847692 **e** kate@cyard.com Ptnr: Chris Hufford.

Covert Music Management 6 Westleigh Court, 28 Birdhurst Rd, South Croydon, Surrey CR2 7EA **t** 07958 958 541 **e** simon@covertmusic.co.uk **w** myspace.com/eddyfink MD: Simon King.

Craig Huxley Management 13 Christchurch Rd, London N8 9QL **t** 020 8374 9133 **f** 020 8292 1205 **e** craighuxleymusic@blueyonder.co.uk Prop: Craig Huxley.

Crashed Music 162 Church Rd, East Wall, Dublin 3, Ireland **t** +353 1 888 1188 **f** +353 1 856 1122 **e** info@crashedmusic.com **w** crashedmusic.com MD: Shay Hennessy.

Creation Management 2 Berkley Grove, Primrose Hill, London NW1 8XY **t** 020 7483 2541 **f** 020 7722 8412 **e** info@creationmngt.com MD: Stephen King.

Creative Music Management Unit 53, Simla House, Weston St, London SE1 3RN **t** 020 7378 1642 **f** 020 7378 1642 **e** general@creativepruk.com CEO: Dave Norton.

Crisis Management 18 Reynard Rd, Manchester M21 8DD **t** 0161 882 0712 or 07771 934 870 **e** firstname@crisismanagement.uk.com **w** crisismanagement.uk.com Dirs: Karen Boardman, Tim Mullett.

Cromwell Management 20 Drayhorse Rd, Ramsey, Cambs PE26 1SD **t** 01487 815 063 **f** 01487 711 896 **e** cromwellmanagement@hotmail.co.uk Managing Partner: Vic Gibbons.

Crown Music Management Services Matrix Complex, 91 Peterborough Rd, London SW6 3BU **t** 020 7371 5444 **f** 020 7371 5454 **e** mark@crownmusic.co.uk MD: Mark Hargreaves.

Cruisin' Music Charlton Farm Studios, Hemington, Bath BA3 5XS **t** 01373 834161 **f** 01373 834164 **e** sil@cruisin.co.uk **w** cruisin.co.uk MD: Sil Willcox.

Cultural Foundation Hollin Bush, Dalehead, Rosedale, N Yorks YO18 8RL **t** 0845 458 4699 or 01751 417 147 **f** 01751 417 804 **e** info@cultfound.org **w** cultfound.org MD: Peter Bell.

D2mm (Direct2 Music Management) 3, 6 Belsize Crescent, Belsize Pk, London NW3 5QU **t** 020 7431 1609 or 07939 028 466 **f** 020 7431 1609 **e** david@d2mm.com **w** d2mm.com Dir: David Otzen.

Daddy Management 15 Holywell Row, London EC2A 4JB **t** 020 7684 5219 **f** 020 7684 5230 **e** paul@daddymanagement.net MD: Paul Benney.

Daisy Management Unit 2 Carriglea, Naas Rd, Dublin 12, Ireland **t** +353 1 429 8600 **f** +353 1 429 8602 **e** daithi@daisydiscs.com **w** daisydiscs.com MD: John Dunford.

The Daniel Azure Music Group 72 New Bond St, London W1S 1RR **t** 07894 702 007 **f** 020 8240 8787 **e** info@jvpr.net **w** danielazure.com CEO: Daniel Azure.

Dara Management Unit 4, Great Ship St, Dublin 8, Ireland **t** +353 1 478 3455 **f** +353 1 478 2143 **e** irishmus@iol.ie **w** irelandcd.com MD: Joe O'Reilly.

Darklight Entertainment 58 Speed House, Barbican, London EC2Y 8AT **t** 020 7628 5180 or 07836 210 926 **f** 020 7681 3588 **e** darklight_entertainment@yahoo.com Contact: James Little.

David Jaymes Associates Ltd Contact: Spirit Music & Media.

Lena Davis John Bishop Associates Cotton's Farmhouse, Whiston Rd, Cogenhoe, Northants NN7 1NL **t** 01604 891487 **f** 01604 890405 Contact: Lena Davis.

Daytime Entertainments The Roundhouse, 91 Saffron Hill, Farringdon, London EC1N 8QP **t** 07973 479 191 **e** diane@daytime-ent.com MD: Diane Young.

Dellphonic Management 112 Bathurst Gardens, London NW10 5HX **t** 020 8969 2657 **f** 020 8969 2657 **e** dickodell@hotmail.com **w** dellphonic.com Artist Mgr: Dick O'Dell.

Deluxxe Management PO Box 373, Teddington, Middx TW11 8ZQ **t** 020 8755 3630 or 07771 861 054 **f** 020 8404 7771 **e** info@deluxxe.co.uk **w** deluxxe.co.uk MD: Diane Wagg.

Tony Denton Promotions Ltd 19 South Molton Lane, London W1K 5LE **t** 020 7629 4666 **f** 020 7629 4777 **e** mail@tdpromo.com **w** tdpromo.com Dir: Tony Denton.

Deuce Management & Promotion 178b Venner Rd, London SE26 5JQ **t** 020 8325 7337 or 07875 245 648 **e** rob@deucemanagementandpromotion.com **w** deucemanagementandpromotion.com MD: Rob Saunders.

Deutsch-Englische Freundschaft 51 Lonsdale Rd, Queens Pk, London NW6 6RA **t** 020 7328 2922 **f** 020 7328 2322 **e** info@d-e-f.com Mgr: Eric Harle.

DGM Management PO Box 1533, Salisbury, Wilts SP5 5ER **t** 01722 780187 **f** 01722 781042 **e** dgm@dgmhq.com **w** disciplineglobalmobile.com MD: David Singleton.

Diamond Sounds Music Management The Fox and Punchbowl, Burfield Rd, Old Windsor, Berks SL4 2RD **t** 01753 855420 **f** 01753 855420 **e** samueldsm@aol.com **w** wildthymeproductions.com Dir: Julie Samuel.

Theobald Dickson Productions The Coach House, Swinhope Hall, Swinhope, Market Rasen, Lincs LN8 6HT **t** 01472 399011 **f** 01472 399025 **e** tdproductions@lineone.net **w** barbaradickson.net MD: Bernard Theobald.

Direct Heat Management PO Box 1345, Worthing, W Sussex BN12 7FB **t** 01903 202426 **f** 01903 202426 **e** dhm@happyvibes.co.uk **w** happyvibes.co.uk MD: Mike Pailthorpe.

Divine Management 1 Cowcross St, London EC1M 6DR **t** 020 7490 7271 **f** 020 7490 7273 **e** info@divinemanagement.co.uk Mgr: Natalie de Pace.

DJT Management Ltd PO Box 229, Sheffield, S Yorks S1 1LY **t** 07778 400 512 **f** 0114 258 3164 **e** david@djtmanagement.co.uk Dir: David Taylor.

DNA Artist Management Unit 3, St Mary Rd, London E17 9RG **t** 020 8520 1188 **f** 020 8520 2514 **e** dna_management@hotmail.com MD: Debra Thompson.

Dogface Management 402 Camden Rd, London N7 0SJ **t** 020 7607 1409 or 07813 897 283 **f** 020 7607 1409 **e** alirawlings@blueyonder.co.uk **w** blackmoses.co.uk Contact: Ali Rawlings.

David Dorrell Management 2nd Floor, Lyme Wharf, 191 Royal College St, London NW1 0SG **t** 0870 420 5088 **f** 0870 420 5188 **e** shane@dorrellmanagement.com Contact: Shane Egan.

Dreamscape Management 40 Wentworth Rd, London NW11 0RL **t** 07832 172 451 **f** 01727 826308 **e** dreamscape25@hotmail.com MD: Adam C Lamb.

Dreem Teem Millmead Business Centre 86, Millmead Ind Estate, Millmead Rd, London N17 9QU **t** 020 8801 8800 **f** 020 8801 4800 **e** viveka@urbanhousemusic.com **w** urbanhousemusic.com Mgr: Viveka Nilsson.

The Dune Music Company 1st Floor, 73 Canning Rd, Harrow, Middx HA3 7SP **t** 020 8424 2807 **f** 020 8861 5371 **e** info@dune-music.com **w** dune-music.com MD: Janine Irons.

Duroc Media Riverside House, 10-12 Victoria Rd, Uxbridge, Middx UB8 2TW **t** 01895 810 831 **f** 01895 231 499 **e** info@durocmedia.com **w** durocmedia.com MD: Simon Porter.

Duty Free Artist Management 3rd Floor, 67 Farringdon Rd, London EC1M 3JB **t** 020 7831 9931 **f** 020 7831 9331 **e** info@dutyfreerecordings.co.uk **w** dutyfreerecords.com Booking Agent: Sacha Hearn.

DWL (Dave Woolf Ltd) 53 Goodge St, London W1T 1TG **t** 020 7436 5529 **f** 020 7637 8776 **e** dave@dwl.uk.net MD: Dave Woolf.

Barry Dye Entertainments PO Box 888, Ipswich, Suffolk IP1 6BU **t** 01473 744287 **f** 01473 745442 **e** barrydye@aol.com Prop: Barry Dye.

Dynamik Music PO Box 32146, London N4 3AX **t** 020 7193 3272 **f** 020 7681 3699 **e** giles@dynamik-music.com **w** dynamik-music.com MD: Giles Goodman.

Earth Music 80 Hadley Rd, Barnet, Herts EN5 5QS **t** 020 8440 0710 **f** 020 8441 8522 **e** ricky@audiojelly.com **w** audiojelly.com Mgr: Ricky Simmonds.

Easy Street Artist Management 333 Millbrook Rd, Southampton, Hants SO15 0HW **t** 023 8078 0088 **f** 023 8078 0099 **e** jay@easyst.co.uk **w** easyst.co.uk Dir: Jason Thomas.

Eclipse-PJM PO Box 3059, South Croydon, Surrey CR2 8TL **t** 020 8657 2627 or 07798 651691 **f** 020 8657 2627 **e** eclipsepjm@btinternet.com MD: Paul Johnson.

Effective Management 185 Ladbroke Grove, London W10 6HH **t** 020 8964 3551 or 07808 741 277 **f** 020 8964 3550 **e** henriette@effectivemusicservices.com **w** effectivemusicservices.com Contact: Henriette Amiel.

EG Management Ltd PO Box 606, London WC2E 7YT **t** 020 8540 9935 A&R: Chris Kettle.

ELA Management Contact: See Wild West Management.

Eleven Clements Yard, Iliffe St, London SE17 3LJ **t** 020 7820 1262 **f** 020 7820 1846 **e** eleven@dsl.pipex.com Contact: Dave Bedford, Ruth Starns.

Elite Music Management Brighton, BN2 4WA 01273 621 **t** 999 **f** 01273 623 999 **e** info@elitemm.co.uk **w** elitemm.co.uk PO Box 3261: Paul Wells, Kirsten Santry.

Elite Squad Management Valtony, Loxwood Rd, Plaistow, W Sussex RH14 0NY **t** 01403 871200 **f** 01403 871334 **e** tony@elitesquad.freeserve.co.uk MD: Tony Nunn.

Emperor Management 2 Brayburne Ave, London SW4 6AA **t** 020 7720 0826 **f** 020 7720 1869 **e** john.empson@btopenworld.com **w** emperormanagement.com MD: John Empson.

Empire Artist Management 36 Uxbridge St, Notting Hill, London W8 7TN **t** 020 7221 1133 **f** 020 7243 1585 **e** info@empire-management.co.uk **w** empire-management.co.uk Dir: Neale Easterby, Richard Ramsey.

Enable Music Ltd 54 Baldry Gardens, London SW16 3DJ **t** 020 8144 0616 or 07775 737 281 **e** mike@enablemusic.co.uk **w** enablemusic.co.uk MD: Mike Andrews.

ePM Unit 204, The Saga Centre, 326 Kensal Rd, London W10 5BZ **t** 020 8964 4900 **f** 020 8964 3600 **e** oliver@electronicpm.co.uk **w** electronicpm.co.uk Ptnr: Oliver Way.

Equator Music 17 Hereford Mansions, Hereford Rd, London W2 5BA **t** 020 7727 5858 **f** 020 7229 5934 **e** info@equatormusic.com **w** equatormusic.com Contact: Ralph Baker.

Escape Music Management 45 Endymion Rd, London SW2 2BU **t** 0871 474 2956 **f** 0870 458 0272 **e** mail@escapeman.com **w** escapeman.com MD: Robert Davies.

Eurock First Floor, 5 Cope St, Temple Bar, Dublin 2, Ireland **t** +353 1 672 8001 **f** +353 1 672 8005 **e** gforce@indigo.ie MD: Brian O'Kelly.

European Arts & Media 11-12 Warrington Pl, Dublin 2, Ireland **t** +353 1 664 4700 **f** +353 1 664 4747 **e** info@euroartsmedia.com **w** euroartsmedia.com Dir: Nigel Tebay.

Everlasting Management 71a Sutton Rd, London N10 1HH **t** 020 8444 8190 **f** 020 8444 9565 **e** info@everlastingmusic.co.uk **w** everlastingmusic.co.uk MD: Danny Parnes.

Evolution Management 13 Haldane Close, London N10 2PB **t** 020 8883 4486 **e** evomgt@aol.com MD: John Brice.

Excession: The Agency Ltd 242 Acklam Rd, London W10 5JJ **t** 020 7524 7676 **f** 020 7524 7677 **e** bookings@excession.co.uk **w** excession.co.uk MD: Tara Morgan.

Extreme Music Production 4-7 Forewoods Common, Holt, Wilts BA14 6PJ **t** 01225 782 984 or 07909 995 011 **e** george@xtrememusic.co.uk **w** xtrememusic.co.uk MD: George Allen.

Face Music 13 Elvendon Rd, London N13 4SJ **t** 020 8889 3969 **f** 020 8889 3969 **e** facemusic@btinternet.com MD: Sue Carling.

Faithless Live PO Box 17336, London NW5 4WP **t** 020 7428 0495 **f** 020 7267 3889 **e** aubrey@faithless.co.uk **w** faithless.co.uk MD: Aubrey Nunn.

Fanatic Management PO Box 153, Stanmore, Middx HA7 2HF **t** 01923 896 975 **f** 01923 896 985 **e** hrano@fan-fair.freeserve.co.uk MD: Mike Hrano.

Fat! Management Unit 36, Battersea Business Centre, 99-109 Lavender Hill, London SW11 5QL **t** 020 7924 1333 **f** 020 7924 1833 **e** info@thefatclub.com **w** thefatclub.com MD: Paul Arnold.

FBI Routenburn House, Routenburn Rd, Largs, Strathclyde KA30 8SQ **t** 01475 673392 or 0795 729 2054 **f** 01475 674075 **e** wbrown8152@aol.com Owner: Willie Brown.

FCM 10 Nightingale Lane, London SW12 8TB
t 020 8675 9233 **e** geoffsmith3@mac.com Mgr: Geoff Smith.

Feedback Communications The Court, Long Sutton,
Hook, Hants RG29 1TA **t** 01256 862865 **f** 01256 862182
e feedback@crapola.com **w** crapola.com Mgmt: Keir Jens-Smith.

Fifth Element Artist Management 45 Poland St,
London W1F 7NA **t** 020 7292 0900 or 07976 758 491
f 020 7734 0764 **e** info@fifthelement.biz **w** fifthelement.biz
Dir: Catherine Hockley.

Fintage House Flat 7 UP, 1 Lexington St, London W1F 9AF
t 020 7727 9126 **f** 020 7220 2945
e firstname.lastname@fintagehouse.com **w** fintagehouse.com
Contact: Bruce Lampcov, Suzanne Plesman.

Firebrand Management 12 Rickett St, London SW6 1RU
t 020 7381 2375 or 07885 282 165 **e** vernfire@aol.com
MD: Mark Vernon.

First Column Management 34 West St, Brighton, E
Sussex BN1 2RE **t** 01273 724710 **f** 01273 736004
e fcm@firstcolumn.co.uk Dir: Phil Nelson.

First Move Management Ltd 137 Shooters Hill Rd,
Blackheath, London SE3 8UQ **t** 020 8305 2077 or
07717 475 433 **f** 020 8305 2077 **e** firstmoves@aol.com
w firstmove.biz Creative Director: Janis MacIlwaine.

First Time Management Sovereign House, 12 Trewartha
Rd, Praa Sands, Penzance, Cornwall TR20 9ST **t** 01736 762 826
or 07721 449 477 **f** 01736 763 328 **e** panamus@aol.com
w songwriters-guild.co.uk MD: Roderick Jones.

Flamecracker Management PO Box 394, Hemel
Hempstead HP3 9WL **t** 01442 403445 **f** 01442 403445
e kdavis@aol.com **w** frantik.org Mgr: Karen Davis.

Flamencovision 54 Windsor Rd, Finchley, London N3 3SS
t 020 8346 4500 **f** 020 8346 2488 **e** hvmartin@dircon.co.uk
w flamencovision.com MD: Helen Martin.

Flamingo Record Management Thornhurst Pl, Rowplatt
Lane, Felbridge, East Grinstead RH19 2PA **t** 01342 317943
f 01342 317943 **e** ed@badgerflamingoanimation.co.uk
w badgerflamingoanimation.co.uk MD: Ed Palmieri.

The Flying Music Company Ltd FM House, 110
Clarendon Rd, London W11 2HR **t** 020 7221 7799
f 020 7221 5016 **e** info@flyingmusic.com **w** flyingmusic.com
Dirs: Paul Walden, Derek Nicol.

Focus Creative Management 2 Arterberry Court, 6
Arterberry Rd, Wimbledon, London SW20 8AB
t 020 8715 0403 **f** 020 8715 0390
e info@focuscreativemanagement.com MD: Brian Oliver.

Fools Paradise 15 Hartland Rd, London NW6 6BG
t 07973 297 124 **e** julian@fools-paradise.co.uk
Mgr: Julian Nugent.

Formidable Management 26 Top Rd, Frodsham, Cheshire
WA6 6SW **t** 07939 140 774 **e** carl@formidable-mgmt.com
w formidable-mgmt.com Dir: Carl Marcantonio.

Four Seasons Management Mulliner House, Flanders Rd,
London W4 1NN **t** 020 8987 2515 or 07841 595 647
e 07841595647 **w** fsmc.co.uk MD: Daryl Costello.

Fox Records Ltd (Management) 62 Lake Rise,
Romford, Essex RM1 4EE **t** 01708 760544 **f** 01708 760563
e foxrecords@talk21.com **w** foxrecordsltd.co.uk Dir: Colin Brewer.

Fredag Artist Management Ltd 39 Palmerston Pl,
Edinburgh EH12 5AU **t** 0131 202 6236 **f** 0131 202 6238
e info@fredagartistmanagement.com
w fredagartistmanagement.com
Managing Consultant: David Murray.

Freedom Management 4 Canalot Studios, 222 Kensal Rd,
London W10 5BN **t** 020 8960 4443 **f** 020 8960 9889
e martyn@frdm.co.uk **w** frdm.co.uk MD: Martyn Barter.

Freshwater Hughes Management PO Box 54,
Northaw, Herts EN6 4PY **t** 01707 661 431 or 020 8360 0505
f 01707 664 141 **e** info@freshwaterhughes.com
w freshwaterhughes.com
Contact: Jackie Hughes, Brian Freshwater.

Friars Management Ltd 33 Alexander Rd, Aylesbury,
Bucks HP20 2NR **t** 01296 434731 **f** 01296 422530
e fmluk@aol.com **w** fmlmusic.com MD: David Stopps.

Fruit Ground Floor, 37 Lonsdale Rd, London NW6 6RA
t 020 7328 0848 **f** 020 7328 8078
e fruitmanagement@btconnect.com Ptnr: Caroline Killoury.

Fruition Management PO Box 10896, Birmingham
B13 0ZU **t** 0121 247 6981 or 07976 215 719 **f** 0121 247 6981
e rod@fruitionmusic.co.uk MD: Rod Thomson.

Fruity Red Inc. Second Floor, The Swiss Center, 10 Wardour
St, London W1D 6QF **t** 020 7864 1300 **f** 020 7437 1029
e info@fruityred.com **w** fruityred.com Dir: Helen Douglas.

The Full 36ixty PO Box 77, Leeds LS13 2WZ
t 08709 905 078 **f** 0113 256 1315 **e** katherine@full360ltd.com
w full360ltd.com MD: Katherine Canoville.

Fundamental Management Ltd Falkland House,
Falkland Rd, London N8 0QY **t** 020 8376 1876
f 020 8808 4413 **e** fundamentaluk@yahoo.co.uk
Mgr: Maria James.

funky star 4 Moray Pl, Glasgow G41 2AQ **t** 0141 424 4703
or 07977 224258 **f** 0141 424 4703 **e** info@funkystar.org.uk
w funkystar.org.uk Dir: alan mccuskerthompson.

Furtive Mass Transit Systems LLP 19b All Saints Rd,
London W11 1HE **t** 020 7727 6664
e tankeelad@furtive-mts.com **w** furtive-mts.com Contact: Tank.

Future Management PO Box 183, Chelmsford, Essex
CM2 9XN **t** 01245 601910 **f** 01245 601048
e Futuremgt@aol.com **w** futuremanagement.co.uk
MD: Joe Ferrari.

G Entertaining 16 Coney Green, Abbotts Barton, Winchester,
Hants SO23 7JB **t** 0845 601 6285
e enquiries@g-entertaining.com **w** g-entertaining.co.uk
MD: Peter Nouwens.

Gailforce Management 55 Fulham High St, London
SW6 3JJ **t** 020 7384 8989 **f** 020 7384 8988
e gail@gailforcemanagement.co.uk MD: Gail Colson.

Ganz Management 88 Calvert Rd, Greenwich, London
SE10 0DF **t** 020 8333 9447 **f** 020 8355 9328
e sam.towers@ganzmanagement.com Mgr: Sam Towers.

Patrick Garvey Management Ltd Top Floor, 59
Lansdowne Pl, Hove, E Sussex BN3 1FL **t** 01273 206623
f 01273 208484 **e** patrick@patrickgarvey.com
w patrickgarvey.com Dir: Andrea McDermott.

Geronimo! Management 15 Canada Copse, Milford,
Surrey GU8 5AL **t** 07960 187529
e barneyjeavons@supanet.com Owner: Barney Jeavons.

Giles Stanley 347-353 Chiswick High Rd, London W4 4HS
t 07718 653 218 **e** giles.stanley@umusic.com
w universalmusic-management.com MD: Giles Stanley.

Global Talent Management 2nd Floor, 53 Frith St,
London W1D 4SN **t** 020 7292 9600 **f** 020 7292 9611
e email@globaltalentgroup.com **w** globaltalentgroup.com
MDs: Ashley Tabor, David Forecast.

Globeshine (UK) Ltd 70A Totteridge Rd, High Wycombe,
Bucks HP13 6EX **t** 01494 528 665 **e** b.hallin@virgin.net
MD: Brian Hallin.

GM Promotions 17 The Athenaeum, 32 Salisbury Rd, Hove,
E. Sussex BN3 3AA **t** 01273 774 469 or 07980 917 056
e info@gmpromotions.co.uk **w** gmpromotions.co.uk
Dir: Laura Ducceschi.

Gol-Don Management 3 Heronwood Rd, Aldershot, Hants.
GU12 4AJ **t** 01252 312 382 or 07904 232 292
e gol-don.music@ntlworld.com **w** goforit-promotions.com
Partners: Golly Gallagher & Don Leach.

Gola Entertainment 7 Crofton Terrace, Dun Laoghaire,
Co.Dublin, Ireland **t** +353 1 202 0909 **f** +353 1 280 1229
e gola@iol.ie **w** moyabrennan.com
Managers: Tim Jarvis & Leon Brennan.

Goldsoul Entertainment Hartford House, Common Rd,
Thorpe Salvin, Notts. S80 3JJ **t** 0870 446 0196
e sales@goldsoul.co.uk **w** goldsoul.co.uk
Sales Manager: Ann Roberts.

Got A Loser Job At The Diner Management 71
Lansdowne Rd, Purley, Surrey CR8 2PD **t** 020 8645 0013
e flamingofleece@yahoo.com **w** geocities.com/flamingofleece
GM: Alvin LeDup.

GR Management 974 Pollokshaws Rd, Shawlands, Glasgow,
Strathclyde G41 2HA **t** 0141 632 1111 **f** 0141 649 0042
e info@grmanagement.co.uk MDs: Rab Andrew, Gerry McElhone.

Graham Peacock Management P.O.Box 84, Hove, W
Sussex BN3 6YP **t** 01273 777409 **f** 01273 777809
e gpmanage@aol.com MD: Graham Peacock.

Grand Union Management 93b Scrubs Lane, London
NW10 6QU **t** 020 8968 7798 **f** 020 8968 3377
e davidbianchi@granduniongroup.com **w** granduniongroup.com
Managers: David Bianchi, Nick Ember.

Grant & Foresight 192D Brooklands Rd, Weybridge, Surrey
KT13 0RJ **t** 01932 855337 **f** 01932 851245 or 020 8232 8160
e davidmanagement@aol.com MD: David Morgan.

Grant Management Dalton House, 60 Windsor Ave,
London SW19 2RR **t** 0845 057 3739 **f** 020 7787 8788
e grant.music@btconnect.com MD: John Watson-Grant.

Grapedime Music 28 Hurst Crescent, Barrowby, Grantham,
Lincs NG32 1TE **t** 01476 560 241 **f** 01476 560 241
e grapedime@pjbray.globalnet.co.uk A&R Manager: Phil Bray.

Graphite Media PO Box 605, Richmond TW9 2YE
t 020 8948 8629 **e** info@graphitemedia.net
w graphitemedia.net Dir: Ben Turner.

Stan Green Management PO Box 4, Dartmouth, Devon
TQ6 0YD **t** 01803 770046 **f** 01803 770075
e tv@stangreen.co.uk **w** keithfloyd.co.uk MD: Stan Green.

Grinning Rat Music Management Brays Cottage,
Bowden Hill, Chilcompton, Somerset BA3 4EN **t** 01761 233555
or 07779 325966 **e** info@grinningrat.co.uk **w** helenaonline.com
MD: Ian Softley.

Peter Haines Management Montfort, The Avenue,
Kingston, Lewes, E Sussex BN7 3LL **t** 01273 475846
e peter@uktourist.freeserve.co.uk Mgr: Peter Haines.

Hal Carter Organisation 72 Borough Way, Potters Bar,
Herts EN6 3HB **t** 01707 649 700 or 07958 252 906
f 01707 657 822 **e** artistes@halcarterorg.com
w halcarterorg.com MD: Abbie Carter.

Handshake Ltd 2 Holly House, Mill St, Uppermill,
Saddleworth, Lancs OL3 6LZ **t** 01457 819 350
f 01457 810 052 **e** info@handshakegroup.com
w handshakegroup.com Dir: Stuart Littlewood.

Hannah Management 102 Dean St, London W1D 3TQ
t 020 7758 1494 **e** hgadsdon@barberamusic.co.uk
Contact: Hugh Gadsdon, Mel Stephenson.

Harmony Entertainment 23 Ruscombe Way, Feltham,
Middx TW14 9NY **t** 020 8751 6060 or 07774 856 679
f 020 8751 6060 **e** harmonyents@hotmail.co.uk
MD: Mike Dixon.

Keith Harris Music PO Box 2290, Maidenhead, Berks
SL6 6WA **t** 01628 674 422 **f** 01628 631 379
e keith@keithharrismusic.co.uk MD: Keith Harris.

Les Hart (Southampton Entertainments) 6
Crookhorn Lane, Purbrook, Waterlooville, Hants PO7 5QE
t 023 9225 8373 or 023 8045 6149 **f** 023 9225 8369
e rod@leshart.co.uk **w** leshart.co.uk Prop: Rod Watts.

Pete Hawkins Management 44 Spar Rd, Weymouth,
Dorset DT3 5EW **t** 020 7193 3617 or 07836 266 328
e ph.uk@tiscali.co.uk MD: Pete Hawkins.

Hazard Chase - Classical Music Management 25
City Rd, Cambridge CB1 1DP **t** 01223 312400 **f** 01223 460827
e info@hazardchase.co.uk **w** hazardchase.co.uk
MD: James Brown.

The Headline Agency 39 Churchfields, Milltown, Dublin 14,
Ireland **t** +353 1 260 2560 **f** +353 1 261 1879
e info@musicheadline.com **w** musicheadline.com
MD: Madeleine Seiler.

Headstone Management 46 Tintagel Way, Woking,
Surrey GU22 7DG **t** 01483 856 760
e colinfwspencer@hotmail.com MD: Colin Spencer.

Dennis Heaney Promotions Whitehall, 8 Ashgrove Rd,
Newry, Co Down BT34 1QN **t** 028 3026 8658
f 028 3026 6673 **e** dennis_heaney@hotmail.com
w susanmccann.com Dir: Dennis Heaney.

Heat Music The Courtyard, Unit A, 42 Colwith Rd,
Hammersmith, London W6 9EY **t** 020 8846 3737
f 020 8846 3738 **e** david@reddmanagement.com
MD: David Moores.

Heavenly Management 47 Frith St, London W1D 4SE
t 020 7494 2998 **f** 020 7437 3317
e lou@heavenlymanagement.com Dir: Martin Kelly.

Heavyweight Management Unit 212, The Saga Centre,
326 Kensal Rd, London W10 5BN **t** 020 8968 0111
f 020 8968 0110 **e** heavyweight@dial.pipex.com
w heavyweightman.com MD: Simon Goffe, Emily Moxon.

Hedgehog 9 Tavistock Court, Tavistock Sq, London WC1H 9HE **t** 020 7387 3220 **f** 020 7383 2832 **e** carol_hodge@hotmail.com Mgr: Carol Hodge.

Henderson Management 51 Promenade North, Cleveleys, Blackpool, Lancs FY5 1LN **t** 01253 863386 **f** 01253 867799 **e** agents@henderson-management.co.uk **w** henderson-management.co.uk MD: John Henderson.

Herotech Management 24-25 Nutford Pl, London W1H 5YN **t** 020 7725 7064 **f** 020 7725 7066 **e** dylan@herotech.co.uk.

Chris Hewlett PR & Artist Management 127 North View Rd, London N8 7LR **t** 020 8348 6767 or 07966 491 786 **e** info@chrishewlett.com **w** chrishewlett.com Contact: Chris Hewlett.

Hope Management Loft 5, The Tobacco Factory, Raleigh Rd, Southville, Bristol BS3 1TF **t** 0117 953 5566 **f** 0117 953 7733 **e** info@hoperecordings.com **w** hoperecordings.com MD: Steve Satterthwaite.

Hug Management .

Hyperactive Music Management PO Box 255, Brentford TW8 0BU **f** 020 8580 4912 **e** teresa@hyperactivemgt.com Contact: Teresa Sutterby.

Idle Eyes Management 81 Sheen Court, Richmond, Surrey TW10 5DF **t** 07866 423 729 or 020 8876 0099 **e** Jon@IdleEyes.co.uk **w** idleeyes.co.uk Dir: Jonathan Rees.

IE Music Ltd 111 Frithville Gardens, London W12 7JG **t** 020 8600 3400 **f** 020 8600 3401 **e** info@iemusic.co.uk **w** iemusic.co.uk MDs: David Enthoven, Tim Clark.

Ignite Marketing Unit 17C Raines Court, Northwold Rd, London N16 7DH **t** 020 7275 8682 **f** 020 7275 0791 **e** paul@ignitemarketing.co.uk **w** ignitemarketing.co.uk MD: Paul West.

Ignition Management 54 Linhope St, London NW1 6HL **t** 020 7298 6000 **f** 020 7258 0962 **e** mail@ignition-man.co.uk.

Illicit Entertainment PO Box 51871, London NW2 9BR **t** 020 8830 7831 **f** 020 8830 7859 **e** ian@illicit.tv **w** mumbojumbo.co.uk MD: Ian Clifford.

Immoral Management PO Box 2643, Reading, Berks RG5 4GF **t** 0118 969 9269 **f** 0118 969 9264 **e** johnjpsuk@aol.com MD: John Saunderson.

Imprint Bookings & Management - DJ Agency Unit 13, Barley Shotts Business Pk, 246 Acklam Rd, London W10 5YG **t** 020 8964 1331 **f** 020 8960 9660 **e** gareth@imprintdjs.com **w** imprintdjs.com Contact: Gareth Rees.

Impro Management 35 Britannia Row, London N1 8QH **t** 020 7704 6206 **e** firstname@impromanagement.com Dirs: Guy Trezise, Steve Baker.

In Phase Management 55A Ditton Rd, Surbiton, Surrey KT6 6RF **t** 020 8390 4583 **f** 020 8288 1597 **e** mail@inphasemanagement.com **w** inphasemanagement.com Mgr: Fay Woolven.

In2music Flat 3, 1 Prince of Wales Rd, London NW5 3LW **t** 020 7428 2604 **f** 020 7424 0183 **e** jessicain2music@aol.com Contact: Jessica Peel.

Incredible Management PO Box 28965, London SW14 7WX **t** 020 8487 8868 **f** 020 8181 6487 **e** graham@incrediblemanagement.com **w** incrediblemanagement.com Dir: Graham Filmer.

Independent Sound Management (ISM) 3rd Floor, 39 Margaret St, London W1G 0JQ **t** 020 7493 9200 **f** 020 7493 9111 **e** alexis@independentsound.net GM: Alexis Vokos.

Indie Music Management 51-55 Highfield St, Liverpool L3 6AA **t** 0151 236 5551 **e** info@indiemusicmanagement.com **w** indiemusicmanagement.com MD: Mark Cowley.

Innocent Management 45 Sylvan Ave, London N22 5JA **t** 07896 428 861 **e** info@innocentmanangement.com **w** innocentmanangement.com Contact: Lise Regan.

Insanity Artists Agency Ltd 8 Duncannon St, London WC2N 4JF **t** 020 7484 5078 **f** 020 7484 5089 **e** info@insanitygroup.com **w** insanitygroup.com MD: Andy Varley.

Instinct Management 10 Nightingale Lane, London SW12 8TB **t** 020 8675 9233 **e** geoffsmith3@mac.com Mgr: Geoff Smith.

Intelligent Music Management Ltd 42A Malden Rd, London NW5 3HG **t** 020 7284 1955 **f** 020 7424 9876 **e** verity.german@glatmanent.com MD: Daniel Glatman.

Interactive Marketing Unit One, 25a Blue Anchor Lane, London SE16 3UL **t** 020 7231 1393 **f** 020 7232 1373 **e** info@interactivem.co.uk **w** interactivem.co.uk MD: Jo Cerrone.

Interactive Music Management 2 Carriglea, Naas Rd, Dublin 12, Ireland **t** +353 1 419 5039 **f** +353 1 419 5409 **e** info@interactive-music.com MD: Oliver Walsh.

Interceptor Enterprises PO Box 46572, London N1 9YL **t** 020 7278 8001 **f** 020 7713 6298 **e** info@interceptor.co.uk Mgr: Charlie Charlton.

International Artists 4th Floor, Holborn Hall, 193-197 High Holborn, London WC1V 7BD **t** 020 7025 0600 **f** 020 7404 9865 **e** reception@intart.co.uk **w** intart.co.uk Dir: Phil Dale.

Interzone Management Interzone House, 74-77 Magdalen Rd, Oxford OX4 1RE **t** 01865 205600 **f** 01865 205700 **e** interzone@rotator.co.uk **w** rotator.co.uk MD: Richard Cotton.

INXS Music Management (London) PO Box 39464, London N10 1WP **t** 07779 340 154 **f** 020 8883 4086 **e** info@inxs.com **w** inxs.com MD: Nathan Hull.

J Management Unit A, The Courtyard, 42 Colwith Rd, London W6 9EY **t** 020 8846 3737 **f** 020 8846 3738 **e** John@jmanagement.co.uk MD: John Arnison.

JACK 'N' JILL ARTISTE MANAGEMENT

F3, 60 West End Lane, London NW6 2NE **t** 07050 056 175 or 07860 232 527 **f** 020 7372 3088 **e** JNJ@mgmt.fsbusiness.co.uk **w** myspace.com/jnjmgmt MD: Joycelyn Phillips. Manager: Chantel Alleyne.

JACKIE DAVIDSON MANAGEMENT

The Business Village, 3 Broomhill Rd, London SW18 4JQ
t 020 8870 8744 **f** 020 8874 1578
e firstname@jdmanagement.co.uk **w** jdmanagement.co.uk MD:
Jackie Davidson. Creative Manager: Seb Monks.

Jamdown Ltd Stanley House Studios, 39 Stanley Gardens,
London W3 7SY **t** 020 8735 0280 **f** 020 8930 1073
e othman@jamdown-music.com **w** jamdown-music.com
MD: Othman Mukhlis.

James Grant Music 94 Strand On The Green, Chiswick,
London W4 3NN **t** 020 8742 4950 **f** 020 8742 4951
e enquiries@jamesgrant.co.uk **w** jamesgrant.co.uk
Co-MDs: Simon Hargreaves, Nick Worsley.

JBS Management UK Apartment 11, Dean Meadow,
Newton-le-Willows, Lancs WA12 9PX **t** 01925 291159
f 01925 291159 **e** xag84@jaybs.freeserve.co.uk
Contact: John Sheffield.

JC Music 84A Strand On The Green, London W4 3PU
t 020 8995 0989 **f** 020 8995 0878 **e** jcmusic@dial.pipex.com
MD: John Campbell.

Jive Entertainments PO Box 5865, Corby, Northants
NN17 5ZT **t** 01536 406406 **f** 01536 400082 **e** hojive@aol.com
MD: Dave Bartram.

JML Management Company Redloh House, 2 Michael
Rd, London SW6 2AD **t** 020 7736 3377 **f** 020 7731 0567
e tash@jjdm.net Contact: Jeremy Marsh, Tash Courage.

John Taylor Management PO Box 272, London
N20 0BY **t** 020 8368 0340 **f** 020 8361 3370
e john@jt-management.demon.co.uk MD: John Taylor.

John Waller Management & Marketing The Old
Truman Brewery, 91 Brick Lane, London E1 6QL
t 020 7247 1057 **f** 020 7377 0732 **e** john@johnwaller.net
MD: John Waller.

Jonny Paul Management 2 Downsbury Studios, 40
Steeles Rd, London NW3 4SA **t** 020 7586 3005
f 020 7586 3005 **e** jonny@paul66.fsworld.co.uk MD: Jonny Paul.

JPR Management PO Box 3062, Brighton, E Sussex
BN50 9EA **t** 01273 779 944 **f** 01273 779 967
e info@jprmanagement.co.uk **w** jprmanagement.co.uk
MD: John Reid.

JPS Management PO Box 2643, Reading, Berks RG5 4GF
t 0118 969 9269 or 07885 058 911 **f** 0118 969 9264
e johnjpsuk@aol.com MD: John Saunderson.

Jukes Productions Ltd PO Box 13995, London W9 2FL
t 020 7286 9532 **f** 020 7286 4739 **e** jukes@easynet.co.uk
w jukesproductions.co.uk MD: Geoff Jukes.

Just Another Management Co Hope House, 40 St
Peters Rd, London W6 9BD **t** 020 8741 6020 **f** 020 8741 8362
e justmusic@justmusic.co.uk Dir: Serena Benedict.

JW Management 380 Longbanks, Harlow, Essex
CM18 7PG **t** 01279 304 526 **f** 01279 304 526
e jpweston@ntlworld.com
Manager/Consultant: John Weston ACCA.

Kabuki 23 Weavers Way, Camden Town, London NW1 0XF
t 020 7916 2142 **e** email@kabuki.co.uk **w** kabuki.co.uk
Mgr: Sheila Naujoks.

KAL Management 95 Gloucester Rd, Hampton, Middlesex
TW12 2UW **t** 020 8783 0039 **f** 020 8979 6487
e kaplan222@aol.com **w** kaplan-kaye.co.uk Dir: Kaplan Kaye.

Kaleidoscope Music Management Suite 215, 535
King's Rd, London SW10 0SZ **t** 020 7351 4877
f 020 7351 4848 **e** ross.fitzsimons@btopenworld.com
Contact: Ross Fitzsimons.

Kamara Artist Management (UK) 81 Carlton Rd,
Boston, Lincs PE21 8LH **t** 07952 289504 **f** 01205 270088
e chriskamara@megahitrecordsuk.co.uk
w megahitrecordsuk.co.uk MD: Chris Kamara.

Karma Entertainment Group Brentwood, Newby,
Middlesbrough TS8 0AQ **t** 07841 622 200
e info@karmaeg.com **w** karmaeg.com Dir: Kevin Parry.

Kartel 13 Milton House Mansions, Shacklewell Lane, London
E8 2EH **t** 020 7159 2498 **f** 020 7159 2498
e info@kartelcreative.co.uk **w** kartel.mu
Artist Manager: Charles Kirby-Welch.

Key Management 20 Lower Stephens St, Dublin 2, Ireland
t +353 1 478 0191 **f** +353 1 475 1324 **e** info@thecube.ie
A&R Director: Mark French.

Key Music Management Edenhurst, 87 Station Rd,
Marple, Cheshire SK6 6NY **t** 0161 221 3681 **f** 0161 221 3682
e keymusicmgmt@aol.com **w** keymusicgroup.com
Artist Mgr: Richard Jones.

Kickstart Management 12 Port House, Square Rigger
Row, Plantation Wharf, London SW11 3TY **t** 020 7223 8666
f 020 7223 8777 **e** info@kickstart.uk.net Dir: Ken Middleton.

Kim Glover Management The White House, 32 Thornton
Hill, Wimbledon, London SW19 4HS **t** 020 8947 5475
f 020 8947 5478 **e** info@bandandbrand.com
w bandandbrand.com MD: Kim Glover.

Kitchenware Management 7 The Stables, Saint Thomas
St, Newcastle upon Tyne, Tyne and Wear NE1 4LE
t 0191 230 1970 **f** 0191 232 0262 **e** info@kware.demon.co.uk
w kitchenwarerecords.com Administration: Nicki Turner.

Krack Music Management E Yorks **t** 01405 861124 or
07881 672 014 **e** alan@krack.prestel.co.uk MD: Alan Lacey.

KSO Records PO Box 159, Chatham, Kent ME5 7AQ
t 07956 120837 **e** ksorecords@hotmail.com
w ksorecords.pwp.blueyonder.co.uk MD: Antonio Sloane.

Kudos Management Crown Studios, 16-18 Crown Rd,
Twickenham, Middx TW1 3EE **t** 020 8891 4233
f 020 8891 2339 **e** kudos@camino.co.uk MD: Billy Budis.

Wolfgang Kuhle Artist Management PO Box 425,
London SW6 3TX **t** 020 7371 0397 **f** 020 7736 9212
e getdown@thepleasuredome.demon.co.uk
Contact: Wolfgang Kuhle.

L25 Entertainment 16 Rowan Walk, London N2 0QJ
t 07973 624 443 or 020 8455 2014
e darren.michaelson@L25entertainment.co.uk
MD: Darren Michaelson.

Lamb Management PO Box 54, Hyde, Cheshire SK16 5FJ
t 07973 724499 or 07789 502877 **f** 0870 164 1848
e john@easylamb.com **w** easylamb.com
Managers: John Leah, Andrew Melchior.

Lateral Artist Management Ltd PO Box 29391, London
W2 1GE **t** 020 8257 9470 **f** 020 8257 9470
e enquiries-information@lateral-am.co.uk **w** lateral-am.co.uk
Dir: David Smith.

Latin Arts Services PO Box 14303, London SE26 4ZH
t 07000 472 572 or 07956 446 342 **f** 07000 472 572 or
020 8291 9236 **e** info@latinartsgroup.com
w latinartsgroup.com Dir: Hector Rosquete.

Lazarus Marlinspike Hall, Walpole Halesworth, Suffolk
IP19 9AR **t** 01986 784 664 **f** 01986 784 666
e cally@thethe.com **w** thethe.com Prop: Cally.

Lazarus Consulting Ltd Cydale House, 249A West End
Lane, London NW6 1XN **t** 020 7794 1666 or 07976 239 140
f 020 7794 1666 **e** info@lazarusconsulting.net
w lazarusconsulting.net MD: Steve Lazarus.

Leafman Reverb House, Bennett St, London W4 2AH
t 020 8747 0660 **f** 020 8747 0880 **e** liam@leafsongs.com
MD: Liam Teeling.

Leap 33 Green Walk, London NW4 2AL **t** 020 8202 4120
f 020 8202 4120 **e** leap@gideonbenaim.com
MD: Gideon Benaim.

Lee & Co 3 Taylor Ave, Silsden, Keighley, West Yorks
B020 0DY **t** 01535 653 139 or 07969 697 660
e erika@letstalkmusic.com Contact: Erika Lee.

The Lemon Group 1st Floor, 17 Bowater Rd, Westminster
Industrial Estate, Woolwich, London SE18 5TF
t 07989 340 593 **e** brian@thelemongroup.com
w thelemongroup.com MD: Brian Allen.

Let It Rock Management PO Box 3, Newport NP20 3YB
t 07973 715 875 **f** 01633 677 672
e alanjones@cmcpromotions.co.uk Principal: Alan Jones.

Level 22 Management 111 Princess Rd, Manchester
M14 4RB **t** 0161 226 9156 or 07950 102 202
e level22uk@yahoo.co.uk Dir: Randolph Mike.

LH Management Studio 205, Westbourne Studios, 242
Acklam Rd, London W10 5JJ **t** 020 8968 0637
e info@lhmanagement.com MD: Lisa Horan.

Liberation Management The Shack at Walnut Cottage,
Walden Rd, Hadstock, Cambs CB1 6NX **t** 01223 890 186 or
07771 506 820 **e** amieintheshack@btinternet.com
Contact: Jamie Spencer.

Liberty City Music PO Box 451, Macclesfield, Cheshire
SK10 3SL **t** 07921 626 900 **e** darren@libertycity.biz
w LibertyCity.Biz Dir: Darren Eager.

Line-Up PMC 9A Tankerville Pl, Newcastle-upon-Tyne, Tyne
and Wear NE2 3AT **t** 0191 281 6449 **f** 0191 212 0913
e chrismurtagh@line-up.co.uk **w** line-up.co.uk
Owner: Christopher Murtagh.

Liquid Management 1st Floor, 139 Sutherland Ave, London
W9 1ES **t** 020 7286 6463 **f** 0709 238 9779
e info@Liquidmanagement.net Contact: David Manders.

Harvey Lisberg Associates Kennedy House, 31 Stamford
St, Altrincham, Cheshire WA14 1ES **f** 0161 980 7100
e harveylisberg@aol.com MD: Harvey Lisberg.

Little Giant Music 2 Hermitage House, Gerrard Rd, London
N1 8AT **t** 07779 616 552 **e** Liza@littlegiantmusic.com
w littlegiantmusic.com Dir: Liza Kumjian-Smith.

Little Piece of Jamaica (LPOJ) 55 Finsbury Park Rd,
Highbury, London N4 2JY **t** 020 7359 0788 or 07973 630 729
e paulhuelpoj@yahoo.co.uk Dir: Paul Hue.

LJE 32 Willesden Lane, London NW6 7ST **t** 020 7625 0231
f 020 7372 6503 **e** lauriejay@btconnect.com MD: Laurie Jay.

LM2 Entertainment Suite 14 Harrow Lodge, St Johns
Wood Rd, London NW8 8HR **t** 020 7286 7470
f 020 7286 7470 **e** brad.lazarus@LM2.co.uk Dir: Brad Lazarus.

LOE Entertainment Ltd LOE House, 159 Broadhurst
Gardens, London NW6 3AU **t** 020 7328 6100
f 020 7624 6384 **e** watanabe@loe.uk.net
Creative Director: Hideto Watanabe.

Rupert Loewenstein 2 King St, St. James's, London
SW1Y 6QU **t** 020 7839 6454 **f** 020 7930 4032
e clare@rll.co.uk Dir: Clare Turner.

Loose PO Box 67, Runcorn, Cheshire WA7 4NL
t 01928 566 261 **e** jaki.florek@virgin.net Mgr: Jaki Florek.

Louis Walsh Management 24 Courtney House, Appian
Way, Dublin 6, Ireland **t** +353 1 668 0309 or +353 1 668 0982
f +353 1 668 0721 **e** info@louiswalsh.net MD: Louis Walsh.

LOW FAT MANAGEMENT

e darron@lowfatmanagement.com **w** lowfatmanagement.com.

M4 Management PO Box 605, Cardiff CF24 3XU
t 02920 317 331 or 07770 988 503
e m4management@btinternet.com Dir: Jo Hunt.

Machine Management 2nd Floor, The Cat & Mutton
Building, 76 Broadway Market, London E8 4QJ **t** 020 7249 1781
f 020 7249 9062 **e** iw@machinemanagement.co.uk
w machinemanagement.co.uk MD: Iain Watt.

Mad Management 7 The Chase, Rayleigh, Essex SS6 8QL
t 01268 771113 **f** 01268 774192
e madmanagementltd@aol.com MD: Alex Rose.

Madison Management 6 Cinnamon Gardens, Guildford,
Surrey GU2 9YZ **t** 07810 540 990
e info@madisonmanagement.co.uk **w** madisonmanagement.co.uk
Artist Manager: Paul Harvey.

magnolia mam 2 Townfield Rd, West Kirby, Merseyside
CH48 7EZ **t** 0151 625 6737 or 07760 170 990
e dave@magnoliamam.co.uk **w** magnoliamam.co.uk
MD: Dave Wibberley.

Mako Music 27 Waverton Rd, London SW18 3BZ
t 020 8870 6790 **e** dombrownlow@tiscali.co.uk
MD: Dominic Brownlow.

The Management Company PO Box 150, Chesterfield
S40 0YT **t** 0870 746 8478
e mail@themanagementcompany.biz
w themanagementcompany.biz MD: Tony Hedley.

Manners McDade Artist Management 4th Floor, 18
Broadwick St, London W1F 8HS **t** 020 7277 8194
e info@mannersmcdade.co.uk **w** mannersmcdade.co.uk
MD: Catherine Manners.

Man's Best Friend The Big White House, Pett Level Rd, Pett
Level, E Sussex TN35 4EH **t** 07830 294 522
e info@the-modern.co.uk **w** the-modern.co.uk
MD: Darron Sven Coppin.

Marko Polo (UK) The Barn, Fordwater Lane, Chichester, W
Sussex PO19 4PT **t** 01243 789786 **f** 01243 789787
e markringwood@btinternet.com **w** markopolo.co.uk
Dir: Mark Ringwood.

Marshall Arts Management Leeder House, 6 Erskine Rd,
London NW3 3AJ **t** 020 7586 3831 **f** 020 7586 1422
e info@marshall-arts.co.uk **w** marshall-arts.co.uk
MD: Barrie Marshall.

Marsupial Management Ltd 63 Sailmakers Court,
William Morris Way, London SW6 2UX **t** 020 7384 9797
e info@marsupialmanagement.com MD: John Brand.

Richard Martin Management Fast Helicopter Building,
Hangar 4, Shoreham Airport, W Sussex BN43 5FF
t 01273 44 64 84 or 07860 722 255 **f** 01273 44 64 94
e ric@ricmartinagency.com **w** hot-chocolate.co.uk
Mgr: Richard Martin.

Nigel Martin-Smith Management Nemesis House, 1
Oxford Court, Bishopsgate, Manchester M2 3WQ
t 0161 228 6465 **e** nigel@nmsmanagement.co.uk
MD: Nigel Martin-Smith.

Martin Wyatt 21c Heathmans Rd, Parsons Green, London
SW6 4TJ **t** 020 7751 9935 **f** 020 7731 9314
e brightmusic@aol.com MD: Martin Wyatt.

MartynLevett.com PO Box 1345, Essex IG4 5FX
t 07050 333 555 **f** 07020 923 292
e martynelevett@hotmail.com **w** MartynLevett.com
Joint MD: Paul Booth.

Matrix Management 91 Peterborough Rd, London
SW6 3BW **t** 020 7384 6400 **f** 020 7384 6401
e flip@matrix-studios.co.uk Mgr: Flip Dewar.

MBL 1 Cowcross St, London EC1M 6DR **t** 020 7253 7755
f 020 7251 8096 MD: Robert Linney.

Michael McDonagh Management The Studio, R.O. 63
Station Rd, Winchmore Hill, London N21 3NB **t** 020 8364 3121
f 020 8364 3090 **e** caramusicltd@dial.pipex.com
Dir: Michael McDonagh.

McLeod Holden Enterprises Ltd Priory House, 1133
Hessle High Rd, Hull, E Yorks HU4 6SB **t** 01482 565444
f 01482 353635 **e** info@mcleod-holden.com
w mcleod-holden.com Chairman: Peter McLeod.

MCM Third Floor, 40 Langham St, London W1N 5RG
t 020 7580 4088 **f** 020 7580 4098 **e** mcmemail@aol.com
Contact: Meredith Cork.

Memnon Entertainment (UK) Ltd Habib House, 3rd
Floor, 9 Stevenson Sq, Piccadilly, Manchester M1 1DB
t 0161 238 8516 **f** 0161 236 6717 **e** memnon@btconnect.com
w memnonentertainment.com Dir of Business Affairs: Rudi Kidd.

Menace Management Ltd. 2 Park Rd, Radlett, Herts
WD7 8EQ **t** 01923 853 789 or 01923 854 789
f 01923 853 318
e menacemusicmanagement@btopenworld.com
MD: Dennis Collopy.

Mental Music Management Email or call for address,
London E3 **t** 020 8981 4888 or 07900 631 883
f 020 8981 4888 **e** mentalmusicmgt@yahoo.co.uk
w myspace.com/mentalmusicmgt Mgr: Gary Heath.

Merlin Elite Ltd 37 Lower Belgrave St, London SW1W 0LS
t 020 7823 5990 **f** 020 7823 5298 **e** info@merlinelite.co.uk
w merlin-elite.com Contact: Richard Thompson, Giles Baxendale.

Metamorphosis Management Matrix Complex, 91
Peterborough Rd, London SW6 3BU **t** 020 7751 2751
f 020 7371 5454 **e** mark@crownmusic.co.uk
Mgr: Mark Hargreaves.

Method Management Matrix Complex, 91 Peterborough
Rd, London SW6 3BU **t** 020 7371 5065 **f** 020 7371 5454
e chloe@crownmusic.co.uk Mgr: Chloe Griffiths.

Metro Associates Latimer Studios, West Kington, Wilts
SN14 7JQ **t** 01249 783 599 **f** 0870 169 8433
e Dolan@metro-associates.co.uk **w** media-print.co.uk
CEO: Mike Dolan.

Midi Management Ltd The Old Barn, Jenkins Lane, Great
Hallingbury, Essex CM22 7QL **t** 01279 759067 **f** 01279 504145
e midi-management@btconnect.com
Manager/Director: Mike Champion.

Midnight To Six Management 4th Floor, 33 Newman
St, London W1T 1PY **t** 020 7462 0026 **f** 020 7462 0012
e harper@midnighttosix.com Dirs: Dave Harper, Tony Crean.

Mighty Music Management 2 Stucley Pl, Camden,
London NW1 8NS **t** 020 7482 6660 **f** 020 7482 6606
e art@mainartery.co.uk Dir: Jo Mirowski.

John Miles Organisation Cadbury Camp Lane, Clapton In
Gordano, Bristol BS20 7SB **t** 01275 854675 or 01275 856770
f 01275 810186 **e** john@johnmiles.org.uk MD: John Miles.

Mimi Music 26-28 Hammersmith Grove, Hammersmith,
London W6 7BA **t** 020 8834 1085 **f** 020 8834 1185
e info@mimi-music.com **w** mimi-music.com MD: Dee Sharma.

Minder Security Services Argentum, 2 Queen Caroline St,
London W6 9DX **t** 020 8323 8013 **f** 020 8323 8080
e info@mindersecurity.com **w** mindersecurity.com
MD: John Giacobbi.

MK Music Ltd PO Box 43312, Highbury, London N5 2XS
t 07939 080 524 **e** debi@mickkarn.net **w** mickkarn.net
Dir: Debi Zornes.

Mobb Rule Management PO Box 26335, London N8 9ZA
t 020 8340 8050 **e** info@mobbrule.com **w** mobbrule.com
MDs: Stewart Pettey, Wayne Clements.

Mockingbird Music PO Box 52, Marlow, Bucks SL7 2YB
t 01491 579214 **f** 01491 579214 **e** mockingbirdmusic@aol.com
Artiste Management: Leon B Fisk.

Modal Management Prospect House, Lower Caldecote, Beds SG18 9BA **t** 01767 601 398 or 07976 254 651 **e** davidsamuel@modalmanagement.co.uk **w** modalmanagement.co.uk MD: David Samuel.

Modernwood Management Cambridge House, Card Hill, Forest Row, E Sussex RH18 5BA **t** 01342 822619 or 020 8947 2224 **f** 01342 822619 **e** mickey.modernwood@virgin.net Senior Partner: Mickey Modern.

Modest! Management Studios 2-3, Matrix Complex, 91 Peterborough Rd, London SW6 3BU **t** 020 7384 6410 **f** 020 7384 6411 **e** firstname@modestentertainment.com Partners: Richard Griffiths, Harry Magee.

Moksha Management Ltd PO Box 102, London E15 2HH **t** 020 8555 5423 **f** 020 8519 6834 **e** info@moksha.co.uk **w** moksha.co.uk MD: Charles Cosh.

Mondo Management Unit 2D, Clapham North Arts Centre, 26-32 Voltaire Rd, London SW4 6DH **t** 020 7720 7411 **f** 020 7720 8095 **e** rob@ihtrecords.com **w** davidgray.com Contact: Rob Holden.

Money Talks Management Cadillac Ranch, Pencraig Uchaf, Cwm Bach, Whitland, Dyfed SA34 0DT **t** 01994 484466 **f** 01994 484294 **e** cadillacranch@telco4u.net **w** nikturner.com Dir: Sid Money.

Moneypenny Management The Stables, Westwood House, Main St, North Dalton, Driffield, East Yorks YO25 9XA **t** 01377 217815 or 07977 455882 **f** 01377 217754 **e** nigel@adastey.demon.co.uk **w** adastra-music.co.uk/moneypenny MD: Nigel Morton.

Monster Music Management 28 Glen View Crescent, Heysham, Lancs LA3 2QW **t** 01524 852037 **f** 01524 852037 **e** croftmc@aol.com Contact: Mike Croft.

Monumental Management Ltd Unit B44A, Eurolink Business Centre, Effra Rd, London SW2 1BZ **t** 020 7871 2803 **e** info@monumentalmanagement.co.uk **w** MonumentalManagement.co.uk MD: Brett Leboff.

David Morgan Management 192D Brooklands Rd, Weybridge, Surrey KT13 0RJ **t** 01932 855337 **f** 01932 851245 or 020 8232 8160 **e** davidmanagement@aol.com MD: David Morgan.

Motive Music Management 93b Scrubs Lane, London NW10 6QU **t** 07808 939 919 **e** nathan@motivemusic.co.uk Contact: Nathan Leeks.

MP Music Services 16 Grosvenor Pl, Oatlands Village, Weybridge, Surrey KT13 9AG **t** 01932 827 224 **f** 01932 827 225 **e** mpmusic@netcomuk.co.uk MD: Mark Plunkett.

MPC Entertainment MPC House, 15-16 Maple Mews, London NW6 5UZ **t** 020 7624 1184 **f** 020 7624 4220 **e** mpc@mpce.com **w** mpce.com Chief Executive: Michael Cohen.

MSM Music Consultants PO Box 10036, Halesowen B62 8WD **t** 07785 506637 **e** trevorlonguk@aol.com MD: Trevor Long.

Muirhead Management Anchor House, 2nd Floor, 15-19 Britten St, London SW3 3TY **t** 020 7351 5167 or 07785 226 542 **f** 020 7000 1227 **e** info@muirheadmanagement.co.uk **w** muirheadmanagement.co.uk CEO: Dennis Muirhead.

Mumbo Jumbo Management Contact: Illicit Entertainment.

The Music & Media Partnership Sanctuary House, 45-53 Sinclair Rd, London W14 0NS **t** 020 7300 6652 **f** 020 7300 1884 **e** firstname@tmmp.co.uk MD: Rick Blaskey.

The Music Management Russell House, 8 Great Russell St, London WC1B 3NH **t** 020 7436 7633 or 020 7255 2260 **e** firstname@themusicmanagement.com **w** themusicmanagement.com Managers: Paul Carey & Caroline McAteer.

The Music Partnership 41 Aldebert Terrace, London SW8 1BH **t** 020 7787 0361 **f** 020 7735 7595 **e** office@musicpartnership.co.uk **w** musicpartnership.co.uk Artist Manager: Louise Badger.

MWM Music Management 11 Great George St, Bristol BS1 5RR **t** 0117 929 2393 **f** 0117 929 2696 **e** office@mwmuk.com Dir: Craig Williams.

Mylestone PO Box 2470, The Studio, Chobham, Surrey GU24 8ZD **t** 01276 855 247 **f** 01276 856 897 **e** myles@mylestoneltd.com MD: Myles Keller.

Native Management Unit 32, Ransomes Dock, 35-37 Parkgate Rd, London SW11 4NP **t** 020 7801 1919 **f** 020 7738 1819 **e** marie.native@19.co.uk **w** nativemanagement.com Contact: Peter Evans.

NBM 43d Ferme Park Rd, London N4 4EB **t** 020 8342 9220 **f** 020 8340 4721 **e** nbengali@lineone.net **w** naive.fr Artist Manager: Neville Bengali.

Necessary Records PO Box 28362, London SE20 7WH **t** 07832 141 503 **e** warren.clarke@necessaryrecords.com **w** necessaryrecords.com Dir: Warren Clarke.

NEM Productions (UK) Priory House, 55 Lawe Rd, South Shields, Tyne and Wear NE33 2AL **t** 0191 427 6207 **f** 0191 427 6323 **e** dave@nemproductions.com **w** nemproductions.com Contact: Dave Smith.

Nettwerk Management UK Clearwater Yard, 35 Inverness St, London NW1 7HB **t** 020 7424 7500 **f** 020 7424 7501 **e** eleanor@nettwerk.com **w** nettwerk.com Contact: Sam Slattery.

No Half Measures Ltd. Studio 19, St. George's Studios, 93-97 St. George's Rd, Glasgow G3 6JA **t** 0141 331 9888 **f** 0141 331 9889 **e** info@nohalfmeasures.com **w** nohalfmeasures.com MD: Dougie Souness.

No Quarter Management Basement, 22a Talbot Rd, London W2 5LJ **t** 07816 870 666 **e** info@noquartermanagement.com **w** noquartermanagement.com Dirs: Christian Miller, Nat Horrocks.

Normal Management 3rd Floor, The Green, 29 Clerkenwell Green, London EC1R 0DU **t** 020 7253 0050 **e** aliceharter@normal-management.com MDs: Alice Harter, Paul Noble.

North Studio 106, Canalot Production Studios, 222 Kensal Rd, London W10 5BN **t** 020 8964 4778 **f** 020 8960 8907 **e** john@nu-song.com **w** nusong.com MD: John MacLennan.

North & South PO Box 1099, London SE5 9HT **t** 020 7326 4824 **f** 020 7535 5901 **e** gamesmaster@chartmoves.com MD: Dave Klein.

Northern Lights Mangement I North Grove, London
N6 4SH **t** 07887 983 452 **e** jonathan.light@virgin.net
Mgr: Jonathan Morley.

Northern Music Company Cheapside Chambers, 43
Cheapside, Bradford, West Yorks BD1 4HP **t** 01274 306361
f 01274 730097 **e** info@northernmusic.co.uk
w northernmusic.co.uk MD: Andy Farrow.

Northstar Artist Management PO Box 458, Rotherham
S66 1YN **t** 01709 709633 or 07740 101347
e Paul.flanaghan1@btinternet.com **w** northstar-management.com
Artist Manager: Paul Flanaghan.

Norwich Artistes Bryden, 115 Holt Rd, Norwich, Norfolk
NR6 6UA **t** 01603 407101 **f** 01603 405314
e brian@norwichartistes.co.uk **w** norwichartistes.co.uk
MD: Brian Russell.

NOW Music 15 Tabbs Lane, Scholes, Cleckheaton, West
Yorks BD19 6DY **t** 01274 851365 **f** 01274 874329
e john@now-music.com **w** now-music.com MD: John Wagstaff.

NoWHere Management 30 Tweedholm Ave East,
Walkerburn, Peeblesshire EH43 6AR **t** 01896 870284 or
07812 818 183 **e** michaelwild@btopenworld.com
Owner: Michael Wild.

NSE Entertainments Minster Cottage, Sincox Lane,
Broomers Corner, Shipley, near Horsham, W Sussex RH13 8PS
t 01403 741321 **e** ian@entertainment-nse.co.uk
w entertainment-nse.co.uk Owner: Ian Long.

Numinous Management Figment House, Church St, Ware,
Herts SG12 9EN **t** 01920 484040 **f** 01920 463883
e jhbee@numinous.biz **w** numinous.biz
Dir, A&R/Management: John Bee.

Nutty Tart Management Call for address.
t 07951 062 566 **e** nuttytartmanagement@hotmail.com
MD: Mandy Freedman.

NVA Management 1 Canada Sq, 29th Floor Canary Wharf
Tower, London E14 5DY **t** 0870 220 0237 **f** 0870 220 0238
e info@nvaentertainment.com **w** nvaentertainment.com
MD: Chris Nathaniel.

NYJO - National Youth Jazz Orchestra 11 Victor Rd,
Harrow, Middx HA2 6PT **t** 020 8863 2717 **f** 020 8863 8685
e bill.ashton@virgin.net **w** NYJO.org.uk Chairman: Bill Ashton.

O-Mix 18 Avonmore Rd, London W14 8RR **t** 020 7622 4176
f 020 7622 4176 **e** info@o-mix.co.uk **w** o-mix.co.uk
Dir: Alex Kerr-Wilson.

Octagon Music Octagon House, 81-83 Fulham High St,
London SW6 3JW **t** 020 7862 0121 **f** 020 7862 0007
e firstname.lastname@octagon.com **w** octagon.com
MD: Peter Rudge.

OMC Management Oxford Music Central, 1st Floor, 9 Park
End St, Oxford OX1 1HH **t** 01865 798 791 **f** 01865 798 792
e firstname@oxfordmusic.net Mgr: Dave Newton.

Omoya Entertainment 26-28 Hammersmith Grove,
London W6 7BA **t** 020 8834 1085 **f** 020 8834 1100
e info@omoya.com **w** omoya.com Contact: Kenneth Omoya.

On 10 Music Entertainment Unit 5, 16-18 Empress Pl,
London SW6 1TT **t** 020 7385 1985 or 07900 055 810
f 020 7385 0676 **e** info@on10music.com **w** on10music.com
MD: Justin Hsu.

One Fifteen 1 Prince Of Orange Lane, Greenwich, London
SE10 8JQ **t** 020 8293 0999 **f** 020 8293 9525
e info@onefifteen.com **w** onefifteen.com MD: Paul Loasby.

Onside Management Suite 6, Alexander House, 15 Ware
Rd, Hertford, Herts. SG13 7DZ **t** 01992 535126 **f** 01992 535127
e mail@onside.co.uk Dir: Nick Boyles.

Opal-Chant Studio 1, 223A Portobello Rd, London W11 1LU
t 020 7221 7239 **f** 020 7727 5404
e opal-chant@dial.pipex.com Dir: Jane Geerts.

Open Top Music Hatch Farm Studios, Hatch Farm, Chertsey
Rd, Addlestone KT15 2EH **t** 01932 828715
e mail@opentopmusic.com **w** opentopmusic.com
Dir: Nick Turner.

Opium (Arts) Ltd 49 Portland Rd, London W11 4LJ
t 020 7229 5080 **f** 020 7229 4841 **e** adrian@opiumarts.com
Contact: Richard Chadwick, Adrian Molloy.

OPL Management 4 The Limes, North End Way, London
NW3 7HG **t** 020 8209 0025 **e** oplmanagement@aol.com
Dir: Miss Sabina Van de Wattyne.

Dee O'Reilly Management 13 Alliance Court, Aliance Rd,
London W3 0RB **t** 020 8993 7441 **f** 020 8992 9993
e info@dorm.co.uk **w** thedormgroup.com GM: John O'Reilly.

Ornadel Management Imperial Works, Top Floor, Perren
St, London NW5 3ED **t** 020 7482 5505 **f** 020 7482 5504
e guy@ornadel.com **w** ornadel.com
Contact: Guy Ornadel, Roman Trystram.

Out There Management Strongroom, 120-124 Curtain
Rd, London EC2A 3SQ **t** 020 7739 6903 **f** 020 7613 2715
e outthere@outthere.co.uk Mgr: Stephen Taverner.

Outerglobe (Global Fusion) 113 Cheesemans Terrace,
London W14 9XH **t** 020 7385 5447 **f** 020 7385 5447
e debbie@outerglobe.com **w** outerglobe.com MD: Debbie Golt.

Outside Management Butler House, 177-178 Tottenham
Court Rd, London W1T 7NY **t** 020 7436 3633 **f** 020 7436 3632
e info@outside-org.co.uk **w** outside-org.co.uk Dir: Alan Edwards.

P3 Music Management Ltd. 4 St Andrew St, Alyth,
Perthshire PH11 8AT **t** 01828 633790 **e** office@p3music.com
w p3music.com Dirs: James Taylor & Alison Burns.

P3M Music Management & Consultancy 126a
Talbot Rd, London W11 1JA **t** 07771 862 401
e paulmoorep3m@aol.com MD: Paul Moore.

Parallel Universe Music 7 Eagle Court, 69 High St, London
N8 7QG **t** 07788 545 112 **f** 020 8340 8031
e carmen@paralleluniversemusic.com
Artist Manager: Carmen Layton-Bennett.

Park Promotions PO Box 651, Oxford OX2 9AZ
t 01865 241717 **f** 01865 204556 **e** info@parkrecords.com
w parkrecords.com MD: John Dagnell.

Parliament Management PO Box 6328, London N2 0UN
t 020 8444 9841 **f** 020 8442 1973
e info@parliament-management.com A&R: Damian Baetens.

Part Rock Management Ltd 1 Conduit St, London
W1S 2XA **t** 020 8207 1418 **e** stewartyoung@mindspring.com
MD: Stewart Young.

Pasadena Roof Orchestra (1997) Priors Hall, Tye
Green, Elsenham, Bishop Stortford, Herts CM22 6DY
t 01279 813 240 or 01279 815 593 **f** 01279 815 895
e procentral@aol.com **w** pasadena.co.uk Dir: David Curtis.

Pat Kane 9 Crown Rd South, Glasgow G12 9DJ
t 07718 588497 **e** patkane@theplayethic.com **w** patkane.com
Singer/Writer: Pat Kane.

Paul Crockford Management (PCM) Latimer House,
272 Latimer Rd, London W10 6QY **t** 020 8962 8272
f 020 8962 8243 **e** pcm.assistant@virgin.net
MD: Paul Crockford.

Pegasus Management 8 Ashington Court, Westwood Hill,
Sydenham, London SE26 6BN **t** 020 8778 9918
f 020 8355 7708 **e** PegasusMgnt@hotmail.com
Dir: James Doheny.

Justin Perry Management PO Box 20242, London
NW1 7FL **t** 020 7485 1113 **e** info@proofsongs.co.uk.

PEZ Management 126 Clonmore St, London SW18 5HB
t 020 8480 4445 or 07831 100 980 **f** 020 8480 4446
e pezmanagement@aol.com Contact: Perry Morgan.

PFB Management 9 Bowmans Lea, London SE23 3TL
t 020 8291 3175 **f** 020 8699 6409 **e** paulbibby@freenet.co.uk
MD: Paul Bibby.

Phantom Music Management Upper Floor, 18 Greek St,
London W1D 4DS **t** 0845 331 3300 **f** 0845 331 3500
e dave.pattenden@phantom-music.com **w** phantom-music.com
Contact: Rod Smallwood, Dave Pattenden.

Phonetic Music Management 12 St Davids Close,
Farnham, Surrey GU9 9DR **t** 01252 330 894 or 07775 515 025
f 01252 330 894 **e** james@phoneticmusic.com
w phoneticmusic.com MD: James Sefton.

Pilot Management 222 Canalot Studios, 222 Kensal Rd,
London W10 5BN **t** 020 7565 2227 **f** 020 7565 2228
e dayo@pilotcreativeagency.com Mgr: Amanda Fairhurst.

PJ Music 156A High St, London Colney, Herts AL2 1QF
t 01727 827017 or 07860 902361 **f** 01727 827017
e pjmusic@ukonline.co.uk **w** schmusicmusic.com
Dir: Paul J Bowrey.

Plan C Management Covetous Corner, Hudnall Common,
Little Gaddesden, Herts HP4 1QW **t** 01442 842851
f 01442 842082 **e** christian.ulf@virgin.net **w** plancmusic.com
Mgr: Christian Ulf-Hansen.

Playpen Management 16a Upper Market St, Hove, E
Sussex BN3 1AS **t** 01273 723 771 or 07932 720 058
e terry@playpen.fsbusiness.co.uk **w** myspace.com/lisaknappmusic
Mgr: Terry O'Brien.

Plus Artist Management 36 Follingham Court, Drysdale
Pl, London N1 6LZ **t** 020 7684 8594 **f** 020 7684 8740
e deschisholm@hotmail.com Contact: Desmond Chisholm.

Popbox Management The Louisiana, Wapping Rd,
Bathurst Terrace, Bristol BS1 6UA **t** 01179 663 615 or
07989 283 253 **e** migstar007@hotmail.com
w myspace.com/popboxmanagement
Dirs: Michael Schillace, Tom Friend.

PopWorks 1 Lopen Rd, Silver St, London N18 1PN
t 020 8807 6268 **f** 020 8351 1497 **e** popworks1@yahoo.com
MD: Linda Duff.

Porcupine Management 33-45 Parr St, Liverpool,
Merseyside L1 4JN **t** 0151 707 1050 **f** 0151 709 4090
e oxygenmusic@btinternet.com Partners: Pete Byrne & Peasy.

POSITIVE MANAGEMENT

POSITIVEMANAGEMENT

41 West Ella Rd, London NW10 9PT **t** 020 8961 6257 or
07966 659 299 **f** 020 8963 1974 **e** Meira@positive-mgmt.co.uk
w positive-mgmt.co.uk MD: Meira Shore.

Power Artist Management 29 Riversdale Rd, Thames
Ditton, Surrey KT7 0QN **t** 020 8398 5236 **f** 020 8398 7901
e barry.l.evans@btinternet.com(DO NOT PUBLISH)
MD: Barry Evans.

Power Music PO Box 734a, Surbiton KT6 6XQ
t 07783 044600 or 07783 555121 **f** 020 8399 5199
e powermusic@hotmail.co.uk **w** power-music.co.uk
Contact: Pauline Nicol, Robert Bicknell.

P&P Music International Crabtree Cottage, Mill Lane,
Kidmore End, Oxon RG4 9HB **t** 0118 972 4356
f 0118 972 4809 **e** ppmusicint@aol.com
w dovehouserecords.com Pres: Thomas Pemberton.

PPM Artist Management 73 Leonard St, London
EC2A 4QS **t** 020 7739 7552 **e** music@ppmlondon.com
w ppmlondon.com MD: Polo Piatti.

pr-ism 2/14 Park Terrace, The Park, Nottingham NG1 5DN
t 0115 947 5440 or 07971 780 821 **f** 0115 947 5440
e phil.long@pipemedia.co.uk **w** pr-ism.co.uk MD: Phil Long.

The Precious Organisation The Townhouse, 1 Park Gate,
Glasgow G3 6DL **t** 0141 353 2255 **f** 0141 353 3545
e elliot@precioustoo.com MD: Elliot Davis.

Prestige Management The Coach House, 3 Royal Drive,
Princess Park Manor, London N11 3FU **t** 020 8248 2020
f 020 8248 2021 **e** info@prestigeuk.com
Partners: Richard Rashman, Matthew Fletcher, Darren Keating.

Principle Management 30-32 Sir John Rogersons Quay,
Dublin 2, Ireland **t** +353 1 677 7330 **f** +353 1 677 7276
e Candida@numb.ie Dir: Paul McGuinness.

Private & Confidential Management Ltd Fairlight
Mews, 15 St. Johns Rd, Kingston upon Thames, Surrey KT1 4AN
t 0208 977 0632 **f** 0870 770 8669 **e** info@pncmusic.com
w pncrecords.com MD: Sir Harry.

Pro-Rock Management Caxton House, Caxton Ave,
Blackpool, Lancs FY2 9AP **t** 01253 508670 **f** 01253 508670
e promidibfp@aol.com **w** members.aol.com/promidibfp
MD: Ron Sharples.

Prodmix International DJ Music Management 98
Edith Grove, Chelsea, London SW10 0NH **t** 020 7565 0324 or
07768 877 426 **f** 020 7168 7257 **e** karen@prodmix.com
w prodmix.com Dir: Karen Goldie Sauve.

Prohibition Management Fulham Palace, Bishops Ave,
London SW6 6EA **t** 020 7384 7372 or 07967 610 877
f 020 7371 7940 **e** Caroline@prohibitiondj.com
w prohibitiondj.com MD: Caroline Prothero.

Prolifica Management Unit 1, 32 Caxton Rd, London
W12 8AJ **t** 020 8740 9920 **f** 020 8743 2976
e colin@prolifica.co.uk Dir: Colin Schaverien.

Psycho Management Company Mill Lane Studio, Mill Lane, Godalming, Surrey GU7 1EY **t** 01483 419429 **f** 01483 419504 **e** patrick@psycho.co.uk **w** psycho.co.uk Dir: Patrick Haveron.

Pure Delinquent 134 Replingham Rd, Southfields, London SW18 5LL **t** 07929 990 321 **f** 020 8870 0790 **e** julie@pure-delinquent.com **w** pure-delinquent.com Dir: Julie Pratt.

Pure Music Management 77 Beak St, No. 306, London W1F 9DB **t** 07766 180 330 **f** 020 7439 3330 **e** puremusicmgmt@yahoo.com Contact: Michael Cox.

Purple Fox Management 19 Hornsey Lane Gardens, London N6 5NX **t** 020 8348 8102 **f** 0871 247 6310 **e** office@purplefoxmanagement.co.uk **w** infadels.co.uk Dirs: Sophie Doel, Mark Henwood.

PVA Ltd 2 High St, Westbury On Trym, Bristol BS9 3DU **t** 0117 950 4504 **f** 0117 959 1786 **e** enquiries@pva.ltd.uk **w** pva.ltd.uk Sales Director: John Hutchinson.

PVA Management Hallow Pk, Worcester WR2 6PG **t** 01905 640663 **f** 01905 641842 **e** pva@pva.co.uk **w** pva.co.uk PA: Cary Taylor.

Qaraj' Ltd 7a Gunter Grove, London SW10 0UN **t** 07768 613 364 **e** info@qaraj.com **w** qaraj.com MD: Michele Baldini.

Quest Management 34 Trinity Crescent, London SW17 7AE **t** 020 8772 7888 **f** 020 8722 7999 **e** info@quest-management.com Managers: Scott Rodger, Stuart Green.

R2 Management PO Box 100, Moreton-in-Marsh, Gloucs GL56 0ZX **t** 01608 651 802 **f** 01608 652 814 **e** editor@jacobsladder.org.uk **w** jacobsladder.org.uk MD: Robb Eden.

Radar Music and Management 31 Lingfield Crescent, Stratford-Upon-Avon, Warcs CV37 9LX **t** 01789 268280 **e** joe@radarmusic.co.uk **w** radarmusic.co.uk Contact: Joe Cooper.

Radius Music PO Box 46770, London SW17 9YH **t** 020 8672 7030 **f** 020 8672 7030 **e** info@radiusmusic.co.uk **w** radiusmusic.co.uk Mgr: Mark Wood.

Rare Management 14 St Peters St, London N1 8JG **t** 07855 494 725 **f** 020 7249 8073 **e** info@rare-management.com Managers: Michelle Curry & Conor McCaughan.

Raygun Music 350 Portland Rd, Hove, E Sussex BN3 5LF **t** 01273 299 452 or 07930 376 810 **e** Julian.deane@btinternet.com **w** myspace.com/raygunmusicmanagment Dir: Julian Deane.

Razzamatazz Management Mulberry Cottage, Park Farm, Haxted Rd, Lingfield, Surrey RH7 6DE **t** 01342 835359 **e** razzamatazzmanagement@btconnect.com Dir: Jill Shirley.

RDPR Music Management The Heritage, Horsley, Stroud, Glocs GL6 0PY **t** 01453 832876 **e** rachel@dunlop4917.freeserve.co.uk Prop: Rachel Dunlop.

ReBjörn Ltd 5 Kimberley Rd, London NW6 7SG **t** 020 7372 6648 **e** enquiries@bjornagain.com **w** bjornagain.com Creator: Rod Leissle.

Reckless 122A Highbury Rd, Kings Heath, Birmingham, W Midlands B14 7QP **t** 0121 443 2186 **e** boblamb@recklessltd.freeserve.co.uk MD: Bob Lamb.

Red Alert Management Sun House, 2 - 4 Little Peter St, Manchester M15 4PS **t** 0161 834 7434 **f** 0161 834 8545 **e** info@redalert.co.uk **w** redalert.co.uk MD: Liam Walsh.

Red Onion Productions 26-28 Hatherley Mews, Walthamstow, London E17 4QP **t** 020 8520 3975 **f** 020 8521 6646 **e** info@redonion.uk.com **w** redonion.uk.com MD: Dee Curtis.

Redd Management The Courtyard, Unit A, 42 Colwith Rd, Hammersmith, London W6 9EY **t** 020 8846 3737 **f** 020 8846 3738 **e** david@reddmanagement.com MD: David Moores.

Represents Artist Management Unit 10 Southam Street Studios, Southam St, London W10 5PH **t** 020 8969 5151 **f** 020 8969 4141 **e** ben@represents.co.uk **w** represents.co.uk MD: Ben King.

Retaliate First Management Unit 9, Darvells Works, Common Rd, Chorleywood, Herts WD3 5LP **t** 01923 286010 **f** 01923 286070 **e** mgmt@retaliatefirst.co.uk **w** ianbrown-online.co.uk MD: Steve Lowes.

Rheoli Ankst Management 104a Cowbridge Road East, Canton, Cardiff CF11 9DX **t** 02920 394200 **f** 02920 372703 **e** rhiannonankst1@aol.com Contact: Alun Llwyd.

Richard Evans Management 15 Chesham St, Belgravia, London SW1X 8ND **t** 020 7235 3929 **e** r.evans@pipemedia.co.uk MD: Richard Evans.

Richard Ogden Management 44 Sillwood Rd, Brighton BN1 2LE **t** 01273 206 111 **f** 01273 205 111 **e** richard@richardogdenmanagement.com **w** richardogdenmanagement.com MD: Richard Ogden.

Richman Management Ltd 66A Highgate High St, London N6 5HX **t** 020 8374 2258 **e** richard@richmanmanagement.com(DO NOT PUBLISH) MD: Richard Shipman.

Right Management 177 High St, Harlesden, London NW10 4TE **t** 020 8961 3889 **f** 020 8951 9955 **e** info@rightrecordings.com **w** rightrecordings.com Dirs: David Landau, John Kaufman.

Riot Club Management Unit 4, 27A Spring Grove Rd, Hounslow, Middx TW3 4BE **t** 020 8572 8809 **f** 020 8572 9590 **e** riot@riotclub.co.uk **w** riotclub.co.uk MD: Lee Farrow.

Riot Management 47 Hay's Mews, London W1J 5QE **t** 020 7499 3993 **f** 020 7499 0219 **e** info@riot-management.com Contact: Matt Page, Ewan Grant.

Riverman Management Top Floor, George House, Brecon Rd, London W6 8PY **t** 020 7381 4000 **f** 020 7381 9666 **e** info@riverman.co.uk **w** riverman.co.uk Dir: David McLean.

Riviera Music Management 83 Dolphin Crescent, Paignton, Devon TQ3 1JZ **t** 07071 226078 **f** 01803 665728 **e** Info@rivieramusic.net **w** rivieramusic.net MD: Kevin Jarvis.

RLM (Richard Law Management) 58 Marylands Rd, Maida Vale, London W9 2DR **t** 020 7286 1706 **f** 020 7266 1293 **e** richard@rlmanagement.co.uk Mgr: Richard Law.

Robert Miller Management Running Media Group Ltd., 14 Victoria Rd, Douglas, Isle of Man IM2 4ER **t** 01624 677214 or 07973 129 068 **e** info@runningmedia.com **w** runningmedia.com MD: Bob Miller.

Robin Morton Consultancy 22 Herbert St, Glasgow G20 6NB **t** 0141 560 2748 or 0141 337 1199 or 07870 590 909 **f** 0141 357 0655 **e** robinmorto@aol.com Contact: Robin Morton.

Rokkpool Artist Management 11 Lawton Rd, London E10 6RR **t** 020 8558 6607 or 07960 442645 **e** rokkpool@tiscali.com **w** myspace.com/rokkpool Contact: Pippa Moye.

Rose Rouge International AWS House, Trinity Sq, St Peter Port, Guernsey, Channel Islands GY1 1LX **t** 01481 728 283 **f** 01481 714 118 **e** awsgroup@cwgsy.net Director/Producer: Steve Free.

Rough Trade Management 66 Golborne Rd, London W10 5PS **t** 020 8960 9888 **f** 020 8968 6715 **e** mog.yoshihara@roughtraderecords.com **w** roughtradeproducers.com Artist Co-ordinator: Mog Yoshihara.

Route One Management 24 Derby St, Edgeley, Stockport, Cheshire SK3 9HF **t** 0161 476 1172 or 07950 119 151 **e** andylacallen@yahoo.co.uk **w** spinning-fields.com Dir: Andy Callen.

RP Management 51A Woodville Rd, Thornton Heath, Surrey CR7 8LN **t** 07956 368 680 **e** R.Pascoe@RPMan.co.uk **w** myspace.com/rpmanagement Contact: Richard Pascoe.

Running Dog Management Whitecroft, Well Lane, Devauden, Monmouthshire NP16 6NX **t** 07831 800 110 **e** runningdogmanagement@yahoo.com **w** bitchpups.com Mgr: Les Modget.

Runrig Management 1 York St, Aberdeen AB11 5DL **t** 01224 573100 **f** 01224 572598 **e** office@runrig.co.uk **w** runrig.co.uk Mgr: Mike Smith.

Billy Russell Management Binny Estate, Ecclesmachan, Edinburgh EH52 6NL **t** 01506 858885 **f** 01506 858155 **e** kitemusic@aol.com **w** kitemusic.com MD: Billy Russell.

Sacred Management 187 Freston Rd, London W10 6TH **t** 020 8969 1323 **f** 020 8969 1363 **e** info@sacred-music.com Mgr: Adjei Amaning.

Safe Management St Ann's House, Guildford Rd, Lightwater, Surrey GU18 5RA **t** 01276 476 676 **f** 01276 451 109 **e** firstname@safemanagement.co.uk Mgr: Chris Herbert.

Safehouse Management Reverb House, Bennett St, London W4 2AH **t** 020 8994 8889 **f** 020 8994 8617 **e** info@safehousemanagement.com **w** safehousemanagement.com Mgr: Ian Hindmarsh.

Saffa Music Ltd Arena House, 12-15 Plough and Harrow Rd, Edgbaston, Birmingham B16 8UR **t** 0121 694 5135 **f** 0121 248 6007 **e** info@safa.co.uk **w** rubyturner.com MD: Geoff Pearce.

Safi Sounds Management & Promotion Po Box 572, Huddersfield HD3 4ZD **t** 01484 340975 **e** info@safisounds.co.uk **w** safisounds.co.uk Mgr: Sarah Hutton.

Sanctuary Artist Management Ltd Sanctuary House, 45-53 Sinclair Rd, London W14 0NS **t** 020 7602 6351 **f** 020 7603 5941 **e** info@sanctuarygroup.com **w** sanctuarygroup.com MD: Martin Hall.

Saphron Management c/o 36 Belgrave Rd, London E17 8QE **t** 020 8521 7764 or 07973 415 167 **e** saphron@msn.com Artist Manager: Annette Bennett MMF.

Satellite Artists Studio House, 34 Salisbury St, London NW8 8QE **t** 020 7402 9111 **f** 020 7723 3064 **e** satellite_artists@hotmail.com MD: Eliot Cohen.

SB Management 2 Barb Mews, London W6 7PA **t** 020 7078 9789 **f** 0871 253 1584 **e** info@sbman.co.uk **w** sbman.co.uk MD: Simon Banks.

Scarlet Management Southview, 68 Siltside, Gosberton Risegate, Lincs PE11 4ET **t** 01755 841750 **f** 01755 841750 **e** info@scarletrecording.co.uk **w** scarletrecording.co.uk MD: Liz Lenten.

Schoolhouse Management Ltd 42 York Pl, Edinburgh EH1 3HU **t** 0131 557 4242 **e** bruce@schoolhousemanagement.co.uk **w** schoolhousemanagement.co.uk MD: Bruce Findlay.

Scruffy Bird The Nest, 205 Victoria St, London SW1E 5NE **t** 020 7931 7990 **e** duncan@scruffybird.com **w** scruffybird.com Head of Management: Duncan Ellis.

Seaview Music 28 Mawson Rd, Cambridge CB1 2EA **t** 01223 508431 **f** 01223 508449 **e** seaview@dial.pipex.com **w** seaviewmusic.co.uk Administrator: Alison Suter.

Alan Seifert Management 1 Winterton House, 24 Park Walk, London SW10 0AQ **t** 020 7795 0321 or 07958 241 733 **e** alanseifert@lineone.net MD: Alan Seifert.

Sentics 18 Coronation Court, London W10 6AL **t** 020 8968 4337 **f** 020 7598 9465 **e** raf.sentics@virgin.net Dir: Raf Edmonds.

Sentinel Management 60 Sellons Ave, London NW10 4HH **t** 020 8961 6992 or 07932 737 547 **e** sentinel7@hotmail.com Dirs: Sandra Scott.

Serious Artist Management PO Box 13143, London N6 5BG **t** 020 8815 5550 **f** 020 8815 5559 **e** sam@seriousworld.com **w** seriousworld.com MD: Sam O'Riordan.

Session Connection PO Box 46307, London SW17 0WS **t** 020 8871 1212 or 07801 070 362 **e** sessionconnection@mac.com **w** thesessionconnection.com MD: Tina Hamilton.

Jon Sexton Management (JSM) 9 Spedan Close, Branch Hill, London NW3 7XF **t** 07855 551 024 **e** copasetik1@aol.com **w** copasetik.com MD: Jon Sexton.

SGO Music Management PO Box 2015, Salisbury SP2 7WU **t** 01264 811 154 **f** 01264 811 172 **e** sgomusic@sgomusic.com **w** sgomusic.com MD: Stuart Ongley.

ShaftRoxy Management PO Box 39464, London N10 1WP **t** 07779 340 154 **f** 020 8883 4086 **e** nathan@shaftroxy.com **w** shaftroxy.com MD: Nathan Hull.

Shalit Global Entertainment & Management 7 Moor St, Soho, London W1D 5NB **t** 020 7851 9155 **f** 020 7851 9156 **e** info@shalitglobal.com MD: Jonathan Shalit.

Shamrock Music Ltd 9, Thornton Pl, Marylebone, London W1H 1FG **t** 020 7935 9719 **f** 020 7935 0241 **e** lindy@celtus.demon.co.uk Mgr: Lindy McManus.

Shavian Enterprises 14 Devonshire Pl, London W1G 6HX **t** 020 7935 6906 **f** 020 7224 6256 **e** info@sandieshaw.com **w** sandieshaw.com Dir: Grace Banks.

Shaw Thing Management 20 Coverdale Rd, London N11 3FG **t** 020 8361 6669 **f** 020 8361 9403 **e** hills@shawthingmanagement.com MD: Hillary Shaw.

Show Business Entertainment The Bungalow, Chatsworth Ave, Long Eaton, Notts NG10 2FL **t** 0115 973 5445 **f** 0115 946 1831 **e** kimholmes@showbusinessagency.freeserve.co.uk MD: Kim Holmes.

Shurwood Management Tote Hill Cottage, Stedham, Midhurst, W Sussex GU29 0PY **t** 01730 817400 **f** 01730 815846 **e** shurley@shurwood.fsnet.co.uk GM: Shurley Selwood.

Sidewalk 7 154 New Kings Rd, London SW6 4LZ **t** 020 7731 3350 **e** info@sidewalk7.com **w** sidewalk7.com MD: Rocco Gardner.

Sidewinder Management 10 Cambridge Mews, Brighton, W Sussex BN3 3EZ **t** 01273 774 460 or 07771 748 666 **e** sdw@SidewinderMgmt.com MD: Simon Watson.

Silentway Management Ltd 1 Chilworth Mews, London W2 3RG **t** 020 7087 8820 **f** 020 7087 8899 **e** tracymenage@silentway.co.uk **w** simplyred.com Mgr: Ian Grenfell.

Silentway Management Ltd. (Manchester) Deansgate Quay, Deansgate, Manchester M3 4LA **t** 0161 832 2111 **f** 0161 832 2333 **e** info@silentway.co.uk **w** simplyred.com.

Silverbird Ltd Amersham Common House, 133 White Lion Rd, Amersham Common, Bucks HP7 9JY **t** 01494 766754 **f** 01494 766745 **e** donatella@silvrbird.demon.co.uk **w** leosayer.com Mgr: Donatella Piccinetti.

Simon Lawlor Management PO Box 18722, Aberdeen AB24 3WX **t** 01224 647 220 or 07792 517 508 **e** simonlawlormanagement@btinternet.com **w** simonlawlor.co.uk MD: Simon Lawlor.

Simple Management 36 Avenue Rd, Brentford, Middx TW8 9NS **t** 020 8560 8402 **f** 020 8560 8402 **e** simonbentley@onetel.net Mgr: Simon Bentley.

Simply Entertainment Ltd Wilson's Corner, 1-5 Ingrave Rd, Brentwood, Essex CM15 8AP **t** 020 7730 2300 **e** anthony@simplyentertainmentltd.com **w** simplyentertainmentltd.com Dir: Anthony Campbell.

Sincere Management 35 Bravington Rd, London W9 3AB **t** 020 8960 4438 **f** 020 8968 8458 **e** office@sinman.co.uk Contact: Peter Jenner & Mushi Jenner.

Sleeper Music Block 2, 6 Erskine Rd, Primrose Hill, London NW3 3AJ **t** 020 7580 3995 **f** 020 7900 6244 **e** info@sleepermusic.co.uk **w** guychambers.com Contact: Dylan Chambers, Louise Jeremy.

Slowburn Productions 18 Eastwick Lodge, 4 Village Rd, Enfield, Middx EN1 2DH **t** 020 8360 4670 **e** Harry@slowburnproductions.co.uk MD: Harry Benjamin.

SMA Talent The Cottage, Church St, Fressingfield, Suffolk IP21 5PA **t** 01379 586 734 **f** 01379 586 131 **e** carolynne@smatalent.com **w** smatalent.com MDs: Carolynne Wyper, Olav Wyper.

SMI/Everyday Productions 33 Mandarin Pl, Grove, Oxon OX12 0QH **t** 01235 771577 or 01235 767171 **e** smi_everyday_productions@yahoo.com Contact: VP A&R.

Doug Smith Associates PO Box 1151, London W3 8HA **t** 020 8993 8436 **f** 020 8896 1778 **e** mail@dougsmithassociates.co.uk **w** dougsmithassociates.co.uk Partners: Doug Smith, Eve Carr.

Social Misfit Entertainment Suite 17 Hunter House, Woodfarrs, London SE5 8HA **t** 020 7924 0565 **e** socialmisfits@hotmail.com **w** social-misfit.com MD: Patrick Waweru.

Soho Artists 1st Floor, 18 Broadwick St, London W1F 8HS **t** 020 7434 0080 **f** 020 7434 0061 **e** mm@sohoartists.co.uk MD: Moshe Morad.

Solar Management 13 Rosemont Rd, London NW3 6NG **t** 020 7794 3388 **f** 020 7794 5588 **e** info@solarmanagement.co.uk **w** solarmanagement.co.uk MD: Carol Crabtree.

Solid Senders 93 Ronald Park Ave, Westcliff On Sea, Essex SS0 9QP **t** 01702 341983 **e** irene@solidsenders.freeserve.co.uk **w** wilkojohnson.co.uk Manager/Agent: Irene Knight.

Son Management 72 Marylebone Lane, London W1U 2PL **t** 020 7486 7458 **f** 020 8467 6997 **e** sam@randm.co.uk Mgr: Sam Eldridge.

Sonic Bang! Management 22B Upland Industrial Estate, Wyton, St Ives, Cambs PE28 2DY **t** 07702 399 798 **e** info@sonicbang.co.uk **w** sonicbang.co.uk MD: Adam J Mills.

Sosusie Music 26 Grenville Rd, London N19 4EH **t** 07951 479 761 **e** info@sosusiemusic.com **w** sosusiemusic.com Contact: Susie Sandford Smith.

Sound Artist Management 192 Portnall Rd, London W9 3BJ **t** 020 8960 9553 **e** info@soundartistmanagement.com **w** soundartistmanagement.com Agents: Edward & Lucy Bigland.

The Sound Foundation The Sound Foundation, PO Box 4900, Earley, Berks RG10 0GA **t** 0118 934 9600 or 07973 559 203 **e** info@soundfoundation.co.uk **w** airplayrecords.co.uk Label Mgr: Hadyn Wood.

Sound Image Unit 2B, Banquay Trading Estate, Slutchers Lane, Warrington, Cheshire WA1 1PJ **t** 01925 445742 **f** 01925 445742 **e** info@soundimageproductionss.co.uk **w** soundimageproductionss.co.uk MD: Steve Millington.

Sound Pets PO Box 158, Twickenham, Middlesex TW2 6RW **t** 07976 577 773 **f** 0871 733 3401 **e** robinhill@soundpets.freeserve.co.uk Dir: Robin Hill.

Southside Management 20 Cromwell Mews, London SW7 2JY **t** 020 7225 1919 **f** 020 7823 7091 **e** kate@southsidemanagement.co.uk MD: Bob Johnson.

Spaced Out Music 8 Southlands Close, Leek, Staffs ST13 8DF **t** 01782 772 989 or 01538 371 418 **e** mike@demon655.freeserve.co.uk **w** the-demon.com MD: Mike Stone.

Sparklestreet HQ 18 Sparkle St, Manchester M1 2NA **t** 0161 273 3435 or 07798 766 861 **f** 0161 273 3695 **e** gary@pd-uk.com **w** sparklestreet.net Dir: Gary McClarnan.

Mal Spence Management Cherry Tree Lodge, Copmanthorpe, York, North Yorks YO23 3SH **t** 01904 703764 **f** 01904 702312 **e** malspence@aol.com **w** sugarstar.com MD: Mal Spence.

Sphinx Management 2 Unity Pl, West Gate, Rotherham, S Yorks S60 1AR **t** 01709 820379 or 01709 820370 **f** 01709 369990 **e** tributebands@btconnect.com **w** tribute-entertainment.co.uk Dir: Anthony French.

Spirit Music & Media PO Box 30884, London W12 9AZ **t** 020 8746 7461 **f** 020 8749 7441 **e** info@spiritmm.com **w** spiritmm.com MD: Tom Haxell.

Splinter Management Terminal Studios, 4-10 Lamb Walk, London SE1 3TT **t** 020 7357 8416 **f** 020 7357 8437 **e** parmesanchic@aol.com **w** sneakerpimps.com MD: Caroline Butler.

Split Music 13 Sandys Rd, Worcester WR1 3HE **t** 01905 613 023 **e** meshmusic@prison-records.com MD: Chris Warren.

Sprint Music High Jarmany Farm, Jarmany Hill, Barton St David, Somerton, Somerset TA11 6DA **t** 01458 851 010 **f** 01458 851 029 **e** info@sprintmusic.co.uk **w** sprintmusic.co.uk Industry Consultant, Producer, Writer: John Ratcliff.

Star Quality Management 50 Anne's Court, 3 Palgrave Gardens, London NW1 6EN **t** 0114 268 5665 **f** 0144 268 4161 **e** bmc@brownmcleod.co.uk MD: John Roddison.

Star-Write Management PO Box 16715, London NW4 1WN **t** 020 8203 5062 **f** 020 8202 3746 **e** starwrite@btinternet.com Dir: John Lisners.

Starwood Management 33 Richmond Pl, Brighton, E Sussex BN2 9NA **t** 01273 675 444 **e** mark@illshows.fsnet.co.uk Co-MD: Mark Nicholson.

Stereophonic Management PO Box 3787, London SE22 9DZ **t** 020 8299 1650 **f** 020 8693 5514 **e** duophonic@btopenworld.com Contact: Martin Pike.

Steve Allen Entertainments 60 Broadway, Peterborough, Cambs PE1 1SU **t** 01733 569 589 **f** 01733 561 854 **e** steve@sallenent.co.uk **w** sallenent.co.uk Principal: Steve Allen.

Steve Harrison Management Lodge Rd, Sandbach, Cheshire CW11 3HP **t** 01270 750448 **f** 01270 750449 **e** info@shmanagement.co.uk **w** shmanagement.co.uk Dir: Steve Harrison.

Stevo Management 14 Tottenham Court Rd, London W1T 1JY **t** 020 7836 9995 **f** 020 8348 2526 **e** stevo@somebizarre.com **w** somebizarre.com Mgr: Stevo.

Stirling Music Limited 25 Heathmans Rd, London SW6 4TJ **t** 020 7371 5756 **f** 020 7371 7731 **e** office@pureuk.com **w** pureuk.com Creative Dir: Billy Royal.

Storm Management 134 Godstone Rd, Caterham, Surrey CR3 6RB **t** 01883 372639 **f** 01883 372639 **e** enquiries@stormmanagement.uk.com **w** stormmanagement.uk.com MD: Stephen Bailey-Johnston.

Streetfeat Management Ltd Unit 105, The Saga Centre, 326 Kensal Rd, London W10 5BZ **t** 020 8969 3370 **f** 020 8960 9971 **e** info@streetfeat.demon.co.uk MD: Colin Schaverien.

Streetside Records 1 Glenthorne Mews, 115a Glenthorne Rd, London W6 0LJ **t** 020 8741 9365 **e** info@streetsiderecords.co.uk Dir: Howard Berman.

Stress Management PO Box 27947, London SE7 8WN **t** 020 8269 0352 or 07778 049 706 **f** 020 8269 0353 **e** suzanne@quixoticrecords.com **w** quixoticrecords.com Dir: Suzanne Hunt.

Strike 3 Management 107 Hamilton Terrace, London NW8 9QY **t** 07787 507 787 or 020 7286 6410 **e** toby@strikeiii.com **w** strikeiii.com Mgr: Toby Harris.

Strike Back Management 271 Royal College St, Camden Town, London NW1 9LU **t** 020 7482 0115 **f** 020 7267 1169 **e** maurice@baconempire.com MD: Maurice Bacon.

Strongroom Management 120-124 Curtain Rd, London EC2A 3SQ **t** 020 7426 5130 **f** 020 7426 5102 **e** coral@strongroom.com **w** strongroom.com/management Dir: Coral Worman.

Sublime Music Brighton Media Centre, 21/22 Old Steyne, Brighton, E Sussex BN1 1EL **t** 01273 648 330 **f** 01273 648 332 **e** info@sublimemusic.co.uk **w** sublimemusic.co.uk MD: Patrick Spinks.

Sugar Shack Management PO Box 73, Fish Ponds, Bristol BS16 7EZ **t** 01179 855092 **f** 01179 855092 **e** mike@sugarshackrecords.co.uk **w** sugarshackrecords.co.uk Dir: Mike Darby.

Sunrise UK Silverdene, Scaleby Hill, Carlisle CA6 4LU **t** 01228 675822 **f** 01228 675822 **e** info@sunriseuk.co.uk **w** sunriseuk.co.uk Prop: Martin Smith.

SuperVision Management Zeppelin Building, 59-61 Farringdon Rd, London EC1M 3JB **t** 020 7916 2146 **f** 020 7691 4666 **e** info@supervisionmgt.com Dirs: Paul Craig & James Sandom.

Sylvantone Promotions 11 Saunton Ave, Redcar, N Yorks TS10 2RL **t** 01642 479898 **f** 0709 235 9333 **e** sylvantone@hotmail.com **w** countrymusic.org.uk/tony-goodacre/index.html Prop: Tony Goodacre.

T2 Management Dolphin Court, 42 Carleton Rd, London N7 0ER **t** 020 7607 6654 or 07971 575810 **e** hilltaryn@hotmail.com Dir: Taryn Hill.

Talent Call Ltd Independent House, 54 Larkshall Rd, Chingford E4 6PD **t** 020 8523 9000 **f** 020 8523 8888 **e** abailey@independentmusicgroup.com **w** independentmusicgroup.com Dir: Andy Bailey.

TARGO Ents Corp Ltd PO Box 1977, Salisbury SP3 5ZW **t** 01722 716716 or 07971 405874 **f** 01722 716413 **e** targo.entscorps@virgin.net Mgr: Mathew Priest.

TCB Group 24 Kimberley Court, Kimberley Rd, Queens Pk, London NW6 7SL **t** 020 7328 7272 **f** 020 7372 0844 **e** stevenhoward@tcbgroup.co.uk **w** tcbgroup.co.uk MD: Steven Howard.

Teleryngg UK 132 Chase Way, London N14 5DH **t** 07050 055167 **f** 0870 741 5252 **e** teleryngg@msn.com **w** teleryngg.com MD: Richard Struple.

Tender Prey Management Studio 4, Ivebury Court, 325 Latimer Rd, London W10 6RA **t** 020 8964 5417 **f** 020 8964 5418 **e** restrictedarea@tenderprey.com Mgr: Rayner Jesson.

Terra Artists The Courtyard, Unit A, 42 Colwith Rd, Hammersmith, London W6 9EY **t** 020 8846 3737 **f** 020 8846 3738 **e** info@terraartists.com MDs: Marc Marot, John Arnison.

TFF Management Lovat House, Gavell Rd, Kilsyth, Glasgow G65 9BS **t** 01236 826555 **f** 01236 825560 **e** tessa@thetffagency.com MD: Tessa Hartmann.

TForce Concorde House, 101 Shepherds Bush Rd, London W6 7LP **t** 020 7602 8822 **f** 020 7603 2352 **e** enquiry@tforce.com **w** tforce.com MD: Tim Byrne.

Tim Prior - Artist & Rights Management The Old Lampworks, Rodney Pl, London SW19 2LQ **t** 020 8542 4222 **f** 020 8540 6056 **e** info@arm-eu.com MD: Tim Prior.

TJM PO Box 46024, London W9 1WW **t** 020 7286 2230 or 07801 702 279 **f** 020 7286 5359 **e** tara@tjm.uk.com Dir: Tara Joseph.

TK1 Management PO Box 38475, London SE16 7XT **t** 020 7481 1411 **f** 020 7481 1411 **e** info@tk1management.com **w** tk1management.com Dirs: Trina Torpey & Kathryn Nash.

Toni Medcalf Management 68 Upper Richmond Road West, London SW14 8DA **t** 020 8876 2421 or 07767 832 260 **e** TTMManagement@aol.com Artist Manager: Toni Medcalf.

Tony Hall Group of Companies Suite 7, 54 Broadwick St, London W1F 7AH **t** 020 7434 7286 **f** 020 7434 7288 **e** tonyhall@btconnect.com MD: Tony Hall.

Top Banana Management Ltd Monomark House, 27 Old Gloucester St, London WC1N 3XX **t** 020 7419 5026 or 07961 056 369 **e** info@topbananaman.com **w** topbananaman.com Contact: Garry Kemp, Nino Pires.

Top Draw Music Management PO Box 21469, Highgate, London N6 4ZG **t** 020 8340 5151 **f** 020 8340 5159 **e** james@tdmm.co.uk **w** tdmm.co.uk Dir: James Hamilton.

Total Management Flat 2, 7 Milnthorpe Rd, Meads Village, Eastbourne, E Sussex BN20 7NS **t** 01323 645879 **f** 01323 728608 **e** chris@totalmgt.biz **w** catherinetran.com MD: Chris McGeever.

Touched Productions 4 Varley House, County St, London SE1 6AL **t** 020 7403 5451 **f** 020 7403 5446 **e** toucheduk@aol.com **w** touched.co.uk Dir: Armorel Weston.

Tour Concepts 123 Hardy St, Hull HU5 2PH **t** 01482 448806 **f** 0870 126 5960 **e** andy.reynolds@tourconcepts.com **w** tourconcepts.com Owner: Andy Reynolds.

Traffik Productions Po Box 23615, Edinburgh EH1 3ZP **t** 0131 524 9591 **f** 0131 524 9581 **e** stuart@traffik.uk.com Mgr: Stuart Duncan.

Transmission Management 79-89 Pentonville Rd, London N1 9LG **t** 020 7993 3316 or 3317 **e** info@transmissionmanagement.com Contact: Adrian Bell, Will Williams.

TRC Management 10c Whitworth Court, Manor Pk, Manor Farm Rd, Runcorn, Cheshire WA7 1TE **t** 01928 571 111 or 07831 803 435 **f** 0871 247 4923 **e** mail@trcmanagement.com MD: Phil Chadwick.

Trinifold Management Third Floor, 12 Oval Rd, London NW1 7DH **t** 020 7419 4300 **f** 020 7419 4325 **e** trinuk@globalnet.co.uk MD: Robert Rosenberg.

Unique & Natural Talent Ltd 57 Elgin Crescent, London W11 2JU **t** 020 7792 1666 **f** 08700 516 570 **e** john@johnirelandandco.net **w** johnirelandandco.net Contact: John Ireland.

Unique Corp Ltd 15 Shaftesbury Centre, 85 Barlby Rd, London W10 6BN **t** 020 8964 9333 **f** 020 8964 9888 **e** info@uniquecorp.co.uk **w** uniquecorp.co.uk MD: Alan Bellman.

Upbeat Classical Management PO Box 479, Uxbridge, Middx UB8 2ZH **t** 01895 259441 **f** 01895 259341 **e** info@upbeatclassical.co.uk **w** upbeatclassical.co.uk Dir: Maureen Phililps.

Upbeat Management PO Box 63, Wallington, Surrey SM6 9YP **t** 020 8773 1223 **f** 020 8669 6752 **e** beryl@upbeat.co.uk **w** upbeat.co.uk MD: Beryl Korman.

Uplifted Management & DJ Agency PO Box 225, Chorlton, Manchester M21 0UH **t** 0161 882 0058 **e** info@upliftedmanagement.com **w** upliftedmanagement.com Mgr: Philip Waterhouse.

Upside Management 14 Clarence Mews, Balham, London SW12 9SR **t** 020 8673 8549 **f** 020 8673 8498 **e** simon@upsideuk.com Co MDs: Simon Jones & Denise Beighton.

Vagabond Management 8th Floor, 245 Blackfriars Rd, London SE1 9UR **t** 020 7921 8353 **e** rubber_road_records@yahoo.co.uk MD: Dexter Charles.

Valley Music Ltd. 11 Cedar Court, Fairmile, Henley-on-Thames, Oxon RG9 2JR **t** 01491 845 840 **f** 01491 413 667 **e** info@valleymusicuk.com **w** tomjones.com MD: Mark Woodward.

Value Added Talent Management (VAT) 1 Purley Pl, London N1 1QA **t** 020 7704 9720 **f** 020 7226 6135 **e** vat@vathq.co.uk **w** vathq.co.uk MD: Dan Silver.

Vashti PO Box 2553, Maidenhead, Berks SL6 1ZJ **t** 01628 620082 **f** 01628 637066 **e** info@sheilaferguson.com **w** sheilaferguson.com MD: Sheila Ferguson.

Denis Vaughan Management PO Box 28286, London N21 3WT **t** 020 7486 5353 **f** 020 8224 0466 **e** dvaughanmusic@dial.pipex.com Dir: Denis Vaughan.

Vex Management 24 Caradoc St, Greenwich, London SE10 9AG **t** 020 8293 9800 **f** 020 8293 9800 **e** paul@vexmanagement.com **w** myspace.com/vex MD: Paul Ablett.

Vibe Artist Management April Cottage, Sea Rd, Winchelsea Beach, E Sussex TN36 4LH **t** 07748 966 241 **e** ryan.farley@vibeartistmgt.com **w** myspace.com/vibeartistmanagement MD: Ryan Farley.

Vine Gate Music 4 Vine Gate, Parsonage Lane, Farnham Common, Bucks SL2 3NX **t** 01753 643696 **f** 01753 642259 **e** vinegate@clara.net **w** salenajones.co.uk Ptnr: Tony Puxley.

Violation Management 26 Mill St, Gamlingay, Sandy, Beds SG19 3JW **t** 01767 651552 or 07768 667076 **f** 01767 651228 **e** dicky_boy@msn.com Mgr: Dick Meredith.

Voicebox PO Box 82, Altrincham, Cheshire WA15 0QD **t** 0161 928 3222 **f** 0161 928 7849 **e** vb@thevoicebox.co.uk **w** thevoicebox.co.uk MD: Vicki Hope-Robinson.

W1 Music Management Munro Studios, 103-105 Holloway Rd, London N7 8LT **t** 07884 430 474 or 07887 531 006 **e** stewart@myhovercraft.co.uk Mgr: Stewart Feeney, Sam Johnson.

War Zones and Associates 33 Kersley Rd, London N16 0NT **t** 020 7249 2894 **f** 020 7254 3729 **e** wz33@aol.com Contact: Richard Hermitage.

Watercress Management The Old Vicerage, Pickering, N Yorks YO18 7AW **t** 01751 475502 **f** 01751 475502 **e** organised@ukonline.co.uk Dir: Ian McDaid.

What Management 3 Belfry Villas, Belfry Ave, Harefield, Uxbridge, Middlesex UB9 6HY **t** 01895 824674 **f** 01895 822994 **e** whatmanagement@blueyonder.co.uk Contact: Mick Cater, David Harper.

White Tiger Management 55 Fawcett Close, London SW16 2QJ **t** 020 8677 5199 or 020 8677 5399 **f** 020 8769 5795 **e** wtm@whitetigermanagement.co.uk MDs: Paul & Corinne White.

Alan Whitehead Management 79 The Ryde, Hatfield, Herts AL9 5DN **t** 01707 267883 **f** 01707 267247 **e** alan_whitehead_uk@yahoo.com MD: Alan Whitehead.

Whitehouse Management PO Box 43829, London NW6 1WN **t** 020 7209 2586 **f** 020 7209 7187 **e** mail@whitehousemanagement.com MD: Sue Whitehouse.

Whitenoise Management PO Box 741, Richmond, Surrey TW9 4HA **t** 020 8878 8550 **f** 020 8878 8550 **e** info@whitenoisemanagement.com MD: Chris Butler.

Wild Honey Management 10 Lansdowne Rd, Hove, E Sussex BN3 3AU **t** 01273 738704 **f** 01273 732112 **e** jimtracey@aol.com **w** wildhoney.co.uk Contact: Jim Tracey.

WILD WEST MANAGEMENT

Argentum, 2 Queen Caroline Street, London W6 9DX **t** 020 8323 8013 **f** 020 8323 8080 **e** ela@ela.co.uk **w** ela.co.uk MD: John Giacobbi. World leaders in business affairs and management consultancy.

Wildlife Entertainment Unit F, 21 Heathmans Rd, London SW6 4TJ **t** 020 7371 7008 **f** 020 7371 7708 **e** info@wildlife-entertainment.com Managing Directors: Ian McAndrew, Colin Lester.

John Williams PO Box 423, Chislehurst, Kent BR7 5TU **t** 020 8295 3639 **f** 020 8295 3641 **e** jrwilliams@lineone.net Contact: John Williams.

Allan Wilson Enterprises Queens House, Chapel Green Rd, Hindley, Wigan, Lancs WN2 3LL **t** 01942 258565 or 01942 255158 **f** 01942 255158 **e** allan@allanwilson.co.uk Owner: Allan Wilson.

Wise Buddah Talent 74 Great Titchfield St, London W1W 7QP **t** 020 7307 1600 **f** 020 7307 1608 **e** nicole.c@wisebuddah.com **w** wisebuddah.com Mgr: Nicole Constantinou.

Wizard Artist Management PO Box 6779, Birmingham B13 9RZ **t** 0121 778 2218 or 07956 984 754 **f** 0121 778 1856 **e** pk.sharma@ukonline.co.uk **w** wizardrecords.co.uk MD: Mambo Sharma.

WonderWorld 55 The Spectacle Works, Jedburgh Rd, London E13 9LX **t** 020 8552 5502 **f** 020 8552 5501 **e** mark@hex-on.com Contact: Mark Shine.

Alan Wood Agency 346 Gleadless Rd, Sheffield, S Yorks S2 3AJ **t** 0114 258 0338 **f** 0114 258 0638 **e** celia@alanwoodagency.co.uk **w** alanwoodagency.co.uk Contact: Alan Wood.

Working Class Music Management 22 Upper Brook St, Mayfair, London W1K 7PZ **t** 020 7491 1060 **f** 020 7491 9996 **e** workingclassmusic@btinternet.com **w** workingclassmanagement.com Contact: Matt Crossey, Lisa Barker.

World Famous Group 467 Fulham Rd, Fulham, London SW6 1HL **t** 020 7385 6838 **f** 020 7385 0999 **e** info@worldfamousgroup.com **w** worldfamousgroup.com Chairman: Alon Shulman.

Worldmaster DJ Management Ltd The Coachhouse, Mansion Farm, Liverton Hill, Sandway, Maidstone, Kent ME17 2NJ **t** 01622 858 300 **f** 01622 858 300 **e** info@eddielock.com **w** eddielock.co.uk Prop: Eddie Lock.

WS Management The Dog House, 32 Sullivan Crescent, Harefield, Uxbridge, Middlesex UB9 6NL **t** 01895 825757 **e** Bill@wsmgt.co.uk **w** wsmgt.co.uk Dir: William L. Langdale-Smith.

X Factor Management Ltd PO Box 44198, London SW6 4XU **t** 0870 251 9540 **f** 0870 251 9560 **e** info@xfactorltd.com **w** xfactorltd.com MD: Natalie Swallow.

XL Talent Reverb House, Bennett St, London W4 2AH **t** 020 8747 0660 **f** 020 8747 0880 **e** management@reverbxl.com **w** reverbxl.com Partners: Ian Wright, Maggi Hickman, Julian Palmer.

X-Rated Management Wimbourne House, 155 New North Rd, London N1 6TA **t** 020 7168 4287 **f** 070 9284 1131 **e** mike@x-rated.me.uk **w** x-rated.me.uk Artist Managers: Michael Hague and Brian Noonan.

Brian Yeates Associates Home Farm House, Canwell, Sutton Coldfield, W Midlands B75 5SH **t** 0121 323 2200 **f** 0121 323 2313 **e** info@brianyeates.co.uk **w** brianyeates.co.uk Ptnr: Ashley Yeates.

Young Guns Ltd 134 Longley Rd, London SW17 9LH **t** 020 8672 7630 or 07980 222 857 **e** enquiries@younggunsuk.com **w** younggunsuk.com Contact: Dom Pecheur.

The Yukon Management Utopia Village, Chalcot Rd, Primrose Hill, London NW1 8LH **t** 020 7242 8408 **e** music@theyukonmusic.com MD: Andrew Maurice.

Z Management The Palm House, PO Box 19734, London SW15 2WU **t** 020 8874 3337 **f** 020 8874 3599 **e** office@zman.co.uk **w** zman.co.uk MD: Zita Wadwa-McQ.

Zeall Management Limited 5A Station Rd, Twickenham, Middx TW1 4LL **t** 020 8607 9401 **e** info@zeall.com **w** zeall.com MD: David McGeachie.

Zen Consultants 27B Felixstowe Rd, London NW10 5SR **t** 020 8960 9171 or 07957 338 525 **e** sacha@zenmedia.net **w** zenmedia.net MD: Sacha Taylor-Cox.

ZincSplash 9 Woodside Lodge, Tivoli Crescent, Brighton BN1 5ND **t** 01273 564 101 or 07970 000 034 **e** theboss@zincsplash.com **w** zincsplash.com Mgr: Craig Tarrant.

Managed Artists

3MI SGO Music Management
4FLAVA Jack 'N' Jill Artiste Management
5 O'CLOCK HEROES A.M.P./TBA
8.58 Fox Records Ltd (Management)
16 HORSEPOWER Tender Prey Management
THE 45S First Column Management
747S Crown Music Management Services
808 STATE North
A Furtive Mass Transit Systems LLP
A-HA Bandana Management
A SILENT FILM On 10 Music Entertainment
A TRIBUTE TO RIVERDANCE Denis Vaughan Management
AADESH Muirhead Management
ABBA GOLD Psycho Management Company

ACOUSTIC ALCHEMY The Art & Music Corporation
ACTOV LIFE Future Management
ACTUAL SIZE ARB Music Management
ADAMS, JUSTIN Spirit Music & Media
ADEM Big Dipper Productions
ADVENTURES OF STEVIE V RDPR Music Management
ADZUKI Avalon Management Group Ltd
AFRO CELT SOUND SYSTEM Impro Management
AFTER EDEN Line-Up PMC
AFTER THE SILENCE Jonny Paul Management
AGENT SUMO Streetfeat Management Ltd
AGUILLERA, CHRISTINA azoffmusic management
AIDAN LAVELLE Effective Management
AIDAN SMITH Sparklestreet HQ
THE AILERONS CMO Management International Ltd
AIRHAMMER Riot Club Management
AKA THE FOX Simon Lawlor Management
ILHAM AL MADFAI Soho Artists
ALAN 'MIDNIGHT' CONNOR First Move Management Ltd
ALBI PopWorks
ALDERGROVE Michael McDonagh Management
ALEX HOLLAND Black Magic Management
ALFIE Steve Harrison Management
ALIEN SEX FIEND 13th Moon Management
ALLEN, ROSS David Dorrell Management
DOT ALLISON Vex Management
ALTERNATIVE 3 CEC Management
A:M LOVERS Clown Management
AMBER MELODY Pilot Management
AMICI FOREVER Paul Crockford Management (PCM)
AMIT PAUL Bandana Management
AMUSEMENT PARKS ON FIRE Bermuda Management
AMY PEPPERCORN PPM Artist Management
AMY WINEHOUSE Brilliant 19 Ltd
ANDERSON NOISE Bulldozer Management
ANDREAS, LISA Fox Records Ltd (Management)
ANDY DUNCAN 7pm Management
ANEMIC Sugar Shack Management
ANGEL OAKS Riviera Music Management
ANIMAL CRUELTY First Time Management
ANNA ANN Stan Green Management
ANNIE CHRISTIAN Schoolhouse Management Ltd
ANT AND DEC James Grant Music
ANTHONY ROTHER Archetype Management
APACHE INDIAN Boom Management & Consultancy
APOLLO 440 XL Talent
APU FROM PERU Line-Up PMC
AQUILINA Automatic Management
ARCADE FIRE Quest Management
ARCH ENEMY Sanctuary Artist Management Ltd
ARCHIVE IE Music Ltd
ARCTIC MONKEYS Wildlife Entertainment
ARENA Billy Russell Management
ROD ARGENT John Waller Management & Marketing
ARNOLD, PETER First Time Management
ASCENSION Earth Music
ASH Out There Management
ASHES OF SOULS Radar Music and Management
ASHLEY Upside Management
ASSASSINS Transmission Management
ASSEMBLY NOW XL Talent
ASWAD J Management
JON ATKINSON CA Management
ATLANTA JBS Management UK
ATLAS, NATACHA CEC Management
ATTAR, STELLA Diamond Sounds Music Management
AUBURN Scarlet Management
AUDIOTWITCH Audio Authority Management
AVALANCHES MBL

B, EMMA Wise Buddah Talent
BACHELOR NUMBER ONE JC Music
BACK DOOR SLAM Robert Miller Management
BAD FIRE QUEEN Simply Entertainment Ltd
BADLY DRAWN BOY Big Life Management
BAGHDADDIES Line-Up PMC
CORINNE BAILEY RAE Robert Miller Management
BAKER, CHERYL Razzamatazz Management
BALBOA Bizarre Management
A BAND CALLED FRANK First Time Management
BAND OF HOLY JOY Charmenko
BANG OUT OF ORDER Direct Heat Management
BAPTISTE, DENYS The Dune Music Company
BARBER'S, CHRIS, JAZZ AND BLUES BAND Cromwell Management
BARCLAY JAMES HARVEST Mad Management
BARKER, SOPHIE Emperor Management
GARY BARLOW Freedom Management
BARRETT, VICKY Jackie Davidson Management
BARTON, DEAN NOW Music
BAY 15 TKL Management
BEATMASTERS X-Rated Management
THE BEAUTY ROOM Consigliari Ltd
JEFF BECK Equator Music
DANIEL BEDINGFIELD Empire Artist Management
BEEDLE, ASHLEY Whitenoise Management
BELARUS Boss Music
BELASCO Mako Music
THE BELLAROSA CONNECTION Solar Management
BELLE Crown Music Management Services
BELLE & SEBASTIAN Banchory Management
FRANCESCA BELMONTE BK 40 Management
BEN & JASON Nettwerk Management UK
BEN ADAMS TForce
BEN `JAMMIN' ROBBINS Private & Confidential Management Ltd
BEN OKAFOR Blue Hippo Management
BENSON, STEPHANIE BK 40 Management
BENSUSAN, PIERRE NEM Productions (UK)
JASON BERKMANN Qaraj' Ltd
BERMUDA TRIANGLE WonderWorld
GEOFF BERNER Sincere Management
CHUCK BERRY Denis Vaughan Management
BERTERO, ROBERTO PVA Management
BETH GIBBONS & RUSTIN MAN Fruit
BETH ORTON azoffmusic management
BETHAN ELFYN Avalon Management Group Ltd
BETTY CURSE Crown Music Management Services
BEULAH Blujay Management
BIG AMONGST THE STARS Rose Rouge International
BIG CHIEF Northstar Artist Management
BIG SUR Retaliate First Management
BILLY BRAGG Sincere Management
BIMBO JONES Ambush Management
BIRD, JEZ Peter Haines Management
BITCH BITCH BITCH Alan Whitehead Management
BITCHPUPS Running Dog Management
BJORK Quest Management
BJORN AGAIN ReBjörn Ltd
BLACK BIKINI ALPHA Arketek Management
BLACK CANDY SMI/Everyday Productions
BLACK DANIEL Terra Artists
THE BLACK DOG Feedback Communications
BLACK HOLES Hannah Management
BLACK LACE NOW Music
BLACK MOSES Dogface Management
BLACK, RICHARD Teleryngg UK
BLACK SIFICHI Feedback Communications
BLACK SMOKE Feedback Communications

BLACK STROBE LH Management
BLACK VELVETS Sanctuary Artist Management Ltd
BLAK TWANG Heavyweight Management
BLAKE, PAUL Little Piece of Jamaica (LPOJ)
BLAKE, PERRY NBM
BLAM, GERI Direct Heat Management
BLAZIN SQUAD Albert Samuel Management
BLING DAWG Jamdown Ltd
BLISS N SCRIPT X-Rated Management
BLOCK 16 Solar Management
BLOCK, RORY NEM Productions (UK)
BLOOD RED SHOES Prolifica Management
BLUE Intelligent Music Management Ltd
BLUE & RED MWM Music Management
BLUE STAR WonderWorld
BLUE SWERVER Plan C Management
COLIN BLUNSTONE John Waller Management & Marketing
BLUR CMO Management International Ltd
BOB BROZMAN & WOODY MANN NEM Productions (UK)
BOBBY O X-Rated Management
BOBBY VALENTINO Firebrand Management
BOG TOWN PLAYBOYS MSM Music Consultants
BOHINTA Ardent Music
BOLA Kamara Artist Management (UK)
BOND, SCOTT Serious Artist Management
BONZO DOG DOO DAH BAND Right Management
BORDER CROSSING Kartel
BOSTON azoffmusic management
BOUJAMAA BOUBOUL Outerglobe (Global Fusion)
BOWIE, DAVID Outside Management
BOYCE, MAX Handshake Ltd
BRASSTOOTH Boom Management & Consultancy
BRAVE CAPTAIN Rheoli Ankst Management
BRAVEHEART TForce
BREEZER, JO B&H Management
BRENDAN BENSON Bermuda Management
BRENNAN, MAIRE Gola Entertainment
BRETT ANDERSON Silentway Management Ltd
BRIAN HARVEY B&H Management
THE BRIDGE Leap
BRIGADE Chuffmedia
BRINKMAN Wildlife Entertainment
BROADCAST Stereophonic Management
BROKEN DOLLS Safehouse Management
BRONZE AGE FOX Rheoli Ankst Management
BROOK, MICHAEL Opium (Arts) Ltd
BROTHERHOOD OF MAN Brotherhood Of Man Management
BROWN, ALEX Escape Music Management
BROWN, IAN Retaliate First Management
BROWN, JOE John Taylor Management
BROWN, JOHN WILLY Show Business Entertainment
BROWN, SAM One Fifteen
BROWN, SARAH Eclipse-PJM
LORNA BROWN Positive Management
BRYAN ZENTZ Archetype Management
BRYDON, MARK Graham Peacock Management
BUDAPEST Easy Street Artist Management
BUDDAHEAD Sanctuary Artist Management Ltd
BUDNUBAC Bermuda Management
BURRIDGE, LEE Excession: The Agency Ltd
CATHY BURTON John Waller Management & Marketing
BUSH azoffmusic management
BUTTABALL Menace Management Ltd.
BYRNE TARGO Ents Corp Ltd
CALDERONE, VICTOR Sanctuary Artist Management Ltd
CALLA PPM Artist Management
TERRY CALLIER Positive Management
CAMPBELL, RUU Rough Trade Management
CAMPI, RAY Paul Barrett (Rock 'n Roll Enterprises)

CANTABILE Seaview Music
CAPALDI, JIM John Taylor Management
CAPTAIN WILBERFORCE Deluxxe Management
CARL PALMER Trinifold Management
BELINDA CARLISLE Sidewinder Management
CARLTON, CARL, & THE SONGDOGS What Management
CARMELO R2 Management
THE CARNIVAL BAND Seaview Music
KENNY CARPENTER Qaraj' Ltd
CARRACK, PAUL Alan Wood Agency
CARROL, CLIVE NEM Productions (UK)
CARTER, JON David Dorrell Management
CARTHY, ELIZA Moneypenny Management
CASABLANCA BOYS McLeod Holden Enterprises Ltd
CASEY, PADDY Principle Management
CASSANDRA FOX Conception Artist Management
CAT THE DOG Starwood Management
CATHEDRAL One Fifteen
CAUTY, JIMMY Feedback Communications
CAVAN, CRAZY, & THE RHYTHM ROCKERS Paul Barrett (Rock 'n Roll Enterprises)
CAVE, NICK, & THE BAD SEEDS Tender Prey Management
CERYS MATTHEWS Rough Trade Management
JAMES CHADWICK Playpen Management
CHAKRA Earth Music
CHARLAMAGNE, DIANE Streetfeat Management Ltd
CHARLIE 3rd Precinct
CHARLOTTE CHURCH Consigliari Ltd
CHEAP HOTEL Hannah Management
CHIKINKI Illicit Entertainment
THE CHILDREN Touched Productions
CHILI MCM
CHILLAGE PEOPLE Northstar Artist Management
CHING Little Piece of Jamaica (LPOJ)
CHRIS SALT Effective Management
CHRIS SMYTH Modal Management
CHRISTIAN, DARREN Duty Free Artist Management
CHRISTOPHER LAWRENCE Represents Artist Management
THE CHUCKER BUTTY OCARINA QUARTET Seaview Music
CHUMBAWAMBA Doug Smith Associates
CHUNGKING CEC Management
CHURCH, CHARLOTTE azoffmusic management
CICCONE Zen Consultants
CINERAMA Globeshine (UK) Ltd
THE CIRCUS OF HORRORS Psycho Management Company
CITIZEN K Red Onion Productions
CJ MACKINTOSH Safehouse Management
CLARE UCHIMA RLM (Richard Law Management)
CLARK, MICHAEL Modernwood Management
CLARK, PETULA Denis Vaughan Management
THE CLASS OF '58 Paul Barrett (Rock 'n Roll Enterprises)
THE CLASSIC BUSKERS Seaview Music
CLAYDERMAN, RICHARD Denis Vaughan Management
CLEA Upside Management
CLOR Big Dipper Productions
COAST Zen Consultants
COCO, CHRIS 7pm Management
COCO VEGA Y LATINOS SALSA BAND Line-Up PMC
COLDPLAY Coldplay Management
COLE, BJ Firebrand Management
COLE, PAULA azoffmusic management
COLIN TEVENDALE (DJ) Traffik Productions
COLLISTER, CHRISTINE Robert Miller Management
COMMONWEALTH Keith Harris Music
CONDEMNED TO DANCE Direct Heat Management
CONVERSATION, THE MCM
COOL BRITANNIA McLeod Holden Enterprises Ltd
THE COOL JERKS Rose Rouge International

COOLIDGE, RITA Numinous Management
CORD SuperVision Management
COSMIC JOKER Future Management
COSMIC ROUGH RIDERS No Half Measures Ltd.
COUSINS, TINA Cruisin' Music
COX, CARL Safehouse Management
CRADLE OF FILTH In Phase Management
CRAIG ARMSTRONG IE Music Ltd
CRAIG GEE (DJ) Traffik Productions
CRAIG SMITH (DJ) Traffik Productions
CRASHLAND CEC Management
CRAY, AARON Easy Street Artist Management
CRAZY Joe Bangay Enterprises
CRAZY PENIS Bond Management
CRISTIAN VARELA Safehouse Management
CROFT NO. FIVE Martin Coull Management
CROSBY, GARY The Dune Music Company
CROSS, CHRISTOPHER azoffmusic management
THE CUBES Everlasting Management
CUD Wild Honey Management
CUNNINGHAM, CARLY SGO Music Management
CURLEY, CARLO PVA Management
CURTIS, MAC Paul Barrett (Rock 'n Roll Enterprises)
CYRKA, JAN Northern Music Company
DA-ESSENCE Social Misfit Entertainment
DAINTIES, PENNY P3 Music Management Ltd.
DAMIEN DEMPSEY Spirit Music & Media
DAMIEN RICE Mondo Management
DANDYLIONS, THE Mighty Music Management
DANKWORTH, JACQUELINE Cromwell Management
DANNHOF, REGINA WonderWorld
DANNY LITCHFIELD Armstrong Academy Artist
Management Ltd
DANNY THOMPSON Paul Crockford Management (PCM)
DARCEY BUSSELL TCB Group
DARIO G Bond Management
DARIUS Brilliant 19 Ltd
DASHBOARD MADONNA Clown Management
DAVE DRESDEN Ornadel Management
DAVE HEMINGWAY 7pm Management
CRAIG DAVID Wildlife Entertainment
DAVID FORD magnolia mam
DAVID GUETTA Prohibition Management
DAVID SAW John Waller Management & Marketing
DAVID THOMAS Charmenko
GREG DAVID Modal Management
DAVIES, DAVE Sanctuary Artist Management Ltd
DAVIES, RAY Octagon Music
DAX O'CALLAGHAN PPM Artist Management
DAY, CHARLOTTE Roger Boden Management
THE DAYS Prolifica Management
DAYWALKERS Crisis Management
DBA Friars Management Ltd
DEACON BLUE CEC Management
DEAF SCHOOL Hannah Management
DEAF SHEPHERD Martin Coull Management
DEATH IN VEGAS Simple Management
DEL AMITRI JPR Management
DELMAR, ELAINE John Williams
DELMONACO Karma Entertainment Group
DEMON Spaced Out Music
DEMPSEY Dellphonic Management
DEREK COX Derek Boulton Management
DEREK MCDONALD Asylum Artists
DEREK MEINS JPR Management
DESCENDANTS OF CAIN Mental Music Management
DES'REE Outside Management
DICKINSON, BRUCE Sanctuary Artist Management Ltd
DICKSON, BARBARA Theobald Dickson Productions

DIDO Nettwerk Management UK
DIGITAL GNAWA Outerglobe (Global Fusion)
DIGWEED, JOHN Safehouse Management
DINNIGAN, SIMON P3 Music Management Ltd.
DINO Jackie Davidson Management
DIRT CANDY Leafman
DIRTY 3 Tender Prey Management
DIRTY HARRY Toni Medcalf Management
DIRTY PERFECT ZincSplash
DIRTY PRETTY THINGS Creation Management
DISCO INFERNO Psycho Management Company
DISCO PARK Graham Peacock Management
DISTOPHIA Necessary Records
DIVA FEVER McLeod Holden Enterprises Ltd
DJ 279 KSO Records
DJ BADLY Bastard Management
DJ DAZEE Hope Management
DJ EXCALIBUR KSO Records
DJ JIMMY KARTIER Sidewalk 7
DJ LADY H BK 40 Management
DJ MARKY Bulldozer Management
DJ PATIFE Bulldozer Management
DJ PLANKTON Graham Peacock Management
DJ TIESTO Represents Artist Management
DO ME BAD THINGS Bermuda Management
CRAIG DODDS Daytime Entertainments
DODGY TARGO Ents Corp Ltd
SIOBHAN DONAGHY CMO Management International Ltd
DONOVAN Denis Vaughan Management
DOPAMINE Idle Eyes Management
DOPE SMUGGLAZ North
DORE, CHARLIE Toni Medcalf Management
DOUGLAS, CRAIG John Williams
DR HAZE Psycho Management Company
DR OCTOPUS Brian Yeates Associates
DR. ROBERT Sincere Management
DR WATSON & SHERLOCK Direct Heat Management
DRACASS, LINDSAY Alan Wood Agency
DRAKE, MOLLY Lazarus
D'RO Blujay Management
DRUMMOND, BILL Lazarus
DUBDADDA Bastard Management
DUBPLATE DIVAS Direct Heat Management
DUELS SuperVision Management
DUFFY, KEITH Carol & Associates
DUM DUMS Modernwood Management
DUNLOP, MARISSA Joe Bangay Enterprises
DUST KAL Management
DUTTY SKILLA BossMedia
DYNAMIC SYNCOPATION KSO Records
DYNAMITE MC Heavyweight Management
DYNAMO DRESDEN Lateral Artist Management Ltd
DYNAMO PRODUCTIONS Fruit
EAR 3rd Stone
THE EARLIES Popbox Management
EARTH THE CALIFORNIAN LOVE DREAM Red Alert
Management
EARTHTONE9 Northern Music Company
EAT STATIC Elite Squad Management
EATON, CHRIS SGO Music Management
ECHO Ardent Music
ECHO AND THE BUNNYMEN Porcupine Management
EDDY TEMPLE-MORRIS Avalon Management Group Ltd
EDDYFINK Covert Music Management
EDEN Hope Management
EDEN, MICHAEL DJT Management Ltd
THE EDEN SESSIONS Emperor Management
THE EDUCATION Sincere Management
EDWARDS, MIKE Gailforce Management

EDWARDS, STEVE Menace Management Ltd.
EL PRESIDENTE GR Management
ELBOW TRC Management
ELECTRIC CIRCUS Kickstart Management
ELESIS Sphinx Management
ELIZABETH HENSHAW - "ZEPHYR" Muirhead Management
ELLA GURU War Zones and Associates
SIMON ELLIS Four Seasons Management
ELROY 'SPOONFACE' POWELL Keith Harris Music
KATE ELSWORTH TJM
ELTON JOHN 21st Artist
EMBER Solar Management
THE EMBEZZLERS Bastard Management
EMBRACE Coalition Management
EMERSON LAKE & PALMER Part Rock Management Ltd
EMMANUEL, TOMMY NEM Productions (UK)
ENGERICA Chuffmedia
ENO, BRIAN Opal-Chant
ENVELOPES Prolifica Management
ENVY Billy Russell Management
ENZO Represents Artist Management
EQUATION NEM Productions (UK)
ESCOFFERY, SHAUN Eclipse-PJM
ESKIMO DISCO Emperor Management
ESP KSO Records
ESSENCE Earth Music
THE ESTATE OF NICK DRAKE Lazarus
ESTELLE Empire Artist Management
EVA ABRAHAM Fruit
EVANS, NIKI Brian Yeates Associates
EVENSTAR Sound Pets
EV.ON KSO Records
THE FABULOUS 50'S Rose Rouge International
FABULOUS THUNDERBIRDS azoffmusic management
FACELIFT WIRED Sunrise UK
FAITHLESS Faithless Live
FARUK GREEN Jon Sexton Management (JSM)
FAT FREDDY'S DROP Kartel
FATAL STAR Sidewinder Management
FBI Psycho Management Company
FC ALLSTARS Escape Music Management
FC KAHUNA Daddy Management
FEEDER Riot Management
FEEL Direct Heat Management
THE FEEL FOUNDATION Direct Heat Management
CATHERINE FEENY Independent Sound Management (ISM)
FELON Armstrong Academy Artist Management Ltd
FERGUSON, SHEILA D Vashti
FERRY, BRYAN TCB Group
FIELD, RS "BOBBY" Muirhead Management
FIGHTCLUB 7pm Management
RICHARD FILE 162a Music
FILTRATE North
FINDLAY WEBSTER Numinous Management
FINGATHING Sparklestreet HQ
FINN, NEIL Ignition Management
FIREWORKS NIGHT Kartel
FIRSTBORN Midnight To Six Management
FISH SWIM NAKED Karma Entertainment Group
FLAM Plus Artist Management
FLAMINGO FLEECE Got A Loser Job At The Diner Management
FLINT, BERNIE McLeod Holden Enterprises Ltd
FLIPPER WonderWorld
FLOYD, KEITH Stan Green Management
FLUKE Fools Paradise
FLYGARRICKS Impro Management
F.O. MACHETE ZincSplash

FOGERTY, JOHN azoffmusic management
FOLDS, BEN CEC Management
CATHERINE FOLEY Pete Hawkins Management
LENNY FONTANA Qaraj' Ltd
FORCE MAJEURE Earth Music
FORD, FRANKIE Paul Barrett (Rock 'n Roll Enterprises)
FOREIGNER Part Rock Management Ltd
4 SENSATIONS McLeod Holden Enterprises Ltd
FOUR STOREYS Atomic Management
FOX, SIMON Kickstart Management
FOXX, JOHN Zeall Management Limited
KARIMA FRANCIS Crisis Management
FRANTIK Flamecracker Management
FRANZ FERDINAND SuperVision Management
LILY FRASER Deluxxe Management
FREAK NASTY Unique Corp Ltd
FREDERIKA BABY DOLL Qaraj' Ltd
FREEFORM FIVE Illicit Entertainment
FREEKSPERT DJT Management Ltd
FREEKSTAR Craig Huxley Management
THE FREELANCE HELLRAISER Big Life Management
FREQ NASTY LH Management
STEPHEN FRETWELL Wildlife Entertainment
FREUD Numinous Management
FREY, GLENN azoffmusic management
FRIDAY HILL Jack 'N' Jill Artiste Management
FRIED GR Management
FRIEDMAN, ARON Kudos Management
FRIENDLY Fat! Management
FRIGID VINEGAR Interzone Management
LIAM FROST & THE SLOWDOWN FAMILY Emperor Management
FROU FROU Modernwood Management
FRUCTUOSO, ISABEL John Waller Management & Marketing
FUME Madison Management
FUN LOVIN' CRIMINALS Sidewinder Management
FUNERAL FOR A FRIEND Sanctuary Artist Management Ltd
FUTURESHOCK Sanctuary Artist Management Ltd
G4 Carol & Associates
GABO Bulldozer Management
GABRIEL & DRESDEN Ornadel Management
GABRIELLE J Management
GAGARIN Charmenko
GANG OF FOUR Big Life Management
GARCIA, FRANCOIS Bodo Music Co
GARRETT, LESLEY The Music Partnership
GARY HOLTON Numinous Management
GAYNOR, RIK Show Business Entertainment
GEEZERS OF NAZARETH North
RAY GELATO LM2 Entertainment
GELDOF, BOB Jukes Productions Ltd
GENASIDE 2 Jon Sexton Management (JSM)
THE GENERAL & DUCHESS COLLINS Automatic Management
GENERAL MIDI Hope Management
GEOFF NICHOLLS Brenda Brooker Enterprises
GEORGE T (DJ) Traffik Productions
THE GHOST FREQUENCY Vex Management
GHOSTLAND Spirit Music & Media
GIBBENS, JOHN Touched Productions
GIBBS, HELEN Monster Music Management
GILMOUR, DAVID One Fifteen
GIRLS ALOUD Shaw Thing Management
GISLI W1 Music Management
GLENN TILBROOK Stress Management
GO HOME PRODUCTIONS Avalon Management Group Ltd
GOLDFRAPP Midnight To Six Management
GOLDIELOCKS Vibe Artist Management
GOOBER PATROL 3rd Stone

GOOD GIRLS GONE BAD Simply Entertainment Ltd
GOOD VIBES NYJO - National Youth Jazz Orchestra
GOODACRE, TONY Sylvantone Promotions
GORILLAZ CMO Management International Ltd
GORKYS ZYGOTIC MYNCI Rheoli Ankst Management
GOTHIC VOICES Seaview Music
GOULDMAN, GRAHAM Harvey Lisberg Associates
GRABOWSKY, PAUL Muirhead Management
GRACE SB Management
TINA GRACE Positive Management
GRAHAM COXON CMO Management International Ltd
GRAHAM, MAX Hope Management
GRAHAM, MIKEY JC Music
GRAMME David Dorrell Management
GRAND DRIVE Wild Honey Management
GRAND NATIONAL Impro Management
GRAND ROSE BAND Liquid Management
GRANT, KATE Hedgehog
GRANT, NOEL Little Piece of Jamaica (LPOJ)
GRAY, DAVID Mondo Management
GRAY, ELIZABETH Sublime Music
GREASED LIGHTNING Psycho Management Company
GREEN, JESSE Satellite Artists
GREEN, LEO LM2 Entertainment
MAX GREENWOOD Positive Management
GREG LAKE Trinifold Management
GREGSON, CLIVE 4 Tunes Management
GROOVE ARMADA Sanctuary Artist Management Ltd
GROOVEZONE Choir Connexion & London Community Gospel
Choir
GUARD, RICK MCM
GUAVA The Dune Music Company
GUY CHAMBERS Sleeper Music
H TForce
HACKETT, STEVE Kudos Management
THE HAIR Vibe Artist Management
HAKEEM Jackie Davidson Management
HAL Independent Sound Management (ISM)
HALL, JOSIE Monster Music Management
HALSTEAD, NEIL Menace Management Ltd.
HAMMILL, PETER Gailforce Management
HANNAH ALETHEA JPS Management
HAPPY DAYS Les Hart (Southampton Entertainments)
THE HAPPY VIBES CORPORATION Direct Heat
Management
HARCOURT, ED Sanctuary Artist Management Ltd
HARD-FI Necessary Records
HARDKNOX Deutsch-Englische Freundschaft
HARRISON, SARAH Fruity Red Inc.
HARRY Seaview Music
JAMIE HARTMAN Safe Management
HARVEY, POLLY Principle Management
HAVE MERCY NoWHere Management
HAWKESTRA Money Talks Management
HAWKWIND MSM Music Consultants
HAYLEY WESTENRA Bedlam Management
HAYMAN, ANDY SMI/Everyday Productions
HAZE VS THE X FACTOR Psycho Management Company
HEADLINERS Satellite Artists
HEADSTAND Incredible Management
HEADWAY 7pm Management
HEAP, IMOGEN Modernwood Management
HEATHER NOVA Bedlam Management
HEATHER SMALL Bandana Management
HEAVEN 17 Sosusie Music
HECKLER Madison Management
THE HEDRONS No Half Measures Ltd.
HEKIMOVA, YANKA PVA Management
HELEN T WonderWorld

HELENA Grinning Rat Music Management
HENLEY, DON azoffmusic management
HERON Porcupine Management
HEWERDINE, BOO Ignition Management
HEYOKA Got A Loser Job At The Diner Management
HEYWARD, NICK Little Giant Music
HILLBILLY BOOGIEMEN Sylvantone Promotions
SOPHIE HILLER BK 40 Management
HINE, RUPERT Jukes Productions Ltd
JADE HOEY Plus Artist Management
HOLLAND, CHRIS One Fifteen
HOLLAND, JOOLS, AND HIS RHYTHM & BLUES
ORCHESTRA One Fifteen
HOMELIFE Sparklestreet HQ
HOODLUM PRIEST DNA Artist Management
HORACE & DUKE Direct Heat Management
HORN, VICTORIA Divine Management
HOT CHOCOLATE Richard Martin Management
HOUSEBREAKERZ Sublime Music
HOWIE B Native Management
HOY, JAYNI Diamond Sounds Music Management
HUDSON, MARK Little Piece of Jamaica (LPOJ)
HUE & CRY No Half Measures Ltd.
HUE, PAUL Little Piece of Jamaica (LPOJ)
HUGGY (DJ) Traffik Productions
THE HUMAN LEAGUE Sidewinder Management
HUNDRED AND 3 Working Class Music Management
HUNDRED REASONS Furtive Mass Transit Systems LLP
HUNT, MILES Spirit Music & Media
HUNTERZ Wizard Artist Management
HUSK Zeall Management Limited
HUSSEY Armstrong Academy Artist Management Ltd
HUTTON, CHRIS Safi Sounds Management & Promotion
HUW STEPHENS Avalon Management Group Ltd
HYBRID Excession: The Agency Ltd
HYPERBOREA Eurock
I MONSTER Menace Management Ltd.
I WANT YOUR SAX Brian Yeates Associates
I'CHELMEE Social Misfit Entertainment
I.D Asylum Artists
IGNITION TECHNICIAN Archetype Management
IL DIVO (US) Octagon Music
INDIAN ROPEMAN CEC Management
INFADELS Purple Fox Management
INJECTORS, THE Teleryngg UK
INME Marsupial Management Ltd
INNER CITY UNIT Money Talks Management
INNER MANTRA BAND Liquid Management
THE INVISIBLES ZincSplash
TONY IOMMI Equator Music
THE IRISH TENORS Pure Music Management
IRON MAIDEN Phantom Music Management
YUSUF ISLAM (CAT STEVENS) Terra Artists
IYNA AK Creative Management
PAUL JACKSON X-Rated Management
JILL JACKSON Giles Stanley
JADE, LEAH Kamara Artist Management (UK)
JAGWA Jamdown Ltd
JAIMESON Bermuda Management
JAKE & ELWOOD McLeod Holden Enterprises Ltd
JAMELIA Shalit Global Entertainment & Management
THE JAMES BROTHERS Direct Heat Management
JAMES CHANT White Tiger Management
JAMES LAVONZ DNA Artist Management
DUNCAN JAMES Merlin Elite Ltd
JAMIE CULLUM Aire International
JAMIE O'NEAL azoffmusic management
JAMIE SCOTT Bamn Management
BERT JANSCH Globeshine (UK) Ltd

JARVIS COCKER Rough Trade Management
JASON JERMAINE Heat Music
JAVINE Shalit Global Entertainment & Management
JAY HARVEY Mental Music Management
JAY, NORMAN Serious Artist Management
JAZZ JAMAICA ALL STARS The Dune Music Company
JAZZUPSTARTS Escape Music Management
JEB LOY NICHOLS Eleven
JEFFERSON Brian Yeates Associates
JEM Method Management
JENGA HEADS North
JENNA G Audio Authority Management
THE JETS Paul Barrett (Rock 'n Roll Enterprises)
JG BROS Qaraj' Ltd
JIM MORAY Playpen Management
JOBE Retaliate First Management
JOHN MATTHIAS LH Management
JOHNSON, HOLLY Wolfgang Kuhle Artist Management
JOHNSON, WILKO Solid Senders
JOI Moksha Management Ltd
JOKER Les Hart (Southampton Entertainments)
JON HOPKINS Just Another Management Co
JONATHAN CZERWIK (SON OF TOM) Parallel Universe Music
THE JONES GANG But! Management
JONES, HOWARD Friars Management Ltd
JONES, JOHN PAUL Opium (Arts) Ltd
JONES, SALENA Vine Gate Music
JONES, WAYNE Kamara Artist Management (UK)
JONNY GREEN & SATELLITE TARGO Ents Corp Ltd
JONNY L Star-Write Management
JONNY MALE Spirit Music & Media
JONT Nettwerk Management UK
JONZ Keith Harris Music
JOOLZ Brian Yeates Associates
JOSIAH Big Brother Management.
JUAN MARTIN'S FLAMENCO DANCE COMPANY Flamencovision
JUDAS PRIEST Trinifold Management
JUDGE, CHRIS Billy Russell Management
JUDGE JULES Serious Artist Management
JUDITH LORDE Omoya Entertainment
JUGGY D 2Point9 Management
JULIA THORNTON Ardent Music
JUPITER ACE Top Draw Music Management
JUSTIN CURRIE JPR Management
JUSTINE FRISCHMANN CMO Management International Ltd
JX Deutsch-Englische Freundschaft
THE KAISER CHIEFS SuperVision Management
KALEIDOSCOPE Bond Management
INI KAMOZE X-Rated Management
KAPITAHL: A Kitchenware Management
KAREN GRACE Alan Whitehead Management
KARIN PARK W1 Music Management
KARINE POLWART Braw Management
KARMENCHEETAH Direct Heat Management
KARN, MICK MK Music Ltd
KASHIWA, JEFF The Art & Music Corporation
KATARZYNA DONDALSKA The Music Partnership
KATE AUMONIER Sanctuary Artist Management Ltd
KATE SULLIVAN Armstrong Academy Artist Management Ltd
KATE WALSH Kitchenware Management
KATHERINE JENKINS Bandana Management
KATHLEEN MCDERMOTT Asylum Artists
KATHRYN ROBERTS & SEAN LAKEMAN NEM Productions (UK)
KEATING, RONAN MP Music Services
KEEP IT UP Martin Coull Management

KEITH FLINT Machine Management
KELLY, JOHN Serious Artist Management
KENNY BALL John Williams
KENNY THOMAS Mental Music Management
CAROL KENYON PEZ Management
KERR, GORDON MCM
KERSHAW, NIK Modernwood Management
KEVIN KENDLE First Time Management
KEVIN SAUNDERSON Safehouse Management
KIDDO Blue Hippo Management
KILLING JOKE Grand Union Management
MK (MARK KINCHEN) X-Rated Management
KINESIS Sanctuary Artist Management Ltd
KING CRIMSON DGM Management
KINGADORA Fruition Management
KINOBE CEC Management
KIONA Strike 3 Management
LINDA KIRALY Shalit Global Entertainment & Management
KIRSTEN Sacred Management
KISH MAUVE Solar Management
KITT, DAVID Interactive Music Management
K+K Mighty Music Management
THE KLAXONS Big Life Management
LISA KNAPP Playpen Management
KNEECAPPED Fat! Management
KNIGHT, BEVERLY DWL (Dave Woolf Ltd), Outside Management
KOBAI Deluxxe Management
THE KOOKS Starwood Management
KOOL & THE GANG Unique Corp Ltd
KOOL KEITH Jon Sexton Management (JSM)
KOOP Impro Management
KOWALSKI Midnight To Six Management
KREEPS Crisis Management
KRISTINA HARVEY Formidable Management
KT TUNSTALL SB Management
KUBANO KICKASSO Money Talks Management
KUBB Conception Artist Management
KUMO O-Mix
BEN KWELLER Nettwerk Management UK
KYM MARSH Safe Management
KYRAH LEONE PPM Artist Management
LACEY, JON Krack Music Management
TIFF LACEY Active Music Management
LAFFERTY, CHRISTOPHER KAL Management
LAGOON WEST Firebrand Management
LAHCEN LAHABIB Outerglobe (Global Fusion)
LAHANNYA Kabuki
LAIBACH Charmenko
LAL Positive Management
LAMACQ, STEVE Wise Buddah Talent
LAMAI Earth Music
LAMB Blue Sky Entertainment
LANTAN Little Piece of Jamaica (LPOJ)
LARUSO Tour Concepts
LASHE WonderWorld
ANNA-MARIA LASPINA Soho Artists
LATE NIGHT MUSIC STORE Lateral Artist Management Ltd
LAURA BETTINSON Big Help Music
LAVELLE, CAROLINE Ardent Music
LAWSON, JAMIE Hedgehog
LEASE OF LIFE Burning Candle Music
LEE, CHRISTOPHER R2 Management
LEE, SHAWN Impro Management
LEE, STEVE Duty Free Artist Management
LEEMING, CAROL O-Mix
LEMON JELLY Terra Artists
LENNOX, ANNIE 19 Management
LEON First Move Management Ltd

LETRIX Parliament Management
YASMIN LEVY Soho Artists
LEWIS, LINDA GALE Paul Barrett (Rock 'n Roll Enterprises)
LICKETY SPLIT Les Hart (Southampton Entertainments)
LIEF X-Rated Management
LIFEHOUSE azoffmusic management
LIFFORD Mimi Music
LIGHTFOOT, TERRY, & HIS BAND Cromwell Management
LIGHTFOOT, TERRY, AND HIS BAND John Williams
LIGHTHOUSE FAMILY Independent Sound Management
(ISM), Kitchenware Management
LILY ALLEN Empire Artist Management
LINOLEUM Brown McLeod Ltd.
LIPSTICK COLOURED MONKEYS Kamara Artist
Management (UK)
LISA LASHES Ornadel Management
LISTER, MICK Modernwood Management
LIZ MITCHELL P&P Music International
LOAFER Hope Management
LOCORRIERE, DENNIS John Taylor Management
LOGANSTONE Bermuda Management
LOGO Red Alert Management
LONDON COMMUNITY GOSPEL CHOIR, THE Choir
Connexion & London Community Gospel Choir
THE LONDON GIRLS Peter Haines Management
LONDON RAGTIME ORCHESTRA Cromwell Management
LONGBONES Coalition Management
LONGRIGG, FRANCESCA One Fifteen
LOOP STORM Onside Management
LOOSE SALUTES Normal Management
LOS PISTOLEROS Firebrand Management
LOST LOVE PROJECT Direct Heat Management
LOUIS ELIOT Spirit Music & Media
LOUISE CANNON The Music Partnership
LOVE BITES TK1 Management
LOVE TO INFINITY JPS Management
LOWCRAFT JC Music
LUCA BRAZZI Kickstart Management
LUCAS, ADRIAN PVA Management
LUCID Black Magic Management
LUCIE SILVAS Empire Artist Management
LUCINDA WILLIAMS azoffmusic management
LUCYS, THE PJ Music
LUIS PARIS Represents Artist Management
LUKE FAIR Safehouse Management
LULU 21st Artist
LUNASA SGO Music Management
LYDIA Little Giant Music
LYONESSE Touched Productions
MAAS, TIMO Hope Management
COLIN MACINTYRE Terra Artists
MACLEAN, DOUGIE NEM Productions (UK)
MACUMBA Line-Up PMC
MAD DOG AND THE SOPHISTICATS McLeod Holden
Enterprises Ltd
MADNESS Hannah Management
MAGDALEN GREEN Plan C Management
MAGNET SuperVision Management
MAGNETIC Normal Management
MAHONEY, GARY JBS Management UK
MAINSTREAM DISTORTION Stevo Management
MAJOR Fruit
MANCHILD Midi Management Ltd
MANDALAY Interceptor Enterprises
MANEKI-NEKO OPL Management
JO MANGO Robin Morton Consultancy
MANHATTAN TRANSFER Denis Vaughan Management
MANIC STREET PREACHERS Sanctuary Artist Management
Ltd

MANNA PRODUCTIONS Bermuda Management
TOM MANSI Kartel
MANSTON, ANDY Duty Free Artist Management
MARA CARLYLE Redd Management
MARC CARROLL Rough Trade Management
MARK ASTON Liquid Management
MARK EVANS The Music Partnership
MARK GARDENER OMC Management
MARK KNOPFLER Paul Crockford Management (PCM)
MARK OWEN 10 Management
MARS BONFIRE Darklight Entertainment
MARSHALL, BEX Numinous Management
MARTHA CHRISTIE MP Music Services
MARTIN BUTTRICH Hope Management
MARTIN, JUAN Flamencovision
MARTIN MORALES Positive Management
MARTIN STEPHENSON & THE DAINTEES NEM
Productions (UK)
ALICE MARTINEAU pr-ism
M*A*S*H JPS Management
M.A.S.S. TARGO Ents Corp Ltd
MASTERSON, ADAM Coalition Management
MATCHBOX Paul Barrett (Rock 'n Roll Enterprises)
MATT BIANCO Denis Vaughan Management
MATTY BENBROOK CMO Management International Ltd
MAXIMO PARK Prolifica Management
SHARONA MAY Split Music
MAZELLE, KYM Soho Artists
MC BUZZ-BEE Omoya Entertainment
MC CHICKABOO Hope Management
MC HARDKAUR Ambush Management
LARA MCALLEN Active Music Management
MCCABE, MARK Ganz Management
MCCALL, GORDON Lena Davis John Bishop Associates
MCCANN, SUSAN Dennis Heaney Promotions
MCEVOY, JONNY Dara Management
MCFLY Prestige Management
MCGOWAN, ALEX WonderWorld
MCLEOD, RORY NEM Productions (UK)
MCLI Little Piece of Jamaica (LPOJ)
JOHN MCMANUS Shamrock Music Ltd
MEDIAEVAL BAEBES Strike Back Management
MEDICINE 8 Terra Artists
MEKA Stevo Management
MEKON Fruit
MELLOTRAUMA Social Misfit Entertainment
MELLOW Fools Paradise
MELYS Rheoli Ankst Management
MERCURY REV Ignition Management
MERKA Fat! Management
METCALFE, BRIDGET Amber
METRO RIOTS Zen Consultants
MICHAEL DEWIS The Music Partnership
MICHAEL ENGLISH Michael McDonagh Management
MICHAEL KILKIE (DJ) Traffik Productions
MICHEL DE HEY Safehouse Management
MICHELLE B Split Music
MICKEY P Jackie Davidson Management
MIDGET Sound Pets
MIKE MONDAY Represents Artist Management
THE MILK & HONEY BAND First Column Management
MILKE Fat! Management
MILLETT, LISA Menace Management Ltd.
DANNII MINOGUE Shaw Thing Management
MINOGUE, KYLIE Terry Blamey Management
MINT ROYALE Nettwerk Management UK
MINUTEMAN A.M.P./TBA
MIRANDA, NINA Evolution Management
MISH MASH 162a Music

MISSISSIPPI FLY Streetfeat Management Ltd
MISTY'S BIG ADVENTURE TARGO Ents Corp Ltd
MITCHELL, ROBERT The Dune Music Company
MOBY Deutsch-Englische Freundschaft
MOGWAI Creation Management
MOHAIR Transmission Management
MOJAVE 3 Menace Management Ltd.
MOKE Elite Squad Management
MOLOKO Graham Peacock Management
MOLVAER, NILS PETTER Tim Prior - Artist & Rights Management
MOMO (MUSIC OF MOROCCAN ORIGIN) Outerglobe (Global Fusion)
MOMY Leap
MONACO Evolution Management
MONKEY FARM FRANKENSTEIN Stevo Management
MONO BAND Liberation Management
MONOMANIA Future Management
GABRIELA MONTERO Big Life Management
MONTGOMERY, ERRINGTON Graham Peacock Management
MOOD INDIGO Brian Yeates Associates
MOORE, GARY Part Rock Management Ltd
MORCHEEBA CMO Management International Ltd
MORE ROCKERS MWM Music Management
MORGAN, JO Streetfeat Management Ltd
MORGAN, TONY PJ Music
MORNING RUNNER Coldplay Management
MORRIS, ANDY 7pm Management
SARAH JANE MORRIS Sincere Management
MORRISEY Sanctuary Artist Management Ltd
THE MOTH LANTERN Automatic Management
MOUSKOURI, NANA Denis Vaughan Management
MOUTH Krack Music Management
MOUTH MUSIC Ardent Music
MR DAVID VINER White Tiger Management
MR ROQUE Just Another Management Co
MR SCRUFF Sparklestreet HQ
MR SMITH But! Management
MRD DNA Artist Management
M&S PRODUCTIONS Ambush Management
MS T REY Little Piece of Jamaica (LPOJ)
MUGENKYO Line-Up PMC
THE MULES Kartel
MULL HISTORICAL SOCIETY Sanctuary Artist Management Ltd
MUMBA, SAMANTHA Louis Walsh Management
MUMM-RA SuperVision Management
MUNGO JERRY Satellite Artists
MURDOCH White Tiger Management
MURPHY, ROISIN Graham Peacock Management
MURRAY TFF Management
MURRAY, STEVE Escape Music Management
MUSAPHIA, JOEY Talent Call Ltd
MUSICA ALHAMBRA Flamencovision
MUST Toni Medcalf Management
MUZZI, MASSIMILIANO PVA Management
MY GIRL SLEEPS 10 Management
MY LUMINARIES Avalon Management Group Ltd
MY SKILLZ & HIS CRAZY GIRLS Shalit Global Entertainment & Management
MYNC PROJECT Represents Artist Management
M.Y.N.C PROJECT Graphite Media
MYONI Peter Haines Management
NAKED INTENTION XL Talent
NARCOTIC THRUST Z Management
NASHER Scarlet Management
KATE NASH ATC Management
NATASHA BEDINGFIELD Empire Artist Management
NATASHA LEE JONES Parallel Universe Music

NATE JAMES >4 Management
NEAT PEOPLE Boss Music
NEBULA, THE Rose Rouge International
NED BIGHAM Hope Management
NEIL JBS Management UK
NEIL BARNES LH Management
NELSON, BILL Opium (Arts) Ltd
NELSON, SHELLEY Fanatic Management
NEMO Boss Music
NEVILLE, LUKE Serious Artist Management
NEW SOUND FOUNDATION McLeod Holden Enterprises Ltd
NEW TELLERS DJT Management Ltd
AMY NEWTON The Sound Foundation
THE NEXT ROOM Split Music
NICK DRESTI Talent Call Ltd
NICK RAPACCIOLI LH Management
NICKELLE Qaraj' Ltd
NICOLA HITCHCOCK Ardent Music
REMI NICOLE Wildlife Entertainment
NIGHTMARES ON WAX LH Management
NINA JAYNE B&H Management
NIO Heat Music
NIXON Arketek Management
NO HOPE IN NEW JERSEY Jonny Paul Management
NO-MAN 3rd Stone
NO PRISONERS Sacred Management
NO SLEEP NIGEL KSO Records
NOBLE, IAN Lena Davis John Bishop Associates
NODDING DOG Marshall Arts Management
NOMAD Strike 3 Management
NORTH EAST Sublime Music
NOTCH, MYKIE Little Piece of Jamaica (LPOJ)
THE NOVA SAINTS Popbox Management
NU TROOP The Dune Music Company
'NUENDO 3rd Precinct
AMY NUTTALL Merlin Elite Ltd
NYJO NYJO - National Youth Jazz Orchestra
NYJO 2 NYJO - National Youth Jazz Orchestra
OAKENFULL, SKI Impro Management
OASIS Ignition Management
OATEN, RICHARD Mal Spence Management
SAM OBERNIK Daytime Entertainments
OBI Mako Music
OBSTOJ, JEANETTE Jukes Productions Ltd
OLIVER LIEB Represents Artist Management
OLIVER MACGREGOR Represents Artist Management
ONE MINUTE SILENCE Northern Music Company
THE ORANGE LIGHTS Graphite Media
ORBITAL Mondo Management
THE ORDINARY BOYS Starwood Management
ORGANIC AUDIO Autonomy Music
OSIBISA Denis Vaughan Management
O'SULLIVAN, GILBERT Park Promotions
OTWAY, JOHN Interzone Management
OUTRAGEOUS BLUES BROTHERS McLeod Holden Enterprises Ltd
OVERSEAS EDITION Social Misfit Entertainment
OVERSEER Sanctuary Artist Management Ltd
OVERVIBE X-Rated Management
OXIDE & NEUTRINO Albert Samuel Management
OXYGEN Bond Management
PACO OSUNA Represents Artist Management
PAGANO, LINDSAY azoffmusic management
PAL JOEY Kickstart Management
PALOMINO funky star
PARADISE LOST Northern Music Company
TIM PARE Illicit Entertainment
PARSONS, GARETH Show Business Entertainment

PASADENA ROOF ORCHESTRA Pasadena Roof Orchestra (1997)
PAUL DALEY LH Management
PAUL DEVLIN Got A Loser Job At The Diner Management
PAUL MASTERSON Top Draw Music Management
PAUL OAKENFOLD Terra Artists
PAULINE SCANLON Spirit Music & Media
PEARCE, DAVE Wise Buddah Talent
PELLOW, MARTI Sanctuary Artist Management Ltd
THE PENKILN BURN Lazarus
PENTANGLE Park Promotions
PEOPLE IN PLANES M4 Management
PERE UBU Charmenko
PERKINS, POLLY Lena Davis John Bishop Associates
THE PERSPIRATIONS Direct Heat Management
PESHAY Evolution Management
PETE SHELLEY Sentics
PHANTOM5000 Lamb Management
PHAT MUSTARD Ambush Management
PHELOUNG, BARRINGTON Barrington Pheloung Management
PHIL LIFE CYPHER KSO Records
PHIL THOMPSON Safehouse Management
PHOR:U TFF Management
PINCH Lazarus
PINE, COURTNEY Collaboration
PINEY GIR Red Alert Management
PLACEBO Riverman Management
PLANET OF WOMEN Liquid Management
PLANT, ROBERT Trinifold Management
PLASTICA Clown Management
PLAYER Mental Music Management
PLEASUREBEACH Mental Music Management
POB WonderWorld
POCOMAN Parliament Management
POLLY PAULUSMA Coldplay Management
POLOROID 7pm Management
SHELLY POOLE Freedom Management
POP! TForce
THE POPES Scarlet Management
PORCUPINE TREE Big Brother Management.
PORNSHOT Evolution Management
PORTISHEAD Fruit
PQ Social Misfit Entertainment
PRAS Cigale Entertainment Ltd
PREFAB SPROUT Kitchenware Management
PRICE, ALAN Cromwell Management
PRIMAL SCREAM GR Management
PRINCESS JULIA X-Rated Management
PRIOR, MADDY Park Promotions
PRODIGAL SUN Top Banana Management Ltd
PRODIGY Midi Management Ltd
PROJECT G Roger Boden Management
PSYCHID Bermuda Management
PSYCHONAUTS MBL
PUBLIC SYMPHONY Safe Management
PURPLE POLO Direct Heat Management
PUSSYCAT DOLLS azoffmusic management
QTEE Pilot Management
QUATRO, SUZI Jive Entertainments
QUAYE, FINLEY Jon Sexton Management (JSM)
QUEMBY, DEE Lena Davis John Bishop Associates
RACHAEL GRAY Easy Street Artist Management
RACHEL FULLER Trinifold Management
RACHEL GOSWELL Menace Management Ltd.
RACHEL MARI KIMBER Marsupial Management Ltd
RACHEL STAMP Cruisin' Music
RACHEL STEVENS 19 Management
RADAR 162a Music

RADIOHEAD Courtyard Management
RADIOTONES Buzz Artist Management
RAFFLES Les Hart (Southampton Entertainments)
RAGING SPEEDHORN Grand Union Management
THE RAILWAY CHILDREN WonderWorld
RAPHIC Sunrise UK
RAPID.LA Fruity Red Inc.
RASCAL Billy Russell Management
RASCO Jon Sexton Management (JSM)
RAT PACK Albert Samuel Management
RAVENHALL, JOHN Right Management
RE4MATION Right Management
REACTOR In Phase Management
THE REALM Earth Music
REBEKAH RAIN O-Mix
RED LAB MCM
RED ORGAN SERPENT SOUND Riverman Management
REDBONE, MARTHA JC Music
LOUISE REDKNAPP Merlin Elite Ltd
REEF In Phase Management
CONNER REEVES Freshwater Hughes Management
REID, DON Show Business Entertainment
REILLY & DURRANT Top Draw Music Management
RELAX Psycho Management Company
RELISH J Management
RENATO COHEN Bulldozer Management
RENBOURN, JOHN NEM Productions (UK)
REO SPEEDWAGON azoffmusic management
RESERVOIR CATS Paul Barrett (Rock 'n Roll Enterprises)
THE REVEREND & THE MAKERS Wildlife Entertainment
RHINO'S REVENGE Fanatic Management
RICCI BENSON Derek Boulton Management
RICHARD A. CHAPMAN Working Class Music Management
RICHARD ROGERS O-Mix
RICHARD SMITH Atrium Music
RICHIE KEYVAN 7pm Management
THE RIFLES ATC Management
RISING SON Unique & Natural Talent Ltd
RISING SON CREW Little Piece of Jamaica (LPOJ)
RITCHIE Rose Rouge International
RIVAL JOUSTAS Incredible Management
THE RIVERS FCM
ROAD Positive Management
ROB DA BANK Graphite Media
ROB SMITH MWM Music Management
ROBBIE RYAN Indie Music Management
ROBERT CLIVILLES Safehouse Management
ROBERT FARNON Derek Boulton Management
ROBERTA ALEXANDER The Music Partnership
ROBERTS, JULIET The Dune Music Company
ROBERTS, MARK WonderWorld
ROLAND SHANKS Emperor Management
ROLLER Key Music Management
ROMONE, PHIL 21st Artist
ROOTS MANUVA LH Management
ROSALIE DEIGHTON Liberation Management
ROUND, CARINA White Tiger Management
ROUSSOS, DEMIS Denis Vaughan Management
ROW Z Atrium Music
ROWE, JASON NBM
ROXY MUSIC TCB Group
ROYKSOPP Deutsch-Englische Freundschaft
ROZALLA J Management
RUBY CRUISER Lateral Artist Management Ltd
RUBY FUSION X Factor Management Ltd
RUFF TOUCH Upside Management
RUMBLE STRIPS Scruffy Bird
RUNRIG Runrig Management
ABI RYAN Shamrock Music Ltd

SABBAMANGALANG Bodo Music Co
SACHA PUTTNAM 7pm Management
SADLER, SOPHIE Joe Bangay Enterprises
SAEED AND PALASH Excession: The Agency Ltd
SAINT ETIENNE Heavenly Management
SALSA CELTICA Playpen Management
SALT TANK Doug Smith Associates
SAMIA Congo Music Ltd
SARAH-ANN WEBB Eclipse-PJM
SARAH LUCIE SHAW Dreamscape Management
SARJANT D O-Mix
SASHA Excession: The Agency Ltd
SAUNA Friars Management Ltd
SAVERS Represents Artist Management
SAXSECTION NYJO - National Youth Jazz Orchestra
SAXSECTION PLUS NYJO - National Youth Jazz Orchestra
SAYER, LEO Silverbird Ltd
SCANNERS Grand Union Management
POLLY SCATTERGOOD Brilliant!
SCATTERGOOD, CAROLINE Lena Davis John Bishop
Associates
SCATTERGOOD, CAZZ Lena Davis John Bishop Associates
SCHMIDT, JAN Les Hart (Southampton Entertainments)
ULRICH SCHNAUSS Machine Management
SCOTT & LEON Boom Management & Consultancy
SCOTT, JACK Paul Barrett (Rock 'n Roll Enterprises)
SCOTT MCKEON Paul Crockford Management (PCM)
SEAL azoffmusic management
SEAMING Sparklestreet HQ
JAY SEAN 2Point9 Management
SEB FONTAINE Represents Artist Management
SECRET KNOWLEDGE Friars Management Ltd
MAX SEDGLEY Sublime Music
SEF TCB Group
SENSER Ignite Marketing
SEVEN CHAIN OCTOPUS Headstone Management
SHAH Unique Corp Ltd
SHAMEN Moksha Management Ltd
SHANE MACGOWAN Michael McDonagh Management
SHANIE CAMPBELL O-Mix
SHAPIRO, HELEN, AND HER BAND John Williams
SHAW, SANDIE Shavian Enterprises
SHAZNAY LEWIS Bamn Management
SHED SEVEN Simon Lawlor Management
SHEILA SOUTHERN Derek Boulton Management
SHEISTY DA GYPSY Social Misfit Entertainment
SHELAN O-Mix
SHINE Martin Coull Management
SHINE, BRENDAN Denis Vaughan Management
SHIT DISCO Big Life Management
SHLOMO CMO Management International Ltd
SHOP Lazarus
SHOWADDYWADDY Jive Entertainments
SIA IE Music Ltd
SIGUR ROS Big Dipper Productions
SILENT FRONT Riot Club Management
RUI DA SILVA X-Rated Management
SILVA, JOY Saphron Management
JIMMY SILVER Plus Artist Management
SIMON, EMELIE NBM
SIMON, VANESSA Congo Music Ltd
SIMPLY RED Silentway Management Ltd
SIOBHAN PARR Stress Management
SIR PRESTIGE Social Misfit Entertainment
SIRENS Kitchenware Management
SIRINU Seaview Music
SISTER SLEDGE Denis Vaughan Management
SISTER SYSTEM Sphinx Management
SIX BY SEVEN Emperor Management

SIZER BARKER Indie Music Management
SKAHANA Ambush Management
SKINDRED Northern Music Company
SKOTT FRANCIS Lee & Co
SKY Little Piece of Jamaica (LPOJ)
SKYE CMO Management International Ltd
SKYMOO Graham Peacock Management
SLAUGHTER, JOHN, BLUES BAND Cromwell Management
SLIGHTLY ALIEN Big Blue Music
SLIP Little Piece of Jamaica (LPOJ)
SLIPSTREAM Pure Delinquent
SM TRAX Unique Corp Ltd
SMITH & MIGHTY MWM Music Management
SMITH, ANDY Fruit
SMITH, 'LEGS' LARRY Right Management
SMOKE THE THIN GLASS BLACK The Yukon Management
SMOKIE NOW Music
SMOOTHIE, JEAN JACQUES Hope Management
SMOTHER Solar Management
SNEAKER PIMPS Splinter Management
SNOW PATROL Big Life Management
SNOWPONY Ardent Music
SO SOLID CREW Albert Samuel Management
THE SOCIAL MISFITS Social Misfit Entertainment
SODA CLUB JPS Management
SOMERVILLE, JIMMY Solar Management
SON OF DAVE Kartel
SON OF DORK Prestige Management
SONIC BLOOM Key Music Management
SONIQUE Deutsch-Englische Freundschaft
SONS & DAUGHTERS Banchory Management
SONS OF JIM TJM
S.O.R. Armstrong Academy Artist Management Ltd
SOSUEME Feedback Communications
SOUL MEKANIK Illicit Entertainment
SOULSAVERS Heavenly Management
THE SOUNDCARRIERS pr-ism
SOUP COLLECTIVE Crisis Management
SPACE Indie Music Management
THE SPACE BROTHERS Earth Music
SPACE COUNTY Toni Medcalf Management
SPACE MONKEEZ Split Music
SPACEMEN 3 3rd Stone
SPEARMINT Charmenko
SPECTRUM 3rd Stone
SPEEDER John Taylor Management
SPENCER DAVIS GROUP Richard Martin Management
JON SPENCER BLUES EXPLOSION Sanctuary Artist
Management Ltd
SPENCER JUDE PEARCE Automatic Management
SPHYNX Money Talks Management
SPIRITUAL BEGGARS Sanctuary Artist Management Ltd
SPIT LIKE THIS But! Management
SPRAGGA BENZ Jamdown Ltd
SQUEEZE Stress Management
S.ROCK LEVINSON Sosusie Music
STARDUST, ALVIN Brian Yeates Associates
STARECASE Hope Management
STARSAILOR Heavenly Management
STARSEEDS WonderWorld
STATELESS Sanctuary Artist Management Ltd
STATUS QUO Duroc Media
PAUL STEEL Raygun Music
STEEL PULSE War Zones and Associates
STEELEYE SPAN Park Promotions
STEEVI JAIMZ Northstar Artist Management
STEINSKI CEC Management
STEPHANIE MCKAY Fruit
STEPHEN JOHN HENRY Little Giant Music

STEPHENS, CARLA Fox Records Ltd (Management)
STEREOLAB Stereophonic Management
STEVE BALSAMO Private & Confidential Management Ltd
STEVE DUB LH Management
STEVE LAWLER Graphite Media
STEWART, ALLAN Handshake Ltd
STEWART, ERIC Harvey Lisberg Associates
STIG Loose
STIVELL, ALAN Denis Vaughan Management
STOCKLEY, MIRIAM Friars Management Ltd
STOKES, DARREN Duty Free Artist Management
STOLEN PEACE Everlasting Management
STONE CIRCLE Social Misfit Entertainment
STONEBRIDGE Talent Call Ltd
STONECOLD ARTISTS Little Piece of Jamaica (LPOJ)
THE STORYS John Waller Management & Marketing
STRETCH & VERN Represents Artist Management
ALEXIS STRUM Safe Management
STUART CABLE Marsupial Management Ltd
SUB-5 Headstone Management
THE SUBWAYS Gailforce Management
SUEDE Interceptor Enterprises
SUGABABES Metamorphosis Management
SUMUDU Incredible Management
SUNGOVER Deuce Management & Promotion
SUNNA A.M.P./TBA
SUPER DELTA THREE Dee O'Reilly Management
SUPER FURRY ANIMALS Rheoli Ankst Management
SUPERGRASS Courtyard Management
SUSAN BLUECHILD JW Management
SUZY WHO? Kickstart Management
SW1 B&H Management
SWAMI Cigale Entertainment Ltd
SWAN, BILLY Muirhead Management
SWAY Heavyweight Management
SWEET DREAMS Direct Heat Management
SWEET SUZI Marsupial Management Ltd
THE SWEET WRAPPERS Plus Artist Management
SYLVIAN, DAVID Opium (Arts) Ltd
SYNTAX Fools Paradise
T-BABE TFF Management
TABOR, JUNE NEM Productions (UK)
TAF OPL Management
TALBOT, JOBY Manners McDade Artist Management
TALI Heavyweight Management
TANIA MANN Top Draw Music Management
TATE, DARREN 7pm Management
TAVENER, SIR JOHN Manners McDade Artist Management
TAYLOR, MARTIN P3 Music Management Ltd.
PAULINE TAYLOR CMO Management International Ltd
BECKY JANE TAYLOR Merlin Elite Ltd
TC CURTIS Right Management
TD LIND Sanctuary Artist Management Ltd
TEALE Top Banana Management Ltd
TEEN SPIRIT Psycho Management Company
TEENIDOL Big Help Music
TEITUR Plan C Management
TENESEE KAIT Buzz Artist Management
TENOR FLY Jamdown Ltd
TEST ICICLES Machine Management
TEXAS GR Management
THE ANSWER Eleven
THE BIG BOSSA Streetfeat Management Ltd
THE BOOKHOUSE BOYS Formidable Management
THE BOY LEAST LIKELY TO Simple Management
THE BRIGHT SPACE Simple Management
THE BUFFSEEDS Simon Lawlor Management
THE BUZZCOCKS Sentics
THE CANDYSKINS Interzone Management

THE CARDINALS Jonny Paul Management
THE CHAMELEONS Simon Lawlor Management
THE CHARLATANS Creation Management
THE CHEMICAL BROTHERS MBL
THE CLIENTS Simon Lawlor Management
THE CRIBS SuperVision Management
THE CRIMEA Out There Management
THE CULT Sanctuary Artist Management Ltd
THE DARKNESS Whitehouse Management
THE DEPARTURE Sanctuary Artist Management Ltd
THE DIVINE COMEDY Divine Management
THE DREEM TEEM Dreem Teem
THE DUKE SPIRIT Heavenly Management
THE EAGLES azoffmusic management
THE FEELING Empire Artist Management
THE FIGHTIN' GATORS OF APALACHICOLA COUNTY
Got A Loser Job At The Diner Management
THE FORTUNES Brian Yeates Associates
THE FREESTYLERS Heavyweight Management
THE FUTUREHEADS Big Life Management
THE GLITTERATI Mondo Management
THE HONEYMOON Sanctuary Artist Management Ltd
THE IDJUT BOYS Solar Management
THE IMMIGRANTS Loose
THE INSPIRAL CARPETS Key Music Management
THE KINKS Sanctuary Artist Management Ltd
THE LEVELLERS First Column Management
THE LOOSE CANNONS Sound Artist Management
THE MACCABEES JPR Management
THE MAGIC NUMBERS Normal Management
THE MAU MAUS Radius Music
THE MISSION Extreme Music Production
THE MITCHELL BROTHERS Cigale Entertainment Ltd
THE-MODERN Man's Best Friend
THE MOHABIR SISTERS Blue Hippo Management
THE MOUNTAINEERS Key Music Management
THE MUSIC Coalition Management
THE NAKED APES The Sound Foundation
THE NEW GODS OF AMERICA Future Management
THE NEXTMEN Leafman
THE OMEGAS JW Management
THE ONE THREE Doug Smith Associates
THE OPERATION Extreme Music Production
THE PADDIES Right Management
THE PADDINGTONS Motive Music Management
THE POUND BOYS D2mm (Direct2 Music Management)
THE PRETENDERS Gailforce Management
THE PROCLAIMERS Braw Management
THE RAIN BAND Steve Harrison Management
THE RAKES CEC Management
THE RESEARCH Prolifica Management
THE ROCK OF TRAVOLTA Interzone Management
THE ROLLING STONES Rupert Loewenstein
THE ROSENBERGS DGM Management
THE SERVANT Firebrand Management
THE SHARP BOYS Ambush Management
THE SOUNDTRACK OF OUR LIVES Sanctuary Artist
Management Ltd
THE SPINNING FIELDS Route One Management
THE STANDS Bermuda Management
THE STEREOPHONICS Nettwerk Management UK
THE STRANGLERS Cruisin' Music
THE STREETS Coalition Management
THE SUNDAYS Raymond Coffer Management Ltd
THE SUNS Arketek Management
THE SUPERBAND Radar Music and Management
THE THE Lazarus
THE TORNADOS John Williams
THE TROGGS Stan Green Management

THE VOOM BLOOMS Motive Music Management
THE WANDERING STEP Steve Harrison Management
THE WANNADIES War Zones and Associates
THE WAYWARD SHEIKS Spirit Music & Media
THE WHO Trinifold Management
THE WURZELS Cruisin' Music
THE X FACTOR TForce
THEE HEAVENLY MUSIC ASSOCIATION Sidewalk 7
THEO First Move Management Ltd
THOMPSON, LINDSEY Dee O'Reilly Management
THUNDER Toni Medcalf Management
TIDEY, DEAN CA Management
TIM BASTMEYER Future Management
TIM BOOTH Octagon Music
TIME MACHINE Psycho Management Company
TINATIN Private & Confidential Management Ltd
TINDERSTICKS Eleven
TOBY GRAFFTEY-SMITH Muirhead Management
TOM JONES Valley Music Ltd.
TOM MIDDLETON Machine Management
THE TOMMIES pr-ism
TOMORROW'S FACE NYJO - National Youth Jazz Orchestra
TONIC azoffmusic management
TOPLEY-BIRD, MARTINA CEC Management
TOURISTE Deluxxe Management
TRAN, CATHERINE Total Management
TRASH PALACE Firebrand Management
TRASHCAN SINATRAS Robin Morton Consultancy
TRAVIS Wildlife Entertainment
TREANA SMI/Everyday Productions
TREVOR NELSON In2music
TRIBE Satellite Artists
TRICIA MCTEAGUE MP Music Services
TRINITY STONE Shalit Global Entertainment & Management
TRUTH Mal Spence Management
T-TOTAL X-Rated Management
AMELIA TUCKER Popbox Management
TUNDE Independent Sound Management (ISM)
TURIN BRAKES CMO Management International Ltd
TURNER, RUBY Saffa Music Ltd
TURNER'S, NIK, FANTASTIC ALL STARS Money Talks Management
TURNER'S, NIK, SPACE RITUAL Money Talks Management
TURTLE K MCM
TUULI Key Music Management
TWINS OF PLEASURE Direct Heat Management
TWIST MSM Music Consultants
2 BANKS OF 4 Impro Management
TWO DAY RULE Sugar Shack Management
TY Sentinel Management
TYLER Four Seasons Management
TZANT PFB Management
U2 Principle Management
UB40 Part Rock Management Ltd
UBERNOISE Mal Spence Management
UFBI Congo Music Ltd
UN-CUT Blue Sky Entertainment
UNA MAS Z Management
UNAMERICAN Richman Management Ltd
UNDERWORLD Jukes Productions Ltd
CHRISTINA UNDHJEM Asylum Artists
UNYSON Boom Management & Consultancy
THE URCHINS Rose Rouge International
UTAH SAINTS North
UTOPIANS Money Talks Management
V-LAW Jack 'N' Jill Artiste Management
VALANCE, RICKY Lena Davis John Bishop Associates
VAN DER GRAAF GENERATOR Gailforce Management
FOY VANCE Freshwater Hughes Management

VANESSA BROWN Empire Artist Management
RUI VARGAS Qaraj' Ltd
VEGA 4 Big Life Management
VELOURIA Sound Pets
THE VENUS EXPERIENCE McLeod Holden Enterprises Ltd
VERONICA 2Point9 Management
VIBEBABY Direct Heat Management
VIBRATION WHITE FINGER Sidewalk 7
VICIOUS CIRCLE MSM Music Consultants
VIENNA McLeod Holden Enterprises Ltd
VIKING SKULL Grand Union Management
VIKKI O'NEILL Heat Music
ST. VINCENT Firebrand Management
VINCENT, JEAN Paul Barrett (Rock 'n Roll Enterprises)
VIOLENT DELIGHT Toni Medcalf Management
THE VISIONS Sonic Bang! Management
VITALITY Uplifted Management & DJ Agency
VOLUME Illicit Entertainment
WADE, COLIN Future Management
TERRI WALKER BossMedia
WANGFORD, HANK Line-Up PMC
WANKDEN Got A Loser Job At The Diner Management
WARD 21 Jamdown Ltd
JEREMY WARMSLEY Solar Management
WASHINGTON, GENO KAL Management
WATERFALL W1 Music Management
RUSSELL WATSON Merlin Elite Ltd
WAXED APPLE GM Promotions
WAYNE HECTOR Jackie Davidson Management
THE WEDDING PRESENT Globeshine (UK) Ltd
WEEKEND PLAYERS Sanctuary Artist Management Ltd
WESTLIFE Louis Walsh Management
WET WET WET No Half Measures Ltd.
WHAM! DURAN Psycho Management Company
MARK WHEAWILL Uplifted Management & DJ Agency
WHEN TRAMS WERE KINGS Dellphonic Management
WHISKYCATS AK Creative Management
WHITE TRASH DJT Management Ltd
WILDE, KIM Onside Management
WILDE, MARTY Big M Productions
WILKIE, IAN Hope Management
WILLIAM TOPLEY Paul Crockford Management (PCM)
KATHRYN WILLIAMS Creation Management
WILLIAMS, ROBBIE IE Music Ltd
WILLOW First Time Management
WILSON, GARY R2 Management
WILT Sanctuary Artist Management Ltd
WINTER ROBERTS Sidewalk 7
WINWOOD, STEVE Atomic Management
WISEGUYS AKA DJ TOUCHE Fruit
WIT Formidable Management
WITHOUT GRACE Indie Music Management
WITHOUT PREJUDICE Kickstart Management
WITNESS Coalition Management
WITNESS Blue Hippo Management
WOMACK, BOBBY David Morgan Management
BILL WYMAN'S RHYTHM KINGS Denis Vaughan Management
X-PRESS 2 Whitenoise Management
THE XCERTS Raygun Music
XCITE Kamara Artist Management (UK)
XRS Bulldozer Management
YELLOWHAND Kickstart Management
YEN SUNG Qaraj' Ltd
YORK, NOLA Chantelle Music
YOUNG, GARETH SMI/Everyday Productions
YOUNG HEART ATTACK Grand Union Management
YOUNG, PAUL What Management
YOUNGSTERS Archetype Management

YOURCODENAMEIS:MILO Sanctuary Artist Management
Ltd
ZABIELA, JAMES Excession: The Agency Ltd
ZERO 7 Solar Management
ZINGER, EARL Impro Management
ZOE Big Help Music
THE ZOMBIES John Waller Management & Marketing

Recruitment Agencies

CAREER MOVES

◇career**moves**
Preferred suppliers to the Music Industry

1-2 Berners Street, London W1T 3LA **t** 020 7908 7900
f 020 7908 7949 **e** jess@cmoves.co.uk **w** cmoves.co.uk. Music
Consultants: Jessica Freeman - jess@cmoves.co.uk; Richard
Watson - richard@cmoves.co.uk; Kate Renwick -
kate@cmoves.co.uk
Specialist Music, Digital Entertainment and Secretarial
recruitment.

Cat Entertainment Search Pinewood Studios, Pinewood
Rd, Iver Heath, Bucks SLO 0NH **t** 01753 630040
f 01753 630830 **e** cat@catentertainmentsearch.com
w catentertainmentsearch.com GM: Catherine Pianta-McGill.

Gottlieb Associates, Executive Search
Consultants Garden Flat, 28 Oakley St, London SW3 5NT
t 020 7351 0717 **f** 020 7351 0604
e stevegottlieb@stevegottlieb.com **w** stevegottlieb.com
MD: Stephen Gottlieb.

Grosvenor Bureau Secretarial Recruitment 22
South Molton St, London W1K 5RB **t** 020 7491 0884
f 020 7409 1524 **e** gb@grosvenorbureau.co.uk
w grosvenorbureau.co.uk MD: Jackie McGurrell.

HANDLE RECRUITMENT

handle
THE MUSIC RECRUITMENT CONSULTANTS

4 Gees Court, London W1U 1JD **t** 020 7569 9999
e music@handle.co.uk **w** handle.co.uk Directors: Stella Walker
and Peter Tafler.
Handle Recruitment is the leading supplier of recruitment
services to every major record company and music related
organisation. We have a team of 24 exceptional consultants
recruiting across every business area and every department
in the music industry.

Kingston Smith Executive Selection Quadrant House,
(Air Street Entrance), 80-82 Regent St, London W1R 5PA
t 020 7306 5670 **f** 020 7306 5682
e jwest@kingstonsmith.co.uk **w** kingstonsmith.co.uk
MD: John West.

MacMillan Davies Hodes 10 Regent's Wharf, All Saints
St, London N1 9RL **t** 020 7551 4732 **f** 020 7551 4682
e jbaker@mdh.co.uk **w** mdh.co.uk Head of Practice: John Baker.

Matchstick Media 1st Floor, 10 Argyll St, London W1F 7TQ
t 020 7297 0030 **e** info@matchstickmedia.co.uk
w matchstickmedia.co.uk Managing Partner: Tim Palmer.

Media Recruitment 1 Parkway, London NW1 7PG
t 020 7267 0555 **f** 020 7482 3666
e tanya@mediarecruitment.co.uk **w** mediarecruitment.co.uk
Senior Consultant: Tanya Ferris.

THE MUSIC MARKET LTD

Lower Ground Floor, 26 Nottingham Place, London W1U 5NN
t 020 7486 9102 **f** 020 7486 7512
e firstname@themusicmarket.co.uk **w** themusicmarket.co.uk MD:
Helen Ward. Recruitment Consultant: Jenny Aston Fleming.
Recruitment Consultant: Christine Babb.
Industry recruitment specialists offering a bespoke
temporary and permanent recruitment service at all levels
within the music and entertainment industries. Placing the
right candidates in the right roles in the right companies at
every level from admin and secretarial through to CEO.

Positive Solutions Recruitment Limited 1 The Mews,
Castle St, Farnham, Surrey GU9 7LP **t** 0871 300 4444 or
07855 395 685 **f** 01252 891 720 **e** info@positivejobs.com
w positivejobs.com Dir: Craig Chuter.

Rose Inc 5th Floor, 133 Long Acre, London WC2E 9DT
t 020 7836 2666 **f** 020 7836 2667 **e** tom@rose-inc.co.uk
w rose-inc.co.uk Managing Partner: Tom Evans.

Event Management

AKlass Event Management PO Box 42371, London
N12 0WS **t** 020 8368 7760 **e** info@aklass.biz **w** aklass.biz
Contact: Patsy McKay.

b-live Entertainment 507 Old York Rd, London SW18 1DJ
t 020 8875 2525 **f** 020 8875 2526 **e** info@b-live.co.uk
w b-live.co.uk MD: Caroline Hollings.

Back Row Productions 71 Endell St, London WC2H 9AJ
t 020 7836 4422 **f** 020 7836 4425
e firstname.lastname@backrow.co.uk **w** backrow.co.uk
Account Mgr, Events: Pippa Rayner-Cook.

Ballistic Events 2nd Floor, 13-19 Vine Hill, London
EC1R 5DX **t** 020 7812 0097 or 020 7812 0096
f 020 7812 0099 **e** info@ballisticevents.com
w ballisticevents.com Contact: Louise Stevens & James Smith.

Barracuda Ltd 3 Delta Way, Thorpe Industrial Pk, Egham,
Surrey TW20 8RX **t** 01784 435 600 **f** 01784 435 700
e info@BarracudaAV.com **w** BarracudaAV.com
Sales/Marketing Dir: Ray Wallace.

Big Cat Group Griffin House, 18-19 Ludgate House,
Birmingham B3 1DW **t** 0121 200 0910 **f** 0121 236 1342
e info@bcguk.com **w** bcguk.com Dir: Nick Morgan.

Big Fish Events Ltd 115 Westbourne Studios, 242 Acklam
Rd, London W10 5JJ **t** 020 7524 7555 **f** 020 7524 7556
e robert@thefishpond.co.uk **w** thefishpond.co.uk
MD: Robert Guterman.

BossMedia Cashmere House, 180 Kensington Church St, Notting Hill, London W8 4DP **t** 020 7727 2727 **e** info@bossmedia.co.uk **w** bossmedia.co.uk Dir: Taharqa Daniel-Rashid.

Brickwerk Suite 33, Barley Mow Centre, 10 Barley Mow Passage, London W4 4PH **t** 020 8995 2258 **e** hello@brickwerk.co.uk **w** brickwerk.co.uk Dir: Jo Brooks-Nevin.

Capitalize Specialist PR and Sponsorship Ltd 52 Thrale St, London SE1 9HW **t** 020 7940 1700 or 020 7940 1739 **e** Info@capitalize.co.uk **w** capitalize.co.uk MD: Richard Moore.

CLOCKWORK ENTERTAINMENTS

Tudor House, Llanvanor Road, London NW2 2AR **t** 020 8731 8899 **f** 020 8455 9555 **e** sales@clockworkentertainment.com **w** clockworkentertainment.com Director: James Miller. Event Manager: Rebecca Warner. **Clockwork Entertainments**

CMPI EVENTS

CMP
United Business Media

CMPi Ltd, Ludgate House, 245 Blackfriars Road, London SE1 9UY **t** 020 7955 3754 **f** 020 7921 8505 **e** lskinner@cmpi.biz **w** cmpi.biz Events Development Manager: Louiza Skinner.
From finding the right venue to onsite delivery, our team of experienced professional organisers will help you to bring all your events to life with flair.

The Day Job 14 Laurel Ave, Twickenham, Middx TW1 4JA **t** 020 8607 9282 **e** nina@thedayjob.com **w** thedayjob.com Contact: Nina Jackson.

Funevents Corporate Services 31 Lower Clapton Rd, London E5 0NS **t** 020 8985 1054 or 020 7987 4385 **f** 020 8985 4334 **e** admin@funevents.com **w** funevents.com Dir: Harv Sethi.

Get Involved Ltd Unit B, Park House, 206-208 Latimer Rd, London W10 6QY **t** 020 8962 8040 **f** 0870 420 4392 **e** info@getinvolvedltd.com **w** getinvolvedltd.com Communications Manager: Clare Woodcock.

Leyline Promotions Studio 24, Westbourne Studios, 242 Acklam Rd, London W10 5JJ **t** 020 7575 3285 **f** 020 7575 3286 **e** firstname@leylinepromotions.com **w** leylinepromotions.com MD: Adrian Leigh.

Mad As Toast 3 Broomlands St, Paisley PA1 2LS **t** 07717 437 148 **f** 0141 887 8888 **e** info@madastoast.com **w** madastoast.com Dirs: John Richardson, George Watson.

Maestro Marketing & Development 62 Naxos Building, 4 Hutchings St, London E14 8JR **t** 07795 358901 **e** info@maestro-marketing.com **w** maestro-marketing.com Dir: Kimberly Davis.

OCTAGON

octagon

Octagon House, 81-83 Fulham High Street, London SW6 3JW **t** 020 7862 0000 **f** 020 7862 0001 **e** firstname.lastname@octagon.com **w** octagon.com VP, Music: Garry Dods. Account Director: Alex Sanders. Account Manager: Joy Campbell. Account Executive: Vanessa Chevalier. **Octagon is a global player in the world of music and brands, creating and implementing music strategies for clients including Vodafone and Coca-Cola. Recent work includes Vodafone TBA and the Vodafone Live Music Awards.**

Osney Media 2 Bath Pl, Rivington St, London EC2A 3DB **t** 0207 880 0000 **f** 0207 880 0010 **e** wendy_fanner@osneymedia.co.uk **w** mobimusicforum.com Marketing Manager: Wendy Fanner.

Shark Media Shark House, 197 Turnpike Link, London CR0 5NW **t** 020 8604 1330 or 07939 220 169 **e** info@shark-media.co.uk **w** shark-media.co.uk MD: Charlotte Clark.

Sugar Events 130 Shaftesbury Ave, London W1D 5EU **t** 020 7031 0975 **e** ian@thesugargroup.com **w** thesugargroup.com Head of Business Dev't: Ian Milne.

TCB Group 24 Kimberley Court, Kimberley Rd, Queens Pk, London NW6 7SL **t** 020 7328 7272 **f** 020 7372 0844 **e** stevenhoward@tcbgroup.co.uk **w** tcbgroup.co.uk MD: Steven Howard.

wildplum Live PO Box 999, Enfield, London EN1 9AD **t** 0777 1777 998 **e** info@wildplum.co.uk **w** wildplum.co.uk Artist Development and Events Manager: AL Douglas.

World Famous Group 467 Fulham Rd, Fulham, London SW6 1HL **t** 020 7385 6838 **f** 020 7385 0999 **e** info@worldfamousgroup.com **w** worldfamousgroup.com Chairman: Alon Shulman.

XRL Events Ltd XRL House, Hatches Barn, Bradden Lane, Gaddesden Row, Hemel Hempstead HP2 6JB **t** 0800 634 0900 **f** 0870 404 4101 **e** events@xrl.co.uk **w** xrl.co.uk Contact: Renu Sen.

Conferences and Exhibitions

Access Events International India House, 2nd Floor, 45 Curlew St, London SE1 2ND **t** 020 7940 7070 **f** 020 7940 7071 **e** info@access-events.com **w** access-events.com Marketing Dir: Paul Gilbertson.

Cup Promotions Ltd Suite 14-16, Marlborough BC, 96 George Lane, South Woodford, London E18 1AD **t** 020 8989 2204 **f** 020 8989 2219 **e** info@cup.uk.com **w** cup.uk.com Dir: Mark Abery.

ESIP Ltd P.O. Box 4702, Summerholme, Henley-on-Thames RG9 9AA **t** 01491 574 717 **f** 0870 122 4634 **e** info@esip.co.uk **w** esip.co.uk Dir: John Ellson.

Event Management Systems (UK) Ltd Unit 100, Rockingham St, London SE1 6PD **t** 020 7407 2115 **f** 020 7407 2132 **e** support@ems-events.co.uk **w** ems-events.co.uk Customer Liaison Mgr: Ms Taly Akiva.

Genesis Trade Shows & Events Merlin House, 6 Boltro Rd, Haywards Heath, W Sussex RH16 1BB **t** 01444 476 120 **f** 01444 476 121 **e** abigail@genesistravel.co.uk **w** genesistravel.co.uk Events Manager: Lorna Milner.

Hawksmere plc 12-18 Grosvenor Gardens, London SW1W 0DH **t** 0845 120 9603 **f** 020 7730 4293 **e** business@hawksmere.co.uk **w** hawksmere.co.uk Event Co-ordinator: Jane Fullbrook.

IAAAM (Int Association Of African American Music) The Business Village, 3-9 Bromhill Rd, London SW18 4JQ **t** 020 8870 8744 **f** 020 8874 1578 **e** info@hardzone.co.uk **w** hardzone.co.uk Co-Founder: Jackie Davidson.

Impact Ventures 38b Brixton Water Lane, London SW2 1QE **t** 020 7274 8509 **f** 020 7274 3543 **e** info@impactventures.co.uk **w** impactventures.co.uk MD: Rachael Bee.

In The City 8 Brewery Yard, Deva Centre, Trinity Way, Salford M3 7BB **t** 0161 839 3930 **f** 0161 839 3940 **e** info@inthecity.co.uk **w** inthecity.co.uk Dir: Anthony Wilson.

International Live Music Conference (ILMC) 2-12 Pentonville Rd, London N1 9PL **t** 020 7833 8998 **f** 020 7833 5992 **e** conference@ilmc.com **w** ilmc.com Producer: Alia Dann.

Jack Morton Worldwide 16-18 Acton Park Estate, Stanley Gardens, London W3 7QE **t** 020 8735 2000 **f** 020 8735 2020 **e** Asitha_Ameresekere@jackmorton.co.uk **w** jackmorton.com Sales/Mkt Dir: Chris Morris.

Lashed Worldwide Events Clearwater Yard, 35 Inverness St, London NW1 7HB **t** 020 7424 7500 **f** 020 7424 7501 **e** roman@ornadel.com Contact: Roman Trystram.

Midem (UK) Walmar House, 296 Regent St, London W1B 3AB **t** 020 7528 0086 **f** 020 7895 0949 **e** javier.lopez@reedmidem.com **w** midem.com Sales Mgr: Javier Lopez.

Mobile Music Retail Forum 2 Bath Pl, Rivington St, London EC2A 3DB **t** 0207 880 0000 **f** 0207 880 0010 **e** wendy_fanner@osneymedia.co.uk **w** mobimusicforum.com Marketing Manager: Wendy Fanner.

MusicWorks 125-129 High St, Glasgow G1 1PH **t** 0141 552 6027 **f** 0141 552 6048 **e** contact@musicworksuk.com **w** musicworksUK.com Producer: Michael Braithwaite.

NUS Ents - Ents Convention 45 Underwood St, London N1 7LG **t** 020 7490 0946 **f** 020 7490 1026 **e** steve@nus-ents.co.uk **w** nus-ents.co.uk NUS Ents Co-ordinator: Steve Hoyland.

onedotzero Unit 212c Curtain House, 136-146 Curtain Rd, London EC2A 3AR **t** 020 7729 0072 **f** 020 7729 0057 **e** info@onedotzero.com **w** onedotzero.com Events Mgr: Anna Doyle.

The Radio Academy 5 Market Pl, London W1W 8AE **t** 020 7255 2010 **f** 020 7255 2029 **e** info@radioacademy.org **w** radioacademy.org Dir: Trevor Dann.

SMi Group Unit 009, Great Guildford Business Sq, 30 Great Guildford St, London SE1 0HS **t** 020 7827 6000 **f** 020 7827 6001 **e** conferences@smi-online.co.uk **w** smi-online.co.uk.

UZ Events 125-129 High St, Glasgow G1 1PH **t** 0141 552 6027 **f** 0141 552 6048 **e** office@uzevents.com **w** uzevents.com Dir: Neil Butler.

Word Of Mouth Events PO Box 31348, London SW11 5ZE **t** 020 8673 3782 **f** 020 8675 6816 **e** info@wordofmouthevents.co.uk **w** wordofmouthevents.co.uk Events Organiser: AJ.

Awards and Memorabilia

AWARD FRAMERS INTERNATIONAL LTD

The Framing Centre, By The Meadow Farm, Steventon, Oxon. OX13 66RP **t** 01235 821 469 **f** 01235 821 427 **e** info@awardframers.com **w** awardframers.com Managing Director: Michael Selway. Production Director: Bryan Barns - Bryan@awardframers.com Sales Manager: Rob Newbould - Rob@awardframers.com
Award Framers International, previously known as Assential Arts, is licensed to design and produce official BPI, Nielsen Music Control and Impala awards.

CENTURY DISPLAYS

CENTURY
CERTIFIED AWARDS SINCE 1973

75, Park Road, Kingston Upon Thames, Surrey KT2 6DE **t** 020 8974 8950 **f** 020 8546 3689 **e** info@centurydisplays.co.uk **w** centurydisplays.co.uk General Manager: Neil Wicks. Accounts Manager: Bryony Caeiro.
Accredited Awards and Presentations – Music / Games / DVD / Corporate / Events • Bespoke Design Service • Merchandise & Memorabilia • 35 years experience •

Framous Unit 12/13 Impress House, Mansell Rd, Acton, London W3 7QH **t** 020 8735 0047 **f** 020 8735 0048 **e** lucy@framous.ltd.uk **w** framous.ltd.uk Office Manager: Lucy Walker.

The Gold Disc.com Moose Towers, 2 Beattie Ave, Newcastle-under-Lyme, Staffs ST5 9LS **t** 0870 855 40 80 **e** sales@thegolddisc.com **w** thegolddisc.com MD: Dave Breese.

Quite Great!

Solutions
Project Management, Design, Marketing, Consultancy

T: 01223 410000
Harvey@quitegreat.co.uk
www.quitegreat.co.uk

Business Consultants

>4 Marketing Consultant PO Box 47163, London
W6 6AS **t** 020 8748 4997 or 07885 512 721
e info@morethan4.com **w** morethan4.com
MD: Anthony Hamer-Hodges.

A Minor Music Consultancy 101 High St, Stetchworth,
Newmarket, Suffolk CB8 9TH **t** 01638 508 582 or
07711 088 972 **e** ed@oneservice.co.uk MD: Edward Ashcroft.

Alice Kendall - Synch Consultant Address on request.
t 07801 179 586 **e** alice.kendall@mac.com MD: Alice Kendall.

Arrowsmith Communications 5 Norfolk Court, Victoria
Park Gardens, Worthing BN11 4ED **t** 01903 200 916 or
07967 102 259 **e** eugeniearrowsmith@yahoo.co.uk
Media Consultant: Eugenie Arrowsmith.

Art & Soul (Consultancy & Catalogue Compilers)
154 Gordon Rd, Camberley, Surrey GU15 2JQ **t** 01276 505030
or 01276 505030 **f** 01276 508819
e davidsmith18@ntlworld.com MD: David Smith.

Blinkhorns Business & Taxation Advisers 27
Mortimer St, London W1T 3BL **t** 020 7636 3702
f 020 7636 0335 **e** Joel.Trott@blinkhorns.co.uk
w blinkhorns.co.uk Senior Manager: Joel Trott.

BossSound - Music Consultancy 4 The Candlemakers,
112 York Rd, London SW11 3RA **t** 07812 349 798 or
07812 349 798 **e** christian@bossSound.co.uk
MD: Christian Siddell.

Caragan Music Agency 5 The Meadows, Worlington,
Suffolk IP28 8SH **t** 01638 717 390 **e** daren@caragan.com
w caragan.com Head of A&R: Daren Walder.

Paul Chantler - Radio Programming Consultant 52
South Block, County Hall, Westminster, London SE1 7GB
t 07788 584 888 **e** chantler@aol.com **w** paulchantler.com
MD: Paul Chantler.

Clancy Webster Partnership Penniwells, Edgwarebury
Lane, Elstree, Herts WD6 3RG **t** 020 8953 8321
f 020 8207 1041 **e** jon@clancywebster.com Ptnr: Jon Webster.

CLEAR FOCUSSED MINDS

195 Micklefield Rd, High Wycombe, Bucks HP13 7HB
t 01494 521 641 **e** kazlanglee@aol.com
w clearfocussedminds.co.uk Consultant: Karen-Joy Langley (Bsc,
BACP Reg.).
**Specialist Music Business Lifestyle Counsellor & Coach;
confidential 1:1 consultation.**

Collective Music Ltd 5 Henchley Dene, Guildford, Surrey
GU4 7BH **t** 01483 431 803 **f** 01483 431 803
e info@collective.mu **w** collective.mu MD: Phil Hardy.

David Bloom Music Sales & Marketing Ltd 5 O'Feld
Terrace, Ferry Rd, Felixstowe, Suffolk IP11 9NA
t 01394 283 712 **f** 01394 283 712 **e** david@dbmusicsales.co.uk
w dbloom.co.uk Dir: David Bloom.

David Newham Associates Windrush, The Ridgeway,
Enfield, Middx EN2 8AN **t** 020 8366 3311
e david.newham@firenet.uk.net **w** davidnewham.co.uk
Contact: David Newham.

Deluxxe Management PO Box 373, Teddington, Middx
TW11 8ZQ **t** 020 8755 3630 or 07771 861 054
f 020 8404 7771 **e** info@deluxxe.co.uk **w** deluxxe.co.uk
MD: Diane Wagg.

Dynamik Music Consultants PO Box 32146, London
N4 3AX **t** 020 7193 3272 **f** 020 7681 3699
e giles@dynamik-music.com **w** dynamik-music.com
MD: Giles Goodman.

Eat Your Greens - Sponsorship Consultants 1 Crane
Cottages, Dudset Lane, Cranford, Middx TW5 9UQ
t 020 8759 2312 **e** info@eatyourgreens.ltd.uk
w eatyourgreens.ltd.uk MD: Denzil Thomas.

Enable Music Ltd 54 Baldry Gardens, London SW16 3DJ
t 020 8144 0616 or 07775 737 281 **e** mike@enablemusic.co.uk
w enablemusic.co.uk MD: Mike Andrews.

EP Music Licensing Consultants 11 Richmond Way,
East Grinstead, W Sussex RH19 4TG **t** 01342 313035
f 01342 313035 **e** clive@epmusic.f2s.com MD: Clive Wills.

Free Associates PO Box 37981, London SW4 0XQ
t 020 8675 4228 or 07818 453 650 **e** jody@freeassociates.org
Dir: Jody Gillett.

Liz Gallacher Music Supervision Suite 1, Buidling 500,
Shepperton Studios, Studios Rd, Shepperton, Middlesex
TW17 0QD **t** 01932 577 880 **f** 01932 569 371 **e** kay@lizg.com
w lizg.com Music Supervisor: Liz Gallacher.

Graham Stokes - Label Management Services 45
Poland St, London W1F 7NA **t** 020 7292 0902
e graham@btdrecords.com MD: Graham Stokes.

Green Consulting 30 Cranley Gardens, Muswell Hill, London
N10 3AP **t** 020 8352 0973 **f** 020 8352 0973
e jonathangreen@blueyonder.co.uk MD: Jonathan Green.

Chris Griffin - Marketing Consultant 69 Shakespeare
Rd, London W7 1LU **t** 07973 883 159 **f** 020 8357 9047
e chris@crgriffin.demon.co.uk Contact: Chris Griffin.

ICP Group (Threat Management & Security) 2 Old
Brompton Rd, London SW1 3DQ **t** 020 7031 4440
e info@icpgroup.ltd.uk **w** icpgroup.ltd.uk MD: Will Geddes.

Immediate Business Management 61 Birch Green,
Hertford, Herts SG14 2LR **t** 01992 550573 **f** 01992 550573
e immediate@onetel.com Ptnr: Derek Jones.

Ingenious Media plc 100 Pall Mall, London SW1Y 5NQ
t 020 7024 3600 **f** 020 7024 3601
e enquiries@ingeniousmedia.co.uk **w** ingeniousmedia.co.uk.

Innate Music Marketing Consultants 18 Drayton
Grove, London W13 0LA **t** 020 8566 9824 **f** 020 8566 9824
e nathan@innate-music.com **w** innate-music.com
Dir: Nathan Graves.

Solutions
Project Management, Design, Marketing, Consultancy

T: 01223 410000
Harvey@quitegreat.co.uk
www.quitegreat.co.uk

Inspiral 6 Cheyne Walk, Hornsea, E Yorks HU18 1BX **t** 01964 536 193 **e** paulcookemusic@btinternet.com **w** paulcookemusic.com MD: Paul Cooke.

JN Promotions (Music Services) PO Box 6879, Wellingborough NN8 3YJ **t** 01933 228 786 **e** jacqui@jnpromotions.biz **w** jnpromotions.biz MD: Jacqui Norton.

John Waller Management & Marketing The Old Truman Brewery, 91 Brick Lane, London E1 6QL **t** 020 7247 1057 **f** 020 7377 0732 **e** john@johnwaller.net MD: John Waller.

Lazarus Consulting Ltd Cydale House, 249A West End Lane, London NW6 1XN **t** 020 7794 1666 or 07976 239 140 **f** 020 7794 1666 **e** info@lazarusconsulting.net **w** lazarusconsulting.net MD: Steve Lazarus.

The Licensing Team Ltd 23 Capel Rd, Watford WD19 4FE **t** 01923 234 021 **f** 020 8421 6590 **e** Info@TheLicensingTeam.com **w** thelicensingteam.com Dir: Lucy Winch.

Lifeco UK PO Box 111, London W13 0ZH **t** 0870 741 5488 **f** 0870 131 5400 **e** info@johnrushton.com **w** johnrushton.com Dir: John S Rushton.

Keith RD Lowde F.C.A. Minoru, Pharaoh's Island, Shepperton, Middx TW17 9LN **t** 01932 222 803 or 0771 444 9765 **f** 01932 222 803 **e** k.lowde@btconnect.com.

Maestro Marketing & Development 62 Naxos Building, 4 Hutchings St, London E14 8JR **t** 07795 358901 **e** info@maestro-marketing.com **w** maestro-marketing.com Dir: Kimberly Davis.

Mandy Haynes Consultancy Covetous Corner, Hudnall Common, Little Gaddesden, Herts HP4 1QW **t** 01442 842039 **f** 01442 842082 **e** mandy@haynesco.fsnet.co.uk MD: Mandy Haynes.

MECS (Music & Entertainment Consultancy Services) 14 Grasmere Ave, Kingston Vale, London SW15 3RB **t** 020 8974 5579 **f** 020 8974 5579 **e** tony@a-b-u.demon.co.uk MD: Tony Watts.

The Music & Media Partnership Sanctuary House, 45-53 Sinclair Rd, London W14 0NS **t** 020 7300 6652 **f** 020 7300 1884 **e** firstname@tmmp.co.uk MD: Rick Blaskey.

Music & Arts Security Ltd 13 Grove Mews, Hammersmith, London W6 7HS **t** 020 8563 9444 **f** 020 8563 9555 **e** sales@musicartssecurity.co.uk **w** music-and-arts-security.co.uk MD: Jerry Judge.

Music & Merit Consultancy 9 Griffin Ave, Kidderminster, Worcs DY10 1NA **t** 07774 117678 **f** 01562 751330 **e** musicalmerit@blueyonder.co.uk Owner/consultant: Robin Vaughan.

Music Business Associates Ltd Apex House, 6 West St, Epsom, Surrey KT18 7RG **t** 01372 840 281 **f** 01372 840 282 **e** johnw@musicbusinessassociates.com **w** musicbusinessassociates.com Contact: Chris or John.

Music Business Services 3 Marlborough Rd, Lancing, W Sussex BN15 8UF **t** 01903 530 005 or 07950 274 224 **e** ray@rowlesmusic.co.uk **w** rowlesmusic.co.uk Contact: Ray Rowles.

Musically Ltd Davina House, 137-149 Goswell Rd, London EC1V 7ET **t** 020 7490 5444 or 07956 579 642 **f** 0870 160 6572 **e** paul@musically.com **w** musically.com MD: Paul Brindley.

Musicare 16 Thorpewood Ave, London SE26 4BX **t** 020 8699 1245 **f** 020 8291 5584 **e** peterfilleul@compuserve.com MDs: Peter Filleul & Sian Wynne.

MusicBusinessCoach.com 39 Palmerston Pl, Edinburgh EH12 5AU **t** 0131 202 6236 **f** 0131 202 6238 **e** info@musicbusinesscoach.com **w** musicbusinesscoach.com Managing Consultant: David Murray.

NiceMan Productions (Licensing & Repertoire Mgmt) 111 Holden Rd, London N12 7DF **t** 020 8445 8766 **e** scott@nicemanproductions.com **w** nicemanproductions.com Licensing Dir: Scott Simons.

One Solution International Group 500 Chiswick High Rd, London W4 5RG **t** 020 8956 2615 **f** 020 8956 2614 **e** info@onesolution-int.com **w** onesolution-int.com Hd, Commercial Services: Alexis Stanislaus.

Platinum Girls Media 1 Queens Walk, Queens Walk House, London W5 1TP **t** 020 8740 7341 or 07956 474 379 **e** lorenzolauren@hotmail.com MD: Lauren Lorenzo.

Pure Delinquent 134 Replingham Rd, Southfields, London SW18 5LL **t** 07929 990 321 **f** 020 8870 0790 **e** julie@pure-delinquent.com **w** pure-delinquent.com Dir: Julie Pratt.

PVA Ltd 2 High St, Westbury On Trym, Bristol BS9 3DU **t** 0117 950 4504 **f** 0117 959 1786 **e** enquiries@pva.ltd.uk **w** pva.ltd.uk Sales Director: John Hutchinson.

Quite Great Solutions Unit D, Magog Court, Shelford Bttm, Cambridge CB2 4AD **t** 01223 410 000 **e** Harvey@quitegreat.co.uk **w** quitegreatsolutions.co.uk MD: Tony Lewis.

R&B Music Consultants The Hoods, High St, Wethersfield, nr Braintree CM7 4BY **t** 01371 850 238 **e** stpierre.roger@dsl.pipex.uk MD: Roger St Pierre.

Rasheed Ogunlaru Life Coaching (for Singers and Performers), The Coaching Studio, 223a Mayall Rd, London SE24 0PS **t** 020 7207 1082 **e** rasaru_coaching@yahoo.com **w** rasaru.com Life & Business Coach: Rasheed Ogunlaru.

Real Time Information The Unit, 2 Manor Gardens, London N7 6ER **t** 020 7561 6700 **f** 020 7561 6701 **e** hq@realtimeinfo.co.uk **w** realtimeinfo.co.uk Dir: Simon Edwards.

Richard Thomas - Music Consultant 42 Geraldine Rd, London SW18 2NT **t** 020 8870 2701 **e** richtt123@yahoo.co.uk Contact: Richard Thomas.

Rightsman The Rights Management and Marketing Group, The Old Lamp Works, Rodney Pl, London SW19 2 LQ **t** 020 8542 4222 **f** 020 8540 6056 **e** dick@rightsman.com **w** rightsman.com Consultants: Tim Prior, Dick Miller.

Siren Productions t 07971 798 393 **f** 0709 200 4055 **e** ellise@sirenproductions.freeserve.co.uk Independent Project Manager and Label Manager: Ellise Fleming.

Skullduggery Services 40a Love Lane, Pinner, Middlesex HA5 3EX **t** 020 8429 0853 **e** xskullduggeryx@btinternet.com MD: Russell Aldrich.

Business Services: Business Consultants

Quite Great! Solutions
Project Management, Design, Marketing, Consultancy

T: 01223 410000
Harvey@quitegreat.co.uk
www.quitegreat.co.uk

Slice Marketing 5 Golden Sq, London W1F 9BS
t 020 7309 5700 **f** 020 7309 5701 **e** firstname@slice.co.uk
w slice.co.uk MD: Damian Mould.

Stuart Batsford - Independent Music Business Consultant 5 Bolton Lodge, 19 Bolton Rd, Chiswick, London W4 3TG **t** 020 8995 3557 or 07870 242 559
e stuart.batsford@btinternet.com Contact: Stuart Batsford.

TCB Group 24 Kimberley Court, Kimberley Rd, Queens Pk, London NW6 7SL **t** 020 7328 7272 **f** 020 7372 0844
e stevenhoward@tcbgroup.co.uk **w** tcbgroup.co.uk
MD: Steven Howard.

Diane Wagg - Coaching Practice & Consultancy
PO Box 373, Teddington TW11 8ZQ **t** 07771 861 054
f 020 8404 7771 **e** info@dianewagg.com **w** dianewagg.com
Contact: Diane Wagg.

Westbury Music Consultants Ltd 72 Marylebone Lane, London W1U 2PL **t** 020 7487 5044 **f** 020 7935 2270
e pcornish@westburymusic.co.uk Consultant: Peter Cornish.

Education

Academy of Contemporary Music (ACM) Rodboro Bld, Bridge St, Guildford, Surrey GU1 4SB **t** 01483 500 800
f 01483 500 801 **e** enquiries@acm.ac.uk **w** acm.ac.uk.

Access To Music Lionel House, 35 Millstone Lane, Leicester LE1 5JN **t** 0800 281 842 or 0116 242 6888 **f** 0116 242 6868
e info@access-to-music.co.uk **w** accesstomusic.co.uk
Head of Admissions: Alan Ramsay.

Alchemea College of Audio Engineering The Windsor Centre, Windsor St, London N1 8QG **t** 020 7359 4035
e info@alchemea.com **w** alchemea.com Contact: Mike Sinnott.

Alternative Display Training 874 Pershore Rd, Selly Pk, Birmingham, W Midlands B29 7LS **t** 0121 414 0436
f 0121 414 0436 **e** pauline@alternatedisplaytraining.com
w alternatedisplaytraining.com MD: Pauline Carr.

Andy's Guitar Workshop 27 Denmark St, London WC2H 8NJ **t** 020 7916 5080 **f** 020 7916 5714
e aguitar@btinternet.com MD: Andy Preston.

Armstrong Multimedia Arts Academy GMC Studio, Hollingbourne, Kent ME17 1UQ **t** 01622 880599
f 01622 880020 **e** records@triple-a.uk.com **w** triple-a.uk.com
CEO: Terry Armstrong.

Associated Board of the Royal Schools of Music
24 Portland Pl, London W1B 1LU **t** 020 7636 5400
f 020 7637 0234 **e** abrsm@abrsm.ac.uk **w** abrsm.ac.uk
Fin Dir: Tim Leats.

Banana Row Drum School 47 Eyre Pl, Edinburgh EH3 5EY **t** 0131 557 2088 **f** 0131 558 9848
e music@bananarow.com MD: Craig Hunter.

Bear Storm South Bank Technopark, 90 London Rd, London SE1 6LN **t** 020 7815 7744 **f** 020 7815 7793
e greg@bearstorm.com Website: **w** bearstorm.com
MD: Greg Tallent.

The Brighton Institute of Modern Music 7 Rock Pl, Brighton, E Sussex BN2 1PF **t** 01273 626 666 **f** 01273 626 626
e info@bimm.co.uk **w** bimm.co.uk
Dirs: Kevin Nixon, Sarah Clayman.

The Brit School for Performing Arts & Technology 60 The Crescent, Croydon, Surrey CR0 2HN
t 020 8665 5242 **f** 020 8665 8676
e admin@brit.croydon.sch.uk **w** brit.croydon.sch.uk
Arts Industy Liason Mgr: Arthur Boulton.

Buckinghamshire Chilterns University College
Wellesbourne Campus, Kingshill Rd, High Wycombe, Bucks HP13 5BB **t** 01494 522141 ex 4020 **f** 01494 465432
e fmacke01@bcuc.ac.uk **w** bcuc.ac.uk HoM: Frazer Mackenzie.

Canford Summer School of Music 5 Bushey Close, Old Barn Lane, Kenley, Surrey CR8 5AU **t** 020 8660 4766
f 020 8668 5273 **e** canfordsummersch@aol.com
w canfordsummerschool.co.uk Director of Music: Malcolm Binney.

Centre For Voice The Tobacco Factory, Raleigh Rd, Bristol BS3 1TF **t** 0117 902 6606 **f** 0117 902 6607
e info@centreforvoice.idps.co.uk **w** centrecords.com
Principal: Andrew Hambly-Smith.

City University Music Department, Northampton Sq, London EC1V 0HB **t** 020 7040 8284 **f** 020 7040 8576
e music@city.ac.uk **w** city.ac.uk/music
Administrator: Andrew Pearce.

Collage Arts The Chocolate Factory, Unit 4, Building B, Clarendon Rd, London N22 6XJ **t** 020 8365 7500
f 020 8365 8686 **e** info@collage-arts.org **w** collage-arts.org
Training Mgr: Preti Dasgupta.

Community Music Wales Unit 8, 24 Norbury Rd, Fairwater, Cardiff CF5 3AU **t** 029 2083 8060
f 029 2056 6573 **e** admin@communitymusicwales.org.uk
w communitymusicwales.org.uk Music Director: Simon Dancey.

Dartington College of Arts Totnes, Devon TQ9 6EJ
t 01803 861 650 **f** 01803 861 685
e enterprise@dartington.ac.uk **w** dartington.ac.uk/enterprise
Director of Enterprise: Adrian Bossey.

David Newham Associates Windrush, The Ridgeway, Enfield, Middx EN2 8AN **t** 020 8366 3311
e david.newham@firenet.uk.net **w** davidnewham.co.uk
Contact: David Newham.

Deep Recording Studios 187 Freston Rd, London W10 6TH **t** 020 8964 8256 **e** deep.studios@virgin.net
w deeprecordingstudios.com Studio Manager: Mark Rose.

Drumtech 76 Stanley Gardens, London W3 7SZ
t 020 8749 3131 **f** 020 8740 8422 **e** info@drum-tech.co.uk
w drum-tech.co.uk GM: Andy Moorhouse.

Ebony and Ivory Vocal Tuition 11 Varley Parade, Edgware Rd, Colindale, Londno NW9 6RR **t** 020 8200 5510
f 020 8205 1907 **e** ajit123@aol.com **w** ebonyivory.co.uk
MD: Ajit Sahajpal.

Gateway School of Recording 16 Bromells Rd, London SW4 0BG **t** 0870 770 8816 **e** info@gsr.org.uk **w** gsr.org.uk
Course Administrator: Hilary Cohen.

Global Entertainment Group Old House, 154 Prince Consort Rd, Gateshead NE8 4DU **t** 0191 469 0100 **f** 0191 469 0001 **e** info@globalmusicbiz.co.uk **w** globalmusicbiz.co.uk Course Co-ordinator: Martin Jones.

Guildhall School of Music & Drama Silk St, Barbican, London EC2Y 8DT **t** 020 7628 2571 **f** 020 7256 9438 **e** music@gsmd.ac.uk **w** gsmd.ac.uk Contact: Principal.

Guitar-X 76 Stanley Gardens, London W3 7SZ **t** 020 8749 3131 **f** 020 8740 8422 **e** info@guitar-x.co.uk **w** guitar-x.co.uk GM: Andy Moorhouse.

Hatchet Music Educational Resources 20 Intwood Rd, Norwich, Norfolk NR4 6AA **t** 01603 458 488 **e** mark@hatchetmusic.co.uk MD: Mark Narayn.

In The Music Biz 108 Oglander Rd, London SE15 4DB **t** 07740 438537 **e** inthemusicbiz@btinternet.com **w** inthemusicbiz.com Course Manager: Amanda Hull.

Institute of Popular Music University of Liverpool, Roxby Building, Chatham St, Liverpool L69 7ZT **t** 0151 794 3101 **f** 0151 794 2566 **e** ipm@liverpool.ac.uk **w** liv.ac.uk/ipm.

iwanttoworkinmusic.com Music Dept., University of Westminster, Watford Rd, Harrow, Middx. HA1 3TP **t** 020 7911 5000 **e** iwanttoworkinmusic@hotmail.com **w** iwanttoworkinmusic.com Contact: Rosie Hartnell.

Sign up to the Free Music Week Daily email news service at www.musicweek.com

Jazzwise Direct 2B Gleneagle Mews, Ambleside Ave, London SW16 6AE **t** 020 8769 7725 **f** 020 8677 7128 **e** admin@jazzwise.com **w** jazzwise.com Operations Mgr: Hugh Gledhill.

Jewel and Esk Valley College 24 Milton Road East, Edinburgh EH15 2PP **t** 0131 657 7321 **f** 0131 657 2276 **e** aduff@jevc.ac.uk **w** jevc.ac.uk Learning Manager: Althea Duff.

Jewish Music Institute School of Oriental & African, Studies, University of London, Thornhaugh St, Russell Sq, London WC1H OXG **t** 020 8909 2445 **f** 020 8909 1030 **e** jewishmusic@jmi.org.uk **w** jmi.org.uk Dir: Geraldine Auerbach MBE.

Leeds University BA Popular and World Musics, School of Music, Leeds LS2 9JT **t** 0113 343 2583 **f** 0113 343 2586 **e** s.r.warner@leeds.ac.uk **w** leeds.ac.uk/music/dept/courses/ug/pwm.htm Senior Teaching Fellow: Simon Warner.

The Liverpool Institute For Performing Arts Mount St, Liverpool, Merseyside L1 9HF **t** 0151 330 3000 **f** 0151 330 3131 **e** admissions@lipa.ac.uk **w** lipa.ac.uk Admissions Manager: Rachel Bradbury.

The London College of Music & Media Thames Valley University, St Mary's Rd, Ealing, London W5 5RF **t** 020 8231 2304 **f** 020 8231 2546 **e** clare.beckett@tvu.ac.uk **w** tvu.ac.uk Marketing Manager: Clare Beckett.

The London Music School Three Mills Film Studios, Unit 20, Sugar House Business Centre, Three Mill Lane, London E3 3DU **t** 020 7247 1311 **f** 020 8555 4577 **e** music@londonmusicschool.com **w** londonmusicschool.com GM: Jo Kemp.

Martin Belmont 101A Cricklewood Broadway, London NW2 3JG **t** 020 8450 2885 Guitar Teacher: Martin Belmont.

MMF Training 14b Turner St, Manchester M4 1DZ **t** 0161 839 7007 **f** 0161 839 6970 **e** admin@mmf-training.com **w** mmf-training.com Head of Training & Education: Stuart Worthington.

Music, Arts & Culture Hiltongrove Business Centre, 25 Hatherley Mews, London E17 4QP **t** 020 8520 3975 **f** 0208520 3975 **e** info@redonion-uk.com Mgr: Dee Curtis.

Music For Youth 102 Point Pleasant, London SW18 1PP **t** 020 8870 9624 **f** 020 8870 9935 **e** mfy@mfy.org.uk **w** mfy.org.uk Executive Director: Larry Westland.

Newark & Sherwood College Friary Rd, Newark, Notts NG24 1PB **t** 01636 680680 **f** 01636 680681 **e** enquiries@newark.ac.uk **w** newark.ac.uk Contact: Customer Services.

Nordoff-Robbins Music Therapy 2 Lissenden Gardens, London NW5 1PP **t** 020 7267 4496 **f** 020 7267 4369 **e** admin@nordoff-robbins.org.uk **w** nordoff-robbins.org.uk Centre Director: Pauline Etkin.

North Glasgow College 110 Flemington St, Glasgow, Lanarkshire G21 4BX **t** 0141 558 9001 **f** 0141 558 9905 **e** hbrankin@north-gla.ac.uk **w** north-gla.ac.uk Snr Lecturer Music: Hugh Brankin.

Orbital Productions 38 Burnfoot Rd, Hawick, Scottish Borders TD9 8EN **t** 01450 378212 **e** info@orbital-productions.com **w** orbital-productions.com MD: Jacqui Gresswell.

Panic Music 14 Trading Estate Rd, Park Royal, London NW10 7LU **t** 020 8961 9540 or 020 8965 1122 **f** 020 8838 2194 **e** mroberts.drums@virgin.net **w** panic-music.co.uk Snr Tutor: Mark Roberts.

Point Blank Music College 23-28 Penn St, London N1 5DL **t** 020 7729 4884 **e** david@pointblanklondon.com **w** pointblanklondon.com Sales & Marketing Mgr: David Reid.

The Recording Workshop Unit 10, Buspace Studios, Conlan St, London W10 5AP **t** 020 8968 8222 **f** 020 7460 3164 **e** info@therecordingworkshop.co.uk **w** therecordingworkshop.co.uk Prop: Jose Gross.

The Royal Academy of Music University of London, Marylebone Rd, London NW1 5HT **t** 020 7873 7373 **f** 020 7873 7374 **e** go@ram.ac.uk **w** ram.ac.uk

The Royal College Of Music Prince Consort Rd, London SW7 2BS **t** 020 7589 3643 **f** 020 7589 7740 **e** info@rcm.ac.uk **w** rcm.ac.uk Secretary & Registrar: Kevin Porter.

The Royal School of Church Music 19 The Close, Salisbury, Wilts SP1 2EB **t** 01722 424 848 **f** 01722 424 849 **e** enquiries@rscm.com **w** rscm.com Contact: Education Administrator.

Royal Welsh College of Music & Drama Castle Grounds, Cathays Pk, Cardiff CF10 3ER **t** 029 2039 1361 **f** 029 2039 1305 **e** music.admissions@rwcmd.ac.uk **w** rwcmd.ac.uk HoM: Jeremy Ward.

SAE Institute United House, North Rd, London N7 9DP **t** 020 7609 2653 **f** 020 7609 6944 **e** saelondon@sae.edu **w** saeuk.com Marketing Mgr: Angi Kuzma.

School Of Sound Recording 10 Tariff St, Manchester M1 2FF **t** 0161 228 1830 **f** 0161 236 0078 **e** ian.hu@s-s-r.com **w** s-s-r.com Principal: Ian Hu.

Sense of Sound Training Parr Street Studios, 33-45 Parr St, Liverpool L1 4JN **t** 0151 707 1050 **f** 0151 709 8612 **e** info@senseofsound.net **w** senseofsound.net Artistic Director: Jennifer John.

Streetlights Contemporary Music School Tally House, Sheepdown Close, Petworth GU28 0BP **t** 01798 343388 **e** streetlights@btconnect.com **w** streetlightsmusicschool.co.uk Principal: Chris Mountford.

Training in Sound Recording The Studio, Tower St, Hartlepool TS24 7HQ **t** 01429 424440 **f** 01429 424441 **e** studiohartlepool@btconnect.com **w** studiohartlepool.com Studio Manager: Liz Carter.

Tribal Tree 66C Chalk Farm Rd, London NW1 8AN **t** 020 7482 6945 **f** 020 7485 9244 **e** enquiries@tribaltreemusic.co.uk **w** tribaltreemusic.co.uk Programme Mgr: Louise Nkosi.

UCC (Warrington Campus) Resolution Records, Crab Lane, Fearnhead, Warrington WA2 0DB **t** 01925 534308 **f** 01925 530001 **e** r.dyson@chester.ac.uk; j.mason@chester.ac.uk **w** chester.ac.uk/media Module Leaders: Russell Dyson, Jim Mason.

University of Surrey School of Performing Arts, Dept of Music, Guildford, Surrey GU2 7XH **t** 01483 686500 **f** 01483 686501 **e** spa@surrey.ac.uk **w** surrey.ac.uk/music.

University Of Westminster University of Westminster, Watford Rd, Harrow, Middlesex HA1 3TP **t** 020 7911 5903 **f** 020 7911 5943 **e** denise.stanley@virgin.net **w** wmin.ac.uk HoM: Denise Stanley.

The Vocal Zone - Vocal Coach PO Box 25269, London N12 9ZT **t** 07970 924 190 **e** info@thevocalzone.co.uk **w** thevocalzone.co.uk Contact: Kenny Thomas.

Vocaltech Vocal School 76 Stanley Gardens, Acton, London W3 7BL **t** 020 8749 3131 **f** 020 8740 8422 **e** enquiries@vocal-tech.co.uk **w** vocal-tech.co.uk Operations Manager: Andy Moorhouse.

Yes! You Can Sing! Vocal & Performance Tuition 32 Bunning Way, London N7 9UP **t** 020 7700 6379 **e** info@yesyoucansing.com **w** yesyoucansing.com MD: Gena Dry.

Zeall Music Business Training 5a Station Rd, Twickenham, Middx TW1 4LL **t** 020 8607 9401 **e** info@zeall.com **w** zeall.com MD: David McGeachie.

Computer Services

Backbeat Solutions 24 Annandale Rd, Greenwich, London SE10 0DA **t** 020 8858 6241 **e** info@backbeatsolutions.com **w** backbeatsolutions.com CEO: Chris Chambers.

Connolly Associates 6 Brookfields, Crickhowell, Powys NP8 1DJ **t** 01873 811633 **f** 01873 811992 **e** info@connolly-associates.co.uk **w** connolly-associates.co.uk MD: Steve Connolly.

Counterpoint Systems 74-80 Camden St, London NW1 0EG **t** 020 7543 7500 **f** 020 7543 7600 **e** info@counterp.com **w** counterp.com CEO: Amos Biegun.

Essential Business Services 131 Clermiston Rd, Edinburgh EH12 6UR **t** 0131 334 3039 or 07774 161536 **f** 0131 334 3055 **e** jackie1ebs@aol.com **w** essentialbusiness.co.uk Owner: Jackie Grant, FIQPS.

MUSICALC SYSTEMS LTD. (ROYALTY ACCOUNTING SOFTWARE)

24 Grove Lane, Kingston-upon-Thames, Surrey KT1 2ST **t** 020 8541 5135 or 07881 913 279 **f** 020 8541 1885 **e** info@musicalc.com **w** musicalc.com Marketing Manager: Asa Palmer.

Portech Systems Ltd 501 The Green House, Gibb St, Birmingham B9 4AA **t** 0121 624 2626 **f** 0121 624 0550 **e** s.naeem@portech.co.uk **w** portech.co.uk Sales Manager: S.Naeem.

Portman Music Services Ltd 38 Osnaburgh St, London NW1 3ND **t** 01962 732033 or 07971 455920 **f** 01962 732032 **e** maria@portmanmusicservices.com Royalty & Copyright Mgr: Maria Comiskey.

Priam Software The Old Telephone Exchange, 32-42 Albert St, Rugby CV21 2SA **t** 01788 558 000 **f** 01788 558 001 **e** contact@priamsoftware.com **w** priamsoftware.com Commercial Manager: Glyn Carvill.

Ranger Computers Ranger House, 2 Meeting Lane, Duston, Northants NN5 6JG **t** 01604 589200 **f** 01604 589505 **e** Postmaster@rangercom.com **w** ranger.demon.co.uk MD: David Viewing.

Spool Multi Media (UK) Unit 30, Deeside Industrial Pk, Deeside, Flintshire CH5 2NU **t** 01244 280602 **f** 01244 288581 **e** rv@smmuk.co.uk **w** smmuk.co.uk MD: Roy Varley.

Summit Services Rosebery Ave, High Wycombe, Bucks HP13 7YZ **t** 01494 447562 **f** 01494 441498 **e** summit@summit-services.co.uk **w** summit-services.co.uk MD: Bob Street.

Sypha 216A Gipsy Rd, London SE27 9RB **t** 020 8761 1042 **e** sypha@syphaonline.com **w** DAWguide.com Ptnr: Yasmin Hashmi.

Willot Kingston Smith Quadrant House, (Air Street Entrance), 80-82 Regent St, London W1B 5RP **t** 020 7304 4646 **f** 020 7304 4647 **e** eb@kingstonsmith.co.uk **w** kingstonsmith.co.uk Dir of IT Dep.: Ed Bayley.

Worldspan Communications Ltd Worldspan House, 80 Red Lion Rd, Surbiton, Surrey KT6 7QW **t** 020 8288 8555 **f** 020 8288 8666 **e** sales@span.com **w** span.com.

Business Services & Miscellaneous

Affinity Music 60 Kingly St, London W1B 5DS **t** 020 7453 4062 **f** 020 7436 3666 **e** info@affinitymusic.co.uk **w** affinitymusic.co.uk MD: Simon Binns.

Aquarius Entertainments 132 Chase Way, London N14 5DH **t** 07958 592 526 or 020 8361 5002 **f** 020 8361 3757 **e** rdldisco@aol.com **w** webvert.co.uk/karaokediscos Mgr: Colin Jacques.

The Arts Clinic 14 Devonshire Pl, London W1G 6HX **t** 020 7935 1242 **f** 020 7224 6256 **e** mail@artsclinic.co.uk **w** artsclinic.co.uk Dir: Sandie Powell.

Assential Arts Coxeter House, 21-27 Ock St, Abingdon, Oxon OX14 3ST **t** 01235 536008 **f** 01235 200700 **e** info@assentialarts.com **w** assentialarts.com MD: Mike Selway.

The Association Of Blind Piano Tuners 31 Wyre Crescent, Lynwood, Darwen, Lancs BB3 0JG **t** 01254 776148 **f** 01254 773158 **e** abpt@uk-piano.org **w** uk-piano.org Secretary: Barrie Heaton.

Blaim 13 Camp View Rd, St Albans AL1 5LN **t** 01727 756 912 **e** stephen@blaim.co.uk **w** blaim.co.uk MD: Stephen Ewashkiw.

Bonhams 65-69 Lots Rd, Chelsea, London SW10 0RN **t** 020 7393 3952 **f** 020 7393 3906 **e** entertainment@bonhams.com **w** bonhams.com/ Entertainment Dept: Niki Roberts.

Caligraving Ltd Brunel Way, Thetford, Norfolk IP24 1HP **t** 01842 752116 **f** 01842 755512 **e** info@caligraving.co.uk **w** caligraving.co.uk Sales Dir: Oliver Makings.

The Chain Music Services Ltd 30 Seby Rise, Uckfield TN22 5EE **t** 01825 769829 **e** mail@chainmusic.com MD: Giorgio Cuppini.

Chapman Freeborn Group 5 Hobart Pl, London SW1W 0HU **t** 020 7393 1234 **f** 020 7393 1275 **e** lon@chapman-freeborn.com **w** chapman-freeborn.com MD: Carol Norman.

Chart Moves-The Game 2 Move 2 PO Box 1099, London SE5 9HT **t** 020 7326 4824 **f** 020 7535 5901 **e** gamesmaster@chartmoves.com **w** chartmoves.com MD: David Klein.

Christian Copyright Licensing (Europe) Ltd PO Box 1339, Eastbourne, E Sussex BN21 4YF **t** 01323 417711 **f** 01323 417722 **e** executive@ccli.co.uk **w** ccli.co.uk Sales Mgr: Chris Williams.

Christie's Pop Memorabilia Auctions 85 Old Brompton Rd, London SW7 3LD **t** 020 7321 3281 or 020 7321 3280 **f** 020 7321 3321 **e** shodgson@christies.com **w** christies.com Head of Dept: Sarah Hodgson.

Churchill Howells Associates Ltd 24 Cornwall Rd, Cheam, Surrey SM2 6DT **t** 020 8643 3353 **f** 020 8643 9423 **e** cha@c-h-a-ltd.demon.co.uk Chairman: Carole Howells.

Essential Business Services 131 Clermiston Rd, Edinburgh EH12 6UR **t** 0131 334 3039 or 07774 161536 **f** 0131 334 3055 **e** jackielebs@aol.com **w** essentialbusiness.co.uk Owner: Jackie Grant, FIQPS.

Hamilton House Mailings Ltd Earlstrees Court, Earlstrees Rd, Corby, Northants NN17 4HH **t** 01536 399000 **f** 01536 399012 **e** sales@hamilton-house.com **w** hamilton-house.com MD: Stephen Mister.

Kaizen Music Services 39 Nunnery St, Castle Hedingham, Essex CO9 3DW **t** 01787 462 312 or 07969 056 052 **f** 01787 462 312 **e** info@kaizenrecords.co.uk **w** kaizenmusic.co.uk Dir: Kenton Mitchell.

Marken Time Critical Express Unit 2, Metro Centre, St Johns Rd, Isleworth, Middlesex TW7 6NJ **t** 020 8388 8555 **f** 020 8388 8666 **e** info@marken.com **w** marken.com Bus Devel Mgr: Rob Paterson.

The Record Factory 38 Wharncliffe Gardens, London SE25 6DQ **t** 020 8239 8464 **f** 020 8239 8464 **e** davemcaleer@blueyonder.co.uk Owner: Dave McAleer.

Rima Travel 10 Angel Gate, City Rd, London EC1V 2PT **t** 020 7833 5071 **f** 020 7278 4700 **e** ernie.garcia@rima-travel.co.uk **w** rimatravel.co.uk MD: Ernie Garcia.

RPM Research Suite 4, 17 Pepper St, London E14 9RP **t** 020 7537 3030 **f** 020 7537 0008 **e** info@rpmresearch.com Partners: Gary Trueman, David Lewis.

S4CDs Music Services 5 Rivett Close, Baldock, Herts SG7 6TW **t** 01462 892181 **e** inquiries@s4cds.co.uk **w** s4cds.co.uk MD: John Hall.

T&S Immigration Services Ltd 118 High St, Kirkcudbright DG6 4JQ **t** 01557 339 123 **f** 01557 330 567 **e** firstname@tandsimmigration.demon.co.uk **w** tandsimmigration.demon.co.uk Work Permit Specialists: Steve & Tina Richard.

ad:tech
EUROPE
EXHIBITION • CONFERENCE • SEMINAR
THE EUROPEAN DIGITAL MARKETING HUB
www.ad-techeurope.com
ad:tech
LONDON
27 - 28 SEPT 2006
ad:tech
HAMBURG
22 - 23 MAY 2007
ad:tech
PARIS
20 - 21 FEB 2007
ad:tech is the premier business platform to
tailor your market expansion throughout Europe

November 2006 | A Music Week Publication

Media

PROMO The First Stop for Music Video

VISIT

www.promonews.co.uk

TO FIND OUT WHY

Media:

Print Media

247 Magazine After Dark Media, Unit 29, Scott Business Pk, Beacon Park Rd, Plymouth PL2 2PB **t** 01752 294 130 **f** 01752 564 010 **e** editorial@afterdarkmedia.com **w** 247mag.co.uk Ed: Lucy Griffiths.

Access All Areas Inside Communications, One Canada Sq, Canary Wharf, London E14 5AP **t** 020 7772 8444 **f** 020 7772 8588 **e** nic_howden@mrn.co.uk **w** access-aa.co.uk Ed: Nic Howden.

Artistes & Agents Richmond House Publishing Co, 70-76 Bell St, Marylebone, London NW1 6SP **t** 020 7224 9666 **f** 020 7224 9688 **e** sales@rhpco.co.uk **w** rhpco.co.uk Mgr: Spencer Block.

Attitude Northern & Shell Tower, 4 Selsdon Way, City Harbour, London E14 9GL **t** 020 7308 5090 **f** 020 7308 5384 **e** attitude@attitudemag.co.uk **w** attitudemag.co.uk Ed: Adam Mattera.

Audience Media Ltd 26 Dorset St, London W1U 8AP **t** 020 7486 7007 **f** 020 7486 2002 **e** info@audience.uk.com **w** audience.uk.com Publisher/Managing Editor: Stephen Parker.

Audio Media Magazine 11 Station Rd, St Ives, Cambs PE27 5BH **t** 01480 461555 **f** 01480 461550 **e** mail@audiomedia.com **w** audiomedia.com Executive Editor: Paul Mac.

Bandit A&R Newsletter PO Box 22, Newport, Isle Of Wight PO30 1LZ **t** 01983 524110 **f** 0870 762 0132 **e** bandit@banditnewsletter.com **w** banditnewsletter.com MD: John Waterman.

Base.ad PO Box 56374, London SE1 3WF **t** 0207 357 8066 **f** 0207 357 8166 **e** london@base.ad **w** base.ad Ed: Tanya Mannar.

BBC Music Magazine Origin Publishing, 14th Floor, Tower House, Fairfax St, Bristol BS1 3BN **t** 0117 927 9009 **f** 0117 934 9008 **e** music.magazine@bbc.co.uk **w** bbcmusicmagazine.co.uk Ed: Oliver Condy.

BBm Magazine Ireland PO Box 49, Lisburn, County Antrim, Northern Ireland BT28 5EF **t** 02892 667000 **f** 02892 668005 **e** judith@bbmag.com **w** bbmag.com Ed: Judith Farrell-Rowan.

The Beat 54 Canterbury Rd, Penn, Wolverhampton, W Midlands WV4 4EH **t** 01902 652759 or 07973 133416 **f** 01902 652759 **e** steve-morris@blueyonder.co.uk **w** http://surf.to/thebeat Ed: Steve Morris.

Between The Grooves 3 Tannsfeld Rd, London SE26 5DQ **t** 020 8488 3677 **f** 020 8333 2572 **e** info@betweenthegrooves.com **w** betweenthegrooves.com Ed: Jonathan Sharif.

The Big Issue 1-5 Wandsworth Rd, London SW8 2LN **t** 020 7526 3201 **f** 020 7526 3301 **e** matt.ford@bigissue.com **w** bigissue.com Ed: Matt Ford.

Billboard Endeavour House, 5th floor, 189 Shaftesbury Ave, London WC2H 8TJ **t** 020 7420 6003 **f** 020 7420 6014 **e** MSutherland@eu.billboard.com **w** billboard.biz Global Editor: Mark Sutherland.

Blag Magazine PO Box 2423, London WC2E 9PG **t** 0870 138 9430 **f** 0870 138 9430 **e** blag@blagmagazine.com **w** blagmagazine.com Dirs: Sarah Edwards & Sally Edwards.

Blues & Soul 153 Praed St, London W2 1RL **t** 020 7402 6869 or 020 7402 7708 **f** 020 7224 8227 **e** editorial@bluesandsoul.com **w** bluesandsoul.com Ed: Bob Killbourn.

Blues Matters! PO Box 18, Bridgend CF33 6YW **t** 01656 743406 **e** editor@bluesmatters.com **w** bluesmatters.co.uk Ed: Alan Pearce.

Border Events 2 Heatherlie Pk, Selkirk, Selkirkshire TD7 5AL **t** 01750 725 480 **e** info@borderevents.com **w** borderevents.com Sales Manager: Andrew Lang.

Brass Band World Peak Press Building, Eccles Rd, Chapel-en-le-Frith, High Peak, Cheshire SK23 9RQ **t** 01298 812816 **f** 01298 812816 **e** advertising@brassbandworld.com **w** brassbandworld.com Ad Mgr: Liz Winter.

British & International Music Yearbook Rhinegold Publishing Ltd, 8 Mansell St, Stratford-upon-Avon, Warks CV37 6NR **t** 01789 209280 **f** 01789 264009 **e** sales@rhinegold.co.uk **w** rhinegold.co.uk Ed: Louise Head.

British Bandsman Harold Charles House, 64 London End, Beaconsfield, Bucks HP9 2JD **t** 01494 674411 **f** 01494 670932 **e** info@britishbandsman.com **w** britishbandsman.com MD: Nicola Bland.

Broadcast Emap Media, 33-39 Bowling Green Lane, London EC1R 0DA **t** 020 7505 8000 **f** 020 7505 8050 **e** admin@broadcastnow.co.uk **w** broadcastnow.co.uk Ed: Conor Dignam.

Campaign 22 Bute Gardens, London W6 7HN **t** 020 8267 4683 **f** 020 8267 4915 **e** campaign@haynet.com Ed: Caroline Marshall.

Celebrity Service 4th Floor, Kingsland House, 122-124 Regent St, London W1B 5SA **t** 020 7439 9840 **f** 020 7494 3500 **e** celebritylondon@aol.com Contact: Diane Oliver.

Chartwatch Magazine 34 Brybank Rd, Hanchett Village, Haverhill, Suffolk CB9 7WD **t** 01440 713859 **e** ndr@sanger.ac.uk **w** chartwatch.co.uk Editors: Neil Rawlings/John Hancock.

City Life 164 Deansgate, Manchester M3 3RN **t** 0161 832 7200 **f** 0161 839 1488 **e** editor@citylife.co.uk **w** citylife.co.uk Ed: David Alan Lloyd.

City Living Magazine 1st Floor, Weaman St, Birmingham B4 6AT **t** 0121 234 5202 **f** 0121 234 5757 **e** jamie_perry@mrn.co.uk **w** icbirmingham.co.uk/cityliving/ Product Mgr: Jamie Perry.

Clash Magazine 143C Nethergate, Dundee DD1 4DP **t** 01382 808808 **f** 01382 909909 **e** info@clashmagazine.com **w** clashmagazine.com MD: John O'Rourke.

Classic FM Magazine Haymarket Publishing, 38-42 Hampton Rd, Teddington, Middx TW11 0JE **t** 020 8267 5180 **f** 020 8267 5150 **e** classicfm@haynet.com **w** classicfm.com Editor in Chief: John Evans.

Classic Rock 99 Baker St, London W1U 6FP
t 020 7317 2600 **f** 020 7317 2686
e firstname.lastname@futurenet.co.uk Ed: Sian Llewellyn.

Classic Rock (UK) Ltd - Classic Rock Society 47
Brecks Lane, Rotherham, S Yorks S65 3JQ **t** 01709 702575
e martin@classicrocksociety.co.uk **w** classicrocksociety.com
MD: Martin Hudson.

Classical Guitar Ashley Mark Publishing Co, 1 & 2 Vance
Court, Trans Britannia Ent Pk, Blaydon On Tyne NE21 5NH
t 0191 414 9000 **f** 0191 414 9001
e classicalguitar@ashleymark.co.uk **w** ashleymark.co.uk
Ed: Colin Cooper.

Classical Music Rhinegold Publishing, 241 Shaftesbury Ave,
London WC2H 8TF **t** 020 7333 1742 (Ed) or
020 7333 1733 (ads) **f** 020 7333 1769 (Ed) or
020 7333 1736 (ads) **e** classical.music@rhinegold.co.uk
w rhinegold.co.uk Ed: Keith Clarke.

CMA Publications Strawberry Holt, Westfield Lane,
Draycott, Somerset BS27 3TN **t** 01934 740270
e grp@cma-publications.co.uk **w** cma-publications.co.uk
MD: Geraldine Russell-Price.

CMU Music Network UnLimited Media, Fl 3, Grampian
House, Meridian Gate, London E14 9YT **t** 0870 744 2643
f 070 9231 4982 **e** cmu@unlimitedmedia.co.uk
w cmumusicnetwork.co.uk
Publishers: Chris Cooke, Caroline Moses.

Comes With A Smile 69 St Mary's Grove, Chiswick,
London W4 3LW **t** 07941 010 250 **e** cwasmatt@yahoo.co.uk
w comeswithasmile.com Ed: Matt Dornan.

Computer Music Future Publishing, 30 Monmouth St, Bath
BA1 2BW **t** 01225 442244 **e** ronan.macdonald@futurenet.co.uk
w computermusic.co.uk Ed: Ronan Macdonald.

Country Music People 1-3 Love Lane, London SE18 6QT
t 020 8854 7217 **f** 020 8855 6370
e info@countrymusicpeople.com **w** countrymusicpeople.com
Ed: Craig Baguley.

Country Music Round Up PO Box 111, Waltham, Grimsby,
NE Lincs DN37 0YN **t** 01472 821808 **f** 01472 821808
e countrymusic_ru@hotmail.com **w** cmru.co.uk
Publisher: John Emptage.

The Crack 1 Pink Lane, Newcastle upon Tyne NE1 5DW
t 0191 230 3038 **f** 0191 230 4484
e rob@thecrackmagazine.com **w** thecrackmagazine.com
Ed: Robert Meddes.

Cuesheet Music Report 23 Belsize Crescent, London
NW3 5QY **t** 020 7794 2540 **f** 020 7794 7393
e cuesheet@songlink.com **w** cuesheet.net
Editor/Publisher: David Stark.

Daily Mail Northcliffe House, 2 Derry St, London W8 5TT
t 020 7938 6000 **f** 020 7937 3251
e editorial@dailymailonline.co.uk **w** dailymail.co.uk.

Daily Record & Sunday Mail 1 Central Quay,
GlasgowGlasgow G3 8DA **t** 0141 309 3000 **f** 0141 309 3340
e reporters@dailyrecord.co.uk **w** dailyrecord.co.uk.

Daily Telegraph 1 Canada Sq, Canary Wharf, London
E14 5DT **t** 020 7538 5000 **f** 020 7538 7650 **w** telegraph.co.uk.

The DAW Buyers Guide Gipsy Rd, London SE27 9RB
t 020 8761 1042 **e** sypha@syphaonline.com **w** syphaonline.com
Ptnr: Yasmin Hashmi.

Dazed & Confused 112 Old St, London EC1V 9BG
t 020 7336 0766 **e** dazed@confused.co.uk **w** confused.co.uk
Ed: Rod Stanley.

Deuce Vision Publishing, 1 Trafalgar Mews, East Way, London
E9 5JG **t** 020 8533 9320 **f** 020 8533 9320
e editor@deucemag.com **w** deucemag.com Ed: Colin Steven.

Diplo Magazine 156-158 Gray's Inn Rd, London WC1X 8ED
t 020 7833 9766 **f** 020 7833 9766
e charlesb@diplo-magazine.co.uk **w** diplo-magazine.co.uk
Editor-in-Chief: Charles Baker.

DJ Magazine Highgate Studios, 53-79 Highgate Rd, London
NW5 1TW **t** 020 7331 1148 **f** 020 7331 1115
e info@djmag.com **w** DJmag.com Deputy Editor: Tom Kihl.

DMC Update DMC Publishing, 62 Lancaster Mews, London
W2 3QG **t** 020 7262 6777 **f** 020 7706 9323 or
020 7706 9310 (ISDN) **e** info@dmcworld.com **w** dmcworld.com
Ad & Sponsorship Mgr: John Saunderson.

Drowned in Sound 1 Chilworth Mews, London W2 3RG
t 020 7087 8880 **f** 020 7087 8899
e editor@drownedinsound.com **w** drownedinsound.com
Ed: Colin Roberts.

Early Music Faculty of Music, University of Cambridge, 11
West Rd, Cambridge CB3 9DP **t** 01223 335 178
f 01223 335 178 **e** earlymusic@oupjournals.org
w em.oupjournals.org Ed: Dr Tess Knighton.

Early Music Today Rhinegold Publishing, 241 Shaftesbury
Ave, London WC2H 8TF **t** 020 7333 1744 **f** 020 7333 1769
e emt@rhinegold.co.uk **w** rhinegold.co.uk Ed: Lucien Jenkins.

Echoes Unit LFB2, The Leathermarket, Weston St, London
SE1 3HN **t** 020 7407 5858 **f** 020 7407 2929
e echoesmusic@aol.com Ed: Chris Wells.

Encyclopedia of Popular Music High Parsons,
Lavenham, Suffolk CO10 9SB **t** 01787 249150
e colinmuze@mac.com **w** muze.com Ed-in-Chief: Colin Larkin.

Essential Newcastle 5-11 Causey St, Newcastle-upon-Tyne
NE3 4DJ **t** 0191 284 9994 **f** 0191 284 9995
e richard.holmes@accentmagazines.co.uk Ed: Richard Holmes.

Evening Standard Northcliffe House, 2 Derry St, London
W8 5TT **t** 020 7938 6000 **f** 020 7937 7392
e editor@thisislondon.co.uk **w** thisislondon.co.uk.

Financial Times 1 Southwark Bridge, London SE1 9HL
t 020 7873 3000 **f** 020 7873 3062 **w** ft.com.

The Fly 59-61 Farringdon Rd, London EC1M 3JB
t 020 7691 4555 **f** 020 7691 4666 **e** editorial@channelfly.com
w channelfly.com Ed: Will Kinsman.

Folk Music Journal 19 Bedford Rd, East Finchley, London
N2 9DB **t** 020 8444 1137 **e** fmj@efdss.org **w** efdss.org
Ed: David Atkinson.

Footloose Magazine 106-108 King St, London W6 0QP
t 020 8563 8174 **f** 020 8563 8175
e info@footloosemagazine.com **w** footloosemagazine.com
Ed: Matt Walker.

Foresight Bulletin/Planner Profile Group, Dragon Court,
27-29 Macklin St, London WC2B 5LX **t** 020 7190 7829
f 020 7190 7858 **e** info@profilegroup.co.uk
w foresightonline.co.uk Ed: Vicki Ormiston.

Fresh Direction c/o Antonville Ltd, Ground Floor, 2 Ella Mews, Cressy Rd, London NW3 2NH **t** 020 7424 0400 **f** 020 7424 0100 **e** editor@freshdirection.co.uk **w** freshdirection.co.uk Ed: Paul Russell.

fRoots c/o Southern Rag Ltd, PO Box 337, London N4 1TW **t** 020 8340 9651 **f** 020 8348 5626 **e** froots@frootsmag.com **w** frootsmag.com Ed: Ian Anderson.

Fused Magazine Studio 315, The Greenhouse, Gibb St, Birmingham B9 4AA **t** 0121 246 1946 or 0121 246 1947 **e** enquiries@fusedmagazine.com **w** fusedmagazine.com Ed: David O'Coy.

Future Music Future Publishing, 30 Monmouth St, Bath, Somerset BA1 2BW **t** 01225 442244 **f** 01225 732353 **e** andy.jones@futurenet.co.uk **w** futuremusic.co.uk Snr Editor: Andy Jones.

G MaG Campro Entertainment, PO Box 18542, London E17 5UY **t** 020 8527 2720 **f** 020 8531 6050 **e** mel@campro.freeserve.co.uk Editor/Publisher: Melissa Sinclair.

The Gen Generator North East, Black Swan Court, 69 Westgate Rd, Newcastle NE1 1SG **t** 0191 245 0099 or 07951 357 549 **f** 0191 245 0144 **e** mail@generator.org.uk **w** generator.org.uk Ed: David John Watton.

GQ Vogue House, Hanover Sq, London W1R 0AD **t** 020 7499 9080 **f** 020 7495 1679 or 020 7629 2093 **e** gqletters@condenast.co.uk **w** gq-magazine.co.uk Ed: Dylan Jones.

Gramophone Haymarket Publications, 38-42 Hampton Rd, Teddington, Middlesex TW11 0JE **t** 020 8267 5050 **f** 020 8267 5844 **e** editor@gramophone.co.uk **w** gramophone.co.uk Deputy Editor: Michael Quinn.

The Grapevine 45 Underwood St, London N1 7LG **t** 020 7490 0946 **f** 020 7490 1026 **e** nick@nus-ents.co.uk **w** nusonline.co.uk Sales Manager: Nick Woodward.

Grove's Dictionaries Of Music The Macmillan Building, Crinan St, London N1 9XW **t** 020 7843 4612 **f** 020 7843 4601 **e** grove@macmillan.com **w** grovemusic.co.uk Marketing Manager: Richard Evans.

The Guardian 119 Farringdon Rd, London EC1R 3ER **t** 020 7278 2332 **f** 020 7713 4366 **e** arts.editor@guardianunlimited.co.uk **w** guardian.co.uk.

The Guide The Guardian, 119 Farringdon Rd, London EC1R 3ER **t** 020 7713 4152 or 020 7239 9980 **f** 020 7713 4346.

Guinness World Records - British Hit Singles & Albums 338 Euston Rd, London NW1 3BD **t** 020 7891 4547 **f** 020 7891 4501 **e** editor@bibleofpop.com **w** bibleofpop.com Ed: David Roberts.

Guitar Magazine Link House, Dingwall Ave, Croydon, Surrey CR9 2TA **t** 020 8774 0600 **f** 020 8774 0934 **e** guitar@ipcmedia.com Ed: Simon Weir.

Guitarist Future Publishing, 30 Monmouth St, Bath, Somerset BA1 2BW **t** 01225 442244 **f** 01225 732285 **e** neville.martin@futurenet.co.uk Ed: Neville Marten.

Heat Endeavor House, 189 Shaftesbury Ave, London WC2H 8JG **t** 020 7295 5000 **f** 020 7859 8670 **e** heat@emap.com Ed: Mark Frith.

The Herald 200 Renfield St, Glasgow G2 3QB **t** 0141 302 7000 **f** 0141 302 7171 or 0141 302 6363 (Ad) **e** arts@theherald.co.uk **w** theherald.co.uk.

Hi-Fi Choice Future Publishing, 99 Baker St, London W1U 6FP **t** 020 7317 2600 **f** 020 7317 0275 **e** tim.bowern@futurenet.co.uk **w** hifichoice.co.uk Dep Ed: Tim Bowern.

Hi-Fi News Leon House, 233 High St, Croydon, Surrey CR9 1HZ **t** 020 8726 8310 **f** 020 8726 8397 **e** hi-finews@ipcmedia.com **w** hifinews.co.uk; avexpo.co.uk Ed: Steve Harris.

Hi-Fi World Audio Publishing, Unit G4, Imex House, Kilburn Park Rd, London W9 1EX **t** 020 7625 3134 **e** edit@hi-fiworld.co.uk **w** hi-fiworld.co.uk Ed: Simon Pulp.

Hip Hop Connection Infamous Ink Ltd, PO Box 392, Cambridge CB1 3WH **t** 01223 210536 **f** 01223 210536 **e** hhc@hiphop.com **w** hiphop.co.uk Ed: Andy Cowan.

Hit Sheet 31 The Birches, London N21 1NJ **t** 020 8360 4088 **f** 020 8360 4088 **e** info@hitsheet.co.uk **w** hitsheet.co.uk Publisher: Paul Kramer.

Hokey Pokey Millham Lane, Dulverton, Somerset TA22 9HQ **t** 01398 324114 or 07831 103194 **f** 01398 324114 **e** hokey.pokey@bigfoot.com Ed: Andrew Quarrie.

The Hollywood Reporter Endeavour House, 189 Shaftesbury Ave, London WC2H 8TJ **t** 020 7420 6004 **f** 020 7420 6015 **e** rbennett@eu.hollywoodreporter.com **w** hollywoodreporter.com European Bureau Chief: Ray Bennett.

Honk Ty Cefn, Rectory Rd, Canton, Cardiff, South Glamorgan CF5 1QL **t** 029 2066 8127 **f** 029 2034 1622 **e** honk@welshmusicfoundation.com **w** welshmusicfoundation.com/honk Ed: James McLaren.

Hot Press Magazine 13 Trinity St, Dublin 2, Ireland **t** +353 1 241 1500 **f** +353 1 241 1538 **e** info@hotpress.ie **w** hotpress.com Ed: Niall Stokes.

i-D Magazine 124 Tabernacle St, London EC2A 4SA **t** 020 7490 9710 **f** 020 7251 2225 **e** editor@i-Dmagazine.co.uk **w** i-dmagazine.co.uk Ed: Avril Mair.

The Independent On Sunday Independent House, 191 Marsh Wall, London E14 9RS **t** 020 7345 2000 **f** 020 7293 2182 **e** arts@independent.co.uk **w** independent.co.uk.

The Independent Independent House, 191 Marsh Wall, London E14 9RS **t** 020 7005 2000 **f** 020 7293 2182 **e** arts@independent.co.uk **w** independent.co.uk Ed: Simon Kelner.

INSTALLATION EUROPE

Installation
EUROPE

1st Floor, Ludgate House, 245 Blackfriars Road, London SE1 9UR **t** 020 7921 8317 **f** 020 7921 8339 **e** dgoldstein@cmpi.biz **w** installationeurope.com Editor: Dan Goldstein. Managing Editor: Sharon Lock.
Installation Europe: the magazine for audio, video and lighting in the built environment.

International Broadcast Engineer BPL Business Media, Brooklyn House, 22 The Green, West Drayton, Middx UB7 7PQ **t** 01737 855102 **e** claresturzaker@dmgbm.com **w** ibeweb.com Publisher: Clare Sturzaker.

IQ Magazine 2-4 Prowse Pl, London NW1 9PH
t 020 7284 5867 **f** 020 7284 1870 **e** greg@iq-mag.net
w iq-mag.net Ed: Greg Parmley.

Irish Music Magazine 11 Clare St, Dublin 2, Ireland
t +353 1 662 2266 **f** +353 1 662 4981
e info@selectmedialtd.com **w** irish-music.net
Publisher: Robert Heuston.

Irish Music Scene Bunbeg, Letterkenny, Co Donegal, Ireland
t +353 7495 31176 **e** donalkoboyle@eircom.net
Ed/Publisher: Donal K O'Boyle.

Irish Times 10-16 D'Olier St, Dublin 2, Ireland
t +353 1 679 2022 **e** (dept)@irish-times.ie **w** ireland.com.

It's Hot! Woodlands, 80 Wood Lane, London W12 0TT
t 020 8433 2447 **f** 020 8433 2763 **e** itshot@bbc.co.uk
PA: Claire Blindell.

Jazz Journal International Jazz Journal Ltd, 3-3A Forest
Rd, Loughton, Essex 1G10 1DR **t** 020 8532 0456 or
020 8532 0678 **f** 020 8532 0440 Publisher/Ed: Eddie Cook.

Jazz Newspapers Limited 26 The Balcony, Castle Arcade,
Cardiff CF10 1BY **t** 029 2066 5161 **f** 029 2066 5160
e jazzuk.cardiff@virgin.net **w** jazzservices.org.uk
Administrator: Carolyn Williams.

The Jazz Rag PO Box 944, Birmingham, W Midlands
B16 8UT **t** 0121 454 7020 **f** 0121 454 9996
e jazzrag@bigbearmusic.com **w** bigbearmusic.com
Ed: Jim Simpson.

Jazzwise Magazine 2B Gleneagle Mews, Ambleside Ave,
London SW16 6AE **t** 020 8664 7222 **f** 020 8677 7128
e jon@jazzwise.com **w** jazzwise.com
Editor & Publisher: Jon Newey.

Kerrang! Emap Metro, Mappin House, 4 Winsley St, London
W1R 7AR **t** 020 7436 1515 or 020 7312 8106
f 020 7312 8910 **e** kerrang@emap.com **w** kerrang.com
Ed: Paul Brannigan.

Keyboard Player 48 Mereway Rd, Twickenham, Middx
TW2 6RG **t** 020 8245 5840 **e** stevemillerkp@blueyonder.co.uk
w keyboardplayer.com Ed: Steve Miller.

Knowledge Magazine Vision Publishing, 1 Trafalgar Mews,
Eastway, London E9 5JG **t** 020 8533 9300
e editor@knowledgemag.co.uk **w** knowledgemag.co.uk
Ed: Colin Steven.

The Knowledge CMP Information Ltd, Info Services,
Riverbank House, Angel Lane, Tonbridge, Kent TN9 1SE
t 01732 362666 **f** 01732 377440
e knowledge@cmpinformation.com **w** theknowledgeonline.com
Grp Mktg Mgr: Katherine Jordan.

Leeds Guide Ltd 30-34 Aire St, Leeds, W Yorks LS1 4HT
t 0113 244 1000 **f** 0113 244 1002 **e** editor@leedsguide.co.uk
Ed: Dan Jeffrey.

The List 14 High St, Edinburgh EH1 1TE **t** 0131 550 3050
f 0131 557 8500 **e** editor@list.co.uk **w** thelist.co.uk
Ed: Nick Barley.

Loaded 26th Floor, Kings Reach Tower, Stamford St, London
SE1 9LS **t** 020 7261 5562 **f** 020 7261 5640
e firstname_lastname@ipcmedia.com **w** loaded.co.uk.

Loud And Quiet Floor 1, 2 Loveridge Mews, Kilburn, London
NW6 2DP **t** 07838 170 171 **e** info@loudandquiet.com
w loudandquiet.com Ed: Stuart Stubbs.

M2F First Floor, 62 Belgrave Gate, Leicester LE1 3GQ
t 0116 251 2233 **f** 0116 299 0077 **e** enquiries@m2fonline.com
w m2fonline.com Ed: Bina 'Bob' Mistry.

Mail On Sunday Northcliffe House, 2 Derry St, London
W8 5TT **t** 020 7938 6000 **f** 020 7937 3829
e editorial@dailymailonline.co.uk **w** mailonsunday.co.uk.

Marketing 174 Hammersmith Rd, London W6 7JP
t 020 8267 4150 **e** Via website **w** marketing.haynet.com
Ed: Craig Smith.

Marketing Week 12-26 Lexington St, 50 Poland St, London
W1R 4 **t** 020 7970 4000 **f** 020 7970 6721
e stuart.smith@centaur.co.uk **w** marketing-week.co.uk
Ed: Stuart Smith.

Maverick 24 Bray Gardens, Maidstone, Kent ME15 9TR
t 01622 744481 **f** 01622 744481
e editor@maverick-country.com **w** maverick-country.com
Ed: Alan Cackett.

Media Research Publishing Ltd Lister House, 117 Milton
Rd, Weston super Mare, Somerset BS23 2UX **t** 01934 644309
f 01934 644402 **e** cliffdane@tiscali.co.uk
w mediaresearchpublishing.com Chairman: Cliff Dane.

MEDIAPACK

MediaPack

CMP Information Ltd, Ludgate House, 245 Blackfriars Rd,
London SE1 9UR **t** 020 7921 8376 **f** 020 7921 8302
e mediapacknews@cmpi.biz **w** mediapack-online.com Editor in
Chief: Paddy Baker. Sales Manager: Lucy Wykes.

M8 Magazine Trojan House, Phoenix Business Pk, Paisley,
Renfrewshire PA1 2BH **t** 0141 840 5980 **f** 0141 840 5995
e info@m8magazine.com **w** m8magazine.co.uk
Ed: Kevin McFarlane.

Metal Hammer Future Publishing, 99 Baker St, London
W1U 6FP **t** 020 7317 2688 **f** 020 7486 5678
e chris.ingham@futurenet.co.uk **w** metalhammer.co.uk
Ed: Chris Ingham.

Metro Scotland 7th Floor, 144 St Vincent St, Glasgow
G2 5LQ **t** 0141 225 3336 **f** 0141 225 3316
e scotlife@ukmetro.co.uk Arts Editor: Rory Weller.

MI Pro (incorporating Audio Pro) Intent Media, St
Andrew House, 46-48 St Andrew St, Hertford SG14 1JA
t 01992 535 646 **e** mipro@intentmedia.co.uk **w** mi-pro.co.uk
Ed: Andy Barrett.

The Mirror 1 Canada Sq, London E14 5AP **t** 020 7293 3000
f 020 7293 3405 **e** feedback@mirror.co.uk **w** mirror.co.uk.

Mixmag Development Hell, 90-92 Pentonville Rd, London
N1 9HS **t** 020 7520 8625 or 020 7078 8423 ads or
020 7323 0276 ads **e** mixmag@mixmag.net **w** mixmag.net
Ed: Andrew Harrison.

Mobile Entertainment Intent Media, St Andrew House,
46-48 St Andrew St, Hertford SG14 1JA **t** 01992 535 646
e stuart.obrien@intentmedia.co.uk **w** mobile-ent.biz
Ed: Stuart O'Brien.

Mojo Emap Performance, Mappin House, 4 Winsley St, London
W1W 8HF **t** 020 7436 1515 **f** 020 7312 8296
e mojo@emap.com **w** mojo4music.com Ed: Phil Alexander.

Music Business Journal 3 Winsdown House, Three Gates Lane, Haslemere, Surrey GU27 2LE **t** 01428 656 442 **e** info@musicjournal.org **w** musicjournal.org Managing Editors: JoJo Gould/Jonathan Little.

Music Education Yearbook (see British Music Yearbook).

Music Journal 10 Stratford Pl, London W1C 1AA **t** 020 7629 4413 **f** 020 7408 1538 **e** membership@ism.org **w** ism.org Ed: Neil Hoyle.

Music Mart Media House, Trafalgar Way, Bar Hill, Cambridge CB3 8SQ **t** 01954 789 888 or 07981 339 109 **e** hannah@musicmart-mag.com **w** musicmart-mag.com Features Editor: Hannah Hamilton.

Music Master Retail Entertainment Data, Paulton House, 8 Shepherdess Walk, London N1 7LB **t** 020 7566 8216 **f** 020 7566 8259 **e** info@redmuze.com **w** redmuze.com.

Music Teacher Rhinegold Publishing, 241 Shaftesbury Ave, London WC2H 8EH **t** 020 7333 1747 **f** 020 7333 1769 **e** music.teacher@rhinegold.co.uk **w** rhinegold.co.uk Ed: Lucien Jenkins.

MUSIC WEEK

CMP Information, Ludgate House, 245 Blackfriars Road, London SE1 9UR **t** 020 7921 8348 **f** 020 7921 8327 **e** firstname@musicweek.com **w** musicweek.com Editor: Martin Talbot. Publisher: Ajax Scott. Managing Editor: Paul Williams. Talent Editor: Stuart Clarke. Database Manager: Nick Tesco. Business Development Manager: Matthew Tyrrell. Advertising Manager: Matt Slade. Senior Advertising Sales Executive: Billy Fahey. Advertising Sales Executive: Dwaine Tyndale. Classified Sales Executive: Maria Edwards.

MUSIC WEEK DIRECTORY

CMP Information, Ludgate House, 245 Blackfriars Road, London SE1 9UR **t** 020 7921 8353 **f** 020 7921 8327 **e** mwdirectory@cmpi.biz **w** musicweekdirectory.com Database Manager: Nick Tesco. Publisher: Ajax Scott. Business Development Manager: Matthew Tyrrell. Advertising Manager: Matt Slade. Senior Advertising Sales Executive: Billy Fahey. Advertising Sales Executive: Dwaine Tyndale. Logo Sales Executive: Maria Edwards.
The definitive contacts directory for the UK music industry.

Music-Zine 3, The Courtyard, Windhill, Bishops Stortford, Herts CM23 2ND **t** 01279 865 070 or 07941 142 779 **f** 0870 486 0812 **e** simon@music-zine.com **w** music-zine.com Ed: Simon Eddie Baker.

Musical Opinion 2 Princes Rd, St Leonards-on-Sea, E Sussex TN37 6EL **t** 01424 715167 **f** 01424 712214 **e** musicalopinion2@aol.com **w** musicalopinion.com Publisher: Denby Richards.

The Musical Times PO Box 464, Berkhamsted, Herts HP4 2UR **t** 01442 879 097 **e** mustimes@aol.com **w** musicaltimes.co.uk Ed: Antony Bye.

Nerve Talbot Campus, Fern Barrow, Poole, Dorset BH12 5BB **t** 01202 965744 **f** 01202 535990 **e** suvpcomms@bournemouth.ac.uk **w** nervemedia.net Ed: Sarah Wiles.

A New Day - The Jethro Tull Magazine 75 Wren Way, Farnborough, Hants GU14 8TA **t** 01252 540270 or 07889 797482 **f** 01252 372001 **e** DAVIDREES1@compuserve.com **w** anewdayrecords.co.uk Ed: Dave Rees.

New Nation Newspaper Unit 2.1, Whitechapel Technology Centre, 65 Whitechapel Rd, London E1 IDU **t** 020 7650 2000 **f** 020 7650 2004 **e** thepulse@newnation.co.uk Music & Ent Ed: Justin Onyeka.

News Of The World News International, 1 Virginia St, London E1 9XR **t** 020 7782 7000 **f** 020 7583 9504 **e** Via website **w** newsoftheworld.co.uk.

Night Magazine Mondiale Publishing Ltd, Waterloo Pl, Watson Sq, Stockport, Cheshire SK1 3AZ **t** 0161 429 7803 **f** 0161 476 0456 **e** night@mondiale.co.uk **w** mondiale.co.uk/night Ed: Ms Alex Eyre.

Nightshift PO Box 312, Kidlington, Oxford OX5 1ZU **t** 01865 372255 **e** nightshift@oxfordmusic.net **w** nightshift.oxfordmusic.net Ed: Ronan Munro.

NME IPC Music Magazines, Kings Reach Tower, Stamford St, London SE1 9LS **t** 020 7261 6472 **f** 020 7261 5185 **e** editor@nme.com **w** nme.com Ed: Conor McNicholas.

The Noise Buckinghamshire College SU, Queen Alexandra Rd, High Wycombe, Bucks HP11 2JZ **t** 01494 446330 **f** 01494 558195 **e** amanda.mcdowall@bcuc.ac.uk **w** bcsu.net Ed: Amanda McDowall.

Northdown Publishing Ltd PO Box 49, Bordon, Hants GU35 0AF **t** 01420 489474 **e** enquiries@northdown.demon.co.uk **w** northdown.demon.co.uk Dir: Michael Heatley.

Notion Studio 2.03, Tea Building, 56 Shoreditch High St, London E1 6JJ **t** 0870 046 6622 **f** 0870 046 6611 **e** info@musichqmedia.com **w** notionmag.com Ed: Bill Hussein.

The Observer 119 Farringdon Rd, London EC1R 3ER **t** 020 7278 2332 or 020 7713 4286 **f** 020 7713 4250 **e** firstname.lastname@observer.co.uk **w** observer.co.uk.

ONE TO ONE

CMP Information, Ludgate House, 245 Blackfriars Road, London SE1 9UR **t** 020 7921 8376 **f** 020 7921 8302 **e** pabaker@cmpi.biz **w** oto-online.com Editor: Paddy Baker. Sales Manager: Lucy Wykes.

onlinePOP PO Box 150, Chesterfield S40 0YT **t** 0870 746 8478 **e** mail@onlinepopnews.com **w** onlinepopnews.com Ed: Tony Hedley.

Opera Now 241 Shaftesbury Ave, London WC2H 8EH **t** 020 7333 1733 or 020 7333 1740 **f** 020 7333 1736 or 020 7333 1769 **e** opera.now@rhinegold.co.uk **w** rhiegold.co.uk Ed: Ashutosh Khandekar.

Organ Suite 212, The Old Gramophone Works, 326 Kensal Rd, London W10 5BZ **t** 020 8964 3066 **e** organ@organart.demon.co.uk **w** organart.com MD: Sean Worrall.

Original British Theatre Directory 70-76 Bell St, Marylebone, London NW1 6SP **t** 020 7224 9666 **f** 020 7224 9688 **e** sales@rhpco.co.uk **w** rhpco.co.uk Mgr: Spencer Block.

Orpheus Publications Ltd 3 Waterhouse Sq, 138-142 Holborn, London EC1N 2NY **t** 020 7882 1040 **f** 020 7882 1020 **w** thestrad.com Ed: Naomi Sadler.

The Piano Rhinegold Publishing, 241 Shaftesbury Ave, London WC2H 8EH **t** 020 7333 1733 or 020 7333 1724 **f** 020 7333 1736 or 020 7333 1769 **e** piano@rhinegold.co.uk **w** rhinegold.co.uk.

Pipeline Instrumental Review 12 Thorkill Gardens, Thames Ditton, Surrey KT7 0UP **t** 020 8398 6684 **f** 020 8398 6684 **e** editor@pipelinemag.co.uk **w** pipelinemag.co.uk Ed: Alan Taylor.

Popular Music Cambridge University Press, The Edinburgh Building, Shaftesbury Rd, Cambridge CB2 2RU **t** 01223 325757 or 01223 325757 **f** 01223 315052 **w** journals.cambridge.org/public/door Eds: Lucy Green, David Laing.

Popworld Pulp Brooklands Media Limited, Westgate, 120-128 Station Rd, Redhill, Surrey RH1 1ET **t** 01737 786 800 **f** 01737 786 801 **e** firstname.lastname@brooklandsgroup.com **w** popworld.com Ed: Hannah Verdier.

Press Association, Rock Listings 4th Floor, 292 Vauxhall Bridge Rd, London SW1V 1AE **t** 020 7963 7749 **f** 020 7963 7800 **e** gigs@pa.press.net Rock & Pop Editor: Delia Barnard.

PRO SOUND NEWS EUROPE

CMP Information Ltd., 1st Floor, Ludgate House, 245 Blackfriars Road, London SE1 9UY **t** 020 7921 8319 **f** 020 7921 8302 **e** david.robinson@cmpi.biz **w** prosoundnewseurope.com Editor: David Robinson. Advertisement Manager: Steve Connolly. Account Executive: Oliver Walker.

PROMO

CMP Information Ltd, Ludgate House, 245 Blackfriars Road, London SE1 9UR **t** 020 7921 8318 **f** 020 7921 8326 **e** davidk@musicweek.com Ed: David Knight. Ad Sales: Maria Edwards.

PSN LIVE

PSNLive

CMP Information Ltd, 1st Floor, Ludgate House, 245 Blackfriars Road, London SE1 9UY **t** 020 7921 8319 **f** 020 7921 8302 **e** david.robinson@cmpi.biz **w** prosoundnewseurope.com Editor: David Robinson. Advertisement Manager: Steve Connolly. Account Executive: Oliver Walker.

Q EMAP Metro, Mappin House, 4 Winsley St, London W1N 7AR **t** 020 7312 8182 **f** 020 7312 8247 **e** q@ecm.emap.com **w** qonline.co.uk Ed: Paul Rees.

QSheet Markettiers 4DC Ltd, 10a Northburgh House, Northburgh St, London EC1V 0AT **t** 020 7253 8888 **f** 020 7253 8885 **e** editor@qsheet.com **w** qsheet.com Music Editor: Nik Harta.

The Radio Magazine Goldcrest Broadcasting, Crown House, 25 High St, Rothwell, Northants NN14 6AD **t** 01536 418558 **f** 01536 418539 **e** radiomagazine-goldcrestbroadcasting@btinternet.com **w** theradiomagazine.co.uk.

Radio Times Woodlands, 80 Wood Lane, London W12 0TT **t** 020 8576 2000 **e** radio.times@bbc.co.uk **w** radiotimes.com.

RAGO Magazine PO Box 1668, Wolverhampton WV2 3WG **t** 07968 295 913 **e** info@ragomagazine.com **w** ragomagazine.com Editors: Tricksta & Late.

Record Collector Room 101, 140 Wales Farm Rd, London W3 6UG **t** 0870 732 8080 **f** 0870 732 6060 **e** firstname.lastname@metropolis.co.uk **w** recordcollectormag.com Ed: Alan Lewis.

Record Information Services Unit 8 (Hasmick), Forest Hill Ind Estate, London SE23 2LX **t** 020 8291 6777 **f** 020 8291 0081 **e** pp@brightguy.demon.co.uk Contact: Paul Pelletier.

Record of the Day PO Box 49554, London E17 9WB **t** 020 8520 2130 (PS) 020 7095 1500 (DB) **f** 020 8520 2130 **e** info@recordoftheday.com **w** recordoftheday.com Eds: Paul Scaife, David Balfour.

Revolutions 211 Western Rd, London SW19 2QD **t** 020 8646 7094 **f** 020 8646 7094 **e** john@revolutionsuk.com **w** revolutionsuk.com Ed: John Lonergan.

Rhythm Future Publishing, 30 Monmouth St, Bath, Somerset BA1 2BW **t** 01225 442244 **f** 01225 732353 **e** louise.king@futurenet.co.uk **w** futurenet.co.uk Ed: Louise King.

rock sound ixo Publishing UK Ltd, 50A Roseberry Ave, London EC1R 4RP **t** 020 7278 5559 **f** 020 7278 4788 **e** rsvp.rocksound@ixopub.co.uk **w** rock-sound.net Publisher: Patrick Napier.

Roots And Branches 54 Canterbury Rd, Penn, Wolverhampton, W Midlands WV4 4EH **t** 07973 133 416 **e** steve-morris@blueyonder.co.uk **w** roots-and-branches.com Ed: Steve Morris.

Rough Guides Ltd Rough Guides, 62-70 Shorts Gardens, London WC2H 9AH **t** 020 7556 5000 **f** 020 7556 5050 **e** mail@roughguides.co.uk **w** roughguides.com Rights/Promo Ass.: Chloe Roberts.

RTE Guide TV Building, Donnybrook, Dublin 4, Ireland
t +353 1 208 2919 **f** +353 1 208 3085 **e** Aoife.Byrne@rte.ie
Ed: Aoife Byrne.

RWD Magazine Suite B3 Lafone House, Leathermarket St,
London SE1 3HN **t** 020 7367 4136 or 07932 636 615
f 020 7367 6184 **e** editor@rwdmag.com **w** rwdmag.com
Ed: Hattie Collins.

Sandman Magazine PO Box 3720, Sheffield S10 9AB
t 0114 278 6727 **e** jan@sandmanmagazine.co.uk
w sandmagazine.co.uk Ed: Jan Webster.

The Scotsman 108 Holyrood Rd, Edinburgh, Midlothian
EH8 8AS **t** 0131 620 8620 **e** enquiries@scotsman.com
w scotsman.com.

Showcase Directory Harlequin House, 7 High St,
Teddington, Middx TW11 8EL **t** 020 8943 3138
f 020 8943 5141 **e** gillie@hollis-pr.co.uk **w** showcase-music.com
Ed: Gillie Mayer.

The Singer 241 Shaftesbury Ave, London WC2H 8TF
t 020 7333 1746 **f** 020 7333 1769 **e** the.singer@rhinegold.co.uk
w rhinegold.co.uk Ed: Antonia Couling.

Sky TV Guide & Digital TV Guide The New Boathouse,
136-142 Bramley Rd, London W10 6SR **t** 020 7565 3000
f 020 7565 3056 **e** skymag@bcp.co.uk.

SongLink International 23 Belsize Crescent, London
NW3 5QY **t** 020 7794 2540 or 07956 270 592
f 020 7794 7393 **e** david@songlink.com **w** songlink.com
Ed/Publisher: David Stark.

Songsearch Monthly Mulberry House, 10 Hedgerows,
Stanway, Colchester, Essex CO3 0GJ **t** 01206 364136
f 01206 364146 **e** songmag@aol.com **w** songwriters-guild.co.uk
Ed: Colin Eade.

Songwriter International Songwriters' Ass, PO Box 46,
Limerick City, Ireland **t** +353 61 228837 **f** +353 61 229464
e jliddane@songwriter.iol.ie **w** songwriter.co.uk
MD: James D Liddane.

Songwriting and Composing Sovereign House, 12
Trewartha Rd, Praa Sands, Penzance, Cornwall TR20 9ST
t 01736 762 826 or 07721 449 477 **f** 01736 763 328
e panamus@aol.com **w** songwriters-guild.co.uk
Ed: Roderick Jones.

Sound Nation Ty Cefn, Rectory Rd, Canton, Cardiff CF5 1QL
t 029 2066 8127 **f** 029 2034 1622 **e** news@soundnation.net
w soundnation.net Ed: James McLaren.

Sound On Sound Media House, Trafalgar Way, Bar Hill,
Cambridge, Cambs CB3 8SQ **t** 01954 789 888
f 01954 789 895 **e** sos@soundonsound.com
w soundonsound.com Publisher: Ian Gilby.

Southern Cross 14-15 Child's Pl, London SW5 9RX
t 020 7373 3377 or 020 7341 6642 **f** 020 7341 6630
e sxeditor@sxmagazine.com **w** tntmagazine.com
Ed: Gordon Glyn-Jones.

The Stage Stage House, 47 Bermondsey St, London SE1 3XT
t 020 7403 1818 **f** 020 7357 9287 **e** editor@thestage.co.uk
w thestage.co.uk.

Stage, Screen & Radio 373 -377 Clapham Rd, London SW9 9BT **t** 020 7346 0900 **f** 020 7346 0901 **e** info@bectu.org.uk **w** bectu.org.uk Ed: Janice Turner.

The Strad Newsquest Specialist Media, 30 Cannon St, London EC4M 6YJ **t** 020 7618 3456 **f** 020 7618 3483 **e** atodes@orpheuspublications.com **w** thestrad.com Ed: Ariane Todes.

Straight No Chaser 17D Ellingfort Rd, London E8 3PA **t** 020 8533 9999 **f** 020 8985 6447 or 020 8525 6647 **e** info@straightnochaser.co.uk **w** straightnochaser.co.uk Ed: Paul Bradshaw.

Sugar 64 North Row, London W1K 7LL **t** 020 7150 7972 **f** 020 7150 7572 **e** lysannecurrie@hf-uk.com **w** hf-uk.com Editorial Dir: Lysanne Currie.

The Sun News International, 1 Virginia St, London E1 9BD **t** 020 7782 4000 **f** 020 7782 4063 **e** talkback@the-sun.co.uk **w** thesun.co.uk.

Sunday Mirror 1 Canada Sq, London E14 5AD **t** 020 7510 3000 **f** 020 7293 3405 **e** Via website **w** sundaymirror.co.uk.

Sunday People 1 Canada Sq, London E14 5AP **t** 020 7293 3000 **f** 020 7293 3810 **e** feedback@mirror.co.uk **w** people.co.uk.

Sunday Telegraph 1 Canada Sq, London E14 5DT **t** 020 7538 5000 **e** firstname.lastname@telegraph.co.uk **w** telegraph.co.uk.

Sunday Times News International, 1 Pennington St, London E1 9XW **t** 020 7782 5000 **f** 020 7782 5658 **e** artsed@thetimes.co.uk **w** timesonline.co.uk.

Tempo (A Quarterly Review of Modern Music) PO Box 171, Herne Bay CT6 6WD **t** 020 7291 7224 **e** tempo2@boosey.com **w** temporeview.com Ed: Calum MacDonald.

Tense Magazine Top Floor, 24 Porden Rd, London SW2 5RT **t** 020 7642 2030 **f** 020 7274 3543 **e** editor@tensemagazine.com **w** tensemagazine.com Ed: Toussaint Davy.

Time Out Universal House, 251 Tottenham Court Rd, London W1T 7AB **t** 020 7813 3000 **f** 020 7813 6158 **e** music@timeout.com **w** timeout.com/london Music Ed: Chris Salmon.

The Times Metro News International, 1 Pennington St, London E98 1TE **t** 020 7782 5000 **f** 020 7782 5525 **e** metro@the-times.co.uk Ed: Rupert Mellor.

The Times 1 Pennington St, London E98 1XY **t** 020 7782 5000 **e** firstname.lastname@thetimes.co.uk **w** timesonline.co.uk.

TNT Magazine 14-15 Childs Pl, London SW5 9RX **t** 020 7341 6685 **f** 0870 752 2717 **e** arts@tntmag.co.uk **w** tntmagazine.com Entertainment Editor: Pierre de Villiers.

Top Of The Pops Magazine Room A1136, 80 Wood Lane, London W12 0TT **t** 020 8433 3910 **f** 020 8433 2763 **e** olivia.mclearon@bbc.co.uk **w** bbc.co.uk/totp PA to Editor: Olivia McLearon.

Transparent Magazine 208 Uxbridge Rd, Southall, Middlesex UB1 3DX **t** 07950 792 422 **e** transparentmagazine@gmail.com **w** transparentmagazine.com Ed: Sahil Varma.

TV Hits 64 North Row, London W1K 7LL **t** 020 7150 7100 **f** 020 7150 7679 **e** tvhits@hf-uk.com **w** tvhits.co.uk Editorial Asst: Ami Neumann.

TV Times IPC Magazines, Kings Reach Tower, Stamford St, London SE1 9LS **t** 020 7261 7740 **e** firstname_lastname@ipcmedia.com **w** ipc.co.uk.

TVB EUROPE

TVBEurope

CMP Information Ltd., Ludgate House, 245 Blackfriars Road, London SE1 9UR **t** 020 7921 8307 **f** 020 7921 8302 **e** sgrice@cmpi.biz **w** tvbeurope.com Grp Sales Mgr: Steve Grice.

Uncut IPC Music Magazines, Kings Reach Tower, Stamford St, London SE1 9LS **t** 020 7261 6992 **f** 020 7261 5573 **e** firstname_lastname@ipcmedia.com **w** uncut.net.

Undercover Undercover Agents Ltd, Basement, 69 Kensington Gardens Sq, London W2 4DG **t** 020 7792 9392 **e** diagnostyx@hotmail.com Editor In Chief: Nat Illumine.

Venue Magazine 64-65 North Rd, St Andrews, Bristol BS6 5AQ **t** 0117 942 8491 **f** 0117 942 0369 **e** music@venue.co.uk **w** venue.co.uk Music Ed: Julian Owen.

Vice Magazine 77 Leonard St, London EC2A 4QS **t** 020 7613 5771 **f** 020 7729 6884 **e** info@viceuk.com **w** viceland.com Ed: Andy R. Capper.

The Voice 8/9th Fl's Bluestar House, 234-244 Stockwell Rd, London SW9 9UG **t** 020 7737 7377 **f** 020 7501 9465 **e** advertising@the-voice.co.uk **w** voice-online.co.uk GM: Simbo Nuga.

Volume10 Online Music Magazine 27 Trent Ave, Liverpool L31 9DE **t** 07779 793 555 **e** team@volume10.com **w** volume10.com Ed: Tony Mooney.

Web User IPC Media, Kings Reach Tower, Stamford St, London SE1 9LS **t** 020 7261 6597 **f** 020 7261 7878 **e** nicola_ponting@ipcmedia.com **w** web-user.co.uk Advertising and Sponsorship Manager: Nicola Ponting.

What Hi-Fi? Haymarket Magazines, 38-42 Hampton Rd, Teddington, Middlesex TW11 0JE **t** 020 8267 5000 **f** 020 8267 5019 **e** whathifi@haynet.com **w** whathifi.com Contact: Ed.

What's On - Birmingham & Central England Weaman St, Birmingham B4 6AT **t** 0121 234 5202 **f** 0121 234 5757 **e** jamie_perry@mrn.co.uk Product Mgr: Jamie Perry.

What's On In London 180-182 Pentonville Rd, London N1 9LB **t** 020 7278 4393 **f** 020 7837 5838 **e** whatson.advertising@virgin.net Ed: Michael Darvell.

The White Book Inside Communications, Bank House, 23 Warwick Rd, Coventry, W Midlands CV1 2EW **t** 024 7657 1171 **f** 024 7657 1172 **e** inside_events@mrn.co.uk **w** whitebook.co.uk Business Manager: Clair Whitecross.

The Wire 2nd Floor East, 88-94 Wentworth St, London E1 7SA **t** 020 7422 5010 **f** 020 7422 5011 **e** listings@thewire.co.uk **w** thewire.co.uk Ed-in-Chief/Publisher: Tony Herrington.

November 2006 | A Music Week Publication

PROMO
The First Stop for Music Video

VISIT
www.promonews.co.uk

TO FIND OUT WHY

Radio Stations by Region

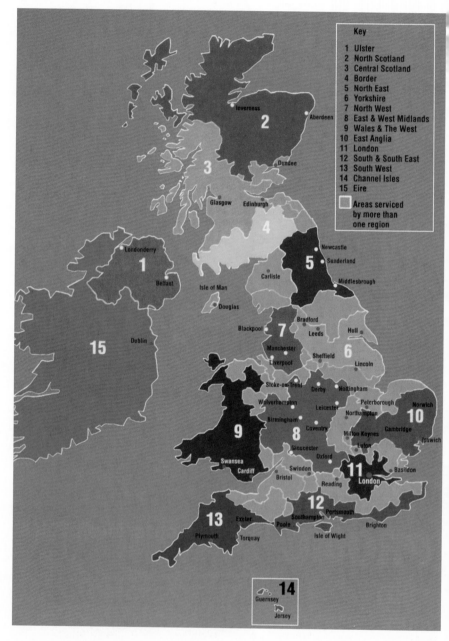

Key

1 Ulster
2 North Scotland
3 Central Scotland
4 Border
5 North East
6 Yorkshire
7 North West
8 East & West Midlands
9 Wales & The West
10 East Anglia
11 London
12 South & South East
13 South West
14 Channel Isles
15 Eire

Areas serviced by more than one region

Radio Stations by Region

Region 1
Belfast Citybeat
Cool FM
Downtown Radio/DTR
Energy FM
Manx Radio
Q101.2FM
Q102.9 FM
Q97.2FM
Seven FM
Six FM
BBC Radio Ulster

Region 2
Central FM
Isles FM 103
Lochbroom FM
Moray Firth Radio
BBC Nan Gaidheal
NECR
Nevis Radio
NorthSound One
NorthSound Two
Radio North Angus FM
River FM
BBC Radio Shetland
SIBC
Tay FM
Tay AM
Wave 102 FM
Waves Radio

Region 3
3C Digital Radio
Argyll FM
Classic VRN 1287
Clyde 1 FM
Clyde 2
107 The Edge
Forth One
Forth 2
Heartland FM
Kingdom FM
Oban FM
Real Radio FM
River FM
96.3 Rock Radio
Saga 105.2
Score Digital Ltd
BBC Scotland

South West Sound
West FM
Westsound AM
Xfm Scotland
Yourradio FM

Region 4
Radio Borders
CFM
BBC Radio Cumbria
Lakeland Radio

Region 5
Alpha 103.2
The Arrow
Century FM
CFM
BBC Radio Cleveland
BBC Radio Cumbria
Durham FM
Fresh Radio
Galaxy 105-106
Magic 1152
Magic 1170
Metro Radio
104.7 Minster FM
BBC Radio Newcastle
Rother FM
103.4 Sun FM
TFM
BBC Radio York
Yorkshire Coast Radio

Region 6
96.3 Radio Aire
BCB
Compass FM 96.4
Dearne FM
Durham FM
Fresh Radio
Galaxy 105
Hallam FM
Home 107.9
BBC Radio Humberside
BBC Radio Leeds
BBC Radio Lincolnshire
Lincs FM 102.2
Magic 1161
Magic 828
Magic AM
104.7 Minster FM
Real Radio (Yorkshire)
Rother FM
BBC Radio Sheffield
97.2 Stray FM

Sunrise FM
radio2XS
96.9 Viking FM
107.2 Wire FM
BBC Radio York
Yorkshire Coast Radio

Region 7
3FM
The Arrow
Asian Sound Radio
The Bay
107 The Bee
Buzz 97.1
Capital Gold - Manchester
105.4 Century FM
Radio City 96.7
Dee 106.3
Dune FM
Energy FM
Galaxy 102 FM
BBC GMR (BBC Greater
Manchester Radio)
Imagine FM
Juice 107.6 FM
Key 103
Lakeland Radio
BBC Radio Lancashire
Magic 1548
Magic 999
Manx Radio
BBC Radio Merseyside
Real Radio Wales
96.2 The Revolution
Ridings FM
97.4 Rock FM
106.7 The Rocket
BBC Radio Shropshire
106.9 Silk FM
Smooth FM
Sunshine 855
107.4 Tower FM
2BR (Two Boroughs Radio)
Wave 96.5
102.4 Wish FM
Wythenshawe FM 97.2
Xfm Manchester

Region 8
107.2 The Wyre
The Arrow
BCR FM
Beacon FM
BBC Radio Berkshire
96.4 FM BRMB
Capital Gold Birmingham
Carillon Radio
Centre FM

Classic Gold 1260
Classic Gold 1359
Classic Gold 1521
Classic Gold 1557
Classic Gold 774
Classic Gold GEM
Classic Gold WABC
Classic Hits 954/1530AM
Herefordshire & Worcester
Connect FM
BBC Coventry &
Warwickshire
BBC Radio Derby
Fosseway Radio
Fox FM
Galaxy 102.2
BBC Radio Gloucestershire
GWR FM
GWR FM.
Heart 106
100.7 Heart FM
BBC Hereford & Worcester
Kerrang! Radio
BBC Leicester
Leicester Sound
BBC Radio Lincolnshire
Lincs FM 102.2
Mansfield 103.2
Mercia FM
BBC Radio Northampton
Northants 96
BBC Radio Nottingham
Oak 107
BBC Radio Oxford
Oxford 107.9FM
Peak FM
Radio Pembrokeshire
RadioXL
102.8 Ram FM
107.1 Rugby FM
Rutland Radio
Sabras Radio
Saga 105.7FM
Saga 106.6 FM
97.5 Scarlet FM
102.4 Severn Sound FM
BBC Radio Shropshire
Signal 2
Signal 1
BBC Somerset Sound
Star 107.5
Star 107.9
BBC Radio Stoke
Sunshine 855
107.4 Telford FM
Touch 107.6
Touch 102
Touch 96.2
Trax FM
Trax FM.
96 Trent FM

BBC Radio Wiltshire
BBC WM
107.7 FM The Wolf
Wyvern FM

Region 9
The Arrow
107.9 Bath FM
106.3 Bridge FM
BBC Radio Bristol
Capital Gold - Red Dragon
Radio Carmarthenshire
Radio Ceredigion
Champion 103 FM
Classic Gold Marcher
Coast 96.3 FM
GTFM
GWR FM
Kiss 101
Radio Maldwyn
MFM 103.4
Radio Pembrokeshire
Red Dragon FM
97.5 Scarlet FM
BBC Radio Shropshire
Star 107.7
Sunshine 855
Swansea Sound 1170 MW
Valleys Radio
BBC Wales/Cymru
96.4FM The Wave

Region 10
103.4 The Beach
Radio Broadland
Cable Radio Milton Keynes
(CRMK) 89.8FM
BBC Radio Cambridgeshire
96.9 Chiltern FM
97.6 Chiltern FM
Classic Gold 1332 AM
Classic Gold 1557
Classic Gold 792/828
Classic Gold Amber
Classic Gold Amber (Suffolk)
Fen Radio 107.5
102.7 Hereward FM
HertBeat FM
FM 103 Horizon
Kiss 105-108
KLFM
Kmfm (Thanet)
Lite FM
MIX 96
BBC Radio Norfolk
North Norfolk Radio
BBC Radio Northampton
Northants 96
Pulse Classic Gold
The Pulse of West Yorkshire

Q103 FM
SGR Colchester
SGR-FM
Star 107
BBC Radio Suffolk
Ten-17
BBC Three Counties Radio

Region 11
2-Ten FM
BBC Radio Berkshire
Capital Radio London
Capital Gold Kent
Capital Gold Network
96.9 Chiltern FM
97.6 Chiltern FM
Choice FM London
Classic Gold 1431/1485
Classic Gold 1521
Classic Gold Breeze
Club Asia Radio London
County Sound 1566 AM
Delta FM 97.1
Dream 100
96.4 The Eagle
Easy Radio DAB
BBC Essex
Essex FM
Heart 106.2
Invicta FM
BBC Radio Kent
107.6 Kestrel FM
Kick FM
Kiss 100 FM
Kmfm (Ashford)
Kmfm (Canterbury, Whitstable
and Herne Bay)
Kmfm (Sheppway &
Whitecliffs Country)
Kmfm (Medway)
Kmfm (Thanet)
Kmfm (West Kent)
Kool AM
LBC 97.3
BBC London
London Greek Radio
London Turkish Radio (LTR)
Magic 105.4
Mercury 96.6
Mix 107
Premier Christian Radio
Radio Jackie
Reading 107FM
SGR Colchester
102.2 Smooth FM
BBC Southern Counties Radio
Spectrum Radio
Sunrise Radio
Ten-17
BBC Three Counties Radio
Time 106.6 FM

Time 107.5
Time 107.3
Time 106.8
Virgin Radio
XFM 104.9

Region 12
2CR FM
3TR FM
Arrow FM
BBC Radio Berkshire
Capital Gold Brighton
Capital Gold Hampshire
Capital Gold Kent
Classic Gold 1260
Classic Gold 828
Classic Gold 936/1161 AM
Dream 107.7FM
Fire 107.6
GWR FM.
Invicta FM
Isle Of Wight Radio
Juice 107.2
BBC Radio Kent
107.6 Kestrel FM
Kick FM
Kmfm (Sheppway &
Whitecliffs Country)
102.7 Mercury FM
Ocean FM
103.2 Power FM
107.4 The Quay
Reading 107FM
The Saint
BBC Radio Solent
BBC Somerset Sound
Southern FM
107.5 Sovereign Radio
Spire FM
Spirit FM
Vale FM
Wave 105.2 FM
BBC Radio Wiltshire
107.2 Win FM

Region 13
107.9 Bath FM
BCR FM
BBC Radio Bristol
Classic Gold 666 & 954
Classic Gold 1152
BBC Radio Cornwall
BBC Radio Devon
Gemini FM
Gemini FM (Torbay)
Kiss 101
Lantern FM
Orchard FM
Pirate FM
97FM Plymouth Sound

Quay FM
South Hams Radio
Star 107.7
Wessex FM

Region 14
Channel 103 FM
BBC Radio Guernsey
Island FM
BBC Radio Jersey

Region 15
Beat 102-103
Clare FM
Cork's 96FM
Dublin's 98 FM
Dublin's Country 106.8FM
East Coast FM
FM104
Galway Bay FM
Highland Radio
Radio Kerry
KFM Radio
Limerick's Live 95FM
LMFM Radio
Mid West Radio
Midlands 103
Raidio na Gaeltachta
Northern Sound Radio
Ocean FM (Ireland)
Q102
Red FM
RTE Radio 1
2FM
Shannonside FM
South East Radio
Spin 103.8
Tipp FM
Tipperary Mid-West
100-102 Today FM
Wired FM
WLR FM

Radio

2-Ten FM, FM:97/102.9/103.4 PO Box 2020, Reading,
Berks RG31 7FG **t** 0118 945 4400 **f** 0118 928 8539
e 2progs@creation.com **w** musicradio.com
Prog Controller: Tim Parker. Head of Music: Ollie Hayes. Sales
Centre Manager: Jo Lee. AC [11]

2CR FM, FM:102.3 5-7 Southcote Rd, Bournemouth, Dorset
BH1 3LR **t** 01202 234900 **f** 01202 234909
e firstname.lastname@gcapmedia.com **w** 2crfm.co.uk
Prog Ctrl: Lucinda Holman. Asst Prog Controller: Martyn Lee.
Sales Centre Manager: Jane Suttie. AC [12]

3C Digital Radio, AM:DAB/Freeview 3 South Ave,
Clydebank Business Pk, Glasgow GB1 2RX **t** 0141 565 2307
f 0141 565 2340 **e** pat.geary@3cdigital.com **w** 3cdigital.com
Station Manager: Pat Geary. Head of Sales: Tracey McNellan.
Contemporary Country [3]

3FM, FM:104-106 45 Victoria St, Douglas, Isle of Man
IM1 3RS **t** 01624 616333 **f** 01624 614333
e moremusic@three.fm **w** three.fm
MD/Programme Dir: Max Hailey. Sales Director: George
Ferguson. AC [7]

3TR FM, FM:107.5 Riverside Studios, Warminster, Wilts.
BA12 9HQ **t** 01985 211111 **f** 01985 211110
e enquiries@3trfm.com **w** 3trfm.com
Programme Controller: Jonathan Fido. Regional MD: John Baker.
Sales Mgr: Will Brougham. AC [12]

107.2 The Wyre, FM:107.2 Foley House, 123 Stourport
Rd, Kidderminster, Worcs. DY11 7BW **t** 01562 641072
f 01562 641073 **e** firstname@thewyre.com **w** thewyre.com
Programme Director: Pete Wagstaff. Head of Sales: Lisa Mahey.
Gold/CHR [8]

96.3 Radio Aire, FM:96.3 51 Burley Rd, Leeds, W Yorks
LS3 1LR **t** 0113 283 5500 **f** 0113 283 5501
e firstname.lastname@radioaire.com **w** radioaire.co.uk
Programme Director: Stuart Baldwin. MD: Alexis Thompson.
Head of Music: Kevin Paver. Commercial Director: Tracy
Eastwood. CHR [6]

Alpha 103.2, FM:103.2 11 Woodland Rd, Darlington, Co
Durham DL3 7BJ **t** 01325 255552 **f** 01325 255551
e studio@alpha1032.com **w** alpha1032.com
Prog Mgr/Head of Music: Emma Hignett. Station & Sales
Manager: Angela Bridgen. Gold [5]

Argyll FM, FM:106.5/107.1/107.7 27/29 Longrow,
Campbeltown, Argyll PA28 6ER **t** 01586 551800
f 01586 551888 **e** studio@argyllfm.co.uk **w** argyllfm.co.uk
Programme Director: Kenny Johnson. Chairman/MD/HoM: Colin
Middleton. Head of Sales: John Armour. Full range [3]

Arrow FM, FM:107.8 Priory Meadow Centre, Hastings, E
Sussex TN34 1PJ **t** 01424 461177 **f** 01424 422662
e firstname.lastname@arrowfm.co.uk **w** arrowfm.co.uk
Programme Controller: Mike Buxton. Station & Sales Manager:
Stuart Woodford. Head of Music: Andy Knight. AC [12]

The Arrow, FM:DAB 1 The Square, 111 Broad St,
Birmingham B15 1AS **t** 0121 695 0000 **f** 0121 695 0055
e feedback@thearrow.co.uk **w** thearrow.co.uk
Programme Director: Alan Carruthers. MD: Paul Fairburn. Head
of Music: Bev Hickman. Head of Sales: Anita Wright. Rock [7, 5,
8, 9]

Asian Sound Radio, AM:1377/963 Globe House,
Southall St, Manchester M3 1LG **t** 0161 288 1000
f 0161 288 9000 **e** info@asiansoundradio.co.uk
w asiansoundradio.co.uk MD/Prog Cont: Shujat Ali. Sales Dir:
Shafat Ali. Asian Film/Asian Dance [7]

107.9 Bath FM, FM:107.9 Station House, Ashley Ave,
Lower Weston, Bath BA1 3DS **t** 01225 471571 **f** 01225 471681
e studio@bath.fm **w** bath.fm Prog Controller: Steve Collins.
Station Manager: Jo Wood. Head of Sales: Richard Thorogood.
AC [13, 9]

The Bay, FM:96.9/102.3/103.2 PO Box 969, St Georges
Quay, Lancaster LA1 3LD **t** 01524 848747 **f** 01524 845969
e firstname.lastname@cnradio.co.uk **w** thebay.fm
HoM: Tony Cookson. Acting Station Director: Rupert Allison.
Programme Controller: Dave Collins. Head of Sales: Cheri Ward.
AC [7]

BBC Asian Network, AM:Various/DAB 9 St Nicholas
Pl, Leicester LE1 5YP **t** 020 8225 6373 **f** 020 857 64196
e Asian.network@bbc.co.uk **w** bbc.co.uk/asiannetwork
Controller: Bob Shennan. Head of Asian Network: Vijay Sharma.
Asian

BCB, FM:96.7 11 Rawson Rd, Bradford, W Yorks BD1 3SH
t 01274 771677 **f** 01274 771680 **e** info@bcb.yorks.com
w bcb.yorks.com MD: Mary Dowson. Broadcast Mgr/Hd of Sales:
Jonathan Pinfield. Head of Music: John Gill. World/Rock/Blues [6]

BCR FM, AM:1 FM:107.4 PO Box 1074, Bridgwater,
Somerset TA6 4WE **t** 01278 727701 **f** 01278 727705
e info@bcrfm.co.uk **w** bcrfm.co.uk
MD/Head of Sales: Steve Bulley. Programming Director/Head of
Music: Dave Englefield. AC/MOR [8, 13]

103.4 The Beach, FM:103.4 PO Box 103.4, Lowestoft,
Suffolk NR32 2TL **t** 0845 345 1035 **f** 0845 345 1036
e info@thebeach.co.uk **w** thebeach.co.uk Prog Contr: Paul Carter.
MD: David Blake. Head of Sales: Syreeta Brighton. AC [10]

Beacon FM, FM:97.2/103.1 267 Tettenhall Rd,
Wolverhampton, W Midlands WV6 0DE **t** 01902 461200
f 01902 461299 **e** firstname.lastname@gcapmedia.com
w beaconradio.co.uk Station Mgr/Prog Cont: Darrell Woodman.
Head of Music: Lisa Gibbons. Head of Sales: Matt Ramsbottom.
CHR [8]

Beat 102-103, FM:102/102.2/102.4/102.8/103.1
The Broadcast Centre, Ardkeen, Dunmore Rd, Waterford, Ireland
t +353 51 849102 **f** +353 51 849103
e reception@beat102103.com **w** beat102103.com
Station Mgr/Prog Dir: Kieran McGeary. Head of Music: Leigh
Doyle. Head of Sales: Karen Cheevers. CHR [15]

107 The Bee, FM:107 8 Dalton Court, Darwen, Lancs
BB3 0DG **t** 01254 778000 **f** 01254 778001
e firstname.lastname@thebee.co.uk **w** thebee.co.uk
Station Manager: Simon Brierley. Head of Music: Martin
Greenwood. Sales Manager: Paul Walsh. AC [7]

Media: Radio

BBC Radio Berkshire, FM:104.1/104.4/95.4/94.6
PO Box 104.4, Reading, Berks RG4 8FH **t** 0118 946 4200
f 0118 946 4555 **e** radio.berkshire@bbc.co.uk
w bbc.co.uk/radioberkshire Managing Editor: Marianne Bell.
Programming Director: Andrew Peach. News [8, 11, 12]

Radio Borders, FM:96.8/97.5/103.1/103.4
Tweedside Pk, Galashiels, Selkirkshire TD1 3TD **t** 01896 759444
f 0845 345 7080 **e** firstname.lastname@radioborders.com
w radioborders.com Station Mgr: Stuart McCulloch. Head of
Music: Keith Clarkson. Head of Sales: Lynsey Graham. AC [4]

106.3 Bridge FM, FM:106.3 PO Box 1063, Bridgend, Mid
Glamorgan CF31 1ED **t** 0845 890 4000 **f** 0845 890 5000
e info@bridge.fm **w** bridge.fm Station Manager: Gillian Boobier.
Prog Cont/Hd of Music: Lee Thomas. AC [9]

Bright 106.4, FM:106.4 Market Place Shopping Centre,
Burgess Hill, W Sussex RH15 9NP **t** 01444 248127
f 01444 248553 **e** reception@bright1064.com
w bright1064.com Prog Dir/Head of Music: Andrew Dancey. MD:
Allan Moulds. Head of Sales: Mak Norman. AC

BBC Radio Bristol, AM:1548 FM:94.9/95.5 PO Box
194, Bristol BS99 7QT **t** 0117 974 1111 **f** 0117 923 8323
e radio.bristol@bbc.co.uk **w** bbc.co.uk/radiobristol
Managing Editor: Tim Burton. Head of Music: Pat Wilson. MOR
[13, 9]

British Forces Broadcasting Service Chalfont Grove,
Narcot Lane, Chalfont St Peter, Gerrards Cross, Bucks SL9 8TN
t 01494 878354 **f** 01494 870552 **e** admin.officer@bfbs.com
w ssvc.com GM: Kal Sutherland. Controller, BFBS Radio: Charles
Foster. Head of Music: Joanne Bell. Programme Planning Admin:
Natalie Peck. CHR

96.4 FM BRMB, FM:96.4 9 Brindley Pl, 4 Oozells Sq,
Birmingham, W Midlands B1 2DJ **t** 0121 245 5000
f 0121 245 5900 **e** info@brmb.co.uk **w** brmb.co.uk
Programme Controller: Adam Bridge. Music Scheduler: Nick
Ralphs. Head of Sales: Jane Davies. CHR [8]

Radio Broadland, FM:102.4 St George's Plain, 47-49
Colegate, Norwich, Norfolk NR3 1DB **t** 01603 630621
f 01603 666252 **e** firstname.lastname@gcapmedia.com
w radiobroadland.co.uk Prog Controller: Steve Martin. Sales
Centre Mgr: Roz Walker. AC [10]

Buzz 97.1, FM:97.1 The Studios, Mold Rd, Wrexham
LL11 4AF **t** 0151 650 1700 **f** 0151 650 8109
e firstname.lastname@musicradio.com **w** wirralsbuzz.co.uk
Programme Controller: Lisa Marrey. MD: Sarah Smithard. Grp
PD: Dirk Anthony. Head of Music: Andy Parry. Head of Sales:
Clive Douthwaite. Chart/Gold [7]

**Cable Radio Milton Keynes (CRMK) 89.8FM,
FM:89.8** 14 Vincent Ave, Crownhill, Milton Keynes, Bucks
MK8 0AB **t** 01908 265 266 **f** 01908 564 893
e phil@crmk.co.uk **w** crmk.co.uk
Programme Controller: Phil Walsh. Station Manager: Dave Watts.
Events Diary: Ron Murch. MD/Head of Sales: Mike Barry. AC [10]

**BBC Radio Cambridgeshire, AM:1026/1449
FM:96/95.7** PO Box 96, 104 Hills Rd, Cambridge CB2 1LD
t 01223 259696 **f** 01223 460832 **e** Cambs@bbc.co.uk
w bbc.co.uk/radiocambridgeshire Music Librarian: Sophie Rowell.
Managing Editor: Jason Horton. MOR [10]

Capital Radio London, FM:95.8 30 Leicester Sq, London
WC2H 7LA **t** 020 7766 6000 **f** 020 7766 6047
e firstname.lastname@gcapmedia.com **w** capitalfm.com
Deputy Programme Controller: Sheena Mason. Programme Dir:
Scott Muller. Commercial Dir: Duncan George. Head of Music:
Rachel Seagrave. CHR [11]

Capital Gold - Red Dragon, AM:1305/1359 Radio
House, Atlantic Wharf, Cardiff, South Glamorgan CF10 4DJ
t 029 2066 2066 **f** 029 2066 2067 **e** info@capitalgold.com
w capitalgold.co.uk Network Station Dir: Andy Turner. Head of
Music: Graham Caplin. Sales Director: Duncan George. Gold [9]

Capital Gold - Manchester, AM:1458 4th Floor, Quay
West, Trafford Wharf Rd, Trafford Pk, Manchester M17 1FL
t 0161 607 0420 **f** 0161 607 0443 **e** info@capitalgold.co.uk
w capitalgold.com Network Station Dir: Andy Turner. Head of
Music: Graham Caplin. Sales Director: Duncan George. Gold [7]

Capital Gold Birmingham, AM:1152 BRMB Radio
Group, Nine Brindley Pl, 4 Oozells Sq, Birmingham B1 2DJ
t 0121 245 5000 **f** 0121 245 5245 **e** info@capitalgold.co.uk
w capitalgold.com Network Station Dir: Andy Turner. Head of
Music: Graham Caplin. Sales Director: Duncan George. Gold [8]

Capital Gold Brighton, AM:945/1323 Radio House, PO
Box 2000, Brighton, E Sussex BN41 2SS **t** 01273 430111
f 01273 430098 **e** info@capitalgold.co.uk **w** capitalgold.com
Network Station Dir: Andy Turner. Head of Music: Graham Caplin.
Sales Director: Duncan George. Gold [12]

Capital Gold Hampshire, AM:1170/1557 Radio House,
Whittle Ave, Segensworth West, Fareham, Hants PO15 5SH
t 01489 589911 **f** 01489 587754 **e** info@capitalgold.com
w capitalgold.com Network Station Dir: Andy Turner. Head of
Music: Graham Caplin. Sales Director: Duncan George. Gold [12]

Capital Gold Kent, AM:1242/603 Radio House, John
Wilson Business Pk, Whitstable, Kent CT5 3QX **t** 01227 772004
f 01227 771560 **e** info@capitalgold.com **w** capitalgold.com
Network Station Dir: Andy Turner. Head of Music: Graham Caplin.
Sales Director: Duncan George. Gold [11, 12]

Capital Gold Network, AM:1548 30 Leicester Sq,
London WC2H 7LA **t** 020 7766 6000 **f** 020 7766 6393
e andy.turner@capitalgold.com **w** capitalgold.com
Network Station Dir: Andy Turner. Head of Music: Graham Caplin.
Sales Director: Duncan George. Gold [11]

Carillon Radio, AM:1386 AM Loughborough General
Hospital, Epinal Way, Loughborough, Leics LE11 5JY
t 01509 564 433 **f** 0870 751 8989 **e** carillonradio@aol.com
Station Sec/Engineer: John Sketchley. Station Manager: Colin
Pytel. [8]

Radio Carmarthenshire, FM:97.1/97.5 14 Old School
Estate, Narbeth SA67 7DU **t** 01834 869384 **f** 01834 861524
e keri@radiocarmarthenshire.com **w** radiocarmarthenshire.com
MD/Prog Dir: Keri Jones. Commercial Director: Esther Morton.
AC [9]

Central FM, FM:103.1 201-203 High St, Falkirk FK1 1DU
t 01324 611164 **f** 01324 611168 **e** mail@centralfm.co.uk
w centralfm.co.uk MD/Prog Dir: Tom Bell. Head of Music: Gavin
Orr. Head of Sales: Anne Marie Miller. AC/GOLD [2]

Centre FM, FM:101.6/102.4 5-6 Aldergate, Tamworth, Staffs B79 7DJ **t** 01827 318000 **f** 01827 318002 **e** firstname.lastname@cnradio.co.uk **w** centrefm.com Programme Controller: Dave James. Station Dir/Hd of Sales: Greg Parker. AC [8]

105.4 Century FM, FM:105.4 Laser House, Waterfront Quay, Salford Quays, Manchester M50 3XW **t** 0161 400 0105 **f** 0161 400 0173 **e** firstname.lastname@gcapmedia.com **w** 1054centuryfm.com Programme Director: Ande Macpherson. MD: Nick Davidson. Head of Music: Mike Walsh. Head of Sales (Local): Allison Forshaw. AC [7]

Century FM, FM:100 - 102 Century House, PO Box 100, Church St, Gateshead, Tyne and Wear NE8 2YY **t** 0191 477 6666 **f** 0191 477 5660 **e** firstname.lastname@gcapmedia.com **w** centuryfm.co.uk Programme Controller: Owen Ryan. Head of Sales: Debbie Bowman. MOR [5]

Radio Ceredigion, FM:103.3/96.6/97.4 Yr Hen Ysgol Gymraeg, Ffordd Alexandra, Aberystwyth, Ceredigion SY23 1LF **t** 01970 627999 **f** 01970 627206 **e** admin@ceredigionfm.co.uk **w** ceredigionradio.co.uk Welsh Prog Cont: Myfanwy Jones. Programme Manager: Eifion Williams. Head of Music: Dylan Williams. Head of Sales: June Forbes. CHR/Welsh/Country/Folk [9]

CFM, FM:96.4/102.2/102.5/103.4 PO Box 964, Carlisle, Cumbria CA1 3NG **t** 01228 818964 **f** 01228 819444 **e** studios@cfmradio.com **w** cfmradio.com Prog Controller: David Bain. MD: Cathy Kirk. Head of Music: Pete Moss. Head of Sales: Julie Currie. AC [5, 4]

Champion 103 FM, FM:103 Unit D1, Llys Y Dderwen, Parc Menai, Bangor, Gwynedd LL57 4BN **t** 01248 671888 **f** 01248 673409 **e** firstname.lastname@creation.com **w** champion103.com Programme Controller: Steve Simms. MD: Sarah Smithard. Head of Sales: Clive Douthwaite. MOR/Welsh [9]

Channel 103 FM, FM:103.7 6 Tunnell St, St Helier, Jersey, Channel Islands JE2 4LU **t** 01534 888103 **f** 01534 887799 **e** firstname@channel103.com **w** channel103.com Programme Controller: Spencer Davies. MD: Linda Burnam. Sales Director: Colin North. AC [14]

96.9 Chiltern FM, FM:96.9 Broadcast Centre, 55 Goldington Rd, Bedford MK40 3LT **t** 01234 272400 **f** 01234 325137 **e** firstname.lastname@gcapmedia.com **w** Chilternfm.com Prog Cont: Stuart Davies. Head of Music: Jono Woodward. Head of Sales: Kris Lingwood. AC [11, 10]

97.6 Chiltern FM, FM:97.6 Chiltern Rd, Dunstable, Beds LU6 1HQ **t** 01582 676200 **f** 01582 676241 **e** firstname.surname@musicradio.com **w** musicradio.com Programme Controller: Stuart Davies. Head of Music: Darren Lee. Head of Sales: Francis Flanagan. AC [11, 10]

Choice FM London, FM:96.9/107.1 30 Leicester Sq, London WC2H 7LA **t** 020 7766 6000 **f** 020 7766 6001 **e** info@choicefm.com **w** choicefm.com Head of Sales: Karina Christiansen. Managing Ed/Programming Controller: Ivor Etienne. Head of Music:Kirk Anthony. Dance/Reggae/Soul/R&B [11]

Radio City 96.7, FM:96.7 St. John's Beacon, 1 Houghton St, Liverpool, Merseyside L1 1RL **t** 0151 472 6800 **f** 0151 472 6821 **e** firstname.lastname@radiocity.co.uk **w** radiocity.co.uk MD: Iain McKenna. Programming Director: Richard Maddock. Sales Director: Mike Sarath. CHR [7]

Belfast Citybeat, FM:96.7 Lamont Buildings, 46, Stranmillis Embankment, Belfast, Co Antrim BT9 5FN **t** 028 9020 5967 **f** 028 9020 0023 **e** firstname.lastname@cnradio.co.uk **w** citybeat967.co.uk Programme Controller: Bill Young. Head of Music: Stuart Robinson. Sales Dir: Dorothy Nixon. MOR [1]

Clare FM, FM:96.4/95.2/95.5/95.9 Abbeyfield Centre, Francis St, Ennis, Co. Clare, Ireland **t** +353 65 682 8888 **f** +353 65 682 9392 **e** info@clarefm.ie **w** clarefm.ie HoM: Andrew Looby. MD: Liam O'Shea. Programme Controller: Colum McGrath. Head of Sales: Susan Murphy. MOR [15]

Classic FM, FM:100.0/102.0 30 Leicester Sq, London WC2H 7LA **t** 020 7343 9000 **f** 020 7344 2783 **e** firstname.lastname@classicfm.com **w** classicfm.com Station Manager: Darren Henley. National Sales Manager: Simon Daglish. Music Manager: Joanna Wilson. Classical

Classic Gold 1260, AM:1260 PO Box 2020, One Passage St, Bristol BS99 7SN **t** 0117 984 3200 **f** 0117 984 3202 **e** admin@classicgolddigital.com **w** classicgolddigital.com Head of Programming: Bill Overton. MD: John Baish. Head of Sponsorship & Sales: Laurette Holmes. AC [8, 12]

Classic Gold 1332 AM, AM:1332 PO Box 225, Queensgate Centre, Peterborough, Cambs PE1 1XJ **t** 01733 460460 **f** 01733 281445 **e** admin@classicgolddigital.com **w** classicgolddigital.com Programme Controller: Bill Overton. MD: John Baish. Head of Sponsorship & Sales: Laurette Holmes. Gold [10]

Classic Gold 1359, AM:1359 Hertford Pl, Coventry, W Midlands CV1 3TT **t** 024 7686 8200 **f** 024 7686 8202 **e** admin@classicgolddigital.com **w** classicgolddigital.com Head of Programmes: Bill Overton. Head of Sponsorship & Sales: Laurette Holmes. Gold [8]

Classic Gold 1431/1485, AM:1431/1485 PO Box 2020, Reading, Berks RG31 7FG **t** 0118 945 4400 **f** 0118 928 8483 **e** admin@classicgolddigital.com **w** classicgolddigital.com Head of Programmes: Bill Overton. Head of Sponsorship & Sales: Laurette Holmes. Gold [11]

Classic Gold 1521, AM:1521 The Stanley Centre, Kelvin Way, Crawley, W Sussex RH10 2SE **t** 01293 519161 **f** 01293 565663 **e** admin@classicgolddigital.com **w** classicgolddigital.com Head of Programmes: Bill Overton. Head of Sponsorship & Sales: Laurette Holmes. Gold [8, 11]

Classic Gold 1557, AM:1557 19-21 St Edmunds Rd, Northampton, Northants. NN1 5DY **t** 01604 795600 **f** 01604 795601 **e** admin@classicgolddigital.com **w** classicgolddigital.com Head of Programmes: Bill Overton. Head of Sponsorship & Sales: Laurette Holmes. Gold [8, 10]

Classic Gold 666 & 954, AM:666/954 Hawthorn House, Exeter Business Pk, Exeter, Devon EX1 3QS **t** 01392 444444 **f** 01392 354202 **e** admin@classicgolddigital.com **w** classicgolddigital.com Head of Programmes: Bill Overton. Head of Sponsorship & Sales: Laurette Holmes. Gold [13]

Classic Gold 774, AM:774 Bridge Studios, Eastgate Centre, Gloucester GL1 1SS **t** 01452 313200 **f** 01452 529446 **e** admin@classicgolddigital.com **w** classicgolddigital.com Head of Programmes: Bill Overton. Head of Sponsorship & Sales: Laurette Holmes. Gold [8]

Classic Gold 792/828, AM:792/828 Broadcast Centre, Chiltern Rd, Dunstable, Beds LU6 1HQ **t** 01582 676200 **f** 01582 676251 **e** admin@classicgolddigital.com **w** classicgolddigital.com Head of Programmes: Bill Overton. Head of Sponsorship & Sales: Laurette Holmes. Gold [10]

Classic Gold 828, AM:828 5-7 Southcote Rd, Bournemouth, Dorset BH1 3LR **t** 01202 234900 **f** 01202 234909 **e** admin@classicgolddigital.com **w** classicgolddigital.com Head of Programmes: Bill Overton. Head of Sponsorship & Sales: Laurette Holmes. Gold [12]

Classic Gold 936/1161 AM, AM:936/1161 PO Box 2000, Swindon, Wilts SN4 7EX **t** 01793 842600 **f** 01793 842602 **e** admin@classicgolddigital.com **w** classicgolddigital.com Head of Programmes: Bill Overton. Head of Sponsorship & Sales: Laurette Holmes. Gold/Chart [12]

Classic Gold Amber, AM:1152 St George's Plain, 47-49 Colegate, Norwich, Norfolk NR3 1DB **t** 01603 666000 **f** 01603 671167 **e** admin@classicgolddigital.com **w** classicgolddigital.com Head of Programmes: Bill Overton. Head of Sponsorship & Sales: Laurette Holmes. Gold [10]

Classic Gold Amber (Suffolk), AM:1170/1251 Alpha Business Pk, 6-12 Whitehouse Rd, Ipswich, Suffolk IP1 5LT **t** 01473 744544 **f** 01473 741200 **e** admin@classicgolddigital.com **w** classicgolddigital.com Head of Programmes: Bill Overton. Head of Sponsorship & Sales: Laurette Holmes. Gold [10]

Classic Gold Breeze, AM:1359/1431 Radio House, 31 Glebe Rd, Chelmsford, Essex CM1 1QG **t** 01245 524500 **f** 01245 524509 **e** admin@classicgolddigital.com **w** classicgolddigital.com Head of Programmes: Bill Overton. Head of Sponsorship & Sales: Laurette Holmes. Gold [11]

Classic Gold 1152, AM:1152 Earls Acre, Alma Rd, Plymouth, Devon PL3 4HX **t** 01752 227272 **f** 01752 670730 **e** admin@classicgolddigital.com **w** classicgolddigital.com Head of Programmes: Bill Overton. Head of Sponsorship & Sales: Laurette Holmes. Gold [13]

Classic Gold GEM, AM:945/999 29-31 Castle Gate, Nottingham NG1 7AP **t** 0115 952 7000 **f** 0115 912 9333 **e** admin@classicgolddigital.com **w** classicgolddigital.com Head of Programmes: Bill Overton. Head of Sponsorship & Sales: Laurette Holmes. Gold [8]

Classic Gold Marcher, AM:1260 The Studios, Mold Rd, Gwersyllt, Wrexham, Clwyd LL11 4AF **t** 01978 571818 **f** 01978 722209 **e** admin@classicgolddigital.com **w** classicgolddigital.com Head of Programmes: Bill Overton. Head of Sponsorship & Sales: Laurette Holmes. Gold [9]

Classic Gold WABC, AM:990/1017 267 Tettenhall Rd, Wolverhampton, W Midlands WV6 0DE **t** 01902 461300 **f** 01902 461299 **e** cgdl@classicgolddigital.com **w** classicgolddigital.com Head of Programmes: Bill Overton. Head of Sponsorship & Sales: Laurette Holmes. Gold [8]

Classic Hits 954/1530AM Herefordshire & Worcester, AM:954/1530 Otherton Lane, Cotheridge, Worcester WR6 5ZE **t** 01905 740600 **f** 01905 740608 **e** studio@classichits.co.uk **w** classichits.co.uk MD: Muff Murfin. Gold/Sport [8]

Classic VRN 1287, AM:1287 PO Box 1287, Kirkcaldy KY2 5SX **t** 01592 654828 **e** info@vrn1287.com **w** vrn1287.com Group Programme Director: Colin Johnston. MD: Hal London. MOR [3]

BBC Radio Cleveland, FM:95.0/95.8 PO Box 95FM, Broadcasting House, Newport Rd, Middlesborough, Cleveland TS1 5DG **t** 01642 225211 **f** 01642 211356 **e** cleveland.studios@bbc.co.uk **w** bbc.co.uk/tees Head of Programmes: Will Banks. Managing Editor: Peter Cook. Gold [5]

Club Asia Radio London, AM:963/972 Asia House, 227-247 Gascoigne Rd, Barking, Essex IG8 8LX **t** 020 8594 6662 **f** 020 8594 3523 **e** info@clubasiaonline.com **w** clubasiaonline.com Programme Dir: Sumerah Ahmad. Asian/Chart [11]

Clyde 1 FM, FM:102.5/97.0/103.3 Clydebank Business Pk, Clydebank, Glasgow G81 2RX **t** 0141 565 2200 **f** 0141 565 2301 **e** Info@RadioClyde.com **w** RadioClyde.com Head of Clyde 1: Paul Saunders. MD: Paul Cooney. Commercial Director: Tracey McNellan. CHR [3]

Clyde 2, AM:1152 Clydebank Business Pk, Clydebank, Glasgow G81 2RX **t** 0141 565 2200 **f** 0141 565 2301 **e** Info@RadioClyde.com **w** RadioClyde.com Acting Head of Clyde 2: Paul Saunders. MD: Paul Cooney. Sales Director: Tracey McNellan. AOR/MOR [3]

Coast 96.3 FM, FM:96.3 PO Box 963, Bangor LL57 4ZR **t** 01248 673272 **f** 01248 673409 **e** firstname.lastname@creation.com **w** coast963.com Programme Controller: Steve Simms. MD: Sarah Smithard. Head of Sales: Clive Douthwaite. AC/CHR [9]

Compass FM 96.4 FM, FM:96.4 26A Wellowgate, Grimsby, NE Lincs DN32 0RA **t** 01472 346666 **f** 01472 508811 **e** enquiries@compassfm.co.uk **w** compassfm.co.uk Programme Mgr: Andy Marsh. Director of Programming: Keith Briggs. Sales Dir: Jeff Harwood. Gold/MOR [6]

Connect FM, FM:97.2/107.4 Unit 1, Robinson Close, Telford Way, Kettering, Northants. NN16 8PU **t** 01536 412413 **f** 01536 517390 **e** info@connectfm.com **w** connectfm.com Programme Manager: Danny Gibson. Station Manager/Hd of Sales: Martyn Parr. AC [1]

Cool FM, FM:97.4 PO Box 974, Belfast, Co Antrim BT1 1RT **t** 028 9181 7181 **f** 028 9181 4974 **e** music@coolfm.co.uk **w** coolfm.co.uk Prog Dir/Head of Music: John Paul Ballantine. MD: David Sloan. Head of Sales: Rodney Bell. CHR/AC [1]

Core, FM:(DAB Digital Radio) PO Box 2269, London W1A 5UQ **t** 020 7911 7300 **f** 020 7911 7369 **e** fresh@corefreshhits.com **w** corefreshhits.com MD: Mark Lee. Programme Controller: Bern Leckie. Head of Sales: Steve Cray. Chart

Cork's 96FM, FM:96.4/103/103.7 Wellington Rd, Patrick's Pl, Cork, Ireland **t** +353 21 4551596 **f** +353 21 4551500 **e** info@96fm.ie **w** 96fm.ie Prog Director: Neil Prendeville. Station Manager: Ronan MacManamy. Head of Music: Steve Hayes. Commercial Director: Sean Barry. Chart/Gold [15]

BBC Radio Cornwall, AM:657/630 FM:95.2/96/103.9 Phoenix Wharf, Truro, Cornwall TR1 1UA **t** 01872 275421 **f** 01872 240679 **e** radio.cornwall@bbc.co.uk **w** bbc.co.uk/radiocornwall Music Librarian: Kath Peters. Managing Editor: Pauline Causey. AC [13]

County Sound 1566 AM, AM:1566 Dolphin House, North St, Guildford, Surrey GU1 4AA **t** 01483 300964 **f** 01483 531612 **e** onair@countysound.co.uk **w** countysound.co.uk Prog Mgr: Dave Johns. PD: Peter Gordon. MD: Val Handley. Head of Music: Mark Chivers. Head of Sales: Mike Craddock. AC/MOR [11]

BBC Coventry & Warwickshire, FM:94.8/103.7/104.0 Holt Court, 1 Greyfriars Rd, Coventry, W Midlands CV1 2WR **t** 024 7655 1000 **f** 024 7655 2000 **e** coventry@bbc.co.uk **w** bbc.co.uk/coventrywarwickshire Assistant Editor: Duncan Jones. Station Manager: David Clargo. AC [8]

CTR 105.6fm, FM:105.6 6-8 Mill St, Maidstone, Kent ME15 6XH **t** 01622 662500 **f** 01622 662501 **e** firstname@ctrfm.com **w** ctrfm.com Programme Manager: Joe Dyer. MD & Sales Dir: Jon Maxfield. Gold

Cuillin FM, FM:106.2 Stormhill Rd, Portree, Isle of Skye IV51 9DT **t** 01478 611 234 **e** info@cuillinfm.co.uk **w** cuillinfm.co.uk HoM: Nick Wakeham. Programme Director: Jim Campbell. Head of Sales: Barbara MacKenzie. Varied

BBC Radio Cumbria, AM:756/837/1458 FM:95.6/96.1/95.2/104.2/104.1 Annetwell St, Carlisle, Cumbria CA3 8BB **t** 01228 592444 **f** 01228 511195 **e** radio.cumbria@bbc.co.uk **w** bbc.co.uk/radiocumbria SBJ/Programmes/Music: Liz Rhodes. Managing Editor: Nigel Dyson. MOR [5, 4]

Dearne FM, FM:97.1/102 Unit 7, Network Centre, Zenith Pk, Whaley Rd, Barnsley S75 1HT **t** 01226 321733 **f** 01226 321755 **e** enquiries@dearnefm.co.uk **w** dearnefm.co.uk Prog Mgr: Matt Jones. Grp Programme Dir: Keith Briggs. Sales Mgr: Sarah Hardy. CHR [6]

Dee 106.3, FM:106.3 2 Chantry Court, Chester CH1 4QN **t** 01244 391000 **f** 01244 391010 **e** studio@dee1063.com **w** dee1063.com Prog Controller: Chris Buckley. Station Dir: Chris Jefferies. Head of Sales: Amanda Hughes. AC [7]

Delta FM 97.1, FM:97.1/101.6/102 65 Weyhill, Haslemere, Surrey GU27 1HN **t** 01428 651971 **f** 01428 658971 **e** studio@deltaradio.co.uk **w** deltaradio.co.uk MD: David Wey. Head of Sales: Andy Wise. AC [11]

BBC Radio Derby, AM:1116 FM:104.5/95.3/96 PO Box 104.5, Derby DE1 3HL **t** 01332 361111 **f** 01332 290794 **e** radio.derby@bbc.co.uk **w** bbc.co.uk/derby Managing Editor: Simon Cornes. Head of Programmes: Anthony Isaacs. Head of Music: Bev Pickles. MOR/Pop [8]

BBC Radio Devon, AM:855/990/1458/801 FM:103.4/104.3/95.8/94.8/96.0 Broadcasting House, Seymour Rd, Plymouth, Devon PL3 5YQ **t** 01752 260323 **f** 01752 234564 **e** radio.devon@bbc.co.uk **w** bbc.co.uk/radiodevon Managing Editor: Robert Wallace. Head of Programmes: Ian Timms. Head of Music: Matt Woodley. MOR [13]

Digital One, FM:Digital 7 Swallow Pl, London W1B 2AG **t** 020 7288 4600 **f** 020 7288 4601 **e** info@digitalone.co.uk **w** ukdigitalradio.com Operations Manager: Dawn Banks. Chief Executive: Quentin Howard.

Downtown Radio/DTR, AM:1026 FM:96.4/96.6/97.1/102.3/102.4 Newtownards, Co Down BT23 4ES **t** 028 9181 5555 **f** 028 9181 5252 **e** firstname.lastname@downtown.co.uk **w** downtown.co.uk HoM: Eddie West. MD/Prog Director: David Sloan. Head of Sales: Rodney Bell. CHR/AC [1]

Dream 100, FM:100.2 Northgate House, St Peter's St, Colchester, Essex CO1 1HT **t** 01206 764466 **f** 01206 715102 **e** info@dream100.com **w** dream100.com Prog Cont/Head of Music: Chris Buckley. MD: Jamie Broadie. Head of Sales: Sarah Head. AC [11]

Dream 107.7FM, FM:107.7 Cater House, High St, Chelmsford, Essex CM1 1AL **t** 01245 259400 **f** 01245 259558 **e** reception@dream107.com **w** dream107.com Station Mgr: Jeff Thomas. Prog Mgr/HoM: Nick Hull. Head of Sales: Annabel Smail. AC [12]

Dublin's 98 FM, FM:98 The Malt House - South Block, Grand Canal Quay, Dublin 2, Ireland **t** +353 1 670 8970 **f** +353 1 670 8969 **e** online@98fm.ie **w** 98fm.ie Programme Director: John Taylor. Station Manager: Ciaran Davis. Head of Sales: Michael Brady. AC [15]

Dublin's Country 106.8FM, FM:106.8 Radio Centre, Killarney Rd, Bray, Co. Wicklow, Ireland **t** +353 1 272 4770 **f** +353 1 272 4753 **e** mail@dublins1068.com **w** perfectstation.com Prog Dir: Jim McCabe. CEO: Sean Ashmore. Head of Sales: Mary O'Sullivan. MOR [15]

Dune FM, FM:107.9 The Power Station, Victoria Way, Southport, Merseyside PR8 1RR **t** 01704 502500 **f** 01704 502540 **e** firstname.lastname@dunefm.co.uk **w** dunefm.co.uk Programme Controller: John Story. Station & Sales Manager: Rachel Barker. AC [7]

Durham FM, FM:102.8, 106.8 3 Framwell House, Framwelgate, Durham, Co Durham DH1 5SU **t** 0191 374 0777 **f** 0191 384 7880 **e** firstname.lastname@durhamfm.net **w** durhamfm.net Station Manager: Peter Grant. Head of Music: Craig Andrews. Sales Manager: Donna Feeney. AC [5, 6]

96.4 The Eagle, FM:96.4 Dolphin House, North St, Guildford, Surrey GU1 4AA **t** 01483 300964 **f** 01483 531612 **e** onair@964eagle.co.uk **w** 964eagle.co.uk Prog Director: Peter Gordon. MD: Val Handley. Head of Music: Mark Chivers. Head of Sales: Mike Craddock. AC [11]

East Coast FM, FM:94.9/96.2/102.9/104.4 Radio Centre, Bray South Business Pk, Bray, Co Wicklow, Ireland **t** +353 1 272 4700 **f** +353 1 272 4701 **e** mail@eastcoast.fm **w** eastcoast.fm Prog Dir/Head of Music: Joe Harrington. Station Manager: Ciara O'Connor. Head of Sales: Paul Bailey. AC [15]

Easy Radio DAB, AM:DAB Radio House, Merrick Rd, Southall UB2 4AU **t** 020 8574 6666 **e** info@easy1035.com **w** easy1035.com Programme Controller: Paul Owens. MD/Sales Dir: Neil Romain. Country [11]

107 The Edge, FM:107.5/107.9 Radio House, Rowantree Ave, Newhouse Industrial Estate, Newhouse, Lanarkshire ML1 5RX **t** 01698 733100 **f** 01698 733318 **e** office@107theedge.co.uk **w** 107theedge.co.uk Prog Cont: Darren Stenhouse. MD: Ian Sewell. AC [3]

Energy FM, FM:98.6/91.2/93.4/98.4/105.2 100 Market St, Douglas, Isle of Man IM1 2PH **t** 01624 611936 **f** 01624 664699 **e** mail@energyfm.net **w** energyfm.net HoM: Jason Quinn. MD: Juan Turner. Head of Sales: Jim Kershaw. CHR [1, 7]

BBC Essex, AM:729/1530/765 FM:103.5/95.3 198 New London Rd, Chelmsford, Essex CM2 9XB **t** 01245 616000 **f** 01245 616025 **e** essex@bbc.co.uk **w** bbc.co.uk/essex Managing Editor: Margaret Hyde. Head of Music: Steve Scruton. Programmes Editor: Tim Gillett. Gold [11]

Essex FM, FM:96.3/102.6 Radio House, 31 Glebe Rd, Chelmsford, Essex CM1 1QG **t** 01245 524 500 **f** 01245 524 509 **e** firstname.lastname@musicradio.com **w** musicradio.com Programming Controller: Chris Cotton. Head of Music: James Bassam. Head of Sales: Brent Coulson. AC/Chart [11]

Fen Radio 107.5, FM:107.5 5 Church Mews, Wisbech, Cambs PE13 1HL **t** 01945 467107 **f** 01945 467464 **e** firstname.lastname@fenradio.co.uk **w** fenradio.co.uk Prog Mgr: Richard Grant. Group Programme Director: Phil Angell. Sales Exec: Kathryn Vithray. Rock [10]

Fire 107.6, FM:107.6 Quadrant Studios, Old Christchurch Rd, Bournemouth, Dorset BH1 2AD **t** 01202 318100 **f** 01202 318110 **e** firstname.lastname@fire1076.com **w** fire1076.com Programme Controller: Paul Gerrard. Station & Sales Manager: tbc. Head of Music: Kelli Nelson. CHR/Rhythmic Contemporary [12]

BBC Radio 5 Live, AM:693/909 Room 2605, BBC TV Centre, London W12 7RJ **t** 020 8743 8000 **f** 020 8624 9588 **e** firstname.lastname@bbc.co.uk **w** bbc.co.uk/radio5live Controller: Bob Shennan. Head of News: Matt Morris. Head of Network Management: Michael Hill. News/Sport

FM104, FM:104.4 Hume House, Pembroke Rd, Balls Bridge, Dublin 4, Ireland **t** +353 1 500 6600 **f** +353 1 668 9401 **e** Firstname+initial@fm104.ie **w** fm104.ie Programme Director: Dave Kelly. Head of Music: Declan Pierce. Head of Sales: Margaret Nelson. CHR [15]

Forth One, FM:97.3/97.6/102.2 Forth House, Forth St, Edinburgh, Lothian EH1 3LE **t** 0131 556 9255 **f** 0131 558 3277 **e** info@forthone.com **w** forthone.com HoM: Sam Jackson. MD: Adam Findlay. Programme Controller: Luke McCullough. Head of Sales: Craig Lumsdaine. CHR [3]

Forth 2, AM:1548 Forth House, Forth St, Edinburgh, Lothian EH1 3LE **t** 0131 556 9255 **f** 0131 558 3277 **e** info@forth2.com **w** forth2.com HoM: Sam Jackson. MD: Adam Findlay. Programme Controller: Luke McCullough. Head of Sales: Craig Lumsdaine. AC/Gold [3]

Fosseway Radio, FM:107.9 1 Castle St, Hinckley, Leics LE10 1DA **t** 01455 614151 **f** 01455 616888 **e** studios@fossewayradio.co.uk **w** fossewayradio.co.uk Station Manager: Ian Ison. Group Programme Dir: Keith Briggs. Group Head of Music: Eddie Shaw. Sales Mgr: Sarah Washington. AC/Gold [8]

BBC Radio 4, FM:92.4/94.6 Broadcasting House, Portland Pl, London W1A 1AA **t** 020 7580 4468 **f** 020 7765 3421 **e** firstname.lastname@bbc.co.uk **w** bbc.co.uk/radio4 Controller: Mark Damazer.

Fox FM, FM:97.4/102.6 Brush House, Pony Rd, Cowley, Oxon OX4 2XR **t** 01865 871000 **f** 01865 871036 **e** reception@foxfm.co.uk **w** foxfm.co.uk Prog Controller: Sam Walker. Commercial Controller: Max Patey. AC [8]

Fresh Radio, AM:936/1413/1431 Firth Mill, Skipton, North Yorks BD23 2PT **t** 01756 799991 **f** 01756 799771 **e** info@freshradio.co.uk **w** freshradio.co.uk MD: Dave Parker. Programme Controller/Head of Music: Nick Bewes. Sales Mgr: Dave Parker. AC [5, 6]

Galaxy 102 FM, FM:102.0 5th Floor, The Triangle, Hanging Ditch, Manchester M4 3TR **t** 0161 279 0300 **f** 0161 279 0303 **e** firstname.surname@galaxymanchester.co.uk **w** galaxy102.co.uk Programme Director: James Brown. MD, Galaxy Group: Martyn Healy. Station Mgr/Head of Sales: Kiron Wood. Dance/Urban [7]

Galaxy 102.2, FM:102.2 1 The Square, 111 Broad St, Birmingham B15 1AS **t** 0121 695 0000 **f** 0121 695 0055 **e** firstname.lastname@galaxy1022.co.uk **w** galaxy1022.co.uk Prog Ctlr/Head of Music: Neil Greenslade. MD: Paul Fairburn. Sales Director: Anita Wright. Urban [8]

Galaxy 105, FM:105.1/105.8 Joseph's Well, Hanover Walk, Leeds, W Yorks LS3 1AB **t** 0113 213 0105 **f** 0113 213 0109 **e** mail@galaxy105.co.uk **w** galaxy105.co.uk Programme Director: Brent Tobin. MD, Galaxy Group: Martyn Healy. Dance/Urban [6]

Galaxy 105-106, FM:105.3/105.6/105.8/106.4 Kingfisher Way, Silverlink Business Pk, Wallsend, Tyne & Wear NE28 9NX **t** 0191 206 8000 **f** 0191 206 8080 **e** reception@galaxy1056.co.uk **w** galaxynortheast.co.uk Programme Director: Matt McClure. MD, Galaxy Group: Martyn Healy. Deputy PD: Tory Miller. Head of Sales: Ian Trotter. Dance [5]

Galway Bay FM, FM:95.8/96.0/96.8/97.4 Sandy Rd, Galway City, Galway, Ireland **t** +353 91 770000 **f** +353 91 752689 **e** info@galwaybayfm.ie **w** gbfm.galway.net CEO: Keith Finnegan. Head of Music: John Richards. Head of Sales: Paddy Madden. MOR/CHR [15]

Gaydar Radio PO Box 113, Twickenham, Middx TW1 4WY **t** 020 8744 1287 **f** 020 8744 1089 **e** studio@gaydarradio.com **w** gaydarradio.com Programme Dir: Jamie Crick. Station Manager: Robin Crowley. Head Of Music: Neil Sexton. Head Of Sales: Alex Friesen.

Gemini FM, FM:97/96.4/103 Hawthorn House, Exeter Business Pk, Exeter, Devon EX1 3QS **t** 01392 444444 **f** 01392 354249 **e** firstname.lastname@gcapmedia.com **w** geminifm.co.uk Acting Prog Cont/HoM: Dani Finch. Sales Centre Manager: Sara Bond. CHR/Gold [13]

Gemini FM (Torbay), FM:96.4, 97.0, 103 Harbour Point, Victoria Parade, Torquay, South Devon TQ21 2RA **t** 01803 202800 **f** 01803 202809 **e** firstname.lastname@gcapmedia.com **w** geminifm.co.uk Acting Programme Cont: Dani Finch. Sales Manager: Sara Bond. AC [13]

**BBC Radio Gloucestershire, AM:1413
FM:104.7/95.8/95** London Rd, Gloucester GL1 1SW
t 01452 308585 **f** 01452 306541
e radio.gloucestershire@bbc.co.uk
w bbc.co.uk/radiogloucestershire Grams Librarian: Chris Fowler.
Managing Editor: Mark Hurell. Head of Programmes: David
Aston. MOR [8]

**BBC GMR (BBC Greater Manchester Radio),
FM:95.1/104.6** PO Box 951, New Broadcasting House,
Oxford Rd, Manchester M60 1SD **t** 0161 200 2020
f 0161 236 5804 **e** manchester.online@bbc.co.uk
w bbc.co.uk/manchester Managing Editor: John Ryan.
Programming Director/Head of Music: Lawrence Mann. AOR [7]

GTFM, FM:106.9 Pinewood Studios, Pinewood Ave,
Rhydyfelin, Pontypridd CF37 5EA **t** 01443 406111
f 01443 492744 **e** andrew@gtfm.co.uk **w** gtfm.co.uk
Station Mgr/Prog Dir: Andrew Jones. CHR [9]

BBC Radio Guernsey, AM:116 FM:93.2 Bulwer Ave,
St Sampsons, Guernsey, Channel Islands GY2 4LA
t 01481 200600 **f** 01481 200361 **e** radio.guernsey@bbc.co.uk
w bbc.co.uk/radioguernsey Ed: David Martin. Head of Music: John
Randall. Gold [14]

GWR FM, FM:96.3/103 PO Box 2000, 1 Passage St,
Bristol BS99 7SN **t** 0117 984 3200 **f** 0117 984 3202
e firstname.lastname@gcapmedia.com **w** gwrfm.co.uk
Programme Controller: Paul Andrew. Group Head of Music:
Caroline Murphy. Head of Sales: David Wenn. AC [8, 9]

GWR FM., FM:103/97.2/102.2 PO Box 2000, Wootton
Bassett, Swindon, Wilts SN4 7EX **t** 01793 663010
f 01793 663009 **e** firstname.lastname@gcapmedia.com
w gwrfm.co.uk Programme Controller: Paul Kaye. Regional Sales
Dir: Steve Jones. CHR [8, 12]

Hallam FM, FM:97.4/102.9/103.4 Radio House, 900
Herries Rd, Sheffield, S Yorks S6 1RH **t** 0114 209 1000
f 0114 285 3159 **e** programmes@hallamfm.co.uk
w hallamfm.co.uk Programme Director: Gary Stein. MD: Iain
Clasper. Head of Music: Chris Straw. Head of Sales: Ev
Mascarhas. CHR [6]

Heart 106, FM:106 City Link, Nottingham NG2 4NG
t 0115 910 6100 **f** 0115 910 6107
e firstname.lastname@chrysalis.com **w** heart106.com
Programme Controller: Anna Riggs. MD: Paul Fairburn. Head of
Music: Jim Davis. Sales Manager: Andrea Olson. AC [8]

Heart 106.2, FM:106.2 The Chrysalis Building, Bramley Rd,
London W10 6SP **t** 020 7468 1062 **f** 020 7465 6196
e firstname.lastname@chrysalis.com **w** heart1062.co.uk
Programme Director: Mark Browning. MD: Barnaby Dawe. Group
PD: Francis Currie. Sales Dir: Gerrard Bridges. Head of Music:
Russ Evans. AC [11]

100.7 Heart FM, FM:100.7 1 The Square, 111 Broad St,
Birmingham, W Midlands B15 1AS **t** 0121 695 0000
f 0121 695 0055 **e** firstname.lastname@heartfm.co.uk
w heartfm.co.uk Programme Dir: Luis Clark. MD: Paul Fairburn.
Head of Music: Mike Zeller. Sales Director: Anita Wright. AC [8]

Heartland FM, FM:97.5 Lower Oakfield, Pitlochry,
Perthshire PH16 5DS **t** 01796 474040 **f** 01796 474007
e mailbox@heartlandfm.co.uk **w** heartlandfm.co.uk
Prog Dir/Head of Music: Pete Ramsden. Head of Sales: Marian
MacDonald. Soft AC/MOR/Speech [3]

**BBC Hereford & Worcester, AM:738
FM:94.7/104/104.6** Hylton Rd, Worcester WR2 5WW
t 01905 748485 **f** 01905 337209 **e** worcester@bbc.co.uk
w bbc.co.uk/herefordandworcester
Managing Editor: James Coghill. Head of Music: Max Thomas.
Programmes Editor: Keith Gooden. AC [8]

102.7 Hereward FM, FM:102.7 PO Box 225, 98
Queensgate Centre, Peterborough, Cambs PE1 1XJ
t 01733 460460 **f** 01733 281379
e firstname.lastname@musicradio.com **w** hereward.co.uk
Prog Ctrl: Tom Haynes. Head of Music: Matt Jarvis. Sales Centre
Mgr: Clive White. Chart/Gold [10]

HertBeat FM, FM:106.9/106.7 The Pump House,
Knebworth Pk, Hertford SG3 6HQ **t** 01438 810900
f 01438 815100 **e** info@hertbeat.com **w** hertbeat.com
Programme Controller: Steve Folland. Station Mgr/Hd of Sales:
Darrell Thomas. Head of Music: Mims Lovelock. AC [10]

Highland Radio, FM:95.2/103.3/94.7 Pine Hill,
Letterkenny, Co Donegal, Ireland **t** +353 74 912 5000
f +353 74 912 5344 **e** enquiries@highlandradio.com
w highlandradio.com Head of Prog & Music: Linda McGroarty.
MD/Head of Sales: Charlie Collins. Head of Promotions: Shaun
Doherty. AC/Gold [15]

Home 107.9, FM:107.9 The Old Stableblock, Brewery
Drive, Lockwood Pk, Huddersfield HD1 3UR **t** 01484 321107
f 01484 311107 **e** firstname.lastname@home1079.co.uk
w home1079.co.uk Station Manager: John Harding. Sales
Manager: Susie Sweeney. Gold [6]

FM 103 Horizon, FM:103.3 14 Vincent Ave, Crownhill,
Milton Keynes, Bucks MK8 0AB **t** 01908 269111
f 01908 591619 **e** firstname.lastname@musicradio.com
w musicradio.com Prog Controller: Trevor Marshall. Sales
Manager: Iam Stuart. CHR [10]

BBC Radio Humberside, AM:1485 FM:95.9 Queens
Court, Queens Gardens, Hull, E Yorks HU1 3RH **t** 01482 323232
f 01482 226409 **e** radio.humberside@bbc.co.uk
w bbc.co.uk/radiohumberside HoM: Richard James. Managing
Editor: Simon Pattern. MOR [6]

Imagine FM, FM:104.9 Regent House, Heaton Lane,
Stockport, Cheshire SK4 1BX **t** 0161 609 1400
f 0161 609 1401 **e** info@imaginefm.net **w** imaginefm.net
Station Dir: Steve Howarth. Programming Controller: Paul Willett.
Head of Music: Wayne Dutton. Sales Dir: Daniel Vincent. AC [7]

Independent Radio News Ltd 200 Gray's Inn Rd,
London WC1X 8XZ **t** 020 7430 4090 **f** 020 7430 4092
e news@irn.co.uk **w** irn.co.uk MD: John Perkins. Senior Editor:
Jon Godel. News

Inflight Productions 15 Stukeley St, London WC2B 5LT
t 020 7400 0700 **f** 020 7400 0707
e firstname.lastname@inflightproductions.com
w inflightproductions.com MD: Steve Harvey. Airline radio progs.

Invicta FM, FM:95.9/96.1/97/102.8/103.1 Radio
House, John Wilson Business Pk, Whitstable, Kent CT5 3QX
t 01227 772004 **f** 01227 774450
e firstname.lastname@invictafm.com **w** invictafm.com
Programme Controller: Craig Boddy. Head of Sales: Emma
Liddiard. Marketing Mgr: Richard Roberts. AC [11, 12]

Media: Radio

Island FM, FM:104.7/93.7 12 Westerbrook, St Sampson, Guernsey GY2 4QQ **t** 01481 242000 **f** 01481 249676 **e** studio@islandfm.guernsey.net **w** islandfm.guernsey.net MD/Prog Controller: Gary Burgess. Head of Music: Carl Ward. Head of Sales: Sue Campanella. CHR/AC [14]

Isle Of Wight Radio, FM:102/107 Dodnor Pk, Newport, Isle Of Wight PO30 5XE **t** 01983 822557 **f** 01983 822109 **e** firstname.lastname@iwradio.co.uk **w** iwradio.co.uk Station Manager: Andy Shier. Programme Controller: Tom Stroud. Head of Sales: Sue Hudson. AC/Gold [12]

Isles FM 103, FM:103 PO Box 333, Stornoway, Isle Of Lewis, Western Isles HS1 2PU **t** 01851 703333 **f** 01851 703322 **e** studio@isles.fm **w** isles.fm Joint Station Co-ordin'r: A.J. Kennedy. Head of Music: Peggy McNeil. Joint Station Co-ordinator: Kathleen Maciver. Operations Director: David Morrison. Head of Sales: Lionel Sewell. MOR/Scottish/Gaelic/News [2]

Ivel FM, FM:105.6/106.6 The Studios, Middle St, Yeovil, Somerset BA20 1DJ **t** 01935 848488 **f** 01935 848489 **e** info@ivelfm.com **w** ivelfm.com Programme Controller: Steve Carpenter. Regional MD: John Baker. Head of Sales: James Richards. CHR

BBC Radio Jersey, AM:1026 FM:88.8 18-21 Parade Rd, St Helier, Jersey, Channel Islands JE2 3PL **t** 01534 870000 **f** 01534 732569 **e** radiojersey@bbc.co.uk **w** bbc.co.uk/jersey Asst. Editor/Programmes: Matthew Price. Managing Editor: Denzil Dudley. Snr Broadcast Journalist/Hd of Music: Roger Bara. MOR/Specialist [14]

Juice 107.2, FM:107.2 170 North St, Brighton, E Sussex BN1 1EA **t** 01273 386107 **f** 01273 273107 **e** info@juicebrighton.com **w** juicebrighton.com MD: Matthew Bashford. Programme Manager: Ms Sam Walker. Head of Music: Mark Wright. Chart/Dance/Indie [12]

Juice 107.6 FM, FM:107.6 27 Fleet St, Liverpool L1 4AR **t** 0151 707 3107 **f** 0871 200 7001 **e** mail@juiceliverpool.com **w** juice.fm Programme Dir: Grainne Landowski. Station Dir: Matthew Allitt. Head of Music: Simon Greening. Sales Mgr: Sue Green. Dance/Indie [7]

BBC Radio Kent, AM:774 FM:96.7/104.2 The Great Hall, Mount Pleasant Rd, Royal Tunbridge Wells, Kent TN1 1QQ **t** 01892 670000 **f** 01892 675644 **e** radio.kent@bbc.co.uk **w** bbc.co.uk/kent Head of Music/SBJ: Lynn Wallis-Eade. Managing Editor: Paul Leaper. SBJ Programmes: Andy Garland. MOR/Chart [11, 12]

Kerrang! Radio, FM:105.2 20 Lionel St, Kerrang! House, Birmingham B3 1AQ **t** 0845 053 1052 **e** firstname.lastname@kerrangradio.co.uk **w** kerrangradio.co.uk HoM: Emma Scrafton. MD: Adrian Serle. Deputy PD: Chris Thorpe. Head of Sales: Marguerite Taylor. Rock [8]

Radio Kerry, FM:96.2/96.6/97.6 Maine St, Tralee, Kerry, Ireland **t** +353 66 712 3666 **f** +353 66 712 2282 **e** martin@radiokerry.ie **w** radiokerry.ie Programme Director: Martin Howard. MD: Paul Byrne. Head of Sales: Melanie O'Sullivan. AC [15]

107.6 Kestrel FM, FM:107.6 2nd Floor, Paddington House, The Walks Shopping Centre, Basingstoke, Hants RG21 7LJ **t** 01256 694000 **f** 01256 694133 **e** studio@kestrelfm.com **w** kestrelfm.com Programme Manager: Pat Sissons. MD: Susan Reynolds. AC [11, 12]

Key 103, FM:103 Castle Quay, Castlefield, Manchester M15 4PR **t** 0161 288 5000 **f** 0161 288 5071 **e** firstname.lastname@key103.co.uk **w** key103.co.uk Prog Dir/Hd of Music: Anthony Gay. MD: Gus MacKenzie. Head of Sales: Tracy Eastwood. AC Chart [7]

KFM Radio, FM:97.3/97.6/107.4 M7 Business Pk, Newhall, Naas, Co Kildare, Ireland **t** +353 4589 8999 **f** +353 4589 8993 **e** info@kfmradio.com **w** kfmradio.com Station Manager: Clem Ryan. Programme Controller: Noel Shannon. Sales Mgr: Trevor Hull. AC [15]

Kick FM, FM:105.6/107.4 The Studios, 42 Bone Lane, Newbury, Berks RG14 5SD **t** 01635 841600 **f** 01635 841010 **e** mail@kickfm.com **w** kickfm.com Programme Mgr: James O'Neill. MD: Sue Reynolds. Soft AC [11, 12]

Kingdom FM, FM:95.2/96.1/96.6/105.4/106.3 Haig House, Balgonie Rd, Markinch, Fife KY7 6AQ **t** 01592 753753 **f** 01592 757788 **e** office@kingdomfm.co.uk **w** kingdomfm.co.uk Station Mgr/Prog Ctrl: Kevin Brady. Chief Executive: Ian Sewell. Head of Sales: Linda McCrabbe. AC [3]

Kiss 100 FM, FM:100 Emap Performance, Mappin House, 4 Winsley St, London W1W 8HF **t** 020 7975 8100 **f** 020 7182 8489 **e** firstname.lastname@totalkiss.com **w** kiss100.com Grp Programme Director: Andy Roberts. Group MD: Bill Griffin. Deputy PD: John Hipper. Group Head of Music: Christian Smith. Head of Sales: Marc Beeney. Sales Co-ordinator: Annie Lewiston. Dance [11]

Kiss 101, FM:97.2/101 26 Baldwin St, Bristol BS1 1FE **t** 0117 901 0101 **f** 0117 930 9149 **e** firstname.lastname@totalkiss.com **w** vibe101.co.uk Sales Dir: Julian Hotchkiss. Prog Mgr: Nathan Thomson. Dance/RnB [13, 9]

Kiss 105-108, FM:105/108 Reflection House, Olding Rd, Bury St Edmunds, Suffolk IP33 3TA **t** 01284 715300 **f** 01284 715329 **e** firstname.lastname@totalkiss.com **w** vibefm.co.uk Programme Mgr: Glen White. Sales Dir: Kelly Snook. Dance [10]

KLFM, FM:96.7 18 Blackfriars St, Kings Lynn, Norfolk PE30 1NN **t** 01553 772777 **f** 01553 766453 **e** admin@klfm967.co.uk **w** klfm967.co.uk Station Mgr: Mark Pryke. Prog Controller: Simon Rowe. Head of Sales: Jason Smith. Gold [10]

Kmfm (Ashford), FM:107.6 Express House, 34-36 North St, Ashford, Kent TN24 8JR **t** 01233 623232 **f** 01233 626545 **e** initial+lastname@kmfm.co.uk **w** kmfm.co.uk/ashford Programme Coordinator: Myrna Seldon. Head of KM Radio: Penny Williams. Grp Prog Cont: Mike Osborne. Grp Head of Music: Toby Mackenzie. Grp Sales & Marketing Controller: Jake Worrall. Regional Sales Mgr, West Kent: Paul Harvey. Gold/CHR [11]

Kmfm (Canterbury, Whitstable and Herne Bay), FM:106 9 St George's Pl, Canterbury, Kent CT1 1UU **t** 01227 786106 **f** 01227 785106 **e** initial+lastname@kmfm.co.uk **w** kmfm.co.uk/canterbury Programme Coordinator: Bob Mower. Group Programming Cont: Mike Osbourne. Grp Head of Music: Toby MacKenzie. Regional Sales Mgr, East Kent: James Colton. AC [11]

Kmfm (Sheppway & Whitecliffs Country), FM:96.4/106.8 93-95 Sandgate Rd, Folkestone, Kent CT20 2BQ **t** 01304 202505 **f** 01304 212717 **e** radams@kmfm.co.uk **w** kmfm.co.uk/shepway Programme Controller: Richard Adams. Grp Prog Cont: Mike Osborne. Grp Head of Music: Toby Mackenzie. Regional Sales Mgr, East Kent: James Colton. AC [11, 12]

Kmfm (Medway), FM:100.4/107.9 Medway House, Ginsbury Close, Sir Thomas Longley Rd, Medway City Estate, Rochester, Kent ME2 4DU **t** 01634 841111 **f** 01634 841122 **e** crance@kmfm.co.uk **w** kentonline.co.uk/kmfm Programme Coordinator: Craig Rance. Group Programme Cont: Mike Osborne. Grp Head of Music: Toby MacKenzie. Regional Sales Mgr, West Kent: Paul Harvey. AC/CHR [11]

Kmfm (Thanet), FM:107.2 Imperial House, 2-14 High St, Margate, Kent CT9 1DH **t** 01843 220222 **f** 01843 299666 **e** tstewart@kmfm.co.uk **w** kmfm.co.uk/thanet Programme Coordinator: Tim Stewart. Grp Prog Cont: Mike Osborne. Grp Head of Music: Toby Mackenzie. Regional Sales Mgr, East Kent: James Colton. AC [11, 10]

Kmfm (West Kent), FM:96.2/101.6 1 East St, Tonbridge, Kent TN9 1AR **t** 01732 369200 **f** 01732 369201 **e** rscott@kmfm.co.uk **w** kmfm.co.uk/westkent Programme Coordinator: Rick Scott. Grp Prog Cont: Mike Osborne. Grp Head of Music: Toby Mackenzie. Sales Manager: Regional Sales Mgr, West Kent: Paul Harvey. AC [11]

Kool AM PO Box 1072, Edmonton, London N9 0WQ **t** 020 8373 1073 **f** 020 8373 1074 **e** info@c4trt.co.uk **w** koolam.co.uk Group Station Manager: Steve Saunders. Programming Director: Joe Bone. Head of Music: Peter Moore. Head of Sales: James Fortune. AC [11]

Lakeland Radio, FM:100.1/100.8 Lakeland Food Pk, Plumgarths, Crook Rd, Kendal, Cumbria LA8 8QJ **t** 01539 737380 **f** 01539 737390 **e** firstname.lastname@lakelandradio.co.uk **w** lakelandradio.co.uk MD: Peter Fletcher. Heads of Music: Steven Bell or Sarah Newman. AC [7, 4]

BBC Radio Lancashire, AM:855/1557 FM:95.5/103.9/104.5 20-26 Darwen St, Blackburn, Lancs BB2 2EA **t** 01254 262411 **f** 01254 680821 **e** radio.lancashire@bbc.co.uk **w** bbc.co.uk/lancashire Managing Editor: John Clayton. Head of Music: Mark Harrison. MOR [7]

Lantern FM, FM:96.2 Unit 2B, Lauder Lane, Barnstable, North Devon EX31 3TA **t** 01271 366370 **f** 01271 366359 **e** firstname.lastname@gcapmedia.com **w** lanternfm.co.uk Prog Cont/Head of Music: Paul Hopper. Head of Sales: Jim Trevelyan. MOR [13]

LBC 97.3, AM:1152 FM:97.3 The Chrysalis Building, 13 Bramley Rd, London W10 6SP **t** 020 7314 7300 **f** 020 7314 7317 **e** firstname.lastname@lbc.co.uk **w** lbc973.co.uk MD: David Lloyd. Head of Sales: Gerrard Bridges. News/Current Affairs [11]

BBC Radio Leeds, AM:774 FM:92.4/95.3/102.7/103.9 2 St Peter's Sq, Leeds, W Yorks LS9 8AH **t** 0113 244 2131 **f** 0113 224 7316 **e** radio.leeds@bbc.co.uk **w** bbc.co.uk/leeds Managing Ed: Phil Roberts. Head of Music: David Crickmore & Stewart Barrett. News/Talk [6]

BBC Leicester, FM:104.9 9 St Nicholas Pl, Leicester LE1 5LB **t** 0116 251 6688 **f** 0116 251 1463 **e** radioleicester@bbc.co.uk **w** bbc.co.uk/radioleicester HoM: Trish Dolman. Managing Editor: Kate Squire. AC [8]

Leicester Sound, FM:105.4 6 Dominus Way, Meridian Business Pk, Leicester, Leics LE19 1RP **t** 0116 256 1300 **f** 0116 256 1303 **e** firstname.lastname@gcapmedia.com **w** leicestersound.co.uk Prog Cont/Head of Music: Simon Ritchie. Sales Centre Mgrs: Leigh Armstrong, Bina Chauhan. AC [8]

Limerick's Live 95FM, FM:95/95.3 Radio House, Richmond Court, Dock Rd, Limerick, Ireland **t** +353 61 400195 **f** +353 61 419595 **e** admin@live95fm.ie **w** live95fm.ie Programme Director: Gary Connor. Chief Exec: David Tighe. Head of Sales: Gerry Long. CHR/AC [15]

BBC Radio Lincolnshire, AM:1368 FM:94.9/104.7 PO Box 219, Newport, Lincoln LN1 3XY **t** 01522 511411 **f** 01522 511058 **e** radio.lincolnshire@bbc.co.uk **w** bbc.co.uk/lincolnshire Managing Editor: Charlie Partridge. Programme Editor: Les Sheehan. Head of Music: Linda Rust. MOR/Gold [6, 8]

Lincs FM 102.2, FM:102.2 Witham Pk, Waterside South, Lincoln LN5 7JN **t** 01522 549900 **f** 01522 549911 **e** enquiries@lincsfm.co.uk **w** lincsfm.co.uk Group Dir of Programming: Keith Briggs. Programme Mgr: John Marshall. Head of Music: Eddie Shaw. Sales Dir: Jeff Harwood. Gold/AC [6, 8]

Lite FM, FM:106.8 2nd Floor, 5 Church St, Peterborough PE1 1XB **t** 01733 898106 **f** 01733 898107 **e** info@Lite1068.com **w** lite1068.com Prog Dir/Head of Music: Kev Lawerence. MD: Dave Myatt. Head of Sales: Dawn Trowsdale. AC [10]

LMFM Radio, FM:95.5/95.8/104.9 Broadcasting House, Rathmullen Rd, Drogheda, Co. Louth, Ireland **t** +353 41 983 2000 **f** +353 41 983 2957 **e** info@lmfm.ie **w** lmfm.ie Programme Director: Eamonn Doyle. MD: Michael Crawley. Head of Sales: Eileen Duggan. Chart/MOR [15]

Lochbroom FM, FM:96.8/102.2 Radio House, Mill St, Ullapool, Ross-shire IV26 2UN **t** 01854 613131 **f** 01854 613132 **e** Lochbroomfm@ecosse.net **w** lochbroomfm.co.uk Station Mgr/Head of Sales: Kevin Guy. Head of Music: Tiffany Macaulay. AOR/Scottish [2]

BBC London, FM:94.9 PO Box 94.9, London W1A 6FL **t** 020 7224 2424 **f** 020 7208 9680 **e** yourlondon@bbc.co.uk **w** bbc.co.uk/london Managing Editor: David Robey. Assistant Editor (Programme Controller): Julia McKenzie. Head of Music: Jim Lahat. AC [11]

London Greek Radio, FM:103.3 LGR House, 437 High Rd, London N12 0AP **t** 020 8349 6950 **f** 020 8349 6960 **e** sales@lgr.co.uk **w** lgr.co.uk Prog Contr/Head of Music: George Gregoriou. Station Manager: Viron Karidis. Head of Sales: Chris Harmandas. Greek [11]

London Turkish Radio (LTR), AM:1584 185B High Rd, London N22 6BA **t** 020 8881 0606 **f** 020 8881 5151 **e** info@londonturkishradio.org **w** londonturkishradio.org MD: Erkhan Pastirmacioglu. Programming Controller: Umit Dandul. Head of Sales: Kelami Dedezade. Turkish [11]

Lyric FM, FM:96/99 Cornmarket Sq, Limerick, Ireland **t** +353 61 207300 **f** +353 61 207390 **e** lyric@rte.ie **w** lyricfm.ie Station Mgr/Prog Dir: Aodan O Dubhghaill. Head of Music: Sean McKenna. Light Classical/Jazz

Magic 105.4, FM:105.4 Emap Performance, Mappin House, 4 Winsley St, London W1W 8HF **t** 020 7182 8000 **f** 020 7182 8165 **e** studio@magic.co.uk **w** magiclondon.co.uk Prog Dir: Richard Park. MD: Andria Vidler. Deputy Prog Dir: Adrian Stewart. Sales Dir: Julieanne Toole. Soft AC [11]

Magic 1152, AM:1152 55 Degress North, Pilgrim St, Newcastle upon Tyne, Tyne and Wear NE1 6BF **t** 0191 230 6100 **f** 0191 279 0288
e enquiries@metroandmagic.com **w** metroradio.co.uk Programme Director: Trevor James. MD: Sally Aitchison. Head of Music: Alex Roland. Head of Sales: Kim Miljus. MOR [5]

Magic 1152 (Manchester), AM:1152 Castle Quay, Castlefield, Manchester M15 4PR **t** 0161 288 5000 **f** 0161 288 5151 **e** firstname.lastname@key103.co.uk **w** key103.co.uk Prog Dir/Head of Music: Anthony Gay. MD: Gus MacKenzie. Head of Sales: Tracy Eastwood. Gold

Magic 1161, AM:1161/258 The Boathouse, Commercial Rd, Hull, E Yorks HU1 2SG **t** 01482 325141 **f** 0845 4580 390 **e** firstname.lastname@vikingfm.co.uk **w** magic1161.co.uk Prog Dir: Darrell Woodman. MD: Mike Bawden. Head of Sales: Steve Allbones. MOR [6]

Magic 1548, AM:1548 St.John's Beacon, 1 Houghton St, Liverpool, Merseyside L1 1RL **t** 0151 472 6800 **f** 0151 472 6821 **e** firstname.lastname@radiocity.co.uk **w** radiocity.co.uk MD: Iain McKenna. Programming Director: Richard Maddock. Sales Director: Mike Sarath. Gold [7]

Magic 828, AM:828 51 Burley Rd, Leeds, W Yorks LS3 1LR **t** 0113 283 5500 **f** 0113 283 5501 **e** firstname.lastname@radioaire.com **w** radioaire.co.uk Head of Magic: Andy Siddell. Programme Director: Stuart Baldwin. Commercial Director: Tracy Eastwood. Soft AC [6]

Magic 999, AM:999 St Paul's Sq, Preston, Lancs PR1 1YE **t** 01772 477700 **f** 01772 477701 **e** firstname.lastname@magic999.com **w** magic999.com Programme Director: Brian Paige. MD: Paul Jordan. Head of Music: Rob Charles. Commercial Director: Rob Kelly. AC [7]

Magic AM, AM:990/1305/1548 Radio House, 900 Herries Rd, Sheffield, South Yorks S6 1RH **t** 0114 209 1000 **f** 0114 285 3159 **e** programmes@magicam.co.uk **w** magicam.co.uk HoM: Chris Straw. MD: Ian Clasper. Head of Sales: Ev Mascarhas. Soft AC [6]

Magic 1170, AM:1170 Radio House, Yales Crescent, Thornaby, Stockton-on-Tees TS17 6AA **t** 01642 888222 **f** 01642 868288 **e** tfm.reception@tfmradio.com Programme Director: Colin Paterson. MD: Catherine Ellington. Head of Music Magic: Peter Grant. Sales Director: Colette Butler. MOR [5]

Radio Maldwyn, AM:756 The Magic 756, The Studios, The Park, Newtown, Powys SY16 2NZ **t** 01686 623555 or 01686 623777 (sales) **f** 01686 623666 **e** radio.maldwyn@ukonline.co.uk **w** magic756.net MD/Prog Controller: Austin Powell. Head of Sales: Martin Adams. AC [9]

Mansfield 103.2, FM:103.2 The Media Suite, Brunts Business Centre, Samuel Brunts Way, Mansfield, Notts NG18 2AH **t** 01623 646666 **f** 01623 660606 **e** info@mansfield103.co.uk **w** mansfield103.co.uk MD: Tony Delahunty. Prog Controller/Head of Music: Katie Trinder. Head of Sales: Gordon Pitman. Chart/Country/Gold [8]

Manx Radio, AM:1368 FM:89/97.2/103.7 PO Box 1368, Broadcasting House, Douglas, Isle Of Man IM99 1SW **t** 01624 682600 **f** 01624 682604 **e** postbox@manxradio.com **w** manxradio.com MD: Anthony Pugh. Programme Dir/HoM: Chris Williams. Business Dir: John Marsom. Dir of Technology: Darren Leeming. MOR [7, 1]

Mercia FM, FM:97.0/102.9/Digital 1359 Hertford Pl, Coventry, W Midlands CV1 3TT **t** 024 7686 8200 **f** 024 7686 8209 **e** firstname.lastname@gcapmedia.com **w** merciafm.co.uk Programme Controller: Russ Williams. Head of Sales: Dave Fisher. CHR [8]

Mercury 96.6, FM:96.6 Unit 5, The Metro Centre, Dwight Rd, Watford WD18 9SS **t** 01923 205470 **f** 01923 205479 **e** firstname.lastname@musicradio.com **w** musicradio.com Programme Controller: Rebecca Dundon. Head of Sales: Kate Fraser. AC [11]

102.7 Mercury FM, FM:102.7/97.5 9 The Stanley Centre, Kelvin Way, Crawley, W Sussex RH10 2SE **t** 01293 519161 **f** 01293 565663 **e** firstname.lastname@gcapmedia.com **w** mercuryfm.co.uk Prog Cont/Head of Music: Dan Jennings. Head of Sales: Amanda Masters. CHR [12]

BBC Radio Merseyside, AM:1485 FM:95.8 55 Paradise St, Liverpool, Merseyside L1 3BP **t** 0151 708 5500 **f** 0151 794 0988 **e** radio.merseyside@bbc.co.uk **w** bbc.co.uk/liverpool HoM: Nickie Mackay. Managing Editor: Mick Ord. MOR [7]

Metro Radio, FM:97.1/102.6/103/103.6 55 Degrees North, Pilgrim St, Newcastle upon Tyne, Tyne and Wear NE1 6BF **t** 0191 230 6100 **f** 0191 279 0288 **e** enquiries@metroandmagic.com **w** metroradio.co.uk Programme Director: Trevor James. MD: Sally Aitchison. Head of Music: Alex Roland. Head of Sales: Kim Miljus. CHR [5]

MFM 103.4, FM:103.4 The Studios, Mold Rd, Gwersyllt, Wrexham, Clwyd LL11 4AF **t** 01978 752202 **f** 01978 722209 **e** admin@mfm.musicradio.com **w** musicradio.com Programme Controller: Lisa Marrey. MD: Sarah Smithard. Grp PD: Dirk Anthony. Head of Music: Andy Parry. Head of Sales: Clive Douthwaite. CHR [9]

Mid West Radio, FM:96.1/97.1 Clare St, Ballyhaunis, Co. Mayo, Ireland **t** +353 94 963 0553 **f** +353 94 963 0285 **e** chris@mnwr.ie **w** mnwrfm.com Station Mgr/Head of Music: Chris Carroll. Programme Director: Paul Claffey. Head of Sales: Tina Mitchell. MOR/Gold [15]

Midlands 103, FM:96.5/102.1/103.5 The Mall, William St, Tullamore, Co Offaly, Ireland **t** +353 506 51333 **f** +353 506 52546 **e** goodcompany@midlandsradio.fm **w** midlandsradio.fm GM Broadcasting: John McDonnell. Station Manager/Hd of Sales: Albert FitzGerald. MOR/Country/Chart [15]

104.7 Minster FM, FM:104.7/102.3 Chessingham House, Dunnington, York, N Yorks YO19 5SE **t** 01904 488888 **f** 01904 488811 **e** studio@minsterfm.com **w** ministerfm.com Acting Prog Cont: Steve Fountain. Head of Sales: Peter Bilsborough. AC [5, 6]

Mix 107, FM:107.4/107.7 PO Box 1107, High Wycombe, Bucks HP13 6WQ **t** 01494 446611 **f** 01494 445400 **e** studio@mix107.co.uk **w** mix107.co.uk Station Manager: Andy Muir. Head of Music: Roy McAllister. Sales Mgr: Bella Campbell. AC [11]

MIX 96, FM:96.2 Friars Square Studios, Bourbon St, Aylesbury, Bucks HP20 2PZ **t** 01296 399396 **f** 01296 398988 **e** studio@mix96.co.uk **w** mix96.co.uk Programme Controller: Matt Faulkner. Station Manager: Rachel Faulkner. Head of Sales: Lydia Flack. AC [10]

Moray Firth Radio, AM:1107 FM:97.4/96.6/96.7/102.5/102.8 PO Box 271, Inverness IV3 8UJ **t** 01463 224433 **f** 01463 243224 **e** mfr@mfr.co.uk **w** mfr.co.uk MD/PC: Danny Gallagher. Head of Music: Tich McCooey. Sales Director: Hilary Cartwright. Chart/Gold/Scot/Country [2]

Music Choice (A member of Music Choice Europe) Fleet House, 57-61 Clerkenwell Rd, London EC1M 5LA **t** 020 7014 8700 **f** 020 7253 8460 **e** contactus@musicchoice.co.uk **w** musicchoice.co.uk CEO: Margot Daly. Director of Music & Marketing: Simon George.

Raidio na Gaeltachta, FM:92-94/102.7 Casla, Conamara, County na Gaillimhe, Ireland **t** +353 91 506677 **f** +353 91 506666 **e** rnag@rte.ie **w** rnag.ie Head of Sales: Mairin Mhic Dhonnchada. Station Manager: Thomas Mac Con Iomaire. Programming Director: Sean O Heanaigh. Head of Music: Mairtin O Fatharta. Gaelic [15]

BBC Nan Gaidheal, FM:103.5-105 52 Church St, Stornoway, Isle of Lewis, Western Isles HS1 2LS **t** 01851 705000 **f** 01851 704633 **e** rapal@bbc.co.uk **w** bbc.co.uk/alba Music Producer: John Murray. Prog Controller/Managing Editor: Marion MacKinnon. AC/Traditional [2]

NECR, FM:97.1/102.1/102.6/103.2 The Shed, School Rd, Kintore, Inverurie, Aberdeenshire AB51 0UX **t** 01467 632878 or 01467 632909 **f** 01467 632969 **e** necrradio102.1fm@supanet.com Prog Controller: John Dean. MD: Colin Strong. Head of Sales: Maggie MacNaughton. Chart/Gold/Specialist [2]

Nevis Radio, FM:96.6/97/102.3/102.4 Ben Nevis Estate, Fort William, Inverness-shire PH33 6PR **t** 01397 700007 **f** 01397 701007 **e** firstname@nevisradio.co.uk **w** nevisradio.co.uk Station Manager: Willie Cameron. Head of Music: Michael McCrae. Head of Sales: David Ogg. Chart/AOR/Specialist [2]

BBC Radio Newcastle, AM:1458 FM:95.4/96/103.7/104.4 Broadcasting Centre, Barrack Rd, Newcastle upon Tyne, Tyne and Wear NE99 1RN **t** 0191 232 4141 **f** 0191 261 8907 **e** radionewcastle.news@bbc.co.uk **w** bbc.co.uk/radionewcastle Senior Producer: Sarah Miller. Managing Editor: Graham Moss. Music Librarian: Michael Poulter. Pop [5]

BBC Radio Norfolk, FM:95.1/104.4 The Forum, Millennium Plain, Norwich, Norfolk NR2 1BH **t** 01603 617411 **f** 01603 633692 **e** radionorfolk@bbc.co.uk **w** bbc.co.uk/radionorfolk Managing Editor: David Clayton. Gold/MOR [10]

North Norfolk Radio, FM:96.2/103.2 The Studio, Breck Farm, Stody, Holt, Norfolk NR24 2ER **t** 01263 860 808 **f** 01263 860 809 **e** info@northnorfolkradio.com **w** northnorfolkradio.com HoM: Bill Johnson. Station Manager/Sales: Colin King. AOR [10]

BBC Radio Northampton, FM:103.6/104.2 Broadcasting House, Abington St, Northampton NN1 2BH **t** 01604 239100 **f** 01604 230709 **e** northamptonshire@bbc.co.uk **w** bbc.co.uk/radionorthampton HoM: Ian Brown. Managing Editor: Laura Moss. Chart/AOR/Gold [10, 8]

Northants 96, FM:96.6 19-21 St Edmunds Rd, Northampton NN1 5DT **t** 01604 795600 **f** 01604 795659 **e** firstname.lastname@gcapmedia.com **w** northants96.co.uk Programme Controller: Chris Rick. Sales Manager: Leigh Armstrong. Chart [10, 8]

Northern Sound Radio, FM:94.8/96.3/97.5 Unit 1E, Mastertech Business Pk, Athlone Rd, Longford, Ireland **t** +353 434 7777 **f** +353 434 9384 **e** info@northernsound.ie **w** northernsound.ie CEO: Richard Devlin. Programming Dir: Joe Finnegan. Head of Sales: Kathy Casey. AC [15]

NorthSound One, FM:96.9/97.6/103 Abbotswell Rd, West Tullos, Aberdeen, Grampian AB12 3AG **t** 01224 337000 **f** 01224 400003 **e** firstname.lastname@northsound.co.uk **w** northsound1.co.uk Prog Controller/HoM: Chris Thomson. MD: tbc. Head of Sales: Joanne Bayliss. CHR [2]

NorthSound Two, AM:1035 Abbotswell Rd, West Tullos, Aberdeen AB12 3AJ **t** 01224 337000 **f** 01224 400222 **e** firstname.lastname@northsound.co.uk **w** northsound2.co.uk Prog Controller/HoM: Chris Thomson. MD: tbc. Head of Sales: Joanne Bayliss. AOR [2]

BBC Radio Nottingham, AM:1584 FM:95.5/103.8 London Rd, Nottingham NG2 4UU **t** 0115 955 0500 **f** 0115 902 1985 **e** radio.nottingham@bbc.co.uk **w** bbc.co.uk/nottingham Managing Editor: Mike Bettison. MOR [8]

Oak 107, FM:107 Waldron Court, Prince William Rd, Loughborough, Leics LE11 5GD **t** 01509 211711 **f** 01509 246107 **e** info@oak107fm.co.uk **w** oak107fm.co.uk Station Director: Greg Parker. Group Programme Dir: Don Douglas. Programme Controller/HoM: Gavin Sanways. Sales Dir: Deborah Nelson. Chart/Gold [8]

Oban FM, FM:103.3 132 George St, Oban, Argyll PA34 5NT **t** 01631 570057 **f** 01631 570530 **e** obanfmradio@btconnect.com Station Manager: Laura Johnston. Programming Director: Tina Robertson. Head of Music: Kyle Lockart. Head of Sales: Ian Simmonds. Various [3]

Ocean FM, FM:96.7/97.5 Radio House, Whittle Ave, Segensworth West, Fareham, Hants PO15 5SH **t** 01489 589911 **f** 01489 587754 **e** firstname.lastname@gcapmedia.com **w** oceanfm.com Programme Controller: Stuart Ellis. Century Group Hd of Music: Mike Walsh. Commercial Controller: Janet Jones. AC [12]

Ocean FM (Ireland), FM:102.5/105 North West Business Pk, Collooney, Co Sligo, Ireland **t** +353 71 911 8100 **f** +353 71 911 8101 **e** studio@oceanfm.ie **w** oceanfm.ie Station Mgr/Programme Dir: Niall Delaney. Head of Sales: Padriag O'Dwyer. MOR/Gold [15]

BBC Radio 1, FM:97-99 Yalding House, 152-156, Gt Portland St, London W1N 6AJ **t** 020 7580 4468 **f** 020 7765 1439 **e** firstname.lastname@bbc.co.uk **w** bbc.co.uk/radio1 Controller 1 & 1Xtra: Andy Parfitt. Editor of Music Policy: George Ergatoudis. CHR

Orchard FM, FM:96.5/97.1/102.6 Haygrove House, Shoreditch Rd, Taunton, Somerset TA3 7BT **t** 01823 338448 **f** 01823 368309 **e** firstname.lastname@gcapmedia.com **w** orchardfm.co.uk Programme Controller: Jon White. Head of Sales: Jim Trevelyan. AC/Gold [13]

BBC Radio Oxford, FM:95.2 269 Banbury Rd, Summertown, Oxford OX2 7DW **t** 08459 311444 **f** 08459 311555 **e** radio.oxford.news@bbc.co.uk **w** bbc.co.uk/oxford Executive Editor: Steve Taschini. Head of Music: Mark Watson. Programme Director: Louisa Hannan. MOR [8]

Oxford 107.9FM, FM:107.9 270 Woodstock Rd, Oxford OX2 7NW **t** 01865 315 982 **f** 01865 553 355 **e** firstname.lastname@fm1079.co.uk **w** fm1079.com Station Mgr/Programme Dir: Ian Walker. Sales Manager: Graham Lysaght. Head of Music: Darren Lee. Hot AC [8]

Peak FM, FM:107.4/102.0 Radio House, Foxwood Rd, Chesterfield, Derbyshire S41 9RF **t** 01246 269107 **f** 01246 269933 **e** studio@peak107.com **w** peak107.com Acting Prog Mgr: Naz Premji. Station & Sales Dir: Chris Overend. Head of Music: Sean Goldsmith. AC [8]

Radio Pembrokeshire, FM:102.5/107.5 14 Old School Estate, Narberth SA67 7DU **t** 01834 869384 **f** 01834 861524 **e** keri@radiopembrokeshire.com **w** radiopembrokeshire.com MD/Prog Dir: Keri Jones. Commercial Director: Esther Morton. AC [8, 9]

Pirate FM, FM:102.2/102.8 Carn Brea Studios, Wilson Way, Redruth, Cornwall TR15 3XX **t** 01209 314400 **f** 01209 315250 **e** onair@piratefm.co.uk **w** piratefm.co.uk Programme Director: Bob McCreadie. Station Manager: Beverley Warne. Head of Music: Neil Caddy. Head of Sales: Colin Halfpenny. AC [13]

97FM Plymouth Sound, FM:97 Earls Acre, Alma Rd, Plymouth, Devon PL3 4HX **t** 01752 275600 **f** 01752 275609 **e** firstname.lastname@gcapmedia.com **w** plymouthsound.co.uk Acting Prog Cont/HoM: Martin Mills. Sales Centre Mgr: Victoria Morrison. AC [13]

103.2 Power FM, FM:103.2 Radio House, Whittle Ave, Segensworth West, Fareham, Hants PO15 5SH **t** 01489 589911 **f** 01489 589453 **e** firstname.lastname@gcapmedia.com **w** powerfm.com Programme Controller: Craig Morris. Head of Music: Jay Smith. Commercial Controller: Janet Jones. CHR [12]

Premier Christian Radio, AM:1305/1332/1413 22 Chapter St, London SW1P 4NP **t** 020 7316 1300 **f** 020 7233 6706 **e** premier@premier.org.uk **w** premier.org.uk Prog Controller: Charmaine Noble-McLean. MD: Peter Kerridge. Head of Sales: Claire Southall. Christian [11]

Pulse Classic Gold, AM:1278/1530 Pennine House, Forster Sq, Bradford, W Yorks BD1 5NE **t** 01274 203040 **f** 01274 203130 **e** westyorkshire@classicgolddigital.com **w** classicgolddigital.com/westyorkshire Head of Programming: Mark Brow. MD: Tony Wilkinson. Head of Music: Steve Buck. Head of Sales: Daniel Goodyear. Gold [10]

The Pulse of West Yorkshire, FM:97.5/102.5 Pennine House, Forster Sq, Bradford, W Yorks BD1 5NE **t** 01274 203040 **f** 01274 203130 **e** firstname.lastname@pulse.co.uk **w** pulse.co.uk Programme Director: Mark Brow. MD: Tony Wilkinson. Head of Music: Jacqui Blay. Head of Sales: Daniel Goodyear. AC [10]

Q101.2FM, FM:101.2 42A Market St, Omagh, Co. Tyrone BT78 1EH **t** 028 6632 0777 **f** 028 8225 9517 **e** manager@q101west.fm **w** q101west.fm Station Manager: Damien Devenney. MD: Frank McLaughlin. AC [1]

Q102, FM:102.2 Glenageary Office Pk, Glenageary, Co. Dublin, Ireland **t** +353 1 662 1022 **f** +353 1 662 9974 **e** admin@q102.ie **w** q102.ie Programme Manager: Ian Walker. MD: Scott Williams. Sales Manager: Chris Maher. Soft AC [15]

Q102.9 FM, FM:102.9 The Riverview Suite, 87 Rossdowney Rd, Waterside, Co Londonderry BT47 5SU **t** 028 7134 4449 **f** 028 7131 1177 **e** manager@q102.fm **w** q102.fm MD/Prog Dir: Frank McLaughlin. Station Manager: David Austin. Head of Music: Steve Kirk. Sales Dir: John O'Connor. CHR/AC [1]

Q103 FM, FM:103 The Vision Pk, Histon, Cambridge CB4 9WW **t** 01223 235255 **f** 01223 235161 **e** firstname.lastname@gcapmedia.com **w** q103.co.uk Prog Controller: James Keen. Head of Sales: Phil Caborn. AC [10]

Q97.2FM, FM:97.2 24 Cloyfin Rd, Coleraine, Co Londonderry BT52 2NU **t** 028 7035 9100 **f** 028 7032 6666 **e** manager@q972.fm **w** q972.fm MD/Programme Director: Frank McLaughlin. Station Manager: Damien Devenney. Head of Music: Kenny Tosh. Sales Dir: John O'Connor. AC/Gold [1]

107.4 The Quay, FM:107.4 PO Box 107.4, Portsmouth, Hants PO2 8YG **t** 023 9236 4141 **f** 023 9236 4151 **e** firstname.lastname@quayradio.com **w** quayradio.com Programme Controller: Sam Matterface. Station Manager: Paul Marcus. Head of Sales: Philippa Atkinson. Gold/Chart/Dance [12]

Quay FM, FM:102.4 Harbour Studios, The Esplande, Watchet, Somerset TA23 0AJ **t** 01984 634900 **f** 01984 634811 **e** studio@quay.fm **w** quay.fm MD/Sales Director: Steve Bulley. Head of Music: Scott Temple. AC [13]

Radio Jackie, FM:107.8 110 Tolworth Broadway, Surbiton, Surrey KT6 7JD **t** 020 8288 1300 **f** 020 8288 1312 **e** info@radiojackie.com **w** radiojackie.com Programme Director: Dave Owen. General Manager: Peter Stremes. Soft AC [11]

Radio North Angus FM, FM:96.6/87.7 Arbroath Infirmary, Rosemount Rd, Arbroath, Angus DD11 2AT **t** 01241 879660 **f** 01241 439664 **e** info@radionorthangus.co.uk **w** radionorthangus.co.uk MD/Prog Dir: Malcolm J.B. Finlayson. News/Healthcare/MOR [2]

RadioXL, AM:1296 KMS House, Bradford St, Birmingham, W Midlands B12 0JD **t** 0121 753 5353 **f** 0121 753 3111 **e** info@radioxl.net **w** radioxl.net Head of Music/Sales: Sukhjinder Ghatoare. MD/Programming Dir: Arun Bajaj. Asian [8]

102.8 Ram FM, FM:102.8 35-36 Irongate, Derby DE1 3GA **t** 01332 324000 **f** 01332 324009 **e** firstname.lastname@gcapmedia.com **w** ramfm.co.uk Prog Cont: James Daniels. Sales Centre Manager: Margaret Dunn. AC [8]

Reading 107FM Radio House, Madejski Stadium, Reading, Berks RG2 0FN **t** 0118 986 2555 **f** 0118 945 0809 **e** studio@reading107fm.com **w** reading107fm.com Prog Controller: Tim Grundy. Head of Sales: Joanna Bishop. [11, 12]

Real Radio Wales, FM:105.4/105.9/106 PO Box 6105, Ty-Nant Court, Cardiff CF15 8YF **t** 02920 315100 **f** 02920 315150 **e** firstname.lastname@realradiofm.com **w** realradiofm.com MD: Andy Carter. Programme Controller: Ricky Durkin. Head of Presentation: Chris Moore. Head of Sales: Tony Dowling. Head of Music Real Group: Terry Underhill. AC [7]

Real Radio FM, FM:100/101 PO Box 101, Glasgow Business Pk, Glasgow G69 6GA **t** 0141 781 1011 **f** 0141 781 1112 **e** firstname.lastname@realradiofm.com **w** realradiofm.com MD: Billy Anderson. Programming Director: Jay Crawford. Head of Sales: Agnes Casssell. Head of Music Real Group: Terry Underhill. AC [3]

Real Radio (Yorkshire), FM:106/108 Sterling Court, Capitol Pk, Leeds WF3 1EL **t** 0113 238 1114 **f** 0113 238 1191 **e** firstname.lastname@realradiofm.com **w** realradiofm.com Prog Dir/Grp Hd of Music: Terry Underhill. MD: Shaun Bowron. Head of Sales: Steve South. AC [6]

Red Dragon FM, FM:97.4/103.2 Atlantic Wharf, Cardiff Bay, South Glamorgan CF10 4DJ **t** 029 2066 2066 **f** 029 2066 2060 **e** firstname.lastname@reddragonfm.com **w** reddragonfm.co.uk Prog Cont: Gavin Marshall. Sales Mgr: Jim Carpenter. Marketing Controller: Kate Novell. CHR/AC [9]

Red FM, FM:104-106 1, UTC, Bishopstown, Cork, Ireland **t** +353 21 486 5500 **f** +353 21 486 5501 **e** info@redfm.ie **w** redfm.ie Programme Dir: Carol O'Beirne. Chief Executive: Henry Condon. Head of Sales: Jim O'Sullivan. CHR [15]

96.2 The Revolution, FM:96.2 PO Box 962, Oldham, Lancs OL1 3JF **t** 0161 621 6500 **f** 0161 621 6521 **e** studio@revolutiononline.co.uk **w** revolutiononline.co.uk Programme Manager: Chris Gregg. Station Manager: Jacquie Sulkowski. Head of Music: Clint Boon. Head of Sales: Nick Rushton. AC [7]

Ridings FM, FM:106.8 PO Box 333, Wakefield, W Yorks WF2 7YQ **t** 01924 367177 **f** 01924 367133 **e** enquiries@ridingsfm.co.uk **w** ridingsfm.co.uk Programme Manager: John Tolson. Group Prog Dir: Keith Briggs. Sales Manager: Sarah Hardy. AC [7]

River FM, FM:103.4/107.7 Stadium House, Alderstone Rd, Livingston, West Lothian EH54 7DN **t** 01506 410 411 **f** 01506 420 972 **e** office@riverfm.co.uk **w** riverfm.co.uk Prog Cont: Donny Hughes. Head of Sales: Susan Dignon. AOR [2, 3]

97.4 Rock FM, FM:97.4 St Paul's Sq, Preston, Lancs PR1 1YE **t** 01772 477700 **f** 01772 477701 **e** firstname.lastname@rockfm.co.uk **w** rockfm.co.uk Programme Dir: Brian Paige. MD: Paul Jordan. Head of Music: Steve Gregory. Commercial Director: Rob Kelly. CHR [7]

96.3 Rock Radio, FM:96.3 Glasgow Business Pk, Glasgow G69 6GA **t** 0141 781 1011 **f** 0141 781 1112 **e** firstname.lastname@realradiofm.com **w** gmgradio.co.uk Programme Director: Jay Crawford. MD: Billy Anderson. AC [3]

106.7 The Rocket, FM:106.7 Cables Retail Pk, Prescot, Merseyside L34 5SW **t** 0151 290 1501 **f** 0151 290 1505 **e** info@1067therocket.com **w** 1067therocket.com Programme Controller: Mike Vitti. MD: Mark Matthews. Head of Sales: Jayne Moore. Gold [7]

Rother FM, FM:96.1 PO Box 622, Rotherham S60 9AY **t** 01709 366080 **e** enquiries@rotherfm.co.uk **w** rotherfm.co.uk AC [6, 5]

RTE Radio 1, FM:88/89/90 Radio Centre, Donnybrook, Dublin 4, Ireland **t** +353 1 208 3111 **f** +353 1 208 4523 **e** radio1@rte.ie **w** rte.ie Head of RTE Radio 1: Eithne Hand. MOR/Country [15]

2FM, FM:90-92 RTE Radio Centre, Donnybrook, Dublin 4, Ireland **t** +353 1 208 3111 or 01850 715922 **f** +353 1 208 3092 **e** info@2fm.ie **w** 2fm.ie Station Mgr/Prog Dir: John Clarke. Head of Music: Aidan Leonard. Group Head of Sales: Antony Whittall. CHR [15]

107.1 Rugby FM, FM:107.1 Suites 4-6, Dunsmore Business Centre, Spring St, Rugby CV21 3HH **t** 01788 541100 **f** 01788 541070 **e** mail@rugbyfm.co.uk **w** rugbyfm.co.uk MD: Julian Hotchkiss. Programme Director: Lee Moulsdale. Head of Sales: Karen Weeson. AC [8]

Rutland Radio, FM:107.2/97.4 40 Melton Rd, Oakham, Rutland LE15 6AY **t** 01572 757868 **f** 01572 757744 **e** enquiries@rutlandradio.co.uk **w** rutlandradio.co.uk Station Mgr: Julie Baker. Grp Programme Dir: Keith Briggs. Grp Head of Music: Eddie Shaw. Sales Manager: Sarah Washington. AC [8]

Sabras Radio, AM:1260 Radio House, 63 Melton Rd, Leicester LE3 6PN **t** 0116 261 0666 **f** 0116 266 7776 **e** news@sabrasradio.com **w** sabrasradio.com Station Mgr/Head of Music: Mark Spokes. Group Head of Sales: Richard Scarle. Asian [8]

Saga 105.2 City Pk, Alexandra Parade, Glasgow G31 3AU **t** 0141 551 1052 **f** 0141 551 1053 **e** firstname.lastname@saga1052fm.co.uk **w** saga1052fm.co.uk MD: Norman Quirk. Programme Dir: Gerry Burke. Sales Dir: Pamela Richardson. [3]

Saga 105.7FM, FM:105.7 Crown House, 123 Hagley Rd, Edgbaston, Birmingham B16 8LD **t** 0121 452 1057 **f** 0121 452 3222 **e** onair@saga1057fm.co.uk **w** saga1057fm.co.uk Grp Programme Director: Paul Robey. MD: Phil Dixon. Director of Sales: Marc Beeney. Gold/MOR [8]

Saga 106.6 FM, FM:106.6 Saga Radio House, Alder Court, Riverside Business Pk, Nottingham NG2 1RX **t** 0115 986 1066 **f** 0115 943 5065 **e** onair@saga1066fm.co.uk **w** saga1066fm.co.uk Grp Programme Dir: Paul Robey. MD: Phil Dixon. Head of Sales: Paul Cranwell. MOR [8]

Media: Radio

The Saint, FM:107.8 The Friends Provident, St Mary's Stadium, Brittania Rd, Southampton, Hants SO14 5fp **t** 023 8033 0300 **f** 023 8020 6400 **e** thesaint@saintsfc.co.uk **w** saintsfc.co.uk Programme Controller: Stewart Dennis. Station Director: Tim Manns. Head of Sales: Ian Wykes. AC [12]

97.5 Scarlet FM, FM:97.5 PO Box 971, Llanelli SA15 1NE **t** 01834 869384 **f** 01834 861524 **e** keri@Scarletfm.com **w** Scarletfm.com MD/Prog Dir: Keri Jones. Commercial Director: Esther Morton. AC [9, 8]

BBC Scotland, FM:92 - 95 Queen Margaret Drive, Glasgow, Strathclyde G12 8DG **t** 0141 338 2000 **f** 0141 338 2657 **e** firstname.lastname@bbc.co.uk **w** bbc.co.uk/scotland Snr Prod Contemp. Music: Stewart Cruickshank. Head of Radio: Jess Zycinski. Indie/Dance/Celtic/Folk [3]

Seven FM, FM:107 1, Millenium Pk, Woodside Industial Estate, Woodside Rd, Ballymena, Co Antrim BT42 4QJ **t** 028 256 48777 **f** 028 256 48778 **e** firstname.lastname@sevenfm.co.uk **w** sevenfm.co.uk Programme Director: Olly Brady. Head of Sales: Fiona Clerkin. AC [1]

102.4 Severn Sound FM, FM:102.4 Bridge Studios, Eastgate Centre, Gloucester GL1 1SS **t** 01452 572400 **f** 01452 572409 **e** firstname.lastname@gcapmedia.com **w** severnsound.co.uk Programme Director: Marcus Langreiter. Sales Manager: Lorraine Milkins. 80s/90s [8]

SGR Colchester, FM:96.1 Abbeygate Two, 9 Whitewell Rd, Colchester, Essex CO2 7DE **t** 01206 575859 **f** 01206 216149 **e** firstname.lastname@gcapmedia.com **w** sgrcolchester.co.uk Programme Director: Jonathan Hemmings. Sales Manager: Purdie Chambers. 80s/90s/Chart [11, 10]

SGR-FM, FM:96.4/97.1 Radio House, Alpha Business Pk, 6-12 White House Rd, Ipswich, Suffolk IP1 5LT **t** 01473 461000 **f** 01473 467549 **e** firstname.lastname@gcapmedia.com **w** sgrfm.co.uk Programme Director: Paul Morris. Sales Manager: Gina Frost. AC [10]

Shannonside FM, FM:94.8/95.7/104.1/103.1/104.8 Unit 1E, Mastertech Business Pk, Athlone Rd, Longford, Ireland **t** +353 43 47777 **f** +353 43 48384 **e** info@shannonside.ie **w** shannonside.ie CEO: Richard Devlin. Programming Controller/Head of Music: Joe Finnegan. Sales Manager: Kathy Casey. MOR/Country [15]

BBC Radio Sheffield, AM:1035 FM:88.6/94.7/104.1 54 Shoreham St, Sheffield, S Yorks S1 4RS **t** 0114 273 1177 **f** 0114 267 5454 **e** radio.sheffield@bbc.co.uk **w** bbc.co.uk/radiosheffield HoM: Jane Kitson. Managing Editor: Gary Keown. MOR/Specialist [6]

BBC Radio Shetland, FM:92.7 Pitt Lane, Lerwick, Shetland Isles ZE1 0DW **t** 01595 694747 **f** 01595 694307 **e** radio.shetland@bbc.co.uk **w** bbc.co.uk/radioscotland Senior Producer: Caroline Moyes. Trad/Country/Some Indie [2]

BBC Radio Shropshire, AM:1584 FM:95/96 2-4 Boscobel Drive, Shrewsbury, Shropshire SY1 3TT **t** 01743 248484 **f** 01743 271702 **e** radio.shropshire@bbc.co.uk **w** bbc.co.uk/england/radioshropshire HoM: Adam Green. SBJ Programmes: Tim Page. MOR [9, 7, 8]

SIBC, FM:96.2/102.2 Market St, Lerwick, Shetland ZE1 0JN **t** 01595 695299 **f** 01595 695696 **e** info@sibc.co.uk **w** sibc.co.uk MD/Prog Controller: Inga Walterson. Head of Sales: Ian Anderson. CHR [2]

Signal 2, AM:1170 Stoke Rd, Stoke-on-Trent, Staffs ST4 2SR **t** 01782 441300 **f** 01782 441301 **e** reception@signalradio.com **w** signal2.co.uk Programme Controller: Kevin Howard. Station Director: Lisa Hughes. Head of Sales: Lee Williams. Gold [8]

Signal 1, FM:96.4/96.9/102.6 Stoke Rd, Stoke-on-Trent, Staffs ST4 2SR **t** 01782 441300 **f** 01782 441301 **e** reception@signalradio.com **w** signal1.com Programme Controller: Kevin Howard. Station Director: Lisa Hughes. Head of Sales: Lee Williams. AC [8]

106.9 Silk FM, FM:106.9 Radio House, Bridge St, Macclesfield, Cheshire SK11 6DJ **t** 01625 268000 **f** 01625 269010 **e** mail@silkfm.com **w** silkfm.com Programme Controller: Andy Bailey. Station & Sales Manager: Rachel Barker. AC [7]

Six FM, FM:106/107.2 2c Park Ave, Burn Rd, Cookstown, Co. Tyrone BT80 8AH **t** 028 8675 8696 **f** 028 8676 1550 **e** firstname.lastname@sixfm.co.uk **w** sixfm.co.uk Launch Director: Robert Walsh. Programme Cont: James Devlin. AOR [1]

102.2 Smooth FM, FM:102.2 26-27 Castlereagh St, London W1H 5DL **t** 020 7706 4100 **f** 020 7723 9742 **e** firstname.lastname@smoothfm.com **w** smoothfm.com Programme Director: Mark Walker. Station Chief Exec: John Myers. MD: Roy Bennett. Jazz/Soul/Blues/R'n'B [11]

Smooth FM, FM:100.4 World Trade Centre, 8 Exchange Quay, Manchester M5 3EJ **t** 0845 050 1004 **f** 0845 054 1005 **e** info@smoothfm.com **w** smoothfm.com Programme Director: Steve Collins. MD: Roy Bennett. Grp Head of Music: Terry Underhill. Sales Director: Joe Radcliffe. Jazz/Soul/Blues/R'n'B [7]

BBC Radio Solent, AM:999/1359 FM:96.1/103.8 Broadcasting House, Havelock Rd, Southampton, Hants SO14 7PW **t** 023 8063 1311 **f** 023 8033 9648 **e** radio.solent.news@bbc.co.uk **w** bbc.co.uk/england/radiosolent Managing Editor: Mia Costello. MOR [12]

BBC Somerset Sound, AM:1323 Broadcasting House, Park St, Taunton, Somerset TA1 4DA **t** 01823 323956 **f** 01823 332539 **e** somerset.sound@bbc.co.uk **w** bbc.co.uk/england/radiobristol/somerset Managing Ed: Simon Clifford. MOR/Specialist [8, 12]

South East Radio, FM:95.6 - 96.4 Custom House Quay, Wexford, Ireland **t** +353 53 45200 **f** +353 53 45295 **e** info@southeastradio.ie **w** southeastradio.ie Prog Dir/Head of Music: Clive Roylance. MD: Eamonn Buttle. Head of Sales: Marion Barry. AC [15]

South Hams Radio, FM:100.5-101.9 Unit 1G, South Hams Business Pk, Churchstow, Kingsbridge, Devon TQ7 3QH **t** 01548 854595 **f** 01548 857345 **e** firstname.lastname@musicradio.com **w** southhamsradio.com Station Mgr/Head of Music: David Fitzgerald. Sales Manager: Alison Anderson. AC/CHR/MOR [13]

South West Sound, FM:97/96.5/103 Unit 40, The Loreburne Centre, High St, Dumfries DG1 2BD **t** 01387 250999 **f** 01387 265629 **e** firstname.lastname@southwestsound.co.uk **w** southwestsound.co.uk Programme Dir/Hd of Music: Alan Toomey. Station Dir/Head of Sales: Fiona Blackwood. MD: Sheena Borthwick. AC/Gold [3]

BBC Southern Counties Radio, FM:104-104.8/95-95.3 Broadcasting Centre, Guildford, Surrey GU6 7AP **t** 01483 306306 **f** 01483 304952 **e** southern.counties.radio@bbc.co.uk **w** bbc.co.uk/southerncounties Managing Editor: Neil Pringle. Head of News: Mark Carter. Assistant Editor: Nick Franklin. AC [11]

Southern FM, FM:102.4/103.5 Radio House, PO Box 2000, Brighton, E Sussex BN41 2SS **t** 01273 430111 **f** 01273 430098 **e** reception@southernfm.com **w** southernfm.com Prog Contr/Head of Music: Tony Aldridge. Head of Sales: Jason Kluver. CHR [12]

107.5 Sovereign Radio, FM:107.5 14 St Mary's Walk, Hailsham, E Sussex BN27 1AF **t** 01323 442700 **f** 01323 442866 **e** info@1075sovereignradio.co.uk **w** 1075sovereignradio.co.uk Station Manager: Nigel Ansell. Head of Music: Andy Knight. Sales Mgr: Karen Dyball. Soft AC [12]

Spectrum Radio, AM:558 4 Ingate Pl, London SW8 3NS **t** 020 7627 4433 **f** 020 7627 3409 **e** enquiries@spectrumradio.net **w** spectrumradio.net Station Mgr: Paul Hogan. Multi Ethnic [11]

Spin 103.8, FM:103.8 Level 3 South Block, The Malt House, Grand Canal Quay, Dublin 2, Ireland **t** +353 1 877 2100 **f** +353 1 855 0711 **e** info@spin1038.com **w** spin1038.com Programme Dir: Liam Thompson. GM: Tom Wright. Music Dir: Chris Doyle. Head of Sales: Joanne Coughlan. Urban [15]

Spire FM, FM:102 City Hall Studios, Salisbury, Wilts SP2 7QQ **t** 01722 416644 **f** 01722 415102 **e** firstname@spirefm.co.uk **w** spirefm.co.uk Station Manager: Ceri Hurford-Jones. Prog Controller: Stuart McGinley. Head of Sales: Karen Bosley. Gold/Chart [12]

Spirit FM, FM:96.6/102.3 9-10 Dukes Court, Bognor Rd, Chichester, W Sussex PO19 8FX **t** 01243 773600 **f** 01243 786464 **e** info@spiritfm.net **w** spiritfm.net Programme Controller: Duncan Barkes. MD: Stephen Oates. Head of Music: Ian Crouch. Head of Sales: Marie Allen. AC [12]

Star 107, FM:107.9/107.1 Radio House, Sturton St, Cambridge CB1 2QF **t** 01223 722300 **f** 01223 577686 **e** studio@star107.co.uk **w** star107.co.uk Prog Controller: Matthew Rowe. Station/Sales Mgr: Darren Taylor. Grp Head of Music: Dave Coull. AC [10]

Star 107.2, FM:107.2 Bristol Evening Post Building, Temple Way, Bristol BS99 7HD **t** 0117 910 6600 **f** 0117 925 0941 **e** firstname.lastname@star1072.co.uk **w** star1072.co.uk Programme Controller: Nick James. Grp Head of Music: Dave Coull. Grp Head of Sales: Campbell Grant. Head of Sales: Paul Kurnyta. AC

Star 107.5, FM:107.5 1st Floor, West Suite, Cheltenham Film Studios, Hatherley Lane, Cheltenham, Gloucs GL51 6PN **t** 01242 699555 **f** 01242 699666 **e** studio@star1075.co.uk **w** star1075.co.uk Programme Controller: Nick James. MD/Head of Sales: Junie Lewis. Head of Music: Dave Coull. AOR [8]

Star 107.7, FM:107.7 11 Beaconsfield Rd, Weston-super-Mare, North Somerset BS23 1YE **t** 01934 624455 **f** 01934 629922 **e** kate@star1077.co.uk **w** star1077.co.uk Station Mgr: Sue Payne. Programme Mgr: Scott Temple. AC [13, 9]

Star 107.9, FM:107.2/107.9 Brunel Mall, London Rd, Stroud, Gloucs GL5 2BP **t** 01453 767369 **f** 01453 757107 **e** programming@star1079.co.uk **w** star1079.co.uk Programme Manager: Marie Greenwood. MD: Junie Lewis. Head of Sales: Rebecca Tansley. (Programme Director & Head of Music based at Star 107.2) AC [8]

BBC Radio Stoke, FM:94.6/104.1 Cheapside, Hanley, Stoke-on-Trent, Staffs ST1 1JJ **t** 01782 208080 **f** 01782 289115 **e** radio.stoke@bbc.co.uk **w** bbc.co.uk/radiostoke Managing Editor: Sue Owen. Head of Programmes: Mary Fox. MOR [8]

97.2 Stray FM, FM:97.2 The Hamlet, Hornbeam Park Ave, Harrogate, N Yorks HG2 8RE **t** 01423 522972 **f** 01423 522922 **e** firstname.lastname@strayfm.com **w** strayfm.com Programme Controller: Mark Brooks. MD: Sarah Barry. Head of Sales: Rebecca Brooks. Hot AC [6]

BBC Radio Suffolk, FM:95.5/103.9/104.6 Broadcasting House, St Matthews St, Ipswich, Suffolk IP1 3EP **t** 01473 250000 **f** 01473 340785 **e** radiosuffolk@bbc.co.uk **w** bbc.co.uk/radiosuffolk HoM: Stephen Foster. Managing Editor: Gerald Main. MOR [10]

103.4 Sun FM, FM:103.4 PO Box 1034, Sunderland, Tyne and Wear SR5 2YL **t** 0191 548 1034 **f** 0191 548 7171 **e** studio@sun-fm.com **w** sun-fm.com Station Manager: Simon Grundy. Grp Head of Sales - North East: Helen Edmondson. AC/CHR [5]

Sunrise FM, FM:103.2 Sunrise House, 30 Chapel St, Little Germany, Bradford, W Yorks BD1 5DN **t** 01274 735043 **f** 01274 728534 **e** info@sunriseradio.fm **w** sunriseradio.fm MD/Prog Controller: Usha Parmar. Head of Sales: Amir Shazad. Asian [6]

Sunrise Radio, AM:1458 Sunrise House, Merrick Rd, Southall, Middlesex UB2 4AU **t** 020 8574 6666 **f** 020 8813 9800 **e** info@sunriseradio.com **w** sunriseradio.com Prog Dir/Head of Music: Tony Patti. MD: Tony Lit. Head of Sales: Kay McCarthy. Asian [11]

Sunshine 855, AM:855 Unit 11, Burway Trading Estate, Bromfield Rd, Ludlow, Shropshire SY8 1EN **t** 01584 873795 **f** 01584 875900 **e** firstname@sunshine855.com **w** sunshine855.com Operations Director: Ginny Murfin. Head of Music: Simon Doe. Head of Sales: Simon Perry. CHR/Gold [9, 8, 7]

Swansea Sound 1170 MW, AM:1170 Victoria Rd, Gowerton, Swansea SA4 3AB **t** 01792 511964 **f** 01792 511171 **e** info@swanseasound.co.uk **w** swanseasound.co.uk Station Director: Carrie Mosley. Programme Controller: Steve Barnes. Head of Music: Andy Miles. Sales Dir: Christine Dunn. AC [9]

Talk Sport, AM:1053/1071/1089/1107 18 Hatfields, London SE1 8DJ **t** 020 7959 7800 **f** 020 7959 7808 **e** firstname.lastname@talksport.co.uk **w** talksport.net Programme Mgr: Matt Smith. Programme Dir: Bill Ridley. Head of Sales: John Howard. Sport/Talk/Phone-ins

Media: Radio

Tay FM, FM:96.4/102.8 6 North Isla St, Dundee, Tayside DD3 7JQ **t** 01382 200800 **f** 01382 423252 **e** firstname.lastname@tayfm.co.uk **w** tayfm.co.uk HoM: Graeme Waggott. MD/Prog Dir: Ally Ballingall. Head of Sales: Ian Reilly. Chart [2]

Tay AM, AM:1161/1584 6 North Isla St, Dundee DD3 7JQ **t** 01382 200800 **f** 01382 423231 **e** firstname.lastname@tayam.co.uk **w** Tayam.co.uk HoM: Richard Allan. MD/Prog Dir: Arthur Ballingall. Head of Sales: Ian Reilly. Gold [2]

107.4 Telford FM, FM:107.4 Shropshire Star Building, Waterloo Rd, Ketley, Telford TF1 5UD **t** 01952 280011 **f** 01952 280010 **e** firstname.lastname@telfordfm.co.uk **w** telfordfm.co.uk MD/Prog Controller: Pete Wagstaff. Head of Music: Paul Shuttleworth. Head of Sales: Lisa Mahey. AC [8]

Ten-17, FM:101.7 Latton Bush Business Centre, Southern Way, Harlow, Essex CM18 7BU **t** 01279 431017 **f** 01279 236659 **e** firstname.lastname@gcapmedia.com **w** ten17.co.uk Programme Controller: Freddie Scherer. Head of Sales: Phil Caborn. AC [11, 10]

TFM, FM:96.6 Yale Crescent, Thornaby, Stockton on Tees, Cleveland TS17 6AA **t** 01642 888222 **f** 01642 868288 **e** tfm.reception@tfmradio.com **w** tfmradio.co.uk Programme Director: Colin Paterson. MD: Catherine Ellington. Head of Music-TFM: Rob Knight. Sales Director: Colette Butler. AC [5]

BBC Radio 3, FM:90 - 93 Room 4119, Broadcasting House, London W1A 1AA **t** 020 7765 2512 **f** 020 7765 2511 **e** firstname.lastname@bbc.co.uk **w** bbc.co.uk/radio3 Controller: Roger Wright. Head of Music Programming: Dr John Evans. Classical

BBC Three Counties Radio, FM:95.5/103.8/104.5 1 Hastings St, Luton, Beds LU1 5XL **t** 01582 637400 **f** 01582 401467 **e** 3cr@bbc.co.uk **w** bbc.co.uk/threecounties Managing Editor: Marc Norman. MOR/Gold [11, 10]

Time 106.6 FM, FM:106.6 The Observatory, Slough, Berks SL1 1LH **t** 01753 551066 **f** 01753 512277 **e** onair@timefm.com **w** timefm.com Programme Director: Mark Watson. MD/Head of Sales: Paul Allen. AC [11]

Time 107.5, FM:107.5 Lambourne House, 7 Western Rd, Romford, Essex RM1 3LD **t** 01708 731 643 **f** 01708 730 383 **e** mdover@timefm.com **w** timefm.com Programme Manager: Mark Dover. Grp Station Dir & Sales Dir: Mark Reason. Soul/RnB [11]

Time 107.3, FM:107.3 2-6 Basildon Rd, London SE2 0EW **t** 020 8311 3112 **f** 020 8312 1930 **e** gary@timefm.com **w** timefm.com Grp Prog Controller: Gary Mulligan. MD: Mike Houston. Grp Station Dir & Sales Dir: Mark Reason. Soul/RnB/Dance/Reggae [11]

Time 106.8, FM:106.8 2-6 Basildon Rd, London SE2 0EW **t** 020 8311 3112 **f** 020 8312 1930 **e** gary@timefm.com **w** timefm.com Grp Prog Cont: Gary Mulligan. Grp MD: Mike Houston. Grp Station Dir & Sales Dir: Mark Reason. Gold [11]

Tipp FM, FM:95.3/97.1/103.9 Davis Rd, Clonmel, Co Tipperary, Ireland **t** +353 52 26222 **f** +353 52 25447 **e** onair@tippfm.com **w** tippfm.com CEO: Ethel Power. Programme Controller: Ollie Brady. Head of Sales: Raymond Mulligan. AC [15]

Tipperary Mid-West, FM:104.8 St Michael St, Tipperary, Ireland **t** +353 62 52555 **f** +353 62 52671 **e** tippmidwest@radio.fm **w** tipperarymidwestradio.com Station Mgr: Anne Power. CEO: Michael Maguire. Head of Music & Sales: Breda Ryan. MOR [15]

100-102 Today FM, FM:100-102 124 Upper Abbey St, Dublin 1, Ireland **t** +353 1 804 9000 **f** +353 1 804 9099 **e** badams@todayfm.com **w** todayfm.com HoM: Brian Adams. Chief Executive: Willie O'Reilly. Associate Programme Manager: Tom Hardy. Head of Sales: Eamon Fitzpatrick. AC [15]

Touch 107.6, FM:107.6 Unit 9, Manor Pk, Banbury, Oxon OX16 3TB **t** 01295 661076 or 01295 661070 **e** firstname.lastname@cnradio.co.uk **w** touchfm1076.co.uk Head of Presenation: Steve Hyden. MD, Touch FM Stations: Christine Arnold. Grp Sales Dir: Natalie Tonner. Grp Programme Dir: Don Douglas. CHR/Gold [8]

Touch 102, FM:102 The Guard House Studios, Banbury Rd, Stratford upon Avon, Warwickshire CV37 7HX **t** 01789 262636 **f** 01789 263102 **e** firstname.lastname@cnradio.co.uk **w** touchfm102.co.uk Head of Presentation: Steve Hyden. MD, Touch FM Stations: Christine Arnold. Sales Dir: Natalie Tonner. Grp Programme Dir: Don Douglas. AC/MOR [8]

Touch 96.2, FM:96.2 Watch Close, Spon St, Coventry, W Midlands CV1 3LN **t** 024 7652 5656 **f** 024 7655 1744 **e** firstname.lastname@cnradio.co.uk **w** touchfm962.co.uk Head of Presentation: Steffan La Touche. MD, Touch FM Stations: Christine Arnold. Sales Dir: Natalie Tonner. Grp Programme Dir: Don Douglas. CHR [8]

107.4 Tower FM, FM:107.4 The Mill, Brownlow Way, Bolton BL1 2RA **t** 01204 387000 **f** 01204 534065 **e** firstname.lastname@towerfm.co.uk **w** towerfm.co.uk Station Dir: Dave Stankler. Programme Mgr: Phil MacKenzie. Head of Sales: Victoria Cullen. AC [7]

Trax FM, FM:107.9 White Hart Yard, Bridge St, Worksop, Notts S80 1HR **t** 01909 500611 **f** 01909 500445 **e** enquiries@traxfm.co.uk **w** traxfm.co.uk Admin Manager: Paula Ingamells. Sales Mgr: Peggy Watson. Programme Manager: Nick Hancock. AC [8]

Trax FM., FM:107.1 5 Sidings Court, White Rose Way, Doncaster, S Yorks DN4 5SE **t** 01302 341166 **f** 01302 326104 **e** enquiries@traxfm.co.uk **w** traxfm.co.uk Admin Manager: Paula Ingamells. Sales Mgr: Peggy Watson. Programme Manager: Nick Hancock. AC/CHR [8]

96 Trent FM, FM:96.2/96.5 29-31 Castle Gate, Nottingham NG1 7AP **t** 0115 873 1500 **f** 0115 873 1509 **e** firstname.lastname@gcapmedia.com **w** trentfm.co.uk Programme Director: Chris Pegg. Sales Manager: Margaret Dunn. AC [8]

BBC Radio 2, FM:88-91 Henry Wood House, 3 and 6 Langham Pl, London W1A 1AA **t** 020 7580 4468 **f** 020 7725 2578 **e** firstname.lastname@bbc.co.uk **w** bbc.co.uk/radio2 Controller: Lesley Douglas. Executive Producer for Music: Colin Martin. AC/Gold/Specialist

2BR (Two Boroughs Radio), FM:99.8 IMEX Spaces, Nelson, Lancs BB9 7DR **t** 01282 690000 **f** 01282 690001 **e** info@2br.co.uk **w** 2br.co.uk Programme Controller: Cliff Brooks. Station & Sales Mgr: Andrea Mercer.. AC [7]

radio2XS, FM:107.8 The Studios, West Handley, Sheffield, S Yorks S21 5RZ **t** 0870 321 1242 **e** programmes@radio2xs.com **w** radio2XS.com MD/Prog Dir: Jeff Cooper. Head of Sales: Paul Chadbourne. New/Alternative [6]

U105, FM:105.8 Ormeau Rd, Belfast BT7 1EB **t** 028 90 332105 **f** 028 90 330105 **e** firstname.lastname@u105.com **w** u105.com HoM: Maurice Jay. MD: John Rossborough. Sales Mgr: Siobhan Lavery. Gold

BBC Radio Ulster, FM:92.4/95.4 Broadcasting House, Ormeau Ave, Belfast, Co Antrim BT2 8HQ **t** 028 9033 8000 **f** 028 9033 8800 **e** firstname.lastname@bbc.co.uk **w** bbc.co.uk/northernireland/atl Senior Producer - Radio: Simon Taylor. All [1]

Unique Production UBC Media Group PLC, 50 Lisson St, London NW1 5DF **t** 020 7453 1600 **f** 020 7453 1665 **e** info1@ubcmedia.com **w** UBCMedia.com Hd of Commercial Prog'g: Andrew Phillips.

Vale FM, FM:96.6/97.4 Longmead Studios, Shaftesbury, Dorset SP7 8QQ **t** 01747 855711 **f** 01747 855722 **e** studio@valefm.co.uk **w** valefm.co.uk Programme Controller: Stewart Smith. Regional MD: John Baker. Head of Sales: Anne Holmes. AC [12]

Valleys Radio, AM:999/1116 PO Box 1116, Ebbw Vale NP23 8XW **t** 01495 301116 **f** 01495 300710 **e** sales@valleysradio.co.uk **w** valleysradio.co.uk Programme Controller: Tony Peters. Station Mgr: Joanne Roberts. Head of Sales: Chris Hurst. AC [9]

96.9 Viking FM, FM:96.9 The Boathouse, Commercial Rd, Hull, E Yorks HU1 2SG **t** 01482 325141 **f** 0845 4580 390 **e** programmes@vikingfm.co.uk **w** vikingfm.co.uk Programme Director: Darrell Woodman. MD: Mike Bawden. Head of Sales: Steve Allbones. AC/Chart [6]

Virgin Radio, AM:1215 FM:105.8 1 Golden Sq, London W1F 9DJ **t** 020 7434 1215 **f** 020 7434 1197 **e** firstname.lastname@virginradio.co.uk **w** virginradio.co.uk HoM: James Curran. Prog Dir: Paul Jackson. MD: Fru Hazlitt. Head of Sales: Nick Hewat. AC/Chart [11]

BBC Wales/Cymru, AM:882/1125/657 FM:92-105 Broadcasting House, Llantrisant Rd, Llandaff, Cardiff, South Glamorgan CF5 2YQ **t** 02920 322000 **f** 02920 323724 **e** radio.wales@bbc.co.uk **w** bbc.co.uk/wales Radio Wales Editor: Julie Barton. Classical/Welsh [9]

96.4FM The Wave, FM:96.4 Victoria Rd, Gowerton, Swansea SA4 3AB **t** 01792 511964 **f** 01792 511965 **e** info@thewave.co.uk **w** thewave.co.uk Station Dir: Carrie Mosley. Programme Controller: Steve Barnes. Head of Music: Andy Miles. Sales Dir: Christine Dunn. CHR [9]

Wave 105.2 FM, FM:105.2/105.8 5 Manor Court, Barnes Wallis Rd, Segensworth East, Fareham, Hants PO15 5TH **t** 01489 481057 **f** 01489 481100 **e** studio@wave105.com **w** wave105.com MD: Martin Ball. Programming Controller: Dave Shearer. AC [12]

Wave 96.5, FM:96.5 965 Mowbray Drive, Blackpool, Lancs FY3 7JR **t** 01253 304965 **f** 01253 301965 **e** info@thewavefm.co.uk **w** wave965.com Station Director: Helen Bowden. Head of Music: Roy Lynch. Head of Sales: Paula Davies. AC [7]

Wave 102 FM, FM:102 8 South Tay St, Dundee DD1 1PA **t** 01382 901000 **f** 01382 900999 **e** studio@wave102.co.uk **w** wave102.co.uk Programme Controller: Peter Mac. Station & Sales Manager: Bill Bowman. Station Dir: Alan Shields. AC [2]

Waves Radio, FM:101.2 7 Blackhouse Circle, Peterhead, Aberdeenshire AB42 1BN **t** 01779 491012 **f** 01779 490802 **e** waves@wavesfm.com **w** wavesfm.com MD: Norman Spence. Prog Dir/Hd of Music: Kenny King. Head of Sales: David Milne. Chart/Gold [2]

Wessex FM, FM:97.2/96 Radio House, Trinity St, Dorchester, Dorset DT1 1DJ **t** 01305 250333 **f** 01305 266486 **e** firstname.lastname@wessexfm.com **w** wessexfm.com Programme Controller: Jason Herbert. Regional MD: John Baker. Sales Manager: Jason Cawley. AC [13]

West FM, FM:96.7 Radio House, 54 Holmston Rd, Ayr KA7 3BE **t** 01292 283662 **f** 01292 283665 **e** info@westfm.co.uk **w** westfm.co.uk Prog Ctrl/Head of Music: Alan Toomey. MD: Sheena Borthwick-Toomey. Head of Sales: Lynne Shirkie. CHR [3]

Westsound AM, AM:1035 Radio House, 54, Holmston Rd, Ayr KA7 3BE **t** 01292 283662 **f** 01292 283665 **e** info@westsound.co.uk **w** west-sound.co.uk Prog Cont/Head of Music: Alan Toomey. MD: Sheena Borthwick-Toomey. Head of Sales: Lynne Shirkie. AC/Gold [3]

BBC Radio Wiltshire, AM:1368/1332 FM:103.6/104.3/103.5/104.9 Broadcasting House, Prospect Pl, Swindon, Wilts SN1 3RW **t** 01793 513626 **f** 01793 513650 **e** radio.wiltshire@bbc.co.uk **w** bbc.co.uk/radiowiltshire HoM: Mark Seaman. Managing Editor: Tony Worgan. Gold/Chart/Classical [8, 12]

107.2 Win FM, FM:107.2 PO Box 1072, The Brooks, Winchester, Hants SO23 8FT **t** 01962 841071 **f** 01962 841079 **e** firstname.lastname@winfm.co.uk **w** winfm.co.uk Programme Controller: Phil Marriott. Station & Sales Mgr: Gordon Drummond. AC [12]

107.2 Wire FM, FM:107.2 Warrington Business Pk, Long Lane, Warrington, Cheshire WA2 8TX **t** 01925 445545 **f** 01925 657705 **e** info@wirefm.com **w** wirefm.com Programme Controller: Paul Holmes. Station Director: Iain Fowler. Head of Music: Pete Pinnington. Senior Sales: Gill Taylor. AC [6]

Wired FM, FM:96.8/106.8 Mary Immaculate College, South Circular Rd, Limerick, Ireland **t** +353 61 315773 **f** +353 61 315776 **e** wiredfm@mic.ul.ie **w** wiredfm.mic.ul.ie Station Manager: Nessa McGann. Programme Director: Miriam Walsh. Indie/Local [15]

102.4 Wish FM, FM:102.4 Orrell Lodge, Orrell Rd, Orrell, Wigan WN5 8HJ **t** 01942 761024 **f** 01942 777694 **e** firstname.lastname@wish-fm.com **w** wishfm.net Programme Mgr: Jo Heuston. Station Director: Danny Holborn. Head of Music: Andy Lawson. Sales Dir: Graham Sarath. AC [7]

WLR FM, FM:95.1/97.5 The Broadcast Centre, Ardkeen, Co Waterford **t** +353 51 872248 **f** +353 51 877420 **e** studio@wlrfm.com **w** wlrfm.com Prog Controller: Billy McCarthy. MD: Des Whelan. Head of Music: Michael Byrne. Head of Sales: Tim Hassett. AC [15]

BBC WM, FM:95.6 The Mailbox, Birmingham, W Midlands B1 1RF **t** 08453 00 99 56 **f** 0121 472 3174 **e** bbcwm@bbc.co.uk **w** bbc.co.uk/radiowm Managing Editor: Keith Beech. Dep Managing Editor: Jeremy Pollock. Head of Music: Steve Woodhall. AOR [8]

107.7 FM The Wolf, FM:107.7 10th Floor, Mander House, Wolverhampton, W Midlands WV1 3NB **t** 01902 571070 **f** 01902 571079 **e** firstname@thewolf.co.uk **w** thewolf.co.uk Programme Controller: Richard Dodd. Station Director: Marie Wright. Regional PD: Kevin Howard. Head of Music: Tim Haycock. Head of Sales: Gisella Wiley. Gold [8]

BBC World Service Room 101, Henry Wood House, 3/6 Portland Pl, London W1A 1AA **t** 020 7765 3938 **f** 020 7765 3945 **e** alan.rowett@bbc.co.uk **w** bbc.co.uk/worldservice HoM: Alan Rowett. Director, World Service: Mark Byford. Programme Director: Phil Harding.

Wythenshawe FM 97.2, FM:97.2 Suite A4, Alderman Gatley House, Hale Top, Manchester M22 5RQ **t** 0161 499 7982 **f** 0161 499 7442 **e** info@wfmradio.org **w** wfmradio.org HoM: Haydn Insley. Station Mgr: Christine Brennan. Programme Cont: Jason Kenyon. AOR [7]

Wyvern FM, FM:96.7/97.6/102.8 First Floor, Kirkham House, John Comyn Drive, Worcester WR3 7NS **t** 01905 545500 **f** 01905 545509 **e** firstname.lastname@gcapmedia.com **w** wyvernfm.co.uk Programme Controller: Rick Simmonds. Sales Manager: Andy McHugh. AC [8]

XFM 104.9, FM:104.9 30 Leicester Sq, London WC2H 7LA **t** 020 7766 6600 **f** 020 7766 6601 **e** firstname.lastname@xfm.co.uk **w** xfm.co.uk Network Programme Controller: Andy Ashton. Network MD: Nick Davidson. Network Head of Music: Mike Walsh. Commercial Director: Duncan George. Alternative [11]

Xfm Manchester, FM:97.7 Laser House, Waterfront Quay, Salford Quays, Manchester M50 3XW **t** 0161 400 0105 **f** 0161 400 1105 **e** firstname.lastname@xfm.co.uk **w** xfmmanchester.co.uk Programme Controller: Matt Whyatt. Network Head of Music: Mike Walsh. Music Scheduler: Kate Beveridge. Sales Exec: Jen Simm. Alternative [7]

Xfm Scotland, FM:106.1/105.7 Four Winds Pavilion, Pacific Quay, Glasgow G51 1EB **t** 0141 566 6106 **f** 0141 566 6110 **e** firstname.lastname@xfm.co.uk **w** xfm.co.uk Prog Controller: Claire Pattenden. Network Head of Music: Mike Walsh. Commercial Controller: Liz Hamilton. Music Manager: John McInally. New Rock/Dance [3]

BBC Radio York, AM:666/1260 FM:95.5/103.7/104.3 20 Bootham Row, York, N Yorks YO30 7BR **t** 01904 641351 **f** 01904 610937 **e** radio.york@bbc.co.uk **w** bbc.co.uk/radioyork Head of Music/Librarian: Jan Moore. Managing Editor: Matt Youdale. Head of Programmes: Bernadette Burbridge. MOR/Specialist [6, 5]

Yorkshire Coast Radio, FM:96.2/103.1 PO Box 962, Scarborough, N Yorks YO11 3ZP **t** 01723 581700 **f** 01723 588990 **e** studio@yorkshirecoastradio.com **w** yorkshirecoastradio.com Station Mgr/Prog Cont: Chris Sigsworth. Head of Sales: tbc. AC [5, 6]

Yourradio FM, FM:103, 106.9 Pioneer Park Studios, 80 Castlegreen St, Dumbarton G82 1JB **t** 01389 734 422 **f** 08454 900 556 **e** firstname@yourradiofm.com **w** yourradiofm.com Prog Controller: Derek McIntyre. MD/Sales Dir: Eddie Startup. CHR, Gold [3]

Digital and Internet Radio

BBC 1Xtra Yalding House, 152-156 Gt Portland St, London W1N 6AJ **t** 020 8743 8000 **f** 020 7765 0759 **e** 1xtra.online@bbc.co.uk **w** bbc.co.uk/1Xtra Station Editor: Ian Parkinson. Programmes Editor: Willber Willberforce. New Urban Music

BBC 6 Music, FM:DAB 5th floor, Western House, 99 Great Portland St, London W1A 1AA **t** 020 7580 4468 **f** 020 7765 4571 **e** firstname.lastname@bbc.co.uk **w** bbc.co.uk/6music Music Manager: Jon Myer. Network Controller: Lesley Douglas. Head Of Programmes: Ric Blaxill. Alternative

Ministry of Sound Radio 103 Gaunt St, London SE1 6DP **t** 0870 060 0010 or 020 7740 8647 **f** 020 7403 5348 **e** studio@ministryofsound.com **w** ministryofsound.com/radio Head of Radio: Oliver Embden.

Planet Rock, FM:(DAB Digital Radio) PO Box 2269, London W1A 5UQ **t** 020 7911 7300 **f** 020 7911 7369 **e** joinus@planetrock.com **w** planetrock.com MD: Mark Lee. Programme Controller: Mark Jeeves. Head of Sales: Steve Cray. Rock

Pulse Rated Enterprise House, Wood Green Industrial Estate, Salhouse, Norwich NR13 6NY **t** 0870 142 3456 **f** 01603 735 160 **e** business@pulserated.com **w** pulserated.com Business Development: Peter Davis.

Score Digital Ltd, AM:Digital Multiplex 3 South Avenues, Clydebank Business Pk, Glasgow G81 2RX **t** 0141 565 2347 **f** 0141 565 2318 **e** firstname.lastname@emap.com **w** scoredigital.co.uk MD: Steve Parkinson. Glasgow: Digital Channel 11C. Edinburgh: Digital Channel 12D. N.Ireland: Digital Channel 12C. [3]

The Storm, FM:(DAB Digital Radio) PO Box 2000, 1, Passage St, Bristol BS99 7SN **t** 020 7911 7300 **f** 020 7911 7369 **e** mail@stormradio.co.uk **w** stormradio.co.uk MD: Mark Lee. Programme Controller: Bern Leckie.

UCB Europe, FM:Sky Digital ch.941 Hanchurch Christian Centre, PO Box 255, Stoke On Trent, Staffs ST4 8YY **t** 01782 642 000 **f** 01782 641 121 **e** ucb@ucb.co.uk **w** ucb.co.uk Station Controller: Andrew Urquhart. Head of Music: Fiona Day. Christian Contemporary/AC

VIP Radio PO Box 909, Thorpe Salvin, Notts. S80 3YZ **t** 01909 774 111 **f** 01909-515171 **e** info@vipradio.net **w** vipradio.net MD: Kev Roberts.

World Radio Network (WRN), AM:Broadcasting on - Sky Digital ch.937 & Telewest Active Digital ch.920 10 Wyvil Court, Wyvil Rd, London SW8 2TG **t** 020 7896 9000 **f** 020 7896 9007 **e** info@wrn.org **w** wrn.org Marketing Manager: Tim Ayris. MD: Gary Edgerton. R&B/World

Television

Anglia Anglia House, Norwich, Norfolk NR1 3JG
t 01603 615151 **f** 01603 631032 **e** duty.office@itv.com
w itvregions.com/Anglia.

At It Productions 68 Salusbury Rd, Queens Pk, London
NW6 6NU **t** 020 7644 0000 **f** 020 7644 0001
e enquiries@atitproductions.com **w** atitproductions.com
MDs: Chris Fouracre, Martin Cunning.

Big Eye Film & Television Lock Keepers Cottage, Century
St, Whitworth Street West, Manchester M3 4QL
t 0161 832 6111 **f** 0161 834 8558 **e** eye@bigeye.u-net.com
Contact: Steven Lock, Mary Richmond.

Blaze TV 43-45 Dorset St, London W1U 7NA
t 020 7664 1600 **f** 020 7935 5907
e firstname.lastname@blaze.tv **w** zenith-enteretainment.com
Dir of Programmes: Conor McAnally.

Border The Television Centre, Carlisle, Cumbria CA1 3NT
t 01228 525101 **f** 01228 541384 **w** border-tv.com.

Bournemouth TV (see Southampton TV).

Brighter Pictures 10th Floor, Blue Star House, 234-244
Stockwell Rd, London SW9 9SP **t** 020 7733 7333
f 020 7733 6333 **e** info@brighter.co.uk **w** brighter.co.uk
MD: Gavin Hay.

Carlton (Central) Carlton Studios, Television House,
Nottingham NG7 2NA **t** 0115 986 3322 **f** 0115 964 5552
w carlton.com/central.

Carlton UK 101 St Martin's Lane, London WC2N 4AZ
t 020 7240 4000 **f** 020 7240 4171 **w** carlton.com.

Carlton (Westcountry) Western Wood Way, Langage
Science Pk, Plymouth, Devon PL7 5BG **t** 01752 333333
f 01752 333444 **w** carlton.com/westcountry.

CC-LAB

5-6 Newman Passage, London W1T 1EH **t** 020 7580 8055
f 020 7637 8350 **e** info@cc-lab.com **w** cc-lab.com Executive
Producer: Justin Rees. MD: Jason Hocking. Creative Director:
Nathan Horrocks. Senior Producer: Celia Moore. Production
Manager: Tori Smith.

Chameleon TV Greatminster House, Lister Hill, Horsforth,
Leeds LS18 5DL **t** 0113 205 0045 **f** 0113 281 9454
e firstname@chameleontv.com **w** chameleontv.com
MD: Allen Jewhurst.

Channel 4 124 Horseferry Rd, London SW1P 2TX
t 020 7396 4444 **f** 020 7306 8630
e Initial+lastname@channel4.co.uk **w** channel4.com
Commissioning Editor, T4 & Music: Neil McCallum.

Channel U PO Box 50239, London EC1V 3YF
t 020 7054 9010 **f** 020 7054 9011 **e** info@vitv.co.uk
w channelu.tv CEO: Stewart Lund.

Chart Show Channels 37 Harwood Rd, London SW6 4QP
t 020 7371 5999 **f** 020 7384 2026 **e** info@chartshow.tv
w chartshow.tv CEO: Gail Screene.

The Chart Show 37 Harwood Rd, London SW6 4QP
t 020 7371 5999 **f** 020 7384 2026 **e** info@chartshow.tv
w chartshow.tv.

Compact Collections Ltd Greenland Pl, 115-123 Bayham
St, London NW1 0AG **t** 020 7446 7420 **f** 020 7446 7424
e info@compactcollections.com **w** compactcollections.com
Contact: John O'Sullivan.

CYP Limited CYP Children's Audio, The Fairway, Bush Fair,
Harlow, Essex CM18 6LY **t** 01279 444707 **f** 01279 445570
e enquiries@kidsmusic.co.uk **w** kidsmusic.co.uk
Contact: John Bassett.

Different Ltd 10 Summerhill Terrace, Summerhill Sq,
Newcastle upon Tyne NE4 6EB **t** 0191 261 0111
f 0191 221 1122 **e** dreid@different-uk.com **w** different-uk.com
Producer: David Reid.

BBC East St Catherine's Close, All Saints Green, Norwich,
Norfolk NR1 3ND **t** 01603 619331 **f** 01603 284455
e look.east@bbc.co.uk **w** bbc.co.uk/england/lookeast.

Emap Performance TV Mappin House, 4 Winsley St,
London W1W 8HF **t** 020 7436 1515 **f** 020 7376 1313
e tv@emap.com **w** emap.com Dir of Music: Simon Sadler.

Endemol UK Productions Shepherds Building Central,
Charecroft Way, London W14 0EE **t** 0870 333 1700
f 0870 333 1800 **e** info@endemoluk.com **w** endemoluk.com
Music Supervisor: Amelia Hartley.

Five 1 Stephen St, London W1T 1AL **t** 020 7691 6610
f 020 7691 6085 **e** firstname.lastname@five.tv **w** five.tv
Mgr, Music Services: Martin Price.

Fizz PO Box 50239, London EC1V 3YF **t** 020 7054 9010
f 020 7054 9011 **e** info@vitv.co.uk **w** fizzmusic.com
CEO: Stewart Lund.

Formosa Films Ltd Sands Film Studios, 119 Rotherhithe St,
London SE16 4NF **t** 020 7237 8070 **f** 020 7681 2567
e info@formosafilms.com **w** formosafilms.com
Producer: Neil Thompson.

GMTV London Television Centre, Upper Ground, London
SE1 9TT **t** 020 7827 7000 **f** 020 7827 7001
e talk2us@gmtv.co.uk **w** gmtv.co.uk Contact: Press Office.

Granada (Manchester) Granada Television, Quay St,
Manchester M60 9EA **t** 0161 832 7211 **f** 0161 953 0298
e officers.duty@granadatv.co.uk **w** granadatv.co.uk
Music & Fim Ent Dept: Louise Wilcockson.

Granada (News Centre) Albert Dock, Liverpool,
Merseyside L3 4BA **t** 0151 709 9393 or 0161 832 7211
f 0151 709 3389 **w** granada.co.uk.

Andy Holland - Independent TV Producer Firedup
TV, 87 Lancaster Rd, London W11 1QQ **t** 020 7313 9156 or
07767 833 603 **e** andy.holland@firedup.tv **w** firedup.tv
Exec Prod: Andy Holland.

Homechoice 205 Holland Park Ave, London W11 4XB
t 020 7348 4000 **f** 020 7348 4370
e lyall.sumner@homechoice.net **w** homechoice.co.uk
Music Channel Manager: Lyall Sumner.

Initial (An Endemol Company) Shepeherds Building Central, Charecroft Way, London W14 OEE **t** 0870 333 1700 **f** 0870 333 1800 **e** info@endemoluk.com **w** endemoluk.com HoM: Phil Mount.

ITV London The London Television Centre, Upper Ground, London SE1 9LT **t** 020 7620 1620 **f** 020 7261 3307 **e** planning@itvlondon.com **w** itvregions.com/london.

ITVWales Television Centre, Culverhouse Cross, Cardiff CF5 6XJ **t** 029 2059 0590 **f** 029 2059 7183 **e** info@itvwales.com **w** itvwales.com.

Landscape Channel Europe Ltd Landscape Studios, Crowhurst, E Sussex TN33 9BX **t** 01424 830900 **f** 01424 830680 **e** info@landscapetv.com **w** landscapetv.com Chairman: Nick Austin.

Later With Jools Holland BBC TV Centre, Wood Lane, London W12 7RJ **t** 020 8743 8000 or 020 8576 0968 **f** 020 8749 4955 **w** bbc.co.uk/later.

Maguffin Ltd 10 Frith St, London W1V 5TZ **t** 020 7437 2526 **f** 020 7437 1516 **e** firstname@maguffin.co.uk **w** maguffin.co.uk MD / Prod: James Chads.

Mike Mansfield Television Ltd 5th Floor, 41-42 Berners St, London W1T 3NB **t** 020 7580 2581 **f** 020 7580 2582 **e** mikemantv@aol.com **w** cyberconcerts.com MD: Mike Mansfield.

Meridian Television Centre, Northam, Southampton, Hants SO14 OPZ **t** 023 8022 2555 **f** 023 8071 2012 **e** viewerliaison@meridiantv.com **w** meridiantv.co.uk.

MTV Base 17-29 Hawley Crescent, London NW1 8TT **t** 020 7284 7777 **f** 020 7284 6466 **e** Lastname.firstname@mtvne.com **w** mtv.co.uk/base Music Ed: Lyndsay Wesker.

MTV Dance Hawley Crescent, London NW1 8TT **t** 020 7284 7777 **f** 020 7284 6466 **e** Lastname.firstname@mtvne.com **w** mtv.co.uk/dance Music Editor: Des Paul.

MTV Flux 17-29 Hawley Crescent, London NW1 8TT **t** 020 7284 7777 **f** 020 7284 6466 **e** Lastname.firstname@mtvne.com **w** mtv.co.uk/base Music Ed: Lyndsay Wesker.

MTV Hits Hawley Crescent, London NW1 8TT **t** 020 7284 7777 **f** 020 7284 6466 **e** Lastname.firstname@mtvne.com **w** mtv.co.uk/hits Music Ed: Des Paul.

MTV UK & Ireland Hawley Crescent, London NW1 OTT **t** 020 7284 7777 **f** 020 7284 6466 **e** lastname.firstname@mtvne.com **w** mtv.co.uk Head of Music Programming: Chris Price.

MTV2 17-29 Hawley Crescent, London NW1 8TT **t** 020 7284 7777 **f** 020 7284 6466 **e** mtv2@mtvne.com **w** mtv2europe.com New Music Editor: Will McGillivray.

Music Box 30 Sackville St, London W1X 1DB **t** 020 7478 7300 **f** 020 7478 7403 **e** reception@sunsetvine.co.uk **w** music-bx.co.uk MD: John Leach.

BBC North BBC Broadcasting Centre, Woodhouse Lane, Leeds, W Yorks LS2 9PX **t** 0113 244 1188 **f** 0113 243 9387 **e** look.north@bbc.co.uk **w** bbc.co.uk/england/looknorthyorkslincs.

BBC North East Broadcasting Centre, Barrack Rd, Newcastle upon Tyne, Tyne and Wear NE99 2NE **t** 0191 232 1313 **f** 0191 221 0112 **e** newcastlenews@bbc.co.uk **w** bbc.co.uk.

BBC North West New Broadcasting House, Oxford Rd, Manchester M60 1SJ **t** 0161 200 2020 **f** 0161 236 1005 **e** nwt@bbc.co.uk **w** bbc.co.uk/england/northwesttonight.

BBC Northern Ireland Ormeau Ave, Belfast, Co Antrim BT2 8HQ **t** 028 9033 8000 **f** 028 9033 8800 **w** bbc.co.uk/northernireland.

Oasis TV 6-7 Great Pulteney St, London W1R 3DF **t** 020 7434 4133 **f** 020 7494 2843 **e** sales@oasistv.co.uk **w** oasistv.co.uk Buisness Dev't Mgr: Matthew Lock.

Off the Radar TV Ltd 20-22 Rosebery Ave, London EC1R 4SX **t** 020 7520 8340 **e** Patrick@offtheradar.tv **w** OfftheRadar.tv Commercial Manager: Patrick Usmar.

Oort Ltd 62 Sprules Rd, London SE4 2NN **t** 020 7635 6765 **e** emma@oortmedia.net **w** oortmedia.net Creative Director: Emma Peters.

Pearson Television Ltd 1 Stephen St, London W1P 1PJ **t** 020 7691 6000 **f** 020 7691 6100 **e** facilites.helpdesk@fremental.com **w** pearsontv.com.

The Pop Factory / Avanti Television Welsh Hills Works, Jenkin St, Porth CF39 9PP **t** 01443 688500 **f** 01443 688501 **e** info@thepopfactory.com **w** thepopfactory.com Contact: Emyr Afan Davies.

Remedy Productions Office 6, 9 Thorpe Close, London W10 5XL **t** 020 8964 4408 **f** 020 8964 4421 **e** info@remedyproductions.tv **w** remedyproductions.tv MD: Toby Dormer.

RTE Network 2 Donnybrook, Dublin 4, Ireland **t** +353 1 208 3111 **f** +353 1 208 2511 **e** television@rte.ie **w** rte.ie.

RTE (Radio-Telefis Eireann) Donnybrook, Dublin 4, Ireland **t** +353 1 208 3111 **f** +353 1 208 3080 **e** webmaster@rte.ie **w** rte.ie.

RTE TG4 Donnybrook, Dublin 4, Ireland **t** +353 1 208 3111 **f** +353 1 208 2511 **w** tg4.ie/tg4.htm.

S4C (Sianel Pedwar Cymru) Parc Ty Glas, Llanishen, Cardiff, South Glamorgan CF4 5DU **t** 029 2074 7444 **f** 029 2074 1457 **e** hotline@s4c.co.uk **w** s4c.co.uk.

SixTV The Oxford Channel 270 Woodstock Rd, Oxford OX2 7NW **t** 01865 557000 **f** 01865 553355 **e** ptv@oxfordchannel.com **w** sixtv.co.uk Producer: Tom Copeland.

Sky Box Office Skt Television, Unit 2, Grant Way, Isleworth, Middlesex TW7 5QD **t** 020 7805 8126 **f** 020 7805 8130 **e** marc.conneely@bskyb.com **w** sky.com Hd of Pay-Per-View Events: Marc Conneely.

Sky Music Channels Unit 4, Grant Way, Isleworth, Middlesex TW7 5QD **t** 020 7805 8526 **f** 020 7805 8522 **e** Ian.Greaves@bskyb.com Music Programming Manager: Ian Greaves.

BBC South Havelock Rd, Southampton, Hants SO1 OXQ **t** 023 8022 6201 **f** 023 8033 9931 **e** spotlight@bbc.co.uk **w** bbc.co.uk.

BBC South West Broadcasting House, Seymour Rd, Plymouth, Devon PL3 5DB **t** 01752 229201 or 01752 234545 **f** 01752 234595 **e** spotlight@bbc.co.uk **w** bbc.co.uk/england/spotlight Press Office: Marlene Crawley.

Southampton Television Sir James Mathews Building, 157-187 Above Bar St, Southampton SO14 7NN **t** 023 8023 2400 **f** 023 8038 6366 **e** James.Rostance@southamptontv.co.uk **w** southamptontv.co.uk Producer, Music & Ent.: James Rostance.

SUBtv 140 Buckingham Palace Rd, London SW1W 9SA **t** 020 7881 2539 or 07771 517 777 **e** jasonbarrett@sub.tv **w** sub.tv/subtv Business Development Mgr: Jason Barrett.

T4 At It Productions, Westbourne Studios, 242 Acklam Rd, London W10 5YG **t** 020 88964 2122 **f** 020 8964 2133 **e** lindsey.brill@atitproductions.com Entertainment Booker: Lindsey Brill.

BBC Television Centre Wood Lane, Shepherd's Bush, London W12 7RJ **t** 020 8743 8000 **f** 020 8749 7520 **e** info@bbc.co.uk **w** bbc.co.uk.

Top Of The Pops Rm 385, Design Building, BBC Television Centre, Wood Lane, London W12 7RJ **t** 020 8743 8000 or 020 8624 8398 (Prod) **f** 020 8624 8395 (Prod) **e** firstname.lastname@bbc.co.uk **w** bbc.co.uk/totp Prod: Sally Wood.

Tyne Tees Television Centre, City Rd, Newcastle upon Tyne, Tyne and Wear NE1 2AL **t** 0191 261 0181 **f** 0191 269 3770 **e** news@tynetees.tv **w** itvregions.com/Tyne_Tees.

Upfront Television 39-41 New Oxford St, London WC1A 1BN **t** 020 7836 7702/3 **f** 020 7836 7701 **e** info@upfronttv.com **w** celebritiesworldwide.com Co-MDs: Claire Nye, Richard Brecker.

UTV (Ulster Television) Havelock House, Ormeau Rd, Belfast, Co Antrim BT7 1EB **t** 028 9032 8122 or 028 9026 2220 **f** 028 9024 6695 or 028 9026 2208 **w** utvlive.com.

VH1/VH1 Classic Hawley Crescent, London NW1 8TT **t** 020 7284 7777 **f** 020 7284 6466 **e** vh1online@mtvne.com **w** vh1online.co.uk Music Editors: Anneli Fairs or Colin Cooper.

Videotech 131-151 Great Titchfield St., London W1W 5BB **t** 020 7665 8200 **f** 020 7665 8213 Producer: Diana Smith.

VMX 205 Holland Park Ave, London W11 4XB **t** 020 7348 4000 **f** 020 7348 4370 **e** vmx@homechoice.net **w** homechoice.co.uk Music Producr Producer: Lyall Sumner.

BBC Wales Broadcasting House, Meirion Rd, Bangor LL57 3BY **t** 01248 370880 **f** 01248 352784 **e** feedback.wales@bbc.co.uk **w** bbc.co.uk/wales.

BBC West Midlands Pebble Mill Rd, Birmingham, W Midlands B5 7QQ **t** 0121 432 8888 **f** 0121 432 8634 **e** midlands.today@bbc.co.uk **w** bbc.co.uk.

Whizz Kid Entertainment 4 Kingly St, Soho, London W1B 5PE **t** 020 7440 2550 **e** firstname@whizzkid.tv **w** whizzkid.tv CEO: Malcolm Gerrie.

Yorkshire Television Ltd Television Centre, Leeds, W Yorks LS3 1JS **t** 0113 243 8283 **f** 0113 244 5107 **w** yorkshiretv.co.uk MD: David Croft.

Broadcast Services

3DD Entertainment Ltd. 190 Camden High St, London NW1 8QP **t** 020 7428 1800 **f** 020 7428 1818 **e** Sales@3dd-entertainment.co.uk **w** 3dd-entertainment.co.uk Publicity Co-ordinator: Sarah Andersen.

Alice Unit 34D, Hobbs Ind Estate, Newchapel, Lingfield, Surrey RH7 6HN **t** 01342 833500 **f** 01342 833350 **e** sales@alice.co.uk **w** alice.co.uk Sales Director: Garry Thompson.

AMI Music Library 34 Salisbury St, London NW8 8QE **t** 020 7402 9111 **f** 020 7723 3064 **e** eliot@amimedia.co.uk **w** amimedia.co.uk MD: Eliot Cohen.

Arcadia Production Music (UK) Greenlands, Payhembury, Devon EX14 3HY **t** 01404 841601 **f** 01404 841687 **e** admin@arcadiamusic.tv **w** arcadiamusic.tv Prop: John Brett.

Audio Processing Technology Edgewater Rd, Belfast, Co Antrim BT3 9JQ **t** 028 9037 1110 **f** 028 9037 1137 **e** jmcclintock@aptx.com **w** aptx.com Sales Dept: Jon McClintock.

Audio Systems Components Ltd 1 Comet House, Calleva Pk, Aldermaston, Berks RG7 8JB **t** 0118 981 1000 or 0118 981 9565 **f** 0118 981 9813 or 0118 981 9687 **e** sales@ascuk.com **w** ascuk.com Contact: Iain Elliott.

Audionics Ltd Petre Drive, Sheffield S4 7PZ **t** 0114 242 2333 **f** 0114 243 3913 **e** online@audionics.co.uk **w** audionics.co.uk Production Director: Phil Myers.

Bomdigi Productions 37 Snowsfields, London SE1 3SU **t** 07949 617863 **f** 0207 4074615 **e** jo@bomdigi.com **w** bomdigi.com Multimedia Producer & Director: Jo Roach.

British Forces Broadcasting Service Chalfont Grove, Narcot Lane, Chalfont St Peter, Gerrards Cross, Bucks SL9 8TN **t** 01494 878354 **f** 01494 870552 **e** admin.officer@bfbs.com **w** ssvc.com GM: Kal Sutherland.

Calrec Audio Ltd Nutclough Mill, Hebden Bridge, W Yorks HX7 8EZ **t** 01422 842159 **f** 01422 845244 **e** enquiries@calrec.com **w** calrec.com Sales & Mkting Dir: John Gluck.

Paul Chantler - Radio Programming Consultant 52 South Block, County Hall, Westminster, London SE1 7GB **t** 07788 584 888 **e** chantler@aol.com **w** paulchantler.com MD: Paul Chantler.

Churches Media Council Box 6613, South Woodham Ferrers, Essex CM3 5DY **t** 01245 322158 **f** 01245 321957 **e** office@churchesmediacouncil.org.uk **w** churchesmediacouncil.org.uk Dir: Peter Blackman.

Community Media Asociation The Workstation, 15 Paternoster Row, Sheffield S1 2BX **t** 0114 279 5219 **f** 0114 279 8976 **e** cma@commedia.org.uk **w** commedia.org.uk Contact: Diane Reid.

Compact Collections Ltd Greenland Pl, 115-123 Bayham St, London NW1 0AG **t** 020 7446 7420 **f** 020 7446 7424 **e** info@compactcollections.com **w** compactcollections.com Contact: John O'Sullivan.

delicious digital Suite GB, 39-40 Warple Way, Acton, London W3 0RG **t** 020 8749 7272 **f** 020 8749 7474 **e** info@deliciousdigital.com **w** deliciousdigital.com Dirs: Ollie Raphael, Ed Moris.

DMX Music Ltd Forest Lodge, Westerham Rd, Keston, Kent BR2 6HE **t** 01689 882 200 **f** 01689 882 288 **e** vanessa.warren@dmxmusic.com **w** dmxmusic.co.uk Marketing Manager: Vanessa Warren.

Doctor Rock The Century, 2A Newlands Rd, Waterlooville, Hants PO7 5NF **t** 023 9225 4426 **e** bob.woodhead@hotmail.co.uk Producer/Presenter: Bob Woodhead.

Document Productions Ltd The Dairy, Main St, Illston, Leics LE7 9EG **t** 01162 599 336 **f** 0870 458 1686 **e** danny.oconnor@documentuk.com **w** documentuk.com MD: Danny O'Connor.

Done and Dusted 3rd Floor, 12 Goslett Yard, London WC2H 0EQ **t** 020 7479 4300 **f** 020 7734 4652 **e** lou@doneanddusted.com **w** doneanddusted.com Producer: Louise Fox.

DT Productions Maygrove House, 67 Maygrove Rd, London NW6 2SP **t** 020 7644 8888 **f** 020 7644 8889 **e** info@dtproductions.co.uk **w** dtproductions.co.uk Music Programming: Lee Taylor.

DTP Radio Production Studios 35 Tower Way, Dunkeswell, Devon EX14 4XH **t** 01404 891598 MD: Don Todd MBE.

Eagle Media Productions Russell House, Ely St, Stratford-upon-Avon, Warcs CV37 6LW **t** 01789 415 187 **f** 01789 415 210 **e** amy@eaglemp.co.uk **w** eagle-rock.com MD: Alan Ravenscroft.

Eagle Vision Eagle House, 22 Armoury Way, London SW18 1EZ **t** 020 8870 5670 **f** 020 8874 2333 **e** mail@eagle-rock.com **w** eagle-rock.com MD of Intl. Television and New Media: Peter Worsley.

Entertainment Media Research Studio One, Charter House, Crown Court, London WC2B 5EX **t** 020 7240 1222 **f** 020 7240 8877 **e** patrick.johnston@entertainmentmediaresearch.com **w** entertainmentmediaresearch.com Dir of Business Devt.: Patrick Johnston.

FASTRAX

IMDFastrax

MOVING SOUND AND VISION

Allan House, 10 John Prince's St, London W1G 0JW **t** 020 7468 6888 **f** 020 7468 6889 **e** info@fastrax.co.uk **w** fastrax.co.uk Contact: Ross Priestley, Sam Bailey, Karina Howe. Fastrax is the leading digital distributor of new release music and music videos to the UK's Radio and TV broadcasters for review and broadcast.

Feltwain 2000 1 Oakwood Parade, London N14 4HY **t** 020 8950 8732 **f** 020 8950 6648 **e** paul.lynton@btopenworld.com MD: Paul Lynton.

Festival Productions PO Box 107, Brighton, E Sussex BN1 1QG **t** 01273 669595 **f** 01273 669596 **e** post@festivalradio.com **w** festivalradio.com MD: Steve Stark.

Freeway Media Services 20 Windmill Rd, Kirkcaldy, Fife KY1 3AQ **t** 01592 655309 or 07973 920488 **f** 01592 596177 **e** cronulla20@aol.com **w** freewaypress.co.uk Dir: John Murray.

G One 50 Lisson St, London NW1 5DF **t** 020 7453 1655 or 020 7453 1619 **f** 020 7453 1665 **e** simon.poole@g-one.co.uk **w** g-one.co.uk Producer: Simon Poole.

The Hobo Partnership 18 Broadwick St, London W1F 8HS **t** 020 7434 2907 **f** 020 7437 9984 **e** info@hobopartnership.com **w** hobopartnership.com MD: Debbie Wheeler.

The Hospital Group 24 Endell St, London WC2H 9HQ **t** 020 7170 9110 **f** 020 7170 9102 **e** studio@thehospital.co.uk **w** thehospital.co.uk Studio Sales Manager: Anne Marie Phelan.

iCast UK Ltd 7 Charteris Rd, London NW6 7EU **t** 020 7624 4605 or 07970 488 179 **e** gill@icast.uk.com **w** icast.uk.com Dir: Gill Mills.

Ig-nite 90 Red Sq, London N16 9AG **t** 07792 017 429 **e** info@ig-nite.com **w** ig-nite.com Multi Media Producer: Kary Stewart.

Immedia Broadcasting 7-9 The Broadway, Newbury, Berks RG14 1AS **t** 01635 572 800 **f** 01635 572 801 **e** customerservices@immediabroadcasting.com **w** immediabroadcasting.com Office Mgr: Lesley Pye.

Independent Television News (ITN) 200 Grays Inn Rd, London WC1X 8XZ **t** 020 7833 3000 **f** 020 7430 4016 **e** press.office@itn.co.uk **w** itn.co.uk Contact: Press Office.

Inner Ear Ltd Argyle House, 16 Argyle Court, 1103 Argyle St, Glasgow G3 8ND **t** 0141 226 8808 **f** 0141 226 8818 **e** dougal@radiomagnetic.com **w** radiomagnetic.com Programme Director: Dougal Perman.

Intelligent Media Clifton Workd, 23 Grove Park Terrace, London W4 3QE **t** 020 8995 0055 **f** 020 8995 9900 **e** jonm@intelligentmedia.com **w** intelligentmedia.com MD: Jon Mais.

The Interview CD Company 3 Haversham Lodge, Melrose Ave, London NW2 4JS **t** 020 8450 8882 **f** 020 8208 4219 **e** sharon@thepublicityconnection.com **w** thepublicityconnection.com MD: Sharon Chevin.

ITV Network Centre Ltd 200 Gray's Inn Rd, London WC1X 8HF **t** 020 7843 8000 **f** 020 7843 8158 **w** itv.co.uk.

JW Media Music 4 Whitfield St, London W1T 2RD **t** 020 7681 8900 **f** 020 7681 8911 **e** salesinfo@jwmediamusic.co.uk **w** jwmediamusic.com MD: George Barker.

Maidstone Studios New Cut Rd, Vinters Pk, Maidstone, Kent ME14 5NZ **t** 01622 691111 **f** 01622 684411 **e** info@maidstonestudios.com **w** maidstonestudios.com Marketing Exec: Sophie Miles.

MediaLane International The Old Garage, The Green, Great Milton, Oxon OX44 7NP **t** 01844 278534 **f** 01844 278538 **e** stratton@medialane-international.com **w** medialane-international.com Dir of Ops: Alan Stratton.

Mediatracks Music Library B.T.M.C., Units 15 / 16, Challenge Way, Blackburn BB1 5QB **t** 01254 691197 **f** 01254 263344 **e** info@mediatracks.co.uk **w** mediatracks.co.uk Proprietor: Steve Johnson.

MetrobroadcastLtd 53 Great Suffolk St, London SE1 0DB **t** 020 7202 2000 **f** 020 7202 2005 **e** info@metrobroadcast.com **w** metrobroadcast.com Dir: Paul Braybrooke.

MUSIC MALL

music mall

1 Upper James St, London W1F 9DE **t** 020 7534 1444 **f** 020 7534 1440 **e** See website for contacts. **w** musicmall.co.uk. One stop music video supply for broadcasters providing a quick, efficient service for content and catalogue titles.

Musicalities Ltd Snows Ride Farm, Snows Ride, Windlesham, Surrey GU20 6LA **t** 01276 474181 **f** 01276 452227 **e** enquiries@musicalities.co.uk **w** musicalities.co.uk MD: Ivan Chandler.

Musicpoint Andrews House, College Rd, Guildford, Surrey GU1 4QB **t** 01483 510 910 **f** 01483 510 911 **e** info@musicpointuk.com **w** musicpointuk.com Business Development Mgr: Jeremy Wood.

NBC News 3 Shortlands, 4th Floor, Hammersmith, London W6 8HX **t** 020 8600 6600 **f** 020 8600 6601 **e** london.newsdesk@nbc.com.

Neon Productions Ltd Studio Two, 19 Marine Crescent, Kinning Pk, Glasgow G51 1HD **t** 0141 429 6366 **f** 0141 429 6377 **e** mail@go2neon.com **w** go2neon.com Contact: Robert Noakes.

Nielsen Music Control (Ireland) Top Floor, 6 Clare St, Dublin 2, Ireland **t** +353 1 605 0686 **f** +353 1 678 5343 **e** f.byrne@nielsenmusiccontrol.com **w** nielsenmusiccontrol.com GM: Feidhlim Byrne.

Nielsen Music Control UK 5th Floor, Endeavour House, 189 Shaftesbury Ave, London WC2H 8TJ **t** 020 7420 9292 **f** 020 7420 9295 **e** info@nielsenmusiccontrol.com **w** nielsenmusiccontrol.com Head of UK Ops: Ray Bonici.

OVC Media Ltd 88 Berkeley Court, Baker St, London NW1 5ND **t** 020 7402 9111 **f** 020 7723 3064 **e** Joanne.ovc@virgin.net MD: Joanne Cohen.

Q Sheet Markettiers 4DC, Northburgh House, 10a Northburgh St, London EC1V 0AT **t** 020 7253 8888 **f** 020 7253 8885 **e** editor@qsheet.com **w** qsheet.com Music Editor: Nik Harta.

Radica Broadcast Systems Ltd 18 Bolney Grange Industrial Pk, Hickstead, Haywards Heath, W Sussex RH17 5PB **t** 01444 258285 **f** 01444 258288 **e** sales@radica.com **w** radica.com/radio Sales Mgr: Graham Sloggett.

The Radio Academy 5 Market Pl, London W1W 8AE **t** 020 7255 2010 **f** 020 7255 2029 **e** info@radioacademy.org **w** radioacademy.org Dir: Trevor Dann.

The Radio Advertising Bureau 77 Shaftesbury Ave, London W1V 5DU **t** 020 7306 2500 **f** 020 7306 2505 **e** aimee@rab.co.uk **w** rab.co.uk Operations Dir: Michael O'Brien.

RadioCentre 77 Shaftesbury Ave, London W1D 5DU **t** 020 7306 2603 **f** 020 7470 0062 **e** info@radiocentre.org **w** radiocentre.org Chairman: Paul Brown.

Rajar (Radio Joint Audience Research) Paramount House, 162-170 Wardour St, London W1F 8ZX **t** 020 7292 9040 **e** info@rajar.co.uk **w** rajar.co.uk MD: Sally de la Bedoyere.

Ricall Limited First Floor, 14 Buckingham Palace Rd, London SW1W 0QP **t** 020 7592 1710 **f** 020 7592 1713 **e** marketing@ricall.com **w** ricall.com MD, Investor Relations: Richard Corbett.

Rock Over London Inc 117 Grove Rd, Sutton, Surrey SM1 2DB **t** 020 8661 2603 **f** 020 8661 2603 **e** psexton@blueyonder.co.uk MD: Paul Sexton.

Satellite Media Services Lawford Heath Teleport, Lawford Heath Lane, Rugby, Warcs CV23 9EU **t** 01788 523000 **f** 01788 523001 **e** sales@sms-internet.net **w** sms-internet.net MD: Tim Whittingham.

Sound Broadcast Services Ltd Lauriston Pk, Pitchill, Evesham, Warcs. WR11 8SN **t** 01386 871 650 **e** sales@sbsfm.com **w** sbsfm.com MD: Marcus Bekker.

Somethin' Else Units 1-4, 1A Old Nichol St, London E2 7HR **t** 020 7613 3211 **f** 020 7739 9799 **e** info@somethin-else.com **w** somethin-else.com Dir: Jez Nelson.

Soundesign Mobiles 20 Heathfield Gardens, London W4 4JY **t** 07973 303 679 **f** 020 8994 0603 **e** conrad@soundesign.co.uk **w** soundesign.co.uk Dir: Conrad Fletcher.

Straight TV Limited 4th Floor, 121 Princess St, Manchester M1 7AG **t** 0161 200 6000 **f** 0161 228 0228 **e** info@straight.tv **w** straight.tv Contact: Clare Winnick.

Student Radio Association The Radio Academy, 5 Market Pl, London W1W 8AE **t** 020 7255 2010 **f** 020 7255 2029 **e** chair@studentradio.org.uk **w** studentradio.org.uk Chair: Talia Kraines.

Talk Of The Devil 5 Ripley Rd, Worthing, W Sussex BN11 5NQ **t** 01903 526515 **f** 01903 539634 **e** steve.power@talk-of-the-devil.com **w** talk-of-the-devil.com MD: Steve Power.

Teletext Building 10, Chiswick Pk, 566 Chiswick High Rd, London W4 5TS **t** 0870 731 3000 **e** listings@teletext.co.uk **w** teletext.co.uk.

Totalrock Ltd 1-6 Denmark Pl, London WC2H 8NL **t** 020 7240 6665 **e** info@totalrock.com **w** totalrock.com Head of Music/Dir of Prog: Tony Wilson.

Transorbital Productions 557 Street Lane, Leeds, W Yorks LS17 6JA **t** 0113 268 7886 or 07836 568 888 **f** 0113 266 0045 **e** carl@carlkingston.co.uk **w** carlkingston.co.uk MD: Carl Kingston.

Unique Facilities (Location Broadcasting Services) 50 Lisson St, London NW1 5DF **t** 020 7723 0322 **f** 020 7453 1666 **e** info@uniquefacilities.com **w** uniquefacilities.com Facilities Mgr: Shane Wall.

Unique Facilities (Radio Production Studios) 50 Lisson St, London NW1 5DF **t** 020 7723 0322 **f** 020 7453 1666 **e** info@uniquefacilities.com **w** uniquefacilities.com Facilities Mgr: Shane Wall.

Victoria Radio Network PO Box 1287, Kirkcaldy, Fife KY2 5ZX **t** 01592 268530 **e** info@vrn1287.com **w** vrn1287.com Group Programme Director: Colin Johnston.

VIP Broadcasting 8 Bunbury Way, Epsom, Surrey KT17 4JP **t** 01372 721196 **f** 01372 726697 **e** mail@vipbroadcasting.co.uk **w** vipbroadcasting.co.uk MD: Chris Vezey.

The Vocal Booth Toxteth TV, 37-45 Windsor St, Liverpool L8 1XE **t** 0151 707 2833 or 07800 993 192 **f** 0151 707 2833 **e** mike.moran@thevocalbooth.com **w** thevocalbooth.com Producer: Mike Moran.

Waterfall Studios 2 Silver Rd, London W12 7SG **t** 020 8746 2000 **f** 020 8746 0180 **e** info@waterfall-studios.com **w** waterfall-studios.com Facilities Mgr: Samantha Leese.

Advertising Agencies

Abbott Mead Vickers BBDO 151 Marylebone Rd, London NW1 5QE **t** 020 7616 3500 **f** 020 7616 3580 **e** linseyf@amvbbdo.com **w** amvbbdo.com Hd of TV Department: Francine Linsey.

adexchange Ltd The Old Garage, Gt Milton, Oxon OX44 7NP **t** 01844 278616 **f** 01844 278611 **e** enquiries@adexchange.co.uk **w** adexchange.co.uk Production Dir: Nick Herbert.

AKA. 115 Shaftesbury Ave, Cambridge Circus, London WC2H 8AF **t** 020 7836 4747 **f** 020 7836 8787 **e** firstnamelastname@akauk.com **w** akauk.com Contact: Adrian Allen, Mike McCraith.

Gavin Anderson & Co 85 Strand, London WC2R 0DW **t** 020 7554 1400 **f** 020 7554 1499 **e** gavinfo@gavinanderson.co.uk **w** gavinanderson.co.uk.

ARC Group Mortimer House, 37-41 Mortimer St, London W1T 3JH **t** 020 7017 5555 **f** 020 7017 5556 **e** info@arcgroup.com **w** argroup.com.

ArtScience Limited 3-5 Hardwidge St, London SE1 3SY **t** 020 7939 9500 **f** 020 7939 9499 **e** lab5@artscience.net **w** artscience.net Dirs: Douglas Coates, Pete Rope.

Bartle Bogle Hegarty 60 Kingly St, London W1B 5DS **t** 020 7734 1677 **f** 020 7437 3666 **e** firstname.lastname@bbh.co.uk **w** bbh.co.uk.

Bartlett Scott Edgar Bartlett House, 65-67 Wilson St, London EC2A 2LT **t** 020 7562 5700 **f** 020 7562 5706 **e** innovate@bartlett.co.uk **w** bartlett.co.uk.

Bates Tavner Resources Int International House, World Trade Centre, 1 St Katharine's Way, London E1W 1UN **t** 020 7481 2000 **f** 020 7702 2271 **e** info@batestavner.co.uk **w** batestavner.co.uk.

BBA Active Ltd 1 Hampstead West, 224 Iverson Rd, London NW6 2HU **t** 020 7625 7575 **f** 020 7625 7007 **e** bba@bbagenius.com **w** bbagenius.com MD: Stephen Benjamin.

Big Blue Star Ltd Dunedin House, Harrow Yard, Akeman St, Tring, Herts HP23 6AA **t** 01442 826 240 **f** 01442 823 076 **e** paulgoodwin@bigbluestar.co.uk **w** bigbluestar.co.uk MD: Paul Goodwin.

BLM Group Eagle House, 50 Marshall St, London W1F 9BQ **t** 020 7437 1317 **f** 020 7437 1287 **e** info@blm.co.uk **w** blm.co.uk.

BMP DDB 12 Bishops Bridge Rd, London W2 6AA **t** 020 7258 3979 **f** 020 7402 4871 **e** name.name@bmpddb.com **w** bmp.co.uk.

Leo Burnett Ltd Warwick Building, Kensington Village, Avonmore Rd, London W14 8HQ **t** 020 7751 1800 **f** 020 7348 3855 **e** firstname.lastname@leoburnett.co.uk **w** leoburnett.com.

CDP-Travis Sully 9 Lower John St, London W1F 9DZ **t** 020 7437 4224 **f** 020 7437 5445 **e** mail@cdp-travissully.com **w** cdp-travissully.com Office Manager: Melody Richards.

The Clinic 32-38 Saffron Hill, London EC1N 8FH **t** 020 7421 9333 **f** 020 7421 9334 **e** firstname.lastname@clinic.co.uk **w** clinic.co.uk Creative Dir: David Dragan.

Cranham Advertising Suite 1, Essex House, Station Rd, Upminster, Essex RM14 2SJ **t** 01708 641164 **f** 01708 220030 **e** cranham@globalnet.co.uk.

Creative Marketing Services Hollinthorpe Hall, Swillington Lane, Leeds LS26 8BZ **t** 0870 381 6222 **f** 0870 381 6333 **e** mail@cmsadvertising.co.uk **w** cmsadvertising.co.uk Contact: Andrew Batty FCIM.

Cunning 192 St John St, London EC1V 4JY **t** 020 7566 5300 **e** info@cunning.com **w** cunning.com MD: Anna Carloss.

Da Costa & Co 9 Gower St, London WC1E 6HA **t** 020 7916 3791 **f** 020 7916 3799 **e** nickdc@dacosta.co.uk **w** dacosta.co.uk.

Delaney Lund Knox Warren 25 Wellington St, London WC2E 7DA **t** 020 7836 3474 **f** 020 7240 8739 **e** info@dlkw.co.uk **w** dlkw.co.uk.

The Design & Advertising Resource 7 Kings Wharf, 301 Kingsland Rd, Hoxton, London E8 4DS **t** 020 7254 3191 **f** 0870 442 5297 **e** info@your-resource.co.uk **w** your-resource.co.uk Account Director: Richard Fearn.

Dewynters 48 Leicester Sq, London WC2H 7QD **t** 020 7321 0488 **f** 020 7321 0104 **e** initial+lastname@dewynters.com **w** dewynters.com Client Management: Richard Abba.

Diabolical Liberties 1 Bayham St, London NW1 0ER **t** 020 7916 5483 **f** 020 7916 5482 **e** sales@diabolical.co.uk **w** diabolical.co.uk HoM: Karl Badger.

Different Ltd 10 Summerhill Terrace, Summerhill Sq, Newcastle upon Tyne NE4 6EB **t** 0191 261 0111 **f** 0191 221 1122 **e** dreid@different-uk.com **w** different-uk.com Producer: David Reid.

DKA 87 New Cavendish St, London171-177 Great Portland S
W1W 6XD **t** 020 7467 7300 **f** 020 7467 7380
e enquiries@dka.uk.com **w** dka.uk.com.

Duke Second Floor, 17-18 Margaret St, London W1W 8RP
t 020 7580 7070 **f** 020 7636 8815 **e** luke@duke.tv **w** duke.tv
Dir: Luke Farrell.

Euro RSCG London Cupola House, 15 Alfred Pl, London
WC1E 7EB **t** 020 7467 9200 **f** 020 7467 9210
e infouk@eurorscg.com **w** eurorscglondon.co.uk.

Exposure (Nation-wide flyer distribution services)
3N Beehive Mill, Jersey St, Manchester M4 6JG
t 0161 950 4241 **f** 0161 950 4240 **e** keith@exposureuk.com
MD: Keith Patterson.

Lee Golding Advertising and Communications Ltd
Edinburgh House, 40 Great Portland St, London W1W 7LZ
t 020 7436 7910 or 020 7436 7978 **f** 020 7636 6091
e carol@leegolding.co.uk Contact: Carol Golding.

Grey London 215-227 Great Portland St, London W1W 5PN
t 020 7636 3399 **f** 020 7637 7473
e firstname.lastname@greyeu.com **w** grey.co.uk.

Hive Associates Ltd Bewlay House, 2 Swallow Pl, London
W1B 2AE **t** 020 7664 0480 **f** 020 7664 0481
e consult@hiveassociates.co.uk **w** hiveassociates.co.uk
Account Director: Alex Moss.

I Like The Sound Of That 79-89 Pentonville Rd, London
N1 9LG **t** 020 7993 3318 **e** sybil@ilikethesoundofthat.com
In Charge: Sybil.

JJ Stereo Units 13-14, Barley Shotts Business Pk, 246 Acklam
Rd, London W10 5YG **t** 020 8969 5444 **f** 020 8969 5544
e info@jjstereo.com **w** jjstereo.com Dir: Ruth Paverly.

Lavery Rowe 69-71 Newington Causeway, London SE1 6BD
t 020 7378 1780 **f** 020 7407 4612 **e** sales@laveryrowe.co.uk.

Leagas Delaney 1 Alfred Pl, London WC1E 7EB
t 020 7758 1758 **f** 020 7758 1760 **e** infouk@leagasdelaney.com
w leagasdelaney.com.

The Leith Agency 37 The Shore, Leith, Edinburgh EH6 6QU
t 0131 561 8600 **f** 0131 561 8601 **e** p.adams@leith.co.uk
w leith.co.uk MD: Phil Adams.

The London Advertising Partnership 61-63 Portobello
Rd, london W11 3DB **t** 020 7229 9755 **f** 020 7229 6720
e london_ad@btinternet.com MD: Simon Dodds.

Lowe & Partners Bowater House, 3rd Floor, 68-114
Knightsbridge, London SW1X 7LT **t** 020 7584 5033
f 020 7581 9027 **e** info@loweworldwide.com
w loweworldwide.com.

Matters Media Ltd 1st Floor, 146 Marylebone Rd, London
NW1 5PH **t** 020 7224 6030 **f** 020 7224 6010
e mark@mattersmedia.co.uk Contact: Mark Riley.

M&C Saatchi 36 Golden Sq, London W1F 9EE
t 020 7543 4500 **f** 020 7543 4501
e firstnameinitialofsurname@mcsaatchi.com **w** mcsaatchi.com
Sponsorship & Events: Georgia Terzis.

McCann-Erickson 7-11 Herbrand St, London WC1N 1EX
t 020 7837 3737 **f** 020 7837 3773
e firstname.lastname@europe.mccann.com **w** mccann.com.

McConnells McConnell House, Charlemont Pl, Dublin, Ireland
t +353 1 478 1544 **f** +353 1 478 0224
e firstname.lastname@mcconnells.ie **w** mcconnells.ie
Contact: John Fanning.

Mearns & Gill Advertising Ltd 7 Carden Pl, Aberdeen,
Grampian AB10 1PP **t** 01224 646311 **f** 01224 631882
e alan@mearns-gill.com **w** mearns-gill.net.

Media Campaign Services - MCS 20 Orange St,
London WC2H 7EW **t** 020 7389 0800 **f** 020 7839 6997
e dwoods@mediacampaign.co.uk **w** mediacampaign.co.uk
Contact: David Woods.

Media Junction 40a Old Compton St, London W1D 4TU
t 020 7434 9919 **f** 020 7439 0794
e media@mediajunction.co.uk **w** mediajunction.co.uk
MD: Giles Cooper.

Mediacom EMG Entertainment Media Group, 180 North
Gower St, London NW1 2NB **t** 020 7874 5500
f 020 7874 5999 **e** martin.cowie@mediacomuk.com
w mediacomuk.com MD: Martin Cowie.

Ogilvy Primary Contact 5 Theobald's Rd, London
WC1X 8SH **t** 020 7468 6900 **f** 020 7468 6950
e firstname.lastname@primary.co.uk **w** primary.co.uk
MD: Gareth Richards.

Pawson Media 207 High Holborn, London WC1V 7BW
t 020 7405 9080 **f** 020 7831 7391
e mail@pawson-media.co.uk Media Director: David Cecil.

PD Communications The Business Village, Broomhill Rd,
London SW18 4JQ **t** 020 8871 5033 **f** 020 8871 5034
e sales@pdcom.net **w** pdcom.net Creative Dir: Peter Saag.

Nick Pease Copywriting Services 290 Elgin Ave, Maida
Vale, London W9 1JS **t** 020 7286 8181 **f** 020 7286 8181
e nickpease@btconnect.com MD: Nick Pease.

Probe Media 2nd Floor, The Hogarth Centre, Hogarth Lane,
London W4 2QN **t** 020 8742 3636 **f** 020 8995 1350
e sanjay@probemedia.co.uk **w** probemedia.co.uk
Account Director: Sanjay Vadher.

Protege Design and Marketing East Dene, 5 Cromer Rd,
Southend on Sea, Essex SS1 2DU **t** 01702 300 176
f 01702 304 028 **e** info@protegedesign.co.uk
w protegedesign.co.uk MD: Nic Cleeve.

Publicis Ltd 82 Baker St, London W1M 2AE
t 020 7935 4426 **f** 020 7487 5351 **e** re-fresh@publicis.co.uk
w publicis.co.uk.

QRBT Ltd Great Guildford Business Sq, 30 Great Guildford St,
London SE1 0HS **t** 020 7921 9292 **f** 020 7921 9342
e qrbt@qrbt.com **w** qrbt.com.

Rainey, Kelly, Camppbell, Rolfe/Y&R Greater London
House, Hampstead Rd, London NW1 7QP **t** 020 7387 9366
f 020 7611 6570 **e** firstname_lastname@uk.yr.com
w rkcryr.com.

Ramp Industry Studio 242, Bon Marche Centre, 241-251
Ferndale Rd, London SW9 8BJ **t** 020 7326 0345
e andy@rampindustry.com **w** rampindustry.com
Managing Partner: Andy Crysell.

Riley Advertising Riley House, 4 Red Lion Court, London EC4A 3EN **t** 020 7353 3223 **f** 020 7353 2338 **e** rileylondon@riley.co.uk **w** riley.co.uk MD: Rob Smith.

Robertson Saxby Associates Standard House, 107-115 Eastmoor St, London SE7 8LX **t** 020 8858 3202 **f** 020 8853 2103 **e** dresource@aol.com Contact: Dick Saxby.

RockBox (A Division of Live Nation) 33 Golden Sq, London W1F 9JT **t** 020 7478 2200 **f** 020 7287 8129 **e** firstname.lastname@livenation.co.uk **w** livenation.co.uk Product Manager: Claire Cooch.

Rowleys:London One Port Hill, Hertford, Herts SG14 1PJ **t** 01992 587350 or 01992 551931 **f** 01992 586059 **e** info@rowleyslondon.co.uk **w** rowleyslondon.co.uk MD: Annie Rowley.

Saatchi & Saatchi plc 80 Charlotte St, London W1A 1AQ **t** 020 7636 5060 **f** 020 7637 8489 **e** fisrtname.surname@saatchi.co.uk **w** saatchi-saatchi.com.

Skinny 4th Floor, 11 D'Arblay St, London W1F 8DT **t** 020 7287 1888 **e** sonya@fullfatskinny.com **w** fullfatskinny.com Dir: Sonya Skinner.

Small Japanese Soldier 32-38 Saffron Hill, London EC1N 8FH **t** 020 7421 9400 **f** 020 7421 9334 **e** Jungle@smallJapanesesoldier.com **w** smalljapanesesoldier.com MD: Andy Hunns.

Sold Out The Windsor Centre, 16-29 Windsor St, London N1 8QG **t** 020 7704 0409 **f** 020 7226 8249 **e** michelle@soldout.co.uk.

Sonic Advertising Ltd The New Boathouse, 136-142 Bramley Rd, London W10 6SR **t** 020 7727 7500 **f** 020 7727 7200 **e** lawrence@sonicadvertising.com **w** sonicadvertising.com Sales Mgr: Lawrence Cooke.

Sowerbykane 12 Burleigh St, Covent Garden, London WC2E 7PX **t** 020 7836 4561 **f** 020 7836 4073 **e** peter@sowerbykane.co.uk **w** sowerbykane.co.uk.

Space Promotions Ltd Unit 12 Wellington St, Unit Factory Development, 74 Eldon St, Sheffield S1 4GT **t** 0114 2729211 **f** 0114 2756220 **e** post@spacegroup.co.uk **w** spacegroup.co.uk MD: Mark Platts.

Spark Marketing Entertainment 16 Winton Ave, London N11 2AT **t** 0870 460 5439 **e** mbauss@spark-me.com **w** spark-me.com Executive Director: Matthias Bauss.

St Luke's Communications Ltd 22 Dukes Rd, London WC1H 9PN **t** 020 7380 8888 **f** 020 7380 8899 **e** initial+lastname@stlukes.co.uk **w** stlukes.co.uk.

Target NMI Middlesex House, 34-42 Cleveland St, London W1T 4JE **t** 020 7462 5800 **f** 020 7462 5799 **e** mail@targetnmi.com **w** targetnmi.com MD: Robert Wilkerson.

TBWA London 76-80 Whitfield St, London W1T 4EZ **t** 020 7573 6666 **f** 020 7573 6728 **e** firstname.lastname@tbwa-london.com **w** tbwa.com Music Director: Dominic Caisley.

TCS Media 35 Garway Rd, London W2 4QF **t** 020 7221 7292 **f** 020 7221 0460 **e** information@tcsmedia.co.uk **w** tcsmedia.com Dir: Mike Ashby.

J Walter Thompson Co Ltd 1 Knightsbridge Green, London SW1X 7NW **t** 020 7656 7000 **f** 020 7656 7010 **e** firstname.lastname@jwt.com **w** jwtworld.com.

TMD Carat 43-49 Parker St, London WC2B 5PS **t** 020 7430 6000 **f** 020 7430 6299 **e** firstname_lastname@carat.co.uk **w** carat.com MD: Colin Mills.

TMP Worldwide Chancery House, 53-64 Chancery Lane, London WC2A 1QS **t** 020 7406 5000 **f** 020 7406 5001 **e** firstname.lastname@tmp.com **w** tmpw.co.uk.

Two:Design Studio 20 The Arches, Hartland Rd, Camden, London NW1 8HR **t** 020 7267 1118 **f** 020 7482 0221 **e** studio@twodesign.net **w** twodesign.net Art Director: Graham Peake.

Martin Waxman Associates 56 St John St, London EC1M 4HG **t** 020 7253 5500 **f** 020 7490 2387 **e** info@waxman.co.uk **w** waxman.co.uk.

Wood Brigdale Nisbet & Robinson Granville House, 132-135 Sloane St, London SW1X 9AX **t** 020 7591 4800 **f** 020 7591 4801.

Wunderman Greater London House, Hampstead Rd, London NW1 7QP **t** 020 7611 6666 **f** 020 7611 6668 **e** firstname_lastname@uk.wunderman.com **w** wunderman.com.

Young Euro RSCG 64 Lower Leeson St, Dublin 2, Ireland **t** +353 1 661 5599 **f** +353 1 661 1992 **e** advertising@young-ad.ie **w** youngeurorscg.ie.

For all the latest directory listings visit www.musicweekdirectory.com

Video Production

The 400 Company B3, The Workshops, 2A, Askew Crescent, London W12 9DP **t** 020 8746 1400 **f** 020 8746 0847 **e** info@the400.co.uk **w** the400.co.uk Production manager: Christian Riou.

422 Studios Battersea Rd, Heaton Mersey, Stockport SK4 3EA **t** 0161 432 9000 **f** 0161 443 1325 **e** rob@gym-tv.com MD: Robert Topliss.

46&2 Films 3 Tennyson Rd, Thatcham, Berks RG18 3FR **t** 01635 868 385 or 07970 182 168 **e** owen@heropr.com **w** 46and2films.com Contact: Owen Packard.

Abbey Road Studios 3 Abbey Rd, London NW8 9AY **t** 020 7266 7366 **f** 020 7266 7367 **e** videoservices@abbeyroad.com **w** abbeyroad.com Video Services Mgr: Tom Williams.

Autopsy Red Bus Studios, 34 Salisbury St, London NW8 8QE **t** 020 7724 2243 **f** 020 7724 2871 **e** info@crimson.globalnet.co.uk MD: Simon Crawley.

Banana Split Productions 11 Carlisle Rd, London NW9 0HD **t** 020 8200 1234 **f** 020 8200 1121 **e** accounts@bananasplitprods.com **w** banana-split.com MD: Steve Kemsley.

Big Talk Productions 83 Great Titchfield St, London W1W 6RH **t** 020 7255 1131 **f** 020 7436 9347 **e** talk@bigtalk.demon.co.uk MD: Nira Park.

The Big Yellow Feet Production Co. Ltd. Dunley Hill Farm, Dorking, Surrey RH5 6SX **t** 01483 285 928 or 07941 318 280 **e** greg@bigyellowfeet.com **w** bigyellowfeet.com Dir: Gregory Mandry.

Black Dog Films Ltd 42-44 Beak St, London W1F 9RH **t** 020 7434 0787 **f** 020 7734 4978 **e** initial+surname@rsafilms.co.uk **w** blackdogfilms.com Rep: Svana Gisla.

Black Shark Media 54 Beltran Rd, London SW6 3AJ **t** 02077316006 **e** jk@blacksharkmedia.com **w** blacksharkmedia.com Dir: James Kibbey.

Blue Planet 96 York St, London W1H 1DP **t** 020 7724 2267 **e** base@blueplanet.co.uk Contact: Bruce Robertson.

Box 5th floor, 121 Princess St, Manchester M1 7AD **t** 0161 228 2399 **e** info@the-box.co.uk **w** the-box.co.uk Dir: Mike Kirwin.

Cara Music Ltd The Studio, rear of 63 Station Rd, Winchmore Hill, London N21 3NB **t** 020 8364 3121 **f** 020 8364 3090 **e** caramusicltd@dial.pipex.com Dir: Michael McDonagh.

Channel 20-20 20-20 House, 26-28 Talbot Lane, Leicester LE1 4LR **t** 0116 233 2220 **f** 0116 222 1113 **e** rob.potter@channel2020.co.uk **w** channel2020.co.uk CEO: Rob Potter.

Cinegenix at PBF Motion Pictures The Little Pickenhanger, Tuckey Grove, Ripley, Surrey GU23 6JG **t** 01483 225179 **f** 01483 224118 **e** image@pbf.co.uk **w** pbf.co.uk Creative Director: Peter Fairbrass.

Condor Post Production 54 Greek St, London W1V 5LR **t** 020 7494 2552 **f** 020 7494 1166 **e** kirsty@condor-post.com **w** condor-post.com Bookings Manager: Kirsty Green.

Cowboy Films 11-29 Smiths Court, Great Windmill St, London W1D 7DP **t** 020 7287 3808 **f** 020 7287 3785 **e** info@cowboyfilms.co.uk **w** cowboyfilms.co.uk Dir: Robert Bray.

D-Fuse 13-14 Gt.Sutton St, London EC1V 0BX **t** 020 7253 3462 **e** info@dfuse.com **w** dfuse.com Dir: Michael Faulkner.

Davey Inc. 4 Dover Mansions, Canterbury Crescent, London SW9 7QF **t** 020 7274 2793 or 07795 220 145 **f** 020 7274 2793 **e** gail@daveyinc.com **w** daveyinc.com Producer: Gail Davey.

DMS Films Ltd 89 Sevington Rd, London NW4 3RU **t** 020 8203 5540 **f** 0870 762 671 **e** danny@dmsfilms.co.uk **w** dmsfilms.co.uk MD: Daniel San.

Done and Dusted 3rd Floor, 12 Goslett Yard, London WC2H 0EQ **t** 020 7479 4300 **f** 020 7734 4652 **e** lou@doneanddusted.com **w** doneanddusted.com Producer: Louise Fox.

DVS Productions Ltd Prospect House, Lower Caldecote, Biggleswade, Beds SG18 9UH **t** 01767 601 398 **f** 0870 706 6257 **e** davysmyth@dvsproductions.com **w** dvsproductions.com Dir: Davy Smyth.

Eagle Eye Productions Eagle House, 22 Armoury Way, London SW18 1EZ **t** 020 8870 5670 **f** 020 8874 2333 **e** mail@eagle-rock.com **w** eagle-rock.com Supervising Producer: Alan Ravenscroft.

Eagle Vision Eagle House, 22 Armoury Way, London SW18 1EZ **t** 020 8870 5670 **f** 020 8874 2333 **e** mail@eagle-rock.com **w** eagle-rock.com Supervising Producer: Alan Ravenscroft.

Exceeda Films 110-116 Elmore St, London N1 3AH **t** 020 7288 0433 **f** 020 7288 0735 **e** contact@exceeda.co.uk **w** exceeda.co.uk Producer: Sarah Davenport.

Factory Films 140 Wardour St, London W1F 8ZT **t** 020 7255 8920 **f** 020 7432 6899 **e** toby@factoryfilms.net **w** factoryfilms.net Head Of Music Video: Toby Hyde.

Filmmaster Clip The Old Lampworks, Rodney Pl, London SW19 2LQ **t** 07870 818 004 **e** luca.legnani@filmmaster.com **w** filmmaster.com UK Representative: Luca Legnani.

Fire House Productions 42 Glasshouse St, London W1B 5DW **t** 020 7439 2220 **f** 020 7439 2210 **e** postie@hellofirehouse.com **w** hellofirehouse.com MD: Julie-Anne Edwards.

Flick Films 15 Golden Sq, London W1F 9JG **t** 020 7734 7979 **f** 020 7287 9495 **e** info@flickmedia.co.uk **w** flickmedia.co.uk Dir: John Deery.

Flicks TV & Video Productions Classlane Studios, Bentley Lodge, Victoria Rd, Beverley, E Yorks HU17 8PJ **t** 01482 873388 **f** 01482 873389 **e** dave_l@classlane.co.uk **w** classlane.co.uk Dir: David Lee.

Flynn Productions Ltd 64 Charlotte Rd, London EC2A 3PE **t** 020 7729 7291 **f** 020 7729 7279 **e** mary@flynnproductions.com **w** flynnproductions.com Exec Producer: Mary Calderwood.

Formosa Films Bridge House, 3 Mills Studios, Three Mill Lane, London E3 3DU **t** 020 8709 8700 or 07973 165 942 **f** 020 8709 8701 **e** info@formosafilms.com **w** formosafilms.com Producer: Neil Thompson.

GALA Productions 25 Stamford Brook Rd, London W6 0XJ **t** 020 8741 4200 or 07768 078 865 **f** 020 8741 2323 **e** beata@galaproductions.co.uk **w** galaproductions.co.uk Executive Producer: Beata Romanowski.

Glassworks 33-34 Great Poulteney St, London W1F 9NP **t** 020 7434 1182 **f** 020 7434 1183 **e** amanda@glassworks.co.uk **w** glassworks.co.uk Joint MD: Amanda Ryan.

Godman Ltd 10A Belmont St, London NW1 8HH **t** 020 7428 2288 **f** 020 7428 2299 **e** promos@godman.co.uk Music Video Rep: Beccy McCray.

Gorgeous Enterprises 11 Portland Mews, London W1F 8JL **t** 020 7287 4060 **f** 020 7287 4994 **e** gorgeous@gorgeous.co.uk **w** gorgeous.co.uk MD: Paul Rothwell.

Great Guns Ltd 43-45 Camden Rd, London NW1 9LR **t** 020 7692 4444 **f** 020 7692 4422 **e** sheridan@greatguns.com **w** greatguns.com Prod Mgr: Sheridan Thomas.

Green Bandana Productions / JLH Music 7 Iron Bridge House, Bridge Approach, London NW1 8BD **t** 020 7722 1081 **f** 020 7483 0028 **e** james.hyman@virgin.net **w** jameshyman.com MD: James Hyman.

Groovy Badger 284a Lee High Rd, London SE13 5PJ **t** 07831 431 019 or 07956 273 883 **f** 0870 124 5135 **e** info@groovybadger.com **w** groovybadger.com Dir: Sebastian Smith.

Gym TV South Manchester Studios, Battersea Rd, Heaton Mersey, Stockport SK4 3EA **t** 0161 442 4205 **f** 0161 442 2677 **e** info@gym-tv.com **w** gym-tv.com MD: Tom Henderson.

Habana Productions PO Box 370, Newquay TR8 5YZ **t** 01637 831 011 **f** 01637 831 037 **e** emmapaterson1@aol.com Mgr: Emma Paterson.

Hangman Studios 111 Frithville Gardens, London W12 7JQ **t** 020 8600 3440 **f** 020 8600 3401 **e** danielle@hangmanstudios.com **w** hangmanstudios.com Studio Mgr: Danielle Edwards.

High Barn The Bardfield Centre, Great Bardfield, Braintree, Essex CM7 4SL **t** 01371 811291 **f** 01371 811404 **e** info@highbarn.eu **w** highbarn.eu MD: Chris Bullen.

HLA 19-21 Great Portland St, London W1W 8QB **t** 020 7299 1000 **f** 020 7299 1001 **e** mike@hla.net **w** hla.net MD: Mike Wells.

The Hold 20 Craigs Pk, Edinburgh EH12 8UL **t** 0131 339 0164 **e** kris@thehold.co.uk **w** thehold.co.uk Dir: Kris Bird.

Illumina 8 Canham Mews, Canham Rd, London W3 7SR **t** 020 8600 9300 **f** 020 8600 9333 **e** matt.jones@illumina.co.uk **w** illumina.co.uk Music Production: Matt Jones.

IMS Interactive Management Services Ltd Unit 19, Price St Business Centre, Birkenhead, Merseyside CH41 4JQ **t** 0151 651 0100 **f** 0151 652 0077 **e** daveims@compuserve.com **w** heritagevideo.co.uk MD: David McWilliam.

Independent Films 3rd Floor, 7A Langley St, London WC2H 9JA **t** 020 7845 7474 **f** 020 7845 7475 **e** mail@independ.net Head of Music Video: Richard Weager.

Influential Films PO Box 141, Manchester M19 2ZW **t** 07050 395 708 **e** info@influentialmedia.co.uk **w** influentialfilms.co.uk MD: Mike Swindells.

IQ Media (Bracknell) Ltd 2 Venture House, Arlington Sq, Bracknell, Berks RG12 1WA **t** 01344 422 551 or 07884 262 755 **f** 01344 453 355 **e** information@iqmedia-uk.com **w** iqmedia-uk.com MD: Tony Bellamy.

JamDVD London **t** 07976 820 774 **f** 07092 003 937 **e** jamdvd@macunlimited.net **w** jamdvd.com Producer: Julie Gardner.

Kyng Films 50A Cross St, London N1 2BA **t** 020 7687 0380 **f** 020 7687 0380 **e** heather@kyngfilms.com MD: Heather Clarke.

Liquid Productions Reverb House, Bennett St, London W4 2AH **t** 020 8995 6799 **f** 020 8995 6899 **e** liquidproductions@btinternet.com Dir: Margot Quinn.

Mad Cow Productions 75 Amberley Rd, London W9 2JL **t** 020 7289 0001 **f** 020 7289 0003 **e** info@madcowfilms.co.uk **w** madcowfilms.co.uk Head of Production: Anwen Rees-Myers.

Maguffin Ltd 10 Frith St, London W1V 5TZ **t** 020 7437 2526 **f** 020 7437 1516 **e** firstname@maguffin.co.uk **w** maguffin.co.uk MD / Prod: James Chads.

Masterpiece Unit 14 The Talina Centre, Bagleys Lane, London SW6 2BW **t** 020 7731 5758 **f** 020 7384 1750 **e** leena.bhatti@masterpiecelondon.com **w** masterpiecelondon.com Sales & Marketing Manager: Leena Bhatti.

Melling White Productions West Hill Dairy, Avington, Winchester, Hants SO21 1DE **t** 01962 779002 **f** 01962 779002 **e** info@mellingwhite.co.uk Head Prod: Carol White.

Metropolis The Power House, 70 Chiswick High Rd, London W4 1SY **t** 020 8742 1111 **f** 020 8742 2626 **e** productions@metropolis-group.co.uk **w** metropolis-group.co.uk Executive Producer: Tessa Watts.

The Mill 40-41 Great Marlborough St, London W1F 7JQ **t** 020 7287 4041 **e** info@mill.co.uk **w** mill.co.uk Mktg Mgr: Emma Shield.

Media: Video Production

The Mob Film Company 10-11 Great Russell St, London WC1B 3NH **t** 020 7580 8142 **f** 020 7255 1721 **e** mail@mobfilm.com Prod: John Brocklehurst.

Mothcatcher Productions 20 Craigs Pk, Edinburgh, Scotland EH12 8UL **t** 0131 3390164 **e** info@mothcatcher.co.uk **w** mothcatcher.co.uk Dirs: Kerry Mullaney & Kris Bird.

The Moving Picture Company 127 Wardour St, London W1F ONL **t** 020 7434 3100 **f** 020 7287 5187 **e** mailbox@moving-picture.co.uk **w** moving-picture.co.uk Snr Prod: Simon Gosling.

Mutiny Films Ltd. 18 Soho Sq, London W1V 3QL **t** 020 7025 8710 **f** 020 7025 8100 **e** info@mutinyfilms.co.uk **w** mutinyfilms.co.uk Company Directors: Adam Wimpenny, Sam Eastall.

Nexus Animation 113-114 Shoreditch High St, London E1 6JN **t** 020 7749 7500 **f** 020 7749 7501 **e** chris@nexuslondon.com Prod: Chris O'Reilly.

Oasis TV 6-7 Great Poultney St, London W1F 9NA **t** 020 7434 4133 **e** sales@oasistv.co.uk **w** oasistv.co.uk Business Dev't Mgr: Matthew Lock.

One Small Step 60 Exmouth Market, London EC1R 4QE **t** 020 7812 1111 **f** 020 7812 1122 **e** info@onesmallstep.tv **w** onesmallstep.tv Music Video Rep: Will McMullan.

OVC Media Ltd 88 Berkeley Court, Baker St, London NW1 5ND **t** 020 7402 9111 **f** 020 7723 3064 **e** Joanne.ovc@virgin.net MD: Joanne Cohen.

Partizan 7 Westbourne Grove Mews, London W11 2RU **t** 020 7792 8483 **f** 020 7792 8870 **e** firstname.surname@partizan.com MD: Georges Bermann.

Passion Pictures 33-34 Rathbone Pl, London W1T 1JN **t** 020 7323 9933 **f** 020 7323 9030 **e** info@passion-pictures.com Producer: Spencer Friend.

Picture Production Company 19-20 Poland St, London W1F 8QF **t** 020 7439 4944 **f** 020 7434 9140 **e** steve@theppc.com **w** theppc.co.uk Sales & Marketing Dir: Steve O`Pray.

Playaville Records Imperial House, 64 Willoughby Lane, London N17 0SP **t** 0870 766 8303 **f** 0870 766 9851 **e** info@playaville.com **w** playaville.com Contact: Stevie Nash.

Poisson Rouge Pictures Ltd 140 Battersea Park Rd, London SW11 4NB **t** 020 7720 5666 **f** 020 7720 5757 **e** info@poissonrougepictures.com **w** poissonrougepictures.com Producer: Christopher Granier-Deferre.

POP @ Paul Weiland Film Co Ltd 14 Newburgh St, London W1V 1LF **t** 020 7494 9600 **f** 020 7434 0146 **e** eatpop@aol.com Producer: Alex Johnson.

PTE Media 123 Regents Park Rd, London NW1 8BE **t** 020 7722 5566 **f** 020 7586 4133 **e** info@ptemedia.com **w** ptemedia.com Contact: Simon Poon Tip.

Pulse Films 36 Berwick St, London W1F 8RR **t** 020 7437 5518 **f** 020 7287 6505 **e** marisa@pulsefilms.co.uk **w** pulsefilms.co.uk Producer: Marisa Clifford.

Punk Films Unit 2A Queens Studios, 121 Salusbury Rd, London NW6 6RG **t** 020 7372 4474 **f** 020 7372 4484 or 020 7328 4447 **e** info@punk.uk.com **w** punk.uk.com Dir: Mark Logue.

QD Productions 93 Great Titchfield St, London W1W 6RP **t** 020 7462 1700 **f** 020 7636 0653 **e** musicvideo@qotd.co.uk **w** qotd.co.uk Head of Music & Video: Andy Leahy.

Rogue 2-3 Bourlet Close, London W1W 7BQ **t** 020 7907 1000 **f** 020 7907 1001 **e** charlie@roguefilms.co.uk **w** roguefilms.com MD: Charlie Crompton.

David & Kathy Rose Productions 159 Earlsfield Rd, London SW18 3DD **t** 020 8874 0744 **f** 020 8874 9136 **e** kathy@theroses.co.uk Ptnr: Kathy Rose.

Science Films Ltd 57 Great Portland St, London W1W 7LH **t** 020 7636 7637 **f** 020 7636 7647 **e** films@sciencefilms.co.uk Exec Prod: Galia Ina.

Scopitone Ltd Tower Bridge Business Complex, Block J - Suite 212, 100 Clements Rd, London SE16 4DG **t** 020 7193 6528 **e** info@scopitone.co.uk **w** scopitone.co.uk Producer: Alex Piot.

Serious Pictures Film Co Ltd 1A Rede Pl, London W2 4TU **t** 020 7792 4477 **f** 020 7792 4488 **e** info@serious-pics.com **w** serious-pics.com Office Mgr: Ann-Marie Morris.

The Showreel Company Ltd. 28 Cleveland Ave, London W4 1SN **t** 020 8525 0058 **e** the.showreelcompany@virgin.net **w** theshowreelcompany.co.uk Dir: John Gugolka.

Single Minded Production 11 Cambridge Court, 210 Shepherds Bush Rd, London W6 7NJ **t** 0870 011 3748 or 07860 391 902 **f** 0870 011 3749 **e** video@singleminded.com **w** singleminded.com MD: Tony Byrne.

Smoke & Mirrors 57-59 Beak St, London W1R 3LF **t** 020 7468 1000 **f** 020 7468 1001 **w** smoke-mirrors.com Office Mgr: Matt Z.

Sounds Good Ltd 12 Chiltern Enterprise Centre, Station Rd, Theale, Reading, Berks RG7 4AA **t** 0118 930 1700 **f** 0118 930 1709 **e** sales-info@sounds-good.co.uk **w** sounds-good.co.uk Dir: Martin Maynard.

Spectre Vision 48 Beak St, London W1F 9RL **t** 020 7851 2000 **e** spectre@spectrevision.com Contact: Janie Balcomb.

Splinter Films Studio 34, Clink St Studios, 1 Clink St, London SE1 9DG **t** 020 7378 9378 **f** 020 7378 9388 **e** splinter@splinterfilms.com **w** splinterfilms.com Producer: Emer Patten.

Stink Ltd 87 Lancaster Rd, London W11 1QQ **t** 020 7908 9400 **f** 020 7908 9400 **e** info@stink.tv **w** stink.tv Head of Promos: Alexa Hayward.

Storm Film Productions Ltd 32 Great Marlborough St, London W1F 7JB **t** 020 7439 1616 **f** 020 7439 4477 **e** sophie.storm@btclick.com Prod Mgr: Sophie Inman.

Straightwire 10 Cranbrook Court, Fleet, Hants GU15 4QA
t 01252 665 873 or 07940 032 286 **f** 01252 665 873
e rob@straightwire.co.uk **w** straightwire.co.uk
Producer: Rob Weston.

Studio Plum 39 Belgrade Rd, London N16 8DH
t 0207 249 8198 **e** jonnie@studioplum.co.uk **w** studioplum.co.uk
Producer: Jonnie Pound.

Stylorouge 57/60 Charlotte Rd, London EC2A 3QT
t 020 7729 1005 **f** 020 7739 7124 **e** rob@stylorouge.co.uk
w stylorouge.co.uk Dir: Rob O'Connor.

Sugar Vision 130 Shaftesbury Ave, London W1D 5EU
t 020 7031 1140 **e** adamglen@thesugargroup.com
w thesugargroup.com Head of Production: Adam Glen.

Swivel Films 23 Denmark St, London WC2H 8NA
t 020 7240 4485 **f** 020 7240 4486
e swivelfilms@btinternet.com Dir's Rep: Sarah Wills.

Syndicate Pictures Truman Brewery, 91-95 Brick Lane,
London E1 6QL **t** 020 7247 7212 **f** 020 7247 7213
e syndicate@dial.pipex.com **w** synpics.com
MD: Jonathan Hercock.

Tele-Cine 48 Charlotte St, London W1T 2NS
t 020 7208 2200 **f** 020 7208 2252 **e** telecine@telecine.co.uk
w telecine.co.uk Music Bking Mgr: Claire Booth.

Ten Grand Films The Dairy, Main St, Illston, Leics LE7 9EG
t 01162 599 336 **f** 0870 458 1686
e karen.craig@documentuk.com **w** tengrandfilms.com
Head of Production: Karen Craig.

TheFireFactory.com 13 William Rd, Westbridgeford,
Nottingham NG3 **t** 07870 553 717 **e** info@thefirefactory.com
w thefirefactory.com Producer: Jake Shaw.

Tom Dick and Debbie Ltd 43A Botley Rd, Oxford
OX2 0BN **t** 01865 201564 **f** 01865 201935
e info@tomdickanddebbie.com **w** tomdickanddebbie.com
Dir: Richard Lewis.

Tomato Films 29-35 Lexington St, London W1R 3HQ
t 020 7434 0955 **f** 020 7434 0255 **e** films@tomato.co.uk
w tomato.co.uk MD: Jeremy Barrett.

Tough Cookie Ltd 3rd Floor, 24 Denmark St, London
WC2H 8NJ **t** 020 8870 9233 or 07977 248 646
f 0871 242 2442 **e** office@tough-cookie.co.uk
w myspace.com/toughcookiemusic Dir: Andy Wood.

TSI Video 10 Grape St, London WC2H 8TG **t** 020 7379 3435
f 020 7379 4589 **e** rwillcocks@tsi.co.uk
Bkings Co-ord: Rebecca Willcocks.

Yawning Dog Productions 70A Uxbridge Rd, London
W12 8LP **t** 020 8742 9067 **f** 020 8742 9118
e nina@yawningdog.fsnet.co.uk Prod: Nina Beck.

Yoyoandco Walnut Tree Cottage, Watercress Lane, Wingham
Well, Canterbury, Kent CT3 1NR **t** 01227 728409
f 01227 728409 **e** info@yoyoand.co.uk MD: Blair Hart.

Video Production Services

Aimimage Unit 5, St. Pancras Commercial Centre, 63 Pratt St,
London NW1 0BY **t** 020 7482 4340 **f** 020 7267 3972
e hire@aimimage.com **w** aimimage.com
Production Manager: Atif Ghani.

Bill Charles London Ltd Unit 3E1 Zetland House, 5-25
Scrutton St, London EC2A 4HJ **t** 020 7033 9284
f 020 7033 9285 **e** dan@billcharles.com **w** billcharles.com
Contact: Daniel Worthington or Olivia Gideon Thomson.

BLACK & BLONDE CREATIVE COMMISSIONING SERVICES

The Primrose Hill Business Centre, 110 Gloucester Avenue,
London NW1 8HX **t** 020 7209 3760 or
07703 201 111 or 07968 499 037 **f** 020 7209 3761
e info@blackandblonde.co.uk **w** blackandblonde.co.uk Directors:
Hermione Ross, Jo Hart.

The Screen Talent Agency 58 Speed House, Barbican,
London EC2Y 8AT **t** 020 7628 5180 or 07836 210 926
f 020 7681 3588 **e** info@screen-talent.com **w** screen-talent.com
Contact: James Little.

Choreography and Styling Services

Bill Charles London Ltd Unit 3E1 Zetland House, 5-25 Scrutton St, London EC2A 4HJ **t** 020 7033 9284 **f** 020 7033 9285 **e** dan@billcharles.com **w** billcharles.com Contact: Daniel Worthington or Olivia Gideon Thomson.

Black & Blonde Creative Commissioning Services The Primrose Hill Business Centre, 110 Gloucester Ave, London NW1 8HX **t** 020 7209 3760 or 07703 201 111 or 07968 499 037 **f** 020 7209 3761 **e** info@blackandblonde.co.uk **w** blackandblonde.co.uk Dirs: Hermione Ross, Jo Hart.

Carol Hayes Management Ltd 5-6 Underhill St, London NW1 7HS **t** 020 7482 3666 **e** ian@carolhayesmanagement.co.uk **w** carolhayesmanagement.co.uk Head Booker: Ian Loughran.

JK Dance South Manchester Film & TV Studios, Studio House, Battersea Rd, Heaton Mersey, Stockport SK4 3EA **t** 0161 4325222 **f** 0161 4326800 **e** info@jkdance.co.uk **w** jkdance.co.uk MD: Julie Kavanagh.

The Screen Talent Agency 58 Speed House, Barbican, London EC2Y 8AT **t** 020 7628 5180 or 07836 210 926 **f** 020 7681 3588 **e** info@screen-talent.com **w** screen-talent.com Contact: James Little.

SR Management Ltd 4 Monkton House, 130A Haverstock Hill, London NW3 2AY **t** 020 7722 4373 **e** srmgmt@aol.com **w** sarahpilates.com MD/Pilates Trainer: Sarah Rosenfield.

Terri Manduca Ltd The Basement, 11 Elvaston Pl, London SW7 5QG **t** 020 7581 5844 **f** 020 7581 5822 **e** sally@terrimanduca.co.uk **w** terrimanduca.co.uk MD: Terri Manduca.

Media Miscellaneous

A United Production (U.P) 6 Shaftesbury Mews, Clapham, London SW4 9BP **t** 020 7720 9624 **f** 020 7720 9624 **e** info@united-productions.co.uk **w** united-productions.co.uk Choreographer: Lyndon Lloyd.

Box Music Ltd 2 Munro Terrace, 112 Cheyne Walk, London SW10 0DL **t** 020 7376 8736 **f** 020 7376 3376 **e** sam@boxmusicltd.com GM: Sam Hilsdon.

Celebrities Worldwide 39-41 New Oxford St, London WC1A 1BN **t** 020 7836 7702/3 **f** 020 7836 7701 **e** info@celebritiesworldwide.com **w** celebritiesworldwide.com Co-MDs: Claire Nye, Richard Brecker.

Constantly Cliff 17 Podsmead Rd, Tuffley, Glos GL1 5PB **t** 01452 306104 **f** 01452 306104 **e** william@constantlycliff.freeserve.co.uk **w** cliffchartsite.co.uk Ed: William Hooper.

Entertainment Press Cuttings Agency Unit 7, Lloyds Wharf, Mill St, London SE1 2BD **t** 020 7237 1717 **f** 020 7237 3388 **e** epca@ukonline.co.uk Mgr: Sally Miller.

Giant Mobile 57 Kingsway, Woking, Surrey GU21 6NS **t** 01483 859 849 **e** mark.studio@ntlworld.com Contact: Mark Taylor.

Green Island Promotions Unit 31, 56 Gloucester Rd, London SW7 4UB **t** 0870 789 3377 **f** 0870 789 3414 **e** greenisland@btinternet.com **w** greenislandpromotions.com Dir: Steve Lucas.

Green Room Productions The Laurels, New Park Rd, Harefield, Middlesex UB9 6EQ **t** 01895 822771 **f** 01895 824880 **e** tony@greenroom2.demon.co.uk **w** auracle.com/greenroom Ptnr: Tony Faulkner.

JN Associates 8 Broxash Rd, London SW11 6AB **t** 020 7223 5280 **f** 020 7223 9493 **e** jonnewey@btinternet.com Research & Archivist Dir: Jon Newey.

Klipjoint - Photo archive service. 25 Plympton Ave, London NW6 7TL **t** 020 8357 3499 **f** 020 7372 2572 **e** mail@klipjoint.info **w** klipjoint.info MD: Duncan Brown.

Hanspeter Kuenzler Journalistic Services 25 Plympton Ave, London NW6 7TL **t** 020 7328 '0052 or 07879 855 126 **e** hpduesi@aol.com **w** hanspeterkuenzler.com Contact: Hanspeter Kuenzler.

Mediamix II - Media planning & buying consultancy 107 Mortlake High St, London SW14 8HQ **t** 020 8392 6885 **f** 020 8392 6803 **e** info@themediamix.co.uk MD: David Collins.

Music & Media Law Services Ltd Wychwood, Kencot, Oxon GL7 3QT **t** 01367 860256 **f** 01367 860116 **e** anicholas@btinternet.com MD: Alastair Nicholas.

Music Innovations 14 Ransomes Dock, 35 - 37 Parkgate Rd, London SW11 4NP **t** 020 7350 5550 **f** 020 7350 5551 **e** firstname@musicinnovations.com MD: Robert Dodds.

Openplay Limited Suite 106, Hiltongrove Business Centre, Hatherley Mews, London E17 4QP **t** 020 8520 6644 **f** 020 8520 7755 **e** info@openplay.co.uk **w** openplay.co.uk Dir: David Hoskins.

Pro-Motion 33 Kendal Rd, Hove, E Sussex BN3 5HZ **t** 01273 327175 **e** info@martinjames.demon.co.uk Executive Producer: Martin James.

Shazam Entertainment 4th Floor, Block F, 375 Kensington High St, London W14 8QH **t** 020 7471 3440 **f** 020 7471 3477 **e** tim.porter@shazamteam.com **w** shazamentertainment.com Marketing Dir: Tim Porter.

Sound Stage Production Music Kerchesters, Waterhouse Lane, Kingswood, Surrey KT20 6HT **t** 01737 832837 **f** 01737 833812 **e** info@amphonic.co.uk **w** amphonic.com MD: Ian Dale.

UK Booking Agency Box 1, 404 Footscray Rd, London SE9 3TU **t** 020 8857 8775 or 07740 351 163 **f** 020 8857 8775 **e** stevegoddardis@aol.com Owner: Steve Goddard.

Upfront Promotions Ltd Unit 217 Buspace Studios, Conlan St, London W10 5AP **t** 020 7565 0050 **f** 020 7565 0049 **e** terence@upfrontpromotions.com **w** upfrontpromotions.com Premiums Manager: Terence Scragg.

XK8 Organisation First Floor, 151 City Rd, London EC1V 1JH **t** 020 7490 0666 **f** 020 7490 0660 **e** roger@xk8organisation.com **w** automaticpromotions.co.uk Dir: Roger Evans.

Are you serious
about a career in music?

Are you a student?
Then subscribe to Music Week at 40% off the normal rate.

Visit www.musicweek.com for details

THE UK'S LEADING RADIO AND TELEVISION PROMOTIONS COMPANY

NATIONAL RADIO
NATIONAL TELEVISION
REGIONAL RADIO
REGIONAL TV
PRESS
MEDIA TRAINING

Clients past and present include

Aaliyah, Ant & Dec, Backstreet Boys, Katie Bush, Enya, Jools Holland, INXS, Janet Jackson, R Kelly, Katie Melua, *NSYNC, OK Go, LeAnn Rimes, Jack Savoretti, Britney Spears, Lisa Stansfield, Steps, Justin Timberlake, TLC, Dionne Warwick.

Press & Promotion

FLEMING CONNOLLY

FLEMING CONNOLLY PR
1st Floor,
45 Poland Street,
London, W1F 7NA
Tel 020 7292 0900
Fax 020 7734 0764

For further information contact
NICK FLEMING nick@fclpr.com
and
MATT CONNOLLY matt@fclpr.com

www.flemingconnolly.com

MUSIC HOUSE GROUP
THE UK'S LEADING RADIO, TV, CLUB AND STUDENT PROMOTIONS COMPANY

SIZE NINE
NATIONAL AND REGIONAL RADIO AND TELEVISION PROMOTION.

HYPERACTIVE
TOP SPECIALIST DANCE & MAINSTREAM CLUB PROMOTION SERVICES.

EUROSOLUTION
COMMERCIAL, UNDER 18, GAY AND URBAN CLUB PROMOTION.

A GUIDE TO **PROMOTION**

HYPER X-CLUSIVE
EXCLUSIVE DIGITAL CLUB & SPECIALIST PROMOTION FOR THE WORLD'S TASTEMAKER DJ'S.

RENEGADE
INDIE / ALTERNATIVE / ROCK CLUB & COLLEGE PROMOTION. STUDENT PRESS & RADIO. BARS / CAFES / RETAIL PROMOTION.

MUSIC HOUSE GROUP
40 ST. PETER'S ROAD
LONDON
W6 9BD

TEL: 020 8563 7788
FAX: 020 8741 9431
www.music-house.co.uk

For further information please contact
Simon Walsh
simon.walsh@music-house.co.uk.

Press & Promotion

Press & Promotion:

Promoters and Pluggers

Absolute PR Hazlehurst Barn, Valley Rd, Hayfield, Derbyshire SK22 2JP **t** 01663 747970 or 07768 652899 **f** 01663 747970 **e** neil@absolutepr.demon.co.uk **w** absolutepr.demon.co.uk Contact: Neil Cossar.

ABSTRAKT 21d Gloucester St, Pimlico, London SW1V 2DB **t** 020 8968 1840 **e** abstrakt@abstraktpublicity.co.uk MD: Anna Goodman.

Aire International 2a Ferry Rd, London SW13 9RX **t** 020 8834 7373 **f** 020 8834 7474 **e** info@airmtm.com **w** airmtm.com Contact: Sheela Bates.

Airplayer Ltd Studio 3, 3a Brackenbury Rd, London W6 0BE **t** 020 8762 9155 or 07795 462 661 **f** 020 8740 0200 **e** rob@airplayer.co.uk Contact: Rob Lynch.

ALL ABOUT PROMOTIONS

ALL ₃OUT PROMOTIONS

27a Kings Gardens, West End Lane, London NW6 4PX **t** 020 7328 4836 **f** 020 7372 3331 **e** info@allaboutpromo.com Prop: Amanda Beel. Contacts: Hayley Codd, Helen Johns, Bobbie Coppen, Lynn Blackwell.

Anglo Plugging Fulham Palace, Bishops Ave, London SW6 6EA **t** 020 7384 7373 **f** 020 7371 9490 **e** firstname@angloplugging.co.uk **w** angloplugging.co.uk Promotions Co-ordinator: Neha Patel.

Avalon Public Relations 4A Exmoor St, London W10 6BD **t** 020 7598 7222 **f** 020 7598 7223 **e** danielb@avalonuk.com Head of PR: Daniel Bee.

Backyard Promotion 106 Great Portland St, London W1W 6PF **t** 020 7722 7522 **e** info@back-yard.co.uk **w** back-yard.co.uk Booker: Mark Ngui.

Beatwax Communications 91 Berwick St, London W1F 0NE **t** 020 7734 1965 **f** 020 7292 8333 **e** michael@beatwax.com **w** beatwax.com MD: Michael Brown.

Big Sister Promotions Studio 3, 3A Brackenbury Rd, London W6 0BE **t** 020 8740 0100 **f** 020 8740 0200 **e** karen@bigsisteruk.com MD: Karen Williams.

Blurb 7 Tower Mansions, 136 West End Lane, West Hampstead, London NW6 1SB **t** 020 7419 1221 **e** hello@blurbpr.com MD: Michael Plumley.

BR-Asian Media Consulting 45 Circus Rd, St Johns Wood, London NW8 9JH **t** 020 8550 9898 **f** 020 7289 9892 **e** moizvas@brasian.com **w** brasian.com MD: Moiz Vas.

Breakout Promotions 36 Durnford St, Basford, Nottingham NG7 7EQ **t** 07961 014 303 **f** 0115 841 5994 **e** holmes_1978@hotmail.com MD: Rachel Holmes.

CD Pool Devonshire House, 223 Upper Richmond Rd, London SW15 6SQ **t** 0845 458 8780 **f** 020 8789 8668 **e** admin@cdpool.co.uk **w** cdpool.com.

Chapple Davies 53 Great Portland St, London W1W 7LG **t** 020 7299 7979 **f** 020 7299 7978 **e** firstname@chapdav.com **w** chapdav.com Partners: Gareth Davies, James C Gill.

CHILLI PR

Clear Water Yard, 35 Inverness St, London NW1 7HB **t** 020 7424 7523/7524 or 07939 150670 **e** firstname@chillipr.com **w** chillipr.com Partners: Helen Jones & Jenni Page.

Chuffmedia Unit 29 Cygnus Business Centre, Dalmeyer Rd, London NW10 2XA **t** 020 8830 0330 or 07762 130 510 **f** 020 8830 0220 **e** warren@chuffmedia.com **w** chuffmedia.com Dir: Warren Higgins.

Content_ Studio 204, Latimer Rd, London W10 6QY **t** 020 8960 1384 or 07976 279 716 **e** gideon@contentunlimited.com **w** independent-music.co.uk MD: Gideon Palmer.

Content PR 223d Canalot Studios, 222 Kensal Rd, London W10 5BN **t** 020 8960 4660 or 07799 882 333 **e** joggs@contentpr.co.uk Dir: Joggs Camfield.

Cool Badge Office 604, Oxford House, 49a Oxford Rd, London N4 3EY **t** 020 7272 8370 or 07766 233 368 **f** 020 7272 8371 **e** music@coolbadge.com **w** coolbadge.com MD: Russell Yates.

Crashed Music 162 Church Rd, East Wall, Dublin 3, Ireland **t** +353 1 888 1188 **f** +353 1 856 1122 **e** info@crashedmusic.com **w** crashedmusic.com MD: Shay Hennessy.

Crunk! Promotions Unit 11 Impress House, Mansell Rd, London W3 7QH **t** 020 8932 3030 **f** 020 8932 3031 **e** duncan@crunk.co.uk **w** power.co.uk/crunk Promotions Mgr: Duncan Stump.

Cypher Press & Promotions Ltd Unit 2A Queens Studios, 121 Salusbury Rd, London NW6 6RG **t** 020 7372 4464 or 020 7372 4474 **f** 020 7328 3808 or 020 7328 4447 **e** info@cypherpress.uk.com **w** cypherpress.uk.com Contact: Simon Ward/Marion Sparks.

DARLING PROMOTIONS

4th floor, 19 Denmark Street, London WC2H 8NA
t 020 7379 8787 **f** 020 7379 5737 **e** info@darlinguk.com
w darlingdepartment.com. Directors: Edward Cartwright & Daniel Stevens.

Lisa Davies Promotions Caravela House, Waterhouse Lane, Kingswood, Surrey KT20 6DT **t** 01737 362444
f 01737 362555 **e** lisa@lisadaviespromotions.co.uk
w lisadaviespromotions.co.uk MD: Lisa Davies.

The Distribution Company ZLR Studios, West Heath Yard, 174 Mill Lane, London NW6 1TB **t** 020 7433 8433
f 020 7433 8434 **e** sales@thedistributionco.co.uk
Senior Account Mgr: Claire Gibson.

Earshot 10-11 Jockey's Fields, London WC1R 4BN
t 020 7400 4560 **f** 020 7400 4561 **e** info@upshotcom.com
w upshotcreek.com Dirs: Stephen Barnes, Tom Roberts.

EURO SOLUTION

Music House Group, 40 St. Peter's Road, London W6 9BD
t 020 8563 3923 **e** craig.eurosolution@music-house.co.uk
w music-house.co.uk Contact: Craig Jones.
Euro Solution provides a full range of commercial, pop & urban club promotion services.

Richard Evans PR 15 Chesham St, Belgravia, London SW1X 8ND **t** 020 7235 3929 **e** r.evans@pipemedia.co.uk.

Exposure (Nation-wide flyer distribution services)
3N Beehive Mill, Jersey St, Manchester M4 6JG
t 0161 950 4241 **f** 0161 950 4240 **e** keith@exposureuk.com
MD: Keith Patterson.

Fake Media May Villas, 50 Main Rd, Naphill, Bucks HP14 4QB
t 07966 233 275 **e** Adam.fisher@fakemedia.com
MD: Adam Fisher.

FFR UK 2 Hastings Terrace, Conway Rd, London N15 3BE
t 020 8826 5900 **f** 020 8826 5902
e fullfrontalrecords@hotmail.com **w** ffruk.com Dir: Tara Rez.

FLEMING CONNOLLY PR

FLEMING CONNOLLY

45 Poland Street, London W1F 7NA **t** 020 7292 0900
f 020 7734 0764 **e** firstname@fclpr.com **w** flemingconnolly.com
Contact: Nick Fleming & Matt Connolly. **NF - 07860 214 837;**
MC - 07801 231 255
National radio & television promotion.

Freeway Press 20 Windmill Rd, Kirkcaldy, Fife KY1 3AQ
t 01592 655309 **f** 01592 596177 **e** cronulla20@aol.com
w freewaypress.co.uk Dir: John Murray.

Frequency Media (FMG UK Ltd) Suite 115 The Greenhouse, Custard Factory 2, Gibb St, Birmingham, W Midlands B9 4AA **t** 0121 224 7450 or 7452 or 07866 422 109
f 0121 224 7451 **e** gerard@fmguk.com **w** fmguk.com
PR Directors: Gerard Franklin & Margaret Murray.

Futureproof Promotions 330 Westbourne Park Rd, London W11 1EQ **t** 020 7792 8597 **f** 020 7221 3694
e info@futureproofrecords.com **w** futureproofrecords.com
MD: Phil Legg.

G Promotions Cambrian Cottage, 3, Trimpley St, Ellesmere, Shropshire SY12 0AD **t** 07855 724 798 or 01691 622 356
e GPromo@btinternet.com Contact: Geraint Jones.

Phil Gibbs Promotes... Faraday Cottage, Faraday Yard, Hampton Court Rd, East Molesey, Surrey KT8 9BW
t 020 8979 3505 or 07767 264154 **f** 08712 215597
e pgibbsprom@tiscali.co.uk Owner: Phil Gibbs.

Go For It Promotions 3 Heronwood Rd, Aldershot, Hants. GU12 4AJ **t** 01252 312 382 or 07904 232 292
e goforit-promotions@ntlworld.com **w** goforit-promotions.com
MD: Golly Gallagher.

Gorgeous Promotions Suite D, 67 Abbey Rd, St John's Wood, London NW8 0AE **t** 020 7724 2635 **f** 020 7724 2635
e promotion@gorgeousmusic.net **w** gorgeousmusic.net
TV/Radio Consultants: David Ross & Victoria Elliott.

Groovefinder Productions 30, Havelock Rd, Southsea, Portsmouth PO5 1RU **t** 07831 450 241
e jeff@groovefinderproductions.com MD: Jeff Powell.

HardZone / Full Service Ltd Gardiner House, The Business Village, 3-9 Broomhill Rd, London SW18 4JQ
t 020 8870 8744 **f** 020 8874 1578
e firstname@hardzone.co.uk **w** hardzone.co.uk
MD: Jackie Davidson.

HART MEDIA LTD.

Primrose Hill Business Centre, 110 Gloucester Avenue, London NW1 8HX **t** 020 7209 3760 **f** 020 7209 3761
e info@hartmedia.co.uk **w** hartmedia.co.uk MD: Jo Hart. Head of Promotions: Sue Reinhardt.

Taryn Hill Promotions Dolphin Court, 42 Carleton Rd, London N7 0ER **t** 07971 575 810 **e** hilltaryn@hotmail.com
Contact: Taryn Hill.

The Howlin' Plugging & Promotion Company 114 Lower Park Rd, Loughton, Essex IG10 4NE **t** 020 8508 4564 or 07831 430080 **e** djone@howardmarks.freeserve.co.uk
Prop: Howard Marks.

Hungry Media Ltd 3 Berkley Grove, London NW1 8XY
t 020 7722 6992 **e** woolfie@hungrylikethewoolf.com
MD: Woolfie.

HYPER ACTIVE

Music House Group, 40 St. Peter's Road, London W6 9BD
t 020 8563 3924 **e** markb@music-house.co.uk
w music-house.co.uk/hyperactive Contact: Mark Bowden.
**Hyper Active provides a full range of upfront & mainstream
club promotion services.**

I Like The Sound Of That 79-89 Pentonville Rd, London
N1 9LG **t** 020 7993 3318 **e** sybil@ilikethesoundofthat.com
In Charge: Sybil.

imPRomptu 10 Stephen Mews, London W1T 1AG
t 020 7307 3162 or 07835 583 883 **e** vic@impromptupr.co.uk
MD: Victoria Gratton.

Indiscreet PR PO Box 48683, London NW8 1AT
t 07813 290 474 or 07930 810 751 **e** alan@indiscreetpr.co.uk
w indiscreetpr.com Dirs: Alan Robinson, Lesley Shone.

INFECTED

18 Eddison Court, 253 Sussex Way, London N19 4DW
t 020 7272 9620 or 07782 269 750
e mike.infected000@btclick.com MD: Mike Gourlay.
**Regional press promotions : Brakes, Coldplay, Dirty Pretty
Things, The Gossip, Graham Coxon, The Holloways, The
Rapture, Razorlight, Richard Ashcroft etc.**

information communication ltd 6 Hornsey Lane
Gardens, London N6 5PB **t** 020 8374 6040
e infocom@dial.pipex.com MD: Michael Thorne.

INTERMEDIA REGIONAL PROMOTIONS

Byron House, 112A Shirland Road, London W9 2EQ
t 020 7266 0777 **f** 020 7266 1293
e info@intermediaregional.com **w** intermediaregional.com MD:
Steve Tandy. GM: Gavin Hughes. Assistant Manager: Stacy
Scurfield. Dance Promotions: Simon Hills. TV & Alternative
Promotions: James Pegrum. Promotions: Polly Roe, Mike Byrne.

ish-media 2, Devonport Mews, Devonport Rd, London
W12 8NG **t** 020 8742 9191 or 07778 263 533
f 020 8742 9102 **e** eden@ish-media.com **w** ish-media.com
Dir: Eden Blackman.

Alan James PR Ground Floor, 60 Weston St, London
SE1 3QJ **t** 020 7403 9999 **f** 020 7403 0000
e promo@ajpr.co.uk **w** ajpr.co.uk MD: Alan James.

James Grant Music 94 Strand On The Green, Chiswick,
London W4 3NN **t** 020 8742 4950 **f** 020 8742 4951
e enquiries@jamesgrant.co.uk **w** jamesgrant.co.uk
Co-MDs: Simon Hargreaves, Nick Worsley.

JBMusicMedia 2, The Bush, Newtown Rd, Awbridge,
Romsey, Hants SO51 0GG **t** 01794 342426 **f** 01794 432426
e jacqui@kwinstanley.free-online.co.uk GM: Jacqui Bateson.

Jeff Chegwin Promotions Suite 139, 2 Lansdowne Row,
Berkeley Sq, London W1H 6JL **t** 020 8579 7997 or
07957 939 072 **e** jeffchegwin@hotmail.com **w** jeffchegwin.com
Dir: Jeff Chegwin.

The Jump Off PO Box 697, Wembley HA9 8WQ
t 020 7253 7766 **f** 020 7681 1007 **e** harry@hiphop.com
w jumpoff.tv CEO: Harold Anthony.

Labels Enabled 1 Romborough Way, London SE13 6NS
t 020 8488 0158 **e** labelsenabled@aol.com
w labelsenabled.co.uk Dir: Neil March.

Press & Promotion: Promoters and Pluggers

NATIONAL TV&RADIO PR

Lander is one of the best-known names in the music industry.

Covering all aspects of music promotion. Including: National & Regional TV/Radio National & Regional press/On Line PR Showcase & Media tours.

LANDER PR can deliver one of the most comprehensive promotion packages, bringing together all the best support services available.

For further information contact:

Judd@landerpr.com

Lander PR & Music

44b The Broadway London NW7 3LH

Tel : 020 8906 9438 Fax: 020 8906 9242

Mail: judd@landerpr.com

www.landerpr.com

Lander PR part of the Lander Music Group

LANDER PR

44B The Broadway, London NW7 3LH **t** 020 8906 9438 **f** 020 8906 9242 **e** judd@landerpr.com **w** landerpr.com Director: Judd Lander. Radio: Mark Gordon - mark@landerpr.com; TV: Nicole Rose - nicole@landerpr.com One of the best-known names in the music business and one of the UK's leading independent promotion companies. Covering all aspects of music promotion, including National TV/Radio - Regional TV/ Radio - On Line PR/Press PR – Dance or Student campaigns.

Large PR Ltd 39 Grafton Way, London W1T 5DE **t** 020 7388 6060 **f** 08700 518 459 **e** info@largepr.com **w** largepr.com Contact: Stuart Emery.

Les Molloy 27 Willesden Lane, London NW6 7RD **t** 07860 389 598 or 07860 389 598 **f** 020 7625 1199 **e** lmolloy@dircon.co.uk Contact: Les Molloy.

LEYLINE PROMOTIONS

Studio 24, Westbourne Studios, 242 Acklam Road, London W10 5JJ **t** 020 7575 3285 **f** 020 7575 3286 **e** firstname@leylinepromotions.com **w** leylinepromotions.com MD: Adrian Leigh. Operations Manager: Ben Steadman. Events Manager: Sarah Ward. PR: Nuala Ginty.

Lucid PR 76 Great Titchfield St, London W1W 7QP **t** 020 7307 7449 **e** firstname.lastname@lucidpr.co.uk **w** lucidpr.co.uk Dirs: Mick Garbutt, Charlie Lycett.

Lisa MacDonald Promotions 155 Jordanhill Drive, Glasgow G13 1UQ **t** 0141 434 0612 or 07836 211 012 **e** lisa_macdonald@btconnect.com Dir: Lisa MacDonald.

Mainstream Promotions The Music Village, 11B Osiers Rd, London SW18 1NL **t** 07000 4 77666 or 020 8870 0011 **f** 020 8870 2101 **e** mainstream@rush-release.co.uk MD: Jo Underwood.

Making Waves Communications 45 Underwood St, London N1 7LG **t** 020 7490 0944 **f** 020 7490 1026 **e** info@makingwaves.co.uk **w** makingwaves.co.uk MD: Matt Williams.

Mocking Bird Music PO Box 52, Marlow, Bucks SL7 2YB **t** 01491 579214 **f** 01491 579214 **e** mockingbirdmusic@aol.com Artiste Management: Leon B Fisk.

Mosquito Media 64a Warwick Ave, Little Venice, London W9 2PU **t** 07813 174 185 **e** mosquitomedia@aol.com **w** mosquito-media.co.uk Contact: Richard Abbott.

Movement London PO Box 31835, London SE11 4WD **t** 020 7735 7255 **f** 020 7793 7225 **e** info@movement.co.uk **w** movement.co.uk Promoter: Nyeleti van Belle Freire.

MP Promotions (MPP) 13 Greave, Romiley, Stockport, Cheshire SK6 4PU **t** 0161 494 7934 **e** maria@mppromotions.co.uk Dir: Maria Philippou.

hart.
media never misses a beat
t. +44 (0) 207 209 3760   info@hartmedia.co.uk
www.hartmedia.co.uk

Music House Group Host Europe House, Kendal Ave, London W3 0TT **t** 020 8896 8200 **f** 020 8896 8201 **e** simon.walsh@music-house.co.uk **w** music-house.co.uk Dir: Simon Walsh.

Music2Mix Unit 16, The Talina Centre, Bagleys Lane, London SW6 2BW **t** 020 7384 3200 **f** 020 7384 2999 **e** eddie@music2mix.com **w** music2mix.com MD: Eddie Gordon.

MVPD Queens House, 1 Leicester Pl, Leicester Sq, London WC2H 7BP **t** 020 7534 3340 **f** 020 7534 3341 **e** chris@mvpd.net **w** mvpd.net Dir: Chris Page.

NoBul Promotions 59 New River Crescent, Palmers Green, London N13 5RD **t** 020 8882 3677 **f** 020 8882 3688 **e** alex@nobul.prestel.co.uk MD: Alex Alexandrou.

NONSTOP PROMOTIONS

Studio 39, Aaron Business Centre, 6 Bardolph Road, Richmond, Surrey TW9 2LS **t** 020 8334 9994 **f** 020 8334 9995 **e** info@nonstop1.co.uk Contact: Niki Sanderson, Stuart Kenning. Contact: Molly Ladbrook-Hutt.

Out Promotion 4th Floor, 33 Newman St, London W1T 1PY **t** 020 7637 3755 **f** 020 7637 3744 **e** caroline@out-london.co.uk Head of Radio & TV: Caroline Poulton.

Outlet Promotions PO Box 2035, Blackpool FY4 1WW **t** 01253 347329 **f** 01253 347329 **e** glenn@outlet-promotions.com **w** outlet-promotions.com MD: Glenn Wilson.

Outpost Unit 20, Acklam Workspace, 10 Acklam Rd, London W10 5QZ **t** 020 8964 8541 **f** 020 8968 7725 **e** david@outpostmedia.co.uk **w** outpostmedia.co.uk Dir: David Silverman.

Overground Promotions PO Box 1NW, Newcastle upon Tyne NE99 1NW **t** 0191 232 6700 **f** 0191 232 6701 **e** lee@overground.co.uk MD: Lee Conlon.

Don Percival Artists' Promotion Shenandoah, Manor Pk, Chislehurst, Kent BR7 5QD **t** 020 8295 0310 **f** 020 8295 0311 **e** donpercival@freenet.co.uk MD: Don Percival.

Phuture Trax Press & Events PR PO Box 48527, London NW4 4ZB **t** 020 8203 3968 **f** 020 8203 3968 **e** nicky@phuturetrax.co.uk **w** phuturetrax.co.uk MD: Nicky Trax.

Pioneer Promotions 5 Emerson House, 14B Ballynahinch Rd, Belfast BT8 8DN **t** 028 9081 7111 **f** 028 9081 7444 **e** ppromo@musicni.co.uk MD: Johnny Davis.

Pivotal PR 4 Heathgate Pl, 75-83 Agincourt Rd, London NW3 2NU **t** 020 7424 8688 **f** 020 7424 8699 **e** bjorn@pivotalpr.co.uk **w** pivotalpr.co.uk Contact: Björn Hall.

Planetlovemusic 2 Gregg St, Lisburn, Co Antrim BT27 5AN **t** 02892 667 000 **f** 02892 668 000 **e** eddie@planetlovemusic.com **w** planetlovemusic.com Dir: Eddie Wray.

The Play Centre Unit 2 Devonport Mews, Shepherd's Bush, London W12 8NG **t** 020 8932 7705 **f** 020 8932 7723 **e** info@theplaycentre.com **w** theplaycentre.com Contact: Shaun "Stuckee" Willoughby.

PlugTwo 133 The Coal Exchange, Cardiff bay, Cardiff CF10 5ED **t** 02920 190151 **e** john@plugtwo.com **w** plugtwo.com Dir: John Rostron.

Poparazzi Unit 11, Impress House, Mansell Rd, London W3 7QH **t** 020 8932 3030 **f** 020 8932 3031 **e** Tracey@power.co.uk **w** power.co.uk Promotions Manager: Tracey Webb.

Power Plugging Power Promotions, Unit 11 Impress Hse, Mansell Rd, London W3 7QH **t** 020 8932 3030 **e** Luke@power.co.uk **w** power.co.uk Contact: Luke Neville.

Power Promotions Unit 11, Impress House, Mansell Rd, London W3 7QH **t** 020 8932 3030 **f** 020 8932 3031 **e** Stimpy@power.co.uk **w** power.co.uk Contact: Steve Stimpson (Stimpy).

pr-ism 2/14 Park Terrace, The Park, Nottingham NG1 5DN **t** 0115 947 5440 or 07971 780 821 **f** 0115 947 5440 **e** phil.long@pipemedia.co.uk **w** pr-ism.co.uk MD: Phil Long.

PRo Promotions Fulham Palace, Bishops Ave, London SW6 6EA **t** 020 7384 7373 **f** 020 7371 7940 **e** caroline@theprogroup.co.uk Dir: Caroline Prothero.

PROHIBITION LTD

PROHIBITION

Fulham Palace, Bishops Avenue, London SW6 6EA
t 020 7384 7372 or 07967 610 877 **f** 020 7371 7940
e Caroline@prohibitiondj.com **w** prohibitiondj.com MD: Caroline
Prothero. Head of Club & Radio Promotions: Steve Wandless –
Wandy@prohibitiondj.com; Club & Radio
Promotions/Management Asst: Annie Mcintyre -
Annie@prohibitiondj.com; International Development/Ibiza
Promotions Manager: Kim Booth - Kim@prohibitiondj.com

RADIO PROMOTIONS

RadioPromotions

PO Box 20, Banbury, Oxon OX17 3YT **t** 0129 581 4995
e music@radiopromotions.co.uk **w** radiopromotions.co.uk
Contact: Steve Betts, Bill Whitney.
Professional regional radio & TV promotion offering an individual service where every record is a priority.

Raised On Radio 23 Handley Court, Aigburth, Liverpool
L19 3QS **t** 0151 427 9884 **f** 0151 427 9884
e steve.raisedonradio@tinyworld.co.uk
Director of Promotion: Steve Dinwoodie.

Red Alert Promotions Sun House, 2 - 4 Little Peter St,
Manchester M15 4PS **t** 0161 834 7434 **f** 0161 834 8545
e info@redalert.co.uk **w** redalert.co.uk MD: Liam Walsh.

Red Shadow Wisteria House, 56 Cole Park Rd, Twickenham,
Middx TW1 1HS **t** 020 8891 3333 **f** 020 8891 3222
e julian@redshadow.co.uk Dir: Julian Spear.

RENEGADE

Music House Group, 40 St. Peter's Road, London W6 9BD
t 020 8563 3929 **e** chris@music-house.co.uk
w music-house.co.uk/renegade Contact: Chris Smith.
Full Range of indie/alternative club & college promotion.
Student press & radio. Music & video Bars/Café's & retail
promotion. Renegade offers the ultimate music marketing
and promotion service to the 18-40 demographic.

Rocket The Brix at St Matthews Church, Brixton Hill, London
SW2 1JF **t** 020 7326 1234 **e** Radio@Rocketpr.co.uk
w rocketpr.co.uk MD: Prudence Trapani.

Rocketscience Media 1st Floor, The Griffin, 93 Leonard St,
London EC2A 4RD **t** 020 7033 4000
e office@rocketsciencemedia.com **w** rocketsciencemedia.com
Dir: Alex Black.

RUSH RELEASE PROMOTIONS LTD

42 Adelaide Road, Surbiton, Surrey KT6 4SS **t** 0845 370 9904
f 0845 370 9905 **e** jo@rushrelease.com **w** rushrelease.com MD:
Jo Titchener.

SCREAM PROMOTIONS

Scream **PROMOTIONS**

4th Floor, 57 Poland St, London W1F 7NW **t** 020 7434 3446 or
07971 859 947 **f** 020 7434 3449
e firstname@screampromotions.co.uk **w** screampromotions.co.uk
Contact: Tony Cooke, Claire Jarvis. Phil Halliday, Scott Bartlett.

Scruffy Bird The Nest, 205 Victoria St, London SW1E 5NE
t 020 7931 7990 **e** emily@scruffybird.com **w** scruffybird.com
Head of Radio & TV: Emily Cooper.

SEESAW PR LTD

seesawᵖʳ

Lower Ground Floor, 22 Tower St, London WC2H 9TW
t 020 7539 8200/03 **f** 020 7836 1167
e firstname@seesawpr.net **w** seesawpr.net Contact: Sam Wright.

Single Minded Promotions 11 Cambridge Court, 210
Shepherds Bush Rd, London W6 7NJ **t** 0870 011 3748 or
07860 391 902 **f** 0870 011 3749 **e** tony@singleminded.com
w singleminded.com MD: Tony Byrne.

SIZE NINE

SiZe*NINE*

Music House Group, 40 St. Peter's Road, London W6 9BD
t 020 8563 3928 **e** simon.walsh@music-house.co.uk
w music-house.co.uk/size9 Contact: Simon Walsh. Regional Radio:
Jonathan Pool **e** jonathan@music-house.co.uk
Size 9 offer a full range of National, Regional & Specialist
Radio Promotion.

Skullduggery Services 40a Love Lane, Pinner, Middlesex
HA5 3EX **t** 020 8429 0853 **e** xskullduggeryx@btinternet.com
MD: Russell Aldrich.

Song And Media Promotions Mulberry House, 10
Hedgerows, Stanway, Colchester, Essex CO3 0GJ
t 01206 364136 **f** 01206 364146 **e** songmag@aol.com
w songwriters-guild.co.uk MD: Colin Eade.

Soulfood Music - Urban Specialists 4 Allen Close, Shenley, Radlett, Herts. WD7 9JS **t** 01923 853737 or 01923 853737 **e** steve@soulfoodmusic.org **w** soulfoodmusic.org MD: Steve Ripley.

Special D (SDDP) 29 St Barnabas St, Belgravia, London SW1W 8QB **t** 020 7730 7697 or 0790 427 2668 **f** 020 7730 7697 **e** steve.stimpy@btinternet.com **w** special-d.com MD: Stimpy.

Steve Osborne Promotions PO Box 69, Daventry, Northants NN11 4SY **t** 01327 703968 or 01327 312545 **f** 0871 2772365 **e** steve@steveosbornemanagement.co.uk **w** steveosbornemanagement.co.uk Prop: Steve Osborne.

Strategic 10 Margaret St, London W1W 8RL **t** 0845 6801 857 **f** 020 3008 6171 **e** info@strategic-trax.com **w** strategic-trax.com Owner: Mal Smith.

Subshot TV - Student Media Promotions 10-11 Jockey's Fields, London WC1R 4BN **t** 020 7400 4560 **f** 020 7400 4561 **e** info@upshotcom.com **w** upshotcreek.com Dirs: Stephen Barnes, Tom Roberts.

Supersonic Publicity 35 Chilcote Rd, Portsmouth PO3 6HY **t** 07866 482 043 **e** Supersonic_Publicity@hotmail.co.uk **w** myspace.com/Supersonic_Publicity MD: Jim Lines.

Swell Music Marketing 2nd Floor, 29 Clerkenwell Green, London EC1R 0DU **t** 020 7490 7911 **f** 020 7490 3693 **e** info@swellmusic.co.uk **w** swellmusic.co.uk Dir: Andrew Grainger.

Terrie Doherty Promotions 40 Princess St, Manchester M1 6DE **t** 0161 234 0044 **e** terriedoherty@zoo.co.uk Dir: Terrie Doherty.

TOMKINS PR

The Old Lampworks, Rodney Place, London SW19 2LQ **t** 020 8540 8166 **f** 020 8540 6056 **e** info@tomkinspr.com **w** tomkinspr.com MD: Susie Tomkins. Promotion Assistant: Luke Tomkins. Finance: Deborah Cutting. **REGIONAL RADIO AND TV PROMOTION**

Upshot Communications 10-11 Jockey's Fields, London WC1R 4BN **t** 020 7400 4560 **f** 020 7400 4561 **e** info@upshotcom.com **w** upshotcreek.com Dirs: Stephen Barnes, Tom Roberts.

Videopops Power Promotions, Unit 11 Impress Hse, Mansell Rd, London W3 7QH **t** 020 8932 3030 **e** Mike@power.co.uk **w** power.co.uk Contact: Mike Mitchell.

VISION PROMOTIONS

22 Upper Grosvenor St, London W1K 7PE **t** 020 7499 8024 **f** 020 7499 8032 **e** vision@visionmusic.co.uk **w** visionmusic.co.uk Head Of Promotions: Rob Dallison. AIM : robvsn - MSN: rob@visionmusic.co.uk

Way to Blue First Floor, 65 Rivington St, London EC2A 3QQ **t** 020 7749 8444 **f** 020 7749 8420 **e** Lee@waytoblue.com **w** waytoblue.com Dir: Lee Henshaw.

Whitenoise Promotions 66 Bacon St, London E2 6DY **t** 020 7729 3320 **f** 020 7729 3321 **e** info@whitenoisepromo.com **w** whitenoisepromo.com MD: Colin Hobbs.

Wild 2B Westpoint, 39-40 Warple Way, London W3 0RG **t** 020 8746 0666 **f** 020 8746 7676 **e** info@wild-uk.com **w** wild-uk.com MD: Dave Roberts.

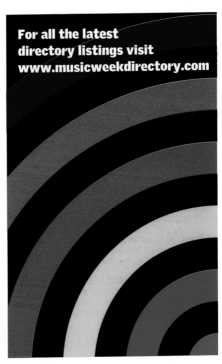

For all the latest directory listings visit www.musicweekdirectory.com

Student Press, Student Radio, Student Marketing, Street Teams

T: 01223 410000
Harvey@quitegreat.co.uk
www.quitegreat.co.uk

Press & Promotion: PR Companies

PR Companies

Ablaze PR Unit 217, Canalot Production Studios, 222 Kensal Rd, London W10 5BN **t** 020 8969 9184 or 07990 680 303 **e** nadia@ablazepr.com Dir: Nadia Khan.

Absolute PR Hazlehurst Barn, Valley Rd, Hayfield, Derbyshire SK22 2JP **t** 01663 747970 or 07768 652899 **f** 01663 747970 **e** neil@absolutepr.demon.co.uk **w** absolutepr.demon.co.uk Contact: Neil Cossar.

Absolute Promotions & PR Ground Floor (Rear), 34 Maple St, London W1T 6HD **t** 020 7323 2238 **f** 020 7323 2239 **e** info@absolutepromo.co.uk Partners: Stuart Emery.

ABSTRAKT

21d Gloucester Street, Pimlico, London SW1V 2DB **t** 020 8968 1840 **e** abstrakt@abstraktpublicity.co.uk MD: Anna Goodman.
Complete promotional service for cutting-edge music and events, World Music, Jazz, Dance, Hip Hop, Spoken Word, Contemporary Dance shows. Clients: Putumayo, Subliminal, Bambossa, Sondos, Ropeadope, Probe, Resist Music, Robert Hylton Urban Classicism, Breakin' Convention, Breaking Cycles.

AFC Publicity 24 Bray Gardens, Maidstone, Kent ME15 9TR **t** 01622 744481 **f** 01622 765014 **e** editor@maverick-country.com **w** maverick-country.com MD: Alan Cackett.

Aire International 2a Ferry Rd, London SW13 9RX **t** 020 8834 7373 **f** 020 8834 7474 **e** info@airmtm.com **w** airmtm.com Contact: Sheela Bates.

Alchemy PR 212a The Bridge, 12-16 Clerkenwell Rd, London EC1M 5PQ **t** 020 7324 6260 **f** 020 7324 6001 **e** mail@alchemypr.com **w** alchemypr.com Dir: Matt Learmouth.

All About Promotions 27a Kings Gardens, West End Lane, London NW6 4PX **t** 020 7328 4836 **f** 020 7372 3331 **e** info@allaboutpromo.com Prop: Amanda Beel.

All Press Unit 13, Acklam Workspace, 10 Acklam Rd, London W10 5QZ **t** 020 8969 3636 or 07931 557 970 **e** nienke.klop@all-press.co.uk **w** all-press.co.uk MD: Nienke Klop.

Stephen Anderson Publicity Cathedral Buildings, 64 Donegall St, Belfast, Co Antrim BT1 2GT **t** 028 9031 0949 **f** 028 9031 5905 **e** stephen_anderson@btconnect.com **w** stephenandersonpublicty.com MD: Stephen Anderson.

APB Studio 18, Westbourne Studios, 242 Acklam Rd, London W10 5JJ **t** 020 8968 9000 **f** 020 8968 8500 **e** apb.press@which.net MD: Gordon Duncan.

Appetite PR 2 Coventry St, Brighton, E. Sussex BN1 5PQ **t** 01273 888099 or 07970 913494 **f** 01273 230189 **e** appetitepr@ntlworld.com MD: Judith Weaterton.

Ark PR The Basement, 11 Old Steine, Brighton, E Sussex BN1 1EJ **t** 01273 696 355 or 07759 528 006 **e** arkpr@tiscali.co.uk MD: Derek Day.

Arrowsmith Communications 5 Norfolk Court, Victoria Park Gardens, Worthing BN11 4ED **t** 01903 200 916 or 07967 102 259 **e** eugeniearrowsmith@yahoo.co.uk Media Consultant: Eugenie Arrowsmith.

ASAP Communications Ltd. Suite One, 2 Tunstall Rd, London SW9 8DA **t** 020 7978 9488 **f** 020 7978 9490 **e** info@asapcomms.co.uk **w** asapcomms.com MD: Yvonne Thompson.

The Associates UK Monticello House, 45 Russell Sq, London WC1B 4JP **t** 020 7907 4770 **f** 020 7907 4771 **e** info@the-associates.co.uk **w** the-associates.co.uk Exec Dir: Lisa Richards.

Bad Moon Publicity 19B All Saints Rd, London W11 1HE **t** 020 7221 0499 **f** 020 7792 0405 **e** press@badmoon.co.uk MD: Anton Brookes.

Badger Promotions PO Box 9121, Birmingham B13 8AU **t** 08712 260 910 **e** info@badgerpromotions.co.uk **w** badgerpromotions.co.uk Promoter: Mark Badger.

Band & Brand The White House, 32 Thornton Hill, Wimbledon, London SW19 4HS **t** 020 8947 5475 **f** 020 8947 5478 **e** info@bandandbrand.com **w** bandandbrand.com MD: Kim Glover.

Bang On - Online PR 41B Ferntower Rd, London N5 2JE **t** 020 7503 4778 **e** info@bangonpr.com **w** bangonpr.com Online Publicists: Leanne Mison, Katie Riding.

Barrington Harvey Troopers Yard, Bancroft, Hitchin, Herts SG5 1JW **t** 01462 456780 **f** 01462 456781 **e** simon@bhpr.co.uk **w** barringtonharvey.co.uk Dir: Simon Harvey.

Beatwax Communications 91 Berwick St, London W1F ONE **t** 020 7734 1965 **f** 020 7292 8333 **e** michael@beatwax.com **w** beatwax.com MD: Michael Brown.

Bestest 3rd Floor, 29-31 Cowper St, London EC2A 4AT **t** 020 7608 4590 **f** 020 7608 4599 **e** beth@bestest.co.uk Head Of Press & Press Officer: Beth Drake, Ruth Clarke.

Beyond Publicity 2nd Floor, 16 - 18 Hollen St, London W1F 8BQ **t** 020 7851 0075 **f** 020 7494 0995 **e** Natasha@beyondpublicity.net **w** myspace.com/beyondpublicity Contact: Angela Robertson & Natasha Mann.

Big Cat Group Griffin House, 18-19 Ludgate House, Birmingham B3 1DW **t** 0121 200 0910 **f** 0121 236 1342 **e** info@bcguk.com **w** bcguk.com Dir: Nick Morgan.

Big Group Ltd 91 Princedale Rd, Holland Pk, London W11 4NS **t** 020 7229 8827 **f** 020 7243 1462 **e** info@biggroup.co.uk **w** biggroup.co.uk Account Director: Simon Broyd.

The No 1 Creative Agency

Est: 2000

With an approachable, dedicated and experienced team of PR and marketing specialists, Zest PR has a reputation for achieving excellent results across all aspects of the arts and entertainment Industry.

Services include:

National & Regional Print & Broadcast Media

Marketing

Media Training

Event Management

Consumer & Brand Management

Crisis & Reputation Management

Zest PR Ltd
Tel: 020 7734 0206
Fax: 020 7734 4084
info@zestpr.com   www.zestpr.com

Hampton Court Palace
FESTIVAL 2005

Quite Great!

Student Press, Student Radio,
Student Marketing, Street Teams

T: 01223 410000
Harvey@quitegreat.co.uk
www.quitegreat.co.uk

Black Arts PR - The Regional Press Specialist The Old Rectory, Mottistone, Isle of Wight PO30 4ED **t** 01983 741 480 or 07973 374 423 **f** 01983 740 052 **e** simonblackmore@blackartspr.com Contact: Simon Blackmore.

Blurb PR 7 Tower Mansions, 136 West End Lane, West Hampstead, London NW6 1SB **t** 020 7419 1221 **e** hello@blurbpr.com MD: Michael Plumley.

Borkowski PR 2nd Floor, 12 Oval Rd, Camden, London NW1 7DH **t** 020 7482 4000 **f** 020 7482 5400 **e** larry@borkowski.co.uk **w** borkowski.co.uk New Bus Dev't Mgr: Larry Franks.

BR-Asian Media Consulting 45 Circus Rd, St Johns Wood, London NW8 9JH **t** 020 8550 9898 **f** 020 7289 9892 **e** moizvas@brasian.com **w** brasian.com MD: Moiz Vas.

Brassneck Publicity 31A Almorah Rd, London N1 3ER **t** 020 7226 3399 **f** 020 7226 7557 **e** brassneckpr@aol.com MD: Mick Houghton.

Burt Greener Communications 6th Floor, 41 St Vincent Pl, Glasgow G1 2ER **t** 0141 248 6007 **f** 0141 248 3322 **e** firstname@burtgreener.co.uk Dirs: Lorna Burt, Janine Greener.

Buzz Publicity 32 Priory Pl, Perth PH2 0DT **t** 01738 638140 **f** 01738 638140 **e** info@thebuzzgroup.co.uk **w** thebuzzgroup.co.uk MD: Dave Arcari.

Cake Group Ltd 10 Stephen Mews, London W1T 1AG **t** 020 7307 3100 **f** 020 7307 3101 **e** andrea@cakegroup.com **w** cakegroup.com Head of Marketing: Andrea Ledsham.

Capitalize Ltd 52 Thrale St, London SE1 9HW **t** 020 7940 1700 **f** 020 7940 1739 **e** Info@capitalize.co.uk **w** capitalize.co.uk MD: Richard Moore.

Caroline Moss PR 50 Marine Parade, Brighton BN2 1PH **t** 01273 689 018 or 07711 961 703 **e** pr@carolinemoss.co.uk **w** carolinemoss.co.uk Dir: Caroline Moss.

Casablanca PR 26 Porchester Sq, London W2 6AN **t** 020 7221 2287 or 07887 610 027 **f** 020 7221 2287 **e** fozia@casablancapr.co.uk MD: Fozia Shah.

Celebration PR Ltd 8 Ashington Court, Westwood Hill, Sydenham, London SE26 6BN **t** 020 8778 9918 **f** 020 8355 7708 **e** celebration@dial.pipex.com Dir: James Doheny.

Chapple Davies 53 Great Portland St, London W1W 7LG **t** 020 7299 7979 **f** 020 7299 7978 **e** firstname@chapdav.com **w** chapdav.com Partners: Gareth Davies, James C Gill.

Ian Cheek Press Suite 5, 51D New Briggate, Leeds, W Yorks LS2 8JD **t** 0113 246 9940 **f** 0113 246 9960 **e** iancheek@talk21.com Head of Press: Ian Cheek.

Sharon Chevin PR (see The Publicity Connection).

CHUFFMEDIA

Unit 29 Cygnus Business Centre, Dalmeyer Road, London NW10 2XA **t** 020 8830 0330 or 07762 130 510 **f** 020 8830 0220 **e** warren@chuffmedia.com **w** chuffmedia.com Director: Warren Higgins. Regional & College Press for acts including +44, The Answer, The Automatic, Breed 77, Brigade, Fall Out Boy, The Horrors, The Hours, Ian Brown, Jamelia, James Morrison, Jurassic 5, Kaiser Chiefs, Klaxons, The Maccabees, The Ordinary Boys, Orson, Parka, Shiny Toy Guns and more...

Circus PR Argo House, Kilburn Park Rd, Maida Vale, London NW6 5LF **t** 020 7644 0267 **f** 020 7644 0698 **e** bernard@circusrecords.net **w** circusrecords.net MD: Bernard MacMahon.

Max Clifford Associates 49-50 New Bond St, London W1Y 9HA **t** 020 7408 2350 **f** 020 7409 2294 **e** max@mcapr.co.uk MD: Max Clifford.

CNC Associates 95 Tantallon Rd, London SW12 8DQ **t** 020 8673 0048 **f** 020 8673 0048 **e** office@cnclimited.co.uk **w** cnclimited.co.uk MD: Conor Nolan.

Coalition Group Devonshire House, 12 Barley Mow Passage, London W4 4PH **t** 020 8987 0123 **f** 020 8987 0345 **e** pr@coalitiongroup.co.uk MD, Music Division: Tony Linkin.

comm:union Criel House, St. Leonards Rd, London W13 8RG **t** 020 8566 3426 **f** 020 8567 3699 **e** mail@comm-union.com **w** comm-union.com Account Dir: Matthew Ryan.

Complete Control PR 178 Seaforth Ave, Motspur Pk, Surrey KT3 6JN **t** 020 8942 9978 or 07958 380 353 **e** polly@completecontrolpr.co.uk **w** completecontrolpr.co.uk MD: Polly Birkbeck.

Complete PR PO Box 34126, London NW10 5BZ **t** 020 8830 3300 **f** 020 8830 0033 **e** alison@completepr.co.uk **w** completepr.co.uk MD: Alison McNichol.

Copperplate Consultants 68 Belleville Rd, London SW11 6PP **t** 020 7585 0357 **f** 020 7585 0357 **e** copperplate2000@yahoo.com **w** copperplateconsultants.com MD: Alan O'Leary.

John Crosby music publicity/PR PO Box 230, Hastings, E Sussex TN34 3XZ **t** 0870 041 0576 **f** 0870 041 0577 **e** johncrosby@pressproms.demon.co.uk **w** pressproms.demon.co.uk MD: John Crosby.

Cunning 192 St John St, London EC1V 4JY **t** 020 7566 5300 **e** info@cunning.com **w** cunning.com MD: Anna Carloss.

Cypher Press & Promotions Unit 2A Queens Studios, 121 Salusbury Rd, London NW6 6RG **t** 020 7372 4464 or 020 7372 4474 **f** 020 7372 4484 or 020 7328 4447 **e** info@cypherpress.uk.com **w** cypherpress.uk.com Dir: Simon Ward.

National, Regional and Online
PR campaigns

T: 01223 410000
Harvey@quitegreat.co.uk
www.quitegreat.co.uk

Darkhorse Music PR 31 Paddington St, London W1U 4HD
t 07740 358 364 or 020 7871 0793
e james@darkhorse-music.com **w** darkhorse-music.com
MD: James Davies.

DARLING DEPARTMENT

4th floor, 19 Denmark Street, London WC2H 8NA
t 020 7379 8787 **f** 020 7379 5737 **e** info@darlinguk.com
w darlingdepartment.com. Directors: Edward Cartwright & Daniel
Stevens.

Delta PR PO Box 25285, London N12 0XD **t** 0845 6801 857
e mal@delta-music.co.uk **w** delta-music.co.uk Owner: Mal Smith.

Diffusion PR PO Box 2610, Mitcham, Surrey CR4 2YH
t 020 7384 3200 **f** 0871 277 3055 **e** jodie@diffusionpr.co.uk
w diffusionpr.co.uk MD: Jodie Stewart.

DMINC

11-15 Betterton St, London WC2 9BP **t** 07786 317 644
e info@dminc.eu **w** dminc.eu MD: Jody Dunleavy.
From print press to podcasts, websites to WAP, tabloids to
tastemakers – DMinc demystifies the rapidly evolving e-
media arena and ensures that every PR avenue is explored.

DNA Publicity Unit 4, Wellington Close, London W11 2AN
t 020 7792 5100 or 020 7792 5200 **e** odaniaud@aol.com
Dir: Olly Daniaud.

Dog Day Press Zeppelin Building, 59-61 Farringdon Rd,
London EC1M 3JB **t** 020 7691 8686 or 07811 159 623
f 020 7691 4666 **e** info@dogdaypress.com **w** dogdaypress.com
Contact: Nathan Beazer, Lauren Zoric.

Dorothy Howe Press & Publicity 41 Hartington Court,
Hartington Rd, Chiswick, London W4 3TT **t** 020 8995 3920
f 020 8994 9963 **e** press@dorothyhowe.co.uk
MD: Dorothy Howe.

Duff Press 411, Riverbank House, 1, Putney Bridge Approach,
London SW6 3JD **t** 020 7736 7611 or 07904 385 308
f 020 7371 9949 **e** duff@duffpress.co.uk **w** duffpress.com
MD: Duff Battye.

DWL (Dave Woolf Ltd) 53 Goodge St, London W1T 1TG
t 020 7436 5529 **f** 020 7637 8776
e kizzi@dwl.uk.net; dave@dwl.uk.net
Account Manager: Kizzi Alleyne-Stewart.

Electric PR 24A, Bartholomew Villas, London NW5 2LL
t 020 7424 0405 **f** 020 7424 0305 **e** electric_pr@hotmail.com
MD: Laurence Verfaillie.

EMMS PUBLICITY

100 Aberdeen House, 22-24 Highbury Grove, London N5 2EA
t 020 7226 0990 **f** 020 7354 8600 **e** info@emmspublicity.com
w emmspublicity.com MD: Stephen Emms. Head Of Press: Junior
Oakes.

Emmsix: Unit A, The Courtyard, 42 Colwith Rd, London
W6 9EY **t** 020 8846 3737 **f** 020 8846 3738
e christianne@emmsix.co.uk MD: Christianne Lambert.

ePM Unit 204, The Saga Centre, 326 Kensal Rd, London
W10 5BZ **t** 020 8964 4900 **f** 020 8964 3600
e jonas@electronicpm.co.uk **w** electronicpm.co.uk
Ptnr: Jonas Stone.

EXCESS PRESS

11 Melville Road, Brighton BN3 1TH **t** 01273 734 141
e info@excesspress.co.uk **w** excesspress.co.uk Dirs: Jayne
Houghton, Alix Wenmouth, Fiona Clarke..

Fake Media May Villas, 50 Main Rd, Naphill, Bucks HP14 4QB
t 07966 233 275 **e** Adam.fisher@fakemedia.com
MD: Adam Fisher.

Ferrara Pr & Management 42 Caliban Tower, Purcell St,
London N1 6PW **t** 07946 523 007 or 020 7729 0147
e rosalia@ferrarapr.com **w** ferrarapr.com MD: Rosalia Ferrara.

FFR UK 2 Hastings Terrace, Conway Rd, London N15 3BE
t 020 8826 5900 **f** 020 8826 5902
e fullfrontalrecords@hotmail.com **w** ffruk.com Dir: Tara Rez.

Fifth Avenue PR 37 Fifth Ave, London W10 4DL
t 020 8960 5802 or 07710 692 023
e fifthavenuepr@googlemail.com Dir: Sarah Lowe.

FIFTH ELEMENT PUBLIC RELATIONS

FIFTH ELEMENT **Pr**
Public Relations and Artist Management

45 Poland Street, London W1F 7NA **t** 020 7292 0900 or
07976 758 491 **f** 020 7734 0764 **e** info@fifthelement.biz
w fifthelement.biz Director: Catherine Hockley.
A friendly, experienced, innovative team covering national,
regional, fanzine and internet press.

Student Press, Student Radio,
Student Marketing, Street Teams

T: 01223 410000
Harvey@quitegreat.co.uk
www.quitegreat.co.uk

Press & Promotion: PR Companies

Connie Filippello Publicity 49 Portland Rd, London W11 4LJ **t** 020 7229 5400 **f** 020 7229 4804 **e** cfpublicity@aol.com **w** cfpublicity.co.uk MD: Connie Filippello.

Fistral PR 114 The Royal, Wilton Pl, Salford, Manchester M3 6FT **t** 0161 835 4142 or 07905 448 607 **e** info@fistralpr.co.uk **w** fistralpr.co.uk MD: Peggy Manning.

Fleming Connolly PR 45 Poland St, London W1F 7NA **t** 020 7292 0900 **f** 020 7734 0764 **e** firstname@fclpr.com **w** flemingconnolly.com Contact: Nick Fleming & Matt Connolly.

Focus Marketing Communications 2 Arterberry Court, 6 Arterberry Rd, Wimbledon, London SW20 8AB **t** 020 8715 0403 **f** 020 8715 0390 **e** info@focusmarketingcommunications.com MD: Brian Oliver.

Free Associates PO Box 37981, London SW4 0XQ **t** 020 8675 4228 or 07818 453 650 **e** jody@freeassociates.org Dir: Jody Gillett.

Freeman PR Room 236, The Bon Marche Centre, 241-251 Ferndale Rd, London SW9 8BJ **e** info@freemanpr.co.uk MD: Amanda Freeman.

Freewheelin' PR 7th Floor, 16 Gresse St, London W1T 1QL **t** 020 7637 4410 **f** 020 7637 4411 **e** Andrea@freewheelinmedia.com **w** freewheelinmedia.com Dir: Andrea Covington.

Frequency Media (FMG UK Ltd) Suite 115 The Greenhouse, Custard Factory 2, Gibb St, Birmingham, W Midlands B9 4AA **t** 0121 224 7450 or 7452 or 07866 422 109 **f** 0121 224 7451 **e** gerard@fmguk.com **w** fmguk.com PR Directors: Gerard Franklin & Margaret Murray.

Frontier Promotions The Grange, Cockley Cley Rd, Hilborough, Thetford, Norfolk IP26 5BT **t** 01760 756394 **f** 01760 756398 **e** frontieruk@btconnect.com MD: Sue Williams.

G Promotions Cambrian Cottage, 3, Trimpley St, Ellesmere, Shropshire SY12 0AD **t** 07855 724 798 or 01691 622 356 **e** GPromo@btinternet.com Contact: Geraint Jones.

Garrett Axford PR Harbour House, 27 High St, Shoreham by Sea, W Sussex BN43 5DD **t** 01273 441200 **f** 01273 441300 **e** mail@garrett-axford.co.uk Partners: Georgina Garrett/Simon Jones.

Gerry Lyseight PR Unit S17, Shakespeare Business Centre, 245a, Coldharbour Lane,, London SW9 8RR **t** 020 7095 8146 **e** gerry@mambo.eclipse.co.uk **w** gerrylyseight.co.uk MD: Gerry Lyseight.

Get Involved Ltd Unit B, Park House, 206-208 Latimer Rd, London W10 6QY **t** 020 8962 8040 **f** 0870 420 4392 **e** info@getinvolvedltd.com **w** getinvolvedltd.com Communications Manager: Clare Woodcock.

Gibson Guitar 3rd Floor, 29-35 Rathbone St, London W1T 1NJ **t** 020 7167 2144 **f** 020 7167 2150 **e** jeremy.singer@gibson.com **w** gibson.com UK PR Mgr: Jeremy Singer.

Glass Ceiling PR 50 Stroud Green Rd, London N4 3ES **t** 020 7263 1240 **f** 020 7281 5671 **e** promo@glassceilingpr.com MD: Harriet Simms.

Global Guest List PR Suite 42, Pall Mall Deposits, 124-128 Barlby Rd, London W10 6BL **t** 020 8962 0601 **f** 020 8962 0575 **e** info@globalguestlist.net **w** globalguestlist.net MD: Babs Epega.

Gold Star Agency PO Box 130, Ross on Wye HR9 6WY **t** 01989 770 105 **f** 01989 770 039 **e** nitagoldstar@btinternet.com MD: Nita Patel.

Greendesk Publicity 29a Waller Rd, London SE14 5LE **t** 07986 235 855 or 07986 235 855 **f** 020 7732 4624 **e** helen@greendesk.demon.co.uk MD: Helen Maleed.

Hackford Jones PR Third Floor, 16 Manette St, London W1D 4AR **t** 020 7287 9788 **f** 020 7287 9731 **e** info@hackfordjonespr.com **w** hackfordjonespr.com Co-MDs: Simon Jones, Jonathan Hackford.

Hall Or Nothing 11 Poplar Mews, Uxbridge Rd, London W12 7JS **t** 020 8740 6288 **f** 020 8749 5982 **e** press@hallornothing.com **w** hallornothing.com MD: Terri Hall.

Jennie Halsall Consultants PO Box 22467, London W6 0SG **t** 020 8741 0003 **f** 020 8846 9652 **e** jhc@dircon.co.uk MD: Jennie Halsall.

HARDZONE / FULL SERVICE LTD

Gardiner House, The Business Village, 3-9 Broomhill Road, London SW18 4JQ **t** 020 8870 8744 **f** 020 8874 1578 **e** firstname@hardzone.co.uk **w** hardzone.co.uk MD: Jackie Davidson. Creative Manager: Seb Monks. Head of Media Street Network: "Chuckie".

Henry's House PR 108 Gt. Russell St, London WC1B 3NA **t** 020 7291 3000 **f** 020 7291 3001 **e** jane@henryshouse.com **w** henryshouse.com Dir: Jane Shaw.

Hermana PR Unit 244, Bon Marche Centre, 241-251 Ferndale Rd, Brixton, London SW9 8BJ **t** 020 7733 8009 **f** 020 7733 0037 **e** ken@hermana.co.uk; pam@hermana.co.uk Dirs: Ken Lower, Pam Ribbeck.

Hero PR 3 Tennyson Rd, Thatcham, Berks RG18 3FR **t** 01635 868 385 **f** 01635 868 385 **e** owen@heropr.com **w** heropr.com MD: Owen Packard.

Chris Hewlett PR & Artist Management 127 North View Rd, London N8 7LR **t** 020 8348 6767 or 07966 491 786 **e** info@chrishewlett.com **w** chrishewlett.com Contact: Chris Hewlett.

Hill & Knowlton (UK) 20 Soho Sq, London W1A 1PR **t** 020 7413 3000 **f** 020 7413 3111 **e** wfick@hillandknowlton.com **w** hillandknowlton.co.uk Brand Mgr: Wayne Fick.

hush-hush Suite 14-15, Old Truman Brewery, 91 Brick Lane, London E1 6QL **t** 020 8989 1726 or 020 7223 7456 **e** danielle@hush-hush.org.uk Press Officer: Danielle Richards.

Hyperactive Publicity Ltd 47 Riverview Gardens, Barnes, London SW13 8QZ **t** 020 8741 7343 **e** info@hyperactive-publicity.com Contact: Caroline Turner.

National, Regional and Online
PR campaigns

T: 01223 410000
Harvey@quitegreat.co.uk
www.quitegreat.co.uk

Hyperlaunch New Media Mardyke House, 16-22 Hotwell Rd, Bristol BS8 4UD **t** 0117 914 0070 **f** 0117 914 0071 **e** don@hyperlaunch.com **w** hyperlaunch.com MD: Don Jenkins.

Ice-Pr Ltd Unit 5, 10 Acklam Rd, London W10 5QZ **t** 020 8968 2222 **f** 020 8968 2220 **e** info@ice-pr.com **w** ice-pr.com Contact: Jason Price.

ID Publicity 25 Britannia Row, London N1 8QH **t** 020 7359 4455 **f** 020 7704 1616 **e** info@idpublicity.com MD: Lisa Moskaluk.

Idea Generation 10 Greenland St, London NW1 0ND **t** 020 7428 4949 **f** 020 7428 4948 **e** frontdoor@ideageneration.co.uk **w** ideageneration.co.uk Dir, Music & Entertainm't: Anita Mackie.

IMD PR Unit 4C, Bannon Court, 54, Michael Rd, London SW6 2EF **t** 020 7371 0995 **f** 020 7751 3095 **e** nikki@imd-info.com **w** imd-info.com Contact: Nikki Wright.

IMPRESSIVE

9 Jeffrey's Place, Camden, London NW1 9PP **t** 020 7284 3444 **f** 020 7284 1840 **e** mel@impressivepr.com **w** impressivepr.com MD: Mel Brown. Senior National PR: Sarah Harries.

In House Press 4th Floor, 20 Dale St, Manchester M1 1EZ **t** 0161 228 2070 **f** 0161 228 3070 **e** info@inhousepress.com **w** inhousepress.com MD: David Cooper.

Indiscreet PR PO Box 48683, London NW8 1AT **t** 07813 290 474 or 07930 810 751 **e** alan@indiscreetpr.co.uk **w** indiscreetpr.com Dirs: Alan Robinson, Lesley Shone.

Infected 18 Eddison Court, 253 Sussex Way, London N19 4DW **t** 020 7272 9620 or 07782 269 750 **e** mike.infected000@btclick.com MD: Mike Gourlay.

inform@tion communication ltd 6 Hornsey Lane Gardens, London N6 5PB **t** 020 8374 6040 **e** infocom@dial.pipex.com MD: Michael Thorne.

Intelligent Media Clifton Works, 23 Grove Park Terrace, London W4 3QE **t** 020 8995 0055 **f** 020 8995 9900 **e** jonm@intelligentmedia.com **w** intelligentmedia.com MD: Jon Mais.

J2PR 1st Floor, 78 Castellain Rd, London W9 1EX **t** 07866 435 876 or 07970 913 494 **e** j2pr@thesundayclub.com Co-MDs: Jude Weaterton,Jamie Stockwood.

Jackie Gill Promotions 3 Warren Mews, London W1T 6AN **t** 020 7383 5550 **f** 020 7383 3020 **e** jackie@jackiegill.co.uk MD: Jackie Gill.

James Grant Music 94 Strand On The Green, Chiswick, London W4 3NN **t** 020 8742 4950 **f** 020 8742 4951 **e** enquiries@jamesgrant.co.uk **w** jamesgrant.co.uk Co-MDs: Simon Hargreaves, Nick Worsley.

Joanna Burns PR LDA House, 44B The Broadway, London NW7 3LH **t** 020 8906 3444 **f** 020 8906 9242 **e** joanna@joannaburnspr.com **w** joannaburnspr.com MD: Joanna Burns.

JS Publicity The Matrix Complex, 91 Peterborough Rd, London SW6 3BU **t** 020 7751 2795 **f** 020 7751 2797 **e** judy@jspublicity.com MD: Judy Shaw.

Karenstringer.pr 18 Landseer Rd, Hove, E Sussex BN3 7AF **t** 01273 240 246 or 07808 404 242 **e** karenstringer.pr@ntlworld.com MD: Karen Stringer.

Katherine Howard PR Eastwick Farm, Clay Lane, Braiseworth, Nr Eye, Suffolk IP23 7DZ **t** 01379 678811 **f** 08700 511 772 **e** khpr@katherinehoward.co.uk **w** katherinehoward.co.uk MD: Katherine Howard.

Kelly Pike Publicity Suite 120, Park Royal Business Centre, 9-17 Park Royal Rd, London NW10 7LQ **t** 020 8621 2345 **f** 020 8621 2344 **e** kpikepr@globalnet.co.uk MD: Kelly Pike.

Lander PR 44B The Broadway, London NW7 3LH **t** 020 8906 9438 **f** 020 8906 9242 **e** judd@landerpr.com **w** landerpr.com Dir: Judd Lander.

Laura Norton PR 105c Finsbury Park Rd, London N4 2JU **t** 020 7359 7745 **e** Laura@lauranortonpr.com **w** lauranortonpr.com Director / Publicist: Laura Norton.

LD Communications 58-59 Gt. Marlborough St, London W1F 7JY **t** 020 7439 7222 **f** 020 7734 2933 **e** info@ldpublicity.com **w** ldpublicity.com CEO: Bernard Doherty.

Leslie Gilotti - Music & New Media Promotions 79 Northcote Rd, London E17 7DT **t** 07867 785 070 **e** info@gilotti.net **w** gilotti.net Dir: Leslie Gilotti.

Leyline Promotions Studio 24, Westbourne Studios, 242 Acklam Rd, London W10 5JJ **t** 020 7575 3285 **f** 020 7575 3286 **e** firstname@leylinepromotions.com **w** leylinepromotions.com MD: Adrian Leigh.

Lucid PR 76 Great Titchfield St, London W1W 7QP **t** 020 7307 7449 **e** firstname.lastname@lucidpr.co.uk **w** lucidpr.co.uk Dirs: Mick Garbutt, Charlie Lycett.

LVPR 51 Tabor Rd, London W6 0BN **t** 020 8741 8374 or 07949 174 811 **e** linda@lindavalentine.biz Publicist: Linda Valentine.

Maestro Marketing & Development 62 Naxos Building, 4 Hutchings St, London E14 8JR **t** 07795 358901 **e** info@maestro-marketing.com **w** maestro-marketing.com Dir: Kimberly Davis.

Magnum PR 41 Halcyon Wharf, 5 Wapping High St, London E1W 1LH **t** 020 7709 0914 or 07956 241542 **e** Tammy@magnumpr.co.uk MD: Tammy Arthur.

Making Waves Communications 45 Underwood St, London N1 7LG **t** 020 7940 0944 **f** 020 7940 1026 **e** info@makingwaves.co.uk **w** makingwaves.co.uk PR Manager: Dan Minty.

Manilla PR 62 Cleveland St, Eston, Middlesbrough TS6 9JR **t** 01642 453 425 **e** tony@manillapr.co.uk **w** manillapr.com MD: Tony McDonagh.

Press & Promotion: PR Companies

MATERIAL MARKETING AND COMMUNICATIONS

m a t e r i a l

Riverside House, 260 Clyde Street, Glasgow G1 4JH
t 0141 204 7970 **f** 0141 221 8643 **e** info@materialmc.co.uk
w materialmc.co.uk Dirs: Colin Spence, Sera Holland.

Matthew Ryan Criel House, St. Leonards Rd, London
W13 8RG **t** 020 8566 3426 **f** 020 8567 3699
e mail@matthewryan.co.uk **w** matthewryan.co.uk
MD: Matthew Ryan.

MBC PR Wellington Building, 28-32 Wellington Rd, London
NW8 9SP **t** 020 7483 9205 **f** 020 7483 9206
e bc@mbcpr.com Co-MDs: Barbara Charone, Moira Bellas.

Mercenary PR Suite 210, Saga Centre, 326 Kensal Rd,
London W10 5BZ **t** 020 8354 4111 or 07904 157 720
f 020 8354 4112 **e** kas@mercenarypublicity.com
w mercenarypublicity.com Dir: Kas Mercer.

Midas Public Relations 7-8 Kendrick Mews, London
SW7 3HG **t** 020 7584 7474 **f** 020 7584 7123
e emma@midaspr.co.uk **w** midaspr.co.uk Dir: Emma Draude.

Midnight Communications 3 Lloyds Wharf, Mill St,
London SE1 2BA **t** 020 7232 4517 **f** 020 7232 4540
e enquiries@midnight.co.uk **w** midnight.co.uk Dir: Vicki Hughes.

Mingo PR Flat 3/1, 19 Duke St, Glasgow G4 0UL
t 0141 552 3623 or 0780 372 8469 **e** mingo@easynet.co.uk
w mingopr.co.uk MD: Jill Mingo.

Momentum PR 83 Great Titchfield St, London W1W 6RH
t 0207 323 9789 or 07973 597 070
e maureen@momentumpr.co.uk MD: Maureen McCann.

Moore Publicity 187 Mackenzie Rd, Beckenham BR3 4SE
t 07809 642 044 or 020 8676 9540
e nik@moorepublicity.co.uk MD: Nik Moore.

Mosquito Media 64a Warwick Ave, Little Venice, London
W9 2PU **t** 07813 174 185 **e** mosquitomedia@aol.com
w mosquito-media.co.uk Contact: Richard Abbott.

Motion 8-10 Rhoda St, London E2 7EF **t** 020 7739 0100
f 020 7739 8571 **e** steven@motiongroup.co.uk
w motiongroup.co.uk
New Media Marketing Manager: Steven Colborne.

MP Promotions 13 Greave, Romiley, Stockport, Cheshire
SK6 4PU **t** 0161 494 7934 **e** maria@mppromotions.co.uk
Dir: Maria Philippou.

Music Company (London) Ltd. 1 Rose Alley, London
SE1 9AS **t** 020 7921 9233 **f** 020 7261 1058
e musicco@musicco.f9.co.uk MD: Melanne Mueller.

Music & Media Consulting Ltd 3 Cypress Close,
Doddington, Cambs PE15 0LE **t** 07774 426 966 or
01354 740 847 **f** 01354 740 847 **e** johnscronin@aol.com
Dir: John S. Cronin.

Music2Mix (M2M) Unit 16, The Talina Centre, Bagleys
Lane, London SW6 2BW **t** 020 7384 3200 **f** 020 7384 2999
e eddie@music2mix.com **w** music2mix.com MD: Eddie Gordon.

MusicPress PR 16 The Green, Wolviston, Co. Durham
TS22 5LN **t** 01740-644453 **e** allan@musicpresspr.com
MD: Allan Glen.

Name Music Innovation Labs, Watford Rd, Harrow, Middx
HA1 3TP **t** 020 8357 7305 **f** 020 8357 7326
e info@namemusic.co.uk MD: Sam Shemtob.

Nelson Bostock Communications Compass House, 22
Redan Pl, London W2 4SA **t** 020 7229 4400 **f** 020 7727 2025
e nbc@nelsonbostock.com **w** nelsonbostock.com
Account Director: Bruce McLachlan.

9PR 65-69 White Lion St, 2nd Floor, London N1 9PR
t 020 7833 9303 **f** 020 7833 9322 **e** julie@9pr.co.uk
w 9pr.co.uk MD: Julie Bland.

No 9 Publicity Suite 216, Bon Marche Building, 241 Ferndale
Rd, London SW9 8BJ **t** 020 7733 1818
e no9@posteverything.com MD: Jim Johnstone.

NOBLE PR

NOBLE**PR**

1 Mercers Mews, London N19 4PL **t** 020 7272 7772
f 020 7272 2227 **e** suzanne@noblepr.co.uk **w** noblepr.co.uk Dirs:
Suzanne & Peter Noble.
Specialists in home entertainment. Clients include Warner
Home Video, Universal, SonyBMG, Demon, Gut. See our
website for current client list and media centre.

National, Regional and Online PR campaigns

T: 01223 410000
Harvey@quitegreat.co.uk
www.quitegreat.co.uk

Press & Promotion: PR Companies

O PR PO Box 34002, London N21 3WX **t** 020 8351 2542 **f** 020 8482 9270 **e** info@o-pr.com **w** o-pr.com MD: Olga Hadjilambri.

Orbit PR Unit 206, 2nd Floor, Curtain House, 134-146 Curtain Rd, London EC2A 3AR **t** 020 7033 4667 or 07930 391 607 **f** 020 7033 4668 **e** karen@orbitpr.net MD: Karen Johnson.

Outerglobe 113 Cheeseman's Terrace, London W14 9XH **t** 020 7385 5447 **f** 020 7385 5447 **e** debbie@outerglobe.com **w** outerglobe.com MD: Debbie Golt.

Outpost Unit 20, Acklam Workspace, 10 Acklam Rd, London W10 5QZ **t** 020 8964 8541 **f** 020 8968 7725 **e** david@outpostmedia.co.uk **w** outpostmedia.co.uk Dir: David Silverman.

The Outside Organisation Ltd. Butler House, 177-178 Tottenham Court Rd, London W1T 7NY **t** 020 7436 3633 **f** 020 7436 3632 **e** info@outside-org.co.uk **w** outside-org.co.uk Chairman: Alan Edwards.

Padcom 11 Junction Works, 40 Ducie St, Manchester M1 2DF **t** 0845 458 8662 **f** 0845 458 8663 **e** info@padcom.co.uk **w** padcom.co.uk MD: Simon Morrison.

Paddy Forwood PR The Studio, Manor Farmhouse, Stubhampton, Blandford, Dorset DT11 8JS **t** 01258 830014 or 07779 606533 **f** 01258 830014 **e** pad.forwood@virgin.net MD: Paddy Forwood.

Palmer Evans Associates 5 Landseer Rd, Hove, E Sussex BN3 7AF **t** 01273 775801 **e** jimevans@talk21.com MD: Jim Evans.

Park Street PR (Specialist Hip-Hop Promotion) PO Box 1668, Wolverhampton WV2 3WG **t** 07968 295 913 **e** info@parkstreetpr.com **w** parkstreetpr GM: Neil Hutchinson.

PB Communications Int 25 Fair Acres, Roehampton Lane, London SW15 5LX **t** 020 8876 9011 **f** 020 8876 9011 CEO: Peter Brown.

Phuture Trax Press & Events PR PO Box 48527, London NW4 4ZB **t** 020 8203 3968 **f** 020 8203 3968 **e** nicky@phuturetrax.co.uk **w** phuturetrax.co.uk MD: Nicky Trax.

Piranha PR Flat 7, 51 The Gardens, London SE22 9QQ **t** 020 8299 1928 or 07956 460 372 **e** rosie@piranha-pr.co.uk **w** piranha-pr.co.uk MD: Rosie Wilby.

Planet Earth Publicity 49 Rylstone Way, Saffron Walden, Essex CB11 3BL **t** 01799 501347 or 07966 557774 **f** 01799 501347 **e** info@planetearthpublicity.com **w** planetearthpublicity.com MD: Dave Clarke.

The Play Centre Unit 2 Devonport Mews, Shepherd's Bush, London W12 8NG **t** 020 8932 7705 **f** 020 8932 7723 **e** info@theplaycentre.com **w** theplaycentre.com Contact: Shaun "Stuckee" Willoughby.

Plus One PR PO Box 11492, Henley in Arden, Warcs B95 6WG **t** 01926 840 394 **f** 01926 840 306 **e** info@plusonepr.com **w** plusonepr.com MD: Claire Ashman.

P&M (Public Relations & Marketing) 3rd Floor, Winchester House, 259-269 Old Marylebone Rd, London NW1 5RA **t** 020 7170 4189 **f** 020 7170 4001 **e** info@pmltd.co.uk **w** pmltd.co.uk Head of PR: Phyllisia Adjei.

Pomona 36 Bridgegate, Hebden Bridge, West Yorks HX7 8EX **t** 01422 846900 **f** 01422 846880 **e** rob@pomonauk.co.uk **w** pomonauk.co.uk Office Manager: Rob Kerford.

Poplicity 100 Aberdeen House, 22-24 Highbury Grove, London N5 2EA **t** 020 7226 0990 **f** 020 7354 8600 **e** info@poplicity.com **w** poplicity.com MD: Stephen Emms.

Porter Frith 26 Danbury St, London N1 8JU **t** 020 7359 3734 **f** 020 7226 5897 **e** porterfrith@hotmail.com MD: Liz Frith.

PPR Rylett Studios, 77 Rylett Crescent, London W12 9RP **t** 020 8746 4600 **f** 020 8746 4618 **e** peteflatt@pprpublicity.com **w** pprpublicity.com MD: Pete Flatt.

The PR Contact Garden Studio, 32 Newman St, London W1T 1PU **t** 020 7323 1200 **f** 020 7323 1070 **e** philsymes@theprcontact.com MD: Phil Symes.

pr-ism 2/14 Park Terrace, The Park, Nottingham NG1 5DN **t** 0115 947 5440 or 07971 780 821 **f** 0115 947 5440 **e** phil.long@pipemedia.co.uk **w** pr-ism.co.uk MD: Phil Long.

Precious PR c/o Cadiz Music Ltd, 2 Greenwich Quay, Clarence Rd, London SE8 3EY **t** 020 8692 3555 or 07958 495 199 **f** 020 8469 3300 **e** jack@preciouspr.plus.com Head Publicist: Jacqueline McKillion.

Press Counsel PR 5-7 Vernon Yard, Off Portobello Rd, London W11 2DX **t** 020 7792 9400 **f** 020 7243 2262 **e** info@presscounsel.com **w** presscounsel.com MD: Charlie Caplowe.

PresStop Creatives 4E Oakdale Rd, London SW16 2HW **t** 020 8677 0193 **f** 0870 163 8615 **e** shazniz@aol.com MD: Shazia Nizam.

Psycho Media 111 Clarence Rd, London SW19 8QB **t** 020 8540 8122 **f** 020 8715 2827 **e** info@psycho.co.uk **w** psycho.co.uk Dir: John Mabley.

Public Eye Communications Ltd Plaza Suite 318, 535 Kings Rd, London SW10 0SZ **t** 020 7351 1555 **f** 020 7351 1010 **e** ciara@publiceye.co.uk Chairman: Ciara Parkes.

The Publicity Connection 3 Haversham Lodge, Melrose Ave, London NW2 4JS **t** 020 8450 8882 **f** 020 8208 4219 **e** sharon@thepublicityconnection.com **w** thepublicityconnection.com MD: Sharon Chevin.

Student Press, Student Radio,
Student Marketing, Street Teams

T: 01223 410000
Harvey@quitegreat.co.uk
www.quitegreat.co.uk

Press & Promotion: PR Companies

PURE PRESS

31 Burnt Oak, Cookham, Berks SL6 9RN **t** 01628 522 603
f 01628 522 603 **e** alison@purepress.co.uk **w** purepress.co.uk
MD: Alison Edwards.
Dedicated Rock, Metal & Alternative publicity agency
offering full specialist PR & Promotions services.

Pure Publicity 31 Mapesbury Rd, London NW2 4HS
t 020 8208 1279 or 07720 941 391
e kim.machray@purepublicity.co.uk **w** purepublicity.co.uk
MD: Kim Machray.

Purple PR (Entertainment) 28 Savile Row, London
W1S 2EU **t** 020 7434 7092 **e** firstname@purplepr.com
w purplepr.com Dirs: William Rice, Carl Fysh.

Quite Great Publicity Unit D, Magog Court, Shelford Bttm,
Cambridge CB2 4AD **t** 01223 410 000
e Harvey@quitegreat.co.uk **w** quitegreat.co.uk MD: Pete Bassett.

Rabbit Publicity Kenilworth House, 79-80 Margaret St,
London W1W 8TA **t** 020 7436 8001 or 020 7299 3685
e caroline@rabbitpublicity.com **w** rabbitpublicity.com
Publicist: Caroline Henshaw.

Radical PR Suite 421, Southbank House, Black Prince Rd,
London SE1 7SJ **t** 020 7463 0678 or 07980 297 759
f 020 7463 0670 **e** radical@radicalpr.com **w** radicalpr.com
Dir: Paul Ruiz.

Random PR 41 Walters Workshop, 249 Kensal Rd, London
W10 5DB **t** 020 8968 1545 **f** 020 8964 1181
e danni@randompr.co.uk **w** randompr.co.uk
Office Manager: Danni Chambers.

Rare Communications 144 Gloucester Ave, Primrose Hill,
London NW1 8JA **t** 020 7483 2500 or 07979 241 458
f 020 7483 3700 **e** louise@rarecommunications.co.uk
w rarecommunications.co.uk Dir: Louise Drabwell.

Razzle PR 66 Red Lion St, Holborn, London WC1R 4NA
t 020 7430 0444 **e** karen@razzlepr.com
Head of Press: Karen Childs.

The Red Consultancy 41-44 Great Windmill St, London
W1D 7NF **t** 020 7465 7700 **f** 020 7025 6500
e red@redconsultancy.com **w** redconsultancy.com
CEO: Mike Morgan.

Red Hot PR 62 Bell St, London NW1 6SP **t** 020 7723 9191
f 020 7723 6423 **e** info@redhotpr.co.uk **w** redhotpr.co.uk
MD: Liz Bolton.

Red Lorry Yellow Lorry 22 Warwick St, London
W1B 5NF **t** 020 7434 2950 **f** 020 7434 2951 **e** robe@rlyl.co.uk
w rlyl.co.uk Dir: Rob Ettridge.

Relatively Entertainment PO Box 1034, Maidstone
ME15 0WZ **t** 07821 357 713 **e** lineage@toucansurf.com
MD: Paul Aaaron.

Renegade Music House Group, 40 St. Peter's Rd, London
W6 9BD **t** 020 8563 3929 **e** chris@music-house.co.uk
w music-house.co.uk/renegade Contact: Chris Smith.

Republic Media Ltd Studio 202, Westbourne Studios, 242
Acklam Rd, London W10 5JJ **t** 020 8960 7449
f 020 8960 7524 **e** info@republicmedia.net **w** republicmedia.net
Dir: Sue Harris.

Revolver Communications Ltd. 1 Sekforde St,
Clerkenwell, London EC1R 0BE **t** 020 7107 2720 or
07717 357 192 **f** 020 7107 2721
e firstname.lastname@revolvercomms.com
w revolvercomms.com Dir: Matt Owen.

RKM Public Relations Suite 201, Erico House, 93-99
Upper Richmond Rd, London SW15 2TG **t** 020 8785 5640
f 020 8785 5641 **e** info@rkmpr.com **w** rkmpr.com
Dir: Rob Montague.

RMP 2C Woodstock Studios, Woodstock Grove, London
W12 8LE **t** 020 8749 7999 **f** 020 8811 8162
e firstname@rmplondon.co.uk MD: Regine Moylett.

Rock Solid PR 11 Downton Ave, Streatham Hill, London
SW2 3TU **t** 020 8674 2224 or 07968 817 359
f 020 8674 2224 **e** rocksolidpr@aol.com MD: John Welsh.

Rocketscience Media 1st Floor, The Griffin, 93 Leonard St,
London EC2A 4RD **t** 020 7033 4000
e office@rocketsciencemedia.com **w** rocketsciencemedia.com
Dir: Alex Black.

Rokkpool PR 11 Lawton Rd, London E10 6RR
t 020 8558 6607 or 07960 442645 **e** rokkpool@tiscali.co.uk
w myspace.com/rokkpool Contact: Pippa Moye.

ROOD MEDIA

PO Box 21469, Highgate, London N6 4ZG **t** 020 8347 7400
e roo@roodmedia.com **w** roodmedia.com Director: Ruchie
Farndon.
Music & Entertainment PR agency covering National,
Regional, Specialist Radio, Online and Student press. Clients
include SonyBMG, One Little Indian, Roger Sanchez, TDK-
Cross Central Festival, Trax2Burn.com, U.D.G/Creator,
Martin Luther (The Roots), Neimo and The Pinker Tones.

RRR Management 96 Wentworth Rd, Birmingham
B17 9SY **t** 0121 426 6820 **f** 0121 426 5700
e enquiries@rrrmanagement.com **w** rrrmanagement.com
MD: Ruby Ryan.

Sainted PR Office 17, Shaftesbury Centre, 85 Barlby Rd,
London W10 6BN **t** 020 8962 5700 **f** 020 8962 5701
e heatherfinlay@saintedpr.com MD: Heather Finlay.

Sally Reeves PR 81 Green End, Landbeach, Cambridge
CB4 8ED **t** 01223 395 133 **e** sallyreeves@btinternet.com
MD: Sally Reeves.

National, Regional and Online
PR campaigns

T: 01223 410000
Harvey@quitegreat.co.uk
www.quitegreat.co.uk

Sarah J. Edwards PR PO Box 2423, London WC2E 9PG **t** 0870 138 9430 **f** 0870 138 9430 **e** blag@blagmagazine.com **w** blagmagazine.com Dir: Sarah J. Edwards.

Phill Savidge PR 8 Denton Rd, London N8 9NS **t** 020 8348 0373 **f** 020 8348 0373 **e** phill.savidge@btinternet.com **w** savagepr.com MD: Phill Savidge.

Scene Not Herd Hillhead Cottage, Avonbridge, Falkirk FK1 2NL. **t** 0870 446 0604 or 07986 527 947 **e** lesley@scenenotherd.co.uk **w** scenenotherd.co.uk Sales & Marketing: Lesley Woodall.

Scruffy Bird The Nest, 205 Victoria St, London SW1E 5NE **t** 020 7931 7990 **e** laura@scruffybird.com **w** scruffybird.com Head of Press: Laura Martin.

Seb & Fiona 3rd Floor, 61-63 Brushfield St, Old Spitalfields Market, London E1 6AA **t** 020 7377 9868 **f** 0870 094 1950 **e** firstname@sebandfiona.com **w** sebandfiona.com Dirs: Fiona Wootton, Seb Emina.

Serious Press and PR 30 West St, Stoke-sub-Hamdon, Somerset TA14 6PZ **t** 01935 823719 **f** 01935 823719 **e** janehamdon@yahoo.co.uk MD: Jane Osborne.

Shark Media Shark House, 197 Turnpike Link, London CRO 5NW **t** 020 8604 1330 or 07939 220 169 **e** info@shark-media.co.uk **w** shark-media.co.uk MD: Charlotte Clark.

Sharp End PR 14/15 Bentinck Mansions, Bentinck St, London W1U 2ER **t** 020 7487 2865 **e** ronmccreight@btinternet.com Contact: Ron McCreight.

Silver PR 41 Lavers Rd, London N16 ODU **t** 020 7502 0240 **f** 020 7502 0240 **e** rachel.silver@silverpr.co.uk **w** silverpr.co.uk Dir: Rachel Silver.

Singsong Ltd Market House, Market Sq, Winslow, Bucks MK18 3AF **t** 01296 715 228 **f** 01296 715 486 **e** peter@singsongpr.biz **w** singsongpr.biz MD: Peter Muir.

Sister PR 1st Floor, 46a Carnaby St, London W1F 9PS **t** 020 7287 9601 **f** 020 7287 9602 **e** rufus@sister-pr.com **w** sister-pr.com Dir: Rufus Stone.

Six07 Press 21 Ferdinand St, London NW1 8EU **t** 020 7428 0933 **f** 020 7428 0919 **e** firstname@six07press.com Dir: Ritu Morton.

Skullduggery Services 40a Love Lane, Pinner, Middlesex HA5 3EX **t** 020 8429 0853 **e** xskullduggeryx@btinternet.com MD: Russell Aldrich.

Slice 5 Golden Sq, London W1F 9BS **t** 020 7309 5700 **f** 020 7309 5701 **e** firstname@slice.co.uk **w** slice.co.uk MD: Damian Mould.

SLIDING DOORS PUBLICITY

PO Box 21469, Highgate, London N6 4ZG **t** 020 8340 3412 **f** 020 8340 5159 **e** info@slidingdoors.biz **w** slidingdoors.biz MD: James Hamilton - james@slidingdoors.biz. PR Account Director: Nicola Freitas - nicola@slidingdoors.biz myspace.com/slidingdoorspublicity

Smash Press 56 Ackroyd Rd, London SE23 1DL **t** 020 8291 6466 or 07721 662 933 **e** smash.press-pr@virgin.net MD: Nick White.

Sofa PR 15 Haynes Lane, London SE19 3AN **t** 07970 551 283 or 0208 771 5354 **e** sofapr@mac.com MD: Simon Ward.

some friendly Unit 5, 5-7 Batemans Row, London EC2 **t** 020 7729 3999 or 07961 436 736 **f** 020 7684 5432 **e** info@somefriendly.co.uk **w** somefriendly.com Dir: Sophie Williams.

Southern PR 6 Stucley Pl, Camden, London NW1 8NT **t** 020 7267 3466 or 020 7267 3498 **e** lisa@southernpr.co.uk MD: Lisa Southern.

Spring PR and Marketing Studio 10, Rose Cottage, Aberdeen Centre, 22-24 Highbury Grove, London N5 2EA **t** 020 7704 0999 **f** 020 7704 6999 **e** rhiannon@spring-pr.com **w** spring-pr.com Dir: Rhiannon Sheehy.

St Pierre Publicity The Hoods, High St, Wethersfield, nr Braintree CM7 4BY **t** 01371 850 238 **e** stpierre.roger@dsl.pipex.uk MD: Roger St Pierre.

Starfish Communications 76 Oxford St, London W1D 1BS **t** 020 7323 2121 **f** 020 7323 0234 **e** fearfield@star-fish.net **w** star-fish.net Managing Partner: Sally Fearfield.

Stay Gold Press Brighton Media Centre, 15 - 17 Middle St, Brighton BN1 1AL **t** 01273 201 327 **e** mel@staygold.co.uk **w** staygold.co.uk 07768 865 737: Mel Thomas.

Stone Immaculate Press Tunstall Studios, 34-44 Tunstall Rd, London SW9 8DA **t** 020 7737 6359 **f** 020 7274 8921 **e** stone@stoneimmaculate.co.uk **w** stoneimmaculate.co.uk MD: Chris Stone.

Storm Interactive Entertainment c/o Sloane & Co., 36-38 Westbourne Grove, Newton Rd, London W2 5SH **t** 020 7099 8849 **f** 020 7099 8850 **e** info@storminteractive.com **w** storminteractive.com MD: Stephen Bayley-Johnston.

Strategic 10 Margaret St, London W1W 8RL **t** 0845 6801 857 **f** 020 3008 6171 **e** info@strategic-pr.org **w** strategic-pr.org Owner: Mal Smith.

Street Life PO Box 23351, London SE16 4YQ **t** 020 7231 1393 **f** 020 7232 1373 **e** info@interactivem.co.uk **w** interactivem.co.uk MD: Jo Cerrone.

Student Press, Student Radio, Student Marketing, Street Teams

T: 01223 410000
Harvey@quitegreat.co.uk
www.quitegreat.co.uk

Press & Promotion: PR Companies

Street Press PR The Top Floor, The Outset Building, 2 Grange Rd, London E17 8AH **t** 020 8509 6073 **f** 020 8509 6021 **e** heather@streetpress.co.uk MD: Heather Moul.

Supersonic Publicity 35 Chilcote Rd, Portsmouth PO3 6HY **t** 07866 482 043 **e** Supersonic_Publicity@hotmail.co.uk **w** myspace.com/Supersonic_Publicity MD: Jim Lines.

Talk Loud PR The Granary, Station Rd, Docking, Norfolk PE31 8LY **t** 07710 329 105 or 01485 518910 **f** 01485 518920 **e** addie@talkloud.co.uk **w** talkloud.co.uk MD: Addie Churchill.

Tara Tomes PR PO Box 6003, Birmingham B45 0AR **t** 0121 477 9553 or 07966 174 319 **f** 0121 693 2954 **e** tara@taratomes.com **w** taratomespr.com MD: Tara Tomes.

Tenacity Po Box 166, Hartlepool, Cleveland TS26 9JA **t** 01429 424 603 or 07951 679 666 **e** info@tenacitymusicpr.co.uk **w** tenacitymusicpr.co.uk Prop: Dave Hill.

Terrie Doherty Promotions 40, Princess St, Manchester M1 6DE **t** 0161 234 0044 **e** terriedoherty@zoo.co.uk Director, Regional Rad/TV: Terrie Doherty.

The Partnership 57-63 Old Church St, London SW3 5BS **t** 020 7761 6005 **f** 020 7761 6035 **e** billy@partnership2.com Ptnr: Billy Macleod.

Peter Thompson Associates Flat 1, 12 Bourchier St., London W1D 4HZ **t** 020 7439 1210 **f** 020 7439 1202 **e** info@ptassociates.co.uk MD: Peter Thompson.

Toast PR Room 210, Bon Marche Building, 241-251 Ferndale Rd, London SW9 8BJ **t** 020 7326 1200 **e** info@toastpress.com **w** toastpress.com MD: Ruth Drake.

Tora! Company Clearwater Yard, 35 Inverness St, London NW1 7HB **t** 020 7424 7500 **f** 020 7424 7501 **e** gary@tora-co.demon.co.uk Dir: Gary Levermore.

Judy Totton Publicity EBC House, Ranelagh Gardens, London SW6 3PA **t** 020 7371 8158 or 020 7371 8159 **f** 020 7371 7862 **e** judy@judytotton.com **w** judytotton.com MD: Judy Totton.

Traffic Marketing 6 Stucley Pl, London NW1 8NS **t** 020 7485 7400 **f** 020 7485 5151 **e** info@trafficmarketing.co.uk **w** trafficmarketing.co.uk MD: Lisa Paulon.

Trailer Suite 36, 99-109 Lavender Hill, London SW11 5QL **t** 020 7924 6443 **f** 020 7733 9966 **e** anton@trailermedia.com MD: Anton Hiscock.

Triad Publicity 27D Lady Somerset Rd, London NW5 1TX **t** 020 7267 5121 or 07711 654 772 **e** info@triadpublicity.co.uk **w** triadpublicity.co.uk Dir: Johnny Hopkins.

Trinity Media Group 72 New Bond St, London W1S 1RR **t** 020 7499 4141 **e** info@trinitymediagroup.net **w** trinitymediagroup.net MD: Peter Murray.

Up-Comms 3rd Floor, 20 Flaxman Terrace, London WC1H 9AT **t** 020 7388 0770 **e** andy@up-comms.com **w** up-comms.com Dir: Andy Crysell.

UP-PR Studio 242, Bon Marche Centre, 241-251 Ferndale Rd, London SW9 8BJ **t** 020 7733 7493 **e** hayley@up-pr.com **w** up-pr.com PR Manager: Hayley Allman.

Uproar Communications The Old Dairy, 35 Little Russell St, London WC1A 2HH **t** 020 7580 1852 **f** 020 7580 1855 **e** julian@uproaruk.com **w** uproaruk.com Chief Urbanaire: Julian Davis.

Upshot Communications 10-11 Jockey's Fields, London WC1R 4BN **t** 020 7400 4560 **f** 020 7400 4561 **e** info@upshotcom.com **w** upshotcreek.com Dirs: Stephen Barnes, Tom Roberts.

VELOCITY COMMUNICATIONS

2nd Floor, Olympic House, 85 Hatton Garden, London EC1N 8JR **t** 020 7430 0200 **f** 020 7430 0204 **e** andy@velocitypr.co.uk **w** velocitypr.co.uk MD: Andy Saunders.
Founded in 2000 Velocity Communications specialise in music industry artist, corporate and new media PR across most genres.

Vision Promotions 22 Upper Grosvenor St, London W1K 7PE **t** 020 7499 8024 **f** 020 7499 8032 **e** vision@visionmusic.co.uk **w** visionmusic.co.uk Head Of Promotions: Rob Dallison.

Wasted Youth 21-22 Great Castle St, London W1G 0HZ **t** 020 7493 5873 **e** sarah@wastedyouthpr.com **w** wastedyouthpr.com MD: Sarah Pearson.

Way to Blue First Floor, 65 Rivington St, London EC2A 3QQ **t** 020 7749 8444 **f** 020 7749 8420 **e** Lee@waytoblue.com **w** waytoblue.com Dir: Lee Henshaw.

Richard Wootton Publicity The Manor House, 120 Kingston Rd, Wimbledon, London SW19 1LY **t** 020 8542 8101 or 07774 111 692 **f** 020 8540 0691 **e** richard@rwpublicity.com **w** rwpublicity.com MD: Richard Wootton.

Work Hard PR 35 Farm Ave, London SW16 2UT **t** 020 8677 8466 or 020 8769 6713 **e** enquiries@workhardpr.com **w** workhardpr.com MD: Roland Hyams.

The Works PR 11 Marshalsea Rd, London SE1 1EN **t** 020 7940 4686 **f** 020 7940 5656 **e** info@theworkspr.com **w** theworkspr.com Press: Judy Lipsey.

Writing Services 20 Rockfield Rd, Monmouth NP25 5BA **t** 01600 713758 **e** anita@writing-services.co.uk **w** writing-services.co.uk Owner/manager: Anita Holford.

Yes Please PR 29 Harford House, 35 Tavistock Crescent, London W11 1AY **t** 020 7792 2843 **e** yespleasepr@btinternet.com MD: Ginny Luckhurst.

National, Regional and Online
PR campaigns

T: 01223 410000
Harvey@quitegreat.co.uk
www.quitegreat.co.uk

Chrissie Yiannou 16-24 Brewery Rd, London N7 9NH
t 020 7607 3608 **f** 020 7607 9608
e chrissie@positivenuisance.com MD: Chrissie Yiannou.

Zen Media Management 27B Felixstowe Rd, London
NW10 5SR **t** 020 8960 9171 or 07957 338 525
e sacha@zenmedia.net **w** zenmedia.net Dir: Sacha Taylor-Cox.

ZEST PR LTD

@ Carnaby Street, 32-34 Great Marlborough Street, London
W1F 7JB **t** 020 7734 0206 **f** 020 7734 4084
e Ian@zestpr.com **w** zestpr.com Managing Director: Ian Roberts.
Senior PR Manager: Jem Bahaijoub - Jem@zestpr.com
**"The No1 Creative Agency" - Covering National & Regional
Press, Broadcast Media, Online, Event Management,
Marketing, Consumer & Brands, Reputation Management
and Media Training.**

ZZonked Unit 348, Stratford Workshops, Burford Rd, London
E15 2SP **t** 020 8503 1880 **f** 020 8534 0603
e info@zzonked.co.uk **w** zzonked.co.uk Contact: Gareth Watkins.

Photographers and Agencies

3D Media Services Seton Lodge, 26 Sutton Ave, Seaford, E
Sussex BN25 4IJ **t** 01323 892 303
e talk2us@3dmediaservices.com **w** 3dmediaservices.com
MDs: Anthony Duke, Kim Duke.

aandr Photographic 16a Crane Grove, Islington, London
N7 8LE **t** 020 7607 3030 **f** 020 7607 2190
e info@aandrphotographic.co.uk **w** aandrphotographic.co.uk
Photographers Agents: Anita Grossman, Rosie Harrison.

Lorenzo Agius Contact: K2>music.

Mark Alesky Contact: Pearce Stoner.

All Action Digital 32 Great Sutton St, London EC1V 0NB
t 020 7608 2988 **f** 020 7336 0491 **e** mo@allaction.co.uk
w allactiondigital.com GM: Isabelle Vialle.

Mark Allan 30 Barry Rd, London SE22 0HU
t 020 8693 6625 or 07836 385352 **f** 020 8299 6566
e mark.allanphotos@btinternet.com.

Ami Barwell - Music Photographer London
t 07787 188 452 **e** ami@musicphotographer.co.uk
w musicphotographer.co.uk Contact: Ami Barwell.

Amit & Naroop Photography Studio 1B, 39 - 40
Westpoint, Warple Way, London W3 0RG **t** 020 8743 4646
e info@amitandnaroop.com **w** amitandnaroop.com
Partners: Amit Amin & Naroop Jhooti.

Andy Fallon Photography 25B Barforth Rd, London
SE15 3PS **t** 07956 303122 **e** andy@andyfallon.co.uk
w andyfallon.co.uk Photographer: Andy Fallon.

Aquarius Picture Library 65 Belvoir Drive, Leicester
LE2 8PB **t** 0116 229 0648 **f** 0116 274 7199
e sales@aquariuscollection.com **w** aquariuscollection.com
Website Manager: Corinne Flint.

Peter Ashworth Photography 107 South Hill Pk, London
NW3 2SP **t** 020 7435 4142 or 07714 952 292
f 020 7435 9988 **e** aaaashy@blueyonder.co.uk
w ashworth-photos.com Contact: Peter Ashworth.

Simon Atlee Contact: Pearce Stoner.

Balcony Jump Management Unit 3, Round House
Studios, 91 Saffron Hill, London EC1N 8PT **t** 020 7831 3355
f 020 7841 1356 **e** info@balconyjump.co.uk **w** balconyjump.co.uk
MD: Tim Paton.

Joe Bangay Photography River House, Riverwoods,
Marlow, Bucks SL7 1QY **t** 01628 486193 or 07860 812529
f 01628 890239 **e** william.b@btclick.com **w** JoeBangay.com
MD: William Bangay.

Sheyi Antony Banks Photography 45 Indigo Mews,
Carysfort Rd, London N16 9AA **t** 020 7254 5352 or
07956 312608 **f** 020 7254 5352 **e** info@sheyiantonybanks.com
w sheyiantonybanks.com Contact: Sheyi Antony Banks.

Colin Bell Contact: K2>music.

Terri Berg Photographic PO Box 20072, London
NW2 3ZU **t** 020 8450 6378 **f** 020 8450 7058
e tnb@dircon.co.uk **w** tbphoto.co.uk Contact: Terri N Berg.

Big Photographic Ltd Unit D4, Metropolitan Wharf,
Wapping Wall, London E1W 3SS **t** 020 7702 9365
f 020 7702 9366 **e** contact@bigactive.com **w** bigactive.com
Directore: Richard Newton/Greg Burne.

Bill Charles London Ltd Unit 3E1 Zetland House, 5-25
Scrutton St, London EC2A 4HJ **t** 020 7033 9284
f 020 7033 9285 **e** dan@billcharles.com **w** billcharles.com
Contact: Daniel Worthington or Olivia Gideon Thomson.

Richard Birch Contact: M Agency.

Black & Blonde Creative Commissioning Services
The Primrose Hill Business Centre, 110 Gloucester Ave, London
NW1 8HX **t** 020 7209 3760 or
07703 201 111 or 07968 499 037 **f** 020 7209 3761
e info@blackandblonde.co.uk **w** blackandblonde.co.uk
Dirs: Hermione Ross, Jo Hart.

Mark Bond Contact: Julie Bramwell Representation.

Harry Borden Contact: K2>music.

Sophie Broadbridge .

Jay Brooks Contact: M Agency.

Ken Browar Contact: Serlin Associates.

Ray Burmiston (see Shoot).

Cableimage **t** 01252 890222 or 07778 156925
e rob@cableimage.com **w** cableimage.com Dir: Rob Cable.

Matt Canon (see Shoot).

Capital Pictures 85 Randolph Ave, London W9 1DL
t 020 7286 2212 **f** 020 7286 3606
e sales@capitalpictures.com **w** capitalpictures.com
Dir: Phil Loftus.

Carlos Cicchelli Photography 42b Medina Rd, London
N7 7LA **t** 07960 726 957 or 020 7686 2324 **f** 020 7686 2324
e Hi@Toshoot.Com **w** Toshoot.Com
Photographer: Carlos Cicchelli.

Andy Carne Photographer Unit 12 Atlas Works, Foundry
Lane, Earls Colne, Essex CO6 2TE **t** 01787 224 464
f 01787 220 055 **e** studio@andycarne.com **w** andycarne.com
Photographer: Andy Carne.

CCPhotoArt.biz 21 New Copper Moss, Moss Lane,
Altrincham, Cheshire WA15 8EG **t** 07799 174 199
e chief@ccphotoart.biz **w** ccphotoart.biz
Contact: Patrick Cusse & Christie Goodwin.

Davide Cernuschi Contact: M Agency.

George Chin Photography **t** 020 8731 9300 or
07876 745943 **f** 020 8731 9290 **e** george@georgechin.com
w georgechin.com MD: George Chin.

Claire Grogan Photography 12 Calverley Grove,
Archway, London N19 3LG **t** 020 7272 1845 or 07932 635 381
e claire@clairegrogan.co.uk **w** clairegrogan.co.uk
Contact: Claire Grogan.

Alan Clarke Contact: Pearce Stoner.

Simon Clemenger Contact: Rockit.

Coochie Management 26 Harcourt St, London W1H 4HW
t 020 7724 9700 or 07802 795 620 **f** 020 7724 2598
e amanda@coochie-management.com
w coochie-management.com MD: Amanda G.

Neil Cooper .

Corinne Day Contact: Susie Babchick Agency.

Pete Cronin 14 Lakes Rd, Keston, Kent BR2 6BN
t 01689 858719 or 07860 391985 **e** pete@petecronin.com
w petecronin.com.

Daniel J.Scott **t** 020 7602 9382 or 07968 191 596
e mail@danieljscott.com **w** danieljscott.com
Photographer: Daniel Scott.

Jack Daniels `The Photographer' Plot 2, The
Plantation, Swanage, Dorset BH19 2TD **t** 07831 356719 or
01929 427429 **f** 01929 427471
e musicweek@jackdaniels.me.uk **w** jackdaniels.me.uk
Contact: Jack Daniels.

Dato Imaging 16A Pavilion Terrace, London W12 0HT
t 07770 946058 **e** info@dato.co.uk **w** dato.co.uk MD: Chris Dato.

Davix Management Suite D, 67 Abbey Rd, St John's Wood,
London NW8 0AE **t** 079 5630 2894 **e** davixuk@hotmail.com
w peromi.co.uk/davidross/ Photographer: David Ross.

Dean Chalkley (see Shoot).

Lou Denim Contact: Rockit.

Dirk Linder Contact: Skinny Dip.

Paul Donohue Contact: Pearce Stoner.

David Drebin .

Liam Duke Contact: Pearce Stoner.

Sandrine Dulermo & Michael Labica
Contact: K2>music.

Giles Duley Contact: K2>music.

Tom Dunkley (see Shoot).

Frederic Duval 6 Dorset Court, Hertford Rd, London N1 4SD
t 020 7503 6870 or 07876 481 279
e jenny_duval@hotmail.com.

Andy Earl 29 Curlew St, London SE1 2ND **t** 020 7403 1156
f 020 7403 1157 **e** mail@andyearl.com **w** andyearl.com.

East Photographic 8 Iron Bridge House, 3 Bridge
Approach, London NW1 8BD **t** 020 7722 3444
f 020 7722 3544 **e** hq@eastphotographic.com
w eastphotographic.com Contact: Nick Selby.

Jude Edginton Contact: P.C.P.

David Ellis Contact: Terri Manduca Ltd.

Eminent Management & Production Ltd The Old
Truman Brewery, 91 Brick Lane, London E1 6QL
t 020 7247 4750 **f** 020 7247 4712
e anita@eminentmanagement.co.uk **w** eminentmanagement.co.uk
MD: Anita Heryet.

McVirn Etienne Contact: Rockit.

Tim Evan-Cook Contact: Serlin Associates.

Famous Pictures & Features Agency 13 Harwood Rd,
London SW6 4QP **t** 020 7731 9333 **f** 020 7731 9330
e info@famous.uk.com **w** famous.uk.com
Library Manager: Rob Howard.

Jim Fiscus Contact: M Agency.

Food 4 Foxes Concert, Event & Studio
Photographers The Studio, 156-158 Grays Inn Rd, London
WC1X 8ED **t** 020 7713 1008
e onethousandwords@food4foxes.co.uk **w** food4foxes.co.uk
MD: Damien Chaos.

Freelance Directory NUJ, Acorn House, 314-320 Gray's Inn
Rd, London WC1X 8DP **t** 020 7843 3703 **f** 020 7278 1812
e pamelam@nuj.org.uk **w** gn.apc.org/media/
Contact: Pamela Morton.

Dean Freeman Contact: Terri Manduca Ltd.

Eric Frideen Contact: Serlin Associates.

Future Earth Photography 59 Fitzwilliam St, Wath upon
Dearne, Rotherham, South Yorks S63 7HG **t** 01709 872875
e david@future-earth.co.uk **w** future-earth.co.uk
MD: David Moffitt.

George Bodnar Productions Churchill House, 137 Brent
St, London NW4 4DJ **t** 020 8457 2757 **f** 020 8457 2602
e george@gbimages.com **w** gbimages.com
Photographer: George Bodnar.

Bob Glanville 77 Shelley House, Churchill Gardens, Pimlico,
London SW1V 3JE **t** 07957 363 472 **e** info@bobglanville.com
w bobglanville.com Photographer: Bob Glanville.

Adrian Green .

Mark Hadley Photography 25A Bridgnorth Ave,
Wombourne, Staffs WV5 0AD **t** 01902 896209
f 01902 896209 **e** thephotoagency@btinternet.com.

Mischa Haller Contact: K2>music.

Cary Hammond .

Trevor Ray Hart Contact: P.C.P.

Jason Hetherington Contact: Pearce Stoner.

Hugo Morris Photography 134 Renfrew St, Glasgow
G3 6ST **t** 07929 194 571 **e** info@XTmedia.co.uk
w hugomorris.com Contact: Hugo Morris.

IDOLS LICENSING AND PUBLICITY LTD

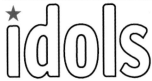

593-599 Fulham Road, London SW6 5UA **t** 020 7385 5121
f 020 7385 5110 **e** info@idols.co.uk **w** idols.co.uk Creative
Liaison: Emma Radford - emma@idols.co.uk. Sales and Marketing
Director and Music/Teen Press: Darren Hendry -
darren@idols.co.ukAE International Press: Tom Wright –
tom@idols.co.ukAE UK Celebrity Press: Malcolm Collins –
malcolm@idols.co.uk

Inoya Photography Flat 23, Key House, Bowling Green St,
London SE11 5TT **t** 020 7091 9015 or 07888 723 197
e info@inoya.co.uk **w** inoya.co.uk Photographer: Zen Inoya.

Justin Jay Contact: Rockit.

J.C.Mac 5 Lawnwood Court, Catteshall Lane, Godalming,
Surrey GU7 1XS **t** 07768 475 622 **e** jcmac@blissmedia.co.uk
w blissmedia.co.uk Photographer: J.C. Mac.

John Beecher Photo Library Rock House, London Rd, St
Mary's, Stroud, Gloucs GL6 8PU **t** 01453 886252 or
0845 456 9759 **f** 01453 885361 or 0845 456 9760
e photo@rollercoasterrecords.com **w** rollercoasterrecords.com
Owner: John Beecher.

Judy Totton Photography EBC House, Ranelagh Gardens,
London SW6 3PA **t** 020 7371 8159 or 07798 806079
f 020 7371 7862 **e** judy@judytotton.com **w** judytotton.com
Photographer: Judy Totton.

Julie Bramwell Representation Holborn Studios, 49-50
Eagle Wharf Rd, London N1 7ED **t** 020 7251 4392
f 020 7251 4393 **e** julie@juliebramwell.com **w** juliebramwell.com
MD: Julie Bramwell.

Junction10 Photography & Design 292-294
Wolverhampton Road West, Bentley, Walsall WS2 0DS
t 0800 019 9726 or 07973 618 503 **f** 0870 760 7654
e jason@junction10.net **w** junction10.net Contact: Jason Sheldon.

Justine Contact: Serlin Associates.

K2>music 109 Clifton St, London EC2A 4LD
t 020 7749 6070 **f** 020 7749 6001 **e** nick@k2creatives.com
w k2creatives.com Contact: Nick Bull.

Katie Kaars Contact: Rockit.

Jason Kelvin Contact: Skinny Dip.

Luke Kirwan Contact: Pearce Stoner.

Kochi Photography 33/37 Hatherley Mews, Walthamstow,
London E17 4QP **t** 020 8521 9227 **f** 020 8520 5553
e xplosive@supanet.com Dir: Terry McLeod.

Kristine Skovli Photography 22a Morval Rd, London
SW2 1DQ **t** 07947 332 514 **e** kristine@kskovli.com
w kskovli.com photographer: Kristine Skovli.

Lacey Contact: Pearce Stoner.

Robert Lakow Contact: M Agency.

Jenny Lewis Contact: PC.P.

Laurie Lewis 176 Camden Rd, London NW1 9HG
t 020 7267 0315 Dir: Topsy Corian.

Link Picture Library 33 Greyhound Rd, London W6 8NH
t 020 7381 2261 or 020 7381 2433 **f** 020 7385 6244
e prints@linkpicturelibrary.com **w** linkpicturelibrary.com
Prop: Orde Eliason.

London Features International Ltd 3 Boscobel St,
London NW8 8PS **t** 020 7723 4204 **f** 020 7723 9201
e john@lfi.co.uk **w** lfi.co.uk Editorial Dir: John Halsall.

Loud Pixels Photography 40 Studland St, London
W6 0JS **t** 07738 920 225 **e** sonicmoo@gmail.com
w loudpixels.net Contact: Marc Broussely.

M Agency 7 Tyers Gate, London SE1 3HX **t** 020 7357 0622
f 020 7403 5424 **e** info@magency.co.uk **w** magency.co.uk
Bookers: Emma Stanton, Grace Holbrook.

Kevin Mackintosh Contact: Pearce Stoner.

Sarah Maingot Contact: Serlin Associates.

Mark McNulty 8E Sunnyside, Princes Pk, Liverpool L8 3TD
t 0151 727 2012 or 07885 847806 **e** mark@mcnulty.co.uk
w mcnulty.co.uk.

Martyn Rose Contact: Rebecca Valentine.

Sean McMenomy Contact: K2>music.

Arthur Meehan Contact: Serlin Associates.

Anne Menke Contact: Serlin Associates.

Michael Taylor Photography 412 Beersbridge Rd,
Belfast BT5 5EB **t** 028 9065 4450 **f** 028 9047 1625
e michael@mtphoto.co.uk **w** mtphoto.co.uk
Photographer: Michael Taylor.

Mitch Jenkins (see Shoot).

One Photographic 4th Floor, 48 Poland St, London
W1F 7ND **t** 020 7287 2311 **f** 020 7287 2313
e harriet@onephotographic.com **w** onephotographic.com
Agents: Belinda Taylor, Harriet Essex.

Scarlet Page Contact: PC.P.

Sue Parkhill .

Ellis Parrinder Contact: PC.P.

Mike Parsons .

Paul Harries Photography Top Floor Office, 95
Waldegrave Rd, Teddington, Middlesex TW11 8LA
t 020 8977 1958 or 07889 767 179 **e** paul@paulharries.co.uk
w paulharries.com Contact: Paul Harries.

PC.P 5-7 Vernon Yard, off Portobello Rd, London W11 2DX
t 020 7313 9100 **f** 020 7313 9109 **e** penny@presscounsel.com
w pcp-agency.com Dir: Penny Caplowe.

Pearce Stoner Associates 12b Links Yard, Spelman St,
London E1 5LX **t** 020 7247 7100 **f** 020 7247 7144
e info@pearcestoner.com **w** pearcestoner.com
Dirs: Eve Stoner, Victoria Pearce.

Rena Pearl 8A The Drive, London NW11 9SR
t 020 8455 7661 or 07798 693756 **f** 020 8381 4050
e rena@renapearl.com **w** renapearl.com Contact: Rena Pearl.

Antonio Petronzio .

Soulla Petrou (see Shoot).

Photo-Stock Library International 14 Neville Ave,
Anchorsholme, Blackpool, Lancs FY5 3BG **t** 01253 864598
f 01253 864598 **e** wayne@photo-stock.co.uk
w photo-stock.co.uk Contact: Wayne Paulo.

Pictorial Press Ltd Unit 1 Market Yard Mews, 194
Bermondsey St, London SE1 3TQ **t** 020 7378 7211
f 020 7378 7194 **e** info@pictorialpress.co.uk
w pictorialpress.co.uk Dir: Tony Gale.

Pilot Creative Agency Unit 208, Canalot Studios, 222
Kensal Rd, London W10 5BN **t** 020 7565 2227
f 020 7565 2228 **e** Beverley@pilotcreativeagency.com
w pilotcreativeagency.com MD: Beverley Kendall.

PR Pictures Ltd Cherry Trees, Loudwater Heights,
Loudwater WD3 4AX **t** 01923 718555 **e** john@prpictures.co.uk
w prpictures.co.uk Contact: John Willan.

Dee Ramadan .

Rebecca Valentine Agency 37 Foley St, London
W1W 7TN **t** 07968 190 411 **e** rebecca@rebeccavalentine.com
w rebeccavalentine.com MD: Rebecca Valentine.

Red represents 98 De Beauvoir Rd, London N1 4EN
t 020 7275 2725 **f** 020 7572 2701 **e** rachel@redrepresents.com
w redrepresents.com Contact: Rachel Thomas.

Redferns Music Picture Library 7 Bramley Rd, London
W10 6SZ **t** 020 7792 9914 **f** 020 7792 0921
e info@redferns.com **w** redferns.com Library Mgr: Jon Wilton.

John Rensten Contact: Rebecca Valentine.

Repfoto 74 Creffield Rd, London W3 9PS **t** 020 8992 2936 **f** 020 8992 9641 **e** repfoto@btinternet.com **w** repfoto.com Ptnr: Robert Ellis.

Retrograph Nostalgia Archive Ltd 10 Hanover Crescent, Brighton, E. Sussex BN2 9SB **t** 01273 687554 **e** retropix1@aol.com **w** Retrograph.com MD: Jilliana Ranicar-Breese.

Rex Features 18 Vine Hill, London EC1R 5DZ **t** 020 7278 7294 **f** 020 7837 4812 **e** rex@rexfeatures.com **w** rexfeatures.com Contact: John Melhuish.

Paul Rider (see Shoot).

Rip Contact: Ripley & Ripley.

Ripley & Ripley The Granary, Park Manor, Donyatt TA19 0RN **t** 07739 745 495 **f** 01460 57330 **e** studio@ripleyandripley.com **w** ripleyandripley.com Contact: Colette Ripley or Rip.

Sheila Rock Contact: Terri Manduca Ltd.

Rood Media PO Box 21469, Highgate, London N6 4ZG **t** 020 8347 7400 **e** roo@roodmedia.com **w** roodmedia.com Dir: Ruchie Farndon.

Yoichiro Sato Contact: Serlin Associates.

Diana Scheunemann Contact: Terri Manduca Ltd.

Grant Scott Contact: Julie Bramwell Representation.

Serlin Associates Unit 445 Highgate Studios, 53-79 Highgate Rd, London NW5 1TL **t** 020 7424 8888 **f** 020 7424 8889 **e** lisa@serlinassociates.com **w** serlinassociates.com Contact: Lisa Hughes.

Jon Shard .

Shoot Production Ltd Unit 2.08, Tea Building, Shoreditch High St, London E1 6JJ **t** 020 7324 7500 **f** 020 7324 7514 **e** production@shootgroup.com **w** shootproduction.com MD: Adele Rider.

Morgan Silk Contact: Rebecca Valentine.

Skinny Dip Studio 301, Westbourne Studios, 242 Acklam Rd, London W10 5JJ **t** 020 7575 3222 **f** 020 8969 8696 **e** info@skinnydip.info **w** skinnydip.info Contact: Amy Foster, Pippa Hall.

Paul Spencer Contact: Rebecca Valentine.

Soren Solkaer Starbird Contact: PC.P.

Stem Agency 1st Floor, 23 Charlotte Rd, London EC2A 3PB **t** 07790 026 628 **f** 020 7729 8258 **e** info@stemagency.com **w** stemagency.com Contact: Will Robinson.

Steve Gullick .

Stewart Birch Photography 30 Kenilworth Rd, Bognor Regis, W Sussex PO21 5NF **t** 07789 648 646 **e** info@stewartbirch.co.uk **w** stewartbirch.co.uk Contact: Stewart Birch.

The Street Studios 2 Dunston St, London E8 4EB **t** 020 7923 9430 **f** 020 7923 9429 **e** mail@streetstudios.co.uk **w** streetstudios.co.uk Studio Manager: Chris Purnell.

Susie Babchick Agency Top Floor, 6 Brewer St, London W1F 0SD **t** 020 7287 1497 **f** 020 7439 6030 **e** susie@susiebabchick.com **w** susiebabchickagency.com Dir: Susie Babchick.

Syndicated International Network 89a North View Rd, London N8 7LR **t** 020 8348 8061 **f** 020 8340 8517 **e** sales@sin-photo.co.uk **w** sin-photo.co.uk Contact: Marianne Lassen.

Nick Tansley Pictures 1 Lopen Rd, London N18 1PN **t** 020 8807 6268 **f** 020 8351 1497 **e** popworks1@yahoo.com Contact: Nick Tansley.

Terri Manduca Ltd The Basement, 11 Elvaston Pl, London SW7 5QG **t** 020 7581 5844 **f** 020 7581 5822 **e** sally@terrimanduca.co.uk **w** terrimanduca.co.uk MD: Terri Manduca.

Alastair Thain Contact: K2>music.

Tina McClelland Photography 34 Ashworth Pl, Harlow, Essex CM17 9PU **t** 07855 715200 **e** tina.mcclelland@photo2000.co.uk **w** photo2000.co.uk Photographer: Tina McClelland.

TPhotographic.com 1 Heathgate Pl, 75-83 Agincourt Rd, London NW3 2NU **t** 020 7428 6070 **f** 020 7428 6079 **e** kitty@tphotographic.com **w** tphotographic.com Senior Producer: Kitty McCorry.

Visualeyes Imaging Services 11 West St, Covent Garden, London WC2H 9NE **t** 020 7836 3004 **f** 020 7240 0079 **e** imaging@visphoto.co.uk **w** visphoto.co.uk Sales & Marketing Manager: Fergal O'Regan.

Jake Walters Contact: Pearce Stoner.

Lawrence Watson Contact: Skinny Dip.

Uli Weber Contact: Terri Manduca Ltd.

WildeHague Ltd Unit 9, The Coach Works, 80 Parsons Green Lane, London SW6 4HU **t** 020 7384 3444 **f** 020 7384 3449 **e** info@wildehague.com **w** wildehague.com Dirs: Janice Hague, Dilys Wilde.

Willy Camden (see Shoot).

Pro Sound News Europe – since 1986 PSNE has remained Europe's leading news-based publication for the professional audio industry. Its comprehensive, independent editorial content is written by some of the finest journalists in Europe, focusing on Recording & Post Production, Audio for Broadcast, Live and Installed Sound.

Installation Europe – Europe's only magazine dedicated to audio, video and lighting in the built environment. For systems designers, integrators, consultants and contractors.

PSN Live is Pro Sound News Europe's new launch dedicated exclusively to the European Live Sound market! PSN Live provides market information never previously published, quantifying and analysing market trends whilst looking at developments in technology within this growing sector.

Look out for the next edition early in 2007.

Advertising sales contact: **Steve Connolly** tel: **+44(0)20 7921 8316**

Live

Sex & Drugs

ROCK

ROLL

PEACE OF MIND

...r made insurance for all live music tours and events. Contact Rick Inglessis: 020 7977 6726.
...ran Mian: 020 7977 6730. rick.inglessis@swinglehurst.co.uk, or kamran.mian@swinglehurst.co.uk.

SWINGLEHURST LTD
INSURANCE

Live:

	Concert Hire Lighting
●	Concert Hire PA
✳	Concert Hire Both

Booking Agents

37 Management - DJ Agency Mare Street Studios, 203-213 Mare St, Hackney, London E8 3QE **t** 020 8525 1188 **f** 020 8525 1188 **e** info@37management.com **w** 37management.com MD: Jermaine Fagan.

ABA Booking 7 North Parade, Bath, Somerset BA2 4DD **t** 01225 428284 **f** 01225 400090 **e** aca_aba@freenet.co.uk MD: Harry Finegold.

ABS Agency 2 Elgin Ave, London W9 3QP **t** 020 7289 1160 **f** 020 7289 1162 **e** nigel@absagency.u-net.com MD: Nigel Kerr.

Acker's International Jazz Agency 53 Cambridge Mansions, Cambridge Rd, London SW11 4RX **t** 020 7978 5885 **e** pamela@ackersmusicagency.co.uk **w** ackersmusicagency.co.uk Prop: Pamela Francesa Sutton.

Adastra 2 Star Row, North Dalton, Driffield, E Yorks YO25 9UX **t** 01377 217662 **f** 01377 217754 **e** adastra@adastra-music.co.uk **w** adastra-music.co.uk Office Manager: Jo Heatley.

African Caribbean Asian Entertainment Agency Stars Building, 10 Silverhill Close, Nottingham NG8 6QL **t** 0870 830 0683 **f** 0115 951 9874 **e** acts@african-caribbean-ents.com **w** african-caribbean-ents.com Contact: Mr LI Sackey.

The Agency Group Ltd 361-373 City Rd, Islington, London EC1V 1PQ **t** 020 7278 3331 **f** 020 7837 4672 **e** agencylondon@theagencygroup.com **w** theagencygroup.com MD: Neil Warnock.

AIR (Artistes International Representation Ltd) AIR House, Spennymoor, Co Durham DL16 7SE **t** 01388 814632 **f** 01388 812445 **e** info@airagency.com **w** airagency.com Dirs: Colin Pearson, John Wray.

Aire International 2a Ferry Rd, London SW13 9RX **t** 020 8834 7373 **f** 020 8834 7474 **e** bethan@airmtm.com **w** airmtm.com Contact: Bethan Hay.

Alan Cottam Agency 8 Cabin End Row, Knuzden, Blackburn BB1 2DP **t** 01254 668471 **f** 01254 697599 **e** alan7000uk@yahoo.com MD: Alan Cottam.

Arcadia Music Agency 1 Felday Glade, Holmbury St Mary, Surrey RH5 6PG **t** 01306 730040 **f** 08700 526969 **e** enquiry@musi.co.uk **w** musi.co.uk MD: Max Rankin.

Asgard Promotions 125 Parkway, London NW1 7PS **t** 020 7387 5090 **f** 020 7387 8740 **e** info@asgard-uk.com Jnt MDs: Paul Fenn, Paul Charles.

Avenue Artistes 8 Winn Rd, Southampton, Hants SO17 1EN **t** 02380 551000 **f** 02380 905703 **e** info@avenueartistes.com **w** avenueartistes.com Dir: Terence A Rolph.

Austin Baptiste Entertainments Agency 29 Courthouse Gardens, London N3 1PU **t** 020 8346 3984 **f** 020 8922 3770 **e** steelbands@aol.com **w** steelbands.uk.com MD: Austin Baptiste.

Barn Dance and Line Dance Agency 62 Beechwood Rd, South Croydon, Surrey CR2 0AA **t** 020 8668 5714 **f** 020 8645 6923 **e** barndanceagency@btinternet.com **w** barn-dance.co.uk Dir: Derek Jones.

Paul Barrett (Rock 'n Roll Enterprises) 21 Grove Terrace, Penarth, South Glamorgan CF64 2NG **t** 029 2070 4279 **f** 029 2070 9989 **e** barrettrocknroll@ntlworld.com MD: Paul Barrett.

Barrucci Leisure Enterprises Ltd 45-47 Cheval Pl, London SW7 1EW **t** 020 7225 2255 **f** 020 7581 2509 **e** barrucci@barrucci.com MD: Bryan Miller.

The Bechhofer Agency 51 Barnton Park View, Edinburgh EH4 6HH **t** 0131 339 4083 **f** 0131 339 9261 **e** agency@bechhofer.demon.co.uk **w** bechhoferagency.com Contact: Frank Bechhofer.

John Bedford Enterprises 40 Stubbington Ave, North End, Portsmouth, Hants PO2 0HY **t** 023 9266 1339 **f** 023 9264 3993 **e** agency@johnbedford.co.uk **w** johnbedford.co.uk Dir: John Bedford.

Tony Bennell Entertainment 10 Manor Way, Kidlington, Oxford, Oxon OX5 2BD **t** 01865 372 645 **f** 01865 372 645 **e** tonybennell@hotmail.com **w** tonybennell.co.uk MD: Tony Bennell.

Best Kept Secret The Basement, 62 Blandford St, London W1U 7JE **t** 020 7935 4044 **f** 020 7935 3799 **e** nick@bestkeptsecret.uk.com **w** bestkeptsecret.uk.com GM: Nick Matthews.

Big Bear Music PO Box 944, Birmingham, W Midlands B16 8UT **t** 0121 454 7020 **f** 0121 454 9996 **e** agency@bigbearmusic.com **w** bigbearmusic.com MD: Jim Simpson.

The Bob Paterson Agency (BPA) PO Box 670, Ipswich, Suffolk IP9 9AU **t** 01473 749 556 or 07946 038 634 **f** 01473 749 556 **e** bp@bobpatersonagency.com **w** bobpatersonagency.com MD: Bob Paterson.

John Boddy Agency 10 Southfield Gardens, Twickenham, Middx TW1 4SZ **t** 020 8892 0133 or 020 8891 3809 **f** 020 8892 4283 **e** jba@johnboddyagency.co.uk **w** johnboddyagency.co.uk MD: John Boddy.

BPR Productions Ltd 36 Como St, Romford, Essex RM7 7DR **t** 01708 725330 **f** 01708 725322 **e** bprmusic@compuserve.com **w** bprmusic.com MD: Brian Theobald.

Brian Gannon Management PO Box 106, Rochdale, Lancs OL15 0HY **t** 01706 374411 **f** 01706 377303 **e** brian@briangannon.co.uk **w** briangannon.co.uk Owner: Brian Gannon.

Garry Brown Associates (International) 27 Downs Side, Cheam, Surrey SM2 7EH **t** 020 8643 3991 or 020 8643 8375 **f** 020 8770 7241 **e** GBALTD@compuserve.com Chairman: Garry Brown.

Celtic Artists - Aisling Entertainments 95 Carshalton Park Rd, Carshalton Beeches, Surrey SM5 3SJ **t** 020 8647 3084 **f** 020 8395 3560 **e** keirajennings@cwcom.net Dir: Keira Jennings.

Central Music Agency Hartfield House, 202 Wells Rd, Malvern Wells, Worcs WR14 4HD **t** 01684 566102 **f** 01684 566100 **e** cmamalvern@aol.com Agent/Promoter: Suzi Glantz.

CNL Touring PO Box 518, Nottingham NG3 6BF **t** 0115 985 6649 **f** 0115 985 7349 **e** info@cnltouring.co.uk **w** cnltouring.co.uk Agent: Jon Barry.

CODA Agency Ltd 81 Rivington St, London EC2A 3AY **t** 020 7012 1555 **f** 020 7012 1566 **e** agents@codaagency.com **w** codaagency.com MD: Phil Banfield.

Barry Collings Entertainments 21A Clifftown Rd, Southend-On-Sea, Essex SS1 1AB **t** 01702 330005 **f** 01702 333309 **e** bcollent@aol.com **w** barrycollings.co.uk Prop: Barry Collings.

Complete Entertainment Services PO Box 112, Seaford, E Sussex BN25 2DQ **t** 0870 755 7610 **f** 0870 755 7613 **e** info@completeentertainment.co.uk **w** completeentertainment.co.uk Events Mgr: Emalee Welsh.

Concorde International Artistes Concorde House, 101 Shepherds Bush Rd, London W6 7LP **t** 020 7602 8822 **f** 020 7603 2352 **e** cia@cia.uk.com MD: Solomon Parker.

Consolidated PO Box 87, Tarporley CW6 9FN **t** 01829 730 488 **f** 01829 730 499 **e** alececonsol@aol.com Agent: Alec Leslie.

Continental Drifts Hilton Grove, Hatherley Mews, London E17 4QP **t** 020 8509 3353 **f** 020 8509 9531 **e** Chris@continentaldrifts.co.uk **w** continentaldrifts.uk.com Dir: Chris Meikan.

Creative Artists Agency UK Ltd 2 Queen Caroline St, Hammersmith, London W6 9DX **t** 020 8323 8016 **e** ebanks@caa.com Agent: Emma Banks.

Creeme Entertainments East Lynne, Harper Green Rd, Doe Hey, Farnworth, Bolton, Lancs BL4 7HT **t** 01204 793441 or 01204 793018 **f** 01204 792655 **e** info@creeme.co.uk **w** creeme.co.uk MD: Tom Ivers.

Crisp Productions PO Box 979, Sheffield, S Yorks S8 8YW **t** 0114 261 1649 **f** 0114 261 1649 **e** dc@cprod.win-uk.net MD: Darren Crisp.

Crown Entertainments 103 Bromley Common, Bromley, Kent BR2 9RN **t** 020 8464 0454 **f** 020 8290 4038 **e** info@crownentertainments.co.uk **w** crownentertainments.co.uk MD: David Nash.

Dark Blues Management Puddephats, Markyate, Herts AL3 8AZ **t** 01582 842226 **f** 01582 840010 **e** info@darkblues.co.uk **w** darkblues.co.uk Office Mgr: Fiona Hewetson.

David Hull Promotions 46 University St, Belfast BT7 1HB **t** 028 9024 0360 **f** 028 9024 7919 **e** info@dhpromotions.com **w** davidhullpromotions.com MD: David Hull.

The Day Job 14 Laurel Ave, Twickenham, Middx TW1 4JA **t** 020 8607 9282 **e** nina@thedayjob.com **w** thedayjob.com Contact: Nina Jackson.

DCM International Suite 3, 294-296 Nether St, Finchley, London N3 1RJ **t** 020 8343 0848 **f** 020 8343 0747 **e** dancecm@aol.com **w** dancecrazy.co.uk MD: Kelly Isaacs.

Decked Out! The Primary Building, 10-11 Jockey's Fields, London WC1R 4BN **t** 020 7400 4500 **f** 020 7400 4501 **e** mail@primary.uk.com **w** primary.uk.com/primary MD: Martin Hopewell.

Denis Vaughan Promotions PO Box 28286, London N21 3WT **t** 020 7486 5353 **f** 020 8224 0466 **e** dvaughanmusic@dial.pipex.com Dir: Denis Vaughan.

Tony Denton Promotions Ltd 19 South Molton Lane, London W1K 5LE **t** 020 7629 4666 **f** 020 7629 4777 **e** mail@tdpromo.com **w** tdpromo.com Dir: Tony Denton.

Derek Block Artistes Agency Ltd 70-76 Bell St, Marylebone, London NW1 6SP **t** 020 7724 2101 **f** 020 7724 2102 **e** dbaa@derekblock.co.uk MD: Derek Block.

Dexnfx Bookings Unit 13-14, Barley Shotts Business Pk, 246 Acklam Rd, London W10 5YG **t** 07773 376 450 or 07855 494 725 **e** jill@dexnfx.com; michelle@dexnfx.com **w** dexnfx.com Agents: Jill Thompson, Michelle Curry.

Dinosaur Promotions/Pulse (The Agency) 5 Heyburn Crescent, Westport Gardens, Stoke On Trent, Staffs ST6 4DL **t** 01782 824051 **f** 01782 761752 **e** mail@dinoprom.com **w** dinoprom.com MD: Alan Dutton.

The Dixon Agency 58 Hedley St, Gosforth, Newcastle upon Tyne, Tyne and Wear NE3 1DL **t** 0191 213 1333 **f** 0191 213 1313 **e** bill@dixon-agency.com **w** dixon-agency.com Owner: Bill Dixon.

Steve Draper Entertainments 2 The Coppice, Beardwood Manor, Blackburn, Lancs BB2 7BQ **t** 01254 679005 **f** 01254 679005 **e** steve@stevedraperents.fsbusiness.co.uk **w** stevedraper.co.uk Prop: Steve Draper.

Duende Music Ltd PO Box 33436, London SW18 3WZ **t** 020 8879 1120 **e** info@duendemusic.co.uk **w** duendemusic.co.uk Creative Manager: Yvonne Mara.

Barry Dye Entertainments PO Box 888, Ipswich, Suffolk IP1 6BU **t** 01473 744287 **f** 01473 745442 **e** barrydye@aol.com Prop: Barry Dye.

Dyfel Management 19 Fontwell Drive, Bickley, Bromley, Kent BR2 8AB **t** 020 8467 9605 **f** 020 8249 1972 **e** jean@dyfel.co.uk **w** dyfel.co.uk Dir: J Dyne.

EC1 Music Agency 1 Cowcross St, London EC1M 6DR **t** 020 7490 8990 **f** 020 7490 8987 **e** jack@ec1music.com MD: Alex Nightingale.

Elastic Artists Agency Flat 5, 3 Newhams Row, London SE1 3UZ **t** 020 7367 6224 **f** 020 7367 6206 **e** info@elasticartists.net **w** elasticartists.net MD: Jon Slade.

Emkay Entertainments Nobel House, Regent Centre, Blackness Rd, Linlithgow, Lothian EH49 7HU **t** 01506 845555 **f** 01506 845566 **e** tom.emkay@btconnect.com **w** emkayentertainments.com Ptnr: Tom Solley.

ePM Unit 204, The Saga Centre, 326 Kensal Rd, London W10 5BZ **t** 020 8964 4900 **f** 020 8964 3600 **e** oliver@electronicpm.co.uk **w** electronicpm.co.uk Ptnr: Oliver Way.

Face Music 13 Elvendon Rd, London N13 4SJ
t 020 8889 3969 **f** 020 8889 3969
e facemusic@btinternet.com MD: Sue Carling.

Fat! Agency Unit 36, Battersea Business Centre, 99-109
Lavender Hill, London SW11 5QL **t** 020 7924 1333
f 020 7924 1833 **e** info@thefatclub.com **w** thefatclub.com
MD: Paul Arnold.

Faze 2 - International DJ Agency PO Box 430,
Manchester M14 0BB **t** 0161 445 6531 **f** 0161 953 4038
e iain@faze2agency.com **w** faze2agency.com Mgr: Iain Taylor.

First Contact Agency Ltd PO Box 35060, Camden,
London NW1 7WD **t** 020 7691 1588 **f** 020 7691 1589
e ae@firstcontactagency.com **w** firstcontactagency.com
Agent: Adam Elfin.

Free Trade Agency Free Trade House, Chapel Pl, Rivington
St, London EC2A 3DQ **t** 020 7739 8872 **f** 020 7739 8862
e enquiries@freetradeagency.co.uk MD: Paul Boswell.

Fruit Pie Music Agency The Shop, 443 Streatham High
Rd, London SW16 3PH **t** 020 8679 9289 **f** 020 8679 9775
e info@fruitpiemusic.com **w** fruitpiemusic.com
MD: Kumar Kamalagharan.

Frusion 1 Holme Rd, Matlock Bath, Derbyshire DE4 3NU
t 07791 699 889 **f** 01629 57082 **e** frusion@mac.com
w frusion.co.uk Contact: Ian Smith.

G Entertainment 16 Coney Green, Abbotts Barton,
Winchester, Hants SO23 7JB **t** 0845 601 6285
e enquiries@g-entertaining.co.uk **w** g-entertaining.co.uk
MD: Peter Nouwens.

GAA (Gold Artist Agency) 16 Princedale Rd, London
W11 4NJ **t** 020 7221 1864 **f** 020 7221 1606
e bob@goldartists.co.uk MD: Bob Gold.

Gentle Fire Music Ltd GFM House, Cox Lane, Chessington,
Surrey KT9 1SD **t** 020 8397 3999 **f** 020 8397 1950
e info@gentlefiremusic.com **w** gentlefiremusic.com
MD: Bill Shannon.

The Groove Company The Coach House, Market Sq,
Bicester, Oxon OX26 6AG **t** 01869 250 647 **f** 01869 321 552
e tracey@groovecompany.co.uk Mgr: Tracey Askem.

HAL CARTER ORGANISATION

72 Borough Way, Potters Bar, Hertfordshire EN6 3HB
t 01707 649 700 or 07958 252 906 **f** 01707 657 822
e artistes@halcarterorg.com **w** halcarterorg.com Managing
Director: Abbie Carter.

Hartbeat Entertainments Ltd PO Box 348, Brixton,
Plymouth, Devon PL8 2ZW **t** 01752 881 155 **f** 01752 880 133
e hartbeat@lineone.net **w** hartbeat.co.uk MD: Mr RJ Hart.

The Headline Agency 39 Churchfields, Milltown, Dublin 14,
Ireland **t** +353 1 260 2560 **f** +353 1 261 1879
e info@musicheadline.com **w** musicheadline.com
MD: Madeleine Seiler.

Helter Skelter The Plaza, 535 Kings Rd, London SW10 0SZ
t 020 7376 8501 **f** 020 7376 8336 or 020 7351 4759
e info@helterskelter.co.uk **w** helterskelter.co.uk
Snr Agent: Paul Franklin.

John Howe Entertainment Agency 2 Meadow Way,
Ferring, Worthing BN12 5LD **t** 01903 249 912
f 01903 507 698 **e** johnhowe@btconnect.com Dir: John Howe.

IMD Ltd PO Box 1200, London SW6 2GH **t** 020 7371 0995
f 020 7751 3095 **e** rachel@imd-info.com **w** imd-info.com
MD: Rachel Birchwood-Gordon.

Imprint Bookings & Management Unit 13, Barley
Shotts Business Pk, 246 Acklam Rd, London W10 5YG
t 020 8964 1331 **f** 020 8960 9660 **e** gareth@imprintdjs.com
w imprintdjs.com Contact: Gareth Rees.

INSANITY ARTISTS AGENCY LTD

insanityartists.

8 Duncannon St, London WC2N 4JF **t** 020 7484 5078
f 020 7484 5089 **e** info@insanitygroup.com
w insanitygroup.com MD: Andy Varley. Agents: Kirsty Williams,
Matt Wynter, Jodi Robins.

International Artists 4th Floor, Holborn Hall, 193-197 High
Holborn, London WC1V 7BD **t** 020 7025 0600
f 020 7404 9865 **e** reception@intart.co.uk **w** intart.co.uk
Dir: Phil Dale.

International Talent Booking (CCE Music) Ariel
House, 74A Charlotte St, London W1T 4QH **t** 020 7637 6979
f 020 7637 6978 **e** mail@itb.co.uk **w** itb.co.uk MD: Barry Dickins.

Jade-Inc Cameo House, 11 Bear St, London WC2H 7AS
t 020 7930 6996 **e** Jade@jade-inc.net **w** jade-inc.net
Music Management: Jade Richardson.

Joe Borrow Agency 2 Conifer Drive, Stockton On Tees,
Cleveland TS19 0LU **t** 01642 616710 **f** 01642 615737
e martintaylor2@netscapeonline.co.uk **w** joeborrowagency.co.uk
Prop: Martin Taylor.

John Osborne Management PO Box 173, New Malden,
Surrey KT3 3YR **t** 020 8949 7730 **f** 020 8949 7798
e john.osb1@btinternet.com Dir: John Osborne.

K2 Agency Suite 402 The Chambers, Chelsea Harbour,
London SW10 0XF **t** 020 7808 9480 **f** 020 7808 9499
e info@k2ours.com MD: John Jackson.

The Leighton-Pope Organisation 8 Glenthorne Mews,
115a Glenthorne Rd, London W6 0LJ **t** 020 8741 4453
f 020 8741 4289 **e** info@l-po.com **w** l-po.com
MD: Carl Leighton-Pope.

Limelight Entertainment 23 Westbury Ave, Droitwich
Spa, Worcs WR9 0RT **t** 01905 796816
e johnandlisanash@hotmail.com Owner: John Nash.

Live Nation 1st Floor, Regent Arcade House, 19-25 Argyll St,
London W1F 7TS **t** 020 7009 3224 **f** 0870 749 0560
e firstname.lastname@livenation.com **w** getlive.co.uk
MD, UK Music: Stuart Galbraith.

Lumin 55 Andrews Rd, London E8 4RL **t** 020 7249 2155
e info@lumin.org **w** lumin.org Bookings: Joana Seguro.

Mainstage Artists Imperial Works, Top Floor, Perren St, London NW5 3ED **t** 020 7482 5505 **f** 020 7482 5504 **e** simon@mainstageartists.com **w** mainstageartists.com MD: Simon Clarkson.

Malcolm Feld Agency Malina House, Sandforth Rd, Liverpool L12 1JY **t** 0151 259 6565 **f** 0151 259 5006 **e** Malcolm@malcolmfeld.co.uk **w** malcolmfeld.co.uk Agent: Malcolm Feld.

Mike Malley Entertainments 10 Holly Park Gardens, Finchley, London N3 3NJ **t** 020 8346 4109 **f** 020 8346 1104 **e** mikemalley@ukstars.co.uk **w** ukstars.co.uk MD: Mike Malley.

Marshall Arts Ltd Leeder House, 6 Erskine Rd, London NW3 3AJ **t** 020 7586 3831 **f** 020 7586 1422 **e** info@marshall-arts.co.uk **w** marshall-arts.co.uk MD: Barrie Marshall.

MassiveUK 36-40 Edge St, Northern Quarter, Manchester M4 1HN **t** 0161 833 4982 **f** 0161 833 4982 **e** info@massiveuk.org.uk **w** massiveuk.org.uk Dir: Jo Fidler.

McLeod Holden Enterprises Priory House, 1133 Hessle Rd, Kingston-upon-Hull, E Yorks HU4 6SB **t** 01482 565444 **f** 01482 353635 **e** Peter.McLeod@mcleod-holden.com **w** mcleod-holden.com Dir: Peter McLeod.

Mi Live 55 St Albans Rd, S.C.R., Dublin 8, Ireland **t** +353 1 416 9418 or +353 (0) 87 9817535 **f** +353 1 416 9418 **e** info@milive.net MD: Bernie McGrath.

Miracle Artists 26 Dorset St, London W1U 8AP **t** 020 7935 9222 **f** 020 7935 6222 **e** info@miracle-artists.com Agency Dir: Steve Parker.

Mission Control Agency 50 City Business Centre, Lower Rd, London SE16 2XB **t** 020 7252 3001 **f** 020 7252 2225 **e** info@missioncontrol.net **w** missioncontrol.net MD: Gary Howard.

Money Talks Agency Cadillac Ranch, Pencraig Uchaf, Cwm Bach, Whitland, Carms. SA34 0DT **t** 01994 484466 **f** 01994 484294 **e** cadillacranch@telco4u.net **w** nikturner.com Dir: Chick Augustino.

Moneypenny Agency The Stables, Westwood House, Main St, North Dalton, Driffield, East Yorks YO25 9XA **t** 01377 217815 or 07977 455882 **f** 01377 217754 **e** nigel@adastey.demon.co.uk **w** adastra-music.co.uk/moneypenny MD: Nigel Morton.

Musicians Inc. 4 Solar Court, 22 Chambers St, London SE16 4XL **t** 0845 450 1962 **e** enquiries@musiciansinc.co.uk **w** musiciansinc.co.uk/musicians.htm MD: Sarah Ings.

NMP Live Ltd PO Box 981, Wallington, Surrey SM6 8JU **t** 020 8669 3128 **f** 020 8404 2621 **e** info@nmp.co.uk **w** nmplive.co.uk Contact: Chris Banks.

Nuphonic Management 93a Rivington St, London EC2A 3AY **t** 020 7739 8757 or 020 7739 8755 **f** 020 7739 8761 **e** james@nuphonic.co.uk **w** nuphonic.co.uk Agents: James Hillard & Bille De Voil.

NVB Entertainments 80 Holywell Rd, Studham, Dunstable, Beds LU6 2PD **t** 01582 873623 **f** 01582 873618 **e** NVBEnts@aol.com Bookers: H Harrison, Frances Harrison.

Peller Artistes Ltd. 39 Princes Ave, London N3 2DA **t** 020 8343 4264 or 0114 247 2365 **f** 07092 808 252 or 0114 247 2156 **e** agent@pellerartistes.com **w** pellerartistes.com MD: Barry Peller.

Gordon Poole Agency Ltd The Limes, Brockley, Bristol, Somerset BS48 3BB **t** 01275 463222 **f** 01275 462252 **e** agents@gordonpoole.com **w** gordonpoole.com MD: Gordon Poole.

Positive Nuisance Booking 16-24 Brewery Rd, London N7 9NH **t** 020 7607 3608 **f** 020 7607 9608 **e** Chrissie@positivenuisance.com MD: Chrissie Yiannou.

Primary Talent International The Primary Building, 10-11 Jockey's Fields, London WC1R 4BN **t** 020 7400 4500 **f** 020 7400 4501 **e** mail@primary.uk.com **w** primary.uk.com/primary MD: Martin Hopewell.

Profile Artists Agency Contact: See Primary Talent Int..

Psycho Management (Tribute & Retro Band Agency) 111 Clarence Rd, London SW19 8QB **t** 020 8540 8122 or 01483 419429 **f** 020 8715 2827 **e** agents@psycho.co.uk **w** psycho.co.uk MD: JH Mabley.

PVA Group Ltd 2 High St, Westbury On Trym, Bristol BS9 3DU **t** 0117 950 4504 **f** 0117 959 1786 **e** enquiries@pva.ltd.uk **w** pva.ltd.uk MD: Pat Vincent.

Red Parrot DJ Management & Agency Unit B204a, Faircharm Studios, 8-10 Creekside, London SE8 3DX **t** 020 8469 3541 **f** 020 8469 3542 **e** red.parrot@virgin.net **w** redparrot.co.uk Contact: Andria Law, Johnston Walker.

Ro-Lo Productions 35 Dillotford Ave, Styvechale, Coventry, W Midlands CV3 5DR **t** 024 7641 0388 or 07711 817475 **f** 024 7641 6615 **e** roger.lomas@virgin.net Prop: Roger Lomas.

RRR Management 96 Wentworth Rd, Birmingham B17 9SY **t** 0121 426 6820 **f** 0121 426 5700 **e** enquiries@rrrmanagement.com **w** rrrmanagement.com MD: Ruby Ryan.

Sasa Music 309, Aberdeen House, 22-24 Highbury Grove, London N5 2EA **t** 020 7359 9232 **f** 020 7359 9233 **e** postroom@sasa.demon.co.uk **w** sasamusic.com MD: David Flower.

Dave Seamer Entertainments 46 Magdalen Rd, Oxford OX4 1RB **t** 0870 756 7382 **f** 0870 756 7383 **e** dave@daveseamer.co.uk **w** daveseamer.co.uk MD: Dave Seamer.

Sensible Events 1st Floor, Regent Arcade House, 19-25 Argyll St, London W1F 7TS **t** 020 7009 3470 **e** Andrew@sensibleevents.com MD: Andrew Zweck.

Serious Ltd 51 Kingsway Pl, Sans Walk, Clerkenwell, London EC1R 0LU **t** 020 7324 1880 **f** 020 7324 1881 **e** david@serious.org.uk **w** serious.org.uk Dir: David Jones.

Solo Agency & Promotions 2nd Floor, 53-55 Fulham High St, London SW6 3JJ **t** 020 7384 6644 **f** 020 3266 1076 **e** soloreception@solo.uk.com **w** solo.uk.com MD: John Giddings.

Sounds Fair Promotions 9 Park Pl, Ashton Keynes, Nr Swindon, Wilts SN6 6NT **t** 01285 861486 **f** 01285 862302 **e** info@soundsfair.freeserve.co.uk **w** soundsfair.freeserve.co.uk Agent: Dave Beckley.

Spun Out 2A Southam St, London W10 5PH **t** 020 8960 3253 **f** 020 8968 5111 **e** caroline@mumbojumbo.co.uk MD: Caroline Hayes.

Steve Allen Entertainments 60 Broadway, Peterborough, Cambs PE1 1SU **t** 01733 569 589 **f** 01733 561 854 **e** steve@sallenent.co.uk **w** sallenent.co.uk Principal: Steve Allen.

Stoneyport Agency 65a Dundas St, Edinburgh EH3 6RS **t** 07968 131 737 **f** 08700 51 05 57 **e** jb@stoneyport.demon.co.uk **w** stoneyport.demon.co.uk MD: John Barrow.

Swamp Music PO Box 94, Derby DE22 1XA **t** 01332 332336 or 07702 564804 **f** 01332 332336 **e** chrishall@swampmusic.co.uk **w** swampmusic.co.uk MD: Chris Hall.

Talking Heads (Voice Agency) 2-4 Noel St, London W1F 8GB **t** 020 7292 7575 **f** 020 7292 7576 **e** voices@talkingheadsvoices.com **w** talkingheadsvoices.com Principal: John Sachs.

13 Artists 34 West St, Brighton BN1 2RE **t** 01273 725 800 **f** 01273 733 247 **e** info@13artists.com MD: Charlie Myatt.

Top Talent Agency Yester Rd, Chiselhurst, Kent BR7 5HN **t** 020 8467 0808 **f** 020 8467 0808 **e** top.talent.agency@virgin.net MD: John Day.

Total Concept Management (TCM) PO Box 128, Dewsbury, West Yorks WF12 9XS **t** 01924 438295 **f** 01924 525378 **e** tcm@totalconceptmanagement.com **w** totalconceptmanagement.com

Vagabond Artists Floor 2, Building B, Tower Bridge Business Complex, 100 Clements Rd, London SE16 1ED **t** 020 7921 8353 **e** rubber_road_records@yahoo.com MD: Dexter Charles.

Value Added Talent 1 Purley Pl, Islington, London N1 1QA **t** 020 7704 9720 **f** 020 7226 6135 **e** vat@vathq.co.uk **w** vathq.co.uk MD: Dan Silver.

Vibe Promotions 91-95 Brick Lane, London E1 6QL **t** 020 7426 0491 **f** 020 7426 0491 **e** info@vibe-bar.co.uk **w** vibe-bar.co.uk Event & Bookings: Adelle Stripe.

Victor Hugo Salsa Show 19, Courtside Dartmouth Rd, London SE26 4RE **t** 020 8291 9236 or 07956 446 342 **e** vhs@victorhugosalsa.com **w** victorhugosalsa.com MD: Victor Hugo.

The Village Agency 43 Brook Green, London W6 7EF **t** 020 7605 5808 **f** 020 7605 5188 **e** firstname@mvillage.co.uk **w** thevillageagency.net Contact: Mary-Anne Costart and Paul Franklyn.

Vision Promotions 22 Upper Grosvenor St, London W1K 7PE **t** 020 7499 8024 **f** 020 7499 8032 **e** vision@visionmusic.co.uk **w** visionmusic.co.uk Head Of Promotions: Rob Dallison.

Vital Edge Artist Agency PO Box 25965, London N18 1YT **t** 0870 350 1045 **f** 0870 350 1046 **e** info@vitaledgeagency.com **w** vitaledgeagency.com Prop: Nicky Jackson.

Wasted 15 Scott St, Bognor Regis, W Sussex PO21 1UH **t** 01243 869115 or 07940 245724 **f** 01243 841252 **e** info@wastedonline.com **w** wastedonline.co.uk Event co-ordinator: Tim Harris.

Jason West Agency Gables House, Saddle Bow, Kings Lynn, Norfolk PE34 3AR **t** 01553 617586 **f** 01553 617734 **e** info@jasonwest.com **w** jasonwest.com MD: Jason West.

X-ray Touring Second Floor, Curtain House, 134-146 Curtain Rd, London EC2A 3AR **t** 020 7920 7666 **f** 020 7920 7663 **e** info@xraytouring.com Contact: Jo Biddiscombe.

XFactory 20 Boughton House, Bowling Green Pl, London SE1 1YF **t** 020 7403 1830 **e** contact@xfactory.co.uk **w** xfactory.co.uk Dir: Nigel Proktor.

X-Rated Management Wimbourne House, 155 New North Rd, London N1 6TA **t** 020 7168 4287 **f** 070 9284 1131 **e** mike@x-rated.me.uk **w** x-rated.me.uk Artist Managers: Michael Hague and Brian Noonan.

Zedfunk Dj's & Artists PO Box 7497, London N21 2DX **t** 07010 714 171 **e** djbookings@zedfunk.com **w** zedfunk.com Mgr: Alice Moles.

Concert Promoters

3A Entertainment Ltd 4 Princeton Court, 53-55 Felsham Rd, London SW15 1AZ **t** 020 8789 6111 **f** 020 8789 6222 **e** aaaents@aol.com Dirs: Pete Wilson, Dennis Arnold, Martyn Stanger.

Active 9 Windy Ridge, Park Farm Rd, Bromley, Kent BR1 2RQ **t** 020 8325 2222 **f** 020 8325 2226 **e** info@active-group.co.uk **w** active-group.co.uk MD: Matthew Lewis.

AEG Live 25 Canada Sq, Canary Wharf, London E14 5LQ **t** 020 7536 2600 **f** 020 7536 2603 **e** info@aegworldwide.co.uk **w** theo2.co.uk CEO: David Campbell.

Aiken Promotions 58-59 Thomas St, Dublin 8, Ireland **t** +353 1 454 6656 **f** +353 1 454 6787 **e** office@aikenpromotions.com **w** aikenpromotions.com Office Mgrs: Mary Kelly / Sorcha.

Aiken Promotions Ltd Marlborough House, 348 Lisburn Rd, Belfast BT9 6GN **t** 028 9068 9090 **f** 028 9068 2091 **e** office@aikenpromotions.com **w** aikenpromotions.com MD: Jim Aiken.

A.M.P. 13-14 Margaret St, London W1W 8RN **t** 020 7224 1992 **f** 020 7224 0111 **e** mail@harveygoldsmith.com MD: Harvey Goldsmith CBE.

Anonymous Groove 186 Town St, Armley, Leeds LS12 3RF **t** 0113 368 9912 or 0793 044 3048 **e** info@anonymous-groove.com **w** anonymous-groove.com MD: Chris Shipton.

Artsun 18 Sparkle St, Manchester M1 2NA **t** 0161 273 3435 **f** 0161 273 3695 **e** mailbox@pd-uk.com MD: Gary McClarnan.

b-live Entertainment 507 Old York Rd, London SW18 1DJ **t** 020 8875 2525 **f** 020 8875 2526 **e** info@b-live.co.uk **w** b-live.co.uk MD: Caroline Hollings.

Back Row Productions 71 Endell St, London WC2H 9AJ **t** 020 7836 4422 **f** 020 7836 4425 **e** firstname.lastname@backrow.co.uk **w** backrow.co.uk Account Mgr, Events: Pippa Rayner-Cook.

Badger Promotions PO Box 9121, Birmingham B13 8AU **t** 08712 260 910 **e** info@badgerpromotions.co.uk **w** badgerpromotions.co.uk Promoter: Mark Badger.

Paul Barrett (Rock 'n Roll Enterprises) 21 Grove Terrace, Penarth, South Glamorgan CF64 2NG **t** 029 2070 4279 **f** 029 2070 9989 **e** barrettrocknroll@ntlworld.com MD: Paul Barrett.

BB Promotions 3 Roberts Rd, Pokesdown, Bournemouth BH7 6LN **t** 07749 768 904 **e** info@bb-promotions.co.uk **w** bb-promotions.co.uk Contact: Bert Burnell.

BDA 32 Chiltern Rd, Culcheth, Warrington, Cheshire WA3 4LL **t** 01925 766655 **f** 01925 765577 **e** brian.durkin@btinternet.com MD: Brian Durkin.

HMV Birmingham International Jazz Festival PO Box 944, Birmingham B16 8UT **t** 0121 454 7020 **f** 0121 454 9996 **e** bigbearmusic@compuserve.com **w** bigbearmusic.com Festival Dir: Jim Simpson.

BKO Productions Ltd The Old Truman Brewery, 91 Brick Lane, London E1 6QL **t** 020 7377 9373 **f** 020 7377 6523 **e** byron@bko-alarcon.co.uk Dir: Byron Orme.

Blow Up PO Box 4961, London W1A 7ZX **t** 020 7636 7744 **f** 020 7636 7755 **e** webmaster@blowup.co.uk **w** blowup.co.uk MD: Paul Tunkin.

Borderline Promotions 157 Charing Cross Rd, London WC2H 0EN **t** 020 7434 9592 **f** 020 7437 1781 **e** beveritt@meanfiddler.co.uk Contact: Barry Marshall Everitt.

Bugbear Promotions 3A Highbury Crescent, London N5 1RN **t** 020 7700 0550 or 020 7700 0880 **e** info@bugbearbookings.com **w** bugbearbookings.com Contact: Jim Mattison, Tony Gleed.

Mel Bush Organization Ltd Tanglewood, Arrowsmith Rd, Wimbourne, Dorset BH21 3BG **t** 01202 691891 **f** 01202 691896 **e** mbobmth@aol.com MD: Mel Bush.

Cathouse Promotions Ltd 21 Sandyford Pl, Glasgow G3 7NG **t** 0141 572 1120 **f** 0141 572 1121 **e** enquire@cplweb.com **w** cplweb.com MD: Donald Macleod.

CC Girlz - Concerts For Causes 17 Thomas More House, Barbican, London EC2Y 8BT **t** 020 7588 6050 or 07952 982 467 **e** anita@ccgirlz.com Contact: Anita Strymowicz, Dom Flewitt.

Channelfly Enterprises 59-61 Farringdon Rd, London EC1M 3JB **t** 020 7691 4555 **f** 020 7691 4666 **e** info@channelfly.net **w** channelfly.com MD: Jason Bick.

Charabanc Promotions 18 Sparkle St, Manchester M1 2NA **t** 0161 273 5554 **f** 0161 273 5554 **e** charabanc@btconnect.com **w** charabanc.net MD: Richard Lynch.

Classic Rock (UK) Ltd 47 Brecks Lane, Rotherham, S Yorks S65 3JQ **t** 01709 702575 **e** martin@classicrocksociety.co.uk **w** classicrocksociety.com MD: Martin Hudson.

CMC PO Box 3, Newport NP20 3YB **t** 07973 715 875 **f** 01633 677 672 **e** alanjones@cmcpromotions.co.uk Principal: Alan Jones.

The Contemporary Music Centre 19 Fishamble St, Temple Bar, Dublin 8, Ireland **t** +353 1 673 1922 **f** +353 1 648 9100 **e** info@cmc.ie **w** cmc.ie Dir: Eve O'Kelly.

Cream Group Cream Office, 1 - 3 Parr St, Wolstenholme Sq, Liverpool L1 4JJ **t** 0151 707 1309 **f** 0151 707 1761 **e** gill@cream.co.uk **w** cream.co.uk Event & PR: Gill Nightingale/James Barton.

DCB Promotions 30 A College Green, Bristol BS1 5TB **t** 0117 9834503 **f** 0117 9042269 **e** dave@dcbpromotions.com **w** dcbpromotions.com MD: Dave Brayley.

Dead Or Alive PO Box 34204, London NW5 1FS **t** 020 7482 3908 **e** gigs@deadoralive.org.uk **w** deadoralive.org.uk MD: Nicholas Barnett.

Denis Vaughan Promotions PO Box 28286, London N21 3WT **t** 020 7486 5353 **f** 020 8224 0466 **e** dvaughanmusic@dial.pipex.com Dir: Denis Vaughan.

Tony Denton Promotions Ltd 19 South Molton Lane, London W1K 5LE **t** 020 7629 4666 **f** 020 7629 4777 **e** mail@tdpromo.com **w** tdpromo.com Dir: Tony Denton.

Derek Block Artistes Agency Ltd 70-76 Bell St, Marylebone, London NW1 6SP **t** 020 7724 2101 **f** 020 7724 2102 **e** dbaa@derekblock.co.uk MD: Derek Block.

DF Concerts 272 St Vincent St, Glasgow G2 5RL **t** 0141 566 4999 **f** 0141 566 4998 **e** admin@dfconcerts.co.uk **w** gigsinscotland.com Promoter: Geoff Ellis.

DMP c/o Dingwalls, Middle Yard, Camden Lock, London NW1 8AB **t** 01920 823 098 **f** 01920 823 098 **e** david@dmpuk.com **w** dmpuk.com MD: David Messer.

Electric Broom Cupboard 2 Lauder Court, Coldharbour, Milborne Port, Dorset DT9 5EL **t** 01963 251407 **e** simon@evolver.org.uk **w** evolver.org.uk MD: Simon Barber.

Eurobiketours Corner House, Pullham Lane, Wetwang, Yorks YO25 8XD **t** 01904 431360 **f** 01904 623660 **e** music@eurobiketours.com **w** eurobiketours.com MD: Phillip Sash.

Flick Productions PO Box 888, Penzance, Cornwall TR20 8ZP **t** 01736 788798 **f** 01736 787898 **e** Flickprouk@aol.com MD: Mark Shaw.

The Flying Music Company Ltd FM House, 110 Clarendon Rd, London W11 2HR **t** 020 7221 7799 **f** 020 7221 5016 **e** info@flyingmusic.com **w** flyingmusic.com Dirs: Paul Walden, Derek Nicol.

Folk in the Fall (see Mrs Casey Music).

Geronimo! 15 Canada Copse, Milford, Surrey GU8 5AL **t** 07960 187529 **e** barneyjeavons@supanet.com Promoter: Barney Jeavons.

Get Real Promotions 141 Malmesbury Pk Rd, Charminster, Bournemouth BH8 8PU **t** 08707 40 65 58 **f** 08707 40 65 59 **e** info@getreal2000.co.uk **w** getreal2000.co.uk Promotions Manager: Andy Freeman.

GM Promotions 17 The Athenaeum, 32 Salisbury Rd, Hove, E. Sussex BN3 3AA **t** 01273 774 469 or 07980 917 056 **e** info@gmpromotions.co.uk **w** gmpromotions.co.uk Dir: Laura Ducceschi.

Hallogen Ltd The Bridgewater Hall, Manchester M2 3WS **t** 0161 950 0000 **f** 0161 950 0001 **e** admin@bridgewater-hall.co.uk **w** bridgewater-hall.co.uk Programming Manager: Sara Unwin.

Jef Hanlon Promotions Ltd 1 York St, London W1U 6PA **t** 020 7487 2558 **f** 020 7487 2584 **e** jhanlon@agents-uk.com MD: Jef Hanlon.

Head Music Ltd 2 Munro Terrace, London SW10 0DL **t** 020 7376 4456 **f** 020 7351 5569 **e** straight@freeuk.com Contact: John Curd.

The Headline Agency 39 Churchfields, Milltown, Dublin 14, Ireland **t** +353 1 260 2560 **f** +353 1 261 1879 **e** info@musicheadline.com **w** musicheadline.com MD: Madeleine Seiler.

Chester Hopkins Int Ltd PO Box 536, Headington, Oxford OX3 7LR **t** 01865 766 766 or 020 8441 1555 **f** 01865 769 736 **e** office@chesterhopkins.co.uk **w** chesterhopkins.co.uk MDs: Adrian Hopkins, Jo Chester.

Infinite Events Ltd 2 Dickson Rd, Blackpool, Lancs FY1 2AA **t** 01253 299 606 **f** 01253 299 454 **e** infinite@mct-online.com Contact: Julian Murray.

Insanity Artists Agency Ltd 8 Duncannon St, London WC2N 4JF **t** 020 7484 5078 **f** 020 7484 5089 **e** info@insanitygroup.com **w** insanitygroup.com MD: Andy Varley.

Jay Taylor Flat 114, India House, 75 Whitworth St, Manchester M1 6HB **t** 0161 278 6087 or 07931 797 982 **e** jaytaylor@cwcom.net **w** bone-box.com Promoter: Jay Taylor.

Just Noize PO Box 84, Bexley, Kent DA5 9AP **t** 07796 288 872 **e** info@justnoize.com **w** justnoize.com Dirs: Laurie Moon & David Howson.

Kennedy Street Enterprises Ltd Kennedy House, 31 Stamford St, Altrincham, Cheshire WA14 1ES **t** 0161 941 5151 **f** 0161 928 9491 **e** kse@kennedystreet.com Dir: Danny Betesh.

King Tut's Wah Wah Hut/DF Concerts 272A St Vincent St, Glasgow G2 5RL **t** 0141 248 5158 **f** 0141 248 5202 **e** kingtuts@dfconcerts.co.uk **w** kingtuts.co.uk Promoter/Venue Manager: Dave McGeachan.

Kingstreet Tours G12 Shepherds Studio, Rockley Rd, London W14 0DA **t** 020 7751 1155 **f** 07092 315 184 **e** info@kingstreetgroup.co.uk **w** kingstreetgroup.co.uk CEO: Andrew Wilkinson.

Line-Up PMC 9A Tankerville Pl, Newcastle-upon-Tyne, Tyne and Wear NE2 3AT **t** 0191 281 6449 **f** 0191 212 0913 **e** chrismurtagh@line-up.co.uk **w** line-up.co.uk Owner: Christopher Murtagh.

Live Nation 1st Floor, Regent Arcade House, 19-25 Argyll St, London W1F 7TS **t** 020 7009 3224 **f** 0870 749 0560 **e** firstname.lastname@livenation.co.uk **w** getlive.co.uk MD, UK Music: Stuart Galbraith.

Scott Mackenzie Associates The Gatehouse, Porlock, Mine, Somerset TA24 8ES **t** 01643 863 330 **f** 01643 863 341 **e** enquiries@scottmackenzie.co.uk **w** scottmackenzie.co.uk MD: Scott Mackenzie.

Marshall Arts Leeder House, 6 Erskine Rd, London NW3 3AJ **t** 020 7586 3831 **f** 020 7586 1422 **e** info@marshall-arts.co.uk **w** marshall-arts.co.uk MD: Barrie Marshall.

Matpro Ltd Cary Point, Babbacombe Downs, Torquay, Devon TQ1 3LU **t** 01803 322 233 **f** 01803 322 244 **e** mail@matpro-show.biz **w** babbacombe-theatre.com MD: Colin Matthews.

Maxrock Masefield House, 271 Four Ashes Rd, Dorridge, Solihull, West Midlands B93 8NR **t** 07801 562801 **f** 01564 77 1078 **e** robert@maxrock.co.uk **w** maxrock.co.uk MD: Robert Smith.

Phil McIntyre Promotions 2nd Floor, 35 Soho Sq, London W1D 3QX **t** 020 7439 2270 **f** 020 7439 2280 **e** reception@mcintyre-ents.com Promoter: Paul Roberts.

McLeod Holden Presentations Ltd Priory House, 1133 Hessle Rd, Kingston-upon-Hull, E Yorks HU4 6SB **t** 01482 565444 **f** 01482 353635 **e** Peter.McLeod@mcleod-holden.com **w** mcleod-holden.com Dir: Peter McLeod.

Mean Fiddler Concerts 16 High St, Harlesden, London NW10 4LX **t** 020 8961 5490 **f** 020 8961 9238 **w** meanfiddler.com.

Metropolis Music 69 Caversham Rd, London NW5 2DR **t** 020 7424 6800 **f** 020 7424 6849 **e** mail@metropolismusic.com **w** gigsandtours.com MD: Bob Angus.

Andrew Miller Promotions Int. Ltd 7 Hazlebury Rd, Fulham, London SW6 2NA **t** 020 7471 4775 **f** 020 7371 5545 **e** info@ampi.co.uk **w** ampi.co.uk Dir: Faye Miller.

Montana Concerts 174 Camden High St, London NW1 0NE **t** 020 7267 3939 **f** 020 7482 1955 **e** jon@theunderworldcamden.co.uk Promoter: Jon Vyner.

Mrs Casey Music PO Box 296, Matlock, Derbyshire DE4 3XU **t** 01629 827012 **f** 01629 821874 **e** office@mrscasey.co.uk **w** mrscasey.co.uk MD: Steve Heap.

Music First PO Box 3418, Sheffield S11 7WJ **t** 0114 268 5441 **e** info@musicfirst.info **w** musicfirst.info Promoter: Barney Vernon.

Musicdash Musicdash, PO Box 1977, Manchester M26 2YB **t** 0787 0727 075 **e** jon@musicdash.co.uk **w** manchestermusic.co.uk Dir: Jon Ashley.

NSMA Concerts PO Box 5413, Bournemouth BH1 4UJ **t** 0870 040 6767 **e** info@nsma.com **w** nsma.com MD: Chris Jenkins.

Orange Promotions 3 Charter Court, Linden Grove, New Malden, Surrey KT3 3BL **t** 020 8942 7722 or 07958 967 666 **e** livegigs@mail.com **w** orangepromotions.com Bookings Manager: Phil Brydon.

Partners In Crime 18 Chenies St, London WC1E 7PA **t** 020 8521 7764 or 07973 415 167 **e** saphron@msn.com Promoter: Annette Bennett.

Perfect Words & Music 2 The Teak House, 37 The Avenue, Branksome Pk, Poole, Dorset BH13 6LJ **t** 01202 763208 or 07810 437179 **e** philmurray.pac@talk21.com Booker: Allison Longstaff.

Performing Arts Management Canal 7, Clarence Mill, Bollington, Macclesfield, Cheshire SK10 5JZ **t** 01625 575681 **f** 01625 572839 **e** info@performingarts.co.uk **w** performingarts.co.uk Marketing Manager: Fifi Butler.

Planet Of Sound - Live (Scotland) 236 High St, Ayr, South Ayrshire KA7 1RN **t** 01292 265913 **f** 01292 265493 **e** planet-of-sound@btconnect.com Dir: Ian Hollins.

Platform Music Bedford Chambers, The Piazza, Covent Garden, London WC2E 8HA **t** 07779 582 927 **f** 020 7379 4793 **e** info@platformmusic.net **w** platformmusic.net Promoter: Lisa Cowan.

Plum Music 56b Farringdon Rd, London EC1R 3BL
t 020 7336 7326 **f** 020 7336 7326 **e** info@plummusic.com
w plummusic.com
Dirs: Allan North, Sarah Thirtle, Matthew Grundy.

Plymouth Music Collective Ltd 21-24 St Johns Rd,
Plymouth PL4 0PA **t** 01752 201275 **e** info@pmc.uk.net
w pmc.uk.net Dir: Oli James.

Pollytone Weekenders PO Box 124, Ruislip, Middx
HA4 9BB **t** 01895 638584 **f** 01895 624793
e val@pollyton.demon.co.uk **w** pollytone.com Owner: Val Bird.

Gordon Poole Agency The Limes, Brockley, Bristol,
Somerset BS48 3BB **t** 01275 463222 **f** 01275 462252
e agents@gordonpoole.com **w** gordonpoole.com
Consultant: James Poole.

Psychic Pig Promotions 46-47 Church St, Trowbridge,
Wilts BA14 8PB **t** 07973 314237 **e** alloutmgmt@hotmail.com
Promotions: George Hodgson.

PVC 51 Bath Rd, Southsea, Portsmouth, Hants PO4 0HX
t 023 9275 2782 **f** 023 9275 2782 **e** ianbpvc@hotmail.com
Contact: Ian Binnington.

Real Promotions 140 Cross Lane, Crookes, Sheffield
S10 1WP **t** 07989 347 645 **e** mark@realpromo.co.uk
w realpromo.co.uk Promoter: Mark Roberts.

Regular Music 42 York Pl, Edinburgh EH1 3HU
t 0131 525 6700 **f** 0131 525 6701 **e** mark@regularmusic.co.uk
w regularmusic.co.uk MDs: Mark Mackie, David McBride.

Richard Ogden Management representing Score
44 Sillwood Rd, Brighton BN1 2LE **t** 01273 206 111
f 01273 205 111 **e** richard@richardogdenmanagement.com
w richardogdenmanagement.com MD: Richard Ogden.

Rideout Lillie House, 1a Conduit St, Leicester LE2 0JN
t 0116 2230318 **e** rideout@stayfree.co.uk
w themusicianpub.co.uk Booker: Darren Nockles.

Riverman Concerts Top Floor, George House, Brecon Rd,
London W6 8PY **t** 020 7381 4000 **f** 020 7381 9666
e info@riverman.co.uk **w** riverman.co.uk Dir: David McLean.

RK Promo 78 Church Rd, Northenden, Manchester M22 4WD
t 0161 998 8903 **f** 0161 998 8903 **e** JasonSingh78@aol.com
w RockKitchen.com Promoter: Jason Singh.

RLM Promotions 2A Old Mill Complex, Brown St, Dundee
DD1 5EG **t** 01382 224405 **f** 01382 224406
e mail@rlm-promotions.com **w** rlm-promotions.com
Owner: John Macdonald.

Rooti-Tooti Music - Festival Planning 6 Princess
Cottages, Coffinswell, Newton Abbot TQ12 4SR
t 01803 875 527 **f** 01803 875 527
e graham@tooti.freeserve.co.uk
Venue Programmer: Graham Radley.

Sedgemoor Contemporary Music Group 21 Kings
Drive, Westonzoyland, Somerset TA7 0HJ **t** 07779 723 061
e matt@midnightmango.co.uk **w** midnightmango.co.uk
MD: Matt Bartlett.

Serious Club Promotions PO Box 13143, London N6 5BG
t 020 8815 5550 **f** 020 8815 5559 **e** sam@seriousworld.com
w seriousworld.com MD: Sam O'Riordan.

Serious Ltd 51 Kingsway Pl, Sans Walk, Clerkenwell, London
EC1R 0LU **t** 020 7324 1880 **f** 020 7324 1881
e david@serious.org.uk **w** serious.org.uk Dir: David Jones.

Shark Promotions 23 Rolls Court Ave, Herne Hill, London
SE24 0EA **t** 020 7737 4580 **f** 020 7737 4580
e mellor@organix.fsbusiness.co.uk MD: MH Mellor.

Shh! Promotions 94 St Andrews Rd, Bridport, Dorset
DT6 3BL **t** 01308 421 340 **e** appliedartists@yahoo.co.uk
MD: Andy Head.

Sidmouth International Festival (see Mrs Casey Music).

Sink And Stove Top Floor Office, 53 Coronation Rd,
Southville, Bristol BS3 1AR **t** 0117 907 6931 **f** 0117 907 6931
e info@sinkandstove.com **w** sinkandstove.co.uk
Promoter: Benjamin Shillabeer.

SJM Concerts St Matthews, Liverpool Rd, Manchester
M3 4NQ **t** 0161 907 3443 **f** 0161 907 3446
e vicky@sjmconcerts.com **w** gigsandtours.com
Office Manager: Vicky Potts.

Solo Agency & Promotions 2nd Floor, 53-55 Fulham
High St, London SW6 3JJ **t** 020 7384 6644 **f** 020 3266 1076
e soloreception@solo.uk.com **w** solo.uk.com MD: John Giddings.

Sonic Arts Network Jerwood Space, 171 Union St, London
SE1 0LN **t** 020 7928 7337 **e** phil@sonicartsnetwork.org
w sonicartsnetwork.org Chief Exec: Phil Hallett.

Sound Advice 30 Artesian Rd, London W2 5DD
t 020 7229 2219 **f** 020 7229 9870 **e** info@soundadvice.uk.com
w soundadvice.uk.com MD: Hugh Phillimore.

South West Artist Network 3 Westend Terrace,
Millbrook, Torpoint, Cornwall PL10 1AL **t** 01752 829 138
e chrisfunkymonkey@hotmail.com MD: Christian Murison.

Straight Music 2 Munro Terrace, London SW10 0DL
t 020 7376 4456 **f** 020 7351 5569
e shelley@straightmusic.com MD: John Curd.

Surface Unsigned Festival 20 Pool St, Walsall WS1 2EN
t 07790 137 091 **e** info@surfaceunsigned.co.uk
w surfaceunsigned.co.uk Events Manager: Jay Mitchell.

The Talent Scout 2nd Floor, Swiss Center, 10 Wardour St,
London W1D 6QF **t** 020 7864 1300 **f** 020 7437 1029
e info@thetalentscout.co.uk **w** thetalentscout.co.uk
Dir: Karen Smyth, Helen Douglas.

Towersey Village Festival (see Mrs Casey Music).

Trailer Park Trash PO Box 2679, Bath BA2 3XS
t 07976 152 694 **e** trailparktrash@hotmail.com
w trailerparktrash.org.uk MD: Lee Cotterell.

Traxxevents 3/2, 1 Kennoway Drive, Glasgow G11 7UA
t 0141 341 0691 **f** 0141 341 0691 **e** info@traxxevents.com
w traxxevents.com Dir: Mark MacKechnie.

Truck 15 Percy St, Oxford OX4 3AA **t** 01865 722333
e paul@truckrecords.com **w** truckrecords.com MD: Paul Bonham.

**Urban Music Entertainment Network (U-Men)
Group** PO Box 7874, London SW20 9XD **t** 07050 605219
f 07050 605239 **e** sam@pan-africa.org **w** umengroup.com
CEO: Oscar Sam Carrol Jnr.

Weekender Promotions PO Box 571, Taunton, Somerset
TA1 3ZW **t** 01823 321605 **e** weekenderlive@btopenworld.com
w weekenderlive.co.uk Dir: Paul Dimond.

The World Music Foundation (WMF) Please, visit website for details **e** events@musicaid.org **w** musicaid.org.

World Unlimited 34, Rothesay Croft, Kitwell, Birmingham, W Midlands B32 4JG **t** 01803 875 527 **f** 01803 875 527 **e** graham@tooti.freeserve.co.uk **w** worldunlimited.freeuk.com Music Programmer: Graham Radley.

Zoot Promotions PO Box 3932, Birmingham B30 2EQ **t** 0121 458 3811 or 07958 340162 **f** 0870 055 7785 **e** jackie@zootmusic.net **w** zootmusic.net Promoter: Jackie Wade.

Club Promoters

Oort Ltd 62 Sprules Rd, London SE4 2NN **t** 020 7635 6765 **e** emma@oortmedia.net **w** oortmedia.net Creative Director: Emma Peters.

Plastic Music Ltd 22 Rutland Gardens, Hove, E Sussex BN3 5PB **t** 01273 779 793 **f** 01273 779 820 **e** enzo@plastic-music.co.uk **w** plastic-music.co.uk MD: Enzo (Vincent Amico).

Concert Hire

A.C. Lighting Ltd (Equipment Supply) Centauri House, Hillbottom Rd, High Wycombe, Bucks HP12 4HQ **t** 01494 446000 **f** 01494 461024 **e** sales@aclighting.com **w** aclighting.com Marketing Director: Glyn O'Donoghue. ▲

A-C Technology Ltd 30 Grove Rd, Pinner, Middlesex HA5 5HW **t** 020 8429 3111 **f** 020 8429 4240 **e** actech@btclick.com MD: George Ashley-Cound. ✱

Adlib Audio Ltd Adlib House, Fleming Rd, Speke, Liverpool L24 9LS **t** 0151 486 2216 **f** 0151 448 1454 **e** hire@adlibaudio.co.uk **w** adlibaudio.co.uk MDs: Andy Dockerty, Dave Kay. ✱

Alliance Music Hire 92A Parchmor Rd, Thornton Heath, Surrey CR7 8LX **t** 020 8239 8815 **f** 020 8239 8816 **e** john@jofish-muzik.com MD: John Fisher. ✱

Aquarius Acoustics Unit 1, Stanley St, Colne, Lancs BB9 8HT **t** 01282 859 797 **f** 01282 863 250 **e** dave@aquariusacoustics.com **w** aquariusacoustics.com MD: Dave Pickering. ✱

Atlantic Hire 4 The Limes, North End Way, London NW3 7HG **t** 020 8209 0025 **e** info@atlantichire.com **w** atlantichire.com Ptnr: Jez Strode. ✱

Audile Unit 110, Cariocca Business Pk, Ardwick, Manchester M12 4AH **t** 0161 272 7883 or 07968 156 499 **f** 0161 272 7883 **e** rob@audile.co.uk **w** audile.co.uk Ptnr: Rob Ashworth. ✱

Audio & Acoustics United House, North Rd, London N7 9DP **t** 020 7700 2900 **f** 020 7700 6900 **e** aaaco@aol.com Dir: Nick Kantoch. ●

Audioforum Ltd Unit 20, Dixon Business Centre, Dixon Rd, Brislington, Bristol BS4 5QW **t** 0870 240 6444 **f** 0117 972 3926 **e** sales@audioforum.co.uk **w** audioforum.co.uk MD: Mike Reeves. ✱

Autograph Sales Ltd. Unit 6, Bush Industrial Estate, Station Rd, London N19 5UN **t** 0207 281 7574 **f** 0207 281 3042 **e** debbiel@autograph.co.uk **w** autograph.co.uk GM: Debbie Lovelock. ✱

Avolites Ltd 184 Park Ave, Park Royal, London NW10 7XL **t** 020 8965 8522 **f** 020 8965 0290 **e** hire@avolites.com **w** avolites.com Sales Manager: May Lee. ▲

Banana Row Backline Hire 47 Eyre Pl, Edinburgh EH3 5EY **t** 0131 557 2088 **f** 0131 558 9848 **e** music@bananarow.com MD: Craig Hunter. ✱

Bandit Lites Ltd Hudson Rd, Elm Farm Industrial Estate, Bedford MK41 0LZ **t** 01234 363 820 **f** 01234 365 382 **e** banditUK@banditlites.com **w** banditlites.com GM: Mark Powell.

Batmink Beckery Rd, Glastonbury, Somerset BA6 9NX **t** 01458 833186 **f** 01458 835320 **e** info@batmink.co.uk **w** batmink.co.uk Dir: D Churches. ✱

Bennett Audio 41 Sherriff Rd, London NW6 2AS **t** 07748 705 067 or 020 7372 1077 **e** bennettaudio@f2s.com **w** bennettaudio.co.uk Dir. and Audio Engineer: Clem Bennett.

B&H Sound Services Ltd The Old School, Crowland Rd, Eye, Peterborough, Cambrigeshire PE6 7TN **t** 01733 223535 **f** 01733 223545 **e** sound@bhsound.co.uk **w** bhsound.co.uk PA Mgr: Julian Stanford.

John Boddy Agency 10 Southfield Gardens, Twickenham, Middx TW1 4SZ **t** 020 8892 0133 or 020 8891 3809 **f** 020 8892 4283 **e** jba@johnboddyagency.co.uk **w** johnboddyagency.co.uk MD: John Boddy. ✱

Bonza Sound Services Ltd Alfriston House, Guildford Rd, Normandy, Surrey GU3 2AR **t** 01483 235313 **f** 01483 236015 **e** ray@bonza.co.uk **w** bonza.co.uk MD: Ray Bradman.

Canegreen Unit 2, 12-48 Northumberland Pk, London N17 0TX **t** 020 8801 8133 **f** 020 8801 8139 **e** yan@canegreen.com **w** canegreen.co.uk MD: Yan Stile.

Capital Sound Hire Abacus House, 60 Weir Rd, London SW19 8UG **t** 020 8944 6777 **f** 020 8944 9477 **e** firstname@capital-productions.co.uk **w** capital-productions.co.uk Owner: Keith Davis. ●

CAV Unit F2, Bath Road Trading Estate, Stroud, Gloucs GL5 3QF **t** 01453 751865 **f** 01453 751866 **e** sales@cav.co.uk **w** cav.co.uk Prop: Hans Beier.

Celco Midas House, Willow Way, London SE26 4QP **t** 020 8699 6788 **f** 020 8699 5056 **e** sales@celco.co.uk **w** celco.co.uk Sales: Mark Buss.

Chameleon Pro Audio & Lighting Ltd Orton Industrial Estate, London Rd, Coalville, Leics LE67 3JA **t** 01530 831337 **f** 01530 838319 **e** info@chameleon-pa.co.uk **w** chameleon-pa.co.uk Dir: Stewart Duckworth. ✱

Chaps Production Co 4 Fairdene Rd, Coulsdon, Surrey CR5 1RA **t** 01737 551144 **f** 01737 552244 **e** hires@chapsproduction.com Dir: Steve Ludlam.

Cheltenham Stage Services ltd Unit 31, Ullenwood Court, Ullenwood, Cheltenham, Gloucs GL53 9QS **t** 01242 244978 **f** 01242 250618 **e** enquiries@ullenwood.co.uk **w** ullenwood.co.uk/css Business Manager: Chris Davey.

The Cloud One Group of Companies 24 Proctor St, Birmingham B7 4EE **t** 0121 333 7711 **f** 0121 333 7799 **e** admin@cloudone.net **w** cloudone.net MD: Paul Stratford.

Coast To Coast 3 Lane Top Cottages, Whalley Lane, Denholme, Bradford, W Yorks BD13 4LE **t** 01274 835558 **f** 01274 835558 **e** gerardrolfe@orange.net Dir: Gerard Rolfe.

Concert Lights (UK) Ltd Undershore Works, Brookside Rd, Bolton, Lancs BL2 2SE **t** 01204 391343 **f** 01204 363238 **e** clightuk@aol.com **w** concertlights.com Hire Manager: Chris Sinnott.

Concert Sound Unit C, Park Avenue Ind Estate, Sundon Park Rd, Luton, Beds LU3 3BP **t** 01582 565855 or 07768 418413 **f** 01582 565856 **e** davec@concert-sound.co.uk **w** concert-sound.co.uk GM: David Catlin.

Concert Systems Unit 4D, Stag Industrial Est, Atlantic St, Altrincham, Cheshire WA14 5DW **t** 0161 927 7700 **f** 0161 927 7722 **e** hire@concert-systems.com **w** concert-systems.com Prop: Paul Tandy.

Corporate Events UK Ltd Gratitude, Foxley Lane, Binfield, Berks RG42 4EE **t** 01344 649549 **f** 01344 649549 **e** info@corporateeventsuk.co.uk **w** corporateeventsuk.co.uk Dir: Paul Donnelly.

CPL 18 St Albans Rd, Dartford, Kent DA1 1TF **t** 01322 229923 or 07860 419728 **f** 01322 284145 **e** cshroff@aol.com Contact: Cyrus Shroff.

Creative Lighting And Sound Unit 6, Spires Business Units, Mugiemoss Rd, Bucksburn, Aberdeen AB21 9NY **t** 01224 683111 **f** 01224 686611 **e** clsabdn@aol.com Owner: Mr Flett.

DHA Lighting 284-302 Waterloo Rd, London SE1 8RQ **t** 020 7771 2900 **f** 020 7771 2901 **e** sales@dhalighting.co.uk **w** dhalighting.co.uk MD: Diane Grant.

Die Hard Productions The Fishergate Centre, 4 Fishergate, York YO10 4FB **t** 0845 226 1923 **f** 0870 705 2958 **e** info@diehardproductions.co.uk **w** diehardproductions.co.uk Dir: John McLean.

Dimension Audio Unit 3, 307-309 Merton Rd, London SW18 5JS **t** 020 8877 3414 **f** 020 8877 3410 **e** mail@dimension.co.uk **w** dimension.co.uk MD: Colin Duncan.

Disaster Area PA 44 Arfryn, Llanrhos, Llandudno, Gwynedd LL30 1PB **t** 01492 584065 or 07778 138463 **f** 01492 584065 **e** berenice.hardman@virgin.net **w** touringproductionservices.co.uk Contact: Berenice Hardman.

DM Audio 22 Duddingston Rd, Edinburgh EH15 1NE **t** 0131 620 0456 **f** 0131 620 1423 **e** info@dmaudio.co.uk **w** dmaudio.co.uk Ptnr: Dino Martino.

DPL Production Lighting Units 2 & 3 Dodds Farm, Hatfield Broad Oak, Bishop's Stortford, Herts CM22 7JX **t** 0870 1610 141 **f** 0870 1610 151 **e** darren@dplighting.com **w** dplighting.com Contact: Darren Parker.

Edwin Shirley Staging (ESS) Marshgate Sidings, Marshgate Lane, London E15 2PB **t** 020 8522 1000 **f** 020 8522 1002 **e** jeffb@ess-uk.com **w** ess-uk.com Dir: Jeff Burke.

Empire Mobile Services 15 Hildens Drive, Tilehurst, Berks RG31 5HW **t** 0118 942 7062 **f** 0118 942 7062 **e** geoffwemp@aol.com Prop: Geoff West.

Enlightened Lighting Ltd 2B - 2C, Bath Riverside Business Pk, Riverside Rd, Bath, Somerset BA2 3DW **t** 01225 311964 **f** 01225 445454 **e** enq@enlightenedlighting.co.uk **w** enlightenedlighting.co.uk Dir: Simon Marcus.

Entec Sound And Light 517 Yeading Lane, Northolt, Middlesex UB5 6LN **t** 020 8842 4004 **f** 020 8842 3310 **e** dick@entec-soundandlight.com **w** entec-soundandlight.com Sound Dept Mgr: Dick Hayes.

The Entertainment Company 13 Appledore, Bracknell, Berks RG12 8QY **t** 01344 867089 **f** 01344 305294 **e** info@entertainmentcompany.co.uk **w** entertainmentcompany.co.uk Dir: Paul James.

ESE Audio Great Job's Cross Farm, Hastings Rd, Rolvenden, Kent TN17 4PL **t** 01580 243330 **f** 01580 243216 **e** janewinterese@hotmail.com Ptnr: Jane Winter.

ESS Unit 14, Bleak Hill Way, Hermitage Lane Ind Estate, Mansfield, Notts NG18 5EZ **t** 01623 647291 **f** 01623 622500 **e** richardjohn@orange.net Ptnr: Richard John.

Eurosound (UK) Unit 12, Station Court, Clayton West, Huddersfield, W Yorks HD8 9XJ **t** 01484 866066 **f** 01484 866299 **e** sales@eurosound.co.uk **w** eurosound.co.uk Prod Mgr: Tony Bottomley.

EVPS White House, Magna Rd, Wimborne, Dorset BH21 3AP **t** 01202 579 675 **f** 01202 579 679 **e** ianw@pepuk.com **w** evpsuk.com Dir: Ian Walker.

Fineline The Old Quarry, Clevedon Rd, Failand, Bristol BS8 3TU **t** 01275 395000 **f** 01275 395001 **e** darren@fineline.uk.com **w** fineline.uk.com MD: Darren Wring.

Futurist Projects 136 Thornes Lane, Wakefield, W Yorks WF2 7RE **t** 01924 298900 **f** 01924 298700 **e** info@futurist.co.uk **w** futurist.co.uk MD: Michael Lister.

FX Music 525 Yeading Lane, Northolt, Middlesex UB5 6LN **t** 020 8841 7666 **f** 020 8841 1333 **e** sales@fx-music.co.uk **w** fx-music.co.uk Hire Mgr: Dave Beck. ✳

FX Rentals 38-40 Telford Way, London W3 7XS **t** 020 8746 2121 **f** 020 8746 4100 **e** info@fxrentals.co.uk **w** fxgroup.net Operations Director: Peter Brooks. ●

GB Audio Unit D, 51 Brunswick Rd, Edinburgh EH7 5PD **t** 0131 661 0022 **f** 0131 661 0022 **e** info@gbaudio.co.uk **w** gbaudio.co.uk Contact: G Bodenham.

Hand Held Audio Unit 2, 12-48 Northumberland Pk, London N17 0TX **t** 020 8880 3243 **f** 020 8365 1131 **e** info@handheldaudio.co.uk **w** handheldaudio.co.uk Dir: Mick Shepherd.

HSL Group Ltd Unit O, Ribble Business Pk, Challenge Way, Blackburn BB1 5RB **t** 01254 698808 **f** 01254 698835 **e** simon@hslgroup.com **w** hslgroup.com MD: Simon Stuart.

IllumiNation 75 Leicester Rd, Quorn, Leics LE12 8BA **t** 01509 415374 **f** 01509 620976 **e** andy@quorndon.com Lighting Designer: Andy Liddle.

Intasound PA (NO THIRD PARTY USE) Unit 15, Highgrove Farm Ind Estate, Pinvin, Pershore, Worcs WR10 2LF **t** 01905 841591 **f** 01905 841590 **e** sales@intasoundpa.co.uk **w** intasoundpa.co.uk Lighting Manager: Chris Dale.

Intrak 6 Delaney Drive, Freckleton, Preston, Lancs PR4 1SJ **t** 01772 633697 **f** 01772 634875 **e** mail@intrak.co.uk **w** intraksoundandlight.co.uk Prop: JA Foley.

Jive Entertainment Services PO Box 5865, Corby, Northants NN17 5ZT **t** 01536 406406 or 07831 835635 **f** 01536 400082 **e** hojive@aol.com MD: Dave Bartram.

John Henry's 16-24 Brewery Rd, London N7 9NH
t 020 7609 9181 **f** 020 7700 7040 **e** johnh@johnhenrys.com
w johnhenrys.com MD: John Henry.

Juice Lighting & Sound 9-10 Gresley Close, Drayton Fields,
Daventry, Northants NN11 5RZ **t** 01327 876883
f 01327 310094 **e** sales@juicesound.co.uk **w** juicesound.co.uk
Prop: John Silk.

Kontakt Productions 44b Whifflet St, Coatbridge
ML5 4EL **t** 01236 434 083 **f** 01236 434 083
e gareth@kontaktproductions.com **w** kontaktproductions.com
Studio Manager: Gareth Whitehead. ●

Lancelyn Theatre Supplies Poulton Rd, Bebington, Wirral,
Cheshire CH63 9LN **t** 0151 334 8991 or 0151 334 3000
f 0151 334 4047 **e** sales@lancelyn.co.uk **w** lancelyn.co.uk
Mgr: Bob Baxter.

Light & Sound Design 201 Coventry Rd, Birmingham
B10 0RA **t** 0121 766 6400 **f** 0121 766 6150
e uksales@lsdicon.com **w** fourthphase.com
Ops Mgr: Kevin Forbes.

Lighting Design Services Ltd Crede Barn, Crede Lane,
Old Bosham, Chichester, W Sussex PO18 8NX **t** 01243 575373
f 01243 572076 **e** jon@light-design.co.uk MD: Jon Pope.

Lite Alternative Unit 4, Shadsworth Business Pk, Duttons
Way, Blackburn, Lancs BB1 2QR **t** 01254 279654
f 01254 278539 **e** anyone@lite-alternative.com
w lite-alternative.com Hire Mgr: Jon Greaves.

LXCO Ltd 32A St Stephens Gardens, London W2 5QX
t 020 7467 0810 **f** 020 7467 0811 **e** info@lxco.co.uk
w lxco.co.uk Dir: James Cobb.

Martin Bradley Sound & Light 69A Broad Lane,
Hampton, Middlesex TW12 3AX **t** 020 8979 0672 or
07973 331 451 **f** 020 8979 0672 **e** mslbradley@aol.com
Contact: Martin Bradley.

MCL 18 Lord Byron Sq, Stowell Technical Pk, Salford Quays,
Manchester M50 2XH **t** 0161 745 9933 **f** 0161 745 9975
e jleah@mcl-manchester.com **w** mclwebsite.com
Marketing Manager: John Leah.

Media Control (UK) Ltd 69 Dartmouth Middleway,
Birmingham, W Midlands B7 4UA **t** 0121 333 3333
f 0121 333 3347 **e** hire@mcl-birmingham.com
w mcl-europe.com MD: Tony Cant.

Midnight Electronics Off Quay Building, Foundry Lane,
Newcastle upon Tyne, Tyne and Wear NE6 1LH
t 0191 224 0088 **f** 0191 224 0080
e info@midnightelectronics.co.uk **w** midnightelectronics.co.uk
Mgr: Dave Cross. ●

Mikam Sound (Ireland) Ltd 38 Parkwest Enterprise
Centre, Park West, Dublin 12, Ireland **t** 00 353 1 623 7277
f 00 353 1 623 7350 **e** mikam@iol.ie Contact: Paul Aungier.

Moonlite Productions 12 Chequers End, Winslow, Bucks
MK18 3HT **t** 07966 331 000 **e** info@moonlite.co.uk
w moonlite.co.uk MD: James Iyengar.

Multiplex Productions 239 Clarendon Park Rd, Leicester
LE2 3AN **t** 0116 270 4007 **f** 0116 270 4007
e dave.davies1@virgin.net Mgr: Teri Wyncoll.

Mushroom Hire & Event Services Ltd 3 Encon Court,
Owl Close, Moulton Park Industrial Estate, Northampton
NN3 6HZ **t** 01604 790900 **f** 01604 491118
e info@mushroomevents.co.uk **w** mushroomevents.co.uk
Hire Mgr: Andy Slevin.

Music Bank (Hire) Ltd Buildings C & D, Tower Bridge
Business Complex, 100 Clement's Rd, London SE16 4DG
t 020 7252 0001 **f** 020 7231 3002 **e** nunu@musicbank.org
w musicbank.org Dir: Nunu Whiting.

Music Room The Old Library, 116-118 New Cross Rd, London
SE14 5BA **t** 020 7252 8271 **f** 020 7252 8252
e sales@musicroom.web.com **w** musicroom.web.com
MD: Gordon Gapper.

Nightair Productions Unit 1, Eastfield Side, Sutton In
Ashfield, Notts NG17 4JW **t** 01623 557040 or 01623 455051
f 01623 555586 **e** sales@nightair.co.uk **w** nightair.co.uk
Prop: Andrew Monk.

Nitelites Unit 3E, Howdon Green Ind Est, Norman Terrace,
Wallsend, Tyne and Wear NE28 6SX **t** 0191 295 0009
f 0191 295 0009 **e** nitelites@onyxnet.co.uk Ptnr: Gordon Reay.

Northern Light 35-41 Assembly St, Leith, Edinburgh, Lothian
EH6 7RG **t** 0131 553 2383 or 0131 440 1771 **f** 0131 553 3296
e enquiries@northernlight.co.uk **w** northernlight.co.uk
Hire Mgr: Gordon Blackburn. ▲

OPTI 38 Cromwell Rd, Luton, Beds LU3 1DN **t** 01582 411413
f 01582 400613 **e** optiuk@optikinetics.com **w** optikinetics.com
Sales Dir: Neil Rice.

The PA Company Unit 7, Ashway Centre, Elm Crescent,
Kingston-Upon-Thames, Surrey KT2 6HH **t** 020 8546 6640 or
07836 600 081 **f** 020 8547 1469 **e** thepacompany@aol.com
MD: Doug Beveridge.

PA Music 172 High Rd, East Finchley, London N2 9AS
t 020 8883 4350 **f** 020 8883 5117 **e** mail@pamusic.net
w pamusic.net Prop: Mr MW Lowe.

Pandora Productions Unit 38 Hallmark Trading Ctr, Fourth
Way, Wembley, Middlesex HA9 0LB **t** 020 8795 2432
f 020 8795 2431 **e** pandoraprods@btconnect.com
Prop: John Montier.

Pearce Hire Unit 27, Second Drove, Industrial Estate, Fengate,
Peterborough, Cambs PE1 5XA **t** 01733 554950 or
07850 363543 **f** 01733 892807 **e** info@pearcehire.co.uk
w pearcehire.co.uk Prop: Shaun Pearce.

Pegasus Sound & Light 23-25 Canongate, The Royal Mile,
Edinburgh, Lothian EH8 8BX **t** 0131 556 1300 **f** 0131 557 6466
e pegasussl@aol.com **w** pegasussl.co.uk Sales Mgr: David Hunter.

PG Stage Electrical Studio House, Northstage, Broadway,
Salford M50 2UW **t** 0161 877 4933 **f** 0161 877 4944
e sales@pgstage.co.uk **w** pgstage.co.uk MD: Paul Holt.

Phase 5 Enterprise (Europe) Ltd **t** 0151 353 8163
f 0151 353 1892 **e** info@phase5.uk.com **w** phase5.uk.com
Dir: Haydn Gregson.

PRG Europe 20-22 Fairway Drive, Greenford, Middlesex
UB6 8PW **t** 020 8575 6666 **f** 020 8575 0424 **e** info@prg.com
w prgeurope.com MD: David Keighley.

Prism Lighting Unit 5A, Hampton Industrial Estate, Malpas,
Cheshire SY14 8JQ **t** 01948 820201 **f** 01948 820480
e sales@prismlighting.co.uk **w** prismlighting.co.uk
Ptnr: John Mellen.

PSL Concert Touring The Heights, Cranborne Industrial Estate, Potters Bar, Herts EN6 3JN **t** 01707 648 120 **f** 01707 648 123 **e** pod.bluman@presservgroup.com **w** presservgroup.com Dir: Pod Bluman. ✳

Pure Energy Production Services Suite 91, 2 Lansdowne Crescent, Bournemouth, Dorset BH1 1SA **t** 01202 579673 **f** 01202 579679 **e** sales@pepuk.com **w** pepuk.com Dir: Ian Walker.

RG Jones Sound Engineering 16 Endeavour Way, London SW19 8UH **t** 020 8971 3100 **f** 020 8971 3101 **e** info@rgjones.co.uk **w** rgjones.co.uk Hire Dept Mgr: John Carroll.

Rhythm Audio Rhythm House, King St, Carlisle, Cumbria CA1 1SJ **t** 01228 515141 **f** 01228 515161 **e** hire@rhythmaudio.co.uk **w** rhythmaudio.co.uk Head of Prod: Ian Howe.

Runway UK 163 Victoria Rd, Horley, Gatwick, Surrey RH6 7BF **t** 01293 820758 **f** 01293 408885 **e** info@runwayuk.com **w** runwayuk.com Prop: Andy Wildy.

SAV Ltd Party House, Mowbray Drive, Blackpool FY3 7JR **t** 01253 302602 **f** 01253 301000 **e** sales@stardream.co.uk Technical Director: Steve Salisbury.

Sensible Music (Ireland) Unit 53, Parkwest Enterprise Centre, Ningor Rd, Dublin 12 Ireland **t** +353 1 620 8321 **f** +353 1 620 8322 **e** info@sensiblemusic.ie **w** sensiblemusic.ie Dir: John Munnis.

Show Presentation Services Unit 6, Northolt Trading Estate, Belvue Rd, Northolt, Middx UB5 5QS **t** 0870 240 0904 **f** 0870 240 0905 **e** info@showpres.com **w** showpres.com Sales Director: Bryan Leathem. ✳

The Small PA Company 49 Liddington Rd, London E15 3PL **t** 020 8536 0649 or 07785 584 273 **f** 07092 022 897 **e** ian@soundengineer.co.uk **w** soundengineer.co.uk MD: Ian Hasell.

Matt Snowball Music Unit 2, 3-9 Brewery Rd, London N7 9QJ **t** 020 7700 6555 **f** 020 7700 6990 **e** enquiries@mattsnowball.com **w** mattsnowball.com Hire/Sales: Kent Jolly.

Sound And Light Productions PO Box 32295, London W5 1WD **t** 0870 066 0272 **f** 0870 066 0273 **e** info@soundandlightproductions.co.uk **w** soundandlightproductions.co.uk Ptnr: John Denby.

Sound Hire Unit 7, Kimpton Trade Business Centre, Minden Rd, Sutton, Surrey SM3 9PF **t** 020 8644 1248 **f** 020 8644 6642 **e** richard@sound-hire.com **w** sound-hire.com MD: Richard Lienard.

Sound of Music 14 Runswick Drive, Wollaton, Nottingham NG8 1JD **t** 0115 875 6359 or 07946 739 384 **e** info@pahire.com **w** pahire.com Mgr: Sash Pochibko.

SouthWestern Management 13 Portland Rd, Street, Somerset BA16 9PX **t** 01458 445186 or 07831 437062 **f** 01458 841186 **e** info@sw-management.co.uk **w** sw-management.co.uk Dir: Chris Hannam.

SRS (Norwich) 59 Darrell Pl, Norwich, Norfolk NR5 8QN **t** 01603 250486 or 07850 235161 **f** 01603 250486 **e** srs@deafgeoff.co.uk Owner: Geoff Lowther.

SSE Hire Ltd Burnt Meadow House, Burnt Meadow Rd, North Moons Moat, Redditch, Worcs B98 9PA **t** 01527 528 822 **f** 01527 528 840 **e** enquiries@sseaudio.com **w** sseaudiogroup.com Dir: John Penn.

Stage Audio Services Unit 2, Bridge St, Wordsley, Stourbridge DY8 5YU **t** 01384 263629 **f** 01384 263620 **e** kevinmobers@aol.com Dir: Kevin Mobberley. ●

Stage Electrics Third Way, Avonmouth, Bristol BS11 9HB **t** 0117 938 4000 **f** 0117 916 2828 **e** sales@stage-electrics.co.uk **w** stage-electrics.co.uk Hire Mgr: Adrian Searle.

Stage Light Design Unit 11, College Fields Business Ctr, Prince George's Rd, London SW19 2PT **t** 020 8640 4100 **f** 020 8640 3400 **e** mw@stagelightdesign.com **w** stagelightdesign.com MD: John Rinaldi.

Stage Two Hire Services Unit J, Penfold Trading Estate, Imperial Way, Watford, Herts WD24 4YY **t** 01923 230789 or 01923 244822 **f** 01923 255048 **e** richard.ford@stage-two.co.uk **w** stagetwo.co.uk Hire Mgr: Richard Ford.

Star Events Group Milton Rd, Thurleigh, Beds MK44 2DG **t** 01234 772233 **f** 01234 772272 **e** firstname.lastname@stareventsgroup.com **w** StarEventsGroup.com Dir: Mark Armstrong.

Stratford Acoustics 24 Procter St, Birmingham B7 4EE **t** 0121 333 7711 **f** 0121 333 7799 **e** admin@cloudone.net **w** cloudone.net MD: Paul Stratford.

STS Touring Productions Ltd Unit 103-104, Cariocca Business Pk, Hellidon Close, Ardwick, Manchester M12 4AH **t** 0161 273 5984 **f** 0161 272 7772 **e** ststouring@aol.com **w** ststouring.co.uk Dir: Peter Dutton. ✳

Sub Zero Music 20-22 Mount Pleasant, Bilston, Wolverhampton, W Midlands WV14 7LJ **t** 01902 405511 **f** 01902 401418 **e** music@therobin.co.uk **w** subzeromusic.com Dir: Mike Hamblett.

System Sound (UK) Ltd 1 Liddall Way, Horton Rd, West Drayton, Middlesex UB7 8PG **t** 01895 432995 **f** 01895 432976 **e** design@systemsound.com **w** systemsound.com Dir: Simon Biddulph.

Tega (Hull) Limited 58 Stockholm Rd, Sutton Fields Ind. Est, Hull, E Yorks HU7 0XW **t** 01482 831 031 or 07900 215 024 **f** 01482 831 331 **e** hire@tega.co.uk **w** tega.co.uk Business Development: Richard Moorhouse. ✳

Terminal Studios 4-10 Lamb Walk, London Bridge, London SE1 3TT **t** 020 7403 3050 **f** 020 7407 6123 **e** info@terminal.co.uk **w** terminal.co.uk Prop: Charlie Barrett.

Tiger Hire Unit 3, Grove Farms, Milton Hill, Abingdon, Oxon OX14 4DP **t** 01235 834000 **f** 01235 820022 **e** jim@tigerhire.com **w** tigerhire.com Owner: Jim Parsons.

TMC Hillam Rd, off Canal Rd, Bradford, W Yorks BD2 1QN **t** 01274 370966 **f** 01274 308706 **e** sales@tmc.ltd.uk **w** tmc.ltd.uk Sales Mgr: Nick Bolton.

TMS Show Services Chichester Rd, Sidlesham Common, Sidlesham, Chichester PO20 7PY **t** 01243 641166 **f** 01243 641888 **e** info@tms1.co.uk Ptnr: Dick Edney.

Tourtech 3 Quarry Park Close, Moulton Park Industrial Estate, Northampton NN3 6QB **t** 01604 494846 **f** 01604 642454 **e** tourtecuk@aol.com **w** tourtech.co.uk MD: Dick Rabel.

Venues

Travelling Light (Birmingham) Ltd Unit 34, Boulton Industrial Centre, Icknield St, Birmingham, W Midlands B18 5AU **t** 0121 523 3297 **f** 0121 551 2360 Dir: Chris Osborn.

Roy Truman Sound Services Unit 23, Atlas Business Centre, Oxgate Lane, London NW2 7HJ **t** 020 8208 2468 **f** 020 8208 3320 **e** rtss@london.com Mgr: Elisabeth Wirrer.

TSProfessional SOUND + LIGHT Unit 6, Avocet Trading Estate, Burgess Hill, W Sussex RH15 9NH **t** 01444 23 30 30 **f** 01444 23 31 59 **e** sales@tsprofessional.co.uk **w** tsprofessional.co.uk MD: Keith Upton. ✳

Up All Night Music 20 Denmark St, London WC2H 8NA **t** 020 7419 4696 **e** info@upallnightmusic.com **w** upallnightmusic.com MD: Phil Taylor.

Utopium Lighting Unit D, The Siston Centre, Station Rd, Kingswood, Bristol BS15 4GQ **t** 0870 950 3399 **f** 0870 950 3355 **e** colin@utopium.co.uk **w** utopium.co.uk Prod Mgr: Colin Bodenham.

Villa Audio Ltd Baileys Yard, Chatham Green, Little Waltham, Essex CM3 3LE **t** 01245 361694 **f** 01245 362281 **e** sales@villa-audio.com **w** villa-audio.com MD: Gareth Jones.

Volume Audio 6 All Saints Crescent, Garston, Watford, Herts WD25 0LU **t** 01923 673027 **f** 01923 893733 **e** david@finn.com Dir: David Finn.

Whitelight Electrics Ltd 20 Merton Park Ind Est, Jubilee Way, London SW19 3WL **t** 020 8254 4820 **f** 020 8254 4821 **e** info@whitelight.ltd.uk **w** whitelight.ltd.uk GM: Bryan Raven.

Wigwam Unit 6, Junction 19 Ind Est, Green Lane, Haywood, Lancs OL10 1NB **t** 01706 363400 or 01706 363800 **f** 01706 363410 **e** events@wigwam.co.uk **w** wigwam.co.uk MD: Mike Spratt. ✳

Zig Zag Lighting (South) 68 Morton Gardens, Wallington, Surrey SM6 8EX **t** 020 8647 1968 **f** 020 8401 2216 **e** kev@zigzag-lighting.com Prop: Kevin Ludlam.

Zique Audio Highfield Works, John St, Hinkley, Leics LE10 1UY **t** 01455 610364 or 07831 342355 **f** 01455 610164 **e** garry@msn.com (DO NOT PUBLISH) Prop: Gary Hargraves.

Zisys AVMN Ltd. 1 Alexander Pl, Irvine, Ayrshire KA12 0UR **t** 01294 204213 **e** danny@zisysavmn.co.uk **w** zisysavmn.co.uk Dir: Danny Anderson.

Sign up to the Free Music Week Daily email news service at www.musicweek.com

3 B's Bar and Cafe Reading Town Hall, Blagrave St, Reading, Berks RG1 1QH **t** 0118 939 9815 **f** 0118 956 6719 **e** andrew.hefferan@reading.gov.uk Bookings Mgr: Andy Hefferan. Seated Capacity: 95 Standing Capacity: 150

12 Bar Club Denmark St, London WC2H 8NL **t** 020 7916 6989 **e** 12barclub@btconnect.com **w** 12barclub.com Bookings Mgr: Andy Lowe.

42nd Street Nightclub 2 Bootle St, off Deansgate, Manchester M2 5GU **t** 0161 831 7108 **f** 0161 831 7108 **e** simon@42ndstreetnightclub.com **w** 42ndstreetnightclub.com Mgr: Simon Jackson.

53 Degrees Brook St, Preston, Lancs PR1 2TQ **t** 01772 894861 **f** 01772 894970 **e** devans@53degrees.net **w** 53degrees.net Ents Mgr: David Evans. Standing Capacity: 1200

100 Club 100 Oxford St, London W1D 1LL **t** 020 7636 0933 **f** 020 7436 1958 **e** info@the100club.co.uk the100club.co.uk Prop: Geoff Horton. Seated Capacity: 290 Standing Capacity: 290

606 Club 90 Lots Rd, London SW10 0QD **t** 020 7352 5953 **f** 020 7349 0655 **e** jazz@606club.co.uk **w** 606club.co.uk Owner: Steve Rubie. Seated Capacity: 130 Standing Capacity: 165

ABC 300 Sauchiehall St, Glasgow GS 3JA **t** 0141 332 2232 or 0141 352 4569 (Bkgs) **e** mig@abcglasgow.com **w** abcglasgow.com Bookings Mgr: Mig. Standing Capacity: 1550

Aberdeen Exhibition and Conference Centre Bridge of Don, Aberdeen AB23 8BL **t** 01224 824824 **f** 01224 825276 **e** firstinitial+surname@aecc.co.uk **w** aecc.co.uk Concert Bookings: Louise Stewart. Seated Capacity: 4700 Standing Capacity: 8000

Aberdeen Music Hall Union St, Aberdeen AB10 1QS **t** 01224 632 080 **f** 01224 632 400 **e** musichallinfo@aberdeenperformingarts.com **w** musichallaberdeen.com Venue Manager: Julie Sinclair. Seated Capacity: 1282 Standing Capacity: 1500

Aberdeen University Union Union Bar, 10 Littlejohn St, Aberdeen AB10 1BA **t** 01224 638 369 **f** 01224 638 369 **e** adg155@abdn.ac.uk **w** abdn.ac.uk\union Ents Mgr: Duncan Stuart. Seated Capacity: 500 Standing Capacity: 600

Aberystwyth Arts Centre Penglais, Aberystwyth, Ceredigion SY23 3DE **t** 01970 622882 **f** 01970 622883 **e** lla@aber.ac.uk **w** aber.ac.uk/artscentre Dir: Alan Hewson. Seated Capacity: 1000 Standing Capacity: 1200

The Academy Cleveland Rd, Uxbridge, Middlesex UB8 3PH **t** 01895 267 447 **f** 01895 462 300 **e** firstname.lastname@brunel.ac.uk **w** brunelstudents.com Promoter: Stephen Dedman. Seated Capacity: 450 Standing Capacity: 600

Accrington Town Hall Blackburn Rd, Accrington, Lancs BB5 1LA **t** 01254 380297 **f** 01254 380291 **e** leisure@hyndburnbc.gov.uk **w** leisureinhyndburn.co.uk Mrktng & Events Officer: Nigel Green. Seated Capacity: 400 Standing Capacity: 360

AK Bell Library York Pl, Perth PH2 8EP **t** 01738 444949 **f** 01738 477010 **e** kmcwilliam@pkc.gov.uk **w** pkc.gov.uk Theatre Mgr: Kenny McWilliam. Seated Capacity: 125

The Alban Arena Civic Centre, St Albans, Herts AL1 3LD **t** 01727 861078 **f** 01727 865755 **e** info@alban-arena.co.uk **w** alban-arena.co.uk GM: Paul McMullen. Seated Capacity: 856 Standing Capacity: 1132

The Albany Douglas Way, London SE8 4AG **t** 020 8692 0231 **f** 020 8469 2253 **e** reception@thealbany.org.uk **w** thealbany.org.uk Programmer: Gavin Barlow. Seated Capacity: 300 Standing Capacity: 425

Albert Halls Dumbarton Rd, Stirling FK8 2QL **t** 01786 473544 **f** 01786 448933 **e** alberthalls@stirling.gov.uk **w** stirling.gov.uk/alberthalls Venues Mgr: Jess Brown. Seated Capacity: 893 Standing Capacity: 1200

Alexandra Palace Alexandra Palace Way, Wood Green, London N22 7AY **t** 020 8365 2121 **f** 020 8365 2662 **e** info@alexandrapalace.com **w** alexandrapalace.com Head of Sales & Mkting: Chris Gothard. Seated Capacity: 7250 Standing Capacity: 7250

Alexandra Theatre Station St, Birmingham, W Midlands B5 4DS **t** 0121 643 5536 **f** 0121 632 6841 **e** firstname.lastname@clearchannel.co.uk **w** getlive.co.uk GM: Andrew Lister. Seated Capacity: 1365

Alloa Town Hall 6 Mars Hill, Alloa, Clackmannan FK10 1AB **t** 01259 222345 **f** 01259 222341 **e** leisure@clacks.gov.uk **w** clacks.gov.uk Activity & Events Coord.. Seated Capacity: 500

Angel Centre Angel Lane, Tonbridge, Kent TN9 1SF **t** 0870 116 1471 **f** 0870 116 1472 **e** angel.leisurecentre@tmbc.gov.uk **w** angelcentre.co.uk Operations Mgr: Sarah Thomas. Seated Capacity: 1100 Standing Capacity: 1500

Anglia Polytechnic University Students Union, East Rd, Cambridge CB1 1PT **t** 01223 460008 **f** 01223 417718 **e** a.tadjrishi@apusu.com **w** apusu.com Ents Mgr: Ash Tadjrishi. Seated Capacity: 230 Standing Capacity: 300

The Anvil Churchill Way, Basingstoke, Hants RG21 7QR **t** 01256 819797 **f** 01256 331733 **e** Ann.Dickson@theanvil.co.uk **w** theanvil.org.uk Prog Mgr: Ann Dickson. Seated Capacity: 1400

Apollo Theatre Shaftesbury Ave, London W1V 7HD **t** 020 7240 0880 **f** 020 7434 1217 **e** info@rutheatres.com **w** rutheatres.com Concerts & Hirings Mgr: Mike Townsend. Seated Capacity: 775

Apollo Victoria 17 Wilton Rd, London SW1V 1LG **t** 020 7834 6318 **f** 08707 492 351 **e** firstname.lastname@livenation.co.uk **w** getlive.co.uk GM: Richard Brown. Seated Capacity: 1564

Aqua Cafe Bar Albion Wharf, Albion St, Manchester M1 5LN **t** 0161 228 1800 Contact: John Houghton. Standing Capacity: 400

The Arches 253 Argyle St, Glasgow, Lanarkshire G1 4PR **t** 0141 565 1009 **f** 0141 565 1001 **e** info@thearches.co.uk **w** thearches.co.uk Music Programmer. Seated Capacity: 330 Standing Capacity: 800

Area Gade House, 46 The Parade, High St, Watford, Herts WD17 1AY **t** 01923 281100 or 01923 281500 **f** 01923 281101 **e** chris@areaclub.com **w** areaclub.com Events & PR Manager: Neil Campbell. Seated Capacity: 1500 Standing Capacity: 1500

The Arena 208 Newport Rd, Middlesbrough TS1 5PS **t** 01642 503128 **f** 01642 503128 **e** info@thearena.co.uk **w** thearena.co.uk Bookings Mgrs: Edzy. Standing Capacity: 600

Artslink Theatre Knoll Rd, Camberley, Surrey GU15 3SY **t** 01276 707612 **f** 01276 707644 Contact: Pat Pembridge. Seated Capacity: 400 Standing Capacity: 600

Ashcroft Theatre Park Lane, Croydon, Surrey CR9 1DG **t** 020 8681 0821 **f** 020 8760 0835 **e** ashcroft@fairfield.co.uk **w** fairfield.co.uk.

Assembly Hall Stoke Abbott Rd, Worthing, W Sussex BN11 1HQ **t** 01903 231 799 **f** 01903 215 337 **e** theatres@worthing.gov.uk **w** worthingtheatres.co.uk Theatres Manager: Peter Bailey. Seated Capacity: 940 Standing Capacity: 1100

Assembly Hall Theatre Crescent Rd, Royal Tunbridge Wells, Kent TN1 2LU **t** 01892 530613 or 01892 532072 **f** 01892 525203 **e** theatreadmin@tunbridgewells.gov.uk **w** assemblyhalltheatre.co.uk Marketing Mgr: Sheila Ryall. Seated Capacity: 930 Standing Capacity: 1000

Assembly Rooms Market Pl, Derby DE1 3AH **t** 01332 255443 **f** 01332 255788 **e** assemblyrooms@derby.gov.uk **w** derby.gov.uk/assembly GM: Peter Ireson. Seated Capacity: 1500 Standing Capacity: 2000

Assembly Rooms 54 George St, Edinburgh, Midlothian EH2 2LR **t** 0131 624 2442 **f** 0131 624 7131 **e** info@assemblyrooms.com **w** assemblyrooms.com GM: Kath M Mainland. Seated Capacity: 700 Standing Capacity: 750

Aston University Students Guild The Triangle, Birmingham B4 7ES **t** 0121 359 6531 **f** 0121 333 4218 **e** l.b.cook@aston.ac.uk **w** astonguild.org.uk Venues Mgr: Larry Cook. Seated Capacity: 400 Standing Capacity: 942

Aylesbury Civic Centre Market Sq, Aylesbury, Bucks HP20 1UF **t** 01296 585527 **f** 01296 392091 **e** aabbott@aylesburyvaledc.gov.uk **w** aylesburycivic.org Mgr: Sam McCaffrey. Seated Capacity: 640 Standing Capacity: 1000

Babbacombe Theatre Babbacombe Downs, Torquay, Devon TQ1 3LU **t** 01803 322233 **f** 01803 322244 **e** colin@matpro-show.biz **w** babbacombe-theatre.com Resident Dir: Colin Matthews. Seated Capacity: 600

BAC Lavender Hill, London SW11 5TN **t** 020 7223 6557 or 020 7223 2223 (box) **f** 020 7978 5207 **e** venues@bac.org.uk **w** bac.org.uk Programme Administrator: Lydia Spry. Seated Capacity: 170

Bar Academy Islington N1 Centre, 16 Parkfield St, London N1 0PS **t** 020 7288 4400 **f** 020 7288 4401 **e** mail@islington-academy.co.uk **w** islington-academy.co.uk. Standing Capacity: 250

Barbican Centre Silk St, Barbican, London EC2Y 8DS
t 020 7638 4141 or 020 7382 7242 **f** 020 7382 7037
e press@barbican.org.uk **w** barbican.org.uk
HoM: Robert Van Leer. Seated Capacity: 1989

Barfly Birmingham 78 Digbeth High St, Birmingham
B5 6DY **t** 0121 633 8311 **f** 0121 633 8344
e Karen.davies@barflyclub.com **w** barflyclub.com
Promoter: Karen Davies.

Barfly Camden The Monarch, 49 Chalk Farm Rd, London
NW1 8AN **t** 020 7691 4244 **f** 020 7691 4243
e Terry.Kirby@Barflyclub.com **w** barflyclub.com
Promoter: Terry Kirby. Standing Capacity: 200

Barfly Cardiff Kingsway, Cardiff CF10 3FD
t 02920 396 589 **f** 02920 396 783
e Mark.Walker@barflyclub.com **w** barflyclub.com
Promoter: Mark Walker. Standing Capacity: 200

Barfly Glasgow Riverside House, 260 Clyde St, Glasgow,
Lanarkshire G1 4JH **t** 0141 204 5700 **f** 0141 204 5711
e Brian.Reynolds@Barflyclub.com **w** barflyclub.com
Promoter: Brian Reynolds. Standing Capacity: 400

Barfly Liverpool 90 Seel St, Liverpool L1 4BH
t 0151 707 6171 **f** 0151 707 9885
e Lyndsey.Boggis@Barflyclub.com **w** barflyclub.com
Promoter: Lyndsey Boggis. Seated Capacity: 225
Standing Capacity: 400

Barrowlands Ballroom 244 Gallowgate, Glasgow,
Lanarkshire G4 0TS **t** 0141 552 4601 **f** 0141 552 4997
e manager@glasgow-barrowland.com
w glasgow-barrowland.com Contact: Stan Riddet.
Standing Capacity: 1900

Bartok 78-79 Chalk Farm Rd, London NW1 8AR
t 020 7916 0595 **w** meanfiddler.com.

The Basement 4-8 Fisher St, Carlisle, Cumbria CA3 8RN
t 01228 510444 **e** Jnightclub@aol.com **w** Jnightclub.com
Promoter/Owner: David Jackson. Standing Capacity: 600

Bath Pavilion North Parade Rd, Bath BA2 4EU
t 01225 486902 **f** 01225 486976
e bath.pavilion@aquaterra.org **w** aquaterra.org GM: Jenny Jacob.
Seated Capacity: 1000 Standing Capacity: 800

Bath Spa University College Students Union, Newton Pk,
Bath BA2 9BN **t** 01225 875588 **f** 01225 874765
e bathspasu@bathspa.ac.uk **w** bathspasu.co.uk
Events: Diane Starling. Standing Capacity: 250

Bath Theatre Royal St John's Pl, Sawclose, Bath BA1 1ET
t 01225 448815 **f** 01225 444080
e firstname.lastname@theatreroyal.org.uk **w** theatreroyal.org.uk
TRB Productions: Nicky Palmer. Seated Capacity: 978

Beach Ballroom Beach Leisure Centre, Beach Promenade,
Aberdeen AB2 1NR **t** 01224 647647 **f** 01224 648693.
Seated Capacity: 1200

Beau Sejour Centre Amherst, St Peter Port, Guernsey,
Channel Islands GY1 2DL **t** 01481 747210 **f** 01481 747298
e cultureleisure@gov.gg **w** freedomzone.gg
Events Mgr: Penny Weaver. Seated Capacity: 1500
Standing Capacity: 2000

Beck Theatre, Hayes Grange Rd, Hayes, Middlesex
UB3 2UE **t** 020 8561 7506 **f** 020 8561 0896
e firstname.lastname@livenation.co.uk **w** getlive.co.uk
GM: Louise Clifford. Seated Capacity: 600

The Bedford Arms 77 Bedford Hill, Balham, London
SW12 9HD **t** 020 8682 8941 **e** info@thebedford.co.uk
w thebedford.co.uk Dir, Music, Art & Dev't: Tony Moore.
Seated Capacity: 250

Bedford Corn Exchange St Paul's Sq, Bedford MK40 1SL
t 01234 344813 **f** 01234 325358
e cornexch-bedford@btinternet.com
w bedfordcornexchange.co.uk Mgr: Carl Amos.
Seated Capacity: 830 Standing Capacity: 1000

Belgrade Theatre Belgrade Sq, Coventry CV1 1GS
t 024 7625 6431 **f** 024 7655 0680 **e** admin@belgrade.co.uk
w belgrade.co.uk Artistic Dir: Hamish Glen. Seated Capacity: 865

The Betsey Trotwood 56 Farringdon Rd, London
EC1R 3BL **t** 020 7336 7326 **e** info@plummusic.com
w plummusic.com Promoters: Sarah Thirtle, Matthew Grundy.
Standing Capacity: 60

The Bierkeller All Saints St, Bristol BS1 2NA
t 0117 926 8514 **f** 0117 925 1347 **e** bs1bierkeller@aol.com
w bristolbierkeller.co.uk Promoter: Dave Hebson.
Standing Capacity: 750

The Big Chill House 257-259 Pentonville Rd, King's Cross,
London N1 9NL **t** 020 7684 2020 **f** 020 7684 2021
e info@bigchill.net **w** bigchill.net Press Manager: Sam Pow.
Seated Capacity: 550

Birkbeck College Student Union, Malet St, London
WC1E 7HX **t** 020 7631 6335 **f** 020 7631 6270
e administrator@bcsu.bbk.ac.uk **w** bbk.ac.uk/su
Contact: Phil Ross. Seated Capacity: 100

Bivouac @ The Duke of Wellington 37 Broadgate,
Lincoln, Lincs LN2 5AE **t** 01522 539883 **f** 01522 528964
e steve.hawkins@easynet.co.uk Booker: Steve Hawkins.
Standing Capacity: 200

Blackheath Halls 23 Lee Rd, London SE3 9RQ
t 020 8318 9758 **f** 020 8852 5154
e co-ordinator@blackheathhalls.com **w** blackheathhalls.com
Operation Mgr: Jenni Darwin. Seated Capacity: 700
Standing Capacity: 1000

**Blackpool Grand Theatre - National Variety
Theatre** 33 Church St, Blackpool, Lancs FY1 1HT
t 01253 290111 **f** 01253 751767
e geninfo@blackpoolgrand.co.uk **w** blackpoolgrand.co.uk
GM: Paul Isles. Seated Capacity: 1192

Blackpool Winter Gardens 97 Church St, Blackpool,
Lancs FY1 1HL **t** 01253 625252 **e** events@leisure-parcs.co.uk
w wintergardensblackpool.co.uk
Sales & Mktg Mgr: Michael Pedley. Seated Capacity: 3250
Standing Capacity: 4000

Bletchley Leisure Centre Princes Way, Bletchley, Milton
Keynes, Bucks MK2 2HQ **t** 01908 377251 **f** 01908 374094
e bletchley@leisureconnection.co.uk **w** bletchleyleisurecentre.co.uk
Mgr: David Taylor. Seated Capacity: 1300
Standing Capacity: 1500

Bloomsbury Theatre 15 Gordon St, London WC1H 0AH
t 020 7679 2777 or 020 7388 8822 **f** 020 7383 4080
e blooms.theatre@ucl.ac.uk **w** thebloomsbury.com
Administrator: Ralph Dartford. Seated Capacity: 550
Standing Capacity: 550

Bluecoat Arts Centre Bluecoat Chambers, School Lane, Liverpool, Merseyside L1 3BX **t** 0151 709 5297 **f** 0151 709 0048 **e** admin@bluecoatartscentre.com **w** bluecoatartscentre.com.

The Boileroom 13 Stokefields, Guildford, Surrey GU1 4LS **t** 01483 440 022 **e** info@theboileroom.net **w** theboileroom.net Venue Manager: Dominique Czopor. Standing Capacity: 200

The Borderline Orange Yard, Off Manette St, Charing Cross Rd, London W1V 5LB **t** 020 7434 9592 or 020 7734 5547 **f** 020 7434 2698 **e** beveritt@meanfiddler.co.uk **w** borderline.co.uk Promoter: Barry Everitt. Standing Capacity: 275

Borough Hall Middlegate, Headland, Hartlepool TS24 0JD **t** 01429 266522 **f** 01429 523005 **e** firstname.lastname@hartlepool.gov.uk GM: Ernie Merrilees.

Bournemouth International Centre (Tregonwell Hall) Exeter Rd, Bournemouth, Dorset BH2 5BH **t** 01202 456400 **f** 01202 456500 **e** chris.jenkins.bic@bournemouth.gov.uk **w** bic.co.uk Entertainment & Events: Chris Jenkins. Standing Capacity: 1202

Bournemouth International Centre (Windsor Hall) Exeter Rd, Bournemouth, Dorset BH2 5BH **t** 01202 456400 **f** 01202 456500 **e** chris.jenkins.bic@bournemouth.gov.uk **w** bic.co.uk Entertainment & Events: Chris Jenkins. Seated Capacity: 3500 Standing Capacity: 4100

Bournemouth Opera House 570 Christchurch Rd, Boscombe, Bournemouth BH1 4BH **t** 01202 399 922 **f** 01202 646 519 **e** info@operahouse.co.uk **w** operahouse.co.uk GM: Paul Marshall. Seated Capacity: 1925

Bournemouth Pavilion Ballroom Westover Rd, Bournemouth, Dorset BH1 2BU **t** 01202 456 400 **f** 01202 451 024 **e** sara.orford.bic@bournemouth.gov.uk **w** bic.co.uk Head of Entertainments: Chris Jenkins. Seated Capacity: 752 Standing Capacity: 900

Bournemouth Pavilion Theatre Westover Rd, Bournemouth, Dorset BH1 2BU **t** 01202 456 400 **f** 01202 451 024 **e** sara.orford.bic@bournemouth.gov.uk **w** bic.co.uk Head of Entertainments: Chris Jenkins. Seated Capacity: 1512

Bournemouth University The Old Fire Station, 36 Holdenhurst Rd, Bournemouth, Dorset BH8 8AD **t** 01202 503888 **f** 01202 503913 **e** info@oldfirestation.co.uk **w** oldfirestation.co.uk Events & Marketing Mgr.: Angus Carter. Seated Capacity: 300 Standing Capacity: 600

Bradford University Commmunal Building Students Union, Richmond Rd, Bradford, W Yorks BD7 1DP **t** 01274 233245 **f** 01274 235530 **e** ubu-ents@bradford.ac.uk **w** ubuonline.co.uk. Standing Capacity: 1300

Braehead Arena Glasgow Braehead, Kings Inch Rd, Glasgow G51 4BN **t** 0141 886 8300 **f** 0141 885 4620 **e** scott-martin@capshop.co.uk **w** braehead.co.uk Arena Manager: Scott Martin. Seated Capacity: 5100

Brangwyn Hall The Guildhall, Swansea SA1 4PE **t** 01792 635489 **f** 01792 635488 **e** brangwyn.hall@swansea.gov.uk **w** swansea.gov.uk/brangwynhall Mgr: Tracy Ellicott. Seated Capacity: 1070 Standing Capacity: 1286

Brel 39 Ashton Lane, Glasgow G12 8SJ **t** 0141 560 2748 or 0141 337 1199 **f** 0141 357 0655 **e** contact@brelbarrestaurant.com **w** brelbarrestaurant.com Booker: Robin Morton. Standing Capacity: 100

Brentford Fountain Leisure Centre 658 Chiswick High Rd, Brentford, Middlesex TW8 0HJ **t** 020 8994 9596 **f** 020 8994 4956 Contact: Alan Boulden. Seated Capacity: 1200 Standing Capacity: 1500

Brentwood Centre Doddinghurst Rd, Brentwood, Essex CM15 9NN **t** 01277 261111 x 381 **f** 01277 200152 Concerts & Promotions Mgr: Steve Allen. Seated Capacity: 1900 Standing Capacity: 1900

Brewery Arts Centre Highgate, Kendal, Cumbria LA9 4HE **t** 01539 725133 **f** 01539 730257 **e** admin@breweryarts.co.uk **w** breweryarts.co.uk Music Officer: Gavin Sharp. Seated Capacity: 300 Standing Capacity: 450

The Brickmakers 496 Sprowston Rd, Norwich, Norfolk NR3 4DY **t** 01603 441 118 **e** info@thebrickmakers.com **w** thebrickmakers.com Bookings Mgr: Charley South. Standing Capacity: 300

The Brickyard Richmond Memorial Hall, 14 Fisher St, Carlisle CA3 8RN **t** 01228 512 220 or 07810 862 455 **e** andy@brick-yard.com **w** brick-yard.com Bookings: Andy McCormack. Standing Capacity: 250

Bridge Lane Theatre Bridge Lane, London SW11 3AD **t** 020 7228 5185 or 020 7228 8828 **f** 020 7262 0090 Artistic Dir: Terry Adams. Seated Capacity: 200

The Bridgewater Hall Lower Mosley St, Manchester M2 3WS **t** 0161 950 0000 **f** 0161 950 0001 **e** admin@bridgewater-hall.co.uk **w** bridgewater-hall.co.uk Programming Manager: Georgina Williamson. Seated Capacity: 2341

Bridgwater Arts Centre 11-13 Castle St, Bridgwater, Somerset TA6 3DD **t** 01278 422700 or 01278 422701 **f** 01278 447402 Contact: Charlie Dearden. Seated Capacity: 196 Standing Capacity: 186

Bridlington Spa Theatre And Royal Hall South Marine Drive, Bridlington, E Yorks YO15 3JH **t** 01262 678255 **f** 01262 604625 Contact: Rob Clutterham. Seated Capacity: 1800 Standing Capacity: 3200

Brighton Centre Kings Rd, Brighton, Sussex BN1 2GR **t** 01273 290131 or 0870 9009100 **f** 01273 779980 **e** b-centre@pavilion.co.uk **w** brightoncentre.co.uk GM: Steve Piper. Seated Capacity: 4273 Standing Capacity: 5127

Brighton Dome 29 New Rd, Brighton, E Sussex BN1 1UG **t** 01273 261530 **f** 01273 261543 **e** events.admin@brighton-dome.org.uk **w** brighton-dome.org.uk GM: Steve Bagnall. Seated Capacity: 1800 Standing Capacity: 1800

Bristol Hippodrome St Augustine's Parade, Bristol BS1 4UZ **t** 0117 926 5524 **f** 0117 925 1661 GM: John Wood. Seated Capacity: 1981

Bristol University, Anson Rooms University of Bristol Union, Queens Rd, Clifton, Bristol BS8 1LN **t** 0117 954 5810 **f** 0117 954 5817 **e** ents-ubu@bristol.ac.uk **w** ubu.org.uk Ents Mgr: Kay Lowrie. Seated Capacity: 600 Standing Capacity: 900

Broadstairs Pavilion Harbour St, Broadstairs, Kent
CT9 1EY **t** 01843 865726. Seated Capacity: 260
Standing Capacity: 340

Broadway Theatre Rushey Green, Catford, London
SE6 4RU **t** 020 8690 2317 or 020 8690 1000
f 020 8314 3144 **e** firstname@broadwaytheatre.org.uk
w broadwaytheatre.org.uk GM: Martin Costello.
Seated Capacity: 855 Standing Capacity: 1000

The Broadway Theatre 46 Broadway, Peterborough
PE1 1RT **t** 01733 316109 **f** 01733 316101
e admin@thebroadwaytheatre.co.uk **w** thebroadwaytheatre.co.uk
GM: Dave King. Seated Capacity: 1168

Brunel University Student Union, Runnymede Campus,
Coopers Hill Lane, Egham, Surrey TW20 0JZ **t** 01784 435508
Ents Officer. Standing Capacity: 320

Brunton Theatre Ladywell Way, Musselburgh, Edinburgh
EH21 6AA **t** 0131 665 9900 **f** 0131 665 7495
Contact: Lesley Smith. Seated Capacity: 302

Buckinghamshire College Newland Park Campus,
Gorelands Lane, Chalfont St Giles, Bucks HP8 4AD
t 01494 871225 **f** 01494 871954.

Buffalo Bar 259 Upper St, London N1 1RU **t** 020 7359 6191
e buffalobars@aol.com **w** buffalobar.co.uk
Bookings: Josh, Michael, Stacey.

Bull & Gate Promotions 389 Kentish Town Rd, London
NW5 2TJ **t** 020 7093 4820 or 020 7485 5358
f 020 7093 4821 **e** info@bullandgate.co.uk **w** bullandgate.co.uk
Booker: Phil Avey. Standing Capacity: 150

The Bullingdon Arms 162 Cowley Rd, Oxford OX4 1UE
t 01865 244516 **f** 01865 202457 **e** info@thebullingdon.com
Mgr: Arron Whan. Seated Capacity: 200 Standing Capacity: 280

Burnley Mechanics Manchester Rd, Burnley, Lancs
BB11 1HH **t** 01282 664411.

Caird Hall Complex City Sq, Dundee, Tayside DD1 3BB
t 01382 434451 **f** 01382 434451 Contact: Susan Pasfield.
Seated Capacity: 2400 Standing Capacity: 2300

Cambridge Arts Theatre 6 St Edward's Passage,
Cambridge CB2 3PJ **t** 01223 578933 **f** 01223 578997
e smarsh@cambridgeartstheatre.com
w cambridgeartstheatre.com Contact: Ian Ross.
Seated Capacity: 660

Cambridge Corn Exchange 3 Parsons Court, Wheeler St,
Cambridge CB2 3QE **t** 01223 457555 admin or 01223 357851
f 01223 457559 admin **e** admin.cornex@cambridge.gov.uk
w cornex.co.uk Asst Head - Arts & Ents: Graham Saxby.
Seated Capacity: 1200 Standing Capacity: 1837

Cambridge Guildhall Cambridge City Council, Market Sq,
Cambridge CB2 3QJ **t** 01223 457000 **f** 01223 463364.
Seated Capacity: 699 Standing Capacity: 400

Cambridge University's Student Union (CUSU)
Student Union, 11-12 Trumpington St, Cambridge CB2 1QA
t 01223 356 454 **f** 01223 323 244
e ents-manager@cusu.cam.ac.uk **w** cusuents.com
Entertainments Mgr: Pete Brizio.

Canterbury Christ Church University College
Student Union, North Holmes Rd, Canterbury, Kent CT1 1QU
t 01227 782080 **f** 01227 458287 **e** ents@cant.ac.uk
w c4online.net Ents & Marketing Mgr: Matt Wynter.
Standing Capacity: 450

Cardiff International Arena Mary Ann St, Cardiff
CF10 2EQ **t** 029 2023 4500 or 029 2023 4600
f 029 2023 4501 **w** sfx-europe.com/cia GM: Graham Walters.
Seated Capacity: 4994 Standing Capacity: 6700

Cardiff University Students Union, Park Pl, Cardiff
CF10 3QN **t** 029 2078 1400 or 029 2078 1456
f 029 2078 1407 **e** westawayj@cardiff.ac.uk
w cardiffstudents.com Ents Mgr: Josh Westaway.
Seated Capacity: 100 Standing Capacity: 300

Cargo Kingsland Viaduct, 83 Rivington St, Shoreditch, London
EC2A 3AY **t** 020 7613 7743 **f** 020 7613 7740
e info@cargo-london.com **w** cargo-london.com
Booking & Event Mgr: Ben Robertson. Seated Capacity: 500

Carling Academy 2 Birmingham 52-54 Dale End,
Birmingham, W Midlands B4 7LS **t** 0121 262 3000
f 0121 236 2241 **e** mail@birmingham-academy.co.uk
w birmingham-academy.co.uk GM: Richard Maides.
Seated Capacity: 400 Standing Capacity: 600

Carling Academy 2 Bristol Frogmore St, Bristol
BS1 5NA **t** 0117 927 9227 **f** 0117 927 9295
e mail@bristol-academy.co.uk **w** bristol-academy.co.uk
GM: Helen Spillane. Standing Capacity: 350

Carling Academy 2 Liverpool 11-13 Hotham St,
Liverpool L3 5UF **t** 0151 707 3200 **f** 0151 707 3201
e mail@liverpool-academy.co.uk **w** liverpool-academy.co.uk
GM: Steve Hoyland. Seated Capacity: 250
Standing Capacity: 500

Carling Academy 2 Newcastle Westgate Rd, Newcastle
NE1 1SW **t** 0191 260 2020 **f** 0191 260 4650
e mail@newcastle-academy.co.uk **w** newcastle-academy.co.uk
GM: Paul Twynham. Standing Capacity: 397

Carling Academy Birmingham 52-54 Dale End,
Birmingham, W Midlands B4 7LS **t** 0121 262 3000
f 0121 236 2241 **e** mail@birmingham-academy.co.uk
w birmingham-academy.co.uk GM: Richard Maides.
Standing Capacity: 2700

Carling Academy Bristol Frogmore St, Bristol BS1 5NA
t 0117 927 9227 **f** 0117 927 9295
e mail@bristol-academy.co.uk **w** bristol-academy.co.uk
GM: Helen Spillane. Standing Capacity: 1900

Carling Academy Brixton 211 Stockwell Rd, Brixton,
London SW9 9SL **t** 020 7771 3000 **f** 020 7738 4427
e mail@brixton-academy.co.uk **w** brixton-academy.co.uk
GM: Nigel Downs. Standing Capacity: 4921

Carling Academy Glasgow 121 Eglinton St, Glasgow
G5 9NT **t** 0141 418 3000 **f** 0141 418 3001
e mail@glasgow-academy.co.uk **w** glasgow-academy.co.uk
GM: David Laing. Standing Capacity: 2500

Carling Academy Islington N1 Centre, 16 Parkfield St,
London N1 0PS **t** 020 7288 4400 **f** 020 7288 4401
e mail@islington-academy.co.uk **w** islington-academy.co.uk
Standing Capacity: 800

Carling Academy Liverpool 11-13 Hotham St, Liverpool L3 5UF **t** 0151 707 3200 **f** 0151 707 3201 **e** mail@liverpool-academy.co.uk **w** liverpool-academy.co.uk GM: Steve Hoyland. Standing Capacity: 1200

Carling Academy Newcastle Westgate Rd, Newcastle NE1 1SW **t** 0191 260 2020 **f** 0191 260 4650 **e** mail@newcastle-academy.co.uk **w** newcastle-academy.co.uk GM: Paul Twynham. Standing Capacity: 2000

Carling Apollo Hammersmith Queen Caroline St, London W6 9QH **t** 020 8748 8660 **f** 08707 490 851 **e** firstname.lastname@livenation.co.uk **w** getlive.co.uk GM: Phil Rodgers. Seated Capacity: 3632 Standing Capacity: 5025

Carling Apollo Manchester Stockport Rd, Ardwick Green, Manchester M12 6AP **t** 0161 273 6921 **f** 0870 749 0779 **e** manchester.apollo@livenation.co.uk **w** getLive.co.uk GM: Phil Sheeran. Seated Capacity: 2693 Standing Capacity: 3500

Carlisle Sands Centre The Sands, Carlisle, Cumbria CA1 1JQ **t** 01228 625208 **f** 01228 625666 **e** ianc@carlisle-city.gov.uk **w** thesandscentre.co.uk Ents Prog Mgr: Ian Congdon. Seated Capacity: 1300 Standing Capacity: 1750

Carnegie Hall East Port, Dunfermline, Fife KY12 7JA **t** 01383 314110 or 01383 314127 **f** 01383 314131 **e** firstname.lastname@fife.gov.uk **w** carnegiehall.co.uk Artistic Dir: Evan Henderson. Seated Capacity: 590

Carnegie Theatre Finkle St, Workington, Cumbria CA14 2BD **t** 01900 602122 **f** 01900 67143 **e** carnegie@allerdale.gov.uk Mgr: Paul Sherwin. Seated Capacity: 354

The Cathouse 15 Union St, Glasgow G1 3RB **t** 0141 248 6606 **f** 0141 248 6741 **e** enquiries@cplweb.com **w** cplweb.com MD: Donald Macleod. Standing Capacity: 400

The Cavern Club 83-84 Queen St, Exeter, Devon EX4 3RP **t** 01392 495370 or 01392 258070 **f** 01392 271625 **e** exetercavern@hotmail.com **w** cavernclub.co.uk Promoters: Pippa, David. Standing Capacity: 250

The Cavern Club. 8-10 Mathew St, Liverpool, Merseyside L2 6RE **t** 0151 236 1965 or 0151 236 9091 **f** 0151 236 8081 **e** cavernnow@gmail.com **w** caverncitytours.com Bookings: Steve Panter. Standing Capacity: 500

Cecil Sharp House 2 Regents Park Rd, London NW1 7AY **t** 020 7485 2206 **f** 020 7284 0534 **e** hire@efdss.org **w** efdss.org Events Mgr: Nicola Elwell. Seated Capacity: 400 Standing Capacity: 450

University of Central England Student Union, Franchise St, Perry Barr, Birmingham B42 2SU **t** 0121 331 6801 **f** 0121 331 6802 **w** uce.ac.uk. Standing Capacity: 350

Central Hall, Westminster Storey's Gate, Westminster, London SW1H 9NH **t** 020 7222 8010 **f** 020 7222 6883 **e** info@c-h-w.co.uk **w** c-h-w.co.uk GM: Michael Sharp. Seated Capacity: 2350

Central Station 15 - 17 Hill St, Wrexham LL11 1SN **t** 01978 358780 **f** 01978 311884 **e** office@yales.fsbusiness.co.uk **w** centralstation-yales.co.uk Promoter: Aled Owens. Seated Capacity: 225 Standing Capacity: 500

The Central Theatre 170 High St, Chatham, Kent ME4 4AS **t** 01634 848584 or 01634 338338 **f** 01634 827711 **e** theatres@medway.gov.uk Contact: Tony Hill. Seated Capacity: 945

The Charlotte 8 Oxford St, Leicester LE1 5XZ **t** 0116 255 3956 **e** charlotte@stayfree.co.uk **w** thecharlotte.co.uk Manager/Owner: Andy Wright. Standing Capacity: 390

Charter Hall Colchester Leisure World, Cowdray Ave, Colchester, Essex CO1 1YH **t** 01206 282946 or 01206 282020 **f** 01206 282916 **e** claire.jackson@colchester.gov.uk **w** colchesterleisureworld.co.uk Event Co-ordinator: Claire Jackson. Seated Capacity: 1216 Standing Capacity: 1216

Cheese & Grain Market Yard, Frome, Somerset BA11 1BE **t** 01373 455768 **f** 01373 455765 **e** office@cheeseandgrain.co.uk **w** cheeseandgrain.co.uk Event Mgr: Nial Joyce. Standing Capacity: 800

Cheltenham Town Hall Imperial Sq, Cheltenham, Gloucs GL50 1QA **t** 01242 521621 or 01242 227979 **f** 01242 573902 **e** townhall@cheltenham.gov.uk **w** cheltenhamfestivals.co.uk Ents & Mktg Mgr: Tim Hulse. Seated Capacity: 1008 Standing Capacity: 1008

Chequer Mead Theatre & Arts Centre De La Warr Rd, East Grinstead, W Sussex RH19 3BS **t** 01342 325577 **f** 01342 301416 **e** info@chequermead.org.uk **w** chequermead.org.uk Administration: Sally Norris. Seated Capacity: 320

Chesterfield Arts Centre Chesterfield College, Sheffield Rd, Chesterfield, Derbyshire S41 7LL **t** 01246 500578 **e** littlewj@chesterfield.ac.uk **w** chesterfield.ac.uk Co-ordinator: Joe Littlewood. Seated Capacity: 250

Chingford Assembly Hall Station Rd, Chingford, London E4 8NU **t** 020 8521 7111 **w** walthamforest.gov.uk Contact: Halls Mgr.

The Citadel Arts Centre Waterloo St, St Helens, Merseyside WA10 1PX **t** 01744 735436 **e** info@citadel.org.uk **w** citadel.org.uk.

City Varieties Music Hall Swan St, Leeds LS1 6LW **t** 0113 391 7777 **f** 0113 234 1800 **e** info@cityvarieties.co.uk **w** CityVarieties.co.uk GM: Peter Sandeman. Seated Capacity: 531

Clair Hall Perrymount Rd, Haywards Heath, W Sussex RH19 3DN **t** 01444 455440 **f** 01444 440041 **e** ClairHall@midsussex.gov.uk.

Clickimin Leisure Complex Lochside, Lerwick, Mainland, Shetland Islands ZE1 0PJ **t** 01595 741000 **f** 01595 741001 **e** mail@srt.org.uk **w** force10.co.uk/srt/pages/clickimin.htm Contact: Mrs Shona Nisbet. Seated Capacity: 1200 Standing Capacity: 1500

Cliffs Pavilion Station Rd, Southend-on-Sea, Essex SS0 7RA **t** 01702 390 657 **f** 01702 391 573 **e** info@cliffspavilion.demon.co.uk **w** thecliffspavilion.co.uk MD: Charles Mumford. Seated Capacity: 1630 Standing Capacity: 2000

Colchester Arts Centre Church St, Colchester, Essex CO1 1NF **t** 01206 500900 **f** 01206 500187 **e** info@colchesterartscentre.com **w** colchesterartscentre.com Dir: Anthony Roberts. Seated Capacity: 300 Standing Capacity: 400

Colne Municipal Hall Bank House, 61 Albert Rd, Colne, Lancs BB8 0PB **t** 01282 661220 **f** 01282 661221 **e** info@pendleleisuretrust.co.uk **w** pendleleisuretrust.co.uk Devel / Mkt Mgr: Gary Hood. Seated Capacity: 600 Standing Capacity: 700

Colston Hall Colston St, Bristol BS1 5AR **t** 0117 922 3693 **f** 0117 922 3681 **e** info@colstonhall.org **w** colstonhall.org Business Development Dir: Graeme Howell. Seated Capacity: 1840 Standing Capacity: 1940

The Comedy 7 Oxendon St, London SW1Y 4EE **t** 020 7482 3908 **e** n_barnett@madasafish.com **w** deadoralive.org.uk Promoter: Nicholas Barnett. Standing Capacity: 100

The Complex 1-5 Parkfield St, London N1 6NU **t** 020 8961 5490 or 020 7288 1986 **f** 020 8961 9238 Contact: David Green. Standing Capacity: 800

Concordia Leisure Centre Forum Way, Cramlington, Northumberland NE23 6YB **t** 01670 717421 **f** 01670 590648 **e** rcalvert@blythvalley.gov.uk **w** blythvalley.gov.uk Centre Mgr: Richard Calvert. Seated Capacity: 920

The Congress Theatre Carlisle Rd, Eastbourne, E Sussex BN21 4BP **t** 01323 415500 **f** 01323 727369 **e** theatres@eastbourne.gov.uk **w** eastbourne.org GM: Chris Jordan. Seated Capacity: 1689

Conway Hall South Place Ethical Society, 25 Red Lion Sq, London WC1R 4RL **t** 020 7242 8032 **f** 020 7242 8036 **e** info@conwayhall.org.uk **w** conwayhall.org.uk Hall Manager: Peter Vlachos. Seated Capacity: 300 Standing Capacity: 500

King's Lynn Corn Exchange Tuseday Market Pl, King's Lynn, Norfolk PE30 1JW **t** 01553 765 565 **f** 01553 762 141 **e** entertainment_admin@west-norfolk.gov.uk **w** kingslynncornexchange.co.uk GM: Ellen McPhillips. Seated Capacity: 738

The Corn Exchange Market Pl, Newbury, Berks RG14 5BD **t** 01635 582666 **f** 01635 582223 **e** admin@cornexchangenew.co.uk **w** cornexchangenew.com Dir: Martin Sutherland. Seated Capacity: 400

The Coronet Theatre 28 New Kent Rd, London SE1 6TJ **t** 020 7701 1500 **f** 020 7701 1300 **e** bookings@coronettheatre.co.uk **w** coronettheatre.co.uk Bookings: Simon Parkes, Marcus Weedon. Seated Capacity: 550 Standing Capacity: 1650

Corporation Milton St, Sheffield, S Yorks S1 4JU **t** 0114 276 0262 **f** 0114 252 7606 **e** enquiries@corporation.org.uk **w** corporation.org.uk Contact: Mr M Hobson. Seated Capacity: 700 Standing Capacity: 700

Coventry University Students Union, Priory St, Coventry, W Midlands CV1 5FJ **t** 024 7679 5200 **f** 024 7679 5239 **e** suexec@coventry.ac.uk **w** cusu.org GM: William Blake. Seated Capacity: 1000

Crawley Leisure Centre Haslett Ave, Crawley, W Sussex RH10 1TS **t** 01293 537431 **f** 01293 523750 **e** enquiries@crawleyleisurecentre.co.uk **w** crawleyleisurecentre.co.uk Promotions & Ents Mgr: David Watmore. Seated Capacity: 1550 Standing Capacity: 2400

The Crypt 53 Robertson St, Hastings, E Sussex TN34 1HY **t** 01424 444675 or 01424 424458 **f** 01424 722847 **e** pete@the-crypt.co.uk **w** the-crypt.co.uk. Seated Capacity: 350

Cumbernauld Theatre Kildrum, Cumbernauld, Glasgow, Lanarkshire G67 2BN **t** 01236 737235 **f** 01236 738408 **e** info@cumbernauldtheatre.co.uk **w** cumbernauldtheatre.co.uk Administrator: Debra Jaffray. Seated Capacity: 258 Standing Capacity: 300

Dancehouse Theatre 10 Oxford Rd, Manchester M1 5QA **t** 0161 237 9753 **f** 0161 237 1408 **e** admin@thedancehouse.co.uk **w** thedancehouse.co.uk Mgr: Chrispin Radcliffe. Seated Capacity: 433

Darlaston Town Hall Victoria Rd, Wednesbury, W Midlands WS10 8AA **t** 01922 650303 **f** 01922 720885 **e** bookings@walsall.gov.uk. Seated Capacity: 300

Darlington Arts Centre Vane Terrace, Darlington, Co Durham DL3 7AX **t** 01325 486555 **f** 01325 365794 **e** info@darlingtonarts.co.uk **w** darlingtonarts.co.uk Music Programmer: Lynda Winstanley. Seated Capacity: 320

Darlington Civic Theatre Parkgate, Darlington, Co Durham DL1 1RR **t** 01325 468555 **f** 01325 368278 **e** info@darlingtonarts.co.uk **w** darlingtonarts.co.uk Head of Theatre & Arts: Peter Cutchie. Seated Capacity: 909

De La Warr Pavilion Marina, Bexhill-on-Sea, E Sussex TN40 1DP **t** 01424 787900 **f** 01424 787940 **e** Ben.Osborne@dlwp.com **w** dlwp.com Head of Live Music: Ben Osborne. Seated Capacity: 1004 Standing Capacity: 800

De Montfort Hall Granville Rd, Leicester LE1 7RU **t** 0116 233 3111 or 0116 233 3113 **f** 0116 233 3182 **w** demontforthall.co.uk Mgr: Richard Haswell. Seated Capacity: 1973 Standing Capacity: 2300

De Montfort Student Union First Floor, Campus Centre Building, Mill Lane, Leicester LE2 7DR **t** 0116 255 5576 **f** 0116 257 6309 **e** initial+surname@dmu.ac.uk **w** mydsu.com. Standing Capacity: 1200

De Montfort University, Bedford Students Union, Pole Hill Ave, Bedford MK41 9EA **t** 01234 793155 **f** 01234 217738 **e** rhurll@dmu.ac.uk **w** mydsu.com Bar & Ents Mgr: Robert Hurll. Standing Capacity: 200

Debates Chamber, Glasgow University Glasgow University, 32 University Ave, Glasgow G12 8LX **t** 0141 339 8697 **f** 0141 339 8931 **e** info@guu.co.uk **w** guu.co.uk Contact: The Porter's Box. Standing Capacity: 900

Deeside Leisure Centre Chester Road West, Queensferry, Deeside, Clwyd CH5 1SA **t** 01244 812311 **f** 01244 836287 **e** deeside_leisure_centre@flintshire.gov.uk **w** flintshire.gov.uk. Seated Capacity: 3500

University of Derby UDSU, Kedleston Rd, Derby DE22 1GB **t** 01332 622238 **f** 01332 348846 **e** m.j.shepherd@derby.ac.uk **w** derby.ac.uk/udsu Ents Mgr: Matt Shepherd. Seated Capacity: 700

Derngate Theatre 19-21 Guildhall Rd, Northampton NN1 1DP **t** 01604 626222 **f** 01604 250901 **e** info@royalandderngate.com **w** royalandderngate.com Contact: Rosemary Jones. Seated Capacity: 1500 Standing Capacity: 1550

Dingwalls Middle Yard, Camden Lock, Camden High St., London NW1 8AB **t** 020 7428 5929 or 01920 823 098 **e** david@dmpuk.com Promoter: David Messer. Standing Capacity: 487

Dominion Theatre 269 Tottenham Court Rd, London W1P 0AQ **t** 020 7580 1889 **f** 020 7580 0246 **e** firstname.lastname@clerchannel.co.uk **w** getlive.co.uk GM: Stephen Murtath. Seated Capacity: 2101

Doncaster Dome Doncaster Leisure Pk, Bawtry Rd, Doncaster, S Yorks DN4 7PD **t** 01302 370777 **f** 01302 379135 **e** info@the-dome.co.uk **w** the-dome.co.uk. Seated Capacity: 1850 Standing Capacity: 3264

Dover Town Hall Biggin St, Dover, Kent CT16 1DL **t** 01304 201200 **f** 01304 201200 **e** townhall@dover.gov.uk **w** dover.gov.uk/townhall Contact: Gen Mgr. Seated Capacity: 500 Standing Capacity: 600

Dublin Castle 94 Parkway, London NW1 7NN **t** 020 8806 2668 or 020 7700 0550 **f** 020 8806 6444 **e** info@bugbearbookings.com **w** bugbearbookings.com Promoters: Jim & Tony. Standing Capacity: 134

Dudley Town Hall St James's Rd, Dudley, W Midlands DY1 1HF **t** 01384 815544 **f** 01384 815534 **e** dudley.townhall@dudley.gov.uk **w** dudley.gov.uk Production Mgr: Tim Jones. Seated Capacity: 1060 Standing Capacity: 1000

Dundee University Student Association, Airlie Pl, Dundee, Tayside DD1 4HP **t** 01382 221841 **f** 01382 227124 **w** dusa.dundee.ac.uk Ents & Publicity Mgr: Trevor San. Seated Capacity: 600 Standing Capacity: 600

Durham University Student Union, Dunelm House, New Elvet, Co Durham DH1 3AN **t** 0191 374 3331 **f** 0191 374 3328 **e** dsu.ents@dur.ac.uk **w** dsu.org.uk Venue Mgr: Jez Light. Seated Capacity: 550 Standing Capacity: 800

Ealing Town Hall Halls & Events, Ground Floor, Perceval House, London W5 2HL **t** 020 8758 5624 or 020 8758 8079 **f** 020 8566 5088 **e** HandM@Ealing.Gov.uk **w** Ealing.Gov.uk/HE&M Head of Halls & Events: M Hand. Seated Capacity: 500 Standing Capacity: 500

Earls Court/Olympia Group Ltd Earls Court Exhibition Centre, Warwick Rd, London SW5 9TA **t** 020 7370 8009 **f** 020 7370 8223 **e** marketing@eco.co.uk **w** eco.co.uk Commercial Director: Nigel Nathan. Seated Capacity: 18000 Standing Capacity: 22000

East Kilbride Civic Centre Andrew St, East Kilbride, Lanarkshire G74 1AB **t** 01355 806000.

East London University Romford Rd, London E15 4LZ **t** 020 8223 3000 **f** 020 8223 3000.

University of East London Union Building, Longbridge Rd, Dagenham, Essex RM8 2AS **t** 020 8590 6017 **f** 020 8597 6987.

Eastbourne Theatres - Winter Garden Compton St, Eastbourne, E Sussex BN21 4BP **t** 01323 415500 **f** 01323 727369 **e** theatres@eastbourne.gov.uk **w** eastbourne.org GM: Chris Jordan. Seated Capacity: 1100 Standing Capacity: 1200

Eden Court Theatre Bishops Rd, Inverness IV3 5SA **t** 01463 239841 or 01463 234234 **f** 01463 713810 **e** admin@eden-court.co.uk **w** eden-court.co.uk. Contact: Colin Marr. Seated Capacity: 810

Edinburgh International Conference Centre The Exchange, Morrison St, Edinburgh EH3 8EE **t** 0131 300 3000 **f** 0131 300 3030 **e** sales@eicc.co.uk **w** eicc.co.uk Snr Sales Team Leader: Lesley Stephen. Seated Capacity: 1200 Standing Capacity: 1200

Edinburgh Playhouse 18-22 Greenside Pl, Edinburgh EH1 3AA **t** 0131 557 2692 **f** 0131 557 6520 **w** edinburgh-playhouse.co.uk GM: Andrew Lyst. Seated Capacity: 3056

Edinburgh University Students Association, Mandela Centre, 5/2 Bristo Sq, Edinburgh EH8 9AL **t** 0131 650 2656 or 0131 650 2649 **f** 0131 668 4177 **e** ian.evans@eusa.ed.ac.uk **w** eusa.ed.ac.uk Entertainments Manager: Ian Evans. Standing Capacity: 1200

Electric Ballroom 184 Camden High St, London NW1 8QP **t** 020 7485 9006 or 020 7485 9007 **f** 020 7284 0745 **e** info@electricballroom.co.uk. Standing Capacity: 1100

Elements Bath University, Students Union, Claverton Down, Bath BA2 7AY **t** 01225 386612 **f** 01225 444061 **e** union@bath.ac.uk **w** bathstudent.com Bars & Ents Co-ordinator: Mike Dalton. Seated Capacity: 250 Standing Capacity: 500

Elgin Town Hall 5 Trinity Pl, Elgin IV30 1VL **t** 01343 543451 **f** 01343 563410 Contact: Eric McGilvery. Seated Capacity: 723

Ellesmere Port Civic Hall Civic Way, Ellesmere Port, South Wirral, Cheshire CH65 0BE **t** 0151 356 6780 or 0151 356 6890 **f** 0151 355 0508 Contact: Miles Veitch. Seated Capacity: 636

Embassy Centre Grand Parade, Skegness, Lincs PE25 2UN **t** 01754 768444 or 01507 329411 **f** 01754 761737 Head of Leisure & Tourism: Bob Suich. Seated Capacity: 1158 Standing Capacity: 1158

The Empire Milton Keynes Leisure Plaza, 1 South Row, Charles Way, Milton Keynes, Bucks MK9 1BL **t** 01908 394 074 **f** 01908 696 768 **e** info@empire-mk.co.uk **w** empire-mk.co.uk Promotions Manager: Nicky Harris. Standing Capacity: 2000

Empire Theatre High Street West, Sunderland, Tyne and Wear SR1 3EX **t** 0191 566 1040 **f** 0191 566 1065 **e** Sarah.b.Clarke@clearchannel.co.uk **w** getlive.co.uk/sunderland GM: Paul Ryan. Seated Capacity: 1875 Standing Capacity: 1875

The English Folk Dance and Song Society Cecil Sharp House, 2 Regent's Park Rd, London NW1 7AY **t** 020 7485 2206 **f** 020 7284 0534 **e** info@efdss.org **w** efdss.org Publications Manager: Felicity Greenland. Seated Capacity: 400 Standing Capacity: 540

English National Opera The London Coliseum, St Martin's Lane, London WC2N 4ES **t** 020 7836 0111 GM: Nicholas Payne. Seated Capacity: 2358

Esquires 60A Bromham Rd, Bedford MK40 2QG **t** 01234 340120 **f** 01234 356630.

The Event II Kingswest, West St, Brighton, E Sussex **t** 01273 732627 **f** 01273 208996 Info Mgr: Dan Boorman. Standing Capacity: 1920

Everyman Theatre 5-9 Hope St, Liverpool, Merseyside **t** 0151 708 0338 **f** 0151 709 0398 **e** info@everymanplayhouse.com **w** everyman.merseyworld.com/ Contact: The General Mgr. Seated Capacity: 450

Evesham Arts Centre Victoria Ave, Evesham, Worcs WR11 4QH **t** 01386 48883 Contact: LA Griffith-Jones. Seated Capacity: 300

Exeter Phoenix Bradninch Pl, Gandy St, Exeter, Devon EX4 3LS **t** 01392 667056 **f** 01392 667599 The Arts Mgr: Andy Morley. Seated Capacity: 216 Standing Capacity: 500

Fairfield Halls Park Lane, Croydon, Surrey CR9 1DG **t** 020 8681 0821 **e** publicity@fairfield.co.uk **w** fairfield.co.uk. Seated Capacity: 1550

Falmouth Arts Centre Church St, Falmouth, Cornwall TR11 3EG **t** 01326 212719 **e** adrian@falmoutharts.org **w** falmoutharts.org GM: Adrian Watts. Seated Capacity: 200

Farnborough Recreation Centre 1 Westmead, Farnborough, Hants GU14 7LD **t** 01252 370411 **f** 01252 372280. Standing Capacity: 2100

Fat Sam's 31 South Ward Rd, Dundee, Angus DD1 1PU **t** 01382 228181 **f** 01382 228181 **e** sam@fatsams.co.uk **w** fatsams.co.uk Mgr: Derek Anderson. Seated Capacity: 480 Standing Capacity: 480

Ferneham Hall, Fareham Osborn Rd, Fareham, Hants PO16 0TL **t** 01329 824864 **f** 01329 281486 **e** rdavies@fareham.gov.uk **w** fareham.gov.uk Head of Arts & Ents: Russell Davies. Seated Capacity: 752 Standing Capacity: 800

Ferry Boat Inn 191 King St, Norwich NR1 2DF **t** 01603 613 553 **e** cummon_lets@rocktheboat.co.uk **w** ferryboat-inn.co.uk Bookings: Alan Thorp. Standing Capacity: 150

The Ferryboat Inn 191 King St, Norwich, Norfolk NR1 2DF **t** 01603 613 553 **f** 01603 613 553 **e** ferryboat_promoter@hotmail.co.uk **w** ferryboat-inn.co.uk Promoter/Landlord: Alan Thorpe. Standing Capacity: 145

Festival City Theatres Trust 13/29 Nicolson St, Edinburgh EH8 9FT **t** 0131 662 1112 **f** 0131 667 0744 **e** empire@eft.co.uk **w** eft.co.uk Acting GM: David W S Todd. Seated Capacity: 1900

Fez Club 5-6 Gun St, Reading RG1 2JR **t** 01189 586 839 **f** 01189 586 796 **e** info@readingfez.com **w** readingfez.com GM: Olly Smith. Standing Capacity: 400

The Fibbers Group Units 8-12, Stonebow House, Stonebow, York, N Yorks YO1 7NP **t** 01904 466148 **f** 01904 675315 **e** fibbers@fibbers.co.uk **w** fibbers.co.uk MD: Tim Hornsby. Seated Capacity: 200 Standing Capacity: 250

Fibbers Stonebow House, The Stonebow, York YO1 7NP **t** 01904 651 250 **f** 01904 670 542 **e** fibbers@fibbers.co.uk **w** fibbers.co.uk Promoter: Tim Hornsby. Standing Capacity: 200

The Fleece 12 St Thomas St, Bristol BS1 6JJ **t** 0117 927 7150 **e** fleece@gigs.demon.co.uk **w** gigs.demon.co.uk Promoter: David Brayley. Standing Capacity: 400

The Fly 36-38 New Oxford St, London WC1A 1EP **t** 020 7631 0862 or 020 7691 4244 **e** ross.grady@barflyclub.com **w** barflyclub.com Promoter: Ross Grady. Standing Capacity: 120

Fort Regent Leisure Centre St Helier, Jersey, Channel Islands JE2 4UX **t** 01534 500009 **f** 01534 500225 **e** c.stanier@gov.je **w** esc.gov.je Marketing & Events Mgr: Colin Stanier. Seated Capacity: 1974 Standing Capacity: 2500

The Forum Fonthill, The Common, Tunbridge Wells, Kent TN4 8YU **t** 08712 777 101 **f** 08712 777 101 **e** twforum@globalnet.co.uk **w** twforum.co.uk Mgr: Mark Davyd. Seated Capacity: 110 Standing Capacity: 250

Forum 28 28 Duke St, Barrow-in-Furness, Cumbria LA14 1HH **t** 01229 820000 **f** 01229 894942 **e** nward@barrowbc.gov.uk **w** barrowbc.gov.uk Bookings Mgr: Neil Ward. Seated Capacity: 485 Standing Capacity: 720

The Forum 9-17 Highgate Rd, London NW5 1JY **t** 020 7284 1001 **f** 020 7284 1102 **w** meanfiddler.com. Seated Capacity: 1400 Standing Capacity: 2110

The Foundry Beak St, Birmingham, W Midlands B1 1LS **t** 0121 622 1894 **w** dr-p.demon.co.uk/foundry.html.

The Fridge 1 Town Hall Parade, Brixton Hill, London SW2 1RJ **t** 020 7326 5100 **f** 020 7274 2879 **e** info@fridge.co.uk **w** fridge.co.uk Mgr: Gary Baker. Seated Capacity: 1100 Standing Capacity: 1100

Futurist Theatre Foreshore Rd, Scarborough, N Yorks YO11 1NT **t** 01723 370742 **f** 01723 365456. Standing Capacity: 2155

Gaiety Theatre Douglas, Isle of Man **t** 01624 620046.

Garage 20-22 Highbury Corner, London N5 1RD **t** 020 8961 5490 or 020 7607 1818 **f** 020 8961 9238 **e** joady@meanfiddler.co.uk Bking Mgr: Joady Thornton. Standing Capacity: 500

The Garage 490 Sauchiehall St, Glasgow G2 3LW **t** 0141 332 1120 **f** 0141 332 1130 **w** cplweb.com MD: Donald Macleod. Standing Capacity: 700

The Gardner Arts Centre University Of Sussex, Falmer, Brighton, E Sussex BN1 9RA **t** 01273 685447 **f** 01273 678551 **e** info@gardnerarts.co.uk **w** gardnerarts.co.uk Dir: Sue Webster. Seated Capacity: 476 Standing Capacity: 476

Garrick Theatre Barrington Rd, Altrincham, Cheshire WA14 1HZ **t** 0161 929 8779 (mktg) or 0161 928 1677 (box). Seated Capacity: 472

Gateshead International Stadium Neilson Rd, Gateshead, Tyne & Wear NE10 0EF **t** 0191 478 1687 **f** 0191 477 1315. Seated Capacity: 11000 Standing Capacity: 38000

Glamorgan University Student Union, Forest Grove, Treforest, Pontypridd, Mid Glamorgan CF37 1UF **t** 01443 408227 **f** 01443 491589 Contact: Jason Crimmins. Seated Capacity: 200 Standing Capacity: 500

Glasgow Caledonian University Students Union, 70 Cowcaddens Rd, Glasgow, Lanarkshire G4 0BA **t** 0141 332 0681 **f** 0141 353 0029 **e** d.mcbride@gcal.ac.uk **w** caledonianstudent.com Venue Mgr: Denis McBride. Standing Capacity: 595

Glasgow City Halls 32 Albion St, Glasgow, Lanarkshire G1 1QU **t** 0141 287 5005 **f** 0141 287 5533 Susan Deighan: Head of Programming. Seated Capacity: 1121 Standing Capacity: 800

Glasgow Garage 490 Sauchiehall St, Glasgow, Lanarkshire G2 3LW **t** 0141 332 1120 **f** 0141 332 1120 Contact: Donald Macleod. Standing Capacity: 600

Glasgow King's Theatre Glasgow City Council, Cultural and Leisure Services, 229 George St, Glasgow G1 1QU **t** 0141 287 3922 **f** 0141 287 5533 Contact: Pauline Murphy. Seated Capacity: 1785

Glasgow Pavilion Theatre 121 Renfield St, Glasgow, Lanarkshire G2 3AX **t** 0141 332 7579 or 0141 332 1846 **f** 0141 331 2745 Theatre Mgr: Iain Gordon. Seated Capacity: 1449

Glasgow Royal Concert Hall 2 Sauchiehall St, Glasgow, Lanarkshire G2 3NY **t** 0141 353 8080 **f** 0141 353 8078 **e** sales@grch.com **w** grch.com Hd of Events: Karen Taylor. Seated Capacity: 2417

Glastonbury Festival Worthy Farm, Pilton, Shepton Mallet, Somerset BA4 4BY **t** 01749 890470 **f** 01749 890285 **e** worthy@glastonbury-festivals.co.uk **w** glastonburyfestivals.co.uk. Standing Capacity: 100000

Glee Club The Arcadian Centre, Hurst St, Birmingham, W Midlands B5 4TD **t** 07973 121 958 **e** markus_sargeant@yahoo.com **w** glee.co.uk Promoter: Markus Sargeant. Seated Capacity: 400 Standing Capacity: 400

The Globe Blackpool Pleasure Beach, Ocean Boulevard, Blackpool, Lancs FY4 1EZ **t** 01253 341033 **f** 01253 401098 Contact: Michelle Barratt. Seated Capacity: 940

Gloucester Leisure Centre Bruton Way, Gloucester GL1 1DT **t** 01452 385310 or 01452 306498. Seated Capacity: 2100 Standing Capacity: 2500

Goldsmiths College Student Union Dixon Rd, New Cross, London SE14 6NW **t** 020 8692 1406 **f** 020 8694 9789 **e** gcsu@gold.ac.uk **w** gcsu.org.uk Entertainment Manager: Barrie Schooling. Seated Capacity: 350 Standing Capacity: 600

The Good Ship 289 Kilburn High Rd, London NW6 7JR **t** 07949 008 253 **e** john@thegoodship.co.uk **w** thegoodship.co.uk Promoter: John McCooke. Standing Capacity: 200

Gordon Craig Theatre Stevenage Arts & Leisure Ctr, Lytton Way, Stevenage, Herts SG1 1LZ **t** 01438 242642 **f** 01438 242342 **e** gordoncraig@stevenage-leisure.co.uk **w** stevenage.gov.uk/GordonCraig Bookings Mgr: Bob Bustance. Standing Capacity: 500

Robert Gordon University Student Union, 60 Schoolhill, Aberdeen, Grampian AB10 1JQ **t** 01224 262262 **f** 01224 262268 **e** rgusa@rgu.ac.uk **w** rgu.ac.uk. Seated Capacity: 150 Standing Capacity: 200

The Grafton West Derby Rd, Liverpool L6 9BY **t** 0151 263 2303 **f** 0151 263 4985. Seated Capacity: 1425

Grand Opera House Great Victoria St, Belfast, Co Antrim BT2 7HR **t** 028 9024 0411 **f** 028 9023 6842 **w** goh.co.uk Contact: Derek Nicholls. Seated Capacity: 1001

Grand Theatre Church St, Blackpool, Lancs FY1 1HT **t** 01253 290111 **f** 01253 751767 **e** gm@blackpoolgrand.co.uk **w** blackpoolgrand.co.uk Contact: Stephanie Sir. Seated Capacity: 1200

Grand Theatre Wolverhampton, W Midlands **t** 01902 429212.

Great Grimsby Town Hall Town Hall Sq, Great Grimsby, North East Lincolnshire DN31 1HX **t** 01472 324109 **f** 01472 324108 Contact: John Callison. Seated Capacity: 350 Standing Capacity: 400

The Green Room 4 West End, Redruth, Cornwall TR15 2RZ **t** 01209 216 626 **f** 01209 315 630 **e** info@greenroomcornwall.com **w** greenroomcornwall.com Promoter: Ben Simpson.

Grimsby Auditorium Cromwell Rd, Grimsby, South Humberside DN31 2BH **t** 01472 323100 **f** 01472 323102 Contact: Mr Morris.

Group Theatre Bedford St, Belfast, Co Antrim BT2 7FF **t** 028 9032 3900 **f** 028 9024 7199 Contact: Pat Falls. Seated Capacity: 221

Guildhall 23 Eastgate St, Gloucester GL1 1QR **t** 01452 505089.

Guildhall Lancaster Rd, Preston, Lancs PR1 1HT **t** 01772 203456.

Hackney Empire Ltd. 291 Mare St, London E8 1EJ **t** 020 8510 4500 **f** 020 8510 4530 **e** frank.sweeney@hackneyempire.co.uk **w** hackneyempire.co.uk Programmer: Frank Sweeney. Seated Capacity: 1300 Standing Capacity: 1500

Halfmoon, Putney 93 Lower Richmond Rd, London SW15 1EU **t** 020 8780 9383 **f** 020 8789 7863 **e** office@halfmoon.co.uk **w** halfmoon.co.uk Bookings/Promotions Mgr: Carrie Davies. Seated Capacity: 150 Standing Capacity: 200

Hammersmith Palais 230 Shepherd's Bush Rd, London W6 7NL **t** 020 8600 2300 **f** 020 8600 2301 **e** info@hammersmithpalais.com **w** hammersmithpalais.com GM: Matt Talbot.

Hare And Hounds High St, King's Heath, Birmingham B14 7JZ **t** 0121 444 2081 or 0121 444 3578 Contact: The Manager. Seated Capacity: 140

Harlow Bandstand Harlow Council Leisure Service, Latton Bush Centre, Southern Way, Harlow, Essex CM18 7BL **t** 01279 446404 **f** 01279 446431 Contact: Recreation Services Officer. Standing Capacity: 5000

Harlow Showground Harlow Council Leisure Service, Latton Bush Centre, Southern Way, Harlow, Essex CM18 7BL **t** 01279 446404 **f** 01279 446431 Contact: Recreation Services Officer. Standing Capacity: 15000

Harrogate International Centre Kings Rd, Harrogate, N Yorks HG1 5LA **t** 01423 500 500 **f** 01423 537 270 **e** sales@harrogateinternationalcentre.co.uk **w** harrogateinternationalcentre.co.uk Dir: Stuart Quin. Seated Capacity: 2009 Standing Capacity: 1431

The Hawth, Crawley Hawth Ave, Crawley, W Sussex RH10 6YZ **t** 01293 552941 **f** 01293 533362 **e** info@hawth.co.uk **w** hawth.co.uk Head Of Arts: Kevin Eason. Seated Capacity: 850 Standing Capacity: 950

Haymarket Theatre 1 Belgrave Gate, Garrick Walk, Leicester LE1 3YQ **t** 0116 253 0021 **f** 0116 251 3310. Seated Capacity: 732

Hazlitt Theatre Earl St, Maidstone, Kent ME14 1PL
t 01622 602178 **f** 01622 602194
e mandyhare@maidstone.gov.uk Mgr: Mandy Hare.
Seated Capacity: 381 Standing Capacity: 400

Heriot-Watt University Students Asso. Students
Association, The Union, Riccarton Campus, Edinburgh EH14 4AS
t 0131 451 5333 **f** 0131 451 5344 **e** K.Easton@hw.ac.uk
w hwusa.org Entertainment Mgr: Keith Easton.
Seated Capacity: 250 Standing Capacity: 450

University of Hertfordshire Student Union, College Lane,
Hatfield, Herts AL10 9AB **t** 01707 285008 or 01707 285000
f 01707 286151 **e** uhsu@herts.ac.uk **w** uhsu.herts.ac.uk/
Contact: Venue Mgr. Seated Capacity: 450
Standing Capacity: 1300

Hexagon Queen's Walk, Reading, Berks RG1 7UA
t 0118 939 0123 **f** 0118 939 0028
e boxoffice@readingarts.com **w** readingarts.com
Prog Co-ordinator: Charity Gordon. Seated Capacity: 1484
Standing Capacity: 1686

Hippodrome Leicester Sq, London WC2 7JH
t 020 7437 4311 **f** 020 7434 4225 **w** londonhippodrome.com
Contact: Annette Morris. Seated Capacity: 700
Standing Capacity: 1945

His Majesty's Theatre Rosemount Viaduct, Aberdeen
AB25 1GL **t** 01224 637788 **f** 01224 632519
e venues@arts-rec.aberdeen.net.uk **w** aberdeencity.gov.uk/venues
GM: Duncan Hendry. Seated Capacity: 1446

The Hive, Glasgow University Glasgow University, 32
University Ave, Glasgow G12 8LX **t** 0141 339 8697
f 0141 339 8931 **e** libraries@guu.co.uk **w** guu.co.uk
Contact: The Porter's Box. Standing Capacity: 1000

The Hope & Anchor 207 Upper St, London N1 1BZ
t 020 7700 0550 or 07956 313 239
e info@bugbearbookings.com **w** bugbearbookings.com
Promoters: Jim & Tony. Standing Capacity: 80

The Horn Victoria St, St Albans, Herts. AL1 3TE
t 01727 844 627 or 01727 853 143 **e** adam@thehorn.co.uk
w thehorn.co.uk Bookings: Adam Foster. Standing Capacity: 350

The Horns 1 Hempstead Rd, Watford, Herts. WD17 3RL
t 01923 225 020 **f** 01923 233 048
e info@thehornswatford.co.uk **w** thehornswatford.co.uk
Bookings: Denis Cook. Standing Capacity: 200

Horseshoe Bar Blackpool Pleasure Beach, Ocean Boulevard,
Blackpool, Lancs FY4 1EZ **t** 01253 341033 **f** 01253 401098
e michelle.barratt@bpbltd.com **w** bpbltd.com
Contact: Michelle Barratt. Seated Capacity: 400

Horsham Arts Centre North St, Horsham, W Sussex
RH12 1RL **t** 01403 259708 or 01403 268689 **f** 01403 211502
Mgr: Michael Gattrell. Seated Capacity: 438

Hove Centre @ Hove Town Hall Norton Rd, Hove, E
Sussex BN3 4AH **t** 01273 292902 **f** 01273 292936
e venuehire@brighton-hove.gov.uk
Admins Officer: Amanda-Jane Stone. Seated Capacity: 1000
Standing Capacity: 1000

Huddersfield Town Hall (also Batley, Dewsbury)
Cultural Services HQ, Red Doles Lane, Huddersfield, W Yorks
HD2 1YF **t** 01484 226300 **f** 01484 221541
e julia.robinson@kirkleesmc.gov.uk
Town Halls Manager: Julia Robinson. Seated Capacity: 1200
Standing Capacity: 700

Huddersfield University Student Union, Queensgate,
Huddersfield HD1 3DH **t** 01484 538156 **f** 01484 432333
e kj.stead@hud.ac.uk **w** huddersfieldstudent.com
Ents Co-ordinator: Kerry Stead. Seated Capacity: 250
Standing Capacity: 300

Hull Arena Kingston St, Hull, E Yorks HU1 2DZ
t 01482 325252 **f** 01482 216066 **w** hullarena.co.uk
Contact: Linda Parker. Seated Capacity: 3250
Standing Capacity: 3750

Hull City Hall Victoria Sq, Hull, E Yorks HU1 3NA
t 01482 613880 **f** 01482 613961
Programming Mgr: Mike Lister. Seated Capacity: 1400
Standing Capacity: 1800

Hull New Theatre Kingston Sq, Kingston Upon Hull, E Yorks
HU1 3HF **t** 01482 613880 **f** 01482 613961
Programming Mgr: Michael Lister. Seated Capacity: 1189

Hull University University House, Cottingham Rd, Hull, E
Yorks HU2 9BT **t** 01482 466253 **f** 01482 466280
e j.a.brooks@hull.ac.uk **w** hull.ac.uk
Ents Co-ordinator: James Brooks. Standing Capacity: 1500

ICA The Mall, London SW1Y 5AH **t** 020 7930 0493 or
020 7766 1444 **e** nickl@ica.org.uk **w** ica.org.uk
Live Music Programmer: Nick Luscombe. Seated Capacity: 167
Standing Capacity: 350

Imperial College Union, Beit Quad, Prince Consort Rd,
London SW7 2BB **t** 020 7594 8068 **f** 020 7594 8065
e ents@ic.ac.uk **w** union.ic.ac.uk Ents Manager: Ham Al-Rubaie.
Seated Capacity: 300 Standing Capacity: 450

Inverurie Town Hall Market Pl, Inverurie, Aberdeenshire
t 01467 621610. Seated Capacity: 400

ION 161-165 Ladbroke Grove, London W10 6HJ
t 020 8960 1702 **w** meanfiddler.com.

Ipswich Corn Exchange King St, Ipswich, Suffolk IP1 1DH
t 01473 433133 **f** 01473 433450
e firstname.lastname@ipswich.gov.uk
w ipswichcornexchange.com
Operations & Events Mgr: Craig Oldfield. Seated Capacity: 900
Standing Capacity: 1000

Ipswich Regent Theatre 3 St Helens St, Ipswich, Suffolk
IP4 1HE **t** 01473 433555 **f** 01473 433727
e firstname.lastname@ipswich.gov.uk **w** ipswichregent.com
Mgr: Hazel Clover. Seated Capacity: 1781
Standing Capacity: 1781

Irish Centre York Rd, Leeds, W Yorks LS9 9NT
t 0113 248 0613.

Isha Lounge Bar 43 Richmond Rd, Kingston Upon Thames,
Surrey KT2 5BW **t** 020 8546 0099 **e** ishalounge@hotmail.com
w ishalounge.com Contact: Titch Deegun. Standing Capacity: 200

The Jaffa Cake 28 Kings Stables Rd, Edinburgh, Lothian
EH1 2JY **t** 0131 229 9438.

JAGZ At the Station, Station Hill, Ascot, Berks SL5 9EG
t 01344 878 100 **e** music@jagz.co.uk **w** jagz.co.uk
Promotions Manager: Miles Gripton. Seated Capacity: 100
Standing Capacity: 150

Jazz Cafe 5 Parkway, Camden Town, London NW1 7PG
t 020 7916 6060 **f** 020 7267 9219 **e** info@jazzcafe.co.uk
w jazzcafe.co.uk Promoter: Adrian Gibson. Seated Capacity: 250
Standing Capacity: 400

Jersey Opera House Gloucester St, St Hellier, Jersey,
Channel Islands JE2 3QL **t** 01534 617521 **f** 01534 610624
Contact: Ian Stephens. Seated Capacity: 680

Joiner's Arms 141 St Mary St, Southampton, Hants
SO14 1NS **t** 023 8022 5612 **f** 01962 878812
e vic@liveattherailway.co.uk **w** joinerslive.com
Promoter: Vic Toms. Standing Capacity: 250

Jug Of Ale 43 Alcester Rd, Moseley, Birmingham, W Midlands
B13 8AA **t** 0121 449 1082.

The Junction Clifton Rd, Cambridge CB1 7GX
t 01223 578000 **f** 01223 565600 **e** spiral@junction.co.uk
w junction.co.uk Commercial Prog Mgr: Rob Tinkler.
Seated Capacity: 278 Standing Capacity: 850

Kartouche Princes St, Ipswich, Suffolk IP2 9TD
t 01473 230666 **f** 01473 232579 **e** info@kartouche.net
w kartouche.net Mgr: Georgie Smith. Standing Capacity: 1450

Keele University Student Union, Keele, Newcastle-under-
Lyme, Staffs ST5 5BJ **t** 01782 583700 **f** 01782 712671
e r.chamberlain@keele.ac.uk; ents@keele.ac.uk **w** kusu.net
Ents Mgr: Rob Chamberlain. Seated Capacity: 400
Standing Capacity: 1100

Kef 9 Belmont St, Aberdeen AB10 1JR **t** 01224 645328 or
01224 648000 **f** 01224 644737 **e** angela_stirling@hotmail.com
Promoter: Paul Stewart. Seated Capacity: 120
Standing Capacity: 150

Kendal Town Hall Highgate, Kendal, Cumbria LA9 4DL
t 01539 725758 **f** 01539 734457 Bookings: Debbie Mckee.
Seated Capacity: 400 Standing Capacity: 400

Town Hall, Kensington Royal Borough Kensington, &
Chelsea, Horton St, London W8 7NX **t** 020 7361 2220
f 020 7361 3442 **e** hall-let@rbkc.gov.uk **w** rbkc.gov.uk
Conference/Events Office: Maxine Howitt. Seated Capacity: 860
Standing Capacity: 900

Kettering Arena Thurston Drive, Kettering, Northants
NN15 6PB **t** 01536 414141 **f** 01536 414334
Contact: Tony Remington. Seated Capacity: 2000
Standing Capacity: 3000

Kidderminster Town Hall Vicar St, Kidderminster, Worcs
DY10 2BL **t** 01562 732158 **f** 01562 750708 Contact: The Mgr.
Seated Capacity: 450

Kilmarnock Palace Theatre 9 Green St, Kilmarnock
KA1 3BN **t** 01563 537710 or 01563 523590 **f** 01563 573047
Asst Theatre & Ents Mgr: Laura Brown. Standing Capacity: 1100

King Georges Hall Northgate, Blackburn, Lancs BB2 1AA
t 01254 582579 **f** 01254 667277
e geoff.peake@blackburn.gov.uk **w** kinggeorgeshall.com
Events/Promo Mgr: Geoff Peake. Seated Capacity: 1853
Standing Capacity: 2000

King Tut's Wah Wah Hut 272A St Vincent St, Glasgow
G2 5RL **t** 0141 248 5158 **f** 0141 248 5202
e kingtuts@dfconcerts.co.uk **w** kingtuts.co.uk
Promoter/Venue Mgr: Dave McGeachan.

King's Hall Exhibition & Conference Centre
Balmoral, Belfast, Co Antrim BT9 6GW **t** 028 9066 5225
f 028 9066 1264 **e** info@kingshall.co.uk **w** kingshall.co.uk
Comm Dir. Seated Capacity: 5000 Standing Capacity: 8000

King's Lynn Arts Centre 27-29 King St, King's Lynn,
Norfolk PE30 1HA **t** 01553 765 565 **f** 01553 762 141
e entertainment_admin@west-norfolk.gov.uk
w west-norfolk.gov.uk GM: Ellen McPhillips. Seated Capacity: 349

King's Theatre Edinburgh 2 Leven St, Edinburgh
EH3 9LQ **t** 0131 662 1112 **f** 0131 667 0744 **e** empire@eft.co.uk
w eft.co.uk Gen Mgr & Chief Exec: Stephen Barry.
Seated Capacity: 1300

King's WC2 King's College London, Students Union, Macadam
Bldg, Surrey St, London WC2R 2NS **t** 020 7836 7132
f 020 7379 9833 **e** Rob.Massy@kclsu.org **w** kclsu.org/events
Events Mgr: Rob Massy. Seated Capacity: 400
Standing Capacity: 620

Kingston University Guild Of Students Penrhyn Rd,
Kingston upon Thames, Surrey KT1 2EE **t** 020 8547 2000
f 020 8255 0032 **w** kingston.ac.uk. Standing Capacity: 700

KoKo (formerly known as The Camden Palace) 1A
Camden High St, London NW1 7JE **t** 0870 432 5527
f 020 7388 4388 **e** info@koko.uk.com **w** koko.uk.com
HoM: Daveid Phillips. Standing Capacity: 1500

Komedia 44-47 Gardner St, Brighton, E Sussex BN1 1KN
t 01273 647100 or 01273 647101 **f** 01273 647102
e admin@komedia.co.uk **w** komedia.co.uk
Venue Manager: Jackie Alexander. Seated Capacity: 210

University of Wales - Lampeter Student Union, Ty
Ceredig, Lampeter, Ceredigion SA48 7ED **t** 01570 422619
f 01570 422480 **e** ents@lamp.ac.uk **w** lamp.ac.uk
Ents Officer: Ian Larsen.

Lancaster University (The Sugar House) Student
Union, Slaidburn House, Lancaster LA1 4YT **t** 01524 593765
f 01524 846732 **e** c.burston@lancaster.ac.uk **w** lancs.ac.uk/lusu.

The Landmark Seafront, Wilder Rd, Ilfracombe, Devon
EX34 9BZ **t** 01271 865655 **f** 01271 867707
e info@northdevontheatres.org.uk **w** northdevontheatres.org.uk
Programming Dir: Karen Turner. Seated Capacity: 483

Larkfield Leisure Centre New Hythe Lane, Larkfield,
Aylesford, Kent ME20 6RH **t** 01622 719345 **f** 01622 710822
Contact: Operations Mgr. Seated Capacity: 600

The Leadmill 6 Leadmill Rd, Sheffield, S Yorks S1 4SE
t 0114 221 2828 **f** 0114 221 2848 **e** promotions@leadmill.co.uk
w leadmill.co.uk Live Promoter: Rupert Dell. Seated Capacity: 500
Standing Capacity: 900

Leas Cliff Hall The Leas, Folkestone, Kent CT20 2DZ
t 01303 228600 **f** 01303 221175 **e** mail@leascliffhall.co.uk
w leascliffhall.co.uk GM: Stephen Levine. Seated Capacity: 1000
Standing Capacity: 1500

Leeds Civic Theatre Cookridge St, Leeds, W Yorks
LS2 8BH **t** 0113 245 6343 **f** 0113 246 5906
w leeds.gov.uk/tourinfo/theatre. Seated Capacity: 521

Leeds Grand Theatre & Opera House 46 New
Briggate, Leeds, W Yorks LS1 6NZ **t** 0113 245 6014
f 0113 246 5906 **w** leeds.gov.uk/GrandTheatre
General Mgr: Warren Smith. Seated Capacity: 1550

Leeds Metropolitan University Student Union, Calverley
St, Leeds, W Yorks LS1 3HE **t** 0113 209 8416 **f** 0113 234 2973
e events@lmusu.org.uk **w** lmusu.org.uk. Seated Capacity: 500
Standing Capacity: 1050

Leeds University PO Box 157, Leeds, W Yorks LS1 1UH
t 0113 380 1334 **f** 0113 380 1336 **e** ents@luu.leeds.ac.uk
w luuonline.com Ents Mgr: Steve Keeble. Standing Capacity: 1750

Leicester University Student Union, University Rd, Leicester
LE1 7RH **t** 0116 223 1169 or 0116 223 1122 **f** 0116 223 1207
e jk69@le.ac.uk **w** le.ac.uk/su Bars & Ents Manager: Jo Kenning.
Seated Capacity: 500 Standing Capacity: 1300

The Lemon Tree 5 West North St, Aberdeen AB24 5AT
t 01224 647999 **f** 01224 630888 **e** info@lemontree.org
w lemontree.org Music Programmer: Andy Shearer.
Seated Capacity: 300 Standing Capacity: 500

Life Cafe 23 Peter St, Manchester M2 5QR **t** 0161 833 3000
f 0161 839 4000 **e** Lifecafe-manchester@luminar.co.uk
w lifecafe.info Promoter: David Potts. Seated Capacity: 950

Lighthouse Pooles' Centre for the Arts, Kingland Rd, Poole,
Dorset BH15 1UG **t** 01202 665 334 **f** 01202 670 016
e jamesg@lighthousepoole.co.uk **w** lighthousepoole.co.uk
Programmer: James Greenwood. Seated Capacity: 1463
Standing Capacity: 2459

Limelight 17 Ormeau Aveue, Belfast, Co Antrim BT2 8HD
t 028 9032 5942 **f** 028 9031 3131
e theoffice@the-limelight.com **w** the-limelight.co.uk
Mgr: David Neeley. Standing Capacity: 500

Limelight Theatre Queens Park Centre, Queens Pk,
Aylesbury, Bucks HP21 7RT **t** 01296 431272 or 01296 424332
f 01296 337363 **e** qpc@ukonline.co.uk **w** qpc.org
Artistic Dir: Amanda Eels. Seated Capacity: 120
Standing Capacity: 120

The Little Civic North St, Wolverhampton, W Midlands
WV1 1RQ **t** 01902 552122 **f** 01902 713665.

Liverpool Academy 1, 2, 3 & 4 (Liverpool Univ)
Guild of Students, 160 Mount Pleasant, Liverpool L69 7BR
t 0151 794 4131 or 0151 794 4143 **f** 0151 794 4144
e ents@liv.ac.uk **w** liverpoolacademy.co.uk
Ents Mgr: Carl Bathgate. Seated Capacity: 700
Standing Capacity: 1530

Liverpool Empire Theatre Lime St, Liverpool, Merseyside
L1 1JE **t** 0151 708 3200 **f** 0151 709 6757
e firstname.lastname@livenation.co.uk **w** liverpool-empire.co.uk
GM: Hannah Collins. Seated Capacity: 2370

Liverpool Students Union 160 Mount Pleasant, Liverpool
L69 7BR **t** 0151 794 4116 or 0151 794 4143 **f** 0151 794 4174
e guild@liv.ac.uk **w** liverpoolguild.org.uk Ents Mgr: Carl Bathgate.
Standing Capacity: 500

Logan Hall Institute of Education, 20 Bedford Way, London
WC1H 0AL **t** 020 7612 6401 **f** 020 7612 6402
e s.nazim@ioe.ac.uk **w** ioe.ac.uk
Conference Office Mgr: Sittika Nazim. Seated Capacity: 933

London Arena Limeharbour, London E14 9TH
t 020 7538 8880 **f** 020 7538 5572 **e** sales@londonarena.co.uk
w londonarena.co.uk Dir of European Events: Eve Hewitt.
Seated Capacity: 11500 Standing Capacity: 12500

London Astoria 157 Charing Cross Rd, London WC2H 0EN
t 020 7434 9592 **f** 020 7437 1781
e calexander@londonastoria.co.uk **w** meanfiddler.com
Bookings Mgr: Chris Alexander. Seated Capacity: 520
Standing Capacity: 2000

London Palladium Argyll St, London W1A 3AB
t 020 7494 5020 or 020 7734 6846 **f** 020 7437 4010
Contact: Gareth Parnell. Seated Capacity: 2291

Loreburn Hall Newall Terrace, Dumfries DG1 1LN
t 01387 260243 **f** 01387 2672255
Area Mgr, East: John MacMillan. Seated Capacity: 800
Standing Capacity: 1400

Loughborough Student Union, Ashby Rd, Loughborough,
Leics LE11 3TT **t** 01509 632020 **f** 01509 235593
e davehowes@lborosu.org.uk **w** lufbra.net
Ents Mgr: Dave Howes. Seated Capacity: 400
Standing Capacity: 2500

The Louisiana Bathurst Parade, Wapping Rd, Bristol
BS1 6UA **t** 0117 926 5978 or 0117 966 3388 **w** thelouisiana.net
Promoter: Michele Schillaci. Standing Capacity: 170

The Lowry Pier 8, Salford Quays, Manchester M50 3AZ
t 0161 876 2020 **f** 0161 876 2021 **e** info@thelowry.com
w thelowry.com.

LSE SU Entertainments LSE SU East Building, East
Building, Houghton St, London WC2A 2AE **t** 020 7955 7136
f 020 7955 6789 **e** su.ents@lse.ac.uk **w** lse.ac.uk/union
Ents Officer: George Ioannou. Seated Capacity: 440
Standing Capacity: 550

LSO St Luke's 161 Old St, London EC1V 9NG
t 020 7490 3939 **f** 020 7566 2881 **e** lsostlukes@lso.co.uk
w lso.co.uk/lsostlukes Centre Director: Simon Wales.
Seated Capacity: 370

The Luminaire 311 Kilburn High Rd, London NW6 7JR
t 020 7372 8668 **e** info@theluminaire.co.uk **w** theluminaire.co.uk
Promoter: Andy Inglis. Standing Capacity: 250

University of Luton Student Union Europa House,
Vicarage St, Luton, Beds LU1 3JU **t** 01582 743272
f 01582 457187 **e** su.entsofficer@luton.ac.uk **w** ulsu.co.uk
Venue & Events Manager: Darren Reed. Seated Capacity: 1000
Standing Capacity: 1000

Lyric Theatre, Hammersmith King St, London W6 0QL
t 020 8741 0824 **f** 020 8741 7694 **e** foh@lyric.co.uk
w lyric.co.uk Theatre Mgr: Howard Meaden.
Seated Capacity: 560

Magnum Theatre Magnum Leisure Centre, Harbourside,
Irvine KA12 8PP **t** 01294 316463 **f** 01294 273172
e wfreckleton@naleisure.co.uk **w** naleisure.co.uk
Ents Officer: Willie Freckleton. Seated Capacity: 1164
Standing Capacity: 1700

Malvern Theatres Grange Rd, Malvern, Worcs WR14 3HB
t 01684 569256 or 01684 892277 **f** 01684 893300
e post@malvern-theatres.co.uk **w** malvern-theaters.co.uk
Chief Exec: Nicolas Lloyd. Seated Capacity: 850

Manchester Academy & University Student Union, Oxford Rd, Manchester M13 9PR **t** 0161 275 2930 **f** 0161 275 2936 **e** maximum@umu.man.ac.uk **w** umu.man.ac.uk Events Manager: Sean Morgan. Standing Capacity: 1800

Manchester Evening News Arena Victoria Station, Manchester M3 1AR **t** 0161 950 5000 **f** 0161 950 6000 **e** info@men-arena.com **w** men-arena.com GM: John Knight. Seated Capacity: 19500

Manchester Met Students' Union 99 Oxford Rd, Manchester M1 7EL **t** 0161 247 6468 **f** 0161 247 6314 **e** s.u.ents@mmu.ac.uk **w** mmsu.com Ents Mgr: Ben Casasola. Seated Capacity: 950 Standing Capacity: 1100

Manchester Opera House Quay St, Manchester M3 3HP **t** 0161 834 1787 **f** 0161 834 5243 **w** manchestertheatres.co.uk Seated Capacity: 1909

Manchester Palace Theatre Oxford St, Manchester M1 6FT **t** 0161 228 6255 **f** 0161 237 5746 **w** manchestertheatres.co.uk Contact: Rachel Miller. Seated Capacity: 1996

Mansfield Leisure Centre Chesterfield Road South, Mansfield, Notts NG19 7BQ **t** 01623 463800 **f** 01623 463912 Mgr: M Darnell. Seated Capacity: 1100 Standing Capacity: 1500

Marco's An Aird Fort William PH33 6AN **t** 01397 700707 **f** 01397 700708. Seated Capacity: 1500 Standing Capacity: 2100

Marcus Garvey Centre Lenton Boulevard, Nottingham NG7 2BY **t** 0115 942 0297 **f** 0115 942 0297 Contact: Mr T Brown.

Margate Winter Gardens Fort Crescent, Margate, Kent CT9 1HX **t** 01843 296111 **f** 01843 295180 Ops Mgr: Mr S Davis. Seated Capacity: 1400 Standing Capacity: 1900

Marina Theatre The Marina, Lowestoft, Suffolk NR32 1HH **t** 01502 533200 (Box) or 01502 533203 **f** 01502 538179 **e** info@marinatheatre.co.uk Venues Mgr: Martin Halliday. Seated Capacity: 751

Marlowe Theatre The Friars, Canterbury, Kent CT1 2AS **t** 01227 763262 **f** 01227 781802 **e** mark.everett@canterbury.gov.uk **w** marlowetheatre.com Theatre Dir: Mark Everett. Seated Capacity: 993

The Marquee Club 1 Leicester Sq, London WC2H 7NA **t** 020 7336 7326 or 020 7734 5467 **e** info@plummusic.com **w** plummusic.com Contact: Allan North.

Maryport Civic Hall Lower Church St, Maryport, Cumbria **t** 01900 812652 Mgr: Margaret Craig. Seated Capacity: 400 Standing Capacity: 600

Mayfield Leisure Centre 10 Mayfield Pl, Mayfield, Dalkeith, Midlothian EH22 5JG **t** 0131 663 2219 **f** 0131 660 9539 Contact: Area Leisure Mgr. Seated Capacity: 400 Standing Capacity: 600

The Mayflower Commercial Rd, Southampton, Hants SO15 1GE **t** 023 8071 1800 **f** 023 8071 1801 **e** Dennis.hall@mayflower.org.uk **w** the-mayflower.com Chief Executive: Dennis Hall. Seated Capacity: 2406

Mean Fiddler 165 Charing Cross Rd, London WC2H 0EN **t** 020 7434 9592 **f** 020 7437 1781 **e** calexander@londonastoria.co.uk **w** meanfiddler.com Promoter: Chris Alexander. Standing Capacity: 1000

Medina Theatre Mountbatten Centre, Fairlee Rd, Newport, Isle of Wight PO30 2DX **t** 01983 527020 **f** 01983 822821 Contact: Paul Broome. Seated Capacity: 425

Mercury Theatre Balkerne Gate, Colchester, Essex CO1 1PT **t** 01206 577006 **f** 01206 769607 **e** info@mercurytheatre.co.uk Marketing Director: Philip Bray. Seated Capacity: 496

The Met Arts Centre Market St, Bury, Lancs BL9 0BW **t** 0161 761 7107 **f** 0161 763 5056 **e** post@themet.biz **w** themet.biz Dir: Ged Kelly. Seated Capacity: 230 Standing Capacity: 300

Metro Club 19-23 Oxford St, London W1D 2DN **t** 020 7636 7744 **f** 020 7636 7755 **e** bookings@blowupmetro.com **w** blowupmetro.com Dirs: Paul Tunkin & Alan Campbell. Standing Capacity: 175

The Metropole Galleries The Metropole Galleries, The Leas, Folkestone, Kent CT20 2LS **t** 01303 255070 **f** 01303 851353 **e** info@metropole.org.uk **w** mertopole.org.uk Dir: Nick Ewbank. Seated Capacity: 140 Standing Capacity: 200

Middlesbrough Town Hall PO Box 69, Albert Rd, Middlesbrough, Cleveland TS1 1EL **t** 01642 263848 or 01642 263850 **f** 01642 221866 Bookings Mgr: Jean Hewitt. Seated Capacity: 1190 Standing Capacity: 1352

Middlesex University Student Union, Bramley Rd, London N14 4YZ **t** 020 8411 6450 **f** 020 8440 5944 **e** d.medawar@mdx.ac.uk **w** musu.mdx.ac.uk VP Ents: David Medawar. Seated Capacity: 400 Standing Capacity: 850

Middleton Civic Hall Fountain St, Middleton, Manchester M24 1AF **t** 0161 643 2470 or 0161 643 2389 **f** 0161 654 0221. Seated Capacity: 565 Standing Capacity: 750

Milton Keynes College Chaffron Way, Leadenhall, Milton Keynes MK6 5LP **t** 01908 230797 **f** 01908 684399.

Ministry of Sound 103 Gaunt St, London SE1 6DP **t** 020 7378 6528 **f** 020 7403 5348 **e** arnie@ministryofsound.com **w** ministryofsound.com GM: Gary Smart. Standing Capacity: 1500

Mitchell Theatre Exchange House, 229 George St, Glasgow, Lanarkshire G1 1QU **t** 0141 287 4855 **f** 0141 221 0695. Seated Capacity: 418

Moles Club 14 George St, Bath BA1 2EN **t** 01225 404445 **f** 01225 404447 **e** kath@moles.co.uk **w** moles.co.uk Bookings Mgr: Kath O'Connor. Standing Capacity: 200

Michael Monroes Bar Carnegie Theatre, Finkle St, Workington, Cumbria CA14 2BD **t** 01900 602122 **f** 01900 67143 Mgr: Paul Sherwin. Standing Capacity: 200

Morfa Stadium Upper Bank, Pentrechwyth, Swansea SA1 7DF **t** 01792 476578 **f** 01792 467995.

Mote Hall Maidstone Leisure Centre, Mote Pk, Maidstone, Kent ME15 7RN **t** 01622 220234 **f** 01622 672462 Events Mgr: Barry Reynolds. Seated Capacity: 1200 Standing Capacity: 1080

Motherwell Concert Hall & Theatre PO Box 14, Civic Centre, Motherwell, Lanarkshire ML1 1TW **t** 01698 267515 **f** 01698 268806 Contact: Theatre Mgr. Seated Capacity: 883 Standing Capacity: 1800

Motherwell Theatre, Civic Centre PO Box 14, Motherwell, North Lanarkshire ML1 1TW **t** 01698 267515 **f** 01698 268806 Theatre Mgr: Lynn McDougal. Seated Capacity: 395

The Musician Clyde St, Leicester LE1 2DE **t** 0116 251 0080 **f** 0116 251 0474 **e** rideout@stayfree.co.uk **w** themusicianpub.co.uk Booker/Mgr: Darren Nockles. Seated Capacity: 120 Standing Capacity: 150

Napier Student Association 12 Merchiston Pl, Edinburgh EH10 4NR **t** 0131 229 8791 **f** 0131 228 3462 **e** e.reynolds@napier.ac.uk **w** napierstudents.com Contact: Ents Officer. Standing Capacity: 100

The National Bowl at Milton Keynes c/o BS Group plc, Abbey Stadium, Lady Lane, Swindon, Wilts SW2 4DW **t** 0117 952 0600 **f** 0117 952 5500 Contact: Gordon Cockhill. Standing Capacity: 65000

National Club 234 Kilburn High Rd, London NW6 4JR **t** 020 7625 4444 or 020 7328 3141 Contact: PJ Carey. Standing Capacity: 1200

The National Indoor Arena King Edward's Rd, Birmingham, W Midlands B1 2AA **t** 0121 780 4141 **e** nia-sales@necgroup.co.uk **w** necgroup.co.uk Dir of Arenas: Linda Barrow. Seated Capacity: 8000 Standing Capacity: 12000

NEC Arena The NEC, Birmingham, W Midlands B40 1NT **t** 0121 767 3981 **f** 0121 767 3858 **e** nec-arena@necgroup.co.uk **w** necgroup.co.uk Dir of Arenas: Linda Barrow.

The Nerve Centre 7-8 Magazine St, Londonderry BT48 6HJ **t** 028 7126 0562 **f** 028 7137 1738 **e** info@nerve-create.org.uk **w** nerve-create.org.uk Promoter: Tony Doherty. Standing Capacity: 600

New Theatre George St, Oxford OX1 2AG **t** 01865 320760 **f** 08707 490 836 **e** firstname.lastname@clearchannel.co.uk **w** getlive.co.uk Theatre Mgr: Anna Charles. Seated Capacity: 1826

New Theatre, Cardiff Park Pl, Cardiff CF10 3LN **t** 029 2087 8787 or 029 2087 8889 **f** 029 2087 8788 Contact: Giles Ballisat. Seated Capacity: 1156

New Theatre Royal Guildhall Walk, Portsmouth, Hants PO1 2DD **t** 01705 646477 or 01705 649000 **f** 01705 646488 Contact: Fiona Cole. Seated Capacity: 320 Standing Capacity: 450

New Victoria Theatre Woking, Surrey **t** 01483 761144.

Newcastle City Hall Northumberland Rd, Newcastle upon Tyne, Tyne and Wear NE1 8SF **t** 0191 222 1778 or 0191 261 2606 **f** 0191 261 8102 Mgr: Peter Brennan. Seated Capacity: 2133

Newcastle University Union Student Union, Kings Walk, Newcastle upon Tyne, Tyne & Wear NE1 8QB **t** 0191 239 3926 **f** 0191 222 1876 **e** union-entertainments@ncl.ac.uk **w** union.ncl.ac.uk/entertainments Entertainments Manager: Polly Woodbridge. Standing Capacity: 1200

Newham Leisure Centre 281 Prince Regent Lane, London E13 8SD **t** 020 7511 4477 **f** 020 7511 6463.

Newman College Of Education Student Union, Genners Lane, Bartley Green, Birmingham B32 3NT **t** 0121 475 6714 **f** 0121 475 6714 **e** ncsu@newman.ac.uk Contact: Louise Beasley. Seated Capacity: 160 Standing Capacity: 300

Newport Centre Kingsway, Newport, Gwent NP20 1UH **t** 01633 662663 **f** 01633 662675 Events Mgr: Roger Broome. Seated Capacity: 2000 Standing Capacity: 1600

Nice 'n' Sleazy 421 Sauchiehall St, Glasgow, Lanarkshire G2 3LG **t** 0141 333 9637 or 0141 333 0900 **f** 0141 333 0900 **e** sleazys@hotmail.com **w** nicensleazy.com Promoter: Mig. Standing Capacity: 200

Night & Day Cafe 26 Oldham St, Northern Quarter, Manchester M1 1JN **t** 0161 236 4597 **f** 0161 236 1822 **e** ben@nightnday.org **w** nightnday.org Promoter/Manager: Ben Taylor. Standing Capacity: 250

North Wales Theatre And Conference Centre The Promenade, Llandudno, Conwy LL30 1BB **t** 01492 872000 **e** admin@nwtheatre.co.uk **w** nwtheatre.co.uk GM: Sarah Ecob. Seated Capacity: 1500 Standing Capacity: 1100

North Worcestershire College Student Union, Burcot Lane, Bromsgrove, Worcs B60 1PQ **t** 01527 570020 **f** 01527 572900.

Northgate Arena Victoria Rd, Chester CH2 2AU **t** 01244 377086 **f** 01244 381693 **e** cadsart@compuserve.com **w** northgatearena.com Business Development Mgr: Jon Kelly. Seated Capacity: 800 Standing Capacity: 1800

Northumbria University Union Building, 2 Sandyford Rd, Newcastle upon Tyne NE1 8SB **t** 0191 227 3791 **f** 0191 227 3776 **e** s.collier@unn.ac.uk Ents Mgr: Sue Collier. Standing Capacity: 1680

Norwich Arts Centre Reeves Yard, St Benedicts, Norfolk NR2 4PG **t** 01603 660387 **f** 01603 660352 Centre Mgr: Pam Reekie. Seated Capacity: 120 Standing Capacity: 250

Norwich City Hall St Peters St, Norwich, Norfolk NR2 1NH **t** 01603 622233 **f** 01603 213000.

Notting Hill Arts Club 21 Notting Hill Gate, London W11 3JQ **t** 020 7460 4459.

Nottingham Albert Hall North Circus St, Off Derby Rd, Notts NG1 5AA **t** 0115 950 0411 **f** 0115 947 6512 Events Mgr: Sarah Robinson. Seated Capacity: 900

Nottingham Trent University Student Union, Byron House, Shakespeare St, Nottingham NG1 4GH **t** 0115 848 6200 **f** 0115 848 6201 **e** ents@su.ntu.ac.uk **w** su.ntu.ac.uk Ents Manager: Alex Ginever. Standing Capacity: 640

University of Nottingham Student Union, Portland Building, University Pk, Nottingham NG7 2RD **t** 0115 935 1100 Social Sec: Tanya Nathan. Seated Capacity: 200

Number10 10 Golborne Rd, London W10 5PE **t** 020 8969 8922 **f** 020 8969 8933 **e** tris@number10london.com **w** number10london.com Events Co-ordinator: Tris Dickin.

The O2 Arena Greenwich Penninsular, London SE10 **t** 020 7536 2630 **e** sales@theo2.co.uk **w** theo2.co.uk Head of Sales - The O2: Caroline McNamara. Seated Capacity: 20000

The O2 Live Music Club Greenwich Penninsular, London SE10 **t** 020 7536 2630 **e** sales@theo2.co.uk **w** theo2.co.uk Head of Sales - The O2: Caroline McNamara. Seated Capacity: 800 Standing Capacity: 2200

Oakengates Theatre Lines Walk, Oakengates, Telford, Shropshire TF2 6EP **t** 01952 619020 **f** 01552 610164 **e** oakthea@telford.gov.uk **w** oakengates.ws Theatre Mgr: Psyche Hudson. Seated Capacity: 650 Standing Capacity: 780

Oasis Leisure Centre North Star Ave, Swindon, Wilts SN2 1EP **t** 01793 445401 or 01793 465173 **f** 01793 445569 **e** mljones@swindon.gov.uk **w** swindon.gov.uk/oasis Bookings Mgr: Michelle Jones. Seated Capacity: 1580 Standing Capacity: 3000

Ocean 270 Mare St, Hackney, London E8 1HE **t** 020 8533 0111 **f** 020 8533 1991 **e** mail@ocean.org.uk **w** ocean.org.uk Venue Manager: Alan Henehan. Seated Capacity: 2100 Standing Capacity: 900

Octagon Theatre Howell Croft South, Bolton, Lancs BL1 1SB **t** 01204 529407 or 01204 520661 **f** 01204 380110 Contact: The Administrator. Seated Capacity: 420

Odyssey Arena 2 Queen's Quay, Belfast BT3 9QQ **t** 028 9076 6000 **f** 028 9076 6111 **e** info@odysseyarena.com **w** odysseyarena.com Executive Director: Nicky Dunn. Seated Capacity: 9500 Standing Capacity: 10000

The Old Institute 9 The Strand, Derby DE1 1BJ **t** 01332 381770 **f** 01332 381745 **e** paul.needham7@btopenworld.com GM/Promoter: Paul Needham. Standing Capacity: 500

The Old Market Upper Market St, Hove, E. Sussex BN3 1AS **t** 01273 736 222 **f** 01273 329 636 **e** carolinebrown@theoldmarket.co.uk **w** theoldmarket.co.uk Artistic Dir: Caroline Brown. Seated Capacity: 300 Standing Capacity: 500

Old Town Hall High St, Hemel Hempstead, Herts HP1 3AE **t** 01442 228097 **f** 01442 234072 **e** othadmin@dacorum.gov.uk **w** oldtownhall.co.uk Marketing & Publicity: Ranjit Atwal. Seated Capacity: 120

The Old Vic The Cut, Waterloo, London SE1 8NB **t** 020 7231 1393 **f** 020 7232 1373 **e** jo@interactivem.co.uk Promoter: Jo Cerrone. Seated Capacity: 1100

Olympia (see Earls Court).

The Orchard Theatre Home Gardens, Dartford, Kent DA1 1ED **t** 01322 220099 **f** 01322 227122 **e** vanessa.hart@dartford.gov.uk **w** orchardtheatre.co.uk Theate Mgr: Vanessa Hart. Seated Capacity: 950

Ormond Multi Media Centre 14 Lower Ormond Quay, Dublin 1, Ireland **t** +353 1 872 3500 **f** +353 1 872 3348.

The Overdraft 300-310 High Rd, Ilford, Essex IG1 1QW **t** 020 8514 4400.

Oxford University Student Union New Barnet House, Little Clarendon St, Oxford OX1 2HU **t** 01865 270777 or 01865 270769 **f** 01865 270776 **e** president@ousu.org **w** ousu.org Pres: Ruth Hunt.

Paisley Arts Centre New St, Paisley, Renfrewshire PA1 1EZ **t** 0141 887 1010 **f** 0141 887 6300 **e** artsinfo@renfrewshire.gov.uk Principle Arts Officer: John Harding. Seated Capacity: 158

University of Paisley - Ayr Campus Student Association, Beech Grove, Ayr KA8 0SR **t** 01292 886330 office or 01292 886362 union **f** 01292 886271 **e** dpa@upsa.org.uk Deputy President: Kim Macintyre. Seated Capacity: 100 Standing Capacity: 200

Paradise Bar 460 New Cross Rd, London SE14 6TJ **t** 020 8692 1530 **f** 020 8691 0445 **w** paradisebar.co.uk Contact: David Roberts. Standing Capacity: 300

The Paradise Room Blackpool Pleasure Peach, Ocean Boulevard, Blackpool, Lancs FY4 1EZ **t** 01253 341033 **f** 01253 407609 **e** debbie.hawksey@bpbltd.com **w** bpbltd.com Contact: Debbie Hawksey. Seated Capacity: 600 Standing Capacity: 750

Parr Hall Palmyra Square South, Warrington, Cheshire WA1 1BL **t** 01925 442345 **f** 01925 443228 **e** parrhall@warrington.gov.uk **w** parrhall.co.uk Arts & Project Mgr: John Perry. Seated Capacity: 1000 Standing Capacity: 1100

Pavilion Argyle St, Rothesay, Isle Of Bute **t** 01546 602127 or 01700 504250 mgr **f** 01700 504225. Seated Capacity: 4100 Standing Capacity: 5250

Pavilion Theatre Marine Parade, Worthing BN11 3PX **t** 01903 231 799 **f** 01903 215 337 **e** theatres@worthing.gov.uk **w** worthingtheatres.co.uk Theatres Manager: Peter Bailey. Seated Capacity: 867 Standing Capacity: 1100

Peacock Arts And Entertainment Centre Victoria Way, Woking, Surrey GU21 1GQ **t** 01483 747422 **f** 01483 770477. Standing Capacity: 500

The Penny 30-31 Northgate, Canterbury, Kent CT1 1BL **t** 01227 450333 or 01227 470512 **f** 01227 450333 Contact: Ian Mills. Seated Capacity: 100 Standing Capacity: 200

Perth City Hall King Edward St, Perth PH1 5UT **t** 01738 624055 **f** 01738 630566 GM: Drew Scott. Seated Capacity: 1350 Standing Capacity: 1627

Philharmonic Hall Hope St, Liverpool, Merseyside L1 9BP **t** 0151 210 2895 **f** 0151 210 2902 **e** hall@liverpoolphil.com **w** liverpoolphil.com Executive Director: Simon Glinn. Seated Capacity: 1682

The Phoenix Phoenix St, Plymouth PL1 3NW **t** 07855 858 086 or 01752 253 334 **e** rachael@plymouthphoenix.co.uk **w** plymouthphoenix.co.uk Promoter: Rachael Easterbrook.

The Platform Old Station Buildings, Central Promenade, Morecambe, Lancs LA4 4DB **t** 01524 582801 **f** 01524 831704 **e** Jharris@lancaster.gov.uk **w** lancaster.gov.uk Head of Arts and Events: Jon Harris. Seated Capacity: 350 Standing Capacity: 1000

The Playhouse Harlow Playhouse Sq, Harlow, Essex CM20 1LS **t** 01279 446760 **f** 01279 424391 **e** playhouse@harlow.gov.uk **w** playhouseharlow.com Theatre Mgr: Phillip Dale. Seated Capacity: 419

Playhouse Theatre High St, Weston-Super-Mare, North Somerset BS23 1HP **t** 01934 627457 **f** 01934 612182 **e** Andy.Jeffrey@n-somerset.gov.uk **w** theplayhouse.co.uk Program'g & Mkt'g Mgr: Andy Jeffery. Seated Capacity: 664

Plug 14-16 Matilda St, Sheffield S1 4QD **t** 0114 249 2200 **f** 0114 249 2209 **e** info@the-plug.com **w** the-plug.com Bookings: Geoff Ticehurst, Ali Peek. Standing Capacity: 1200

Plymouth College Of Art & Design Student Union, Tavistock Pl, Plymouth, Devon PL4 8AT **t** 01752 203434 **f** 01752 203444.

Plymouth Pavilions Millbay Rd, Plymouth, Devon PL1 3LF **t** 01752 222200 **f** 01752 262226 **e** enquiries@plymouthpavilions.com **w** plymouthpavilions.com Mktg Mgr: Sarah Weeks. Seated Capacity: 2400 Standing Capacity: 4000

Plymouth University Student Union, Drake Circus, Plymouth, Devon PL4 8AA **t** 01752 663337 **f** 01752 251669 Contact: Mark Witherall. Standing Capacity: 600

The Point - Cardiff Bay Mount Stuart Sq, Cardiff Bay, Cardiff CF10 6EB **t** 029 2046 0873 **f** 029 2048 8535 **e** info@thepointcardiffbay.com **w** thepointcardiffbay.com Contact: Mike Johnson. Seated Capacity: 200 Standing Capacity: 280

The Point Arena and Theatre East Link Bridge, Dublin 1, Ireland **t** 00 353 1 836 6777 **f** 00 353 1 836 6422 GM: Cormal Rennick. Seated Capacity: 6500 Standing Capacity: 8500

The Point Cardiff Bay Mount Stuart Sq, Cardiff Bay, Cardiff CF10 6EB **t** 029 2046 0873 **f** 029 2048 8535 **e** info@thepointcardiffbay.com **w** thepointcardiffbay.com Venue Manager: Ceri Whitehead.

The Point The Plain, Oxford OX4 1EA **t** 01865 798794 **f** 01865 798794 **e** mac@thepoint.oxfordmusic.net **w** thepoint.oxfordmusic.net Promoter: Mac. Seated Capacity: 220 Standing Capacity: 220

The Pop Factory Welsh Hills Works, Jenkin St, Porth CF39 9PP **t** 01443 688500 or 01443 688504 **f** 01443 688501 **e** info@thepopfactory.com **w** thepopfactory.com Contact: Mair Afan Davies. Standing Capacity: 300

The Porter Cellar Bar 15 George St, Bath BA1 2QS **t** 01225 424104 **f** 01225 404447 **e** steve@moles.co.uk **w** moles.co.uk Booker: Steve Wheadon. Seated Capacity: 150 Standing Capacity: 150

Portobello Town Hall 147 Portobello High St, Edinburgh, Lothian EH15 1AF **t** 0131 669 5800 **f** 0131 669 5800 Hall Keeper: Andrew Crazy. Seated Capacity: 771

Portsmouth Guildhall Guildhall Sq, Portsmouth, Hants PO1 2AB **t** 01705 834146 **f** 01705 834177 GM: Martin Dodd. Seated Capacity: 2017 Standing Capacity: 2228

Portsmouth University The Student Centre, Cambridge Rd, Portsmouth, Hants PO1 2EF **t** 02392 843640 **f** 02392 843667 **e** janet.hillier@port.ac.uk **w** upsu.net Trad Op's Exec: Janet Hillier. Standing Capacity: 450

Pressure Point 33 Richmond Pl, Brighton BN2 9NA **t** 01273 684 501 **e** gareth@pressurepoint.me.uk **w** pressurepoint.me.uk Bookings Mgr: Simon Parker. Standing Capacity: 210

Prince of Wales Theatre Coventry St, London W1V 8AS **t** 020 7930 9901 **f** 020 7976 1336 Contact: George Biggs. Seated Capacity: 1100 Standing Capacity: 100

Princes Hall Princes Way, Aldershot, Hants GU11 1NX **t** 01252 327671 **f** 01252 320269 **w** rushmoor.gov.uk/princes/index.htm GM: Steven Pugh. Seated Capacity: 700 Standing Capacity: 700

Princes Theatre Station Rd, Clacton-on-Sea, Essex CO15 1SE **t** 01255 253208 **f** 01255 253200 **e** rfoster@tendringdc.gov.uk **w** tendringdc.gov.uk Ents Officer: Bob Foster. Seated Capacity: 820 Standing Capacity: 800

Princess Pavilion Theatre & Gyllyndune Gardens 41 Melvill Rd, Falmouth, Cornwall TR11 4AR **t** 01326 311277 or 01326 211222 **f** 01326 315382 Contact: Mr RHD Phipps. Seated Capacity: 400 Standing Capacity: 400

Princess Theatre Torbay Rd, Torquay, Devon TQ2 5EZ **t** 01803 290288 or 01803 290290 (BO) **f** 01803 290170 GM: Wendy Bennett. Seated Capacity: 1487

Purcell Room Royal Festival Hall, Belvedere Rd, London SE1 8XX **t** 020 7921 0952 **f** 020 7928 2049 **e** Initial+surname@rfh.org.uk **w** rfh.org.uk Prog Planning Mgr: Liz Sweetland. Seated Capacity: 367

Purple Turtle 9 Gunn St, Reading, Berks RG1 2JR **t** 0118 959 7196 **f** 0118 958 3142 **e** andy@purpleturtlebar.com **w** purpleturtlebar.com Bookings Manager: Andy Churchill. Standing Capacity: 470

Quay Arts Centre Sea St, Newport Harbour, Isle Of Wight PO30 5BD **t** 01983 822490 **f** 01938 526606 **e** info@quayarts.org **w** quayarts.org Dir/Programming: Stephen Munn. Seated Capacity: 130

Queen Elizabeth Hall Belvedere Rd, London SE1 8XX **t** 020 7921 0815 **f** 020 7928 2049 **e** Initial+lastname@rfh.org.uk **w** rfh.org.uk Hd of Hall Program'g: Pam Chowhan. Seated Capacity: 902

Queen Elizabeth Hall West St, Oldham, Lancs OL1 1UT **t** 0161 911 4071 **f** 0161 911 3094 Admin Mgr: Shelagh Malley. Seated Capacity: 1300 Standing Capacity: 2000

Queen Margaret University College Student's Union, 36 Clerwood Terrace, Edinburgh EH12 8TS **t** 0131 317 3403 **f** 0131 317 3402 **e** union@qmuc.ac.uk **w** qmucsu.org.uk Ents Mgr: Matt Zitron. Seated Capacity: 300 Standing Capacity: 400

Queen's Hall Arts Centre Beaumont St, Hexham, Northumberland NE46 3LS **t** 01434 606787 or 01434 607272 **f** 01434 606043 Arts Mgr: Geoff Keys. Seated Capacity: 399

Queen's Hall Victoria Rd, Widnes, Cheshire WA8 7RF **t** 0151 424 2339 **f** 0151 420 5762 Contact: Brian Pridmore. Seated Capacity: 640 Standing Capacity: 810

Queens Hall Victoria Rd, Widnes, Cheshire WA8 7RF **t** 0151 424 2339 **f** 0151 420 5762 **e** queenshall@halton-borough.gov.uk **w** queenshall-widnes.com Entertainments Manager: Brian Pridmore. Seated Capacity: 640 Standing Capacity: 810

The Queens Hall Edinburgh Clerk St, Edinburgh, Lothian EH8 9JG **t** 0131 668 3456 **f** 0131 668 2656 Hall Mgr: Iain McQueen. Seated Capacity: 868 Standing Capacity: 900

Queen's Theatre Boutport St, Barnstaple, Devon EX31 1SY **t** 01271 327357 or 01271 865655 **f** 01271 326412 **e** info@northdevontheatres.org.uk **w** northdevontheatres.org.uk Karen Turner: Programming Dir. Seated Capacity: 688

Queens University Students Union, 79-81 University Rd, Belfast, Co Antrim BT7 1PE **t** 028 9032 4803 **f** 028 9023 6900 **e** info@qubsu-ents.com **w** qubsu-ents.com. Standing Capacity: 800

Queensway Hall Vernon Pl, Dunstable, Beds LU5 4EU
t 01582 603326 **f** 01582 471190 GM: Yvonne Mullens.
Seated Capacity: 900 Standing Capacity: 1200

Rada Bar Malet St, London WC1E 7PA **t** 020 7636 7076
f 020 7908 4895 **e** finance@rada.ac.uk **w** rada.ac.uk
Mgr: Annette Bennett. Standing Capacity: 100

Reading University PO Box 230, Whiteknights, Reading,
Berks RG6 2AZ **t** 0118 986 0222 **f** 0118 975 5283.
Standing Capacity: 1400

The Red Brick Theatre Aqueduct Rd, Blackburn, Lancs
BB2 4HT **t** 01254 698859 or 01254 265566 **f** 01254 265640
Contact: Miss C Kay. Seated Capacity: 380

Redditch Palace Theatre Alcester St, Redditch, Worcs
B98 8AE **t** 01527 61544 or 01527 65203 **f** 01527 60243
Bookings Mgr: Michael Dyer. Seated Capacity: 399

The Rex 361 Stratford High St, London E15 4QZ
t 020 8215 6003 **f** 020 8215 6004 **w** meanfiddler.com.

The Rhythm Station Station House, Station Court,
Newhallhey Rd, Rawtenstall, Rossendale, Lancs BB4 6AJ
t 01706 214039.

The Richmond 10 Fisher St, Carlisle, Cumbria CA3 8R
t 01228 512220 **f** 01228 534168 **e** Rvenue@aol.com
w jnightclub.co.uk Promoter/Owner: David Jackson.
Standing Capacity: 325

Richmond Theatre The Green, Richmond, Surrey TW9 1QJ
t 020 8940 0220 **f** 020 8948 3601 Theatre Dir: Karin Gartzke.
Seated Capacity: 830

The Ritz Ballroom Whitworth Street West, Manchester
M1 5NQ **t** 0161 236 4355 **f** 0161 236 7515
e eddieritz@hotmail.com GM: Eddie Challiner.
Standing Capacity: 1500

Rivermead Leisure Complex Richfield Ave, Reading,
Berks RG1 8EQ **t** 0118 901 5014 **f** 0118 901 5006.
Seated Capacity: 2400 Standing Capacity: 3000

Riverside Studios Crisp Rd, Hammersmith, London W6 9RL
t 020 8237 1000 **f** 020 8237 1011
e jonfawcett@riversidestudios.co.uk **w** riversidestudios.co.uk
Hires Mgr: Jon Fawcett. Seated Capacity: 500
Standing Capacity: 500

The Roadhouse 8 Newton St, Piccadilly, Manchester
M1 2AN **t** 0161 237 9789 or 0161 228 1789 **f** 0161 236 9289
e kris@theroadhouselive.co.uk **w** theroadhouselive.co.uk
Promoter: Kris Reid. Standing Capacity: 350

The Roadmender 1 Ladys Lane, Northampton NN1 3AH
t 01604 604 603 **f** 01604 603 166 **w** roadmender.uk
Contact: Jon Dunn. Seated Capacity: 300 Standing Capacity: 900

The Robin 2 26-28 Mount Pleasant, Bilston, Wolverhampton,
W Midlands WV14 7LJ **t** 01902 405 511 or 01902 401 211
f 01902 401 418 **e** music@therobin.co.uk **w** therobin.co.uk
Dir: Mike Hamblett. Standing Capacity: 700

Rock City 8 Talbot St, Nottingham NG1 5GG
t 0115 941 2544 **f** 0115 941 8438 **e** boxoffice@rock-city.co.uk
w rock-city.co.uk Dir: George Akins. Standing Capacity: 1900

The Rock Garden/Gardening Club Bedford Chambers,
The Piazza, Covent Garden, London WC2E 8HA
t 07779 582 927 **f** 020 7379 4793 **e** info@platformmusic.net
w rockgarden.co.uk Platform Promoter: Lisa Cowan.
Standing Capacity: 250

The Rocket Complex 166-220 Holloway Rd, London
N7 8DB **t** 020 7133 2238 **e** info.rocket@londonmet.ac.uk
w rocket-complex.net Event Mgr: Geoff Barnett.
Standing Capacity: 1200

Ronnie Scott's 47 Frith St, London W1D 4HT
t 020 7439 0747 **f** 020 7437 5081
e ronniescotts@ronniescotts.co.uk **w** ronniescotts.co.uk
Owner/Club Director: Pete King. Seated Capacity: 300
Standing Capacity: 100

Rotherham Civic Theatre Catherine St, Rotherham, S
Yorks S65 1EB **t** 01709 823640 **f** 01709 823638.
Seated Capacity: 357

Rothes Halls The Kingdom Centre, Glenrothes, Fife KY7 5NX
t 01592 612121 or 01592 611101 (box) **f** 01592 612220
e admin@rotheshalls.org.uk **w** rotheshalls.org.uk
Halls Mgr: Frank Chinn. Seated Capacity: 706
Standing Capacity: 1500

Roundhouse Chalk Farm Rd, London NW1 8EH
t 020 7424 6774 **f** 020 7424 9992
e kate.lewis@roundhouse.org.uk **w** roundhouse.org.uk
PR & Events Manager: Kate Lewis. Standing Capacity: 3000

Royal Albert Hall Kensington Gore, London SW7 2AP
t 020 7589 3203 **f** 020 7823 7725 **e** sales@royalalberthall.com
w royalalberthall.com Head of Sales & Mkting: Tracy Cooper.
Seated Capacity: 5266

Royal Centre Theatre Sq, Nottingham NG1 5ND
t 0115 989 5500 **f** 0115 947 4218
e enquiry@royalcentre-nottingham.co.uk
w royalcentre-nottingham.co.uk
Acting Director: James Ashworth. Seated Capacity: 2499

Royal Concert Hall Theatre Sq, Nottingham NG1 5ND
t 0115 989 5500 **f** 0115 947 4218
e mgrayson@royalcentre.co.uk **w** royalcentre-nottingham.co.uk
MD: J Michael Grayson. Seated Capacity: 2499
Standing Capacity: 10000

Royal Court Theatre 1 Roe St, Liverpool, Merseyside
L1 1HL **t** 0151 709 1808 or 0151 709 4321 **f** 0151 709 7611
e Richard.Maides@iclway.co.uk **w** royalcourttheatre.net
Theatre Manager: Richard Maides. Seated Capacity: 1525
Standing Capacity: 1796

Royal Court Theatre Sloane Sq, London SW1W 8AS
t 020 7565 5050 **f** 020 7565 5001
e info@royalcourttheatre.com **w** royalcourttheatre.com
Exec Dir: Vikki Heywood. Seated Capacity: 396

Royal Exchange Theatre St Ann's Sq, Manchester
M2 7DH **t** 0161 833 9333 **f** 0161 832 0881
e philip.lord@royalexchange.co.uk **w** royalexchange.co.uk
Contact: Philip Lord. Seated Capacity: 700

Royal Festival Hall Belvedere Rd, London SE1 8XX
t 0870 380 4300 **f** 020 7928 2049
e Initial+lastname@rfh.org.uk **w** rfh.org.uk
Project 2007 Dir: Elspeth McBain. Seated Capacity: 2900

Royal Highland Centre Ingliston, Edinburgh EH28 8NF
t 0131 335 6200 **f** 0131 333 5236 **e** info@rhass.org.uk
w royalhighlandcentre.com Dir: Grant Knight.

Royal Lyceum Theatre Grindlay St, Edinburgh EH3 9AX
t 0131 248 4800 or 0131 248 4848 **f** 0131 228 3955
e info@lyceum.org.uk **w** lyceum.org.uk
Admin Mgr: Ruth Butterworth. Seated Capacity: 658

Royal Spa Centre Newbold Terrace, Leamington Spa,
Warcs CV32 4HN **t** 01926 334418 **f** 01926 832054
GM: Peter Nicholson. Seated Capacity: 800
Standing Capacity: 800

The Royal Pall Mall, Hanley, Stoke On Trent, Staffs ST1 1EE
t 01782 206000 or 01782 207777 box off **f** 01782 204955
w webfactory.co.uk/theroyal/ Dir: Mike Lloyd.
Seated Capacity: 1451 Standing Capacity: 1900

Royal Victoria Hall London Rd, Southborough, Tunbridge
Wells, Kent TN4 0ND **t** 01892 529176 **f** 01892 541402.
Seated Capacity: 322

St David's Hall The Hayes, Cardiff CF10 1SH
t 029 2087 8500 **f** 029 2087 8599
Head Arts & Cultural Serv: Judi Richards. Seated Capacity: 1956

St George's Concert Hall Bridge St, Bradford, W Yorks
BD1 1JS **t** 01274 752186 **f** 01274 720736
e christine.raby@bradford.gov.uk **w** bradford-theatres.co.uk
Programme Booking Admin.: Christine Raby.
Seated Capacity: 1574 Standing Capacity: 1872

St George's Hall Market St, Exeter, Devon EX1 1BU
t 01392 665 866 **f** 01392 665 940
e halls.events@exeter.gov.uk **w** exeter.gov.uk/stgeorgeshall
Mgr: David Lewis. Seated Capacity: 500 Standing Capacity: 500

St James Concert & Assembly Hall College St, St
Peter Port, Guernsey, Channel Islands GY1 2NZ **t** 01481 711360
f 01481 711364 Contact: Miss KR Simon. Seated Capacity: 480
Standing Capacity: 350

St John's Tavern 91 Junction Rd, London N19 5QU
t 020 7272 1587 **f** 020 7371 8797 Contact: Nick Sharpe.

St Mary's College Student Union, Waldergrave Rd,
Strawberry Hill, Twickenham, Middlesex TW1 4SX
t 020 8240 4314 **f** 020 8744 1700 Contact: Kieran Renihan.
Seated Capacity: 300 Standing Capacity: 600

Salford University Student Union, University House, The
Crescent, Salford, Greater Manchester M5 4WT **t** 0161 736 7811
f 0161 737 1633 **e** Entsorg-ussu@salford.ac.uk
w salfordstudents.com.

Salisbury Arts Centre Bedwin St, Salisbury, Wilts
SP1 3UT **t** 01722 430700 **f** 01722 331742
e info@salisburyarts.co.uk **w** salisburyarts.co.uk
Centre Mgr: Catherine Sandbook. Seated Capacity: 300
Standing Capacity: 400

Salisbury City Hall Malthouse Lane, Salisbury, Wilts
SP2 7TU **t** 01722 334432 **f** 01722 337059
e gpettifer@salisbury.gov.uk
Sales & Marketing Mgr: Gail Pettifer. Seated Capacity: 953
Standing Capacity: 1116

Scala 275 Pentonville Rd, London N1 9NL **t** 020 7833 2022
f 020 7520 0045 **e** lee@scala-london.co.uk **w** scala-london.co.uk
GM: Lee Hazell. Standing Capacity: 1145

Scarborough Univerity College Student Union, Filey Rd,
Scarborough, N Yorks YO11 3AZ **t** 01723 362392
f 01723 370815 Contact: Nick Evans. Standing Capacity: 250

Scottish Exhibition & Conference Centre Glasgow,
Lanarkshire G3 8YW **t** 0141 248 3000 **f** 0141 226 3423
Acct Mgr, Concerts: Susan Verlaque. Seated Capacity: 9300
Standing Capacity: 10000

Shanklin Theatre Prospect Rd, Shanklin, Isle of Wight
PO37 6AJ **t** 01983 862739 **f** 01983 867682
Contact: David Redston. Seated Capacity: 472

Sheffield Arena Broughton Lane, Sheffield, S Yorks S9 2DF
t 0114 256 2002 **f** 0114 256 5520 **e** info@clearchannel.co.uk
w sheffield-arena.co.uk GM: David Vickers.
Seated Capacity: 12500

Sheffield City Hall Barkers Pool, Sheffield, S Yorks S1 2JA
t 0114 223 3834 **e** c.procter@sheffieldcityhall.co.uk
w sheffieldcityhall.com Bookings: Carol Procter.
Seated Capacity: 2346

Sheffield Hallam University Student's Union, Nelson
Mandela Building, Pond St, Sheffield, South Yorksire S1 2BW
t 0114 225 4122 **f** 0114 225 4140 **e** a.sewell@shu.ac.uk
w shu.ac.uk/su Ents Co-ordinator: Alice Sewell.
Seated Capacity: 250 Standing Capacity: 900

Sheffield University Students Union, Western Bank,
Sheffield, S Yorks S10 2TG **t** 0114 222 8556 **f** 0114 222 8574
e c.white@sheffield.ac.uk **w** sheffieldunion.com
Ents Manager: Chris White. Seated Capacity: 1000
Standing Capacity: 1500

Shepherds Bush Empire Shepherds Bush Green, London
W12 8TT **t** 020 8354 3300 **f** 020 8743 3218
e mail@shepherds-bush-empire.co.uk
w shepherds-bush-empire.co.uk GM: Bill Marshall.
Seated Capacity: 1278 Standing Capacity: 2000

Shrewsbury Music Hall The Square, Shrewsbury,
Shropshire SY1 1LH **t** 01743 281281 **f** 01743 281283
e mail@musichall.co.uk **w** musichall.co.uk
Programming & Mktg Mgr: Adam Burgan. Seated Capacity: 384
Standing Capacity: 500

Snape Maltings Concert Hall High St, Aldeburgh, Suffolk
IP15 5AX **t** 01728 687100 **f** 01728 687120
e enquiries@aldeburghfestivals.org **w** aldeburgh.co.uk
Concert Mgr: Sharon Godard. Seated Capacity: 820

Sound Swiss Centre, 10 Wardour St, London W1V 3HG
t 020 7287 1010 **f** 020 7437 1029 **e** info@soundlondon.com
w soundlondon.com Head of Corporate: Phil Bridges.
Seated Capacity: 300 Standing Capacity: 1335

South Bank University Student Union, Keyworth St,
London SE1 6NG **t** 020 7815 6060 **f** 020 7815 6061
Ents Mgr: Tom Dinnis. Seated Capacity: 400
Standing Capacity: 800

South Hill Park Arts Centre Ringmead, Birch Hill,
Bracknell, Berks RG12 7PA **t** 01344 484858 **f** 01344 411427
e music@southhillpark.org.uk **w** southhillpark.org.uk
Music Officer: Simon Chatterton. Seated Capacity: 330
Standing Capacity: 600

South Holland Centre 23 Market Pl, Spalding, Lincs
PE11 1SS **t** 01775 725031.

South Street 21 South St, Reading, Berks RG1 4QU
t 0118 901 5234 **f** 0118 901 5235
e 21southstreet@reading.gov.uk **w** readingarts.com
Venue Mgr: John Luther. Seated Capacity: 125
Standing Capacity: 200

Southampton Guildhall Civic Centre, Southampton, Hants
SO14 7LP **t** 023 8083 2453 **f** 023 8023 3359
e h.richardson@southampton.gov.uk **w** southampton.gov.uk
Events/Ents Services Mgr: Sue Cheriton. Seated Capacity: 1350
Standing Capacity: 1700

Southampton University Student Union, Highfield
Campus, University Rd, Southampton SO17 1BJ
t 023 8059 5213 or 023 8059 5221 **f** 023 8059 5245
e em@susu.org **w** susu.org
Entertainments Manager: Melissa Taylor. Standing Capacity: 800

Southport Arts Centre Lord St, Southport, Merseyside
PR8 1DB **t** 0151 934 2134 **f** 0151 934 2126
e jake.roney@leisure.sefton.gov.uk **w** seftonarts.co.uk
Programme Mgr: Jake Roney. Seated Capacity: 472

Southport Theatre & Floral Hall Promenade, Southport,
Merseyside PR9 0DZ **t** 01704 540454 **f** 01704 536841
Contact: Lisa Chu. Seated Capacity: 1631

Spa Pavilion Theatre Seafront, Felixstowe, Suffolk
IP11 8AQ **t** 01394 282126 **f** 01394 278978.

The Spitz 109 Commercial St, Old Spitalfields Market, London
E1 6BG **t** 020 7392 9034 **f** 020 7377 8915
e booking@spitz.co.uk **w** spitz.co.uk
Live Music Programmer: Marie McPartlin. Seated Capacity: 180
Standing Capacity: 250

The Square Fourth Ave, Harlow, Essex CM20 1DW
t 01279 305000 **f** 01279 866151
e promotion@harlowsquare.com **w** harlowsquare.com
Music Promoter: Tom Hawkins. Standing Capacity: 325

St Andrews Music Centre North St, St Andrews, Fife
KY16 9AJ **t** 01334 462226 **e** music@st-andrews.ac.uk
w st-andrews.ac.uk/services/music
Office Manager: Alison Malcolm. Seated Capacity: 450
Standing Capacity: 1000

St Andrews University - Venue 1, Venue 2 Student
Union, St Mary's Pl, St Andrews KY16 9UZ **t** 01334 462700
f 01334 462740 **e** doserv@st-and.ac.uk **w** yourunion.net
Building Supervisor: Bruce Turner. Seated Capacity: 450
Standing Capacity: 1000

St George's Bristol Great George St, (off Park Street),
Bristol BS1 5RR **t** 0117 929 4929 **f** 0117 927 6537
e administration@stgeorgesbristol.co.uk **w** stgeorgesbristol.co.uk
Dir: Suzanne Rolt. Seated Capacity: 562

The St Helens Citadel Waterloo St, St Helens, Merseyside
WA10 1PX **t** 01744 735436 **f** 01744 20836
Contact: Jake Roney. Seated Capacity: 172
Standing Capacity: 300

Stables Theatre Stockwell Lane, Wavendon, Milton Keynes,
Bucks MK17 8LU **t** 01908 280814 **f** 01908 280827
e stables@stables.org **w** stables.org Programmer: Penny Griffiths.
Seated Capacity: 396

Stafford Gatehouse Eastgate St, Stafford ST16 2LT
t 01785 253595 **f** 01785 225622 Mgr: Daniel Shaw.
Seated Capacity: 564

Staffordshire University, Legends Nightclub
Student Union, Beaconside, Stafford, Staffs ST18 0AD
t 01782 294582 **f** 01785 353599 **e** b.clements@staffs.ac.uk
w staffs.ac.uk Ents & Venues Manager: Ben Clements.
Standing Capacity: 500

Staffordshire University, Stoke On Trent Student
Union, College Rd, Stoke On Trent, Staffs ST4 2DE
t 01782 294582 **f** 01782 295736 **e** b.clements@staffs.ac.uk
w staffsunion.com Ents & Venues Manager: Ben Clements.

The Standard Music Venue 1 Blackhorse Lane, London
E17 6DS **t** 020 8503 2523 or 020 8527 1966
f 020 8527 1944 **e** thestandard@btinternet.com
w standardmusicvenue.co.uk Contact: Nigel Henson.
Standing Capacity: 400

Stantonbury Leisure Centre Purbeck, Stantonbury,
Milton Keynes, Bucks MK14 6BN **t** 01908 314466
f 01908 318754 Mgr: Matthew Partridge.
Seated Capacity: 1000 Standing Capacity: 1000

Stirling University Students Association Student
Union, The Robbins Centre, Stirling University, Stirling FK9 4LA
t 01786 467189 **f** 01786 467190 **e** susa-services@stir.ac.uk
w susaonline.org.uk VP Services: Robert Hudd.
Seated Capacity: 1100

Stour Centre Tannery Lane, Ashford, Kent TN23 1PL
t 01233 625801 **f** 01233 645654. Seated Capacity: 1500
Standing Capacity: 1800

Stourbridge Town Hall Crown Centre, Stourbridge, W
Midlands DY8 1YE **t** 01384 812948 or 01384 812960
f 01384 812963 Contact: Laurence Hanna. Seated Capacity: 300
Standing Capacity: 650

University of Strathcylde Students Association, 90 John
St, Glasgow, Lanarkshire G1 1JH **t** 0141 567 5023
f 0141 567 5033 **e** a.j.mawn@strath.ac.uk. Seated Capacity: 300
Standing Capacity: 700

The Studio Tower St, Hartlepool TS24 7HQ **t** 01429 424440
f 01429 424441 **e** studiohartlepool@btconnect.com
w studiohartlepool.com Studio Manager: Liz Carter.
Standing Capacity: 300

The Sub Club 2 Goulston St, Aldgate, London E1 7TP
t 020 7133 2238 **e** info.rocket@londonmet.ac.uk
Events Mgr: Geoff Barnett. Seated Capacity: 150
Standing Capacity: 300

Subterania 12 Acklam Rd, London W10 5QZ
t 020 8960 4590 **f** 020 8961 9238
Promoter: Poorang Shahabi. Standing Capacity: 600

Suga Suga 187 Wardour St, London W1 8ZB
t 020 7434 2118 **e** eunica@sugasuga.co.uk **w** sugasuga.co.uk
Promoter: Jade Richardson. Standing Capacity: 150

Sunderland University Student Union, Manor Quay,
Charles St, Sunderland SR6 0AN **t** 0191 515 3583
f 0191 515 2499 **e** andy.fitzpatrick@sunderland.ac.uk
w mq@sunderland.co.uk Contact: A Fitzpatrick.
Seated Capacity: 1200 Standing Capacity: 1200

The Superdome Ocean Boulevard, Blackpool, Lancs FY4 1EZ
t 01253 341033 **f** 01253 401098. Seated Capacity: 1000

University of Surrey Union Club Union House, University
of Surrey, Guildford, Surrey GU2 7XH **t** 01483 689983
e ents@ussu.co.uk **w** ussu.co.uk Events Mgr: Alan Roy.
Standing Capacity: 1600

Sussex University Student Union, Falmer House, Falmer, Brighton BN1 9QF **t** 01273 678555 **f** 01273 678875 Contact: Entertainments Dept.

The Swan 215 Clapham Rd, London SW9 91E **t** 020 7978 9778 or 020 7738 3065 **f** 020 7738 6722 **w** swanstockwell.com Contact: John McCormack. Seated Capacity: 300 Standing Capacity: 500

The Swan Abbey Barn Rd, High Wycombe, Bucks HP11 1RS **t** 01494 539482.

University of Wales - Swansea Student Union, Fulton House, Singleton Pk, Swansea SA2 8PP **t** 01792 295485 **f** 01792 513006 **e** suents@swansea.ac.uk **w** swansea-union.co.uk/ents Ents Mgr. Seated Capacity: 800 Standing Capacity: 800

Symphony Hall International Convention Ctr, Broad St, Birmingham B1 2EA **t** 0121 200 2000 **f** 0121 212 1982 **e** symphony-hall@necgroup.co.uk **w** necgroup.co.uk MD: Andrew Jowett. Seated Capacity: 2260

Tait Hall Edenside Rd, Kelso, Roxburgh TD5 7BS **t** 01573 224233. Seated Capacity: 700

Tameside Hippodrome Oldham Rd, Ashton-under-Lyne, Tameside OL6 7SE **t** 0161 330 2095 **f** 0161 343 5839 **e** stuart.dornford-May@clearchannel.co.uk **w** getlive.co.uk Theatre Manager: Stuart Dornford-May. Seated Capacity: 1262

Tamworth Arts Centre Church St, Tamworth, Staffs B79 7BX **t** 01827 53092 **f** 01827 53092 Contact: The Arts Venue Mgr. Seated Capacity: 360 Standing Capacity: 200

Teesside University University of Teesside Union, Southfield Rd, Middlesbrough, Cleveland TS1 3BA **t** 01642 342234 **f** 01642 342241 **e** L.Stretton@utsu.org.uk **w** utsu.org.uk Ent & Promotions Mgr: Luke Stretton. Seated Capacity: 450 Standing Capacity: 1000

Telewest Arena Arena Way, Newcastle upon Tyne NE4 7NA **t** 0191 260 6002 **f** 0191 260 2200 **w** telewestarena.co.uk Exec Dir: Colin Revel. Seated Capacity: 9700 Standing Capacity: 11321

Telford Ice Rink Telford Town Centre, Telford, Shropshire TF3 4JQ **t** 01952 291511 **f** 01952 291543 Mgr: Robert Fountain. Seated Capacity: 3300 Standing Capacity: 4000

Thames Valley University Students Union, St Mary's Rd, London W5 5RF **t** 020 8231 2531 **f** 020 8231 2589.

Theatre Royal 282 Hope St, Glasgow G2 3QA **t** 0141 332 3321 admin or 0141 332 9000 box **f** 0141 332 4477 **w** theatreroyalglasgow.com Theatre Mgr: Martin Ritchie. Seated Capacity: 1555

Theatre Royal Grey St, Newcastle upon Tyne, Tyne and Wear NE1 6BR **t** 0191 232 0997 **f** 0191 261 1906 Contact: Peter Sarah. Seated Capacity: 1294

Theatre Royal Norwich Theatre St, Norwich, Norfolk NR2 1RL **t** 01603 598500 **f** 01603 598501 **e** j.walsh@theatreroyalnorwich.co.uk **w** theatreroyalnorwich.co.uk Bookings: Jane Walsh. Seated Capacity: 1314

Theatre Royal Theatre Sq, Nottingham NG1 5ND **t** 0115 989 5500 **f** 0115 947 4218 **e** enquiry@royalcentre.co.uk **w** royalcentre-nottingham.co.uk MD: JM Grayson. Seated Capacity: 1135

Theatre Royal Royal Parade, Plymouth, Devon PL1 2TR **t** 01752 668282 or 01752 267222 **f** 01752 671179 **e** info@theatreroyal.com **w** theatreroyal.com Chief Exec: Adrian Vinken. Seated Capacity: 1296

Theatre Royal Corporation St, St Helens, Merseyside WA10 1LQ **t** 01744 756333 admin or 01744 756000 bo **f** 01744 756777 GM: Basil Soper. Seated Capacity: 698

Time Club Bangor Student Union, Deiniol Rd, Bangor, Gwynedd LL57 2TH **t** 01248 388033 **f** 01248 388031 **e** adami@undeb.bangor.ac.uk **w** undeb.bangor.ac.uk Ents Mgr: Adam Isbell. Standing Capacity: 700

Tiverton New Hall Barrington St, Tiverton, Devon, Exeter EX16 6QP **t** 01884 253404 **f** 01884 243677 Town Clerk: B Lough. Seated Capacity: 222 Standing Capacity: 300

TJ's Disco 16-18 Clarence Pl, Newport, South Wales NP19 0AE **t** 01633 216608 **e** sam@tjs-newport.demon.co.uk **w** tjs-newport.demon.co.uk Mgr: John Sicolo. Seated Capacity: 500

The Top of Reilly's 10 Thurland St, Nottingham NG1 3DR **t** 0115 941 7709 **f** 0115 941 5604. Standing Capacity: 450

Torbay Leisure Centre Clennon Valley, Penwill Way, Paignton, Devon TQ4 5JR **t** 01803 522240 **w** torbay.gov.uk. Seated Capacity: 2000 Standing Capacity: 3400

Torquay Town Hall Lymington Rd, Torquay, Devon TQ1 3DR **t** 01803 201201 **f** 01803 208856 **e** pete.carpenter@torbay.gov.uk Contact: Mr P Carpenter. Seated Capacity: 1000 Standing Capacity: 1000

The Tower Ballroom Reservoir Rd, Edgbaston, Birmingham, W Midlands B16 9EE **t** 0121 454 0107 **f** 0121 455 9313 **e** tower@zanzibar.co.uk **w** zanzibar.co.uk MD: Susan Prince. Seated Capacity: 1000 Standing Capacity: 1200

The Tower Ballroom Blackpool Tower, Promenade, Blackpool, Lancs FY1 4BJ **t** 01253 629600 **f** 01253 629700 **e** firstname+lastname@leisure-parcs.co.uk **w** blackpooltower.co.uk Entertainments Co-ord: Donna Molyneaux. Seated Capacity: 1650 Standing Capacity: 1700

Town Hall High St, Hawick TD9 9EF **t** 01450 364743 Contact: Alister Murdie. Seated Capacity: 600 Standing Capacity: 900

Town Hall Birmingham Paradise St, Birmingham B3 3DQ **t** 0121 644 6157 **f** 0121 212 1982 **e** simon.wales@symphonyhall.co.uk **w** townhall.org.uk GM: Simon Wales. Seated Capacity: 1100

Tramway 25 Albert Drive, Pollockshields, Glasgow, Lanarkshire G41 2PE **t** 0141 422 2023 **f** 0141 423 1194 **e** info@tramway.org **w** tramway.org Administrator: Margaret Dalzell. Seated Capacity: 1000 Standing Capacity: 1500

Trinity & All Saints College The Base, Brownberrie Lane, Horsforth, Leeds, W Yorks LS18 5HD **t** 0113 283 7241 **f** 0113 283 7283 **e** president@tasc.ac.uk **w** tasc.ac.uk Standing Capacity: 600

The Trinity Centre Trinity Rd, Bristol BS2 0NW **t** 0117 9351200 **e** info@3ca.org.uk **w** 3ca.org.uk Activities Coordinator: Melanie West. Seated Capacity: 225 Standing Capacity: 500

Truro Hall for Cornwall Back Quay, Truro, Cornwall
TR1 2LL **t** 01872 262465 **f** 01872 260246
e admin@hallforcornwall.org.uk **w** hallforcornwall.co.uk.
Seated Capacity: 1000 Standing Capacity: 1700

Tufnells 162, Tufnell Park Rd, London N7 0EE
t 020 7272 2078 **f** 020 8546 3689 **e** tufnellsclub@yahoo.co.uk
Bookings: Chris Larsen. Standing Capacity: 500

The Tunnels Carnegie's Brae, Aberdeen AB10 1BF
t 01224 211 121 **e** info@thetunnels.co.uk **w** thetunnels.co.uk
Bookings Mgr: Hen Beverly. Standing Capacity: 300

Turnmills 63b Clerkenwell Rd, London EC1M 5NP
t 020 7250 3409 **f** 020 7250 1046 **e** info@turnmills.co.uk
w turnmills.co.uk Corporate Events Mgr: Linda Ransome.

University of Ulster Cromore Rd, Coleraine, Co Antrim
BT52 1SA **t** 028 9036 5121 **f** 028 9036 6817.

Ulster Hall Bedford St, Belfast, Co Antrim BT2 7FF
t 028 9032 3900 **f** 028 9024 7199
e ulsterhall@belfastcity.gov.uk **w** ulsterhall.co.uk Mgr: Pat Falls.
Seated Capacity: 1600 Standing Capacity: 1800

Ulster University Students' Association, York St, Belfast, Co
Antrim BT15 1ED **t** 028 9032 8515 **f** 028 9026 7351
e info@uusu.org **w** uusu.org Club Sec. Standing Capacity: 450

ULU (University of London Union) Malet St, London
WC1E 7HY **t** 020 7664 2022 or 020 7664 2092
f 020 7436 4604 **e** entsinfo@ulu.lon.ac.uk **w** Ulu.co.uk/ululive
Venue Manager: Laurie Pegg. Seated Capacity: 320
Standing Capacity: 828

UMIST Union PO Box 88, Sackville St, Manchester M60 1QD
t 0161 200 3286 or 0161 200 3276 **f** 0161 200 3268
e paul.parkes@su.umist.ac.uk Contact: Paul Parkes.
Seated Capacity: 350 Standing Capacity: 600

The Underworld 174 Camden High St, London NW1 0NE
t 020 7267 3939 **f** 020 7482 1955
e contact@theunderworldcamden.co.uk
w theunderworldcamden.co.uk Bookings Mgr: Jon Vyner.
Seated Capacity: 500 Standing Capacity: 500

Unex Towerlands Arena Panfield Rd, Braintree, Essex
CM7 5BJ **t** 01376 326802 **f** 01376 552487
e info@unextowerlands.com **w** unextowerlands.com
Mktg Mgr: Holly Gredley. Seated Capacity: 3600
Standing Capacity: 4000

Union Chapel Project Compton Ave, London N1 2XD
t 020 7226 1686 or 020 7226 3750 **f** 020 7354 8343
e events@unionchapel.org.uk **w** unionchapel.org.uk
Venue Mgr: Pete Stapleton. Seated Capacity: 500

University College London Student Union, 25 Gordon St,
London WC1H 0AH **t** 020 7387 3611 **f** 020 7383 3937
e A.davis@ucl.ac.uk Contact: Andy Davis. Standing Capacity: 600

University College Of St Martin Student Union, Rydal
Rd, Ambleside, Cumbria LA22 9BB **t** 01539 430216
f 01539 430309.

University of Chester - Warrington Campus
Student Union, Crab Lane, Warrington, Cheshire WA2 0DB
t 01925 534375 **f** 01925 534267 **e** csuw.ents@chester.ac.uk
w chestersu.com Entertainments Officer: David Cowell.
Seated Capacity: 400 Standing Capacity: 500

University of East Anglia Students Union, University Plain,
Norwich, Norfolk NR4 7TJ **t** 01603 505401 or 01603 593460
f 01603 593465 **e** ents@uea.ac.uk **w** ueaticketbookings.co.uk
Ents Mgr: Nick Rayns. Seated Capacity: 780
Standing Capacity: 1470

University of Essex Students' Union Students' Union,
Uni of Essex, Colchester, Essex CO4 3SQ **t** 01206 863211
f 01206 870915 **e** ents@essex.ac.uk **w** essexentsonline.com
Ents & Venues Mgr: Lee Pugh. Seated Capacity: 400
Standing Capacity: 1000

University of Gloucestershire Students' Union
Student Union, PO Box 220, The Park, Cheltenham GL52 2EH
t 01242 532848 **f** 01242 361381 **e** union@ugsu.org **w** ugsu.org
VP Communications: John Webb. Seated Capacity: 600
Standing Capacity: 1200

University of Greenwich Student Union, Bathway,
Woolwich, London SE18 6QX **t** 020 8331 8268
f 020 8331 8591.

University of the Arts London Student Union, 2-6
Catton St, Holborn, London WC1R 4AA **t** 020 7514 6270
f 020 7514 7838 **e** a.lukes@su.arts.ac.uk **w** thestudentsunion.info
Ents Manager: Adrian Lukes.

Upstairs @ Garage 20/22 Highbury Corner, London
N5 1RD **t** 020 7607 1818 or 020 8961 5490 **f** 020 7609 0846
e joady@meanfiddler.co.uk Bking Mgr: Joady Thornton.
Standing Capacity: 150

Usher Hall Lothian Rd, Edinburgh EH1 2EA **t** 0131 228 8616
f 0131 228 8848 Mgr: Moira McKenzie. Seated Capacity: 2200
Standing Capacity: 2737

The Venue at Kent University Kent Student Union,
Mandela Building, Canterbury, Kent CT2 7NW **t** 01227 824235
f 01227 824207 **e** g.newlands@kent.ac.uk **w** kentunion.co.uk
Entertainments Manager: Graham Newlands.
Seated Capacity: 1500 Standing Capacity: 1500

The Venue 15-21 Calton Rd, Edinburgh EH8 8DL
t 0131 557 3073 **e** info@edinvenue.com **w** edinvenue.co.uk
Live Bookings Mgr: Jaq Findlayson. Standing Capacity: 400

Vibe Bar 91-95 Brick Lane, London E1 6QL **t** 020 7247 3479
f 020 7426 0641 **e** info@vibe-bar.co.uk **w** vibe-bar.co.uk
Events Manager: Adelle Stripe.

Victoria Community Centre Oakley Building, West St,
Crewe, Cheshire CW1 2PZ **t** 01270 211422 **f** 01270 537960
Centre Mgr: Mrs E McFahn. Seated Capacity: 550
Standing Capacity: 1000

The Victoria Hall Bagnall St, Hanley, Stoke-on-Trent, Staffs
ST1 3AD **t** 01782 213808 **f** 01782 214 738
e Firstname+lastname@theambassadors.com **w** victoria-hall.info
GM: Mike Keane. Seated Capacity: 1700 Standing Capacity: 637

Victoria Hall Akeman St, Tring, Herts HP23 6AA
t 01442 228951. Seated Capacity: 250 Standing Capacity: 250

The Victoria Inn 12 Midland Pl, Derby DE1 2RR
t 01332 740 091 **e** thevicinn@hotmail.com **w** thevicinn.co.uk
Promoters: Micky Sheehan, Andy Sewell. Standing Capacity: 150

Victoria Theatre Wards End, Halifax, W Yorks HX1 1BU
t 01422 351156 or 01422 351158 **f** 01422 320552
e victoriatheatre@calderdale.gov.uk
w calderdale.gov.uk/tourism/victoriatheatre
Contact: George Candler. Seated Capacity: 1585
Standing Capacity: 1585

Vivid & Elite Atlanta Boulevard, Romford, Essex RM1 1TB
t 01708 742289 **f** 01708 733905
e vividelite.romford@firstleisure.com **w** applebelly.com
GM: John Mercer. Seated Capacity: 1625
Standing Capacity: 1300

Wakefield Theatre Royal & Opera House Drury Lane,
Wakefield, West Yorks WF1 2TE **t** 01924 215531
f 01924 215525 **e** mail@wakefieldtheatres.co.uk
w wakefieldtheatres.co.uk GM: Murray Edwards.
Seated Capacity: 509 Standing Capacity: 509

Warwick Arts Centre University Of Warwick, Coventry, W
Midlands CV4 7AL **t** 024 7652 4524 **f** 024 4652 4777
e box.office@warwick.ac.uk **w** warwickartscentre.co.uk
Dir: Alan Rivett. Seated Capacity: 1462 Standing Capacity: 1462

Warwick University Student Union, Gibbet Hill Rd,
Coventry, W Midlands CV4 7AL **t** 024 7657 3056
t 024 7657 3070 **e** dwalter@sunion.warwick.ac.uk
w sunion.warwick.ac.uk/ents
Entertainments Manager: Darren Walter.
Standing Capacity: 2700

The Water Rats 328 Grays Inn Rd, Kings Cross, London
WC1X 8BZ **t** 020 7336 7326 **e** info@plummusic.com
w plummusic.com Contact: Allan North, Sarah Thirtle.
Standing Capacity: 100

The Waterfront 139 King St, Norwich, Norfolk NR1 1QH
t 01603 632717 **f** 01603 615463 **e** p.ingleby@uea.ac.uk
w ueaticketbookings.co.uk Programmer: Paul Ingleby.
Standing Capacity: 700

Watermans Arts Centre 40 High St, Brentford, Middlesex
TW8 0DS **t** 020 8847 5651 **f** 020 8569 8592
Contact: Lorna O'Leary. Standing Capacity: 500

Watford Colosseum Rickmansworth Rd, Watford, Herts
WD1 7JN **t** 01923 445300 **f** 01923 445225
Contact: John Wallace. Seated Capacity: 1440
Standing Capacity: 1800

The Wedgewood Rooms 147B Albert Rd, Southsea,
Portsmouth, Hants PO4 0JW **t** 023 9286 3911
f 023 9285 1326 **e** tickets@wedgewood-rooms.co.uk
w wedgewood-rooms.co.uk GM: Geoff Priestley.
Seated Capacity: 300 Standing Capacity: 400

The Welly Club 105-107 Beverley Rd, Hull HU3 1TS
t 01482 221113 **f** 01482 221113 **e** thewelly@hull24.com
w yo-yo-indie.com Promotions Mgr: Andrew Coe.

Wembley Arena Arena Sq, Engineers Way, Wembley,
London HA9 0DH **t** 020 8782 5624
e katie.musham@livenation.co.uk **w** LiveNation.co.uk/wembley
Venue Bookings: Katie Musham. Seated Capacity: 12000
Standing Capacity: 12500

Wembley Stadium Empire Way, Wembley HA9 0WS
t 020 8795 9696 or 020 8795 9618
e jim.frayling@wembleystadium.com **w** wembleystadium.com
Head of PR & Music: Jim Frayling. Seated Capacity: 90000

West End Centre Queens Rd, Aldershot, Hants GU11 3JD
t 01252 408040 **f** 01252 408041
e westendcentre@hants.gov.uk **w** westendcentre.co.uk
Centre Dir: Barney Jeavons. Seated Capacity: 150
Standing Capacity: 200

University of West England Student Union, Coldharbour
Lane, Frenchay, Bristol B16 1QY **t** 0117 965 6261 x 2580
f 0117 976 3909 **e** union@uwe.ac.uk
w gate.uwe.ac.uk:8000/union/ents/index.html
Contact: Programming Asst. Seated Capacity: 400
Standing Capacity: 1500

West One Four 3 North End Crescent, North End Rd, West
Kensington, London W14 8TG **t** 020 7751 1044
e livegigs@mail.com **w** orangepromotions.com
Booker/Promoter: Phil Brydon. Seated Capacity: 300
Standing Capacity: 300

Westex Royal Bath & West Showground, Shepton Mallet,
Somerset BA4 6QN **t** 01749 822219 **f** 01749 823134
e bwwestex@ukonline.co.uk **w** westex.uk.com GM: Jo Perry.
Seated Capacity: 4000 Standing Capacity: 5250

University of Westminster Student Union, 32 Wells St,
London W1T 3UW **t** 020 7911 5000 x 2306 **f** 020 7911 5848
e edfrith@hotmail.com Events Mgr: Ed Frith.
Seated Capacity: 150 Standing Capacity: 450

Westpoint Arena Clyst St Mary, Exeter, Devon EX5 1DJ
t 01392 446000 **f** 01392 445843
e info@westpoint-devonshow.co.uk
w westpoint-devonshow.co.uk Events Mgr: Sarah Symons.
Seated Capacity: 6000 Standing Capacity: 7500

Weymouth Pavilion The Esplanade, Weymouth, Dorset
DT4 8ED **t** 01305 765218 or 01305 765214 **f** 01305 789922
Arts & Entertainments Mgr: Stephen Young.
Seated Capacity: 1000

The Wheatsheaf Live Music Venue Church St, Stoke
On Trent, Staffs ST4 1BU **t** 01782 844438 **f** 01782 410340
Contact: Anne Riddle. Standing Capacity: 400

White Rock Theatre White Rock, Hastings, E Sussex
TN34 1JX **t** 01424 781010 or 01424 781000 **f** 01424 781170
Contact: Andy Mould. Seated Capacity: 1165
Standing Capacity: 1500

Whitehaven Civic Hall Lowther St, Whitehaven, Cumbria
CA28 7SH **t** 01946 852 821 **e** civichalls@copelandbc.gov.uk
w copelandbc.gov.uk Marketing Officer: Paul Tomlinson.
Standing Capacity: 600

Whitley Bay Ice Rink Hillheads Rd, Whitley Bay, Tyne and
Wear NE25 8HP **t** 0191 291 1000 **f** 0191 291 1001
Contact: Francis Smith. Seated Capacity: 6000
Standing Capacity: 6000

Wigmore Hall 36 Wigmore St, London W1H 0BP
t 020 7258 8200 **f** 020 7258 8201
e info@wigmore-hall.org.uk **w** wigmore-hall.org.uk
Contact: Management Office. Seated Capacity: 540

Wimbledon Theatre 93 The Broadway, London SW19 1QG
t 020 8543 4549 **f** 020 8543 6637
e maralynsarrington@theambassadors.com
w newwimbledontheatre.co.uk GM: Maralyn Sarrington.
Seated Capacity: 1665

Winchester Guildhall The Broadway, High St, Winchester,
Hants SO23 9GH **t** 01962 840 820 **f** 01962 878 458
e guildhall@winchester.gov.uk **w** winchesterguildhall.co.uk
GM: Andrew Jacques. Seated Capacity: 600
Standing Capacity: 800

Winchester School Of Art Student Union, Park Ave, Winchester, Hants SO23 8DL **t** 01962 840772 **f** 01962 840772 **e** cvasudev@hotmail.com **w** soton.ac.uk/~wsasu Pres: Chetan. Seated Capacity: 250 Standing Capacity: 250

Windmill Brixton 22 Blenheim Gardens, (off Brixton Hill), London SW2 5BZ **t** 020 8674 0055 or 07931 351 971 **e** windmillbrixton@yahoo.co.uk **w** windmillbrixton.co.uk Booker: Tim Perry. Standing Capacity: 120

Windsor Arts Centre St Leonard's Rd, Windsor, Berks SL4 3BL **t** 01753 859421 or 01753 859336 **f** 01753 621527 Contact: Debbie Stubbs. Seated Capacity: 179 Standing Capacity: 100

The Winter Gardens - Opera House, Empress Ballroom Church St, Blackpool FY1 3PL **t** 01253 625 252 **f** 01253 751 203 **e** events@leisure-parcs.co.uk **w** wintergardensblackpool.co.uk Contact: Events Team.

The Winter Gardens Pavilion Royal Parade, Weston-super-Mare, Somerset BS23 1AJ **t** 01934 417117 **f** 01934 612323 **e** Peter.Undery@n-somerset.gov.uk **w** thewintergardens.com GM: Peter Undery. Seated Capacity: 500 Standing Capacity: 550

Wolverhampton Civic Halls North St, Wolverhampton, W Midlands WV1 1RQ **t** 01902 552122 **f** 01902 552123 **e** markblackstock@wolvescivic.co.uk **w** wolvescivic.co.uk GM: Mark Blackstock. Seated Capacity: 2200 Standing Capacity: 3000

Wolverhampton University Students Union, Wulfruna St, Wolverhampton, W Midlands WV1 1LY **t** 01902 322021 **f** 01902 322020 **w** wlv.ac.uk. Seated Capacity: 200 Standing Capacity: 600

WOMAD Festival (see Rivermead Leisure Complex,).

Woodville Halls Theatre Woodville Pl, Gravesend, Kent DA12 1DD **t** 01474 337456 or 01474 337611 **f** 01474 337458 **e** woodville.halls@gravesham.gov.uk **w** gravesham.gov.uk/woodvillehalls.htm Contact: Rob Allen. Seated Capacity: 814 Standing Capacity: 1000

Wyvern Theatre Theatre Sq, Swindon, Wilts SN1 1QN **t** 01865 782900 **f** 01865 782910 Contact: Nicky Monk. Seated Capacity: 617

Yeovil Octagon Theatre Hendford, Yeovil, Somerset BA20 1UX **t** 01935 422836 or 01935 422720 **f** 01935 475281 GM: John G White. Seated Capacity: 625

York Barbican Centre Barbican Rd, York, N Yorks YO10 9AJ **t** 01904 628991 or 01904 621477 **f** 01904 628227 **e** craig.smart@york.gov.uk **w** fibbers.co.uk/barbican Contact: Craig Smart. Seated Capacity: 1500 Standing Capacity: 1860

York University Students Union, Goodricke College, Heslington, York, N Yorks YO1 5DD **t** 01904 433724 **f** 01904 434664 **e** ents@york.ac.uk **w** york.ac.uk/student/su/index.shtml Andrew Windsor: Entertainments Officer. Seated Capacity: 300 Standing Capacity: 540

Younger Graduation Hall North St, St Andrews KY16 9AJ **t** 01334 462226 **f** 01334 462570 **e** music@st-and.ac.uk **w** st-and.ac.uk/services/music Contact: The Secretary. Seated Capacity: 900

Zanzibar 43 Seel St, Liverpool, Merseyside L1 4AZ **t** 0151 707 0633 **f** 0151 707 0633.

The Zodiac 190 Cowley Rd, Oxford OX4 1UE **t** 01895 42 00 42 **f** 01895 42 00 45 **e** info@the-zodiac.co.uk **w** the-zodiac.co.uk GM: Carl Bathgate. Standing Capacity: 750

Ticketing Services

Aloud.com Emap, Mappin House, 4 Winsley St, London W1W 8HF **t** 020 7182 8360 **f** 020 7182 8918 **e** sales@aloud.com **w** aloud.com Hd Ticket'g & Co-Prom'ns: GiGi Dryer.

Needtickets.com 17 Lloyd Villas, Lewisham Way, London SE4 1US **t** 020 8320 2060 **e** editor@needtickets.com **w** Needtickets.com MD: Simon Harper.

Ticket Zone Unit 3 Barum Gate, Whiddon Valley, Barnstaple, Devon EX32 8QD **t** 01271 323 355 **f** 01271 375 902 **e** customerservices@ticketzone.co.uk **w** ticketzone.co.uk Contact: Domingo Tjornelund.

TICKETMASTER UK

ticketmaster

48 Leicester Square, London WC2H 7LR **t** 020 7344 4000 **f** 020 7915 0411 **e** sales@ticketmaster.co.uk **w** ticketmaster.co.uk MD: Chris Edmonds. Group Sales Director: Paul Williamson. General Manager: John Gibson. Regional Sales Manager, North: Ian Sanders. Regional Sales Manager, South: Andrew Parsons. Regional Sales Manager, Scotland: Colette Grufferty.
Ticketmaster is the world's leading ticketing company, providing ticket sales and distribution though Ticketmaster.co.uk.

TICKETWEB (UK) LTD

TICKETWEB

48 Leicester Square, London WC2H 7LR **t** 020 7344 4000 **f** 020 7915 0411 **e** clients@ticketweb.co.uk **w** ticketweb.co.uk General Manager: Sam Arnold. Client Services Manager: Janine Douglas-Hall. Regional Sales Manager, South: Andrew Parsons. Regional Sales Manager, Scotland: Colette Grufferty. Regional Sales Manager, North: Ian Sanders.
TicketWeb is a self-service, fully functioned box-office system available for use by venues and event organisers at potentially no cost.

WeGotTickets.com 9 Park End St, Oxford OX1 1HH **t** 01865 798 797 **f** 01865 798 792 **e** info@wegottickets.com **w** WeGotTickets.com Marketing Dir: Laura Kramer.

Touring and Stage Services

5 Star Cases Broad End Industrial Estate, Broad End Rd, Walsoken, Wisbech, Cambs PE14 7BQ **t** 01945 427000 **f** 01945 427015 **e** info@5star-cases.com **w** 5star-cases.com MD: Keith Sykes.

23 Management **t** 07785 228000 or +61 415 498 955 **f** 0870 130 5365 **e** ifan@23management.com **w** 23management.com Tour Manager: Ifan Thomas.

Air Partner Platinum House, Gatwick Rd, Crawley, W Sussex RH10 9RP **t** 01293 844 855 **f** 01293 844 859 **e** travel@airpartner.com **w** airpartner.com Contact: Sarah Jamieson.

Band Pass Ltd 1st Floor, 20 Sunnydown, Witley, Surrey GU8 5RP **t** 01428 684 926 **f** 01428 683 501 **e** maxine@band-pass.co.uk **w** band-pass.co.uk Dir: Maxine Gale.

Beat The Street UK (Tour Coaches) Unit 103, Cariocca Business Pk, Helldon Close, Ardwick, Manchester M12 4AH **t** 0161 273 5984 **f** 0161 272 7772 **e** beatthestreetuk@aol.com **w** beatthestreet.net Mgr: Paul Collis.

Bennett Audio 41 Sherriff Rd, London NW6 2AS **t** 07748 705 067 or 020 7372 1077 **e** bennettaudio@f2s.com **w** bennettaudio.co.uk Dir. and Audio Engineer: Clem Bennett.

Blackout Ltd 280 Western Rd, London SW19 2QA **t** 020 8687 8400 **f** 020 8687 8500 **e** sales@blackout-ltd.com **w** blackout-ltd.com Contact: Sales.

BossMedia Cashmere House, 180 Kensington Church St, Notting Hill, London W8 4DP **t** 020 7727 2727 **e** info@bossmedia.co.uk **w** bossmedia.co.uk Dir: Taharqa Daniel-Rashid.

Capes UK Security Services Ltd Unit 1, West Street Business Pk, Stamford, Lincs PE9 2PR **t** 01780 480712 **f** 01780 480824.

Capital Productions Abacus House, 60 Weir Rd, London SW19 8UG **t** 020 8944 6777 **f** 020 8944 9477 **e** firstname@capital-productions.co.uk **w** capital-productions.co.uk Owner: Keith Davis.

Lee Charteris Associates 10 Marco Rd, London W6 0PN **t** 020 8741 2500 or 07801 663 700 **f** 020 8741 2577 **e** mail@LeeCharteris.com Production Mgr: Lee Charteris.

David Lawrence Tour Mgmt & Security Solutions Suite 358, 78 Marylebone High St, London W1U 5AP **t** 0870 443 5494 **f** 020 8884 0454 **e** lawrence@davidlawrence.org.uk **w** davidlawrence.org.uk MD: Lawrence Levy.

Extreme Music Production - Tour Management 4-7 Forewoods Common, Holt, Wilts BA14 6PJ **t** 01225 782 984 or 07909 995 011 **e** george@xtrememusic.co.uk **w** xtrememusic.co.uk MD: George Allen.

Fruit Pie Music Productions Ltd The Shop, 443 Streatham High Rd, London SW16 3PH **t** 020 8679 9289 **f** 020 8679 9775 **e** info@fruitpiemusic.com **w** fruitpiemusic.com MD: Kumar Kamalagharan.

ICP Group (Threat Management & Security) 2 Old Brompton Rd, London SW1 3DQ **t** 020 7031 4440 **e** info@icpgroup.ltd.uk **w** icpgroup.ltd.uk MD: Will Geddes.

Mad As Toast 3 Broomlands St, Paisley PA1 2LS **t** 07717 437 148 **f** 0141 887 8888 **e** info@madastoast.com **w** madastoast.com Dirs: John Richardson, George Watson.

Music & Arts Security Ltd 13 Grove Mews, Hammersmith, London W6 7HS **t** 020 8563 9444 **f** 020 8563 9555 **e** sales@musicartssecurity.co.uk **w** music-and-arts-security.co.uk MD: Jerry Judge.

NPB Group (Instrument Repair & Servicing) Electron House 2, Landmere Close, Ilkeston, Derbyshire DE7 9HQ **t** 01159 321447 **f** 01159 321447 **e** npbelectronics@btinternet.com **w** npbgroup.net Contact: Pauline Barker.

The Production Office Ltd 18 Fleet St, Beaminster, Dorset DT8 3EF **t** 01308 861 374 **f** 01308 861 375 **e** Theproductionoffice@mac.com Dirs: Chris Vaughan, Keely Myers.

Sound Moves (UK) Ltd Abbeygate House, Challenge Rd, Ashford, Middx TW15 1AX **t** 01784 424 470 or 01784 424 489 **f** 01784 424 490 or 01784 424499 **e** london@soundmoves.com **w** soundmoves.com MD: Martin Corr.

Vans For Bands Ltd 161 Woodstock Rd, Oxford OX2 7NA **t** 01865 559 574 or 07886 684 140 **e** info@vansforbands.co.uk **w** vansforbands.co.uk MD: Tarrant Anderson.

Violation Tour Production 26 Mill St, Gamlingay, Sandy, Beds SG19 3JW **t** 07768 667 076 or 01767 651 552 **f** 01767 651 228 **e** dickmeredith@mac.com Mgr: Dick Meredith.

The Vocal Zone - Vocal Coach PO Box 25269, London N12 9ZT **t** 07970 924 190 **e** info@thevocalzone.co.uk **w** thevocalzone.co.uk Contact: Kenny Thomas.

Travel and Transport Services

Air Brokers International Charity Farm, Fulborough Rd, Parham, Sussex RH20 4HP **t** 01903 740 200 **f** 01903 740 102 **e** bugle@instoneair.com Contact: Mike Bugle.

AIR CHARTER SERVICE PLC

Brentham House, 45C High Street, Hampton Wick, Kingston upon Thames, Surrey KT1 4DG **t** 020 8614 6299 **f** 020 8943 1062 **e** carmen.vanegas@aircharter.co.uk **w** aircharter.co.uk Senior Charter Analyst: Carmen Vanegas. Air Charter Service are specialists in providing air charters to the music industry - including VIP jets, helicopters and airliners.

Air Partner (Charter Services) Platinum House, Gatwick Rd, Crawley, W Sussex RH10 9RP **t** 01293 844 812 **f** 01293 844 859 **e** arts@airpartner.com **w** airpartner.com Contact: Ian Browne.

Anglo Pacific International Units 1 & 2, Bush Industrial Estate, Standard Rd, London NW10 6DF **t** 020 8965 1234 **f** 020 8965 4954 **e** info@anglopacific.co.uk **w** anglopacific.co.uk MD: Steve Perry.

Beat The Street UK (Tour Coaches) Unit 103, Cariocca Business Pk, Hellidon Close, Ardwick, Manchester M12 4AH **t** 0161 273 5984 **f** 0161 272 7772 **e** beatthestreetuk@aol.com **w** beatthestreet.net Mgr: Paul Collis.

Civilised Car Hire Company Ltd. 50 Parsons Green Lane, London SW6 4HU **t** 020 7703 3737 or 020 7384 1133 **f** 020 7384 3366 **e** mail@londoncarhire.com **w** londoncarhire.com MD: Toby Hobson.

The Concert Travel Company Unit 3, Barum Gate, Widdon Valley, Barnstaple, Devon EX32 8QD **t** 01271 323 355 **f** 01271 375 902 **e** sales@ticketzone.co.uk **w** ticketzone.co.uk Contact: Robert Cotton.

Crawfords Luxury Cars And Coaches 8 Concord Business Centre, Concord Rd, London W3 0TJ **t** 020 8896 3030 **f** 020 8896 3300 **e** crawfords@btconnect.com **w** crawfordscars.co.uk Divisional Manager: Ivor Davies.

DETONATE MUSIC & ENTERTAINMENT TRAVEL SERVICES

104-105 High Street, Eton, Windsor, Berks SL4 6AF **t** 01753 801 200 **f** 01753 672 710 **e** Detonate@eton-travel.co.uk **w** detonatetravel.com. **Manager: Alison Rodgers.**

DJB Passports & Visas 1st Floor, 16-20 Kingsland Rd, Shoreditch, London E2 8DA **t** 020 7684 6242 **f** 020 7739 5244 **e** info@djbvisas.com **w** djbvisas.com Accounts Manager: James Cox.

Dunn-Line Travel Dunn-Line Holdings, Beechdale Rd, Nottingham, Notts NG8 3EU **t** 0870 012 1212 **f** 0115 900 7051 **e** enquiries@dunn-line.com **w** dunn-line.com MD: Scott Dunn.

ET Travel 35 Britannia Row, Islington, London N1 8QH **t** 020 7359 7161 **f** 020 7354 3270 **e** info@ettravel.co.uk **w** ettravel.co.uk Dir: Melanie Weston.

EXECUTOURS

Tour Management / Ground Transport & Logistics **e** info@executours.co.uk **w** executours.co.uk Contact: Guy Anderson. **(UK) 07774 137 910 (US) +1 973 262 5068 (AUS) + 61 423 193866**

Fineminster - Air Charter Ltd. Worth Corner, Pound Hill, Crawley, W Sussex RH10 7SL **t** 01293 885888 **f** 01293 883238 **e** charter@fineminster.com **w** fineminster.com MD: Graham Plunkett.

Genesis Trade Shows & Events Merlin House, 6 Boltro Rd, Haywards Heath, W Sussex RH16 1BB **t** 01444 476 120 **f** 01444 476 121 **e** abigail@genesistravel.co.uk **w** genesistravel.co.uk Events Manager: Lorna Milner.

Marken Time Critical Express Unit 2, Metro Centre, St Johns Rd, Isleworth, Middlesex TW7 6NJ **t** 020 8388 8555 **f** 020 8388 8666 **e** info@marken.com **w** marken.com Bus Devel Mgr: Rob Paterson.

MEDIA TRAVEL LTD

mediatravel ★
travel management for the entertainment industry

Studio 1, Cloisters House, 8 Battersea Park Rd, London SW8 4BG **t** 020 7627 2200 **f** 020 7627 2221 **e** fran@mediatravel.com **w** mediatravel.com MD: Fran Green.

Millennium Concert Travel 1a Dickson Rd, Blackpool, Lancs FY1 2AX **t** 01253 299 266 **f** 01253 299 454 **e** sales@mct-online.com **w** mct-online.com Contact: Julian Murray.

Movin' Music Ltd (London) Suite 1, 52 Highfield Rd, Purley, Surrey CRB 2JG **t** 020 8763 0767 **f** 020 8668 2214 **e** info@movinmusic.net **w** movinmusic.net Dir: Brenda Lillywhite.

Music By Appointment (MBA) - Tour Travel Agents The Linen House, 253 Kilburn Lane, London W10 4BQ **t** 020 8960 1600 **f** 020 8960 1255 **e** byron.carr@appointmentgroup.com **w** appointmentgroup.com GM: Byron Carr.

Nightsky Travel Ltd Starcloth Way, Mullacott Ind. Est, Ilfracombe, Devon EX34 8AY **t** 01271 855 138 **f** 01271 867 120 **e** info@nightskytravel.com **w** nightskytravel.com Dir: Danny Hudson.

Nova Travel 20 Old Lydd Rd, Camber, E Sussex TN31 7RH **t** 08452 300 039 **e** peter@sleepercoaches.co.uk **w** sleepercoaches.co.uk Contact: Peter Davie.

Pinnacle Chauffeur Transport London North 14 Lucerne Close, London N13 4QJ **t** 0870 752 3385 **e** info@yourchauffeur.co.uk **w** yourchauffeur.co.uk Dir: Alan D Pinner.

Premier Aviation UK Ltd 2 Newhouse Business Centre, Old Crawley Rd, Faygate, Horsham, W Sussex RH12 4RU **t** 01293 852688 **f** 01293 852699 **e** operations@premieraviation.com **w** premieraviation.com MD: Adrian Whitmarsh.

Rima Travel 10 Angel Gate, City Rd, London EC1V 2PT **t** 020 7833 5071 **f** 020 7278 4700 **e** ernie.garcia@rima-travel.co.uk **w** rimatravel.co.uk MD: Ernie Garcia.

SAMSON TRAVEL

Samson.*Travel*
TAILOR-MADE TRAVEL & EVENTS

Fun Events Corporate Services

31 Lower Clapton Road, London E5 0NS **t** 020 8985 1054 or 020 7987 4385 **f** 020 8985 4334 **e** admin@funevents.com **w** samsontravel.co.uk Director: Harv Sethi.

Screen And Music Travel Ltd Colne House, High St, Colnebrook, Middx SL3 0LX **t** 01753 764 050 **f** 01753 764 051 **w** screenandmusictravel.co.uk Special Proj Mgr: Colin Doran.

Sound Moves (UK) Ltd Abbeygate House, Challenge Rd, Ashford, Middx TW15 1AX **t** 01784 424 470 or 01784 424 489 **f** 01784 424 490 or 01784 424499 **e** london@soundmoves.com **w** soundmoves.com MD: Martin Corr.

T&S Immigration Services Ltd 118 High St, Kirkcudbright DG6 4JQ **t** 01557 339 123 **f** 01557 330 567 **e** firstname@tandsimmigration.demon.co.uk **w** tandsimmigration.demon.co.uk Work Permit Specialists: Steve & Tina Richard.

Vans For Bands Ltd 161 Woodstock Rd, Oxford OX2 7NA **t** 01865 559 574 or 07886 684 140 **e** info@vansforbands.co.uk **w** vansforbands.co.uk MD: Tarrant Anderson.

Tour Miscellaneous

Audile Unit 110, Cariocca Business Pk, Ardwick, Manchester M12 4AH **t** 0161 272 7883 or 07968 156 499 **f** 0161 272 7883 **e** rob@audile.co.uk **w** audile.co.uk Ptnr: Rob Ashworth. ✳

BCS Multi Media (Computer Visuals) Grantham House, Macclesfield, Cheshire SK10 3NP **t** 01625 615 379 **f** 01625 429 667 **e** dpl@bcsmm.fsnet.co.uk **w** bcsmm.fsnet.co.uk Dir: Duncan Latham.

Calma - Complementary Therapies PO Box 49669, London N8 4YU **t** 07973 887 520 **e** caroline@calma.biz **w** calma.biz Therapist: Caroline Dapre.

Lee Charteris Associates 10 Marco Rd, London W6 0PN **t** 020 8741 2500 or 07801 663 700 **f** 020 8741 2577 **e** mail@LeeCharteris.com Production Mgr: Lee Charteris.

The Chevalier Catering Company Studio 4-5, Garnet Close, Watford, Herts WD24 7GN **t** 020 8950 8998 or 01923 211703 **f** 01923 211704 **e** bonnie@chevalier.co.uk **w** chevalier.co.uk Ops Manager: Sarah 'Bonnie' May.

Crisp Productions Tour Mgmt & Support Services, 21 Stupton Rd, Sheffield S9 1BQ **t** 0114 261 1649 **f** 0114 261 1649 **e** dc@cprod.win-uk.net MD: Darren Crisp.

The Departure Lounge 29 Kingdon Rd, London NW6 1PJ **t** 020 7431 2070 **f** 020 7431 2070 Contact: Susan Ransom.

Detonate Music & Entertainment Travel Services 104-105 High St, Eton, Windsor, Berks SL4 6AF **t** 01753 801 200 **f** 01753 672 710 **e** Detonate@eton-travel.co.uk **w** detonatetravel.com.

Eat To The Beat Studio 4-5, Garnet Close, Greycaine Rd, Watford, Herts WD2 4JN **t** 01923 211702 **f** 01923 211704 **e** catering@eattothebeat.com **w** eattothebeat.com Ops Manager: Mary Shelley-Smith.

Eat Your Hearts Out Basement Flat, 108A Elgin Ave, London W9 2HD **t** 020 7289 9446 **f** 020 7266 3160 **e** eyho@dial.pipex.com MD: Kim Davenport.

EST Ltd Marshgate Sidings, Marshgate Lane, London E15 2PB **t** 020 8522 1000 **f** 020 8522 1002 **e** delr@est-uk.com **w** yourock-weroll.co.uk Dir: Del Roll.

Event Experts 3 Walpole Court, Ealing Green, London W5 5ED **t** 020 8326 3290 **f** 020 8326 3299 **e** info@event-experts.co.uk **w** event-experts.co.uk Production Manager: John Denby.

Fexx Live Sound 159A High Rd, Romford, Essex RM6 6NL **t** 07931 752641 **e** adamfexx@yahoo.co.uk **w** fexx.co.uk Sound Engineer: Adam Taylor.

FM Productions Great Bossinghamn Farmhouse, Bossingham, Kent CT4 6EB **t** 01227 709790 **f** 01227 709730 **e** kenfmprod@aol.com Prod Designer/Mgr: Ken Watts.

Front Of House Productions 81 Harriet St, Trecynon, Aberdare, Rhondda Cynon Taff CF44 8PL **t** 01685 881006 **f** 01685 881006 **e** info@fohproductions.co.uk **w** fohproductions.co.uk Production Mgr: Jules Jones.

Fruition Chestnut Farm, Frodsham, Cheshire **t** 01928 734422 or 020 7430 0700 **f** 01928 734433 or 020 7430 2122 **e** musicevents@fruition.co.uk **w** fruition.co.uk Contact: Mark Tasker.

Future Management & Tour Logistics PO Box 183, Chelmsford, Essex CM2 9XN **t** 01245 601910 **f** 01245 601048 **e** Futuremgt@aol.com **w** futuremanagement.co.uk MD: Joe Ferrari.

Grand Tours 93b Scrubs Lane, London NW10 6QU **t** 020 8968 7798 **f** 020 8968 3377 **e** johndawkins@granduniongroup.com **w** grand-tours.net Mgr: John Dawkins.

Health & Safety Advice PO Box 32295, London W5 1WD **t** 0870 066 0272 **f** 0870 066 0273 **e** info@health-safetyadvice.co.uk **w** health-safetyadvice.co.uk Dir: Jan Goodwin.

Jaguar Chauffeur t 07921 777 611 **e** info@jaguarchauffeur.com **w** jaguarchauffeur.com MD: Emily M. Bingham.

Judgeday Ltd The Manor House, Box, Corsham, Wilts SN13 8NF **t** 01225 744226 **f** 01225 742155 **e** judgedaybeck@dial.pipex.com Contact: Dave T.

K West Hotel & Spa Richmond Way, London W14 0AX **t** 087 00 27 43 43 **f** 087 08 11 26 12 **e** ces@k-west.co.uk **w** k-west.co.uk Senior Sales Manager: Clara Saffer.

Key Cargo International 7 Millbrook Business Centre, Floats Rd, Roundthorn, Manchester M23 9YJ **t** 0161 283 2471 **f** 0161 283 2472 **e** info@keycargo.net Operations Director: Steve Plant.

Knights Guitar Electronics and Flight Cases 28 Hill Grove, Romford, Essex RM1 4JP **t** 07788 740793 **f** 07092 231176 **e** kge@freeuk.com **w** http://welcome.to/kge MD: Ron Knights.

MDMA 1A, 1 Adelaide Mansions, Hove, Sussex BN3 2FD **t** 01273 321602 **f** 0870 1213472 **e** tourmanric@aol.com Mgr: Rick French.

Midland Custom Cases 24 Proctor St, Birmingham B7 4EE **t** 0121 333 7711 **f** 0121 333 7799 **e** admin@cloudone.net **w** cloudone.net MD: Paul Stratford.

Midnight Costume Design & Wardrobe t 07941 313 223 **e** Midnight_wardrobe@hotmail.com Designer/Wardrobe: Midnight.

Millsea Production Services 2A Rotherwood Mansion, 78 Madeira Rd, Streatham, London SW16 2DE **t** 020 8677 2370 or 07770 428 096 **f** 020 8677 8690 **e** millsea@aol.com Tour Manager: Caron Malcolm.

Movin' Music Ltd (London) Suite 1, 52 Highfield Rd, Purley, Surrey CRB 2JG **t** 020 8763 0767 **f** 020 8668 2214 **e** info@movinmusic.net **w** movinmusic.net Dir: Brenda Lillywhite.

Movin' Music Ltd (Manchester) Studio 2, 33 Albany Rd, Chorlton, Manchester M21 0BH **t** 0161 881 9227 **f** 0161 881 9089 **e** info@movinmusic.net **w** movinmusic.net Dir: Nick Robinson.

Moving Space Rentals 93b Scrubs Lane, London NW10 6QU **t** 020 8968 7798 **f** 020 8968 3377 **e** nickyeatman@granduniongroup.com **w** movingspaceuk.co.uk Mgr: Nick Yeatman, John Dawkins.

MTFX Velt House, Velt House Lane, Elmore, Gloucester GL2 3NY **t** 01452 729903 **f** 01452 729904 **e** info@mtfx.com **w** mtfx.com MD: Mark Turner.

Pa-Boom Phenomenal Fireworks Ltd 49 Carters Close, Sherington, Bucks MK16 9NW **t** 01908 612 593 or 0860 439 380 **f** 01908 216 400 **e** pa@boom.demon.co.uk **w** pa-boom.com Contact: Neil Canham.

Packhorse Case Co 9 Stapledon Rd, Orton Southgate, Peterborough, Cambs PE2 6TB **t** 01733 232440 **f** 01733 232556 Contact: Sam Robinson.

Pod Bluman 65 Coppetts Rd, London N10 1JH **t** 020 8374 8400 **f** 020 8374 2982 **e** pod.projects@blueyonder.co.uk (Projection Specialist).

Polar Arts Ltd Corbett Cottage, The Street, Castle Combe, Wilts SN14 7HU **t** 01249 783850 **f** 020 7681 1900 **e** juliette@polararts.com **w** polararts.com Dir: Juliette Slater.

Premier Aviation UK Ltd 2 Newhouse Business Centre, Old Crawley Rd, Faygate, Horsham, W Sussex RH12 4RU **t** 01293 852688 **f** 01293 852699 **e** operations@premieraviation.com **w** premieraviation.com MD: Adrian Whitmarsh.

Pure Energy Productions Services Suite 91, 2 Lansdowne Crescent, Bournemouth, Dorset BH1 1SA **t** 01202 579673 **f** 01202 579679 **e** sales@pepuk.com **w** pepuk.com Dir: Ian Walker.

Pyramid Productions & Promotions Cadillac Ranch, Pencraig Uchaf, Cwm Bach, Whitland, Carms. SA34 0DT **t** 01994 484466 **f** 01994 484294 **e** cadillacranch@telco4u.net Dir: Weepy Moyer.

Rhythm Of Life Ltd Rhythm House, King St, Carlisle, Cumbria CA1 1SJ **t** 01228 515141 **f** 01228 515161 **e** events@rhythm.co.uk **w** rhythm.co.uk MD: Andrew Lennie.

Saucery Catering Watchcott, Nordan, Leominster, Herefordshire HR6 0AJ **t** 01568 614221 **f** 01568 610256 **e** saucery@aol.com MD: Alison Taylor.

Shell Shock Firework Ltd Furze Hill Farm, Knossington, Oakham, Leics LE15 8LX **t** 01664 454 994 **f** 01664 454 995 **e** zoe@shell-shock.co.uk **w** shell-shock.co.uk Dir: Zoe Gibson.

Showsec Head Office, Phoenix Yard, 1st & 2nd Floor, Block C, Upper Brown St, Leicester LE1 5TE **t** 01162 043 333 **e** mark.harding@crowd-management.com **w** crowd-management.com MD: Mark Harding.

So Touring Services PO Box 20750, London E3 2YU **t** 020 8573 6652 **f** 020 8573 6784 **e** sotouring@aol.com Contact: Sean O'Neill.

Sonic Movement Flat 2, 110 Chepstow Rd, London W2 5QS **t** 020 7229 0196 **f** 020 7691 7276 **e** JOwens666@btinternet.com Tour Manager: Jamie Owens.

Sound & Light Productions PO Box 32295, London W5 1WD **t** 0870 066 0272 **f** 0870 066 0273 **e** info@soundandlightproductions.co.uk **w** soundandlightproductions.co.uk Contact: John Denby.

SPA Catering Services 44 Oak Hill Rd, London SW15 2QR **t** 020 7563 2550 or 07788 785 493 **f** 020 8871 4579 **e** spacatering@hotmail.com MD: Simon Peter.

Stardes Ashes Buildings, Old Lane, Holbrook Industrial Estate, Halfway, Sheffield S20 3GZ **t** 0114 251 0051 **f** 0114 251 0555 **e** info@stardes.co.uk **w** stardes.co.uk Contact: David Harvey-Steinberg.

Taurus Self Drive Ltd 55 Wyverne Rd, Chorlton, Manchester M21 0ZW **t** 0161 434 9823 or 020 7434 9823 **f** 0161 434 9823 or 020 7434 9823 Contact: Sean Shannon.

TCP International Ltd 101 Shepherds Bush Rd, London W6 7LP **t** 020 7602 8822 **f** 020 7603 2352 Live Manager/Event Prod: John Fairs.

Teri Wyncoll Tour Management 239 Clarendon Park Rd, Leicester LE2 3AN **t** 0116 270 4007 **f** 0116 270 4007 **e** dave.davies1@virgin.net MD: Teri Wyncoll.

That's EnTEEtainment 59 Prince St, Bristol BS1 4QH **t** 0117 904 4116 **f** 0117 904 4117 **e** dick@dicktee.com **w** dicktee.com MD: Dick Tee.

TM International 4 Badby Rd, Newnham, Northants NN11 3HE **t** 01327 705032 or 07785 267751 **f** 01327 300037 **e** hotel.india@virgin.net MD: Harry Isles.

The Tough Enough Touring Company Tour Mngmt & Splitter Van Hire, 88 Calvert Rd, Greenwich, London SE10 0DF **t** 020 8333 9447 or 07985 142 193 **e** sam.towers@ganzmanagement.com Contact: Sam Towers.

The Tour Company Studio 19, St Georges Studios, 93-97 St Georges Rd, Glasgow G3 6JA **t** 0141 353 8800 **f** 0141 353 8801 **e** admin@thetourcompany.co.uk **w** thetourcompany.co.uk MD: Tina Waters.

Tour Concepts - Tour Management 123 Hardy St, Hull HU5 2PH **t** 01482 448806 **f** 0870 126 5960 **e** andy.reynolds@tourconcepts.com **w** tourconcepts.com Owner: Andy Reynolds.

Len Wright Band Services 9 Elton Way, Watford, Herts WD2 8HH **t** 01923 238611 or 07831 811201 **f** 01923 230134 **e** lwbs1@aol.com Contact: Les Collins.

one to one

The world's leading information source for media manufacturers

www.oto-online.com

Recording Studios & Services:

 APRS studio members

Recording Studios

▲ **2KHz Studios** 97a Scrubs Lane, London NW10 6QU
t 020 8960 1331 **f** 020 8968 3377 **e** info@2khzstudios.co.uk
w 2khzstudios.co.uk Studio Manager: Mike Nelson.

10th Planet 40 Newman St, London W1T 1QJ
t 020 7637 9500 **f** 020 7637 9599 **e** studio@10thplanet.net
w 10thplanet.net Dirs: Ben Woolley & Jon Voda.

45 RPM 45 Royal Parade Mews, Blackheath, London SE3 0PA
t 020 8852 4664 **f** 020 8269 0353
e suzanne@quixoticrecords.com
Contact: Suzanne Hunt, Glenn Tilbrook.

▲ **Abbey Road Studios** 3 Abbey Rd, London NW8 9AY
t 020 7266 7000 **f** 020 7266 7250
e bookings@abbeyroad.com **w** abbeyroad.com
Studio Mgr: Colette Barber.

AGM Studios 1927 Building, 2 Michael Rd, London
SW6 2AD **t** 020 7371 0234 **e** contacts@agmstudios.com
w agmstudios.com MD: Alex Golding.

▲ **Air-Edel Recording Studios** 18 Rodmarton St, London
W1U 8BJ **t** 020 7486 6466 **f** 020 7224 0344
t trevorbest@air-edel.co.uk **w** air-edel.co.uk
In-house Production and Studio Manager: Trevor Best.

▲ **Air Studios (Lyndhurst)** Lyndhurst Hall, Lyndhurst Rd,
London NW3 5NG **t** 020 7794 0660 **f** 020 7794 8518
e info@airstudios.com **w** airstudios.com
Bookings Mgr: Alison Burton.

Airtight Productions Unit 16, Albany Rd Trading Estate,
Albany Rd, Chorlton M21 0AZ **t** 0161 881 5157
e info@airtightproductions.co.uk **w** airtightproductions.co.uk
Dir: Anthony Davey.

Alaska @ Waterloo Bridge Studios 127-129 Alaska
St, London SE1 8XE **t** 020 7928 7440 **f** 020 7928 8070
e blodge_uk@yahoo.com **w** alaskastudio.co.uk
Studio Mgr: Beverley Lodge.

Albert Studios Unit 29, Cygnus Business Centre, Dalmeyer
Rd, London NW10 2XA **t** 020 8830 0330 **f** 020 8830 0220
e info@alberts.co.uk **w** albertmusic.co.uk
Studio Manager: Paul Hoare.

All of Music PO Box 2361, Romford, Essex RM2 6EZ
t 01708 688 088 **f** 020 7691 9508 **e** michelle@allofmusic.co.uk
w allofmusic.co.uk MD: Danielle Barnett. [Budget Rate]

Angel Recording Studios Ltd 311 Upper St, London
N1 2TU **t** 020 7354 2525 **f** 020 7226 9624
e angel@angelstudios.co.uk **w** angelstudios.co.uk
Studio Mgr: Lucy Jones.

Mark Angelo Studios Unit 13, Impress House, Mansell Rd,
London W3 7QH **t** 020 8735 0040 **f** 020 8735 0041
e mimi@markangelo.co.uk **w** markangelo.co.uk
Studio Manager: Mimi Kerns.

APE Recording 19 Market St, Castle Donington, Derby
DE74 2JB **t** 01332 810933 **f** 01332 850123 **e** info@APE.co.uk
w APE.co.uk Studio Mgr: Nira Amba.

Apollo Studio (see Temple Lane Recording).

Arclite Studios The Grove Music Studios, Unit 10, Latimer
Ind. Estate, Latimer Rd, London W10 6RQ **t** 020 8964 9047
e Info@arcliteproductions.com **w** arcliteproductions.com
Studio Mgrs: Alan Bleay, Laurie Jenkins.

Arcsound Studio 443, New Cross Rd, London SE14 6TA
t 020 8691 8161 **e** info@arcsound.co.uk **w** arcsound.co.uk
Studio Manager: James Dougill. [Budget Rate]

Are We Mad? Studios 34 Whitehorse Lane, London
SE25 6RE **t** 020 8653 7744 or 020 8771 1470
f 020 8771 1911 **e** info@ariwa.com **w** ariwa.com
Studio Mgr: Kamal Fraser.

Ariwa Sounds 34 Whitehorse Lane, London SE25 6RE
t 020 8653 7744 or 020 8771 1470 **f** 020 8771 1911
e info@ariwa.com **w** ariwa.com Studio Mgr: Joseph Fraser.

Arriba Studios 256-258 Gray's Inn Rd, London WC1X 8ED
t 020 7713 0998 **e** info@arriba-records.com
w arriba-records.com Contact: SJ/Baby Doc.

The Audio Workshop 217 Askew Rd, London W12 9AZ
t 020 8742 9242 **f** 020 8743 4231
e info@theaudioworkshop.co.uk **w** theaudioworkshop.co.uk
MD: Martin Cook.

Band On The Wall Studio 25 Swan St, Northern Quarter,
Manchester M4 5JZ **t** 0161 834 1786 **f** 0161 834 2559
w bandonthewall.org Promotions: Gavin Sharp.

Bandwagon Studios Westfield Folkhouse, Westfield Lane,
Mansfield, Notts NG18 1TL **t** 01623 422962 **f** 01623 633449
e info@bandwagonstudios.co.uk **w** bandwagonstudios.co.uk
Studio Mgr: Andy Dawson.

▲ **Bark Studio** 1A Blenheim Rd, London E17 6HS
t 020 8523 0110 **f** 020 8523 0110 **e** Brian@barkstudio.co.uk
w barkstudio.co.uk Studio Manager: Brian O'Shaughnessy.

BBC Resources (London) Maida Vale Music Studios,
Delaware Rd, London W9 2LH **t** 020 7765 3374
f 020 7765 3203 **e** adam.askew@bbc.co.uk
Ops Mgr: Adam Askew.

Be-Bop Recording Studio Unit 4 Indian Queens
Workshops, Moorland Rd, Indian Queens, Cornwall TR9 6JP
t 01726 861068 **e** sales@be-bop.co.uk **w** be-bop.co.uk
Prop: Steve White.

Beaumont Street Studios Ltd St Peters Chambers, St
Peters St, Huddersfield, W Yorks HD1 1RA **t** 01484 452013
f 01484 435861 **e** info@beaumontstreet.co.uk
Studio Mgr: Sam Roberts.

Beechpark Studios Newtown, Rathcoole, Co Dublin, Ireland
t +353 1 458 8500 **f** +353 1 458 8577 **e** info@beechpark.com
w beechpark.com Studio Manager: Dara Winston.

Berlin Recording Studios Caxton House, Caxton Ave,
Blackpool, Lancs FY2 9AP **t** 01253 591 169 **f** 01253 508 670
e info@berlinstudios.co.uk **w** berlinstudios.co.uk
MD: Ron Sharples.

Berry Street Studio 1 Berry St, London EC1V 0AA
t 020 7253 5885 or 020 7608 3977
e kp@berrystreetstudio.com **w** berrystreetstudio.com
MD: Kevin Poree.

Big Noise Recordings 12 Gregory St, Northampton
NN1 1TA **t** 01604 634455 **w** myspace.com/bignoisestudio
Studio Mgr: Ben Gordelier.

Blah Street Studios The Hop Kiln, Hillside, Odiham, Hants
RG29 1HX **t** 01256 701112 **f** 01256 701106
e studio@blahstreet.co.uk **w** blahstreet.co.uk
Producer: Nick Hannan.

Blakamix International Garvey House, 42 Margetts Rd,
Bedford MK42 8DS **t** 01234 302115 **f** 01234 854344
e blakamix@aol.com **w** blakamix.co.uk MD: Dennis Bedeau.

Blossom Studio Station Rd, Blaina, Gwent NP13 3PW
t 01495 290 960 or 07932 377 109
e info@blossomstudio.co.uk **w** blossomstudio.co.uk
Proprietor & Engineer: Noel Watson.

Blueprint Studios Elizabeth House, 39 Queen St, Salford,
Manchester M3 4DQ **t** 0161 835 3088 **f** 08700 11 27 80
e tim@blueprint-studios.com **w** blueprint-studios.com
Studio Manager: Tim Thomas.

BonaFideStudio Burbage House, 83-85 Curtain Rd, London
EC2A 3BS **t** 020 7684 5350 or 020 7684 5351
f 020 7613 1185 **e** info@bonafidestudio.co.uk
w bonafidestudio.co.uk Studio Director: Deanna Gardner.

Born To Dance Studios Unit 34, DRCA Business Centre,
Charlotte Despard Ave, Battersea, London SW11 5JH
t 01273 301555 **f** 01273 305266 **e** studio@borntodance.com
w borntodance.com Studio Mgr: Gavin McCall.

The Bridge Facilities Ltd 55-57 Great Marlborough St,
London W1F 7JX **t** 020 7434 9861 **f** 020 7494 4658
e bookings@thebridge.co.uk **w** thebridge.co.uk
Facilities Mgr: Tom McConville.

Britannia Row Studios 3 Bridge Studios, 318-326
Wandsworth Bridge Rd, London SW6 2TZ **t** 020 7371 5872
f 020 7371 8641 **e** info@britanniarowstudios.co.uk
w britanniarowstudios.co.uk Studio Manager: Jamie Lane.

Broadley Studios Broadley House, 48 Broadley Terrace,
London NW1 6LG **t** 020 7258 0324 **f** 020 7724 2361
e admin@broadleystudios.com **w** broadleystudios.com
MD: Ellis Elias.

Bryn Derwen Studio Coed-y-Parc, Bethesda, Gwynedd
LL57 4YW **t** 01248 600234 **f** 01248 601933
e Laurie@brynderwen.co.uk **w** brynderwen.co.uk
Mgr: Laurie Gane.

The Building 37 Rowley St, Stafford, Staffs ST16 2RH
t 01785 245649 or 07866 718010 **e** info@thebuilding.co.uk
w thebuilding.co.uk Studio Mgr: Tim Simmons.

The Bunker Recording Studio Borras Rd, Borras,
Wrexham LL13 9TW **t** 01978 263295 **f** 01978 263295
e kklass@btconnect.com **w** k-klass.com
Contact: Andrew Willimas.

Ca Va Sound 30 Bentinck St, Kelvingrove, Glasgow,
Strathclyde G3 7TT **t** 0141 334 5099 **f** 0141 339 0271
e cavasound@mac.com **w** cavasound.com
Studio Mgr: Brian Young.

Cabin Studios 82 London Rd, Coventry, W Midlands
CV1 2JT **t** 024 7622 0749 **e** office@sonar-records.demon.co.uk
w cabinstudio.co.uk Studio Mgr: Jon Lord.

Cadillac Ranch Recording Studio Cadillac Ranch,
Pencraig Uchaf, Cwmbach, Whitland, Carms. SA34 0DT
t 01994 484466 **f** 01994 48446 **e** cadillacranch@telco4u.net
w nikturner.com Dir: Moose Magoon.

CAP Recording Studios Crask Of Aigas, By Beauly,
Inverness-Shire IV4 7AD **t** 01463 782364 **f** 01463 782525
e capdonna@cali.co.uk Studio/Bkings Mgr: Donna Cunningham.

Castlesound Studios The Old School, Park View,
Pencaitland, East Lothian EH34 5DW **t** 0131 666 1024
f 0131 666 1024 **w** castlesound.co.uk
Studio & Bookings Mgr: Freeland Barbour.

The Cave Studio 155 Acton Lane, Park Royal, London
NW10 7NJ **t** 020 8961 5818 **f** 020 8965 7008
e dannyray@jetstar.co.uk Contact: Danny Ray.

Cent Music Melbourne House, Chamberlain St, Wells
BA5 2PJ **t** 01749 689074 **f** 01749 670315
e kevin@centrecords.com **w** centrecords.com MD: Kevin Newton.

Chamber Recording Studio 120A West Granton Rd,
Edinburgh, Midlothian EH5 1PF **t** 0131 551 6632
f 0131 551 6632 **e** mail@humancondition.co.uk
w chamberstudio.co.uk Studio Mgr: Jamie Watson.

Chem19 Recording Studios Unit 51B, South Ave,
Blantyre Industrial Estate, Blantyre G72 0XB **t** 01698 324 246
f 01698 327 979 **e** jim@chemikal.co.uk **w** chem19studios.co.uk
Dir: Jim Savage.

Chestnut Studios 17 Barons Court Rd, West Kensington,
London W14 9DP **t** 020 7384 5960
e info@chestnutstudios.com **w** chestnutstudios.com
Studio Manager: Chris Young. [Standard Rate]

The Church Road Recording Company 197-201 Church Rd, Hove, E Sussex BN3 2AH **t** 01273 327 889 or 07803 173 003 **e** info@churchroad.net **w** churchroad.net Producer/Engineer: Julian Tardo.

▲ **Classic Sound** 5 Falcon Pk, Neasden Lane, London NW10 1RZ **t** 020 8208 8100 **f** 020 8208 8111 **e** info@classicsound.net **w** classicsound.net Dir: Neil Hutchinson. [Standard Rate]

CMS Studios The Millennium Centre, 11-13 Clearwell Drive, London W9 2JZ **t** 020 7641 3679 or 07747 451 704 **e** john@miller9878.fsnet.co.uk Contact: John Miller. [Budget Rate]

Compression Studios 56 Frazer Rd, Perivale, Middlesex UB6 7AL **t** 020 8723 6158 **e** suli.hirani@btinternet.com Studio Manager: Suli.

Contour Studios Unit 4 Hallam Mill, Hallam St, Stockport, Cheshire **t** 07974 236 275 **e** danfunk@breathe.com **w** contourstudios.co.uk Producer: Daniel Broad.

Conversion Studios Woolfields, Milton On Stour, Gillingham, Dorset **t** 01747 824729 **e** info@conversionstudios.co.uk **w** conversionstudios.co.uk Studio Manager: Owen Thomas.

Cordella Music Alhambra, High St, Shirrell Heath, Southampton, Hants SO32 2JH **t** 08450 616 616 **f** 01329 833 433 **e** barry@cordellamusic.co.uk **w** cordellamusic.co.uk MD: Barry Upton. [Budget Rate]

Core Studios Kings Court, 7 Osborne St, Glasgow G1 5QN **t** 0141 552 6677 **f** 0141 552 1354 **e** mail@corestudios.co.uk **w** corestudios.co.uk Co-Dir: Alan Walsh.

Cottage Recording Studios 2 Gawsworth Rd, Macclesfield, Cheshire SK11 8UE **t** 01625 420 163 **f** 01625 420 168 **e** info@cottagegroup.co.uk **w** cottagegroup.co.uk MD: Roger Boden. [Budget Rate]

Courtyard Recording Studios Gorsey Mount St, Waterloo Rd, Stockport, Cheshire SK1 3BU **t** 0161 477 6531 **e** tim@courtyardrecordingstudios.co.uk **w** courtyardrecordingstudios.co.uk Studio Mgr: Tim Woodward.

Courtyard Studio 21 The Nursery, Sutton Courtenay, Abingdon, Oxon OX14 4UA **t** 01235 845800 **f** 0870 0510183 **e** pippa@cyard.com Studio Mgr: Pippa Mole.

Cuan Studios Spiddal, Conamara, Co Galway, Ireland **t** +353 91 553838 **f** +353 91 553837 **e** info@cuan.com **w** cuan.com Studio Director: Eilis Lennon.

The Cutting Rooms Abraham Moss Centre, Crescent Rd, Manchester M8 5UF **t** 0161 740 9438 **f** 0161 740 9438 **e** cuttingrooms@hotmail.com **w** citycol.com/cuttingrooms Studio Mgr: Andrew Harris.

Dada Studios 157A Hubert Grove, Stockwell, London SW9 9NZ **t** 020 7501 9545 or 07956 945 417 **f** 020 7501 9216 **e** dadastudios@mac.com **w** dadastudios.co.uk Studio Manager: George Holt. [Budget Rate]

▲ **The Dairy** 43-45 Tunstall Rd, London SW9 8BZ **t** 020 7738 7777 **f** 020 7738 7007 **e** info@thedairy.co.uk **w** thedairy.co.uk Contact: Emily Taylor.

deBrett Studios 42 Wood Vale, Muswell Hill, London N10 3DP **t** 020 8372 6179 or 07814 267 792 **e** jwest@debrett41.freeserve.co.uk Prop: Jon West.

Deep Blue Recording Studio 38 Looe St, Plymouth, Devon PL4 0EB **t** 01752 601462 **e** dbs@deepbluesound.co.uk. **w** deepbluestudio.co.uk Studio Mgr: Matt Bernard.

Deep Recording Studios 187 Freston Rd, London W10 6TH **t** 020 8964 8256 **e** deep.studios@virgin.net **w** deeprecordingstudios.com Studio Manager: Mark Rose. [Budget Rate]

Delta Recording Studios Deanery Farm, Bolts Hill, Chatham, Kent CT4 7LD **t** 01227 732140 **f** 01227 732140 **e** deltastudios@btconnect.com **w** deltastudios.co.uk Contact: Julian Whitfield.

DEP International Studios 1 Andover St, Birmingham, W Midlands B5 5RG **t** 0121 633 4742 **f** 0121 643 4904 **e** enquiries@ub40.co.uk **w** ub40.co.uk Bkngs/Studio Mgr: Dan Sprigg.

Dreamhouse Studio (Right Bank Music UK) Home Park House, Hampton Court Rd, Kingston Upon Thames, Surrey KT1 4AE **t** 020 8977 0666 **f** 020 8977 0660 **e** rightbankmusicuk@rightbankmusicuk.com **w** rightbankmusicuk.com VP: Ian Mack.

Earth Productions 163 Gerrard St, Birmingham, W Midlands B19 2AP **t** 0121 554 7424 **f** 0121 551 9250 **e** info@earthproductions.co.uk **w** earthproductions.co.uk Studio Mgr: Lorna Williams.

Earthworks Music Studios 62 The Rear, Barnet High St, Herts EN5 5SL **t** 020 8449 2258 or 07989 549 730 **e** ljdarlow@aol.com **w** earthworksstudio.co.uk Head Engineer: Leigh Darlow.

Eastcote Studios Ltd 249 Kensal Rd, London W10 5DB **t** 020 8969 3739 **f** 020 8960 1836 **e** peggy@eastcotestudios.co.uk **w** eastcotestudios.co.uk Studio Mgr: Peggy Fussell.

Ebony & Ivory Productions 11 Varley Parade, Edgware Rd, Colindale, London NW9 6RR **t** 020 8200 7090 **e** SVLProds@aol.com Studio Manager: Alan Bradshaw.

▲ **Eden Studios Ltd** 20-24 Beaumont Rd, Chiswick, London W4 5AP **t** 020 8995 5432 **f** 020 8747 1931 **e** eden@edenstudios.com **w** edenstudios.com Studio Mgr: Natalie Horton.

Elektra Studio (see Temple Lane Recording).

EMS Audio Ltd 12 Balloo Ave, Bangor, Co Down BT19 7QT **t** 028 9127 4411 **f** 028 9127 4412 **e** info@musicshop.to **w** musicshop.to Dir: William Thompson.

The Factory Sound (Woldingham) Toftrees, Church Rd, Woldingham, Surrey CR3 7JX **t** 01883 652386 **f** 01883 652457 **e** david@mackay99.plus.com Producer/Engineer: David Mackay.

Fairlight Mews Studios 15 St. Johns Rd, Kingston upon Thames, Surrey KT1 4AN **t** 0208 977 0632 **f** 0870 770 8669 **e** info@pncmusic.com **w** pncrecords.com MD: Sir Harry. [Budget Rate]

Fat Fox Studios 24a Radley Mews, Kensington, London W8 6JP **t** 020 7376 9666 **f** 020 7937 6246 **e** info@fatfox.co.uk **w** fatfoxstudios.co.uk Studio Manager: Richie Kayvan.

Firebird Studios Kyrle House Studios, Edde Cross St, Ross-on-Wye, Herefordshire HR9 7BZ **t** 01989 762269 **e** info@firebird **w** firebird.com CEO: Peter Martin.

Foel Studio Llanfair, Caereinion, Powys SY21 0DS
t 01938 810 758 **f** 01938 810 758 **e** foel.studio@dial.pipex.com
w foelstudio.co.uk MD: Dave Anderson. [Budget Rate]

Freak'n See Music Ltd Suite C, 19 Heathmans Rd, London
SW6 4TJ **t** 020 7384 2429 **f** 020 7384 2429
e firstname@freaknsee.com **w** freaknsee.com
MD: Jimmy Mikaoui.

Frog Studios Unit 2B, Banquay Trading Estate, Slutchers
Lane, Warrington, Cheshire WA1 1PJ **t** 01925 445742
f 01925 445742 **e** info@frogstudios.co.uk **w** frogstudios.co.uk
Studio Mgr: Steve Millington.

The Funky Bunker Recording Studios Unit 5, 10
Acklam Rd, London W10 5QZ **t** 020 8968 2222
f 020 8968 2220 **e** info@ice-pr.com **w** ice-pr.com
Contact: Jason Price.

The Garage Workshop 1st Floor Office Suite, 122
Montague St, Worthing, W Sussex BN11 3HG **t** 01903 606 513
or 07861 232 006 **e** Owen.thegarageworkshop@gmail.com
w thegarageworkshop.com Producer: Owen A Smith.

▲ **Gateway Studio** Pinewood Studios, Pinewood Rd, Iver
Heath, Bucks SL0 0NH **t** 01753 785 495 **f** 01753 656 153
e info@phoenixsound.net **w** phoenixsound.net
Studio Mgr: Pete Fielder. [Standard Rate]

Giginabox 444 Shoreham St, Sheffield S2 4FD
t 0114 221 6283 or 07960 510 889
e davecarrick@googlemail.com **w** giginabox.com
Contact: Dave Carrick. [Budget Rate]

Jeffrey Ginn 11 Haycroft, Wootton, Bedford MK43 9PB
t 01234 765602 **f** 01234 765602 **e** jeffginn@onetel.net.

The Granary Studio Bewlbridge Farm, Lamberhurst, Kent
TN3 8JJ **t** 01892 891128 **e** thegranarystudio@btconnect.com
w thegranarystudio.co.uk Studio Mgr: Guy Denning.

Grand Central Studios 25-32 Marshall St, London
W1F 7ES **t** 020 7306 5600 **f** 020 7306 5616
e info@grand-central-studios.com **w** grand-central-studios.com
MD: Carole Humphrey.

Gravity Shack Studio Unit 3, Rear of 328 Balham High Rd,
London SW17 7AA **t** 020 8767 1125
e jessica@gubbinsproductions.co.uk **w** gravityshackstudios.com
Producer/Engineer: Jessica Corcoran. [Standard Rate]

▲ **Great Linford Manor** Great Linford, Milton Keynes,
Bucks MK14 5AX **t** 01908 667432 **f** 01908 668164
e bookings@greatlinfordmanor.com **w** greatlinfordmanor.com
Studio Manager: Sue Dawson.

Greystoke Studios 39 Greystoke Park Terrace, Ealing,
London W5 1JL **t** 020 8998 5529 or 07850 735591
e andy@greystokeproductions.co.uk
w greystokeproductions.co.uk Owner/Director: Andy Whitmore.

Groovestyle Recording Studio 33 Upper Holt St, Earls
Colne, Colchester, Essex CO6 2PG **t** 01787 220326
e info@groovewithus.com **w** groovewithus.com
Owner: Graham Game. [Budget Rate]

Ground Zero Studios 43-45 Coombe Terrace, Lewes Rd,
Brighton BN2 4AD **t** 01273 819 617 **f** 01273 272 830
e james@g-zero.co.uk **w** g-zero.co.uk
Studio Mgr: James Stringfellow.

Grouse Lodge Residential Studios Rosemount, Co
Westmeath, Ireland **t** +353 906 436 175 or +353 87 253 0180
f +353 906 436 131 **e** info@grouselodge.com
w grouselodge.com Bookings Mgr: Tracy Bolger.

H2O Enterprises Sphere Studios, 2 Shuttleworth Rd,
Battersea, London SW11 3EA **t** 020 7326 9460
f 020 7326 9499 **e** simonb@h2o.co.uk **w** h2o.co.uk
Bkngs/Studio Mgr: Simon Bohannon.

Happybeat Studios 101 Greenway Rd, Higher Tranmere,
Merseyside CH42 0NE **t** 0151 653 3463
e happybeatstudios@yahoo.co.uk **w** happybeat.net
Contact: Fran Ashcroft.

Harewood Farm Studios Harewood Farm Studios, Little
Harewood Farm, Clamgoose Lane, Kingsley, Staffs ST10 2EG
t 07973 157 920 **f** 01538 755 735
e kristian@harewoodfarmstudios.com
w harewoodfarmstudios.com Producer: Kristian Gilroy.

Hatch Farm Studios Chertsey Rd, Addlestone, Surrey
KT15 2EH **t** 01932 828715 **f** 01932 828717
e brian.adams@dial.pipex.com MD: Brian Adams.

Heartbeat Recording Studio Guildie House Farm, North
Middleton, Gorbridge, Mid Lothian EH23 4QP **t** 01875 821102
f 01875 821102 **e** eddie@logane.freeserve.co.uk
Engineer/Prod: David L Valentine.

Hi Street 25 Churchfield Rd, London W3 6BD
t 020 8896 1925 Studio Manager: Gareth Redfarn.

High Barn Studio The Bardfield Centre, Great Bardfield,
Braintree, Essex CM7 4SL **t** 01371 811 291 **f** 01371 811 404
e info@high-barn.com **w** highbarnstudio.com
Studio Manager: Simon Allen.

▲ **ICC Studios** 4 Regency Mews, Silverdale Rd, Eastbourne,
E Sussex BN20 7AB **t** 01323 643341 **f** 01323 649240
e info@iccstudios.co.uk **w** iccstudios.co.uk
Studio & Bookings Mgr: Neil Costello.

The ICE Group 3 St Andrews St, Lincoln, Lincs LN5 7NE
t 01522 539883 **f** 01522 528964
e steve.hawkins@easynet.co.uk **w** icegroup.co.uk
MD: Steve Hawkins.

▲ **Iguana Studios** Unit 1, 88a Acre Lane, London
SW2 5QN **t** 020 7924 0496 **e** info@iguanastudio.co.uk
w iguanastudio.co.uk MD: Andrea Terrano.

Impulse Studio 71 High Street East, Wallsend, Tyne and
Wear NE28 7RJ **t** 0191 262 4999 **f** 0191 263 7082
MD: David Wood.

In A City Studio Unit 49, Carlisle Business Centre, 60
Carlisle Rd, Bradford BD8 8BD **t** 01274 223251 or
01377 236395 b'kgs **f** 01904 623660
e music@projectmanager.co.uk **w** inacity.co.uk MD: Carl Stipetic.

Influential Studios Unit 46 - Wenta Business Centre, Colne
Way, Watford, Herts WD24 7ND **t** 01923 801 635 or
07738 475 246 **f** 020 8421 5155
e andy@influentialstudios.co.uk **w** influentialstudios.co.uk
Principal Producer: Andy Smith. [Standard Rate]

INFX Recording Studios Wellesbourne Campus, Kingshill
Rd, High Wycombe, Bucks HP13 5BB **t** 01494 522141 ex 4020
f 01494 465432 **e** fmacke01@bcuc.ac.uk
Studio Manager: Frazer Mackenzie.

Bunker A: The Universe Room

Live Room

Bunker B: The Bubblin' Room

Vocal Booth

Funky Bunker Studios

Bunker A: The Universe Room
Apple Macintosh G4 80G Drive
ORAM Series 24 BEQ 40 Channel Console
iZ RADAR
Pro Tools / Logic

Live Room
10.2msq. Variable Acoustic Panels

Bunker B: The Bubblin' Room
Apple Macintosh G4 Processor
Yamaha 24 Track Console
iZ RADAR
Pro Tools / Logic 5

Full specifications available on website
www.ice-pr.com

Studio Services Include
Production
Engineering
Session Musicians
Video Editing
Graphic Design
Web Design
Studio Design

APRS
the professional recording association
M E M B E R

Unit 5 Acklam Workspace
10 Acklam Rd
London
W10 5QZ
Ph: +44 (0) 208 968 2222
Fax: +44 (0) 208 968 2220
Email: info@ice-pr.com
www.myspace.com/innercirtcleuniversalrecords

Jam Central Studio P.O. Box 230, Aylesbury, Bucks HP21 9WA **t** 07765 258 225 **e** stuart@jamcentralrecords.co.uk **w** jamcentralrecords.co.uk MD: Stuart Robb.

KD's Studio see Saturn Music Group..

Kenwood Studios 23 Kenwood Park Rd, Sheffield S7 1NE **t** 0114 249 9222 **f** 0114 249 9333 **e** adam@kenwoodstudios.co.uk **w** kenwoodstudios.co.uk Studio Manager: Adam Dowding.

▲ **Keynote Studios** Burghfield Bridge, Green Lane, Burghfield, Reading RG30 3XN **t** 01189 599 944 **f** 01189 596 442 **e** tom@keynotestudios.com **w** keynotestudios.com Studio Mgr: Tom Languish.

▲ **Konk Studios** 84-86 Tottenham Lane, London N8 7EE **t** 020 8340 4757 or 020 8340 7873 **f** 020 8348 3952 **e** linda@konkstudio.com Studio Mgr: Sarah Lockwood.

Kontakt Productions 44b Whifflet St, Coatbridge ML5 4EL **t** 01236 434 083 **f** 01236 434 083 **e** gareth@kontaktproductions.com **w** kontaktproductions.com Studio Manager: Gareth Whitehead. [Budget Rate]

The Lab Music Studio Unit J, Blackhorse Mews, off Blackhorse Lane, London E17 6SL **t** 020 8527 7300 **e** info@thelabmusicstudio.com **w** thelabmusicstudio.com Studio Manager: Mikee Hughes. [Budget Rate]

Lab 24 346 Kingsland Rd, Ground Floor, London E8 4DA **t** 07970 309470 Studio Mgr: Hamish Dzewu.

Bob Lamb's Recording Studio 122A Highbury Rd, Kings Heath, Birmingham, W Midlands B14 7QP **t** 0121 443 2186 **e** boblamb@recklessltd.com Studio Mgr/Prop: Bob Lamb.

Lansdowne Recording Studios (incorporating CTS) Rickmansworth Rd, Watford WD17 3JN **t** 020 8846 9444 **f** 05601 155 009 **e** info@cts-lansdowne.co.uk **w** cts-lansdowne.co.uk Bookings Enquiries: Sharon Rose. [Standard Rate]

Larry Lush Studio The Studio, 2 Faygate Rd, Streatham, London SW2 3AR **t** 07716 887 576 **e** Laurence.e.p@gmail.com **w** larrylush.co.uk Producer/Engineer/Arranger: Laurence Elliott-Potter. [Budget Rate]

The Leisure Factory Ltd 20-22 Mount Pleasant, Bilston, Wolverhampton, W Midlands WV14 7LJ **t** 01902 405511 **f** 01902 401418 **e** Music@therobin.co.uk **w** theleisurefactory.com Dir: Mike Hamblett.

The Library 2 Sybil Mews, London N4 1EP **t** 07956 412 209 **e** jules@librarystudio.com **w** librarystudio.com Owner: Julian Standen.

Lime Street Sound 3 Lime Court, Lime St, Dublin 2, Ireland **t** +353 1 671 7271 **f** +353 1 670 7639 **e** limesound@eircom.net **w** limesound.com Dir: Steve McGrath.

LimeTree Studios Welgate, Mattishall, Dereham, Norfolk NR20 3PJ **t** 01362 858015 **f** 01362 858016 **e** info@limetreestudios.com **w** limetreestudios.com Prop: Stephen Pitkethly.

Linden Studio High Bankhill, Kirkoswald, Penrith, Cumbria CA10 1EZ **t** 01768 870353 **e** guy@lindenstudio.co.uk **w** lindenstudio.co.uk Producer/Engineer: Guy Forrester. [Budget Rate]

Livingston Recording Studios Brook Rd, off Mayes Rd, London N22 6TR **t** 020 8889 6558 **f** 020 8888 2698 **e** mail@livingstonstudios.co.uk **w** livingstonstudios.co.uk Bkings/Studio Mgrs: Lise Regan & Verity Boys.

The Lodge 23 Abington Sq, Northampton NN1 4AE **t** 01604 475399 **f** 01604 516999 **e** studio@lodgstud.demon.co.uk **w** demon.co.uk/lodgstud Snr Engineer/Owner: Max Read.

London Recording Studios 9-13 Osborn St, London E1 6TD **t** 020 7247 5862 **e** info@thelondonrecordingstudios.com **w** thelondonrecordingstudios.com Studio Manager: Jasmin Lee. [Budget Rate]

Loose Ingledene, 94, Holloway, Runcorn, Cheshire WA7 4TJ **t** 01928 566261 **e** william.leach1@virgin.net Studio Manager: Bill Leach. [Budget Rate]

Lost Boys Studio Hillgreen Farm, Bourne End, Cranfield, Beds MK43 0AX **t** 01234 750 730 **f** 01234 751 277 **e** lostboysstudio@onetel.com **w** lostboysstudio.com Studio Mgr: Rupert Cook. [Budget Rate]

MA Music Studios PO Box 106, Potton, Beds. SG19 2ZS **t** 01767 262040 **e** info@mamusicstudios.co.uk **w** mamusicstudios.co.uk Studio MGR: Noel Rafferty.

Manic One Studio PO Box 2251, London SE1 2FH **t** 020 7252 2661 **f** 0870 0512594 **e** manicone@movingshadow.com **w** movingshadow.com Studio Mgr: Gavin Johnson.

Mayfair Recording Studios 11A Sharpleshall St, London NW1 8YN **t** 020 7586 7746 **f** 020 7586 9721 **e** bookings@mayfair-studios.co.uk **w** mayfair-studios.co.uk Bkings/Studio Mgr: Daniel Mills.

▲ **Metropolis Studios** The Power House, 70 Chiswick High Rd, London W4 1SY **t** 020 8742 1111 **f** 020 8742 2626 **e** studios@metropolis-group.co.uk **w** metropolis-group.co.uk Business Dev't Studios: Alison Hussey.

Metway Studios 55 Canning St, Brighton, E Sussex BN2 2EF **t** 01273 698171 **f** 01273 624884 **e** lois@levellers.co.uk **w** metwaystudios.co.uk Studio Manager: Lois Teague.

Mews Productions The Hiltongrove Business Center, Hatherley Mews, London E17 4QP **t** 020 8520 3949 **e** nick@mewsproductions.com **w** mewsproductions.com Dir: Nick Michaels. [Budget Rate]

Mex One Recordings The Basement, 3 Eaton Pl, Brighton, E Sussex BN2 1EH **t** 01273 572090 **f** 01273 572090 **e** mexone@mexone.co.uk **w** mexonerecordings.co.uk MD: Paul Mex.

Mighty Atom Studios Dylan Thomas House, 32 Alexandra Rd, Swansea SA1 5DT **t** 01792 476567 **f** 01792 476564 **e** joe@mightyatom.co.uk **w** mightyatom.co.uk Producer/Engineer: Joe Gibb.

Mill Hill Recording Company Ltd Unit 7, Bunns Lane Works, Bunns Lane, Mill Hill, London NW7 2AJ **t** 020 8906 5038 **f** 020 8906 9991 **e** enquiries@millhillmusic.co.uk **w** millhillmusic.co.uk MD: Roger Tichborne.

MILOCO
36 Leroy St, London SE1 4SP **t** 020 7232 0008
f 020 7237 6109 **e** info@miloco.co.uk **w** miloco.co.uk Studio
Manager: Sophie Nathan. Operations Manager: Nick Young.
[Standard Rate] Studio 1: Neve VR, Munro M4, 1031A, S3A,
NS10 M, Protools HD3, Otari 2", Ampex 1/2". Studio 2: DDA
QMR, Genelec 1031A, Yamaha NS10M, Protools HD2 Accel.
Studio 3: Amek G2520, ATC SCM200, 1031A, Yamaha
NS10M, Protools HD3, Otari 2". Studio 4: Neve V3, Boxer
Series 5, 1031A, Yamaha NS10M, Protools HD3, Studer 2",
Otari 1/2". Studio 5: SSL G, Boxer T2, NS10M, Protools HD3.
Studio 6: Long term rental. Studio 7: Harrison Series 10, ATC
SCM300A, NS10M, Protools. Studio 8: 1800 sq ft all-in-one
live room/studio. Complete with a one-off collection of
vintage gear (and can also be used as an additional live room
with Studios 1 & 2).

MIX Records North Lodge, Auchineden, Blanefield, Glasgow
G63 9AX **t** 01360 771 069 or 07968 240 958
e andy@mixrecords.com **w** mixrecords.com
Studio Manager: Andy Malkin. [Budget Rate]

Mixing Rooms 222-226 West Regent St, Glasgow G2 4DQ
t 0141 221 7795 **f** 0141 847 0495
e chris_h@mixingrooms.co.uk **w** mixingrooms.co.uk
Assistant Studio Manager: Chris Hely. [Budget Rate Standard
Rate]

Moles Studio 14 George St, Bath BA1 2EN **t** 01225 404446
f 01225 404447 **e** paul@moles.co.uk **w** moles.co.uk
Studio Mgr: Paul Corkett.

Monkey Puzzle House: Residential Studio Monkey
Puzzle House, Heath Rd, Woolpit, Bury St Edmunds, Suffolk
IP30 9RJ **t** 01359 245050 **f** 01359 245060
e studio@monkeypuzzlehouse.com **w** monkeypuzzlehouse.com
Studio Owner: Rupert Matthews. [Standard Rate]

Monnow Valley Studio Old Mill House, Rockfield Rd,
Monmouth NP25 5QE **t** 01600 712761 or 07770 988503
f 01600 715039 **e** enquiries@monnowvalleystudio.com
w monnowvalleystudio.com Bookings Mgr: Jo Hunt.

Monroe Production Co 103-105 Holloway Rd, London
N7 8LT **t** 020 7700 1411 **e** monroehq@netscapeonline.co.uk
Studio Mgr: Halina Ciechanowska.

Mother Digital Studio 30 Redchurch St, Shoreditch,
London E2 7DP **t** 020 7739 8887
e studio@motherdigitalstudio.com **w** motherdigitalstudio.com
Owner: Justin Morey.

The Motor Museum Studios 1 Hesketh St, Liverpool,
Merseyside L17 8XJ **t** 0151 726 9808 **f** 0151 222 0190
e info@themotormuseum.co.uk **w** themotormuseum.co.uk
Studio Manager: Julia Jeory.

The Music Barn PO Box 92, Gloucester GL4 8HW
t 01452 814321 **f** 01452 812106
e vic_coppersmith@hotmail.com MD: Vic Coppersmith-Heaven.

The Music Factory Hawthorne House, Fitzwilliam St,
Parkgate, Rotherham, S Yorks S62 6EP **t** 01709 710022
f 01709 523141 **e** info@musicfactory.co.uk **w** mfeg.com
CEO: Andy Pickles.

▲ **MUSIC 4/MUSIC4 STUDIOS**

41-42 Berners Street, London W1T 3NB **t** 020 7016 2000
e studios@music4.com **w** music4.com MD: Sandy Beech. Studio
Manager: Sarah Davis. Senior Post-Production Engineer: Lee Kerr.
State-of-the-art facility with latest Pro-Tools HD
systems/Logic Pro/Final Cut Studio/superb client lounge
area. Audio/sound to picture; ISDN links for interviews/radio
edits/podcast creation.

MVD Studios Unit 4, Rampart Business Pk, Greenbank Ind,
Estate, Newry, Co Down BT34 2QU **t** 028 3026 2926
f 028 3026 2671 **e** mail@wren.ie **w** soundsirish.com
Studio Manager: Jim McGirr.

MWA Studios 20 Middle Row, Ladbroke Grove, London
W10 5AT **t** 020 8964 4555 **f** 020 8964 4666
e studios@musicwithattitude.com **w** musicwithattitude.com
Studio Engineer: Matt Foster.

MySoundRules Croydon Hse, 1 Peall Rd, Croydon, Surrey
CR0 3EX **t** 07985 733 177 or 07737 143 181
e mysoundrules@yahoo.co.uk **w** myspace.com/mysoundrules
Contact: Mike Sogga. [Budget Rate]

Natural Grooves Studio 3 Tannsfeld, London SE26 5DQ
t 020 8488 3677 **f** 020 8333 2572 **e** jon@naturalgrooves.co.uk
w naturalgrooves.co.uk Studio Manager: Jonathan Sharif.

The Next Room Studios 5B Oakleigh Mews, Whetstone,
London N20 9HQ **t** 020 8343 9971 **e** studio@thenextroom.com
w thenextroom.com Studio Mgr: Bob Wainwright.

Nimbus Performing Arts Centre Wyastone Leys,
Monmouth, Monmouthshire NP25 3SR **t** 01600 890 007
f 01600 891 052 **e** antony@wyastone.co.uk **w** wyastone.co.uk
Dir: Antony Smith.

Nucool Studios 34 Beaumont Rd, London W4 5AP
t 020 8248 2157 **e** r.niles@richardniles.com **w** richardniles.com
Dir: Richard Niles.

Odessa Wharf Studios 38 Upper Clapton Rd, London
E5 8BQ **t** 020 8806 5508 **f** 020 8806 5508
e odessa@mathias.idps.co.uk **w** surf.to/odessa
MD: Gwyn Mathias.

Old Smithy Recording Studio 1 Post Office Lane,
Kempsey, Worcs WR5 3NS **t** 01905 820659 **f** 01905 820015
e muffmurfin@btconnect.com Bookings Mgr: Janet Allsopp.

▲ **Olympic Studios** 117 Church Rd, Barnes, London
SW13 9HL **t** 020 8286 8600 **f** 020 8286 8625
e siobhan@olympicstudios.co.uk **w** olympicstudios.co.uk
Studio Mgr: Siobhan Paine.

Online Studios Unit 18-19 Croydon House, 1 Peall Rd,
Croydon, Surrey CR0 3EX **t** 020 8287 8585 **f** 020 8287 0220
e info@onlinestudios.co.uk **w** onlinestudios.co.uk
MD: Rob Pearson.

OTR Studios Ltd 143 Mare St, Hackney, London E8 3RH
t 020 8985 9880 or 07956 450 607
e info@otrstudios.wanadoo.co.uk **w** otrstudios.co.uk
Dir: Paul Lewis. [Budget Rate]

Out Of Eden 20-24 Beaumont Rd, Chiswick, London W4 5AP
t 020 8995 5432 **f** 020 8747 1931 **e** natalie@edenstudios.com
w andyrichards.com/outofeden Studio Mgr: Natalie Horton.

Overtones Recording Studio 14-15 Lambs Conduit
Passage, London WC1R 4RH **t** 020 7404 6006
f 020 7404 6060 **e** paul@overtones.co.uk **w** overtones.co.uk
Studio Manager: Paul Kennedy. [Budget Rate]

OxRecs Digital 37 Inkerman Close, Abingdon, Oxon
OX14 1NH **t** 01235 550589 **e** info@oxrecs.com **w** oxrecs.com
Dir: Bernard Martin.

Panther Recording Studios 5 Doods Rd, Reigate, Surrey
RH2 0NT **t** 01737 210848 **f** 01737 210848
e studios@dial.pipex.com **w** ds.dial.pipex.com/sema/panther.htm
Studio Manager: Richard Coppen.

Park Lane 974 Pollokshaws Rd, Glasgow, Strathclyde
G41 2HA **t** 0141 636 1218 **f** 0141 649 0042
e alan@parklanestudio.com **w** parklanestudio.com
Studio Mgr: Alan Connell.

Parkgate Studios Catsfield, Battle, E Sussex TN33 9DT
t 01424 774088 **f** 01424 774810
e parkgatestudio@hotmail.com **w** parkgatestudio.co.uk
Contact: Dan Priest.

Parkland Studios The Old Garage, 37a Grosvenor St, Hull
HU3 1RU **t** 01482 211 529 **e** suzanne@thedeebees.com
Studio Manager: Suzanne Pinder.

Parr Street Studios 33-45 Parr St, Liverpool L1 4JN
t 0151 707 1050 **f** 0151 709 4090
e info@parrstreetstudios.com **w** parrstreetstudios.com
Bookings: Pete or Peasy. [Standard Rate]

The Pierce Rooms Pierce House, London Apollo Complex,
Queen Caroline St, London W6 9QH **t** 020 8563 1234
f 020 8563 1337 **e** meredith@pierce-entertainment.com
w pierce-entertainment.com Studio Mgr: Meredith Leung.

Pisces Studios 20 Middle Row, Ladbroke Grove, London
W10 5AT **t** 020 8964 4555 **f** 020 8964 4666
e matt@musicwithattitude.com **w** musicwithattitude.com
Head Engineer: Matt Foster.

Planet Audio Studios 33 Bournehall Ave, Bushey, Herts
WD23 3AU **t** 08707 605 365 **f** 020 8950 1294
e mix@planetaudiostudios.com **w** planetaudiostudios.com
GM: Helen Gammons.

Pluto Studios Hulgrave Hall, Tiverton, Tarporley, Cheshire
CW6 9UQ **t** 01829 732427 **f** 01829 733802
e info@plutomusic.com **w** plutomusic.com
Studio Mgr: Keith Hopwood.

PM Muzik Studio 226 Seven Sisters Rd, London N4 3GG.
t 020 7372 6806 **f** 020 7372 0969 **e** info@pmmuzik.com
w pmmuzik.com Bookings: Mikey Campbell.

Point Blank 23-28 Penn St, Hoxton, London N1 5DL
t 020 7729 4884 **f** 020 7729 8789
e studio@pointblanklondon.com **w** pointblanklondon.com
CEO: Rob Cowan.

Pollen Studios 97 Main St, Bishop Wilton, York, N Yorks
YO42 1SQ **t** 01759 368223 **e** sales@pollenstudio.co.uk
w pollenstudio.co.uk Prop: Dick Sefton.

The Pop Factory Welsh Hills Works, Jenkin St, Porth
CF39 9PP **t** 01443 688500 **f** 01443 688501
e info@thepopfactory.com **w** thepopfactory.com
Contact: Emyr Afan Davies.

Power Recording Studios Unit 11, Impress House, Mansell
Rd, London W3 7QH **t** 020 8932 3033 **f** 0870 139 3608
e Keith@power.co.uk **w** power.co.uk Studio Mgr: Keith Neill.

The Premises Studios Ltd 201-205 Hackney Rd,
Shoreditch, London E2 8JL **t** 020 7729 7593 **f** 020 7739 5600
e info@premises.demon.co.uk **w** premises.demon.co.uk
CEO: Viv Broughton.

Presshouse PO Box 6, Colyton, Devon EX24 6YS
t 01297 553508 **f** 01297 553709 **e** presshouse@zetnet.co.uk
Studio Mgr: Mark Tucker.

Priderock Recording Studios Deppers Bridge Farm,
Southam, Warwicks CV47 2SZ **t** 01926 614640 or
07782 172 101 **e** studio@bighelpmusic.com **w** bighelpmusic.com
MD: Dutch Van Spall.

Priory Recording Studios 3 The Priory, London Rd,
Canwell, Sutton Coldfield, W Midlands B75 5SH
t 0121 323 3332 **f** 0121 308 8815
e greg@prioryrecordingstudios.co.uk
w prioryrecordingstudios.co.uk Studio Mgr: Greg Chandler.

The Propagation House Studios East Lodge, Ogbeare,
North Tamerton, Holsworthy, Devon EX22 6SE **t** 01409 271111
f 01409 271111 **e** office@propagationhouse.com
w propagationhouse.com Studio Mgr: Mark Ellis.

Pulse Recording Studios 67 Pleasants Pl, Dublin 8, Ireland
t +353 1 478 4045 **f** +353 1 475 8730 **e** pulse@clubi.ie
w pulserecording.com Studio Mgr: Tony Perrey.

Quince Recording Studio 62a Balcombe St, Marylebone,
London NW1 6NE **t** 020 7723 4196 or 07810 752 765
f 020 7723 1010 **e** info@quincestudios.co.uk
w quincestudios.co.uk Dir: Matt Walters.

Quo Vadis Recording Studio Unit 1 Morrison Yard, 551A High Rd, London N17 6SB **t** 020 8365 1999 **e** quovadis_2002@yahoo.co.uk **w** quovadisstudios.com Studio Mgr: Don MacKenzie.

Raezor Studio 25 Frogmore, London SW18 1JA **t** 020 8870 4036 **f** 020 8874 4133 Studio Mgr: Ian Wilkinson.

Rainmaker Music Music Bank, Building D, Tower Bridge Business Complex, 100 Clements Rd, London SE16 4DG **t** 020 7252 0001 or 07980 607 808 **f** 020 7231 3002 **e** rainmakermusic@aol.com **w** rainmakermusic.com MD: Chris Tsangarides.

▲ **RAK Recording Studios** 42-48 Charlbert St, London NW8 7BU **t** 020 7586 2012 **f** 020 7722 5823 **e** trisha@rakstudios.co.uk **w** rakstudios.co.uk Bookings Mgr: Trisha Wegg.

Raya Recording Studios Unit 6, The Saga Centre, 326 Kensal Rd, London W10 5BZ **t** 020 7240 8055 **f** 020 7379 3653 **e** RRS@plasticfantastic.co.uk **w** rayarecordingstudios.co.uk Studio Manager: Luis Paris.

The Real Stereo Recording Company 14 Moorend Crescent, Cheltenham, Gloucs GL53 OEL **t** 01242 523304 **f** 01242 523304 **e** martin@instantmusic.co.uk **w** instantmusic.co.uk Prod Mgr: Martin Mitchell.

▲ **Real World Studios** Box Mill, Mill Lane, Box, Corsham, Wilts SN13 8PL **t** 01225 743188 **f** 01225 743787 **e** owenl@realworld.co.uk **w** realworldstudios.com Studio Mgr: Owen Leech.

Red Bus Recording Studios 34 Salisbury St, London NW8 8QE **t** 020 7402 9111 **f** 020 7723 3064 **e** eliot@amimedia.co.uk **w** amimedia.co.uk MD: Eliot Cohen.

Red Fort The Sight And Sound Centre, Priory Way, Southall, Middlesex UB2 5EB **t** 020 8843 1546 **f** 020 8574 4243 **e** kuljit@compuserve.com **w** keda.co.uk MD: Kuljit Bhamra.

Red Kite Studio Cwmargenau, Llanwrda, Carms SA19 8AP **t** 01550 722 000 **f** 01550 722 022 **e** info@redkiterecords.co.uk **w** redkiterecords.co.uk Contact: Ron Dukelow.

Red Rhythm Productions 2 Longlane, Staines, Middlesex TW19 7AA **t** 01784 255629 **e** cliffrandall@telco4u.net Studio Mgr: Cliff Randall.

Redwood Studios 20 Great Chapel St, London W1F 8FW **t** 020 7287 3799 **e** andrestudios@yahoo.co.uk **w** sound-design.net MD/Producer: Andre Jacquemin.

Revolution Studios 11 Church Rd, Cheadle Hulme, Cheadle, Cheshire SK8 6LS **t** 0161 485 8942 or 0161 486 6903 **f** 0161 485 8942 **e** revolution@wahtup.com Prop: Andrew MacPherson.

Ride Studio 9 Coach Ride, Marlow, Bucks SL7 3BN **t** 07734 975 576 **e** info@ridestudio.co.uk **w** ridestudio.co.uk Studio Manager: Pete Hutchins. [Budget Rate]

Ridge Farm Studio Rusper Rd, Capel, Dorking, Surrey RH5 5HG **t** 01306 711202 **e** info@ridgefarmstudio.com **w** ridgefarmstudio.com Bookings & Admin. Mgr: Ann Needham.

Riff Raff Studios Penvale Cottage, Siliverwell, Truro, Cornwall TR4 8JE **t** 01872 561 331 **e** info@Riffraffmusic.co.uk **w** riffraffmusic.net Studio Manager: Baz Cox.

RMS Studios 43-45 Clifton Rd, London SE25 6PX **t** 020 8653 4965 **f** 020 8653 4965 **e** rmsstudios@blueyonder.co.uk **w** rms-studios.co.uk Bookings Mgr: Alan Jones.

RNT Studios Pinetree Farm, Cranborne, Dorset BH21 5RR **t** 01725 517204 **f** 01725 517801 **e** info@rntstudios.com **w** rntstudios.com Studio Manager: Rick Parkhouse.

▲ **Rockfield Studios** Amberley Court, Rockfield Rd, Monmouth, Monmouthshire NP25 5ST **t** 01600 712449 **f** 01600 714421 **e** rockfieldstudios@compuserve.com **w** rockfieldstudios.com Contact: Lisa Ward.

Rogue Studios RA 4 Bermondsey Trading Estate, Rotherhithe New Rd, London SE16 3LL **t** 020 7231 3257 **f** 020 7231 7358 **e** info@RogueStudios.co.uk **w** roguestudios.co.uk Contact: Jon Paul Harper/Jim Down.

Rollover Studios 29 Beethoven St, London W10 4LJ **t** 020 8969 0299 **f** 020 8968 1047 **e** bookings@rollover.co.uk Studio Mgr: Phillip Jacobs.

Room With A View 167, Ringwood Rd, St. Leonards, Ringwood, Hants BH24 2NP **t** 01425 473432 **f** 01425 473432 **e** info@rwav.co.uk **w** rwav.co.uk Studio Manager: Bonnie Smith.

Rooster 117 Sinclair Rd, London W14 0NP **t** 020 7602 2881 **e** roosteraud@aol.com **w** roosterstudios.com Prop: Nick Sykes.

Rotator Studios Ltd Interzone House, 74-77 Magdalen Rd, Oxford OX4 1RE **t** 01865 205600 **f** 01865 205700 **e** studios@rotator.co.uk **w** rotator.co.uk MD: Richard Cotton.

Roundhouse Recording Studios 91 Saffron Hill, Clerkenwell, London EC1N 8PT **t** 020 7404 3333 **f** 020 7404 2947 **e** roundhouse@stardiamond.com **w** stardiamond.com/roundhouse Studio Managers: Lisa Gunther & Maddy Clarke.

Sahara Sound Unit 18a/b, Farm Lane Trading Estate, 101 Farm Lane, London SW6 1QJ **t** 020 7386 2400 **f** 020 7386 2401 **e** info@saharasound.com **w** saharasound.com Contact: Cath Cloherty, Javier Weyler.

▲ **Sain** Canolfan Sain, Llandwrog, Caernarfon, Gwynedd LL54 5TG **t** 01286 831111 **f** 01286 831497 **e** studio@sain.wales.com **w** sain.wales.com Studio Mgr: Eryl Davies.

▲ **Sarm Hook End** Hook End Manor, Checkendon, Nr Reading, Berks RG8 0UE **t** 020 7229 1229 **f** 020 7221 9247 **e** roxanna@spz.com **w** sarmstudios.com Studio Mgr: Roxanna Ashton.

▲ **Sarm West** 8-10 Basing St, London W11 1ET **t** 020 7229 1229 **f** 020 7221 9247 **e** roxanna@spz.com **w** sarmstudios.com Studio Mgr: Roxanna Ashton.

Saturn Music Group Unit 1-133 Clarence Rd, London E5 8EE **t** 020 8533 1067 or 07904 773 908 **f** 020 8533 1067 **e** info@saturn-web.co.uk Contact: Chris Harraway.

▲ **Sawmills Studio** Golant, Fowey, Cornwall PL23 1LW **t** 01726 833338 or 01726 833752 **f** 01726 832015 **e** ruth@sawmills.co.uk **w** sawmills.co.uk Studio Mgr: Ruth Taylor. [Standard Rate]

School of Sound Recording 10 Tariff St, Manchester M1 2FF **t** 0161 228 1830 **f** 0161 236 0078 **e** ian.hu@s-s-r.com **w** s-s-r.com Principal: Ian Hu.

Sensible Music Studios 90-96 Brewery Rd, London N7 9NT **t** 020 7700 9900 **f** 020 7700 4802 **e** studio@sensible-music.co.uk **w** sensible-music.co.uk Studio Manager: Pat Tate.

Silk Sound Ltd 13 Berwick St, London W1F 0PW **t** 020 7434 3461 **f** 020 7494 1748 **e** bookings@silk.co.uk **w** silk.co.uk Studio Mgr: Paula Ryman.

Silk Studios 23 New Mount St, Manchester M4 4DE **t** 0161 953 4045 or 07887 564 485 **f** 0161 953 4001 **e** leestanley@silkstudios.co.uk Dir: Lee Stanley.

▲ **Soho Recording Studios** The Heals Building, 22-24 Torrington Pl, London WC2E 7AJ **t** 020 7419 2444 or 020 7419 2555 **f** 020 7419 2333 **e** dominic@sohostudios.co.uk **w** sohostudios.co.uk Bkngs/Studio Mgr: Dominic Sanders.

Soleil Studios Unit 10, Buspace Studios, Conlan St, London W10 5AP **t** 020 7460 2117 **f** 020 7460 3164 **e** soleil@trwuk.com Prop: Jose Gross.

Solitaire Recording Studio 3 The Collops, Kingscourt, Co. Cavan, Ireland **t** +353 42 966 8793 **f** +353 42 966 8793 **e** info@solitairestudio.com **w** solitairestudio.com MD: Alan Whelan.

Songwriting & Musical Productions Sovereign House, 12 Trewartha Rd, Praa Sands, Penzance, Cornwall TR20 9ST **t** 01736 762826 or 07721 449477 **f** 01736 763328 **e** panamus@aol.com **w** songwriters-guild.co.uk MD: Colin Eade.

Soul II Soul Studios 36-38 Rochester Pl, London NW1 9JX **t** 020 7284 0393 **f** 020 7284 2290 **e** sales@soul2soul.co.uk **w** soul2soul.co.uk Contact: Louise Howells/Ed Colman.

The Sound Suite 92 Camden Mews, London NW1 9AG **t** 020 7485 4881 **f** 020 7482 2210 **e** peterrackham@soundsuite.freeserve.co.uk Studio Mgr: Peter Rackham.

Southern Studios 10 Myddleton Rd, London N22 8NS **t** 020 8888 8036 **f** 020 8889 6166 **e** studio@southern.com **w** southern.com/studio Studio Manager/Engineer: Harvey Birrell.

Southside Studios Ltd 8 Southside, Clapham Common, London SW4 7AA **t** 020 7627 2086 or 07939 564 832 **e** pbarraclough@claranet.co.uk **w** southsidestudios.eu Director/Studio Manager: Peter Barraclough. [Budget Rate]

Space Eko Recording Studio Unit 42, 72 Farm Lane, London SW6 1QA **t** 020 7381 0059 **e** alex@thefutureshapeofsound.com **w** thefutureshapeofsound.com Contact: Alex McGowan. [Budget Rate]

Space Facilities 16 Dufours Pl, London W1F 7SP **t** 020 7494 1020 **f** 020 7494 2861 **e** bookings@space.co.uk **w** space.co.uk Facility Manager: Tom McConville.

Spatial Audio Theatre 8, Pinewood Studios, Iver, Bucks SL0 0NH **t** 01753 654 288 or 07802 657 258 **f** 020 8932 3465 **e** gerry@spatial-audio.co.uk **w** spatial-audio.co.uk Chief Engineer: Gerry O'Riordan.

▲ **Sphere Studios** 2 Shuttleworth Rd, London SW11 3EA **t** 020 7326 9450 **f** 020 7326 9499 **e** inform@spherestudios.com **w** spherestudios.com Studio Mgr: Nikki Affleck. [Premium Rate]

SPM Studios 9 Lichfield Way, South Croydon, Surrey CR2 8SD **t** 020 8657 8363 or 07970 646 166 **f** 020 8657 8380 **e** steve@spmstudios.co.uk **w** spmstudios.co.uk Prop: Steve Parkes.

SPRINT STUDIOS

Sprint Studios
Creative atmosphere
Great engineers
Luxurious & spacious layout
Only 2 hours from London

High Jarmany Farm, Jarmany Hill, Barton St David, Somerton, Somerset TA11 6DA **t** 01458 851 010 **f** 01458 851 029 **e** info@sprintmusic.co.uk **w** sprintmusic.co.uk Industry Consultant, Producer, Writer: John Ratcliff. Engineer, Producer, Programmer: Mark Chamberlain. Art & Design Consultant: Cecilia Welch. [Standard Rate]

St George's Bristol Great George St, (off Park Street), Bristol BS1 5RR **t** 0117 929 4929 **f** 0117 927 6537 **e** administration@stgeorgesbristol.co.uk **w** stgeorgesbristol.co.uk Dir: Suzanne Rolt.

Stanley House Stanley House, 39 Stanley Gardens, London W3 7SY **t** 020 8735 0280 **f** 020 8743 6365 **e** sh@stanley-house.co.uk Studio & Bookings Mgr: Jess Gentle.

Steelworks Studio Unit D, 3 Brown St, Sheffield S1 2BS **t** 0114 272 0300 **f** 0114 272 0303 **e** steelworksmu@aol.com **w** steelworks-studios.com Studio Mgr: Dan Panton.

Sticky Studios Great Oaks Granary, Kennel Lane, Windlesham, Surrey GU20 6AA **t** 01276 479255 **f** 01276 479255 **e** admin@stickycompany.com **w** stickycompany.com MDs: Jay Mein, Jake Gosling.

Street Level Studios 1st Floor, 17 Bowater Rd, Westminster Industrial Estate, Woolwich, London SE18 5TF **t** 07886 260 686 **e** ceo@streetlevelenterprises.co.uk **w** streetlevelenterprises.com MD: Sam Crawford. [Budget Rate]

▲ **Strongroom Ltd** 120-124 Curtain Rd, London EC2A 3SQ **t** 020 7426 5100 **f** 020 7426 5102 **e** mix@strongroom.com **w** strongroom.com General-Studio Manager and Bookings: Nina Mistry and Linda Dixon

Studio 17 17 David's Rd, London SE23 3EP **t** 020 8291 6253 **f** 020 8291 1097 **e** chris@dubvendor.co.uk Dir: Chris Lane.

Studio 24 60 Benedict Close, Romsey, Hants SO51 8PN **t** 01794 501774 **f** 01794 501774 **e** info@s24.uk.net **w** audio-production.co.uk Studio Manager: Alan Cotty.

Studio Sonic Enterprise Studios, 1-6 Denmark Pl, London WC2H 8NL **t** 020 7379 1155 or 020 7379 1166 **e** info@studio-sonic.co.uk **w** studio-sonic.co.uk Studio Manager: Andy Brook.

The Studio Tower St, Hartlepool TS24 7HQ **t** 01429 424440 **f** 01429 424441 **e** studiohartlepool@btconnect.com **w** studiohartlepool.com Studio Manager: Liz Carter.

Sun Studios - 1 & 2 8 Crow St, Dublin 2, Ireland **t** +353 1 677 7255 **f** +353 1 679 1968 **e** apollo@templelanestudios.com **w** templelanestudios.com Studio Mgr: John Hanley.

Sweet Georgia Browns Unit 12, 407 Hornsey Rd, London N19 4DX **t** 020 7263 1219 **f** 020 7263 3270 **e** info@sweetgeorgiabrowns.co.uk **w** sweetgeorgiabrowns.co.uk Studio Mgr: Dani.

Sync City Media Ltd 16-18 Millmead Business Centre, Millmead Rd, Tottenham Hale, London N17 9QU **t** 020 8808 0472 **e** sales@synccity.co.uk **w** synccity.co.uk Studio Manager: Ron Niblett.

Temple Lane Recording Studios 8 Crow St, Temple Bar, Dublin 2, Ireland **t** +353 1 677 7255 **f** +353 1 670 9042 **e** info@templelanestudios.com Studio Mgr: John Hanley.

Temple Music Studios 48 The Ridgway, Sutton, Surrey SM2 5JU **t** 020 8642 3210 or 07802 822 006 **f** 020 8642 8692 **e** jh@temple-music.com **w** temple-music.com Chief Bottlewasher: Jon Hiseman.

Temple Records Shillinghill, Temple, Midlothian EH23 4SH **t** 01875 830328 **f** 01875 825390 **e** info@templerecords.co.uk **w** templerecords.co.uk Studio Mgr: Robin Morton.

▲ **Ten21** Little Milgate, Otham Lane, Bearsted, Maidstone, Kent ME15 8SJ **t** 01622 735 200 **f** 01622 735 200 **e** info@ten21.biz **w** ten21.biz Owner: Sean Kenny.

Tin Pan Alley Studio 22 Denmark St, London WC2H 8NG **t** 020 7240 0816 **e** info@tinpanalleystudio.com **w** tinpanalleystudio.com Studio Mgr: Alexandra Fry.

Toerag Studios 166A Glyn Rd, London E5 0JE **t** 020 8985 8862 **e** toeragstudios1@hotmail.com MD: Liam Watson.

Touchwood Audio Productions 6 Hyde Park Terrace, Leeds, W Yorks LS6 1BJ **t** 0113 278 7180 **f** 0113 278 7180 **e** bruce.w@appleonline.net **w** touchwood/20m.com Studio Mgr: Bruce Wood.

▲ **Townhouse Studios** 150 Goldhawk Rd, London W12 8HH **t** 020 8932 3200 **f** 020 8932 3207 **e** info@townhousestudios.co.uk **w** townhousestudios.co.uk MD: Al Stone. [Premium Rate]

Tribal Tree Studios 66c Chalk Farm Rd, Camden, London NW1 8AN **t** 020 7482 6945 **e** info@triangle-records.co.uk **w** tribaltreestudios.co.uk Studio Manager: Chris Lock. [Budget Rate]

Tweeters Unit C1, Business Park 7, Brookway, Kingston Rd, Leatherhead, Surrey KT22 7NA **t** 01372 386592 **e** info@tweeters2studios.co.uk **w** tweeters2studios.co.uk Studio Eng: Nigel Wade.

Twin Peaks Studio Ty Neuadd, Torpantau, Brecon Beacons, Mid Glamorgan CF48 2UT **t** 01685 359932 **e** twinpeaksstudio@btconnect.com **w** TwinPeaksStudio.com Dir: Adele Nozedar.

Unit Q Studio Unit Q The Maltings, Station Rd, Sawbridgeworth, Herts CM21 9JX **t** 01279 600078 **e** unitq@orgyrecords.com **w** orgyrecords.com Ptnr: Darren Bazzoni.

Univibe Audio 20 Pool St, Walsall, Birmingham, W Midlands WS1 2EN **t** 01922 709 152 or 07734 151 589 **e** info@univibeaudio.co.uk **w** univibeaudio.co.uk Owners/Engineers: Joel Spencer, Phil Penn. [Budget Rate]

Vertical Rooms Road Farm, Ermine Way, Arrington, Herts SG8 3YY **t** 01223 207007 **f** 01223 207007 **e** info@verticalrooms.com **w** verticalrooms.com Studio Manager: Phil Culbertson.

Vital Spark Studios 1 Waterloo, Breakish, Isle Of Skye IV42 8QE **t** 01471 822 484 or 07768 031 060 **e** chris@vitalsparkmusic.demon.co.uk **w** hi-arts.co.uk/studios1.htm Mgr: Chris Harley.

Warehouse 60 Sandford Lane, Kennington, Oxford OX1 5RW **t** 01865 736411 **e** info@warehousestudios.com **w** warehousestudios.com Studio Mgr: Steve Watkins.

Waterfront Studios Riverside House, 260 Clyde St, Glasgow G1 4JH **t** 0141 248 9100 **f** 0141 248 5020 **e** waterfront@picardy.co.uk **w** picardy.co.uk.

WaterRat Music Studios Unit 2 Monument Way East, Woking, Surrey GU21 5LY **t** 01483 764444 **e** jayne@waterrat.co.uk **w** waterrat.co.uk Prop: Jayne Wallis.

West Orange Unit 1, 16B Pechell St, Ashton, Preston, Lancs PR2 2RN **t** 01772 722626 **f** 01772 722626 **e** westorange@btclick.com Studio Mgr: Alan Gregson.

West Street Studios 3 West St, Buckingham, Bucks MK18 1HL **t** 01280 822814 **f** 01280 822814 **e** jamie@weststreetstudios.co.uk **w** weststreetstudios.co.uk Studio Manager: Jamie Masters.

Westland Studios 5-6 Lombard Street East, Dublin 2, Ireland **t** +353 1 677 9762 **f** +353 1 671 0421 **e** westland@indigo.ie **w** westlandstudios.ie Studio Mgr: Deirdre Costello.

Westpoint Studio Unit GA, Westpoint, 39-40 Warple Way, London W3 0RG **t** 020 8740 1616 **f** 020 8740 4488 **e** respect@mailbox.co.uk **w** westpointstudio.co.uk Studio Manager: Ian Sherwin. [Standard Rate]

Westsound 95 Carshalton Park Rd, Carshalton Beeches, Surrey SM5 3SJ **t** 020 8647 3084 **f** 020 8395 3560 **e** tomjennings@cwcom.net Studio Mgr: Tom Jennings.

White's Farm Studios Whites Farm, Wilton Lane, Kenyon Culcheth WA3 4BA **t** 0161 790 4830 **f** 0161 703 8521 **e** whitesfarmstudio@aol.com **w** whitesfarmstudios.com Dir: Gary Hastings.

Windmill Lane Studios 20 Ringsend Rd, Dublin 4, Ireland **t** +353 1 668 5567 **f** +353 1 668 5352 **e** info@windmill.ie **w** windmill.ie Mktg: Sinead Slattery.

Wired Studios Ltd 26-28 Silver St, Reading, Berks RG1 2ST **t** 0118 986 0973 **e** office@wiredstudios.demon.co.uk **w** wiredstudios.demon.co.uk Mgr: Chris Britton.

Wise Buddah Creative 74 Great Titchfield St, London W1W 7QP **t** 020 7307 1600 **f** 020 7307 1601 **e** paul.plant@wisebuddah.com **w** wisebuddah.com GM: Paul Plant.

Wizard Sound Studios Prospect House, Lower Caldecote, Biggleswade, Beds SG18 9UH **t** 01767 601 398 **f** 0870 706 6257 **e** davysmyth@wizardsoundstudios.com **w** wizardsoundstudios.com Producer: Davy Smyth. [Budget Rate]

Wolf Studios 83 Brixton Water Lane, London SW2 1PH **t** 020 7733 8088 **f** 020 7326 4016 **e** brethes@mac.com **w** wolfstudios.co.uk Dir: Dominique Brethes.

Woodbine Street Recording Studio 1 St Mary's
Crescent, Leamington Spa, Warcs CV31 1JL **t** 01926 338 971
e jony2r@ntlworld.com **w** woodbinestreet.com
MD/Studio Mgr: John A Rivers.

Woodlands Recording Perseverance Works, Morrison St,
Castleford, W Yorks WF10 4BE **t** 01977 556868
f 01977 603180 **e** sales@jarberry-music.co.uk
w woodlandsrecording.co.uk Studio Mgr: Simon Humphrey.

Woodside Studio Woodside, Eason's Green, Framfield, Nr.
Uckfield, E Sussex TN22 5RE **t** 01825 841484 **f** 01825 880019
e woodsidestudios@btconnect.com **w** woodsidestudios.com
Studio Manager: Terri Myles.

Xplosive Studios 33/37 Hatherley Mews, Walthamstow,
London E17 4QP **t** 020 8521 9227 **f** 020 8520 5553
e postmaster@xplosiverecords.co.uk **w** xplosiverecords.co.uk
Dirs: Terry McLeod/Tapps Bandawe.

Zoo Studios 145 Wardour St, London W1F 8WB
t 020 7734 2000 **f** 020 7734 2200 **e** mail@zoostudios.co.uk
Bking Mgr: Danielle Jones.

Mobile Studios

Abbey Road Mobiles 3 Abbey Rd, London NW8 9AY
t 020 7266 7000 **f** 020 7266 7250
e bookings@abbeyroad.com **w** abbeyroad.com
Studio Mgr: Colette Barber.

As The Crow Flies The Retreat, Pidney, Hazlebury Bryan,
Dorset DT10 2EB **t** 01258 817214 or 07971 686961
f 01258 817207 **e** PeteFreshney@compuserve.com
w petefreshney.co.uk Contact: Pete Freshney.

The Audiomobile 30 Bentinck St, Kelvingrove, Glasgow,
Strathclyde G3 7TT **t** 0141 334 5099 **f** 0141 339 0271
e cavasound@mac.com **w** cavasound.com
Studio Mgr: Brian Young.

BBC Radio Outside Broadcasts (London) Brock
House, 19 Langham St, London W1A 1AA **t** 020 7765 4888
f 020 7765 5504 **e** will.garnett@bbc.co.uk
Operations Mgr: Will Garnett.

Black Mountain Mobile 1 Squire Court, The Marina,
Swansea SA1 3XB **t** 01792 301 500 **f** 01792 301 500
e info@blackmountainmobile.co.uk **w** blackmountainmobile.co.uk
MD: Michael Evans.

▲ **Circle Sound Services** Circle House, 14 Waveney Close,
Bicester, Oxon OX26 2GP **t** 01869 240051 **f** 0870 7059679
e sound@circlesound.net **w** circlesound.net Owner: John Willett.

▲ **Classic Sound** 5 Falcon Pk, Neasden Lane, London
NW10 1RZ **t** 020 8208 8100 **f** 020 8208 8111
e info@classicsound.net **w** classicsound.net Dir: Neil Hutchinson.

The Classical Recording Co.Ltd 16-17 Wolsey Mews,
Kentish Town, London NW5 2DX **t** 020 7482 2303
f 020 7482 2302 **e** info@classicalrecording.com
w classicalrecording.com Snr Producer: Simon Weir.

Doyen Recordings Ltd The Doyen Centre, Vulcan St,
Oldham, Lancs OL1 4EP **t** 0161 628 3799 **f** 0161 628 0177
e sales@doyen-recordings.co.uk **w** doyen-recordings.co.uk
MD: Nicholas J Childs.

Emglow Records

Norton Cottage, Colchester Road, Wivenhoe, Essex CO7 9HT
t 01206 826 342 or 07974 677 532 **e** emglorecs@aspects.net
Contact: Marcel Glover.

The Eureka Factor 12 Laxford House, Cundy St, London
SW1W 9JU **t** 020 7259 9903 **f** 020 7259 9903
e info@theeurekafactor.com **w** theeurekafactor.com
Recording Engineer: Mike Jeremiah.

Fleetwood Mobiles Denham Media Pk, North Orbital Rd,
Denham, Bucks UB9 5HQ **t** 08700 771071 **f** 08700 771068
e ian.d@fleetwoodmobiles.com **w** fleetwoodmobiles.com
MD: Ian Dyckhoff.

Floating Earth Ltd Unit 14, 21 Wadsworth Rd, Perivale,
Middx UB6 7JD **t** 020 8997 4000 **f** 020 8998 5767
e record@floatingearth.com **w** floatingearth.com Dir: Steve Long.

K&A Productions 5 Wyllyotts Pl, Potters Bar, Herts
EN6 2HN **t** 01707 661200 **f** 01707 661400
e info@kaproductions.co.uk **w** kaproductions.co.uk
MD: Andrew Walton.

Leapfrog Audiovisual 1 Currievale Farm Cottages, Currie,
Midlothian EH14 4AA **t** 0131 449 5808 or 07941 346813
e claudeharper@supanet.com Prop: Claude Harper.

MACH2 412 Beersbridge Rd, Belfast BT5 5EB
t 08707 300 030 or 07850 663 089 **f** 08707 300 040
e michael@machtwo.co.uk **w** machtwo.co.uk Dir: Michael Taylor.

Make Some Noise Recording & Mastering PO Box
792, Maidstone, Kent ME14 5LG **t** 01622 691 106
f 01622 691 106 **e** info@makesomenoiserecords.com
w makesomenoiserecords.com Mgr: Clive Austen.

Manor Mobiles Denham Media Pk, North Orbital Rd,
Denham, Bucks UB9 5HQ **t** 08700 771071 **f** 08700 771068
e ian.d@fleetwoodmobiles.com **w** fleetwoodmobiles.com
MD: Ian Dyckhoff.

Ninth Wave Audio 46 Elizabeth Rd, Moseley, Birmingham,
W Midlands B13 8QJ **t** 0121 442 2276 or 07770 364 464
f 0121 689 1902 **e** ninthwave@blueyonder.co.uk
Studio Mgr: Tony Wass.

Regent Records PO Box 528, Wolverhampton, W Midlands
WV3 9YW **t** 01902 424377 **f** 01902 717661
e regent.records@btinternet.com **w** regentrecords.com
Contact: Gary Cole.

Silk Recordings 65 High St, Kings Langley, Herts. WD4 9HU
t 01923 270 852 or 07812 602 535 **e** info@silkrecordings.com
w silkrecordings.com MD: Bob Whitney.

Sound Moves The Oaks, Cross Lane, Smallfield, Horley, Surrey
RH6 9SA **t** 01342 844 190 **f** 01342 844 290
e steve@sound-moves.com **w** sound-moves.com
Prop: Steve Williams.

Soundesign Mobiles 20 Heathfield Gardens, London
W4 4JY **t** 07973 303 679 **f** 020 8994 0603
e conrad@soundesign.co.uk **w** soundesign.co.uk
Dir: Conrad Fletcher.

Strongroom Mobile 120-124 Curtain Rd, London
EC2A 3SQ **t** 020 7426 5150 or 07980 552 425
f 020 7426 5102 **e** hire@stronghire.com **w** stronghire.com
Bookings: Phil Sisson, Alex Green.

Producers and Producer Management

2am Productions Contact The Lemon Group

2B3 Productions Suite B, 2 Tunstall Rd, London SW9 8DA
t 020 7733 5400 **f** 020 7733 4449
e paulette@westburymusic.net Producer: Neville Thomas.

2Point9 Management PO Box 44607, London N16 0YP
t 07801 033 741 **e** Office@2point9.com **w** 2point9.com
Dirs: Billy Grant, Rob Stuart.

3D Media Services Seton Lodge, 26 Sutton Ave, Seaford, E
Sussex BN25 4IJ **t** 01323 892 303
e talk2us@3dmediaservices.com **w** 3dmediaservices.com
MDs: Anthony Duke, Kim Duke.

3kHz 54 Pentney Rd, London SW12 0NY **t** 020 8772 0108
f 020 8675 1636 **e** threekhz@hotmail.com
Mgr: Jessica Norbury.

3rd Precinct 34 Wroxham Ave, Hemel Hempstead, Herts
HP3 9HF **t** 01442 265 415 **f** 01442 265 415
e charlotte@3rdprecinct.co.uk **w** 3rdprecinct.co.uk
CEO: Charlotte Roel.

4 Tunes Management PO Box 36534, London W4 3XE
t 020 8293 0999 **f** 020 8293 9525 **e** andy@4-tunes.com
w 4-tunes.com MD: Andy Murray.

19 Management 33 Ransomes Dock, 35-37 Parkgate Rd,
London SW11 4NP **t** 020 7801 1919 **f** 020 7801 1920
e reception@19.co.uk **w** 19.co.uk MD: Simon Fuller.

24 Management Westfield Cottage, Scragged Oak Rd,
Maidstone, Kent ME143HA **t** 01622 632 634 **f** 01622 632 634
e info@24twentyfour.com MD: Andy Rutherford.

140dB Management 133 Kilburn Lane, London W10 4AN
t 020 8354 2900 **f** 020 8354 2091 **e** firstname@140db.co.uk
w 140db.co.uk Managers: Ros Earls or Katrina Berry.

365 Artists Ltd 91 Peterborough Rd, London SW6 3BU
t 020 7384 6500 **f** 020 7384 6504 **e** info@365artists.com
w 365artists.com Dir: Adam Clough.

A Cool Dry Place Productions 24 Tennyson Rd, London
SW19 8SH **t** 07834 556 506 **f** 020 8715 9898
e info@acooldryplace.co.uk **w** acooldryplace.co.uk
Audio Engineer/Sound Designer: Chris Hill.

A Side Productions Contact XL Talent

Jim Abbiss Contact This Much Talent

Absolute Contact Native Management

Active Music Management (AMM) Suite 401, 29
Margaret St, London W1B 3HH **t** 0870 120 7668
f 0870 120 9880 **e** activemm@btopenworld.com
w activemm.co.uk MD: Mark Winters.

Adage Music 22 Gravesend Rd, London W12 0SZ
t 07973 295 113 **e** dobs@adagemusic.co.uk **w** adagemusic.com
MD: Dobs Vye.

Justin Adams Contact Spirit Music & Media

Adrian Newton Contact Chunk Management

Afreex Contact Stephen Budd Management

Afrikan Cowboy 33 Colomb St, London SE10 9HA
t 07957 391 418 or 020 8305 2448
e info@afrikancowboy.com **w** afrikancowboy.com Dir: Dean Hart.

AGM Studios 1927 Building, 2 Michael Rd, London
SW6 2AD **t** 020 7371 0234 **e** contacts@agmstudios.com
w agmstudios.com MD: Alex Golding.

ah! Contact 3rd Precinct

Matt Aitken Contact Menace Management

Alan Cowderoy Management 2 Devonport Mews,
London W12 8NG **t** 020 8743 9336 **f** 020 8743 9809
e alan@producermanagement.co.uk
w producermanagement.co.uk MD: Alan Cowderoy.

Alchemy Remix Management PO Box 53353, London
NW10 4UW **t** 020 8965 7600 **f** 020 8965 7600
e info@alchemy-remix.com **w** alchemy-remix.com
Owner: Howie Martinez.

Alex Golding Contact AGM Studios

The All Seeing I Contact Menace Management

Chris Allison c/o Sonic360, 33 Riding House St, London
W1W 7DZ **t** 020 7636 3939 **f** 020 7636 0033
e info@sonic360.com Contact: Chris Allison.

John Altman Contact SMA Talent

Ambush Management 32 Ransome's Dock, 35-37
Parkgate Rd, London SW11 4NP **t** 020 7801 1919
f 020 7738 1819 **e** alambush.native@19.co.uk
w ambushgroup.co.uk MD: Alister Jamieson.

Amco Music Productions 2 Gawsworth Rd, Macclesfield,
Cheshire SK11 8UE **t** 01625 420 163 **f** 01625 420 168
e info@cottagegroup.co.uk **w** cottagegroup.co.uk
MD: Roger Boden.

Andy Whitmore Productions 39 Greystoke Park Terrace,
London W5 1JL **t** 020 8998 5529 or 07850 735591
e andy@greystokeproductions.co.uk
w greystokeproductions.co.uk Prod: Andy Whitmore.

Archangel Management UK PO Box 1013, Woking
GU22 7ZD **t** 01483 729 447
e info@archangelmanagement.co.uk
w archangelmanagement.co.uk A&R: Bruce Elliott-Smith.

The Animal Farm Atomic Studios, Block B, Tower Bridge
Business Complex, 100 Clements Rd, London SE16 4DG
t 020 7237 8768 **e** ville@theanimalfarm.co.uk
w theanimalfarm.co.uk MD: Ville Leppanen.

Anu Pillai Contact Illicit Entertainment

Apollo 440 Contact XL Talent

Peter Arnold Contact Panama Productions

Artfield 5 Grosvenor Sq, London W1K 4AF **t** 020 7499 9941 **f** 020 7499 5519 **e** info@artfieldmusic.com **w** bbcooper.com MD: BB Cooper.

Artist, Music & Talent International PO Box 43, Manchester M8 0BB **t** 0161 795 7717 or 07905 001 687 **f** 0161 795 7717 **e** amti@btconnect.com MD: Peter Lewyckyj.

Jon Astley Contact Pachuco Management

Asylum Artists PO Box 121, Hove, E Sussex BN3 4YY **t** 01273 774 468 **f** 08709 223 099 **e** info@AsylumGroup.com **w** AsylumGroup.com Dirs: Bob James, Scott Chester.

Atlas Realisations Music Trendalls Cottage, Beacons Bottom, Bucks HP14 3XF **t** 01494 483 121 **f** 01494 484 303 **e** info@craigleon.com **w** craigleon.com Producer: Craig Leon.

Audio Authority Management 1, Sherwood Oaks, Frensham Rd, Kenley, Surrey CR8 5NS **t** 020 7101 2880 or 07980 607 808 **e** tim.hole@audioauthority.co.uk **w** audioauthority.co.uk Contact: Tim Hole.

Dan Austin Contact 140dB Management

David Ayers and Felix Tod Contact Giles Stanley

Baby Ash Contact This Much Talent

Bacon & Quarmby Contact Alan Cowderoy Management

Arthur Baker Contact Stephen Budd Management

James Banbury Contact Giles Stanley

Lucas Banker Contact XL Talent

Barny Contact This Much Talent

Dave Bascombe Contact Alan Cowderoy Management

Beat Factory Productions PO Box 189, Hastings TN34 2WE **t** 01424 435 693 **f** 01424 461 058 **e** jimsrbmusic@aol.com **w** myspace.com/jimbeadle Dir: Jim Beadle.

Joe Belmaati Contact XL Talent

Haydn Bendall Contact Duncan Management

Vito Benito Contact Nuff Productions

Richard Bennett Contact Muirhead Management

Gary Benson Contact Menace Management

Biffco representing Richard "Biff" Stannard **t** 01273 607 484 or +353 87 2780233 **e** Ejbiffco@mac.com **w** biffco.net Contact: Emma Jane Lennon.

Big George and Sons PO Box 7094, Kiln Farm MK11 1LL **t** 01908 566 453 **e** big.george@btinternet.com **w** biggeorge.co.uk Mgr: Big George Webley.

BIG LIFE PRODUCER MANAGEMENT

«biglife»

67-69 Chalton Street, London NW1 1HY **t** 020 7554 2100 **f** 020 7554 2154 **e** reception@biglifemanagement.com **w** biglifemanagement.com Producer Management: Jill Hollywood & Nikki Harris. MD: Jazz Summers. Tim Parry, Tony Beard & Tara Richardson.
BIG LIFE PRODUCER MANAGEMENT REPRESENTS : Jacknife Lee, Andy Gill, Youth, Nick Franglen, Jagz Kooner, Jon Gray, Hugo Nicolson, Freelance Hellraiser (as artist & producer).

Big Lion Productions 30 Holgate, Pitsea, Basildon, Essex SS13 1JD **t** 01268 728 274 or 0956 887 162 **f** 01268 728 274 **e** leo294@dircon.co.uk **w** biglionproductions.com Dir: Phillip Leo.

Big M Productions Thatched Rest, Queen Hoo Lane, Tewin, Herts AL6 0LT **t** 01438 798 395 **f** 01438 798 395 **e** joyce@bigmgroup.freeserve.co.uk **w** martywilde.com MD: Joyce Wilde.

Big M Productions Contact Marty Wilde Productions

Big Out Ltd 27 Smithwood Close, Wimbledon, London SW19 6JL **t** 020 8780 0085 or 07703 165146 **f** 020 8785 4004 **e** BigOutLtd@aol.com **w** mis-teeq.com MD: Louise Porter.

Peter Biker Contact 365 Artists Ltd

Henry Binns Contact Solar Management Ltd

BJ Contact Zomba Management

Black Man Jack Productions The Garage Workshop Ltd, 1st Floor Office Suit, 122 Montague St, Worthing, West Sussex BN11 3HG **t** 01903 606 513 or 07861 232 006 **e** Owen.thegarageworkshop@gmail.com **w** thegarageworkshop.com Producer: Owen A Smith.

Robin Black Contact Deluxxe Management

Blah Street Productions The Hop Kiln, Hillside, Odiham, Hants RG29 1HX **t** 01256 701112 **f** 01256 701106 **e** studio@blahstreet.co.uk **w** blahstreet.co.uk Contact: John Stimpson/Patch Hannan.

Blinkered Vision 4-10 Lamb Walk, London SE1 3TT **t** 020 7921 8353 **f** 020 7407 7081 **e** Info@blinkvis.co.uk **w** blinkvis.co.uk Creative Director: Fabian Enculez.

Blueprint Management PO Box 593, Woking, Surrey GU23 7YF **t** 01483 7153363 **f** 01483 7574904 **e** blueprint@lineone.net Contact: John Glover.

Bob Lamb 122A Highbury Rd, Kings Heath, Birmingham, W Midlands B14 7QP **t** 0121 443 2186 **e** boblamb@recklessltd.co.uk Studio Mgr/Prop: Bob Lamb.

Bob Noxious Contact Extreme Music Productions

Bobfalola Music Production 628 Old Kent Rd, London SE15 1JB **t** 07989 471263 **e** bobfalola@aol.com Dir: Bob Falola.

Roger Boden Contact Amco Music Productions

Phil Bodger Contact Pachuco Management

Bodyrockers Contact 24 Management

Boomin' System Contact Asylum Artists

Daniel Boone Contact Value Added Talent

David Bottril Contact Paul Brown Management Ltd

Julian Bown (see Alan Bown Mgmt).

Br1 Productions 30 Highland Rd, Bromley BR1 4AD
t 07802 723 124 or 020 8249 9683
e alan@br1productions.co.uk **w** br1productions.co.uk
Producer: Alan Little.

Andy Bradfield Contact 365 Artists Ltd

Derek Bramble Contact Freshwater Hughes Management

David Brant Contact XL Talent

Brenda Brooker Enterprises 9 Cork St, Mayfair, London
W1S 3LL **t** 020 7544 2893 **e** BrookerB@aol.com
MD: Brenda Brooker.

Brian Rawling Productions 78 Portland Rd, London
W11 4LQ **t** 01483 225226 **f** 01483 479606
e mail@metrophonic.com **w** metrophonic.com
MD: Brian Rawling.

Greg Brimson Contact Audio Authority Management

Pete Briquette Contact Pachuco Management

Michael Brook Contact Opium (Arts) Ltd

Ian Broudie Contact Alan Cowderoy Management

James Brown Contact Smoothside Organisation

Paul Brown Management Ltd Knightsbridge House, 229
Acton Lane, London W4 5DD **t** 020 8994 8887 or
07715 541 676 **e** paulb@pbmanagement.co.uk
w pbmanagement.co.uk MD: Paul Brown.

Phill Brown Contact CEC Producer Management

Wayne Brown Contact LJE

STEPHEN BUDD MANAGEMENT

The Zeppelin Building, 59-61 Farringdon Road, London
EC1M 3JB **t** 020 7916 3303 **f** 020 7916 3302
e info@record-producers.com **w** record-producers.com MD:
Stephen Budd. GM: Simon Dix & Jo Beckett.
Representing producers including: Rick Nowels, Tore
Johansson, Simon Gogerly, Stephen Hague, Arthur Baker,
Jon Kelly, Greg Haver, Steve Lironi, KK, Carsten Kroeyer,
Mark Wallis, Colin Emmanuel (C Swing), Ian Grimble, Steve
Lyon, Teo Miller, Martijn Ten Velden, Valgeir Sigurdsson,
Steve Hilton, Rik Simpson, Richard Robson, Jay Reynolds,
Afreex, James Lewis, Kenisha and Billy Steinberg.

Bukowski Productions PO Box 33849, London N8 9XJ
t 07092 047 780 **e** bukowskiproductions@btinternet.com
Contact: Michael Bukowski.

Lukas Burton Contact XL Talent

Steve Bush Contact Paul Brown Management Ltd

Adrian Bushby Contact This Much Talent

Bernard Butler Contact Rough Trade Producer Management

Ian John Button Contact The Day Job

Buzz-erk Music 17 Villers Rd, Kingston Upon Thames, Surrey
KT1 3AP **t** 020 8931 1044 **e** info@buzz-erk.com
w buzz-erk.com Dir: Niraj Chag.

CA Management Southpark Studios, 88 Peterborough Rd,
London SW6 3HH **t** 0207 384 9575
e adam@camanagement.co.uk **w** camanagement.co.uk
MD: Adam Sharp.

Cameron Craig Contact The Day Job

Colin Campsie Contact WG Stonebridge Producer
Management

Cargogold Productions 39 Clitterhouse Crescent,
Cricklewood, London NW2 1DB **t** 020 8458 1020
f 020 8458 1020 **e** mike@mikecarr.co.uk **w** mikecarr.co.uk
MD: Mike Carr.

Carl Stipetic Contact In A City Producer Management

Carpe Diem Contact Worldmaster Dj Management Ltd

Nick Carpenter PO Box 22626, London N15 3WW
t 020 8211 0272 **f** 020 8211 0272.

Cavemen Contact Rough Trade Producer Management

CEC Producer Management 65-69 White Lion St,
London N1 9PP **t** 020 7837 2517 **f** 020 7278 5915
e jess@cecmanagement.com
Managers: Jess Gerry or Claire Southwick.

Guy Chambers Contact Sleeper Music

Change of Weather Productions 29 Gladwell Rd,
London N8 9AA **t** 020 8245 2136 or 07974 070 880
e pcarmichael@changeofweather.com **w** changeofweather.com
MD: Paul Carmichael.

Chunk Management 97a Scrubs Lane, London NW10 6QU
t 020 8960 1331 **f** 020 8968 3377
e info@chunkmanagement.com **w** chunkmanagement.com
MD: Mike Nelson.

Simon Climie Contact Signia Productions

Claudio Coccoluto Contact Prodmix International

Coda Recordings 141, Wren Wood, Welwyn Garden City,
Herts AL7 1QF **t** 01707 331771 **e** coda@coda-uk.co.uk
w coda-uk.co.uk MD: Colin Frechter.

BJ Cole Contact Firebrand Management

Jon Collyer Contact Strongroom Management

Con Fitzpatrick Productions Unit 3, Gravity Shack, Rear
of 328 Balham High Rd, London SW17 7AA **t** 020 8672 4772
e con.fitzpatrick@virgin.net Contact: Con Fitzpatrick.

Steve Constantine Contact SCO Productions

Cordella Music Alhambra, High St, Shirrell Heath,
Southampton, Hants SO32 2JH **t** 08450 616 616
f 01329 833 433 **e** barry@cordellamusic.co.uk
w cordellamusic.co.uk MD: Barry Upton.

John Cornfield Contact Dangerous Management

Rich Costey Contact 140dB Management

Courtyard Productions Ltd 22 The Nursery, Sutton Courtenay, Oxon OX14 4UA **t** 01235 845800 **f** 0870 0510183 **e** kate@cyard.com Dir: Chris Hufford & Bryce Edge.

Craig Leon Contact Atlas Realisations Music

Pete Craigie (see Z Mgmt).

Craigie Dodds Contact Native Management

Creation Management 2 Berkley Grove, Primrose Hill, London NW1 8XY **t** 020 7483 2541 **f** 020 7722 8412 **e** info@creationmngt.com Office Manager: Peter Jackson.

Creative Productions (UK) Ltd 1 Roundtown, Aynho, Oxon OX17 3BG **t** 01869 810956 **e** guy@creativeproductionsuk.com Contact: Guy Stanway, Gary Stevenson.

Stuart Crichton Contact Z Management

Crisis Media The Old Granary, Ammerham, Somerset TA20 4LB **t** 01460 30846 **e** ronnie@crisismedia.co.uk Dirs: Ronnie Gleeson, Meredith Cork.

Crocodile Music 431 Linen Hall, 162-168 Regent St, London W1B 5TE **t** 020 7580 0080 **f** 020 7637 0097 **e** music@crocodilemusic.com **w** crocodilemusic.com Contact: Malcolm Ironton, Ray Tattle.

Mike Crossey Contact Alan Cowderoy Management

Ross Cullum Contact FKM

Ian Curnow Contact Z Management

Cutfather Contact XL Talent

The Cutting Room Abraham Moss Centre, Crescent Centre, Manchester M8 5UF **t** 0161 740 9438 **f** 0161 740 0583.

Da3rd Contact 3rd Precinct

Dan Grech-Marguerat Contact Solar Management Ltd

Graham D'Ancey Contact Panama Productions

D&S Contact 365 Artists Ltd

Dangerous Management South Down, Sandwell Manor, Totnes, Devon TQ9 7LN **t** 01803 867 850 or 07738 543 746 **e** info@dangerousmanagement.com **w** dangerousmanagement.com Contact: Mike Audley or Liam Smith.

Danny D Contact 19 Management

Darah Music 21C Heathmans Rd, Parsons Green, London SW6 4TJ **t** 020 7731 9313 **f** 020 7731 9314 **e** mail@darah.co.uk MD: David Howells.

David Jaymes Associates Ltd PO Box 30884, London W12 9AZ **t** 020 8746 7461 **f** 020 8749 7441 **e** info@spiritmm.com **w** spiritmm.com Dirs: David Jaymes, Tom Haxell.

Pete Davis Contact Native Management

Charlotte Day Contact Amco Music Productions

The Day Job 14 Laurel Ave, Twickenham, Middx TW1 4JA **t** 020 8607 9282 **e** nina@thedayjob.com **w** thedayjob.com Contact: Nina Jackson.

dB Entertainments PO Box 147, Peterborough, Cambs. PE1 4XU **t** 01733 311755 **f** 01733 709449 **e** info@dbentertainments.com **w** dbentertainments.com Director/Producer: Russell Dawson-Butterworth.

Edward de Bono Contact Wingfoot Productions

John de Bono Contact Wingfoot Productions

Ted de Bono 41A Cavendish Rd, London NW6 7XR **t** 020 8459 2833 or 07958 521 099 **e** edwarddebono@f2s.com Contact: Ted de Bono.

Marius De Vries Contact Native Management

DeeKay Contact Asylum Artists

DeepFrost Contact Asylum Artists

Delta Rhythm Contact The Day Job

Deluxxe Management PO Box 373, Teddington, Middx TW11 8ZQ **t** 020 8755 3630 or 07771 861 054 **f** 020 8404 7771 **e** info@deluxxe.co.uk **w** deluxxe.co.uk MD: Diane Wagg.

Gez Dewar Contact XL Talent

Dionne Contact Shalit Global Entertainment & Management

Disclab Contact Zomba Management

Ben Dobie Contact Strongroom Management

Dobs Vye Contact Adage Music

Sean Doherty see Roundhouse Mgmnt.

Graham Dominy Contact Innocent Management

Tim Dorney Contact Spirit Music & Media

Double Jointed Productions (address witheld by request) **t** 020 7836 7553 **e** djp@musicard.co.uk Production Mgr: David Newell.

Johnny Douglas Contact Twenty Four Seven Music Management

Dreamscape Music 36 Eastcastle St, London W1W 8DP **t** 020 7631 1799 or 07767 771 157 **f** 020 7631 1720 **e** lester@lesterbarnes.com **w** lesterbarnes.com Composer: Lester Barnes.

Dave Dresden Contact Ornadel Management

Richard Drummie Contact Blueprint Mgmt

Dub Organiser Contact Fashion Productions

Duncan Management 29 Lansdowne Crescent, London W11 2NS **t** 020 7165 1810 or 07990 550 001 **e** rebecca@duncanmanagement.com **w** duncanmanagement.com MD: Rebecca Duncan.

Matt Dunkley Contact SMA Talent

Duran Duran Productions 55 Loudoun Rd, London NW8 0DL **t** 020 7625 3555 **e** evon@ddproductions.easynet.co.uk **w** duranduran.com Programmer/Engineer: Mark Tinley.

Floyd Dyce Onward House, 11 Uxbridge St, London W8 7TQ
t 020 7221 4275 **f** 020 7229 6893
e info@bucksmusicgroup.co.uk **w** bucksmusicgroup.co.uk
Publisher: Simon Platz.

Colin Eade Contact Panama Productions

Eclectic Method Contact The Day Job

Steve Edwards Contact Menace Management

Finn Eiles Contact Miloco Management

Bruno Ellingham Contact Illicit Entertainment

Colin Elliot Contact 365 Artists Ltd

Jorgen Elofsson Contact XL Talent

Colin Emmanuel (C Swing) Contact Stephen Budd
Management

David Eriksen Contact Freedom Management

Dave Eringa Contact Solar Management Ltd

Richard Evans Contact Polar Arts Ltd

Extreme Music Productions 4-7 Forewoods Common,
Holt, Wilts BA14 6PJ **t** 01225 782984 **f** 01255 782281
e george@xtrememusic.co.uk **w** xtrememusic.co.uk
MD: George D Allen.

Jean-Louis Fargier Contact Loriana Music

Fashion Productions 17 Davids Rd, London SE23 3EP
t 020 8291 6253 **f** 020 8291 1097
e chrislane@dubvendor.co.uk **w** dubvendor.co.uk
Studio Manager: Chris Lane.

Fathead Contact Multiplay Music Management

The Fern Organisation Fern Studios, 5 Low Rd,
Conisbrough, Doncaster, S Yorks DN12 3AB **t** 01709 868511
f 01709 867274 Contact: Howard Johnson.

Pedro Ferreira Contact Strongroom Management

Fexx 159A High Rd, Chadwell Heath, Romford, Essex RM6 6NL
t 07931 752641 **e** adamfexx@yahoo.co.uk **w** fexx.co.uk
Prod/Engineer: Adam Taylor.

RS "Bobby" Field Contact Muirhead Management

Magnus Fiennes The Lansdowne Suite, Lansdowne House,
Lansdowne Rd, London W11 3LP **t** 020 7727 4214 or
07880 865 754 **e** magnus@beatguru.com
Contact: Magnus Fiennes.

Daniel Figgis Contact The Day Job

Benedict Findlay Contact Polar Arts Ltd

Fingaz Contact Shalit Global Entertainment & Management

Firebrand Management 12 Rickett St, London SW6 1RU
t 020 7381 2375 or 07885 282 165 **e** vernfire@aol.com
MD: Mark Vernon.

Greg Fitzgerald Contact Freedom Management

Stephen Fitzmaurice Contact Native Management

Guy Fixsen Contact Deluxxe Management

FKM PO Box 242, Haslemere, Surrey GU26 6ZT
t 01428 608 149 **e** fken10353@aol.com
Chairman: Fraser Kennedy.

Andrew Flintham Productions Titlow Rd, Harleston,
Norfolk IP20 9DH **t** 01379 853982
e andrew.flintham@talk21.com
Freelance Producer: Andrew Flintham.

Flood Contact 140dB Management

Sergio Flores Contact Active Music Management (AMM)

John Fortis Contact XL Talent

Matt Foster Contact Miloco Management

FourFives Productions 21d Heathman's Rd, London
SW6 4TJ **t** 020 7731 6555 **f** 020 7371 5005
e mp@fourfives-music.com **w** fourfives-music.com
Dir: Andrew Greasley.

Charlie Francis Contact Paul Brown Management Ltd

Freak'n See Music Ltd Suite C, 19 Heathmans Rd, London
SW6 4TJ **t** 020 7384 2429 **f** 020 7384 2429
e firstname@freaknsee.com **w** freaknsee.com
MD: Jimmy Mikaoui.

Freedom Management 4 Canalot Studios, 222 Kensal Rd,
London W10 5BN **t** 020 8960 4443 **f** 020 8960 9889
e martyn@frdm.co.uk **w** frdm.co.uk MD: Martyn Barter.

Freeform Five Contact Illicit Entertainment

Mark Freegard Flat 2/1, 91 Oban Drive, Glasgow G20 6AB
t 0141 533 1837 or 07977 101 081 **e** info@markfreegard.com
w markfreegard.com Contact: Mark Freegard.

Freelance Hellraiser Contact Big Life Producer
Management

Freshwater Hughes Management PO Box 54,
Northaw, Herts EN6 4PY **t** 01707 661 431 or 020 8360 0505
f 01707 664 141 **e** info@freshwaterhughes.com
w freshwaterhughes.com
Contact: Jackie Hughes, Brian Freshwater.

Aron Friedman Contact Kudos Management

Mark Frith Contact Positive Management

Fume Productions 30 Kilburn Lane, Kensal Green, London
W10 4AH **t** 020 8969 2909 **f** 020 8969 3825
e info@fume.co.uk **w** fume.co.uk MD: Seamus Morley.

Fundamental Music 64 Manor Rd, Wheathampstead, Herts
AL4 8JD **t** 01582 622 757 **f** 01582 621 718
e chickers@ntlworld.com Mgr: Karen Ciccone.

Pascal Gabriel Contact This Much Talent

Toby Gafftey-Smith Contact Muirhead Management

Pete Gage Production 47 Prout Grove, London NW10 1PU
t 020 8450 5789 **f** 020 8450 0150 MD: Pete Gage.

Gailforce Management 55 Fulham High St, London
SW6 3JJ **t** 020 7384 8989 **f** 020 7384 8988
e gail@gailforcemanagement.co.uk MD: Gail Colson.

Galaxy P Contact Jamdown Ltd

Julian Gallagher Contact Native Management

Sergio Galoyan Contact Paul Brown Management Ltd

Rod Gammons c/o G2 Music, 33 Bournehall Ave, Bushey, Herts WD23 3AU **t** 020 8950 1485 **f** 020 8950 1294 **e** rod@planetaudiogroup.com **w** g2-music.com Contact: Rod Gammons.

Gaudi Contact The Lemon Group

Sean Genockey Contact Solar Management Ltd

Karen Gibbs Contact Active Music Management (AMM)

Brad Gilderman Contact Pachuco Management

Andy Gill Contact Big Life Producer Management

Kristian Gilroy Harewood Farm Studios, Little Harewood Farm, Clamgoose Lane, Kingsley, Staffs ST10 2EG **t** 07973 157 920 **f** 01538 755 735 **e** kristian@harewoodfarmstudios.com **w** harewoodfarmstudios.com Producer: Kristian Gilroy.

Junior Giscombe Contact P3M Music Management & Consultancy

Mick Glossop Contact Giles Stanley

Go Crazy Music The Studio, Penybryn, Tydcombe Rd, Warlingham, Surrey CR6 9LU **t** 01883 626859 **e** gocrazymusic@aol.com GM: Sara Watts.

Goetz B Contact 365 Artists Ltd

Simon Gogerly Contact Stephen Budd Management

Goldie Contact X-Rated Management

Goldman Associates 16 Red Hill Lane, Great Shelford, Cambridge CB2 5JR **t** 01223 840416 **f** 01223 840436 **e** dox@goldman.co.uk **w** goldman.co.uk Contact: Martin Goldman.

Nigel Godrich Contact Solar Management Ltd

Tim Gordine Contact This Much Talent

Paul Grabowsky Contact Muirhead Management

Graeme Stewart Contact Solar Management Ltd

Noel Grant Contact Little Piece of Jamaica (LPOJ)

Howard Gray Contact XL Talent

Jon Gray Contact Big Life Producer Management

Andy Green Contact Giles Stanley

Drew Griffiths Contact Duncan Management

Ian Grimble Contact Stephen Budd Management

Raj Gupta Contact Solar Management Ltd

Robin Guthrie Contact The Day Job

Guy Massey Contact 140dB Management

DJ H (Queasyrider) Contact The Day Job

Steve Hackett Contact Kudos Management

Ryan Hadlock Contact CEC Producer Management

Stephen Hague Contact Stephen Budd Management

Hannah Management 102 Dean St, London W1D 3TQ **t** 020 7758 1494 **e** hgadsdon@barberamusic.co.uk Contact: Hugh Gadsdon, Mel Stephenson.

Happybeat 101 Greenway Rd, Higher Tranmere, Merseyside CH42 ONE **t** 0151 653 3463 **e** happybeatstudios@yahoo.co.uk **w** happybeat.net Contact: Fran Ashcroft.

Phil Harding Contact P.J. Music

Martin Harrington Contact Native Management

Simon Harris Unit 9b, Wingbury Business Village, Upper Wingbury Farm, Wingrave, Bucks HP11 4LW **t** 07770 364 268 **e** chris@musicoflife.com **w** musicoflife.com Contact: Chris France.

Iain Harvie Contact JPR Management

Mads Hauge Contact WG Stonebridge Producer Management

Greg Haver Contact Stephen Budd Management

Head Contact Paul Brown Management Ltd

Hearsay Contact Multiplay Music Management

Heat Music The Courtyard, Unit A, 42 Colwith Rd, Hammersmith, London W6 9EY **t** 020 8846 3737 **f** 020 8846 3738 **e** david@reddmanagement.com MD: David Moores.

Heatwave Productions Contact Mental Music Management

Mike Hedges Contact 3kHz

Elizabeth Henshaw Contact Muirhead Management

Sally Herbert Contact Solar Management Ltd

Max Heyes Contact Z Management

Paul Hicks Contact 3kHz

Ben Hillier Contact 140dB Management

Paul Hillyer Contact Asylum Artists

Steve Hilton Contact Stephen Budd Management

Hip-Hop Cow Management Ltd 27 Church Drive, North Harrow, Middx HA2 7NR **t** 020 8866 2454 **e** hiphopcow@aol.com **w** hiphopcow.com MD: Andrew East.

Joe Hirst Contact Miloco Management

Pete Hofmann Contact Miloco Management

Jimmy Hogarth Contact Native Management

Tim Holmes Contact Strongroom Management

Holyrood Recording & Film Productions 86 Causewayside, Edinburgh EH9 1PY **t** 0131 668 3366 **f** 0131 662 4463 **e** neil@holyroodproductions.com MD: Neil Ross.

Dean Honer Contact Menace Management

Trevor Horn Contact Sarm Management

Hot Source Productions Island Cottage, Rod Eyot, Wargrave Rd, Henley-on-Thames, Oxon RG9 3JD **t** 01491 412 946 **e** Jay-F@hotsourceproductions.com Contact: Jay-F.

Howard Hughes 8 Mentmore Terrace, London E8 3PN **t** 020 8525 4179 or 07714 202 435 **e** exbetts@aol.com **w** howardhughes.co.uk Contact: Producer.

Howarth & Johnston **t** 0131 555 2288 or 07976 209105 **e** h+j@daveandmax.co.uk **w** daveandmax.co.uk Contact: Max Howarth, David Johnston.

Liam Howe Contact This Much Talent

Ash Howes Contact Native Management

Howie B Contact Native Management

Hoxton Whores Contact 24 Management

Mark Hudson Contact Little Piece of Jamaica (LPOJ)

Paul Hue Contact Little Piece of Jamaica (LPOJ)

Chris Hughes Contact Positive Management

Miles Hunt Contact Spirit Music & Media

Matt Hyde Contact Miloco Management

I Monster Contact Menace Management

Illicit Entertainment PO Box 51871, London NW2 9BR **t** 020 8830 7831 **f** 020 8830 7859 **e** ian@illicit.tv **w** mumbojumbo.co.uk MD: Ian Clifford.

In A City Producer Management Unit 49, Carlisle Business Centre, 60 Carlisle Rd, Bradford BD8 8BD **t** 01274 223 251 or 01377 236 395 **f** 01377 236 397 **e** music@projectmanager.co.uk **w** inacity.co.uk MD: Carl Stipetic.

Innocent Management 45 Sylvan Ave, London N22 5JA **t** 07896 428 861 **e** info@innocentmanangement.com **w** innocentmanangement.com Contact: Lise Regan.

The Insects Contact Paul Brown Management Ltd

Jacknife Lee Contact Big Life Producer Management

Jon Jacobs Contact Giles Stanley

Andre Jacquemin Contact Redwood Studios

Mark Jaimes and Danny Saxon Contact Smoothside Organisation

Jamdown Ltd Stanley House Studios, 39 Stanley Gardens, London W3 7SY **t** 020 8735 0280 **f** 020 8930 1073 **e** othman@jamdown-music.com **w** jamdown-music.com MD: Othman Mukhlis.

JamDVD London **t** 07976 820 774 **f** 07092 003 937 **e** jamdvd@macunlimited.net **w** jamdvd.com Producer: Julie Gardner.

Stewart & Bradley James 223b Victoria Park Rd, London E9 7HD **t** 020 8985 1115 **f** 020 8985 1113 **e** brad.james@virgin.net Contact: Bradley James.

Eliot James Contact Audio Authority Management

Jeff Jarratt Hotrock Music, Forestdene, Barnet, Herts EN5 4PP **t** 020 8449 0830 **f** 020 8447 1210 **e** jeff@abbeyroadcafe.com MD: Jeff Jarratt.

JAY Productions 107 Kentish Town Rd, London NW1 8PD **t** 020 7485 9593 **f** 020 7485 2282 **e** john@jayrecords.com **w** jayrecords.com Producer: John Yap.

Jazzwad Contact Jamdown Ltd

Martin Jenkins Contact Miloco Management

Jewels & Stone Contact Freedom Management

Jimmy Thomas PO Box 38805, London W12 7XL **t** 020 8740 8898 **e** jimmythomas@osceolarecords.com **w** osceolarecords.com Record Producer.

Joe Brown Productions Ltd PO Box 272, London N20 0BY **t** 020 8368 0340 **f** 020 8361 3370 **e** john@jt-management.demon.co.uk MD: John Taylor.

Thomas Johansen Contact Chunk Management

Tore Johansson Contact Stephen Budd Management

Gary Johnson Contact Asylum Artists

Cliff Jones Contact Audio Authority Management

David Jones Contact Panama Productions

Hugh Jones Contact Alan Cowderoy Management

John Paul Jones Contact Opium (Arts) Ltd

Roderick Jones Contact Panama Productions

Jonesey Ltd 50 Pentstemon Drive, Neptune Pk, Swanscombe, Kent DA10 0NJ **t** 07866 523 691 **e** jonesey@jonesey.com **w** jonesey.com Contact: Jonesey.

JPR Management PO Box 3062, Brighton, E Sussex BN50 9EA **t** 01273 779 944 **f** 01273 779 967 **e** info@jprmanagement.co.uk **w** jprmanagement.co.uk MD: John Reid.

The Jump Off PO Box 697, Wembley HA9 8WQ **t** 020 7253 7766 **f** 020 7681 1007 **e** harry@hiphop.com **w** jumpoff.tv CEO: Harold Anthony.

June Productions Ltd Toftrees, Church Rd, Woldingham, Surrey CR3 7JX **t** 01883 652386 **f** 01883 652457 **e** david@mackay99.plus.com Producer: David Mackay.

Junior Dubbs Contact Fashion Productions

Junk Scientist Contact Giles Stanley

K-Gee Contact Redd Management

K-Klass The Bunker Recording Studio, Borras Rd, Borras, Wrexham LL13 9TW **t** 01978 263295 **f** 01978 263295 **e** kklass@btconnect.com **w** k-klass.com Contact: Andrew Willimas/Carl Thomas.

Karon Productions 20 Radstone Court, Hillview Rd, Woking, Surrey GU22 7NB **t** 01483 755 153 **e** ron.roker@ntlworld.com MD: Ron Roker.

Phil Kay (Dekko) Contact CEC Producer Management

Jon Kelly Contact Stephen Budd Management

Kevin Kendle Contact Panama Productions

Kenisha Contact Stephen Budd Management

Eliot Kennedy Contact Freedom Management

Kick Production The Carriage House, 26B Dunstable Rd, Richmond upon Thames, Surrey TW9 1UH **t** 020 8332 7525 **f** 020 8332 7527 **e** firstname@kickproduction.co.uk **w** kickproduction.com Contact: Terry J Neale.

Kidz Contact 365 Artists Ltd

Chris Kimsey Contact Giles Stanley

King Unique Contact 24 Management

Rob Kirwan Contact 140dB Management

KK Contact Stephen Budd Management

Kookie Contact XL Talent

Jagz Kooner Contact Big Life Producer Management

Bob Kraushaar 24 Arlington Gardens, London W4 4EY **t** 020 8995 0676 **f** 020 8987 9656 **e** mail@bobkraushaar.com **w** bobkraushaar.com.

Carsten Kroeyer Contact Stephen Budd Management

Kudos Management Crown Studios, 16-18 Crown Rd, Twickenham, Middx TW1 3EE **t** 020 8891 4233 **f** 020 8891 2339 **e** kudos@camino.co.uk MD: Billy Budis.

Stan Kybert Contact CEC Producer Management

Kynance Cove Ltd 58-60 Berners St, London W1P 4JS **t** 020 7747 4296 **f** 020 7747 4470 **e** max.hole@umusic.com Contact: Rhona Levene.

Mutt Lange Contact Zomba Management

Clive Langer Contact Hannah Management

Laurie Latham Contact SJP/Dodgy Productions

Simon Law & Lee Hamblin Contact Z Management

Peter Lawlor c/o Water Music Productions, 1st Floor, Block 2, 6 Erskine Rd, London NW3 3AJ **t** 020 7722 3478 **f** 020 7722 6605 Contact: Tessa Sturridge.

Matt Lawrence Contact Audio Authority Management

Mike Lawson Contact Value Added Talent

Graham Le Fevre 59 Park View Rd, London NW10 1AJ **t** 020 8450 5154 **f** 020 8452 0187 **e** rubiconrecords@btopenworld.com **w** rubiconrecords.co.uk Founder: Graham Le Fevre.

Leafman Reverb House, Bennett St, London W4 2AH **t** 020 8747 0660 **f** 020 8747 0880 **e** liam@leafsongs.com MD: Liam Teeling.

John Leckie Contact SJP/Dodgy Productions

Lee Management 9A Nettleton Rd, London SE14 5UJ **t** 020 7732 4335 or 07808 489553 **e** jazzlb@leemanagement.co.uk MD: Jasmin Lee.

Colin Leggett Flat 20, 24 Bemerton St, Islington, London N1 0BT **t** 07712 583 331 **e** colin@usrecords.co.uk **w** usrecords.co.uk Contact: Colin Leggett.

The Lemon Group 1st Floor, 17 Bowater Rd, Westminster Industrial Estate, Woolwich, London SE18 5TF **t** 07989 340 593 **e** brian@thelemongroup.com **w** thelemongroup.com MD: Brian Allen.

Dino Lenny Contact Prodmix International

Paul Leonard-Morgan Contact SMA Talent

Lester Barnes Contact Dreamscape Music

Tim Lever Contact Freedom Management

James Lewis Contact Stephen Budd Management

The Liaison and Promotion Company 124 Great Portland St, London W1W 6PP **t** 020 7636 2345 **f** 020 7580 0045 **e** garydavison@fmware.com Dir: Gary Davison.

Chris Liberator Contact Tortured Artists Ltd

Linus Loves Contact Illicit Entertainment

Stephen Lipson Contact Native Management

Steve Lironi Contact Stephen Budd Management

Robert Lissalde Contact Loriana Music

Little Piece of Jamaica (LPOJ) 55 Finsbury Park Rd, Highbury, London N4 2JY **t** 020 7359 0788 or 07973 630 729 **e** paulhuelpoj@yahoo.co.uk Dir: Paul Hue.

Living Productions 39 Tadorne Rd, Tadworth, Surrey KT20 5TF **t** 01737 812922 **f** 01737 812922 **e** livingprods@ukgateway.net Dir: Norma Camby.

LJE 32 Willesden Lane, London NW6 7ST **t** 020 7625 0231 **f** 020 7372 6503 **e** lauriejay@btconnect.com MD: Laurie Jay.

Nick Lloyd Contact Paul Brown Management Ltd

Lo Fidelity Allstars Contact The Day Job

Eddie Lock Contact Worldmaster Dj Management Ltd

Roger Lomas Ro-Lo Productions, 35 Dillotford Ave, Styvechale, Coventry, W Midlands CV3 5DR **t** 024 7641 0388 or 07711 817475 **f** 024 7641 6615 **e** roger.lomas@virgin.net.

Loriana Music PO Box 2731, Romford RM7 1AD **t** 01708 750 185 or 07748 343 363 **f** 01708 750 185 **e** info@lorianamusic.com **w** lorianamusic.com Owner: Jean-Louis Fargier.

James Lott Contact Muirhead Management

Jim Lowe Contact Dangerous Management

Larry Lush The Studio, 2 Faygate Rd, Streatham, London SW2 3AR **t** 07716 887 576 **e** Laurence.e.p@gmail.com **w** larrylush.com Producer/Engineer/Arranger: Laurence Elliott-Potter.

Brendan Lynch Contact CEC Producer Management

Steve Lyon Contact Stephen Budd Management

Steve Mac Contact Darah Music

Calum MacColl Contact CEC Producer Management

Neill MacColl Contact CEC Producer Management

Steve Mackey Contact Rough Trade Producer Management

Logan Mader Contact XL Talent

Per Magnusson & David Kreuger Contact XL Talent

Majic Productions PO Box 66, Manchester M12 4XJ
t 0161 225 9991 **e** info@majicmusic.co.uk **w** sirenstorm.com
Dir: Mike Coppock.

Major Seven Ltd 47 Combemartin Rd, London SW18 5PP
t 020 8788 9147 **f** 020 8785 7291 **e** major.seven@virgin.net
Dir: Jane Wingfield.

Makis G Contact The Lemon Group

Jonny Male Contact Spirit Music & Media

Richard Manwaring 25 Waldeck Rd, London W13 8LY
t 020 8991 0495.

MAP Productions 27 Abercorn Pl, London NW8 9DX
t 07905 116 455 **f** 020 7624 7219 **e** hkhan@greycoat.co.uk
Contact: Helen Khan.

Pete `Boxsta' Martin Contact 365 Artists Ltd

Sir George Martin Contact CA Management

Giles Martin Contact CA Management

Mike Mason Contact The Day Job

Matpro Ltd Cary Point, Babbacombe Downs, Torquay, Devon
TQ1 3LU **t** 01803 322 233 **f** 01803 322 244
e mail@matpro-show.biz **w** babbacombe-theatre.com
MD: Colin Matthews.

Richard Matthews Contact Chunk Management

Guy Mcaffer Contact Tortured Artists Ltd

Dave McCracken Contact 140dB Management

Reg McLean RMO Music, 37 Philip Close, carshalton, Surrey
SM5 2FE **t** 020 8646 3378 **f** 020 8646 3376.

Neil McLellan Contact This Much Talent

James McMillan Contact Giles Stanley

Dave Meegan Contact Z Management

Menace Management 2 Park Rd, Radlett, Herts WD7 8EQ
t 01923 853 789 **f** 01923 853 318
e menacemusicmanagement@btopenworld.com
MD: Dennis Collopy.

Mental Music Management Email or call for address,
London E3 **t** 020 8981 4888 or 07900 631 883
f 020 8981 4888 **e** mentalmusicmgt@yahoo.co.uk
w myspace.com/mentalmusicmgt Mgr: Gary Heath.

Mentor Kolktiv Contact 2Point9 Management

Messy Productions Studio 2, Soho Recording Studios, 22-
24 Torrington Pl, London WC1E 7HJ **t** 020 7813 7202
f 020 7419 2333 **e** info@messypro.com **w** messypro.com
MD: Zak Vracelli.

Mews Productions The Hiltongrove Business Center,
Hatherley Mews, London E17 4QP **t** 020 8520 3949
e nick@mewsproductions.com **w** mewsproductions.com
Dir: Nick Michaels.

Teo Miller Contact Stephen Budd Management

Miloco Management 36 Leroy St, London SE1 4SP
t 020 7232 0008 **f** 020 7237 6109 **e** info@miloco.co.uk
w miloco.co.uk Studio Manager: Sophie Nathan.

Grant Mitchell Contact Sarm Management

Martin Mitchell Commercial Music Productions 14
Moorend Crescent, Cheltenham, Gloucs GL53 OEL
t 01242 523304 **f** 01242 523304 **e** mmitchell@hrpl.u-net.com
MD: Martin Mitchell.

Mobb Rule Productions PO Box 26335, London N8 9ZA
t 020 8340 8050 **e** info@mobbrule.com **w** mobbrule.com
MDs: Stewart Pettey, Wayne Clements.

Micky Modelle Contact Tortured Artists Ltd

Moneypenny The Stables, Westwood House, Main St, North
Dalton, Driffield, E Yorks YO25 9XA **t** 01377 217815
f 01377 217754 **e** nigel@adastey.demon.co.uk MD: Nigel Morton.

Mike Moran Contact SMA Talent

Owen Morris Contact Nomadic Music

Ian Morrow Contact Sarm Management

Motive Music Management 93b Scrubs Lane, London
NW10 6QU **t** 07808 939 919 **e** nathan@motivemusic.co.uk
Contact: Nathan Leeks.

Alan Moulder Contact Fundamental Music

MPG (The Music Producers Guild Ltd.) PO Box
29912, London SW6 4FR **t** 020 7371 8888 **f** 020 7371 8887
e office@mpg.org.uk **w** mpg.org.uk
Office Manager: Susie Sparrow.

Muirhead Management Anchor House, 2nd Floor, 15-19
Britten St, London SW3 3TY **t** 020 7351 5167 or
07785 226 542 **f** 020 7000 1227
e info@muirheadmanagement.co.uk
w muirheadmanagement.co.uk CEO: Dennis Muirhead.

Multiplay Music Management 19 Eagle Way, Harrold,
Bedford MK43 7EW **t** 01234 720 785 or 07971 885 375
f 01234 720 664 **e** kevin@multiplaymusic.com
w multiplaymusic.com MD: Kevin White.

Mumbo Jumbo Management
Contact: Illicit Entertainment.

Music Factory Entertainment Group Hawthorne
House, Fitzwilliam St, Parkgate, Rotherham, S Yorks S62 6EP
t 01709 710 022 **f** 01709 523 141 **e** info@musicfactory.co.uk
w musicfactory.co.uk Contact: Andy Pickles.

Music Masters Ltd Orchard End, Upper Oddington,
Moreton-in-Marsh, Gloucs GL56 OXH **t** 01451 812288
f 01451 870702 **e** info@music-masters.co.uk
w music-masters.co.uk MD: Nick John.

The Music Sculptors 32-34 Rathbone Pl, London W1P 1AD
t 020 7636 1001 **f** 020 7636 1506.

Music 4/Music4 41-42 Berners St, London W1T 3NB
t 020 7016 2000 **e** studios@music4.com **w** music4.com
MD: Sandy Beech.

Native Management Unit 32, Ransomes Dock, 35-37
Parkgate Rd, London SW11 4NP **t** 020 7801 1919
f 020 7738 1819 **e** marie.native@19.co.uk
w nativemanagement.com Contact: Peter Evans.

Ned Bigham Contact Ocean Bloem Productions

Negus-Fancey Company 78 Portland Rd, London W11 4LQ **t** 020 7727 2063 **f** 020 7229 4188 **e** negfan@aol.com Contact: Charles Negus-Fancey.

Bill Nelson Contact Opium (Arts) Ltd

Ken Nelson Contact Oxygen Music Management

The Next Room 5B Oakleigh Mews, Whetstone, London N20 9HQ **t** 020 8343 9971 **e** studio@thenextroom.com **w** thenextroom.com Studio Mgr: Bob Wainwright.

The Nextmen Contact: Leafman.

Tom Nichols Contact Freedom Management

Nick Franglen Contact Big Life Producer Management

Hugo Nicolson Contact Big Life Producer Management

Mike Nielsen Contact Strongroom Management

Nightmoves Contact Illicit Entertainment

Niles Productions 34 Beaumont Rd, London W4 5AP **t** 020 8248 2157 **e** r.niles@richardniles.com **w** richardniles.com Dir: Richard Niles.

Richard Niles Contact Niles Productions

Rab Noakes Studio 1, 19 Marine Crescent, Kinning Pk, Glasgow G51 1HD **t** 0141 423 9811 **f** 0141 423 9811 **e** stephy@go2neon.com **w** rabnoakes.com Production Organiser: Stephanie Pordage.

Noiz Studios 1 Sutherland House, 2 Greencroft Gardens, London NW6 3LR **t** 0870 240 7596 **f** 0787 686 7836 **e** info@noizstudios.co.uk **w** noizstudios.co.uk Producer: Noel da Costa.

Noko Contact XL Talent

Nomadic Music Unit 18, Farm Lane Trading Estate, 101 Farm Lane, London SW6 1QJ **t** 020 7386 6800 or 07779 257 577 **f** 020 7386 2401 **e** info@nomadicmusic.net **w** nomadicmusic.net Label Head: Paul Flanagan.

Chuck Norman Contact Solar Management Ltd

North Star Music PO Box 868, Cambridge CB1 6SJ **t** 01787 278256 **f** 01787 279069 **e** info@northstarmusic.co.uk **w** northstarmusic.co.uk MD: Grahame Maclean.

Gil Norton Contact JPR Management

Erik Nova Contact Multiplay Music Management

Rick Nowels Contact Stephen Budd Management

Nuff Productions 139 Whitfield St, London W1T 5EN **t** 020 7380 1000 **f** 020 7380 1000 **e** neil@nuff.co.uk **w** nuff.co.uk Contact: Neil 'Nuff' Stainton.

Nursery Cottage Productions PO Box 370, Newquay, Cornwall TR8 5YZ **t** 01637 831011 **f** 01637 831037 **e** nurseryco@aol.com Mgr: Rod Buckle.

Obi & Josh Contact Asylum Artists

Ocean Bloem Productions Unit 127, Canalot Production Studios, 222 Kensal Rd, London W10 5BN **t** 020 8960 3888 **e** ned@oceanbloem.com **w** oceanbloem.com Producer: Ned Bigham.

OD Hunte Contact Treasure Hunte Productions

Paul Staveley O'Duffy Contact 365 Artists Ltd

Tim Oliver Contact Positive Management

Opium (Arts) Ltd 49 Portland Rd, London W11 4LJ **t** 020 7229 5080 **f** 020 7229 4841 **e** adrian@opiumarts.com Contact: Richard Chadwick, Adrian Molloy.

Ornadel Management Imperial Works, Top Floor, Perren St, London NW5 3ED **t** 020 7482 5505 **f** 020 7482 5504 **e** guy@ornadel.com **w** ornadel.com Contact: Guy Ornadel, Roman Trystram.

Shinichi Osawa (Mondo Grosso) Contact CEC Producer Management

Steve Osborne Contact 140dB Management

osOHso Limited PO Box 50690, London SW6 4YW **t** 020 3080 1010 **e** ronnie@osohso.com **w** osohso.com Mgr: Ronnie Elmhirst.

The Outfit Productions Sherwood Plaza, 530a Mansfield Rd, Sherwood, Nottingham NG5 2FR **t** 07798 902 749 **e** info@theoutfitproductions.com **w** theoutfitproductions.com Producer: James Hancock.

Oven Ready Productions 10 Cedar Rd, London NW2 6SR **t** 07050 803 933 **f** 07050 693 471 **e** info@ovenready.net **w** ovenready.net MD: Moussa Clarke.

Ovni Audio 33-37 Hatherley Mews, London E17 4QP **t** 020 8521 9595 or 07967 615647 **f** 020 8521 6363 **e** flavio.uk@ukonline.co.uk **w** curiousyellow.co.uk Owner: Flavio Curras.

Gorwel Owen Ein Hoff Le, Llanfaelog, Ty Croes, Ynys Mon LL63 5TN **t** 01407 810 742 or 07987 672 824 **f** 01407 810 742 **e** besyn.digwydd@virgin.net.

Oxbridge Records (Classical, Choral & Organ only) 1 Abbey St, Eynsham, Oxford OX8 1HR **t** 01865 880240 **f** 01865 880240 MD: HF Mudd.

Oxygen Music Management 33-45 Parr St, Liverpool, Merseyside L1 4JN **t** 0151 707 1050 **f** 0151 709 4090 **e** oxygenmusic@btinternet.com MD: Pete Byrne.

P3M Music Management & Consultancy 126a Talbot Rd, London W11 1JA **t** 07771 862 401 **e** paulmoorep3m@aol.com MD: Paul Moore.

Pachuco Management Priestlands, Letchmore Heath, Herts WD2 8EW **t** 01923 854 334 **f** 01923 857 884 **e** grahamcarpenter@hotmail.com MD: Graham Carpenter.

Hugh Padgham Contact Giles Stanley

Panama Productions Sovereign House, 12 Trewartha Rd, Praa Sands, Penzance, Cornwall TR20 9ST **t** 01736 762 826 or 07721 449477 **f** 01736 763 328 **e** panamus@aol.com **w** panamamusic.co.uk MD: Roderick Jones.

P+E Music Contact P.J. Music

Paradigm Productions Ltd 143 West Vale, Neston, South Wirral, Cheshire CM64 0TJ **t** 0151 336 6657 or 07974 900740 **f** 0151 336 6657 **e** paraprod@cwcom.net **w** mp3.com/subsymphonic MD: Andy Williams.

Nick Patrick Contact Giles Stanley

Kevin Paul Contact Audio Authority Management

Ewan Pearson Contact Illicit Entertainment

Mike Peden Contact Native Management

Mike Pela Contact Giles Stanley

Mike Pelanconi Contact Motive Music Management

Dave Pemberton Contact Strongroom Management

Mike Percy Contact Freedom Management

PHAB High Notes, Sheerwater Ave, Woodham, Surrey KT15 3DS **t** 019323 48174 **f** 019323 40921 MD: Philip HA Bailey.

Mark Phythian Contact Innocent Management

Pierce c/o Pierce Ent., Pierce House, Hammersmith Apollo, Queen Caroline St, London W6 9QH **t** 020 8563 1234 **f** 020 8563 1337 Contact: Deborah Cable.

Pivotal Music Management 4 Heathgate Pl, 75-83 Agincourt Rd, London NW3 2NU **t** 020 7424 8688 **f** 020 7424 8699 **e** info@pivotalmusic.co.uk Contact: Björn Hall.

P.J. Music Willow Barn, Wrenshall Farm, Walsham-Le-Willows, Bury St Edmunds, Suffolk IP31 3AS **t** 01359 258 686 **f** 01359 258 686 **e** phill-harding@btconnect.com **w** myspace.com/philthepowerharding MD: Phil Harding.

Platinum Tones Productions Ltd PO Box 5935, Towcester, Northants NN12 7ZL **t** 01327 811 618 **f** 0871 242 2890 **e** tp@platinumtones.com MD: Tony Platt.

Tony Platt Contact Platinum Tones Productions Ltd

Poet Name Life Contact Audio Authority Management

Point4 Productions Unit 16 Talina Centre, Bagleys Lane, Fulham, London SW6 2BW **t** 07788 420 315 **e** info@point4music.com **w** point4music.com Dirs: Paul Newton, Peter Day.

Polar Arts Ltd Corbett Cottage, The Street, Castle Combe, Wilts SN14 7HU **t** 01249 783850 **f** 020 7681 1900 **e** juliette@polararts.com **w** polararts.com Dir: Juliette Slater.

Pop Muzik Haslemere, 40 Broomfield Rd, Henfield, W. Sussex BN5 9UA **t** 01273 491 416 **f** 01273 491 417 **e** robin@robinscott.org **w** robinscott.org Dir: Robin Scott.

Positive Management 4th Floor Studio, 16 Abbey Churchyard, Bath BA1 1LY **t** 01225 311 661 **f** 01225 482 013 **e** carole@helium.co.uk **w** positivebiz.com Mgr: Carole Davies.

Chris Potter Contact Z Management

Steve Power Contact Zomba Management

Matt Prime Contact Native Management

Principle Management 30-32 Sir John Rogersons Quay, Dublin 2, Ireland **t** +353 1 677 7330 **f** +353 1 677 7276 **e** Candida@numb.ie Dir: Paul McGuinness.

Prodmix International 98 Edith Grove, Chelsea, London SW10 ONH **t** 020 7565 0324 or 07768 877 426 **f** 020 7168 7257 **e** karen@prodmix.com **w** prodmix.com Dir: Karen Goldie Sauve.

Prohibition Management Fulham Palace, Bishops Ave, London SW6 6EA **t** 020 7384 7372 or 07967 610 877 **f** 020 7371 7940 **e** Caroline@prohibitiondj.com **w** prohibitiondj.com MD: Caroline Prothero.

Project G Contact Amco Music Productions

Craig Pruess Contact SMA Talent

Q Productions The Red Cottage, East Tytherley Rd, East Tytherley, Hants SO51 OLW **t** 01794 341181 **f** 01794 511810 Contact: Ian Baddon.

QD Music 72A Lilyville Rd, London SW6 5DW **t** 07779 653930 **f** 0870 0511 879 **e** drewtodd@qdmusic.co.uk **w** koolesac.com MD: Drew Todd.

QFM PO Box 77, Leeds LS13 2WZ **t** 08709 905 078 **f** 0113 256 1315 **e** info@qfm.com MD: Katherine Canoville.

Quince Productions 62a Balcombe St, Marylebone, London NW1 6NE **t** 020 7723 4196 or 07810 752 765 **f** 020 7723 1010 **e** info@quincestudios.co.uk **w** quincestudios.co.uk Dir: Matt Walters.

Quintessential Music PO Box 546, Bromley, Kent BR2 ORS **t** 020 8402 1984 **f** 020 8325 0708 Contact: Quincey.

Quiz & Larossi Contact XL Talent

Q-Zone 21C Heathmans Rd, Parsons Green, London SW6 4TJ **t** 020 7731 9313 **f** 020 7731 9314 **e** mail@darah.co.uk Contact: Nicki L'Amy.

Peter Raeburn Contact Soundtree Music

RandM Productions 72 Marylebone Lane, London W1U 2PL **t** 020 7486 7458 **f** 020 8467 6997 **e** mike@randm.co.uk **w** randm.co.uk MDs: Mike Andrews, Roy Eldridge.

Mark Rankin Contact Miloco Management

Simon Raymonde Contact CEC Producer Management

Louis Read Contact Alan Cowderoy Management

Realsound Nottingham NG5 1JU **t** 0115 978 7745 or 07973 279 652 **f** 0115 978 7745 **e** john@realsound.fsnet.co.uk **w** realsound-live.co.uk Engineer: John Mison.

Red Fort Studios The Sight And Sound Centre, Priory Way, Southall, Middlesex UB2 5EB **t** 020 8843 1546 **f** 020 8574 4243 Contact: Kuljit Bhamra.

Red Parrrot Management B114 Faircharm Studios, 8-10 Creekside, London SE8 3DX **t** 020 8469 3541 **f** 020 8469 3542 **e** red.parrot@virgin.net **w** redparrot.co.uk Contact: John Cecchini.

Red Rhythm Productions Red Rhythm Towers, 2 Longlane, Stains, Middlesex TW19 7AA **t** 01784 255629 **e** cliffrandall@telco4u.net Ace Production Team: Cliff Randall.

Red Sky Records PO Box 27, Stroud, Gloucs GL6 0YQ **t** 0845 644 1447 **f** 01453 836877 **e** info@redskyrecords.co.uk **w** redskyrecords.co.uk MD: Johnny Coppin.

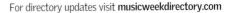

Redd Management The Courtyard, Unit A, 42 Colwith Rd, Hammersmith, London W6 9EY **t** 020 8846 3737
f 020 8846 3738 **e** david@reddmanagement.com
MD: David Moores.

Redemption Music Management 13 Bexhill Rd, London SW14 7NF **t** 07779 257 577
e info@redemptionmusicmanagement.co.uk Mgr: Paul Flanagan.

Redwood Studios 20 Great Chapel St, London W1F 8FW
t 020 7287 3799 **e** andrestudios@yahoo.co.uk
w sound-design.net MD/Producer: Andre Jacquemin.

Respect Productions Ltd Unit GA, 39-40 Westpoint, Warple Way, London W3 0RG **t** 020 8740 1616
f 020 8740 4488 **e** respect@mailbox.co.uk
w westpointstudio.co.uk Studio Manager: Ian Sherwin.

Jay Reynolds Contact Stephen Budd Management

John Reynolds Contact Spirit Music & Media

Rhythm of Life Ltd Lazonby, Penrith CA10 1BG
t 01768 898888 **f** 01768 898809 **e** events@rhythm.co.uk
w rhythm.co.uk MD: Andrew Lennie.

Rishi Rich Contact 2Point9 Management

Richard Lightman Productions 353 St. Margaret's Rd, Twickenham, Middx TW1 1PW **t** 020 8891 3293
f 020 8744 0811 **e** richard@lightman.demon.co.uk
Producer: Richard Lightman.

Richard Rainey Contact Duncan Management

Richard Robson Contact Stephen Budd Management

James Richards Contact Big M Productions

Neil Richmond 12 Fairwall House, Peckham Rd, London SE5 8QW **t** 020 7703 4668 or 0799 0932850
f 020 7703 4668.

Max Richter Contact Stephen Budd Management

Riff Raff Music Ltd Stanley House, 39 Stanley Gardens, Acton, London W3 7SY **t** 020 8735 0280
e roy@riffraffmanagement.com **w** riffraffmusic.net
Director/Producer: Roy Jackson/ Gareth Young.

Right Bank Music Productions Home Park House, Hampton Court Rd, Kingston upon Thames, Surrey KT1 4AE
t 020 8977 0666 **f** 020 8977 0660
e rightbankmusicuk@rightbankmusicuk.com
w rightbankmusicuk.com VP: Ian Mack.

John A Rivers 1 St Mary's Crescent, Leamington Spa, Warcs CV31 1JL **t** 01926 338 971 **e** jony2r@ntlworld.com
w woodbinestreet.com MD/Studio Mgr: John A Rivers.

Riviera Music Productions 83 Dolphin Crescent, Paignton, Devon TQ3 1JZ **t** 07071 226078 **f** 01803 665728
e Info@rivieramusic.net **w** rivieramusic.net MD: Kevin Jarvis.

Tom Rixton Contact The Day Job

RNT Music Ltd Pinetree Farm, Cranborne, Dorset BH21 5RR
t 01725 517204 **f** 01725 517801 **e** info@rntmusic.com
w rntmusic.com Producers: Rick & Tim Parkhouse.

Iain Roberton Contact Sarm Management

Jimmy Robertson Contact CEC Producer Management

Robot Club Contact Smoothside Organisation

Jony Rockstar Contact Z Management

Jarrad Rogers Contact Twenty Four Seven Music Management

Roll Over Productions 29 Beethoven St, London W10 4LJ
t 020 8968 0299 **f** 020 8968 1047 **w** rollover.co.uk
Contact: Phil Jacobs.

Mike Rose Contact Native Management

Rose Rouge International AWS House, Trinity Sq, St Peter Port, Guernsey, Channel Islands GY1 1LX **t** 01481 728 283
f 01481 714 118 **e** awsgroup@cwgsy.net
Director/Producer: Steve Free.

Rough Trade Producer Management 66 Golborne Rd, London W10 5PS **t** 020 8960 9888 **f** 020 8968 6715
e mog.yoshihara@roughtraderecords.com
w roughtradeproducers.com Artist Co-ordinator: Mog Yoshihara.

Matt Rowe Contact Native Management

RP Management 51A Woodville Rd, Thornton Heath, Surrey CR7 8LN **t** 07956 368 680 **e** R.Pascoe@RPMan.co.uk
w myspace.com/rpmanagement Contact: Richard Pascoe.

RPM Management Ltd Pierce House, London Apollo Complex, Queen Caroline St, London W6 9QU **t** 020 8741 5557
f 020 8741 5888 **e** marlene-rpm@pierce-entertainment.com
w pierce-entertainment.com MD: Marlene Gaynor.

Rufus Stone: Producer 1st Floor, 35 Marshall St, London W1F 7EX **t** 020 7287 9601 **f** 020 7287 9602
e rufus@sister-pr.com.

Ralph P Ruppert 23 Gatton Rd, Bristol BS2 9TF
t 0117 983 8050 **f** 0117 983 8063
e ralphruppert@onetel.net.uk.

Russ Russell Contact Audio Authority Management

Ron Saint Germain Contact SJP/Dodgy Productions

Johnny Sandlin Contact Zane Productions

James Sanger Contact Z Management

Sarm Management The Blue Building, 8-10 Basing St, London W11 1ET **t** 020 7229 1229 **f** 020 7221 9247
e jill@spz.com **w** sarm.com MD: Jill Sinclair.

Mike Satori Management Email for address, London
t 07963 011 302 or +43 650 407 1527
e office@deep9music.com **w** martin101.com Mgr: Mike Satori.

Andy Saunders Contact CEC Producer Management

The Schizofreniks PO Box 12, 499 Uper Richmond Rd, London SW14 7DE **t** 07766 064468
e niki@theschizofreniks.com **w** theschizofreniks.com
Producer/Managing Director: Niki Clarke.

Schmusicmusic 156a High St, London Colney, Herts AL2 1QF **t** 01727 827017 or 07860 902361 **f** 01727 827017
e pjmusic@ukonline.co.uk **w** shmusicmusic.com
Dir: Paul J Bowrey.

SCO Productions 29 Oakroyd Ave, Potters Bar, Herts EN6 2EL **t** 01707 651 439 **f** 01707 651 439
e constantine@steveconstantine.freeserve.co.uk
MD: Steve Constantine.

Sentinel Management 60 Sellons Ave, London NW10 4HH **t** 020 8961 6992 or 07932 737 547 **e** sentinel7@hotmail.com Dirs: Sandra Scott.

Session Connection PO Box 46307, London SW17 0WS **t** 020 8871 1212 or 07801 070 362 **e** sessionconnection@mac.com **w** thesessionconnection.com MD: Tina Hamilton.

Shake Up Music Ickenham Manor, Ickenham, Uxbridge, Middx UB10 8QT **t** 01895 672994 **f** 01895 633264 **e** mail@shakeupmusic.co.uk Dir: Joanna Tizard.

Shalit Global Entertainment & Management 7 Moor St, Soho, London W1D 5NB **t** 020 7851 9155 **f** 020 7851 9156 **e** info@shalitglobal.com MD: Jonathan Shalit.

Chris Sheldon Contact Alan Cowderoy Management

George Shilling Contact SJP/Dodgy Productions

Kevin Shirley Contact Duncan Management

Signia Productions 44 Edith Rd, London W14 9BB **t** 020 7371 2137 **e** dee@signiamusic.com **w** signiamusic.com MD: Dee Harrington.

Valgeir Sigurdsson Contact Stephen Budd Management

Stuart Sikes Contact Rough Trade Producer Management

Silver Lion Productions 10 Oakwood Rd, London NW11 6QX **t** 07937 345368 Contact: Tony Wilson.

Craig Silvey Contact Smoothside Organisation

Victor Simonelli Contact X-Rated Management

Rik Simpson Contact Stephen Budd Management

SJP/Dodgy Productions 263 Putney Bridge Rd, London SW15 2PU **t** 020 8780 3311 **f** 020 8785 9894 **e** laurie@tastemusic.com **w** sjpdodgy.co.uk Creative Mgr: Laurie Latham Jnr.

Skatta Cordel Burrell Contact Jamdown Ltd

Skillz Contact Shalit Global Entertainment & Management

Skylark Contact 24 Management

Slave Productions (UK) PO Box 200, South Shore, Blackpool, Lancs FY1 6GR **t** 07714 910257 **e** sploj3@yahoo.co.uk Contact: Rob Powell.

Sleeper Music Block 2, 6 Erskine Rd, Primrose Hill, London NW3 3AJ **t** 020 7580 3995 **f** 020 7900 6244 **e** info@sleepermusic.co.uk **w** guychambers.com Contact: Dylan Chambers, Louise Jeremy.

SMA Talent The Cottage, Church St, Fressingfield, Suffolk IP21 5PA **t** 01379 586 734 **f** 01379 586 131 **e** carolynne@smatalent.com **w** smatalent.com MDs: Carolynne Wyper, Olav Wyper.

Small World 18A Farm Lane Trading Centre, 101 Farm Lane, London SW6 1QJ **t** 020 7385 3233 **f** 020 7386 0473 **e** tina@smallworldmanagement.com MD: Tina Matthews.

Alexis Smith Contact 365 Artists Ltd

Fraser T Smith Contact Twenty Four Seven Music Management

Smoothside Organisation Stoke House, South Green, Kirtlington, Oxford OX5 3HJ **t** 01869 351096 **f** 01869 351097 **e** info@smoothside.com **w** smoothside.com MD: Barbara Jeffries.

Sniffy Dog 26 Harcourt St, London W1H 4HW **t** 020 7724 9700 **f** 020 7724 2598 **e** amanda@coochie-management.com **w** sniffy-dog.com Contact: Michael Blainey.

Solar Management Ltd 13 Rosemont Rd, London NW3 6NG **t** 020 7794 3388 **f** 020 7794 5588 **e** info@solarmanagement.co.uk **w** solarmanagement.co.uk MD: Carol Crabtree.

Sonic Music Production Building 348a, Westcott Venture Pk, Westcott, Aylesbury, Bucks HP18 0XB **t** 01296 655 880 **e** reception@sonic.uk.com **w** sonic.uk.com MD: Adrienne Aiken.

Sonny Contact Innocent Management

Soul Mekanik Contact Illicit Entertainment

Soulem Productions The Cabin Studios, 24a Coleridge Rd, Crouch End, London N8 8ED **t** 07906 172 455 **e** soulemproductions@yahoo.co.uk Contact: Mathieu Karsenti.

Soulfood Music - Urban Specialists 4 Allen Close, Shenley, Radlett, Herts. WD7 9JS **t** 01923 853737 or 01923 853737 **e** steve@soulfoodmusic.org **w** soulfoodmusic.org MD: Steve Ripley.

Sound Alibi Productions 92 Hartley Ave, Leeds, W Yorks LS6 2HZ **t** 0113 243 0177 **f** 0113 243 0177 **e** andy@soundalibi.co.uk **w** soundalibi.co.uk Ptnr: Andy Wood.

Sound Image Productions Unit 2B, Bankquay Trading Estate, Slutchers Lane, Warrington, Cheshire WA1 1PJ **t** 01925 445742 **f** 01925 445742 **e** info@soundimageproductionss.co.uk **w** soundimageproductionss.co.uk MD: Steve Millington.

Soundcakes 14A Hornsey Rise, London N19 3SB **t** 020 7281 0018 **f** 020 7272 9609 GM: Kris Hoffmann.

Soundtree Music Unit 124, Canalot Studios, 222 Kensal Rd, London W10 5BN **t** 020 8968 1449 **f** 020 8968 1500 **e** post@soundtree.co.uk **w** soundtree.co.uk GM: Jay James.

Soundz Of Muzik Ltd The Courtyard, 42 Colwith Rd, London W6 9EY **t** 020 8741 1419 **f** 020 8741 3289 **e** firstname@evolverecords.co.uk Dir: Trevor Porter.

Sam Spacey Contact Tortured Artists Ltd

John Spence - Freelance Engineer/Producer 20 Churchside, Appleby, North Lincs DN15 0AJ **t** 01724 732062 or 07718 061 297 **e** john@spence252.wanadoo.co.uk.

Jim Spencer Contact Paul Brown Management Ltd

Spirit Music & Media PO Box 30884, London W12 9AZ **t** 020 8746 7461 **f** 020 8749 7441 **e** info@spiritmm.com **w** spiritmm.com MD: Tom Haxell.

John Springate 61 Lansdowne Lane, London SE7 8TN **t** 020 8853 0728 **f** 020 8853 0728 **e** handbagmusic@cwcom.net **w** starguitar.mcmail.com/johnspring.html.

SRB Music PO Box 189, Hastings TN34 2WE **t** 01424 435 693 **f** 01424 461 058 **e** jimsrbmusic@aol.com **w** myspace.com/jimbeadle Dir: Jim Beadle.

Jeremy Stacey Contact Sarm Management

Giles Stanley 347-353 Chiswick High Rd, London W4 4HS **t** 07718 653 218 **e** giles.stanley@umusic.com **w** universalmusic-management.com MD: Giles Stanley.

Ian Stanley Contact Alan Cowderoy Management

Paul Statham Contact This Much Talent

Ali Staton Contact Alan Cowderoy Management

Billy Steinberg Contact Stephen Budd Management

Mark 'Spike' Stent Contact TLS Music Management

Steve Smith 167, Ringwood Rd, St. Leonards, Ringwood, Hants BH24 2NP **t** 01425 473432 **f** 01425 473432 **e** info@rwav.co.uk **w** rwav.co.uk.

Al Stone Contact Smoothside Organisation

WG Stonebridge Producer Management PO Box 49155, London SW20 0YL **t** 020 8946 7242 **f** 020 8946 7242 **e** w.stonebridge@btopenworld.com Contact: Bill Stonebridge.

Andy Strange Contact 365 Artists Ltd

Street Level Contact Street Level Management Ltd

Street Level Management Ltd 1st Floor, 17 Bowater Rd, Westminster Industrial Estate, Woolwich, London SE18 5TF **t** 07886 260 686 **e** ceo@streetlevelenterprises.co.uk **w** streetlevelenterprises.com MD: Sam Crawford.

Stephen Street Contact Gailforce Management

Streetfeat Management 26 Bradmore Park Rd, London W6 0DT **t** 020 8846 9984.

Stress Management PO Box 27947, London SE7 8WN **t** 020 8269 0352 or 07778 049 706 **f** 020 8269 0353 **e** suzanne@quixoticrecords.com **w** quixoticrecords.com Dir: Suzanne Hunt.

Strongroom Management 120-124 Curtain Rd, London EC2A 3SQ **t** 020 7426 5130 **f** 020 7426 5102 **e** coral@strongroom.com **w** strongroom.com/management Dir: Coral Worman.

Studio 24 Production 60 Benedict Close, Romsey, Hants SO51 8PN **t** 01794 501774 or 07754 969326 **f** 01794 501774 **e** info@studiotwentyfour.co.uk **w** studiotwentyfour.co.uk Producer: Alan Cotty.

Subsymphonic 143 West Vale, Neston, South Wirral, Cheshire CH64 0TJ **t** 0151 336 6657 **e** andy@subsymphonic.com **w** subsymphonic.com Producer: Andy Williams.

Sugarcane Music The Shed, Cooper House, 2 Michael Rd, London SW6 2AD **t** 020 8847 2695 **f** 020 8847 2695 Contact: Richard Bailey.

Suli n' Stef Productions Ltd. 56 Fraser Rd, Perivale, Middlesex UB6 7AL **t** 020 8723 6158 **f** 020 7738 1764 **e** suli.hirani@btinternet.com Producer: Suli.

Sunship Contact Jamdown Ltd

Danton Supple Contact 140dB Management

Graham Sutton Contact Rough Trade Producer Management

Martin Sutton Contact WG Stonebridge Producer Management

Billy Swan Contact Muirhead Management

Dan Swift Contact Z Management

Syze-up Contact Smoothside Organisation

Brio Taliaferro Contact 365 Artists Ltd

Shel Talmy Productions 14 Raynham Rd, London W6 0HY **t** 020 8846 9912 **f** 020 8748 6683 Contact: Judy Lipson.

TAT Productions Contact 2B3 Productions

Damian Taylor Contact This Much Talent

Temple Studios 97A Kenilworth Rd, Edgware, Middlesex HA8 8XB **t** 020 8958 4332 or 07956 510620 **f** 020 8958 4332 **e** contact@templestudios.co.uk **w** templestudios.co.uk Producer: Howard Temple.

J Templeman Contact Respect Productions Ltd

Ten21 Little Milgate, Otham Lane, Bearsted, Maidstone, Kent ME15 8SJ **t** 01622 735 200 **f** 01622 735 200 **e** info@ten21.biz **w** ten21.biz Owner: Sean Kenny.

Terpsichord PO Box 794, High Wycombe, Bucks HP10 9FD **t** 01628 667515 **f** 01628 667515 **e** paul@terpsichord.com **w** terpsichord.com Producer: Paul Dakeyne.

Ben Thackeray Contact Miloco Management

This Much Talent The Fan Club, 133 Kilburn Lane, London W10 4AN **t** 020 8354 2900 **f** 020 8354 2095 **e** contact@ThisMuchTalent.co.uk **w** ThisMuchTalent.co.uk MD: Sandy Dworniak.

Chris Thomas Contact Rough Trade Producer Management

Ken Thomas Contact Strongroom Management

Peter Thompson Contact Zane Productions

Rod Thompson Music 73 Bromfelde Rd, London SW4 6PP **t** 020 7720 0866 **f** 020 7720 0866.

Ali Thomson Contact Sarm Management

Phil Thornalley Contact WG Stonebridge Producer Management

Darrell Thorp Contact Solar Management Ltd

TidyTrax Contact Music Factory Entertainment Group

Dimitri Tikovoi Contact 140dB Management

Glenn Tilbrook Contact Stress Management

Mark Tinley Unit 462, 405 Kings Rd, London SW10 0BB **t** 0709 212 6916 **f** 0709 212 6916 **e** marktinley@hotmail.com **w** tinley.net/mark Producer: Mark Tinley.

Paul Tipler Contact Motive Music Management

TLS Music Management London **t** 07785 706 565 **e** tracy@tlsmanagement.com Contact: Tracey Slater.

TMC Records PO Box 150, Chesterfield, Derbyshire S40 0YT **t** 01246 236667 or 07711 774369 **f** 01246 236667.

Tortured Artists Ltd 19F Tower Workshops, Riley Rd, London SE1 3DG **t** 020 7252 2900 **f** 020 7252 2890 **e** business@truelove.co.uk **w** truelove.co.uk Contact: John Truelove, Brian Roach.

Cenzo Townshend Contact Alan Cowderoy Management

Toy Productions see Principle Management.

Traxx Music Production 6 Lillie Yard, London SW6 1UB **t** 020 7385 9000 **f** 020 7385 0700 **e** sharonrose@traxx.co.uk **w** traxx.co.uk Contact: Sharon Rose.

Treasure Hunte Productions Suite 6, Cross House, Cross Lane, London N8 7SA **t** 07774 265 211 **e** odhunte@thp-online.com **w** thp-online.com Producer: OD Hunte.

Triple X + Bassman Contact Simon Harris

Tropical Fish Music 351 Long Lane, London N2 8JW **t** 0870 444 5468 or 07973 386 279 **f** 0870 132 3318 **e** info@tropicalfishmusic.com **w** tropicalfishmusic.com MD: Grishma Jashapara.

John Truelove Contact Tortured Artists Ltd

Chris Tsangarides Contact Audio Authority Management

Dan Turner Contact Muirhead Management

Twenty Four Seven Music Management PO Box 2470, The Studio, Chobham, Surrey GU24 8ZD **t** 01276 855 247 **f** 01276 856 897 **e** info@24-7musicmanagement.com **w** 24-7musicmanagement.com MD: Craig Logan.

Ty Contact Sentinel Management

U-Freqs 20 Athol Court, 13 Pine Grove, London N4 3GU **t** 07831 770 394 **f** 0870 131 0432 **e** info@u-freqs.com **w** u-freqs.com Ptnr: Stevino.

The Umbrella Group Call for address. **t** 07802 535 696 **f** 020 7603 9930 **e** Tommy@Umbrella-Group.com **w** Umbrella-Group.com Dir: Tommy Manzi.

UMU Productions 144 Princes Ave, London W3 8LT **t** 020 8992 7351 **f** 020 8400 4931 **e** promo@ciscoeurope.co.uk MD: Mimi Kobayashi.

Barry Upton Contact Cordella Music

Utopia Records/Video Utopia Village, 7 Chalcot Rd, London NW1 8LH **t** 020 7586 3434 **f** 020 7586 3438 **e** utopiarec@aol.com MD: Phil Wainman.

Pete Vale Contact Freshwater Hughes Management

Value Added Talent 1 Purley Pl, Islington, London N1 1QA **t** 020 7704 9720 **f** 020 7226 6135 **e** vat@vathq.co.uk **w** vathq.co.uk MD: Dan Silver.

Matthew Vaughan Contact Smoothside Organisation

Martijn Ten Velden Contact Stephen Budd Management

Vernandaz Productions 15 St Johns Church Rd, Folkestone, Kent CT19 5BQ **t** 01303 257714 or 01303 257285 **e** vernon@songlife.co.uk MD: Vernon Woodward.

Peter-John Vettese Contact FKM

Dan Vickers Contact Sarm Management

Phil Vinall Contact Deluxxe Management

Tony Visconti Tony Visconte Productions Inc, PO Box 314, Pomona, NY, USA 10970 **t** 001 845 362 8876 **f** 001 845 362 9190 **w** tonyvisconti.com Contact: May Pang.

Vision Discs PO Box 92, Gloucester GL4 8HW **t** 01452 814321 **f** 01452 812106 **e** vic_coppersmith@hotmail.com **w** visiondiscs.com MD: Vic Coppersmith-Heaven.

Mark Wallis Contact Stephen Budd Management

Greg Walsh Contact The Liaison and Promotion Company

Peter Walsh Contact The Liaison and Promotion Company

Rik Walton Giffords Oasthouse, Battle Rd, Dallington, E Sussex TN21 9LH **t** 01424 838148 or 07808 453321 **f** 01424 838148 **e** rik.walton@virgin.net Producer/Engineer: Rik Walton.

Ward 21 Contact Jamdown Ltd

Jeremy Wheatley Contact 365 Artists Ltd

David White Contact The Liaison and Promotion Company

Adam Whittaker Contact Smoothside Organisation

Ricki Wilde Contact Big M Productions

Mark Williams Contact 140dB Management

Sam Williams Contact Alan Cowderoy Management

Tim Wills Contact Z Management

Pete Wingfield Contact Major Seven Ltd

Wingfoot Productions 15 Flower Lane, London NW7 2JA **t** 020 8959 5913 **f** 020 8959 5913 **e** info@wingfoot.co.uk **w** wingfoot.co.uk MD: John de Bono.

Alan Winstanley Contact Hannah Management

Tim Woodcock Contact Freedom Management

Nina Woodford Contact Twenty Four Seven Music Management

Denis Woods Contact Muirhead Management

Woolven Productions 55a Ditton Rd, Surbiton, Surrey KT6 6RF **t** 020 8390 4583 **f** 020 8390 4583 **e** kitw@cygnet.co.uk Producer/engineer: Kit Woolven.

Worldmaster Dj Management Ltd The Coachhouse, Mansion Farm, Liverton Hill, Sandway, Maidstone, Kent ME17 2NJ **t** 01622 858 300 **f** 01622 858 300 **e** info@eddielock.com **w** eddielock.co.uk Prop: Eddie Lock.

XL Talent Reverb House, Bennett St, London W4 2AH **t** 020 8747 0660 **f** 020 8747 0880 **e** management@reverbxl.com **w** reverbxl.com Partners: Ian Wright, Maggi Hickman, Julian Palmer.

X-Rated Management Wimbourne House, 155 New North Rd, London N1 6TA **t** 020 7168 4287 **f** 070 9284 1131 **e** mike@x-rated.me.uk **w** x-rated.me.uk Artist Managers: Michael Hague and Brian Noonan.

Gota Yashiki Contact Respect Productions Ltd

Yazuka Productions 30 West Block, Rosebery Sq, London EC1A 4PT **t** 020 7916 9205 Contact: Brett Hunter.

Gareth Young Contact Heat Music

Youth Contact Big Life Producer Management

Z Management The Palm House, PO Box 19734, London SW15 2WU **t** 020 8874 3337 **f** 020 8874 3599 **e** office@zman.co.uk **w** zman.co.uk MD: Zita Wadwa-McQ.

Zane Productions 162 Castle Hill, Reading, Berks RG1 7RP **t** 0118 957 4567 **f** 0118 956 1261 **e** info@zaneproductions.demon.co.uk **w** zanerecords.com Contact: Peter Thompson.

Zomba Management 20 Fulham Broadway, London SW6 1AH **t** 020 7835 5260 **f** 020 7835 5261 **e** tim.smith@zomba.co.uk GM: Tim Smith.

Rehearsal Studios

Achieve Fitness New Islington Mill, Regent Trading Estate, Oldfield Rd, Manchester M5 7DE **t** 0161 832 9310 **f** 0161 832 9310 Prop: Glenn Ashton.

Alaska @ Waterloo Bridge Studios 127-129 Alaska St, London SE1 8XE **t** 020 7928 7440 **f** 020 7928 8070 **e** blodge_uk@yahoo.com **w** alaskastudio.co.uk Studio Mgr: Beverley Lodge.

All of Music PO Box 2361, Romford, Essex RM2 6EZ **t** 01708 688 088 **f** 020 7691 9508 **e** michelle@allofmusic.co.uk **w** allofmusic.co.uk MD: Danielle Barnett.

Arcsound Studio 443, New Cross Rd, London SE14 6TA **t** 020 8691 8161 **e** info@arcsound.co.uk **w** arcsound.co.uk Studio Manager: James Dougill.

Ariwa Rehearsal Studios 34 Whitehorse Lane, London SE25 6RE **t** 020 8653 7744 or 020 8771 1470 **f** 020 8771 1911 **e** info@ariwa.com **w** ariwa.com Studio Manager: Joseph Fraser.

Backstreet Rehearsal Studios 313 Holloway Rd, London N7 9SU **t** 020 7609 1313 **f** 020 7609 5229 **e** backstreet.studios@virgin.net **w** backstreet.co.uk Prop: John Dalligan.

Banana Row Rehearsal Studios 47 Eyre Pl, Edinburgh EH3 5EY **t** 0131 557 2088 **f** 0131 558 9848 **e** music@bananarow.com MD: Craig Hunter.

Berkeley 2 54 Washington St, Glasgow G3 8AZ **t** 0141 248 7290 **f** 0141 204 1138 **w** berkeley2.co.uk Prop: Steve Cheyne.

Big City Studios (Dance only) 159-161 Balls Pond Rd, London N1 4BG **t** 020 7241 6655 **f** 020 7241 3006 **e** pineapple.agency@btinternet.com **w** pineapple-agency.com Prop: Rebecca Paton.

Big Noise 12 Gregory St, Northampton NN1 1TA **t** 01604 634455 **e** bignoisestudios@hotmail.com Studio Mgr: Kim Gordelier.

BonaFideStudio Burbage House, 83-85 Curtain Rd, London EC2A 3BS **t** 020 7684 5350 or 020 7684 5351 **f** 020 7613 1185 **e** info@bonafidestudio.com **w** bonafidestudio.co.uk Studio Director: Deanna Gardner.

Charlton Farm Rehearsal Solutions (Residential) Charlton Farm, Hemington, Bath BA3 5XS **t** 01373 834161 **f** 01373 834167 **e** al@cruisin.co.uk **w** cruisin.co.uk GM: Al Hale.

Chem19 Rehearsal Studios Unit 5C, Peacock Cross Trading Estate, Burnbank Rd, Hamilton ML3 9AY **t** 01698 286 882 **f** 01698 327 979 **e** jim@chemikal.co.uk **w** chem19studios.co.uk Dir: Jim Savage.

Colorsound Audio 68 Fountainbridge, Edinburgh, Midlothian EH3 9PY **t** 0131 229 3588 **f** 0131 221 1454 **e** r.heatlie@virgin.net **w** colorsound.mu MD: Bob Heatlie.

Crash Rehearsal Studios Imperial Warehouse, 11 Davies St, Liverpool, Merseyside L1 6HB **t** 0151 236 0989 **f** 0151 236 0989 Dirs: John White, Mark Davies.

Cruisin' Music Charlton Farm, Hemington, Bath BA3 5XS **t** 01373 834161 **f** 01373 834164 **e** sil@cruisin.co.uk **w** cruisin.co.uk MD: Sil Wilcox.

Downs Sounds Studio Units 3-4 New Southgate Industrial Estate, Lower Park Rd, London N11 1QD **t** 020 8211 3656 **e** info@downssounds.co.uk **w** downssounds.co.uk Prop: Adam Downs.

Falling Anvil Studios Unit 114 Stratford Workshops, Burford Rd, London E15 2SP **t** 020 8503 0415 **e** necker@falling-anvil.freeserve.co.uk **w** fallinganvil.co.uk Studio Mgr: Necker.

Gracelands East Acton Lane, London W3 7HD **t** 020 8740 8922 **f** 020 8740 8922 Prop: Paul Burrows.

Groovestyle Recording Studio 33 Upper Holt St, Earls Colne, Colchester, Essex CO6 2PG **t** 01787 220326 **e** info@groovewithus.com **w** groovewithus.com Owner: Graham Game.

House of Mook Studios Unit 1, Authorpe Works, Authorpe Rd, Leeds LS6 4JB **t** 0113 230 4008 **e** mail@mookhouse.ndo.co.uk **w** mookhouse.ndo.co.uk Studio Mgr: Phil Mayne.

Islington Arts Factory 2 Parkhurst Rd, Holloway, London N7 0SF **t** 020 7607 0561 **f** 020 7700 7229 **e** IAF@islingtonartsfactory.fsnet.co.uk **w** islingtonartsfactory.org.uk Bookings: Mathew Coates.

JJM Studios 20 Pool St, Walsall, W Midlands WS1 2EN **t** 01922 629 700 **e** info@jjmstudios.com **w** jjmstudios.com Contact: Jay Mitchell.

John Henry's 16-24 Brewery Rd, London N7 9NH **t** 020 7609 9181 **f** 020 7700 7040 **e** johnh@johnhenrys.com **w** johnhenrys.com MD: John Henry.

Kontakt Productions 44b Whifflet St, Coatbridge ML5 4EL **t** 01236 434 083 **f** 01236 434 083 **e** gareth@kontaktproductions.com **w** kontaktproductions.com Studio Manager: Gareth Whitehead.

OTR Studios Ltd 143 Mare St, Hackney, London E8 3RH **t** 020 8985 9880 or 07956 450 607 **e** info@otrstudios.wanadoo.co.uk **w** otrstudios.co.uk Dir: Paul Lewis.

Panic Rehearsal Studios 14 Trading Estate Rd, Park Royal, London NW10 7LU **t** 020 8961 9540 or 020 8965 1122 **f** 020 8838 2194 **e** mroberts.drums@virgin.net **w** panic-music.co.uk Studio Mgr: Mark Roberts.

The Premises Studios 201-205 Hackney Rd, Shoreditch, London E2 8JL **t** 020 7729 7593 **f** 020 7739 5600 **e** info@premises.demon.co.uk **w** premises.demon.co.uk CEO: Viv Broughton.

React Studios 3 Fleece Yard, Market Hill, Buckingham MK18 1JX **t** 01280 821840 or 01280 823546 **f** 01280 821840 **e** info@reactstudios.co.uk **w** reactstudios.co.uk Studio Mgr: Tom Thackwray.

Red Onion Rehearsal Studios 26-28 Hatherley Mews, Walthamstow, London E17 4QP **t** 020 8520 3975 **f** 020 8521 6646 **e** info@redonion.uk.com **w** redonion.uk.com MD: Dee Curtis.

Rich Bitch 505 Bristol Rd, Selly Oak, Birmingham, W Midlands B29 6AU **t** 0121 471 1339 **f** 0121 471 2070 **e** richbitchstudios@aol.com **w** rich-bitch.co.uk Owner: Rob Bruce.

Riot Club Unit 4, 27A Spring Grove Rd, Hounslow, Middx TW3 4BE **t** 020 8572 8809 **f** 020 8572 9590 **e** riot@riotclub.co.uk **w** riotclub.co.uk Studio Manager: Ben Smith.

Ritz Studios 110-112 Disraeli Rd, Putney, London SW15 2DX **t** 020 8870 1335 **f** 020 8877 1036 **e** lee.webber@virgin.net Dir: Lee Webber.

Rogue Studios RA 4, Bermondsey Trading Estate, Rotherhithe New Rd, London SE16 3LL **t** 020 7231 3257 **f** 020 7231 7358 **e** info@roguestudios.co.uk **w** roguestudios.co.uk Contact: Jon-Paul Harper/Jim Down.

The Rooms Rehearsal Studios Lynchford Lane, North Camp, Farnborough, Hants GU14 6JD **t** 01252 371177 **e** minister.g@ntlworld.com **w** theroomsstudios.com Dirs: Gerry Bryant/Shaun Streams.

Rooz Studios 2A Corsham St, London N1 6DP **t** 020 7490 1919 Studio Mgr: Graham Clarke.

Rotator Rehearsal Studios 74-77 Magdalen Rd, Oxford OX4 1RE **t** 01865 205600 **f** 01865 205700 **e** rehearse@rotator.co.uk **w** rotator.co.uk Senior Manager: Phill Honey.

Soundbite Studios Unit 32, 17 Cumberland Business Pk, Cumberland Ave, London NW10 7RG **t** 020 8961 8509 **f** 020 8961 8994 Owner: Ranj Kumar.

The Studio Tower St, Hartlepool TS24 7HQ **t** 01429 424440 **f** 01429 424441 **e** studiohartlepool@btconnect.com **w** studiohartlepool.com Studio Manager: Liz Carter.

Survival Studios Unit B18, Acton Business Centre, School Rd, London NW10 6TD **t** 020 8961 1977 Mgr: Simon Elson.

Unit 25 - Mill Hill Music Complex Bunns Lane Works, Bunns Lane, London NW7 2AJ **t** 020 8906 9991 **f** 020 8906 9991 **e** enquiries@millhillmusic.co.uk **w** millhillmusic.co.uk Dir: Roger Tichbourne.

Warwick Hall of Sound Banastre Ave, Heath, Cardiff CF14 3NR **t** 029 2069 4455 **f** 029 2069 4450 **e** booking@ffvinyl.co.uk **w** warwickhall.co.uk MD: Martin Bowen.

Waterloo Sunset Tower Bridge Business Complex, 100 Clements Rd, London SE16 4DG **t** 020 7252 0001 **f** 020 7231 3002 **e** nunu@musicbank.org **w** musicbank.org/waterloo.html Studio Mgr: Dave Whiting.

WaterRat Rehearsal Unit 2 Monument Way East, Woking, Surrey GU21 5LY **t** 01483 764444 **e** jayne@waterrat.co.uk **w** waterrat.co.uk Prop: Jayne Wallis.

WESTBOURNE REHEARSAL STUDIOS

The Rear Basement, 92-98 Bourne Terrace, Little Venice, London W2 5TH **t** 020 7289 8142 **f** 020 7289 8142 **w** myspace.com/westbournerehearsals Studio Mgr: Chris Thomas.
Large, air-conditioned mirrored studios. Acoustically conditioned rooms with superb PA. Back line. Free parking. Refreshments. Storage. Shop. Special Solo Musician rates+++newly decorated 16' x 6' workspace for hire. Suit music related business. Mention Music Week for extra discount.

White Rooms Rehearsal Studios Roden House, Alfred St South, Nottingham NG3 1JH **t** 0115 932 2802 **e** whiterooms@btinternet.com **w** npbgroup.net Prop: Pauline Barker.

Session Fixers

AKLASS "THE ENTERTAINER'S AGENCY"

PO Box 42371, London N12 0WS **t** 020 8368 7760 **e** info@aklass.biz **w** aklass.biz Contact: Patsy McKay.
First class service for providing musicians, singers, gospel singers, jazz, latin, funk bands, dancers, strings and more...

B&H Management/B&H Musicians PO Box 1162, Bovingdon, Herts. HP1 9DE **t** 01442 832 010 **f** 01442 834 910 **e** simon@bandhmanagement.demon.co.uk **w** myspace.com/bandhmanagement MD: Simon Harrison.

Choir Connexion Brookdale House, 75 Brookdale Rd, Walthamstow, London E17 6QH **t** 020 8509 7288 **f** 020 8509 7299 **e** choirconnexion@btconnect.com **w** lcgc.org.uk Principal: Bazil Meade.

Citizen K Gospel Choir Suite 100, Hilton Grove Business Centre, Hatherley Mews, London E17 4QP **t** 020 8520 3975 **f** 020 8521 6646 **e** citizenk@ukf.net **w** citizenk.co.uk MD: Dee Curtis.

Cool Music Ltd 62A Warwick Gardens, London W14 8PP **t** 020 7565 2665 **f** 020 7603 8431 **e** enquiries@coolmusicltd.com **w** coolmusicltd.com Musicians Contractor: Richard Nelson.

CyberStrings (Powerbase) Limited 1 Norlington Rd, London E11 4BE **t** 020 8279 8286 **f** 020 8928 0613 **e** rjwardroden@argonet.co.uk MD: Richard Ward-Roden.

Eclipse-PJM (Vocalists) PO Box 3059, South Croydon, Surrey CR2 8TL **t** 020 8657 2627 or 07798 651691 **f** 020 8657 2627 **e** Eclipsepjm@btinternet.com Mgr & PA: Paul Johnson & Iris Sutherland.

First Move Management 137 Shooters Hill Rd, Blackheath, London SE3 8UQ **t** 020 8305 2077 or 0771 473 433 **f** 020 8305 2077 **e** firstmoves@aol.com **w** firstmove.biz Creative Dir: Janis MacIlwaine.

Isobel Griffiths **t** 020 7351 7383 **f** 020 7376 3034 **e** isobel@isobelgriffiths.co.uk Contact: MD.

Hornography 180 Lyndhurst Rd, London N22 5AU **t** 020 8365 8862 or 07956 510 112 **e** mat@hornography.freeserve.co.uk Contact: Mat Colman.

In A City Session Fixers Unit 49, Carlisle Business Centre, Carlisle Rd, Bradford BD8 8BD **t** 01274 223251 or 01377 236395 **f** 01904 623660 **e** music@projectmanager.co.uk **w** inacity.co.uk MD: Carl Stipetic.

Kick Horns 158 Upland Rd, London SE22 0DQ **t** 020 8693 5991 or 07931 776155 **f** 020 8693 5991 **e** info@kickhorns.com **w** kickhorns.com Dir: Simon C Clarke.

Knifedge 57b Riding House St, London W1W 7EF **t** 020 7436 5434 **f** 020 7436 5431 **e** info@knifedge.net **w** knifedge.net Dir: Jonathan Brigden.

Lager Productions 10 Barley Rise, Baldock, Herts SG7 6RT **t** 01462 636799 **f** 01462 636799 **e** dan@Lockupmusic.co.uk Dir: Steve Knight.

London Musicians Ltd Cedar House, Vine Lane, Hillingdon, Middlesex UB10 0BX **t** 01895 252555 **f** 01895 252556 **e** mail@lonmus.demon.co.uk MD: David White.

London Symphony Orchestra Barbican Centre, Silk St, London EC2Y 8DS **t** 020 7588 1116 **f** 020 7374 0127 **e** smallet@lso.co.uk **w** lso.co.uk Director of Planning: Sue Mallet.

More Music PO Box 306, Harrow, Middlesex HA2 0XL **t** 020 8423 1078 or 07721 623171 **f** 020 8423 1078 **e** info@moremusicagency.com Contact: Debra Williams.

Red Onion Productions 26-28 Hatherley Mews, Walthamstow, London E17 4QP **t** 020 8520 3975 **f** 020 8521 6646 **e** info@redonion.uk.com **w** redonion.uk.com MD: Dee Curtis.

Rhythm & Bookings Ltd Townhouse Studios, 150 Goldhawk Rd, London W12 8HH **t** 020 8354 1726 **f** 020 8354 1719 **e** randb@pennies.demon.co.uk **w** rhythmandbookings.com Booker/Contractor: Graeme Perkins.

Royal Philharmonic Orchestra 16 Clerkenwell Green, London EC1R 0QT **t** 020 7608 8800 **f** 020 7608 8801 **e** info@rpo.co.uk **w** rpo.co.uk MD: Ian Maclay.

SD Creative 113b Leander Rd, London SW2 2NB **t** 020 7652 9676 **e** office@sdcreative.co.uk Session Coordinator: Suzann Douglas.

Sense of Sound Training Parr Street Studios, 33-45 Parr St, Liverpool L1 4JN **t** 0151 707 1050 **f** 0151 709 8612 **e** info@senseofsound.net **w** senseofsound.net Artistic Director: Jennifer John.

SESSION CONNECTION

SESSION CONNECTION

PO Box 46307, London SW17 0WS **t** 020 8871 1212 or 07801 070 362 **e** sessionconnection@mac.com **w** thesessionconnection.com MD: Tina Hamilton. **Top session fixers. Providing Session Musicians and Singers for tours, recording sessions, TV's, video and commercials. Pop/Soul/Rock etc.**

Tuff The Session Agency Ltd Unit 15, Millmead Business Centre, Millmead Rd, London N17 9QU **t** 0870 8030 672 **f** 0870 8030 692 **e** info@tuffsessions.com **w** tuffsessions.com Business Manager: Joanne Costello.

Wired Strings 92 Uplands Rd, London N8 9NJ **t** 07976 157 277 **f** 020 8347 8455 **e** rosie@wiredstrings.com **w** wiredstrings.com Dir: Rosie Wetters.

The Wrecking Crew 15 Westmeads Rd, Whitstable, Kent CT5 1LP **t** 01227 264 966 or 07957 686 152 **f** 01227 264 966 **e** sophie@thewreckingcrew.co.uk **w** thewreckingcrew.co.uk Bookings: Sophie Sirota.

XFactory 20 Boughton House, Bowling Green Pl, London SE1 1YF **t** 020 7403 1830 **e** contact@xfactory.co.uk **w** xfactory.co.uk Dir: Nigel Proktor.

Young Guns Ltd 134 Longley Rd, London SW17 9LH **t** 020 8672 7630 or 07980 222 857 **e** enquiries@younggunsuk.com **w** younggunsuk.com Contact: Dom Pecheur.

Studio Equipment Hire and Sales

20th Century Vintage and Rare Guitars Ltd 6 Denmark St, London WC2 8LX **t** 020 7240 7500 **f** 020 7240 8900 **e** enquiries@vintageandrareguitars.com **w** vintageandrareguitars.com Mgr: Adam Newman.

Absolute Music Solutions (Audio Sales) 58 Nuffield Rd, Poole, Dorset BH17 0RT **t** 0845 025 55 55 **f** 0845 025 55 56 **e** sales@absolute.ms **w** absolute.ms Pro Audio Sales: Andy Legg.

Advanced Sounds Ltd Admin address on request. **t** 01305 757088 **f** 01305 268947 **e** advancedsoundsltd@btinternet.com **w** advancedsounds.co.uk Hire, Sales & Repairs: Mike Moreton.

Arcsound Studio 443, New Cross Rd, London SE14 6TA **t** 020 8691 8161 **e** info@arcsound.co.uk **w** arcsound.co.uk Studio Manager: James Dougill.

Audile Unit 110, Cariocca Business Pk, Ardwick, Manchester M12 4AH **t** 0161 272 7883 or 07968 156 499 **f** 0161 272 7883 **e** rob@audile.co.uk **w** audile.co.uk Ptnr: Rob Ashworth. ✱

Audiohire Ltd The Old Dairy, 133-137 Kilburn Lane, London W10 4AN **t** 020 8960 4466 **f** 020 8964 0343 **e** admin@audiohire.co.uk **w** audiohire.co.uk Mgr: Richard Zamet.

Delta Concert Systems Unit 4, Springside, Trinity, Jersey, Channel Islands JE3 5DG **t** 01534 865885 **f** 01534 863759 **e** hire@delta-av.com **w** delta-av.com Dir: Cristin Bouchet.

FX Rentals 38-40 Telford Way, London W3 7XS **t** 020 8746 2121 **f** 020 8746 4100 **e** info@fxrentals.co.uk **w** fxgroup.net Operations Director: Peter Brooks.

GearBox Express (Soho) 36-44 Brewer St, Entrance 1 Lexington St, London W1F 9LX **t** 020 7437 4832 **f** 020 7437 5402 **e** express@gearbox.com **w** gearbox.com Contact: Danny Simmonds.

GearBox (Sound and Vision) Unit 15 Alliance Court, Alliance Rd, London W3 0RB **t** 020 8992 4499 **f** 020 8992 4466 **e** mail@gearbox.com **w** gearbox.com Contact: Danny Simmonds.

GWH Backline Rental GWH, Hillcroft Business Pk, Whisby Rd, Lincoln LN6 3QT **t** 01522 501815 **f** 01522 501816 **e** gary@gwhmusic.com **w** gwhmusic.com Dir: Gary Weight.

Harris Hire 49 Hayes Way, Park Langley, Beckenham, Kent BR3 6RR **t** 020 8663 1807 **f** 020 8658 2803 **e** info@harris-hire.co.uk **w** harris-hire.co.uk MD: Mr P Harris.

The M Corporation (Audio Sales) 58 Nuffield Rd, Poole, Dorset BH17 0RT **t** 0845 025 55 55 **f** 0845 025 55 56 **e** sales@absolute.ms **w** theMcorporation.com Pro Audio Sales: Andy Legg.

Midnight Electronics Off Quay Building, Foundry Lane, Newcastle upon Tyne, Tyne and Wear NE6 1LH **t** 0191 224 0088 **f** 0191 224 0080 **e** info@midnightelectronics.co.uk **w** midnightelectronics.co.uk Mgr: Dave Cross. ●

Music Room Hire The Old Library, 116-118 New Cross Rd, London SE14 5BA **t** 020 7252 8271 **f** 020 7252 8252 **e** sales@musicroom.web.com **w** musicroom.web.com MD: Gordon Gapper.

Sensible Rentals 88 Brewery Rd, London N7 9NT **t** 020 7700 6655 **f** 020 7609 9478 **e** johnnyh@sensiblerentals.com **w** sensiblerentals.com Hire Mgr: Johnny Henry.

Strong Hire 120-124 Curtain Rd, London EC2A 3SQ **t** 020 7426 5150 or 07980 552 425 **f** 020 7426 5102 **e** hire@stronghire.com **w** stronghire.com Bookings: Phil Sisson, Alex Green.

Studiocare Professional Audio Ltd Unit 9 Century Building, Brunswick Business Pk, Summers Rd, Liverpool L3 4BL **t** 0845 345 8910 **f** 0845 345 8911 **e** hire@studiocare.com **w** studiocare.com Hire Department Manager: Andrew Culshaw.

Studiohire 8 Daleham Mews, London NW3 5DB **t** 020 7431 0212 **f** 020 7431 1134 **e** mail@studiohire.net **w** studiohire.net GM: Sam Thomas.

Terminal Studios Hire 4-10 Lamb Walk, London SE1 3TT **t** 020 7403 3050 **f** 020 7407 6123 **e** info@terminal.co.uk **w** terminal.co.uk MD: Charlie Barrett.

Tickle Music Hire Ltd The Old Dairy, 133-137 Kilburn Lane, London W10 4AN **t** 020 8964 3399 **f** 020 8964 0343 **e** hire@ticklemusichire.com Dir: Tad Barker.

TL Commerce Unit 2 Iceni Court, Icknield Way, Letchworth SG6 1TN **t** 01462 492095 **f** 01462 492097 **e** info@tlcommerce.co.uk **w** tlcommerce.co.uk MD: Tony Larking.

Peter Webber Hire 110-112 Disraeli Rd, Putney, London SW15 2DX **t** 020 8870 1335 **f** 020 8877 1036 **e** lee.webber@virgin.net Dir: Lee Webber.

Studio Equipment Manufacture and Distribution

AES Pro Audio North Lodge, Stonehill Rd, Ottershaw, Surrey KT16 0AQ **t** 01932 872672 **f** 01932 874364 **e** aesaudio@intonet.co.uk **w** aesproaudio.com Dir: Mike Stockdale.

Allen & Heath Ltd Kernick Industrial Estate, Penryn, Cornwall TR10 9LU **t** 01326 372070 **f** 01326 377097 **e** sales@allen-heath.com **w** allen-heath.com Sales Dir: Bob Goleniowski.

AMG Electronics 2 High St, Haslemere, Surrey GU27 2LR **t** 01428 658775 **f** 01428 658438 **e** amg@c-ducer.com **w** c-ducer.com Prop: AW French.

AMS Neve plc Billington Rd, Burnley, Lancs BB11 5UB **t** 01282 457011 **f** 01282 417282 **e** enquiry@ams-neve.com **w** ams-neve.com Dir of Commercial Oper.: Greg Cluskey.

Arbiter Group Atlantic House, Stirling Way, Borehamwood, Herts WD6 2BT **t** 020 8207 7860 **e** mtsales@arbitergroup.com **w** arbitergroup.com Mktg Mgr: Nick Sharples.

Audio Agency PO Box 4601, Kiln Farm, Milton Keynes, Bucks MK19 7ZN **t** 01908 510123 **f** 01908 511123 **w** audioagency.co.uk Sales Mgr: Paul Eastwood.

Audio & Design Reading Ltd 51 Padick Drive, Lower Earley, Reading, Berks RG6 4HF **t** 0118 324 0046 **f** 0118 324 0048 **e** sales@adrl.co.uk **w** adrl.co.uk Sales Manager: Ian Harley.

Audio Developments Ltd Hall Lane, Walsall Wood, Walsall, W Midlands WS9 9AU **t** 01543 375351 **f** 01543 361051 **e** sales@audio.co.uk **w** audio.co.uk Sales Director: Antony Levesley.

Audio Digital Technology Ltd Manor Rd, Teddington, Middx TW11 8BG **t** 020 8977 4546 **f** 020 8977 4576 **e** info@audiodigitaltech.com **w** audiodigitaltech.com Dir: Jim Dowler.

Audio Technica Technica House, Royal London Ind Est, Old Lane, Leeds LS11 8AG **t** 0113 277 1441 **f** 0113 270 4836 **e** sales@audio-technica.co.uk **w** audio-technica.co.uk Sales Manager UK & Export: Tony Cooper.

Audio-Technica Technica House, Royal London Industrial Estate, Old Lane, Leeds, W Yorks LS11 8AG **t** 0113 277 1441 **f** 0113 270 4836 **e** sales@audio-technica.co.uk **w** audio-technica.co.uk UK Marketing Manager: Tony Cooper.

Audionics Petre Drive, Sheffield, S Yorks S4 7PZ **t** 0114 242 2333 **f** 0114 243 3913 **e** info@audionics.co.uk **w** audionics.co.uk Prod Dir: Phil Myers.

BBM Electronics Group Ltd Kestrel House, Garth Rd, Morden, Surrey SM4 4LP **t** 020 8330 3111 **f** 020 8330 3222 **e** sales@trantec.co.uk **w** trantec.co.uk Dir: Steve Baker.

Beyerdynamic GB Ltd 17 Albert Drive, Burgess Hill, W Sussex RH15 9TN **t** 01444 258258 **f** 01444 258444 **e** sales@beyerdynamic.co.uk **w** beyerdynamic.co.uk MD: John Midgley.

BSS Audio Cranbourne House, Cranbourne Rd, Potters Bar, Herts EN6 3JN **t** 01707 660667 **f** 01707 660755 **e** info@bss.co.uk **w** bss.co.uk Marketing Manager: David Neal.

Canford Audio plc Crowther Industrial Estate, Crowther Rd, Washington, Tyne and Wear NE38 0BW **t** 0191 418 1000 **f** 0191 418 1001 **e** info@canford.co.uk **w** canford.co.uk Sales & Mktg Director: Barry Revels.

Chevin Research Ltd 4A Ilkley Rd, Otley, W Yorks LS21 3JP **t** 01943 466060 **f** 01943 466020 **e** sales@chevin-research.com **w** chevin-research.com MD: Martin Clinch.

Chiswick Reach Ltd TBA **t** 07977 427535 **e** chiswick.reach@virgin.net **w** chiswickreach.co.uk MD: Nigel Woodward.

ComSec Int. 26 Penwinnick Rd, St Austell, Cornwall PL25 5DS **t** 01726 874180 or 01235 550791 (Sales) **f** 01726 874185 or 01235 550874 (Sales) **e** steve@comsecint.com **w** comsecint.com Sales Manager: Steve Smith.

Connectronics PO Box 22618, London N4 1LZ **t** 07000 422253 **f** 07000 283461 **e** sales@connectronics.co.uk **w** connectronics.co.uk Sales Manager: Gary Ash.

Cunnings Recording Associates Brodrick Hall, Brodrick Rd, London SW17 7DY **t** 0870 90 66 44 0 **f** 020 8767 8525 **e** info@cunnings.co.uk **w** cunnings.co.uk Prop: Malcolm J Cunnings.

dBm Ltd. The Loft, Mill Lane, Little Hallingbury, Bishop's Stortford, Herts CM22 7QT **t** 01279 721434 **f** 01279 721391 **e** info@dbmltd.com **w** dbmltd.com Sales & Marketing Dirs.: Janice Glen, Richard Watts.

dCS Ltd Mull House, Great Chesterford Court, Great Chesterford, Saffron Walden, Essex CB10 1PF **t** 01799 531999 **f** 01799 531681 **e** sales@dcsltd.co.uk **w** dcsltd.co.uk Mktg Mgr: Robert Kelly.

Deltron Emcon Ltd Deltron Emcon House, Hargreaves Way,, Scunthorpe, N. Lincs DN15 8RF **t** 01724 273200 **f** 01724 270230 **e** media@deltron-emcon.com **w** deltron-emcon.com Mktng Co-ord: Diane Kilminster.

Digidesign UK Westside Complex, Pinewood Studios, Pinewood Rd, Iver Heath, Bucks SL0 0QF **t** 01753 655999 **e** euro_presales_uk@digidesign.com **w** digidesign.com UK Sales Specialist: Alex Keane.

Direct Distribution Unit 6 Belfont Trading Estate, Mucklow Hill, Halesowen, W Midlands B62 8DR **t** 0121 550 2777 **f** 0121 585 8003 **e** info@directdistribution.uk.com **w** directdistribution.uk.com UK Manager: Andrew Scott.

D&M Professional Chiltern Hill, Chalfont St Peter, Bucks SL9 9UG **t** 01753 888447 **f** 01753 880109 **e** info@d-mpro.eu.com **w** d-mpro.eu.com Sales & Marketing Mgr: Simon Curtis.

Dolby Laboratories, Inc. Interface, Wootton Bassett, Wilts SN4 8QJ **t** 01793 842100 **f** 01793 842101 **e** info@dolby.co.uk **w** dolby.com Sound Consultant: Andrea Borgato.

Drawmer Distribution Ltd Charlotte St Business Centre, Charlotte St, Wakefield, W Yorks WF1 1UH **t** 01924 378669 **f** 01924 290460 **e** sales@drawmer.com **w** drawmer.com MD: Ken Giles.

eJay Empire Interactive Europe Ltd., The Spires, 677 High Rd, North Finchley, London N12 0DA **t** 020 8492 1049 **f** 020 8343 7447 **e** cate@empire.co.uk **w** eJay.com Brand Manager: Cate Swift.

Euphonix Europe Ltd Linton House, 39-51 Highgate Rd, London NW5 1RS **t** 020 7267 1226 **f** 020 7267 1227 **e** mhosking@euphonix.com **w** euphonix.com Sales Manager: Mark Hosking.

Focusrite Audio Engineering 19 Lincoln Rd, Cressex Business Pk, High Wycombe, Bucks HP12 3FX **t** 01494 462246 **f** 01494 459920 **e** sales@focusrite.com **w** focusrite.com Marketing Manager: Giles Orford.

Graff Electronic Machines Ltd Wood Hill Rd, Collingham, Newark, Notts NG23 7NR **t** 01636 893036 **f** 01636 893317 **e** sales@graffelectronics.co.uk **w** graffelectronics.co.uk Sales Mgr: Roger Platts.

Groove Tubes Europe - Guitar XS 12a Waterside, Upper Brents, Faversham, Kent ME13 7AU **t** 01795 538877 **f** 01795 538877 **e** sales@guitarXS.com **w** guitarXS.com Contact: Doug Chandler, Tina Sharpe.

Harbeth Audio Ltd Unit 3, Enterprise Pk, Lindfield, W Sussex RH16 2LH **t** 01444 484371 **f** 01444 487629 **e** sound@harbeth.com **w** harbeth.com MD: Alan Shaw.

HHB Communications 73-75 Scrubs Lane, London NW10 6QU **t** 020 8962 5000 **f** 020 8962 5050 **e** sales@hhb.co.uk **w** hhb.co.uk Sales & Marketing Dir.: Steve Angel.

HIQ Sound Units 2 & 3, Cedars Farm, South Carlton, Lincs LN1 2RH **t** 01522 730810 **f** 01522 731055 **e** sales@hiqsound.co.uk **w** hiqsound.co.uk Contact: Tony Hopkinson.

Jarberry Pro Audio Perseverance Works, Morrison St, Castleford WF10 4BE **t** 01977 556868 **f** 01977 603180 **e** sales@jarberry-music.co.uk **w** jarberry-music.co.uk Dir: Ryan Davis.

Junger Audio Invicta Works, Elliott Rd, Bromley, Kent BR2 9NT **t** 020 8460 7299 **f** 020 8460 0499 **e** sales@michael-stevens.com **w** michael-stevens.com UL Sales Mgr: Simon Adamson.

Kelsey Acoustics 9 Lyon Rd, Walton on Thames, Surrey KT12 3PU **t** 01932 886060 **f** 01932 885565 **e** kelsey@yahoo.com Op's Mgr: Michael Whiteside.

Klark Teknik Telex Communications (UK) Ltd, Klark Teknik Building, Walter Nash Rd, Kidderminster, Worcs DY11 7HJ **t** 01562 741 515 **f** 01562 745 371 **e** firstname.lastname@uk.telex.com **w** klarkteknik.com Marketing Manager: James Godbehear.

Logic System Pro Audio Ltd Unit 46, Corringham Road Industrial Est, Gainsborough, Lincs DN21 1QB **t** 01427 611791 **f** 01427 677008 **e** sales@logic-system.co.uk **w** logic-system.co.uk MD: Chris Scott.

Mackie 2 Blenheim Court, Hurricane Way, Wickford, Essex SS11 8YT **t** 01268 571212 **f** 01268 570809 **e** martin.warr@loudtechnologies.com **w** mackie.com UK Sales Manager: Martin Warr.

Marquee Audio Shepperton Film Studios, Studio Rd, Shepperton, Middlesex TW17 0QD **t** 01932 566 777 **f** 01932 565 861 **e** info@marqueeaudio.co.uk **w** marqueeaudio.co.uk Office Mgr: Tim Cowling.

A & F McKay Audio Ltd/Oktava The Studios, Hoe Farm, Hascombe, Surrey GU8 4JQ **t** 01483 208511 **f** 01483 208538 **e** fergus@mckay.org **w** oktava.net Contact: Fergus McKay.

MC2 Audio Ltd Units 6 & 7 Kingsgate, Heathpark Industrial Estate, Honiton, Devon EX14 1YG **t** 01404 44633 **f** 01404 44660 **e** mc2@mc2-audio.co.uk **w** mc2-audio.co.uk MD: Ian McCarthy.

Mitsubishi Electric UK Travellers Lane, Hatfield, Herts AL10 8XB **t** 01707 276100 **f** 01707 278690 **e** yoshinori.miyata@meuk.mee.com **w** meuk.mee.com Pres: Yoshinori Miyata.

MJQ Ltd (Studio Consultants) Swillett House, 52 Heronsgate Rd, Chorleywood, Herts WD3 5BB **t** 01923 285266 **f** 01923 285168 **e** sales@mjq.co.uk **w** mjq.co.uk MD: Malcolm Jackson.

MTR Ltd Ford House, 58 Cross Rd, Bushey, Herts WD19 4DQ **t** 01923 234050 **f** 01923 255746 **e** mtrltd@aol.com **w** mtraudio.com MD: Tony Reeves.

Munro Acoustics Unit 21, Riverside Studios, 28 Park St, London SE1 9EQ **t** 020 7403 3808 **f** 020 7403 0957 **e** info@munro.co.uk **w** munro.co.uk Prop: Andy Munro.

Musisca (Music Stands & Accessories) Piccaddilly Mill, Lower St, Stroud, Glos. GL5 2HT **t** 01453 751911 **f** 01453 751911 **e** info@musisca.co.uk **w** musisca.co.uk Dir: Marc Oboussier.

Mutronics Unit 12 Impress House, Mansell Rd, London W3 7QH **t** 020 8735 0042 **f** 020 8735 0041 **e** mutronics@mutronics.co.uk **w** mutronics.co.uk Technical Dir: James Dunbar.

Nemesis Professional Audio Products Ltd (see SHEP Associates).

Ohm (UK) Ltd Wellington Close, Parkgate, Knutsford, Cheshire WA16 8XL **t** 01565 654641 **f** 01565 755641 **e** info@ohm.co.uk **w** ohm.co.uk Dir: Paul Adamson.

Orange Amplifiers Ltd T/A Omec Ltd, 4th Floor, 28 Denmark St, London WC2H 8NJ **t** 020 7240 8292 **f** 020 7240 8112 **e** info@orange-amps.com **w** orangeamps.com Marketing/Press: Michelle Printer.

Peavey Electronics Great Folds Rd, Oakley Hay, Corby, Northants NN18 9ET **t** 01536 461234 **f** 01536 747222 **e** sales@peavey-eu.com **w** peavey-eu.com Contact: Ken Achard.

Penny & Giles Controls Ltd Nine Mile Point Ind Estate, Cwmfelinfach, Gwent NP1 7HZ **t** 01495 202000 **f** 01495 202006 **e** sales@pennyandgiles.com **w** pennyandgiles.com Product Manager: Andrew Clarke.

Planet Audio Systems 33 Bournehall Ave, Bushey, Herts WD23 3AU **t** 08707 605 365 **f** 020 8950 1294 **e** proaudiosales@planetaudiosystems.com **w** planetaudiosystems.com MD: Rod Gammons.

PRECO (Broadcast Systems) Ltd 3 Four Seasons Crescent, Kimpton Rd, Sutton, Surrey SM3 9QR **t** 020 8644 4447 **f** 020 8644 0474 **e** sales@preco.co.uk **w** preco.co.uk MD: Tony Costello.

Quantegy Europa Ltd Unit 3, Commerce Pk, Brunel Rd, Theale, Reading, Berks RG7 4AB **t** 0118 930 2240 **f** 0118 930 2235 **e** sales.uk/eire@quantegy-eu.com **w** quantegy.com Sales Co-ordinator: Rose McCormack.

Quested Monitoring Systems Ltd Units 6&7 Kingsgate, Heathpark Industrial Estate, Honiton, Devon EX14 1YG **t** (0)1404 41500 **f** (0)1404 44660 **e** sales@quested.com **w** quested.com MD: Ian McCarthy.

Ridge Farm Industries Rusper Rd, Capel, Surrey RH5 5HG **t** 01306 711202 **e** info@ridgefarmindustries.com **w** ridgefarmindustries.com MD: Frank Andrews.

River Pro Audio Unit 6a, Juno Way, London SE14 5RW **t** 020 3183 0000 **f** 020 3183 0006 **e** sales@riverproaudio.co.uk **w** riverproaudio.com Contact: Joel Monger.

RMPA & Rauch Amplification 42 Lower Ferry Lane, Callow End, Worcester WR2 4UN **t** 01905 831877 or 07836 617158 **f** 01905 830906 **e** rmpaworcester@aol.com **w** rmpa.co.uk Owner: Richard Bailey.

Roland (UK) Ltd Atlantic Close, Swansea Enterprise Pk, Swansea, West Glamorgan SA7 9FJ **t** 01792 515 020 **f** 01792 600 527 **e** customers@roland.co.uk **w** roland.co.uk.

SADiE UK The Old School, Stretham, Ely, Cambs CB6 3LD **t** 01353 648 888 **f** 01353 648 867 **e** sales@sadie.com **w** sadie.com Sales & Mkt Mgr: Geoff Calver.

SCV London 40 Chigwell Lane, Oakwood Hill Ind. Estate, Loughton, Essex IG10 3NY **t** 020 8418 0778 **f** 020 8418 0624 **e** orders@scvlondon.co.uk **w** scvlondon.co.uk Marketing Manager: Steve McDonald.

Sennheiser UK 3 Century Point, Halifax Rd, High Wycombe, Bucks HP12 3SL **t** 01494 551 551 **f** 01494 551 550 **e** info@sennheiser.co.uk **w** sennheiser.co.uk Director of Marketing: John Steven.

Shep Associates Long Barn, North End, Meldrith, Royston, Herts SG8 6NT **t** 01763 261 686 **f** 01763 262 154 **e** info@shep.co.uk **w** shep.co.uk MD: Derek Stoddart.

Shure Distribution UK 167-171 Willoughby Lane, London N17 0SB **t** 020 8808 2222 **f** 020 8808 5599 **e** info@shuredistribution.co.uk **w** shuredistribution.co.uk Sales Manager: Mike Gibson.

Shuttlesound 4 The Willows Centre, Willow Lane, Mitcham, Surrey CR4 4NX **t** 020 8646 7114 **f** 020 8254 5666 **e** info@shuttlesound.com **w** shuttlesound.com MD: Paul Barretta.

Silver Productions Ltd 29 Castle St, Salisbury, Wilts SP1 1TT **t** 01722 336221 **f** 01722 336227 **e** info@silver.co.uk **w** silver.co.uk IT & Systems Director: Riza Pacalioglu.

Solid State Logic Spring Hill Rd, Oxford OX5 1RU **t** 01865 842300 **f** 01865 842118 **e** info@solid-state-logic.com **w** solid-state-logic.com Sales Dir: Niall Feldman.

The Solutions Company (TSC) 1 Amalgamated Drive, West Cross Centre, Great West Rd, London TW8 9EZ **t** 020 8400 4333 **f** 020 8400 9444 **e** andy.campbell@gotsc.com **w** gotsc.com Sales Director: Andrew Campbell.

Sound and Video Services UK Ltd Shentonfield Rd, Sharston Industrial Estate, Manchester M22 4RW **t** 0161 491 6660 **f** 0161 491 6669 **e** sales@svsmedia.com **w** svsmedia.com Dir: Mike Glasspole.

Sound Control 61 Jamaica St, Glasgow G1 4NN **t** 0141 204 2774 or 0141 204 0322 **f** 0141 204 0614 **e** sales@soundcontrol.co.uk **w** soundcontrol.co.uk GM: Kenny Graham.

Sound Technology plc 17 Letchworth Point, Letchworth, Herts SG6 1ND **t** 01462 480000 **f** 01462 480800 **e** info@soundtech.co.uk **w** soundtech.co.uk Sales Office Manager: Colin Haines.

Soundcraft, Harman Pro UK Cranborne House, Cranborne Rd, Potters Bar, Herts EN6 3JN **t** 01707 665 000 **f** 01707 660 482 **e** info@harmanpro.com **w** soundcraft.com VP, Sales: Adrian Curtis.

Soundtracs DiGiCo Unit 10, Silverglade Buisness Pk, Leatherhead Rd, Chessington, Surrey KT18 7LX **t** 01372 845 600 **f** 01372 845 656 **e** uk@digiconsoles.com **w** soundtracs.co.uk Sales Dir: James Gordon.

EA Sowter Ltd The Boatyard, Cullingham Rd, Suffolk IP1 2EL **t** 01473 252794 **f** 01473 236188 **e** sales@sowter.co.uk **w** sowter.co.uk MD: Brian W Last.

Speed Music PLC 195 Caerleon Rd, Newport, South Wales NP19 7HA **t** 01633 215577 **f** 01633 213214 **e** info@speedmusic.co.uk **w** speedmusic.co.uk Dir: Nick Fowler.

Michael Stevens & Partners Ltd Invicta Works, Elliott Rd, Bromley, Kent BR2 9NT **t** 020 8460 7299 **f** 020 8460 0499 **e** sales@michael-stevens.com **w** michael-stevens.com UL Sales Mgr: Simon Adamson.

Stirling Trading (UK) 5 The Chase Centre, Chase Rd, London NW10 6QD **t** 020 8963 4790 **f** 020 8963 4799 **e** info@stirlingtrading.com **w** stirlingaudio.com MD: Andrew Stirling.

Straight Edge Manufacturing Ltd Bladewater Marina, The Esplanade, Mayland, Chelmsford, Essex CM3 6FD **t** 01621 742000 **f** 01621 742222 **e** info@straight-edge.co.uk **w** straight-edge.co.uk MD: Ian Wilson.

Studer UK Ltd Cranbourne House, Cranborne Rd, Potters Bar, Herts EN6 3JN **t** 01635 254 719 **e** andrew@studer.co.uk **w** studer.ch Sales: Andrew Hills.

Studiospares Ltd 964 North Circular Rd, London NW2 7JR **t** 08456 441 020 or 020 8208 9930 **f** 020 8208 9930 **e** sales@studiospares.com **w** studiospares.com Mgrs: Richard Venables/Mike Dowsett.

Tannoy Professional Rosehall Industrial Estate, Coatbridge, Strathclyde ML5 4TF **t** 01236 420199 **f** 01236 428230 **e** prosales@tannoy.com **w** tannoy.com Sales Mgr: Sean Martin.

Tapematic UK Unit 13 Hurricane Close, Hurricane Way, Wickford, Essex SS11 8YR **t** 01268 561999 **f** 01268 561709 **e** uk@tapematic.com **w** tapematic.com MD: David Hill.

TDK UK Ltd TDK House, 5-7 Queensway, Redhill, Surrey RH1 1YB **t** 01737 773773 **f** 01737 773809 or 01737 773805 **w** tdk-europe.com Brand Dev Mgr: Donna de Souza.

TEAC UK Limited (TASCAM) Marlin House, The Croxley Centre, Watford, Herts WD18 8TE **t** 01923 438880 **f** 01923 236290 **e** info@teac.co.uk **w** teac.co.uk Sales Mgr: Neil Wells.

Thurlby Thandar Instruments Ltd Glebe Rd, Huntingdon, Cambs PE29 7DR **t** 01480 412451 **f** 01480 450409 **e** sales@tti-test.com **w** tti-test.com Dir: John Cornwell.

TL Audio Sonic Touch, ICENI Court, Icknield Way, Letchworth, Herts SG6 1TN **t** 01462 492 090 **f** 01462 492 097 **e** info@tlaudio.co.uk **w** tlaudio.co.uk MD: Tony Larkin.

Turbosound Star Rd, Partridge Green, W Sussex RH13 8RY **t** 01403 711 447 **f** 01403 710 155 **e** sales@turbosound.com **w** turbosound.com Sales Dir: Rik Kirby.

Denis Tyler Ltd 59 High St, Great Missenden, Bucks HP16 0AL **t** 01494 866262 **f** 01494 864959 **e** denistylerlimited@btinternet.com **w** denistyler.com MD: Elizabeth Tyler.

Vestax (Europe) Ltd Unit 5, Riverwey Industrial Pk, Alton, Hants GU34 2QL **t** 01420 83000 **f** 01420 80040 **e** sales@vestax.co.uk **w** vestax.co.uk MD: Andy Williams.

Volt Loudspeakers Ltd Enterprise House, Blyth Rd, Hayes, Middlesex UB3 1DD **t** 020 8573 4260 **f** 020 8813 7551 **e** info@voltloudspeakers.co.uk **w** voltloudspeakers.co.uk MD: David Lyth.

Wharfedale Professional Ltd IAG House, Sovereign Court, Ermine Business Pk, Huntingdon, Cambs PE29 6XU **t** 01480 447709 **f** 01480 431767 **e** marketing@wharfedale.co.uk **w** wharfedalepro.com Int'l Marketing Manager: Lisa Fletcher.

Yamaha-Kemble Music (UK) Sherbourne Drive, Tilbrook, Milton Keynes, Bucks MK7 8BL **t** 01908 366700 **f** 01908 368872 **w** yamaha-music.co.uk MD: Andrew Kemble.

Studio Design and Construction

Acoustics Design Group 30 Pewley Hill, Guildford, Surrey GU1 3SN **t** 01483 503681 **f** 01483 303217 **e** acousticsdesign@aol.com Prop: John Flynn.

Asadul Ltd Hophouse, Colchester Rd, West Bergholt, Colchester, Essex CO6 3TJ **t** 01206 241600 **f** 01206 241988 **e** 2cv@Beeb.net Dir: Stuart Bailey.

The Audionet Unit 13 Impress House, Mansell Rd, London W3 7QH **t** 020 8735 0040 **f** 020 8735 0041 **e** james@theaudionet.ltd.uk MD: Mark Lusardi.

Autograph Sales Ltd. Unit 6, Bush Industrial Estate, Station Rd, London N19 5UN **t** 0207 281 7574 **f** 0207 281 3042 **e** debbiel@autograph.co.uk **w** autograph.co.uk GM: Debbie Lovelock.

AVD (FM) Ltd PO Box 15, Swaffham, Norfolk PE37 8JE **t** 01362 822444 **f** 01362 822488 **e** info@avdco.com **w** avdco.com Dir: Alan Stewart.

Black Box Ltd (UK) 1 Greenwich Quay, London SE8 3EY **t** 020 8858 6883 **f** 020 8692 6957 **e** info@blackbox-design.com **w** blackbox-design.com Dir: Hugh Flynn.

Cablesystems 8 Woodend, London SE19 3NU **t** 020 8653 5451 or 07771 755 339 **e** cablesystems@yahoo.com Owner: Alan Maskall.

J Decor Interiors 159-161 High St, Epsom, Kent KT19 8EW **t** 01372 721773 **f** 01372 742765 **e** jdecor@btconnect.com Dir: Judith Newbit.

Eastlake Audio (UK) PO Box 6016, London W2 1WH **t** 020 7262 3198 **f** 020 7706 1918 **e** info@eastlake-audio.co.uk **w** eastlake-audio.co.uk Dir: David Hawkins.

Hi-Fi Services - Studio Electronics White House Farm, Shropshire TF9 4HA **t** 01630 647374 **f** 01630 647612 Service Mgr: Don Stewart.

IAC IAC House, Moorside Rd, Winchester, Hants SO23 7US **t** 01962 873000 **f** 01962 873111 **e** info@iacl.co.uk **w** iacl.co.uk Sales Manager: Ian Rich.

Kelsey Acoustics (Cables & Interconnections) 9 Lyon Rd, Walton On Thames, Surrey KT12 3PU **t** 01932 886060 **f** 01932 885565 **e** kelsey@fuzion.co.uk **w** kelseyweb.co.uk Op's Mgr: Michael Whiteside.

Munro Acoustics Unit 21, Riverside Studios, 28 Park St, London SE1 9EQ **t** 020 7403 3808 **f** 020 7403 0957 **e** info@munro.co.uk **w** munro.co.uk Prop: Andy Munro.

Recording Architecture Ltd (UK) 1 Greenwich Quay, Greenwich, London SE8 3EY **t** 020 8692 6992 **f** 020 8692 6957 **e** ra@aaa-design.com **w** aaa-design.com MD: Roger D'Arcy.

R&W Sound Engineering Unit 7u, Long Spring, Porters Wood, St Albans AL3 6EN **t** 01727 756999 **f** 01737 765777 **e** enquiries@rwsound.co.uk **w** rwsound.co.uk Technical Director: Jon Raper.

Sacred Space Design 28 Hollerith Rise, Bracknell, Berks RG12 7TJ **t** 0845 345 2750 or 07734 513 345 **e** info@sacredspacedesign.ltd.uk **w** sacredspacedesign.ltd.uk Senior Designer: Daphne Rotenberg.

Sound Workshop (Sound System Design/Installation) 19-21 Queens Rd, Halifax, W Yorks HX1 3NS **t** 01422 345021 **f** 01422 360440 **e** enquiries@thesoundworkshop.co.uk **w** thesoundworkshop.co.uk MD: David Mitchell.

The Studio Wizard Organisation Sawmill Cottage, Melton Pk, Melton Constable, Norfolk NR24 2NJ **t** 07092 123 666 or 01263 862999 **f** 07092 123 666 **e** info@studiowizard.com **w** studiowizard.com MD: Howard Turner.

Veale Associates 16 North Rd, Stevenage, Herts SG1 4AL **t** 01438 747666 **f** 01438 742500 **e** info@vealea.com **w** vealea.com MD: Edward Veale.

Studio Miscellaneous

Audio Motion Ltd Osney Mead House, Osney Mead, Oxford, Oxon OX2 0ES **t** 08701 600 504 **f** 01865 728 319 **e** info@audiomotion.com **w** audiomotion.com Audio Mgr: Des Tong.

Audio Transfers @ Inflight Studios 15 Stukeley St, Covent Garden, London WC2B 5LT **t** 020 7400 8569 or 020 7400 0725 **e** keith.knowles@inflightstudios.com **w** ifsaudiotransfers.com Facility Mgr: Keith Knowles.

Casmara 16 West Pk, Mottingham, London SE9 4RQ **t** 020 8857 3213 **f** 020 8857 0731 **e** mail@meridian-records.co.uk **w** casmara.supanet.com Owner: Richard Hughes.

5 Star Cases Broad End Industrial Estate, Broad End Rd, Walsoken, Wisbech, Cambs PE14 7BQ **t** 01945 427000 **f** 01945 427015 **e** info@5star-cases.com **w** 5star-cases.com MD: Keith Sykes.

GTek The Barley Mow Centre, 10, Barley Mow Passage, Chiswick, London W4 4PH **t** 020 8994 6477 x3069 **e** gtek@jgtek.demon.co.uk Prop: Jon Griffin.

Melissa Miguel Vocal Training 33/37 Hatherley Mews, Walthamstow, London E17 4QP **t** 020 8521 9227 **f** 020 8520 5553 **e** xplosive@supanet.com Vocal Trainer.

Speed Music PLC 195 Caerleon Rd, Newport, South Wales NP19 7HA **t** 01633 215577 **f** 01633 213214 **e** info@speedmusic.co.uk **w** speedmusic.co.uk Dir: Nick Fowler.

Studio Electronics- Hi Fi Services White House Farm, Shropshire TF9 4HA **t** 01630 647374 **f** 01630 647612 Service Mgr: Don Stewart.

Advertisers Index